ST. MARTIN'S

MINOTAUR

MYSTERIES

GET A CLUE!

Be the first to hear the latest mystery book news...

With the St. Martin's Minotaur monthly newsletter, you'll learn about the hottest new Minotaur books, receive advance excerpts from newly published works, read exclusive original material from featured mystery writers, and be able to enter to win free books!

Sign up on the Minotaur Web site at:
www.minotaurbooks.com

**ALSO BY
JULIA SPENCER-FLEMING**

OUT OF THE DEEP I CRY

A FOUNTAIN FILLED WITH BLOOD

IN THE BLEAK MIDWINTER

AVAILABLE FROM ST. MARTIN'S/MINOTAUR PAPERBACKS

In the Bleak Midwinter

Julia Spencer-Fleming

St. Martin's Paperbacks

IN THE BLEAK MIDWINTER

Copyright © 2002 by Julia Spencer-Fleming.
Excerpt from *To Darkness and to Death* © 2005 by Julia Spencer-Fleming.

Cover photo of house © Layne Kennedy/Corbis.
Photo of tree by Linda Raskin/Jupiterimages.

Hymn on page xi, "In the Bleak Midwinter," from *The Hymnal 1982*, published by The Publishing Co.

Hymn on page 79, "The King Shall Come When Morning Dawns," from *The Hymnal 1982*, published by The Publishing Co.

Library of Congress Catalog Card Number: 2001051303

ISBN: 0-312-94055-6
EAN: 80312-94055-3

Printed in the United States of America

St. Martin's hardcover edition / March 2002
St. Martin's Paperbacks edition / March 2003

St. Martin's Paperbacks are published by St. Martin's Press, 175 Fifth Avenue, New York, NY 10010.

10 9 8 7 6 5 4

–To Leslie–

WINTER MUST BE COLD FOR THOSE WITH NO
WARM MEMORIES.

—DELMER DAVES AND LEO McCARY

ACKNOWLEDGMENTS

Thanks to Ruth Cavin, Julie Sullivan, and everyone at St. Martin's Press for making my first time so much fun, and thanks to Luci Zahray for discovering me. This book was immeasurably improved by the critiques of those who read it as a work-in-progress: Adele Hutchinson; my father, John Fleming; Karen Fletcher; Les Smith; and Anne Steele Zembala. I had expert help from the clergy of the Cathedral Church of St. Luke, Portland, Maine, and from Timothy J. LaMar, formerly of the U.S. Army Infantry, who took me shooting and explained what it sounds like when you bash in someone's head with a rock. Thanks to my mother, Lois Fleming, my first and best writing instructor, editor, critic, and fan. Finally, thanks to my husband, Ross Hugo-Vidal, who went through everything but a plague of locusts during the writing of this book and lived to tell the tale.

IN THE BLEAK MIDWINTER
LYRICS BY CHRISTINA GEORGINA ROSSETTI

In the bleak midwinter, frosty wind made moan,
Earth stood hard as iron, water like a stone;
Snow had fallen, snow on snow, snow on snow,
In the bleak midwinter, long ago.

Our God, heaven cannot hold him, nor earth sustain;
Heaven and earth shall flee away when he comes to reign;
In the bleak midwinter a stable place sufficed
The Lord God incarnate, Jesus Christ.

Angels and archangels may have gathered there,
Cherubim and seraphim thronged the air;
But his mother, in her maiden bliss,
Worshiped the beloved with a kiss.

What can I give him, poor as I am?
If I were a shepherd, I would bring a lamb;
If I were a wise man, I would do my part;
Yet what I can give him: give him my heart.

CHAPTER 1

It was one hell of a night to throw away a baby. The cold pinched at Russ Van Alstyne's nose and made him jam his hands deep into his coat pockets, grateful that the Washington County Hospital had a police parking spot just a few yards from the ER doors. A flare of red startled him, and he watched as an ambulance backed out of its bay silently, lights flashing. The driver leaned out of his window, craning to see his way between cement rails.

"Kurt! Hey! Anything for me?"

The driver waved at Russ. "Hey, Chief. Nope. Heart attack stabilized and heading for Glens Falls. You heard about the baby?"

"That's why I'm here."

Kurt continued to back out, almost to the end of the parking lot. "Jesum, hard to imagine sumpin' like that here in Millers Kill—" The rest of his commentary was lost as he heeled the ambulance into the road. Russ waved, then pushed open the antiquated double doors to the emergency department.

His glasses fogged up within seconds in the moist heat of the foyer. He pulled off the wire frames and rubbed them with the end of his scarf, mentally cursing the myopia that had finally led him, at forty-eight, to cave in and wear the damn things full time. His stomach ached and his knee was bothering him and for a moment he wished he had taken that security consulting job in Phoenix like his wife had wanted.

"Hey! Chief!" A blurry form in brown approached him. Russ tucked his glasses over his ears and Mark Durkee, one of his three night-shift officers, snapped into focus. As usual, the younger man was spit-and-polished within an inch of his life, making Russ acutely aware of his own non-standard-issue appearance: wrinkled wool pants shoved into salt-stained hunting boots, his oversized tartan muffler clashing with his regulation brown parka. Hell, Mark was probably too young to get a cold neck, even with the back of his head shaved almost bald.

"Hey, Mark," Russ said. "Talk to me."

The officer waved his chief down the drab green hallway toward the emergency room. The place smelled of disinfectant and bodies, with a whiff of cow manure left over by the last farmer who had come in straight from the barn. "Man, it's like something out of an old Bing Crosby movie, Chief. The priest at Saint Alban's found the little guy bundled up at the door of the church. The doctor's checking him out now."

"How's the baby look?"

"Fine, as far as they can tell. He was wrapped up real well, and the doc says he probably wasn't out in the cold more'n a half hour or so." Russ's sore stomach eased up. He'd seen a lot over the years, but nothing shook him as much as an abused child. He'd had one baby-stuffed-in-a-garbage-bag case when he'd been an MP in Germany, and he didn't care to ever see one again.

Mark and Russ nodded to the admissions nurse standing guard between the ER waiting room and the blue-curtained alcove where patients got their first look-see. "Evening, Alta," Russ said. "How's business?" The waiting room, decorated with swags of tired tinsel and a matching silver tree, was empty except for a teenager sprawled over one of the low sofas.

"Slow," the nurse said, buzzing them into the emergency treatment area. "Typical Monday night." The old linoleum floors carried the rattle of gurney wheels and the squeak of rubber-soled shoes.

"Over there," Mark said, pointing. Framed by limp white curtains dangling from ceiling tracks, an athletic-looking woman in gray sweats was leaning on a plastic incubator, writing in a pocket-sized notebook.

"Who the hell's that?" Russ asked. "I swear, if they let a reporter in here before we've cleared the facts I'll—" he strode toward the incubator. "Hey, you," he said.

His challenge brought the woman's chin up, and she snapped her head around, zeroing in on the two policemen. She was plain, no makeup and nondescript dark blond hair scraped back in a ponytail. She had that overbred look he associated with rich women from the north side of town: high cheekbones and a long thin nose that was perfect for looking down at folks. Mark grabbed his arm, grinning. "No, no. That's the priest, Chief." He laughed out loud at the expression on Russ's face. The priest? Christ on a bicycle. She gave Russ a look that said, "Wanna make something of it?" He felt himself coloring. Her eyes were the only exceptional thing about her, true hazel, like granite seen under green water.

"Officer Durkee," she said, her gaze sliding off Russ as if she had already weighed and found him wanting. "Any word yet from the Department of Human Services?" There was the barest trace of a Southern accent in her no-nonsense voice.

"No, ma'am," Mark said, rocking back and forth on his heels. "But I'd expect that. They got a lot of ground to cover around here, and not many people to cover it with." He was still grinning like a greased hyena.

Russ decided the best defense was a good offense. "I'm

Russell Van Alstyne, Millers Kill chief of police." He held out his hand. She shook firm, like a guy.

"Clare Fergusson," she said. "I'm the new priest at Saint Alban's. That's the Episcopal Church. At the corner of Elm and Church." There was a faint testiness in her voice. Russ relaxed a fraction. A woman priest. If that didn't beat all.

"I know which it is. There are only four churches in town." He saw the fog creeping along the edges of his glasses again and snatched them off, fishing for a tissue in his pocket. "Can you tell me what happened, um . . ." What was he supposed to call her? "Mother?"

"I go by Reverend, Chief. Ms. is fine, too."

"Oh. Sorry. I never met a woman priest before."

"We're just like the men priests, except we're willing to pull over and ask directions."

A laugh escaped him. Okay. He wasn't going to feel like an unwashed heathen around her.

"I was leaving the church through the kitchen door in the back, which is sunken below street level. There are stairs rising to a little parking area, tucked between the parish hall and the rectory, not big, just room enough for a couple cars. I was going for a run." She looked down and waggled one sneaker-shod foot. Her sweatshirt read ARMY. "The box was on the steps. I thought maybe someone had left off a donation at first, because all I could see were the blankets. When I picked it up, though, I could feel something shifting inside." She looked through the plastic into the incubator, shaking her head. "The poor thing was so still when I unwrapped him I thought he was already dead." She looked up at Russ. "Imagine how troubled and desperate someone would have to be to leave a baby out in the cold like that."

Russ grunted. "Anything else that might give us an idea of who left him there?"

"No. Just the baby, and the blankets, and the note inside."

Russ frowned at Mark. "You didn't tell me about any note," he said.

The officer shrugged, pulling a glassine envelope out of his jacket pocket. "Reverend Fergusson didn't mention it until after I had called you," he explained. He handed Russ the plastic-encased paper.

"That's my fault, yeah," said the priest, not sounding at all apologetic. Russ held the clear envelope at arm's length to get a better view. "I didn't call DSS until I was over here, and I wanted to make sure they knew what the baby's parents intended." She looked over his arm at the note. "I'm sorry, but I handled it without thinking about any fingerprints or anything."

It was an eight-by-eleven sheet of paper ripped from a spiral-bound notebook, the kind that you could get anywhere. The handwriting, in blue ink, was blocky, extremely child-like. Russ guessed that the note's author had held the pen in her left hand to disguise her printing. "This is our baby, Cody," it read. "Please give him to Mr. and Mrs. Burns here at St. Alban's. We both agree they should have him, so there won't be any trouble later on with the adoption. Tell our baby we love him."

Russ lowered the note and met the priest's green-brown eyes. "Kids," he said.

"That would be my guess," she said.

"Who are the Burnses?"

"Geoffrey and Karen Burns."

"The lawyers," Russ said, surprised.

"They're parishioners of St. Alban's. I understand they've been seeking adoption for over two years now. They've been on the Prayers of the People list for the past two weeks, and as I recall, our secretary told me that's a regular thing for them."

"This is something published? Or what?"

"Prayed out loud, every Sunday during the service."

He looked closely at her. "Sounds like at least one of the baby's parents might go to your church."

She looked uncomfortable. "Yeah. Although I'm sure that everyone who knows the Burnses also knows they're looking for a baby."

"Why leave it at St. Alban's then? Why not on the Burnses' doorstep?"

Reverend Fergusson swept her hands open wide.

Russ handed the note back to Mark. "What time did you find the baby?" he asked the priest.

"About . . . nine-thirty, quarter to ten," she said. "There was a welcoming reception from the vestry tonight that finished up around nine. I changed in my office, checked messages, and then headed out. I already gave Officer Durkee the names of the people who were there."

Russ squinted, trying for a mental picture of the area where Elm branched off the curve of Church Street. One of Tick Soley's parking lots was across the street from the church, one light on the corner but nothing further up where the houses started. "What did you say was behind the little parking area?"

"The rectory, where I live. There's a tall hedge, and then my side yard. My driveway is on the other side of the house."

Russ sighed. "The kids—the parents—could have parked in any one of those spots and snuck over to the stairs with the baby. I somehow doubt we're gonna get an eyewitness with a license number and a description of the driver."

The priest tapped the glassine envelope. "Chief Van Alstyne, exactly how hard do you have to look for the parents of this baby?" For the first time Russ let himself take a long look into the portable incubator. The sleeping baby didn't look any different from every other newborn he had ever seen, all fat burnished cheeks and almond-shaped eyes. He wondered how hard up or screwed up or roughed up a girl would have to be to pull a perfect little thing like that out of her body and then leave him in a cardboard box. In the dark. On a night when the windchill hovered at zero degrees.

He looked back at the priest. She was leaning toward him slightly, focusing on him as if he were the only person in the whole hospital. "I don't need to tell you that leaving a baby like that is called endangering a child," he said. She nodded. "And of course, if we can't find the parents, it's going to take longer for DSS to actually get the baby out of foster care and into an adoptive home. But the thing is to find out how voluntary this really was, giving up the baby."

Her mouth opened and then snapped shut. He continued. "When a woman really wants to give up her kid for adoption, she usually gets in touch with an agency, or a lawyer, or somebody, well before the baby is born. These throwaway situations—"

"She didn't throw Cody away. Whoever she is."

"No, she didn't. Which makes me think it's not one of those times when the mother is a druggie or a drunk or a psycho. But it does make me wonder if her boyfriend or her father forced her into it. And if she's not already regretting what she did, but is too scared of us or of him to come forward and reclaim her son."

"I never thought of that," Reverend Fergusson said, biting her lower lip. "Oh dear. Maybe I shouldn't have—"

The emergency room doors opened with a hydraulic pouf. Russ recognized the small, bearded man in the expensive topcoat and the striking brunette woman at his side, but he'd know who they were even if he had never seen them in the Washington County Courthouse before, just from the look on Reverend Fergusson's face.

"We got here as soon as we could," Geoffrey Burns said. His voice was tight. His glance flicked around the treatment area, lighting on the incubator. His wife saw it at the same time.

"Oh . . ." she said, pressing one perfectly manicured hand to her mouth. "Oh. Is that him?"

The priest nodded. She stepped aside, allowing the Burnses a clear view of the sleeping baby. "Oh, Geoff, just look at him . . ." Karen Burns hesitated, as if showing too much eagerness might cause the incubator to vanish.

Her husband stared at the baby for a long moment. "Where's the doctor who's been treating him?" he said. He looked at Russ. "Chief Van Alstyne. I take it the Department of Social Services hasn't seen fit to send anyone over yet."

"Mr. Burns." Russ nodded. "I expect we'll see somebody soon. They're a little overwhelmed over there, you know."

"Oh, don't I just," Geoff Burns said.

"I take it Reverend Fergusson called you about the note that was found with the baby?" Russ glanced pointedly toward the priest, who lifted her chin in response. "You folks know that it's way too early to start thinking of this boy as your own. No matter what the parents wrote."

Karen Burns turned toward him. "Of course, Chief. But we are licensed foster parents without any children in our home right now, and we intend to press DSS to place Cody with us." Mrs. Burns had a voice so perfectly modulated she could have been selling him something on the radio. Russ glanced at Burns, thin and short, and wondered at the attraction. His own wife was one hell of a good-looking woman, but Karen Burns would put her in the shade.

"Under the standard of the best interests of the child, it's preferable that a pre-adoptive child be fostered with the would-be adoptive parents, if there are no natural relatives able to care for the child. Young v. The Department of Social Services."

Russ blinked at the lawyer's aggressively set brows. "I'm not contesting you in court, Mr. Burns," he said. "But we don't know that there aren't any natural relatives. We don't

know if the mother gave him up of her own free will or not."
He shifted his weight forward, deliberately using his six-foot-
three-inches as a visual reminder of his authority here. "Isn't
it a little odd for a professional couple like you to be foster
parents?"

Karen Burns laid her hand on her husband's arm, cutting
off whatever he was about to say. "I work from home as well
as from my office, part time. On those times we've had a
child in our care, I just cut way back."

"I assure you we're properly licensed and have passed all
the state requirements," Burns said, his face tight. "We are
fully prepared to make the sacrifices necessary to care for a
child. Unlike the biological parents of this boy."

Karen Burns twisted a single gold bangle around her wrist.
"Of course you have to look for the parents, Chief Van Alstyne. And I'm sure that anyone who took such care to make
sure their baby would be found immediately, and left a note
asking us to be his adoptive parents, would only confirm that
request."

Her husband spoke almost at the same time. "We intend
to file for TPR immediately, on grounds of abandonment and
endangerment." There was a pause. The Burnses looked at
each other, then at Russ. They both spoke at once.

"I hope you do find her. She undoubtedly needs help and
counseling."

"I hope you don't find her, to be frank. It'll be better for
the baby all around."

Reverend Fergusson broke the awkward silence. "What's
TPR mean?"

"Termination of parental rights," Russ answered. "Usually
happens after the court takes a DSS caseworker's recommendation that there's no way the child ought to go back to the
parent. Takes months, sometimes years, if DSS is trying to
reunite the family." He rubbed his forehead with the palm of

his hand. "During which time the kid is in foster care."

"Unless, as in this case, the child is an abandoned infant and the parents can't be found," Geoff Burns said, tapping his finger into his palm in time to his words.

"Uh huh," Russ agreed. "Unless they can't be found."

CHAPTER 2

The pediatric resident, bright-eyed and way too young for comfort, entered the treatment area from behind a blue baize curtain. "Oh, hey!" he said. "You must be the Burnses! Your priest here told me about you. Hey, you wanna hold Cody here or what?" He unlatched the top of the incubator and scooped up the baby expertly, placing him in Karen Burns's arms before she had a chance to respond.

"Oh," she said. "Oh." Her husband put his arm around her, turning her away from the others. Russ, rubbing away at the headache building behind his eyebrows, felt the weight of attention on him. He glanced down at Reverend Fergusson, who was looking at him instead of at the would-be-parents. It took him a moment to identify the expression on her face, it had been so long since he'd seen it directed at him. Sympathy.

The resident was trying to give his report to Durkee, who was just as doggedly pointing him in Russ's direction. "Hey," he said, "You're the police chief? Really neat."

"I think so." Over the doctor's shoulder, Russ could see Reverend Fergusson's lips twitch.

"The baby's in real good shape," the doctor said, pulling out several sheets of paper stapled together. "Here's a copy of his tests and the examination results. I place the time of birth within the last two or three days. No drugs in his system, no signs of fetal alcohol syndrome, no signs of abuse. His cord was cut and wrapped inexpertly, but somebody kept it nice and clean. We'll have to wait until he's had a bowel movement, but I'm guessing he's been fed formula."

Russ scanned the report, noting the blood group—AB positive—and the notation that the baby had been bathed at some point in his brief life. "Okay," he said. "Mark, get me the box and the blankets, we'll see if we can get anything from those. I want you to stay here until somebody from DSS arrives, unless you get a squawk." Mark nodded and disappeared into the examination cubby. Russ folded the medical report and tucked it into his jacket pocket.

"Here you go, Chief," Mark said, returning with the box. He passed it to Russ, who examined it without much hope of anything useful. It was sturdy, new-looking, marked with the logo of a Finger Lakes orchard. Lane's IGA and the Grand Union probably had hundreds just like it tossed in their storerooms. The blankets were a mix: an old, well-worn gold polyester thing, a heavy woolen horse blanket in plaid, and what looked like two brand-new flannel baby blankets, the kind his sister had by the dozens. Russ had a sudden image of himself going door-to-door, asking, "Ma'am? Do you recognize any of these blankets? And has anyone in your household given birth lately?"

Reverend Fergusson had gone over to the Burnses and was talking softly to them. Karen Burns said something, looking at her husband, and he nodded. All three of them bent their heads. Russ realized with a shock that they were praying. Openly displayed religion made him as uncomfortable as hell, and it didn't help when the priest signed the cross over both of them and then laid her hands on the baby and blessed him. She really was a priest. Jesus Christ. A woman priest. Were Episcopalians like Catholics? He'd have to ask his mother, she'd know.

When Reverend Fergusson broke away from the Burnses and walked straight toward him, he thought for one guilty moment she must have read his mind and was coming over to give him what for.

"Chief Van Alstyne, will you be leaving soon?" she asked.

"Yeah," he said, warily. Did she want to pray over him, too?

"Ah. Well, Karen and Geoff are going to stay here until after the caseworker arrives, and I, um . . ." She worried her lower lip some, hesitating. "I called an ambulance, you see, 'cause I thought Cody ought to be seen as soon as possible, and I, I don't have . . ."

The light dawned. "Do you need a ride home, Reverend?" Russ said.

"I don't want to impose . . ."

"I'd be glad to give you a lift, if you don't mind me stopping by the station to drop this off before we get to your house. I want to make sure our fingerprint guy has it first thing in the morning." He hefted the box.

"I'm not in any hurry," she said. "On the other hand, I did want to get to the rectory sometime tonight, and I understand that the taxis in Millers Kill aren't the quickest to respond to a call . . ."

Russ snorted. "If you're talking about In-Town Taxi, you're right. One car is their whole fleet, and when the driver decides he's done for the day, you're outta luck." He waved good-bye to Mark and gestured for the priest to precede him through the emergency department doors.

" 'Night, Chief," the admitting nurse called.

" 'Night, Alta," he said.

The dry, cold air outside the overheated hospital was like a good stiff drink after a hard day. Russ breathed deeply. He noticed the priest wasn't carrying a coat. "Hey, Reverend, you can't go outside in just sweats this time of year. Where are you from, anyway?"

She looked down at her unseasonable outfit. "It shows, huh? Southern Virginia. And when I was in the army, I managed to never get myself stationed any place where the temperature dipped to below freezing."

"Neat trick," he said. In the army? A woman priest in the army. What next? She parachute out of planes dropping bibles?

"I was a helicopter pilot," she said. "Late of the Eighteenth Airborne Corps. You'd be surprised how often we needed to drop men and gear into overheated climates."

"No, I wouldn't," he said. "I was career army. First in the infantry, then an MP. I retired about four years ago."

"Really?" She stopped in her tracks. "We'll have to compare postings." She looked up at him curiously. "It's just that the way you knew everybody, I assumed you'd lived in Millers Kill all your life."

Russ pulled open the passenger-side door of his cruiser. She slid into the seat, yelping at the chilly vinyl. He crossed to the other side, dropped the box into the backseat, and got behind the wheel. "I was born here, lived here my first eighteen years." He started up the car, turned on the radio, and grabbed the mike. "Ten-fifty, this is Ten-fifty-seven. I'm rolling, en route from the hospital to the station." The radio crackled and Harlene's voice came on the line. "Ten-fifty-seven, this is Ten-fifty. Acknowledged you en route from the hospital to the station. We'll see you soon."

The woman beside him was shivering, her arms clasped around herself, her knees drawn up. "Sorry," he said. "The heater in the old whore takes a long time to warm up." A second after he spoke, he remembered he was talking to a priest. "Oh, Jesus," he said, caught himself, then blurted out, "Christ!" at his own stupidity before he could help it. He hung his head, laughing and groaning at the same time.

"You! Swearing in front of a priest!" She pointed her finger at his chest. "Drop and gimme twenty!" He stared at her, not sure he was hearing right. She smiled slowly, her eyes half-closing. "Gotcha."

Russ shook his head, laughing. "Okay, okay. Sorry." He shifted the cruiser into gear and eased it out of the hospital parking lot onto Burgoyne Avenue. Nearing midnight on a Monday, there was hardly any traffic on the normally busy road.

Reverend Fergusson shifted in her seat, exclaiming briefly when she hit a particularly cold spot. "You were telling me you were born and raised right here . . ."

"Oh, yeah," he sighed. "Probably would have gotten a job at the mill and never left town. But I got out of high school in 'sixty-nine and my number came up in the Instant Loser Lottery. Next thing I knew, it was good-bye New York State, hello Southeast Asia."

He checked the gauge on the heater. "Turned out the army and I made a pretty good match. We went from Vietnam to the Gulf together." He switched the blower to high and the interior began to warm up. "After I retired,"—no need to go into detail about that phase of his life—"I decided the time was right to finally come home. The old chief was retiring, and they needed someone with experience who wanted to live the quiet life up here in Washington county. It's a good outfit, eight officers and four part-timers, and I liked they way everyone worked together. My wife, Linda, loved the idea of us finally settling down somewhere other than a big city or busy post"—well, that was half-true, she *had* wanted him to settle down—"and she likes being so close to my mother and my sister." Now that was a whopper. But it was the party line, and he stuck to it. "So that's how I wound up back in my old home town a quarter-century after I left."

"Does your wife work?"

"Oh, yeah." He swung into the right-hand lane and turned onto Morningside Drive. The lights from the new Wal-Mart turned the night sodium orange. "She has her own business, making custom curtains. It's been more successful than either of us imagined." He slowed, checking out the cars in the parking lot. He didn't like all-night stores, they were targets for trouble. "She's getting into mail orders now, says she wants to make up a whole catalogue. It's great, it's been really just great."

"Sounds like she found her vocation. Good for her. It can be hard for some military families to readjust to civilian life. You two have any kids?"

"No," he said. "What's your story? You came from Virginia originally?"

"Born and bred in a small town outside of Norfolk," she said. "My family owns a charter and commercial air business. I had always thought I wanted to be part of it someday, so after college, I joined the army as a helo jock. The military is still the best way to train for a career as a pilot, you know. And the army was putting on a big push to get female recruits into non-traditional fields. I was the only woman in my unit."

"Must have been tough," he said. Now that he thought about it, she did seem less like a bible-tosser and more like the type to be dropping arms in an LZ.

"At times, yeah. It was good though." Taking his eyes off the road for a second, he could see a one-sided smile flash across her face. "But, as it turned out, I had to put my piloting plans aside when I was called to the priesthood. I went back to Virginia to go to seminary, which was really good for my parents."

Russ didn't want to get into the murky mystical depths of how someone was "called to the priesthood." "How'd you wind up here?" he asked.

"I spent a summer as an assistant curate in the Berkshires. I had never been in this part of the country before, and I just fell in love with it. I started looking for a position somewhere in New England, and when St. Alban's came open, I thought, well, it's only a half-hour drive from Vermont . . ."

"Ah ha," Russ said. "So you haven't experienced a North-country winter yet." The light at the intersection with Radcliff Street turned red, and he pumped his brakes to avoid skidding on the icy spots.

"Therein lies the rub, as they say. My internship ran from May through September, so I was a little unprepared for six inches of snow before the end of November. I've only been here for three weeks, so I'm not exactly acclimated yet. I do have a coat, though. But when I stumbled over the baby, I was on my way out for a run."

He looked at her again. She was obviously fit, but she wasn't a big woman, scarcely up to his shoulder standing. "Just because this is a small city and we look like Bedford Falls from *It's a Wonderful Life*, don't be fooled into thinking bad things can't happen here. They can, and do, so watch where you run if you're out at night alone."

She waved a hand, unconcerned. "I can take care of my-self," she said.

"Lemme guess, you know karate, you're trained in the art of self-defense . . ."

"Nothing formal. But the army made sure I could break somebody's arm if I needed to."

The light turned green. He rolled onto Radcliff, causing an ancient Chevy Nova that had been barreling down the street to brake hard in an attempt to get under the thirty-five-mile-an-hour speed limit. "Lemme tell you, Reverend, somebody tries to mug you, they aren't gonna get close enough for you to break their arm. Every ass—uh, jerk on the streets today's got a gun. Even up here. They come up outta New York City, just like the drugs do."

He glanced at her when he made a left turn onto Main. She was studying the peaceful storefronts and frowning, ab-sently rubbing her forearm with one long-fingered hand. "Is that a big problem in Millers Kill? Drugs?" she asked.

Russ sighed. He knew when he was being side-stepped.

"Not too bad, no. Alcohol is the number one drug of choice up here, like you'll find in a lot of rural areas. My biggest single crime problem is domestic violence, and nine times out of ten there's alcohol involved."

He pulled the cruiser up in front of the station. "I'll leave the car running for you," he said. "Be back in a minute." He grabbed the box and took off through the icy air, bounding up the stairs two at a time. There was nobody at the front desk at this hour. Instead, he loped into the dispatch room, where Harlene was just pouring herself a cup of coffee. "Harlene, you good lookin' woman!" he said. Harlene was some ten years his elder, a big, square woman with an uncannily organized mind and a photographic memory of every highway, lane, and dirt road in three counties.

"One of these days, I'm going to slap you with a sexual harassment lawsuit," she said, hefting herself into her chair and curling her headset over her springy gray hair.

"And let Harold know how much fun you're having over here? No way." Her husband Harold had recently retired, and was riding Harlene pretty hard to quit work and stay at home with him. "I'm gonna lock this into evidence," Russ said, waggling the box. "Will you leave a note for Phil to get on it first thing in the morning? Prints, hairs, anything he can come up with."

Harlene peered at the cardboard. "You want him to send it on to the state if nothing pans out?"

"No. No need to spend the money. This is that abandoned baby Mark called in. More likely than not the mother'll surface within a week or so. You know how these things run."

Harlene nodded. The teenager wound up in the hospital with post-partum complications. Or she broke down and told a friend, who told another, until there wasn't any secret anymore.

"Okay, Chief, you got it." She pointed to the coffeemaker. "Just brewed a fresh pot," she said.

"Gotta haul it," Russ said, stuffing the ends of his scarf back into his jacket. "I'm giving the priest who found the baby a ride back to St. Alban's rectory."

"You and a priest." Harlene snorted. "I'd give good money to hear how that conversation goes."

"Actually," Russ said, enjoying his moment as much as Mark had his, "She's very easy to talk to. She's old army, too."

Harlene was gratifyingly surprised. "Well! Didn't know they could *have* women priests." She looked into the middle distance for a moment. "Ask her what she thinks of my sexual harassment suit," she said.

Russ bit back a laugh and grabbed the locker key off the hook on the wall. He clattered downstairs and unlocked the evidence cage, tagging the box and scribbling his entry information in the dog-eared logbook. Within two minutes he was running back upstairs, shouting a good-night to Harlene, and out the front door again.

When he got into the cruiser, Reverend Fergusson jerked her hand away from the radio. "Sorry," she said. "I couldn't resist. I wanted to see if it sounded like it does on all those television shows."

"And?" Russ said, backing the car out of his parking spot.

"And it sounds like the state police have wa-a-a-ay too much time on their hands," she said. "One guy was going on and on about some fishing tournament he'd gone to. It sounded more like *Bassmasters* than *Dragnet*."

They both laughed. "Yeah, well . . ." Russ said. "Mondays are the quietest night of the week. You come cruising with me on Friday, then you'll really hear something."

She pinned him with those clear hazel eyes. "Could I?"

Startled, he almost ran a red light. He looked at her. "Reverend, why on earth would you want to do something like that?" he said.

"Because I want to get a feel for the problems of Millers

Kill that I won't get in a vestry reception," she said. "Because I need to figure out what kind of outreach ministry my church ought to be doing, instead of just what my parishioners feel comfortable doing right now. And because," she grinned, a reckless, one-sided grin that made him think she must be mistaken about a priestly calling, "I'm a recovering adrenaline addict. Who hasn't had a fix in a while. Green light."

"Huh." He drove on. "Doesn't your church have a mass or whatever it is on Fridays? I recall seeing cars there in the evening. And besides, I'm out pretty late. Don't you, I dunno, get up early to pray or something?"

She made an amused sound in the back of her throat. "Saturday's a day off for me. At least, it's supposed to be. So I can sleep in. If worse comes to worse, I can double up. Praise God while I'm making pancakes, thank the Lord while I'm doing the week's shopping." She began to sing almost inaudibly, "And He walks with me, and He talks with me . . ."

"Uh-huh. I may not know much about religion, but I can tell when I'm being sold a bill of goods."

"So can I come?"

How do I get myself into these situations? he thought. "Okay, yeah," he said finally. "But you do what I say, when I say it, and if I decide for whatever reason that it's not safe, you get left behind. No arguments."

"Do I strike you as the argumentative type?" she asked. He snorted. Along Church Street, the municipal Christmas decorations had been hung on the lampposts. Same fuzzy plastic candy canes and reindeer that had been there when he was a kid. Same fake greenery around the poles, same fat outdoor bulbs. He wondered where they got replacements from. No way anyone was still making lights like that. He turned onto Elm. The rectory was a pretty Dutch Colonial from the turn of the century.

"Here it is, on the left."

"Nice," Russ said, parking in the drive. "Bet you've got great woodwork in there."

The priest groaned. "I can't tell," she said. "The place is all over boxes, most of 'em completely unlabeled, so I have no idea what's in there. I have some I filled before my last posting to Fort Rucker and haven't unpacked in seven years. They could contain anything from 'eighties-style miniskirts to relics of the True Cross for all I can remember. Somehow, there always seems to be something more interesting to do than unpacking and housecleaning . . ."

He slung his arm over the seat and turned toward her. "You gotta get one of those ladies' committees over to do their thing. Have you set up and sparkling in no time."

"Oh, yeah," she said. "And they'd do a great job, too. But you know, you get the place clean and organized at the start and forever after, whenever one of my parishioners came over for a visit, they'd be thinking, My! She certainly didn't keep this up very well!" She looked up the drive to her house, smiling a little. "Ah, it's just the new-posting blues. A new town, all new faces. It can get . . ."

"Lonely."

"Yeah."

They sat in companionable silence, not in any hurry to end the ride.

The radio squawked. "Ten-fifty-seven, this is Ten-fifty. I've got an accident reported out on Route Thirty-Five, at mile fifteen."

Russ clicked in the mike. "Ten-fifty, this is Ten-fifty-seven. Acknowledged. I'm rolling to Route Thirty-Five, mile fifteen." He spread his hands apologetically. "Duty calls. Good-night, Reverend Fergusson."

"Oh, for heaven's sake, call me Clare." She opened her door and slid out, leaning down to keep him in view.

"Clare," he said. "And you can call me Chief." She

laughed loudly. "No, no, call me Russ. After all, if we're going to be partners next Friday . . ."

She nodded. "I'll be there. Russ. Good night, now." She slammed the door. He waited until she had reached her front door and let herself in. Without keys. He made a mental note to get on her about that come Friday. He backed out of her drive and hit his lights, unaccountably smiling all the way to Route Thirty-Five.

The girl unlocked the deadbolt and turned the latch. It was cold in the kitchen, but then again, she had been desperately cold all night long. A light had been left on for her in the hall. She walked to the stairs and tried to remember what she was supposed to be doing. Concentrate. Upstairs. She hefted her overnight bag and gasped as a cramping pain shot through her abdomen. She stopped, pressed her fist against her belly. Nothing to worry about. It was normal. The book had said it was normal to have cramps for several days afterwards.

She picked up her bag again and trudged up the bare wooden stairway. In the upstairs hall, she stared stupidly at the closed doors. Everything was totally foreign to her. Her breasts were aching and damp. She shut her eyes and breathed in deeply, and when she looked again, she saw her own bedroom door in front of her.

Inside, she dropped her luggage and sagged onto the bed. The springs creaked loudly. "Mmmm," came a voice from the other side of the room. "Katie, is that you? Geez, it's late."

"Yeah, Emily," she whispered. "It's me." From across the street, she heard a dog barking and barking. It would go on for an hour or more some nights, a frustrated sheepdog chained to a barren circle of dirt.

"That damn dog," groaned Emily. "Why don't they do it a favor and take it out to the country and let it go?"

"It's not that . . . it's not that . . ." Katie gulped loudly and began to cry.

"Katie, honey, what's wrong?" Emily snapped on a tiny bedside lamp. "Oh sweetie, tell me what's wrong."

Katie shook her head, crying harder. Emily crossed to her bed and sat beside her, hugging her tight. Katie leaned on her shoulder, sobbing open-mouthed, while outside the dog barked and howled into the freezing air.

CHAPTER 3

The case clock in St. Alban's meeting room rang twelve slow, ceremonious hours. The donation of a grateful parishioner who had made a fortune carpetbagging in the post–Civil War South and returned to retire in his native eastern New York, it had a place of honor between two enormous diamond-paned windows. Where, Clare reflected, it had undoubtedly sat un-moved since 1882. She was beginning to suspect the congregation of St. Alban's didn't exactly embrace novelty and innovation. Hiring the first female head of a parish in this area may have exhausted their reserves of daring for the next ten years.

Norm Madsen, a basset-faced gentleman in his seventies, tapped the sheet of paper before him reproachfully. "This isn't an agenda, Reverend Fergusson. We always have an agenda for the vestry meetings."

"And the Wednesday lunch meeting is always financials, to get anything ready to pass on to the stewardship committee Thursday night." Terence McKellan, the head of commercial loans at AllBanc—until recently The First Alleghany Farmers and Merchants Bank, he had taken pains to tell her—laced his hands across his commodious middle. "No offense, but articles about unwed mothers ought to go before the activities committee."

"What sort of activity do you want them to take up, Terry?" Robert Corlew snorted with laughter. The wide-shouldered, bull-necked developer had an improbable mass of hair that Clare was sure must be a toupee.

Mrs. Henry Marshall, the only woman on the vestry board, looked quellingly at Corlew. "Since most of the ladies on activities are my age, Bob," she poked a pencil at her silver waves, "I expect they won't be adding to the unwed mother population any time soon. Though most of them are unwed by now," she said thoughtfully.

Clare breathed slowly and deeply. In. Out. "I'm sorry I didn't compile an agenda. I'll be sure to do that next meeting. As for the newspaper article and the figures sheet in front of you," she leaned forward, resting her arms on the massive black oak table that dominated the room, "you all know about the baby found abandoned here Monday night. That inspired me to do some research into what facilites are available to help single teen mothers."

"There's plenty of aid in Millers Kill," Vaughn Fowler said, popping an antacid tablet into his mouth. "Welfare and low-income housing and a Goodwill store. We even support a soup kitchen with the other churches in town." The retired colonel rapped the table with his chunky West Point ring as he enumerated each item.

"That's true, Mr. Fowler. No teenager with a baby is going to starve here. But did you know seventy percent of the girls who get pregnant in their teens drop out of Millers Kill High?"

"Not to sound unsympathetic," Fowler said, "but what makes you think these girls would have finished high school in the first place?"

Clare had seen that question coming since yesterday, when she had woken up with her inspired idea. "If you look to page four, you'll see an article I copied from *The Washington Post*, about a Junior League program I helped with when I was a seminarian."

"Junior League?" Mrs. Marshall adjusted her reading glasses and bent to the paper. "That's always a good recommendation."

"In their area, the League had found that one of two things tended to happen when a girl had a baby. Either she dropped out of high school to care for the child or her mother stopped working, and often went on to welfare, to care for the child." Terry McKellan read along, his plump cheeks quivering as he nodded. "Drop-outs were at very high risk for further pregnancies, drug abuse, and domestic abuse. Girls whose mothers gave up work to stay at home with the baby finished high school in higher numbers, but few of them found work afterwards, leading to the same sort of dependencies as their sisters with no diploma."

Corlew frowned. "Couldn't find work? Or didn't look for it?"

"Most of these girls had no experience with or example of combining motherhood and work. That's what the Junior League program did. It partnered girls with mentors, who tutored them in everything from parenting skills to how to interview for a job. It provided free day care for the girls during the school day and a quiet space for them to do homework after school. Girls who went through the program not only had a ninety percent graduation rate, but most of them then went on to either community college or to work."

Fowler rapped the table with his ring. "Funding?"

Clare quelled the urge to respond, "Yes, sir." Colonel Fowler was the double of several commanding officers she had served under, complete with graying brush cut and age-defying figure. He expected her to assess problems, devise solutions, and act. Or at least, that's what he had told her during the interview process for this parish. She flipped open to the last page. "Initial funding came from the League, who paid for the day-care workers, some equipment and baby supplies, and a part-time grant writer to raise money independently. Area churches donated the space. Girls who used the facilities after they had started working paid an hourly fee, adjusted to their income." She looked around the table, meeting the eyes of every man and woman, gathering each vestry member in. "I propose St. Alban's start a similar project here. To be funded out of the general funds, using either the parish hall or the old nursery room for the day care. We could have a powerful effect on the lives of young women and children who otherwise don't have much of a future."

The room was silent for a moment. "You want us to be a home for unwed mothers?" Sterling Sumner raised his bushy eyebrows in disbelief. "Outrageous." He flipped the ends of one of the English-school scarves he always affected.

"How much would this cost us?" Terry McKellan asked, scribbling some notes on the margin.

"What about insurance? State licensing requirements for running a day-care facility? Transportation to and from the school and the girls' homes?" Fowler rapped his ring on every point. "This isn't like opening our nursery for members' children during the Sunday services."

"No, si—no, it's not. All of those are issues that will have to be researched. I don't have a whole, detailed proposal to present yet. But I would like the approval and support of the vestry before I call up a committee or start running down licensing requirements. I'd like to know this project has your support so long as the general fund isn't unduly strained by it." Nervous energy forced her out of her seat to stride around the table. "It's innovative, it's meeting an unmet need in the community, it will open St. Alban's doors to new faces, young faces. It exemplifies Christ's charge to us to be his disciples by serving others." She reached her chair and leaned against the worn green velvet back. "I believe those were some of the things you said you wanted me to accomplish as your priest."

Vaughn Fowler's bright blue eyes seemed to be assessing her for leadership potential. "One of the most important goals we set for you was to grow St. Alban's. Bring in new families. Kids."

"More pledges," Corlew muttered.

Fowler shot him a curt glance. "This . . . unwed mother outreach sounds commendable. But will it attract more of the kind of members we want? Or will it scare some families away?"

Clare went blank. "What?"

"In other words," Sterling Sumner said, "will the quality families we want to attract stay away because we've filled our landmark Eighteen-fifty Gothic Revival sanctuary with Daisy Mae and Queen Latisha!" He swiped at the table with one end of his scarf, as if wiping away contamination.

"My grandfather would have been more blunt," Clare said, crossing her arms. "He would have come right out and said 'poor white trash' and 'uppity coloreds.' "

Fowler held up one hand. "No name calling. Reverend Clare, please." He gestured, flat-handed, for her to resume her seat. She did so, ungraciously. "Sterling was being melodramatic, as usual. But the core of the thing is a matter of concern. St. Alban's was one of the first Episcopal churches in this area. We've been able to draw members from even beyond the Millers Kill-Cossayaharie-Fort Henry townships because we have traditional worship with wonderful music in a beautiful setting. Many of us," his gesture encompassed the rest of the vestry, "are from families that have been congregants for generations." Clare opened her mouth. "Let me finish. The parish needs to grow. It needs new blood and, realistically, new money. Before you plunge ahead with your teen-mother project, I'd like to see you do something to encourage families in. Something to draw favorable attention to St. Alban's."

Around the table the other vestry members were nodding. Clare folded her hands. "I can handle two assignments simultaneously, si—Mr. Fowler."

His mouth tilted in the suggestion of a smile. "I'm sure you can."

"Perhaps organizing some meet-the-parishioners teas?" Mrs. Marshall said.

"No, no, no." Robert Corlew shook his head. His hair did not move. "We need something that'll get us in the papers. Free advertising."

"Tours of the church? An evening organ concert series!" Sterling Sumner brightened.

"You were inspired, you said, by the baby abandoned at our back door. I suggest you help the Burnses to foster him. That's—" Fowler's ring rapped for emphasis, "the kind of image and publicity that says we're a family-friendly place. Helping a couple become a family by supporting their efforts to adopt."

"But—not that I wouldn't want to focus my time and effort on the Burnses, but isn't that up to the Department of Social Services? And the legal system? And as much as I'm sure we'd all like to see them become parents, I don't see how that will help us attract new members."

"You don't know what this town is like." Terry McKellan laughed. "Word of mouth is a way of life here. Plus, the news about the baby is already in the paper. Why the heck not make sure they say a few nice things about us, huh?"

Clare looked out a leaded-glass window to where snow flurries were spinning through the air. Ideas crowded her mind, far-fetched, practical, too expensive, possible—"We could start by enlisting parish support," she said. She returned her attention to the table. "A letter-writing campaign to the DSS and the governor's office. Get volunteers to help them transition from a couple to foster parents. Hold a Blessing of Adoption and invite the local press. Invite adoption support groups to meet at St. Alban's."

"Good! Excellent! Knew you would be the priest for us," Fowler said.

Clare looked sharply at him. "What about my mother-baby project?"

"You show us you can organize and get results on the Burnses' adoption, and we'll back you to the hilt on day care for unwed teens." Fowler glanced around the table, registering assent from the rest of the vestry. "Agreed? Agreed."

Clare blew out her breath in a puff. "Then let's adjourn." *Before anyone can think of something else to keep out the undesirables,* she thought. Everyone stood, stacking papers and collecting coats.

"I've gotta make it to Fort Henry Ford by one-thirty," Terry McKellan said, buttoning his wool coat across a wide expanse of midsection. "My daughter blew out the electrical system in her Taurus, so we swapped her my wife's Mazda while she was home for Thanksgiving. Now she wants to keep it. Can you imagine what our insurance is gonna be with her driving in Boston?" He looked at Fowler. "What did you get Wes?"

"A Jeep Wrangler. Good in the snow, appeals to an eighteen-year-old's idea of 'cool.' Unfortunately, it couldn't carry all his stuff down. I'm off to West Point tomorrow with another load. We should have just traded the Expedition with him during the holiday." Clare attempted to edge past the men as they drifted toward the hallway. "And speaking of vehicles, Reverend Clare, that car of yours is totally impractical."

Clare had already heard several people's opinion of her bright red '82 MG. She smiled brightly. "Your son goes to West Point? And you're a graduate, too. You must be very proud."

Terry McKellan roared with laughter. "It was a disappointment to them when he couldn't get into the Culinary Institute . . ."

Vaughn Fowler ignored the witticism. "He's the fifth generation of Fowlers to be an Academy man. Edie and I are very proud, yes."

Clare touched his arm. "Wonderful." She glanced at her watch. "Oh, look at the time. Gentlemen, I've got to run." She waved to the remaining vestry members and quick-stepped down the hall before the subject of her car could come up again.

She ducked into the parish office and caught her secretary, Lois, with a mouthful of nonfat yogurt and raw bran. Lois looked like a strawberry-blond Nancy Reagan, and she kept her size-two figure, as near as Clare could tell, by eating less than any other human being she had ever seen.

"Mmph!" Lois put down the yogurt and waved her hands.

"I'm escaping comments about my car," Clare explained.

"Mmmm," Lois said, swallowing. "It's too tiny. A Lincoln Town Car, that's comfort and styling. And if you have blond hair, you can get the leather seats to match."

Clare made a face. "I'm a dirty blond. I'd have to have dirty seats. Besides, I'm too young for a Town Car."

Lois made a noncommittal noise.

Clare poked at the Rolodex next to Lois' white-and-pink book of message slips. "The vestry says they'll support my young mother's outreach project if I can help the Burnses successfully adopt Cody."

Lois sniffed.

"Now I just have to figure out how to influence New York State's Department of Human Services."

Lois' eyebrows arched.

"I think I'm going to need some help on this one."

"I think you might," Lois agreed.

*   *   *

Her desk chair creaked as Clare tilted back, looking out the window. Flurries swirled through the air outside, making tiny ticking noises as they hit the glass. The only help she could think of was Chief Van Alstyne. Whom she had already impositioned for a ride from the hospital and bulldozed into offering to take her along on his Friday-night patrol. He was going to think she was only ever after him for something at this rate. Which was a shame, because she had really liked him. He was good people, as grandmother Fergusson would say. He reminded her of friends she had in the army, friends who could always see her, no matter what uniform she was wearing at the time.

Okay. She could ask how the search for Cody's birth mother was going. Find out what was happening with DSS—surely he'd be up to date on that. And if she gave him a chance to change his mind about Friday night, it would probably be the right thing to do. She should do that. Well. Maybe. She picked up the receiver in one hand and the Millers Kill directory in the other.

Russ was having one of those days that, if it were on video, you'd fast-forward through until you got to a good part. One of his officers had called in with a suspiciously early-in-the-season flu that was probably being treated with shots of cherry brandy and a long ride on a snowmobile. When Russ had taken a break from patrolling and shown up for an unexpected lunch at home, Linda had been too busy sewing up another order of curtains to eat with him. And she had asked him to drop off her loan application at the bank, when she knew he hated running personal errands in uniform. He always ran into somebody who would make some crack about how he was using the taxpayer's dime.

He had a mountain of paperwork covering his ugly gray metal desk, stuff he'd been putting off and putting off until it had become a full day's job. When he'd bitched about it to Harlene, she told him if he'd worked at it a little at a time, he wouldn't be staring down the barrel now, which he already knew, which made him even more pissy.

And now this little gem. Circled in red in the *Post-Star* courtesy of Officer Pollack, who always brought in his copy before his shift. Russ had been expecting the article about the baby, of course. He'd given the beat reporter an interview, explaining what the police were doing to find the mother, saying the boy had been found "outside an area church" and omitting all mention of the note tucked in the box with the baby. She had gotten the resident from the hospital to describe the overall good health of the child. And a line from the Department of Social Services confirming the baby was being placed with an experienced foster mother.

The usual stuff. What was making him grip his coffee mug to keep from throwing it across the room was the paragraph devoted to the Burnses. How the hell the reporter had found out about them he didn't know, but there it all was, in glorious black and white: Saint Alban's, the note, Burns complaining about DSS, and a plea to the mother to contact the couple directly. "We only want to help," Karen Burns was quoted. "We believe what the mother did was courageous, not criminal."

He looked out his window, almost lost between the bulletins and WANTED posters and advisories taped up all over his wall, and watched the hard, dry snow spitting through the air. Temperature dropping, cold night tonight. He thought about Cody-No-Last-Name, thought about what might have happened if Reverend Fergusson hadn't been heading out for a run that night. Maybe whoever had left the baby had been nearby, watching and waiting for someone to discover the box. Maybe not. Courageous. Yeah.

The phone rang. Through the frosted glass window in his door, he could see Harlene's outline as she crossed the office to pick it up. A moment later his line buzzed. "Hey, Harlene, can you get me some more coffee while I take this?" he yelled. He couldn't hear her reply distinctly, but he thought it was something about being the dispatcher, not a geisha girl. He lifted the receiver.

"Chief Van Alstyne? Clare Fergusson. I hope I'm not calling at a bad time."

"No, no," he said, "Not at all. I'm staring at about a thousand state and county reports I'm supposed to have filled out sometime in November and I'm contemplating whether I can throw Geoff Burns in jail for interfering with an investigation. I can use a break."

"You're contemplating what?"

"I take it you haven't read today's paper. The article about the abandoned baby."

"No. It's here somewhere . . ." There was a rustling and a thumping sound. "Got it. Where is it?"

"Right on page three. Take a look at where Geoff Burns offers his protection and free legal services to the mother!"

There was silence on the other end of the line. "Holy crow," Clare said after a moment.

"Yeah. After I had deliberately left out the note and the location where Cody was found. It'll serve that little weasel right when he starts getting crank calls from half the teenagers in the county, claiming to be the baby's mother."

"Is that what you mean by interfering with an investigation? Because, you know, if the reporter had come to me, I wouldn't have known I wasn't supposed to say anything about the note."

"It's not just that, Reverend . . . Clare. This crap about protecting the mother from misguided officials. Burns might as well come right out and say 'Come to us, and we'll see the police never lay a hand on you.' What are they gonna do, give her ten thousand and ship her off to Bolivia? Geez, that really frosts my cookies." There was a strangled sound from the other end of the line. After a moment, he realized Clare was trying not to laugh. "Well, it does."

"I'm sorry, it's really not funny." She snickered. " 'Frosts my cookies'?"

"Now you know one of our quaint local expressions." The sound of her muffled laughter took the edge off his anger. He sighed.

"Okay. Do you really think that Karen and Geoff might make contact with the mother and not tell you?"

"Yes."

Now she sighed. "Me, too. Is there anything you can do now the information about where Cody was found is out in the open? You can't really mean to arrest the Burnses."

"I'd like to. At least, I'd like to arrest Geoff Burns. Jesus Christ, what an arrogant little snot. Sorry." Russ held the newspaper out at arm's length to reread the paragraph. "But no, I don't have any grounds. As much as he's pushing the line, he hasn't gone over it. There's nothing illegal about giving your opinion on what the mother did or in offering free legal aid."

"So you can't put the proverbial cat back in the bag. That leaves the problem of the mother turning to the Burnses for help instead of turning herself in to the police."

"There is that problem, yes."

"What if you offered to help them get the baby?"

"What?"

"They want to be Cody's foster parents now. Think about it. That way, they not only have the note in their favor, they also will have bonded with Cody. They'll be able to argue it's in his best interests to stay with them."

"Yeah, but . . ."

"I think they'll be less anxious about who finds the mother first if they have Cody already. You can offer to use your influence with the Department of Social Services to get the baby assigned to them. In exchange, they promise to let you know right away if the mother contacts them."

"My influence with DSS, huh?"

"Oh, c'mon. You must know a few people." Her slight Southern drawl was more noticable over the phone, he thought. "I'll tell you, I'm under the gun here, too. My vestry wants St. Alban's to pitch in and help the Burnses. I've decided to get a letter-writing campaign going among the parishioners. All the well-heeled Republicans here? There must be a few who've donated enough to make some politicians sit up and listen when they ask for a little consideration for this deserving couple, who have waited so patiently for so long to be a family."

He whistled. "You're good. You ever think of running for office?"

She snorted. "Preachers and politicians are kissin' cousins, didn't you know that?"

"I guess it's worth a try. Anything's better than waiting for Geoff Burns to get ahold of some scared kid and wave money in her face to make her disappear. When were you planning to enlist your letter-writing troops?"

"Putting it into my sermon this Sunday would be the simplest thing. Dang, and I was going to preach on what I saw going on patrol with you this Friday. Maybe I can work them both in . . ." There was a pause. "Um . . . you haven't changed your mind, have you? About taking me?"

"If I had, I've been effectively wangled into taking you now, huh?"

Clare groaned. "I didn't mean it that way . . ."

Russ laughed. "Guess I'd better keep my end of the bargain, or you might get your parishioners to write to the aldermen and have me tossed out on my ear. What time can I pick you up?"

"Evening Prayer's at five-fifteen, so I'll be free by six."

"Six is good. Wear a coat this time, okay? And some heavy boots."

"I'll bring two pair of mittens and electric socks. I'm really looking forward to seeing the authentic Millers Kill, Chief. Thank you."

"It's Russ, remember? And don't thank me until the night's over. You may be so bored, collecting stacks of letters might seem like a big thrill."

Standing behind the patrol car's open door, Clare banged her knees together and kicked her feet against the front tire, hoping to keep her circulation going. Wishing she were in her office, writing letters.

"I didn't do nuthin'! Get your hands off me!" In front of a large video arcade, Russ was toe to toe with an angry, drunken young man. The kid was several inches over six feet, as tall as the police chief, and beefy. Clare glanced at the radio. On television cop shows, people were always calling for backup. Was she supposed to do that? How? She stomped her feet a few more times. If she had stayed home, she could be sitting down to the ten o'clock news with a cup of hot chocolate right now.

Teens were crowded along the sidewalk outside the arcade. Its huge picture windows blazed with neon signs and the hypnotic flash of the cruiser's red lights, giving the place a cinematic, high-tech look that jarred badly with the no-nonsense blue-collar bars and the depressed little shops that were its neighbors. The chief was leaning forward, talking to the kid in low tones. Not touching him, but ready to move if he had to. She couldn't hear what he was saying over the insistent bass thumping from the inside of the arcade.

Clare scanned the crowd, looking for any sign of someone else willing to take on trouble. She shivered inside the roomy police parka that Russ had loaned her. When she had stepped out of the church in her leather bomber jacket, he had laughed at it. Sure enough, within an hour she was begging for something warmer. At the station house, where they dropped off a drunk driver Russ had arrested, Harlene dug through the lockers and emerged with a regulation brown parka large enough to fit a moose. Or the young man who had been brawling in the arcade.

Russ leaned back, said something, crossed his arms. The kid hung his head, and for the first time, Clare could see an oversized boy instead of a threat. From the crowd, another boy sporting several piercings said something she couldn't make out. The kids around him laughed. Russ snapped his head around and pointed a finger at them, bellowing, "You damn well bet he is. And that's what's gonna keep him alive past seventeen. How about you, mister?" The boys in the group visibly shrank back. "I don't want to hear any more from you, got it?" A few nods.

Russ beckoned to two teens who had been hovering near him during the confrontation. Clare couldn't make out his words, but it looked as if he was putting the troublemaker in their care. One of the boys clapped an arm around his ine-briated friend. Russ pinned the big kid with a glare, raising his voice so everyone could hear. "If I have to come here again tonight, I'm arresting anybody involved. Got it?" There was a shuffle-footed assent from the crowd. "Good. Now get inside or go home. It's too damn cold to be hanging out here on the sidewalk."

Russ trudged through the slush at the curbside and tugged open his door. He looked wearily across the roof at Clare, the whirling lights emphasizing the lines in his face. He seemed older than he had at the start of the night's patrol. "Idiot kids," he muttered, sliding behind the wheel. Clare gently kicked against her door, knocking snow off her boots before joining him inside the car.

"You're not going to arrest the boy who was fighting?"

"Ethan? Naw. He didn't hurt anybody." Russ reached for the radio. "Ten-fifty, this is Ten-fifty-seven."

"Come in, Ten-fifty-seven."

"Harlene, will you call the Stoners and tell them to pick up Ethan at Videotek? And tell 'em he missed a drunk and disorderly by the skin of his teeth."

"Will do, Chief."

"We're headed out to the kill. See if there are any other kids out tonight making fools of themselves. Ten-fifty-seven out."

"At the kill. Ten-fifty out."

He hung up the microphone and fastened his seatbelt.

"You have got to tell me something." Clare buckled herself in. "What, exactly, is the kill?"

"Huh?" He glanced at her. "You mean, like in Millers Kill?"

"Yeah. What is it?"

"Kill's the old Dutch name for a shallow river or a big creek. Lotta towns around upstate have 'kill' in their names—Fishes Kill, Eddys Kill . . . our kill runs from the Hudson to the Mohawk Canal."

"A big creek? I've crossed over it a few times and it looks more like a full-fledged river."

"It was dredged out during the building of the canal system in the early eighteen hundreds. Between the river traffic and the mills, it made the town. Geez, you're gonna live here, you need to learn some geography and history. I'll see if I can find you a few books to read."

He shifted and pulled into traffic. They headed west, cruising slowly down the strip, past bars, a liquor store, a tightly shuttered pawn shop. No candy canes and reindeer hanging from the battered old light poles here.

"Why didn't you take the boy in?" she asked.

"I know the Stoners. His dad has a thirty-five, forty acre dairy farm that barely supports the family. Ethan's not a bad kid." Russ signaled, turned down a narrow street, and drove past two dark, boarded-up warehouses. Another turn took them into the parking lots behind the buildings. The head-

lights picked out churned-up snow and tire tracks crisscrossing randomly. "He's just like a hundred other kids in this
area. They drink, they do drugs, they get into car wrecks and
fights because they've got nothing to do with their lives."

Russ swung the cruiser slowly out of the shadowy parking
lot. The rear of the car slid in the snow, and he eased into
the skid. "Nothing around here for average kids with high
school diplomas and no money for college." Back on Mill
Street, the cruiser turned west again. Clare watched through
the window as the commercial buildings gave way to shabby-
genteel houses. Homemade signs hammered into snow-
covered lawns gave mute testimony to the struggle to make
ends meet: LITTLE LAMBS DAY CARE. DOLLHOUSES BUILT TO
ORDER. PLOWING AND HAULING. DEER DRESSED OUT.

"Thirty years ago, that boy could have gone straight into
one of the textile mills and made a good wage. Or gone to
work for one of the big dairy farms in the area, saved up his
money to buy land of his own. Or gone into the army." Russ
pinched the bridge of his nose beneath his glasses. "Voluntarily or not, it gave a guy a chance to learn a trade or get
money for college."

The houses were fewer and farther apart. They drove past
the last streetlight into the darkness. "This is Route One-
Thirty-Seven. We call it the Cossayaharie Road," he said. The
pines and alders crowded in along the road, and beyond the
trees, the Adirondack piedmont closed the horizon around
them. The dark bulk of the hills looked like breaching whales
outlined in starlight, old and powerful.

The car cocooned them in warmth, made them fellow trav-
elers into the wilderness. Clare unzipped her parka and
stretched her legs. The glow from the dashboard picked out
Russ's large, blunt hands, securely controlling the steering
wheel. "Thirty years ago, you could get married and buy a
house and have a family once you got out of school. And
you didn't have to leave the area to do it. But nowadays,

there's nothing for Ethan Stoner to do when he graduates next spring except maybe flip burgers part time. So he drives his old beater too fast and gets into fights and goes down to Albany to party with his buddies who've already left for good."

He turned the cruiser into a narrow lane overhung with snowy branches. The road was noticeably bumpier. They were silent, Russ peering forward to negotiate the barely plowed road, Clare considering Ethan Stoner. They came to a dead end in a clearing marked by a few tire tracks.

She stared into the snow and darkness. "Where are we?"

Russ opened the door. Cold air rushed around the unzipped edges of her parka. "This is the lot for Payson's Park," he said, reaching behind her seat for two long, heavy flashlights. "In the summertime, the town puts out picnic benches and grills, and somebody always ties a few tire swings to the big branches overhanging the kill. It's real nice."

She accepted a flashlight and got out. "There aren't any cars here," she pointed out. "Don't tell me your young lovers are rolling in the snow somewhere. I know teenagers are hot-blooded, but . . ."

Russ walked through the beams from the headlight toward the edge of the clearing. "There's a trail that runs along the river for several miles. When I was a kid, you went on foot or you didn't go at all, but nowadays everybody's got four-wheel drive. And here we are, tire tracks."

He aimed the light into the woods and Clare could see where the trail ran past the open picnic area and over a rise. They tromped forward, following the tire tracks marring the otherwise untouched snow.

"Half a mile upstream there's an abandoned railroad bridge that crosses over the kill. That's another spot we like to keep an eye on, for drinking or doing drugs. There's a sheer slate embankment from the old train bed to underneath the bridge.

A lot of people would rather get there by driving the trail instead of risking the climb down."

"I can't help think there must be more comfortable places to have a drink," she said. Her breath hung in the air, glowing in the reflected light of her flashlight.

"Oh, yeah," he said, ducking to avoid a snow-heavy branch. "But Napoli's Discount Liquors and the infamous Dew Drop Inn are less than a mile up the road, offering a last crack at booze before you cross the town line into Cossayaharie. Which is one of the last dry towns in New York State."

"So the good people of Cossayaharie drink here in the park instead?"

"Don't know if I'd say the *good* people, but—"

Clare slipped where the trail took a downward turn, and Russ caught her arm, steadying her. She added boots with serious treads to her growing list of things to buy.

"Watch it," he said, pointing his light to the left. The land sloped steeply down to the half-frozen edge of the river, visible between tangled bushes and slim stands of trees. "You don't want to fall in in this weather." She nodded and walked more slowly, staying between the tire tracks, emulating Russ's steady tread. "I remember last year, some idiot came out here to jack deer, fell in the kill instead, and nearly died from the hypothermia. 'Course, it didn't help that he'd been keeping himself entertained with blackberry brandy."

"Jack deer?" She caught a flash of something dark and gleaming near the water. A deer? She aimed her flashlight toward the thicket it might be hiding in.

"Poaching. At night. If you shine a light into a deer's eyes you can freeze it long enough to shoot."

The gleam looked funny, familiar but out of place. She moved the beam of light to the right. And saw a hand, barely distinguishable from the snow it rested on. The dark gleam, that was hair. That was someone's long, dark—

"Russ," she said.

"What?"

"Russ," she repeated. She pointed, part of her amazed at how steadily she was holding the flashlight. "Down there."

"Oh my God!" he said. He scrambled down the slope, falling and sliding and catching at trees. "Oh Jesus, oh God, oh Jesus, no." He yanked a bush almost out of the ground, stopping his headlong descent before he plunged into the water. Clare held her light tightly. She wasn't sure if she could move it at this point. Russ squatted in the snow and bent over the . . . her mind tried to slide over the word "body."

"Oh no. Oh, Jesus, oh no." He hunkered down for a moment. She could see him backlit by the glow of his flashlight, shaking his head over and over. Then he straightened, wiped his face. Turned toward her. "It's a girl. She's dead."

CHAPTER 4

Clare pressed her gloved fist against her mouth. Her flashlight never wavered. Russ pointed his light up at her, making her eyes sting and blink. "Clare? Are you okay?"

She nodded. She couldn't see him, but she could feel him looking at her, realized he might not see the small movement.

"Yes. I'm okay," she said. "What do you want me to do?"

"Can you make it back up the trail to the car and call for help? I'm going to have to secure the area now, see if I can find anything before—before they get here to take her out."

"Turn on the radio and ask for Harlene?"

"Yeah. Tell her we've found a body off the trail, about a quarter mile upstream from Payson's Park. Can you do that?" She nodded again. "Good girl," he said.

Clare couldn't stop herself from looking at that hand once more, so pale and still it might have been carved out of snow. Snow on snow, the old hymn went. Snow on snow. She could make out some kind of sleeve, disappearing into the tangled brush. Whoever it was must be half in the water. Did she jump? Had she changed her mind and tried to crawl out? Clare blinked the blurriness out of her eyes and filled her lungs with sharp, dry air. She headed up the trail, jogging as quickly as she could in the snow. The trees crowded in against the path. She slipped and slid, trying to keep her footing and not break her pace. There was an explosion of snow from her left. She yelped and almost dropped her flashlight. A doe leaped into the beam of light and vanished again in another shower of snow. Clare staggered, her heart about to hammer its way out of her chest.

She made it to the cruiser finally, her knees aching from several falls, sweaty and hot under her borrowed parka. She slid into the car and flicked on the radio, and when she heard the dispatcher's hail she keyed the mike and said exactly what Russ had told her. Harlene put her on hold for what seemed like an eternity.

"Okay, Reverend, I've got an ambulance on the way and I've notified Doctor Dvorak. He'll be waiting at the county morgue. Officer Flynn is headed out to lend a hand, and the state troopers are sending a technician along with a crime scene van. Can you sit tight and lead them to the chief when they get there?"

Clare keyed the mike again. "Yes, I'll be here."

"Are you okay, Reverend?"

"Yeah, Harlene. Thanks for asking. I'll be fine."

"Good girl. Dispatch out."

Clare stripped off her gloves and blew on her fingers. She could remember the time when she would have torn into anyone who called her a girl. At thirty-five she was finally mellowing. Had Russ seen a woman down there in the snow and ice? Or was it really a girl? She yanked her coat around her, her exercise-induced heat seeping away in the chill of the car. As cold and as still as the grave.

Clare leaned her cheek against the rigid vinyl of the car seat. She shut her eyes very tightly, trying to put the sight of that white hand, that dark hair somewhere she could bear it. Did something drive that woman out here to end her own life? Something inside her so dark and cold that the moonless night and the icy water seemed preferable? Merciful God. That was the start of the collect she would pray tomorrow, looking at the comfortable, satisfied faces of her congregation. Merciful God, who sent your messengers the prophets to preach repentance and prepare the way for our salvation: Give us grace . . . Give us Grace . . . she felt hot tears behind her eyelids. Give us grace to heed their warnings and forsake our sins . . .

She was exhausted, numb and sleepy when the squad car and ambulance pulled into the lot. The flare of red lights against her closed eyes jerked her into alertness and prodded her out of the car before her mind had caught up with her body. She shuffled through the snow, waving to a uniformed man who must have been Officer Flynn levering himself from his squad car. Next to the car, two paramedics in bulky snowsuits jumped from the ambulance. Clare slogged over to the officer.

"Ma'am," Flynn greeted her. "I'm awful sorry you had to see something like this." She echoed the sentiment silently. The doors to the ambulance clanged open. The EMTs hauled a rescue pallet off the van bed.

"If you follow me, I can take you to the chief," she said. Her voice seemed unnaturally loud in the still, cold air. Flynn opened the trunk of his car and hefted a canvas bag over his shoulder. As they began their slippery processional, he fished into the bag and retrieved a self-starting flare. He yanked the tab and the clearing lit up with a harsh chemical glare. Flynn stuck the flare butt-end into the snow beside the trail.

The EMTs balanced the pallet between them, picking their way through snow as they pushed on toward the water. Every few yards Flynn lit another flare. The trail resembled a nightmare version of a garden walkway illuminated by torches for the benefit of evening strollers. Clare kept her eyes on the tracks as they walked, tire marks crisscrossing at the edges of the trail, two sets of boot prints leading downward, small, deep holes left by deer hooves, and blurry disturbances where she had fallen in her headlong rush to get back to the cruiser.

"There," she said, pointing down the steep slope where a single flashlight beam appeared and disappeared through the pines.

"Chief?" yelled Officer Flynn. Clare pointed her flashlight toward the water.

"Yeah!"

She shifted her light toward his voice and nailed him straight on with the light. Russ threw his hand in front of his face. "I'll come up! Don't anybody climb down until we've gotten some photographs of the tracks."

Flynn pulled the tab on another flare. The trail sprang into high relief. The trees cast hard, dark shadows downslope, concealing and revealing glimpses of Russ's brown parka as he clambered back up the hill. Clare could hear him grunting with effort. By the time he reached them, he was breathing hard.

"Are you all right?" she asked, peering up into his face.

He leaned against a birch tree, panting. "Been up and down this damn stretch of ground about six times already," he said. "Jesus, I'm getting too old for this kind of thing. Sorry, Clare." He sketched a wave to the two paramedics. "Guys, you can retrieve the body just as soon as the state crime lab gets here."

Flynn stared down at the water's edge, craning his neck for a better view. "What's it look like, Chief? Not a jumper moved downstream?"

Russ tilted his head toward Clare. "Every once in a while somebody decides to check out by jumping off the old railroad bridge," he explained. He turned away from the officer and shone his flashlight a couple of yards up the trail. Clare could see where the tire tracks they had been following came to an end. "Somebody drove in to this point and then backed up again." He shifted the light to the edge of the trail closest to the water.

"What's that?" Clare asked. The snow was heavily churned.

"That is where the girl slid all the way down the slope." Russ sounded worn down. "I followed the trail she left back up to the car tracks. Looks just like when little kids roll themselves down a hill."

Flynn whistled, a high, excited sound. Russ glared at him. "Sorry, Chief," the young officer replied. "Just . . . I haven't done a homicide yet."

"Homicide?" Clare looked down toward the water. "Someone killed her?"

"Looks that way," Russ said.

Clare touched Russ's arm, heavy glove over thick parka. "Any clear tracks from whoever drove the car away?" she said.

He shook his head. "Nope. Could be whoever it was threw her body down the hill, hoping she'd land in the kill and disappear for a while. Or it could be she and the driver got into a fight while they were standing here, he hauls off and clips her one, and she falls down the hill. He panics and drives away."

Clare shook her head. "Dear God." She shivered. "Imagine lying there hurt, unable to move or help yourself, and seeing the car lights disappearing . . ."

"Don't. Don't think about it too much," Russ broke in. "We won't know anything until the coroner's report. Don't start speculating or you'll make yourself crazy."

She looked up at him. "The voice of experience?"

"The voice of experience," he agreed. They both looked into the darkness at the creek's edge. Impossible to tell, from here, what was rock and what was shadow and what was water. "There's something else," Russ said.

"What?"

"I think this murder may be connected to the baby you found."

"What? Why on earth would you—"

"Because I have two unusual, unexplainable events happening back to back. A girl abandons a baby. Now a girl shows up dead. This isn't New York City, where kids are stuffed into trash cans and Jane Does turn up twice a week. This is my town. This sort of thing doesn't happen in my town." She cocked an eye at him. He swung his arms wide in frustration. "I mean, of course it happens, obviously it has, but it sure as hell makes the back of my neck crawl. Which is my brain's way of telling me to keep my eyes open."

A halloo echoed further up the trail. A state trooper, bundled up to his ears and wearing his distinctive hat over a knit balaclava, heaved into view around the bend, lugging a chest. "Chief Van Alstyne?" he shouted.

"Yeah, here," Russ called. "Kevin, go on and help him with that." Flynn loped back up the trail and took one end of the box. When they reached the chief, they dropped the chest, stenciled PROPERTY NYSP CRIME SCENE UNIT and the trooper pulled off a glove to shake hands with Russ.

"Sergeant Hayes," he said. "How can I help you, Chief?"

"We need photos, mostly, starting here, where the tire tracks terminate," Russ led the technician toward the site of the disturbance, careful to put his feet into his old boot prints, "and here, where she fell, or they fought, and the slope . . ." he pointed down toward where the body lay hidden. Hayes nodded. "And then let's get her in situ as quickly as we can, so these fellows can take her over to the morgue and our doctor can take a look at her."

They backtracked to the others. Hayes opened the crime-scene chest and began digging out lights and camera parts. Russ pulled Clare to one side. "Why don't you take my keys and go back to the car," he said. "At least one of us can stay warm. I'd have Kevin drive you back, but I may need him here . . ."

Clare shook her head. "I'd rather stay. At least until you

bring her up. I'll walk with her back to the ambulance."

"You don't have to do that."

"I know I don't have to. I need to."

He looked at her for a long moment. The reddish lights from the flares were like the last glorious minutes of a sunset falling across his face.

He smiled faintly. "I think I like the way you work, Reverend." Clare shrugged one shoulder and looked away, embarrassed at getting extra credit for just doing the right thing. "Okay," he said. "Stay back out of the way and don't let your feet get numb."

By the time Sergeant Hayes had photographed every mark in the snow, and the chief and Officer Flynn had gone over every branch and every tree for hairs and fibers, Clare had stomped a circle of snow into packed ice. No wonder cop shows never portrayed this part of the job. It was mind-alteringly dull to watch. If she hadn't had to keep moving in order not to freeze, she might have fallen asleep. Hard to keep that edge of horror over the death of another human being when it was surrounded by so much tedious scutwork.

The paramedics, who had waited a lot more comfortably thanks to their arctic-weight snowsuits, skidded down the slope in a zigzag pattern, dragging the pallet behind them. Clare watched as they conferred with the police officers at the water's edge.

"Okay," someone said, "let's do it."

"One . . . two . . . three . . ." said another voice. There was a cracking sound. Someone grunted.

"Watch the water, watch the water!"

"Got 'er. Okay, okay, let go now."

Russ detached himself from the group and hiked up the slope to Clare. The paramedics followed, with Hayes and Flynn behind them in case they slipped. The figure strapped onto the pallet looked like something out of a fairy tale, white skin and dark hair, a train of servants and attendants. The flares' glow gave the scene an otherworldly cast.

When they reached the trail, the paramedics came close to tipping the pallet as they slipped carrying harnesses over their shoulders. "Be careful with her," Russ snapped. Clare had been bracing herself for a disfigured death, but the body was more like a statue of a pretty, round-faced girl, asleep with her head fallen to one side. There were leaves frozen into her long hair. Clare looked at Russ. "May I touch her?" she asked.

He nodded. "Carefully. Don't move her." Clare made the sign of the cross on the girl's marble forehead.

Hayes leaned over toward Russ. "Thought you said she wasn't related to the decedent," he whispered too loudly.

"She's a priest," Russ whispered back.

The state trooper looked at Clare, startled. "Ma'am?" he said. "I mean, Reverend." Clare closed her eyes for a moment. She really, really didn't want to do her song and dance about women priests at this point. "I'm a Christian, ma'am," he continued, "and I'd be glad to join you in prayer."

She looked up to meet Russ's gaze straight on. She wasn't going to ask permission. Their eyes locked for a moment before he nodded almost imperceptibly. "Thank you, Sergeant Hayes," she said. She spread her arms wide across the girl's body. "Let us pray," she said. The men bowed their heads. "Depart, O soul, out of this world; in the name of the Creator who first made you; in the name of the Redeemer who ransomed you; in the name of the Sustainer who sanctifies you." She laid her hand across the girl's icy chest. "May your rest this day be in peace, and your dwelling place in the Paradise of God."

There was a ragged chorus of "Amens." Russ reached past one of the EMTs and pulled a blanket free from the foot of the pallet.

"Chief?" Flynn said.

Russ shook out the blanket and laid it over the girl.

"Okay," he said. "Let's all get out of here." Clare let Hayes and Flynn take the lead up the trail, following behind the paramedics and their burden. Russ fell into step beside her. "Don't believe in God, you know," he said.

"Mmmm hmmm," she said.

"Never saw any use for organized religion, either," he said.

"No," she said.

"But I do believe that everybody deserves a basic respect as a human being."

"Even the dead."

They trudged on silently. "Maybe especially the dead," Russ said at last.

Clare nodded. "I like the way you pray," she said. Russ shook his head, smiling faintly. "The last thing any of us can do for the dead is to show respect."

"No. The last thing any of us can do for the dead is give them justice."

She breathed in sharply and scrubbed the back of her glove against the sudden prickle of tears stinging her eyes. "Yes," she said, after she knew her voice would be steady. "You're right. We owe the dead justice."

CHAPTER 5

The Burnses' Range Rover was already parked in the lot across the street by the time Clare arrived to unlock the parish hall for their nine o'clock meeting. Fumbling with the heavy chain of keys, she paused to check her watch. She knew she was running behind, but even so, she prided herself on always being prompt. Her old steel Seiko, hanging from its olive-twill strap, read 8:55. The Burnses must not have wanted to linger around the house this morning. Well, neither had she.

Last night, Clare had slept badly, dreaming of Grace for the first time in seven or eight months. When she dragged herself out of bed, still aching with weariness, she went for a long run along Route 51, the river running slow and wide to the old mills on her left, the mountains in front of her, shell-pink and cotton-candy blue in the first light. She ran herself hard in an attempt to outpace the images of angry teenagers, surly drunks, and most of all, the snow-white face of the dead girl. Later, in her shower, she let the hot water soak into her bones, trying to quiet her mind enough to hear the small, inward voice that would tell her which way to go. What to do. In her experience, hard knowledge, painful knowledge, was a gift. God's way of pushing aside the distractions, the self-centeredness, leaving the right way clear, open, marked for travel.

The heavy chunk of the Range Rover doors brought her back to the moment. The Burnses headed across the parking lot toward the back of the church. In their casual coats, jeans, and sweaters, they looked perfectly turned out for a Saturday morning, like models on the cover of a J. Crew catalogue. Younger, and more vulnerable than they seemed in their weekday suits or Sunday clothes. Clare succeeded in unlocking the medieval-looking door and bumped it open with her hip.

"Good morning," she said, juggling her thermos to shake hands.

The Burnses returned her greeting, looking at her attire curiously. "Reverend Clare," Karen asked, "are you moonlighting with the police department?"

Clare plucked at the large brown parka she was wearing. "Oh. This. Chief Van Alstyne loaned this to me last night. I forgot to return it. I have to confess, it's so much warmer than any of the coats I brought with me, I'm tempted to permanently forget to return it."

Karen nodded. "You used to have to go into Saratoga to get anything to wear," she said, "but in the past few years some wonderful stores have moved into Millers Kill. I'd be happy to take you shopping some time if you like."

Clare looked at the lawyer's beautifully-made felt coat, which appeared to have been hand-appliqued by Austrian nuns. Probably the same nuns who did the detailed knitting on her designer sweater. Clare had the feeling she couldn't afford Karen's wonderful little stores.

"Shall we go inside?" Geoff asked. "Ladies?" he tacked on a moment later. They scuffed their boots on the protective mats that reached six feet into the parish hall.

"I brought some breakfast pastries," Karen said, holding up a neatly folded white bag. "There's a place on Main Street called 'In the Dough' that does the most wonderful croissants. Not to mention real bagels."

Clare thought of the donut shop Russ had insisted on taking her to last night. "You can't be a cop if you don't eat donuts," he had said, ushering her into the Kreemie Kakes Diner. He had spun out an elaborate theory that people's personalities could be revealed by the type of donuts they ate. That the choice of jelly donut versus French cruller could unveil the secrets of a person's soul. She had laughed at the time, but watching Karen pull an exquisitely puffed mini-muffin out of the bag, she wondered if he might not be on to something after all. She opened her door and let the Burnses precede her into her office.

"Oh, my," Karen said. They both stopped inside the doorway and looked around slowly. "It certainly is different from when Father Hames was here."

"Yes," Clare agreed, thinking of the unrelieved English-country style that had been her predecessor's office. "It's a nice space to display some of my collections." Over the fireplace that dominated the wall opposite the door, she had hung an intricately carved fragment from a Spanish rood screen, brightly colored Southwestern santos, olivewood bas-reliefs from the Middle East, and Pacific Island fabric-printing blocks. A pair of leather chairs that had originally furnished the admiral's wardroom of a World War Two destroyer—her most spectacular military surplus find ever—were pulled up cozily in front of the fireplace. The large Victorian desk against the far wall was a hand-me-down from Father Hames, but Clare had replaced his oil paintings of stags and spaniels with aeronautical sectional charts and aircraft design blueprints. They shared space on the wall opposite the fireplace with several gilt-framed flea-market mirrors. Clare was very pleased with that touch, since they reflected the light from the west-facing windows flanking the chimneypiece and made the whole room glow at sunset.

"Huh," Geoff Burns said.

"How unique," Karen added quickly.

To the left of the door, a slightly saggy love seat faced the leather chairs. It was a donation Clare suspected hadn't moved at the church's last rummage sale. "Please, sit down," she said, hanging her borrowed parka on the coatrack behind the door. The Burnses followed suit.

Clare dropped her bag on her desk and unscrewed the top from her thermos. In front of the built-in bookcase, Geoff Burns was staring at an Apache helicopter clock her brother Brian had given her for a gag, and Karen was peering at a photo of Clare in T-shirt and camouflage pants. "Is this . . . you?" she asked.

Clare smoothly pushed a mug decorated with a flying rattlesnake and the logo: DEATH FROM THE SKY! out of sight and poured her coffee into a Virginia Seminary mug instead. "That was me," she said. "Several years ago." She sat in a leather chair. "Let's talk about this idea Chief Van Alstyne had for getting Cody into your foster care."

Geoff took the love seat. "Van Alstyne's idea? When he called me, it sounded like your idea. He made it pretty clear that the only reason he was behind it was to make sure we would let him know if Cody's mother contacted us."

"We were both thinking along the same lines, then."

Karen sat down in the other leather chair. "I talked to Chief Van Alstyne, too, and I'll tell you what I told him. There's nothing wrong, or illegal, about Geoff and me helping out Cody's birth mother."

"I'm not suggesting there is. You two want Cody. From all we know, the mother—the birth mother—wants you to have Cody. And we all want to ensure that Cody has a good home with loving parents and that the girl who gave birth to him gets whatever help she needs, whether it be medical, or legal, or counseling. It would be an untruth to say we can guarantee a win-win situation—"

"Of course not!" Geoff interrupted. "What's to prevent a scatter-brained teenager who put him in a box in the first place from deciding, on a whim, that she wants him back? You've never dealt with DSS, Reverend Clare. You have no idea what those people are like. They act as if genetics were sacred destiny. If they get their hands on the birth mother, they'll do everything in their power to persuade her to hang onto the baby. It doesn't matter to them if she's underaged, if she lives in a dump, if she's going to be a welfare breeder all her life. In their book, providing the egg and sperm for a child is more important than providing him with a good life. I'm sick of it."

Clare sat back, blinking.

"Geoff is so right," Karen said. "We've been up one side and down another with them." She opened her arms, encompassing herself and her husband. "Just as a logical starting point, wouldn't you say we were better parent prospects than a girl who would leave a baby out in the cold on the back steps to the church kitchen?"

Clare nodded. "As a logical starting point. Yes." She took a sip of her coffee. "Why do you think DSS hasn't given you Cody to foster at this time?"

"Because we've put up a stink before," Geoff said. "When they returned that baby girl we told you about to her abusive mother, we went to the press, we took them to court—"

"It was a nightmare," Karen said.

"If you kowtow to DSS, they might throw you a bone now and again, but if you stand up to their fascist bureaucracy and let others know what they're doing wrong, you get on their enemies' list."

"We knew a couple, the Baldaccis, who ran a home for pregnant teens, a wonderful, caring place. They'd help these girls adopt out or find help for them if they wanted to keep their babies. A few years ago, they fostered a very troubled girl who kept her baby after it was born. She got into trouble later, DSS took the child away, and then, after one of their so-called parental re-education courses, they reunited mother and child. The Baldaccis wrote the caseworker and called her, they sent letters to everyone they knew in DSS warning them that the girl was unstable and the baby would be in danger. Six weeks after what DSS deemed a successful reunification, she murdered the baby."

"Oh, my God. How horrible!"

"Yes, but that's not the end of it. The Baldaccis were so outraged at this utterly needless death, they went public with the whole story. Despite the fact that they were the only home for pregnant teens in Washington county, DSS yanked their license and shut them down."

"That's outrageous," Clare said.

"So you can see why we're not eager for them to get their hands on the birth mother," Geoff said.

"We've already filed suit requesting temporary custody of Cody," Karen said, "but we talked it over, and we think it might be helpful to have members of the congregation write letters in our favor to DSS."

"Especially if anyone knows someone personally they can write to, or call. A state senator, or a member of the governor's staff, or someone on the board of governors for Social Services." Geoff braced his elbows on his knees and cracked his knuckles. "You know, Reverend, when we first started trying to have a baby, I swore we'd do it ourselves, with no help from anybody, doctor or adoption agency. But now?" He scowled. "What the hell. Let's get everyone involved. Maybe someone in the congregation has a friend of a friend who knows Senator Schumer. Whatever it takes to get the baby into our home as soon as possible."

"Okay," Clare said. "At the end of my sermon tomorrow, I'll ask the congregation for help. We'll need some sort of directory, something that gives addresses that people can write to." She reached for one of the croissants Karen had laid out on the flattened bag. "We can just squeak it into the December newsletter if you can get the information to Lois by Monday." She bit off a chunk of croissant, showering her lap with buttery flakes. Her eyes widened at the taste.

"Wonderful," Karen said. For a moment, Clare didn't know if she was talking about the bread or the plan. "I have a good feeling about this. I think having the backing of the whole congregation will make this time different."

Clare devoured the rest of the croissant and brushed the flakes off her lap. "I'd like to talk about the other half of this matter. The part that Chief Van Alstyne brought up with you. Have you thought about what happens when Cody's mother shows up? From what I understand, the mothers in this sort of abandonment case are almost always caught, or turn themselves in."

"That's why we need custody now," Geoff said. "We'll need to be able to argue that the baby has bonded with us, that she is an unfit mother, and that the child's best interests will be served by remaining with us."

"That's a little harsh, isn't it?"

"Reverend, finding a healthy white infant in this country is a harsh business. It's not for the squeamish, or for people who aren't willing to play hardball."

"And besides, maybe the mother won't turn up." Geoff and Clare both looked at Karen.

"That's an unrealistic attitude to take, Kar. We have to position ourselves strategically to win against her, not cross our fingers and hope she's disappeared for good."

There was one more croissant left, and Clare snagged it, wondering what it said about her personality.

"Of course. You're right. It's just I believe that Cody is the one. I just know he's meant to be ours." Karen beamed. Clare hoped that all their focus and intensity wouldn't end in disappointment. Who could say? If passion and commitment made for good parents, the Burnses would be the best thing that could happen to Cody.

"Then we'd better be prepared to do what we have to to ensure that he stays ours," Geoff said.

Russ resignedly contemplated the old glass-fronted vending machine in the hallway between the coroner's office and the mortuary, where he was reluctantly spending his Saturday afternoon. EAT-A-TERIA it proclaimed in vintage fifties lettering. HOT—COLD—TASTY—CONVENIENT! For a buck in change, you could get one of several sandwiches alleged to be turkey, ham, or cheese, and for fifty cents more you could make your meal complete with chicken soup, which poured out of a spout to the right of the sandwiches.

Everything tasted as if it had been made sometime last summer and had been left in the machine since then. The idea of a limp mystery-meat sandwich and soup with more salt than chicken in it was pretty damned unappealing, but it was closing in on one o'clock, and if he didn't get some food in him he was going to collapse. He was thinking longingly of lunch at his mom's place when Dr. Dvorak came through the heavy wooden doors of the mortuary.

"Don't tell me you're actually going to consume some of that swill," the M.E. said.

Russ snorted. "It's your machine."

Dvorak shrugged off his lab coat and slung it over his arm. "It's the county's machine, my friend, probably put there to ensure a steady supply of customers to the hospital." He headed up the short hallway to his office. Russ fell into step alongside him. "I tell you, Chief, in seven years I don't think I've ever actually seen anyone refill that thing." Dvorak opened his door, solid wood and frosted glass, just like the one to Russ's office. "You didn't need to come here, you know. Right now all I have is my preliminary report. We'll have to wait on the state lab for toxicology."

Dvorak sat down at a desk considerably neater than Russ's. The preliminary report, already color-coded, went on top of a thin stack of similar files, squared to the edge of the desk. A large desktop calendar was filled with precisely lettered notes and reminders, its edges held down with a pencil cup of identically sharpened pencils and a marble-based pen set from the New York State Association of Medical Examiners. The leather cup matched the framed photo of Dvorak, the heavyset, bearded man who was his partner, and their two border collies.

The coroner, who also worked as a pathologist at the county hospital, was a compact man in his fifties, with close-cropped, grizzled hair and pale blue eyes that peered at Russ over the top of his trifocals.

"Of course I needed to stay," Russ said. "A Jane Doe that's a possible murder? You're lucky I didn't sit in on the autopsy."

Dvorak looked askance. "Mmmm. As I recall, the last time you did that you—"

"Don't remind me. What do you know?"

"The basics. From her teeth, she's somewhere between sixteen and twenty-four. She was hit with a heavy, blunt object at the base of her skull, crushing in part of her medulla and causing swelling and hemorrhaging in her brain. It would have rendered her unconscious, and could have led to her death eventually."

"Eventually?"

"My guess is she died of exposure. Based on her lividity, she hadn't been dead more than four hours before you found her. But the body temperature taken by the paramedics was very low, the sort of thing you see a day or so after death. There's no sign of frostbite, which means she was dead before any damage to the skin could occur."

Russ nodded. "Her killer whacked her and then dumped her. And she froze to death."

"In the vernacular, yes."

Russ remembered Clare's voice, shaky with horror, asking

what it would be like, watching the car drive away, leaving you alone in the cold and the dark. "Did she ever regain consciousness?"

"No."

He wondered if Clare would think this a mercy from her God. He rubbed his eyes underneath his glasses. "Anything else?"

"No other injuries. No distinguishing marks. The lab work from the state should be back by Monday afternoon, Tuesday at the latest. Then I can let you know if there were any alcohol or drugs involved." The pathologist opened the folder he had carried from the mortuary and slid a paper across the desktop to Russ. "Here are her prints." A set of X-rays. "Her dental profile." A few Polaroids followed. "Pictures for identification purposes. I hope for her family's sake you find out who she was quickly." Russ turned the photos over in his hands, trying to lay the color and expression of life over the pale, fixed mask of death. "She had a baby recently, poor thing."

"What?" Russ jerked his attention back to the doctor. "God damn. I was right. You sure?"

Dvorak gave him a quelling look. "Am I sure? Of course I'm sure. She's about a week, ten days post-partum. Why?"

"Because six days ago we found an abandoned infant we've been trying to place ever since. And when Jane Doe turned up, I had this feeling . . . You got her blood type?"

The doctor looked at his sheet. "AB negative."

"Hot damn. The baby is AB positive. That means she could be its mother, right?"

"Sure. It simply means the father would have to have a positive blood type." Dr. Dvorak steepled his fingers together. "I take it this wasn't a hospital birth?"

"Not that we can track down, no."

"Well, then, if this girl gave birth to a baby with a different rhesus factor, and she didn't receive an antigen shot afterwards, she'll have Rh antibodies swimming in her blood. I can test for that."

"Do it." Russ stood, anxious to get to the station and put her prints into the database. "Would you give me a call when you have the results?"

The pathologist stood as well. "Of course." They shook hands.

Russ glanced back at the report. "Damn. We really don't have a whole hell of a lot here, do we?"

Dvorak shrugged. "She could have been killed by almost anything: a baseball bat, a small log, a tire iron, the leg off a barstool . . ." he opened his hands apologetically. "And the injury could have been done by almost any healthy adult. Sorry I can't make it any easier for you."

"It would be nice if you could have told me it was 'a left-handed man under five-feet-six who pumps iron, wielding a barbell,' but I'll work with whatever you give me."

"You don't want a pathologist, you want a game of Clue. It was Miss Scarlet, in the Conservatory, with the candlestick."

Russ scooped up the photographs, the X-rays, and the print sheet and put them into the empty folder Dvorak proffered him. The two men walked down the short hallway to the waiting room.

"You think there's a connection between this girl having a baby and being murdered?" Dvorak patted his pockets absentmindedly, searching for the keys to unlock the door to the public area of the morgue. "Seems hard to imagine in this day and age."

"I know. What's the big deal about an unmarried girl having a baby these days? Not like when we were young." Russ shook his head as the pathologist ushered him through the empty waiting room to the entrance.

"There are a lot of people willing to kill to get rid of an

unwanted baby," Dvorak said, smiling sourly. "It's called abortion, and it's perfectly legal."

Russ did not want to go down that road. "What I need to know is who would be willing to kill to get rid of an unwanted mother." Bright sunshine spilled over the buffed wooden floorboards when he opened the door. "Warmed up. Must be over forty."

"Nice," the pathologist agreed. "As long as you don't count on it lasting."

CHAPTER 6

Dvorak was right, Russ thought. As soon as the sun dropped behind the mountains, the mercury plummeted. Turning onto Church Street, he could see the time and temperature sign outside of Farmer's and Merchant's Savings and Loan. Twenty-one degrees, and with the air so clear it was bound to keep on dropping overnight. At least they were done with snow for awhile. Hell of a lot of snow for the beginning of December. Lousy for driving, but good for all the bed-and-breakfasts catering to skiers.

At a red light, his gaze dropped to the folder on the seat beside him. He'd spent the rest of his Saturday afternoon showing the X-rays to all three dentists in town, with no results. He didn't want to consider the possibility that she might have been a tourist. Somebody who had come up to Millers Kill for antiquing or leaf-peeping or skiing and decided it would be the ideal place to drop her baby. If she was an out-of-towner, he might never be able to get an I.D. on her.

He drove past St. Alban's, onto Elm, and pulled into Clare's driveway. The connection to the church. That was the key, his best lead so far. Either the dead girl or the man who had impregnated her had some tie to St. Alban's, and he needed the priest's help to find out what it was. He killed the engine and sat for a moment, looking at the glow of lights through the windows, the intermittent puffs of smoke from the stone chimney. Admitted to himself that he wanted to check up on Clare, too. Not that she'd appreciate the idea. Russ got out of the car and crunched his way across her snow-covered lawn. The Dutch-Colonial house had a deep-hipped roof and a wide porch supported by four plain columns. He swept his boot back and forth as he climbed the stone steps up to the porch, clearing off a little of the snow. There must be another doorway out back by the ramshackle garage that she'd been using. Kind of a shame, because the double front door, with its small, stained-glass windows, was one fine piece of woodworking. He loved old houses.

He tried the wrought-iron door handles. They turned easily. After what she had seen, she still wasn't locking her door. He sighed, rang the bell. From inside, he could hear a muffled lumping, then a faint "Coming!"

The left door opened wide, framing Clare in a swirl of smoke. She coughed. "Russ!" she said. "I didn't expect you. Do you know anything about fires?" He followed her into a roomy foyer, wiping his boots on a worse-for-wear rag rug stretched out in front of the door. The air was acrid, making his eyes sting.

"Holy cow, Clare. What're you doing, burning wet leaves?"

She reached for his coat. "I tried to get a fire going in the fireplace in the living room. But something went wrong." He shrugged out of the bulky nylon parka and she hung it on an old coatrack.

On either side of the door were broad archways. From the size of the brass chandelier hanging in the room to his left, Russ guessed it was meant to be a dining room, although it looked more like a warehouse at the moment, with boxes and mismatched wooden chairs taking up most of the space. He bit back a smile. Evidently even the prospect of living out of cardboard hadn't made the Reverend any more receptive to the idea of the church ladies swarming through her things, doing up the house for her.

Through the right arch, he could see the source of the problem. The Colonial-style brick fireplace in the center of the wall held a pile of overly large logs that were sputtering flames. Smoke curled under the mantel and filled the room. Since he didn't hear anything, he guessed the quaint rectory had never been fitted out with anything as modern and useful as smoke alarms. "Let me see what I can do," he said. "You open a few windows."

The first thing he saw once he was on his knees on the flagstone hearth was that the flue was closed. He pulled its handle forward, opening it. The air rushed up the chimney with a sucking sound, drawing the smoke with it. There was an iron woodbox to the left of the fireplace and a wrought iron carrier holding kindling. "You got a newspaper handy?" he asked. She scooped yesterday's *Post-Star* off a pine coffee table. He knocked the slightly singed logs to one side and replaced them with crumpled wads of paper, then laid on several small pieces of kindling and a quarter-split log. She had one of those silly brass canisters with foot-long match sticks on the mantelpiece.

"You're supposed to use newspaper?" she asked, as the fire caught cleanly and began to burn. "I didn't know that."

"Where did you learn to make a fire?" Russ asked.

"Survival training," she admitted. "You know, using pine needles, branches, a gum wrapper . . ."

"Do yourself a favor," he said, grinning. "Use paper instead. And start small. Don't pile on the big logs until you've got a roaring fire going."

"I did have a roaring fire going!" she said. "For a minute or two."

"What, when the pinecones caught on fire?" Russ laughed.

"The smoke's cleared out," she said with dignity. "I'll close the windows."

Russ took in the room while Clare cranked the casement windows shut. There was an overstuffed sofa and a few fat chairs with faded chintz covers grouped in front of the fireplace, and a needlepoint rug over the floorboards. The low built-in bookcases on either side of the fireplace were piled with haphazardly arranged books, pictures, and plants, and topped by two narrow clerestory windows.

"So what brings you here? Besides saving my bacon from getting smoked."

"Wanted to talk about the case."

"Ah," she said. "Then why don't I get us some coffee first? Make yourself at home."

"Coffee would be great. This is quite a place you have here. Do you know when it was built?"

She disappeared through a swinging door in the back of the room, but her voice floated out to him. "Nineteen-twelve. It's very Arts-and-Crafts, isn't it?"

"Oh, yeah." He walked back to the foyer and pulled off his wet boots. "Linda and I have an eighteenth-century farmhouse out near Fort Henry. No closets, eleven rooms and not a level wall or floor in any of them."

"Must take a lot of work," Clare shouted from the kitchen.

"Yeah, but I like it. Pretending I'm Bob Vila is a hobby of mine."

She had set up a square chest on legs under the big front window and put it to work as the bar. Nice decanters. Russ uncorked one and took a sniff of Scotch. The smell was enough to make his mouth water. Sighing, he replaced the top. The little cane-seat chairs on either side didn't look as if they could hold his weight, but he liked the plain, bare window, showing off the small panes of glass that ran along the edges. That was the one thing that drove him nuts about his wife's custom curtain business—every window in his house was swagged and draped and ruffled with about fifty-seven yards of fabric.

Two standing lamps flanked a folded gateleg table behind the sofa. There was an assortment of family pictures, some in fancy silver frames, others in good-quality wood. He picked up the largest photo, taken on a beach somewhere. An older couple who must be Clare's parents sitting on a driftwood log. A younger Clare in shorts and cotton sweater, her arm around a similarly dressed blond girl of eye-catching good looks. Two blond guys flanking them, not much taller than the girls but broad-shouldered and big. Which would explain the two separate photos of men in UVA football uniforms.

A smaller picture in an elaborate frame caught his eye. Mom and Dad dressed like one of those rich couples in a Cadillac ad, and Clare, who was decked out in a heavily embroidered robe, smiling and teary-eyed. Inside a church somewhere, from the looks of it. The two beefy brothers were accompanied by two cheerleader types, one of whom held a baby.

"Here you go," Clare announced, backing through the door at the rear of the room. She lowered a tray containing two plain crockery mugs and a sugar bowl onto the coffee table. The smell was incredible.

"Damn, that is one good-smelling coffee. 'Scuse my French."

She sat in one of the plump chairs and picked up a mug. "Why thank you. I grind my own mix. Jamaican Blue roast, Colombian . . . I put in a little ground hazelnut and cinnamon . . ." She smiled, the smile of a really good cook attempting without success to look modest. "The secret is to use fresh-roasted beans and fresh spices, and to grind 'em yourself. Don't bother with the stuff in the supermarket that's been sitting around in a bag for who knows how long."

Russ took the other chair. "I'll keep that in mind. Next time I have a spare half hour to make a cup of coffee."

She laughed. "I didn't know how you take it, so . . ." she

said, waving a hand over the sugar bowl, packets of artificial sweetener, and creamer.

"I should probably be a macho guy and say I drink it black, but the truth is, I like it real sweet."

"Oh, yeah. I drink mine sweet, too, but I'm always a little embarrassed by it. I used to stash sugar in my pockets and slip it in on the sly at briefings. Hey. Do you think how people drink their coffee reveals their personality?"

Russ stirred sugar into his mug and took a sip. He closed his eyes. "This is good. I needed this." He opened his eyes and looked at Clare. "No. How you drink your coffee while you're eating donuts, that reveals your personality." She was wearing a woolly turtleneck tucked into a pair of khakis and what looked like some New York designer's idea of army boots. She was curvier than he had thought when he had seen her in baggy sweats and thick outdoors clothes. "You run today?" he asked.

She nodded. "Six miles. I needed it, too, after last night."

"Yeah. I've seen my share of dead bodies, and I've never gotten used to it. To tell you the truth, I hope I never do. Seeing someone who's been murdered . . . that should make you lose sleep at night."

Clare sat up a little straighter. "She was definitely murdered? It wasn't a suicide?"

"Oh, no, it was murder, all right." He told her Dr. Dvorak's findings. When he got to the part about giving birth recently, her eyes went wide.

"Cody's mother," she said. "Good Lord. I have to admit, when you said it was too much of a coincidence last night, I chalked it down to, um . . . paranoia."

"Thanks a lot. If I were a woman, you'd have called it intuition." She made a face at him. He continued, "Dvorak is going to send DNA samples to Albany, along with some of Cody's, to make sure. Of course, that will take up to four months."

"That poor girl. I can't imagine . . ." Clare looked into the fire. "I wish she could have known Cody was settled with the couple she had picked out for him. Before she died. Was killed."

He got up and laid another two logs on the fire. "Don't be wishing that so quick. As far as I'm concerned, Geoff Burns is my number one suspect. With Karen Burns following close behind."

"You must be joking! The Burnses? You're just saying that because you don't like Geoff."

"I admit that. I don't like Geoff Burns. He's an arrogant, self-important, humorless pain in the butt." He sat down on the edge of his chair, leaning across the table. "But think about it, Clare. Who else has a better motive? The father of the baby? He's gonna kill to avoid a few bucks child support a month? Or the Burnses, who have been trying for years to get a child, and are running out of resources and time and have no friends at DSS?"

She crossed her feet under her, tailor style. "You know nothing about this girl. What if Cody's father was a married man, with a family, and she was going to blackmail him? Or what if her boyfriend killed her because Cody wasn't his? Or . . . or . . ."

"Or what if she was a hit-woman for the Mafia and they rubbed her out before she could testify to the Feds?"

"Don't be smart. You see what I'm saying, here. You can't pin a murder on the Burnses without doing a lot more legwork. Just because they're convenient."

"Legwork?"

"Well . . . that's what they say on TV."

"I'm not going to cut the investigation short, no. In fact, I want you to help us with something."

She shifted forward in her chair. "Yeah?"

"The one thing we do know about the girl is that she knew

the Burnses were looking for a baby, and that she left Cody at the church."

"Or she agreed to let someone leave him at the church."

"Right. Somewhere, there's a connection. She was either a member of your congregation, or she worked there, or the father of the baby did, or she had friends there."

"You think someone in my parish will be able to identify her?"

"Yeah." He leaned back into his chair. "How would you feel about arranging for people to take a look at some photos tomorrow?"

She tucked a strand of hair behind her ear and bit her lip. In the warm light, her hair was the color of honey and molasses. Russ looked into his coffee.

"What do you mean by 'arranging' for people to look at the photographs? Flash them in front of every member of the congregation as they leave the church?"

"Well . . . yeah."

"I can't do that, Russ. Even if I were inclined to try to order them to do something, I'm their priest, not their commanding officer. Besides, you ever hear of a little thing called 'separation of church and state'?"

"Oh, c'mon, Clare, I'm not asking you to march 'em all past a lineup at gunpoint. There are how many members of St. Alban's?"

"Around two hundred families. We'll get maybe a hundred folks at the ten o'clock service, and thirty or so at seven-thirty."

"I've got an eight-man force that has to cover three towns as well as investigate this murder. Can you imagine what going door-to-door with every member of St. Alban's will cost us in lost hours? I can't spare the time this case will take me as it is. You know domestics, drunk driving, and shoplifting all increase around Christmas. Gimme a break. Help me out." She crossed her arms and worried her lower lip. He pressed his point. "Neither of us wants to see something preventable happen because my officers were canvassing your congregation."

She rolled her eyes. "Spare me. Next you'll be trotting out a poor orphan boy and his sick dog. Just because I wear a collar doesn't mean I'm a soft touch."

"Okay, okay, scratch the last. Please. I'll go by your rules, Clare, whatever you say. I need your help."

She crossed her ankle over her knee, like a guy, and rested her mug on her leg. "This is what I can do. I'll explain that your Jane Doe may have had some connection to the church. I'll offer anyone who's willing to help the chance to look at the photographs." She looked into the fire. "I'll remind them that somewhere she's got parents, or brothers and sisters, who don't know where she is or what's happened to her." She paused for a moment, then looked back at him. "You can take down the names of anyone who views the pictures, and I'll have Lois give you a copy of our membership directory." She smiled a one-sided smile. "The rest, I'm afraid, will have to be legwork."

"You really like that word, don't you?"

"Yes, I do."

"Okay. Thank you. I know this is a lot to throw on you, this being your, what, third week? Thank you. For everything."

"Oh, lord. My sermon was going to be on Cody, and then the announcement about the Burnses' attempt to have him fostered with them. Do I have to tell everyone we think this girl is his mother? Not that I want to sweep it under the rug, far from it, but it will make things sound awfully odd. 'Here's the baby, here are the adoptive parents, and, oh, by the way, will you all look at pictures of the dead mother?' "

"No. As a matter of fact, I'd rather play that piece of information close to my vest. Let's just say I have reason to believe the dead girl had some connection to St. Alban's and leave it at that."

Clare leaned forward, resting her elbows on her knees. "I'm still going ahead with my announcement after the sermon, asking the congregation to write letters in support of the Burnses. I cannot believe they had anything to do with that girl's death." She shook her head. "Oh, for heaven's sake, I hope you can find out her name soon. It sounds so callous to keep calling her 'that girl.'"

He nodded. "I know. I want you to ask yourself if you can't believe the Burnses might have done it because they really haven't ever given you any cause to think they might be capable of such a thing, or if you can't believe it because you've met them, they belong to your church, and they're 'nice people.'"

She frowned, bit her lower lip again. "They're very intense, very focused on getting Cody. But anyone who's been trying to have a baby for so long would be that way, I think. And they strike me more as the types who would throw money or the force of law at a problem and expect it to go away." She looked at Russ. "I met with them just this morning, did I mention that?"

"Last night you told me you had an appointment with them. How did it go?"

"Fine. Karen was all bubbly and hopeful, and Geoff was . . . his usual self. They certainly didn't behave like a couple who committed murder the night before."

"Have you ever seen anyone after they committed murder?"

"Um." She looked into the fireplace.

"Um?"

"I've seen people after they've killed. How's that?"

Russ retreated from the sharpness in her voice. "I didn't mean to be flip. What I'm saying is that you can't always tell by someone's behavior afterwards."

She waved a hand. "No, no, I'm sorry. Sensitive area. You're right." She looked into his eyes. "I do recognize that part of me doesn't want anyone from my parish to be involved. That I can't believe that one of my . . ."

"Nice, white-collar Episcopalians?"

She smiled ruefully. "One of my nice Episcopalians could do something so brutal. Now, if someone had been murdered with poisoned sherry . . ."

"Or clubbed to death with a nine-iron . . ."

"Or strangled with a shetland sweater from Talbots . . ." They both laughed. Clare smiled at him. "I'm really glad you came over." She pushed her hair back with one hand. "Finding her has been weighing on my mind all day, but there was no one I could talk with about it."

Russ removed his glasses and rubbed them on his shirt. "Yeah. You need to talk to someone who's been there. That's why cops tend to go off-duty straight to the nearest bar instead of going home. It's not any different than coming off patrol someplace, you and your buddies getting together to drink too much and tell lousy jokes and talk about what happened over and over again."

"Because nobody else will understand."

"Yeah." They looked at each other in agreement, then she turned to the fire. He rolled the mug between his palms, watching the play of firelight over the many textures in the room. They sat for awhile, the fire hissing and popping occasionally, comfortable with not talking. Russ finished off his coffee and smiled to himself. It was so many years since he had made a new friend, he'd forgotten how enjoyable it could be, getting to know someone whose mind was both fresh and familiar.

"What?" Clare asked.

He hadn't realized he had been smiling at her. "Oh, just that you remind me of myself. Cops and priests have a lot in common, don't you think? Confessions, sin, helping folks no one else wants to help . . ."

"Funny uniforms, working odd hours, lousy pay . . ."

He grinned. "Laughing at things no one else could laugh at . . ."

"Heck," she said, "it's just like the army, except without free medical coverage."

Russ groaned and pulled himself out of his chair. "Speaking of odd hours, I'd better head home before Linda decides I'm out on a call and puts my dinner back in the freezer." He glanced at the fire, burning bright and clean. "Make sure you bank that fire before you go to bed. You don't want to have the volunteer fire department out here in the middle of the night."

"I promise." Clare got up and headed for the foyer. "So, I'll see you tomorrow at church?"

He snorted. "Maybe not for the whole service. That might blow a gasket on this old unbeliever." She handed him his parka. "What's the best way to make sure everyone has the chance to look at the photos?"

"Hmmm. If you station an officer near the main door of the church, and you take the parish hall, we should be able to ensure anyone who wants to help out will be able to get ahold of a picture." She looked up at him while he shrugged on his coat. "Can we try to keep this as low-key as possible? There will be little kids there, you realize."

Russ paused from tugging on his heavy boots. "I realize that. I'll take care to be as unobtrusive as possible. I promise."

"Just promise me you'll look into every possibility, and not just focus on the Burnses." She touched his arm briefly. "As far as we know, the last thing she wanted in life was for her baby to be settled with them. I'd really like to see that happen."

"I promise I'll conduct a thorough investigation. Don't worry, my own theory won't stop me from chasing down any other leads. It's not so much that I want to nail Geoff Burns, Clare, it's that I want to catch whoever did this. Do you realize that if I'd started Friday night's patrol at the kill instead of ending up there, that girl would be alive today?" He kept his eyes on his gloves as he pulled them over his hands.

She rested her hand on his arm again, saying nothing, looking at him with those clear, bright eyes. They were more brown than green tonight. He shook his head sharply.

"Oh, shit, I know I can't stop bad things from happening. But I don't have to like it. Excuse my French. This is my town. My home, where I grew up. They could have hired anybody to do my job, but they gave it to me, and sometimes I get the feeling, Clare, I tell you, like when I first held my sister's newborn, like I had been given something amazing and valuable, and it was up to me to guard her and protect her." He let out his breath explosively. "Am I making any sense at all?"

Clare nodded. "Yes."

"Sorry. I didn't mean to . . . I'm not the sort to usually get melodramatic."

She shook her head. "Telling the truth isn't melodramatic. And I certainly don't think taking your responsibilities seriously is melodramatic." She smiled up at him, a small, thoughtful smile. "Sounds to me like you have a vocation, Russ. You're called to your profession."

"Huh." He thrust his hands in his pockets. "If that's a calling, it's a damned uncomfortable feeling."

"It can be, at times. Other times, it carries you on like nothing else in the world, because you're doing what you know you're meant to do."

He grinned at her. "Are you going to bring God into it, now?"

She crossed her arms. "No, you'll have to wait for tomorrow for that. And don't forget something for the collection plate."

He laughed. "I'll be there." He held his hand out, and she shook it in her firm, no-nonsense way. "See you in church, Reverend."

"Police work in the parish hall. It should make for an interesting Sunday."

CHAPTER 7

Waiting her turn to recess down the center aisle behind the choir, Clare inspected the crowd, taking the emotional temperature of her flock. The Right Reverend Malcom Steptoe, one of her teachers, had pounded in the importance of seeing the congregation as a whole. "You'll meet with individuals and small groups all the time," he would say. "Once a week, you have a chance to see the whole family of communicants together. Are they peaceable? Satisfied? Discontent? Angry? You must know!"

Right now, at the end of the Eucharist, several of her family looked entirely disapproving. It wasn't from her homily on Cody, she knew. That had been a tight piece of writing, comparing the baby to the infant Jesus, and his waiting for a family to the Christian waiting for the advent of Christ on Earth. It segued nicely into her plea for help for the Burnses. And it was under fifteen minutes long, always a plus for a sermon.

The last of the choir crossed the chancel. Nathan Andernach, the deacon, lined up shoulder to shoulder with Sabrina Campbell, today's reader, and Clare took her place at the end of the line. "The king shall come when morning dawns," the choir and congregation thundered, "and earth's dark night is past." The three trod slowly down the steps, past the altar rail, into the aisle. "O haste the rising of that morn, the day that aye shall last." From her unquestioned place in the front pew, Mrs. Marshall gave Clare a look that said, "This is *not* the way we do, things, young lady."

No, this was definitely about the two police officers in the back of the church. During announcements, in between calls for donations to the soup kitchen and volunteers for the Christmas Eve greening of the church, she had outlined the situation as briefly as possible and asked for everyone's co-operation with Chief Van Alstyne, who had risen from his seat in the last pew and nodded soberly to the crowd. There had been a buzz of conversation, cut short by the offertory and the celebration of the Eucharist. "And let the endless bliss begin, by weary saints foretold," the congregation sang. Sterling Sumner tugged the end of his scarf around his throat and glared at her as she marched past his pew. "When right shall triumph over wrong, and truth shall be extolled." Vaughn Fowler was scanning the congregation, frowning slightly. Probably picking out who was going to be most disturbed by looking at pictures of a dead body.

The choir fanned out in two lines against the back of the church. "The king shall come when morning dawns, and light and beauty brings." Their harmony soared above the congregation's melody. Russ Van Alstyne was singing along, his finger tracing across the hymnal, following the words. Now that was a surprise. Nice baritone too, from what she could hear with the choir reverberating only a few feet away. "Hail, Christ the Lord! Thy people pray, come quickly, King of kings."

Clare held the heavily embroidered floor-length cope—a literal mantle of priestly authority—out with one arm so she could turn without tangling. She drew a deep breath, letting the words come from a place deep inside herself. "Go in peace, to love and serve the Lord," she said, projecting her voice so that it echoed back enthusiastically from the stone walls. "Alleluia, alleluia!"

"Thanks be to God," the congregation responded, "Alleluia, alleluia!" It was an immensely satisfying moment, even if all hell was about to break loose. A polite, Episcopalian sort of hell, of course. She grinned.

The choir members headed back up the aisles in groups of two or three. Parishioners were rising from their seats, drifting toward the parish hall, putting on coats, collecting squirming children. The din of voices made it hard to hear, so she nearly jumped when Russ spoke quietly in her ear.

"Nice sermon. In fact, the whole thing was pretty cool. Very ritualistic."

"Isn't it? Come for one of the big feast days. You'll get to see me cense the altar."

"Uh huh. Sounds interesting."

"Colorful natives practicing their quaint rituals in their natural habitat."

"Speaking of colorful natives, where should I . . . ?"

"I have to stay here and greet everyone leaving now. You head back to the parish hall, right through those doors there," she pointed to the front of the church, "down the hall to the right." The officer Russ had brought with him slipped through the inner doorway into the vestibule. He carried a plain manila folder. "Do me a favor," she said to Russ, "give people a chance to grab a cup of coffee and have a cookie before you start flashing the photos, okay?"

"Okay." He tapped his own folder and pushed his way through the crowded center aisle, apparently not noticing the round-eyed glances directed at him. It must be hard, being a cop, she thought. Always either a hero or a bad guy to the public, never just another human being.

"Reverend Fergusson!" Mr. Sumner's preemptory tone jerked her away from her thoughts. "Don't you think asking the congregation to view pictures of murdered women in the sanctity of their own church is the height of poor taste?"

Clare's spine stiffened. It was going to be a long Sunday.

"No, I don't think we'll be called upon to help the investigation again, Mr. Fitzpatrick. That would mean the Millers Kill police couldn't find the killer, and I'm sure that won't happen."

"Wouldn't count on that. When I was an alderman, I told 'em we needed another trained investigator. Too many people coming up from the cities these days! It's getting so you can't walk down Main Street without tripping over some newcomer from New York or Albany." The octogenarian wheezed indignantly. Clare laid a steadying hand on his arm, and he responded by seizing her hand and pumping it in time to his words. "Told 'em we'd be needing more investigators, but they wanted to save money, so what do they do? Hire a detective as chief and send one of the boys off to the state troopers for the summer. I blame Harold Collins, that cheapskate. You haven't met Harold Collins, yet, have you? You know how he voted when we had that water treatment problem?"

"I really have to get back to the parish hall, Mr. Fitzpatrick. It's been great talking with you, and I hope that bursitis calms down soon. How about I plan on making a visit later this week? I'll give you a call Monday. Take care!" Clare deftly pried her hand from the former alderman's clutches and trotted down the aisle as fast as her dignity and her flapping alb would allow. She made it to the sacristy without having to speak to anyone else. She unknotted the cincture around her waist, a rope-like belt symbolizing her vows, and removed her stole, kissing the embroidered cross at its center with a hasty reverence. During the four years she had served the church as a deacon, she had worn the rectangular scarf across her chest, and it still thrilled her to feel it in the ordained priest's position, hanging squarely around her neck, falling over both shoulders. She yanked the alb over her head in a billow of white linen, shook it with a snap she hoped would take out most of the wrinkles, and hung it. On a wire hanger. Her conscience pricked her. It didn't make much of a symbol of purity with one sleeve inside out, ready to slip to the floor at any moment. She pulled it off and rehung it on its own wooden hanger.

In one of her less-mottled mirrors, she was amazed to see herself so collected. Not a hair was out of place in her French twist. After listening to complaints and denials and gasps of horror and agreeing over and over and over again that yes, it was a terrible shame, and no, the police didn't suspect anyone in their congregation, and what was the world coming to, she felt her hair should be standing away from her scalp in a frizzled heap, the ends smoking.

There was a knock on the door. Clare sighed. *Not another round of questions, please.* The door cracked open, admitting a hand holding a very full, very enticing sherry glass.

Lois sidled into the room. "I asked the refreshment ladies to bring up the sherry from the kitchen. I thought you might need it."

Clare held the glass to her nose and sniffed deeply. "Ahhhh . . ." She took a larger-than-recommended swallow. "God bless you, Lois."

"Is that official?"

"You bet. How's it going in there?"

"I heard a few comments about priests overstepping the bounds, but so far no one's used the phrase 'meddling woman.' "

"Oh. Great."

"Chief Van Alstyne is being quite charming. He hasn't started waving eight-by-ten glossies of murder victims around, so people are feeling a tad more relaxed."

"Encouraged by the sherry?"

"I brought up the second bottle myself. I thought the chief

might like some as well, but he turned me down. No drinking on duty, I suppose." Clare finished off her glass and sighed again, this time with contentment. The secretary went on. "He's really quite attractive, don't you think?"

"Who?"

"Chief Van Alstyne. All that tousled hair and those sexy lines at the corners of his eyes. He has that rugged, all-American look, like the kind Ralph Lauren puts in his ads, except his models always have this slightly gay edge to them. The chief is very . . . heterosexual."

Clare laughed. "The chief is also very married, Lois. Just how much of the sherry have you had?"

"Don't worry," Lois said, floating back into the hall. Clare followed her. "I'm sure there's enough left to rustle up another glass for you."

In the large, sunlit parish hall, things did seem almost normal. Clare worked her way back to the white-draped refreshment table, greeting the people she knew by name and smiling at those she didn't know yet. Mae Bristol, as plump and pale as an over-risen bun, was serving up coffee and tea from the church's silver service. She always wore a printed silk dress with a matching hat—this Sunday it was cabbages in shades of blue. The sherry bottles were between the creamer and the coffee cups. They looked seriously depleted.

"This is stupid, Miss Bristol. My parents let me drink wine at home!" A slim girl in a fashionably skinny velvet-and-patchwork dress leaned across the white tablecloth. Her hair was perfectly retro-seventies, straight and shining and parted in the middle. She reminded Clare of the girls at her old high school whose outfits always looked like they were straight off the pages of *Seventeen* magazine and whose hair was always blown dry to frothy perfection. She could still remember feeling angular and underdeveloped and unfeminine next to them, a jock whose clothes never looked right off the basketball court or the track, a girl whose fingernails were always lined with grease because she'd been helping her dad with airplane maintenance. It had been—what?—seventeen or eighteen years since she graduated? Funny how the individuals changed, but the type remained. There would always be girls who had been blessed by the gods of adolescence, and girls like Clare. She reached around the latest version of the homecoming queen and snagged one of the sherry bottles. Age, thank heavens, most definitely hath its privileges. The girl flashed her a well-polished look of teenage disdain.

"Then your mother can come over here and get a glass for you, Alyson. I'm not giving you any sherry until then, and that's final." The girl flipped her dazzling hair in annoyance and flounced away as well as she could in her high-heeled platform boots.

"The difficult age," Clare said, filling her glass to the top and handing the bottle back to Miss Bristol.

The elderly lady fixed Clare with her black-currant eyes. "That girl is spoiled rotten," she said. "I had her in my fourth-grade class, and she was spoiled then. Alyson will always be at the difficult age, whether she's seventeen or seventy."

"Ah," Clare said. "Well."

"Oh, don't mind me, Reverend. I never felt I could speak my mind when I was teaching, so now that I'm retired, I'm making up for lost time. Which reminds me. Some of those men who believe they run the church undoubtedly want to let you know their opinions about this police business. You stand your ground. I think you're doing a splendid job."

"Goodness," Clare said. "Thank you, Miss Bristol." She turned away, feeling as if she'd been given a sticker for good behavior from an otherwise strict teacher. She took a sip of her sherry, spotting Russ standing by the door to the street. Casual, not obviously blocking it, but making it impossible to get past him without at least making an excuse. He really was tall, several inches above anyone else in the room. It was more noticeable in a group. She wended her way toward him through the crowd, careful not to spill any of her drink on the faded rose-patterned carpet. As she nodded and smiled at her congregants, Vaughn Fowler fell in beside her.

"Any luck with identifying the victim?" he asked.

"At the church door? No,—no." She had to forcibly restrain herself from adding "sir" every time she spoke to Colonel Fowler. Mr. Fowler.

"Let's hope someone here will be able to help the police, then. Speaking as a vestry member, I don't like it. The sooner we get this off church property the better. You do realize there could be a question of liability for St. Alban's?"

"Liability? For a murder? I don't see how."

"If there was some connection. Do the police have a suspect yet? If it's a member of our congregation, we may need to consult the diocesan attorney to ensure that the church, as a corporate entity, has no responsibility."

"Ah . . . as far as I know, Chief Van Alstyne hasn't singled out any one person as a suspect. After all, finding out who she was is a very preliminary step."

"I'm thinking about the next step. Suppose he arrests someone from St. Alban's. It's in the *Post-Star*. It's on the news. Then the real murderer turns up. That leaves us wide open to a lawsuit. Contributing to defamation of character or some such. Lawyers. You have to think of the ramifications of everything you do these days."

Millers Kill's chief of police was smiling reassuringly to a young couple wrestling their two little girls into snowsuits. "Mama," the older child said, "is that Officer Friendly?"

"I was wondering when you'd get over here. I wanted to wait for you before I started showing the pictures around." Russ reached behind him and swept the folder off an unused *prie-dieu* standing beside the door. He looked keenly at Mr. Fowler. Clare introduced the two men.

"I recall reading about you in the *Post-Star* around the time you were appointed police chief, Van Alstyne. You were in the Eighty-ninth MP brigade weren't you? I was chief of staff at Fort Hood during their deployment there in 'eighty-seven."

The chief blinked and straightened slightly. "Yes, sir, I was in the Eighty-ninth." Clare bit back a smile. Evidently she wasn't the only one to have a hard time treating the colonel as a civilian. "I'm surprised you'd remember something like that," Russ went on.

"Military service is something I always look for. It's what makes a man." He frowned. "Or woman." Clare felt her cheeks flush. Fowler pointed to the folder. "You ready to start this, Chief?"

"Yessir," Russ said.

"Then I might as well be the first. Set an example, let everyone know what's expected of them. Nothing to be afraid of, after all." Russ looked at Clare. She nodded. He flipped open the folder. Clare had avoided looking at the photographs when she had been saying good-bye to parishioners at the front door, but now she took a long, steady look at the face of the unknown. Four shots, face front, profiles, and full body, covered with an institutional green sheet. She was struck by how much less real the girl looked, laid out on a steel table, lit by fluorescents and flashbulbs. Not at all like the sleeping princess, leaves frozen into her long hair, that she had stood over on the bank of the creek.

"Sorry," Fowler said. "Don't know her." He frowned. "Where did you say it happened?"

"I didn't," Russ said. "We found her body just upstream from Payson's Park."

The colonel glanced at Russ. "Kids still go there to get away from their parents?" He shook his head. "I used to skinny dip in the river there. Jump off the old trestle bridge and swim downstream. It was a more innocent time. . . . Sorry I can't be of any help."

"Thank you anyway," Russ said.

Fowler nodded, slipping on his overcoat. "Reverend, I'll

be seeing you at the next vestry meeting. Chief Van Alstyne, good to meet you." When he opened the door, the sunlight and snowlight flooded the parish hall, drawing glances from the rest of the room.

Clare held up her hands. "May I have your attention, please? For those of you willing to help with the police investigation, Chief Van Alstyne is ready to have you look at the photographs. If you could give him your name before leaving, he'll be able to keep track of which members of our congregation have seen the pictures. I know it's an unpleasant task, but it's important that we all do our part to help the police catch whoever is responsible for this crime. Thank you."

There was a surge of bodies toward them. "Good heavens." Clare murmured. "They don't seem to be too horrified at the prospect of autopsy shots, do they?"

"Reality TV," Russ whispered. "If you've seen all those specials on serial killers, this is pretty tame." He raised his voice. "If you could form a line there, we can get you all out of here quickly."

It was a repeat of the earlier scene in the vestibule of the church, with more people. The same exclamations, expressions of sympathy, philosophical mutterings. No one recognized her. There was a moment of excitement when Mae Bristol's turn came up. She held two of the photos in her hands, looking slowly from one to the other. "I feel as if I should know her," she said. "I just can't place her. But I'm sure I've seen her before." She shook her head and smiled apologetically at Russ and Clare. "Too many years of too many young people, I suppose."

The tedium of the whole process reminded Clare of how she had felt waiting on the trail for the evidence to be photographed. Police work was a lot like combat, she decided, hours and days of boredom punctuated by moments of sheer terror.

"Oh! My! God!" The squeal brought her mind back to the scene at hand. Alyson what's-her-name stood in front of Russ, flanked by two well-dressed adults who were presumably the parents who had spoiled her. "I know her! That's Katie McWhorter! I know her!"

CHAPTER 8

Clare had offered her office to the Shatthams, figuring it would be a comfortable spot for their daughter to talk with the police chief, but they were insistent that Clare be there for Alyson's statement, so the five of them wound up clustered at one end of the massive oak table in the vestry meeting room. Clare wasn't sure what role the Shatthams wanted her to play. Counsel? Witness? Maybe they hoped she would put the fear of God into Alyson, who, after her first emotional outburst, had reassumed her pose of pseudo-sophistication and contempt. Clare was out to sea when it came to adolescents, which she'd freely admit if anyone bothered to ask. The only teens she had known in recent years had been in the army, and she didn't think telling Alyson to keep her weapon grounded and her hands inside the bird would be useful in this situation.

The girl sat in a chair facing away from one of the windows, her hair a blond nimbus, her face shadowed. Her parents had dithered for a few moments before taking up seats on either side of her. Russ sized up his choices and sat down directly opposite Alyson, leaving the chair at the head of the table for Clare. She took it, wishing she had brought her glass of sherry along, wondering how Russ could let the seconds roll on by without demanding Alyson tell them everything she knew.

He flipped open the folder again, arranged the photos against the creamy manila, and slid it across the table to Alyson. The teen's eyes flickered to the pictures and then returned to the chief. Russ reached inside his shirt pocket, removed a pair of sunglasses, and swapped his glasses for the shades. They were mirrored. Clare rested a finger against her lips to keep from making a crack about Cool Hand Luke.

"Katie McWhorter," he said. "What can you tell me about her, Alyson?"

"She was just a girl who went to school with me, that's all. She graduated last year."

"Did she stay in town after she graduated? Or did she move away?"

The girl shifted slightly in her seat. "She went off to college. Somewhere. I'm not sure. It's not like we were friends or anything."

"No?"

"No. She was like, living somewhere around Depot Street? My parents sure don't want me going there. And she didn't exactly hang out at Smoky Joe's drinking cappuccino."

"Who did she hang with, Alyson? Before she went to college."

"Nobody much. She was a brainiac, really smart, so she knew a lot of the geeks. I know she had a job at the Infirmary." She paused, frowning. "She had a boyfriend."

Clare wanted to yell, "Yes! Now we're getting somewhere!" Russ didn't twitch. "A boyfriend?" he asked, with no particular emphasis.

"Yeah. Ethan Stoner. They were like, a weird combination, what with her being a brain and him being a head." The unintentional pun made Alyson smile at her own wit. "I think they knew each other from way back, like in grade school or something. He was held back a year someplace, otherwise he would have graduated last year with Katie. They were a pretty hot and heavy item."

"Had you seen her since she went away to school?"

"Had I seen her? What do you mean?" Clare wished there was more light on Alyson's face. She couldn't tell if her voice was strained because it was finally sinking in that an acquaintance, someone her own age, was dead, or if she knew more than she was letting on. Or if she was just hostile to Russ's authority.

"Did you see her back in Millers Kill at any time?"

"No. But like I said, we weren't friends. So if she came back to visit Ethan, I wouldn't have known about it."

"Or her parents."

"Huh?"

"She might have come back to visit her parents."

"Oh. Yeah." Alyson looked at her own parents at this. "Can I go now? I really don't know anything else."

"Can you think of any reason, anything at all, why someone might have wanted Katie dead?"

"God, no. I think it must be one of those random violence things, don't you? Some stranger coming into town and raping and murdering the first girl he can lure into his car?" She shuddered visibly and dramatically.

Her mother whimpered. "Chief Van Alstyne, do we need to be worried about the safety of our daughter?"

"My God, what if it's one of those serial killers, like the one over in Rochester a few years back?" Mr. Shattham put his arm around his daughter's thin shoulders.

"Dad-dy . . ." she said, her voice rising in a whine.

"I can't rule out a stranger killing in this case," Russ said, "but I doubt that's what we have here. And Katie was never raped." He folded his fingers together and leaned his chin on his hands. "She had recently had a baby, though."

Alyson's mouth dropped open. Dust motes rose through the air on thermals caused by the sunlight puddling on the floor and the table. "What?" she finally choked out. "She was pregnant?" It was the first genuine emotion Clare had seen from the girl since she laid eyes on the photos of Katie's body.

"She had been pregnant. The doctor who autopsied her says she gave birth within the last two weeks."

"Pregnant. Holy shit."

"Alyson!"

"Oh, Mummy, don't have a cow." Alyson's shaded face stilled, only a small frown marring the blankness of hard thought. "It must have been Ethan," she said finally. "He knocked her up and then killed her. It must have been Ethan."

"Why do you say that?" Russ leaned back in his chair.

"Like, who else would it be? He was seriously in love with her. Aren't most women murdered by their husbands or boyfriends? I remember discussing that in my health class."

Clare thought back to health class at Hopewell High School. The only thing dangerous she had discussed was venereal disease, which over 50 percent of the male population was afflicted with, according to her teacher.

"Maybe he wanted her to, like, have an abortion and she wouldn't. Or maybe he wanted her to marry him and she wouldn't. Whatever."

"Whatever," Clare said under her breath.

"Wow. Ethan and Katie. And I know both of them. That's like, creepy."

"Alyson," Russ asked, "do you remember Katie's parents' address? Was it on Depot Street?"

"No. I don't know her parents' names. Oh, whoa, she has a big sister, though. She was a senior when I was a freshman. Kristen. She works at Fleet Bank as a teller."

"The branch here in town?"

"Yeah. I know because that's our bank."

"Okay, Alyson." Russ gathered up the photos and closed

the folder. "Thank you for your cooperation. You've been a big help."

"I can go? I'm done?"

"That's right. I don't need a formal statement from you, there's no need to go to the station." He pulled off his shades and stared into her eyes. "Remember that we're just gathering information at this point. I appreciate your, ah, insight into Katie's relationship with Ethan Stoner, but none of us can draw any conclusions from that." The girl gaped, a blank expression on her beautiful face. Russ sighed. "Don't go telling everyone you meet that Katie's dead and Ethan murdered her. Got it?" He turned to Alyson's parents. "Mr. and Mrs. Shattham, thank you."

"You will let us know if you come to suspect this was the work of some . . . some . . ."

"Wandering serial killer? I certainly will, Mr. Shattham."

Russ and the Shatthams looked at Clare. She rose from her seat, gesturing toward the door. "Let me walk you out," she said to the Shatthams. They got up, taking coats off the other chairs, and preceded her into the hall. Somehow, she assumed Russ would remain behind, sitting in the sunlight, thinking. Probably the same way he was assuming she'd come back as soon as she had seen the Shatthams off, to talk things over with him.

This time, she did bring her glass, as well as the remaining bottle. "Want a slug?" she asked, brandishing the cream sherry in her fist.

"I don't think you can have a slug of sherry," Russ said. "No, thank you."

Clare sat down in the seat she had vacated, thought for a moment, then moved to where Alyson had been sitting, turning that chair sideways to catch more of the sun. "Lord, it gets cold in this room," she said, pouring herself a measure of sherry. "I must say, though, the sun makes it almost bearable."

"You've got thin Southern blood, that's your problem. Keep your thermostat set at sixty and always wear no more than two layers of clothing. That'll toughen you up."

"Ugh." She took a sip of sherry. "My mamma would call this a little tot." She drawled the expression. "Every drink to my mamma is either a little tot or a splash. A tot of wine. A splash of bourbon." She took another small sip. "So. What do you think?"

"What do you think?" Russ countered.

"I think Alyson's not being entirely honest. I can't say why. It's not as if I know her or her family. It was just . . . something off."

"Mmmm. I agree. You notice that we still don't know what Katie's connection to St. Alban's is. Alyson only mentioned knowing her from school. Maybe that's what she's hiding."

"Why, though? I mean, if you consider Alyson as a suspect, which I find very difficult to do, what possible motive could she have?"

"Jealousy? Rivalry?"

"They moved in entirely different circles, it sounds like. I remember Ethan Stoner from that fight you broke up on Friday. I realize he wasn't showing at his best, but I find it hard to believe that even cleaned up and sober, he'd appeal to Alyson."

"Hmmm mmmm. Ethan Stoner. I hate to think he could do something as bad as this. He was awful edgy and upset that night, wasn't he?" Abstracted by thought, his upstate accent thickened, so that "wasn't he" came out "wun't he?" "Maybe he had real reason to be so upset."

"Are you going to go out and talk to him this afternoon?"

"No. If I'm going to move him onto the list of possibles, I want more information first. There's a good piece of advice about interrogating suspects: never ask a question you don't already know the answer to. Not that you ever know all the answers. But if I haul Ethan in now, I'll be working in the dark. No, I'm going to find Katie's parents first, if I can, or her sister. Get a handle on who she was, what she was about."

"What do you mean, find her parents if you can? There can't be that many McWhorters on or around Depot Street."

"You haven't seen the area. It's our own quaint, rural version of a rat-infested slum. Mostly six- or eight- or ten-unit apartment buildings, falling down around the tenant's ears. Not that most of 'em would notice if a place came down. Half the residents of that area don't have telephones. They have twenty-four-inch TVs and satellite reception, but no phones."

"Being poor doesn't make a person bad, Russ. Just as being rich doesn't make a person good."

"I don't blame anyone for being poor. Hell, my mother was poor after my father passed on. I blame people who could change their condition but are too lazy or too attached to drugs or booze or who just plain don't care that they live like pigs and suck off the public teat."

Clare dropped her glass to the table and stared at him incredulously. "Maybe, if instead of being angry at them, you got angry at the forces that shaped their lives, you might find yourself an instrument of change, rather than just a complainer. Maybe if you tried seeing individuals instead of some amorphous 'them,' you'd see people with problems, not just people who are problems."

"Of all the—'scuse me for being blunt, Clare, but that's naive."

"No, it's not. Reaching out to people who may not even realize what sort of help they need is hard, thankless work. I've met men and women who've dedicated their lives to it, and they're some of the toughest, least starry-eyed people I know."

"I notice you're not doing that inner city thing, though."

She threw up her hands. "I think you've pretty well proved that Millers Kill has the full compliment of modern problems, even without an 'inner city.' Part of my work here is going to be to lead my congregation into service. To get them to open their eyes and see the need all around them."

"And do what?"

Clare tucked a strand fallen from her French twist behind her ear. "To start, I want us to reach out to girls like Katie McWhorter, girls whose pregnancies would otherwise mean a lifetime sentence of dependancy and bad relationships. Help them to stay in school. Teach them how to find a job, be a better mother. Mentor them so they know there are other ways they have value besides producing babies. Support them in changing their lives."

"You haven't seen the ingrained pockets of country poverty yet, Clare. Folks who've never held a job, or lived in a house where some man wasn't beating on a woman, or gotten through a day without pounding down enough booze to make 'em forget their hardscrabble life. I've been there, and I've seen it all and cleaned up after the messes, and I'm here to tell you, you're gonna break your heart if you try to change people like that."

She smiled at him. Maybe not such a hard case after all. "I don't have a choice, Russ. We're all called to see the Christ in all people. Even a down-and-dirty atheist like you must have heard of 'Love thy neighbor as thyself.' "

"Oh. Well, hell, if you're gonna bring God into it . . ."

"You know, I like that about you."

"What?"

"You've just seen me celebrate the Eucharist, I'm sitting here in my cassock and collar, and you still manage to forget that I'm a priest. You argue with me like I'm . . . just me. I like that."

Russ shifted in his chair. "No big deal. I'm just too ignorant to know there's a way I'm supposed to treat a priest, that's all."

Clare smiled into her sherry. Russ spun the manila folder around on the tabletop.

"Katie McWhorter."

"Yes." Clare dropped her glass on the table and rose from her chair. "We can check right now to see if there are any McWhorters listed in the phone book. C'mon into my office."

Russ studied Clare's eclectic decor while she paged through the Millers Kill directory. "No McWhorters listed for Depot Street. Or for South Street or Beale Avenue. No Kristen McWhorter, no K. McWhorter." She flopped the book shut. "Now what?"

"Now, tomorrow morning I go to the bank and see if I can find the sister. The best way to a positive I.D. will be to have a family member identify her at the morgue. Failing that, I'll head for the high school. They should still have Katie's records."

"Would you like me to come along to the bank? Or to the morgue? To be there when you break the news to Katie's sister?"

"To what, comfort her in her hour of need? We don't know if she's religious or not, Clare. Maybe she wouldn't want a priest hanging around."

"Maybe not. But I'll bet she'll want to speak to the woman who was there when her sister's body was recovered. And you'd be better off having someone from St. Alban's there when you ask her about Katie's connection to the church."

"I will, huh? And this wouldn't have anything to do with you wanting to be in on the investigation?"

"I'm already in on the investigation," Clare pointed out. "This simply saves some time and lets me hear what she has to say firsthand. And if you'd like, I could help you tell her what happened to her sister. I'm . . . I took a course in grief work at the seminary."

"Well, I never took any course. But I've broken this kind

of news enough times to know what to do. The trick is to not leave 'em hanging. Get to the worst of it fast."

Get to the worst of it fast, Russ reminded himself. He arrived Monday morning right at nine o'clock, opening time. He found the branch manager first off and filled her in on the situation. She expressed sympathy, and welcomed him to use her office when he told Kristen the bad news. She left for the service counter and came back with a young woman in tow.

"Kristen McWhorter?" Russ asked. The branch manager silently shut the door behind herself on the way out.

"Yes . . ." Kristen said, frowning. She was pretty, in a milkmaid sort of way that even her ink-dark punk hairstyle and thick black eyeliner couldn't conceal. "Did my father do something?" she asked.

"Your father? No. I have some very bad news for you, Kristen. This past Friday we discovered your sister Katie's body near the kill, about a quarter-mile upstream from Payson's Park. She had been murdered."

Kristen stood perfectly still, blinking. "No," she said. "You're mistaken. Katie's in Albany. She's a freshman at SUNY-Albany, and she hasn't been home since school started. She's in Albany."

"She was identified in a photograph by someone who knew her in high school. We'd like you or your parents to view the body to make a positive identification."

"I'll go. I'll go right now. It's not Katie. She's in Albany. I'll get my coat right now. You have the wrong person. Oh, no, I'm starting my shift right now. I have to talk with Rosaline about getting off."

Russ gestured through the glass walls at the manager. "I've already spoken with your boss, Kristen. Everything's set."

The manager came in carrying a heavy coat and a purse. "I brought these from the break room. They're Kristen's."

Kristen grabbed at the purse and started scrabbling through

it. "Wait! Wait! I can prove to you it isn't Katie. I can call her house. I have her number. I have it here." She dug through the purse like a small, desperate animal digging for shelter. She fished out a plastic address book the size of a box of cigarettes. "Here. Her number's here. I can call her, she's in Albany." She looked around the office, frowning. "It's a long distance number, though. Can I use your phone to make a long distance call, Rosaline?"

"Of course you can," the manager said. She took Kristen by the shoulders and steered her to the phone on the laminate desk. "Go right ahead, Kristen." She looked behind the girl's back at Russ, asking him wordlessly for guidance. Kristen hammered out the number.

Russ made a smoothing gesture with his hands to let the manager know she was doing fine. "C'mon, c'mon . . ." Kristen said. "Pick up." Her face brightened. "Emily!" she said. "It's Kristen, Katie's sister. Can I speak to Katie?" There was a pause. "Is she in class?" There was an even longer pause. Kristen's eyes filled with tears and she pressed her palm against her mouth. She looked up at Russ. "She says Katie took a bus to Millers Kill on Friday morning. She hasn't seen her since." She blinked and the tears spilled over her cheeks. "Oh God, oh God . . ."

Russ held out his hand for the receiver. "Let me talk with her," he said. Kristen surrendered the phone. "Hello, this is Russ Van Alstyne, Millers Kill Police. Who is this, please?"

"I'm Emily Colbaum. Katie's housemate." The voice on the other end of the line was shaky. "Has something happened to Katie?"

"I'm sorry, Miss Colbaum. We believe she was killed Friday night. Can I ask you a few—"

The sound of wailing cut him off. He waited. Kristen was leaning against the branch manager, mopping her eyes with a wad of damp tissues. She had black makeup smeared on her cheeks and her dried-blood-red lipstick had come off entirely. "Emily? Miss Colbaum?" he tried again. He was answered with more sobbing. He put his hand over the receiver. "Kristen, will you come over to the morgue with me now? Or do you need more time?"

She shook her head. "No," she whispered. "If it's her, I want to know. Let's go."

He tried the phone again. "Miss Colbaum? Emily, do you think you can talk with me? Or do you need some time to get yourself together?" She sobbed out something about feeling light-headed. "Emily, listen to me. Are you listening? Is there anyone else there at the house with you? Another roommate?"

There was a confusing sentence about Heather, who had missed an organic chemistry final.

"Good. I want you to give her a yell—" he held the phone away from his ear as she did just that. "Uh . . . good girl. You make sure she stays with you until you're feeling calmer, okay? If you need to, you go on over to the university clinic and tell 'em what happened. There'll be someone you can talk with there, maybe fix you up with a sedative if you need one." Wet, weepy snuffles. "I'm going to give you the number of the police station here in Millers Kill. You got a pen and paper? Good girl." He told her his direct office line. "I'll be calling you to talk later, Emily, but in the meanwhile, if you think of anything, anything at all, call that number. If I'm not there, you can talk to our dispatcher, Harlene."

Emily blubbed a watery thank you and hung up, promising to call with any information she might have.

Kristen was gamely struggling her way into her long black coat, crying soundlessly, mopping her face with the ineffectual tissues. "Would you like me to come with her?" the manager asked, her face creased with what Russ judged to be equal parts worry over her employee and the prospect of leaving the bank unattended on a Monday morning.

"No, I have a, um, grief specialist waiting for us at the

morgue. We'll make sure Miss McWhorter's taken care of."

He held the office door open for the women. "Kristen, don't worry about coming in to work tomorrow," the manager said. "I'll make sure your shifts are covered. Take all the time you need, honey." She hugged the girl awkwardly.

Outside, it was another bitterly cold and clear day. Kristen rubbed her gloved hands over her cheeks as they drove. The heater wheezed and complained and started warming the car minutes before they reached the county morgue's parking lot. Clare was already there, waiting in an older-model cherry-red MG that was going to give her more trouble than she could imagine on the winter roads. She got out as he parked the cruiser.

"Let's get inside before we do introductions," he yelled across the lot. She nodded and disappeared into the building, climbing the steps two at a time. He held Kristen's arm to steady her until they got into the waiting room, then released her to help her out of her enormous coat. She had stopped crying and was looking around her with the same absorption she would have shown watching a fascinating movie. Not that there was anything fascinating about the dun-colored walls that someone had attempted to brighten with scenic travel posters. He had seen that look before, many times. It was the look you got when the bottom fell out of your world, and your own life seemed as distant and unreal as any big-screen fantasy.

"Kristen?" Clare took the girl's coat from Russ and tossed it on a chair next to her own. "I'm Clare Fergusson." She held out a hand to Kristen, who took it mechanically. "I was there when your sister's body was discovered." Kristen's lips flexed and quivered. "I'm also a priest." Given the clerical collar peeking out from underneath her black sweater, Russ thought that was pretty self-evident. He went to the window separating the waiting room from records storage. Tapping the bell three times brought the morgue assistant, who took in the scene in the waiting room and went to unlock the inner doors without a word. "Would you like me to come with you?" Clare went on, gently leading Kristen to the hallway. "Sometimes, it can make it less scary to be with someone else."

Kristen stopped, looked into Clare's face. "I've never seen a body before," she said. "Isn't that strange?"

"No, not strange at all," Clare said, linking her arm through the girl's. "It's not bad, like you might think. Death looks different from life, from sleeping, but it's not ugly."

Russ had seen more than a few ugly deaths in his time, but he knew enough to keep his mouth shut. The attendant paused at a small desk outside of the body storage room. "We're here to identify the Jane Doe," Russ said quietly.

The attendant made a note in the log book. "She's in number three," he said, looking at Kristen's black-smeared face. "You can go in alone, miss, or I could come with you, or . . . ?"

She shook her head at the young man and tightened her hold on Clare's arm. "Will you come?" she asked. "I forgot your name."

"I'm Clare. Yes, I'll come with you."

The attendant opened the dull metal door. Russ caught a glimpse of white tile and harsh fluorescent lighting before the door closed again, Clare and Kristen on the other side. It was a lousy place for a person to end up, laid out naked in a stainless steel drawer. Of course, there were worse ways to finish it. Zippered inside a body bag and hustled into a refrigerated cargo hold, for instance. He shut his hand reflexively. At times like these, he could still feel the material they made those bags from. He stilled his breathing, forcing himself not to get impatient to leave Death's waiting room. What the hell was taking them so long?

Clare pushed the door open, letting Kristen pass through first. The girl looked into Russ's eyes, her own dazed, full of clouds. "It's her. It's my sister." She bit down hard on her lip. "I thought . . . I thought she'd finally be safe once she was in Albany. Once she was away. Why did she come back?" Fresh tears rose in her eyes. "Why did she come back?"

CHAPTER 9

"Kristen, what did you mean when you said you thought your sister would be safe once she was away at school?" Russ handed Kristen black coffee in a mug decorated with fat country sheep and geese, part of a set his sister had given them one Christmas that he and Linda had agreed were too damn cutesie-poo to keep at home. He hated Styrofoam cups: too small, too fragile, and too wasteful.

Kristen bent over the mug until her face was almost obscured by ink-colored hair and steam. "Nothing. I don't know. I don't know what I was thinking."

He dumped three teaspoons of sugar into another mug and handed it to Clare. She was sitting kitty-corner to Kristen, a Millers Kill P.D. tape recorder at her left hand. After Kristen had identified her sister's body, the girl couldn't get out of the morgue fast enough. She had agreed to give her statement at the police station, where Harlene, in full mother-hen mode, had fussed over her, fetching coffee and strudel from the dispatch room, opening the shades in the briefing room to let in the sunlight.

"You know, sometimes, the first thing that comes to mind is the right thing, no matter how bizarre or improbable it seems," Clare said. "It could be your intuition was trying to tell you something. What was it, Kristen?"

The young woman put down her mug and smoothed her hands over her face. She had washed up in the station's unisex bathroom—unisex by virtue of having both urinals and a tampon machine—and without her black and purple and red makeup, she looked like one of the pretty country girls from up the hills past Cossayaharie. Katie must have borne a strong resemblance to her sister before her death.

"Can you tell me how she died?"

Russ sat down in a red leatherette chair, cradling his coffee to warm his hands. "She was hit in the back of the head by something heavy and blunt, hard enough to make her unconscious. Then she was rolled off the trail downhill, to the edge of the kill. The medical examiner believes she died of hypothermia, that she never woke up."

"How did she get out there? Do you know?"

"Only that it was a four-wheel-drive vehicle with all-weather tires. The wheel width indicates a truck or a sport-utility vehicle. We don't know if your sister was conscious when she reached the trail, or if her killer drove her there after she had been knocked out."

Kristen closed her hands over her face again for a moment. "What a weird thing to say," she said. "Her killer. Like, her sister, her teacher, her boyfriend. Her killer. Somebody with a relationship to her." She frowned. "Was she molested? Had she been, you know . . ."

"No," Russ said. He glanced at Clare.

"What? What is it?" Kristen's gaze flickered between the two of them. He tilted his head, passing the job of telling about the baby to the one who had found him.

"There is something else, Kristen," Clare said. "According to the medical report, Katie had a baby within the past two weeks. We have strong reason to believe that she, or someone, left the baby on the back steps of St. Alban's church a week ago. He's in foster care right now."

"He?"

"A little boy, yes. She left a note, naming him Cody."

Kristen's face contorted. "Oh . . . she always loved that name. She used to say if she had a boy, she'd name him Cody, and if she had a girl, she'd name her Corinne." She squeezed her nose and eyes, trying to stifle more tears. "I can't believe Katie would give her baby away. I just can't believe it. Unless he made her!"

"Who made her, Kristen?"

She was crying openly now, shaking her head. "Our father."

Clare and Russ looked at each other. "Your father would've made her give up her child because she wasn't married?" Clare asked.

"No, no . . ." Kristen blew her nose on one of the paper napkins Harlene had piled next to the strudel. She took a shaky breath. "My father would have forced her to give up a baby if he was its father."

Russ felt as if someone had thrown a bucket of the kill's icy water over him. Clare was pale, but calm. "Kristen, what are you saying? Did your father sexually abuse Katie?"

Kristen pushed her hands through her short hair. "I don't know. I really don't know. But he used to do it to me."

"Jesus," Russ exclaimed, under his breath.

"Can you tell us, Kristen?"

The girl looked at Clare, indecision and grief warring on her features. "It's hard. It's hard to talk about."

"Listen, Kristen," Russ said, "You don't have to be afraid of your father. Give me his name and address and he'll be in the county jail before five o'clock." With maybe an unscheduled stop on the way, where the bastard could fall down a few flights of stairs by accident. Nobody at the jail would make a comment.

"No, please!" Kristen said. "I don't want to press charges. I got away, and that's all I wanted. I thought Katie had escaped, too . . ."

"Tell us, Kristen. You don't have to sign out a complaint against your father if you don't want to." Clare forestalled Russ's complaint with a swift glance that said, "Back off."

"I . . . I . . ."

Clare held out her hand, flat on the tabletop. "Take my hand and tell me. If it gets too hard, just squeeze as tightly as you can."

The girl tentatively placed her hand in the priest's. She took another breath heavy with unshed tears. "Okay. I'll try." She shut her eyes. "My father started in on me when I was around fourteen or so. Katie would have been twelve. I wasn't dumb, I knew that what he was doing was wrong. But I was afraid to tell anyone, because without him, how would we live? He had his business—and he's got disability and social security money. Mom was useless. Worse than useless. She would have denied he was fooling with me up one side and down another. Besides, she would have fallen apart without him. So I just . . . hung on. I knew girls who dropped out of school, or got pregnant to get a boy or the state to take care of them, but I wanted something more than that. I knew that if I could just last until I finished high school, I could get a decent job, make enough money to live on. So that's what I did."

"For four years?" Clare asked quietly.

"Uh huh."

Russ felt sick. His muscles shook from the effort of sitting still and not pacing around the room, pounding on the walls.

"I started working at the bank the day after I graduated, and as soon as I had my first paycheck, I was out of there. I begged Katie to come with me, but she wouldn't. She said Mom needed her." She bit down on her lip. "I think she was worried that it would be too much, me trying to support the two of us until Katie finished high school. And she was really ambitious, too. She was so smart, her teachers all said she could get a scholarship. She wanted a college degree more than anything."

"That's how she got to the State University at Albany? A scholarship?"

"For her tuition, yeah. She's been covering her room and board with student loans, and working for her book and spending money." Russ could see Kristen's hand tighten over Clare's. "I didn't know—before I left home, he never touched her. And she didn't mention anything to me. But maybe she wouldn't have. She was, I don't know, sort of distant her last semester in high school. We didn't get together as much. But I knew she was busy, working at the Infirmary and studying and all that." She looked at Russ, pleading. "I mean, she would have told me if he was, was after her, wouldn't she?"

"You never saw any signs of her pregnancy?" he asked.

She shook her head. "She went to Albany in June, right after she graduated. The university had given her a work-study job in the computer center, and they needed her there for the summer. At least, that's what she told me. We talked on the phone at least once a week. She sounded so good! I never guessed. I never would have guessed." She released Clare's hand to pick up her coffee.

"The girl who first identified Katie for us said she's had a boyfriend, Ethan Stoner. Is there any possibility that he could be Cody's father?"

"Ethan? Geez, that's hard to imagine. They did go out for a long time in high school, but Katie broke it off senior year."

"She broke it off? How did Ethan take that?"

"I don't know. Probably not too well. Katie was . . ." she gestured widely, ". . . more than anything else he had in his life. I know she didn't break up with him over any bad feelings. She just felt they had really grown apart over the years."

"She was college-bound, and Ethan was going to wind up on a dairy farm, is that it?" Clare asked.

"Yeah. Plus, Katie is really smart. She used to like to talk about books and poetry and stuff like that. Ethan wasn't much of a talker, and what he did have to say was usually about some TV show or the Nine Inch Nails. You know what I mean?"

Clare nodded. "Did she have any other boyfriends, then? Maybe someone more like her?"

"No. It was hard for Katie. She didn't fit in very well. She didn't have new clothes and money for fun things like the other college-track kids in school, but she didn't have anything in common with the grounders, either."

"The grounders?"

"You know, like Ethan. The kids who are hanging on 'til they graduate and then get married right off the bat and go to work for a gas station."

Russ got up. "Anyone want some more?" he asked. The women both declined. "Kristen," he said, his eyes on the hot coffee flowing out of the pot, "why do you think it was your father who got Katie pregnant, and not Ethan?"

She swiveled around to where she could see him. "I . . . I guess one is as likely as the other. She never said anything to me about sleeping with anyone. As far as I knew, she was still a virgin." She pushed her fingers through her hair. "I guess that's a pretty naive thing to say, isn't it? But I'll tell you something. I can't imagine Ethan getting violent with Katie. But I sure as hell can picture my father doing it. He's an evil man. An evil man. He could have killed Katie and gone home the same night and slept . . . and slept like a baby."

The chief of police stared up at the windows of number 162 South Street from the relative warmth of his car. He had been to this address many times before, though never to the fourth floor apartment of Darrell McWhorter. Unlike his neighbors, who drank and partied and beat each other up where everybody could see, Darrell McWhorter did his lawbreaking in private.

Russ opened the door, wincing as the cold pinched his nostrils shut and stung his eyes. From the second floor, a curtain flapped aside for a moment and then fell. Cops were not welcome to this flat-faced yellow building, and he wondered how many baggies were being flushed down the john even as he crossed the sidewalk, opened the chain-link gate, and walked up the sagging steps to the front door. He ran his finger down a double row of tarnished door buzzers. MCWHORTER: 3D. He pressed the bell and waited.

"What is it?" a voice crackled indistinctly over the intercom.

"Mr. McWhorter? Chief Van Alstyne, Millers Kill Police. I need to speak with you, please."

Russ looked at a small plastic slide and trike half-buried under the snow covering what passed for a yard in this place. On the sidewalk, a pair of teenage girls with teased-up hair were smoking and gabbing despite the cold, while two toddlers in snowsuits waited, ignored. One of them stared at Russ, slack-faced and runny-nosed. How could anyone believe in a God who let some kids grow up with everything, and other kids live out their whole lives in poverty and neglect? Or worse.

"What do you want?"

"We don't want to discuss this over the intercom, sir. It's about your daughter Katie."

"Katie?" The voice, as distorted as it was, sounded surprised. The buzzer sounded, cracking the front door open. Russ climbed the stairs to the fourth floor, not holding the banister because he was resting his hand on his holster. Habit. Not a bad one.

The door was open when he reached the fourth-floor landing. "What is it about Katie?" Darrell McWhorter was no more than five-ten, squared off, with the look of a high school jock run to flab. His dark hair was pretty well thinned out on top, and he had it combed over in what Linda would describe

as a spider-holding-a-billiard-ball style. He looked unthrea-
tening and unremarkable, a cigarette smouldering between his
fingers, the kind of guy you'd pass a hundred times in the
A&P and never think, "That one's screwing his own
daughter."

Russ tamped down the heat behind his eyes. Kristen had
emphatically refused to swear out a complaint against her
father when she gave his name and address. Until he had
something linking the sonofabitch to Katie's death, Russ
couldn't touch him. Officially, he was here to break the bad
news to Mr. and Mrs. McWhorter. Unofficially, he was here
to see if he could shake something loose.

"May I come in?" he asked.

"Sure, sure, come on in," McWhorter said, stepping aside.
The apartment reeked of cigarette smoke, but it was well kept,
especially compared to the dumps some other tenants inhab-
ited. The furniture was mostly old, too big and too dark for
the living room. It had the look of family hand-me-downs
rather than Goodwill. The TV in the corner was a built-in in
a blond wood cabinet, pure Danish Modern circa 1965. His
mom had had one just like it. The picture was surprisingly
good for something that old. He could count every tooth in
the oversized smile of the game-show hostess twirling around
a shiny new car.

"Great, innit?" McWhorter thumbed toward the set.
"That's what I do, TVs and small electronics. My wife says
she wants one of those big-screen jobs, but I figure, as long
as I can keep this one running cherry . . ." He took a last drag
on his cigarette and stabbed it out in a pedestal ashtray.

Russ turned to face McWhorter. "Is your wife here, Mr.
McWhorter?"

"Yeah, yeah, she's in the bedroom. Brenda!" he yelled
down the darkened hallway between the living room and the
gallery kitchen. "Get out here! There's a cop here with news
about Katie."

"About Katie?" An enormous woman lumbered up the hall. "What about my little girl?" She looked like her daughters, blown up to Macy's parade size, their rounded cheeks and soft chins expanded into a fleshy mask through which once-pretty eyes peered at him suspiciously.

Get to the worst of it fast, he thought. "I have very bad news for you folks. Your daughter, Katie McWhorter, was found dead out past Payson's Park last Friday night." Darrell McWhorter stared at him blankly. Brenda McWhorter screamed.

"My baby! My baby!" She staggered around like an elephant with a tranquillizer dart before slipping to the floor. Her husband caught her under her arms and hefted her onto an elaborately carved Victorian sofa. A man would have to be pretty damn strong to help get that woman up. Russ wondered what sort of disability kept him from working.

"How did it happen?" Darrell McWhorter asked.

Russ recounted what the coroner had found out about Katie's death. Brenda McWhorter continued wailing, punctuating her cries with, "My poor baby! My poor little girl!" Her husband listened without comment, frowning.

"There's one more important thing I have to tell you," Russ concluded. "Katie had a child within a week or so of her death. DHS has custody of the baby right now."

Brenda's wails cut off abruptly. Darrell looked as if he were trying to get the final *Jeopardy!* answer within thirty seconds. "A baby?" he said.

"A little boy. Did either of you know or suspect she was pregnant?"

Brenda shook her head, her mouth still half open.

"Do either of you know what connection Katie might have had to Saint Alban's church?"

"Saint Alban's?" Darrell still looked as if he wasn't going to make the buzzer before Alex Trebeck called time. "What's that? The fancy looking church across from the old band-stand?"

The small park at the end of Church Street was a popular summer spot. The town still put on dances and concerts there, just like when Russ was a young man. "That's the one."

Darrell thought for a few seconds more. "A baby," he said. Then, "No, I don't know nothing that Katie would of been up to involving a church. How come?"

"Katie, or someone, left the baby on the back steps of St. Alban's, with a note directing that the boy go to the Burnses, a couple from the church that've been looking to adopt for several years. Would you or Katie have known them some other way? They're lawyers here in town."

The McWhorters looked at each other.

"A lawyer?" Brenda said. "We don't know no lawyers. 'Cept that one who settled my dad's estate, but that was ten years back, and he was old then. He wouldn't be looking for no baby."

Darrell reached for a pack of cigarettes lying atop a *Soap Opera Digest* magazine. "These lawyers go to that fancy church?" he asked.

"Yes sir, they do."

"But they don't got the baby yet?"

"No. There are several legal issues to sort out, from what I understand. For instance, we don't know who the father of the child is." Russ fixed Darrell with a level stare. "I had a long talk with her sister this morning, who told me Katie broke up with her boyfriend in her senior year. Kristen hadn't heard of anyone else who might have been going out with Katie."

Darrell lit his cigarette and took a drag. "Can't put much store by what Kristen says. We wouldn't help her out with money she wanted after she was out of school, and since then, she's been bad-mouthing us something awful."

"Never comes to see us," his wife chimed in. "Not in al-

most two years. It was like we lost her. And now Katie . . ."
She started wailing anew.

Russ was tempted, sorely tempted, to ask Darrell to come
to the hospital right now for a blood test and cell scraping.
But he didn't want anything questioned and possibly thrown
out if it went to court.

"Had either of you seen Katie recently?"

"Nope," Darrell said. Brenda shook her head.

"Where were you two last Friday?"

"Why?" Darrell frowned. "You asking if we had anything
to do with it?"

Damn right I am, thought Russ. "I'm trying to get a fix
on Katie's movements, to see where she might have gone and
who she might have seen."

"We went out to that new Long John Silver's at the County
Road shopping center," Brenda said. "We had coupons."

"Then we went to the Dew Drop for a few. Met up with
some friends. We must of been there until eleven o'clock."

"We come straight home after that. I remember, 'cause it
was awful cold and I was worried I had left the bathroom
window cracked open and things would start freezing in the
bath."

Russ never trusted people who could recall and retell their
every movement without having to stop and think about it.
Most folks' lives weren't that memorable. On the other hand,
first Friday of the month, after the social security check had
come in, it might be their big night out.

"You wouldn't happen to remember the names of the
friends you were with, would you?" He tried to make his
question as inoffensive as possible.

"Sure we do," Darrell said, "It was the Jacksons, Dave and
Tessa. They live out to Cossayaharie, where we used to. You
wanna phone number so you can check up on them or something?"

"That won't be necessary," Russ said, omitting the "yet."

"While I'm here, do you have a sample of Katie's handwriting I could take with me? Printing would be best. I'll send it on to the state lab to see if they can match it to the note that was found with the baby."

"Let me check her room," Brenda said, hoisting herself from the couch.

"Why d'you need that if you know the baby is Katie's?" Darrell said.

"Just another way of making sure. The medical examiner sent a scraping of Katie's genetic material down to Albany for DNA testing. That will prove Cody is her son. That's the baby's name, by the way. Cody."

Darrell rubbed his lips with the edge of his hand. "I heard about that DNA testing on some news report."

"It's one hundred percent accurate. Once we have an idea who the father is, we can do the same thing. It takes a few months to get the lab work back, but there's no way to fudge your DNA. It either matches, or it doesn't." He paused, let that one sink in. "What kind of car do you drive, Mr. McWhorter?"

"Huh? An 'eighty Ford Ranger pickup." He ground the cigarette stub out in the standing ashtray. "Look, Chief, I don't know what Kristen told you and I don't care, I ain't seen Katie since she left for Albany this summer. And neither has my wife."

Brenda hurried into the room, puffing from the exertion. "Here. It's a college application she didn't finish. She printed it, like it says on the form."

Russ took the thin sheaf of papers from Brenda. "Thank you."

"What do you need to find the father for, anyway?" Darrell asked.

"In the first place, the father has rights to the child. Either to take custody of the boy, or to consent to adoption. Understand, we were looking for Cody's parents before we discovered Katie's body. More important, now we're working on the theory that the man who fathered Katie's child either killed her, or has knowledge that could lead to her murderer."

"And if the father ain't found, we're the closest relatives of the baby, right?" Darrell's eyes lit up with the greatest interest he had shown so far during the interview. The thought of placing a baby with this pair started the acid sizzling along the nerve edges in Russ's stomach. The Burnses would be Parents of the Year material compared to these two.

"Right," he said.

"So, we should get custody of the boy, right?"

At this, Darrell's wife frowned. "Honey, we're kinda old to be having a baby around again."

"Naw, naw, that baby belongs to us. How do we get ahold of the people who got him now?"

Russ pulled one of his cards out of his breast pocket. "I'll write down the number at DHS you can call." He leaned over an oblong table reeking of ashes and dusting spray, fishing for his pen. "The other side of this card has my number on it. Call me if you think of anything that might have slipped your mind. I know it's been a shock." Though they seemed to have recovered mighty quick.

"A shock," Brenda agreed. Darrell took the card, reaching out his hand to Russ, who gritted his teeth and shook hands.

"Thank you for telling us about Katie," Darrell said. "And about our grandson. We'll call DHS right away and see about that little boy."

Russ paused at the door. "DHS hasn't gotten my paperwork yet, identifying Katie as Cody's mother. You may have to wait a day or two." Maybe he could lose it. Not that it would do Cody any good in the long run. Just give him an extra week with the foster mother before McWhorter got his hands on him.

Brenda looked distinctly unhappy. Darrell smiled. "It'll be

worth the wait. It'll be just like having a little piece of Katie back with us again."

Clumping down the stairs, Russ was in what his mother would have called "an old cow stew." When a door inched open, revealing a bearded man with spectacularly bad teeth, Russ glared at him with such venom the man nearly caught his facial hair in the frame as he slammed the door shut. Russ toyed with the idea of shouting "Washington County Probation Department!" to see how many residents would cut and run. It would feel good to do something constructive, even if it did mean filling out packets of forms at the county jail.

What would the McWhorters want with Cody? More accurately, what would Darrell want with Cody? The monthly foster child support check from the state? Jesus Christ, what if Darrell's tastes ran to little boys? It was a stretch, but, still . . . Russ wiped the hand Darrell had shaken on his parka before opening the outside door. Either he convinced Kristen to make a complaint against Darrell McWhorter, or he had better find another candidate as the baby's father right quick. Because if he didn't, Cody would be one of those slack-faced little kids sentenced to poverty and neglect. Or worse.

CHAPTER 10

Russ's wave of determination to help Cody broke apart on that jagged rock of modern life, the telephone answering machine. He tried to reach Kristen at her apartment and was met with a blast of unintelligible music that sounded like jackhammers destroying a guitar shop, followed by a half-screamed order to leave a name and message. Saint Alban's office had on a machine, too, asking him to call between the hours of eight-thirty and three. In case of pastoral emergency, you can reach Reverend Clare Fergusson at the rectory. Except he couldn't. On her message Clare sounded too enthusiastic to make her apology for not picking up the phone believable. In case of pastoral emergency, her pager number was . . . Russ began to wonder about these pastoral emergencies. What were they, deathbed confessions? Emergency baptisms?

He weighed the idea of paging her, but decided against it. Instead, he left a message describing his meeting with the McWhorters and asked her to call him back. He slapped his chest and rummaged through his pockets until he found the paper with Emily Colbaum's number, then sat through a recording featuring a whole flock of giggling females telling him he had reached "the girlz in the house!" He left his name and number and tried the DSS case worker's office next, only to get caught up in a voicemail system. He tried following the automated directions—press two, press the pound sign twice, if you know your party's extension—and wound up in the mailbox of the educational scheduling department. He banged the receiver down and unloaded a piece of army vocabulary on the person who had first replaced an operator with a machine.

He stomped into the dispatch room, hoping Harlene would ask him what was wrong so he could let loose his opinion of people who were never at the damn phone when you needed them. Harlene wasn't there. He followed her voice into the squad room, a kind of big-city name for a cluster of six desks and a water cooler. Lyle MacAuley and Noble Entwhistle must have just checked in at the end of their shifts, but instead of filling out their incident reports, they were huddled with Harlene over a big red camping cooler.

"Hey, Chief!" Noble said.

"Oh, here he is, you can give it to him now," Harlene said, elbowing Lyle. Lyle dug into the cooler, emerging with a large package neatly wrapped in butcher's paper.

"For you, Chief," he said, grinning. "Steaks and the round. I hit the jackpot with a twelve-point stag the day before season close."

Twelve-point antlers. Russ tried to suppress his pangs of envy. At least Lyle was being liberal with the venison. God damn, a whole deer season come and gone and he had been too busy working to ever get out and—the day before season close? When Lyle had been scheduled on the duty roster? "Weren't you sick with the flu for two days before Thanksgiving?" Russ asked. "What did he do, walk into your yard and have a heart attack?"

Lyle smiled more broadly. "I guess that's the way it happened, Chief."

Russ looked at Harlene and Noble, both of them grinning their fool heads off. Russ pulled himself up to his full height and tucked the package of venison under his arm. "Then I'm sure it will be good and tender, Lyle, seeing as how he died peaceful-like, of natural causes."

Their laughter followed him back to his office where he put on his parka and turned out the lights. At the door, he paused, thinking, before wheeling and scooping up the Katie McWhorter file. He returned to the squad room and laid it on Noble Entwhistle's desk. "Noble, you read the file on our homicide yet?" he asked.

Noble ambled to his desk and flipped open the folder. "Nope," he said.

"Take a look at it tonight before you go home. Tomorrow, I want you to get a life picture of the victim from her sister and start making the rounds of all the motels and bed-and-breakfasts and whatall. See if you can find someone who remembers a pregnant young woman checking in. We're especially interested in any man who might have been with her. Get the bus station, too, see if anyone picked her up when she arrived in town Friday."

The officer ran his finger down the case entry form. "Yup."

"Thanks. Good night, all." Noble was the right man for this job. Unimaginative, not the sharpest pencil in the box, but methodical, with an ability to put people at ease and get them to open up. Russ pulled his knit cap firmly over his head before braving the cold. Outdoors, the temperature had fallen still further. Thank God he had the Ford pickup tonight, with its fast-working heater, and not the old whore. He'd stop at his mother's, give her the venison, and wangle a dinner invitation for later in the week, when Linda was away on her buying trip to the city. Maybe he ought to introduce Mom to Clare. Interesting to see how they'd get along.

It was out of the way to his mother's, but he drove by the rectory just to make sure everything was all right. The lights were all off. Had he left her his number at home so she could reach him? Yeah, he had. His dashboard clock glowed. Geez, he'd better hurry, or he'd miss another dinner.

Clare folded her hands together and bowed her head. "Lord God," she said, "for the blessings of food and fellowship we are about to receive, make us truly thankful. Open our hearts so that in the midst of plenty, we are aware of those who hunger, and in the midst of friends, we remember those who are friendless. Give us a hunger to do your will, and an appetite to see your kingdom, here and in the world to come. We ask this in Jesus' name, Amen."

"Amen," the rest of the room said. The silence was broken by the clatter and ring of utensils and glasses, the scrape of chairs and the sound of eleven voices, all asking to pass this and that at the same time.

The first Monday of the month was the Foyers dinner, an informal gathering of members of the parish, offering a chance to eat and get to know each other outside of the confines of Sunday service or a committee meeting. Tonight's meal was at the home of Chris Ellis and his wife, Anne Vining-Ellis. Anne was a physician practicing in Glens Falls, and everyone, including her own husband, referred to her as Doctor Anne. The Ellises were practically neighbors of Clare's, only three blocks away on Washington Avenue. Their huge Victorian house would have been imposing if it weren't for the obvious wear and tear on the place from their three teenage boys. The formal dining room, where two round tables held tonight's guests, was decorated with a chandelier, a Boaz Persian carpet, several sets of skis propped up in the corner, and a deep gash in the wall, approximately hockey-helmet high. One of the boys, pressed into service as a waiter for the evening, shambled back and forth from the kitchen to the tables on overlarge feet.

Doctor Anne, sitting on her right, passed Clare a bowl of rice. "I recommend starting with this if you plan on having

Phoebe's green chile stew," she said. "Hot? I can't begin to describe it. I think she brings it to these things in order to hear people gasping and crying out for water."

"Thanks for the warning," Clare said. "Maybe I should go for that casserole over there instead?"

"Judy Morrison's tuna hot dish," Doctor Anne said. "Judy converted from Lutheranism." She looked meaningfully at the casserole. "After she learned to cook."

"This is a veritable culinary minefield, isn't it? Just waiting for a wrong step. Tell me, am I supposed to take at least a taste of everyone's offering?"

"Only if you want to gain thirty pounds in the next year. I keep trying to get people to bring light dishes to these dinners, but do they listen? Look at Sterling's Swedish meatballs. I happen to know he uses the fattiest ground chuck he can get and then lards it with several eggs before cooking it in a butter-based sauce. Is it a miracle that man's not dead of a heart attack? You be the judge."

Clare laughed. She could feel the tension that had caught in her shoulders dissipating under Doctor Anne's acidic humor. It had been a difficult day all the way around, first in the morgue and the police station, then helping Kristen at Ruyter's Funeral Home. Ignoring the ache of old pain while Kristen ricocheted between anger and bewilderment and grief with the speed of someone fast forwarding through cable channels.

It was good to lean back and listen to the stream of culinary critiques and gossip, and have nothing more taxing to look forward to than a walk home and an early bedtime. "The only thing that could make this any better would be a cold beer," she murmured.

"That's definitely the missing element, isn't it? It would certainly help wash down Phoebe's chili." Doctor Anne passed Clare a basket of rolls. "Sometimes there will be wine at one of these dinners. No one bothers when Chris and I play host, because I'm such a fanatic about drinking and driving I practically give Breathalyzer tests at the door."

"We had sangria at the Foyers dinner I went to in August," Clare said. "A barbecue."

"This was when? During the selection process?"

"Uh huh. And it was about as comfortable a meal as one can get, when you're eating with your prospective employers. I dreaded spilling something and making a horrible stain on myself, so I stuck to smoked turkey on a dry roll." She made a face. "I'm surprised no one concluded I was anorexic."

Doctor Anne laughed. "Where was this?"

"The Fowlers."

"Oh, my lord, and you had to listen to Vaughn speechifying about the charm, intelligence, good looks, and record-breaking success of his kids, did you?" She rolled her eyes. "Me, I figure if the police aren't actively looking for my sons, they're doing okay. Vaughn and Edie, they'll take the family to the beach because they want to see their children walk on water." She laughed. "Oh, come here, darling, say hello to Reverend Fergusson." Doctor Anne snagged her son as he shuffled past with an empty water pitcher. "I was just telling the Reverend how highly accomplished you are. This is my oldest boy, Anderson." The teen ducked his head awkwardly, setting his long blond hair swinging around his face. He mumbled hello. "Anderson's in his last year of school at Millers Kill High. When he's done, we're throwing him out of the house and forcing him to support himself as a karaoke singer in nightclubs."

"Ma!" the boy protested. "She says that because I'm in the drama society. I'm going to Brown. I got my early acceptance," he told Clare.

"Congratulations. That's a great university. It'll be a big change from Millers Kill High School, won't it?" she asked.

"You bet. I can't wait. Hey, they were talking about our church today, did I tell you?" Anderson looked at his mother.

"It was all over the place that Ethan Stoner killed his old girlfriend and Alyson Shattham identified her from a picture right in St. Alban's! That was way cool."

"What?" Clare looked from Doctor Anne to her son. "Anderson, there's no evidence that Ethan Stoner killed anyone. The police are looking for anybody who knew Katie McWhorter and who might be able to give some information on the case."

"That's not how I heard it. It sounded like the cops were ready to haul old Ethan into the county jail and charge him with murder. You mean like somebody else might have done it?" He sounded disappointed. "Shoot. If it was Ethan, it would have been the biggest thing to hit the high school since girls' basketball took the state championship."

Of course it would be, in a town of eight thousand. An awful, low, unworthy thought occurred to Clare. What if Geoff Burns *was* guilty of Katie's murder? She could see the headlines in every paper in eastern New York state: SAINT ALBAN'S PARISHIONER SLAYS MOTHER OF ADOPTED SON! And in smaller type: PRIEST SPEARHEADED EFFORT TO PLACE INFANT WITH MURDERER! She shook her head. No. She knew the Geoff Burns type. All the heat and fire came right out, up front, leaving behind nothing more menacing than low-level discontent and grumbling.

"I think we'll have to wait and see what Chief Van Alstyne comes up with in his investigation before we can make any reasonable guesses about Katie's murderer," she said. "Did you know Katie McWhorter, Anderson?"

He draped a gangly arm across the back of his mother's chair. "No, not really. I knew who she was, 'cause she was in Honors track, like me, but she was a year ahead of me."

"Millers Kill High is a big school, too," Doctor Anne said. "It's got the kids from this town, Cossayaharie, and Fort Henry."

"I know most of the other seniors," Anderson said. He

pounded his fist against his forehead. "Oh, duh, I should have known Alyson was exaggerating about Ethan. She's, like, 'I'm the center of attention and the rest of you aren't.' I think she's still fried about not getting elected to the student council in September. So now she's like, 'Ethan's O. J. Simpson and I brought him down.' " He looked at his mother. "She never got it that the reason she was in with everyone last year was because she was going out with Wesley. But now, she wants to buddy up with the jocks or the brains—"

"Anderson is a brain-slash-jock," Doctor Anne interrupted.

"—and they're, like, go back to the mall girls, Alyson."

"Do you need that translated?" Doctor Anne smiled wryly.

"I think I got the gist of it," Clare said.

"Wesley is Wesley Fowler, he-who-walks-on-water."

"Ma!"

"Okay, okay, Wes is a perfectly nice boy who helped you a lot last year in the plays you were in together, and the musical, in which he was, of course, the lead." She leaned over in an exaggerated aside to Clare. "I suppose it's not his fault his father made a golden statue of him and put it on his front lawn."

"Ma!"

Doctor Anne laughed. "Me, I practice the traditional Chinese method of child rearing, I never say anything nice about my kids. That way, they avoid the notice of evil spirits." She wrapped an arm around Anderson's waist and hugged him hard.

"Ma, you are so weird," he said. The boy picked up his pitcher and scuffled off toward the kitchen.

"That means, 'I love you,' in seventeen-ese," his mother said.

Clare laughed. "He's a nice kid. You must be very proud of him."

"Very," Doctor Anne said. She leaned toward Clare. "So

tell me, Reverend, *do* you have the inside scoop on this murder? Since you've been helping the police?"

Clare shook her head. "I don't know much more than you do," she said. "I'm sure Ethan will be brought in for questioning, but I don't think Chief Van Alstyne is anywhere near to arresting a suspect yet." She took a bite of her roll. "Hard to believe that something like this happened here, isn't it?"

Doctor Anne shook her head. "After thirteen years working the emergency rooms in Washington County and Glens Falls hospitals, I've seen way too much to think we're invulnerable just because we're small. Small towns have the same evils that big cities do, just in smaller numbers. And instead of some anonymous stranger, the evil is always someone's neighbor or husband or friend. That's the hard part, that you can't blame some 'other' when awful things happen. The 'other' is one of us."

CHAPTER 11

When her pager beeped in the middle of one of Mrs. DeWitt's rambling stories about the Depression, Clare expected it to be the hospital. She was chaplain-on-call this Tuesday, responsible for the spiritual needs that might arise in the intersections between health and sickness and birth and death. Clare lowered her teacup gingerly onto the hand-tatted lace of the table runner.

"Mrs. DeWitt? May I use your phone for a moment? I have to see what this is."

"Of course, Reverend," the elderly woman said. "I left it . . . where did I leave it? Try the kitchen table."

Clare would have sworn that not a thing in Mrs. DeWitt's house, other than herself, had been made after 1935, so she almost laughed when she found the latest Toshiba micro-cell phone lying on the metal cherry-painted table. She punched in the number.

"Burns and Burns," a pleasant voice replied.

"Uh . . . this is the Reverend Fergusson. I got a pager message to call here?"

"Oh, let me connect you with Ms. Burns, Reverend." The voice was replaced by a symphonic rendering of "I Can't Get No Satisfaction." The Burnses. Now what? Oh heck, she had tried reaching Russ that morning before setting out on her home visits, but he had already left for the courthouse. Had he found something linking the Burnses to Katie's death?

"Reverend? Karen Burns. Thank you for getting back to me so quickly."

"What's up, Karen?"

"It's complicated." Karen laughed humorlessly. "It's about Cody, so of course it's complicated. Could we meet? As soon as possible?"

"Sure. I'm at Mrs. DeWitt's right now. I have one more home visit to make, and I can keep it brief . . . how about an hour, an hour and a half from now? I can come to your office, that'll be closer than the church."

"Oh, wonderful. Thank you, Reverend. We'll see you in an hour or so."

Clare brought the cell phone back into the living room, her mind caught up in possible scenarios involving Cody.

"Everything all right, Reverend?" Mrs. DeWitt's heavily wrinkled face creased with concern.

"I hope so, ma'am. But I'll have to be going soon."

"Well then," her hostess said, levering herself out of her faded Morris chair with the help of her cane, "before you go, let me show you an idea I had for the church." Mrs. DeWitt braced herself against a Philco radio set as she hobbled toward the hall. "The computer room is right down here."

"The—you have a computer, ma'am?"

"Oh, my, yes. It's the latest Gateway, customized for me. I ordered it over the Internet. Special-ordered cable access for my modem, too. At my age, I can't afford to wait around all day for files to download, can I?" She paused, flicked a bit of dust off a Boston fern sitting on a plant stand. "I've been fooling around with a Web site for Saint Alban's, and I want you to tell me what you think."

Russ picked up his receiver. Put it down. Picked it up. Put it down. "What the heck are you doing in there?" Harlene yelled from the dispatch room.

"What are you doing, spying on me?" he yelled back.

"I can see the active light on the phone, you cranky old buzzard," she said, appearing in his doorway.

He tapped the folded legal papers lying next to the crumpled remains of his lunch bag. "Judge Ryswick gave me the warrants."

"For the blood tests on McWhorter and the Stoner boy? Good. Why don't you go on out and serve 'em, then, and leave the phone system to those of us who understand it."

He sighed. "I want to talk to Cody's caseworker at DSS first. If this test clears McWhorter as the baby's father, he and his wife will get Cody faster than you can say 'closest living relative.' I want to try to persuade DSS to keep the baby in his current foster home."

"They'll have to do a home visit," Harlene pointed out. "Maybe they'll find some reason not to place the baby there."

"Aw, Harlene, you have to have shit smeared on the walls to get the state to take a kid out of his home. This place looked . . . respectable. Clean. Probably a fridge full of food and the rent all paid on time."

"So tell them about Kristen."

"I don't know if I can! She won't make a complaint against her father. I can't tell them something she told me in an interview if she won't back it up."

"You know, they encourage citizens to call in and report suspected child abuse."

"Not when the child is twenty and hasn't lived with the parents for two years. Then it becomes our business, not DSS's. Besides, I'm not a citizen. I'm a law enforcement official. An agent of the state."

"Look, Mr. State Representative. Call up. Let them know Grandpa McWhorter is under criminal investigation and that you have a warrant—which means Judge Ryswick thought you had probable cause—to test his blood and see if he's the baby's father. That alone should tell them to put the brakes on changing the baby's custody. You don't need to mention Kristen."

"Damn, Harlene, you're right!"

"Uh huh. Like usual."

"Why don't you leave that switchboard and become an officer, huh?"

"Because you need a mastermind sitting here in this office more than you need another uniform out there, driving around with nothing to do."

"Something to do now," he said, waggling the papers in the air.

"Delivering orders to get a blood test. There's a thrilling day's work. No thanks, I'll stick with the phones." She grimaced. "Besides, I look terrible-bad in brown."

From the address, Clare had expected the Burnses' office to be in one of the late-nineteenth century brick commercial buildings that gave upper Main Street the genteel air of another century. Instead, she found herself in a brand new post-and-beam construction that looked as if it had been lifted straight from the pages of *Architectural Digest*. Climbing to the second floor law office, she caught disorienting glimpses of the Christmas decorations on the street below through odd, geometric windows.

The reception area was an uneven pentagon, with narrow I-beams crisscrossing the ceiling and large, dramatically colored abstracts on the walls. No wonder Karen and Geoff had goggled at her office. It looked like a curiosity shop next to this place.

"Hello," she said to the receptionist. "I'm the Reverend Clare Fergusson. The Burnses are expecting me."

"Please take a seat, Reverend," the young woman said. "Ms. Burns will be with you in a moment." Clare sat in one of the plump chairs covered in what looked like hand-loomed upholstery and wondered when she'd stop getting the urge to whirl around looking for the real priest whenever she was called "Reverend." When she was a kid, of course, it had always been "Father" Such-and-so, and that title still sounded more . . . authentic to her ear. *Reverend is an adjective after "the," not a title after "hello,"* Grandmother Fergusson sniffed. A proper word for female priests corresponding with "Father" had been on her wish list for years. She supposed they'd think up one right about the time the Roman Catholics began ordaining women.

"Reverend Clare!" Karen strode across the reception floor, her hands outstretched. Clare rose. "I'm so glad you could come on such short notice. Come on into my office, please. Geoff is still stuck in court, I'm afraid."

Karen Burns's office was clean and spare, with more abstract artwork that blended perfectly with the Shaker-style furnishings. Clare sat in a severely cut chair across from the desk, surprised at how comfortable it was. The lawyer went to the window, then toward the door, then back to her desk.

"Can I get you some coffee? Tea? Water?" Karen was too elegant a woman to actually bustle, but she was close to it now.

"Karen," Clare said. "Sit down. Tell me what's happened."

"Oh, God," Karen exhaled, collapsing in her chair. "We got a call this morning from a man named Darrell Mc-Whorter. He claims to be Cody's grandfather, and said that he had already talked to DHS and was pressing for custody of the baby."

Clare shook her head. "I'm sorry, I should have called you yesterday. Yes, he is Cody's biological grandfather." Should she say anything about Kristen's accusations?

"Presuming that the murdered girl was Cody's mother. That won't be conclusive until the DNA results come in." Karen's shoulders sagged. "That's the law, anyway. Cold comfort. We all know Katie McWhorter gave birth to Cody."

"Why was Mr. McWhorter calling you, Karen?"

The lawyer sat bolt upright. "He wanted us to buy Cody, that's why."

"What!"

"Oh, he didn't come right out and say it. He's smart enough to know that baby selling is against the law. He could land himself in jail for the offense, and lose his chance at custody."

"You didn't . . . you didn't agree, did you?"

"God, no. If it ever got out, it would render any adoption null and void. We'd face jail, the loss of our licenses . . . no." She paused, took a deep breath. "But we did ask him to meet with us on neutral territory, as it were, and see if we could try to work out some sort of . . . accommodation."

Clare frowned. "What sort of accommodation, Karen?"

Karen leaned forward, forearms against her desk. "We need your help. He's agreed to accept you as a mediator if we can get you."

"Get me? Mediating what?"

"We can't pay the man off, not directly. But we can re-imburse him for expenses, offer to pay for, say, improvements to his house in order to make it a better place for Cody to visit, things of that nature. And I thought, what if Geoff and I make a large donation to the church, dedicated to helping lower-income residents of Millers Kill? And what if one of the recipients of this aid is McWhorter?"

"What? You're asking me to make the church your money launderer?" Clare stood up, pushing the chair away. "In a scheme that boils down to you paying for another human being. No. I won't do it. It's immoral, even if it is legal." Karen looked up at her, stricken. Clare sat back down. "Karen," she said, more gently, "you can't buy motherhood. I know how much you want that baby. But this . . . this wouldn't work. What's badly begun has a way of turning out badly. Imagine Cody as an older child, finding out that his grandfather had essentially sold him to his parents. Imagine how he would feel about himself."

Karen folded her arms tightly around herself. "Do you think he'd be better off being raised by the man who's willing to sell him?"

Clare shook her head, laid her hands palm up on the desk. "No. I'll do everything I can to help you. Let's go ahead and set up a meeting with McWhorter, see what we can accomplish."

"With what? Earnest entreaties and prayer? Somehow, I don't think he'll respond very well to that."

"Nope. We offer him what assistance you can legally and ethically," Clare emphasized the word, "provide. That's the carrot. Then, we show him the stick."

When Russ turned his cruiser onto Main Street at the end of a long day, his lights picked out Clare's MG half in and half out of the police station's driveway. Grinning, he pulled up behind the little car and gave it a hit of his flashers. The door opened, and the Reverend Clare Fergusson got out, reluctantly turned around, and spread-eagled against the side of her car. Russ was laughing so hard it took him two tries to find his seatbelt latch.

"What are you doing here?" he asked, once he had managed to get out of his cruiser.

"I was dropping by to speak to you between home visits, and my . . . dang . . . car got stuck."

He looked down at the scant two inches of snow and ice the plow had thrown up on the lip of the driveway. "In that? Heck, my niece's trike could drive through that." The old snow had been churned to dirty slush by her spinning tires. "You gotta get yourself a real car for this climate. Not an itty-bitty wind-up toy like that one."

"This car," she told him, "is a marvel of precision engineering. Zero to sixty in ten point seven seconds. It handles like a dream, and it can drive a mountain road at sixty miles an hour without a shimmy across the yellow line."

"Yeah? Well if I ever catch it doing that, it can also get impounded. C'mon, I'll help you push it out." He braced himself against the back fender. Clare leaned into the edge of the door, one hand on the wheel. "Okay, push," Russ said. They heaved together. The MG slid over the low snowbank and rolled forward a foot.

"Thanks." Clare looked at the tire marks in the snow, thrown into high relief by the streetlights. "That is an embarrassingly small amount of snow to get stuck in, isn't it?"

"You need something heavy, with front-wheel-drive," Russ said, opening the door to his cruiser. "Four-wheel-drive is better. Until you get that, load up the trunk with bags of kitty litter. It'll give some weight to your rear and if you get stuck, you can always sprinkle some around for traction."

"Great. I can see it now. I'll get my car free just in time to run over some old lady's cat who's come to investigate."

He grinned. "Why don't you park that thing. Let me get the cruiser in, and I'll stand you a cup of coffee."

"Any of Harlene's strudel left?"

"I might be able to rustle something up." She nodded approvingly, slid into her car, and pulled it forward. *A strudel person,* he thought, shifting the cruiser into first. *Should have guessed that.*

In the briefing room, two of the sheep-and-geese mugs at hand and nothing left of the last slice of strudel except crumbs, he told her about delivering the warrant to Darrell McWhorter. "You should have seen him. So cool. The nicest guy about it you could imagine. He drove himself over to the hospital, with me following, thank God, because I sure didn't want to have to make conversation with him in my car. Got his blood drawn and went home."

"That doesn't sound like a man who's afraid the test will show something incriminating."

"AB negative. Same as Katie's."

"And Cody's father has to be Rh positive, doesn't he?"

"You've got it. I'd love to be able to put the sonofabitch away for molesting his daughters, 'scuse my French, but there's no evidence he abused Katie and Kristen still refuses to cooperate. I spoke to a caseworker at DSS and told her about the warrant and everything, but she said after the home study was completed, they could only delay giving Cody to his grandparents as long as the question of whether McWhorter had been abusing Katie remained open."

"But if he's not Cody's father, there isn't any other evidence of that."

"Right. It'll be a happy family reunion." He licked his finger and picked up a few strudel crumbs.

"I found out why McWhorter is so eager to get his hands on Cody." Russ's eyebrows went up. Clare told him about the offer to the Burnses and the meeting scheduled for tomorrow.

"You really think you can convince this guy to allow the Burnses to adopt the baby?"

"I don't know. I can get him to think twice about taking Cody. It's worth a try."

"Be careful, okay? I don't like the idea of you drawing McWhorter's attention. We don't know what he's capable of."

"He sounds like a bully to me, plain and simple." Clare propped her chin on her fist. "I'm not an easy person to bully. Besides, if the blood tests show nothing, he'll be out of the running as a suspect in the murder, right?"

"Well . . . I'll have to drop him back to third place. I haven't forgotten the Burnses."

Clare waved her hand dismissively. "You don't seriously think they did it. You're thinking it was Ethan."

"Yeah," he admitted.

"Are you going to serve him the warrant to test his blood

type tonight?" she asked, glancing out into the darkness.

"No. I have to pick up Linda and get her on the six-fifteen train. There's a big fabric convention or something in New York, and she's buying stock for her curtains." He took a sip of coffee. "I'll drive over to the Stoner's farm tomorrow after school, bring him in then. That'll give me enough time to question him and then decide whether to arrest him or not."

"You're not worried he might take off someplace?"

Russ shook his head. "His whole life's right here. All his family and friends. I'll bet the farthest he's ever traveled has been New York City on the junior class trip. Where's he gonna go?"

CHAPTER 12

"Mr. McWhorter, Karen and Geoff can't solve your problems for you. But they can help prevent further problems." Clare took a deep breath and thought of the Wednesday Eucharist she would be celebrating a few hours away at noon. The prospect helped her keep her cool. The Burnses shifted on her small office sofa and glowered at her, obviously frustrated and out of temper with McWhorter's continual sad narrative about his financial woes and his declarations of affection for his dear, departed Katie. So far, he had been skirting the out-right offering of Cody in exchange for cash, but the implication was clear enough. Karen and Geoff had outlined the benefits they could give Cody; the excellent home, the education, the love and attention, even the puppy dog in the back-yard. McWhorter countered with how ashamed the boy would be of his poor grandparents, how he would reject his own flesh and blood, living in a shabby apartment and eating beans and rice at the end of the month when the money ran low.

When Karen asked him if he wanted to bring up Cody in that shabby apartment, he went into a song-and-dance about poor but honest hearts that could have come straight out of *Little Nell*. Clare, who had held Kristen's hand until she thought her bones would grind together while the girl stammered out her story of abuse, kept her peace by picturing herself snapping McWhorter's kneecap with a well-placed kick. It wasn't very Christian, and she wasn't proud of herself, but there it was. They had tried the carrot. Now it was time for the stick.

"What further problems?" McWhorter said.

Clare rose from her admiral's chair. "Are you aware of the average cost of rearing a child these days, Mr. McWhorter?" She retrieved several sheets of paper from her desktop. "I asked a parishioner to do some research for me on the Internet, and she found several articles giving parents the costs for the first year." She handed McWhorter a paper. "Take a look. Diapers. Formula. The medical visits. That's going to be a sizable chunk for a couple living on disability and a pension."

She dropped another paper into his lap. "Here's the monthly stipend you'll be getting as foster parents. Falls a little short of the expenses, doesn't it?"

Clare handed McWhorter more papers. "Unless your pension stretches quite a bit further, I imagine you or your wife will have to go back to work. Child care and baby-sitters are expensive." She gave him another paper. "Here's the average cost of infant care in the tri-county area." She turned to the Burnses. "Mrs. DeWitt did a great job. She's very thorough." The couple were sitting up straight now, staring at her with twin expressions of unconcealed surprise. McWhorter shuffled through the papers, frowning.

"You'll be taking on a big responsibility, Mr. McWhorter. A big, expensive, time-consuming responsibility. And we'll make sure you're doing your job." She smiled blindingly. "We all feel connected to Cody here at Saint Alban's. So we'll be keeping an eye on him. Not just Geoff and Karen, but a whole lot of us. Dropping by to see how he's doing. Talking to the neighbors. Checking him out when he's at the grocery store and the bank and the pediatrician's office." She could hear her voice loosen into a light Virginia drawl. "Chief Van Alstyne is interested, too, and I'll bet he'd be happy to arrange for police drive-bys every day. We'll all be watching out for little Cody. And at the first hint of neglect or abuse one of us will have DSS on you like fleas on a hound."

"Hey!" McWhorter crumpled the paper he was holding. "You saying I'm gonna beat this kid or starve him or something? Where do you get off saying that?"

"I'm not saying what you will or will not do, Mr. Mc-Whorter. I'm telling you what we all are going to do. I'm telling you, realistically, that you are not going to make one dime off that baby. To the contrary, you can look forward to spending a lot more than you're used to on the child. Or, you can authorize the Burnses to take custody of your grandson, and accept their more than generous offer to pay any debts Katie left behind."

"You're threatening me, aren't you? I'm being threatened by a priest and a couple of rich lawyers. For trying to give my grandson a good life and a family he can be proud of."

Clare drank some coffee. She balanced the mug casually in her hand, where McWhorter could see the flying rattlesnake and the motto DEATH FROM THE SKY! She looked at him levelly. "I never threaten, Mr. McWhorter." His eyes flickered from the coffee cup to her face. "You have a chance to save yourself considerable trouble and to do the right thing for your grandson. Why don't you take it?" The Burnses were still staring at her. *Yes*, she thought, *I am a very different priest from Father Hames. Get used to it.*

McWhorter looked at the papers on his lap. He shuffled them together in a messy pile and rolled them up. "I . . ." He looked over to the Burnses, frowning. "Maybe. I'll take this home and show it to my wife. Talk it over with her. She had her heart set on having that baby come live with us, you understand."

"She can visit with Cody as much as she wants," Karen said. "I'll drive her myself if need be."

McWhorter rose, and they all rose with him. "Maybe." He

headed into the hallway, Clare and the Burnses close on his heels. "So," he said, eyeing the carpet and the woodwork and the prints hanging from the walls as if he were casing the joint, "Cody would come to this church if he were your kid?"

"That's right," Karen said. "It's a wonderful community. Not many children now, but we expect that to change over the next few years."

McWhorter stopped in front of the parish family bulletin board, looking at the snapshots of congregants and their families. "Hey, here's you." He stabbed a finger at the picture neatly labeled "Geoff Burns and Karen Otis-Burns."

"Many of those pictures were taken during the parish picnic last June," Karen said, her voice unnaturally cheery and light. "Maybe you and Mrs. McWhorter could come along with Geoff and me next summer. We could all show off Cody together."

McWhorter continued to study the wall of photographs. Clare felt the back of her neck prickle. Something about the way McWhorter was acting didn't fit with a man who had been closed into a corner. "Why don't we all—" she began.

McWhorter shifted to face them. "I don't think so."

"What?" Karen's voice was polite, but shaky.

"I've thought about it, and I can't give him up. He's the only thing I have left of my Katie. He stays with me and my wife."

"What sort of game are you playing, McWhorter?" Geoff Burns crowded the taller man against the wall. "We aren't going to come back with an offer of money, so you can just forget it!"

McWhorter sidled past Geoff and retreated to the parish hall. "No. Sorry. I'm keeping him."

"Wait!" Karen said "Maybe we can work something out! What if we got you a new car, so you could drive over to see Cody?"

She tried to follow after McWhorter, snapping to a halt

when her husband jerked back on her upper arm. "Stop it, Karen," he said. "Let him go."

"Wait," she said. "Wait!" McWhorter reached for the doors. "God damn you!" Karen's voice thickened. "God damn you!" Clare put her arm around the other woman. She met Geoff's eyes and tried not to flinch away from the resigned pain she saw there. Together, they held Karen tightly as her body heaved with the effort to expel tears and venom. "I could kill you, you bastard!" she shouted after the vanished man. She laid her head against her husband, weeping with rage. "I could kill him," she whispered. "I could kill him."

A mid-week drive up to Cossayaharie usually relaxed Russ. Although Millers Kill policed the rural township, he seldom patrolled the mountain roads and tiny village himself. So his associations with the area were mostly good ones: visits to his sister's farm, fishing up at the lake, hiking into the hills, or picnicking in the Muster Field, where militiamen had gathered during the French and Indian War and the Revolution after that. Returning from Cossayaharie you could drive through almost every war the men from this area had taken part in. There were the crumbling granite stones in the Muster Field, and then a big marble obelisk at the front of the old Cossayaharie cemetery, a memorial for two brothers who had drowned in the War of 1812. Before you reached Millers Kill, you passed by its cemetery, guarded by a droopy-mustached Union soldier holding a rifle and forever looking South to where his fallen brothers lay. Then over the bridge, stone cairns carrying brass plaques dedicating it to the sacred memory of those who fell in the Great War, and on into town, where a four-sided plinth listed the names of those who had served in each branch of the armed forces during World War Two. If you finished your journey at the post office, you could run your fingers over the bronze plaque memorializing men who had died on the Korean peninsula while he had been in diapers.

There was nothing marking his war. He didn't know how he felt about that, and he didn't want to think about it long enough to make up his mind one way or the other. There had been what his mother described as one almighty patriotic hot flash over Desert Storm, and since then, there had been talk on and off of putting up something for the rest of the veterans. He stayed away from it. He didn't want to become one of those big-bellied guys down at the American Legion, droning on about their war adventures as if they had forgotten what it was really like. Probably file clerks and car-pool mechanics, anyway. The ones who knew what it was really like hardly ever talked about it, not in the Legion Hall bar and not in front of some committee to erect a monument.

He passed the obelisk to the brothers who had died in the waters of Lake Erie and took the next right turn. A dense stand of spruce and hemlock crowded in on either side of the road. As it wound its way into the hills, the evergreens petered out and the scenery opened up onto sprawling, uneven grazing fields bordered by bare-branched hardwoods. The road dipped and twisted, past sheltered hayfields, farmhouses, and an occasional trailer. For a mile or so, a stony creek ran alongside the road, black water barely visible under the heavy banks of snow. He drove past sleeping orchards of dwarf apple trees, modern feed silos, and century-old barns. At Jock Montgomery's place, he saw two of the kids making a snowman in the front yard, and he slowed down, tooted, and waved.

The Stoner's farm was a mile past the Montgomerys'. He crunched into the drive, parking next to Mindy's Chevelle. He was relieved to see Ethan's old pickup by the road leading up the hill toward the cow barn.

Mindy Stoner came out on the porch, wiping her hands on a dishcloth. "Russ," she said. "What brings you up this way?"

She was a tall, raw-boned woman, whose square, strong features had looked almost homely back when she was a schoolgirl. Time had refined her so that now, in her forties, she had the spare beauty of a mountaintop blown clean of snow.

He held up the folded paper. "I'm afraid I'm here on business, Mindy. Can I come in?"

She looked back toward the kitchen, then opened the door. "You might as well. No need to freeze out here in the dooryard." Russ scraped the slush off his boots and followed her through the mudroom into the kitchen, a large room of wooden cupboards, blue-and-white dish towel fabrics, and children's papers and artwork tacked up everywhere. The woodstove between the mudroom and the pantry was throwing off heat, and the overhead lamp had been lit in preparation for the four o'clock twilight. Their thirteen-year-old—her name escaped him for the moment—was sitting at the round, oilcloth-covered table, doing homework. "Hannah," Mindy said, "run up to the barn and tell your father Chief Van Alstyne's here and needs to speak with him."

The girl gaped, her too-large eyes widening with a mix of excitement and apprehension. "Is Daddy in trouble?"

Russ shook his head. "No. But I am going to have to speak with Ethan, too."

"He's out in the barn with Wayne, hooking up for the milking. Hannah, fetch 'em both in."

At the mention of her brother's name, the girl had relaxed. "Oh, Ethan," she said, heading for the mudroom. "That figures."

Her mother sighed. "What's he gone and done now, Russ?"

He laid the papers on the kitchen table. "Have you heard about the girl found murdered by the kill last week?"

"Of course. It was on the news. Unidentified body fished out of the kill, that's not something you see everyday around here." Mindy's eyes widened as she listened to herself. She clapped her hands over her stomach. "God in heaven, don't tell me you think my boy had something to do with that!"

"Calm down, Mindy, I'm not here to arrest him for murder. This is a warrant for a blood test. The murdered girl had a baby about a week before she was killed, and I have reason to suspect that Ethan may be the father."

Mindy sank into a ladderback chair. "Dear Lord," she said. "Dear Lord." She looked up at him. "Who . . . ?"

"It was Katie McWhorter."

Mindy pressed her hands more tightly to her stomach. "Oh. No. Oh, no. That sweet girl." She shook her head back and forth. "That sweet girl . . ." She covered her eyes with one hand, screening any tears from his view. Russ's hands twitched, caught between maintaining some sort of professional detachment and reaching out to comfort this woman he had known since his high school days.

She slapped her hand on the oilcloth suddenly, startling Russ into stepping back. "As far as I knew, Ethan broke up with Katie last year. If he was sneaking around without us knowing, and got her pregnant, we'll have the truth out. And he'll take responsibility for it." She rose slowly from her chair, glaring at Russ. "But you listen to me, Russ Van Alstyne. My boy didn't have anything to do with killing anybody, least of all Katie McWhorter."

"What's going on?" Wayne Stoner stood in the mudroom door, prying off his boots with the jack. "Russ?" Wayne had the round reddened cheeks and the ice-pale blue eyes that marked so many people of Dutch descent in the county. He reached out and shook Russ's hand firmly before he crossed to his wife's side. "What's that boy gotten into now?"

"Russ wants to take Ethan for a blood test," Mindy said. "Seems Katie McWhorter had a baby a few weeks back and Ethan might be responsible."

"Aw, Christ," Wayne said, pulling off his hat and slapping it onto the table. "What a damn fool thing to do. Jesus, you can practically buy condoms at the feed store nowadays!"

Hannah had slipped in and was watching round-eyed from beside the woodstove. "Did Ethan get some girl pregnant?" she asked. "Whoa. No wonder he's been acting so weird."

"There's more," Mindy said to her husband, ignoring her daughter. "Katie is the girl they found dead down by the kill. The one that was in the news?"

Wayne shook his head as if he were checking it for loose wiring. He shook it again. He squinted at Russ. "You think Ethan had something to do with that?"

Russ spread his hands. "Wayne, I don't know. First step is to get this blood test and see if he could be the baby's father. Then we'll take if from there."

"I'm calling our lawyer," Wayne said. "I don't want Ethan leaving this property until I've talked to him." He pivoted to the phone table between the two windows looking out onto the dooryard. Russ heard the slap of the phone book opening.

"Wait a minute," Mindy said, "wasn't she killed on Friday? Isn't that what it said on the news? You saw Ethan on Friday. Remember? We had to come pick him up from that video game place. He couldn't possibly have . . . he didn't kill Katie."

"The girl died sometime after sundown, Mindy. I didn't see Ethan until well after ten o'clock." He looked out the windows. The sky was darkening, blue to lavender, masses of pink clouds floating on the icy air. He turned to Hannah, who had lost the gloating look of a younger sister seeing her big brother about to get it from the grown-ups. It was sinking in that Ethan might be in a whole lot more trouble than she had ever imagined. "Hannah, did you tell Ethan I was here when you got your father?"

She nodded. "He said he'd be right down."

Russ looked up to the barn. It wasn't dark enough yet to need lights on, but it would be in half an hour or so. He wanted to get this over with. "I guess I'd better walk up there myself."

"I'll come with you," Mindy said, pulling on her jacket. Outside, they crossed the path separating the barn drive from the house driveway and tramped up the well-plowed gravel road. To the northwest, the clouds were dark blue and heavy, rising from behind the mountains in a solid mass. Snow later tonight or tomorrow.

"You can't tell for sure from a blood test if Ethan's the father," Mindy said.

"No. It's more in the way of eliminating or confirming him as a possibility. If he has the right blood type, they'll send his sample down to a lab in Albany that can compare his DNA to the baby's."

Mindy opened the cattle gate to the barnyard. "If he has the right blood type, what are you going to do?"

"Ask him some questions. He can have a lawyer present. Depending on what he tells me, we'll go from there." He stepped carefully, avoiding half-frozen cow patties.

"Ethan!" Mindy called. The road ended at the gaping two-story-high entrance to the old barn. Even in the antiseptic winter air, the smell of manure and hay and machine oil was strong. "Ethan!"

"Maybe you ought to stay out here," he said.

"Don't be ridiculous. This is my son we're talking about." Inside, the barn was warm with animal heat. The cows on the left-hand stalls had all been hooked up to their milkers, while the ones on the right waited their turn with bovine patience. The machinery was silent, however, and Ethan was nowhere in sight. The low ceiling was punctuated by four trap doors that Russ could see, leading up to the huge hayloft. The back of his neck felt hot and prickly. Something in the situation read wrong, very wrong.

"Where's that lead to?" He pointed to the door at the opposite end of the barn.

"The tank room. See where the tubing goes in through the collars on the wall?"

"Anything after that?"

"Storage. We have a machinery shed for our tractors and such, but that's not connected to the barn. Ethan must be having some problem in the tank room. The pressure valves have been acting up lately. Ethan!"

The tank room door bounced open. Ethan stood framed in the doorway, a big, scared young man with a shotgun pointed straight at Russ.

Russ shoved Mindy into a stall and dove in beside her. "Ethan!" she screamed. The cow sharing the space tried to turn her head around to see what was going on, but her bit chains held her to the feed trough. Mindy jumped up. "Ethan, what are you doing?!?"

Russ yanked her down so hard she hit the floor and lost her breath for a moment. "Shut up, Mindy," he hissed.

"Get out of here, Mom!"

"Ethan?" Russ said, projecting a calm he didn't feel into his voice. "Your mother is going to get out of this stall and walk out of the barn. She'll be alone. Then you and I can talk. Is that okay?"

"I'm not leaving!" Mindy whispered.

"Both of you get out of here!"

"You get out and run to the house and call nine-one-one. Tell them what's happened. Then keep Wayne and your girl away from here. Let me handle this."

"You'll shoot him! You'll shoot him!"

"What are you doing?" Ethan shouted.

"Mindy, I haven't fired my gun off the range in over four years, and I don't intend to start now. Let me talk to the boy." He raised his voice. "Ethan? Your mom's coming out of the stall now. Don't shoot." He hauled Mindy to the edge of the wooden wall. "Go, goddamnit."

She stood shakily. "Ethan, please, don't do this."

"Get out, Mom. This doesn't have anything to do with you." Mindy looked back at Russ.

"Go!" he hissed. "Go, go!" She stumbled back a few steps, moving to the doorway while still facing her son. Russ nodded encouragement. Even when you trust someone, it takes a steel sphincter to turn your back on a loaded weapon pointed at you. When she disappeared into the barnyard, he rested his forehead against the low wooden wall for a few seconds worth of sheer relief.

"Ethan? How about you and me talk now? Okay? Let's work this out."

Mindy Stoner was scrambling up her porch steps two at a time when she heard the shot fired.

CHAPTER 13

Mark Durkee had his head in between two half-unscrewed pipes when the phone rang. "Daddy, issa phone," Madeline said helpfully.

"Yeah, cupcake, Daddy hears it." He backed out from under the kitchen sink carefully. The phone kept ringing as he wiped off his hands and moved his toolbox out of Maddy's reach. He hoped it wasn't Rachel with more car problems. He'd have to leave an hour early if he wanted to fetch her home from work and still make his shift on time.

"Yeah," he answered. Maddy was trying to pick up some of the washers he had left on the floor. Were those small enough for her to swallow?

"Mark, it's Harlene. Listen, we've got an officer in distress in Cossayaharie and I want you there."

His first thought was that it must be some sort of prank. Except Harlene sounded dead serious. "What's going on?" He'd have to get Maddy into her snowsuit. Where could he leave her until Rachel got home?

"The Chief went to Wayne Stoner's to serve a warrant on his boy, Ethan. Ethan's holding the chief in the barn with one of their hunting rifles. At least one shot has been fired."

"Shit! The chief?"

"We don't know. The state troopers are sending a squad

there, and I've called Lyle and Ed off patrol, but you're closest."

He was. Maybe a ten-minute drive from the Stoner's farm. He knew from experience that it would take the troopers at least thirty minutes or more to reach Cossayaharie. A man who'd been rifle shot could bleed to death in fifteen minutes. Less.

"Harlene, I'm gonna drop Maddy off with the Slingers, next door. Will you call my wife and let her know? I'll call you on the situation when I get there."

"Be careful. You know what Russ would say. Don't try to be a hero, okay?"

"Yeah." He hung up. No squad car, no shotgun, no spray, no vest. Shit. He scooped up Maddy, who squealed in delight. "Come on, cupcake. Daddy's going to work early tonight."

Old instinct had sent Russ flat into the straw and the cowshit when Ethan's shotgun went off. A second later, he was back up, crouching against the wall, where he had a chance of keeping the terrified Holstein from crushing him. Throughout the barn, he could hear disturbed lowing and thuds and clanks as the agitated cows tried to flee their stalls.

Ethan couldn't reach him from that tank room door. The boy would have to shoot directly into the stall, opening himself up to Russ's fire. So as long as they both stayed put, they were safe. The cow's white-rimmed eye rolled back and fixed on him. She kicked ineffectually, then tried to rid herself of the intruder by leaning against the wall. Russ rolled into a ball and went underneath her, hitting his head on her udder. She bellowed and stamped, narrowly missing taking the fingers off his left hand. He imagined his obituary in tomorrow's *Post-Star*: POLICE CHIEF SLAIN BY COW. He rolled out the other side of her and stood up as far as he could without exposing himself to Ethan's fire. He hit the cow hard with the flat of his hand, as he'd seen his brother-in-law do when his stock got unruly.

She bellowed again, but it seemed to settle her. "Good girl," he said, thumping her a few more times for good measure. "Ethan!" He raised his voice to be heard down the dimming length of the barn. "I'm willing to say that gun went off by accident. Right now, you're facing resisting arrest and threatening a police officer. Don't make it attempted murder. Put the shotgun down and walk out of the barn with your hands on top of your head."

"Don't jerk with me! I know you came here to arrest me for Katie's murder! I didn't do it!" Ethan's voice had the shaky, defiant sound young men get when they're half-wild with fear and half-drunk on the power of the weapon in their hands. Russ had heard it in jungles and in Third World cities and in squad cars and coming from his own mouth.

"If you say you didn't do it, Ethan, I'll believe you. I came here to ask you to take a blood test, to see if Katie's baby was yours."

"You lie! Everybody thinks I did it! I didn't! I could never hurt her! I loved her!"

"Then let's go to someplace more comfortable than this, and you can clear everything up for me. If you loved Katie, help me find who did kill her."

"I can't clear anything up, you asshole! I was drinking alone in my car before I went to Videotek that night. I know I don't have any damn alibi. Nobody saw me, I got no one who can say I didn't do it. You don't give two shits about who really killed her. You just want to arrest someone, and I'm the easy suspect. You think I'm just a punk anyway."

"I think you're a guy who's in trouble and who needs someone to listen to him seriously. Look, Ethan, you know me. I don't come off like Joe Friday." Jesus, had this kid ever heard of Joe Friday? "I cut you a break last week, when I knew you'd been drinking. Because I'm not interested in an arrest record. I want to help people keep out of trouble. Let me help you now."

"You can help me by getting the hell out of here and leaving me alone! I didn't kill her!"

Russ spread his hands against the cow's warm flank. Somewhere, there was a magic combination of words that would get the kid to lay down his gun and walk out with no one hurt. All he had to do was find them. "Ethan, I'm not gonna tell you what to do. I am going to give you the facts, so that you can make an informed decision. Fact. You picked up a shotgun and fired on a peace officer. That's not going to go away. Fact. Right now, there are cops from the town and the sheriff's department and the state all converging on your farm. Some of them aren't gonna be too particular if you leave this barn walking or feet-first. Fact. I will listen to anything you have to say about Katie and the night she died with an open mind, and I will pursue this investigation until I'm satisfied we have the real killer. Fact. You've got the power, right here and now, to stop this thing. You can put down your weapon, walk out of here, and make your parents the happiest people alive tonight. Or you can choose to shoot it out with a state SWAT team. What do you think the outcome of that will be?"

The cows lowed. Chains rattled. Somewhere, water dripped from a faucet.

"This is Officer Durkee of the Millers Kill Police," a voice shouted from outside the barn.

"Mark! This is Russ! I'm okay!" Now. Now was the moment to take a chance. He eased his 9mm Glock out of its holster. The click of a round chambering sounded as loud as a gunshot in his ears. Keeping the weapon down by his side, he straightened to his full height, shoulders and head above the cow's broad back. In the fading twilight, he could see Ethan's outline at the back of the barn. "Stay where you are, Mark," he shouted. "I think Ethan's going to put down his gun and come out." He ignored the feeling like ants crawling up his neck and through his hair. Ethan could blow his head off before he'd be able to get his piece up past the cow. "Aren't you, Ethan?"

The boy was a space of stillness in the dark. Hay rustled. A cow kicked against her stall with a loud thump. "Yeah," Ethan said.

Russ hadn't realized he was holding his breath until he let it out in a whoosh. "Okay. Put the gun on the floor, then lace your fingers together and put your hands on top of your head. We want to make sure everyone can see you're unarmed when you leave the barn."

When Ethan walked past him, hands on head, Russ slipped from the stall and fell in behind him. He holstered his gun, but left it unfastened. Just in case.

Mark Durkee was beside the barn door. He leveled his gun at Ethan. "Ethan Stoner, you're under arrest," he said. His glance flickered to Russ. "Chief?"

"I'm fine, Mark. Take Ethan to the car while I go talk to his parents, please." He let himself through the cattle gate while Mark read the boy his rights. A Millers Kill squad car flashed its red lights at the base of the driveway. Lyle and Ed were getting out. On the porch, Wayne and Mindy stood with their arms wrapped around each other, straining to see the barnyard in the twilight. Far down the road, he could hear another siren approaching. Russ felt flushed and shaky, his legs almost too heavy to carry him down the barn drive and across the dooryard. The bite of the December air, the dazzle of the house lights on the snow, the sound of people's voices all flooded his senses. It was good to be alive. He forced a smile to his face and began the long, long climb up the porch steps.

Clare smiled when she saw that the driveway to the police station had been thoroughly plowed. She eased her car over the sidewalk and into a parking space. She really was going to need a vehicle that wouldn't get stuck if someone threw a snowball under its tires. Problem was, the only way she could afford a new car was to sell the old one. The thought of which sent her into a blue funk. This MG was the closest she had ever gotten to flying on the ground. She thought of the dark, mid-sized anonymous American cars so many of her teachers at the seminary had driven. Clergymobiles. "Baby, climb inside my car," she sang as she strolled up the sidewalk. A municipal employee leaving City Hall next door looked pointedly at her collar and frowned. Probably a Baptist. Clare winked at him before charging up the steps to the police station.

Inside, she shucked off her jacket. "Harlene?" she said, approaching the dispatch room. "Has the chief left yet? I was hoping to—" She shut up when she saw Harlene's face. "What is it?"

"I really shouldn't talk to civilians yet," Harlene said, her crumpled expression at odds with her formal words.

"Harlene, is anyone hurt? Please . . ."

The dispatcher pushed her headset further back over her springy gray curls. "The chief went to bring Ethan Stoner in for his blood test and the boy pulled a shotgun on him."

The rest of the room faded to a blur, and Harlene's face came into exquisite focus. Clare could see every mole, every hair, the wrinkles around her lips as she pursed them together, the light on her lashes as she blinked quickly, over and over again.

"What happened?" Clare's voice was even.

"I don't know. They're both in the barn. Mindy Stoner heard a gunshot, but I haven't had any news since then."

Clare nodded. She kept nodding as the possibilities flitted through her mind. "Harlene," she said, "I'd be grateful if you'd let me stay. I'd like to find out if . . . if anything has happened."

Harlene held her hand out toward an old office chair next to the filing cabinet. "You just sit right down. I'd be glad for the company, to tell the truth." Clare tossed her coat under the chair and sat. The two women looked at each other.

"Who has—" Clare began.

"Do you—" Harlene said. They smiled weakly at one another. "Go on," said Harlene.

"Who has been sent out to help? With the situation?"

"Three of our own officers. The sheriff's department is sending a car or two, and the state troopers are mustering their SWAT team." She worried at the inside of her cheek. "And an ambulance."

"Oh. Of course." Clare looked at her hands. "What was it you were going to say?"

Harlene looked embarrassed. "I was going to ask if you believe praying can really help at a time like this."

Clare folded her hands together and pressed them to her lips. She paused. "I believe that prayer focuses our human thoughts and energies, sends them to the people we're praying for. I believe that helps, in ways we can't yet understand." Harlene looked surprised. She had probably expected a quick yes. Followed by an exhortation to the Almighty to keep everyone safe. "I believe that God hears our prayers, and cherishes them. I believe He answers by sending us His spirit, giving us strength, and peace, and insight. I don't think He responds by turning away bullets and curing cancer. Though sometimes that does happen."

Harlene frowned. "In other words, sometimes, the answer is no?"

"No. Sometimes the answer is 'This is life, in all its variety. Make your way through it with grace, and never forget that I love you.' "

Harlene creaked back in her wheeled dispatcher's chair. "You're not one of those strict fundamentalist preachers, are you?"

Clare laughed. The phone rang. Harlene had it off the hook before the sound died away. "Millers Kill Police," she said. There was a pause. Her face crinkled up into a huge smile. "Oh, it's good to hear your voice, too."

"Is it him?" Clare whispered. "Is he okay? Is the boy all right?"

Harlene nodded. "No, no, he's absolutely right. You let them handle the arrest and the initial report. You go home!" Another pause. "Then go to your mother's house. I don't care. If you show up here, I'll chase you off myself." She laughed, then listened for awhile. "Are you really okay? You sound kinda funny." Harlene glanced over at Clare again. "Hold on, there's somebody who's been waiting here to find out how you are. Do you feel like speaking to Reverend Fergusson?" She nodded to the phone and held it out to Clare.

"Hello," she said, feeling unaccountably shy.

"Hi," Russ said.

"Remember when you warned me Millers Kill wasn't a sleepy little town? I believe you now."

He laughed. "Good."

"So, it sounds like you're under strict orders not to come into the office."

He sighed. "I guess I should go home. Linda's out of town. And my mother . . . she doesn't need to hear about this just yet. I'm still . . ." he drifted off.

"I know."

"You know?" He sounded surprised.

"I know that you're still . . ." She let her voice trail off, echoing his. "Meet me for a drink somewhere. We can talk."

"Oh, God. I don't think I can handle going out in public right now. Besides, I smell like cowshit and the scared-cold sweats."

"Then tell me where you'll be, and I'll come to you."

"Do you think . . . would my place be okay? I could

shower and change, rustle up some burgers or something. Would that be, um, unpriestly or anything?"

She laughed softly. "I think what would be unpriestly would be to let a friend sit at home all alone with no one to talk to. Give me directions and tell me when to be there. Preferably after you no longer smell like cowshit, et cetera."

He laughed. After she had his address, she handed the phone back to Harlene, who said into it, "You gonna confess your sins to Reverend Fergusson? Make sure she has a few hours." She listened, snorted at something he said. "Okay. Yes, I will. Yes, I promise. Don't you trust me? Wait, don't answer that." Harlene laughed. "Good. I hope you feel good about this, Chief. You just captured Katie's killer." There was a pause. Her smile faded. "Well . . . 'Bye then. See you tomorrow." She hung up.

"What did he say?" Clare asked.

"Said he didn't know about that. He didn't know what he had just done."

CHAPTER 14

When Russ opened the door to her knock, he looked . . . different. It was . . . it was . . . the jeans and a sweater. "You're in civvies!" she said. "I was beginning to think of you like the sheriff of Mayberry, you know, always dressed in brown poly."

He laughed. "You obviously didn't watch enough. He had a plaid shirt and jeans he wore fishing." He looked over her shoulder. "Where's your car?"

She grimaced. "I didn't want to risk getting stuck, so I left it parked at the base of the drive and walked up."

He moved out of the way and let her enter the mudroom. "In that leather jacket and your oh-so-practical boots, too." She looked down at her soggy, salt-stained suede half-boots. "Talk about unprepared for the weather. You're worse than a little kid. I'm gonna get you a pair of mittens with a string attached, so at least your hands will stay warm."

"I remembered the important stuff," she said, holding up a six-pack of micro-brewed beer. She dropped it with a thud and bent to remove her boots. "And I could have worn my warm parka. Unfortunately, it actually belongs to the police, and I'm afraid if you see it, you'll confiscate it." She handed him her jacket.

"Stolen property." He hung it up on one of the many hooks running along the wall.

"I prefer to think of it as permanently on loan."

"Situational ethics." He opened the door to the kitchen.

"Oh. A wood cooking-stove!" she said. "I always wanted one of those. They're supposed to be great for baking bread."

"I hate to disillusion you, but the only thing we make on that stove is hot water." He unhooked a bottle of beer from the cardboard container and opened a paneled pine cabinet to get a couple of glasses.

"I thought your house was two hundred years old," Clare said as Russ retrieved a liter bottle of soda from the fridge. "This kitchen looks kind of forties." The floor was an old linoleum patterned with big flowers, the walls and floor-to-ceiling cupboards warm, glowing pine. The windows over the sink and in front of the table were hung with layer after layer of fruit and flower prints that reminded Clare of the old dish towels in her grandmother Avery's kitchen. Matching fabric-covered balls hung from the evergreen ropes swagged along the cornice.

"You have a good eye," Russ said, pouring their drinks. "The first modern kitchen was built here in the mid-forties. Before that, there was just the summer kitchen, which is on the other side of the mudroom, and a keeping room. I put in the brick wall and hearth for the wood stove, but other than that, we just peeled away the so-called improvements the last owners had made to get to this." He handed her her beer. "You should have seen it. Vinyl flooring and all the wood-work painted in southwestern colors. Took me three months to get down to the pine."

She sat at the round oak table and touched a finger to the tiny Christmas tree serving as a centerpiece. "I like it like this. It's like a bright, warm quilt keeping out the cold."

"Huh." He sat opposite her. "I'll pass that on to Linda. She does the decorating. I'm just the hired help." He drank from a tall glass of soda. She propped her chin in her hand and studied him. He had a fit, outdoors look to him, still slightly tan from last summer, his dark brown hair picked out with gold and copper. She'd have to disagree with Lois, his nose was too big and his lips were too nonexistent to call him handsome. But he looked like a man who had lived comfortably within his skin for the past forty-odd years.

"So," she said.

"So," he agreed. His eyes were Fourth-of-July blue, high and bright with the snap of a flag in the wind. But behind them she could see something moving, like pages turning in a book no one was allowed to read.

"How do you feel?" she asked.

He took another sip of soda. "Fine. No one got hurt, and Ethan's in jail. I count it as a victory for the good guys."

"Have you called your wife yet? To let her know what happened?"

He shook his head emphatically. "No."

"Don't want to scare her?"

"No, it's my mother who gets scared." He smiled wryly. "I figured something might be on the news by tonight, so I called my sister Janet and asked her to talk to Mom. I'll still have to face one of her 'Why can't you get into some other line of work' lectures, but I can duck it for a few days until she's cooled off."

"Uh huh. And you didn't talk to Linda because . . ."

He frowned. She kept her face open, waiting. He glanced around the kitchen, shifted in his chair, cleared his throat. She sat still, her hand lying palm up on the table. "So this is like PTSD counseling?" He laughed a little. She tilted her head a fraction of an inch. Listening. No threat. "Okay. Linda and I have been married sixteen years now. So she's been with me through a lot of shit. Armed deployments, police work, bullets flying, the whole nine yards. And, I don't know if she started out like this or if she cultivated it, but she thinks I'm invulnerable. I've learned that I can't go to her and say, 'I was frightened out of my wits today,' because she won't understand why. What I do, what I've done in the past, is like an action-adventure movie or a television show to her. Nothing's quite real, so why should it bother me?" He flicked a tiny calico ornament on the tabletop tree, then looked at Clare and smiled slightly. "Did I just do an elaborate version of 'my wife doesn't understand me'?"

She smiled. "Uh huh. But you don't have your shirt unbuttoned halfway down your chest to show off your gold chains, so it's legitimate."

"Oh, God save me from male menopause." He laughed a little, shaking his head.

She leaned forward, crossing her arms on the table. "You know, it's not unusual, being unable to share that kind of thing with your wife or your family. I used to see a lot of that, guys who had spent time in very intense, very dangerous situations, couldn't talk about it with their wives. Couldn't admit to being scared to their buddies, of course, except when it's a joke. It builds up after a while, all that stuff inside and no way to let it out. I think that's why there's so much drinking and wild-ass behavior in some units." She dropped her glance to his glass. "Are you an alcoholic?"

He choked on a mouthful of soda. "Holy shit! You don't beat around the bush, do you? 'Scuse my French."

She looked at him mildly. "You don't need to be handled with kid gloves. Answer me."

"Christ on a crutch. Yes, I'm a recovering alcoholic. I've been dry for five years now. What the hell does that have to do with anything?"

"I'm just wondering, if you can't talk about it with your wife, and you can't pour it into a bottle, who do you talk with? Where do you go?"

He crossed his arms against his chest and leaned back in his chair, looking up toward the ceiling. "I don't, I guess," he said, finally. He looked at her. "But let's face it, it's not like I'm a homicide detective in the city. I'm not looking at dead bodies week after week, or having guns pointed at me on a regular basis. I'm just the chief of an eight-man police force in little ol' Millers Kill. Hell, the entire three town area we're responsible for doesn't have more than twelve thousand people, tops."

"Twelve thousand people for whom you feel personally responsible." She pointed one blunt-nailed finger at him. "Tell me, what feels the worst about what happened today? Being scared you might die?"

"No." He braced his elbows on the table. "Only an idiot isn't scared when somebody pulls a gun on him. I'm not ashamed of it. Not inclined to think about it too much afterwards."

"The rush you get when you walk away and you haven't died? Do you like that?"

"No! I mean, yes, I like walking away, but no, I'm not an adrenaline junkie. I'd be perfectly happy if the most action I ever saw was being dunked at the police booth during the county fair, believe me."

"Is it the fact that you should have known that Ethan was on edge and ready to blow? That if you had handled the situation differently, he never would have picked up that shotgun?"

He dropped back into his chair, his face paling. "Holy shit! Do you believe that?"

"Do you?" She leaned farther across the table, crowding him against the truth.

"When you put it that way . . . shit." He swallowed. "Yeah, I do feel responsible. It was a stupid situation to get into. I kept thinking, what a piss-awful waste it would be if Ethan didn't make it, because I hadn't taken the time to find out the kids in his school already had him tried and convicted and on death row. Instead, I waltzed in there with my patrol car and my service piece and my warrant. Not even a phone call ahead of time so his parents could set him straight about what would happen. That's just plain careless. Careless and lazy and stupid." He clenched the edge of the table tightly.

"I knew about what the kids were saying at the high school. Heard about it on Monday night. I didn't do anything about it."

He scowled at her. "That's different."

She scowled back. "Why? Because it's not my job to know everything about everybody? Because I'm not personally responsible every time one of the citizens of Millers Kill falls off the straight and narrow? Because I shouldn't do all I can to . . . to . . . to protect and to serve?"

He laughed quietly. "That's the LAPD, not Millers Kill."

"No, that's you." She took a drink of her beer. "The angel at the gate with the flaming sword, that's you. Guarding your own little paradise from the evil of a fallen world."

He closed his hand around air as if he were holding something in front of him. "A flaming sword, huh?"

"Yep."

"So you think I should—what? Stop caring so much?"

She slid her elbow next to her glass and leaned her cheek on her hand. "No. Not at all. I think it's a fine thing that you bring such dedication and passion to your work. But I think you should stop beating yourself up when you fall short of some imagined standard of perfection." She smiled lopsided at him. "Come talk to me next time, instead. I'd be happy to point out the flaws in your image of yourself."

"As opposed to pointing out my actual flaws."

"I think I need to know you better before I start in on those."

He smiled at her. "Seems like you already know me a little too well for comfort."

She shook her head, smiling, dropping her gaze to the table. She traced meaningless designs on the tabletop with the water condensation that had dripped from her glass. There was a muffled mechanical roar as the furnace kicked in. The thermostat must have been set high, because the kitchen was plenty warm already. A clock ticked in the next room.

"Would you—" he began.

"Now we've—" she said at the same time. They both laughed.

"You first," he said.

"I was going to say, now we've solved all your problems, how about that burger I was promised?"

"And I was going to ask you if you'd like dinner. Another example of great minds thinking alike."

"More like hungry stomachs rumbling in unison, but, yeah."

Russ made what Clare always thought of as he-man burgers, the same three-inch thick monstrosities her brothers would put together at family cookouts. She asked to be made useful, and he put her to work on a salad, although when she started rummaging through the pantry, pulling out cans of artichoke hearts and mandarin oranges, he looked as if he might have regretted not limiting her to setting the table. They talked about cooking as a chore and as a means of expression, and argued about which state had the greatest barbecue, and agreed that vinegar-and-salt potato chips were better with burgers than home fries, and a lot faster, too.

She would have pegged him as a paper-plate-and-napkin guy when his wife wasn't around, but he surprised her by laying out beautifully pieced place mats and huge cloth napkins, along with old ironware that could have come from the earliest years of the kitchen. As they ate, he listened very patiently when she got carried away describing all her gadgets from Williams-Sonoma, only laughing once, when she told him about her latest acquisition, a shrimp de-veiner. She asked him plainly if he ever missed wine with a meal, and he raised his eyebrow at her and said he had never been a wine drinker, but he sometimes missed a bottle of whisky after.

"You mean a glass," she said.

"I mean a bottle," he corrected. Afterwards, he washed and she dried. She made several pointed comments about historical authenticity nuts who wouldn't have a dishwasher because it didn't fit with the kitchen's time period. He smiled serenely and reminded her not to leave any water spots on the glasses. When the kitchen had been restored to its pristine state—she could hardly believe it looked like this all the time, since hers wasn't as immaculate even when it had been scrubbed for company—she grabbed another bottle of beer and he gave her the grand tour.

It was a jewel-box of a house, small and beautifully crafted. Russ told her funny stories about all the mistakes he made and had to redo when he first began its restoration. She oohed and aahed over the elaborate draperies and slipcovers and pillows, so he took her upstairs to where he had built an enormous workroom for Linda out of the old under-the-eaves space. He showed her the half-finished bathroom that was his latest project, and complained about his inability to find a tub anywhere near long enough for him.

She told him about her father, whose mechanical expertise began and ended with aircraft, and who persisted in do-it-yourself projects that had become family legends. Or horror stories. That led to a discussion on the workshop as a sacred place for the American male, and he trotted her all the way down to the cellar, where his impressive collection of power tools looked like high-tech instruments of torture hanging on metal gridwork over the original hewn-rock foundation. Just like her dad's, Russ's workshop had a TV and a suspiciously comfortable chair, although it lacked the dozens of model planes that hung from her father's ceiling.

"How come I've never seen any pinups in one of these

workrooms?" she asked. "I'd think that would be the perfect place for a little cheesecake."

"Introducing the feminine would disrupt the whole Iron Male, sweat lodge, men's-only aspect of the space, though," he said. "For instance, what kind of calendar does your dad have in his workshop?"

"Uh . . . World War Two nose art."

"Nose art?"

"Paintings on the noses of planes. Please don't ask me to explain."

Russ opened one of the cabinet doors. Inside was a glossy calendar showing a man in blaze orange creeping up on a twelve-point stag, who seemed to be waiting patiently to meet his fate. "See? All male, all the time."

Clare laughed. "Okay, I get it. Do you have to blow smoke around the room when I leave, to purify it?"

"No, but if you reveal any of our secrets, the Society of Masks comes to your house in the middle of the night and plays 'Louie, Louie' until you repent."

"Society of Masks?"

"Iroquois ceremonial group. Don't tell me you don't know anything about the Iroquois?" She went back upstairs to a lecture on Iroquois history. She snagged another beer while hearing about their political structure and made herself comfortable on the Chippendale sofa in the living room while learning about their culture, past and present. When she confessed to her abysmal ignorance on anything that had happened in the Adirondack region before, say, last March, Russ rummaged about making disapproving noises until he came up with five books she had to read, to get a grounding in her new home.

"History! That's what it's all about," he said.

"I guess so," she said, craning her neck to look at all the history titles jammed into the bookcase.

"I see a lot of police work as a kind of history," he said,

flopping into a high-backed Martha Washington chair.

"Really?" she said, her attention drawn away from the books he had handed her. "How so?"

He propped his sock-clad feet on a footstool. "First, you have to recreate the history of the crime. Who did it, when, where, all that. Then, it's usually the history of the individuals involved that helps you to understand why. This guy was molested as a kid, so he, in turn, molests other kids once he's grown."

Clare made a face. "Like Darrell McWhorter, you mean? I don't get it. I can see where knowing his history would help if he were in counseling. But what effect does it have on your ability to put him behind bars?"

"If you know a person's history, you can use it to help predict what that person might do. A person's history can be the key to understanding his motivation for committing a crime. For instance, in Katie's murder." Russ leaned forward, feet hitting the floor, elbows on his knees. "We know Ethan may be Cody's father. But why would he kill Katie? Is there something in his past or in their history together that would make him likely to do it? What about McWhorter? Apparently, he'd be willing to kill Katie to cover up his molestation of her. But it looks damn sure that the baby isn't his. What's in his history that makes him a suspect?"

"A need to control his daughters?" she suggested. "Katie demonstrated her control of her own body by having another man's child, so he killed her in a rage?"

"Maybe. But compare that to the Burnses' history. A couple tries for years to get a baby, stressing their marriage and their financial resources in the meanwhile, and then a kid falls in their laps. But, the mother shows up and says it was all a mistake, she wants Cody back now. I think that's damn good motive for murder."

"Except for one thing." Clare scooted to the edge of the

loveseat and skewered the air with her finger. "If Katie had wanted Cody back, she could have just gone to DSS. She's the birth mother, she doesn't need to deal with the Burnses to get him back."

"Okay, she doesn't want him back. She wants money to stay away."

"Now you're ignoring history. Does that sound like the Katie McWhorter we've been hearing about? And anyway, the Burnses wouldn't pay to get Cody. This morning they—"

The phone rang, cutting her off. "I gotta get this." Russ vaulted out of his chair. "I'm expecting word on the blood test results and how Ethan's interrogation went." He glanced at his watch. "Geez, it's almost ten o'clock! Where did the evening go?"

She rose and followed him into the kitchen. "I'll take that as a compliment on my ability to be a distraction."

He grinned. "You are that," he said, picking up the receiver. "Hello?"

Clare went into the chilly mudroom to retrieve her boots and jacket. She looked glumly out the window. When had it started to snow? *Please God, let the plows be out and the roads clear.* She didn't relish the idea of getting stuck between here and the town. She carried her things back into the kitchen. "Russ?" she asked.

He waved her off, still holding the phone. "Okay," he said. "Okay. I'll be there. Half an hour, forty-five minutes at the most." He hung up the phone and leaned on it, shaking his head.

"I was going to impose on you for a ride into town, since it's really coming down out there. But I can see it's a bad time . . ." She bit her lower lip, unsure if she should ask what was wrong or not.

He passed a hand over his face. "That was the night dispatch out of Glens Falls. A motorist called in what he thought was a deer beside the road. It was a body. Durkee and Flynn went to check it out. Wallet was in the guy's pants." He looked at her. "It's Darrell McWhorter. He's been shot to death."

CHAPTER 15

If Katie McWhorter had resembled a frozen story-book princess in death, her father looked like roadkill. Russ tried to summon some basic human identity with the corpse, but the only emotion he could come up with was irritation that Darrell had died before Russ had had a chance to dig any more information out of him. That, and the conviction that the world—or at least his small corner of it—was a slightly cleaner place tonight.

He and Clare had been the last to arrive at the scene on the old Schuylerville Road. Durkee and Flynn had done a good job securing the area, with tape and flares and cones to redirect the infrequent traffic to the other side of the road. The state crime scene unit was already in place. Two technicians this time, since it wasn't a matter of humping the equipment a half-mile into the woods. They were working as fast as they could, racing the snow that had already covered up tire tracks and footprints, turning Darrell into a blurred heap. Russ turned his collar up against the thick flakes melting along the back of his neck, and wished he had stopped to get his hat. The snow was wetting his unprotected glasses, turning the scene into a kaleidoscope of splashing red lights and a blur of white.

Darrell had died from a single gunshot at the back of his

head, delivered only inches away. He had died with his coat on, unzipped, falling face forward onto the narrow pull-off, just missing the guardrail. He had died with a half-smoked cigarette in his fingers. The soggy butt was in a plastic baggy in the evidence box right now.

"Whaddya think?" Mark Durkee swung his flashlight in the direction of the state trooper who was methodically combing through the snow between the body and the road.

"I think he has a better chance of finding the winning lottery ticket than finding a shell casing in all that," Russ said. "We'll just have to cross our fingers and hope Dvorak can give us ballistics information from the autopsy."

"Actually, I meant, what do you think happened?"

Russ glanced down the road, past the ambulance with its anonymous, snow-suited paramedics, past his pickup, where Clare sat steaming at his orders not to leave the cab. "He was in a car," Russ said, recreating the scene in his mind. "Not his car. The killer was driving. McWhorter wants a smoke. They're going someplace . . . not local. He doesn't want to wait for his nic fix until they get there. The killer says, no smoking in my car. But I'll pull off up ahead, you can get out, have one there. McWhorter gets out. The killer gets out, maybe to brush snow off the rear window or snap the wiper blades. There aren't any cars going by. It's an opening, and the killer takes it. Bang, he does McWhorter, gets back in the car, and drives off. Anybody hears the gunshot, they'd think it was backfire, or someone jacking deer." He looked past the guardrail, where a few stunted sumacs thinned out as the land fell away into a sloping valley. On the opposite hillside, a mile or so away, he could see the lights of two or three farms. "It's been coming down hard. If the killer had been a little luckier, Darrell here would have been a mound of snow covered up by the plows when they came through."

"That's somebody very cool. Somebody who can put it all together fast."

"Yeah. Or somebody who has fantasized about killing McWhorter so often that when the opportunity arose, she was ready to snatch it."

"She?"

"Sure. Don't be a sexist, Mark. You think only men can kill?"

"Hell, no. I'm a married man."

Russ laughed. The technician waved at them. "We've got all we're going to get," he shouted. "Tell the medics they can bag him." Durkee nodded and trudged off through the growing drifts toward the ambulance.

A van was coming up the road, slowing down, then pulling in past the crime scene. CHANNEL 7: LIVE! LATE BREAKING! Russ read on its side. He knew it was fashionable to bash the press, but publicity could be a big assist in a case. There was a reason the FBI fought to keep *America's Most Wanted* on the air. He watched a burly guy unload a hand-held camera. He'd have to give them the usual speech about not releasing the identity until the family had been notified. Would anything be likely to shake loose if he mentioned the probable connection to the previous murder and the abandoned baby?

He waved Durkee over again. "Mark, as soon as you can wrap this up, I want you to head over to Geoffrey and Karen Burnses' house and find out where they've been this evening. Do they own a gun, all that. Ask to see the inside of their cars. If they give you any problems, call me. We'll get a warrant tonight, if necessary."

"Okay. Want me to bring them in for questioning?"

"Go with your gut. You get a reasonable suspicion, go ahead. But remember, these two are the sort to sue the department for false arrest, so make sure you cross your T's and dot your I's."

"Will do, Chief."

"As soon as I'm done with the TV crew, I'm going to pay a visit to McWhorter's daughter Kristen. See if after two years, she finally agreed to meet with her dear old dad tonight."

"I've been thinking," Clare announced when Russ climbed into his truck.

"Congratulations," he said, tossing his parka in the back. The cab was almost too warm, undoubtedly the result of leaving Clare in possession of the keys.

"I'm going to come with you when you go to talk with Kristen."

Russ buckled his seatbelt and shifted the pickup into gear. "No, you're not. I said I'd drop you home, and I will. I didn't say anything about making you junior deputy. And what makes you think I'm going to talk with Kristen anyway?"

"She's a logical suspect, isn't she?"

"So are the Burnses." He cautiously pulled into the road. The slap of the wipers barely kept up with the pelting snow. "As a matter of fact, they're the only ones I can think of who had reason to kill both Katie and her father. McWhorter did say he wouldn't let them have custody of Cody this morning, right?"

Silence. He risked letting his eyes leave the road and glanced over at Clare. She was limned by the dashboard light, arms wrapped around herself, frowning. "What?" he said.

She hummed in the back of her throat.

"What, Clare?"

Out of the corner of his eye, he could see her turn toward him. "I've been debating telling you something. I'm not sure if it's covered by pastoral confidence or not, since it was kind of in a public place. Heck, for all I know, Lois could have overheard it."

"What?"

"This morning, things seemed to be going well at first. I thought we had convinced McWhorter to release Cody to the Burnses. But then, just like that, he changed his mind. Karen went absolutely wild. She was yelling, 'I could kill you' at McWhorter." Clare hunched her shoulders and sighed.

"They do start to look more and more like couple number one, don't they?"

"Was McWhorter killed and then dumped?" she asked abruptly.

"Nope. He got out of the car and was shot there on the side of the road." Flashing yellow lights up ahead. Plows and sanders were out, trying to keep up with the relentless accumulation of snow.

"Why would he be in a car with the Burnses? Where does this road go?"

"Away from town, it heads toward Schuylerville and Saratoga and the Northway. As for why he'd be in the car with them, I'd guess they were making a payoff."

Clare shook her head. "No. Even if they were going to exchange money for the baby, which would be a complete turnaround from their earlier position, why would they be heading out of town together? McWhorter was . . . not smart, exactly, but crafty. Looking out for himself as well as the main chance. Why agree to go off on a lonely road with someone who'd been screaming she was going to kill him this morning?"

He tried to come up with a reason that made sense. The frustrating feeling that this case was getting more complicated rather than less was creeping up like a fog around his head. It had been a long, hard day, and he wanted to go home and tumble into bed and forget half-frozen corpses and bloody snow and shotgun-toting teens and sisters who cried until their cheeks ran black.

"The Northway—that's the highway that runs the length of the state, right?"

"Route Eighty-seven, right."

"That's how you get to Albany."

"Yeah . . ." he nodded. His head was working slowly, but

it was working. "Katie's things. McWhorter and whoever killed him could have been headed for Albany to get something from the house she lived in."

"You haven't been there, yet, have you?"

"No, the Albany P.D. is supposed to cover that." His numb brain finally sparked the right connections. "Shee—it!" he said, snatching at the radio. "Do you remember the address?"

Clare spread her hands helplessly. Russ clicked on the mike. "Dispatch, this is Chief Van Alstyne of the Millers Kill P.D. Can you connect me direct to cruiser Fifty-seven-fifteen?"

There was a blare of static and then Kevin Flynn's voice from the speaker. "Fifty-seven-fifteen. Go ahead."

"Kevin? This is the chief. Cancel the Burnses. I want you and Mark to go to the station, get the Katie McWhorter file, and find the address of her student digs in Albany. Then get on the horn to Albany and have them send someone there immediately. I think whoever killed McWhorter may be headed for that house."

"Ten-four, Chief. Fifty-seven-fifteen out."

Clare looked out the window at the snow-blotched roadway. "You think they might catch the killer?"

"Maybe. The paramedics weren't sure about the time of death, 'cause the cold and the snow do funny things to body temperature. But McWhorter wasn't killed much more than three hours ago, I'll bet. If the snow slowed his killer down enough, and if he takes his time at Katie's house, maybe the Albany P.D. will walk in on him. Worth a shot."

"What are you going to do now?"

"Now? Now I'm going to drop you off at the rectory. What do you think, you've got a free pass to tag along every step of the way?"

Evidently, she did. It wasn't that her arguments for coming with him were irrefutable. She didn't actually refuse to get out of the truck. But somehow, she was still there when he cruised past the Burnses, noting the lit windows and the two vehicles in the driveway. "That doesn't mean they're not involved," he said to her smug smile. "It just means they aren't in Albany right now." He put another call through to the station, asking Durkee and Flynn to head over to the Burnses after they had gotten hold of the Albany police. "And for god's sake make sure someone in Albany calls me if they manage to collar anyone!" he concluded.

Clare's smile disappeared when they drove up to the tiny rental park where Kristen McWhorter lived. "What's she drive?" Russ asked as they cruised slowly along a row of tightly packed, two-story town houses.

"An 'eighty-nine Honda Civic," she said, rubbing condensation off the window, trying to spot Kristen's car somewhere in the parking lot. "Black."

"I don't see it."

They parked in the first available space and waited. After a while, he turned on the truck's radio and fiddled until he had the all-talk station. A gravelly-voiced man was dispensing investment and business advice to callers who identified themselves with names like "Randy from Salt Lake City" and who started each conversation with "I have an extra thirty thousand dollars in convertible debentures to invest . . ." The show broke frequently for mutual fund advertisements and the local weather, which could be summed up as deep and getting deeper.

"I can't believe Kristen had something to do with her father's death." Clare's voice broke in on a guy complaining about his wife sheltering her income in off-shore banks.

"I think you can't imagine people you like doing bad things, that's what I think," Russ said. "You said the same thing about Karen and Geoff and Ethan."

"I never said I liked Geoff Burns," she said, grinning.

"Too bad it wasn't McWhorter," he said. "He made such a satisfying heavy." She nodded. "Too bad it isn't like ninety percent of murders," he continued, "where the husband or the wife or the friend is standing there with the weapon in hand when the cops arrive, saying, 'But I didn't mean to do it!' "

Headlights gleamed at the entrance to the parking lot. A small car crept in, tires churning against the snow. The black Honda Civic pulled in a few spaces away from the pickup. Its interior light flashed weakly as someone opened and shut the door. Russ could barely make out the figure struggling up the sidewalk through the screen of heavy snow, something sizable clutched in her arms. He and Clare both opened their doors, the contrast between the almost too-warm cab and the bone-chilling wind taking his breath away for a moment. He could hear the noise Clare made as her stupid little indoor boots sank into five inches of fresh snow.

"Kristen?" he called.

She whirled, bringing her fist up. Her keys stuck up between her fingers like stubby claws. She held a bulky knapsack against her chest.

Russ raised his hands. "It's me, Chief Van Alstyne. Reverend Fergusson is with me."

"What? What's going on? Is it Katie's baby?"

"We need to talk to you. May we come in?"

Under her black knit cap, Kristen looked at them suspiciously. "Okay." She waded through the snow drifting across her walkway and unlocked the town house door. She kicked her boots against the side of the door to knock off the snow. Russ and Clare followed suit. Inside, they all crammed together on a tiny patch of tile, trying to wrestle off jackets and tug off boots without spreading any more snow than necessary onto the pale green wall-to-wall carpet.

Kristen's place was not what he'd expected from her all-black wardrobe and gothic hair. Instead of vinyl upholstery and posters of thrash groups on the walls, she had import-shop bamboo furniture in white with flowery pastel fabric. Reproductions of gauzy paintings of ballerinas hung over shelves filled with thin paperbacks and stuffed animals. The room of a young girl. One more thing Darrell McWhorter had taken away from her.

"What are you doing out here so late?" Kristen asked, dropping the knapsack on a glass-topped coffee table. "Is there news on Katie's case?"

Clare looked at him as if to say, okay, how do you do this? Damned if he knew. *Your father's had his brains blown out tonight. And by the way, did you do it?* If she didn't have anything to do with McWhorter's murder, he was going to start to look like her personal angel of death. First her sister, then her dad. "Where've you been for the last few hours, Kristen?" he asked.

She raked her hand through her ink-black hair, ruffling it upwards. "I went out for some 'za with my friends tonight after class. I'm studying for my CPA at WCCC." At Clare's raised eyebrows, she explained, "The community college." Russ suspected Clare had been reacting to the idea of Kristen as an accountant rather than puzzling over the acronym. "Look," Kristen said, "Will you please tell me what all this is about?"

The college class and the pizza joint should be easy to check out. "How long did it take you from the time you left the pizza place to the time you arrived here?" he said.

Her face shifted, from annoyed and curious to alarmed and cautious. "Maybe half an hour," she said. "Has something happened?"

Clare stepped close to Kristen and laid a hand on the girl's arm. "Kristen, your father was found dead tonight. He's been murdered. If you know anything about it, please tell us." She cut to the chase as quick as any cop he'd ever seen. Somehow, he'd thought a priest would be more . . . euphemistic.

Kristen gaped. "He's *dead*?" she asked in a shrill voice. Then she burst into tears.

CHAPTER 16

Russ felt like he was in a rerun of a bad television show. Kristen, sobbing and bleeding out her makeup, Clare holding the girl's hand . . . if he wasn't so goddamn tired he'd swear it was Monday morning instead of the middle of Wednesday night.

"Why's she broken up over this guy?" he half-whispered to Clare.

She glared at him from over Kristen's shoulder. "She's not broken up like she was for Katie, for heaven's sake. She's angry."

Kristen wailed. "Now I'll never get a chance to tell him what I thought of him!" She sucked air in great noisy gulps. "Now I'll never know about Katie!"

"If your father killed her, Kristen, he's already paid for it. And if he didn't, we'll find who did. I promise you." He watched Clare rock the girl in her arms and wondered if she would come to distance herself more from the people she wanted to help. She was going to crash and burn in a few years if she kept wading right in and feeling all this personally.

She met his gaze and he saw how tired she was, smudgy dark circles under her eyes, the fine lines on either side of her mouth noticeable. "Kristen," she said, "do you have any idea who your father was meeting tonight? Do you have any ideas who might have killed him?" Russ wasn't entirely convinced Kristen was innocent, for all that her tears might be real. But until her alibi checked out one way or another, he'd go with it.

Kristen shook her head. "I told you, I haven't spoken to him since I left home. I got an unlisted number so he can't call me. I was working up the nerve to call him and Mom about Katie's funeral." She jerked her head up, blinking swollen eyes at Clare. "Oh, God, now I'm going to have to make arrangements for him, too! Mom won't be able to handle it." She closed her hands over her face and wept, frustrated, angry tears that even Russ, who had learned to ignore crying from witnesses, could recognize.

"I can help you," Clare said, rubbing her hands briskly along Kristen's upper arms. "I can help."

Kristen shook her head, dumb animal grief, over and over. "All I wanted was some peace to bury my sister in. Now he's even taken that, the bastard. Why couldn't he leave me and my sister alone. My sisterrrr . . ."

Russ mumbled his excuses and went into the kitchen to look for a telephone and to escape the pain and anger ricocheting through the living room. He suppressed a twinge of guilt at letting Clare take on all the burden of dealing with the girl. There wasn't anything useful to be had out of her, not tonight, and maybe a priest was what she needed now, anyway.

He dialed the station first, and when the message to dial 911 clicked on, he hung up and called the Glens Falls dispatcher. She had the number of the detective in Albany who had been sent out with the black and white to Katie's former home. In Albany, they got cell phones. Better pension plans, too, he'd bet.

Two rings and a brisk, feminine voice answered, "Ramirez here."

"Uh . . . Detective Ramirez?"

"The one and only."

"Detective, this is Chief Van Alstyne, from Millers Kill. I understand you're assisting with a murder we've had up here."

"Chief Van Alstyne. Yeah, I spoke with your man, what's his name? Doofee?"

"Durkee," he said. She owed him that for his obvious surprise at hearing a woman's voice.

"We got a unit here right after we got your message, but your man had already been and gone."

Russ slapped the receiver against his thigh and swore quietly. He jerked the phone back up to his ear in time to hear Detective Ramirez say, ". . . identified himself to the girl as your decedent's father."

"There's a witness?"

"For what it's worth. We've got her downtown with an artist right now, but I wouldn't hold your breath. She's eighteen, she'd had a few beers earlier in the evening, and she thinks everyone over the age of twenty-eight is, and I quote, a wrinkly."

Russ laughed in spite of himself.

"The description we have so far is average height, average weight, no discernible identifying features except for a bushy mustache, which may be fake, and that he was one of the previously mentioned 'wrinklies.' "

Geoff Burns was what, forty? forty-two? Certainly would look like a wrinkly to Emily Colbaum or one of her housemates. And "average" would describe him to a T, until he opened his mouth. Russ sighed. "So, what did the perp do at the house?"

"According to the witness, there had been a call earlier from someone identifying himself as the murder victim's father. Said he was coming down to get some of the girl's things. This guy shows up around nine-thirty, goes to her room, and comes back out ten or fifteen minutes later with a backpack. It's hard to tell at this point if the room was left messy or if he tossed it. We're hoping for prints, of course."

"I know this is a long shot, but do you have any idea what he took from the room?"

"Something that could fit into a student backpack?" Ramirez snorted. "Sorry, Chief. Could be almost anything. Was your girl into drugs?"

"Not that we know," he said. "Was there anything pregnancy-related there?"

"Yeah, there was, as a matter of fact. Couple of books stashed under the bed. *What To Expect When You're Expecting*, that sort of thing. Some used feminine napkins in the wastebasket, but that could have been her period. Look, give me your fax number, and I'll have the complete report and the artist's sketch to you by tomorrow morning. Uh, make that later this morning."

Russ looked at his watch. Christ, it was after twelve. He was going to have to switch shifts with Lyle MacAuley. No way he could be working this case and still be alert enough to pull Friday night patrol tomorrow. He told Detective Ramirez the station's fax number, thanked her for her help, and hung up.

In the living room, Kristen was sitting quietly, her head dropped back against the top of her flowery love seat, staring vacantly at the ceiling. Clare, in the bamboo chair next to her, looked up as he walked in. She asked a question with her eyebrows.

He shrugged. "Someone showed up at Katie's house tonight claiming to be her father. He took something out of her room in a knapsack. One of her housemates was there, she's talking to a police artist right now, trying to give us a description."

Clare glanced at Kristen, who didn't move. "Any chance it was Darrell?" she asked.

"Doesn't sound it. Supposedly an older man with a mustache. I'm not discounting the idea that it might have been a disguise."

Clare looked skeptical. "Who the heck could it be? Ethan? He's in jail."

"Kristen," he said, then again, louder, "Kristen?" She rolled her head to face him without stirring from her position on the love seat. "I've asked you this before, but was there anyone else your sister might have been seeing? Maybe an older man?"

"I told you," she said, her voice raw and tired. "If she was seeing someone else, she never let on to me."

He glanced over to Clare. "The detective in Albany asked if Katie might have been into drugs. Maybe we're on the wrong track, thinking her murder had something to do with the baby. Maybe she got on the wrong side of some bad people."

Clare opened her mouth to respond, but she was cut off by Kristen. "My sister didn't do drugs! Or kiddie porn or illegal adoptions or passing bad checks or anything else! She was a good person. A good person! If you weren't such a cluck-ass small town cop you might have caught the man who did this to her by now!" She lurched upright in the middle of her tirade and stood pointing a shaking finger at Russ.

"Kristen!" Clare jumped to her feet. "That's not fair."

Kristen jerked her head around to face the priest. "What do you know about it! My sister is dead! And the best this guy can do is come here and ask me if I know any reason why she might deserve it? Oh, and by the way, did you kill your father tonight? Well, Chief Van Alstyne," she made his name an insult, "if my sister's murder didn't have anything to do with her baby, maybe some nut case is out to kill off all the McWhorters! Who's gonna be next? Me? Cody?"

"That's enough, Kristen." Clare's voice cut through the air like a helicopter blade, sharp and no-nonsense. "You're exhausted and upset and not thinking." She moved to the door, pulling her coat off the rack and finding her boots with her feet, her eyes never leaving the angry young woman twisting her hands back and forth in front of the loveseat. "You call me tomorrow if you want any help with the arrangements."

She waved a hand at Russ, who was still standing, stocking-footed and wool-headed, in the doorway between the kitchen and the living room. He switched into motion, getting his coat and boots while Clare continued. "Chief Van Alstyne will let you know as soon as he finds out anything about the murders." She laid her hands on Kristen's shoulders and shook her once, like a mother cat settling a kitten. "In the meanwhile, I want you to get yourself something hot to drink and go straight to bed. Try to get a good night's sleep and make sure you eat something in the morning. You have my number." Kristen nodded. "Then we'll say good night." Her voice softened. "I'm sorry, Kristen. About everything." Clare opened the door and jerked her head at Russ. "Time to go." He kept himself from saying, "Ma'am, yes ma'am," but he hustled out the door just the same.

"Good night, Kristen. We'll talk tomorrow." She shut the town house door and hunched her shoulders against the pelting snow, high-stepping past him to the truck in a futile effort to keep her boots from getting even more wet. She was inside, brushing off her jacket, by the time he climbed up into the cab, wincing a little at the ache in his hip. Definitely too long a day. He fired up the engine and sat for a moment, too wiped out to shift into gear and begin the long, slow ride back home. He rubbed his forehead with the palm of his hand. Back to the rectory, that was. Had to take Clare home first. On the radio, a psychiatrist was incredulously quizzing her caller who had fallen in love with her sister's husband. "Reality Check!" Dr. Adele barked like a drill instructor.

He smiled as he reversed out of the parking space, his four-wheel drive chugging against the accumulated snow. "So you really were an officer," he said.

"Sorry if I rolled over you in there, but I—"

"No, no, I appreciate it, really. I never know the right way to handle these scenes. Try to comfort someone and you're just as likely to get an ashtray over the head. Hang tough and be professional, and next thing you know you've got a reputation as a heartless monster or worse, there's a suit for police brutality on your desk."

"Mmmm." She turned her face away from him and leaned against the window.

He concentrated on the road, turning the defroster on full to clear the steam from his windshield. The snow came at him horizontally as he drove, as if nature were trying to sandblast his truck with the icy flakes. Traction was bad, even with his weight and the four-wheel drive. It had been a hell of a night. Thank god he hadn't let Clare drive home in that ridiculous little mosquito of hers.

Between the roar of the heater and the annoying jingle for an auto dealership on the radio—"Fort Henry Ford for Quick Credit Cash Back Cars!"—he missed the first two or three muffled gulps from the other side of the cab. He risked taking his eyes off the road for a moment. Clare was twisted so he couldn't see her face, her arms wrapped tightly around her midsection. He heard her again, the sound of something noisy being swallowed.

"Clare?" For a selfish second, he thought please, please, not another distressed woman. I can't handle any more today. "Are you okay?" The back of her head jerked up and down. He saw the bank of yellow lights ahead and coasted to a slow stop well before the oddly angled intersection of Route 39 and Tanco Road. He had once waited here while the Millers Kill fire department used the jaws of life to remove three mangled bodies from a station wagon that had tried to beat the light in bad weather. The driver had been a guy his age.

"Clare," he said, turning toward her, "if you're okay, will you please look at me?"

The back of her head jerked back and forth. "Clare?" He thought back to how he felt earlier this evening, the weight and tension dropping off of him as he sat across from her at the kitchen table, talking. "Clare, who do you talk to? You asked me that, remember? Who do you talk to, Clare?"

Her voice was thick and tight. "I'll be all right. It's just been a long—" she couldn't continue. The lights turned green. He didn't move. "It's just—" she tried again. "She makes me think of my sister," she finally got out.

"Your sister," he said. "The blond girl in those pictures on your table? What about your sister?"

She turned to him, her eyes bright, her face drawn and pinched. "She died. Five years ago this Thanksgiving." She scrubbed her face with her open hands.

In the mirror, he could see distant lights headed up Route 39. He shifted the truck into gear and carefully drove on through the icy intersection. "Tell me," he said, wondering as he said it why he was asking. He respected people's privacy more than most, and this was clearly a private pain. "What was her name?"

"Grace. She was . . ." She coughed. "She was like a beautiful decoration on a Christmas tree. Funny and loving and frivolous. She was the sweet little sister and I was the tomboy know-it-all big sister. She was the beautiful one and I was the smart one." One side of her mouth crooked up. "She was always trying to get me more interested in clothes and makeup and dating and all that girl stuff that came so naturally to her." She plucked at the leather sleeve of her coat. "She gave me this jacket when I made first lieutenant, because she thought it looked like something a dashing aviatrix would wear."

"She sounds like a very special person," he said quietly.

"She was to us," Clare said. "She never did anything that

would make you stand up and take notice. She worked for our parents' aviation company, secretarial work and book-keeping. Enough to make minimum payments on her credit cards, she used to say. Mostly, she wanted to get married and have lots of kids. She would have, too. She had guys left, right, and center." Clare smiled, a small, inward smile. "She volunteered at the local hospital because she wanted to meet a doctor."

Russ didn't want to hear more. He hated the dread creeping along the edges of his nerves, knowing how the story ended. He wanted the details left off, so he wouldn't have to feel the ache under his sternum that had already begun. Aching for Clare, who had dried her eyes and was speaking in a low, thick voice.

"She was four years younger than me. Twenty-five when she—when it happened. She had had this pain on and off in her abdomen, thought it was indigestion or gas. It finally got bad enough for her to have it checked out." She closed her eyes. "It was colo-rectal cancer, well advanced. She didn't suspect. No one suspected. No one in our family had ever had cancer. She went in for a checkup in the morning and by that evening she was under a death sentence. In one day."

He made the left-hand turn onto Main Street, the truck's rear fishtailing gently before he got it straightened out. The shop lights were almost invisible in the snowy haze.

"I was stationed at Fort Bragg at the time, about four hours from home, so I didn't ask for compassionate leave. Grace moved back into our parents' house and I visited them every weekend. For awhile, I really thought she was going to get better. They treated it very, very aggressively, and I thought, she's twenty-five, she's under the best medical care possible, she has people all over the country praying for her, writing her letters, of course she can't die. Of course she can't die." She folded her hands and pressed them to her mouth as if she were pushing a prayer back into her throat. "Four months.

After four months, 'she can't die' became the problem, not the expectation. Do you know anything about colo-rectal cancer?"

He shook his head.

"She was in agony. She was half-dead from the chemo and the half of her that was alive was suffering every day, all day. The fact that she was young and strong became a . . . a curse, because her body hung on, and hung on . . ." She rested her chin on her tightly clasped hands. "There was an intern she had dated, a friend of hers. Harry Jussawala. He would visit her, sometimes stay with her during treatments in the hospital." She breathed deeply. "He came for Thanksgiving dinner. My folks always have friends as well as family for Thanksgiving. Their house is always open. I wasn't there, I was on duty so one of the married guys could be at home with his family. Anyway, while the rest of them were in the kitchen or outside, Harry went into Grace's room and gave her fifty crushed Valium pills suspended in a solution of cranberry juice and vodka." She looked at Russ. "Does that sound stiff? That's how I always think of it, you know, because that's how I first heard about it from the investigators." Her mouth quirked. "It was a Cape Codder, get it? Her favorite drink. She died within a half hour. She was dead when my mom went in to check on her."

He didn't know what to say. His heart hurt for her. "Oh, Clare. I'm so sorry."

"Harry was never arrested. They talked about murder, then about manslaughter, but in the end, no one could prove anything except that he had brought the crushed Valium to her room. His medical license was revoked. I still don't know, to this day, if it was really her idea to kill herself or if he acted out of his own sense of compassion. She didn't leave a note or anything." Her face crumpled at last. "I never got to say good-bye to her." She furiously blinked back tears. "And you know what's awful? To this day, I don't know whether to curse him or bless him. She was suffering, I know that, and it was going to end in her death. But she was alive! To be put down like a hurting dog . . ." she shook her head sharply, her lips closing tightly over her grief. She rubbed her face again, hard, and sniffled wetly. "I'm sorry. I never talk about this, I don't know what got into me."

He turned onto Church Street, swerving to one side to let a snow plow get by in the other lane. "It's late and you're tired," he said. "Fatigue is like a truth drug, you know. Makes you do and say things you ordinarily wouldn't consider." He stopped at a red light and looked at her. "I think with all this stuff about Kristen and her sister, you needed to talk about Grace, and you needed a friend. I like to think I qualify there."

She wiped a finger under her nose, smiling a little at him. "You do. You surely do. Thanks."

He drove forward, past the park, past St. Alban's, onto Elm Street. Over her protests about not trying to make it into her driveway, he shifted into second and churned a path up to her kitchen door. He was damned if he'd make her walk any farther than she had to in those skimpy boots she had on.

The truck idled quietly. "The guys on the graveyard shift always swing by my place around dawn," he said. "Give me your key. I'll radio them tonight before I turn in, ask if one of them will drive your car back into town if the roads are plowed by then." She nodded, rubbing her eyes once more before fishing a key chain out of her pocket. She looked like a little kid at the end of an overlong day, all flushed cheeks and exhausted, tear-bright eyes. She pulled a key off the ring and handed it to him. "You need me to come in?" he asked.

She shook her head. "I started out this evening hoping I could help you get it all off your chest," she said, smiling. "Didn't expect to be on the receiving end."

He draped his arm over the back of the seat. "Will I embarrass you if I tell you I admire you? The way you listen to people, the way you want to help?"

She smiled more emphatically. "Yes, you will. But thanks. For everything. You're right, you know. I do need a friend." She looked at him seriously. "Thanks. For letting me be just Clare. Instead of the Reverend Fergusson. It's been a long time since I—it's a rare thing to have someone you can just be yourself with, you know. Your whole self."

He was going to make a crack about hanging out with heathens more, but he couldn't, not with her looking at him that way. He shifted his gaze to the dashboard, unable to meet her eyes. "Good night, Clare."

"Good night, Russ." She opened the door and slipped from the cab.

"Clare—" he said. She paused, her hand on the door, the snow swirling around her and into the passenger seat. Her hair stirred in the wind, already hung with feathery snow-flakes.

"Nothing," he said. "Talk to you tomorrow." He waited until he had seen her inside the kitchen before he shifted the truck into gear. She waved at him from the window. He pulled out of her snow-drifted driveway and drove away from the rectory at a much faster speed than was safe.

CHAPTER 17

Clare paused in front of the parish bulletin board, a packing box of Christmas banners propped against one hip. Still woolly-headed from the late night and high emotion, she had tackled the messy, mindless task of digging the church's Christmas decorations out of the undercroft this morning. The Sunday-best of her parishioners' photographs contrasted with her rumpled, sweaty, dusty state and reminded her that she would have to wash and change in order to be presentable. The picture of Karen and Geoffrey Burns caught her eye. They looked so happy and relaxed in the photo, with the kind of sleek contentment that more than enough money brings.

For all of Geoff's raging and Karen's desperation, Clare still couldn't believe that their desire for a child could lead them into murder. She had seen them with that baby in the hospital, seen the instant love and tenderness that was ordinarily lost in the brassy blare of their personalities. Within their small universe of two, they were gentle, caring people. It struck her that perhaps they needed a child most of all so they could show that vulnerable side to another human being.

"Reverend Clare?" Lois's voice broke her concentration. She hoisted the box higher and walked into the secretary's office.

"A few messages for you," Lois said. "Karen Burns called,

and Mr. Felton's daughter, to reschedule your visit. He's going in for some tests and he won't be back to the Infirmary until tomorrow."

"Anything serious?"

"She didn't sound too concerned. The last one was Kristen McWhorter. Is she related to the—"

"Her sister. What did she say?"

"She's going to see her mother, and wondered if you'd come along." Lois pushed the pink message memos across her desk. "Her number's there."

"Thanks." Clare dropped the box against the wall and took the paper slips. "Say, Lois, you don't know anyone who could get the mold spots out of these felt banners, do you?"

The church secretary sniffed a few times. "That's what that smell is." She tilted her head so that her perfectly cut bob swung sideways. "You've come to the right person. Not that I ever have to deal with mold, you understand, but I do know the best dry cleaner in the three-county area."

"Somehow, I knew you would."

In her office, Clare flung herself into her chair with a creak and a snap. She picked up two of the pink papers and held them up, one in each hand, as if weighing Karen Burns against Kristen McWhorter. She looked out the window at the diamond-pieced sky, longing for a four-hour nap. Steam off the smell of moldy old boxes, burrow under her grandmother's quilt, turn her Thelonious Monk CD on low and forget about the world for awhile.

Too bad the inward voice that gently and relentlessly urged her on could find her, even under a Baltimore quilt. And make itself heard even over jazz from the '68 Monmartre session. Heck, God was probably playing at that session. She picked up the phone and dialed.

"Kristen? It's Clare Fergusson. You left a message for me?"

"Yeah. I was hoping . . . I have to go see my mom today

to start sorting things out. I was wondering . . . would you come with me?"

"Are you sure you don't want some privacy with your mother? I mean, if you want to do more than go over the funeral plans with her. You two have some very intense issues to discuss."

Kristen groaned over the phone. "Yeah. The thing is, I think if you were there I'd, you know, be more likely to get to the tough stuff. I know it's asking a lot . . ."

"No, I'd be more than happy to come if I can be helpful, Kristen. It's not asking a lot. I'm glad you thought to call me."

There was a pause. "About last night? I'm sorry I got all weird on you. I was just . . . it was all too much, you know?"

"I know. Believe me, I understand." Clare pulled her over-sized agenda toward her. "I've got a counseling session at three, but I'm free until then. Give me the directions to your mother's apartment, and I'll meet you there." She scribbled the address on a piece of scrap paper and wrote KRISTEN: NOON in the agenda. "Okay. See you in about half an hour."

Someone had hung a pair of plastic wreaths on the front doors of 162 South Street. The peeling apartment facades must have been workingman's flats a hundred years ago. Utilitarian and cheap back then, and not improved by the last thirty years of unemployment and neglect. Still, Clare could see evidence of the coming Christmas as she fishtailed slowly down the street. Crayon-colored reindeer taped in windows, strings of fairy lights wrapped around the posts of one battered and sagging porch.

She parked as close to the curb as she could. No sign of Kristen's black Civic. She kept her engine running to ward off the cold and turned up the Top Forty station on her radio. Everything was calm in the afternoon's watery sunlight, but she couldn't be far from where Russ had answered a domestic disturbance call last Friday when she had gone on patrol with him.

A girl with a toddler balanced on her hip trudged past Clare, ignoring the unusual sports car, intent on keeping her cigarette ash from blowing into the child's face. She couldn't have been more than sixteen, and Clare wondered if it was choice or a lack of them that kept her out of school. This was the sort of young woman and child her proposed program could help, if she could only get the vestry behind her. She blew out her breath in frustration.

A slamming door jerked her back to the here and now. Kristen had arrived. Clare killed the engine and slid out of her car. Kristen walked around the MG, her eyes wide, nodding. "This is your car?" she said.

"Yeah."

"Wow. Way cool. I didn't think priests had enough money for this sort of thing."

Clare laughed. "I don't. I've had it for seven years and if something big goes, I'll be in deep pockets. I really ought to sell it and get something more practical."

"Must be lousy in the snow." Kristen opened the passenger-side door and peered in at the leather interior. "But, oh, man, it sure has some style."

Clare caressed the curve of the hood. "It sure does, doesn't it?"

Kristen clicked the lock and slammed the door shut. She pointed to Clare's side. "You oughtta lock up around here." She glanced up at the third story windows while Clare complied.

"Are you ready for this, Kristen?" Clare asked, picking her way over the sidewalk snowbank to keep her boots dry.

"No. I feel kinda sick to my stomach, to tell you the truth. But I'm here, so hey. Let's do it."

Mrs. McWhorter buzzed them up without comment. The stairs were steep and poorly lit, and Clare wondered if this place could pass a municipal safety inspection. Did Millers Kill have safety inspectors?

The door to 4A swung open at Kristen's knock.

"Hello, Ma," she said, her voice forcibly calm. Clare tried to school her shock at the size of the woman who embraced the ramrod-stiff girl.

Brenda McWhorter pulled away from her surviving daughter, her expression a mixture of hurt and frustration. "Aw, Kristen, don't be like that." Her eyes flickered to where Clare stood in the hall. "Aw, now don't tell me you've brought a cop with you. Krissie . . ."

"She's not a cop, Ma, she's a priest. She's the one who was there the night they found Katie's—the night they found Katie. She's been helping me out. This is Reverend Clare Fergusson."

Clare stuck out her hand. "Mrs. McWhorter," she said, rummaging for something to say. "Pleased to meet you" and "Sorry about your husband" seemed grotesquely inappropriate under the circumstances. "I'm so very sorry about your recent losses," she said. "From everything I've heard, Katie was an exceptional girl. She'll be missed." *And as for your husband, good riddance to bad rubbish*, Grandmother Fergusson added.

Brenda McWhorter shook hands and led Kristen and Clare into the apartment. They bunched awkwardly in front of a massive maple sideboard. "Well, go ahead, take your coats off," Mrs. McWhorter said, gesturing toward a row of hooks by the door. "Same place, nothin's changed since you left."

Kristen rolled her eyes but obediently gathered up Clare's bomber jacket and hung it alongside her own bulky coat.

"What interesting pieces you have," Clare said. "They look like antiques."

Brenda surveyed her kingdom. "They were my parents'. Came from the big farmhouse we had out toward Cossayaharie. We had to sell it when my dad passed, but I kept some of the furniture."

Kristen plunked herself into the narrow Victorian settee and crossed her arms. "What are you gonna do now that he's gone, Ma? Move back out to Aunt Pat's? Get a job? What?"

Her mother sat, an operation that required her to lower her center of gravity over a well-used, well-sprung chair and then drop in a controlled fall. "Well, honey, I thought I'd stay right here. I know that we've had some problems in the past, but I figured now your daddy's gone you and I can take up again, get to be friends. I got enough money to keep me . . ."

Clare sat on a cane-seated ladder chair, her face composed and pleasant, wondering how another human being could let herself get that large. She shifted in her chair. No, that wasn't fair. Not everyone grew up in an active family and started off in a career that demanded physical fitness. On the other hand, basic self-respect should get you off the sofa and on your feet—she twitched. She didn't call alcoholism a lack of self-respect. She shouldn't see obesity that way, either. If some people didn't have the discipline to push away from the table after a third helping—her cheeks warmed at her persistent failure of compassion. Dear God, she thought, help me to accept as Christ accepted. Keep my mind on helping, not judging. And remind me to put in a five-mile run this evening.

Kristen was going over her mother's financial situation, asking to look over the pension and insurance documents, quizzing her on any other benefits. Mrs. McWhorter was at best vague about money matters.

"Ma, you're going to have to learn to keep a checkbook now. Come on down to the bank tomorrow and I'll set you up. That way, I can help you balance your account for awhile. You got the information on the CDs and the savings? Can I see it, please?"

Mrs. McWhorter heaved herself up from her chair and waddled down the hall. "Isn't she smart?" she tossed back to Clare.

Clare turned to Kristen, still sitting back with her arms

crossed defensively over her chest. "You are smart about finances," she said.

"Everybody's good about something, they say. I like it. I like numbers."

"So consistent, aren't they? So easy to control." Kristen shot her a look. Clare went on. "It can be a lot easier to throw yourself into your work than to face personal problems, have you noticed that? It's comfortable and distracting."

Kristen shot up from the settee and threaded her way through the heavy furniture to the pass-through kitchen. "You want something to drink? I know Ma's got soda in here."

"I'm fine. Are you going to ask your mother about what she'd like for the funerals?"

Brenda McWhorter lumbered up the hallway, a sheaf of papers and envelopes in her hand. She stopped dead at Clare's words. "Aw, Krissie," she said. "We do gotta talk about that. You're gonna take care of the details, aren't you, honey? You know I'm no good at that sort of thing."

Kristen slammed the refrigerator door with enough force to set the contents rattling. "Yeah, Ma, I'm gonna take care of the details. I know you're no good at that sort of thing." Her voice began to crack. "You don't like to deal with life's crappy little details." She slammed a liter bottle of orange soda on the counter and knocked over two plastic glasses in the drainboard before grabbing hold of one.

"Krissie . . ."

"Ma, I'm the kid here, remember? You're the mom. You're supposed to be taking care of me, not the other way around." The soda slopped over the pebbled sides of the glass. "You were supposed to take care of me and Katie and I gotta tell you, Ma, you did a piss-poor job of it." A barking sob escaped her before she covered her mouth.

"Krissie . . ." Brenda's hands fluttered ineffectually. Clare suddenly saw, very clearly, the small woman inside that bulky disguise. Had she done that to herself? Or was it more of

Darrell's handiwork? "I tried . . . you don't understand. You never understood what it was like to need someone." She looked down at the paperwork charting how her and Darrell's money had grown over the years. She looked beseechingly toward Clare. "In a lot of ways, he was a real good husband and father."

Clare clenched her teeth tightly to keep her gorge down.

"Ma, I gotta know. Was he doing Katie? Did he start messing with her after I moved out?"

"Kristen! How can you say that!"

Her daughter leaned over the speckled countertop, hands braced. "I know. We never say that, do we? We none of us ever came right out and said what was happening, did we? Not even Katie and me. Did he, Ma? Did he?"

Brenda dropped her gaze to the carpet and shook her head. "He . . . I dunno if Katie told him something or if it was . . . if it was just you. He was good around Katie." She looked up at her daughter again. "I couldn't lose him, Krissie. I didn't think . . ." She looked at the papers in her hand. "I didn't think about it, that's all. You gotta learn to overlook some things when you're married. He took good care of me, and he loved me." She started to cry.

"Aw, Ma. Jesus, Ma. You didn't think about it." Kristen plodded around the counter and put her arms as far around her mother as she could. "Ma, he used all of us." Her voice cracked, but she went on, "I made myself into the kind of person who will never get used again, and you can, too. It's not too late."

Her mother shook her head. "I ain't tough like you nor smart like Katie. I've always needed somebody to help me get along. I know you hate him, and I can't blame you, you got that right. But I don't know what I'll do without him. God damn him for thinking he could make one last big deal."

Clare stepped forward involuntarily. *What?*

Kristen wiped her eyes and nose with her sleeve. "Geez, him and his big deals . . ."

"Kristen." The girl looked at Clare, red-nosed and blotchy-eyed. "If your father was killed while involved in one last 'big deal,' whoever he was dealing with may have been his killer." Brenda jerked her head off her daughter's shoulder. "It may have been Katie's killer."

Kristen and Clare both looked at Brenda, who stepped back out of her daughter's hold. "No," she said. "I don't wanna borrow trouble, Krissie, and neither do you." She darted a glance at Clare. "I already said my piece to the cops, I don't got anything else to say."

"Ma . . ." Brenda shook her head, backing away another step. Kristen's eyes narrowed. "Ma," she hissed, "if you know something and don't tell me, I'm heading out this door and you can bury Dad in a shoebox by yourself for all the help you'll get from me."

Clare laid a hand on the girl's arm. "I don't think your mother's reluctant so much as she's scared. Is that it, Mrs. McWhorter?"

The woman shifted from foot to foot, her gaze darting from Kristen to Clare to Kristen again, her face a mask of misery. "I don't want no trouble from the police," she said.

"The police will have to know what you tell us," Clare said, "but I don't see that they need to know who told us." She caught Brenda's eyes, wide and white, and made herself still, wiping out everything she already knew about the woman, her whole body open, listening.

Clare held Brenda's gaze until the older woman sighed and quivered in relaxation. "Darrell said he knew who the baby's father was. Said he had surprised Katie and him together last winter, in a car." She looked at the sheaf of papers trembling in her hand. "He said he could get money from the guy. He called him that afternoon, that last afternoon."

"Darrell called someone?"

"Oh my God, Ma, do you know the phone number? Do you know his name?"

Brenda's face quivered. "He didn't tell me none of the details, honey. You know I'm not good—"

"Not good with details. Yeah, I know."

"There was a phone number written down." Clare's heart squeezed with excitement. Now they were getting somewhere. "I thought about doing something with it, but I wound up throwing it into the disposal." Clare couldn't help a small groan of frustration. "I was scared. I figured whoever this man was, he'd killed your father and maybe your sister and who's to say he couldn't kill me, too. I may not be smart, but I know when to keep my mouth shut."

"Mrs. McWhorter, when Darrell told you that he was going to get in touch with this man, did either one of you consider that you were going to be making a deal with the man who probably killed your daughter?" Clare knew she was speaking too sharply, but Brenda's monstrous self-absorption was sucking the patience out of her.

"Well . . ." Brenda looked uncertainly at Clare. "You know, there wasn't nothin' gonna bring Katie back, was there? And maybe Darrell would have turned him in after he'd gotten what he wanted." She opened her hands. "I didn't really . . . think about it."

CHAPTER 18

Russ was dropping piles of papers on the big scarred-oak table in the briefing room when Mark Durkee strolled in, fifteen minutes early for the evening shift. "Hey, Chief. How y'doing?"

"This goddamn case is giving me a goddamn headache," Russ informed him, slapping down a manila folder next to a reprint of Katie McWhorter's high school photo.

"Actually, I was thinking more like, how are you feeling after that shootout at the Stoner's place yesterday? Everything cool?"

Lyle MacAuley stopped in the doorway, already changed into his civvies. "Yeah, Chief. That post-cow stress disorder can be a killer." Mark laughed. "Maybe you ought to have yourself checked out," Lyle went on helpfully, "make sure you didn't pick up any hoof-and-mouth disease."

Russ gave both of them what he hoped was a killing look.

Mark laughed harder. "Really, Chief, we were worried about you."

Lyle nudged past the younger officer. "Hell, Mark, it'll take a lot more than some pumped-up kid with a shotgun to take out the chief here. It takes a solid ton of muscle, hide, and milk to make the man sweat." He leaned over the assorted folders and files, his bushy, graying eyebrows rising in interest. "Whatcha got here?"

"I'm drowning in reports on the McWhorter case. I'm sorting everything out, trying to shake something loose." Russ slid a broken stick of chalk across the table to Lyle. "Get up to the board there, Lyle, help me time line this thing out."

Lyle moved to the school-room sized blackboard hanging on the windowless wall of the briefing room.

Russ opened the medical examiner's report on Katie McWhorter. "Friday, December fourth." Lyle chalked the date in the upper left-hand corner. "Sometime between seven and nine o'clock, the killer—no, wait, better make that killer A—bashes Katie's head in and drives off." Underneath the time, Lyle added "A→Katie McW."

"A could be one or both of the Burnses. They have no alibi other than each other for Friday night. It could have been Darrell McWhorter—"

"Those names he gave you checked out, though," Lyle reminded him. "Dave Jackson?" He stepped back to the table and ran his finger over the single-sheeted investigative reports. "Here it is. He was ready to affidavit that he and his wife had been with the McWhorters from seven to eleven that night."

"Yeah, I know. Okay, erase McWhorter. Ethan Stoner could have done it, too. He had the truck, he had the time, and he was mighty riled up about something that night when I saw him around ten or so."

"I took his initial statement," Mark said. "He said his friends would testify that he'd been with them all that evening."

Lyle and Russ looked at each other. "Is it me, or does that boy seem awful young to you?" Lyle asked.

Russ pushed the bridge of his glasses up his nose. "I'm sure his friends would say just that, Mark. And I'm just as sure that five minutes of grilling would bust that story wide open if the Stoner boy hadn't been babysat all night by his buddies."

Lyle wrote down the name.

"Ethan's blood type checks out as the possible father of Katie's baby. But," Russ tapped the hospital's test report, "Noble showed Katie's picture around to the local motel owners and found that the guy who runs the Sleeping Hollow Motor Inn saw Katie with some man who wasn't Ethan Stoner right around Thanksgiving. Had a record of the car and everything. We ran a match on the '86 Nova they were driving. Turns out it's one of Katie's roommate's cars. We haven't been able to match the name and the numbers on the license the guy showed the clerk, which leads me to believe it's a fake I.D. So, Katie and whoever stayed three days, and when they left, they took a blanket with them that's an exact match to one of the blankets the baby was wrapped in."

"So Ethan's not the father?" Mark hitched a hip onto a wide sill and leaned back against the wire mesh covering the lower half of the tall, turn-of-the-century window.

"I don't like Ethan as the father," Russ said. "It doesn't fit with what we know about Katie. She broke up with him clean, and according to her sister, she was nice to him, but not friends with him, after that. She doesn't strike me as a girl who'd have jumped in the sack with her old boyfriend on a whim."

"Doesn't mean Ethan couldn't have killed her when he found out about the baby," Lyle said. "He wouldn't be the first rejected guy to build up a fantasy about getting together with a girl and then turn violent when reality intrudes. And let's face it, we've seen he's capable of picking up a gun and threatening to kill someone."

"I know. That's why I haven't discounted him as her murderer." Russ flipped open the medical examiner's report on Darrell McWhorter. "Let's take a look at the next one. Darrell McWhorter meets with the Burnses on the morning of December eight." Lyle noted the date. "He tells them he and his wife are keeping the baby, because it's the last link to their little girl or some cowpuckie like that. Sometime between eight and ten that night, he's shot to death by the side of the Old Schuylerville Road. Probably while on his way down to Albany. In Albany, some man shows up at Katie's house around ten o'clock, says he's her father and ransacks her room."

"It couldn't have been Ethan Stoner, because he was sitting in the county jail in Glens Falls at the time," Mark reminded him.

Lyle tapped the chalk stick against the Burnses' names. "How 'bout these two?"

"How 'bout them?" Russ said. "Again, no alibi except each other. Reverend Fergusson and I drove past their place at eleven-thirty that night, and both cars were in the drive."

"It only takes an hour to get to Albany," Lyle said. "An hour and a half in bad weather."

"Was the Northway speed limit reduced to forty-five last night?" Russ asked.

"Nope. Snow wasn't that bad, the plows kept up with it."

"So it'd be tight, but possible."

"Maybe they have a winter rat," Mark said.

Lyle and Russ looked at each other again. Lyle nodded thoughtfully. It was a common practice for people to protect their good cars from the ravages of rock salt, potholes, and cycles of freezing and thawing water by garaging them between December and March and driving a winter rat instead; any junky old heap with a heater and a defroster that worked.

"If they did," Mark went on, "One of them could have taken it out while the other one stayed home, parking the cars in the drive, turning on the lights, maybe even making phone calls to establish an alibi."

"Is it just me, or does that boy seem awfully smart to you?" Russ asked. Lyle grinned. "Okay, Mark," Russ continued, "run with it. Get into the DMV records and find out how many vehicles are registered to Mr. and Mrs. Burns. Don't forget to check any that might be under her maiden name. Or registered to their law practice instead of to them as individuals."

"If it was Geoff Burns who tossed the student apartment in Albany," Lyle said, "what was he after?"

"Maybe there was something there that would tie him to Katie's murder," Russ said. "A letter, a note she wrote to herself—something." He leaned one-handed against the table and tapped the folder containing the Burnses' statements. "The way I see it, during the negotiations with the Burnses, Darrell thinks of whatever it is that could prove Geoff Burns killed his daughter. So he calls everything off. Tightens the screws, makes the Burnses see he's going to play hardball. Then he calls Burns later, tells him about the evidence or whatever, and arranges the meeting. On the way to Albany, Burns shoots him."

"Burns shoots him because . . ."

"Hell, I don't know. To cover up the blackmail? Because Darrell pissed him off bad enough? Geoff Burns has a temper like a bantam rooster, and believe me, Darrell McWhorter was the kind of guy you could easily get pissed off at."

Lyle took aim at Mark with a half-cocked finger. "Did you ask 'em about owning any firearms when you spoke with 'em last night?"

"She's got a nine-millimeter Smith and Wesson registered in her name. Said she keeps it in the trunk of her car for when she's traveling long distances alone. I didn't even ask to see it at the time. It was late, and the chief had said to go real carefully."

Russ nodded. "We're gonna need a warrant to be able to test that weapon, sure enough."

Lyle crossed his arms over his flannel shirt and looked at the worn-down green chalkboard, where abbreviations and arrows connected the Burnses to Katie and Darrell Mc-Whorter. "You think you got enough to convince Judge Ryswick to let you take a look at that gun? These are a couple of lawyers, remember. People like him. Not the usual type to get hauled up on a murder charge."

Russ sighed. "Dunno. Maybe." He pointed at the three events Lyle had written down and circled. "We've got an abandoned baby. We've got a dead mother and a dead grandfather. So, do we have three separate suspects, one who fathered the baby, one who killed Katie, and one who killed Darrell?"

"Too complicated. I don't like it," Lyle said.

"So maybe we have one suspect. The same man who was at the motel with Katie when her baby was presumably born, later killed her and her father. It's a lot neater, but we've got squat evidence." He rapped his knuckles on Katie McWhorter's autopsy report. "Or we have one man, identity unknown, who is Cody's father, and one other suspect who did both the McWhorters." He smiled one-sided at Mark, who squinted up at the blackboard's crisscrossing lines. "Maybe I should take the chalkboard in with me to Ryswick, you think?"

"I think finding another car will help." Lyle dropped the chalk into Russ's hand and headed for the door. "Maybe we'll luck out and find a bloody baseball bat locked in the trunk."

"Oh, yeah," Russ said. "A signed confession, too. Get out of here, stop bucking for overtime."

Lyle rounded the corner, waving good-bye. Over the sound of his boots clumping down the wooden stairs, Russ could hear him mooing.

"That guy," he said to Mark. "Tell you what, you do the run-down on the Burnses' registration, and I'll cover your patrol time until you're done. I'll just drive the squad car home afterwards if I'm not near the station."

"You don't have to be home?"

"Nope. I'm batching it until Linda gets back on Saturday."

"You got a deal."

The streets had been plowed clear early in the morning, and the day's sun, though intermittant, had warmed things up enough to dry up the slush. It was a pleasure to drive without having to pay too much attention to the condition of the road. Russ headed south, where the scenery opened up into long valleys between easy, rolling hills. The lights of farmhouses and barnyards scattered across the landscape, familiar and comforting. To the west, and behind him, to the north, the Piedmont rose in wave after rounded wave. The great hills broke the sky into two darknesses, the one above glittering with stars, the one below glowing, here and there, with snow.

He loved this part of the world more than any other, loved the sight of those old hills surrounding him. There was something unknowable about them, a mystery that had been there when the first Dutch and Scottish settlers had carved farms for themselves along the rivers running out of the vast wilderness. With the dark hills looming and the lights few and far between, it was easy to imagine what it had been like nearly three hundred years ago. The Adirondacks were still a wild and sometimes dangerous place, sparsely settled, with few roads in and out of the great Adirondack Park, a wilderness stretching thousands of square miles over ten counties. Every year, a few unprepared or incautious people went into these mountains and never came out.

He thought about that fight he had had with Linda their first winter here, when she was planning on driving up to Gore Mountain to consult on a curtain order for somebody's chalet. He had insisted she pack the car with a blanket, a self-heater, a flare, and even rations. She couldn't believe a stalled engine or a car in a snow-covered ditch could be fatal. He had won that one, and was rewarded, when she got back, by her casual observation that the chalet hadn't had another neighbor within twenty miles. Twenty steep, single-lane, hardly plowed miles.

"Ten-fifty to Ten-fifty-seven, over." The crackle of the radio brought him back to his squad car.

"Ten-fifty-seven, go," he said.

"Mark's all done, Chief," Harlene said, "and he says to tell you he hit the jackpot. There is another car."

"Yes!" He pumped the radio receiver in truimph. "Give that man a kiss, Harlene."

"Well, if I gotta . . ."

"I'll sign off and take this unit back to my house if he's ready to roll."

"Okay, I'll log you off duty. You had a phone call a while back. Reverend Fergusson."

"Clare called?"

"Ayeh. Said she wanted to talk with you about the McWhorter case."

"Oh. That all?"

"Yes, that's all. She's a smart girl, she knows better than to waste a police dispatcher's time with a lot of chit-chat."

"Uh huh. Don't forget who signs your paychecks, honey."

"The town clerk. I won't."

He laughed. "Okay, thanks, Harlene. I'll see you tomorrow." He realized a second after he clicked the unit off that he didn't have Clare's number on him. He thought about calling Harlene back and getting it, but it was only fifteen, twenty minutes into town. He'd feel better if he could check up on her, make sure she was doing okay after everything that had happened last night. And while he was there, it would be worthwhile checking that MG of hers, making sure she was prepared for a winter breakdown. He swung the squad car across lanes and headed back north, toward the ancient hills half-hiding the winter stars.

*　　*　　*

St. Alban's was dark when he swung past it from Church Street onto Elm. For a moment, he thought the rectory was dark, too, until he saw the lights shining out the back of the house. Of course, it was seven o'clock. She was probably making dinner. Nothing like showing up uninvited and unexpected at suppertime. He parked behind her car and trudged along the beaten-down snow. Didn't she have anyone to plow for her? He kicked his boots against the lowest stairstep before mounting to the door.

The kitchen door was as uncurtained as the rest of the house, and Russ could see the rector of St. Alban's sipping red wine and cooking up a storm on her gas stove. She was wearing jeans and a University of Virgina sweatshirt hacked off around the waist. From the bulk of the sleeves pushed up her arms, it must have belonged to one of her hulking brothers at one point. He could hear music through the glass, the pounding of the bass vibrating throught his palm when he touched it. Some group from the 'eighties, Sons of the West or something, singing, "Live it up, live it up, Ronnie's got a new gun," and as he watched, smiling helplessly, Clare shimmied back and forth shaking some sort of dried herb from a little glass bottle into an enameled pot on the stove. He started laughing at the point where the music blasted, "You can take all your flags and march 'em up and down," because she did just that, swinging her hips and jabbing a wooden spoon in the air. Russ knocked loudly on the door before he could scare her by suddenly appearing in her window when she turned around.

He startled her anyway. She spun at the sound, dropping the spoon, her stockinged feet slipping on the floor. She didn't screech, but she did clap a hand dramatically to her chest as she reached for the door. "Holy cow, you nearly gave me a heart attack," she said, standing in the doorway.

"Sorry." He retreated down a step, so her eyes were almost level with his. Coming over in person suddenly seemed intrusive. "I'm sorry, I should have just called."

"I tried to reach you at the station," she said, crossing her arms around herself against the cold. A gust of wind stirred her hair. "Good lord, it's freezing out here. Please, come in."

He paused. "Just for a minute." He stomped more snow off on the top step. There was a wide rubber mat inside the door and beside it, a cardboard moving box held rubber rain-boots and a pair of wet running shoes. A coat tree tilted pre-cariously toward the telephone, weighed down by the Millers Kill police-issue parka she still hadn't returned.

She shut the door behind him. Her arms were still crossed, the wooden spoon clenched in one fist. "Please. Take your things off. Can I—oh, dang!" A dollop of tomato sauce had dripped off the spoon onto the worn white linoleum. Clare grabbed a rag and swiped at it while Russ shucked off his parka and hung it on the opposite side of the tree. There was a calendar thumbtacked into the wall next to the phone, pic-turing a stained glass window. There were saints listed in most of the days, and each Sunday was highlighted in red.

Clare tossed the rag into a bland, stainless steel sink, and replaced the spoon in the pot. She leaned one hip against the counter, her arms crossed again, while Russ rocked back and forth in his boots, reluctant to tread muck all over her floor, hesitant about taking them off.

"Oh, take off your boots and sit a spell," Clare said, as if he were a book she could read. Bent over unlacing, he could hear her deep breath. "I wanted to apologize for last night," she said. "I never just break down like that. It was inappro-priate and poorly timed and I'm sorry." It sounded as if she had practiced the speech.

Russ straightened, sliding his boots off heel by heel. "Never? You never break down and cry?"

A flush rose in her cheeks. "Okay, almost never. Certainly not with someone I haven't known for very long." She clapped her hands to her cheeks. "Oh, this is embarrassing."

He sat in one of the four wooden chairs clustered around the kitchen table. "Funny. It doesn't feel as if we haven't known each other for very long. Does it?"

She blinked. "Honestly? No. It doesn't."

He spread his hands. "Remember what you asked me last night? 'Who do you go to when you feel this way?' "

She smiled faintly, then laughed, a breathing out kind of laugh. "You're doing me, aren't you? That's supposed to be me. Okay, okay, you're right. I guess I don't need to apologize for dumping on you."

"I bet you'd call it 'sharing' or 'venting' if somebody did it to you."

"Hmmmm." She turned to the stove to transfer sauteed mushrooms from an iron skillet to the sauce pot.

The rectory kitchen was a faded white, with a dull and unpolished white linoleum floor, unornamented white cupboard doors, a serviceable white refrigerator, and a matching dishwasher next to the sink. The whole room had been turned out as cheaply and inoffensively as possible around fifteen or twenty years ago, he guessed. Reminded him of army housing.

Clare had evidently dealt with the blandness by littering the refrigerator door with photos, clippings, and cartoons, and hanging up a series of framed prints, each one featuring a single vegetable: an improbably wide carrot, a voluptuous eggplant, an aggressive tomato.

Crimson and yellow canisters marched across the white and gray-veined countertops, accompanied by thick glass jars filled with exotically shaped pastas. The sauce pot she was vigorously stirring was a startling cobalt blue, and whatever was in it, it smelled to him like he had died and gone to Provence.

She turned back to him in time to see the expression on his face. She laughed. "Hungry? Why don't you stay for supper?"

"Oh, no. No, I couldn't," he said, as unconvincingly as possible.

She opened the refrigerator door, retrieved a wedge of cheese and plunked it on a cutting board in front of him. "You can grate the Parmesan," she said. She rummaged in one of the drawers a moment before handing him what looked like the top of an egg beater with no beaters attached. "Just stick a chunk of cheese in that opening there and turn the handle," she said, pointing. "It does all the work. Grates hazelnuts, too."

She opened the oven door, releasing a cloud of bread-flavored steam. His stomach rumbled at the smell like a dog whining to be fed. "Almost done," she said, shutting the door and retrieving her wine glass. She leaned against the counter. "I went with Kristen McWhorter today to her parent's apartment."

"That dump? Jesus, you—sorry—you shouldn't be wandering around that neighborhood by yourself. And for God's sake, stay away from that family until we've closed on whoever killed McWhorter."

"For God's sake? For God's sake I should stay away?" She grinned at him hugely. He shook his head, pushed his glasses up his nose and applied himself to the over-complicated grating gadget she had stuck him with.

"As I was saying, I met Brenda McWhorter, and she told me that between the time I saw him at St. Alban's and the time he showed up dead, Darrell McWhorter got in touch with the man he said was Cody's father. Evidently, he had seen the two of them together some time before Katie left for college, although Brenda didn't know anything about it. Obviously, he thought he could get money out of the guy by threatening to reveal his identity."

"What?" He let the grater drop to the cutting board, a pungent chunk of Parmesan still stuck in its basket. "He made a call to Cody's father? Was she sure? It couldn't have been to

Katie's killer? Darrell knew who had killed her and was preparing to blackmail him?"

She tucked her hair behind her ears. "He told Brenda he knew who had fathered Katie's baby. She didn't know his name or their plans for meeting." She grimaced. "The woman was so self-absorbed, it was scary. She hadn't even been bothered that Darrell was going to cut a deal with the man who might very well be her daughter's killer."

He picked up the grater and pressed the cheese further into the opening. "That's assuming we're dealing with one person. That Katie's lover was also her killer. And Darrell's."

She sipped her wine. "It certainly indicates they were one and the same."

He finally jammed the Parmesan in and slid the cover shut. He cranked hard, nearly wrenching the gadget from his hand. He gripped it more tightly and tried again. The nutty-sweet smell of Parmesan burst from the grater as he showered the cutting board with fine shavings. "I was going with this scenario: Geoff Burns killed Katie, Darrell had something that linked Burns to her murder and threatened him, Burns met with Darrell and iced him. Literally."

"But if Darrell was blackmailing the father of the baby, and not Geoff Burns . . ."

"Maybe he was working both of them. There's no guarantee whoever it was met with Darrell, after all. Maybe he had the wrong guy, anyway. What if he was thinking of some boy she walked home from school with, or went to the sock hop with?"

Clare pulled a chair from under the table and straddled it backwards, still holding her wine glass. "Listen to you. Have you ever heard of Occam's Razor?"

"No. What is it, like a Columbian necktie?"

"It's a principle of logic that says that the simplest theory is usually the right one. Which is simpler, that Geoff Burns killed Katie, negotiated with Darrell, was blackmailed by Darrell who also and at the same time was blackmailing Cody's biological father, and shot him? Oh, also rifling Katie's student digs and returning home in time for us to see both their cars in their driveway at eleven thirty?" She pointed a finger at him. "Or is it simpler to say there's one man, who fathered Katie's child, and in a panic to cover it up, killed both Katie and her dad, the only two people who could reveal his identity?"

"Murder isn't something you can apply principals of logic to, Clare. Bad guys kill people for reasons that are too stupid to believe."

"I'm not saying his reasoning was logical. I'm saying we need to be logical."

"We do?" He shook a last few flakes of Parmesan free and laid the grater on the board. "We?"

She pushed back her chair and took the cutting board to the counter. "You know what I mean." She pointed to one of the cupboards. "Plates are in there."

Dinner was a lamb stew thick with winter vegetables, garnished with Parmesan. He went through half the loaf of golden-crusted bread sopping up the sauce. "Where'd you learn to cook like this?" he asked between mouthfuls.

"My grandmother Fergusson. We went to live with her and Pawpaw when I was seven. I was a handful. A tomboy in a household of Southern ladies and mad at the world to boot. One day she caught me dropping eggs off the veranda to see what would happen to 'em. She marched me into the kitchen and tied about an acre of apron around me and said, 'I'm going to teach you to put those eggs to better use, missy.' " She smiled. "First thing she taught me to make was meringue. Talk about starting at the top."

He grinned. "I can just see you. You must have been a cute kid."

"Lord, no. I was a homely little girl. My sister got the looks."

He shook his head. "There isn't such a thing as a homely little girl." He tore off another hunk of bread. "And I've seen pictures of your sister. She was pretty, yeah, but pretty like hundreds of other girls. You," he dabbed the bread in the air as if sketching her, "you're . . . memorable. Who you are just shines through your face." He popped the bread in his mouth and watched, amused, as she blushed bright red. "You're one fine-looking woman, Reverend." She clapped her hands over her cheeks. He laughed.

She snorted loudly and jumped up from the table to ladle more stew into her bowl. "I should have you meet my mother. She loooves," she drawled out the word, "a flatterin' man." She turned and batted her eyelashes hard enough to create a breeze. "More stew, Chief?"

He surrendered his bowl. "Yeah. Sounds like you miss your family."

"Sometimes." She put his stew in front of him and sat down. "Sometimes I'm glad we have some distance between us. My decision to enter the priesthood, coming on the heels of Grace's death, was hard for them. It wasn't what they had wanted for me."

"You can't blame them. It's a lot to give up." He blew on a spoonful of stew. "All parents want their kids to have the same things they had. Marriage and a family. I know my mom regrets that Linda and I never had any children."

She leaned back in her chair, her head cocked. "Marriage and a family?"

"You know, giving that up to be a priest."

She grinned, then quickly covered her smile with her hand. "I think you're under some misapprehension here. Episcopal priests don't take a vow of chastity. We can get married, have kids, the whole nine yards."

"What?" He dropped his spoon into the bowl and stared at her. "But the old priest, the one you replaced, he was there forever and he never—"

"Some priests choose to remain celibate. But it's just that, a choice. Not an obligation."

"Huh. If that don't beat all." He watched as she devoured a wad of sauce-soaked bread. He felt unsettled and annoyed, as if she had deliberately kept the truth from him. He tried to picture her going out for a night on the town with a man and his mind drew a blank. "You'd think they'd just call you ministers, then, instead of all this priest business and the white collar and all."

She sighed, pushed her chair back and headed for the living room. "Hang on," she said. She reemerged a minute later to hand him a large paperback.

"*The History and Customs of the Episcopal Church in America*," he read. "Sounds like a real page turner."

"If I can read up on the Iroquois Nation, you can read up on my church. Now, finish that stew up and you can have some pumpkin roll for dessert."

He declined dessert on behalf of his waistband, which had a tendency to shrink in the wash when he ate too much. She turned down his offer to help wash the pots and pans, but she did let him load the dishwasher.

"Would you like some coffee?"

"No, I'd better get going. It's late." He climbed back into his boots and parka. "Thanks for the dinner."

"It was my pleasure. Company makes the meal, Grandmother Fergusson used to say."

He stuck out his hand just as she wrapped her arms around herself. Like an idiot, he shoved his hands into his pockets just as she reached out to shake. Finally, he slapped his hand around hers and pumped her arm like he was at a Rotary Club Meeting. Over the lingering odors of dinner, he could smell her, fresh and green, like new-mown hay in his brother-in-law's field. "Night, now," he said, and yanked open the door so hard he could hear the hinges bite into wood. They both looked at the door frame. He turned to her, frowning. "And for God's sake, lock your doors."

The squad car was freezing. He cursed the heater, cursed the weather, cursed the drive back to a dark and empty house. Why the hell had Linda gone on this fabric-buying trip anyway? He wanted her home. Only two more days. Then he'd feel better.

CHAPTER 19

Clare knew she ought to be more interested in the boiler. She flexed her chilly fingers together and glanced at the papers on the black oak table, listening for the telltale hiss and rattle of the radiators. She seemed to be the only one who noticed that the meeting room—the entire parish hall—never warmed up, so Robert Corlew's projections on repairing the aging water heater ought to have her spellbound. Contractors, unfortunately, rarely made compelling speakers.

"—rests directly on blocks, so that the insulation can be applied—"

She needed to be getting more sleep. Through diamond-paned windows, she could see the front corner of St. Alban's, its stone walls massed like a storm front against the wan December light. So little daylight on a Friday afternoon, she thought, already noon and only four more hours 'til sunset. A month or more until she could see longer days. She flexed her shoulders back, stretching the neckline of her thick wool sweater, causing her collar to tug against her throat. She turned her attention back to the table, where Vaughn Fowler was calling the vote.

"Aye," she said, copying the rest of the votes. Had she just agreed to replacing the hot water heater with a nuclear powered furnace?

"All right, then, we're agreed to hold off replacing Old Bessy until the replacement prices go down this summer."

Serves you right, missy, she could hear her grandmother Fergusson say. *If you're cold, put on another sweater.*

Terence McKellan and Mrs. Marshall pushed their high-backed chairs away from the table. "Before you go," Clare said, "I'd like to update you on the Burnses' situation. The letter-writing campaign is going very well, with lots of participation. The police have a strong lead on the identity of Cody's father, and as soon as he's identified, we're going to try to persuade him to sign adoption papers naming the Burnses as parents." At least she hoped someone would be able to get the paperwork in front of him before Russ hauled him off to jail. "With that in mind, I have some more facts and figures about the mother-and-baby outreach project that I intend to present at our next meeting."

Sterling Sumner harrumphed, but the rest of the board managed at least polite expressions of interest. The meeting adjourned. Clare headed straight for the coffee machine. She poured herself a cup, yawning convulsively.

"Tired?" Terry McKellan grinned. His coat's moulton collar, the same color as his moustache, made his fat, friendly face look like Mr. Badger in *Wind in the Willows*.

Clare nodded. "You'd think with sixteen hours of night, I'd be getting more sleep, wouldn't you?"

He grinned. "Only if you're not up on police business."

Clare started. She hadn't told anyone about chasing down Darrell McWhorter's murder scene or questioning Kristen. "What? I'm sorry, I don't . . . ?"

"I understand there was a cop car in your driveway last night." He winked. "And your car was at the police chief's all night Wednesday. Small town, Reverend Clare."

She gaped. "Good heavens." Gossip had simply never occured to her. Especially when the whole thing was so innocent.

McKellan grinned again, wiggling his badger-colored eyebrows for effect. "May be time to trade that MG of yours for something less conspicuous. Come to my bank, I'll make sure you get a great rate on a loan."

"Mr. McKellan! Chief Van Alstyne is a married man!"

"So?"

She sighed with exasperation. "He had been in an armed confrontation earlier that day. I was at his place Wednesday for counseling." *Stretch the truth too far, missy, and it'll snap back to hit you in the nose*, her grandmother said. She ignored the waspish voice. "It was snowing hard by the time I left, so he drove me home instead of me taking my car, which, as everyone keeps pointing out, is terrible in winter driving conditions."

McKellan looked disappointed.

"Last night, he stopped by around dinner and I invited him to share a little stew with me while we discussed the Burnses and the baby." It really had been entirely innocent. She had never done or said anything to Russ that she couldn't have done or said in front of the entire vestry. So why did she feel like she was lying to Terry McKellan?

He squeezed her sweatered arm. "I'm suitably chastized. Next person I hear talking about it, I'll set him straight."

"Thank you."

"You should still come in and see me about a car loan, though."

In the parish office, Clare hitched one hip onto the unnaturally neat desk. "Lois, have you heard any gossip about—" she looked at the secretary's disdainful expression. "Never mind."

Lois tore off a pink memo slip and handed it to the priest. "Gossip." She sniffed. "Never listen to it, never repeat it."

Clare glanced at Lois's Parker-penmanship writing. "The Department of Social Services? For me? How did—" she looked at the memo again, "—Ms. Dunkling sound?"

"Ms. Dunkling sounded just a tad put out."

"Just a tad, huh? Guess that means the letter-writing campaign is having some effect."

Lois lowered her reading glasses and raised her eyebrows. "Uh-huh."

"No sense putting it off. Better beard the lion in her den. Lioness." Clare reversed step in the hall and poked her head back through the door. "And can you speak to Mr. Hadley about getting some wood and kindling into my office? I don't intend to shiver all winter long with a perfectly good fireplace just sitting there."

She pretended to ignore the warning that floated down the hallway after her. "Winter hasn't even begun yet, Reverend . . ."

The radiator was wheezing under its window in a respectable effort to take the chill off. Clare slipped her copy of Mr. Corlew's report in the "Building Maintenance" file, which already took up an entire desk drawer and threatened to spill over into a cardboard filing box at any moment. She poured a cup of coffee from her thermos, grimaced at the taste, and abandoned it on the bookshelf cabinet. Her desk chair creaked and snapped as she sat down and reached for the phone. Waiting for Ms. Dunkling to come on the line, she flipped through her calendar. Infirmary visits. Music meeting. Stewardship committee. Marriage counseling. "Yes, hello. Angela Dunkling, please. Clare Fergusson." She frowned and jotted down a note to call Kristen McWhorter about the funerals. "Ms. Dunkling? This is Clare Fergusson of St. Alban's."

"Yes, Ms. Fergusson. I called you about these letters I've been getting from your membership." The voice on the other end of the line sounded nasal and inflectionless, like someone who had long ago memorized her speech and could recite it without thought or effort. "DSS is not an organization you can lobby, Ms. Fergusson. We have a legislative mandate to answer only to the best interests of the families we serve.

Taking time out to read and answer a bunch of letters only results in less time and resources for our vital mission to protect the children of New York."

Clare frowned. "Are you saying that getting information about Cody's prospective adoptive parents isn't an important part of your job?"

Angela Dunkling let out an irritated snort. "Of course it is. Believe me, we have considerable information on the Burnses already. We don't need to hear from everybody who goes to church with them about what a great couple they are."

Clare tucked a strand of hair behind her ear. If the letters were so ineffective, why was she getting this call from a DSS caseworker? "Why not simply file the letters in with the other information you have, then? Why are you answering them?"

"Let's not pussyfoot around this, okay? Your people are sending us letters, and they're getting their state legislators and senators to send us letters, too. I don't need some House Rep breathing down my neck over this just because some supporter of his has decided the Burnses would make ideal parents. It's our job to determine what living arrangements will serve the best interest of the child. We're still waiting on the police investigation to try to track down the biological parents of the child."

"Parent. His mother is dead."

"Father, then. The child can't be cleared for adoption until we've made a final determination of his status vis-à-vis his father or living relatives."

"So meanwhile, Cody spends his first formative year in a foster home instead of with his future parents?"

"Ms. Fergusson, he's in a perfectly good home with a caring, experienced foster mom. I'll give you her number and you can check her out yourself if you're so concerned." There was a pause, the faint sound of a Filofax flipping. "Deborah McDonald. 555-9385. Believe me, we're not running orphanages out of Charles Dickens." Ms. Dunkling sighed exasperatedly. "Do you have any idea how many prospective parents are out there looking for the Great White Baby? There are couples who've been on lists a lot longer than the Burnses. Why should they get to jump line?"

"Because Cody's biological parents left a note saying so?"

"Forget it. Call off your hounds, Ms. Fergusson. We don't need the additional headache and believe me, it's not going to alter our final disposition in the case. If you want to help the Burnses, tell them to settle down and learn to work with the system instead of trying to manipulate it to serve their own purposes. And tell them to stop making unauthorized visits to Mrs. McDonald. They know the rules."

"What—they've been just stopping by to see Cody? That's a problem?"

"Yeah, it is a problem. As prospective adoptive parents, they shouldn't be seeing the child without DSS supervision. Call Mrs. McDonald, she'll tell you. Wednesday, Geoff Burns showed up without so much as a phone call at eight o'clock at night. Believe me, stunts like that aren't going to help their application any."

Clare rested a hand on her open calendar. "This past Wednesday? The eighth?" The night Darrell McWhorter was killed.

"Yeah. Why?"

"No reason. Yes, I'll talk with them about that."

"And you'll stop the letters?"

Clare paused for a fraction of a second. "I'll pass on your comments to my parishioners. I can only suggest, I can't order them to do anything."

The DSS caseworker grunted. "I'll look forward to being able to get back to work without attempts at coercion, then."

Clare rang off quickly. She tapped a finger on the square labeled "Wednesday, 8th." Eight o'clock. Russ said they had told his officers they had been home all night. Perhaps Geoff Burns considered that to be the end of the workday and not the night? Maybe he stopped by Mrs. McDonald's on his way home and hadn't thought to mention it. Maybe he had driven straight home and spent the rest of the night watching TV with his wife. Maybe he had a passenger in his car when he visited Cody. Maybe he killed Darrell McWhorter, drove to Albany, rifled Katie's room and returned to Millers Kill with no one the wiser.

Clare folded her arms against her desk and slid flat until her head was resting on her arms. Dear Lord. She closed her eyes. Please, please don't let me have been wrong about them.

CHAPTER 20

Clare grimaced at the back of the eighteen-wheeler spraying dirty slush over her windshield. The plows had cleared the roads efficiently after Wednesday's snowfall, but the same wet combination of grit and salt that gave her enough traction to navigate through the winding hills to Fort Henry had turned her car's Scarlet Metallic Special Lacquer finish—for which she had paid an extra seven hundred dollars in the days when she was young and flush—into a drab sparrow color identical to every other car she passed. She wondered how Russ and his officers identified vehicles when they all looked as if they'd been spray-painted with industrial waste. He was right, she was going to have to get another car. She could almost hear the salt eating away at the undercarriage as she drove.

She glanced down at the directions Deborah McDonald had given her. "I'd be happy for you to come call, Reverend," the foster mother had told her in their brief phone call. "All the ways I've had babies come into my care, and never by being dropped at a church doorstep. It's a miracle you were there, that's what I believe. A miracle." Clare gripped her steering wheel more tightly and thumbed a spray of blue antifreeze across the windshield.

The McDonald's vinyl-sided garrison looked as if it had been plucked from some densely populated suburb and capriciously planted on a windy hillside surrounded by pasturage. Two life-sized plastic snowmen flanking the front steps and a plyboard Santa-with-reindeer did nothing to ease the loneliness of the house, whose only neighbor was a dairy farm a half mile down the twisting road.

The woman who opened the door to Clare's knock was like her home, a disconcerting blend of bare-bones plainness and cozy domesticity. Angular, unhandsome, with tightly permed hair and coffee colored eyes, wearing double-knit polyester pants and a sweatshirt decorated with puffy bears. Deborah McDonald smiled widely and took both Clare's hands in her own.

"You must be the minister. I'm so glad to meet you. Come in, come in!" Her kitchen was country cute and immaculate. "I was saying to Keith, that's my husband, that of all the babies I took in, there never was one left on the church steps. Thank goodness you were there. Take off your coat! Can I offer you some coffee? Hot cocoa? You have to tell me what to call you. Our minister goes by the name of Mr. Simms— we're Church of Christ—but I know you folks may do differently. We have lady ministers, too, you know. Not here, of course, but other places. I seem to recall reading in the *Evangel* there was one in New Jersey."

Clare accepted the proffered coffee. The geese marching around the rim reminded her of the mugs in Russ's office. "Call me Clare. Please. I appreciate you seeing me, Mrs. McDonald."

"Deborah, call me Deborah. All these years and 'Mrs. McDonald' still sounds like my mother-in-law, though she's eighty and living up at the Infirmary now." She tilted her head toward a bulletin board covered with photographs of infants, children, teens, and young adults. "After all the kids I've had, 'Mom' seems more natural than my own name."

Clare examined the faces on the wall. "Looks like quite a crew. They must have kept you busy."

Deborah laughed. "Still do. I make it my business to knit something for each one of my kids for Christmas. Hats, scarves, mittens, the like. I start in January. I'm down to just three more to go. Four, including Cody. I'm doing up a little hat for him."

Clare, whose only craft accomplishment was refinishing furniture, almost missed the baby's name while contemplating the scope of the foster mother's gift-making project. Cody. Right. "Is the baby asleep?"

"Lord, yes, you'd be able to hear him if he wasn't. He's a noisy boy, that one, always wanting to talk with us." Deborah gestured Clare through the archway leading from the kitchen into the living room. "He gets the cutest expression, too, like he's thinking, 'Who said that?' whenever he makes a noise." She led Clare through a carpeted hallway into a white-walled nursery with two cribs. The windows and cribs were swathed with petticoat fabric, and dancing bears lined the walls like gingerbread men.

Cody sprawled in the middle of one of the cribs, his round tummy pushing out his fuzzy blue sleeper. "Gosh. He's gotten bigger. I can't believe it's only been ten days since I saw him last." Clare found it hard to connect this fat and contented infant with the bundle she had unwrapped that night in the parish kitchen.

"He's close to ten pounds. The doctor's very pleased."

Ten pounds must be good. "Shouldn't he be sleeping on his stomach?"

"Oh, no. Only on the back, we know that these days. Cuts down on the instances of crib death." Deborah smiled at Cody, the chocolate-sundae smile people get around babies. "We don't want anything happening to this little guy."

Clare reached inside the crib. "May I?"

"Touch him? Go ahead, until he's hungry again nothing's going to wake him up."

Clare settled her whole hand over Cody's head and blessed

him with an inarticulate surge of tenderness and amazement that the most helpless of creatures were caught and held by God. As she signed the cross on his forehead, Deborah nudged her arm and pointed to a needlepoint hanging near the window. HE KEEPS HIS EYE ON THE SPARROW it read. "Yes," Clare said. "Yes, he does."

In the living room, Clare admired more pictures of graduations and proms and weddings before getting to the point. "I understand the Burnses have been visiting Cody. Did Ms. Dunkling from DSS tell you about the note that was left with Cody?"

"Ayuh, she did, she's kept me up to date on everything about Cody. She's wonderful that way."

"Is it true Mr. Burns was here this past Wednesday? In the evening?"

"Ayuh, though that's not the only time it's happened. Mrs. Burns showed up at the pediatrician's office when I took Cody in for his checkup. And they came 'round unsupervised a day or two after I got him, although to be fair, there hadn't been much time to arrange a proper visitation and they did call first."

"Did Mr. Burns call before he stopped by that night?"

Deborah crossed her legs, a slither of polyester. "No, he didn't, and to tell you the truth, the whole visit made me nervous. I won't say he was drunk, because he wasn't, but he smelled like he had definitely dropped off at the Dew Drop Inn for a few after work."

Clare shook her head. "After work?"

"I figured he must have left his office, gone out for a beer or two and then hit on the bright idea to visit Cody. He was still in his coat and tie. Really, I don't like to complain. I understand how hard it is for the adoptive parents to wait, and I'm not against a few visits. I like the company, and it's good for the kids and the parents. But, Lord!" She threw her hands in the air. "I can't have folks showing up here at eight o'clock at night, sulking all over my living room and disturbing the baby's routine."

"Geoff Burns seemed sulky?"

"I guess angry would be a better word. He showed up without so much as a by-your-leave, invited himself in just as I was getting ready for Cody's eight o'clock feeding, and acted mad at the whole world. Insisted on holding the baby, but he was so mad or tense or something that he got Cody all riled up and the poor thing wouldn't settle down to his bottle for over half an hour." She leaned forward. "Babies can sense people's moods very well in their body language, you know."

Clare took a drink of coffee. The newspaper headline she envisioned, PRIEST SUPPORTS MURDERER'S ATTEMPT TO ADOPT VICTIM'S CHILD had been joined by a subsidiary lead: DIOCESE SUED BY DEPARTMENT OF HUMAN SERVICES.

"Deborah," she said, "how long does it take to get to the Old Schuylerville Road from here?"

"Hmmm? Are you heading that way next? Let's see, if you take the turn at Power's Corners and then use old Route eleven, you can reach it in about ten minutes."

"Ten minutes." Long enough to get to the spot where Darrell McWhorter's body had been dumped, take off for Albany, and still be home in time to meet the Millers Kill police at his front door. Clare had a sudden urge to drive to the Burnses' office right that minute. She wanted the truth from them, no matter how wrong it might prove her instincts.

She put her coffee on a needlepoint coaster. "Deborah, thank you so much for having me over to take a look at Cody and chat." She stood. "I'd like to stop by and see him again sometime, if you wouldn't mind."

Deborah McDonald stood, gathering the mugs in one hand. "Not at all. I'm glad of the company, like I said."

The two women walked to the kitchen. "I promise you I'll talk to the Burnses and mention your concerns."

The foster mother unhooked Clare's coat from the rack. "I appreciate the chance to let 'em know without having to go through DHS and making it all official. I'm sure they're perfectly nice people. Just terrible eager for their baby by this point, I imagine. I've seen it before. Waiting on a baby when you can't have one of your own makes folks a little crazy at times."

Clare had to drive around the block three times before a parking space opened up. It looked as if the boutique owners at this end of Main Street would have a merry Christmas. She could have found a space more readily a few blocks away, but she still hadn't gotten around to shopping for new boots and her low suede ones had already seen more than enough snow and salt.

The Burnses' receptionist looked up, startled, when Clare came through the stairwell door.

"Ummm . . . can I help you?"

"Yes. I'm Clare Fergusson. I need to see Mr. Burns right away. Or Mrs. Burns, if he's unavailable." Clare unzipped her coat and let it drop onto the asymmetrically striped sofa.

"I'm sorry, Mr. Burns is in court all afternoon and Mrs. Burns is working out of her home today. I could make you an appointment for tomorrow . . . ?"

"Oh—" Clare bit down hard on what she had been about to say, "—gosh darn." She snatched up her coat again. "No, thanks. I'll try to get Mrs. Burns at home."

On the drive to the Burnses' house, Clare tried out what she might say. Karen, did your husband shoot Darrell McWhorter? Or how about, Karen, did your husband father a child and try to cover it up with this abandoned-at-the-church-doorstep scheme and when that fell through, did he start killing everyone else involved? "Oh, shoot me now," Clare groaned.

The Burnses' house was a brick Italianate revival with

five-foot-high windows and a cupola that must have given them a view of the entire town. Wreaths decorated with wooden fruits hung from the deeply-paneled front doors, which had the look of an unused entrance. Down the long drive, by the separate garage at the corner of the house, Clare found the back door.

Karen Burns opened at the second ring. "Reverend Fergusson? What brings you out here?"

"Well, I—" Clare stamped her boots on the welcome mat.

"Please, come on in. No need to stand in the cold to talk."

Clare pushed into the narrow hall lined with hanging coats, boots, shelves of hats and gloves. She left her coat, following Karen into the kitchen.

"Is this about the letter-writing campaign? I've gotten some wonderfully supportive notes and phone calls from people, you know. Mrs. Strathclyde told me she actually called our congressman's office to complain. Can you believe it?" Karen led Clare through a high-ceilinged, granite-countered kitchen into a small den done up in burgundy and hunter green. Karen waved at the glass-fronted barrister's bookcases and the computer centered on a wide mahogany desk. "My home office. I work here about seventy-five percent of the time, now. When we adopt Cody, I'll be able to switch to a twenty-hour-a-week schedule without making any drastic changes." She gestured toward a tapestry-covered love seat.

Clare sat. She took a steadying breath. "Karen, I didn't come to discuss the letters."

Karen sank gracefully into a green leather chair. "You didn't."

"I know that the police have been asking you about the night Darrell McWhorter was killed. I know you both claim to have come straight home from work."

"Claim?"

Clare leaned forward, trying to meet the other woman's eyes. Karen tilted her head, examining her hands. Her fingernail polish matched the study's rug. "I know Geoff wasn't at home at eight o'clock that night. He was at Cody's foster mother's house. Wearing a suit and tie, as if he'd come straight from work, and smelling as if he'd had a drink or two."

The lawyer looked straight at Clare, her beautiful face calm. "What are you suggesting?"

"It looks bad, that's what I'm suggesting! Karen, you two have got to tell the police the truth. What happened that night?"

Karen looked toward the bookcase. "Nothing." She compressed her lips into a tight line. "I don't know."

Clare slid to the end of the love seat until their knees almost touched. "Tell me what you do know."

The other woman continued staring at the bookcase. Clare touched her arm. "Please, Karen. I want to help you. And Geoff. But you have to be honest with me."

There was a pause. Slowly, Karen turned her head to face the priest. "We had a horrible fight that afternoon in the office. We had been arguing about what approach to take with McWhorter all day long and we got . . . it just . . . anyway, I told him what he could do, and took off. I was so angry with him I wanted to . . ." She blew out a breath. "I did a little shopping, I called my mother, I fixed some stir fry for dinner—you know, working the mad off." She laced her fingers together. "Dinnertime came and went, with no Geoff, and no phone call. I started to get worried. I mean, really worried; the weather was bad and he was driving the little Honda Civic. Finally, finally he showed up around ten or so." She shook her head. "I didn't know whether to kill him or kiss him. Turns out he'd been out at the Dew Drop Inn most of the night. I don't know how he managed to get himself home, he was in no condition to drive. I was horrified! He could have killed himself. Not to mention the damage to his reputation if he had been picked up. The last thing we need is a morals censure from the Bar Association or a D.U.I. conviction on his record."

Clare pressed her forefingers against her mouth to refrain from mentioning that Geoff could just as well have killed other people out on the roads that night. "Does this sort of thing happen often?" she asked, her voice neutral.

"God, no. Geoff's idea of a blowout indulgence is a bottle of Nouveaux Beaujolais the week it hits the stores. So you can imagine how I felt when those two officers showed up at the door asking where we had been that evening! All I could think of was Geoff being hauled in for questioning. So I told them we'd been home all night, having a few drinks and watching TV." She sagged back into her chair. "Geoff just went along with my story." Her gaze went to the ceiling, as if looking for the Fates lurking there. "Yesterday, when we learned that McWhorter had been killed, it was too damn late to recant. There wasn't anyone except a few anonymous bar patrons to say he'd been at the Dew Drop instead of . . ."

"Instead of taking Darrell McWhorter on his last drive to Albany?"

"Yes. We had already lied to the police. As you said, it looks bad."

Clare tilted her head back, closing her eyes. Did she believe Karen Burns? Yes? The question was, did she believe Geoff Burns told the truth to his wife? "You've got to tell this to the police. You and Geoff."

"No!"

"Do you believe your husband's story about what happened Wednesday night?"

"Yes, of course. He would never lie to me."

"Then tell Chief Van Alstyne. Geoff's absence that night is going to come out sooner or later. If you wait until the police find out on their own, the two of you are going to look guilty as sin. Go to Van Alstyne's office, tell him what you've just told me, admit that you were both royal idiots to lie about it, and offer to enroll Geoff in one of those driver education courses. Voluntarily."

"What? There's no way they can prove drunk driving after the fact—"

"We're not talking about legalities, Karen, we're talking about admitting you did something wrong and setting it right. Confession and repentance." She braced her elbows on her knees. "Because on a moral and emotional level, you aren't going to be able to continue on with this lie weighing you down. And because on a practical level, if you don't cop to the drinking and driving and lying, your husband's going to look like a murderer when the police do find out."

Karen pressed the palm of her hand to her forehead, half-shielding her face from Clare's direct stare. "There's a good chance they won't find out," she said, trying the idea on for size.

Clare exploded out of the love seat. "There's no chance Chief Van Alstyne won't find out, Karen, because if you don't tell him, I will!"

"You can't do that!"

"I can't tell him anything of this conversation we're having right now, no. I can certainly tell him Ms. Dunkling of the Department of Human Services called me to complain that your husband was at Cody's foster mother's house Wednesday night. And I can tell him Deborah McDonald confirmed Geoff was upset and smelled like he'd been drinking."

Clare collapsed back into the love seat. "I'll do everything I can to help you talk to the police. I'll do everything I can to help you become Cody's parents. But I won't compromise the truth for you. I won't help you stand in the way of finding Katie McWhorter's killer. We owe her that. We all owe her that."

"You're lucky he's in. Five minutes more and you would have missed him." Harlene punched the intercom button on her heavy, licorice-colored telephone. "Chief? Reverend Clare's here to see you. And Karen Burns."

The door to his office banged open and the chief of police strode out. His gaze flicked between Clare and Karen, back to Clare, finally settling on Mrs. Burns. "What can I do for you ladies?"

Clare tucked a strand of hair behind her ear, suddenly aware of the effortless chic of the woman standing beside her. She looked like a badly tailored crow next to Karen's drapey wool separates and hundred-dollar haircut. Which was ridiculous. Appearance was not what was important here. She tugged her bulky, faded sweater down, revealing more of her clerical collar.

"Mrs. Burns?" Russ said. "Reverend Fergusson?"

Karen looked uneasily at Clare. "I . . . uh . . . was going to wait for my husband, but he's being held over in a deposition . . ."

Russ tilted his head a little to the side. His eyes narrowed thoughtfully. "Why don't you come into the interview room with me. We can be more private there."

Karen nodded. "Clare, will you stay with me?"

"Of course."

Russ looked at her hard while pulling out a chair for Karen, asking what was going on as clearly as if he'd said it. Clare raised her eyebrows, radiating encouragement. He rolled his eyes at her before crossing the room and taking a seat opposite Karen. Clare seated herself.

"Mind if I tape this? I hate to have misunderstandings later on because we're remembering different things." He rested his hand easily on a cheap portable tape recorder.

Karen frowned. "As long as you make it clear I'm speaking without an attorney."

"Oh? Do you need one?"

Karen flushed. "As you say, I'd just hate to have misunderstandings later on."

He nodded, turning on the tape machine. "This is Chief Van Alstyne, interviewing Karen Burns." He glanced at Clare. "Accompanied by her priest, Reverend Clare Fergusson. Ms. Burns is unrepresented by legal counsel." He looked at Karen. She nodded. "The date is Friday, December tenth, and the time is . . ." he glanced at his watch, "six P.M."

Karen took a deep breath and began. Clare listened to her voice, calm and orderly. Her recounting of the events of Wednesday night was organized, yet compelling. Clare propped her chin in her hand, struck by Karen's poise. She must make a dynamic advocate in court. Russ, on the other hand, looked less than impressed. He sat with one hand resting on the tape recorder and the other splayed across a pad of paper. Clare supposed his expression could qualify as neutral, but she could see something underneath. Disapproval? Skepticism? She bit her lower lip. It was important that he treat Karen right. How else could he encourage this kind of honesty?

When she concluded her story, Karen folded her hands, as if waiting for comment. Russ chewed the inside of his cheek for a moment. He tapped the tape machine a few times. "Your husband was driving a Honda Civic that night?"

"That's correct. He uses it instead of his Saab when the roads are salty."

"Has he driven it anywhere since that night?"

"Yes . . . he's got it today. He likes me to keep the Land Rover, in case I need the four-wheel-drive. Why?"

"Was he drinking at the Dew Drop Inn before he went to Mrs. McDonald's?"

"No, that's in the opposite direction from our office and her house. Um . . . he didn't actually say, but I assumed he'd gone to the Sign of the Musket after work. That's where we usually go for Happy Hour."

"Mrs. Burns, when you spoke to Officer Entwhistle Wednesday night, you said you own a nine millimeter Smith

and Wesson, registered to yourself, and that you keep it in
your Land Rover for times when you're on the road by yourself."

"That's . . . correct. I have clients spread out between Albany and Plattsburgh, and a woman traveling alone can be
vulnerable. What relevance does this have, Chief?"

"Is that gun still in your Land Rover?"

"Yes."

"You sure?"

"Yes!"

Russ nodded. He popped the tape from the machine and
rose from the table. "Will you wait here for a moment? I'll
be right back." He closed the door on his way out.

Karen jerked around in her seat. "Clare, I don't like this.
I do not like this at all."

Clare rested her hand on the other woman's forearm.
"Karen, we knew he'd be suspicious. After all, you did lie
before. I'm sure Chief Van Alstyne wants to check with
someone at the, what was it? Sign of the Musket? And at the
Dew Drop Inn."

"You're right." Karen sighed. "He's going to want to talk
to Geoff, too. Oh, God, I should have just waited for him to
get back from that damn deposition. We could have done this
tomorrow."

By which time, Geoff could have argued her out of talking
to the police. Clare patted Karen's arm and tried not to doubt
Geoff Burns when she hadn't even had the chance to talk
with him.

The women sat in silence as the minutes crawled by. Clare
got up and checked the coffeemaker, but it was cold and dry.
The plate beside it was empty. No homemade strudel today.

"What on earth is taking him so long?" Karen demanded.
She pushed her chair back and stood. "I'm going to find a
phone. I want to call the office and see if Geoff's there yet."

"Maybe you should wait until you hear what Chief Van Alstyne has to—"

The door opened. Russ and Officer Durkee walked in. The young man smiled discreetly at Clare, who waggled her fingers at him. He'd been good company at the hospital the night she'd found Cody.

Russ cleared his throat. Officer Durkee fell in, his face serious. Russ held up a curling sheet of fax paper. "Karen Burns," he began formally. "I have here a copy of a warrant executed by Judge Ryswick granting us permission to search your cars and to confiscate any firearms in your or your husband's possession for testing. We are also warranted to search your house for any materials possibly related to the deaths of Katie McWhorter and Darrell McWhorter." He folded the piece of paper carefully, creasing it with finger and thumb pressed tightly together. "Judge Ryswick thought our new information was sufficient to issue a separate warrant for your husband's arrest."

Karen's posture went rigid, and her arm, still holding the back of the chair, trembled slightly. She made no other sign or sound.

"However, I won't execute the arrest if Geoff presents himself to the station for questioning within the next two hours. I've sent someone to your office to let him know. If he comes home first, of course, we'll have someone there," Russ said. "Officer Durkee will accompany you to your vehicle. If you'll hand over your keys?"

"I want to call my lawyer. Now."

"There's a phone at the main desk. Mark, will you escort Mrs. Burns to the phone?"

Karen shot Clare a venomous glance. "Confession and repentance?" Her voice hissed like caustic lye. She turned and swept out of the interview room, Officer Durkee close on her heels.

Clare faced Russ. "This is absolutely outrageous!"

"Stay out of it, Clare."

"Stay out of it? I'm the one who persuaded her to come in her and tell you the truth! How you can twist that around in order to search her car and her house. . . . Are you going to arrest Geoff Burns?"

"Depends on whether he shows up or not. What he says in the interview. I may very well hold him overnight while we test the gun."

Clare clenched her teeth to keep her voice from rising. "*I* brought Karen Burns in here. *I* persuaded her to come clean with you. *I* assured her you would listen to her. I thought—"

"No, you didn't think. You just jumped in feet first without looking where you were going or considering the consequences. I'm a cop, Clare! What the hell did you expect me to do when a woman I suspect is an accessory to two murders walks in and tells me her husband was drunk and unaccounted for during the time Darrell McWhorter was killed? Shake her hand and give her a good citizenship badge? Get real!"

Clare pressed her hands flat against the table to keep them from shaking. "I was trying to help—"

"You were trying to help the Burnses, yeah, I know. And you're trying to help Kristen McWhorter, and the baby, and the unwed mothers of the world, and every damn soul you come across. That's why you're a priest, Clare. I, on the other hand, am a cop. The only thing I'm trying to do is catch the sonofabitch who killed Katie McWhorter and her father and send him to the chair. And I will do anything—anything within the law—if it means getting closer to that arrest." He spread his legs slightly and hooked his thumbs into his belt, an archetype of law enforcement authority. "If that interferes with your agenda, I'm sorry. But don't act the outraged innocent with me when I'm doing my job."

Clare flushed hotly. "You! Can kiss my ass!"

"Oh, very nice. They teach you that in seminary?"

She spun on her heel and stalked out of the room, past an embarrassed-looking Harlene, past the abandoned main desk. Behind her, she could hear Russ's voice, exasperated, angry. "Clare. Clare!"

She took the stairs two at a time and burst out into the icy night air. She interlaced her fingers tightly and took a deep breath. The cold, dry air made her cough. She clattered down the front steps, almost losing her footing, and swung around the corner into the station parking lot.

Karen was standing next to her Range Rover, arms folded. Officer Durkee was inside, his flashlight bouncing off the windows and mirrors. Karen's lips pinched together when she saw Clare. "I'm not going to be able to give you a lift back to my place. My vehicle's going to be out of commission for awhile. And I have to wait for our lawyer to get here." She glanced at Durkee's shadowy form. "I've asked him to try to get a stay on the warrant."

"Karen," Clare began. "I'm so sorry . . ."

The other woman pulled a knit hat from her coat pocket and twisted her hair underneath it. Automatically, she pulled a few loose curls down here and there, framing her face. "I'm sure you are. And I'm sure that when this is all over, I'll be able to listen to your apology. But right now, I'd rather you just leave me and my husband alone."

Clare dropped her arms to her sides. She could feel a hot pricking behind her eyes. "Of course. I'm . . . I'm so sorry. I didn't think . . ." Karen's scornful look told her it was obvious she hadn't thought. Clare bobbed her head and left the parking lot as fast as she could, wanting nothing so much as to put the fiasco behind her. What had she been thinking? Her mind drew a blank. She had been dismayed that the Burnses had lied to the police. She had been hopeful that Karen's confession would finally clear them in the investigation. She had been . . . pleased with herself, bringing a new piece of information to Russ, like some attention-starved dog showing off a trick. She jammed her hands deep into her pockets in disgust. She hadn't been thinking, just feeling. And reacting.

She stopped at an intersection and waited for cars to pass. Damn, it was cold. Her ears already ached and it was another mile at least to the Burnses house, where her car was parked. Why hadn't she worn a hat? *A stitch in time saves nine*, her grandmother said. *Proper prior planning prevents piss-poor performance*. That voice belonged to the warrant officer who had taught her survival course. They were evidently in agreement with Russ.

The light turned green and she crossed. But, dammit, he was so focused on the Burnses he couldn't consider any other possibility. Why would Karen have told her about Geoff's absence the night Darrell was murdered if it wasn't to exculpate him? It was so obvious! But Russ couldn't entertain the notion that he might be wrong. Him and his 'Me cop, you priest' routine. Patronizing jerk.

The flash of red lights and brief blurp of a siren jerked her attention to the road. A cruiser was pacing her, its passenger-side window unrolled.

"Get in, I'll drive you."

"No," she told the car.

"For God's sake, Clare, just because you were wrong about the Burnses doesn't mean you have to sulk like a little kid. It's a long walk to their house."

"I can use the exercise."

"Clare, get in the goddamn car!"

"No."

"I won't ask again!"

She remained silent, facing in the direction she was walking, her eyes fixed on the building across the next intersection.

"Fine, dammit. Be that way!" The cruiser picked up speed and drove off.

In the fading rumble of its engine and the accelerating

swish swish swish of its tires, she could hear her grandmother Fergusson's voice. *Self-righteousness won't mend any shoe leather, missy, and pride won't put a meal on the table.* Wrapping her arms and her self-righteousness around her, Clare trudged on into the night.

CHAPTER 21

Weekends were peak time for the Millers Kill Infirmary. Children and grandchildren and great-grandchildren, busy from Monday through Friday, would come for visits Saturday and Sunday, bringing magazines, photographs, and potted plants that the staff would labor to keep alive. So far, Clare had kept her visits to weekdays, when the corridors were largely quiet and the oldest members of her congregation were happy to see someone from the outside.

But Mr. Howard's niece had asked her to stop by to encourage the old gentleman, who had just gotten back to the Infirmary after a rough bout of pneumonia, so here she was, hoping that by showing up first thing in the morning she could avoid the sullen teenagers and guilty-looking adults who populated the corridors on Saturdays.

Mr. Howard looked weak and washed-out but seemed to be in high spirits. Clare had visited with him once before, and found what he most wanted was an audience for his stories of the Great Depression and his never-ending string of dreadful puns. He didn't acknowledge she was a priest: whether that was from faulty memory or a politely unvoiced disagreement with the ordination of women, she didn't know. They did pray together at the end of her half-hour visit, though. She wondered, leaving him with a promise to say hello to his niece, if the prayers of a man of ninety were somehow more easily heard by God. After that many years, God must seem like just one more old friend living on the other side of the divide.

At the unmanned nurses' station, Clare tucked her brown police parka under her arm and flipped through the roster of residents, finding names she knew, reading the brief notes to see if anyone was doing poorly or heading for the hospital. The sound of muffled crying caught her attention. She dropped the notebook and stepped around the counter into the corridor. An old woman dressed in a heavy floor-length robe leaned against the wall, her fist jammed into her mouth, her eyes wide and frightened.

"Hello," Clare said quietly. "Can I help you?"

"I—I don't know," the woman said. She looked about her. "I don't know where . . ."

Clare held her hand out. "Are you lost? Let me help you find out where your room is." She tucked the woman's arm under her own and craned her neck, looking for a nurse or aide.

"Do you know my husband? I'm looking for my husband." She held tightly to Clare's arm.

"I don't work here, I'm just visiting. Let's find someone who can help us."

"I'm all runny," the woman said, touching her eyes. "I need a . . . a . . ."

Clare tugged a tissue out of its box at the nurses' station. Behind a partial wall, she spotted a door marked DIRECTOR OF NURSING. "Let's try over here. Can you walk this way with me? That's great." She knocked at the door.

Nothing. Clare was about to try the nurses' station on the next floor when the door opened. "Yes?" a deep voice rumbled. The doorway was filled with an enormous bear of a man, tall, broad, well-padded, luxuriously bearded. His gaze immediately fell onto the woman clinging to Clare. "Oh, Mrs.

Ausberger. Did you get lost again, dear?" He draped a massive arm around the frail lady's shoulders and guided her back to the nurses' station. He picked up a handset and punched in a number. "Staci? Can you come to three, please? Mrs. Ausberger is here." There was a pause. "Yes, probably."

Mrs. Ausberger patted the man's tweed jacket, visibly calmed by his presence. "Oh, you smell just like my husband. Just like my husband."

The man grinned sheepishly at Clare. "You two caught me smoking a pipe in my office. I know I'm not supposed to, but I hate going outside to puff away on these cold days. Takes all the pleasure out of it, reminds me that it's really just a filthy addiction." He reached out with his right hand. "I'm Paul Foubert. Director of Nursing."

"Clare Fergusson. I'm the new priest at St. Alban's."

"Yep, the collar kind of gives you away. Thanks for rescuing Mrs. Ausberger. She's been known to wander pretty far afield. Hey, Staci, great."

A cute young woman barely out of her teens clattered down the corridor. "Sorry, Paul. I was fixing Mrs. Meerkill's hair in the bathroom and didn't realize she had slipped out." She took Mrs. Augsberger's hand. "C'mon, Mrs. A. How 'bout we get you washed up and I'll make your hair pretty."

"My husband likes my hair down."

"You're not going to be seeing your husband today, Mrs. A. But your grandson Nicholas will be visiting with his family. Won't that be nice?" The girl's cheerful voice faded as the pair turned the corner.

Clare looked up at Paul Foubert. "Her husband?"

"Dead ten years." They both looked down the empty corridor. Foubert idly slapped his hands against his coat pockets. "Damn. Left my lighter in the office. Why don't you come in for a minute or two?"

The director of nursing's office was appropriately den-like in brick and wood. Tall shelves crammed with books and memorabilia lined one wall, facing a collection of obviously amateur artwork, undoubtedly done by residents of the Infirmary. Foubert gestured to one of the comfortable chairs facing his generously cluttered desk before settling himself into a well-sprung leather armchair.

"So, how long have you been at St. Alban's?"

Clare propped her leg on the opposite knee. "A little over a month. It's been . . . hectic. I'm still trying to get to the point where I don't have to have a directory to remember my parishioners' names and a map spread over my legs when I go out for a drive."

Foubert picked up a pipe from a lumpy, half-glazed ashtray. "Do you mind?"

"Not at all."

He tamped in fresh tobacco. "What do you think of our Infirmary?"

"It seems like a good facility. The staff members I've met have all been pleasant and helpful. Caring. I imagine the small size helps. I did some work at a nursing home in Virginia while I was at seminary. It was huge. Well-run, but impersonal."

"Mmmm. I've been fortunate to be able to get good people, both staff and volunteers. You're right, being small does help. Makes it more like family. Before we moved here, I was at a large facility in New York City, and Lord, sometimes it felt like a body warehouse."

"You're not from here?"

He lit the pipe. The rich tobacco tang filled the room. "I am, originally. My dad worked in the mill. I escaped to the big city like a lot of kids and didn't return until I was a burnout case, with nowhere else to go. I've been here eight years now."

Clare glanced at the multiple diplomas hanging on the wall opposite the windows. "Some people would say running a nursing home is a burnout job."

"Oh, no. Caring for men struck down in the prime of their lives, watching a dozen of your best friends die, that's burn-out." He waved his pipe toward the rest of the Infirmary. "This is much more peaceful. It's—you'll pardon the slightly facist sound of this—the natural order. It's a privilege to help our oldest through the ends of their lives. I try to impress that on everyone who works here, because I've found folks who don't feel that way tend to get depressed and impatient with our residents."

Clare nodded. "I'll consider myself impressed upon." The diploma wall also held a photo collage that stretched a good three feet square. She could pick out shots of parties and Christmas celebrations, elderly residents surrounded by three and four generations of family, doctors in white lab coats and nurses in cheerful-print smocks. A very large Easter Bunny in one picture turned out to be Foubert himself. She laughed.

"My Hall of Fame. Or Shame, as the case may be."

"We have a similar one hanging outside our parish hall. But your pictures are definitely more fun than ours." She opened her mouth soundlessly, struck by a sudden thought. "Are there pictures of all your volunteers here?"

"There sure are. We couldn't run this place without them. I can't afford to hire LPNs to do what they're willing to do for free."

"You must have a photo of Katie McWhorter, then."

Foubert's pleasant expression tightened under his bushy eyebrows. "I read about her in the paper." He looked down at the pipe in his hand. The tobacco smouldered fragrantly. "She was such a wonderful kid. A little too much on the serious side for her age, but a damn hard worker. And smart." He shook his head. "What a waste." He looked up. "You leave the city to get away from that sort of thing, but it's everywhere nowadays, isn't it? There isn't any safe spot any-more." He rose from behind his desk and hunkered down in front of the collage. "Here she is. This was taken last year, at the Christmas party. She was prettier than she photographed. It was her expression, I think."

Clare got out of her chair for a better view.

"The residents loved her. She never got antsy around them, the way some of our teenage volunteers do. She liked being here."

"Who's the boy with his arm around her? He looks sort of . . . have I seen him here during one of my visits?"

"No, he's off to college as well. That's her sweetheart, Wes Fowler. He was another volunteer." Foubert laughed softly. "They used to take breaks together, go out to his car. Later I'd see them come in all pinked up and grinning. Kids." His smile faded. "What a waste. What a terrible waste. I remember once when—"

Clare sat back in her chair. Foubert's voice seemed to come from far away, as if he were on the radio in another room. Her ears buzzed.

Wes Fowler.

What had Doctor Anne's son said about the boy? Serious, studious, hard working. Just like Katie.

Golden boy. From a family that had everything the McWhorter's didn't. The Fowlers three-thousand-square-foot dream home was maybe ten miles from the apartment on Depot Street, but it could just as well have been on the other side of the planet.

A boy who had everything going for him, including an appointment to West Point and a beautiful girlfriend from a family as well-respected as his own. What would a boy like that do to hide a screwup? A really big, life-altering, won't-go-away-for-the-next-eighteen-years screwup?

Wes Fowler.

The boy Katie didn't want her family to know about. He evidently felt the same way about keeping it secret.

She was going to have to tell Vaughn Fowler and his wife about this. Oh, God.

"—you'd think, wouldn't you? Reverend Fergusson?"

"Huh?"

"Are you okay? You look odd."

"I feel odd. I mean—yes, I'm okay."

She stood up. Foubert rose with her, clasping one huge paw around her arm. "Are you sure?"

"Yes, thank you." She smiled at him, a kind of social grimace. "I do need to be going, though. I just remembered something important."

"Alright, then." He cradled his pipe in the ashtray. "I wish I knew who to send my condolences to about Katie. She never talked about her family."

"She has a sister, Kristen. She's asked me to perform the burial service, as it happens. If you'd like, I'll let you know when and where. She has to wait until the police, um . . ."

"Yeah. I do. I'd like that, please." Foubert plucked a business card off his desk and handed it to her.

Hand halfway to her pocket, Clare stopped. "Paul, could I borrow the photograph of Katie? I'll return it."

He squatted and peeled the picture off the board, balling up sticky gum between his fingers before giving it to Clare.

"Thank you."

He opened the office door and ushered her out. "I'll be hearing from you, then. Stop by the next time you're visiting, will you?"

"I sure will do that, yes." She took off with indecent haste. The photograph of the young couple, projections for the cost of the church roof, Karen Burns's angry face, all jostled for space at the front of her consciousness.

Wes Fowler! My God!

There was a Pathfinder parked next to the Fowler's Explorer at the top of their long, well-plowed drive. Clare pulled in close behind them and killed her engine. The two hulking SUVs could probably four-wheel-drive straight over her windshield and down the back of her car without noticing more than a little bump. She rested her head on the steering wheel for a moment, reaching for the sense of someone outside her and within her, looking for strength, looking for courage. Asking for the right words to come when she needed them.

Gravel and snow crunched underfoot as she walked up to the side porch. The Fowler's home was a modern interpretation of a Georgian house, a sweep of white clapboard frequently broken by double-glazed windows with Palladian arches. At some point, the rolling acreage upon which the house sat must have been a farm, but it was all pleasure land now, the pastures used only for cross-country skiing and snowmobiling. Idyllic spot to be a retired gentleman. Pressing on the bell, Clare felt like the angel with the flaming sword, sent to roust the inhabitants out of their Eden.

"Reverend Fergusson! What brings you out here?"

Edith Fowler was a horsy-looking woman whose extreme slenderness was beginning to look bony with age. Her short brown hair was clipped to a sporty, no-nonsense length and she wore pearls and a shetland sweater over a monogrammed turtleneck. Clare pulled her hat off. *If someone had been strangled with a shetland sweater from Talbots*, she had said to Russ, laughing at the idea of one of her congregants commiting murder.

"Honey? Who is it?" Vaughn Fowler crowded around his wife's shoulder as she was standing back to let Clare in the door. "Clare. This is an unexpected pleasure."

Clare stuffed her gloves into the pockets of her oversized parka and pulled it off. "I apologize for intruding, but I needed to speak with you." Edith Fowler took the coat and hung it in the hall closet. "Both of you."

The couple looked at each other. "We're entertaining right now . . ." Edith said hesitantly.

"It shouldn't take long. It is important."

Vaughn gestured her through the kitchen door. "Of course." Inside the kitchen, preparations for a brunch were obviously in progress. Bowls of batter, a carton of eggs, cutting boards of chopped vegetables. And, sipping what looked like mimosas, were the Shatthams. Clare smiled feebly. Great. They were probably getting ready to toast Wes and Alyson's engagement or something.

The Shatthams greeted her warmly, which made her feel even guiltier for what she was about to lay on the Fowlers. "Clare needs to speak with me and Edith for a few minutes," Vaughn said. "I know you two can entertain yourselves."

"Barb, give a quick poke to the sausages, will you?" Edith asked.

"In here's my study. Right next to the kitchen in case I get a snack attack while working." Vaughn let Clare and his wife enter the room, then shut the door behind them. The study was a monument to Fowler's family and military career. Photos and maps and trophies and a few threadbare battalion flags.

"Working?" Clare asked, temporizing the moment of truth.

"On a history of Washington county." He waved toward a pigeonholed desk, where an electric Remington typewriter sat next to several hardbound books. "It's going to fill in the gaps other histories leave out." Clare bent down to examine a black-and-white photograph of a lean young man in fatigues standing next to a general with a whole salad of ribbons on his chest. Both men were squinting into the sun, smiling stiffly.

"Sir. Is that you?"

"With my father. 1965. Day before I shipped to Vietnam."

"You look just like him." Clare straightened. Edith Fowler looked at her husband, who cocked his head toward Clare.

"You needed to speak with us about . . ."

She took a deep breath. "Sir . . . Vaughn . . . you recall when Chief Van Alstyne was showing the photographs of the dead girl in the parish hall? You said you'd never seen her before."

"Of course I remember. That's not the sort of everyday Sunday you're likely to forget."

"We know the girl's identity now."

"Yes, I know. Mitch and Barb told us all about it. Alyson identified her as one of her classmates."

"Yes, sir. Her name was Katie McWhorter." Clare clasped her hands behind her back. "Did your son ever mention that name?"

Fowler looked at his wife. "No," she said. "What on earth does this have to do with Wes?"

"Today I discovered your son was seeing Katie McWhorter secretly. They were volunteers at the Infirmary together, as well as being in the same class at the high school. The director of nursing told me he used to see them sneaking off to neck. Whatever it was, it probably started in the fall, when Katie broke up with her boyfriend. It was certainly going on at Christmastime last year."

"Wait a minute," Fowler said, turning toward his wife again. "Wasn't he going out with Alyson last year?"

"Of course he was." Edith Fowler frowned at Clare. "If you had to speak with us about our son cheating on his girlfriend, Reverend Fergusson, I'm afraid I don't see the point. Nor do I see that it's any business of yours."

Clare bit the tip of her tongue. "Katie McWhorter had a baby just a week or so before she was killed. So far, the police haven't been able to identify the baby's father."

"So far? Are you suggesting—"

"Calm down, Edie. Clare, you don't know our son. If anything, he's overly responsible. And devoted to Alyson. Maybe he did have a little romance with this girl, but there's no way he'd be so thoughtless as to risk a pregnancy."

"This is ridiculous. How do you know it's not some other boy anyway?"

"I have a photograph of them taken at the Infirmary Christmas party last year. It's—" she reached into her pants pockets, coming up with nothing more than a fistful of change and a wadded tissue. "I left it in my coat pocket." She let her hands drop. "I'm not saying that your son is involved in Katie McWhorter's murder. I'm suggesting that he may have fathered her child. We know she had a boyfriend that she didn't want her family to know about. Somebody accompanied her to a local motel around Thanksgiving and stayed with her while she had the baby. She named him Cody, wrote a note asking that he be adopted by Geoff and Karen Burns, and left him on the kitchen steps at St. Alban's, despite having no connection to the church." She flipped her hands open. "Don't you see? Wes had a reason to want to stay anonymous. He was home around Thanksgiving, right?"

Vaughn Fowler nodded.

"And he's a member of the church. He would have known about the Burnses looking for a child."

Edith Fowler covered her mouth for a moment. "Oh, dear God. Vaughn, do you think . . . ?"

"I don't know. It's a long chain of supposition from just one link." He looked at the floor, frowning. "Have you been to the police with this, yet?"

"No. Chief Van Alstyne is . . ." she paused, reining in the anger she still felt from yesterday. ". . . anxious to find the killer. He's been frustrated so far, and he's pouncing on possibilities without giving them much thought." Had Geoff Burns been arrested yet? Not that Karen would call and tell her. "I'm afraid that if he hears about the connection between Wes and Katie, he'll leap straight to the conclusion that Wes murdered her. And probably Darrell McWhorter as well." Darrell had looked at the parish bulletin board before changing his mind about giving Cody to the Burnses. He had seen Wes's picture there, with his family. And made a phone call that afternoon. "Does Wes have access to any money?" she asked.

"What?"

"Certainly. He has an account with a bank in West Point."

"Sorry, I was just thinking." A scared kid with his own cash made an easy target for blackmail. She glanced at Mrs. Fowler, leaning against her husband. Maybe their son was a murderer. One way or another, though, she was going to make damn sure she had gathered some evidence before handing the boy over to Russ's tender mercies. "Let me check this out some before we involve the police," she said.

Vaughn nodded. "I want Wes here to answer questions." He looked at his watch. "I can head for West Point later this afternoon and bring him back tomorrow morning first thing."

"Good. I'm going down to Albany. Katie's sister gave me the address yesterday. I'll talk to Katie's housemates, and see what they remember. Do you have a picture of Wes I could borrow?" She looked around the room. All the family photos were framed and hanging on the walls.

"Here, take this." Edith Fowler grabbed a large bound volume off the coffee table. "It's his high school yearbook."

"Thank you. I—"

"I'd like to see that photograph you have," Edith went on. "Just to make sure there's no mix-up."

"Of course."

Vaughn opened the door. In the kitchen, the Shatthams were intently poring over cookbooks. Clare wondered how soundproof the study door was.

"All set. We'll just see Reverend Fergusson out."

In the hall foyer, Edith handed Clare her coat. "Thank you. It's—" Clare yanked her gloves from the pocket and dug inside. "—right here."

The Fowlers examined the Polaroid. Edith made a soft noise.

"It's him, all right," Vaughn said, his voice gravelly. "I'll get him on the phone right away. I want to get to the bottom of this." He shook his head. "May we keep this?"

Clare reached for the picture. "I'd like to take it with me to Albany. I hope it's nothing, but it may need to go to the police." She deposited it back into her pocket.

There was a noise from the kitchen entrance. "We wanted to say good-bye," Mitchell Shattham said hesitantly.

"Edie, are you all right?" his wife asked. Edith Fowler shook her head.

"We'll want to get in touch with you as soon as you're back from Albany," Vaughn said.

"I'll stop by my office. You can leave me a message and I'll call you from there." She tucked the yearbook under her arm and shook hands with the Fowlers. "I'm sorry to lay all this on you this morning. I sincerely hope I'm wrong." She waved to the Shatthams as she stepped off the porch. Before the door closed, she could see Barbara Shattham embracing Edith Fowler.

In her car, Clare let her head drop back against the headrest and closed her eyes, boneless. She opened them again. Through steel and glass, she could hear the familiar flat pulsing of rotors. She pressed her face against the chilly window. There it was, at maybe eight hundred feet, flying northwest. Maybe a skiing trip. She squinted. Looked like a Bell AH-51. Good ship, fast, reliable. Before she left Virginia, she had been trying to talk her dad into replacing his old OH-50.

Shifting, she flipped open the glove compartment and flicked through the maps there. Eastern New York State, with a city map of Albany. She folded the heavy paper into a manageable size and started the engine. She could see the helicopter in the passenger-side window now. As she watched, unable to look away, it heeled its tail rotor up, accelerating toward the Adirondacks. She rubbed a gloved hand over her dry lips. God. She wished she were up there right now.

CHAPTER 22

Emily Colbaum was a tiny, fey girl with huge brown eyes and a close-cropped haircut that looked like Audrey Hepburn on speed. She stood in the doorway of the room she had once shared with Katie McWhorter, crossing and uncrossing her arms. "You see, Reverend? I mean, I'm not a complete slob, but it would be hard to know what went missing."

Clare crawled backwards from underneath Katie's bed. "I'm really not so concerned about what the man took. I was hoping maybe there was something left behind. A photograph, a note from a phone message . . . something." She grunted in frustration as she clambered to her feet.

"The cops were pretty thorough. Of course, I think they were thinking, like, drugs, or something bad like that, like the only thing that could get a girl killed was either a rapist or being mixed up in something bad." Emily crossed her arms around herself again. "Katie wasn't like that."

"I know." Clare sat on the bed that had been Katie's. The posters on her half of the room ran heavily to cute kittens with inspirational sayings and landscapes with greeting-card poetry. There was nothing hinting of a secret life in her messy desk and overstuffed bookcase. Clare brushed a piece of a dust bunny off her nose. She was eighteen, and pregnant.

Let's say by Wes Fowler. She didn't want anyone to know. Why?

"Emily, did Katie ever talk about what she wanted to do after college?"

"Oh, sure. She wanted to get into computers. Maybe Web designing, SYSOP, she had lots of ideas. She wanted her own business, to work for herself. She could have done it, too. She was just amazingly hardworking. She was like, never partying or blowing off class."

"So getting married or having children right away wasn't in her plan."

"No way. I couldn't believe it when they told me she'd had a baby. I just couldn't believe it."

"Hey, who's here?" A black girl trailing layers of knitwear sidled around Emily into the room. She had multiple earrings and a small stud set in one nostril. "Hi, I'm Ebony."

"Ebony rooms with Sara, across the hall."

"Yeah, the room where you don't have to listen to that nasty dog next door."

"Yeah, but you get the street lamp all night long. This is Reverend Clare, from Katie's hometown. She's kind of helping Katie's sister."

"Hi, Ebony." Clare rose and shook the girl's hand. "I have a picture I already showed Emily, of Katie with a boy. I think he might be the father of her baby." She dug into her pants pocket, grateful she was wearing off-duty khakis and a wool turtleneck instead of her usual garb. "Have you ever seen him?"

Ebony studied the photograph. She shook her head. "No. I'm sorry. I don't think I ever saw any guy with Katie, you know? She was . . . focused. She wanted to hit the ground running."

"I was telling the Rev how I was, like, in disbelief when I heard she had had a baby."

"Oh, yeah," Ebony agreed, handing the photo back to

Clare. "I thought she was just putting on weight. We all were complaining about the food, and the freshman fifteen and all that stuff. Most of us eat at the dining halls, and man, that stuff is nasty for your figure."

"I remember," Clare said, smiling a little. "Look, I left a yearbook from Katie's high school downstairs. There are some more pictures of the boy—his name is Wes. Did she ever mention that name?"

Ebony and Emily looked at each other.

"You ever hear that?"

"Nope."

"Me, neither."

"Would you take a look at the yearbook? Just in case?"

The living room of the group house was cheerfully ram-shackle, furnished with someone's old family-room sofa, crate-style and director's chairs, an elaborately carved coffee table that had been the height of Mediterranean chic in 1972, and the ubiquitous cinder-block-and-board shelving. The girls sat on the sofa together. Clare retrieved the yearbook from the coffee table.

"This is his senior picture." Wes was a good-looking boy, square-jawed and athletic, a young version of his father.

"What is this, skinhead hair?"

"No, he's in the U.S. Military Academy."

"And he got an early start on the buzzcut thing. No, I've never seen this guy." Ebony leafed through a few pages. "Here's Katie." She read the script below the photograph. " 'SUNY Albany. Favorite memory of MKHS, the junior trip car wash fund-raiser, and Mr. Delogue's class. Quote: I think I can, I think I can.' " She flipped through a few more pages. "Man, I knew she came from a small town. Look at these folks. What's the matter, they don't allow black people in Millers Kill?"

"Ebony!" Emily squealed.

Clare smiled crookedly. "Let's just say that diversity is not their strong suit."

"No lie. Hey, Em. Isn't this that girl who came to see Katie at the beginning of the year?"

"What? Who?" Clare leaned over the coffee table to see.

"This blonde copping an attitude. Remember her, Em?"

On a page of candid photographs, Ebony had one finger squarely on a *Seventeen* magazine blonde with perfect skin and a form-fitting tie-dyed dress.

"Alyson Shattham was here visiting Katie?" Clare blinked in disbelief.

"It wasn't like, a social call." Emily said. "She was a bitch on wheels."

"She had some sort of problem with Katie. Actually, she had a problem with all of us. Acted like her shit didn't smell." Ebony looked at Clare, biting her lip. "Oh. Sorry, Reverend. I forgot."

"That's okay. Tell me what you remember about Alyson's visit."

"She wanted to speak with Katie. She was, like, very rude. They went into the kitchen to talk and shut the door."

"She was definitely riding Katie. But Katie, she could hold her own. I don't know what they went on about while they were in the kitchen, but blondie flounced out of here like somebody had caught her tail in a crack."

"Did Katie ever tell you what they talked about?"

"No. She was, like, very private with stuff bothering her. She would smile and change the subject if you asked if she was okay. Like, she didn't want to burden anybody."

Ebony nodded in agreement.

"Did either of you ever see Alyson here again? Or did Katie mention she saw her again?"

Ebony and Emily looked at each other.

"You ever see her after that time?"

"Nope."

"Me, neither."

Clare stood up straight and rubbed her forefinger across her lips. Alyson Shattham. Now that was interesting.

Clare picked up the yearbook. "I think I'll show this around at the computer center where Katie worked. Maybe someone there overheard her or saw her with either Wes or Alyson." She glanced out the window. "Then I'd better head back home. I don't want to get caught in any more of this upstate weather. I have a friend who doesn't trust my car in the snow."

Clare checked her rearview mirror, changed lanes, and wedged her soda between her thighs. She adjusted the radio tuner as an eighteen-wheeler passed her. Traffic was light on the Northway this Saturday afternoon.

"WNCR's accu-weather update!" the speakers blared. She turned the volume down. "A low pressure system continues to move in fast from the northeast," the announcer said portentously. "I'm looking for snow to start mid-afternoon, with temperatures falling into the single digits by nightfall and increasing storm intensity. Accumulations from four to six inches along the Hudson Valley areas, higher in the mountains. Get out those skis if you haven't already, because it's prime time at the peaks!" The weather report broke for an ad extolling snowboarding at Hidden Valley Ski Area.

"Wonderful," Clare muttered. She ate a few more french fries. She was a long way from being able to "smell snow" as Russ claimed he could do, but even she could tell the lead-gray clouds darkening the sky to the north meant another snowstorm. Didn't it ever stop snowing up here?

"Is it my imagination, or is this a really snowy December?" the DJ asked.

"It's not your imagination, Lisa, this is the third snowiest December since 1957," the smooth-voiced weatherman said. "And with the storms now forming over the Rockies and the

Canadian plains, we may set a new record before the month is over."

Clare groaned.

"So get out and get that Christmas shopping done before you're stuck indoors waiting for the plows, right, Dave?"

"That's right, Lisa!"

"Let's have something seasonal, then!"

Harry Connick, Jr.'s voice filled the car. "I'm dreaming of a white Christmas . . ." Clare picked her bacon burger off the yearbook cover. She might as well have left Albany right after talking with Emily and Ebony, instead of waiting until the afternoon, risking driving into the storm. No one at the university's computer center could recall seeing Katie with Wes or Alyson.

She chewed her rapidly cooling burger thoughtfully. Alyson had lied straight out to her, Russ, and her parents. Maybe Wes had thrown her over for Katie. Could she have murdered in a fit of jealousy? What could she have said to have lured Katie back to Millers Kill? Had she found out about the baby, somehow?

Keeping her eyes on the highway, Clare groped for a napkin and wiped her mouth. She found it easy to think the worst of Alyson. Something about that girl got under her skin. Who would have guessed she still had unresolved issues from her high-school days as an ugly duckling? She frowned. Maybe Alyson and Wes both did it, like that high-school couple out in Texas, who had murdered a girl who threatened their romance.

She sighed. She was going to have to call Russ and tell him everything she'd found out. The convoluted strands of this case twisted around like bad wiring, an offense to her pilot's sense of order. Maybe he had been right to jump on the Burnses. Not because they had been guilty, but because trying to put together the events of the crime with only pieces of motivation and insight into the human heart was hopeless.

Real, physical evidence, that's what pointed the finger at the guilty. Besides, how was she going to get Alyson to talk to her? Russ was . . . was . . . not entirely right. But he was a little right when he told her to leave it to the professionals. Although if he thought she was going to admit that over the phone, he had another think coming.

She pulled into the tiny parking area behind St. Alban's an hour or so before sunset, grateful to have beaten out the storm. She had no illusions about her winter driving skills. She unlocked the back door and made her way up to her office, pausing to plug in the coffeemaker. Lois must have turned down the thermostat when she left at noon, since the parish hall was even colder than usual. Clare could up the setting by a few degrees, but her first good look at the yearly oil bills a few days ago had shown her exactly why the church was rarely warmer than 62 degrees, even in the coldest weather. She sighed. Mr. Hadley would be in at 5:30 tomorrow morning to turn the heat up before the services. She could tough it out for a few hours this afternoon.

She carried her coffee into her office. As if in answer to her virtuous intentions, there was an iron carrier overflowing with split logs and a basket of kindling next to the fireplace. "Mr. Hadley!" she said. "You dear, sweet man!"

She had once read that a fire actually takes warm air out of a room, but you couldn't prove it by her. With flames popping the logs and the iron fire-back radiating heat, she finally felt warm enough to take off her parka. Reaching for the phone, she shook her head in bemusement. Computers and cell phones and nuclear power and space shuttles, and here she was, heating herself like a curate in a Dickens novel.

"Millers Kill Police. May I help you?"

"Harlene? It's Clare Fergusson. Is the chief in?"

"He sure isn't, Clare. But I know he's been trying to get

ahold of you. I expect him back within an hour or so. Want
to leave a message?"

"He's been trying to reach me? Okay. Yes ... tell him I
called, and that I'll be here at my office for a couple of hours.
I need to speak with him about Katie McWhorter's case."

"I'll do that. Have a good one."

"Thanks, Harlene. You, too."

She clunked down the receiver. Tapped a pencil against
her lips. May as well get the messages and start returning
calls. Maybe the Fowlers had spoken to Wes and persuaded
him to tell the truth about his relationship with Katie. And
there was Alyson to consider. It was probably a bad idea to
talk with the Shatthams before she heard back from Russ.

She retraced her steps to the main office and pressed the
messages button on Lois's phone. The first message was from
Russ. "Just calling to see how everything's going. Give me a
call when you get in." The second was someone asking about
early-morning services, the third was from the Cutlers, wanting to know their pledge balance. The forth and fifth were
also from Russ. "I've tried calling your home. Are you out,
or what? Give me a call when you get this, will you?" The
last message was from Edith Fowler. "Reverend Clare?
Vaughn and I spoke briefly with Wes this morning. I don't
want to go into it over the machine, I'm sure you'll understand. Vaughn called the Commandant and has permission to
pick up Wes for the rest of the weekend. If the driving's not
too bad, they'll be back late tonight, otherwise he'll stay over
and they'll return tomorrow. Can we all meet tomorrow afternoon? Let me know. 555-1903."

Six or seven pink memo slips poked out of her mail cubbie
on the wall. She squinted against the growing dimness in the
hall, reading them on the way back to her room. Inquiry about
a christening. Possible new members. Sterling Sumner wants
another meeting about the boiler. Chief Van Alstyne called,
no message.

Kristen McWhorter called, left no return number. Most urgent, underscored by Lois's confident pen. Has info re: who killed her father. She and mother are hiding out—here Lois had made a big, black question mark and exclamation—at cousin's hunting cabin. Please come at once. Mother does not trust police. The detailed directions to the cabin covered the rest of the pink slip and continued onto another.

"Lois!" Clare said to her fireplace. "Couldn't you put the 'most urgent' one on top? Holy cow." Too many years as a church secretary undoubtedly gave a person a jaundiced view of others' emergencies. She took a quick gulp of coffee and donned the police parka. She really did need to get her own someday soon. She stuffed the directions into her pocket and pulled on her gloves. Kristen's call had come in just at noon, three and a half hours ago. She must be frantic by now.

Outside, snow was showering down in tiny, dry flakes, freckling her cheeks and nose as she brushed off her windshield. There wasn't that much accumulation yet. If it took her less than an hour to reach the cabin, she shouldn't have too much difficulty with the roads. The MG's engine roared to life reassuringly. Of course, she might not be able to get back out until the storm finished up. She used the last napkin to wipe the melted snow off her face. When she had been young and romantic, she had fantasized about being snowbound in a rustic cabin. But she had for sure never pictured Brenda McWhorter in there with her.

Route 9 North was well-trafficked and easy to drive, even though the plows hadn't been out yet. She exited near Lake Lucerne and took River Road south. To her left, the Hudson River ran high and fast, carrying away clots of snow and ice in its gray waters. Far fewer cars kept her company here. Snakes of snow slithered across the road, obscuring the macadam. She glanced at her directions. The right onto Tenant Mountain Road turned her due west, but there was no sign of impending sunset behind the hills ascending in front of her, only an iron shell of sky and the snow, falling faster and harder against her windshield. Infrequently, she passed houses, their lights glowing through the swirling flakes like figures inside glass snow globes. Beautiful and unreachable. The sense of isolation pricked at her. Skittered. She turned the radio up for its illusion of company.

She spotted Alan's Gas and Grocery, the landmark mentioned in her directions. From here it was two miles to the road leading directly up into the mountains. It was a small general store with lighted signs blazing cheerfully if commercially through the storm. COCA COLA! BUDWEISER! DIESEL, $1.00! She almost pulled over. It would be dry and safe, there would be a phone, she could admit she was too inexperienced to be driving in this weather and call—who? One of the congregation? A taxi?

She gritted her teeth. Russ was the only person she considered enough of a friend to ask for a favor like that. She drove past the entrance to the grocery's tiny parking lot. How could she come begging for a ride like a stranded teenager after yesterday? She blew out a gusty breath. Her inexperience at winter driving, and the unfamiliar landscape, were making her jittery. If she calmed down, drove carefully, and didn't run scared to the nearest big, strong man to save her, she'd be fine. Alan's Gas and Grocery disappeared from her rearview mirror. Two miles to the turnoff. Six miles to the camp road. Less than a mile to the cabin. Even if she had to drop down from her current speed of thirty miles an hour, it shouldn't take her more than twenty minutes. Then she would whap Kristen upside the head for not leaving a phone number where she could be reached.

She slowed as she hit the two-mile mark. Her headlights shone blurrily through the gathering dark, their edges softened by the snowfall, their light swallowed up in the storm. Two large stone cairns marked the otherwise signless road. Hidden under white, they looked like lean and misshapen snowmen, and she was suddenly sorry she had thought Mrs. McDonald's plastic snowmen were tacky. On a night like this, they would be beacons of hospitality, marking the boundary between safety and the storm.

She set the trip odometer to zero, turned, fishtailed, overcompensated, then recovered. The MG pulled steadily along the line of ascent. The trees closed in heavily, shrouding the road, giving some protection against the full force of the snowfall. The twilight turned the sky, the air, the snow shades of underwater blue, as if she were piloting through a drowned world. She downshifted, and the engine growled as her tires churned through the light, dry snow. The headlights picked out a few well-covered tracks, but no one had driven through recently enough to compact the snow, which made it easier for her front wheels to get the traction she needed.

The road wound its way up the mountain, never stretching more than a few car-lengths before disappearing around another bend. There was still light enough to clearly see the outlines of the culverts on either side and Clare kept her speed to a steady twenty-five miles an hour, grateful she wasn't trying to navigate the twisty turns in total darkness. She passed an opening in the trees and realized it must be another camp road. She bit her lip. Kristen had better have been dead-on accurate about the miles to the turnoff, or she was going to be lost but good on this God-forsaken road.

Rounding the next bend, she saw twin lights, small and bright as halogen bulbs, windshield-high in the middle of the road. She slammed on the brakes at the same moment the lights resolved themselves into eyes and her car skidded past harmlessly as a buck bounded off the road into the cover of the brush. She swore out loud for the first time in three weeks and it felt so good she continued to rain down curses on every deer in New York State as she coaxed her car into a straight line and slowly, slowly accelerated.

A mile up the mountain, there was another narrow, unmarked road, barely visible through the encroaching trees. Unplowed, of course. She was beginning to worry about getting through the camp road to Kristen's cousin's cabin. The snow was piling higher with every minute, deep enough to seriously impede her car, deep enough to make the mile walk an unthinkable misery in her lightweight boots. She turned off the radio, the better to hear the sound of her tires slurring through snow. She would just have to chance making it as far as she could toward the cabin, and if she got stuck, she would lay on the horn until Kristen came. Let her bear the burden of finding some decent footwear for slogging through the rest of the way.

The trip odometer crawled toward the six-mile mark. She speeded up the wipers, peering through the curtain of snow for the entrance to the camp road. The light had leached almost entirely away by now. She tried switching her high-beams on, but the dizzying flurry of snowflakes through the field of light and the reflected glare from the snow on the road was disorienting.

Up ahead there was a gap in the wall of trees. She slowed, and unrolled her window for a better look. It was hard to tell, but the faint depressions under the new-fallen snow seemed to be tire tracks from earlier in the day. She rolled the window back up and carefully turned onto the camp road.

Thankfully, it sloped downhill in a gentle, hillside hugging curve. Nothing requiring agile maneuvering from the already-overtaxed car. She glanced at the odometer. Almost there, although between the watery blue darkness and the screen of trees and brush and the snow, she could probably drive into the front door before spotting it. Ahead, the road rose along a lengthy, uneven incline. She groaned. On a clear fall day, that hill would be nothing but a pleasant surge under her tires and the fun of watching the leaves scatter. Now . . .

She clutched the steering wheel more firmly, downshifted again, and stepped on the gas. Hard. The back end shimmied, then lurched forward, pulling hard. Clare leaned toward the windshield, as if shifting her body weight could tip the balance in favor of an uphill climb. The engine keened.

"Come on. Come on," Clare hissed between gritted teeth. The car crept upward. "Almost there, almost there . . ." She tromped down on the gas pedal a final time, laughing in triumph as the front wheels dug in, held, and hauled her over the crest of the hill. She instantly surged downhill, the car twisting violently to the left, as if the roadbed were half eaten away. The steering wheel nearly jerked from her grasp. Clare yanked her foot off the gas and slammed on her brakes. The front wheels locked. She skidded downhill, the car swinging sideways, tipping. Clare fought for control, pumping the brakes, steering out of the high-velocity skid.

She shrieked involuntarily as the car's undercarriage slammed into something low and hard, then shrieked again, louder and longer, as she tipped for real this time, crashing and bouncing and crunching over and over.

CHAPTER 23

Stillness and dark. She heaved for air, shuddering gasps sounding abnormally loud in the silent aftermath. She hung from her shoulder belt, her left arm pressing against shattered glass and smeared snow. Her car had come to rest on its side. The remains of the driver's side window showed slaggy rock. The windshield was intact, but half popped out of its rubber and chrome frame. Above her, like some crazy-cracked skylight, what had been the passenger-side window was slowly whiting out under the falling snow.

She breathed in deeper and more deeply, feeling for pain in her lungs or ribs. She shifted her legs carefully. Her knees felt like someone had been hammering on them, but all her joints moved and nothing seemed to be grinding or poking out. She reached for the door handle above her. Something twinged nastily in her side. Her gloved hand came short. She swallowed. She had to get out of the car. Hitching her hip up, she fumbled at her seatbelt latch. As she slowly shifted her weight, leading headfirst toward the passenger-side door, the car shivered. Metal screeched. Clare flung herself against the seats, clinging to the leather while the vehicle slid downward another half-foot, stopping with a kidney-bruising crunch. She was canted at an easier angle now, some of the car's weight resting on its upslope side. She pulled at the passenger door latch. It stuck. She braced her boots on the remains of the driver's door and yanked at the latch again, hunching over and throwing her shoulder against the door at the same time. It popped open with the scrape of metal against raw metal. Clare scrambled out.

She balanced unsteadily on a steep field of boulders and jagged rock, halfway down a crevasse that cut through the mountain as far as she could see upslope and down. Five or six yards beneath her it bottomed out in a wide stream, whose black waters ran fast enough to have kept it from icing over despite the past three days of below-freezing temperatures. Above her, the camp road slanted down to two blocky cement pilings and then vanished into thin air. Her car had gouged a scar along the snow, the pilings, the rubble, and scree. Reluctantly, she looked at the MG. She made a small noise in the back of her throat, resolutely turned away, and picked her way uphill slowly, testing each foothold as she climbed. When she reached the cement pilings, she propped her backside against one and rubbed her knees vigorously. Across the gorge, there might have been twin pilings underneath the unmarked snow. Hard to tell. There was certainly more road there. She could see the cleared width of it between the trees. A bridge had been here. Once.

Clare stamped her feet, knocking away some of the snow clinging to her boots. If there was a cabin in the woods over there, no one had gotten to it by this road. Which meant either the directions got garbled between Kristen and Lois, or she had taken a wrong turn somewhere, or . . . she looked again at where the road simply vanished. Or someone had sent her here. Deliberately. The thought made her stomach clench and her skin prickle coldly.

She pushed herself away from the piling and hiked the rest of the way up to the crest of the road. Whichever it was, mistake or malice, she was in a bad way. She was close to ten miles away from the last outpost of civilization she'd seen, and although her parka and sweater were keeping her upper body warm, she could already feel goose bumps beneath her cotton khakis. Her boots were a bigger problem. Even with heavy woolen socks, her toes ached with cold. How would she feel after one mile in the snow? After five? At what point would she stop hurting and start permanently damaging her flesh?

She pulled the parka hood up and tied it under her chin. The fake fur edging tickled her cheeks. Normally, she could walk a mile easy in fifteen minutes. She started down the road, stepping inside the rapidly filling tire tracks. Fresh snow, packed snow, uneven terrain—say it would take half again as long to go a mile. Twenty-two minutes or so.

Her heel came down on something slippery and loose. She skidded, flailed, and landed hard on her backside, grunting. She picked herself up, beating snow off her pants. Make that twenty-two minutes plus time to fall down and get back up again.

At the side of the road, a dead branch was wedged between the fork of a tree. Clare yanked it loose. It was straight and spar-like, thin enough for her to grasp in one hand and long enough to test the depth of snow a few feet ahead of her. She knocked off the snow crusting its bark and continued on, bracing her steps with the stick.

All right. Ten miles to Alan's Gas and Grocery would take her four to five hours. What about another cabin? She could hike down the mountain until she reached the closest camp road. She had passed one two or three miles before reaching her turnoff. If it was another mile to a cabin it would still be less than half the distance to the store. She could have shelter. Blankets. Probably a fireplace. Maybe even, God willing, a working telephone.

Snow collected on her cheeks and chin. She scrubbed her face with her glove, trying to dry her skin as much as possible. Not heading straight for the Gas and Grocery would be risky, of course. If she couldn't find a place within a mile of the main road, she would have to retrace her steps. She pulled the parka sleeve away from her wrist and lit up her watch. Almost five o'clock. By the time she reached the next camp road, it would be full dark. Could she trust herself to stay on a narrow, unplowed road at night with a heavy snow falling? Already the underwater blueness was thickening, making distance impossible to judge, swallowing the details of the forest only a few yards away.

The thought she had been pushing aside crystalized, unavoidable. *I could die out here.* Her stomach lurched as if she'd dropped a thousand feet of altitude in a few seconds. She could become just one more missing person, her whereabouts a mystery to her family and friends, until some autumn day who-knew-how-many-years in the future, when hunters stumbled over her bones wrapped in a Millers Kill police parka.

"God," she said, her voice very small in the immense quiet of the woods, "I don't want to die. Please help me."

She poked her walking stick into a particularly deep depression one of her tires had spun into the snow. There didn't seem to be much more she could add to that prayer, unless it was, "and let me find the so-and-so who sent me directions to this place so I can throttle him or her." No, that wouldn't do.

She braced and stepped, braced and stepped. The 139th Psalm. It had been a dim twilight, like this one, the sky dark with rain instead of lit by snow. She had been sitting by Grace's bedside, her sister's hand resting weightlessly in hers because it hurt Grace to be touched firmly. Their father had read the 139th Psalm in his deep, soft voice. "If I say, surely, the darkness shall cover me; even the night shall be light about me. Yea, the darkness hideth not from thee, but the night shineth as the day. The darkness and the light are both alike to thee." It had been the last time they had all been together. In the silence and the dark, so far from where Grace had lived and died, she felt an urgent closeness to her sister, a moment of absolute certainty that death was just a pocket-trick, that the dead were all around her, supporting her, giving her strength, pricking her with warnings to watch the road, watch the road—

A dark shape emerged from the bend in the road before her.

Clare blinked. Her heart thumped once, hard. She tightened her grip on her walking stick, wondering, even as she halted in her tracks, muscles tensing, why she wasn't running forward.

The bulky figure moved ahead another step. It was a person in a jumpsuit, one of those allover padded things they wore snowmobiling around here. Clare eased a fraction and opened her mouth to speak when a flashlight beam suddenly speared her.

"Take off your coat," a voice hissed.

Clare squinted, dazzled by the sudden light, trying to make sense out of this bizarre sequence of events.

"What?"

"Off!" The voice was guttural, deep, like a man's, but as unidentifiable as the figure behind it. The flashlight beam dipped low, as if the person had shifted it in his grasp, and Clare heard the distinctive sound of a round being chambered in an automatic pistol.

Her throat closed. Heat surged through her body. She hurled her walking stick as hard as she could toward the flashlight and dove headfirst for the brush at the side of the road.

The gun went off, shattering the stillness like an axe through thin ice, dwarfing a strangled scream of "Goddamnit!" A trio of deer exploded from a thicket of trees, careening into the camp road, the beating of their hooves echoed by wings everywhere overhead, winter birds fleeing in terror.

Sprawled beneath a fir tree, Clare saw the flashlight beam arch crazily into the sky and took off, scrambling hand and foot downslope, away from the sounds of thrashing and swearing. She made it to her feet and ran a yard, two yards, three, before tripping over something buried in the snow and tumbling. She kept her momentum going, rolling forward, regaining her footing, dodging ancient oaks and dense, matted stands of fir, steadying herself on deadwood and saplings. Branches whipped her face. She changed direction, ran until she fell, pawed the snow from her face and shifted direction again. A long-thorned bush scratched and caught at her parka. She plunged through snow up to her thighs, hauled up a slide of scree and branches, her heart pounding and her breath sawing in her ears as loud as jet exhaust.

At a slight rise, she climbed a toppled pine tree and stood, gasping, to get her bearings. She couldn't see any light from where she had come. Where she thought she had come from. She shook her head, disoriented. If, as she thought, her attacker had dropped his flashlight, as soon as he found it he'd be on her trail. Her all-too-obvious trail. She gulped air, turning away from where she'd been, staking out the lay of the land ahead. Somewhere to her left, hopefully not too far, was the mountain road. If she lost that, she was dead, whether the shadowy man in the snowmobile suit caught up with her or not.

She struck out for where she thought the road must be at a diagonal, picking her route more slowly and carefully, jumping from treefall to treefall and squeezing under the thick shelter of hemlocks and firs whenever possible. She couldn't leave a clean trail, but she could put breaks in it, make it hard to follow, slow him down.

If she went straight for the road, it would only make it easier for him to catch her. Even if she could manage to run in the slippery snow, he must have a vehicle somewhere, not too far from where he ran into her, near the junction of the camp road and the mountain road.

He had a gun. He had a flashlight, was dressed for the

environment, was bigger and probably heavier than she was. He wanted her dead.

She had . . . a branch of feathery needles whacked Clare in the face. She spat out the taste of pine tar. She had a head start. She would be able to see his flashlight a long way before he saw her. Her night vision would be sharper, not relying on artificial light. He was carrying something small-caliber, without much stopping power, so he'd have to get right in close to her in order to drop her. And one other advantage: he had underestimated her, and chances were he'd keep on underestimating her. Her survival school instructor at Egeland AFB, a shiny-headed old warrant officer nicknamed "Hardball" for obvious reasons, told them, "Biggest advantage any woman's got in an escape and evasion situation is the fact that ninety-nine percent of the men she runs into won't look past the fact she's a girl! So don't use your tits for brains!" The first time she had given up in an exercise, he made her do push-ups in the mucky Florida swamp water until she threw up. She had never surrendered again.

She could use some Florida heat right now. Her feet felt like they were being squeezed in an icy vise. She paused near an old hemlock, its trunk studded with dozens of branches starting only a few feet from the ground. She looked up, the snow pelting her eyelashes, blinking furiously. Time for her to locate an ambush site. The only way out of this forest now would be over the body of the man hunting her.

She went up the tree hand over foot, showering down snow and the odd abandoned nest. Small branches broke against her arms, smearing her coat with gummy pine tar. She climbed as high as she could, until the tree trunk shivered beneath her weight, and bent back a heavily needled branch to take in the view.

Through the murky underlight, too close for comfort, she could see the bobbing and twitching of a flashlight. Her St. Elmo's Fire, heralding death and disaster. She shifted another branch, straining to see through the snow and the darkness. She needed to find high ground. Someplace she could lure him up to, bringing him to her, letting him tire himself out.

To her right, at a distance impossible to judge in the gloom, a series of steep little hillocks rose from the general downward slope of the mountain. It would mean heading away from the road, which was a disadvantage, but there were thickets of evergreens mixed in with the birch and maples, perfect for what she had in mind. She clung to the hemlock trunk and swiveled around. If she were quick enough, she could backtrack to the small ridge she had stumbled over and make her trail from there, something big and obvious to lead him to the ambush. And her real route . . . she squinted, willing in that moment to trade a year's pay for a single set of binoculars. The last hillock was cut by a darker gash. She followed it as far as she could with her eyes. It looked as if it might be part of the crevasse that had taken her car. Running water would explain the little hills, harder stone rising from the softer earth of the mountain, eroded away each spring.

She bit her lip. The crevasse it would be. She descended from the hemlock gracelessly, crashing and dropping as fast as possible. If her assailant caught her out in the open, all the clever plans in the world wouldn't amount to a snowball in hell. She retraced her trail to the spot beneath the lip of a ridge where she had stumbled and fallen. From the well-thrashed disturbance in the snow, she set out for her ambush site, trotting in a fast, low shuffle that left a clear path plowed through the snow. She took the most direct route possible, avoiding any cover, arrowing straight for the thickest clump of fir trees at the edge of the first small hill.

It would look, she hoped, as if she had seen a potential hide and bolted. She turned and shuffled back the fifty yards or so to the ridge, more slowly, careful not to stray outside the path she had laid down. She was damp with sweat under her parka, her heart rattling the cage of her ribs from exertion and fear. Back at her starting point, she picked her way downhill, stepping on fallen branches as much as possible, swinging around tree trunks to conceal her footprints from her hunter's view. She wanted him to see nothing but the dense clumps of evergreens, see that she would have picked it as a good hidey-hole, see there were more places to huddle unseen at the top of the hill, where a frightened woman could crouch and pray to be overlooked.

From behind her, she heard a noise. She froze, crouching, her gloved hands folded against her mouth to still her breathing. It came again, a crackling. Then a scrape. She fought the urge to close her eyes like a little kid, hiding from the monsters' sight by refusing to see. There was a rushing, a clap of air, and from the corner of her eye she saw a snowy owl take wing. Her lungs wrung every ounce of oxygen from her body. For a second, she couldn't move while she tried to remember how to breathe.

She headed downhill again, moving faster as she got farther away from her starting point at the ridge, risking obvious footprints in order to gain time.

She hit the crevasse unexpectedly and nearly went headfirst to the bottom when she fell short of the rocky outcrop she had picked for her next foothold. She slid belly-down a few uncomfortable yards before hooking onto an exposed root, breaking her fall. She grimaced at the wide trail she had left. Just like her car. She would simply have to hope he wouldn't track her this way, because she was committed now. No time to make alternative plans. She clambered down the remaining length of the crevasse, wincing at the feel of snow-dampened pants clinging to her legs.

Balanced on a rock edging the black, rushing water, she hesitated for only a heartbeat. She might have been able to make it all the way to the hillocks hopping from stone to stone, never wetting her feet, if she had half an hour. But her time was measured in minutes and seconds now. She stepped in. The water was shallow, rising just over her ankles, but so cold, it brought tears to her eyes. She jogged downstream, slowly at first, picking up speed as she got her footing on the smooth cobbled stones lining the stream. It felt as if she had two great toothaches at the ends of her legs, and every joint in her body throbbed with sympathetic pain.

She kept jogging, her teeth gritted hard against any sounds she might make, her arms held away from her body for balance. On and on she sloshed through the almost-freezing water, unable to think of anything except her misery. It wasn't until she looked up and saw the darker outcropping of heavy stone that she realized she had reached the hillocks. She thrashed her way to the shore and leaped out of the stream, shaking and kicking each foot to expel as much water from her boots as possible.

Between the water and the snow was a tumble of smooth stones, wet but still free of ice, varying in size from hail to small boulders. Clare bent over and picked one up. It hefted well, about five pounds, flat enough so she could hold its edge with one hand if necessary. It was as close as she was going to get to an offensive weapon, unless she could take the gun off the man in the snowmobile suit. She stowed it in one of the parka's cargo pockets, where it banged against her thigh every time she drew her leg up to climb the hillside. The ascent was difficult. She couldn't flex her feet enough to get toeholds, so she had to use the outside edge of her boots and hang on, hoping she wouldn't topple back to the bottom of the crevasse.

At the top of the hill she collapsed beneath the shelter of a pine tree. No light bobbing in the distance, yet. The rush of elation was enough to get her back on her feet. She looked at the hill she had just climbed. This way back would be her escape route if her ambush didn't come off. She could roll down the crevasse within seconds and be headed in either direction quick enough to vanish. For awhile.

She squelched through the snow, keeping to the far side of the slope, her head a handsbreadth above the crest of the hill. She wanted a clear view of that flashlight. She teetered down one hill and trudged up another, looking for the trees she had marked in her mind. Surprisingly, her feet didn't feel so bad. They prickled a little, but she didn't feel the cold as keenly as she had.

By a cluster of tall firs, she went over the top, crawling on her elbows and knees to keep her profile low. The pines she had made a path to were a dozen yards away and almost directly below. He would step around them, careful to keep his gun between himself and the trees, and when he found she wasn't there he would want to head up to the next obvious hidey-hole, the firs near the crest of the hill. On his left, he would see birch growing too thickly together to make an easy route up the hill. So he would go to the left of the firs. She hoped. With no time to create an obstacle to channel him toward her ambush, it would have to be nature or nothing.

She reversed direction, up over the top, backtracking a half-dozen steps. From this spot, she walked, crouching low, taking long steps, leaving as little trace of herself as possible. A little more than halfway between the two clusters of evergreens she spotted what she wanted. A birch sapling, almost branchless, a couple feet taller than her head and slim enough to wrap her hand around. She yanked open the bow beneath her chin and pulled the long drawstring out of the parka's hood. Reaching as high as she could along the sapling, she drew its slender length down, holding hard against its springy recoil. She looped one end of the drawstring around a pair of miniature branches near the top of the sapling's trunk and tied off tightly.

Scarcely two yards away lay the brown remains of a toppled fir, spiky, tangled branches and dead needles rising less than a foot out of the snow. Low cover, enough to keep her out of sight—barely—if she dug down and stayed flat. Low cover her hunter might overlook while he kept his gun and flashlight trained on better hiding places. Only problem was, the drawstring wouldn't reach that far.

In the distance, a light winked. Clare's stomach squeezed. Time. No time. She abandoned the sapling, string dangling, for the nearest shaggy hemlock. She grabbed a flexible, living branch from low near the ground, pulled it taut, and smashed her heel over the juncture where it grew from the trunk. The branch snapped free. Clare teetered for balance. She had scarcely felt the blow with her foot. That had to be a bad sign.

The light flashed again and again in the darkness. She retrieved the loose end of the drawstring and tied it with the feathery tip of the branch in a double knot. She pulled down on her string and branch. It held. She pulled farther, bringing the sapling over in an arch, retreating toward the desiccated corpse of the fir. The branch and the drawstring held. The birch sapling trembled, and Clare twisted the whip-thin fir branch several times around her fist, straining to bring the sapling closer and closer to the ground. One-handed, she tossed the heavy river stone beneath the dead fir and knelt, quickly pawing away some of the snow. She settled down flat on her belly, wiggling herself as far into the painfully sharp needles as she could go.

She pulled on the birch with two hands now, the effort shaking her shoulders, the tension in the branch cutting into her gloves. The sapling was almost buried in the snow now, a few feet of its trunk bowed up into view. It looked, she hoped, like a large fallen branch. Something a tired and angry man wouldn't think twice about stepping over. Or at least stepping near. She couldn't see the light anymore from her hiding place, but he was out there. Close by. On her trail.

She counted her own heartbeats, willing them to slow, disciplining her breath to a deep, even relaxation. She held perfectly still except for an involuntary twitch or shiver, letting herself be covered by a gentle layer of falling snow. The muscles in her arms and shoulders ached from the effort of keeping the springy sapling arched taut. Her feet seemed detached from her legs, which stung and burned from the cold radiating out of the frozen ground. Even the heavy parka wasn't enough to keep her warm, lying motionless in a bed of snow.

Below her, she heard a noise. A slight snagging sound, the liquid slide of nylon dragged over something sharp. She gripped the branch more tightly. Tilting her head a fraction of an inch, she saw the faint glow of the flashlight beam playing over the tops of the fir trees, as if someone were crouched low at the base of the hill, training his light up underneath the first cluster of trees. The light shifted, disappeared.

Clare swallowed. Her heart felt as if it were trying to force sludge through her veins. The light reappeared, clearer now, sweeping across the hillside. It hit the birch trees, canted to the left, and then swung straight across toward her hiding place. She shut her eyes and held her breath. When she dared crack open an eyelid, the light had moved on. The flashlight was rocking, coming closer, the round brightness of it shockingly brilliant in the nighttime darkness. There was no sound of footsteps, no telltale crunch or snap or rustle. The thick, dry snow swallowed everything. He was nearing the kill zone. Cutting a zigzag path up the hill, pausing every few steps, shining his flashlight into the brush and evergreens.

Clare's jaw clenched, excitement and adrenaline warring with fear until her muscles shook. She could make him out behind the light, now, the padded outline of a man, larger than she had thought on the camp road, face concealed behind an enveloping ski mask. He held the flashlight high, over his head, where the reflected light would least impair his own vision. His other arm pointed down, away from his side. Keeping the gun muzzle away from his body. He was cocked and locked then, ready to roll as soon as he caught sight of her.

A few more steps would bring him into range. His caution was the wariness of a hunter afraid of scaring off the game. Underestimating her. She was the hunter here. He had become the game the moment he stepped onto her hill. Everything except her awareness of him faded away, and she watched intently as he moved closer and closer toward the kill. Just a few more steps.

The flashlight beam played over the trees at the top of the hill. He took a step. He took another. Clare squeezed her hands around the branch. Waiting for him to give himself up to her. He shifted the flashlight away from the crest of the hill and scanned the first group of trees again. He paused, searching slowly and carefully with the light. Clare's lungs burned, reminding her to breathe. One. More. Step. One more. Step. One more step. His face still turned downhill, he walked into her trap.

CHAPTER 24

Clare let go the draw. She heard, rather than saw, the swish of the sapling, the snap of the draw whipping the air, the shower of displaced snow. She seized the river rock and was on her feet before the full force of the young tree caught her assailant across the shoulders and back. The gun went off with a deafening hammerclap. His yell of pain cut off abruptly as he crashed belly-first into the snow. She launched herself into the air, smashed full-length onto his back, levered herself to a straddle and raised the rock over the back of his wool-covered skull. He bucked hard as she clubbed downward. Her killing blow fell off-center with a sound like rotten wood breaking open. He gurgled and sagged limply beneath her thighs.

She scrambled backwards, off his body, the rock banging and bruising her fingers as she staggered into a standing position. Crouching, she raised the rock again for the strike that would split his skull open. *If you kill him while he's unconscious, you'll be a murderer*. The thought seemed to come from outside herself. The rock trembled between her hands. *If you aren't gonna do him, at least make sure he's not playin' with you*, the old warrant officer drawled in her ear. She drew back one ice-stiffened boot and kicked the sprawling form as hard as she could between his legs. No reaction. He was for sure either dead or unconscious.

She dropped to her knees and shoved both hands underneath him, flipping him with a grunt. She tugged her gloves off with her teeth and unsnapped the big pockets on his thighs, digging frantically for keys to a car, a truck, a snowmobile. At his waist the pockets had zippers with freezing cold tangs that bit into her fingers as she yanked and wiggled and pried them open. Nothing. The zippers on his arms were the same way, sticking tight, either frozen shut or jammed. She gave up trying to open them, instead compressing and sliding the fabric between her fingertips, hoping for something small and metallic. One pocket held a pencil or pen inside that rolled under her thumb, the other was empty.

Clare squatted back on unfeeling heels, her wet pants clinging to her thighs. Whatever he drove, the keys must still be in it. She pulled her gloves back on. She would have to make her way back to the junction of the camp and mountain roads. He had to have parked somewhere within walking distance of where he first assaulted her. He had to. She breathed deeply, striving for calm.

She looked about for the gun. The flashlight was lighting up a snowbank halfway down the hill, but she didn't see a weapon anywhere. She stood up and circled around her opponent, casting about for a hole in the snow that could hold a firearm. She bounded loosely down the hill, retrieved the flashlight, and played the light over the snow while she hiked back to the unconscious body. Nothing. She blew out a breath in frustration. She was zero for zero. No, that wasn't true. She was awake, on her feet, and had the flashlight. That put her way on top, for the time being.

She crouched at his head and tugged at the ski mask covering everything except his closed eyes. It was a long one, the dark wool disappearing into the zippered and snapped neck of his snowmobile suit. It stretched slightly, but stayed on. She tugged harder. It obscured his eyelids as it slid, then pulled up tight against her grasp. It was either caught in the zipper or fastened inside somehow. Clare tugged again, harder, and his head tilted. He moaned.

She leaped to her feet, raising the flashlight as if to club him senseless again. Except there was no way to ensure that hitting him on the head hard enough to put him out wouldn't also kill him. She didn't want to kill him. She didn't have to kill him. He breathed out, a sigh. All she had to do was make sure she got to his vehicle before he did.

She circled around him and crouched just below his feet. He wore leather and rubber hunting boots, the kind LL Bean made, tucked beneath the elastic opening of his snowmobile suit. Clare pushed the padded nylon up his calf. His boot was laced and knotted tightly to a good five inches above his ankle. She yanked her gloves off again, stuffed them into her pocket, and picked at the double-knotted bow on top. It fell apart under her fingers. She hurriedly unhooked the laces from the endless series of hooks on either side of the tongue, then undid another double-knotted bow. Cradling the heel and toe between her hands, she wrenched the boot off. She wrinkled her nose at the sour smell. He moaned. Louder than the first time.

Clare shoved the other snowmobile suit leg up out of the way and tore at the top knot of his left boot. He moaned again. His leg twitched. She unlaced as quickly as she could down the rows of hooks, her fingers clumsy with tension and cold. She heard his head shift slightly. She scrabbled at the second knot, her fingernails shredding, her heart thumping in her ears. She loosened the knot a few inches before it caught and tightened again. She dug her hands into the boot's tread and yanked, getting her legs under her. She landed on her backside, boot in hand.

Her assailant cried out something unintelligible. Clare dropped the flashlight into one of her cargo pockets, tucked a boot under each arm, and scrambled downhill, slipping and sliding. It took her several seconds to find the false trail she had laid down. Night was no longer imminent, it had arrived, and details that had stood out in the twilight blueness were completely obscured by the darkness and the relentlessly falling snow.

She jogged off at a fast shuffle, headed for the spot beneath the ridge where she had started her ambush trail. If she had kept the relative directions straight in her mind, that ridge should lead toward the mountain road. The flashlight in her pocket banged heavily against her thigh. Useless for finding a way to the mountain road through the trees and the storm. She would use it only as a last resort, if she had to retrace her route all the way from here to the spot on the camp road where the man had tried to shoot her. Otherwise, it would only make her an easy target. She hugged the boots more tightly under her arms. Not that she thought he'd be able to catch up with her now.

From the hillside behind her, she heard an enraged bellow. She skidded to a halt. She turned around, her feet deadened, her legs burning and stinging with cold, her arms cramped and aching. She clutched the boots in her stiff, clumsy hands and shook them over her head.

"Suck wind, you loser! I'm gonna put your boots over my fireplace and laugh at you every time I see 'em!" She spun around and bounded away. Another garbled, angry cry. She could make out, "Bitch!" and "kill you . . ." There was a sound of branches cracking, a deep whumpf as a heavy load of snow slid off an evergreen. Was he coming after her? Clare churned through the snow, blinking away the flakes that landed on her eyelashes, desperate to find that ridge.

She fell onto it, face first, when her nerveless feet rolled over a branch hidden underfoot and sent her sprawling. She swiped at her face, a hopeless gesture of drying, and groped for the boots. Dangling one glove from her teeth, she knotted the laces together and hung them over her shoulder. She went up the ridge soundlessly, listening for any indications that her attacker was on her trail. The huge silence of the forest was disorienting; she had no way of knowing if he had given up on catching her or if the sounds of his pursuit were being muffled by the snow and the trees.

At the top of the ridge, Clare crouched, looking for her old tracks. She finally found a few, frighteningly indiscernable, already vanishing under the falling snow. She stood up, thighs and back complaining, and pressed a gloved thumb hard between her eyes. Risk that the ridge would lead her to the road? Or backtrack along to the camp road, hoping that there was enough of a trail left to follow?

There was a sharp crack followed by a rustle. Impossible to tell how far away. Her heart seized hard, trying to send the icy slurry that was her blood into her frozen extremities. Time to fish or cut bait. She took one last look at the blurred marks she had left climbing up the ridge during her flight from the camp road. She stamped her boots and waded into the virgin snow to her right.

It was slow going. Plodding over branches and around trees, stumbling down one side or another and scrambling back up to the narrow ridge crest, misstepping again and again because she felt as if she were walking on wooden boxes, unable to read the terrain under her feet.

The cold stole inside quietly, implacably. Her legs had gone numb. Beneath her parka, she shivered spasmodically, violent quakes that did nothing to dispel the damp chill of her skin. Her face felt raw, her hands distant and unwieldy. Even her brain seemed stiff with cold. Instead of listening alertly for any noise from her attacker, she found herself drifting, mesmerized by her legs breaking the snow, by the constant movement of the flakes filling the air, by the patterns of the trees she slapped against as she plowed onward. Birch, pine, birch, unknown, fir, fir, hemlock.

With a start, she realized she had run out of ridge. The thin spine of rock had melded seamlessly into the forest floor, no slope on either side of her to keep her headed in one direction. No indication of which way she should continue. Nothing to keep her from wandering in circles until she surrendered to the cold. *They say hypothermia is a happy death*, the old warrant officer observed. Angry, frustrated tears flooded her eyes and spilled over, hot against her raw skin. She took off a glove and wiped them away with the heel of her hand. Breathed in shakily. Okay. She would navigate by line-sighting between trees, even if she could only see a few feet ahead. Tree by tree, she would try to keep to a straight path. If she didn't reach the road within . . . a half hour, she would dig in. Branches and evergreen boughs were sure to provide her with some protection. Snow itself was an insulating material.

She had to force her spine to straighten, her legs to move forward. Her fear had cooled, too, to chilly despair. She sighted a marker tree and stumbled through the snow. When she reached it, she did it again. And again. And again.

When she caught the first flash of light from the corner of her eye, it almost didn't register. It flashed again, and she jerked her head left, her mouth dropping open. It was a flashlight beam, a strong one, casting through the forest from some distance away. She steadied herself against a birch. Either she was saved, or there were two of them. All she had to do was find out which.

She giggled involuntarily. All she had to do was stalk this one, knock him down and whack him with her flashlight. Then she could take his car keys. She giggled again, shrilly, unable to stop herself. *Stress and tension*, the warrant officer drawled. *Screws up your thinkin'*. She swallowed a giggle, hiccuped, giggled some more. Hit herself three times hard in the midsection. When she was silent again, she set out for the light in the distance.

* * *

"Dispatch ten-fifteen, this is unit ten-fifty-seven." Russ gingerly picked up the Styrofoam cup of hot cocoa and blew on it.

"Unit ten-fifty-seven, this is dispatch."

"Hey, Harlene. You get ahold of Lyle and Noble yet?"

"I reached Lyle, he said he can come on in. Haven't been able to find Noble yet."

Russ took a sip and swiped whipped cream off his upper lip. His arteries were probably clogging even as he idled in the Kreemie Kakes parking lot, but on a stormy winter afternoon, nothing beat their homemade hot chocolate. He'd do penance later tonight when Linda served up frozen diet dinners. "Keep trying. Two Saturdays before Christmas, nobody's gonna let a snowstorm stop 'em from shopping. I want to make sure we have enough men on the road once folks start plowing into each other."

"That's why I'm doing all my Christmas shopping over the phone this year."

Russ took another sip before keying his mike. "Did you know Linda wants to put out a catalogue?" It was all she could talk about when he had picked her up at the train station noontime.

"Does she? Good for her! Sell enough of those fancy curtains and you can retire a rich man. Let her support you."

"That's the plan." He slid the hot chocolate into a plastic cup holder. The prices she had been quoting for publishing the damn thing would have made his eyes pop out if he hadn't been wearing his glasses, but she was convinced the increased sales would make it worthwhile. Linda knew a damn sight more about the care and feeding of money than he ever would. He hadn't asked if increased sales would make their lives more worthwhile.

"Dispatch, I'm rolling out of Main and Canal, heading for Route forty-seven. Anything else?"

"Reverend Fergusson called a half hour ago. Said she'd be in her office in the church until five thirty or so. Want me to raise her for you?"

He tapped the microphone against his chin. "No," he said, "I'll swing by that way. Let me know if you can't get Noble, we may have to call in one of the part-time guys. It's gonna be a mess out here within a few hours."

The church was dark when Russ pulled into the tiny parking area out back, but he could see lights shining from the attached building that housed the offices and parish hall. The kitchen door was locked tight. He followed the walkway shoveled around the parish hall until he reached the big double doors. Open, of course. He shook his head. It wouldn't occur to her to lock the door behind her.

"Clare? Hey, Clare, it's me. Russ." He brushed snow off his parka. The coffeemaker squatting on the table was on. So were the hall lights. In Clare's office, the remains of a fire burned low on the brick hearth. Her appointment book, a fistful of pink phone message slips and a half-full mug of cold coffee sat on her desk.

"Clare? You here?" Maybe she had run over to the rectory? He backtracked outside, crossed the parking area and craned to see over the tall boxwood hedge separating Clare's driveway from the church grounds. The rectory was dark. No tire tracks or footprints marred the fresh snow on her steps.

Frowning, he returned to her office. What the hell had taken her in such an all-fired hurry she couldn't bank the fire or turn off the coffeemaker? He glanced at her appointment book. Nothing for Saturday except a morning visit to the Infirmary. He flipped through the pink phone message slips. Nothing. He walked down the shadowy hall to the cold, dark church. A single votive candle hung in a red glass container to the left of the altar, washing a carved wooden cabinet with a ruddy glow. "Clare?" he called. His voice echoed back from hard lines of stone.

He slapped his gloves against one thigh, talking himself out of the unease creeping up the base of his skull. She had probably been called away on one of those mysterious "pastoral emergencies." No big deal. There was nothing compelling him to find out what it was. Of course, if he listened to the answering machine, he might be able to figure out where she had gone without making an ass of himself calling around. He stalked back up the hall, annoyed at Clare for being so damn hard to get hold of, annoyed even more at himself for wasting time worrying about it.

The main office was as dark as the church. He snapped on the lights, dropped into the secretary's chair, punched the blinking red button on the answering machine. It beeped and obediently began reciting its messages. Next to the phone was a spiral-bound book for written messages, yellow carbon copies, and unused pink tear-out squares. He sat up straighter. There were carbon records of his calls, that one about the baptism, a meeting, and there, slopping over two spaces, a detailed message he hadn't seen on Clare's desk.

Russ held the memorandum book at arm's length, tilting his head back to make out the words. A meeting with Kristen McWhorter up in the mountains? He closed his eyes, envisioning the route described on the message copy. Somewhere around Tenant or Buck Mountain? West of Lake Lucerne. Wherever this cabin was, it would be one hell of a tough drive for Clare's car. He cut off the recording in the middle of some woman going on about her son and dialed the station. "Harlene? I need you to find a phone number for me. Kristen McWhorter. It'll be in either McWhorter file."

He traced the slashes underlining URGENT! while waiting for Harlene to return with the number. Jumping into that piece of flashy junk and driving into the mountains without stopping to think about the consequences sounded just like Clare. Somebody needed to teach that woman to measure twice and cut once.

"Chief?" Harlene rattled off Kristen's number. "Anything I can help with?"

"Nah. I'm just trying to track down Reverend Fergusson. She's not here at the church. If she happens to call in, make sure you find out how I can reach her."

"You got it."

He hung up and immediately dialed Kristen's apartment. It rang once. Twice. Three times.

"Hello?"

"Kristen? This is Chief Van Alstyne."

"Oh, Christ. What is it now? You find something new?"

"No. Kristen, did you call Reverend Fergusson earlier today and ask her to meet you and your mother at a cousin's cabin? Someplace near Tenant Mountain?"

There was a blank pause. "What? I'm sorry, Chief, my cousins live in trailers, not mountain cabins. I haven't spoken with Clare since the day before yesterday. What's going on?"

The unease Russ had been fending off jelled into a solid icy mass of dread. "I'll get back to you."

"Can you—"

He dropped the receiver in its cradle, rubbing his forehead with his fist. Christ on a bicycle. The question of who had set out to lure Clare into the Adirondack wilds would have to be put on hold. Whatever was waiting for her there was more important.

He tore the yellow carbon sheet out of the memorandum book and left the church office at a fast dogtrot. In his cruiser, he radioed Harlene while firing the engine up and maneuvering out of the tiny parking area. "Ten-fifteen, this is ten-fifty-seven, come in."

"Ten-fifty-seven, this is dispatch, come back."

"Harlene, I want you to call in Tim and Duane for traffic duty. Somebody pretending to be Kristen McWhorter conned Reverend Fergusson into driving up into the mountains." Squinting at the yellow sheet, he read the directions to Harlene. "I'm heading after her. I'm inbound to the station, gonna switch this cruiser for my truck. She'll handle the roads up there better." He slowed to take the left onto Main.

"Do you want me to send backup along?"

He frowned at the snow spattering against his windshield. "No. I have a feeling we're going to be short-handed as it is. I can handle this. Ten-fifty-seven out."

He pulled into the station's parking lot as he hung up his mike. His truck was parked in the rear, already blanketed with snow. He killed the cruiser's engine, got out, unlocked the trunk. From its locked safety box, he removed the rifle and a box of shells. He cracked the magazine. The chambers were loaded.

Russ laid the rifle and the ammunition in the backseat of the pickup before starting it up. It roared to life reassuringly, warming up fast as Russ swept the dry powdery snow off the windows and headlights. By the time he hiked himself up into the cab, warm air was blasting from the vents. He tossed his gloves onto the yellow memorandum sheet, reversed, and rolled out of the lot, the four-wheel-drive gripping tight to the packed-down snow.

He made good time, considering the roads. Traffic was heavy on Route 9, as he had predicted, shoppers heading home to fix dinner passing shoppers just hitting the stores. The evening trade would be starting soon, maybe not dinners-out so much in this storm, but worse, habitual drinkers who spent every Saturday night on a barstool, Christmas party-goers who wouldn't see anything wrong in having just one more cup of rum and eggnog.

The driving was trickier once he had taken the exit to Tenant Road. His truck held well to the road, but it was a bad surface, driven over just enough to be slushy and half-frozen. His windshield wipers beat away steadily at the spitting snow. The sound made him think of Wednesday night, driving through the last storm, Clare in the passenger seat, exhausted and weeping. Paying attention to everyone's feelings except her own, until they snuck up and blindsided her. A single car approached. He squinted to make it out, snorting as it crept past slowly. Some Subaru. God damn, he should have dragged her to the Fort Henry dealership and made her lease something winter-worthy.

He passed a mom-and-pop store. Once its lights had dwindled in his rearview mirror, there was nothing except rising country and snow. His headlights tunneled through the dark, barely reaching two or three truck lengths before vanishing in the storm. The touch of light on each snowflake was as distracting as popping flashbulbs. Long habit helped him ignore the show, concentrating instead on what he could see of the road ahead.

Even so, he overshot the mountain road. The gap in the trees and the blank white roadbed registered a few seconds after he had seen it. He slowed carefully, taking his time before finally stopping and turning the truck around. Too many people forgot four-wheel-drive was meant to help acceleration, not braking. He had cleaned up too many of their accidents to make the same mistake.

His pickup ground slowly up the mountain road. He shook his head, trying to imagine Clare making it up here in her featherweight car. If she had made it. The snow had covered any traces of tire tracks that might show her route up the narrow, twisting road. He checked the trip odometer against the numbers on the directions. He ought to be getting close. If there was no sign of her at the cabin, he didn't know what the hell he was going to do.

The unmistakable sound of a shot made him jerk reflexively, swearing. He slammed on his brakes, sending the truck into an angled skid. Twisted off the heat and killed the engine, rolling down his window clumsily. There was a bump, and the silent truck slid backwards and down slightly, its rear wheels coming to rest in the snow-covered gully at the edge of the road. Russ thrust his head through the window, straining to hear any other noise through the darkness.

CHAPTER 25

The slithery hissing of dry snow meeting snow. Everything else was an immense silence. He didn't realize he had been holding his breath until it rushed out of his chest. He opened the glove compartment and removed his flashlight, long and heavy, a weapon in itself. Reaching into the backseat, he retrieved the box of shells and the rifle. He poured a good handful of shells into his coat pocket before tugging on his hat and gloves and stepping out of the cab.

He hesitated at the edge of the trees. He didn't dare go more than a dozen yards from the road in the dark with no compass. He tugged his knit hat lower on his forehead. The thought of walking toward an unknown shooter shining a light and calling out made his nuts want to crawl back up inside his body. But if Clare had been—if she couldn't see him, he could search for a week without stumbling over her. He cradled the rifle and thumbed his flashlight on. What the hell. Either the shooter wasn't interested, or he was going to get drilled. Either way, he wasn't walking out of here without doing everything he could to bring Clare with him.

He waded into the forest, sweeping his light around in 180 degree arcs, listening for anything that might indicate the presence of another human being. The cold pinched at his face. He thought of Clare, underdressed for the weather as usual, slogging deeper and deeper into the woods, slowly freezing to death. A hundred paces into the trees, he angled back toward the road, traveling downhill. If someone had been shooting, she must be around here. Noise traveled far in the mountains, but that shot had been close. Too damn close. He held up his arm to fend off lashing branches of bittersweet, trying not to picture her lying in a crumpled heap, her blood staining the snow red.

He angled again, away from the road, pushing through pines and hemlock. It was important to be methodical, not to give into the urge to run around yelling. A long zigzag pattern, working his way downhill because that's the direction most lost folks take, his light shining like a beacon.

He heard nothing except his own breathing and the sweep and stretch of snow over the mountain. His throat closed over the fear rising in his gorge. Not the fear that he might get drilled by whoever else was out here with a gun. Fear that Clare was gone for good.

The flashlight beam hit him straight in the eyes, blinding him. He yelped involuntarily, so startled his mind went blank. His body knew how to think for him, though, dropping into the snow and sighting the rifle toward the other light.

"Russ?" Her voice was weak and cracking from the cold.

"Clare?" He scrambled back to his feet, swinging his flashlight in her direction. "Oh, my God. Clare." She staggered toward him. He crossed the distance first, catching her in his arms, the rifle and flashlight clunking together as he picked her up off the ground. "Clare. Jesus, are you all right? Were you hit?"

"My feet . . . I can't feel my feet anymore."

He released her to shine the light over her again. Her face was raw, chapped and scratched. Thank God she had been wearing a departmental parka. It looked as if it were holding up, but her pants were wet up to her thighs and chunks of ice and caked snow were frozen to her flimsy boots. He flashed the light up again.

"What the hell are you doing with hunting boots hung over your shoulder?" She opened her mouth. "No, don't tell me now. My truck's about seventy yards away. I can carry you, but I think we'll be faster and steadier if you can walk."

She nodded. "I can walk," she said.

He looked around them. "The shooter—is he close? Did you get a look at him?"

She shook her head. "I couldn't see his face. He's—" She rubbed her eyes with a snow-clotted glove and blinked hard. "I don't know if he's close by. He's unarmed, though. He lost his gun when I took him out."

He hung the rifle strap on his shoulder and took her arm, shining his flashlight toward the way out of the woods. "You took him out? What do you mean?"

She clutched at his arm, but otherwise walked steadily. "I knocked him down with a sapling tree and bashed him with a rock. I couldn't find his gun, but I took his flashlight and his boots."

He helped her over a fallen log. "You took his flashlight and his boots."

"I wanted to find his car keys but he wasn't carrying them. I was . . ." She gulped air. "I was working my way back to the road. To find his car or whatever. Snowmobile." He tightened his grip on her arm. She gulped again. "But I was going the other way when I saw your light, Russ. I was going the wrong way." Her voice cracked. "I thought I was headed for the road, but I must have gotten turned around. I would have . . . I would have just kept on walking . . ."

Up ahead, he saw a flash where the light caught metal. "Almost there." He couldn't see her face. Only the fur encircling the hood. He forced himself to speak confidently. "You wouldn't have kept on walking, darlin'. You're too smart. You would have dug in, covered yourself up. Probably figured out some way to build a fire. With pine needles and a gum wrapper."

She made a dry sound, halfway between a laugh and a sob. He could see his truck clearly now. "C'mon, let me take you up." He picked her off the ground and settled her against his shoulder, grunting with the effort. "Good God, woman, what are you wearing, lead-lined pants?" She made the sound again, this time more a laugh.

At the truck, he opened the passenger's door first and helped her in. Climbing into the driver's side, he almost laid the rifle in the backseat again, then thought better and slid it bore-down next to the door, within a moment's reach. He fired up the engine and turned on the dome light before rummaging in the back for his two spare blankets. "Okay, darlin', let's get your wet things off."

She nodded jerkily. She pulled off her sodden gloves and dropped them on the floor, but she couldn't manage the snap and zipper at her neck. "My fingers," she said.

He nodded. "We need to take a look at your feet first anyway." He lifted her stiff, ice-encrusted boots into his lap. "What the hell did you do to get these so wet?" The laces were unmanagable. He flipped open the glove compartment and removed his knife.

"I . . . ran through a stream. Only fast way to . . . get to the spot I picked to . . . ambush him." She shivered violently as he sliced her laces away and gently wiggled each boot off. "I'm so cold . . ."

He adjusted the vents to blow on her. The hot air was already blasting at top speed. He carefully peeled away her socks, sucking in his breath at the sight of the blotchy white patches mottling blueish skin. Jesus. How had she hiked through the woods like this? Under his hands the flesh felt like heavy clay that had been stored in a refrigerator. "Oh, darlin'," he said.

"Is it bad?" He looked at her. "Tell me the truth, Russ."

"It doesn't look like frostbite, but we're going to have to

soak your feet in cool water and bring 'em up to temperature slowly. Here, let's get those pants off you." He tried to be gentle, but he had to tug and wrestle the stiff, wet khaki off her, each jerk and twist causing her to gasp. "I'm sorry, I'm so sorry, Clare."

She shook her head. "No, it's good. It's burning. That's a good sign, isn't it?"

"Yeah. Means the blood is coming back." The skin on her legs was alarmingly cold and pale, but there were no signs of frostbite there, either. He cocooned her feet and legs in one of the blankets. "It's gonna hurt like a bitch when you get circulation going. Like when your leg falls asleep, but lots worse." He kept her legs resting on his thighs while he went to work on the parka, unbuttoning and unzipping. Underneath, her woolly turtleneck was dry. He wrapped the second blanket around her, chafed her hands between his own. "How do they feel?"

"Cold. Like the rest of me."

"Can you feel this?" He ran his fingertips lightly down her fingers and across her palm.

She looked at him. Her eyes were huge and dark. Her fingers flexed over his. "Yes," she whispered. The hot air roared past him, stirring staticky cobwebs of her hair. He opened his mouth to speak, then shut it again. She raised her free hand as if she would touch his cheek, then let it fall. "I'm so glad you're here," she said. She blinked against the watery light in her eyes. "I was such a jerk last night. I'm sorry, you were right, you were right about everything."

He dropped his gaze to her hand, picked up the other one and began rubbing them vigorously. "Maybe. But I shouldn't have been such a hard ass about it." He smiled at her. "And I wasn't right about everything. Ballistics came back negative on their gun. We're still waiting to hear about the hair and fiber samples from their cars." He looked at her extraordinary face, laced by angry scratches and chafed raw by the snow and cold. He squeezed her hands hard. "I was right about one thing, though. This isn't any business of yours. Jesus, Clare, you could have died out there!"

She smiled waveringly. "Not me. I'm too smart."

He released her hands, swinging her feet to the floor. He reached around her and buckled her in. "Let's get you someplace warm, smart girl."

The truck strained and groaned before lurching from the ditch and turning slowly back down the road. "What about the man who attacked me?" Clare asked.

Russ kept his attention on the road. "What about him?"

"Aren't you going to try to find him? Or at least find his vehicle?"

He spared her a glance. "Do you have any idea where he is? Or where his truck or snowmobile is?"

"No."

"And he doesn't have any boots on?"

"No."

"You said you couldn't see his face?"

"No! He had one of those face masks on, and I tried to get it off, but the damn thing was stuck!" She snorted. "Then he started to wake up and I thought I'd be better served getting the heck out of there."

"Good girl. And the answer is no, I'm not going after him. I could turn out the National Guard and we'd still never find him in this weather. My first priority is to get you thawed out. We can be at the Glens Falls Hospital in half an hour if the county's gotten the plows out."

"No. No hospital. I don't like hospitals."

"You go to hospitals all the time, for Chrissake!"

"Not for myself!" She had an edge of hysteria to her voice. He shut up. "Just take me home, Russ," she said. "Please."

"Okay, darlin'. Home it is." He downshifted in preparation for churning the truck out of the snow and leaf-filled gully. *And then I'm going to get someone to take a look at you if I have to knock you down and sit on you to do it.*

CHAPTER 26

They didn't talk much on the ride back to Millers Kill. Clare leaned back against the seat, exhausted, her mouth thinning occasionally when they went over a bump. He knew her legs must be hurting. Despite his sensible words, he was sorely tempted to round up as many men as he could and scour the mountain for the sonofabitch who had done this to her. But he had been right, it would be a waste of time at this point. Either the guy had found his way back to his vehicle or he was losing his feet to exposure someplace.

He glanced over at Clare. Knocked him down with a tree and bashed him with a rock. Jesus. He smiled a little.

When they pulled into her driveway, he said, "Keys?"

"I left them in my car. But don't worry, it's—"

"Unlocked. Of course." She didn't argue when he opened her door and picked her up to carry her inside. He grunted as they went up the steps. "Don't make a habit of this, Clare, or I'm going to have to buy a truss."

Inside, he deposited her blanket-wrapped form on the sofa and cranked up the thermostat. "Okay," he said, "You need dry clothes, a tub of tepid water to soak those feet in—" She groaned loudly at the suggestion. "—and something warm to drink. Not coffee, the caffeine's bad for your circulation."

"Hot cocoa?"

"That's fine. Where can I find stuff?"

She gave him directions. Her bedroom was spartan, nothing but bed, dresser, and her Army sweats tossed over some wooden kneeler-prayer-thingy in front of the uncurtained window. He grabbed the sweats and dropped them next to her on the sofa before hitting the kitchen to find the cocoa ingredients. No bags of instant, of course. He put the milk on to heat and rummaged beneath the sink for a plastic tub, which he filled with lukewarm water.

"You decent?" he called from the kitchen.

"Yeah."

He walked slowly, careful not to slosh the water. "Stick your feet in there," he said, settling the tub in front of the sofa. She pulled the legs of her sweatpants up a bit and complied.

"It feels warm." She looked surprised.

"That's because your feet are so damn cold. I don't have to do anything like hand-grate imported bittersweet chocolate and hazelnuts for this hot cocoa, do I?"

She made a face. "Just sugar and cocoa. Oh, and a drop of vanilla extract is nice."

"I have to introduce you to the Kreemie Kakes Diner version of hot chocolate." He found everything quickly. Like her office, her kitchen was orderly and well-organized. She was a woman who had her priorities, no doubt about it.

"Here you go." He put two mugs on the coffee table, then crossed to the front window and tested to see if the tops locked.

She craned her neck to see what he was up to. "What are you doing?"

"Locking you in." He moved to the front door, threw the bolt and latched it at the top. "Who can I call to come and stay with you tonight?"

"Russ!" She sounded scandalized. "I couldn't impose on anyone like that."

He turned to her. "Clare, someone put a lot of effort into killing you tonight. Let's not make it any easier for him to take a second crack at you."

"But he's—"

"We don't know what he is. The guy who attacked you might be a Popsicle right now. Or he might have gotten onto his snowmobile and ridden away. And don't forget whoever that woman was who called the church to get you out there."

She worried her lower lip. "All right. You can make sure the doors and windows are all locked," she said. "But I don't know anyone well enough to ask over. It would be an imposition."

"Your mother teach you that? You sound very Southern when you say 'an imposition.' " He crossed the room to stand in front of her sofa. "You're exhausted and you can barely walk. You think of someone you can 'impose' on right quick like or I'll station one of my officers here." She glared at him. "Which will mean taking someone away from traffic duty during a major storm."

Her face melted into a look of concern. She gnawed on her lower lip again. "Doctor Anne," she said finally. "Anne Vining-Ellis. She lives a couple blocks away."

"She the same Doctor Anne who works the Glens Falls emergency room?" Clare nodded. "I've met her. I'll give her a call." There was a cordless phone on the table behind the sofa. He dialed information, punched in the number and headed for the stairs. "I'm going to check the upstairs windows," he told Clare.

"I can't believe I'm letting you do this," she said.

"Hello, Ellis residence." He jiggled the latches in Clare's bedroom. Locked.

"Hi, is this Dr. Vining-Ellis?"

"Sure is."

Another bedroom was empty except for a Nordictrak exercise machine and a floormat. The windows were locked.

"This is Chief Van Alstyne of the Millers Kill Police Department. We've met a few times before—"

"Over a few drunk drivers. Of course. How can I help you, Chief?"

He sketched out the situation while testing the latches in the next bedroom. It looked as if it had been a guest room for the former priest, and nothing had been removed. He was pretty sure the gun and dog prints and the dark Depression-era furniture weren't Clare's. Doctor Anne was horrified at the story of her priest's ordeal. "Of course I'll come over and stay with her," she said. "It's absolutely no trouble at all. I'll bring my kit and give her a going-over, too, just to make sure she doesn't need to be admitted to the hospital."

He thanked the doctor and rang off. One of the windows in the bathroom was propped open a sliver. A fine line of snow had accumulated on the sill. He shut and locked it. The toilet was running, and he couldn't get it to stop by jiggling the handle. Inside the cistern, the plunging apparatus was falling apart. He frowned. Couldn't her parishioners pay for a plumber, for Chrissakes? Well, he could pick up something at Tim's Hardware, put it in for her next time he was around this way.

"Doctor Anne's on her way over," he announced as he reentered the living room. Clare groaned. "And she said to tell you it was not an imposition." He stuck his hand in the water her feet were soaking in. Cooling. "So, you wanna tell me about what happened?" He headed into the kitchen for more hot water.

"Master Sergeant Ashley 'Hardball' Wright saved my sorry ass," she called after him.

He poked his head through the swinging doors before emerging with a teakettle of hot water. "Hey! I thought I saved your sorry ass."

She smiled faintly. "You helped. You surely did help." She sipped her hot cocoa and dabbled her feet while he poured a thin stream of steaming hot water into the tub. "How on earth did you know I was out there?"

He told her about finding the paper trail at St. Alban's and calling Kristen.

"So she didn't have anything to do with it. Well, I didn't think so, not after that guy took a shot at me." She tipped her head back and closed her eyes. "Although before that, when I drove my car over a cliff, I had my doubts. Maybe she was just really bad at directions."

"You drove your car over a cliff? Christ."

She frowned.

"Sorry."

"Well, maybe it wasn't quite a cliff. A big gorge. My car is totaled." She compressed her lips in an expression he was beginning to recognize. "I loved that car. I don't get attached to many material things, but I really loved that car."

"You have any idea who could have been behind this?"

"How about this? This morning, I found out that Katie's secret lover was Wesley Fowler. His family are members of the congregation. And about as far from the McWhorter's as you can get, socially, culturally, economically . . ."

"How the hell did you get that piece of information?"

She told him about her visit to Paul's office at the Infirmary and the photograph. "It's still in the pocket of my parka. Your parka," she amended. "I visited the Fowlers to see if they knew anything about it, which they didn't, unsurprisingly. Then I went to Albany."

"Albany?"

"I wanted to see if Katie's roommates might recognize Wesley's picture."

He rolled his eyes. "You know, Clare, the Albany PD already questioned at least two of the roommates."

"But they didn't have a picture, and I did. And I had his

yearbook." She twisted on the sofa to face him more fully. "Ow! You were right about the hot prickles. Anyway, at first I thought it was a bust, because none of the girls recognized Wes. But then, just by chance, they spotted a picture of Alyson Shattham. And guess what? She had been to see Katie. It was not a cheerful social visit. They had a fight."

"When was this?" He swept the newspaper off one overstuffed armchair and perched on the edge.

"Beginning of the school year. September."

"Huh. Little Alyson Shattam. Who said she hadn't seen Katie since graduation."

"Guess who Alyson's boyfriend was all through last year."

He smiled slowly. "Wesley Fowler."

"Ten points."

"Where is this kid? Still in town?"

"No, he's a plebe at West Point. His father's gone down to bring him back, though. They should be here tomorrow."

He began twisting the sheets of newspaper into kindling. "Want a fire?"

"Please."

He raked the old ashes to one side and laid splitwood from a big basket over the paper. He crossed two small logs over the kindling and struck one of her silly six-inch-long matches. "Alyson and Wes," he said, tossing the match on the fire with five inches left unburnt. "A boy and a girl. Go to the same church. Are their families friends?"

"Oh yes," she said. He sprawled back onto the armchair. "Oh, I feel warmer already. I may become addicted to fires."

"Yeah, the Shattams were with the Fowlers this morning when I went over. I knew about Alyson and Wes before, though. Dr. Anne's son gave me the inside scoop on all the high school gossip this past Monday. Sounded like they were the classic king and queen of the prom pair."

"You sound a tad disenchanted, there."

"Oh . . . that's just an old high school outsider looking in,

I suppose." She crossed her arms over her chest. "You've met Alyson. She clearly believes that the world owes it to her to treat her like the princess she is. And from what I've heard of Wes Fowler, he's the same type, a golden boy who's never had anything bad happen to him."

"So what do you think? Did Alyson know Wes was seeing Katie on the side? Maybe she wouldn't put out and Katie would? So she let Katie keep Wesley-boy happy?"

"There's no doubt that Katie did, as you oh-so-tastefully phrased it, 'put out.' But honestly, I can't see Alyson Shattham standing by while her boyfriend gets . . . serviced. She strikes me more as the kind of girl to keep him on as tight a leash as possible."

"Yeah, I know that type. Gets her kicks from making some poor slob jump through hoops for the promise of some—" Clare was looking at him with undisguised interest. He felt the tips of his ears redden. "Never mind. I agree, it's more likely Alyson didn't know that Katie was sleeping with Wes."

"But then, at some point, it's more than just sleeping with her. He gets her pregnant. Could he have come running to Alyson then?"

"What for?"

"Help. Advice. Forgiveness. Knowing a little bit about the psychology of teenage boys, I'm willing to bet a non-pregnant girlfriend suddenly looked a lot more appealing to him."

"She looked genuinely surprised to me that morning at your church. Of course, I've been fooled before." He watched Clare twist a strand of hair around her finger and chew her lip. "Okay. Let's say he did tell her. What do the king and queen of the prom do when he's gotten another girl knocked up?"

"They make the problem disappear?"

"Let's say Wesley persuades Katie to give away the baby."

"That could explain Alyson's visit to Albany. Maybe she was the go-between, trying to talk Katie into it."

"But a few days after leaving the baby at your back door, Katie gets back in touch with Wesley. She says she can't stand it, she wants the baby back."

"I don't think Wes Fowler would have been too keen to have it come out that he got a girl from Depot Street pregnant and then abandoned the baby outside St. Alban's on a freezing winter's night. The West Point commandant and the ethics commission take a dim view of that sort of thing."

Russ snorted.

"And there had already been a story in the paper, remember? The day after we found the baby? There wouldn't have been much chance of him keeping it quiet if Katie tried to reclaim Cody."

"So one of them—Wesley or Alyson—decides to stop Katie before she can tell anyone she's the baby's mom. One of them gets her out by the kill and cracks her head open and leaves her there to die."

She swished her feet through the water.

"But then another problem rears its ugly head," he said. "Darrell, who evidently once saw Katie and Wes together."

"He must have seen the Fowlers' family picture on our parish bulletin board Wednesday morning when he met with me and the Burnses. That would explain why he broke off the discussion so quickly, if he had a name to put with a face, finally." She shook her head, silent for a moment.

"If he did, it's not your fault, Clare." She glanced up at him. "You've got your responsible look on," he explained. She gave him a half smile. "We know he called somebody. Maybe he was putting the squeeze on Wesley, and the kid high-tailed it back to town and put a bullet through Darrell's slimy little brain."

"Or Alyson did."

He looked at her, nonplused. She spread her hands. "You think she couldn't? Maybe she's the shooter while Wes went to the house in Albany to collect any incriminating evidence."

"The guy who said he was Katie's father? The roommate described him as older, with a mustache."

"According to Dr. Anne's boy, Wes Fowler was in the Millers Kill High School Drama Society. He appeared in several plays and in the yearly musical. A little left-over gray tint in his hair, a fake moustache . . . it might been enough to fool a couple of freshmen who had had a few too many beers."

Russ slid out of his chair and squatted on the floor in front of her. "Let's have a foot." She lifted one, dripping, out of the water and let him squeeze it. "Need to heat it up a bit," he said. He held a hand against the copper teakettle, checking to make sure it was still warm before pouring a stream of warm water into the tub.

She made a noise in the back of her throat, flexing her toes. "If he did kill Darrell and clean out Katie's room, he must have thought at that point he had covered all the bases. There wasn't anything to link him to Katie except Cody himself, and who would think to ask for Wes Fowler's DNA to test for paternity of poor Katie McWhorter's abandoned child?"

"Nobody, until the Reverend Fergusson got her hands on a photo of the two of them together and immediately rushed over to confront his proud parents with evidence that one plus one makes three." He turned to the fireplace and tossed another log in. "Holy Christ, Clare. You really could have died up on that mountain. You were supposed to have died." He rubbed the back of his neck.

"Would he have had time to get from West Point to here and set up that ambush for me?"

He stood slowly, turning around, scanning the dark corners of the room without meaning to. "I don't see why not. It's a three-hour drive at most, another hour to get himself parked somewhere safe on a camp road on Tenant Mountain. It's not as if he needed to come up with an elaborate way to trap you.

All he needed was a good way to get you up to that mountain and someone pretending to be Kristen McWhorter."

"Which brings us back to Alyson."

"She knew you were helping Kristen, didn't she?"

Clare nodded.

"And she must have known you're the sort to charge off to help first, without asking questions until later."

She cocked her head at him. "You make me sound like the Lone Ranger."

"Doesn't make it untrue. The fact that you're impulsive is not a deeply hidden character trait."

"I prefer to think of it as making decisions quickly."

"I'm sure you do. Prefer to think of it that way."

The doorbell chimed. He headed for the kitchen to admit a snow-dusted Dr. Anne.

"My car's blocking you in, so we'll have to switch," she said, unwinding an immense scarf from her neck. "How is she?"

"I've got her soaking in a tub of lukewarm water that I've been heating up gradually." The doctor stared at him. The tips of his ears reddened. "I mean, her feet. She's soaking her feet. In there." He led Dr. Anne into the living room in time to see Clare standing wobbly-legged, clutching at the back of the sofa. "What the hell do you think you're doing?" he said, more loudly than he intended.

She grinned at him tensely. "I believe it's called 'walking.' It's all the rage of the over-one-year-old set. Hi, Dr. Anne."

"Sit down, you damn fool woman."

She straightened, releasing the sofa. The lines and planes of her face tightened. "I have things to do," she said through gritted teeth. "I have to call Kristen, and Mrs. Fowler. And the deacons, to let them know I may not be able to celebrate seven A.M. Eucharist tomorrow morning."

He reached over the sofa and wrapped his hand around her

arm. "You don't need to prove how tough you are. I already know. Clare, please. Sit down."

She looked at him, then sat.

Dr. Anne dropped her medical bag on the sofa next to Clare. "As soon as I've checked you out, I'll help you make those phone calls." She glanced at Russ. "Anything in particular I need to watch out for?"

"You see anything, or hear anything that makes you feel uneasy, call the station. No, give me a call." He scrawled his home number on the scratch pad next to the cordless phone base.

"I will, Chief. Let's move those cars so you can get out."

He looked down at Clare. She smiled crookedly. "Thank you. It seems inadequate, but thank you."

He crossed his arms over his chest. "Just take care of yourself. I'll see you tomorrow. Try not to get into any trouble until then, okay?"

"Okay."

Dr. Anne waited while he pulled on his boots and coat. Outside, snow still fell furiously. His truck was already blanketed again. "I can't thank you enough for coming to stay with her," he said. "She's so damn busy taking care of other people's needs she completely ignores her own."

Dr. Anne smiled knowingly. "Mmmm. Yes, I know the type." She paused, one hip bumped against her car door. "Chief? I don't mean to pry, but I heard Clare's car was parked at the foot of your drive all night Wednesday."

"What? That's ridiculous! I mean, yeah, it was there, but that's because it was snowing and I drove her home."

Dr. Anne raised her hands placatingly. "I'm not trying to imply anything. I just wanted you to know that if I've heard talk, other people have too. It's a small town."

Russ hauled open his truck door. "Christ, isn't that the truth. If folks are so interested in the whereabouts of Clare's car, let's hope somebody saw something that'll tell us who wanted to dump it into a gorge. With her along for the ride."

CHAPTER 27

Clare looked out at her congregation as the last notes from the communion hymn faded and wondered if one of the people looking back at her wanted her dead. Alyson Shattham and her mother were in their usual spots, but the Fowlers, who usually sat nearby, were missing. As were the Burnses. Sterling Sumner was glaring at her again while Doctor Anne, who last night had argued strenuously against her celebrating the nine o'clock Eucharist, was frowning in concern.

Ronnie Allbright, her acolyte, turned a page in the huge presentation prayer book that lay propped open on the altar. Clare glanced at the text of the post-communion prayer and took a deep, slow breath, focusing on the clear channel of the words. "Almighty God," she began, and the voice of the congregation joined her in a rumble, "We thank you for giving us the most precious body and blood of your son, Jesus Christ . . ." She knew the prayer like she knew the names of her family. It settled and centered her, so that when she raised her hands to bless the congregation, she could feel an honest surge of affection and support for them all.

Martin Burr attacked the organ, pumping out the opening strains of "On Jordan's Bank the Baptist's Cry." The torch-bearers and the crucifer assembled in front of the altar to begin the recessional. Clare glanced up from her hymnal just in time to see the inner vestibule door opening at the end of the church. Russ Van Alstyne slipped inside. Across the length of the nave, his eyes met hers.

The calm and centered feeling she had been nursing vaporized. She joined the recessional, last in line, inadvertently wincing at the ache that intensified every time she put a foot down. She kept her gaze fixed on the hymnal in order to remember a song she had known by heart since childhood. At the conclusion of the hymn, she stood for a beat too long, unable to dredge up the simple words to dismiss the congregation. She could see the back of Alyson Shattham's hair, immaculate and shining. Finally she blurted out, "Go in peace to love and serve the Lord, Alleluia, Alleluia," and bolted toward the door while everyone else was still responding with their own Alleluias.

"What are you doing here?" she hissed at Russ.

"I'm going to talk to Alyson," he said, bending down to keep his voice close to her ear. "What are you doing up and walking around? How do your feet feel?"

"They hurt. But not bad enough to miss the Eucharist. Why here?"

"Because I want her comfortable enough to talk, of course. You'd be amazed at how many people clam up and call for a lawyer when you haul 'em into the station for questioning."

"The whole 'separation of church and state' thing doesn't carry much weight for you, does it?"

"I think the church-as-sanctuary rule went out a few centuries ago."

One of the ushers bumped past them. "Excuse me, Reverend, but I have to get these doors open."

Clare and Russ stepped out of the way. Parishioners clad in bulky winter wools and chain-tread boots jostled each other on the way down the aisle. "I have to do the receiving line," she said. "I want to be there when you talk to her."

"I figured you would."

She pasted on a pleasant expression, shaking hands, exclaim-

ing over bits of news, thanking those who offered to volunteer
for the Christmas preparations, all the while watching as Russ
intercepted Alyson and her mother in their pew and spoke with
them. Alyson shook her head. Russ jerked his thumb toward
the door. Alyson said something to her mother, who fluttered
her hands like a bird afraid to fly. Russ leaned forward. When
he stepped back, both the Shatthams collected their things and
followed him up the side aisle toward the parish hall.

Clare had no idea there were so many people in her congregation. She felt as if she had shaken five hundred hands
and listened to at least that many comments about yesterday's
storm before the last of them left the vestibule and she could
painfully stump her way up the aisle, through the hall, and
into the meeting room.

This time, Russ was the one sitting with his back to the
window. Brilliant sunshine from a sky swept clean by the
storm glowed around him, partially obscuring his face. Alyson slouched in the chair opposite him, twisting a strand of
hair around two fingers.

Clare shut the door against the hum of conversation and
the clink of coffee cups coming from the parish hall. "Good
morning, Alyson, Mrs. Shattham."

"Reverend Clare," Barbara Shattham said, "Chief Van Alstyne says he needs more information about the dead girl.
And that we've been waiting for you?"

Russ rose and ceremoniously pulled out a chair. Clare
cocked an eyebrow at him. "I know your feet must be hurting
you after your ordeal last night," he said.

"Ah." She got it. "Yes, thank you." She hobbled more
obviously toward the table and sat down.

"Where's your husband, Mrs. Shattham?"

She frowned. "At home. He's not feeling well. He went
cross country skiing yesterday and overdid it."

Clare shot a glance at Russ, but his eyes never left Barbara
Shattham's face.

"Did you go with him?"

"It's not a sport I enjoy." She turned to Clare. "Reverend Fergusson—"

"Did he get home early or late?"

"What?"

"From skiing. Did Mr. Shattham get home early or late?"

"I don't know! Early evening. Seven or eight o'clock. What's this all about?"

Now Russ looked at Clare. She bit her lip, thinking. Could Mitch Shattham have been the man who attacked her? He was about the right height and size, inasmuch as she could tell from a bulky snowsuit. Just how much would he do for his little girl?

"Yesterday evening," she turned toward the Shatthams, "there was a phone message waiting for me when I got back from Albany. I believe you knew I was going to Albany, Mrs. Shattham."

Barbara Shattham blinked, then nodded.

"And you told Alyson about what had happened at the Fowlers. That I discovered Wes and Katie McWhorter had been dating."

"Yes, I did. It concerned her, after all."

Clare looked directly at Alyson. "But you weren't surprised when your mother told you that Wes had had another girlfriend last year, were you? You already knew about him and Katie."

Alyson's fingers twitched at her hair. "No, I didn't." Sweet. Simple. A child who had never been called on cookie-stealing or missing homework.

"Katie has three roommates who have identified you from photographs as having visited her at the beginning of the school year." Russ's voice was calm. "Now, we can have them all come up for a live lineup—"

"A lineup? You mean as in arresting my daughter?"

Alyson's mouth dropped open. Her hair fell from between her fingers.

"She could do the lineup voluntarily. Or, she could do it after we've arrested her." He stared at the girl. "Or, she could tell us what she knows right here."

"I didn't do anything! Mummy, honestly, I didn't hurt anyone!" Her blue eyes swam soft and liquid with tears.

"There, you see?" her mother began.

Russ rose from his seat. "Alyson Shattham, I'm placing you—"

Alyson squealed. Russ sank back into his seat, slowly. The girl glanced at Clare and dropped her eyes. "Okay, I did know Wes was hanging around with Katie. I didn't have anything to do with what happened to her, okay? I only went down to Albany to tell her to lay off because it was like, time for the school-year fling to be over." She turned to her mother. "I mean, can you really see some chunky girl from Depot Street going with Wes to the Academy Ball? She was like, so wrong for him."

Clare leaned into the table. "You didn't know she was pregnant when you fought with her in Albany, did you?"

"God, no! That's so gross!" She raised her eyebrows. "I think Katie must have done it on purpose. Like to get him to marry her. Or for the welfare money. You know what those girls are like."

Clare opened her mouth but Russ stopped her with an upraised hand, shaking his head minutely.

"Why did you lie to us about not having seen Katie, Alyson?"

The girl glanced at her lap. Her shoulders twitched in what might have been a shrug. "I . . . um . . ."

"Where were you yesterday evening?"

"Huh?"

Mrs. Shattham frowned. "She was at home all afternoon and evening."

"Did she receive any phone calls?"

"Are you kidding? Of course she did. If Mitch and I didn't have our own line, we'd never be able to use the phone."

Russ removed a small notepad from his chest pocket. "Can you give me her number, please?"

"Why?"

"It'll make things go faster Monday morning when we contact the phone company for a record of all her outgoing calls."

Clare watched Alyson. She had never seen anyone actually go white before. Barbara Shattham started to protest. Clare laid a hand over her arm, stilling her. "Last night," she said, "a young woman claiming to be Kristen McWhorter called the church and left an urgent message for me to join her." She looked steadily at Alyson. "This young woman left directions for me to drive. I'm not very familiar with this area yet, as you know, so it helps a lot if I have directions. These ones weren't so good, however. They led to a washed-out road crossing a gorge. My car went in. I was fortunate—very fortunate—to walk away. My car was totaled."

"Dear God," Barbara Shattham said. "Are you suggesting my daughter had a hand in this? That's outrageous."

Alyson's gaze darted between Clare and Russ.

"I was stranded on Tenant Mountain with no vehicle and no cold-weather gear," Clare went on. "But that wasn't the worst. The worst was when a man in a snowmobile suit began shooting at me."

Everyone was silent for a moment. Russ clicked his pen and poised it over the notepad. "We can get a list of Alyson's calls first thing tomorrow morning," he said. "We'll be able to see right away if she called the church office yesterday."

Barbara Shattham stood abruptly. "She's not saying anything else until we see our attorney."

Russ leaned back, crossing his arms. "Well, that's certainly your right, ma'am. I was hoping we could sort things out right now, though." He shifted, splaying his hands on the table. "Let me make my position clear. Katie McWhorter and her father are both dead. Your daughter was seen arguing with Katie, who was poaching on her territory with Wes Fowler. She has access to a four-wheel-drive vehicle, she was in town during both murders, and when Reverend Clare found out about Katie and Wes, I believe your daughter sent her off on a wild goose chase designed to get her killed." He pinned Alyson with a level stare. "Either you give up a better suspect, Alyson, or I'll arrest you on two counts of murder and one of attempted murder."

The girl let out a nasal whine. "It wasn't me!"

"Alyson, don't—"

She swung her head violently, her perfect hair cascading everywhere. "I'm not going to jail for Wesley Fucking Fowler, Mother! Not after the way he's blown me off!" She reached across the table toward Russ. "He sent me an e-mail yesterday afternoon. Asked me to call and say I was Kristen. He was all sweet, just like he used to be, you know? It was just, like, a joke, because the Reverend had been poking around. I didn't know anyone was going to be hurt. I swear! I should have known he was yanking my chain. He's been, like, thanks but no thanks ever since he started sneaking around with that bitch."

Barbara Shattham sat down heavily. "Alyson," Clare said, "What about Katie?"

"I didn't have anything to do with that. And you can bet Wes didn't say anything to me. Except for a family get-together around Thanksgiving, he hasn't said shit to me since he left for the Academy."

"Alyson, your language . . ." Mrs. Shattham's voice trailed off.

"When was the last time you saw Katie?" Russ asked. "For real, this time."

"When I went to her house in Albany that time. I didn't

know she was pregnant, I swear. I kept thinking, like, how could he prefer her to me? She was like, a size fourteen, for God's sake."

"Did Wesley ever indicate that he was having problems, or that he was troubled about his relationship with Katie?"

"He was weirding out before he went away to the Academy, but when I tried to talk with him, he blew me off. I had already figured it out, him and her, for God's sake. But he goes, 'just don't tell anyone.' Like I would. That's why I went to see her. And that's the last time I saw her. Alive or dead."

Russ and Clare looked at each other. He nodded slowly. "Thank you, Alyson. Mrs. Shattham, I suggest Alyson stay close to home."

"What do you think she's going to do, run to Canada?"

"I'm not worried she's going to flee jurisdiction. I'm worried because she knows something about Katie and Wesley. Just like Clare and Darrell McWhorter did. And look what happened to them."

Barbara Shattham clutched her daughter's sleeve. "Dear God." She glared at Russ. "She's in trouble because she's spoken to you. I expect you to provide us with police protection."

Russ pinched the bridge of his nose beneath his glasses. "Mrs. Shattham, she's in trouble because she's an accomplice to attempted murder. I'm not going to arrest her now. I may not ever arrest her, depending on what the district attorney has to say. I will," he stressed, "take any attempt to get in touch with Wes Fowler as a sign that she's actively assisting him. So take her home and keep an eye on her."

After the Shatthams left in a swirl of silky hair and tearful glares, Russ shook his head. "Girl like that makes me grateful I never had kids. Holy shit. What a self-centered little monster. Excuse my French."

"You wouldn't have a girl like that."

"I can understand why kids from crappy neighborhoods

with piss-poor parents get into trouble. But how can kids with every advantage turn out so badly?"

Clare leaned forward. "Because the things you have, and the neighborhood you live in, doesn't have anything to do with what kind of human being you are. As I've said before."

"As you've said before." He smiled slightly. "What do you think? Was she telling the truth?"

"I don't know. She sure sounded pi—peeved at Wesley, though. I'd swear she was genuinely surprised that first time you questioned her, when she found out about Katie being pregnant."

"Well, that shoots my boy-and-girl-did-it-together theory."

"Vaughn Fowler should be back home with Wesley by now."

"That's assuming he wasn't already back home last night, trying to shoot you." From the open door, Clare could hear the sounds of coffee hour. "You probably have to go join your flock."

"Oh, no." She sank back into her seat. "I missed the Christmas cookie sale." At Russ's look she explained, "Fund-raiser for the choir. Everyone brings in cookies and you mix and match what you want to buy. I was going to show the flag by getting two bags' worth." She tried to pile her hair atop her head, but it was already in a French twist. She settled for pushing at the bobby pins. "I guess I may as well bow out entirely and come with you to see the Fowlers. Give me ten minutes to change out of my vestments and say good-bye."

He looked at the ceiling. "Why don't I just deputize you and issue you a gun, while I'm at it?"

Clare rose from the table. "No, thanks. But if there's a paying position as departmental chaplain, I'll take that. I'm going to need some extra money if I ever hope to replace my car."

CHAPTER 28

It was a short drive from St. Alban's to the Fowlers, but it was long enough for Clare to work up a full head of nerves and excitement. Fortunately, Russ was an easy person to be keyed up with; he listened to her ramble on about her ideas for the mother-and-baby outreach program, interjecting a question every time she stalled out over the realization that they were minutes away from confronting the young man who might be Katie's killer.

As they turned down the long country road that led to the Fowler's house, she confessed, "I'm a little tense about all this."

"Oh? I never would have guessed."

She punched him in the arm.

"Ow!"

"Don't you feel it, too? This may be it! Finally."

"I've done this a few more times than you, Reverend. Questioning someone doesn't get me all worked up." He glanced over to see her scowling. "Of course, it's different if I think the person I want to question is going to start shooting at me. I remember one time, I was working the violent crimes unit at Mannheim, we were investigating a series of rapes. Chief suspect was a ranger who taught hand-to-hand combat. One of these guys who can disable you with his forefinger and kill you with one hand tied behind his back. Walking up to his quarters to question him, I thought I was going to piss my pants, I was so scared."

"What happened?"

"I talked him into coming with me to the M.P. post. That's ninety percent of police work, you know, being able to talk and keep on talking until the problem is defused."

She pointed to a neatly plowed gravel drive. "Here it is." She recognized the Fowlers' Explorer and Volvo sedan. There was also a brand new Jeep Wrangler parked in front of the barn. "That must be Wesley's truck."

Russ parked the patrol car behind the Jeep and took a slow walk alongside it on his way to the door. Clare, staring into the windows, caught sight of herself and quirked her mouth. What did she think she was going to see, the abandoned snowmobile suit and a gun? She stepped lively to catch up with Russ, who had mounted the front steps.

Edith Fowler opened the door. Her deep-set eyes showed stark and white in her narrow face, like a spooked horse trapped in its stall.

"Mrs. Fowler? I'm Chief Van Alstyne. May I come in?"

Her social graces kicked in and her face relaxed. She opened the door widely. "Certainly, Chief. Reverend Clare, I'm glad to see you here as well." In the foyer, she took their coats. "I'm sorry we missed church this morning, but it's been . . . well . . ." She gestured down the hall. "They're in the family room."

Clare stepped out of rubber rainboots, the only foul-weather footwear she owned since trashing her leather boots last night. She was glad she hadn't changed into civvies. Her collar and black blouse created a shield dividing the woman who had slogged through an icy stream from the priest who was here to counsel and support this morning. *You are what you wear*, she could hear her grandmother lecture, stuffing Clare-the-tomboy into a ladylike dress. She plucked a piece

of fluff from her ankle-length black wool skirt and followed
Russ through the door.

The family room had obviously been a later addition to
the old house. Its cathedral ceiling allowed for a Christmas
tree that was easily twelve feet high, and the sweep of windows created an unbroken vista of snow and hills. The Fowler
men were rising from a cluster of leather-covered love seats
and chairs.

"Chief Van Alstyne." Vaughn Fowler didn't sound surprised to see a uniformed officer in his home at eleven o'clock
on a Sunday morning.

Wesley looked startlingly like his father: same height,
same strong features, same heavily-muscled build. His hair
was shorter than even his father's military clip, shaved down
to a bare fuzz. His face was strained and weary. He looked
older than his eighteen or nineteen years, and Clare thought
it entirely possible he could have been the "older man" Katie's roommates had seen.

"This is my son, Wesley."

"Sir." Wesley pumped Russ's hand.

Vaughn waved Clare over. "Wes, I don't think you've had
the chance to meet our new priest yet. This is the Reverend
Clare Fergusson."

"Ma'am." Clare and Wesley studied each other while shaking hands. He was definitely discomfited to see her. Was it
because she was the one who had brought his connection to
Katie out in the open? Or because she had brained him with
a rock last night? A tough, strong kid like him could have
recovered enough from last night's violence to appear this
morning as if nothing had happened.

"Let's all sit down." Vaughn gestured Clare to one of the
caramel-colored chairs. He was looking the worse for wear,
too. As the men took their seats, she wondered if his control
of the situation was what was keeping him together. "I've
been talking with Wes." Vaughn said, before Russ could

speak. "He has something to say to you, Chief."

The young man stood. "Sir, I am—I was Katie's boy-friend. I am the baby's father. There's no need to do a blood test. I'm responsible."

Russ laced his hands across his belt. "Sit down, Wes, you're not on report." The boy sat, spine held straight and away from the back of the love seat. "So you're Cody's father. Were you with her when she had the baby?"

"Yes sir. It was just after Thanksgiving." He glanced at his father. "I told my folks I was spending a few days with a friend. I took Katie to the Sleeping Hollow Motel, and she . . . she had the baby there."

"What happened after Katie gave birth?" Clare said.

"We waited a day to make sure he was, you know, okay, then we left him on the steps at St. Alban's."

She leaned forward. "Why?"

He glanced at her and then focused his gaze at a point two inches to the left of her head. "Ma'am, we agreed with each other to give the baby up. We thought—I thought, with the Burnses looking to adopt for so long, that it would be easy. Make sure they had the baby and then Katie and I could get back to our lives."

Clare steepled her fingers against her lips, holding back her reaction to such raw thoughtlessness.

"I didn't know the police would get involved!" he said. "I didn't know she would—" he caught his breath. "I just found out last week she had been, had been, killed. Alyson called me." Clare noticed a distinct lack of warmth when he mentioned his official girlfriend's name. "She said Ethan had been arrested for the murder."

"Ethan Stoner was arrested for threatening an officer and resisting arrest." Russ said. "He's no longer a suspect in the murders."

Wesley drew a deep breath. "I didn't kill Katie or her father. Sir. I—" his voice broke, a reminder that he was barely more than a boy after all. "I cared for her very much." He looked at Clare, square on. "I guess it was stupid to just leave the baby. But I knew there was a meeting that night, and that somebody would find him quickly. I thought once he was gone everything could be normal again."

His distress caught at Clare. "Pretending nothing happened can't right the world again, though, can it?"

He shook his head. "I want to do the right thing. Even though it's too late for . . . Katie. I'm ready to take care of the baby, to be his father." He glanced at his own father. "I've discussed it with my folks."

"That's a very stirring sentiment from a boy facing a double murder rap," Russ said.

Vaughn laid a hand on Wesley's shoulder. "My son has said he had nothing to do with the murders of the girl or her father, and I believe him. He's a Fowler. He wasn't raised to tell lies."

Russ unlaced his hands. "No offense, Mr. Fowler, but your son has already lied through omission about a lot of things, including his relationship with Katie, his whereabouts, and the fact that he's now a father. You'll understand why I have to take what he says with a grain of salt." He turned to Wesley. "The way I see it, you were desperate to keep the existence of Katie and Cody under wraps. You thought the Burnses would step in and take care of your responsibilities for you. My guess is, sometime between the night you dropped Cody off at the church and the night Katie's body was found, she got in touch with you and said she had changed her mind." The young man's face flinched almost imperceptibly. "Your plan for getting on with your life was about to be royally screwed. So you told Katie to meet you back in Millers Kill, drove her out to Payson's Park to discuss things, brained her with a tire iron, and rolled her down the hill into the river."

"No!"

"It wasn't the blow to the head that killed her, you know. She froze to death."

"No!" Wesley erupted from his chair, lurching toward Russ.

His father moved like an uncoiling spring, seizing his son by the arms. "Stop it, Wes! Stop it."

"This is what we're going to do," Russ said, standing slowly. "Wesley, you and I are going to the station, where we'll have a talk with Mr. Kaminsky of the D.A.'s office. If we decide we have enough to hold you on, we're going to charge you." Russ's gaze flicked from the young man's pale face to that of his father. "Mr. Fowler, I suggest you call your lawyer and meet us at the station."

"You can't question him without the presence of one of his parents."

"He's over eighteen."

"I didn't do it," Wesley said. "I didn't do it." He shook himself free of his father's restraint and turned to the older man. "What if I refuse to go?"

Russ broke in. "I'll arrest you right here."

Vaughn looked at his son for a long moment. "You go with him, Wes." The young man opened his mouth in protest. "It'll be for the best. We'll get a lawyer over there and have you back out by dinnertime."

"I didn't kill her, Dad. I couldn't have."

Vaughn squeezed his son's shoulders. "I know you didn't, Wes."

"Let's get your coat, Wesley." Russ stepped out of the way, keeping behind and to the side of the young man. He looked as if he sorely wanted to use his handcuffs.

"Mr. Fowler," Clare said quietly, "I didn't drive myself here. If you'd like me to, I'd be happy to stay here with you and Mrs. Fowler and come back to town with you. If you think I could be of some help."

Vaughn Fowler looked toward her, his gaze already a thousand yards ahead of him. He shook his head. "Thank you, Reverend, but under the circumstances . . ."

"Of course. The last thing I want to do is be intrusive." She impulsively took one of his hands between hers. "If I can do anything, please. Please give me a call."

From the hallway, Mrs. Fowler wailed. Vaughn Fowler jerked his hand from Clare's grasp and strode toward the sound.

"No, no, no," Wesley's mother said, clutching at her parka-clad son. "You can't take him! You can't take him!"

"Edith!" Vaughn Fowler grasped her upper arms firmly and tugged her away from Wesley. "Edith." He spoke quietly, almost intimately. "I'm calling the lawyer right now. Wes will be back home with us tonight."

"Mom, I'll be okay. Please."

"This can't be happening, not to us, not to our son—" Edith Fowler pressed one hand over her mouth, shuddering. She blinked hard, but no tears fell.

Her husband glared at Russ. "If anything happens to my son while he's in your care, I'll have your job."

Russ bristled. "I don't allow police brutality in my force, Mr. Fowler. Come on, Wesley. Clare, are you riding with me?"

She snatched her coat from the hall closet.

"Don't say anything until our lawyer gets there, Wes. Understand me?" Wesley nodded to his father as Russ led him down the steps toward the squad car.

Clare stood on the threshold. She spread her hands, miserably aware of how much she had contributed to these people's unhappiness and how little she could do to comfort them. "I'm so sorry. At times like these, it's tempting to feel as if you've been abandoned, by God and by your friends. Please remember that's not true."

Edith Fowler blinked again and wiped her eyes. "This whole thing is like a nightmare." She looked at her husband.

"My God, Vaughn, do you realize we're grandparents?"

"I guess you're right." His face tightened. "Clare, will we be able to see the child? Or do we have to jump through some bureaucratic hoops now that he's in foster care? Where is he?"

"I don't know what sort of requirements the Department of Human Services will have. I suspect that if you two feel up to it, they'd be happy to have you serve as Cody's foster parents. His caseworker's name is Angela Dunkling, and right now he's fostering with Deborah McDonald, out toward Ft. Henry. I'll call you with their phone numbers as soon as I get back to my office."

Behind her, Russ tapped on the horn. "Meanwhile, I hope you'll reach out for some support and not try to go it alone."

Edith nodded. "I'll call Barb and Mitch. After all, they're involved too, in a way."

Clare opened her mouth and closed it again. If she got into exactly how involved the Shatthams had become last night, she could be here all afternoon. They'd find out their son's latest attempt to get out from under his problem soon enough.

"You do that." She retreated down the steps. "We'll speak soon."

She tugged on the car door, only to find it locked. Russ leaned over and let her in. Sliding into her seat, she glanced through the clear Plexiglas screen at Wesley, sitting perfect-postured in the back. The small sliding door that allowed for communication between front and back was latched shut. Clare reached for it.

Russ shifted the car into gear. "Clare, I'd rather not have any more questions until we get to the station. I want to do this by the book." He backed slowly out of the Fowler's drive. "I want his voluntary statement on the record, not in a car where his lawyer will be able to get it thrown out at trial."

She cast one more look back at the young man. He met her eyes, bleak and hopeless. She had wanted to feel a sense of triumph, of justice, when they caught up with Katie's killer. Instead she felt an ache in the pit of her stomach. So much damage. To so many lives. And it wasn't over yet.

CHAPTER 29

At the station, Russ escorted Wesley into the interrogation room and latched the door behind him. "I'm going to make a pot of coffee," he said to Clare. "I don't know about you, but I could use a cup right now."

"Please. What happens now?"

"I already talked with Kaminsky last night, so he'll be expecting my call. He's going to be here to listen in to the questioning. I want to charge this kid some bad, but I want it to stick." He squinted into the distance. "We'll need a cross-jurisdiction warrant to search his room at the Academy. And I want his truck . . ."

Clare cut him off. "Can I speak with him now? Not as part of this, but as priest to parishioner?"

Russ frowned. "You just met him this morning. How much of a pastoral relationship can you have?"

"That's not the point, Russ. I want to help him if I can. He's obviously very troubled."

"He's very troubled because he carefully planned and executed two cold-blooded murders and now I've caught his ass, excuse my French. And let's not forget he would have done the same to you if you hadn't escaped him. Jesu—um Crow, Clare, you'd try to make excuses for Charles Manson!"

"I'm not making excuses for anything he may have done."

She crossed her arms. "No one is beyond forgiveness, Russ. Or beyond asking for forgiveness. I have to believe that."

He pulled off his glasses and polished them on his shirt front. "I don't even know why you're here. After I speak with Kaminsky, I want you to take my truck and go home." He rapped on the door to the interrogation room. "Wesley? Reverend Clare here would like to speak with you as your—" he glanced at Clare, "—spiritual advisor. You want to talk with her?"

There was a pause. "I guess so. Okay."

Russ unlatched the door. "There's an alarm buzzer on the wall. If he makes any moves on you, use it. I'll be back in a few minutes."

Clare nodded. The room was a smaller version of the meeting room, albeit without windows. Heavy, well-worn wooden table and chairs, tired institutional green walls. She had thought there would be one of those two-way mirrors like in the movies, but it looked like the Millers Kill police department wasn't quite up to cinematic standards yet.

Wesley was standing at the far end of the room, his back against the wall, his eyes shadowed and suspicious. She tugged at a chair. It was bolted to the floor. She sat down and propped her chin in her hand. "I'm the one who found Cody, you know."

Wesley looked at his boots. "Yeah, I know." He darted a glance at her. "My dad says you've been working hard to see that the Burnses get to adopt him."

She nodded. "You could help with that. As his father, you can authorize a legal adoption just by signing over the papers. They wouldn't have to wait and wonder the way they are doing now."

He brushed the speckled vinyl floor with the toe of his boot. "I guess we never realized that you couldn't just give away a baby. I didn't mean to have them wait. We just—it was easier to not think about it. The fact that there was a baby on the way. We never exactly planned any of it."

"What about the motel? The fake I.D.? That must have taken some planning."

"I already had an old I.D. I had doctored up so I could, um, get into bars." He looked at the wall opposite him. "I met her at her school—she had her roommate's car—and we stopped at the first place that was open. We weren't even sure if she was going to have the baby then or not. She'd been having those, you know, fake contractions." He tilted his head back. "It all seemed so unreal. Being there, the baby, everything. I just wanted things to go back to the way they were. Without our parents finding out."

"Why did you leave the baby at the church instead of at the Burnses' house?"

"They weren't home when we drove by. Then I remembered my parents talking about the reception for the new priest that night. We figured somebody would find the baby and read the note and hand him over to the Burnses. Pretty dumb, huh?"

She bit her lower lip. "It wasn't the smartest thing, no."

He glanced at her. "Hey, do you think if I help the Burnses adopt the baby quickly, it'll help me with the cops?"

"I don't think so. It might help you with your own conscience, though."

He dropped into a chair opposite her. "What we're talking about here, you can't tell that to anyone, right?"

"No, I can't. What we say here is just between you and me and God."

"I didn't do it."

"Wesley . . ."

"Reverend, I didn't kill her. Or her rotten father. And it's been driving me crazy, because I don't know who could have done it. She was so . . . she was so special. Sweet. Funny. She didn't like me because of my family or my car. She didn't care if I got into student council or West Point. She liked me because of who I was. Not who I was supposed to be. You know?" He rubbed his hands back and forth against the tabletop. "I didn't want to have a baby. And I didn't want to get married. But it wasn't her, it was just . . . it was too soon. You know what I mean?"

"Yes."

"And I don't think she really wanted to get married and keep the baby, either. She sent me a long e-mail about how she did, after we had both gotten back to school, but I don't think it was something she had thought out. My dad said that after-pregnancy hormones can make a woman kind of crazy, and if I just let it be for awhile, she'd realize that rushing into marriage would be a bad idea."

"Your dad said that?"

"Yeah. I figured, if she really couldn't stand not having the baby, I could transfer from the Academy to SUNY Albany. Forget the whole military thing and go for a business degree, something so I could support them as soon as I graduated. But I didn't know how I'd swing it financially." He looked up at her. "You don't have to pay to go to West Point, you know, so I didn't have anything saved. I didn't know if my parents could help us out. I wanted to talk about it with Dad before I suggested it to Katie."

She took a slow, deep breath to keep her voice even. "You offered to leave West Point? You spoke with your father before Katie was killed?"

"Yeah. I didn't want to let him know how bad I screwed up, but I had to. I mean, if we had taken Cody back and gotten married, Katie would have had to drop out if she joined me at the Academy. Lose her scholarship. That would have been a total waste. She was so smart. God, I can't believe she's actually dead." Wesley buried his face in his hands.

Clare sucked in air and held her breath for a moment. "Wes? This is going to sound strange, but can I touch the back of your head?"

He looked at her as if she had lost her mind. "Uh . . . this isn't some sort of faith-healing thing, is it?"

"No." She rose partway from her chair, extending her arm toward his close-cropped hair. "May I?"

He shrugged. "Sure."

She ran her hand lightly over the crown and back of his skull, then pressed more firmly with her fingers. Nothing. No bump, no swelling, no soft spot. "Does this hurt anywhere?"

"No. What are you doing, Reverend?"

"Feeling my way toward the truth." She sank into her chair again. "You weren't out in the woods last night trying to kill me."

He reared back. "Are you crazy? Of course I wasn't out trying to kill you. I wasn't trying to kill anyone! I was in my dorm room, studying."

"What time did your dad pick you up to bring you home?"

"Early this morning. There must have been a dozen guys who saw me there last night, in my room, in the hall, in the john. You can ask them. I wasn't out trying to kill anyone. I'm not a killer!"

Clare looked at her hands, flat on the table. She flipped them over and studied her palms. "Anyone can be a killer, Wes. All it takes is the right training. And enough motivation." She blew out her breath. "Could your father access your e-mail account?"

"Huh? Not my account at the Academy. He could send stuff from my old address at home, he knew my password for that." Clare stood, wrapping her arms around herself. "Why? What the hell does this have to do with—" his face changed suddenly.

"Your father," she said.

"No," he said.

She felt as if she had just flown into a strong thermal and gained a thousand feet of altitude in a few seconds. Dizzy. Disoriented. From where she was now, everything was the

same, but everything looked different. "Your father, Wesley."
She looked down at the young man. His face was a mask of
absolute denial. "Your father is so proud of you. And so determined that you go to West Point and have a brilliant military career. What wouldn't he do to protect you from 'ruining
your life' with some white-trash girl and her baby?"

"No," he said.

"He must have contacted her and invited her to Millers
Kill. Maybe he tried to bribe her into forgetting about you
and Cody first. But that didn't work. He wouldn't have known
that that wouldn't work with someone like Katie. So he got
rid of the problem another way."

"No!"

She paced around the table, talking as much to herself as
to Wesley. "We assumed that Darrell McWhorter threatened
to blackmail Cody's father. But why go to a kid in college
when you can tap into so much more money from his dad?"
She leaned over the table. "He saw you two together, didn't
he? Darrell."

Wesley hesitated, then nodded. "I drove her home from
the library late once. She used to have me leave her at the
intersection, but it was dark and starting to snow, so I took
her right to her apartment house instead. She was always
scared that her dad would find out about us. He was just
getting back from a bar or something that night, and got a
real good look at me." He leaned back in his chair and
scrubbed at his face with his hands. "Katie said he asked her
a lot of questions about me, but she convinced him I was just
a guy in her study group."

"Darrell was smarter than any of us gave him credit for.
As soon as he saw your family photo on the parish bulletin
board, he put all the pieces together. When he called your
father, they must have agreed to ride down to Albany to get
any incriminating stuff left in Katie's room as part of the deal.
And when your father saw his chance to get rid of Darrell,

he acted quickly and decisively." She straightened. "Wesley, your father's been methodically removing every person who might interfere with you becoming the fifth generation of Fowlers to graduate from West Point."

"This is insane. My dad wouldn't kill anybody! And if he's willing to do anything to protect me, why the hell wouldn't he confess instead of letting the cops cart me off to jail?"

"Your dad could kill somebody, Wes. He's done it before, lots of times. It's just not in the line of duty this time." She paused. "Or maybe for him it is." She crossed her arms and blew out a frustrated breath. "But you're right, it doesn't make sense that he'd let you be convicted of—" her stomach clenched into a tight ball. "Oh, my God. The baby."

"What? What do you mean?"

"The baby, Wes, the baby! The one you told him you were ready to raise as a single father? The baby who is the root of all his troubles? Oh, holy God, I told him where to find him. I told him." She slammed her palm against the alarm button, setting off an electronic siren that made the edge of her back teeth ache.

The door rattled and then Russ was inside the room, crouching low, his gun drilled at Wesley. "Down on the floor! Now!" Wesley fell out of his chair, flat and spread-eagled. Russ didn't look away from him. "Clare? Are you okay?"

The siren made it impossible to talk. "Yes!" she shouted. "I just needed to get out of the room!"

"What?" Russ straightened and stalked over to the alarm. He twisted a knob. It fell silent, leaving sound-echos ringing in her ears. "What the hell did you mean, setting off an alarm just to get out? You don't move until I say you do, mister!" He swiveled his gun back toward Wesley, who had levered himself up on his arms.

Clare opened her mouth to tell Russ everything, then shut it again. What we say here is just between you and me and

God. Priestly confidence. Her throat and chest felt as if they would burst with her discovery. A discovery she couldn't share with anyone. She groaned.

"Clare?"

"Give me your truck keys. Now."

"What's—"

"Now, Russ!" He fished his keys out of his pocket.

"I'm going to Deborah McDonald's house out on Aubry Road near the intersection of old Route One Hundred." She jabbed a finger at Wesley. "You! Tell the chief everything!" She pelted through the door before Russ could stop her with any more unanswerable questions.

After her speedy little MG, driving Russ's pickup felt like piloting a C-130 Hercules transport down the runway. She rolled over the corner curb getting out of the parking lot and nearly sideswiped a carload of Christmas shoppers. Fortunately, the route to Deborah McDonald's was mostly through countryside. As soon as she hit the town limits, she tromped on the accelerator. "Let's see how fast you can go, big guy," she said to the speedometer. She knew her way from Millers Kill to both the Fowlers' and the McDonalds', but she had no idea how long it might take Vaughn Fowler to get from his place to Cody's foster mother's. She pressed harder on the gas pedal. Maybe she was wrong, and she'd find the baby napping peacefully. Maybe the McDonalds were out shopping. Maybe Wesley's father was too busy rousting out a lawyer on a Sunday afternoon to think of Cody. Maybe.

Just past the turnoff from old Route 100, she went over the ridge and around the corner way too fast, overcorrected, and would have hit an Explorer heading up the hill if it hadn't slid into the shoulder. Its horn blared as she went past, her heart beating out of her chest. The next corner she took slow and safe, cresting the top carefully until the valley stretched out before her like a Christmas card. Everything looked peaceful in the McDonalds' yard as she pulled in.

As she jumped down from the truck, the front door flew open to reveal Deborah McDonald. Today's sweatshirt pictured two kittens playing with mistletoe. "Oh, my goodness," Deborah said, "you're that lady priest. Are you with the family? Do you know where he's gone?"

Clare's skin prickled. "What's happened, Mrs. McDonald?"

"I just had a visit from Cody's grandfather. At least, he said he was Cody's grandfather. He knew who Angela Dunkling was—"

"What happened?"

"He was with the baby in the living room while I went to get some pictures, and when I came back, they were gone! I wasn't sure what to do. I was about to call the folks at DHS . . ."

Clare took the front steps two at a time. "You need to call the police. Tell them Vaughn Fowler has the baby. What was he driving?"

"A big, blue sport-utility truck."

The Explorer! "Tell them he's in a dark blue Ford Explorer. I passed him on the curve before this. I didn't notice the driver." God had better forgive her for being such an idiot, because she wasn't about to. She swung around to dash down the steps again.

"Wait! Where are you going? Where did he take Cody?"

Clare closed her eyes. *Where.* "Let me use your phone for one moment before you call the police," she said.

Deborah McDonald pointed through the door. Clare strode through the living room, snatched up the receiver and dialed Information for the Fowler's number, which she punched in before the electronic voice was finished with the last digit.

The phone rang. And rang. And rang. Clare thought she might scream.

"Hello?" It was Edith Fowler.

"Mrs. Fowler, this is Clare Fergusson. Do you know where your husband is?"

"He's not here, Reverend. He asked me to call our lawyer and left right after you did. Why? Nothing's happened to Wes, has it?"

"No, no. Did Vaughn have his gun with him?"

"His gun?"

"Is there any way to check? Please, it's important."

"Why on earth—"

"Please! It's important."

"Let me look in the gun case . . ." over the phone, Clare could hear the sounds of a door opening and shutting. "I'm right here in his study. His rifles are all here, but his Colt is missing."

Clare would have bet a year's salary the Colt was buried in a snowdrift somewhere on Tenant Mountain. "Listen, Mrs. Fowler. I'm calling from Cody's foster mother's house. Your husband has taken the baby. If he comes back home or contacts you, try to keep him calm and get the baby away from him. Let the police know right away."

It was so silent Clare thought for a moment the line had gone dead. "I understand," Edith Fowler said finally. "I will."

Clare rang off and headed back outside. Vaughn Fowler was unarmed. But she couldn't shake the conviction that he meant to dispose of Cody once and for all.

"Did she know where he went?" Deborah McDonald asked as Clare hauled herself into the truck's cab.

Where would he go? Where, when it was so easy to kill an infant? Clare pressed her fingers to her forehead. *When you are threatened and on the run, you will tend to return to the same base of operations,* "Hardball" Wright drawled. *If not to the same spot, then to the same sort of terrain. Remember that. The enemy will.* She opened her eyes. "I think he's headed for the river. The trail from Payson's Park or the old railroad bridge. I'm going to head there. Let the police know." If Russ had any better ideas, he could chase after them without her. She ground the gears and backed out of the driveway, catching the McDonald's mailbox with the rear bumper and setting it swinging wildly.

Traffic through the north end of town was agonizingly slow, but she didn't know any other way toward where she and Russ had discovered Katie's body. She swung onto the Cossayaharie road, Route 137, driving carefully, tamping down the urge to go faster and faster, afraid she might miss the turnoff to the park.

She nearly did miss it, mistaking the newly plowed entrance for a driveway. At the last moment, she turned the truck into a frame-shuddering turn and rolled down the lane toward the parking area. The county plow had cleared a large U out of the fresh snow before heading back to the main road. She couldn't tell from where she sat if there were tracks heading down the trail. Leaving the truck running, she jumped from the cab and ran to the edge of the parking lot. Behind the ridge of snow thrown up by the plow, the trail leading down to the kill was unbroken by footprints or tire tracks. "Vaughn Fowler," she hissed from between clenched teeth, "where are you?"

CHAPTER 30

Clare ranged up and down the edge of the parking lot to make sure Fowler hadn't cut through the woods to join the trail further down. Her rubber boots weren't meant for snow, and the treads slipped and slid as she searched for any sign of the man. Nothing. She muttered obscenities she hadn't allowed herself to use in several years and climbed back into the truck. The engine on, she rested her head against the steering wheel and breathed deeply to calm herself. Could she be wrong about where Fowler was headed? After all, it would be easy to kill a baby anywhere—a story where ancient Romans had disposed of infants by smacking them into walls thrust itself into her consciousness. She wrenched her mind away from the horrific image and concentrated on Vaughn Fowler.

The riverside bank, the rest stop on a remote stretch of highway, an abandoned camp road high on a mountain. Every place he had killed or tried to kill had been isolated, a place where a body could disappear for hours. Or years. She sat up, rubbing at the crease in her forehead left by the wheel. Her instructor from Survival School had been right. Fowler was returning to the same sort of terrain. She had to try the abandoned railroad bridge.

She swung the pickup through the plowed area, turning left when she reached the road. Where was she going to find the thing? Russ had told her it was a half-mile upstream from the trail, but that didn't necessarily translate into a half-mile drive up the road. There must have been train tracks leading straight toward the river, but where were they?

Ahead of her, high-voltage lines crossed Route 137, sparking memories of the times she had navigated small planes by following the clearly visible paths maintained by electric companies. She slowed the truck, then pulled over onto the shoulder. Metal transmission towers marched in a receding line down a wide right-of-way through the forest. It vanished over a gentle rise that led, if she wasn't mistaken, toward the river. The kill. She couldn't see any train tracks under the snow, but there were clear marks of snowmobiles crisscrossing beneath the towers and there, ahead of her and to the right, tire tracks along what must be the electric company's access road.

She fumbled with a dial on the steering column, engaging the four-wheel-drive. She downshifted and rolled onto the snow, following the other tracks as closely as possible, praying hard that she wasn't chasing after some die-hard fisherman or snowmobiling enthusiast.

The truck growled up the access road, crunching snow beneath its big tires, carrying her forward surely and steadily. As she crested the rise, it struck her that none of the squad cars would be able to follow her. Hot prickles ran up the insides of her arms and she bit her lip. Some of the officers had better have four-wheel-drive vehicles or she was going to be in a world of trouble. She refused to think about the possibility that the police might not be following her at all.

The right-of-way, and the tire tracks, curved gently to the left, disappearing from view in the thick stand of trees. She accelerated slightly, the rear tires whining a complaint. As she rounded the bend, the landscape opened startlingly before her: blue sky, white snow, black water. Dark green bridge. Dark blue Ford Explorer.

She slammed on the brakes, sending the truck into a skid that ended with a jarringly abrupt stop. She almost fell from the cab in her frantic need to get out. She could see him, perhaps halfway along the span of the bridge, silhouetted against the sky. Well-bundled up against the cold, carrying something.

"Mr. Fowler!" she screamed. Running through the snow to the bridge was like running in a nightmare, slipping and dragging and making almost no headway despite the efforts that left sweat running down her spine. "Stop!"

He did. She thrashed through the remaining few feet to the bridge and staggered onto the rails. She saw why he had been walking so slowly: the train track was supported on a huge trestle but open to the air. On either side of the railbed was a riveted steel walkway and parapet, something the rail workers must have crossed on decades ago. Between the scanty patches of snow that hadn't been scoured off by the wind, she could see patches of rust eating away the green-painted metal. She decided to stay right where she was, on the half-foot-wide wooden ties.

Vaughn Fowler was facing her now, cradling a blanket-wrapped bundle with one arm. "I can't say I'm surprised to see you, Reverend," he said, his voice carrying clearly through the cold air. "As president of the vestry, I'm disappointed in your performance so far. Way too much time spent on a situation that is out of your area of concern."

She heard nothing from inside the blanket. Shouldn't the baby be crying after all this? She pressed her lips tightly together. Dear God, don't let him be already dead. "My area of concern? It's the people around me. The McWhorters. The Burnses." She picked her way along another few crossbars, moving closer. "Your son. Your grandson. You." She looked steadily at Fowler, searching his face for something she could reach with her words. "Let me help you."

"Very comforting, coming from a woman who tried to kill

me last night." He held out a hand. "Stop there, Reverend."

She stopped, her arms spread for balance. Beneath her feet, she could see the kill, black and glittering in the pale sunlight. Chunks of ice bobbed lazily in the slow current. "Are you going to try to shoot me again?" she asked.

Fowler laughed, a short, coughing sound. "Hardly. I lost my side arm when you ambushed me. Carried that Colt for twenty years, and lost it to a damn woman. A priest to boot. Damn, I liked that piece." He narrowed his eyes. "You were good out there. I'm lucky to have survived with my feet and my balls intact."

"I'm so sorry. I didn't mean to hurt you—"

"Bullshit. You meant to hurt me, and you did. I underestimated you, and I paid the price. Don't apologize for being successful."

"No, sir." The acknowledgment was an automatic response to his tone of voice. She sure wasn't going to reach him by appealing to him as a priest, but maybe she could engage him officer to officer. The longer they kept talking, the more likely it was Russ and his men could find them. "I thought taking your boots and flashlight to keep you from reaching your vehicle was good strategy, but obviously, it didn't work."

"I had a penlight in my snowmobile suit. Always carry backup equipment when you're in the woods. As soon as I'd assessed the situation, I stopped chasing after you and headed straight for my snowmobile."

"But . . . your feet . . ."

"Were damn cold by the time I reached my friend's cabin. However, I was wearing insulated hunting socks. Next time you try to cripple someone, make sure you leave him with bare feet. Better still, just split his head open."

"Sir, my objective was to slow you down, not to kill you."

"Stupid objective. The only way to deal with an enemy is to take him out. Period. Otherwise, you'll never know when he'll jump back up and bite you in the ass."

"Like Darrell McWhorter?"

His face crinkled in disgust. "Slimy bastard. Called me up and said he'd tell the cops about Wesley and his daughter if I didn't pay him off. Ten thousand dollars. He thought Wes had killed her and he was still willing to overlook it for money. What a scumbag."

A raven flew past the bridge, cawing loudly. She took another step along the railroad ties. "How did you persuade him to come with you to Albany, sir?"

"I told him I'd pay if he'd collect any telltale evidence from the girl's apartment and hand it over. I knew he'd jump at the chance to find something more substantial to hold over my head." He gave her a look that invited her to agree that the late Darrell McWhorter was an idiot. "I planned on getting rid of him in Albany; as it happened, a better opportunity presented itself."

"So that was you who rifled through Katie's things."

He tucked his head in assent. "With some of last year's Halloween costume stuck to my face. Crude, but effective."

From below, Clare could hear the flat lapping of the river against its rock-and-snow-covered banks. Would dropping Cody in also qualify as crude, but effective? She glanced at the bundle in Fowler's arm.

"Oh, he's alive. The little bastard fell sound asleep in my truck, can you believe it?"

"What is it you're looking for here, Colonel? What outcome are you after?" She let a note of challenge creep into her voice. "Wesley's already off the hook for the murders. What do you hope to accomplish out here?"

"I'm trying to save my son from himself. He's already fumbled badly, getting that girl pregnant in the first place and then not insisting she have an abortion. He was going to walk away from everything, just because she decided at the last minute she didn't want to give it up. Can you believe that?"

Clare bit her lip. "There's no chance of that now, though, is there? You took care of that."

"You mean the girl? I didn't set out to eliminate her. If she had just taken the money I'd offered—Christ, she could have paid her way through the state school and had a nest egg left over! She was too stupid to do what was best for her."

"Some people might say she was too principled to trade money for her child."

"Bullshit. She saw an opportunity to trap a boy from a decent family who could be counted on to earn a good paycheck." He glared at her. "If Wes had quit school to marry her, if he takes on her—" he glanced at the blankets in his arm, "—kid, he'd regret it for the rest of his life. I'm not going to let that happen." His face tightened. "Wes is still too soft, yet. It's up to me to protect him."

"By killing his son and sending his father to death row? Do you really think that's going to protect him? That he won't regret it for the rest of his life?" She stepped toward Fowler, never taking her eyes off him, feeling out the ties through her boots. "Wesley's ready to sign the boy over to the Burnses. He told me so himself." She balanced on one leg, bumping her other boot against a wooden tie until she had a foothold. "He's a good kid. Sensitive, responsible, caring. You can stop this right here without damaging him any further." She stretched out her arms. "Give me the baby. The other two you . . . eliminated, those were on the spur of the moment, unplanned, right? That's manslaughter. You can plead to diminished capacity or temporary insanity or . . . or . . . something."

She kept her arms open. Her chest and throat ached. From a distance, she could hear the sound of a motor. A snowmobile, maybe. She wanted it to be help. She wasn't up to this. She couldn't do this all by herself.

You aren't all by yourself, the thought came, from inside and outside all at once. She breathed in sharply. "Give me the baby, Colonel. Don't burden the rest of Wesley's life with the knowledge that he was the reason you did this terrible thing."

He frowned, pressing his lips together. Considering. Poised between two ties, she held herself absolutely still, arms burning, reaching.

Behind them, the sound of an engine cut through the air. Fowler looked past her. "Ah. Reinforcements," he said. He hefted the blanket-wrapped parcel higher.

Clare couldn't look back. She heard thudding doors and the faint squawk of a walkie-talkie. "They don't change anything," she said. "This is still your call."

"Vaughn." Russ's voice was measured, temperate. The sound of it was like seeing the landing lights at the end of a long night's flight. "How 'bout I walk onto this bridge and we all try to resolve this situation?"

Fowler raised his bundle higher. From within the blanket, the baby began to cry, short, sharp squalls demanding attention. "Stay where you are, Chief, or I toss this into the kill."

"No!" Clare's hands clutched around empty air. Beneath them, she heard the motor coming closer, a spluttering roar.

"You're not going to walk away from this, Vaughn. That's a police boat covering the water. The state troopers will be moving men in on the other side of the kill, and they're going to be bringing a sharpshooter with them. Give the baby to Clare, and let's all get out of the cold. Your son is waiting to see you. He's worried sick about you."

Fowler shook his head. "I didn't plan to walk away from this, Chief. I knew when I moved decisively to save my son from dropping out and marrying that trailer trash that I would have to be an acceptable loss."

"No. Colonel." Clare moved forward another shaky step. "Think what you'll be doing to your family."

"I have. I'm saving them the embarrassment of a trial and incarceration. Don't you think I considered how this would look? No one understands sacrifice these days. No one appreciates what it is to put your duty to your family or your service first."

In her peripheral vision, Clare caught a glimpse of the boat, motoring slowly upstream toward the bridge. She took another step. Fowler began to unwind the blanket from the wailing infant. She knew, at that moment, he would toss Cody into the kill, no matter what they said or did. She unzipped her parka and peeled it off. "Give me the baby, Colonel," she said, holding out her coat. "You can put him right in here." She balanced on a single tie, feet together, pressing down on the back of one rubber boot. "I promise you, I'll see that the Burnses get him. He won't interfere with Wesley's schooling ever again." Her stockinged foot slid free. She wavered, one-legged, almost losing her balance. She didn't take her eyes off Vaughn Fowler's face.

He looked down at the angry baby kicking in the crook of his arm. "He's such a responsible kid, that's part of the problem." Clare found her footing again. Her toes curled over the edge of the tie as she lifted her other leg and shook the boot free. It hit one of the ties and fell off her foot. A moment later, she heard a splash.

"Give her the baby, Vaughn, and let's get out of here. Your son needs you." Russ's voice sounded much closer now. She could feel him, radiating strength and reassurance, almost close enough to reach back and touch.

Vaughn drew a deep breath, as if savoring the taste of the air. "Wes is the fifth generation of my family to attend West Point, did I tell you that?"

Clare nodded. "Yes, sir, you did."

He looked into her eyes, soberly, measuring. "It's a good thing to live as a soldier." With a shrug and a twist of his arms, he tossed Cody over the parapet.

Russ shouted, "Get down, Clare!" as the parka tumbled from her arms. She went over the side before she had a chance to think about it, her shins scraping the iron, the wind tearing up her eyes and blinding her, and then she was under the water, and it was cold, cold beyond any definition of cold, burning her skin like acid. She followed her bubbles up to the pale sunshine, broke the surface, unable to breathe, the shock of it seizing her lungs. She heard yelling, a motor gunning, shots. It was hard to think, impossible to focus. She couldn't see Cody. She gulped in air with a sob, forcing her chest to work, went under again. The boat motor throbbed through her nerves. Her body felt like one huge tooth ache. She spiraled through the clear water. There was a flash of white ahead, but when she broke surface, it was a clump of snow and ice. Someone was yelling her name. She went under again, the ache intensifying, although she couldn't have imagined it could get any worse.

She saw him. Floating so near the surface his ice-blue sleeper was dappled with sunlight. She stroked through the water, kicking against the drag of her skirt, time slipping past her like bubbles, until she reached the tiny form. She surfaced again, hauling Cody up with her, holding his head out of the water one-handed while she tread in place. "Here!" she screamed. "I've got him! Here!"

The sound of the boat was everywhere, but she was still surprised when she turned and it was there; cutting engines, sliding alongside her. Hands reached out, so many hands, and she held up Cody and let him be whisked out of view. She reached for the side, but she was too weak to hold on. More hands grasped her, grabbed her arms, and she was hauled in like a fish, flopping and twitching on the bottom of the boat until someone tossed a thermal blanket over her and rolled her in it. Through the press of parkas, she saw a man half-dressed in diving gear resuscitating Cody, his mouth covering half the baby's face.

"Breathe."

"For Christ's sake, take us over to the shore so we can

pick up the chief, he's going to freeze to death."

"Get on that radio to County Hospital, tell 'em we're coming in with possible hypothermias."

"Miss, I have another blanket. Can you get your clothes off under there?"

"What about the perp's body? Are we fishing him out?"

Cody's tiny fist jerked in the air. The diver pulled away, rolling the baby onto his side. Cody coughed, vomited up a stream of water, and began to cry. Everyone cheered except Clare, who squeezed her eyes shut against hot tears.

The boat bumped and scraped against rock. She opened her eyes in time to see Russ wading through the water. The boat tipped hard to one side as he heaved himself in. "Come back here, Chief," the voice beside her said. "I've got a blanket for you. Jeez, you tore the hell out of your pants, didn't you? What the hell were you thinking of? We had them."

Clare focused on the man who had been helping her, and recognized Kevin Flynn. The engine kicked in again, pulling them steadily away from the shore, gaining speed as they motored downstream.

"Shove it over, Kevin," Russ said, his voice thick. The young officer handed him a blanket and carefully shifted down the bench. Russ wrapped himself from the waist down and sat heavily. "Lyle, you notify the hospital we're coming in?"

"I sure did, Chief."

"Call the staties, let 'em know we're going to need a diving team and a water search to recover Fowler's body."

"What happened?" Clare asked, her teeth clicking together.

"You mean after you did your swan dive? Fowler fired on me."

"Oh, no. Oh no. Were you the one who—"

"No, my gun was still holstered. Mark was my backup. He's a damn good shot." He shook his head. "Fowler was hit. He went between the ties." He looked at her, his eyes so deep she thought she could dive in and touch the bottom of him.

"I'm so sorry," she said.

"For Fowler or for Mark?" He raised a hand. "No, don't tell me. I know. For both of them." He took off his glasses and wiped them on a corner of the blanket. "When I saw you go over the edge like that . . ." He shook his head. "I took the fast route down by sliding down that goddamn slate embankment. My ass is going to feel that one for a month. 'Scuse my French." He threw his arm around Clare and pulled her blanket-wrapped form tightly to his side. "Jesus Christ, Clare, what were you thinking of? Do you have any idea how fast you can die in water that cold? We had a diver standing by, for chrissakes."

"I didn't know it was going to be that cold," she said, shaking uncontrollably against him. She jerked her chin toward the squalling baby. "It was worth it."

He nodded. "Yeah, I guess it was." He smiled a bit. Then he started to laugh softly.

"What?"

"Damn, I sure had you pegged when I said you jumped in feet-first without thinking . . ."

CHAPTER 31

At twilight, the small parking area behind St. Alban's was already filled. Well, he should have expected that on Christmas Eve. Russ parked in the lot across the street, collected his package, and trudged across Elm toward the Gothic double doors hung with wreaths. The pavilion in the square was glowing with Christmas lights and the shining windows of the last stores open, and for a moment he could have been back in 1962, when everything in his world was safe and understandable. Where businesses never closed and marriages were forever and no one ever died.

He shook his head at his sentimentality and hauled on one of the elaborately cast bronze door pulls. Inside the church, his glasses fogged over, blinding him. The smell of pine and beeswax filled the shadowy air. From the choir stalls a soloist was singing, then stopping, going back and repeating her phrase.

"Hey. Chief Van Alstyne. Are you here to help, too?"

He popped his glasses back on. A startlingly well-scrubbed Kristen McWhorter faced him, carrying a box of tall white candles.

"Kristen. Hi. I'm surprised to see you here."

She jiggled the box. "Reverend Clare talked me into help-

ing with the decorating. I'm sprigging the candles. Don't
ask."

He grinned. "Okay. How is everything?"

"Pretty good. The funerals were hard. Hard to get through.
But knowing what happened to her helped. I still haven't
spoken with Wes Fowler. Which I can understand. But I have
been seeing Cody." She smiled. "The Burnses have asked me
to be a godmother, isn't that cool? He's going to be baptized
here in January."

"That's very cool, yeah. I'm glad for you." He glanced
around the church. A woman was twining greenery around
huge standing candelabras and an elderly man was wedging
votive lights into recesses in the windowsills. "Where's the
Reverend?"

"I heard her muttering something about coffee. I'd check
in her office."

The hallway was dim and quiet. He knocked on her door
frame. "Anyone in?"

"Russ! Well, isn't this a nice surprise. If you're here for
the seven o'clock service, you're a few hours early." Clare
rose from one of her odd-looking admiral's chairs, elegant in
a tailored black blouse and long skirt. "Let me get you a cup
of coffee." She poured from her Thermos into a Virginia
Seminary mug. The coffee was hot and sweet and tasted of
cinnamon. He dropped his package on the shabby love seat
and laid his parka over it before sitting down.

"I meant to call when I saw the notice about Fowler's
funeral in the paper."

"I didn't officiate. I asked Clifton Whiting from St. Ann's
in Saratoga. I thought my presence would be more of a hurt
than a help." She looked into her coffee. "I can't help but
think that if I'd been a little more on the ball—"

"You could have stopped Fowler from destroying himself?
Someone once told me you can't take responsibility for everyone around you. Seems like a pretty smart observation."

She smiled crookedly at him. "I should have had you around to put in a good word for me when the vestry called me on the carpet to explain what had been going on. I don't know who shocked them more, me or Vaughn Fowler."

He slipped off his glasses and polished them on his scarf. "If you need me to let them know what a genuine help you were—"

"No, no. They just need time to readjust their worldview. I'm taking advantage of the confusion to push forward my young mothers' mentoring program. For which, by the way, I have the support of the Burnses, who have forgiven me for narcing on Geoff's drunk driving episode."

"Let me get my glasses back on. Whenever I think about Geoff as a father, I get a headache."

"It's given him a sense of humor. He told me they were signing Cody up for infant swim classes." Her eyes glinted. "At least, I think he was trying to be funny."

He almost snorted coffee out his nose. He put the mug down. "I'm really here to give you this." He pulled the wide, foil-wrapped package from beneath his coat. "Happy Holidays."

"For me? You shouldn't have!" She tore into the paper eagerly. "Oh, Russ." She started laughing. "Thank you. They're just what I needed." She held up the waterproof, insulated, chain-tread-soled boots. "How did you know?"

He laughed. "Lucky guess?" She turned the boots back and forth, admiring them.

"I love them." She dropped them into the box. "I'll wear them tonight after midnight mass."

"It must get crazy for you on Christmas Eve. Everyone else is having a holiday and you're working your tail off."

"Like a cop."

"Like a cop."

"It easy for me to lose all sense of what I'm here for and turn into this grumpy, harried martinet, obsessing with getting everything done right and on time. That's why I'm hiding out in my office."

"Oh. I didn't mean to interrupt."

"Oh, no, I'm glad you came. I haven't seen you since they hustled you off to get your backside dressed at the hospital." The last light of the sunset was flooding the room, from windows and mirrors. Her hair, caught up in its usual twist, had already come loose, strands the color of gingerbread and fire floating around her face.

"Seems like a long time, yeah."

"I've really missed having you to talk with." Her words hung in the air.

"Me, too." There was a long pause. He had a sudden, lung-constricting conviction that coming here had been a mistake, that he had to leave right away, had to climb back into his truck and go home. "I ought to be going."

"Oh." She looked at the coffee mug in her hand. "Of course." She placed it carefully on the desk. "Thank you. Thank you for my favorite present." They both stood. She reached out and they clasped hands, squeezing hard. She smiled brightly. "Merry Christmas, Russ."

He pulled her to him without conscious thought and she came, settling against him, their arms wrapped around each other. He held her pressed tightly against his heart. "Merry Christmas," he said into her hair. It smelled of beeswax and cinnamon.

She looked up at him. Her eyes were very large.

"Clare," he said.

She swallowed.

"Clare . . ."

She shook her head. "No."

He touched her face. She closed her eyes and for a moment, pressed her cheek into his palm. Then she opened her eyes and stepped backwards, breaking his hold. He reached for her. She threw up both hands, a barricade against him. "Leave. Now. Go home to your wife."

He let his hands drop, heavy and useless. "I wouldn't—"

"Yes, you would. And God help me, so would I. Go. Please."

He nodded, turned, walked away, through the dim hall, through the scent of pine and beeswax, through the haunting voice of the soloist, singing. "Earth stood hard as iron, water like a stone. Snow had fallen, snow on snow, snow on snow. In the bleak midwinter, long ago."

Around the square, the remaining shops were closing, employees chattering down the sidewalks, last-minute shoppers slipping and sliding under the weight of bags and boxes. The fuzzy candy canes and reindeer, the fat lightbulbs, everything the same as it always was, as it always had been. Everything the same. Everything different. Everything.

He climbed into his truck and headed home.

Keep reading for an excerpt from
Julia Spencer-Fleming's latest mystery:

To Darkness and to Death

Coming in June 2006
from St. Martin's/Minotaur Paperbacks

MORNING PRAYER

When the wicked man turneth away from his wickedness that he hath committed, and doeth that which is lawful and right, he shall save his soul alive.

Ezek. 18:27

SATURDAY, NOVEMBER 14, 5:00 A.M.

Cold. The cold awoke her, creeping underneath her blanket, spreading like an ache along her hip. She tried to move, to burrow into some warm space, but the cold was beneath her, and then there was a hard, hot twinge of pain in her shoulders and she had a panicky moment of *Where? What?* She tried again. She couldn't move her arms. They were pinned behind her back, her wrists fastened by something sticky and implacable.

Scream. Her cheeks and lips didn't move. Her eyelids felt glued together, but she blinked and blinked until the sting of cold air brought tears to her eyes. Open, closed, the darkness was the same. The darkness, and the cold.

Her brain didn't want to make sense of anything she was feeling. Was she drunk? Was this some sort of game? What had she done? She couldn't remember. She remembered dinner. She had chickpea stew. Homemade bread. Red wine. She could picture the table, laid with her mother's best china. She could remember looking down the long table to where her father's picture hung on the wall, thinking, *I know he'd approve. I know he would.* But then what? Nothing. A blankness more frightening than the cold blackness around her. Because it was inside her. A hole in her mind.

She suddenly remembered a trip to Italy they had taken. She had been ten or eleven then. It was the summer after Gene's mother had died, the only summer they didn't come up to the camp. Daddy had hired a driver to take them on the drive through the mountains to Lake Como, but the morning they were to leave Pisa, he had canceled. An American had been kidnapped. She had been whiny, bored with the university town, eager for the water-skiing and boat rides she had been promised. Daddy pulled up a chair and explained they couldn't risk it. That they would make very good targets. That was the word he used, targets. *Because we're American?* She had asked. *Because we're rich,* he had answered. It was the first time, the only time he had ever said that. *Because we're rich.*

Kidnapped. Oh, God. She squeezed her eyes shut against a spill of hot tears and wished, for the thousandth time, that her father was still alive. To make everything all right.

5:15 A.M.

Ring. Ring. The phone. She snarled, rolled onto her stomach, and pulled her pillow over her head, but the damn thing wouldn't give up. Once. Twice. Three times. With an inarticulate curse, she reached out from under the covers and grabbed the receiver. "H'lo," she said.

"Reverend Fergusson? Did I wake you?" She was spared coming up with an answer worthy of the question, because her caller went on. "It's John Huggins, Millers Kill Search and Rescue. I'm calling you on official business."

I'm so glad it's not personal, she thought, but the only thing her mouth could manage was "Me?"

"You signed up, didn't you?" She could hear the rustle of paper over the line. "Air force training in survival, search, and rescue? Nine years army helicopter pilot? Physically fit, has own gear?"

She shoved the pillow beneath her and propped herself up on her elbows. The only word her sleep-sodden brain latched on to was "pilot". "You want me to fly?"

"Not hardly. We got a young woman reported missing. Went out for a walk last night, never returned. Her brother called it in this morning after he discovered her bed hadn't been slept in."

This morning? She squinted at the blackness outside her window. Didn't look like morning to her. "Why me?"

"Because we're down to the bottom of the list." Huggins said, his voice laced with exasperation. "Two-thirds of the crew are off on loan to the Plattsburgh mountain rescue. They got an old lady wandered away from her home and a pair of hunters who haven't reported in for three days. Can you do it or not?"

The bishop's visit. She pushed away the last of her muzzy-headedness. Half the congregation of St. Alban's would be at the church today, preparing for the dog-and-pony show that was the bishop's annual visit. She should be there. But . . . the search and rescue team needed her. She did sign up. *And hiking through the woods is a lot more appealing than counting napkins and polishing silver,* a treacherously seductive voice inside her pointed out. "Sure, I can do it," she said. "Where should I meet you?"

"A place called Haudenosaunee."

"What's that? A town?"

"Naw, it's an old-time estate. What they call a great camp. Inside the Blue Line."

"The Blue Line?"

"Inside the boundary of the Adirondack State Park." Huggins sounded as if he were having second, maybe third thoughts about calling her.

She rolled out of bed. There was a pencil and a pad of paper on her nightstand. "Give me the directions," she said. "I'll be there as soon as I can."

5:15 A.M.

Ed Castle was sitting in the dark. There was no reason for it, really. He had crept out of his unlit bedroom to avoid waking his wife, but with their door safely shut, he could have snapped the hall lights on. Or turned on one of the lamps in the living room when he unlocked the gun cabinet and tucked his rifle under his arm.

Maybe it was because for so many years he had been up early winter mornings, long gone before his family awoke or the sun rose. Tiptoeing past the doors that had once led to his daughters' bedrooms, he felt a tug, like a hook from out of the past embedded in his heart, and he had wanted to open the doors once again to see them sleeping, all silky hair and boneless limbs.

In the kitchen, he had started the coffee and found his Thermos by touch and the green glow of the microwave clock. He thought maybe he'd need some light to find the box of cartridges he kept hidden behind Suzanne's baking tins on the top shelf, but he hadn't. Now he sat in the dark and thought about the years of his life, which were doled out, it seemed to him, winter by winter, tree by tree, marked by a chain tread and a scarred path leading into the woods. Leading to where he could not see.

The light snapped on, starting him upright in his chair. Suzanne stood in the orange and gold halo of the hanging tulip lamp, zipped into her velour robe, her graying hair every which way. "What on earth are you doing here, sitting around with no lights on?" She stepped toward him, her slippers shush-shushing over the vinyl floor. "You didn't get a call about a fire, did you?" Ed was a member of the Millers Kill Volunteer Fire Department.

"No." He shrugged. "I was thinking about when the girls were little. This was the only quiet time I had back then."

"Well, you're going to get a chance to relive those days." She crossed to the counter and opened a cupboard to retrieve her coffee cup. "I'm watching Bonnie's boys while she's finishing up that big sewing job, and Becky's coming home for the weekend."

He grunted. She waved the pot in his direction, and he held out his mug. "She coming up here to gloat?"

"Stop that," Suzanne said sharply. "She didn't force you to put the business up for sale. You can't make the Adirondack Conservancy Corporation the bad guy in all this. It was your decision."

"I wouldn't have had to make any decision if the ACC wasn't going to cut off my lumbering license." He buried his nose in his coffee cup. "I can't believe my own daughter turned into a damn tree hugger."

Suzanne seated herself at the table. "It's your own fault. You used to sneak her out to your cut sites when she wasn't big enough to tie her own shoes."

One half of a smile crooked his cheek. "You used to carry on something fierce about that."

"A lumbering camp is no place for a four-year-old."

He laughed. "Remember how she would stomp around in a fit if she couldn't come with me?"

"Uh-huh." Suzanne looked at him pointedly over the rim of her cup. "So now she's grown up into someone who loves the woods, is hot-tempered, always speaks her mind—and you can't figure out where she gets it from." She snorted. "The only thing she doesn't favor you in is her hair."

Ed ran his hand over his nearly bald scalp and grinned.

Suzanne rolled her white crockery mug between her hands, a gesture he had seen her make on a thousand cold mornings like this one. "What's really bothering you?"

"Sellin' off the business."

"Thought so."

"I know it makes sense. If this land trade-off goes ahead like it's supposed to, by this time tomorrow the van der Hoeven wood lot is gonna be off-limits to lumbering. By this time next week, the crew and I'd have to head fifty miles north to the nearest open woods. A hundred extra miles a day. Six hundred a week. With fuel prices the way they are, Suze—"

"I know."

"Not to mention the increase in the insurance premium once we start putting that many open-road miles on our trucks."

"I know."

"And we'll be getting hit with more maintenance on the trucks."

"I know."

"I just don't see how we can take the increased cost and survive." He looked down at the rifle resting in his lap. It had been his dad's, along with the timber business. For a moment, he felt cut loose in time, unsure if he was sixty or sixteen. The gun, the woods, the coffee, even. All the same in his father's time. In his grandfather's.

"I always hoped to keep it in the family somehow. Maybe leave it to Bonnie's boys. They love the woods."

She nodded. "They do. On the other hand, do you want them risking their necks sixty hours a week to bring home twenty-five thousand a year?"

He looked at her, surprised. "You never complained."

She laughed quietly. "I was a lumberman's daughter. I knew what I was getting into when I married you."

He put down his coffee and took her hand. The feel of her skin under his thumb was another bright spot against time and the dark. "I called the boys on the crew yesterday. Told 'em I wasn't going out this winter. It's a hell of a thing to do, to tell a man he ain't got the job he's been counting on. But if I sell out now to one of the larger companies, I can get a good price for the equipment. Not great, not with fuel prices high and interest rates low, but decent. Good enough so's we could get a place in Florida. Become snowbirds. Would you like that?"

He watched her roll the thought around in her mouth, tasting it. "It'd be nice," she finally said. "Wearing short sleeves all the time. Gardening year-round."

"No more dark mornings," he said.

She smiled a bit at that. "I'd miss seeing Bonnie and the

boys, though. And it would be odd having Christmas where it's sunny and warm." She looked at him more closely. "What are you going to do? I can't imagine you not timbering."

He glanced down at the old rifle in his lap. That was the question, wasn't it? "Man and boy, I've hauled wood out of those mountains forty years now. I don't know what I'll do if I'm not a lumberman. But change is coming, Suze." He rubbed his thumb over her hand again. "And if we don't change with it, we'll get left behind."

5:30 A.M.

Dressed in insulated camos and a blaze-orange vest, Russ Van Alstyne padded downstairs in his stocking feet. Every chair, sofa, and table in the parlor was piled high with meticulously folded draperies, glossy stripes and chintzes that made the room look like a dressmaker's shop gone mad. He shifted a deeply ruffled swag to grab the new Lee Child novel he'd been reading last night and heard the dry crunch of tissue paper stuffed into the folds. No wrinkles for these babies. Unlike him. Straightening, he caught sight of himself in the mirror above the mantel. *I don't look a half-century old,* he thought. *Do I?*

The smell of coffee drew him on to the kitchen. Even in heavy wool socks, the drafts along the two hundred-year-old farmhouse's floor chilled his feet. He stepped into the unlaced boots waiting for him by the mudroom door before pouring himself another cup from the coffeemaker. Boxes of rings and hooks and other curtain-hanging hardware took up all the available space on the kitchen table, so he stood by the sink, looking out the window into the pale darkness, Jack Reacher's adventures abandoned on the counter.

Upstairs, a whirring sewing machine fell silent. A moment later, he heard the stairs creak. "Can I help you load any of this stuff in the car?" he called out.

"Not yet," his wife said, toting what looked like a ball gown through the kitchen. "Let me get rid of this, and I'll be right back." She kneed open the mudroom door and clattered down the steps into the unheated summer kitchen they used for storage. That room led to the barn, where Russ had spent most of the last summer prying up the uneven plank flooring and laying down heavy-duty joists, making it a usable garage for the first time since the horse-and-buggy days. He was actually looking forward to the first big storm of the season, just for the novelty of getting into his truck without knocking snow off first.

"Okay, birthday boy, you ready?" Linda Van Alstyne peeked around the mudroom door. "I couldn't wrap it, so this is all the surprise you get." She emerged into the kitchen cradling a pristine quilted canvas rifle case.

"Whoa," he said.

"Take a look inside." She handed it to him. He unzipped the case. Nestled in the well-padded interior was a .378 Weatherby Mark V.

"Oh, Honey." He drew it out reverently, running a hand along the gunstock walnut, smooth and warm to the touch, like a living thing. "It's beautiful." Rosewood and maple gleamed in the kitchen light. He drew his fingers across the bolt sleeve, etched with scrollwork from another century. "I don't know what to say. This is amazing."

Linda dimpled at him, glowing with cleverness. Dressed in a sweatsuit, her face showing the strain of the past weeks' work, she was still gorgeous, all extravagant curves and tousled blond curls. His very own Marilyn Monroe. "How on earth did you know what to get?" he asked.

"I asked Lyle MacAuley for a list of recommendations." His deputy chief was an avid hunter. "Last time I went to New York to buy fabric, I got it. I'm glad you like it."

"Like it? I love it. I didn't think I'd ever handle a Weatherby outside of a gun shop." He glanced up at her. "Are you sure we can afford it?"

Her dimples vanished. "Russ."

"Don't get me wrong. I love it, I really do. But Weatherbys

cost an arm and a leg. I don't want you to be shorting your budget just to get me a pretty gun."

"Stop worrying about the money. I've got more business than I can handle right now with this commission from the Algonquin Waters resort. And if I can pull it all off in time for their grand opening tonight, I'll be able to pick up tons more business."

"Yeah." He replaced the gun in the carrying case. "If that's what you want."

She tugged a dishrag off the faucet and swiped the immaculate counter. "Don't start with me. This is absolutely the right direction to take the business. No more running up curtains for one room or even one house at a time. The spa has almost five hundred installations, counting the interior accent decorations. That's a year's worth of work. It's my chance to step up to a whole different level."

"I just don't like to see you working so hard—"

"Russell! Hello! Is this the man who can't take a vacation because the police department might fall apart without him?" She tossed the rag into the sink and faced him head-on. "For years, I've been supportive and understanding when you've left dinner on the table to run to a crime scene, or when you've stayed out until 4:00 A.M. working a case, or when you've missed Thanksgiving or Christmas because you're taking someone else's shift. Now it's your turn. I've finally found something I love to do, something I'm good at, something people will pay me for. You've always had that. I haven't. You should be happy for me."

"I am. I know when we retired from the army it was hard on you. I'm glad you've found something to do with yourself." She opened her mouth disbelievingly, and he winced. "I didn't mean it like that. It's just . . . you're spending all your time at the spa these days."

"Have you run out of groceries? Is the house a filthy mess? Are the monthly bills unpaid? I'm keeping up my end, so get off my back."

"Linda," He was making a hash of this, but some shambling monster of marital discord made him open his mouth and wedge his foot deeper in. "It's not the time. You're . . . I hate that you're working with John Opperman." He couldn't stop his voice from tightening when he said the resort developer's name.

She shoved one of the wooden chairs against the table. "Mr. Opperman has been both a perfect gentleman and a generous employer who's committed to hiring locally. If he had gone with a big commercial furnishings company, he'd have his curtains up this morning, instead of having to wait and wonder if I can pull it off before the opening ceremonies tonight." She stalked into the living room. "I have to load the rest of this into my car. You can help, or you can go. Whatever." She scooped up a stack of quilted shades piled so high they looked like bedding for a princess and a pea.

"For chrissakes, give me those. They must weigh a ton." He relieved her of the stack. "I've dealt with Opperman. He smiles at you and he talks real smooth, and all the time he's got the knife out, waiting to stick it in."

"You haven't dealt with him. You've investigated him. Of course you think he's the bogeyman." She shook out a plastic bag and slid several tissue-stiffened swags inside. "One of his business partners was murdered. His other partner tried to kill him. I'm sorry if the case didn't turn out like you thought it would, but honey, it's been over a year. The trial has come and gone, and Mr. Opperman wasn't implicated in any way. Don't you think it's time to let it go already?"

He stomped through the kitchen with unnecessary force.

"He could have taken the insurance money and run," Linda went on. "Instead, he built the resort. He gave a lot of local people jobs, including yours truly." She trailed him through the open mudroom door into the unheated summer kitchen. "Let's face it, honey, you divide the world into two categories, criminals and potential criminals." Her words made vapor puffs in the cold air. "I've worked with him. Believe me. He has a clear conscience."

In the barn, Russ lifted the back gate of her boxy old Volvo wagon and slid the quilted shades in. "Careful of those sheets," she said.

"Jeffrey Dahmer had a clear conscience, too, you know."

She dropped her swags in the back and slammed the tailgate. "You. Are. Impossible." She stomped up the barn steps, strode through the summer kitchen, and let the mudroom door swing in his face.

"Honey?" he started, but she held up her hand.

"I don't know why you've been such a grouchy old bastard lately, but it's going to stop." She threw open the refrigerator and pulled out an insulated lunchbox. "Here, I made you a lunch. Take your pretty new gun and go shoot something."

"Honey . . ." He tried again.

She paused in the doorway between the kitchen and the living room. "And don't think all this talk about how terrible Mr. Opperman is will get you out of going to the grand-opening party tonight. I expect you to be here, wearing your tux, car keys in hand, by seven-thirty tonight. Do us both a favor and work out your aggressions on the deer, okay?" She leaned against the doorjamb, crossing her arms over her chest. "Okay?"

He was rewarded with the dimples again. "You're impossible, but I love you."

"I am impossible," he agreed.

"And . . ."

"And I love you, too."

She disappeared into the living room. God, she was still so beautiful. When he had married her twenty-five years ago, he had wanted nothing else than to grow old with her. And now, that had happened. He was fifty years old today. Fifty years old, and in love with another woman.

ELTON
JOHN

PHILIP NORMAN

A   FIRESIDE   BOOK
Published by Simon & Schuster
New York London Toronto Sydney Tokyo Singapore

Contents

Acknowledgements

Permission to reproduce the photographs in this book is gratefully acknowledged as follows:

First section:

p. 1 Roy Dwight (both); p. 2 Geoff Dyson (top), Arnold Tendler (bottom); p. 3 Philip Gotlop Photographs Ltd (bottom); p. 4 Bryan Forbes; p. 5 Richard Young and Rex Features (both); p. 6 Bryan Forbes (top), Rex Features (bottom); p. 7 Terry O'Neill, Camera Press (both); p. 8 Terry O'Neill (top) and David White (bottom), both Camera Press.

Second section:

p. 1 Sotheby's; p. 2 Janet Edroff (top); all other photos Rex Features.

Third section:

p. 1 Terry O'Neill, Camera Press (top), Rex Features (bottom); p. 2 Rex Features (top); David White and Camera Press (bottom); p. 3 Camera Press (top), David White and Camera Press (bottom); p. 4 Terry O'Neill and Camera Press (top left), Rex Features (all others); p. 5 Norman Parkinson and Camera Press (top right, bottom left), Camera Press (top left), Rex Features (bottom right); p. 6 Rex Features; p. 7 Syndication International (top), Michael B. Lippman and Aurum Press (bottom); p. 8 Camera Press (top), Rex Features/*The Sun* (bottom).

Thanks are also due to *Rolling Stone* for permission to quote from their interview with Elton John.

Contents

Acknowledgements

Permission to reproduce the photographs in this book is gratefully acknowledged as follows:

First section:

p. 1 Roy Dwight (both); p. 2 Geoff Dyson (top), Arnold Tendler (bottom); p. 3 Philip Gotlop Photographs Ltd (bottom); p. 4 Bryan Forbes; p. 5 Richard Young and Rex Features (both); p. 6 Bryan Forbes (top), Rex Features (bottom); p. 7 Terry O'Neill, Camera Press (both); p. 8 Terry O'Neill (top) and David White (bottom), both Camera Press.

Second section:

p. 1 Sotheby's; p. 2 Janet Edroff (top); all other photos Rex Features.

Third section:

p. 1 Terry O'Neill, Camera Press (top), Rex Features (bottom); p. 2 Rex Features (top); David White and Camera Press (bottom); p. 3 Camera Press (top), David White and Camera Press (bottom); p. 4 Terry O'Neill and Camera Press (top left), Rex Features (all others); p. 5 Norman Parkinson and Camera Press (top right, bottom left), Camera Press (top left), Rex Features (bottom right); p. 6 Rex Features; p. 7 Syndication International (top), Michael B. Lippman and Aurum Press (bottom); p. 8 Camera Press (top), Rex Features/*The Sun* (bottom).

Thanks are also due to *Rolling Stone* for permission to quote from their interview with Elton John.

Author's Note

THIS is not an authorised biography of Elton John. His manager, John Reid, declined to make it so, on the grounds that Elton intended to write his own memoirs some time in the future. However, by the winks and nods that pass for communication in the pop music world, I was given to understand that he did not disapprove of my project. I even briefly became an official Boswell, writing the programme notes for his 1989 North American tour.

From the early to middle Seventies, as Elton rose to fame, I was covering pop music for *The Times* and the *Sunday Times Magazine*. Much first-hand observation can therefore be found in the pages that follow. I have drawn extensively on newspaper archives, despite an inherent mistrust of 'yellowed cuttings'. From the very start of his career, Elton was an outstandingly articulate and truthful interviewee. Especially in encounters with Britain's now vanished literate music papers, and the famous confessional sessions with *Playboy* and *Rolling Stone*, his voice rings loud and clear.

Though denied direct access, I have received help from many of his closest friends and associates, and members of his family. My overwhelming debt is to his lyricist Bernie Taupin, who generously granted me many hours of interview in London and Miami. My grateful thanks also to Sue Ayton, Long John Baldry, Clive Banks, Jack Baverstock, Andrew Bendel, Don Black, Caroline Boucher, Sally Brompton, Paul Buckmaster, Eric Clapton, Ray Coleman, David Croker, Elton Dean, Gus Dudgeon, Kirk Duncan, Roy Dwight, Geoff Dyson, Mick Eaves, Janet Edrof, Geoffrey Ellis, Peter Emery, Bryan Forbes and Nanette Newman, Cyril Gee, Harvey Goldsmith, Roger Greenaway, John Gunnell, John Hall, Linda Hannon, John Harvey, Pat Higgs, Andrew Hill, George Hill, Neil Hubbard, Nicky James, Stephen James, Bill Johnson, Tony King, David Larkham, Sharon Lawrence, Joan Lewis, Vic Lewis, Kenny Lynch, Linda Mallarkey, Bob Miller, Dee Murray, Nina Myskow, Yoko Ono, Helen Piena, Caleb Quaye, Terri Quaye, Annie Reavey,

Russ Regan, Tommy Roberts, Paul Robinson, Johnny Rogan, Ken Russell, Gill Saitch, Gay Search, Neil and Leba Sedaka, Margo Stevens, Rod Stewart, Robert and Daphne Taupin, Alistair Taylor, Arnold Tendler, Penny Valentine, Helen Walters, Michael Watts, Jack Westgate Smith, Doug Weston, Ray Williams, Richard Williams, Chris Wilson, Norm Winter, Al Woodrow and Neil Woodrow.

I owe much to my two editors, Gail Rebuck – whose idea this book was – and Robyn Sisman. My agent, Michael Sissons, has been enthusiastic and supportive, as always. Chris Carne of Calancraft Computers was a saviour at moments of technical panic. In helping me on discographical matters and tracking down obscure sources, Mark Lewisohn constantly proved himself a researcher of true brilliance. Nor could I have gone the distance without Sue, my energy and inspiration on so many disgruntled summer mornings.

Philip Norman
London, 1991.

Prologue
'Feeling like a true survivor'

Wembley, North London, 22 May, 1989

WEMBLEY is a suburb in terminal exhaustion. The streets have a fragile, overwrought air, as if the year-round tramp of feet has almost shaken them to pieces. The shops, pubs and Indian restaurants look wearied to death by the battening and unbattening of protective boards. The gardens of the 1930s houses, accepting their fate as rubbish-dumps and urinals, are desolate and denuded as no-man's-land on the Somme. Especially on Saturdays, the despair is almost audible, as if a suburb could sigh. Not another soccer match, Wembley seems to be praying. Please God, not another rock concert!

British sport had always lacked the heroic element, being played for the most part on small rectangular fields set about by low-rise seating. Wembley's mixed blessing is to possess the only stadium deserving the name in the entire United Kingdom. Built for the 1923 Empire Exhibition, it is a massive Art Deco period piece, lying at the end of a half-mile triumphal avenue. Flanking its main gate are two white towers with pistachio-green facings and Moorish domes from which green flags permanently fly. Even today, the whole thing looks like nothing so much as an illustration in some sixty-year-old *Boys' Own Annual*. One can almost see the twin towers set about with Bugatti racing cars, Schneider Trophy-winning seaplanes and other brand-new marvels from that age when everything just got better and better.

Wembley, to most British ears, means Wembley Stadium, not the long-suffering district round about. It means the place where the climactic event of Britain's football season annually takes place before a capacity 88,000 crowd, on an oval greensward rolled into immaculate green stripes. Since 1923, the FA Cup Final has been played here, frequently watched by the King, and later the Queen, in a ritual owing something to Roman games. The competing teams arrive down the long avenue in almost gladiatorial progress. Later, the winning captain receives the great, studded chalice, then turns to flourish it aloft for the crowd like an exultant Spartacus.

In the 1970s, however, Wembley had to recognise a source of mass joy and excitement greater even than football. The stadium, while retaining its yearly Cup Final glory, is also Britain's largest and most prestigious open-air rock music venue. The adjacent 12,000-seat Wembley Arena is London's most prestigious covered rock music venue. While football is a seasonal happening at Wembley complex, rock is year-round mega-business. A night seldom falls in any season when local residents are not lulled to sleep by distant electronic thunder.

There are two Englishmen named Dwight in whose careers Wembley has loomed large. The elder, Roy Dwight, was a professional footballer who scored a goal for Nottingham Forest against Luton in the Cup Final of 1959. Minutes later, he had the bad luck to break his leg, so effectively ending a brilliant First Division career.

Roy's younger cousin, christened Reginald Kenneth Dwight, grew up only a few miles across Middlesex from here. Reggie Dwight also longed to be a pro footballer and caper out on to the hallowed stadium turf as part of some brilliant eleven. Disappointed in that, he had to come up with alternative ways of filling Wembley's giant spaces and making the crowd roar.

As a rule, any major rock concert attraction can be immediately identified by its audience. Hippies with paunches and bald patches mean Bob Dylan or the Grateful Dead. Black leather, gaunt cheekbones, studs and chains mean heavy metal, Def Leppard, Iron Maiden or ZZ Top. Fat boys in porkpie hats mean rap. Girls wearing fingerless gloves and brassieres on the outside mean Madonna. Children with junk-food-perfect complexions mean Jason or Kylie.

But what is one to make of the crowd streaming into Wembley Arena this balmy spring evening? They seem drawn from every British age-group, culture, style and class. There are today's high fashion young men, with slicked-back hair, knee-length shorts and white ankle socks. There are today's high fashion young women, in brass-buttoned bellboy jackets and microskirts. There are today's high fashion grandmothers, with *Dynasty*-coiffed hair and stone-washed blue jeans. There are today's high fashion fathers, in designer stubble and Mickey Mouse T-shirts, shepherding today's high fashion small boys, in baseball caps, Day-Glo knickerbockers and wedgy training shoes. Now and again, one glimpses an archaic silhouette, flaring where it should be straight, waisted where it should hang loose, its hair not teased into spikes or flattened with gel, but still an obdurate, bubbly Afro perm. This is a night, above all, when Seventies children may briefly rise from the grave and walk.

Normally, an audience entering Wembley Arena must pass through a cordon of shifty-looking men offering tickets at eight or nine times their face value (very often producing them from the recesses of yellowish underpants). But tonight few, if any, ticket touts seem to be on station. Similar restraint is noticeable in the police, who have held back their customary dog teams, armoured cars and snatch squads, deploying barely a dozen officers in sherbet lime flak jackets. Even the stewards who examine handbags for bombs seem calm and avuncular. We are at a thoroughly wholesome family event, closer in spirit to one of Wembley's Boy Scout shows, model-railway-fests or international stamp fairs.

Amazing to consider the social emancipation of rock music these past two decades! One does not have to be so old to remember when it was merely the aberrant taste of teenagers, condemned and mocked by virtually everyone over twenty-one. Now it covers the earth, an element second only to oxygen. Children grow up dancing to it. Old age pensioners keep themselves supple with it. Newspapers that once barred it now contain intelligence of little else. Whether or not one enjoys it is irrelevant since it permeates every facet of life, the same mass placebo and seducer in every country and language, riveting the ear to TV sales pitches for cars, chocolate, shampoo, banks and insurance companies; playing behind movie credits; wafting among supermarket shelves; blurring from above station concourses and escalators; racketing in shops; thudding from cars; hissing from personal stereos; whispering from lifts and tinkling out of telephones.

Amazing, too, to recollect when the species known as 'rock stars' lived apart from most normal codes of human decency. In those not far-off days, being a rock star meant getting drunk, taking drugs, screwing groupies and throwing television sets through the windows of hotel rooms. Now it is more likely to mean appearing in society columns, collecting antique silver, hunting with the Quorn and being on friendly terms with Prince Charles. Once, rock stardom spelt reclusiveness, monomaniacal selfishness and monster ego. Now it spells togetherness, social conscience and public spirit: helping out on one another's records; appearing as modest walk-ons in one another's concerts; being healthy, 'clean' and happily married, with children; caring about rain forests and food additives; lending one's name to anti-drink and anti-drug programmes; speaking out against nuclear arms, rape and racism; and periodically joining one's superstar brothers in charity galas for the starving of Ethiopia or research into AIDS.

In the huge normalisation process that rock has undergone, no one has been more influential than the star playing Wembley Arena tonight. At the same time, no one has more poignantly shown what an abnormal, unreal – and sometimes terrifying – thing rock stardom still can be.

His career virtually spans rock music history as we know it. When he started on the piano, Little Richard and Jerry Lee Lewis were in their keyboard-punishing prime. When he was a teenager, Bobby Vee and Fabian lisped their cow-eyed ballads to Venuses in blue jeans and Mona Lisas with pony-tails. When he first went on the road, the Beatles were mop-topped, Bob Dylan was a folkie, Stevie Wonder was 'Little Stevie Wonder' and Brian Jones the pre-eminent Rolling Stone. When he had his first hit, Jimi Hendrix was at Middle Earth, Sam and Dave were at the Albert Hall, Jefferson Airplane were at the Fillmore East and Blind Faith were in Hyde Park.

He became the definitive rock star of the Seventies, as big in that unsteadily shod era as the Beatles in the Sixties, bigger than any solo artist before or since, with the single exception of Elvis Presley. He became so, moreover, with none of the visual attributes that rock stars ordinarily possess; without physical beauty, commanding height or very much hair; with nothing on his side but talent, energy, stamina and sheer wanting to.

He was a peerless live performer whose shows sated even the Seventies' vast appetite for flamboyance and excess. At the same time, he was a recording prodigy whose dominance of the Top 20 charts in America and Britain is unequalled to this day. Between 1972 and 1977, a week seldom passed when he did not have an album or a single, or both, in the charts on both sides of the Atlantic. No one else, singer or band, has matched his mid-Seventies run of seven consecutive American number one albums, four of them at number one simultaneously in America and Britain. He was hugely over-productive and many of his songs can safely be consigned to history's black rubbish bag. But the numerous best are classics and mirrors of their time: 'Your Song', 'Rocket Man', 'Daniel', 'Bennie and the Jets', 'Goodbye Yellow Brick Road', 'Candle in the Wind'.

A decade and a half on, at the age of forty-two, his fame is Himalayan. He belongs to the tiny handful of rock star names – Presley, Dylan, Beatles, Stones – who have risen above the screaming adoration of their own sphere to become embedded in the general consciousness. Like them, he transcends his own particular decade with an attraction that has been proof against ten more years of rock's multitudinous fashions and fads. He remains rock music's highest-grossing performer, able to pack out any stadium throughout Europe, the Americas, the Far East or Australasia, for however many straight nights he cares to appear. As tonight's audience shows, his appeal is timeless, ageless and classless, embracing both acmes of modern style and untrendy nostalgics, both nymphets and grannies, both fathers who remember and small boys who don't. Of the thirty-odd record albums he has made since 1969, twenty-four are now certified to have 'gone platinum' with sales of more than one million copies. His total record sales are hazily estimated to be somewhere around 100 million. A music trade paper recently computed that he accounts for 3 per cent of all albums, singles, compact discs and tapes purchased annually throughout the world.

He is a musician's musician, respected throughout the rock industry, not only for his talent and wild inventiveness but also for being a professional to his hardened fingertips, schooled and seasoned in every department of recording and performing. His knowledge of popular music is encyclopedic, his personal record collection possibly the world's largest. The roster of his friends, admirers and sometime collaborators includes everyone who has been anyone in rock these past twenty years, from John Lennon, George Harrison, Eric Clapton, Mick Jagger and David Bowie to Phil Collins, Tina Turner, Paul Young, George Michael, Billy Joel, Michael Jackson and Prince. The youngest musicians of the late Eighties acknowledge his influence on their writing, phrasing and wardrobe, and clamour for the opportunity of sharing a stage with him.

He is also a celebrity's celebrity, having learned the social graces a good decade in advance of any other rock star. The famous names he has courted, or who have cultivated him, would make a surreal assembly for a *Sgt. Pepper*-style album-cover: Elizabeth Taylor, Mae West, Groucho Marx, Billie-Jean King, Liberace, Katharine Hepburn, Jimmy Connors, Hugh M. Hefner, Shirley MacLaine, Lech Walesa, Martina Navratilova. He was the first rock personage to be taken up by the British royal family, his palace-based fans over the years having included Princess Margaret, the Duke and Duchess of York, the Princess of Wales and Queen Elizabeth the Queen Mother.

For all that, the shiny crust of stardom has never completely hardened around him. Despite his huge fame and wealth, he has contrived to remain – at least, to outward appearance – simple, straightforward and down to earth. Despite his displays of excess, on- and offstage, he remains paradoxically self-effacing and shy. As well as the most instinctive he is also the most intelligent of rock musicians. Only John Lennon was ever his equal for honesty, articulateness and humour.

He was the first rock star to adopt a clean and wholesome, as opposed to a frowsty and depraved, life style, and to spend his leisure hours, not lying comatose in unlit rooms, but engaged in energetic outdoor sports. To this day, he is the only member of his profession to have played tennis with Wimbledon champions and cricket on the sacred wicket at Lord's. A constant counterpart to his Carmen Miranda wildness has been his rosette-wearing, rattle-waving, schoolboyish passion for football. In Britain, a huge parallel public knows and admires him for the money and personal commitment he has invested in the game, as though in consolation for the star player he himself could never be. Thirteen years ago he became Chairman of his boyhood's local club, Watford, thereafter spending several million pounds to lift them from Fourth Division no-hopers to contenders in the 1984 Cup Final. It was for him a moment of pride far eclipsing any musical achievement, and one which caused him to weep unashamedly before the Wembley Stadium crowd.

He is also a model for hedonism, a spender and self-indulger on an epic scale, who can strip a Cartier showcase bare in seconds and always returns from foreign travels loaded with souvenirs that have caught his fancy, such as a set of six-ton Imperial Chinese stone lions or a Melbourne tram. Despite being a self-confessed 'looter' of anything buyable anywhere, he is also a connoisseur and art collector of fine discrimination. In an industry whose great stars tend to be Scrooges, his generosity is legendary. Like the late Nubar Gulbenkian, he possesses the knack of flaunting his wealth in a way that amuses the British rather than rousing them to their usual transports of vindictive envy. It helps that he is a notable philanthropist, who espoused good causes and began giving concerts for charity a decade and a half ahead of the Live Aid cult. By the standard that gave Bob Geldof a knighthood, he should have received a peerage.

Together with his triumphs, his audience has always shared his keen sense of his own deficiencies. Of these, the most painful is his hair, which began to disappear in his late teens and has continued to do so despite an expensive and painful programme of surgical transplants. Nearly as vexatious is the tendency of his stocky physique to put on weight, and retain it, no matter how many pounds he may seem to sweat off in performance. Only a heroic series of crash diets down the years has prevented his collapse into his predestined shape: that of Billy Bunter, the Fat Owl of Greyfriars school.

Nor have his celebrity and his millions ever made a protective carapace. Stupendously rich as he is, he also is known not to be outstandingly happy. Surrounded though he is by famous friends and obedient servants, he has often seemed withdrawn and lonely. Notwithstanding the vast pile-up of success behind him, he suffers chronic self-doubt and insecurity, periodic nervous prostration, attacks of self-destructive anger and dark fits of fathomless despair. In 1976, he confessed in a magazine interview that he was bisexual. Since then, as his fame and wealth and popularity have doubled and redoubled, contentment and stability have visibly receded from his grasp. On two occasions, at least, he has attempted suicide.

Middle age, and his vast sophistication, have brought no stability to his personal life. The past five years, which should have seen him at an unassailable professional and social pinnacle, have instead proved the most torn and traumatic of his career. He has made an impulsive and hugely publicised marriage and, a few months later, undergone an anguished, remorseful parting from his new wife. He has had surgery for a throat ailment, rumoured to be cancer. He has fought a High Court battle with his former song publisher, which not only failed to win him what he wanted but also, some maintain, led directly to the publisher's death. Latterly and climactically, he has been the subject of a tabloid newspaper 'exposé' of his private life worse than anything even in Fleet Street's long history of victimisation and untruth. The paper was eventually forced to apologise in three-inch banner headlines and pay him one million pounds, the largest libel settlement in British legal history, though whether even that compensated for his internal devastation remains questionable.

The star has come through these ordeals, however, not only surviving but determined they shall mark a watershed in his life. His twenty-fifth year as a rock musician, he has announced, will be a totally new start, both professionally and mentally. As an earnest of that, in typical all-or-nothing fashion, he has decided to dispose of all his labyrinthine possessions. The latest headline was the auction sale where the contents of his stately home, and all the myriad treasures and relics of his career – saving only his works of art and his cars – were put under the hammer by Sotheby's.

The new start is also a return to what he understands best: a year-long tour, taking in Europe, the UK, the USA and South America. His best refuge from trouble – and from himself – has always been to appear in a different huge black space, to new applause every night. He admitted it, with his familiar candour, to *Paris-Match* magazine not long ago. 'The stage is about the only place where I feel safe.'

Of all previous world-class performers, only Judy Garland has generated the mixed emotions of the crowd streaming to Wembley Arena this evening. There is excitement of course, on the threshold of matchless entertainment. But, more than that, there is solicitude. They have all been very worried about him.

Among the audience taking their seats – and among those who examine tickets by torchlight or sell bottled beer, soft drinks and food out in the concourse – a particular kind of face often recurs. It is a very English pug dog face with its domed forehead and large glasses, its button nose and drawn-in upper lip. Just as typically English is its expression of shyness yet brashness; of hesitancy and uncertainty mingled with a certain obscure dogged determination.

It is the face one has already met on the concert poster, multiplied a thousand times under a tilted white fedora hat. This is the star above all in whom his fans recognise themselves, both as they wish they were and wish they weren't. Especially on this night so crucial to his wellbeing, one seems to see Elton John everywhere.

The blocks of scarlet chairs over the Arena floor, and its steep scarlet tiers, seethe with a resigned, unresentful murmur. Rock fans, whatever their age or allegiance, grow accustomed to the convention that performances almost never start on time. From barn-like rafters, midway back, hangs an enormous screen showing a little-heeded cavalcade of pop videos and advertisements. High on the distant back wall, a sign says ELTON JOHN in the same electric mosaic one might see above Piccadilly Circus or Times Square, advertising Budweiser beer or Kentucky Fried Chicken.

Suspended over the stage is a mass of what look like half-melted and clotted-up silver saxophones. In the twilight below, a dozen indistinct figures still hurry back and forth, making final adjustments to the batteries of amplifiers and drums. The centre is a thin keyboard instrument set between a pair of Art Deco wings vaguely – and, if one knew the whole story, ironically – recalling the insignia of the Royal Air Force. The keyboard has its own attendant, not a 'roadie' but an earnest-looking girl in black, who can be seen wiping it as carefully and scientifically as if engaged on the restoration of some Old Master.

How to arrive onstage is a major problem for someone whose entrances are a part, not merely of rock, but of show business history. What compère's superlatives could surpass, for example, Linda Lovelace, the Seventies porno queen, calling him down into cicada-buzzy night at Hollywood Bowl, in terms that might have embarrassed Jehovah? What could ever surpass that 1973 entrance, down a

Busby Berkeley staircase to the strains of the Twentieth Century-Fox theme music, as flocks of white doves were let fly, and the lids of five grand pianos opened to spell out his Christian name? What weirder blend of ultra-modern glamour with period kitsch, of impossible hubris with self-knowing humour, could ever be devised to bring a balding singer-pianist of sturdily unromantic build face-to-face with his paying customers?

These days, the device is gargantuan modesty; colossal understatement. First, a roll of Vesuvian thunder on electronic synthesisers. Up in the roof, the clotted saxophones pour down many-directional shafts of light. Five musicians hurry out to their places as side and rear lights explode into purple spokes and red flashing T-shapes, and dry ice smoke pours from vents. The electronic thunder dwindles under a louder human roar. There he suddenly is, materialised from some central trapdoor, walking up and down and bowing inside a thin spotlight.

What to wear is still more hideously problematic for someone who, over the years, has perpetually surpassed himself in extravagance, implausibility and idiocy of stage costume. After the glitter suits and platform shoes; the outsize top hats and stage-filling cloaks; the jumpsuits, leotards, hot pants and ladies' tights; the jerkins, blousons and jerseys; the tracksuits, tail suits, baseball, football and toreador outfits; the semblances of Uncle Sam, Prince Charming, Donald Duck, Lady Bracknell, Ronald McDonald, Mozart and Santa Claus; the knickers, breeches, plus-fours, pantaloons and puttees; the bowlers, boaters, bonnets, tammies and stetsons; the feather boas, Ziegfeld showgirl plumes and necklets of outsize bananas, there would seem to be no article of human or quasi-human apparel left that the stocky body has not draped about itself.

Tonight's outfit is so muted and miscellaneous as to hint at an underlying fatigue with the whole subject. A purple satin dress suit, cut in the baggy mode that so benefits ampler figures. A heavy waistcoat, worked in scarlet and gold, that Louis XVI might have selected to wear to the scaffold. Wrap-around Rommel sunglasses which, from a distance, all but conceal his face. A tipped-down black porkpie hat, to one side of which adheres a large jewelled device in dark, quivery red, like something hurled with expert aim from a restaurant dessert trolley. Always the hat to hide the wisps of transplanted hair, whose few visible areas, on his temples and neck, are now an eerie platinum white.

For a long time, the roaring does not stop. He walks to and fro, substantial in the narrow light, his little hat and bulky suit giving him a transient look of the boogieing bear that advertises Hofmeister lager.

'Hello, Wembley,' he says in his light, well-brought-up voice. 'It's good to be back. Thank you.'

He climbs between the Art Deco wings, which have begun to glow vaguely pink, like stove burners getting warm. He lowers himself behind his keyboard, facing the audience, his stout purple knees visible underneath. He flips his satin lapels from his French aristo's waistcoat and flexes his pudgy hands, not quite rubbing them together.

Downstage left, an additional figure stands in darkness, its burden poised, water-carrier-style, on one shoulder. This is the cameraman who will film the performance for instantaneous transmission up to the giant video screen. Conditions have improved since the days when those in far seats at rock concerts could see little but lights and the odd flash of a guitar. Those in really good seats can see, as well, the video cameraman, moving about in determined indifference to the music, genuflecting before the fingers of guitarists, clambering up and down from the drummer's podium, always returning to different close-up angles of Elton, there to kneel, long-muzzled burden on bowed back, a humble, self-denying votary.

The image projected on the video-screen is as different from reality as public life from private. Up there, his stage suit is not purple but pale candyfloss pink. A face becomes discernible, under its hatbrim and sunglasses, next to a single silver drop earring. Its trademark spectacles have always given it a blank, nerdish look, like 'Brains' in *Thunderbirds*. One must catch it without glasses to see the deep-set, dark-browed eyes, which suddenly make sense of the firmly cleft upper lip, and the jutting determination of the chin.

The puggy face has, understandably, aged of late, filling to a margin that crash diets can no longer help, taking on the unhealthily vivacious bloom of the confirmed drinker. His latest formal portrait – by Lord Snowdon, ex-husband of his old friend Princess Margaret – shows him in Chairman Mao cap and plain blue fatigues, ruefully taciturn like some long-banished Manchurian exile about to be permitted back into the fold. But there is still, now and then, the familiar broad grin, showing the gap between his two top front teeth, and unusually long and pointed canines.

He has begun with 'Sixty Years On', an early song whose portentous opening chords underline a moment of general tension. Rumours are rife that his voice might be permanently impaired, if not by laser throat surgery then by the jugular-rippings of *The Sun* newspaper. True, in the interim there has been an album, *Reg Strikes Back* – defiantly dropping his alias of twenty-one years – on which he sounds perfectly restored. But albums, everyone knows, can sometimes mislead.

The first verse of 'Sixty Years On' banishes all such fears. It is the Elton voice of old, blown over flawless channels of digitalised sound. The voice like none other in its erratic register, that at one moment keens and howls in flamenco wildness, at the next bluesily bites off and swallows its words. The voice, soaked through in Deep Southern soul, whose vital essence remains that of the streets outside this hall: the semi-detached houses with sunrise gates, the little trees in squares of earth, the Co-op bakeries, Finlay's sweetshops and Odeon cinemas.

The words are the very last one would expect from that carnival-coloured, jewel-encrusted figure. 'Walk me down to church when I'm sixty years of age . . .' It is a song about fear of growing old, sung as if by one of the war veterans who parade on English Remembrance Sundays in campaign-ribbons and bowler hats. Two lines later, it becomes a cowboy ballad, after 'The Streets of Laredo' or Marty Robbins's 'El Paso'. The narrator switches continents and centuries from English village green to Mexican *cantina*, where a dark-eyed *señorita* moves among the tables, playing a guitar. The C-of-E old soldier is now a Catholic *vaquero* who, in a sudden Grahame Greene touch, finds his 'rosary has broken . . . its beads have all slipped through'.

The song's unabashed stylistic borrowing, its weighty confessional thoughts, its air of melancholy, all seem as quintessentially Elton as his spectacles, earrings and hats. Even among his aficionados, there are some who do not realise a curious fact about a performer whose susceptibilities are impressed upon continents. He has not, or scarcely ever, written the words he sings. Twenty-two years ago, unable as he thought to write pop-lyrics, he joined forces with a young would-be poet from the Lincolnshire countryside named Bernie Taupin. The words to every colossal hit were written by Bernie first, then handed to Elton to be wrapped in a tune. While seeming to bare his soul in dozens of anthems, eulogies and laments, the superstar has in reality told us almost nothing about himself.

He says no more for now but 'Thank you. We're going to start with some of the old songs.' A solid wedge of them follows, recalling his first great breakthrough, nineteen years ago. 'I Need You To Turn To' and 'The King Must Die', from the original, famous *Elton John* album; 'Burn Down The Mission' from *Tumbleweed Connection* in 1970. Songs remarkable in their day for venturing outside the boy-girl idiom of pop, into literature, history and the celluloid dreams of Hollywood. Echoes of Tennyson, Lord Macaulay, Mary Renault, T. H. White's *Sword in the Stone* and Lerner and Loewe's *Camelot*.

Simplistic rock chords, mixed into cathedral-like settings, after Beethoven, Wagner or Purcell. Songs of chivalrous love, idealistic love, disillusioned or despairing love, but never one hint of the lust that is rock's basic fuel. Smoke and darkness, melodrama, quasi-literacy and high seriousness. Herbal breaths of a far-off time when boy's shirts had high collars with rounded ends, when girls' hair suddenly grew short and their winter coats grew long, when every student sitting-room had an outsize paper dragonfly on the wall above the couch and every right-thinking bathroom a full-length poster of Lenin behind the door.

Around the porkpie hat, everything looks as the most up-to-date rock concert should. Atop the high plinth, the drummer labours and smashes in his silvery den, sometimes ostentatiously spinning both sticks up into the air. Two backup keyboard players work with the inspired fervour of scientists on the edge of reproducing life. A white-trousered black bass-player sashays to and fro, grinning at how ridiculously simple his job is. Elton's long-time lead guitarist, Davey Johnstone – a stunning Seventies artefact with shoulder-length blond hair, sunbed tan and ferocious white-ruffled *décolletage* – strikes every pose known to rock-performance ecstasy on a computerised guitar whose lack of tuning pegs gives it a curious, unsatisfactory appearance, like a length of vacuum-cleaner pipe. A couple of songs in, three black girl singers materialise on the left, emitting mellifluous 'Oohs' and 'Aahs', swaying and pointing each index finger in unison, as if to say 'You're a naughty boy . . . and *you're* a naughty boy.'

The next song starts with a massed piano and synthesiser riff that sounds like Eric Clapton's intro to 'Layla', except that it's twice as fast, three times as loud and four times as long. From its initial frenetic speed, it then grinds down as slowly and tortuously as some great ramshackle oil-tanker trying to stop in mid-ocean. At last, only the voice is left, spelling out each line with slow anguish that displays all its own special peculiarities of articulation and phrasing:

> Oh haveyuh heard . . . the dogs . . . at ny-eet
> A-somewhere awn . . . thuh hill . . .

The song is 'Have Mercy on the Criminal', another composite image from the poems, stories and B-movies of Bernie Taupin's boyhood. Remember all those sub-Steinbeck films about runaways from Deep South prison farms, plunging through swamp and bayou, pursued by cowboy-hatted guards with Winchester rifles and ravening bloodhounds? 'Have Mercy on the Criminal' lasts fourteen minutes, in the process awakening every memory of what made early Seventies stadium rock pretentious, self-indulgent and insufferable. Up on the video screen, the face, beside its pendant earring, is blunted with ersatz agony. Davey Johnstone, with his tossing blond locks and length of vacuum-cleaner pipe, enters a creative rapture that might have moved Michelangelo. Overhead, the clotted silver saxophones pour down light in designer shades of Lincoln green, moleskin grey, desert-khaki brown, Air Force blue, plasma red and burnt orange. Shorter, lateral beams of white project turning windmill-sails, Daliesque spheres and elongated waffle-grids. Thick white smoke billows out afresh as from New York manholes. For pity's sake, let the bloodhounds tear the fugitive to pieces and make an end of it!

To outward appearance, he holds Wembley Arena spellbound. Each song is greeted with applause as it begins; with panoramic whistles, cheers and whoops as it cymbal-crashes to its eventual end. But this is no more than protocol between a star of uttermost magnitude and people who have paid up to £50 apiece to see him. Despite each wild ovation, despite each smile and gratified 'Thank you' from him, something, on either side, is palpably being held back. Those *Sun* headlines, though long discredited, still exert a powerful malignity. It is as if old friends are meeting in the shadow of some tragedy or deep embarrassment that neither is willing to mention first.

The turning-point is 'Philadelphia Freedom', a song from 1975, written under the influence of Thom Bell's Philadelphia sound – Harold Melvin, The O'Jays, Three Degrees et al. – and, as powerfully, recalling the high season of Elton's infatuation with world champion tennis stars. He would play singles with Jimmy Connors or Billie Jean King; they in turn would join the onstage party at Dodger Stadium or Carnegie Hall.

'Philadelphia Freedom' was never designed to be a show-stopper. But tonight, its mild, tracksuit-jogging tempo is exactly what is needed to break through the mutual reserve. With an explosion of relief the whole of Wembley Arena is on its feet, dancing, singing and waving acclamatory arms. On each chorus of 'Shine a light', powerful lamps are turned from the stage, revealing the full multitudinous range of age, style and figure. An elderly Elton look-alike in black satin blouson and baseball cap stands next to a hair-gelled acme of modern fashion in black coat, couture shorts, sandals and white socks. Both boogie the same as they echo the same words, arms swaying together in the upstretched forest:

> Phil-a-delphia Freedom, I lu-hu-uv you.
> Yes I do!

From here on, the ice is broken. He takes a moment to pause, sip water and let some air get beneath the porkpie hat that is the object of so much apologetic fascination. After all the inundations of pink, green and silver or crimson dye, the puncturing, gouging, seeding and stitching, what can it possibly be like now under there? One thinks of some Vietnamese paddy field laid scorching waste by years of American helicopter gunships, flame-throwers and Agent Orange.

He is talking more intimately, in the accentless voice that, for all its sophistication, still runs words together in nervous, hurried little groups. 'I expect you've heard I don't play the piano any more . . . I've got a three-hundred-thousand-pound organ . . . Actually, this is a digital piano . . . I always thought my organ was worth at least a million.' This highly condensed joke refers to the million pounds which *The Sun* was obliged to pay him in out-of-court damages after publishing a photograph of him nude on its front page.

'Here's a song from the last album, which didn't do so well over here . . . but we liked a few things on it, anyway.' There is probably no other rock star alive who would admit before such a company that his last album 'didn't do so well'. Marvelling at the unpretentiousness, one almost overlooks the use of the royal 'we'. Doubtless, he just meant the other guys in the studio.

It becomes clear he is a great performer in spite of, not because of, the Seventies. The best moment tonight is a simple nugget, revealed only after all the hippy and post-hippy fool's gold has been panned away. It starts as another dreary celestial sequence, filled with more mock-heavenly synthesisers and the head-tossing tedium of Davey Johnstone's vacuum-cleaner pipe. Suddenly, from under the flare-trousered clichés, there escapes a long piano solo, jumping with echoes of blues and barrelhouse, strung together with the technique of the long-ago Royal Academy student, but above all evoking scuffed brown linoleum, pink Formica tables, wet glass rings and tin ashtrays loaded with cigarette-ends. The face and darting fat hands up on the video screen look exactly as they must have done twenty-six years ago, at the Northwood Hills Hotel, Middlesex. For all his megastardom, he remains essentially what he was back then: a terrific Saturday-night pub pianist. The only difference is that now his saloon bar encircles the world.

He stops again for the MC-ish ritual of introducing the members of his band, soliciting for each an individual round of applause. These demonstrations of love and solidarity, as important in rock as in the theatre, have special significance at present. Still in the guise of genial host, he crosses to the three black girl singers on the left. He kisses the slender one in the microskirt, and the middle-sized one in the

Chanel cocktail sheath. He pretends to quail as the large, ebullient one seizes his face and plants an outsize lipstick cupid's-bow on his cheek. He bends and receives from the audience a red baseball cap and a scroll of flowers in coloured paper, which he slips to someone offstage, the way one has seen royalty politely dispose of gifts. 'Thank you for the hat,' he does not forget to say as he climbs back over the Art Deco wings. No one, as usual, bothers to introduce the video cameraman.

The imponderable pains of his life are replaced by the mild, almost pleasant aches of his later slow ballads. 'Nikita', 'A Word in Spanish', 'I Guess That's Why They Call It The Blues', 'Sorry Seems To Be The Hardest Word'. Postcards from Bernie Taupin, to unknown girlfriends or wives, that one could decipher as Elton, if one knew no better. Sensible footnotes to an ongoing relationship. Messages for the card accompanying the flowers. Nothing here about trying to commit suicide with gas ovens or pills. Or being so flattened by despair at the epicentre of your millions, you can only lie in bed all day, watching TV and sucking ice lollies.

Most agreeably sad of all is 'Sad Songs', a jaunty end-of-tether lament that has become his biggest singalong favourite. As a prelude tonight, each of the backing trio sings the title words in her own tear-'em-up gospel recitative. Thence to a white voice, just as steeped in tent-show revivalist fervour, for all its early nurturing among C-of-E Harvest Festivals, summer fêtes and vicars' Bright Hours. 'Sad songs . . . mm-hmm . . . Won't you gimme those sad songs, yeah . . .' On the video screen, the pudgy hands stretch to even tricksier chord-shapes of make-believe agony. The gap-toothed smile is broader than we have yet seen.

'Sad Songs' brings all Wembley Arena to its feet again, swaying and clapping in unison; his voice augmented by 12,000 others, all word-perfect, Elton-accented and in tune. Towards the end, the elderly Elton lookalike turns to the acme of Eighties fashion beside him, and offers a cigarette. A struck match passes; a smile is given and returned. It is a moment of communion across galaxies, hardly bettered by Stephen Spielberg's *ET*.

For most people now, music measures life. Not national events but pop songs make milestones of their progress from youth to age, their joys and sorrows, triumphs and disasters. Even those with no special keenness of memory can hear a record and create a world around it as instantly as Proust with his madeleine. Here's 'Border Song': 1970, free festivals, maxicoats, fruit-gum sweaters, the Tories unbelievably back in power. Here's 'Daniel': 1972, the Vietnam War, hijacking, split skirts, Dustin Hoffman in *Straw Dogs*. Here's 'Island Girl': 1976,

Hyde Park parched like an African game reserve. Here's 'Little Jeannie': 1980, High Tech, Afghanistan, Lennon's death. Here's 'Blue Eyes', 1982; 'Nikita', 1986. Here are incalculable numbers of first kisses and divorces, of babies born and parents dead, of meetings and partings, adventures and boredoms, treats and penances, liberations and imprisonments, remembered in the earnestly listening dark.

During this quiet passage, an extra spectator appears in a side balcony near the stage, sitting on the steps halfway down. Those who notice him see a slightly built man of about forty in a conventional dark suit, a gingham shirt and tie fixed in a fastidious Windsor knot. His pointed face, turned intently sideways, has the smooth impassivity of a china doll's. His name is John Reid; he has been Elton's friend and manager for eighteen years. With a personal fortune estimated at twelve million pounds, he ranks as Britain's 176th-richest person. That doll-like face, with its staring dark eyes, was most recently seen in the British press making towards a photographer who had tried to snatch a picture of Elton. The photographer withdrew, not wishing to join the considerable number of people whom Reid, over those eighteen years, has publicly clouted.

Only once in the whole show does Elton himself make any direct reference to recent events. 'I want to thank you all for your support over the past two years. It means a hell of a lot.' He flips off his porkpie hat, affording a brief glimpse of the platinum-white fuzz beneath. As if it were an extra star soloist onstage, the hair-transplant is given a rousing cheer.

He returns to his primary talent, playing a long nocturne-ish sequence that finally turns to the quickening heartbeat chords of 'I'm Still Standing'. Once or twice, in their enormous joint oeuvre, Bernie Taupin produced a lyric that exactly chimed with Elton's mood and emotions at a given moment. Nowhere was the symbiosis ever more perfect than in this triumphant hymn to his own longevity. 'I'm Still Standing' is his answer, not only to *The Sun* but to every other cut and buffet of the last twenty-five years, both from without and within; every ecstatic and miserable love affair; every pound gained and hairline lost; every cruel headline, snide reviewer, peeping Tom photographer and crazy high or low in the charts. They're all past and forgotten, but he's still here, 'Looking like a true survivor . . . feeling like a little kid . . . ' Not since Bernie ironically dubbed him 'Captain Fantastic' have words so well summed up the contradictions of that shy, irrepressible English face. 'I'm still standing!' he ululates. 'Yeah, yeah, yeah,' his 12,000 close friends agree.

The stage empties, amid confident cheers and whistles for more. It is the dummy ending: another time-honoured rock concert tradition. With Elton there is always the additional chance of a surprise encore guest from among his huge circle of music business friends. It could be some Sixties hero-giant, Eric Clapton or Pete Townshend. It could be some old Seventies rival, Rod Stewart or Freddy Mercury. It could be anyone across the whole spectrum of contemporary pop, from teenybop idols like Debbie Gibson to heavy-metal kids like Jon Bon Jovi.

Tonight, however, he comes back alone, wearing a top hat now, and a gold tail-suit which shows pale primrose yellow up on the video screen. He has exchanged the wrap-around Rommel shades for ordinary glasses with grey frames. His friends can look him straight in the eye again.

The band and its bristling hardware fade into obscurity. Silence falls as his lone Pickwick figure plays the rippling elegiac chords that form one of the best-known introductions in all pop music. It is 'Candle in the Wind', Bernie Taupin's requiem for Marilyn Monroe, written for the *Goodbye Yellow Brick Road* album, sixteen years ago. The ultimate Elton John 'standard', it focuses all the qualities associated with him: sensitivity, sympathy, infinite nostalgia and an ability, unique in his milieu, to treat women with chivalry and respect. He sings of Marilyn not as the masturbation aid she usually represents, but from the viewpoint of a pure and high-minded 'young man in the twenty-second row . . . who thinks of you as something more than sexual . . . ' The tribute to an even greater media victim than himself seems especially kind and ennobling tonight. From his valedictory 'Good- bye, Norma Jean . . . ' the audience sings along with each verse in a soft, word-perfect echo. Following time-honoured tradition, matches and cigarette lighters are struck and held up, flickering like an army of fireflies in the cavernous dark.

As the applause erupts, he jumps down from his keyboard, pulls his band and girl singers into a line and leads them in a deep flourishing bow. But everyone knows it can't be over yet. He still has to give them 'Saturday Night's Alright For Fighting', that brawling ton-up rocker which, by inexplicable means, has turned into a family chorus as harmless as 'Old Macdonald's Farm'.

He walks to and fro in his top hat and gold suit, bowing as delightedly and confusedly as if it were the first ovation he'd ever received. From the forests of waving arms, a hand comes up to grab his, and hold it tight for a long moment. He bows again, lets some air under his top hat, then climbs back through the Art Deco wings to his keyboard.

*

Two nights later, after the dummy ending, his friend George Michael, the ex-Wham! star, is waiting backstage to join him in his encore. But something about the performance or the audience response has upset Elton. He walks offstage furious and, without a word to George Michael, goes straight out to his limousine and is driven away.

I
MR FRANTIC

1

The Buttoned-up Boy

'LIVERPOOL!' Dick James the music publisher exclaimed quizzically on a famous occasion. 'So what's from Liverpool?' His power of prophecy would have been still more profoundly paralysed by Pinner.

In 1930s Britain, the future advanced with audible tread. From grubby, cramped Victorian London, the brand-new suburbs ribboned out along brand-new carriageways, lined with brand-new factories making aeroplanes, motor cars, electric stoves and vacuum cleaners, punctuated by new shopping 'parades', recreation grounds, hotels, pubs and quasi-Elizabethan roadhouses. At regular intervals along the blowy way to a brave new world stood the monumental redbrick tower and circular portals of an Underground station.

It was the world named 'Metroland' after its vital artery and chief cultural influence, the Metropolitan Line. These were days when public transport was a public pride, and each Underground line gave a distinct character and voice to the area it served. Especially the Metropolitan Line, whose posters and brochures exhorted migration to the new Middlesex dormitory suburbs in an accent of deep-piled cosiness. If the London office-worker would choose Metroland, what best of all worlds would be his! In the morning, abundant trains could whisk him in no time up to his City desk. At night, equally abundant trains would carry him home to his Olde English Nirvana of leafy woods and quiet avenues, box hedges and box Brownies. Pipe, tobacco and plaid slippers before the Magicoal fire. Hot Horlicks or Bournevita, then up the wooden hill to Bedfordshire. English order and normality at its best!

Pinner lies on the Metropolitan Line's north-westerly branch, where the station-names are like a row of leather-bound volumes in an Art Deco book-case. Before Pinner come Jane Austeny Northwick Park and Surtees-flavoured Harrow-on-the-Hill; after it come Wild West-sounding Northwood Hills, Enid Blytonish Chorleywood, the Walter Scott-like heraldic grandeur of Chalfont and Latimer. Three subsequent branch-lines extend into authentic countryside, penetrating Buckinghamshire as far as Chesham and Amersham, and Hertfordshire as far as Watford.

Though the future never did arrive, and the Metropolitan Line is sunken into squalor like all the rest, Metroland lives on a little in Pinner. There is still the broad shopping parade where fortunate Metro-landers foregathered on Saturday mornings for Camp coffee and Fuller's cakes, ordered their *Daily Sketch*, *Woman's Weekly* and *Everybody's*, purchased their Bird's Custard, Symington's soups and Bile Beans and entrusted their dry-cleaning to the winged pageboy of Achille Serre. Order and decorum endure in the police station's neo-Gothic flourishes. Beyond lie wide verges and topiary-trim hedges, bordering the mock-Tudor gables and Art Deco apartment 'courts' of prewar Elysium.

Pinner Hill Road, where Elton was born and spent his earliest years, is an ascending way, as long as the avenue where two hooded and gaitered toddlers walked in the old Tube-wall poster for Start-Rite Shoes. On the left stands a tall, dark clock tower, remnant of some local squire's 'folly' back in the pre-commuter dark age. Isolated among the gabled roofs and neat gardens, it seems to feel Pinner's crushing disapproval of anything ostentatious or flamboyant.

A hundred years ago there was no fast train between Chesham and Pinner, nor any but the most limited concept of social mobility. The place you were born was the place where you died. Your station – especially if it was low – bound you eternally to a horizon of a mile or two.

The Dwight family first surfaces up there in Buckinghamshire, in the vast permanence of the late nineteenth century. William Dwight, Elton's great-grandfather was – by a coincidence the future platform-heeled wonder would appreciate – a shoemaker, of Waterside, Chesham. His wife Jane, *née* Palmer, like many a dutiful Victorian wife, was unable to write her own name. An X marks her signature on her marriage lines and the birth certificate of her son, Edwin.

The quickened industrial pace of the early twentieth century was what finally set the Buckinghamshire Dwights in motion, though still not towards leafy Metroland. Elton's grandfather Edwin Dwight, a cable factory worker, moved forty-odd miles due south to join the cable firm of Callendar's in Belvedere, Kent. Callendar's was an old-fashioned patriarchal employer, solicitous for the recreation as well as sweated labour of its workforce. The firm had a name for music, boasting a brass band that won many a silver cup and rosette in interfactory competitions. It also offered good facilities for sport, especially football, a passion with all Dwights, past and to come.

Edwin and Ellen Dwight – he, small and inoffensive; she, large and voluble – had six children, five sons and a daughter. Their youngest son, born in 1925, was Elton's father, Stanley.

The household at 6 Stapley Road was further increased by family tragedy. Edwin and Ellen's son Ted lost his young wife after the birth of their daughter, Susan; then Ted himself fell mortally ill with tuberculosis. He and his two small sons, Roy and Dave, came to live at Edwin's tiny house, where the only place to nurse an invalid was a couch in the walk-in living room. When Ted died, aged only thirty-four, his sons stayed on with their grandparents.

For Roy and Dave, growing up with old people, themselves not in the best of health, could occasionally be dull and stifling. The consolation was their uncle Stan, still living at home and young enough to seem more like an elder brother and ally than a censorious adult.

He was, indeed, rather a glamorous figure to the boys, though – like his father – quiet and reserved. His great friend Bob Miller, who lived two doors away, was mad about American dance music and had formed an amateur swing band which played for dances and club socials in the district. With Bob Miller's encouragement, Stan had taken up the trumpet. Roy Dwight remembers often hearing him 'have a blow' in his room, the notes mingling with the sound of a circular saw in the adjoining woodyard.

Stan was as keen on football as all the family, and shared their intrigued realisation that young Roy seemed a better than ordinary player. Money being too short to buy him proper equipment, he would turn out with books pushed down his socks as shin-pads. His grandfather Edwin – who repaired all the family's shoes – fitted some leather strips under his boots to make up for the absent metal studs.

In those days, Stanley Dwight seemed an archetypal young man of his class. After leaving Northumberland Heath Secondary School, he became a milkman, making rounds with an old-fashioned horse-drawn cart. He joined his friend Bob Miller's grey-jacketed Miller-men, playing trumpet in Benny Goodmanish versions of 'Me and My Shadow' at dances organised by Plumstead Social Club. On special occasions, they would fill in for big names like the Oscar Rabin Orchestra at grand London venues like the Lyceum Ballroom, off the Strand.

Still only fifteen at the outbreak of World War II, Stanley did not become eligible for military service until – as was then perceived – 'the tide had turned'. He joined the Royal Air Force, seemingly bound for the life of an ordinary conscripted aircraftsman. Instead, his astonished family learned he had been given a commission.

Even in the vast social shake-up of war, this was far from usual. Air Force officers were a dandy élite in whom Battle of Britain and Dam Buster heroism combined with almost film star glamour. And no film star or combat hero of the Forties was lower class. The young men who sat outside Nissen huts in deck chairs, waiting for the 'scramble', represented the high-born cream of Oxford, Cambridge and the Inns of Court. In Bomber and Fighter Command, as in Victorian cavalry regiments, a private income was highly desirable.

It was the end of Stan Dwight, the milkman who had made his round with rattling crates in the long streets abutting Woolwich. Now he belonged to the world of silk scarves and handlebar moustaches, of 'stoogeing' and 'kites', open-top sports cars, black labradors and batmen. He was accustomed to command and be instantly obeyed, to insist on efficiency and conformity, and mingle with confidence at functions in the officers' mess. Even his nephew Roy, who remained hugely fond of him, noticed the pronounced personality change. 'Somehow from then on, Stan always seemed to talk a bit louder than he needed to.'

Towards the war's end, he met a dark-haired, petite girl named Sheila Eileen Harris, then working as a clerk at RAF Coastal Command's complex in Northwood, Middlesex. Twenty-year-old Stanley and nineteen-year-old Sheila were married at Pinner Parish Church in January, 1945.

Sheila came of south London stock. Her father, Fred Harris, served with the Welsh Guards in World War I, afterwards becoming groundsman at Hatch End Tennis Club, Middlesex. For the sake of the job, Fred's guardsmanlike figure cycled forty miles each day, from home in Peckham to Hatch End and back again. Eventually, with his wife Ivy and three children, he migrated to Middlesex, living first at Kenton, then Hatch End and finally Pinner Green.

The Harris family home was 55 Pinner Hill Road, a semi-detached council house in the row just south of that Victorian clock tower which looks over Metroland. In the style of late-Thirties municipal housing, number 55 was solid, even spacious, with a back garden that Fred lovingly tended, along with two vegetable allotments. Beyond the hedge lay the green turf and metal scoreboard of Pinner Cricket Club.

For their first few years of married life, Stanley and Sheila lived with Fred and Ivy Harris at 55 Pinner Hill Road. Finding a place of their own was a problem for any young couple in the immediate postwar years. Besides, Stanley's service duties frequently took him away from home. Sheila needed the company of her parents, her younger sister, Win, and her brother, Reg.

Stanley Dwight's RAF commission was not merely a temporary elevation. At the war's end, he stayed on in the Volunteer Reserve, a sign of indispensability, confirmed by rapid promotion. By the time his son was born in 1947, he had become a flight lieutenant. The glamour and egalitarianism of the war receded into the past. Stanley remained firmly rooted in a class above his parents, his wife and his new in-laws.

He began to receive postings abroad, on which he would go alone. Sheila was not cut out to be a service wife, attending bridge parties and taking sherry with the CO.

They had only one child, Reginald Kenneth Dwight, the future Elton Hercules John, born at his grandparents' council house, 55 Pinner Hill Road, on March 25, 1947.

The deep, sometimes not quite explicable, bitterness which Elton would afterwards cherish against his father can be traced right back to what he believed a slight on his very birth. The story – still capable of making the millionaire superstar boil over in resentment thirty years later – was that, when Sheila went into labour, Stanley was absent overseas on RAF service. 'I was two years old when he came home. Mother said "Do you want to see him?" He said "No, I'll wait till morning." He'd been in Aden or somewhere, and he came home after two years, after not seeing me born or anything.' This is unfair to Stanley, whom the birth certificate proves to have registered his son's arrival only a day afterwards.

It was well-known in the family that Sheila had really been hoping for a girl. Baby Reggie very nearly granted her wish. Early photographs show an infant of radiant beauty, with massed golden curls that Shirley Temple might have envied. Sheila was a devoted and also fastidious mother. The baby possessed innumerable changes of outfit.

The world he first saw about him was anything but a colourful one. Though the war had been over for two years, Britain remained in the grip of food-shortages and rationing, a chill, grey place under officially prescribed 'austerity' where any self-indulgence or surfeit was accounted downright sinful. In ordinary households, the only respite was 'the wireless', from which the BBC Light Programme poured out an unrestricted supply of morale-boosting variety shows, like *Stand Easy* and *Workers' Playtime*, and the turbaned housewife's mid-morning portion of *Music While You Work*.

Music was the taste Stanley and Sheila Dwight had most in

common – he from his pre-RAF stint with Bob Miller's Millermen, she as the natural outflow of her warm, expansive nature. Among the future superstar's earliest memories was to be his parents' collection of big, breakable 78 rpm records, and the American stars of that pre-pop era: Guy Mitchell, breathy and good-humoured, on 'Red Feathers' or 'Truly Fair', Kay Starr, lovelorn and lingering on 'Wheel of Fortune', Les Paul and Mary Ford, a girl whispering in harmony with what few people then could identify as an electric guitar. Almost before Reggie learned to read, he could recognise all the different record labels. He also possessed the aesthetic sense that many children have at a young age, but can find no words to express. He still remembers vaguely resenting the dull, muddy liveries most of the labels wore and his pleasure in the one great exception, MGM's bright yellow and black.

Reggie's first years were spent in an atmosphere almost exclusively feminine. His father, the young flight-lieutenant, was constantly away from home. His grandfather, Fred Harris, died when he was five. Ivy, his beloved Nan, subsequently married a man named Horace, who had lost a leg in World War I. A silent man – but for his artificial leg, which squeaked when he walked – Horace did not interfere with the adoring axis of mother and grandmother who brought up Reggie. A neighbour in Pinner Hill Road, Jacky Reppington, remembers him as an overprotected toddler, not allowed to run riot with other children on the field behind the council houses. He would usually be in the garden by himself, playing with his many toys, carefully and decorously.

Like many ordinary households in that pre-television era, 55 Pinner Hill Road had a piano. To keep Reggie quiet while she did the housework, Sheila would encourage him to bang on the keys. One day – the family legend goes – he astonished her by suddenly starting to pick out the melody of 'The Skaters' Waltz'.

The marginal family talent that had drawn his grandfather to factory brass bands, and his father to Benny Goodman nights at Plumstead Social Club, was finally manifested in a perfect musical ear. Even as a toddler, Reggie Dwight could hear a piece of music once, then instantly sit at a piano and play it.

His early schooling reflected the disparate social elements in his background. At the age of four he started at the local state primary school, Pinner Wood Junior and Mixed Infants. After only a year he was taken away and sent to Reddiford School, a small private academy of about a hundred pupils run, in their back garden, by an elderly man named Mr White and his spinster sister. By the age of six, he was also having piano lessons from a Pinner woman named

Jones, whose husband was an accomplished classical musician. A Reddiford classmate, David Lewis, remembers walking home with Reggie one day and asking him what he wanted to be when he grew up. 'A concert pianist' was the firm reply.

The life of a small boy who plays the piano is, to a large degree, pre-ordained. At school he is a celebrity, older than his years as he arrives with his adult briefcase full of music, grave in his demeanour as he settles down to perform. His skill is frequently co-opted by authority, to show the school off at concerts and open days, perhaps even play the hymn for morning assembly when the music teacher is indisposed. Preoccupied with his staves and rests, he has little time or opportunity to be other than utterly conformist and conventional. The small boy who plays the piano tends to be a very good boy indeed.

To his family he is a live-in entertainer, called upon whenever grown-up conversation falters. The first of many times this happened to Reggie was when he was seven, at the wedding of his grown-up cousin Roy Dwight. 'Stan was my best man,' Roy remembers, 'and Reggie was a page boy. After the wedding breakfast we'd got a band booked, but they were a bit late in turning up. So Reggie was put on the piano in his little white tail suit and bow tie. He kept things going until the real band arrived.'

An early snapshot – destined to be many times reproduced – sums up everything that could possibly be said about his early childhood. A plump small boy with a round pug face sits at an upright piano, hands poised on white notes, looking over his left shoulder. Even at seven or eight his chubby-cheeked smile has the resigned quality of the pro who must perform whether he feels like it or not. There is an implicit air of celebrity but, even more, of virtue. Hair neatly slicked down and parted where other boys' would be tousled. Plump knees peeping from traditional flannel shorts where other boys would demand blue jeans. Neat white shirts and starched handkerchieves. Socks correctly pulled up and polished shoes. Framed certificates and silver cups. His name in the local paper every now and then. A very, very good boy.

But not a particularly happy one. By the time Reggie began grammar school, it had become clear that Stanley and Sheila Dwight's marriage was in trouble. Easy and fun-loving enough when Sheila first met him, Stanley had grown stiffer and more formal as his Air Force career progressed. In its own way, his was a personality change as total as his son would undergo, fifteen years afterwards. Alas, in Stanley's case there remained the all-too-visible former milieu of working-class family, council houses and lively, down-to-earth young wife who wished no part of the rules and traditions that now governed him. Arriving home on leave each time must have seemed to Stanley like coming down in the world. To Sheila – and to Reggie – these became occasions to dread.

They now had their own house, number 111 Potter Street, Northwood Hills. So uncomfortable were the associations of that modest detached villa that later, when Reggie's past life became of interest to journalists, he would always omit it from the chronology.

The larger family, however, was happy on both sides. Reggie tended to see less of his Dwight relations, far away in Kent. But the Harris side all lived around Pinner: his Nan in Pinner Hill Road, his namesake Uncle Reg and two cousins, John and Cath. The circle increased when Sheila's younger sister, Win Robinson, returned from overseas, bringing her baby son, Paul. They were the kind of family that always got together at Christmas and even took their summer holiday together. One such perfect Fifties box Brownie scene was a camping expedition to Ilfracombe, Uncle Reg in charge, Sheila and Win hooting with laughter together, baby Paul bedded down each night on the back seat of the car.

The abiding influence on Reggie was Sheila, his champion, protector and constant encourager. One needs no better picture of the relationship than those early Fifties mornings, with Reggie at the piano and Sheila doing the housework. Brasso, fire tongs and Min Cream. Milk for Camp coffee heating on the stove and *Music While You Work* on an old-fashioned dial-lit radio. His every new finger-step into melody given a rousing cheer amid her scrubbing and polishing.

His father, by contrast, had become a remote figure whose infrequent spells at home broke up the cosy mother-and-son routine, and made everything turn tense, anxious and tight-lipped. Stanley and Sheila had resolved to stay together, as unhappy marrieds used to 'for the child's sake'. One has to have lived in such a household to know what a chill wind always blows.

Though still only in his early thirties, Stanley had reached the rank of squadron leader, equivalent to a major in the army or lieutenant commander in the navy. With him he brought a CO's manner that found much fault even with so good a boy. At meals Reggie would be reproved for not sitting up straight, putting elbows on the table, talking with his mouth full, even biting into celery with too loud a crunch. In the garden, he was not allowed to kick his ball around in case it damaged the rose bushes.

He was consequently a boy of almost painful self-restraint – careful, neat, methodical and anxiously polite. His nature was considerate and thoughtful, punctilious about writing Christmas and birthday thank-you letters and buying gifts for his mother and family. His only fault was a tendency to temper tantrums, usually arising from the stress and fatigue of piano practice. These would blow up in a moment, and usually disappear as quickly as they had come.

In one department at least, he wholeheartedly took after his father. He was as keen on football as all the Dwights, and – like Stanley – became a devoted follower of Pinner's local club, Watford. What few harmonious moments father and son shared mostly took place on the terraces at Watford's Vicarage Road ground.

The family's interest was further sharpened by what had happened to Roy, the orphan nephew whom Stanley had befriended in prewar days down in Kent. At the age of fourteen, while playing in a kick-around on Dartford Heath, Roy had been spotted by a talent scout for Fulham, the celebrated Second Division club. After a probationary period on Fulham's ground staff, he had turned professional (signing on the same day as future England manager Bobby Robson). In his debut season, he had been picked to replace Bedford Jezzard in the star centre-forward spot. He had scored in each of his first eight games, culminating with a four-goal tally against Sheffield United.

In mid-Fifties Britain, professional footballers were national pin-ups – none more so than Roy's Fulham colleague Johnny Haynes, who combed back his hair with a smug smile in advertisements for Brylcreem. Reggie's greatest excitement as a small boy was to be taken to see Haynes and Co. play in their brilliantine and baggy shorts at Fulham's Craven Cottage ground. Sometimes as a special treat Roy would arrange for him to watch the match sitting on the touchline.

Break-time games in Reddiford School's garden had shown that Reggie himself, though keen and energetic, possessed no comparable spark. He was more useful at tennis, for which many openings existed in leafy Metroland. But, most of all, he was a boy who practised long hours alone, whose briefcase bulged with grown-up names like Chopin and Brahms, and whose puggy, patient face was turned towards the next, more arduous grade examination set by the Royal Academy of Music in London.

Radio – and now television – presented his chosen instrument in very different guise. It was the great age of star piano entertainers: Semprini with his Viennese charm, Joe 'Mr Piano' Henderson with his oleaginous charm, Russ Conway with his dour charm. Most of all, beamed from America, Liberace with the oozing charm no one yet recognised as high camp; his lace ruffs, duck-egg-sized diamond rings, piano-top candelabra and violin-playing 'brother George'.

The performer of later life would owe a manifest stylistic debt to Liberace. But more influential still was Winifred Atwell, an amiable black entertainer who, in the middle and late Fifties, enjoyed a string of massive piano hits like 'Coronation Rag' and 'The Poor People of Paris'. All Reggie liked that was both extrovert and good-natured seemed to be in that glossy, overflowing figure – on Jack Payne's TV show, or Billy Cotton's – switching from Bechstein grand to her honky-tonkish 'other piano', smiling and roguishly winking as her jewel-studded fingers dashed to and fro.

The one instance of outrageous live performance his childhood witnessed was at a Saturday night variety show at the London Palladium, starring the 'Red Feathers' man Guy Mitchell. 'At the end of his set, he took off his sock and whirled it round his head. I thought, "What a funny guy!" And, do you know, I always remembered that.'

When rock-'n'-roll music first hit Britain in 1955, Reggie Dwight was not yet nine years old. He was far too young – and, in any case, Metroland saw little of those first surreal moments when close-cropped and tweed-jacketed English youths suddenly grew sideburns like Mississippi cardsharps, put on cylindrical coats with velvet collars, thick-soled 'brothel-creepers' and bootlace ties, and mumbled their knee-trembling worship of an unfathomable American song entitled 'Houn' Dog'. Nor, as a pianist, was he swept up by the related skiffle phenomenon, when English boys – who hitherto would sooner have disembowelled themselves than be caught singing in public – rushed to form groups with cheap guitars, tea-chest basses and kitchen washboards, and discordantly chorus hobo and work songs written by impoverished black men half a century earlier in the obscurity of America's Deep South.

Stanley Dwight, the former swing trumpeter, predictably discouraged his son from all interest in the raucous new music. For Reggie's ninth birthday, in the year of Bill Haley's 'Rock Around The Clock' and Lonnie Donegan's 'Rock Island Line', Stanley presented him with a long-playing record by the cocktail jazz pianist George Shearing. Twenty years later, the superstar would still be simmering against his father for having made so utterly wrong a choice.

It was Sheila Dwight – then only just turned thirty – who became the household's prototype rock-'n'-roll fan. The first Reggie knew of it was when his mother brought home two new 78s – 'Houn' Dog' by Elvis Presley and 'ABC Boogie' by Bill Haley and his Comets. The boy with the doggedly virtuous face and the head full of theory listened in amazement to these wildly pulsing and pounding intimations of how different a piano-player's life could be.

In September 1958, he joined the brown-blazered throng at Pinner County Grammar School. A boy named Peter Emery sat next to him in the first music lesson when the teacher, Mr Stoupe, asked each pupil in turn about his musical interests and attainments. 'A few of us said we played the piano,' Peter Emery remembers. 'One or two said they'd done Junior Royal Academy to Grade 5. When Mr Stoupe got to Reggie, he said he was Grade 8. Stoupe didn't realise what he'd said at first – he carried on for a moment, then did a huge double-take.'

Pinner County Grammar was another perfect manifestation of Metroland. Built in 1937, its streamlined frontage and square central tower epitomised Art Deco futurism and environmental progress for all. Save that boys and girls occupied segregated quarters, its air was more that of an American high school. No more cinder playgrounds, pothooks and squeaky slates but a veritable campus amid the trees and bulbous Morris Minor cars of Beaulieu Drive.

Behind the Norman Rockwell façade lay an ethos more like that of some exclusive fee-paying school: a heraldic badge of a stag rampant with the motto 'Honour Before Honours'; a house and prefectorial system; a sixth-form club, The Stag, owing something to the Pop fraternity at Eton; even pointless but rigid 'traditions', like that forbidding all but sixth formers to cross the frontage from girls' side to boys'. The headmaster, Jack Westgate Smith, was a teacher of the best old-fashioned sort, a stern but just disciplinarian with the gift of maintaining order through affection rather than fear. Pinner County Grammar could boast a record of scholastic and sporting achievement second to none among Middlesex state schools. It was also a tolerant place, free from bullying and with no hidebound view that all children ought to be the same. Under Jack Westgate Smith, the singular or eccentric pupil received equal interest and encouragement.

Music was one of the school's greater strengths. Mr Westgate Smith was himself a classical pianist, a frequent performer as soloist or in duet with the music teacher, W. G. Stoupe. The history master, Bill ('Scruff') Johnson was a blues enthusiast, a friend of the music historian Paul Oliver. The school's concerts and recitals were famous throughout the district. Among its proudest possessions was the Steinway grand piano in its assembly hall.

R. K. Dwight of Downfield House initially seemed set fair to add further lustre to Pinner County's musical prestige. At the age of eleven, he had been interviewed at the Royal Academy of Music in London for possible enrolment on its Junior Exhibitioners – i.e. part-time scholarship – scheme. Not only did he win the scholarship but the course director, Margaret Donington, recommended him to Sub-professor Helen Piena as a piano student of special interest.

Helen Piena taught him at the Royal Academy of Music for the next four years. The classes were every Saturday morning at the Academy's Gothic building in Marylebone Road: schoolroom tuition in theory and composition, choir practice and a forty-five-minute individual lesson.

The first thing Helen Piena noticed – and set out firmly to thwart – was his astounding natural ear. 'I remember once playing him a prelude by Handel, four pages long. As soon as I'd finished, he played it straight back to me just like a gramophone.'

That annoying facility aside, she remembers him as a model pupil, hard-working, punctilious and polite. 'I always called him by his full name, Reginald. But he was very affectionate, too. He'd send me letters with kisses on the bottom. Once he sent me an embroidered skullcap from Switzerland, where he'd gone on holiday with his school.'

At Pinner County Grammar, he was making no such mark. Fifteen years later, when his flashing reincarnation bestrode the world, the same astonished question would be asked by almost everyone who had known him at school. 'That can't be Reg Dwight, can it?'

Then he was a boy of such averageness and conventionality as to be almost invisible. Though imaginative and quick-witted, with an excellent memory, he did not shine in class. Even with his best subjects, like English and languages, he followed a line of least resistance, doing only just enough to satisfy his teachers and get by in examinations. 'Satisfactory', 'Of average achievement', 'Not particularly distinguished' were common judgements in his end-of-term reports.

His fondness for sport was hampered by the school's pretensions. At Pinner County Grammar they did not play football, but the more upper-class game of rugby. Where Reggie longed to dribble the ball like his famous cousin Roy, his small stature and bullet head made him a natural for hooker in the thick of the set scrum. There, at least, his dogged determination earned some notice. 'He'd come out, looking like a chewed-up monster,' Peter Emery says. 'But he'd always go back in again for more.'

Even his musical talent and status as a Royal Academy exhibitioner did not win him unstinted praise. Mr Stoupe the music teacher – a New Zealander afflicted with an unfortunately appropriate stoop

– seemed almost resentful of this extracurricular distinction. When Reggie produced composition homework better than anyone else's, and instantly hummable, he would risk censure for having done it too easily; the schoolmaster's crime of being 'casual'.

Musically, too, he preferred to be just one of the crowd. In a typical school concert, R. Dwight's rendering of 'Les Petites Litanies de Dieu' by Groylez was buried in a full programme that also included Patricia Corry's violin performance of Bach's 'Gavotte in D'; M. Wheeler's cello rendering of Mozart's 'Ave Verum'; T. White's trumpet solo, Allegro from Haydn's 'Concerto in E flat'; and Messrs Stoupe and Westgate Smith's piano duet in Arthur Benjamin's 'Jamaican Rumba' and the Polka from Weinberger's 'Schwanda the Bagpiper'.

In appearance he was equally unexceptional, a neat, orderly boy whose school uniform bore no trace of the Teddy-boy flourishes that even Metroland youth was starting to sport. Such was the edict of his father, Squadron Leader Dwight, backed up by the normally indulgent Sheila. Both were determined Reggie should not become a Teddy boy, and insisted that even his non-school clothes be of utterly conventional style and cut. On Reggie Dwight, one never saw drainpipe trousers, Slim Jim ties, suede or yellow knitted waistcoats, or socks other than kitbag regulation grey. The summit of his modest Beau Brummel ambitions was to possess a pair of the newly fashionable suede shoes called Hush Puppies. It was a moment that would have repercussions all through the next decade but one when Stanley told him even Hush Puppies were 'Teddyish'.

A school group photograph, taken when he was about thirteen, shows a boy no longer just chubby or plump, but unequivocally fat, his hair mousy dark, his round pug face resignedly studious in half-frame glasses. He wore glasses not because he needed them but in homage to Buddy Holly, rock music's first four-eyes, who died in a plane crash in 1959. Alas, in Reggie's case the resemblance would often seem closer to Billy Bunter, the Owl of the Remove in Frank Richards's stories of Greyfriars school. But he persisted in imagining himself Buddy, not Billy, and in the process managed to make himself genuinely myopic.

By now, like virtually every other blazered and cricket-capped British schoolboy, he was possessed and besotted by rock 'n' roll. One has to have been there to fully appreciate its brilliant presence amid the boredoms of adolescence in late-Fifties Britain. On the one hand, Mr Macmillan and Mr Gaitskell; on the other, Elvis Presley's 'King Creole'. On the one hand Purchase Tax and the Motor Show; on the other, Danny and the Juniors' 'At the Hop'. On the one hand,

Prince Philip inaugurating International Geophysical Year; on the
other, Marvin Rainwater's 'Whole Lotta Woman'. On the one hand,
black-and-white TV, red phone boxes, brown GPO vans and beige
Austin saloon cars. On the other, Johnny Otis and his Three Tons of
Joy. Disapproving adults used to condemn rock 'n' roll as sexually
suggestive, but actually it was utterly childish; the ultimate form of
play, with its silly names, silly voices, silly words like 'bop-shoowop'
and 'rama-lama-ding-dong'. Reggie Dwight, in Pinner, was one of
the generation it would spare from ever having to grow up.

The taste in Britain now was for softer pop, like the hiccupping
Buddy Holly parodies of Adam Faith. But Reggie remained true to
the prototypes his mother had first brought home. Reggie – not
entirely fashionably – was a true rock-'n'-roll fan.

His idols were the two wildest, freakiest stars of the genre, both
brilliant piano players as well as inimitable vocalists. He had all
Little Richard's records: 'Tutti Frutti', 'Long Tall Sally', 'Lucille' and
'Good Golly Miss Molly' – stentorian shrieks of joyous gibberish
accompanied by manic pounding on innocent keys. As well as the
madness, he loved the theatricality of the tiny dervish figure with its
lounge-lizard moustache and wobbling drape suit. He managed to
see it 'live' just once, in a package show at Harrow's Granada
cinema. As Little Richard jumped over his piano, the virtuous fat boy
had a spellbinding thought: 'I wish that was me.'

Even his switched-on mother drew the line at Jerry Lee Lewis,
whose 1958 British tour was cut short when it emerged that he had
married his thirteen-year-old cousin. The 'Killer' was rock-'n'-roll
outrage personified with his permed hair, his cherry-red suit, his habit
of concluding a session at the piano by dousing it in petrol and setting
it alight. Reggie was entranced by Jerry Lee Lewis, and struggled to
stretch his own small hands into the same wicked rippling runs that
tore up piano keyboards like rotten linoleum.

Other teenagers could socialise over music at youth clubs and
coffee bars. But Reggie was cut off from most friends and after-school
activities by his parallel career at the Royal Academy of Music. With
school and piano practice every day, the Academy on Saturdays and
homework on Sundays for the next Monday morning, he scarcely had
an hour to himself in the whole week.

Almost all his spare time was spent in his bedroom at 111 Potter
Street. He would be hours up there alone, tending his record
collection, already considerable. Each single, LP and EP had its own
protective brown-paper cover and was meticulously catalogued. As
much as the music, he loved records as physical things: their labels
and covers, back as well as front; the madly hip language of their

meagre liner-notes, even the addresses of the pressing plants, like EMI, Hayes, Middlesex. The shine of the velvety blackness as it turned, the playing-arm's little click as it moved across, were almost living things, keeping him company. As the future stupendous hoarder of possessions would admit, 'I grew up with inanimate objects as my friends.'

Loneliness combined with obsessiveness made him a born fan, able to derive almost complete happiness and fulfilment from following and extolling the achievements of others. As well as a rock-'n'-roll fan he was a sports fan, keen on cricket and tennis, a football fanatic like all males on the Dwight side of his family. After music, he gave greatest fervour to supporting his local team, Watford, attending as many home games as possible at the modest Vicarage Road ground, using their triumphs and disasters, their ups and downs in the Football League, as a surrogate for his own uneventful, unexpectant life.

The only small fame he seemed destined ever to enjoy was as cousin to a famous footballer. For Roy Dwight was still going from strength to strength. Having helped take Fulham to the FA Cup semi-final in 1957–8, Roy had been signed by First Division Nottingham Forest for the then hefty transfer fee of £15,500. Among the trophies of his growing fame was a wallet autographed by Hollywood's blonde bombshell, Jayne Mansfield. 'I was judging a beauty contest in Mansfield, Notts., and they somehow got Jayne Mansfield to judge it as well.'

The 1958–9 season began as a magic one for Roy Dwight. Not only did he score four hat-tricks in as many matches, but at the end came the climax of which every player dreams. Nottingham Forest made it through to the FA Cup Final, playing Luton at Wembley Stadium, watched by the Queen and the Duke of Edinburgh.

Roy, at outside-right, scored in the ninth minute, confirming his reputation as an audacious goal-snatcher. Then in the thirty-third minute, he was heavily blocked by Luton's full back, Brendan McNally, and rolled on the Wembley turf clutching his right leg. When his team trainer attempted to manipulate the leg, Roy gave a yell of agony. His tibia, the shin bone, had sustained a compound fracture.

Rushed to a local hospital, Roy showed his own measure of Dwight doggedness by refusing to be X-rayed until he had seen the remainder of the match. Still in his player's gear, he was put in a wheelchair and pushed into a ward to join a circle of astonished old men round a TV set which, only minutes before, had shown him being carried from the Wembley turf.

*

One Saturday, during Reggie's piano tutorial with Helen Piena, he told her he might have to give up his scholarship at the Royal Academy. Naturally perturbed, Helen asked him why. Reggie answered that his parents were about to get divorced.

Stanley and Sheila Dwight had, in truth, been divorced for years in everything but name and strained outward appearance. The void at the centre of Reggie's life was as familiar to him as sleeping or waking. Low-burning chronic unhappiness is, however, infinitely preferable to unhappiness dragged out under a spotlight and minutely examined. A home in any state is better than one finally and irrevocably broken.

The long-delayed breaking point was Sheila's friendship with a local painter and decorator named Fred Farebrother. In 1962 Stanley petitioned for divorce on the grounds of adultery, citing Farebrother as co-respondent.

Even as it was going on, Reggie spoke about it to almost no one. Divorce makes every child feel a criminal. Greater even than unhappiness was his dread of the untidiness about to be caused. 'He told me that he needed a new piano, but he didn't think he'd be able to have it now,' Helen Piena remembers. Subsequently she was rung up by Stanley, who told her Reggie could have his piano, and could continue with his Royal Academy scholarship. Helen reacted with the feminine protectiveness Reggie always would seem to arouse. 'I told him it wasn't up to him whether Reginald continued at the Royal Academy or not.'

Reggie's wholehearted support for Sheila did not lessen the rending effect on him. He hated the fact that, though his mother was now free, she seemed to have been made the guilty party in the matter. Relieved that the strict squadron leader would no longer be coming home, he also felt hurt and rejected by his father as never before. Eighteen months after divorcing Sheila, Stanley began seeing Edna Clough, a thirty-three-year-old laboratory technician. They married, and in rapid succession Edna bore Stanley four baby boys. 'My pride was really snipped, because he was always supposed to hate kids,' the future star would say bitterly. 'I guess I was just a mistake in the first place.'

Much healing was done by his mother's man-friend, Fred Farebrother, a figure who could easily have deepened Reggie's sense of isolation and insecurity but who, instead, became an anchor for him almost as much as for Sheila. Homely and artisan, without a breath of squadron leader in his whole body, Fred took pains to be a friend and ally to Reggie. He was, indeed, more like an elder brother, liberal with pocket money and lifts in his ex-Post-Office van, enthusiastic about music and Hush Puppies, so amiable and easy-going he did not even mind Reggie's schoolboy joke of reversing his name to Derf.

For Reggie, the divorce also meant goodbye to the unhappy house in Potter Street. He and Sheila were now living in Frome Court, one of the several colonies of maisonettes on the long, leafy road between Pinner and its adjacent suburb, Northwood Hills. Though technically an apartment block, Frome Court was more like a large, double-winged Metroland villa, with stained glass heraldry set into the windows and front doors of mock-Tudor design. Reggie and Sheila lived in number 30a, on the ground floor to the left. There Derf also became a fixture, and was generally referred to by Reggie as 'my dad', though he and Sheila would not marry for another ten years.

Moving to a new home and new neighbourhood increased Reggie's solitariness. His world was still mainly his bedroom – an even smaller one now in the tiny Frome Court maisonette. His best friends remained his records in their brown-paper covers, his books on sport and the movable counters of his Football League chart.

He was fond of his Auntie Win's son Paul, a cheerful little boy who used to bring Sheila her newspapers every Sunday. Paul would be allowed into his room to look at his League table and hear about a wonderful new group called the Beatles. 'He said they were the greatest thing there'd ever been,' Paul remembers. 'We'd sit there with an album-cover and he'd tell me which one was John, Paul, George and Ringo.'

He was galvanised by the Beatles, their energy and humour and also the extraordinary possibilities they opened up to all such bedroom-bound British youth. The songs with which they turned the charts upside-down were not cover versions of American hits, but had been written by two of them, Lennon and McCartney. It was a transfixing thought to a boy with a musical ear that had always made tunes spontaneously dance in his head. With everything else, the Beatles were themselves record fans, acknowledging a debt to backwaters of American blues and soul known only to serious aficionados like Reggie Dwight. In particular he watched the Beatle named John Lennon, whose shadow of a cynical smile first hinted to him that rock-'n'-roll performance need not be entirely in earnest.

'He took me to a Beatles concert once,' his cousin, Paul Robinson, remembers. 'We'd gone up to London to see a schoolboys' exhibition. That was boring, so Reg said, "Do you fancy seeing The Beatles?" They were doing one of their Christmas shows at Hammersmith Odeon.' Another great eye-opener was to see John, Paul, George and Ringo prancing around the stage in pantomime fancy dress, even coming on in drag. No one had thought of putting pop together with slapstick fun before.

He was unusual in liking female pop singers, a tiny faction then. His particular favourite was Dusty Springfield, who left a folk trio to find solo success in 1963. Not since Winifred Atwell had a female performer so interested Reggie. Along with a smoky gospel-edged voice went over-the-top Barbie Doll glamour: spun-up bouffant hair, bow-tied balloon-skirt dresses and enormous black-smeared eyes. Despite apparently singing straightforward love songs to straight-forward men, she also projected a curious sense of uninvolvement and aloneness. Reggie had pictures of Dusty Springfield, cut from *Reveille* magazine, pinned all round his bedroom wall.

The usual pains and tensions of puberty seemed to trouble him remarkably little. He had the advantage of attending a co-educational school, where girls were a daily fact rather than, as for so many English boys, distant figures of fantasy and speculation. Despite his podgy build and puggy, four-eyed face, he had a good rating on Pinner County Grammar girls' grapevine. He was funny and interesting; he possessed the unusual attributes of good manners and politeness, and the still more unusual one of knowing how to be friends with girls. Going on a date with Reg Dwight was totally free of the usual physical unease. He was happy to see a film or a pop show, walk his partner home, then say goodnight. Girls were relieved to know someone with whom they could spend an evening, free from the ultimate dread of a spotty lunge or a knee driven into their layered petticoats.

Julie Westaway, the daughter of his English teacher in the fifth year, was one of several such regular female 'mates'. Another was Janet Ritchie, who had known him since they both started at Pinner County. Reggie was a regular visitor at both their houses, approved of for his punctilious good manners. Even in 1963 it was becoming rare to find a boy like this, who got up when a lady entered the room, and addressed all older men as 'sir'.

Janet became a particular mate because her uncle was secretary of Chelsea Football Club and she a comparable football enthusiast. Reggie and she would go together to Chelsea matches and to pop shows at the Harrow Granada. She also was one of the few school-friends, of either sex, he ever liked and trusted enough to invite home to Frome Court. He even took her into his room to show her his precious brown-paper-covered record collection and the meticulous cataloguing system that went with it. But he'd never lend a record, even to Janet, for fear it might come back scratched.

At school, she was one of a clique who went in for Goonish humour and conversed in a private vocabulary largely invented by Reggie. A favourite trick was to drop initial letters, so that the class lookout would signal a teacher's approach by a hiss of 'She's 'oming'. Anything good was termed 'dos muchos', 'diode' or 'small'. The height of understated enthusiasm was to look momentarily shame-faced, as Reggie did so well, and apologetically murmur 'small hyperbole there'.

He also was a gifted mimic, able to bend his light, accentless voice to almost any timbre, male or female. He could recite whole segments of TV and radio comedy shows back through his childhood: *The Goon Show, Hancock's Half-hour, Round The Horne, Take It From Here*. Most of all he loved *Steptoe and Son*, Galton and Simpson's classic sitcom about a genteel rag-and-bone dealer, his evil old father and their patient horse, Hercules.

Thanks to far happier home circumstances, Reggie became noticeably more relaxed and happy during his last two years at Pinner County Grammar. In his fourth year, one of the Downfield House sixth-formers was a girl named Gay Search, later to become a successful journalist and broadcaster. 'Yes, Dwight – I can see him now with his blazer buttoned across his chest and his bum sticking out. He had a walk that I won't put an adult gloss on and call "mincing", but it was an odd little walk, special to him. I remember him as being totally different from the general rabble of younger boys. He had an air of being far more grown-up, more civilised. He wasn't a sycophant, he didn't creep, but as a fourth-former he was someone a prefect or sixth-former could talk to on equal terms.'

Pinner County Grammar now knew R. K. Dwight for something other than 'Les Petites Litanies de Dieu'. That beautiful Steinway piano in the assembly hall felt a very different pressure on its immaculate keys. To the amazement of his peers, the earnest Royal Academy student also could play like Jerry Lee Lewis, or nearly, rippling with a manic index finger to and fro, kicking away the piano stool to stand there and hammer, duck-like rear thrust out under his blazer hem. To still greater general astonishment, the buttoned-up fat boy revealed he could sing, and even sing while playing just like the crazy drape-suited figures up on the cinema screen in *High School Confidential* and *Disc Jockey Jamboree*. It was the last kind of voice anyone had expected from that shy dumpling face – keening rock-'n'-roll gibberish in a flamenco-high tenor, bursting every tight stitch of his former self-consciousness and reserve.

He would perform at end-of-term socials and at odd moments in term-time when the sacred Steinway was unsupervised. In these dull interludes of school, any entertainer is highly prized. And Reggie did not just entertain. He astonished. He excited. He drew crowds. It was an authentic marvel, how dumpy R. K. Dwight had somehow emerged from his bedroom, spinning off 'Great Balls of Fire'.

A star among his classmates, he now found himself against the grain of authority for the first time in his life. Mr Stoupe the music master had a loudly-vented hatred of all pop music, and bitterly upbraided him for so wasting his abilities. Bill Johnson the history master, and blues buff, was more sympathetic. 'I remember at one end-of-term party he wanted to rig up a microphone at the piano. I found him a bit of wood that he could nail it to.' The first in a multitude of increasingly long-suffering roadies.

As rock 'n' roll took stronger and stronger hold, his interest in his classical studies dwindled to vanishing point. In his Royal Academy class with Helen Piena, the once model pupil grew casual and slapdash. Some Saturday mornings he would leave home with his briefcase, but never arrive at the Academy. As the star would admit in later life, 'I'd come up to Baker Street, get on the Circle Line and stay there for three hours, then go home again.'

In his fourth year, a school group including Janet Westaway, Peter Emery and Reggie went on a trip to Annecy in France. During the week of educational visits, their itinerary somehow became combined with that of some girls from a French lycée. 'These lycée girls literally used to clamour to be on the same coach as Reg,' Peter Emery remembers. 'I can see him now, sitting at the back, with French schoolgirls all round him, beating out rhythm on the seat-back and singing Elvis Presley songs.'

George Hill was among the most go-ahead landlords in the chain of pubs operated by Benskins brewery. He and his wife, Ann, had made such a success of the Hare, at Harrow Weald, that Benskins offered them a place more than twice as large, though not as immediately attractive. In 1961, therefore, with many misgivings, George and Ann Hill accepted tenancy of the Northwood Hills Hotel, just outside Pinner.

The Northwood Hills bore little resemblance to their previous idyllically pretty country inn. Situated immediately opposite Northwood Hills tube station, it was a large detached building, in size and gloomy aspect more like some abandoned Rural District Council offices. It had, indeed, been built as a hotel in the years of Metroland expansion, but all the room-and-board side had long ago vanished.

Within were three enormous bars lined in dark Olde English oak panelling, with heavy, knobby furniture and drab brown industrial linoleum. Six sad cheese rolls under a plastic dome represented the only catering. When the new tenants arrived, trade was so slight that one person could easily tend all three bars at once.

George and Ann Hill set out to change all that. They reopened the defunct dining-room, putting on special lunches for employees of the nearby headquarters of Vehicle and General Insurance. For the evenings, George saw he must appeal to the growing teenage element. He therefore decided to have live music in the saloon bar on Friday and Saturday nights.

Among the benefits of the Hills' previous pub had been two highly popular saloon-bar pianists. 'One was an old lady who used to play the honky-tonk style,' George Hill remembers. 'Then we had Bob. He was an albino who just turned up one day with his white walking-stick. But he was a marvellous pianist – and a real showman. He used to jump up and down, get really carried away. The customers loved him.'

Bob followed the Hills to their new pub, played there a couple of weekends, but said he'd have to stop as the travelling was too much for him. George still had not found a satisfactory replacement when a man he had not seen before came into the saloon bar and asked for a word with him. 'It was Reggie's father. He asked me if I needed a pianist, because his boy wanted to have a go. I said, "All right. I don't mind having a look at him."'

Reggie's 'father' was, in fact, Sheila's man-friend Fred Fare-brother, who not only got Reggie his try-out at the Northwood Hills but also delivered him there, along with a rudimentary microphone system to augment the saloon bar's decrepit upright piano.

The initial impression was hardly that of a Saturday-night show-stopper. 'He was only about fifteen, still at school,' George's wife, Ann, remembers. 'His hair was cut very short. He wore a collar and tie, and grey flannel trousers. And this Harris tweed sports jacket that was a kind of gingery colour. He was very shy. But he did tell us he'd written a song that was called "Come Back, Baby".'

Picture the scene, that inaugural night in the Northwood Hills saloon bar. The sprawling old bar, still more full of echoes than people, with its dingy panelled walls and faded lampshades, its brown lino worn by generations of feet and supine dogs. The brightly lit bar-counter with a go-ahead new husband-and-wife team, pulling Benskins pints or turning for push-ups at the spirit optics. A few incurious eyes turn to the piano, where a bespectacled boy in a ginger tweed sports jacket is setting up some kind of microphone and loudspeaker, helped by a man and a petite, vociferous woman, plainly his mother. Man and woman retire to a side table, leaving boy alone. Dogged bespectacled face nerves itself as for plunge into cold swimming-bath. A sudden passionate salvo from the yellow piano-keys. A voice from the loudspeaker fabric, keening the lovelorn words of Ray Charles's Country and Western hit:

> Take these chains from my heart and set me free.
> You've grown cold and no longer care for me . . .

To begin with, the customers didn't appreciate it. 'They gave him terrible stick,' George Hill remembers. 'They'd shout "Get off!" or "Turn it down!" He'd have empty crisp packets and ashtrays thrown at him – we only had tin ones, so they didn't hurt. Or somebody would sneak up and unplug the leads of his PA system. I think he had quite a few pints emptied into that piano as well.'

But, with the ringside support of his mother and Fred Farebrother, Reggie stuck it out. And after a few nights, the hail of scrunched-up crisp packets and tin ashtrays was somewhat moderated. The leads from the mike were left alone, and the piano innards spared their baptism of Benskins best bitter. Here and there, under a knobby oak table, a foot began to tap on the old brown lino. Hands even loosened their grip on pints and gin glasses to clap along in time.

Enormously in the boy's favour was that he did not only do 'modern stuff'. Like his early exemplar Winifred Atwell, he would play anything his listeners showed the smallest signs of liking. If he could not reach them with Ray Charles or Jim Reeves, then he would try with English bar-room evergreens like 'Roll Out the Barrel' or 'Bye Bye Blackbird'. Some nights, he would be joined in performance by the amateur vocalists every English pub can produce. 'There was one old girl from the East End, called Mary Whitmarsh,' George Hill remembers. 'She used to like to get up and do all the traditional Cockney things, like "The Old Bull and Bush". And there was a bloke named Toby Barry, who really fancied his voice. He'd play the spoons on his knee as well, or beat time on a tray.'

After a few weeks, George was forced to admit he had found an attraction at least the equal of albino Bob. 'But I still don't think Reggie was as good a piano-player,' he insists to this day. 'As far as I'm concerned, Bob was the one who ought to have become a star.'

George Hill's object of drawing 'the young crowd' worked, if anything rather too well. 'It was quite a hard pub, actually. We used to get this crowd in from South Ruislip who had a scrap every

Friday night. I remember a punch-up starting one night while Reg was playing. There was a window near the piano, and he just went out through that like a flash.'

Reggie was the Northwood Hills' weekend pianist for almost two years. His pay was £1 10s a night, plus the collection which Mary Whitmarsh, the old Cockney lady, would make for him on a glass-ringed tin tray. In all that time, he did not ask for a rise, or for his name to be displayed outside the Northwood Hills Hotel, as indeed it never was.

While the boy in the Harris tweed jacket pounded the yellowed piano-keys, Britain was in the grip of Beatlemania and its vast cultural backwash. If Liverpool could have an internationally popular and commercial sound, then why not any other hitherto remote, unfashionable British city or town? Consequently, there was soon a Manchester sound, spearheaded by the amiable, sub-Beatle-ish Hollies. There was a Birmingham Sound, represented by the Applejacks, with their amazing novelty of a girl bass-player. There was even a Tottenham Sound, briefly incarnate in the white-trousered Dave Clark Five. There were potentially Scottish, Irish, Welsh and West Country Sounds. But never in the keenest entrepreneurial eye the smallest glimmer of a Middlesex and, especially not, a Pinner Sound.

To date, Reggie Dwight's home area had produced only one pop musical attraction, of somewhat special appeal. This was Screaming Lord Sutch, a Medusa-haired rock maniac whose stage properties included Viking horns, a coffin and a Jack-the-Ripper-style Gladstone bag, and whose family home was in Northolt Road, Harrow-on-the-Hill.

It was in these decorous London suburbs, however, that the next great musical generation was taking shape. Across in Ealing, in a packed club room under the ABC teashop, Alexis Korner's Blues Incorporated presented a roster of unknown young vocalists including Rod Stewart and Long John Baldry. In front of the grandstand at Richmond's Old Deer Park, cord-clad boys and girls jazz-stomped to an unregenerate rhythm-and-blues band called the Rolling Stones. Southward, at the Wooden Bridge Hotel, Guildford, you could hear Rhode Island Red and the Roosters, featuring Eric Clapton. At the Railway Hotel, Harrow and Wealdstone, just down the road from Pinner, one would soon be able to catch the Mann-Hugg Blues Brothers, later Manfred Mann, and a wild West London Mod group called the Detours, soon to be transmogrified into the High Numbers and finally the Who.

In his fourth year at Pinner County Grammar, Reggie had gained admittance to a local amateur group named the Corvettes. Its founders were two Northwood Secondary School boys, Stuart Brown and Geoff Dyson, on guitar and bass respectively. The drummer's father ran a pub, The Gate, near Mount Vernon Hospital. Their name was inspired by the Chevy Corvette sports car driven by two young freebooting heroes in an American TV series, *Route 66*.

The Corvettes played a mixture of blues and rock 'n' roll. Stuart Brown, who had a huskily soulful voice, did the blues numbers. Reggie Dwight, at the piano, did the Jerry Lee Lewis 'shouters'. Their celebrity was not great. The most Geoff Dyson ever remembers them being paid was £2 a night at the youth club in St Edmund's Roman Catholic Hall, Pinner Road. 'Reggie had to play whatever piano was there, which nearly always would be horribly out of tune. Stuart and I used to try to tune our guitars to the piano. The other thing I remember was how dapper and conventional-looking he always was. While the rest of us would be in jeans, he'd be in grey flannels.'

The Corvettes disbanded after a few unspectacular months, and Geoff Dyson took his bass guitar to another local group, the Mockingbirds, good enough to 'open' for big-time R & B bands like the Yardbirds. Then he met up with Stuart Brown and Reggie Dwight again. They told him they were starting afresh, with a new name and new serious intent. They were now Bluesology, in homage to a number by the gipsy jazz guitarist Django Reinhardt.

Geoff Dyson agreed to rejoin them on bass guitar, though there was another role in which he could be still more useful. While with the Mockingbirds, he had played at glamorous Soho music venues like the Marquee Club. With his contacts there, he could act informally as Bluesology's booking manager.

Not that Bluesology would show much sign of promise, for quite a long time yet. Most of its personnel were more interested in chasing girls and fooling around. 'But we always knew Reg was going to make it,' Geoff Dyson says. 'He'd look at the rest of us sometimes, and say "Oooh, you lot! But I'm going places."'

2

A Bit of Outrage

H E had reached that stage of school life when a Careers Advisory Officer arrived in the late afternoon period to conduct individual interviews amid piles of helpful literature about opportunities in banking, insurance or the Forestry Commission. For male Grammar School leavers in those monochrome early Sixties, official advice was virtually always the same. A good all-round GCE, followed by college or, at least, technical college. Your place thus assured on the morning platform for the Metropolitan Line train up to town. Work, a cheese roll lunch, and more work. Home at five to your pipe, slippers and Ovaltine in Metroland.

Among the new generations of prospective commuters there were always a few renegades, inquiring about offbeat jobs for which the careers Advisory Officer possessed no official literature. One such at Pinner County Grammar School was a portly fifth-former named R. K. Dwight, who had announced that he wanted to go into the 'music business'.

Viewed from rural Middlesex in 1964, the 'music business' was a mystery as remote and impenetrable as the diplomatic service or the BBC. Music was not, as it is today, a visible, pullulating industry. Pop was a barely emancipated part of a tiny professional enclave, ruled by dynasties and nepotism and centred on a couple of streets in London's West End. As with the film business, you got in by grabbing any opening, wherever it occurred. Being in that old-fashioned music business for Reggie Dwight could have meant managing the Royal Philharmonic Orchestra or selling pianos in a department store. It could have meant cutting records in a factory, etching sheet music or filing and cataloguing in the BBC Gramophone Library.

The last thing he thought it might mean was becoming a professional performer, rather than a busy amateur. He had turned his back on a classical career, and pop did not seem a possibility. Pop performers of late 1964 were match-thin northerners with glossy fringes, chain-smoking fingers and long-toed goblin boots. They were not portly boys from Middlesex, in spectacles, ginger tweed sports jackets and grey flannel trousers, who got up when a lady entered the room.

What Reggie aimed for was some conventional career, rubbing against the magic and glamour of pop. Perhaps a job with a music publisher – Novello & Co., Francis Day & Hunter – names familiar from the covers of his piano sheet-music. Or with one of the record-companies whose labels the lonely, bedroom-bound boy would lie and recite to himself – 'Decca, Parlophone, HMV, London, Fontana, Liberty.'

Looking at R. K. Dwight, the Careers Officer could see nothing exceptional. He had sat his GCE Ordinary Level exam at sixteen, passing in only four subjects: English Language, English Literature, French and Music. It was the typical result of the clever but torpid pupil who had done next to no work, merely getting by in those subjects where he possessed innate ability. Even in Music, he had reached only the lowest pass grade. He was now in the sixth form, the only one in his year to be studying music at A-Level. But his teacher, Mr Stoupe, complained that he wasted his ability – and unconscionable amounts of study-time – in messing around with a pop group. Clearly, not a boy destined to set the world alight. A boy who might possibly get his wish and find a minor niche in some office, shop or outlet connected with music. But where?

Of all unlikely people, it was Reggie's footballer cousin Roy who found that elusive opening. Roy's 1959 Cup Final accident had put paid to his stardom, though he played on for a while, first with Fulham, then under Jimmy Hill at Coventry. From playing he would move into coaching, and tireless work with young people in several departments of sport which continues to this day.

Roy had stayed on friendly terms with Sheila Dwight after her divorce from Stanley, and had good-naturedly promised to help Reggie if possible via his many contacts in the sporting and showbiz world. It happened that a football friend of Roy's knew Pat Sherlock, who worked for the West End song publishers Mills Music. Roy arranged for Sherlock to interview Reggie, and himself conscientiously accompanied the lad up to town for the occasion.

'I can see him now, sitting in my office,' Pat Sherlock remembers. 'I remember thinking what small hands he had for a piano-player. He had this nervous mannerism of pushing his glasses back up his nose. And a funny little pouting look.' Reggie was, of course, an excellent interviewee with his shy and studious air and his habit of addressing older men as 'sir'. A further interview with Mills' managing director, Cyril Gee, confirmed the favourable impression. He was offered a job as Mills Music's office boy at a starting salary of £5 per week.

His decision to leave school in early 1965, a term before his A-Level exams, caused universal protest. As well as being the school's only A-Level Music pupil, he had also been due to take English, a subject in which he could be brilliant when he chose. With two A-Levels added to his four O-Level passes, he could have competed for admittance at several redbrick universities, if not the Royal Academy of Music. His Academy tutor Helen Piena was particularly dismayed at what seemed a perverse squandering of promise, academic as well as musical. 'I remember sitting with him for about three-quarters of an hour, trying to talk him into going to university. All he said was that he wouldn't because no one in his family ever had before.'

Stanley Dwight – now living with his new wife and family in Cheshire – also weighed in, reproaching his nephew Roy for having set up the Mills Music interview. Stanley thought that Reggie should go into government service, a bank or, failing that, follow some currently prestigious young man's vocation like cabin steward on British European Airways.

The stumbling-block most to be feared was Pinner County's stern head, Jack Westgate Smith. Reggie broke the news to him in trepidation, well aware that Mr Westgate Smith had the power to jinx the plan if he chose. 'He asked me if it was really what I wanted to do,' the star would remember later. 'I said "Yes", and he said "All right. You have my blessing." I was flabbergasted.'

R. K. Dwight's last recorded attendance at Pinner County Grammar School was on 5 March, 1965. Bill Johnson, his history master, delivered a philosophical farewell. 'I told him if he really wanted to be in the music business, this was probably the most sensible way. "When you're forty," I told him, "you'll either be some sort of glorified office-boy or you'll be a millionaire."'

Denmark Street, London's version of Tin Pan Alley, is a brief thoroughfare between Charing Cross Road and the sour, windy wastes under the Centre Point skyscraper. When Reggie Dwight arrived there twenty-five years ago, the days were long gone when songwriters in poky offices would try out a tune on any old 'tin pan' or rush into the street to see if some passing tramp could instantly whistle it back (hence 'the old grey whistle test'). But Denmark Street in 1965 remained the hub of what was still not quite the British music industry.

Here, as half a century before, any composer must come to have his work published, in sheet-music form, the words even of wildest rock-'n'-roll numbers written below the notes with archaic hyphens and accents. Here, before the age of private recording studios, aspiring groups must come to make their 'demos' in eggbox-lined confessionals at £5 per hour. Here, among shades of Music Hall and Variety and smells of jangly upright pianos and violin-dust, the next week's teenage Top 10 was still put together by men in their late forties and early fifties, chain-smoking Player's or chewing on wet Wills 'Whiff' cigars.

In barely a hundred yards could be found all one needed to get on in pop music. Publishing houses like Southern, Pickwick, Grosvenor, Mills and KPM. Recording studios like Regent Sound, where the first ever Rolling Stones sides were cut. Promotion men like Brian Sommerville, who had first taken the Beatles to America. Film and variety agents like Lipton and Andy Lothian. Not to mention L. Lennox, the music-engravers; the Tin Pan Alley Club; and Musical Exchange with its window full of Fender and Gretsch guitars, black Vox amps, organs and zebra-skin-covered bongo drums.

Though thrustful new Tin Pan Alleyites were to be seen everywhere in their Carnaby Street clothes, the monarchs were still figures embodying continuity and tradition. Of these none was greater than Dick James, once a small-time danceband crooner, now the Beatles' music-publisher. It had been in Tin Pan Alley, or not many yards away, that Brian Epstein had been stood up by another publisher, then walked into Dick James's hole-in-the-wall office to find James fortuitously at his desk. Since then, of course, Dick James had risen to far more sumptuous offices, in nearby New Oxford Street. But his regal promenades through Denmark Street and his regular court at the Gioconda coffee bar remained a symbol and affirmation of just how lucky a man in this business could get.

Mills Music was an American firm, born in New York's original Tin Pan Alley, whose catalogue included such illustrious names as Fats Waller, Duke Ellington and Leroy Anderson. Its UK catalogue, though more modest, covered the spectrum of British pop, from Cliff Richard's 'Move It' to 'Side Saddle', 'Snow Coach' and other piano hits by the dour Russ Conway. Not that Reggie Dwight put so much as a toe on the ladder to such things. His job was in the warehouse at the rear of Mills' premises, in Denmark Place, filling casual orders for sheet-music, brewing tea, packing parcels and wheeling them on an old-fashioned hand-barrow to the Post Office depot in Kingsway. His closest brush with celebrity would be when he was sent with a piece of music or a message to the Regent Street office of the veteran bandleader Joe Loss.

On his Tin Pan Alley bosses he seems to have made scarcely more impact than on his schoolteachers. Cyril Gee, the managing director, was aware only of 'this podgy kid' who persisted in calling him 'sir'. 'I remember him coming to me one day and asking if he could play one of the arrangers' pianos in the lunch hour.' Even his original mentor, Pat Sherlock, knew little about him, save that he played piano at every moment he was not packing parcels or hunting for something or other among the dusty catalogue shelves. 'That Christmas, we had a party in the office, with a lot of Chelsea football players. We kept Reggie back after work, playing a lot of Cockney things like "The Old Bull and Bush".' Cousin Roy's wedding all over again.

As well as being poorly paid, menial, boring and submerged, the job entailed frequent leg-pulling from the far more sassy and streetwise boys who constituted Tin Pan Alley's messenger class. One such was Caleb Quaye, office boy for Paxton's wholesale music-delivery firm in Old Compton Street, who used to call at Mills every day on his rounds. The son of prewar bandleader Cab Quaye, himself flashily proficient on guitar, piano and drums, Caleb at this stage spotted no fellow spirit in Reggie Dwight. 'I just used to laugh at him because he looked so much like Billy Bunter.'

But Reggie was starting to change. His girl 'mate' Janet Ritchie received another privileged invitation into his bedroom at Frome Court to try on some new things he had bought in the trendy boutiques and second-hand clothes shops around Carnaby Street. 'I remember, he'd got a fur coat. One of the short ladies' ones all the boys were starting to wear. And a Mickey Mouse T-shirt. I'd never seen such way-out stuff before. "I like a bit of outrage," he said.

Meanwhile, his new group, Bluesology, struggled in continuing birth-pangs. Their style was meant to be cool, sophisticated and worldly, something like the hugely popular Georgie Fame and the Blue Flames. Putting aside simple rock and even simple blues, they experimented with the more complex, less cheerful repertoire of Mose Allison and Jimmy Witherspoon. As the star himself would later admit, this was usually far over the heads of teenage audiences at dances in the Pinner area. 'We were always playing the wrong stuff, trying to appeal to minority tastes. Bluesology were either two months too late or three years too early.'

Despite being largely held in church halls and British Legion clubs, their gigs were not immune from excitement or physical danger. One night at South Harrow British Legion, a squad of black-clad 'rockers' rode their motorbikes into the club and demanded that Bluesology call a halt to Jimmy Witherspoon and do some old-fashioned rock 'n' roll. On that terrifying occasion, the least terrified was Reggie Dwight. He did not mind at all going back to being Jerry Lee Lewis. And he secretly loved the 'bit of outrage' that turned the flag-hung war veterans' hall into a scene Marlon Brando might have played in *The Wild One*.

Bluesology now numbered five. With Reggie on piano and Stuart A. Brown on guitar and vocals, there was Mick Inkpen on drums and Rex Bishop, replacing Geoff Dyson, on bass. Emulating the Blue Flames, they also acquired a tenor-sax player named Mike, somewhat older than the others, as brass sidemen then tended to be. In nearly every teenage R & B outfit there would be one member who looked like the others' big brother, if not father.

With the elder Mike among them, blowing lustily if erratically, Bluesology now felt ready to move up another notch. They began to enter for the amateur talent contests that, in the beat-group craze of 1965, were frequently put on by dance halls and clubs. Though large entertainment chains like Mecca did offer alluring prizes – even recording contracts – most were simply a wheeze to get five or six hopeful bands to perform free of charge. Bluesology entered one contest at the Wimbledon Palais, another at Rory Blackwell's club in Islington. In both they were beaten by more practised groups with material more accessible than Jimmy Witherspoon.

On Sunday afternoons they would meet to practise in the big back bar of the Northwood Hills Hotel. Though ready enough to grant that favour George Hill remained deaf to any hints that he might allow Bluesology to augment Reggie's weekend piano spot, or possibly put up money for new equipment. 'I never knew what went on when Reggie brought them all in,' Hill remembers now. 'I just knew there was always a hell of a noise.'

Georgie Fame's number one hit 'Yeh Yeh' had made the electric piano massively popular. Geoff Dyson remembers that at the Wimbledon Palais talent contest, one of the groups who trounced Bluesology already possessed this treasure. 'Reggie was allowed to have a go on it. He thought it was wonderful.' Shortly afterwards he approached George Hill at the Northwood Hills and asked for the loan of £200 to buy an electric piano for Bluesology. 'I had to say "No",' Hill remembers. 'I hadn't got two hundred pounds to lend him.'

A more serious patron was acquired through their drummer Mick Inkpen, who worked as an apprentice to a jewellery manufacturer in Bond Street. Inkpen persuaded his employer, Arnold Tendler, to come and see Bluesology at one of their Pinner church-hall gigs. 'After having had my arm twisted to go and see them, I was really bowled over,' Tendler remembers now. 'At the piano there was this little roly-poly boy in clothes even I called square. But when he played, he was marvellous. Even then he used to kick away the piano-stool and play sitting on the floor.'

Arnold Tendler became Bluesology's first real manager, putting up money for new instruments, stage uniforms and a Ford Thames van. At the same time, using every penny of his savings and pub earnings, Reggie managed to raise the price of a Hohner 'Planet' electric piano and amplifier.

Between Bluesology's good-looking vocalist and its owlish tweed-jacketed one, there was no contest as far as Arnold was concerned. 'No matter what he looked like, Reg was the one who made that group. Stu Brown had a good voice, but it could be flat. And it always took him a bit of time to get going. Whereas Reg just had to open his mouth, and there it was.'

Despite being well into his thirties – an almost prehistoric age to sixteen- and seventeen-year-olds – Arnold Tendler entered into the spirit of Bluesology, accompanying them on most of their outings to disappointing talent competitions. 'And I used to go down and watch Reggie play at that pub in Northwood Hills, even though there'd be a fracas most weekends. At the time, I remember, he had a girl friend with red hair, called Gipsy.'

The jeweller's money also financed the making of a two-side demo record at a studio in Rickmansworth operated by the son of bandleader Jack Jackson. On one side Bluesology did Reggie's song 'Come Back, Baby', with the composer himself on vocal. The other side featured Stuart Brown's soulful voice in Jimmy Witherspoon's 'Times Getting Tougher Than Tough'. Armed with this, Arnold Tendler made the rounds of the London record companies. He struck gold – or, at least, rolled gold – at Philips, whose head of Artist and Repertoire, Jack Baverstock, was sufficiently impressed to offer a recording contract with Philips' associated label, Fontana.

Tendler had not pulled off such a marvellous coup. In that post-Beatlemania spring of 1965, record companies would sign up virtually anything, so long as it featured long hair, hipster trousers and guitars. Bluesology were just one of hundreds of amateur bands from all over the United Kingdom, contracted on royalty rates of fractions of a penny and run quickly through the system, like baggage through an X-ray machine, to see if they might be a Fab Four, Five or Six.

But for the band concerned, it was still a thrilling moment. Most thrilling was it for Reggie Dwight, who would feature on the A-side of the debut single, singing his own song, 'Come Back, Baby'. To complete his triumph, 'Come Back, Baby' was also accepted for publication by his daytime employers, Mills Music.

Actually, it was a measure of Fontana's perfunctoriness merely to let Bluesology re-record the two sides they had cut as demos in Rickmansworth. The recording took place at Philips' London studios, under Jack Baverstock's supervision, on 3 June, 1965. It speaks volumes for Reggie's self-effacing manner in those days that Baverstock does not remember noticing him during the three-hour session.

The future Elton's debut on record is a half-pint ballad, full of the sidelong chords and macho wistfulness of the Merseybeat era. Its lyric is lifted complete from the songwriter's phrasebook: 'Come back, I'll treat you right. Come back, I'll hold you tight.' The voice is recognisably Elton's, clearer and higher than almost any dared be in those days, holding together the cheap blur of sound and Mike's lone, off-key saxophone. The piano chords give the good value one would expect from a Royal Academy junior exhibitioner. Key changes are heralded by emotional pounding, as in the very best of Bobby Vee. The B-side version of 'Times Getting Tougher Than Tough' might have been thought marginally more commercial in those rhythm-and-blues-crazy days. Stuart Brown's husky café-au-lait voice has more than a touch of Georgie Fame. Reggie is represented by piano boogie infillings and a long middle solo in the groove of a Northwood Hills Saturday night.

The single came out in July, in company with the cream of the British and American beat boom. Also released, that twangling Op-Art midsummer, were the Rolling Stones' 'Satisfaction', the Hollies' 'I'm Alive', the Animals' 'We Gotta Get Out Of This Place', the Byrds' 'Mr Tambourine Man', the Kinks' 'Set Me Free', the Yardbirds' 'Heart Full of Soul' and the Who's 'Anyway, Anyhow, Anywhere'.

The star still remembers the thrill of hearing his voice crackling on a car-radio, when 'Come Back, Baby' got its first play on Radio Luxembourg. After that, it rapidly sank under the thousand-watt tank-tracks of the Yardbirds and the Stones. There was not even the faintest seismic hint of an appearance in the charts.

Nevertheless, a watershed had been reached. Bluesology were no longer an amateur group, playing for school hops and Catholic socials. As 'Fontana recording artists', they could aspire to serious London R & B venues like the Last Chance and the 100 Club. When they played, it was in the uniform of dark blue pants, red polo shirts and blue-and-white blazers bought for them by Arnold Tendler at Irvine Sellars's Carnaby Street boutique.

On 22 July, they received their first national publicity – a story in the trade paper *Record Retailer and Music Industry News*:

Bluesology, a group of five talented young musicians, take their name from the title of a record by the famous French jazz guitarist Django Reinhardt. Their first Fontana record release was 'Come Back Baby', composed by the group's singer-pianist, Reg Dwight. 'We play blues music mainly after the style of Jimmy Witherspoon, Memphis Slim and Muddy Waters with, dare I say it, a slight jazz flavour,' says spokesman drummer Mick Inkpen (17).

Above was a minuscule picture of the 'talented young musicians' – four of them slim, hollow-cheeked and fashionably handsome, the fifth bespectacled, his face set in the glower of a Bunter who has just learned that the Greyfriars tuck shop is out of cream buns.

Arnold Tendler was successful in getting them bookings, though of a somewhat variable and unpredictable kind. 'One was at the Phoenix Theatre, in Charing Cross Road, supporting Eric Burdon and the Animals. The audience threw so much stuff at the stage that Eric had to go out, sheltering behind a dustbin lid, and threaten no one would play if it didn't stop. Another time, I got them in at the restaurant on top of the Hilton Hotel in Park Lane. When we arrived, the lady in charge said "We like it very quiet." So the lads played just one number, "The Girl From Ipanema", making it last about twenty minutes.'

Towards the end of 1965 Pat Higgs, an experienced dance band trumpeter, read in a music press ad that an up-and-coming blues band sought recruits for its newly inaugurated horn section. The only slightly disconcerting thing was that auditions were to take place in Pinner, Middlesex.

Pat Higgs made it out to Pinner, and found Bluesology. They told him they had to get a proper brass section before they could make their next record. Though several years older than any of the personnel, Higgs thought he might as well join up. The same auditions produced tenor saxophonist Dave Murphy, another noticeably older recruit whose previous experience had been mainly in theatre orchestra-pits.

The expanded Bluesology's first major foray was to a talent contest-cum-audition for bands, run by a contact of Arnold's named Trevor Witchelo. The venue was the State, a huge circuit cinema modelled on New York's Empire State Building in the heart of Irish Kilburn. After their three numbers, they were approached by a representative of the Roy Tempest Agency, which at that time handled a large number of touring pop package shows. The Tempest man asked if they would be interested in backing American R & B solo performers on tour in Britain. If they were to accept, it was obvious that Reggie Dwight could not continue in a daytime clerical job, as he had previously managed to do. He therefore turned fully professional, handing in his notice at Mills Music and exchanging a regular £5 pay packet for the excitement and uncertainty of life on the road. Little did he guess where that road would lead – or that he was destined never to get off it again.

The first American R & B artist to whom Bluesology were offered as sidemen was Wilson Pickett, born in Pratville, Alabama, singer of 'Mustang Sally', 'In The Midnight Hour' and 'Land of 1,000 Dances', most aggressive of the new funky generation on the Memphis Stax label, and a difficult companion in almost any circumstances.

Alas, Bluesology were not to experience life on the road with 'the Wicked Pickett'. At the audition, his guitarist took against them and ordered Roy Tempest to find Pickett another backing band. 'All those American acts used to be very organised,' Pat Higgs remembers. 'They'd have their song-arrangements all written out, and expect the backing band to be the same. Bluesology had never used arrangements. Before we went up for the next audition, I had to try to scribble a few out.'

Their first successful audition was with Major Lance, a high-register soul man, named in the grand tradition of the Duke of Earl, whose best-remembered song bears the title 'Um Um Um Um Um Um'. Pat Higgs having got the horn arrangement down on paper, Bluesology were booked for their first fully pro tour in December 1965.

For Reggie Dwight, who naturally knew every word of 'Um Um Um Um Um Um', the next two weeks were unforgettable. Merely to shake hands with Major Lance was a thrill almost beyond expression by the shy, pug face. Never mind to travel and socialise with him and, each night, gamely try to reproduce his original arrangements on the stage of some noisy little club. The ultimate music fan had found a way of being closer to his idols than the very best seat in the front row. Twenty-five years later that same, undiminished music fan would still maintain, 'Backing Major Lance was probably the biggest thing that ever happened to me.'

More idols followed, from the mainstream and also the backwaters of Reggie's record-collection. During early 1966, Bluesology toured as backing band for the Drifters, the Ink Spots, Billy Stewart, Doris Troy and Patti LaBelle and the Bluebells – or 'Blue Bellies', as one provincial club poster announced them.

Working for the Roy Tempest Organisation was no rest cure. As well as importing genuine veteran US groups like the Drifters and Ink Spots, Tempest also put on groups of the same name who, at the most charitable estimate, were no closer than fourth or fifth cousins to the originals. Most of the groups stayed in a flat owned by Roy Tempest, for which they were charged a hefty rent. 'Tempest used to con us, really,' Pat Higgs says. 'We'd be shown a two-week tour sheet with just a few dates, and proper rest days. Then when we started, all the spaces would have been filled in. We'd find ourselves doing two, sometimes three gigs in a day.'

The future star's memory would also be of virtual slave labour. 'There was one day with Billy Stewart we did four gigs – in London and Birmingham. We started off in the afternoon, playing an American servicemen's club in Lancaster Gate, finished that at four, raced up to Birmingham and played the Ritz and Plaza there, then came back to London and played the Cue Club in Praed Street the same night. And we never had road managers in those days. At the time we didn't think anything of it, humping our equipment up and down all the stairs.'

Arnold Tendler, the Bond Street jeweller, continued as their manager, patiently bailing them out when equipment was lost or stolen, even forking out for a new van when the other was wrecked on a trip to Norway. 'I think Arnold was having a bit of financial trouble at the time,' Pat Higgs remembers. 'Still, he always paid us all right. Sometimes he'd open his car boot and it'd be full of watches. He'd dole out one to each of us, so that we could go off and sell that.'

Not all the American stars Bluesology backed had the cult status of Major Lance. The Ink Spots were the original late Forties vocal group, combining pre-doowop harmonies with an archaic comedy routine. 'I remember we went with them to this really hip black club around Liverpool Street,' Pat Higgs says. 'Suddenly in the middle of the number, one of these Ink Spots starts taking his clarinet to pieces. The audience nearly pulled us off the stage.'

The star's own fondest recollection would be of Patti LaBelle, who both mothered him with home cooking and took a small fortune from him at suitcase-top cards. And of Billy Stewart, another hero of Reggie's for his gymnastic scat versions of 'Summertime' and 'Sitting in the Park'. 'He died very shortly after he left us – was shot to death back in America. An enormous man. I mean, I remember stopping alongside the motorway on the M1, waiting for him to relieve himself, and it was like waiting for a train.'

In between, Bluesology would do gigs on their own at London

clubs like the Cromwellian in South Kensington, or the highly fashionable Scotch of St James's. At the latter, Reggie had a traumatic experience with his new acquisition, a Vox AC 30 electric organ, painted a lurid shade of orange. 'In the very first number, one of the notes got stuck. I was so embarrassed. But later on, Eric Burdon of the Animals came up and said "Never mind, lad. That happened to us once, too."'

The Vox became hallowed on a later night at the Cromwellian, when Stevie Wonder, the Motown prodigy – then only just metamorphosed from 'Little Stevie Wonder' – borrowed it for an entire set. Reggie was still a starstruck fan above all, thrilled that music could smuggle him in to places like the Scotch, where the faint profile of a Beatle or, at least, a Gene Pitney, might glimmer through the high-priced darkness.

Bluesology's second single for Fontana, recorded the previous November, was released in February 1966. The A-side, 'Mr Frantic', was another Reggie Dwight composition, a soul number rather oddly slow and tentative, befitting this nearest-ever approach to self-portraiture. The B-side was a traditional R & B boogie, 'Every Day I Have the Blues', sung by Stuart Brown. Despite the vastly fatter, more confident sound of the new horn section, airplay was minimal and chart-action nil.

At this point, something strange happened to Reggie Dwight. From being undisputed front man in the group he had co-founded, he was relegated – or relegated himself – further and further into Bluesology's background. A mixture of chagrin and guilt at having failed to sing a hit seemed to undermine his confidence, his extrovert showmanship and determination to 'go places'. The lead singer became merely the Vox organist, loyally backing up this or that American star, on solo gigs giving up his limelight to the handsome, husky Stuart A. Brown. That he still passionately wanted to sing could be divined by an anguished flash in his glasses whenever Stu Brown started giving it hot. But, in some obscure self-destructive mood, he felt he couldn't, or shouldn't.

It was enough for him to be in a busy band, with regular money and a full engagement book. In the new van financed by the long-suffering Arnold Tendler, Bluesology voyaged to Britain's further-most music venues, like the Whisky-à-Go-Go, Newcastle-upon-Tyne. With Doris Troy they even played the Cavern Club in Liverpool, dank subterranean birthplace of the Beatles. Reggie's Pinner friend Janet Ritchie, who was doing teacher training in Liverpool, hitched a ride in the van and helped carry their equipment down the eighteen famous steps from Mathew Street.

In the six-strong line-up, fat Reggie was odd man out – quiet, neat and self-contained, inhabiting his own little patch of order amid the travelling chaos. Most indulgences of a blues musician's life seemed to pass him by. He barely drank and didn't smoke, either cigarettes or marijuana. He showed no interest in the girls who clustered at Bluesology's feet as they played and followed them backstage or to the pub afterwards if they liked. Reggie's only interest in girls seemed to be for conversation. 'If nothing was happening, he'd just go to sleep,' Pat Higgs remembers. 'He had a special little pillow that he used to carry round with him.'

Within the group he was the comedian and clown, the one most likely to raise a laugh from their punishing itinerant life. On long road journeys he would entertain the others with streams of punning wordplay, or his wide repertoire of funny voices from radio and TV shows: Eric Morecambe, 'Professor' Stanley Unwin, Bloodnock and Bluebottle from the Goons. 'And when we broke down – which was a lot – we'd say "Come on, Reg. Do us your little dance",' Pat Higgs remembers. 'He'd get out and do this special little dance for us on the hard shoulder of the motorway.'

There was also the other Reggie, troubled, bashful and unconfident, buttoned up inside a mod jacket as tightly as he once had been in his brown school blazer. His hair had already become a problem, receding from the temples and thinning at the crown, so that his regulation Beatle busby required more and more elaborate maintenance with shampoo, hair-dryer and comb. In 1966 the idea of going bald was a pop musician's ultimate nightmare. Ghastly to end up like the Hollies' drummer, who was forced to hide his terrible affliction under a wide-brimmed cowboy hat.

The other torment was his chronic weight problem. He had chosen the very worst life to keep slim, eating as he most often did in pull-up musicians' cafés like the Blue Boar, whose walls were like action paintings, zigzagged with the tomato and egg stains of late-night food fights. Not that he was gluttonous like the real Billy Bunter; as he often remarked bitterly, he had only to look at a doughnut for the pounds to pile on. In desperation, he started to take amphetamine slimming pills, the kind that promote weight loss by speeding up the metabolism. 'He said he'd pinched them from his mum,' Pat Higgs remembers. 'He handed them out to the rest of us, too, to help us stay awake.'

Following the Beatles' path, five years too late, Bluesology even did a stint on the Hamburg Reeperbahn, playing at the selfsame club, the Top Ten, where Beatlemania had first taken root. 'Though Reg usually didn't drink much, he did have a bit of a go in Hamburg,'

Pat Higgs says. 'I remember him dancing among the traffic out on the Reeperbahn.'

It was the summer of 1966. The Beatles were far away from grubby Hamburg with their chastely black-and-white-jacketed album *Revolver*. *Time* magazine had dubbed London 'The Style Capital of Europe'. England won the World Cup, snatching the vital goal from West Germany in the last minutes of extra time. Girls' bumblebee-striped dresses climbed four inches above the knee. England was drunk with sunshine, football and sounds. Bluesology still couldn't get a hit.

In a single day they did three London gigs, then drove straight down to the South of France to play for a month at the St Tropez Papagayo Club. When they arrived, the accommodation to which they were shown was a completely bare room. The club owner explained that his previous resident band had destroyed all the beds and furniture. 'I remember the Papagayo because Reg electrocuted himself on his gear one night,' Pat Higgs says. 'He was out for quite a few minutes. We had to call a doctor to give him an injection in his bum. The rest of us stood round the bed and watched.'

Among British blues singers of this era, none was so distinctive as Long John Baldry. A London policeman's son, six foot seven and a half inches tall, blond of hair and pink of face, he combined a voice oozing Southern molasses and hominy grits with a manner which, in either sense, could accurately be termed high camp.

Camp was not a thing much encountered in blues circles then, and Long John's appearance made it the more striking. As well as being immensely tall, he was a notable dandy, fond of flipping open his jacket to display the LJB monogram patterned over its silk lining. The Deep Southern voice that growled macho blues ballads each night was by day exercised in all the parodied gambits of a screaming 'old queen'. Whereas other musicians called each other 'man' or 'cat', Long John preferred the appellation 'dear' or 'she', as in 'She's bold today!' A saxophone player who travelled with him remembers once passing a full troop of Boy Scouts, trudging along replete with Baden-Powell hats, khaki shorts, woggles and toggles. A satirical cry from Long John Baldry rang out in tones to curdle the blood of any scoutmaster. 'Ooh look, dear! Trade!'

Onstage he was equally unlikely, his immaculate figure towering through the cigarette smoke, a Savile Row suit straight out of some Mississippi bayou. To his teenage audiences his manner was at best caustic, at worst downright testy. On one famous night, he actually tapped an inattentive girl spectator on the head with his microphone.

When feminine chatter interrupted his emotional rendering of 'Black Is The Colour of My True Love's Hair', Long John broke off to shout that they were 'just a lot of Woolworth's shop girls'.

Like Mick Jagger, Long John got his big break as a singer with Alexis Korner's Blues Incorporated under the ABC teashop in Ealing. He had subsequently joined another great British blues eccentric, the harmonica-playing Cyril Davies. When Davies died in early 1964, Long John took over his backing band, renaming them the Hoochie Coochie Men and bringing in a sandpaper-voiced youth named Rod Stewart as second vocalist.

Unlike most blues purists, Long John Baldry had his eye firmly fixed on commercial success. His next venture was Steampacket, an early 'supergroup' combining Rod Stewart with Julie Driscoll and Brian Auger, the duo who would later produce a classic Sixties single, 'This Wheel's on Fire'. There were, indeed, too many potential stars in Steam Packet for it to last, and by late 1966 Long John was looking for another backup band.

Dropping in at the Cromwellian Club, South Kensington, one night, he happened to catch Bluesology playing in the basement. 'They were a good tight band,' Long John remembers now, 'though they didn't have a guitarist. And the Vox Continental their organist was playing looked rather hideous.' There and then Long John Baldry offered them the job of backing group to himself, paying them a flat weekly wage via his managers. Though Bluesology were already under contract to the jeweller Arnold Tendler, they instantly accepted what promised to be a far more attractive offer.

Long John's managers at the time were John and Rik Gunnell, sharp-operating brothers who had started the famous Flamingo Club in Soho and now had a virtual monopoly of white blues and soul acts, from Georgie Fame and Alan Price to Chris Farlowe and P. J. Proby. As well as the Flamingo, they ran the Bag o' Nails in Kingly Street, currently the in-club for London's rock-music aristocracy. Their reputation as tough guys was considerable. Arnold Tendler did not try to resist the poaching of his boys.

As Long John Baldry's sidemen, Bluesology were re-outfitted in yellow shirts with frilly fronts and cuffs, and green John Stephen suits whose double-breasted jackets buttoned from left shoulder to right hip. There was also an influx of bigger-time musicians, all but obliterating the original Pinner line-up. Mick Inkpen and Rex Bishop were replaced on drums and bass respectively by Pete Gavin and Freddy Gandy. A talented boy named Neil Hubbard took over from Stuart Brown on lead guitar. A clean sweep of the horn section brought in Marc Charig on trumpet and a tenor sax-player with an unusual Christian name, deriving from ancestors in Nottinghamshire. His name – half of it destined for immortality – was Elton Dean.

The new style was that Long John took the spotlight in his monogrammed silk suit, with husky-voiced Stuart Brown demoted to backup vocalist, and Reggie Dwight to backup backup vocalist. After a few weeks, Long John brought in another singer, Alan Walker, to harmonise with Stu Brown. Now Reggie wasn't even needed to do 'Oohs' and 'Aahs'.

A photograph of him in this period shows a figure anything but fulfilled, happy or comfortable. His hair is wedged into a Beatle fringe, as rigid and unnatural as the strip of handkerchief in his breast pocket. His pug face, with its unfashionable half-frame spectacles, is set in a resigned glower. His high-lapel jacket visibly strains at all three of its buttons. His discontent and frustration are almost ectoplasmic.

Long John says now he was not aware that Reggie ever nurtured ambitions as a vocalist. 'As far as I was concerned when I took on the group, Stuart Brown was the leader and the one with the voice. Later on, I even produced Stuart on a couple of demos of songs that Reggie had written.'

Elton Dean first noticed Reggie as a dispirited, silent figure out on the margin, not playing conspicuously well. Despite the modish prestige of the Vox organ, he never felt comfortable on it, or properly mastered its fingering. 'He didn't make mistakes. He didn't inspire you particularly, either,' Elton Dean remembers. 'He was just Reggie – or Bunter, I used to call him, 'cos he was a little bit portly and always used to wear striped blazers.'

To newcomers like Dean he seemed more like the band's archivist, the one who would find out-of-the-way blues numbers on forgotten labels to bolster their repertoire. 'He'd write songs and bring them to rehearsals, but none ever got done onstage. I never even knew he sang until I heard him do a number one day at a sound-check. Then I thought he sounded great. Just like José Feliciano.'

His frustrations became harder to restrain, especially under the influence of the amphetamine pills he was still taking in an effort to control his weight. The sudden squalls of his childhood reappeared, in what Long John satirically described as 'screaming fits'. Elton Dean remembers how, in a moment, the band's cheery fall-guy and one-man *Goon Show* could change to a glowering dressing-room recluse. Another couple of minutes and he'd be himself again. His fellow musicians used to call them Reggie's Little Moments.

3
'I feel lost'

EVERY so often Britain's TV audience is treated to selected re-runs of the Sixties TV pop programme, *Ready Steady Go!* Modern music fans can look back, with amusement or nostalgia, to a quintessential expression of Swinging London. They can see the stuffy old Rediffusion studio at the Aldwych end of Kingsway, which, each Friday just after tea, became as 'in' as the trendiest West End club. They can see the format, so daring for those primitive black-and-white days, that put musicians and audience together in open plan with the unconcealed hardware and freneticism of the studio floor. Everyone from polo-necked Beatles and barefoot Sandie Shaw to Martha and the Vandellas and James Brown's Famous Flames, surrounded by Mod crowds of their near-equals dancing along industrial catwalks or draped around iron fire escapes. A poignant monochrome memento of the last days when pop didn't have a care in the world.

The audience is of equal fascination, fresh-trawled from Carnaby Street or King's Road, in its hipsters and Mary Quant bobs, shaking, frugging, ponying, monkeying or hullygullying among the sound-booms and trundling cameras. Especially those young men one glimpses alone in the crowd, running combs through their Ringo mops and staring round them with eyes as bright and unblinking as baby piranha fish. The next generation of hustlers, entrepreneurs and tycoons is watching and waiting to get a fingernail or squared-off boot-toe into the business, anywhere.

Ray Williams first went to *RSG* as a fifteen-year-old fan from the Heathrow, Middlesex, area, following his local soul band, Cliff Bennett and the Rebel Rousers. When the band did well enough to be asked back, so was their loyal entourage. As Cliff and the boys belted out their first chart success, 'One Way Love', Ray appeared on camera, dancing in a gallery.

The decisive thing about Ray Williams was his almost ludicrous handsomeness. His hair was thick gold, his skin liqueur honey brown, his Delft china-blue eyes as wide open and ingenuous as Christopher Robin's. It was inevitable that, after a couple of weeks frugging with the extras on *Ready Steady Go!*, he should come to the notice of the show's presenter, Cathy McGowan. She made him her unofficial assistant, helping audition other girls and boys who hoped to feature as dancers. When he arrived at the TV studios on Friday nights, screaming girls would mob him as if he, too, were a pop star.

It was the high summer of Mod style, striped box jackets, peg-top trousers, button-down shirts and fringed faces composed into becoming scowls. Ray Williams grew famous as the ultimate specimen, regularly featured in *Mods Monthly* magazine. When any foreign camera team came to London to report on 'the scene', they usually ended up interviewing and photographing Ray.

At *Ready Steady Go!* he met a great many useful people, notably Brian Epstein, the Beatles' famous manager, and Brian Sommerville, their original public-relations man. The golden good looks were again decisive. He became Brian Sommerville's assistant, working out of a Tin Pan Alley office only yards from where Reggie Dwight was making tea and packing parcels. Not that anyone suggested that so gildedly handsome and right-looking a youth as Ray Williams should ever dampen his Mod blazer on an electric kettle or soil his mitred shirt cuffs with anything so mundane as brown paper and string.

At barely sixteen he was doing PR work for the Kinks, Sonny and Cher and Tommy Roe, a Buddy Holly clone who spirited him off to work in America. Thence, with a single Cuban-heeled leap, into publishing, running Lowry Music for Tommy Roe's manager. Thence into corporate life with his own organisation, Mayfair Public Relations, working with two young partners, Simon Hayes and Allan McDougall, from a house in Bruton Mews, off Berkeley Square. He was not yet quite eighteen. So things went in the summer of 1966.

Mayfair Public Relations represented Sonny and Cher, Buffalo Springfield, the Hollies and Cream. Simon Hayes also did some PR work for Brian Epstein, at that time becoming estranged from the Beatles and attempting to console himself with management of a West End theatre, the Saville.

The defection of Simon Hayes, in 1966, brought an end to Mayfair Public Relations. With the company went most of Ray Williams's resources, including the briefcase Tommy Roe had given him and the camera that had been a present from Sonny and Cher. But he retained his matchlessly good contacts, most crucially with Allan Clarke, Graham Nash and Tony Hicks of the Hollies.

In 1967, the American Liberty record label, previously licensed through British EMI, decided to set up its own self-contained European operation. By thought processes utterly logical to that youth-obsessed time, eighteen-year-old Ray Williams was appointed Liberty's European head of Artist and Repertoire, and installed behind an executive desk in Albemarle Street, Mayfair.

Two slight snags lay in this. The first was that Williams had no experience whatever in A & R, a job combining talent scout and record producer. The second was that Liberty – famed as the label of transatlantic legends like Bobby Vee and the Chipmunks – had virtually no artists under contract outside America.

The blond teenage tycoon was entirely undaunted. On his executive desk he drafted an advertisement, inviting would-be recording talent to come and audition for him at Liberty. The ad ran as a quarter-page in the *New Musical Express*, on 17 June, 1967. The aureoled face of New York's Statue of Liberty and her upheld torch drew attention to the enticing words:

LIBERTY

WANTS TALENT

ARTISTES / COMPOSERS / SINGERS / MUSICIANS

TO FORM NEW GROUP

Call or write Ray Williams for appointment or mail audition tape or disc to 11 Albemarle Street, London W1. Tel. Mayfair 7362.

Among the flood of applicants was one whom Ray Williams would have special cause to remember. 'This little dumpy guy came into my office,' Williams recalls. 'He was a bit fat, a bit forlorn-looking, dressed in blue denim, with all his stuff in a carrier bag, like Tiny Tim.' It was Reggie Dwight, of Pinner, Middlesex.

Reggie had seen the advertisement while gigging with Bluesology in Newcastle-on-Tyne. To an unhappy organ-player, somewhere to the rear of Long John Baldry's coat tails, it had seemed too good to be true. Liberty Records – another name of magic from his lonely bedroom hops – were not full to capacity with talent like Bobby Vee and the Chipmunks. In some humble or invisible capacity, there might be room for him, too.

Ray Williams's lordly title and letterhead had led him to expect some senior, intimidating management figure. Instead, he beheld the goldenly handsome young man of his own age, beautifully dressed, impressively secretaried but otherwise friendly, pleasant and sympathetic. 'We got on well from the start,' Williams remembers. 'We started talking like mates, really. He told me he was in a band, backing John Baldry, that he really wanted to sing, but Baldry wouldn't let him. "I feel lost" he said. What struck me most was how unloved he seemed. Plus coming out with a thing like that, which you'd hardly say even to a very close friend. I just felt so sorry for him.'

The Liberty advertisement, indeed, had come at a moment of terminal despair for Reggie. With no chance to sing in Bluesology, and no alternative prospects, he was thinking of quitting stage-performance altogether. He had even secretly gone to Philips Records and asked for a job as a record plugger, back in the painless faint glamour of Tin Pan Alley. Time and again through these early years, a kindly Providence would thwart his instinct to do exactly the wrong thing. Philips turned his application down. His mother bolstered his confidence and resolve yet again, helping him draft a reply to the *NME* ad in his neat music-student's writing.

Here he was, as a result, seated at Ray Williams's office piano, twitching his spectacles back up his nose and spreading his diminutive hands. At this crucial opportunity to display his talents, all memory of upbeat Bluesology material fled from Reggie's mind. Instead, he chose a slow country-and-western number, Jim Reeves's 'He'll Have To Go', charging its mournful, fatalistic words with all his own feelings of frustration and hopelessness.

The keening voice was like none in pop, save perhaps the young Latin-American José Feliciano. The song, in that time of Monkees and flower power, was practically an antique. That he was clearly an excellent pianist did not help at all. Under the long-running dominance of four-man guitar groups, the piano had been relegated to an old-fashioned parlour joke. A solo singer-pianist was as archaic a notion as Russ Conway or Winifred Atwell. Ray Williams could barely count the ways in which he was totally unhip.

A string of similar numbers followed in the same lachrymose vein from the Jim Reeves and Ray Charles song books, each as far as it could possibly be from current pop fashion. The climax was a plaintively whiteface version of Al Jolson's 'Mammy'. Williams still remembers how the forlorn figure changed completely as the music took hold. 'He didn't look sad and lost any more, but totally in command and relaxed.'

Despite the unsuitable songs and passionately non-commercial performance, Ray Williams was impressed. He suggested that, as Reggie had brought no audition tape, he should make a demo record. This Williams promised to play at the first opportunity to his American boss, Bob Reisdorf. For, despite the grandeur of his title, he himself had no power to sign talent on his own direct authority.

The demo was made at Regent Sound in Denmark Street, the studio where Andrew Loog Oldham had first recorded the Rolling Stones. 'Reggie just did the same numbers he'd already played in my office,' Williams remembers. 'At Regent, studio time still only cost five pounds an hour. I think we did it all inside one hour, with another hour for the mixing.'

In the course of that afternoon, Reggie admitted a further handicap. Though he could write tunes almost instantly and ad lib, he said he was 'no good' at lyrics. This even though song-lyrics by him had already been recorded, and even published as sheet-music.

Then Ray Williams remembered a letter from the huge shoal he had received after his *NME* advertisement. It was from another would-be songwriter with a handicap as large as Reggie's, in that he could not write music, only words. With the letter had come a sheaf of lyrics, typed on an ancient faint-ribboned machine. Quirkily interesting as Williams found them, he had seen no immediate practical use for them. Now his entrepreneurial instinct went to work, putting two and two – or, rather, one and one – together. He found the letter, handed it over with the lyrics that were enclosed, and suggested that Reggie have a crack at putting them to music. If there were any justice in the world the making of this one connection would have given Ray Williams riches for life. But, we can be assured, there is no justice in the world.

The letter had come from Lincolnshire, that slightly mysterious eastern county of flat farmland, mists, gypsies, medieval stone gargoyles and village names outlandish even by the standard of the English gazetteer. The address at the top of the page was 'Maltkiln Farm, Owmby-by-Spital'. The signature also was exotic: Bernard Taupin.

The name familiarly pronounced 'Torpin' by a generation of pop fans is, in fact, French, deriving from *taupe*, a mole, or *taupinière*, a molehill. It is a suitable trick of etymology for French stock that became transplanted to the deepest English countryside. Not bad, either, in its later twentieth-century meaning, for someone destined to be the supreme underground worker of popular music. Working silently as he has behind a blazing frontal talent, pursuing his own private, subterranean paths, shunning the light and limelight, Bernie

Taupin could very well be classified as a 'mole'.

The Taupin family originated in Burgundy. Bernie's paternal grandfather was a wine shipper who set up business in London but still preferred to raise his four sons and one daughter in wholly French style. Robert Taupin, Bernie's father, was born in London but sent to boarding school in Dijon. He intended to be a lawyer, but poor health interrupted his studies at the London School of Economics. Instead, the lycée-educated Frenchman decided to become an English farmer.

The literature and learning that were to influence Bernie's life came largely from his mother's people, the Corts, originally a family of Anglican clergymen in north-west England. His maternal great-great-grandfather and great-grandfather both served as vicar of the parish of St Anne's, in Sale, Cheshire. His grandfather, John Leonard Patchett Cort, was a schoolmaster, a Cambridge MA who taught on the naval training ship HMS *Conway* and later co-owned a private prep school in Reigate, Surrey.

His mother, Daphne, was academically gifted, although circumstances ruled out the university degree she might otherwise have taken. Just before World War II, the Corts moved to Switzerland, hoping to find a cure for Daphne's mother's acute asthma. There Daphne became fluent in French and studied French literature and Russian. On her mother's death, her father returned to England, but Daphne stayed in Switzerland throughout the war. There she became involved with the relief organisations bringing both Swiss and French children over the frontier for brief respite from the privations of Nazi-occupied France. Daphne herself would cross to the German side, risking internment as an enemy alien.

She met Robert Taupin in London just after the war, while working as children's nanny for his brother Henry. They married in 1947, and immediately set forth on Robert's farming career. Their first son, Tony, was born in 1948. Their second, Bernard, arrived in 1950. A third, Kit, was to follow eleven years later.

Bernie's memory of his early upbringing has the roseate glow of Laurie Lee's *Cider with Rosie*. Robert Taupin worked as a stockman for a large farm estate near Sleaford. The family lived in feudally tied accommodation, first a farm then a rambling old house named Rowston Manor, full of nooks and passageways that were paradise to an imaginative small boy.

The great influence on Bernie and his elder brother, Tony, was their grandfather Cort, the classics master, now both widowed and retired. 'Poppy', as the boys called him, fostered their interest in nature, teaching them to recognise plants, birds and butterflies. He also read them the great poems of English literature: Tennyson's 'Charge of the Light Brigade', Coleridge's 'Rime of the Ancient Mariner', Lord Macaulay's 'Lays of Ancient Rome'. While other village boys played simple cowboys and Indians, Bernie's infant games were all based on schoolroom classics, Scott's Lochinvar and Macaulay's epic tale of Horatius. 'Whenever I charged down a field, I was always Lochinvar. I'd take my friends down to the little stream we called the beck, which had a tiny bridge over it. I'd make them be the Tuscan hordes while I was Horatius, keeping them at bay while I recited the poem. I knew every stanza, word-perfect.'

His other initiation was into *Winnie-the-Pooh*. He loved A. A. Milne's archly *faux-naïf* tales of the Bear of Very Little Brain, Piglet, Rabbit and Eeyore. His great treat with Poppy was to play 'Poohsticks' – throwing twigs into the stream off one side of the bridge, and seeing which twig would come out first on the opposite side. Little did Bernie Taupin then dream his future destiny as Pigletish accomplice to a Pooh colourful beyond any illustration by E. H. Shepard.

The move to Owmby-by-Spital marked Robert Taupin's first independent farming venture as a smallholder and battery-chicken farmer. Maltkiln Farm comprised two dilapidated houses in the dead centre of the tiny hamlet, keeping company with its marshy field, a single barn and the chicken battery-house. In the beginning, there was neither running water nor mains sewerage. Baths had to be taken in a tin tub before the fire. The only lavatory was a chemical closet in the cellar.

Yet in this austere English setting, the habits of Robert's French upbringing prevailed, with evening dinner instead of high tea, oil-and-vinegar dressing instead of salad cream and wine served on occasions when Lincolnshire neighbours would have had bitter beer or sticky sweet sherry. Where other families went to church or 'chapel', Robert and the boys attended the Catholic church in nearby Market Rasen, where Bernie served as an altar-boy.

Encouraged both by his grandfather and his mother, he absorbed books through every pore: *Winnie-the-Pooh*, *The Wind in the Willows*, the Narnia stories of C. S. Lewis. He became fascinated by the American West, going beyond the pasteboard Hollywood version to read the true-life, often squalid adventures of Jesse James, Billy the Kid and Wyatt Earp. His parents had by now moved from their draughty, inconvenient farmhouse to a new bungalow a few yards away. Bernie used a room in the old house to create a museum of the fall of the Alamo, with a broken breadknife doubling as Jim

Bowie's eponymous blade, an old fur coat as Davy Crockett's coonskin cap, copper pennies as Colonel Travis's uniform buttons and bits of boundary-railing as Mexican lance-heads.

Almost as soon as he could read he had begun to write, stories and poetry. At the age of ten he decided to write a book on the American West, filling half a dozen pages of a school jotter and sending it boldly off to a publisher in London. 'I got a very sweet letter back, saying "There's nothing we can do with this at the present time",' Bernie remembers now. 'I was as thrilled by that as if they'd said they'd publish it.'

Like many another super-imaginative Fifties child, he was considered academically dull. While his brother Tony attained the glory of De Aston Grammar School, Bernie was relegated to Market Rasen Secondary Modern, a Treblinka-like establishment largely attended by half-witted farm boys whose hobnailed boots struck sparks off the concrete paths. Much of his first term was spent in hiding, to avoid the ritual initiation of having his head dunked in a toilet bowl.

Music was added to his excitements long before the onset of adolescence. On a visit to his father's brother Henry, in Putney, he discovered a stack of dusty 78 records by Woody Guthrie, 'Leadbelly' and their English interpreter Lonnie Donegan. For Bernie, it was a perfect extension of his fascination with Americana. In particular he loved Donegan's 'Rock Island Line', its story in droll recitative, building up to a triumphant comic pay-off. 'It was American history, the kind I could never get enough of from books. I loved the grittiness and reality of it.'

As a teenager he was still small and slight, with looks that seemed to come less from his French ancestors than from the gypsies that haunt Lincolnshire's roads and fens. His face, habitually shy and downcast, could break into a grin that was wolfish, even faintly dangerous. With the dreamy, romantic eyes went a libido that was active – even hyperactive – though his virginity was to remain intact until well after he had left Lincolnshire behind.

Living in Owmby-by-Spital meant being roughly two years to the rear of current teenage fashion. For a long time, Bernie's only contact with developing pop culture was a battered transistor radio his father used around the farm in the daytime. On this, after dark, he would listen to Radio Luxembourg or AFN, the American Forces Network, broadcast to the many US bases throughout East Anglia. Much as he loved rock 'n' roll, his preference was always for songs with a cowboyish, narrative feel: Johnny Cash's 'Ring of Fire', Johnny Horton's 'North to Alaska', especially Marty Robbins's doomy Mexican-flavoured ballads, 'El Paso' and 'Devil Woman'.

With pop to help him, the Catholic altar-boy grew up rough, racy and rash. He abandoned literature, birds and butterflies for the more dubious charms of Market Rasen, hanging out at a clothes boutique named Banger Hall's which kept its catalogue for winklepicker shoes chained to the counter. His appearance changed constantly, varying from Mod high collars to the blue jeans and patches of a Woody Guthrie hobo. He went with a gang that indulged in petty burglary of mobile shops and fish-and-chip vans, and was himself not above vandalising contraceptive machines, even filching the occasional five-pound note from his hard-working father's wallet. In pursuit of girls, he frequented all the toughest Saturday night dances, relying on luck or fast-talking chutzpah to avoid trouble with Lincolnshire's archaic but no less frightening Teddy boys. 'If you said you liked the same music they did, that always helped. In a tight spot, you could try mentioning Little Richard or Jerry Lee Lewis. It was like taking the thorn out of the lion's paw.'

His interest in writing flared up and lapsed erratically until one memorable night under the covers with his father's transistor radio. On crackly Radio Luxembourg, he heard Bob Dylan's 'The Times They Are a-Changin''. 'I'd only seen Bob Dylan's name written down before. I didn't even know how to pronounce it. Suddenly through the static comes this plaintive guitar and this amazing voice. To me, folk music had always meant tunes you heard on BBC *Children's Favourites* – Burl Ives or "An English Country Garden". This voice was like broken glass, like spitting. The words were like arrows, being shot straight into the heart of the Establishment. That was what made me realise what the words of a song could do.'

Not that the lesson seemed of any practical use. Leaving school at fifteen, he tried to get a job as a reporter on a local paper, the *Lincolnshire Standard*, but instead found himself apprenticed in the printroom. It was a steady job, such as was then prized, with ancillary night-school courses leading to a diploma five years hence. To alleviate the boredom and hatred of setting up wedding invitations and raffle-tickets on an antiquated Heidelberg press, he took to drinking heavily. One night he was discovered in a field near his home, trying to feed crème de menthe to cows in order to produce green milk.

From here on, as in some eighteenth-century poem heard at his grandfather's knee, Bernie started to go to the bad. Tempted by a job as a fruit-machine mechanic, he threw up his printer's apprenticeship, badmouthing the foreman and tossing a valedictory ink trowel into the Heidelberg press. When the slot machine life did not materialise, he frowsted at home, living off his parents, contemplating no career beyond vague notions of life as a professional housebreaker.

It was early 1967. In the world always tantalisingly two years ahead of Owmby-by-Spital, pop songs now teemed with words and images such as had always filled Bernie Taupin's head. He himself was working as a labourer on a chicken farm, carting hundreds of corpses to be incinerated during an outbreak of fowl pest. 'I've got a photograph of myself bundled up against the wind, surrounded by all these dead bodies, looking like some scene from *The Killing Fields*.'

At night in his bedroom he would scribble endless, yearning parodies of the Beatles' 'Strawberry Fields Forever', Bob Dylan's 'Rainy Day Woman', the Byrds' 'Mr Tambourine Man', Procol Harum's 'A Whiter Shade of Pale'. That June, when he chanced on Ray Williams's advertisement in the *New Musical Express*, Bernie had been fired from the chicken farm and was 'literally at a dead end'. In common with another pessimistic youth a hundred miles away, he could not imagine that 'talent wanted' meant what it said. 'I was so far from the centre of everything. I had no idea how record companies or songwriters worked. I just thought that maybe something I'd written might be of some use to someone, somewhere down the line.'

On an ancient portable typewriter he picked out a letter to Ray Williams and enclosed a sheaf of his newest poems. He then put it on the living-room mantelpiece and, by his own account, 'forgot all about it'. Fortunately, his mother noticed it there and posted it for him.

The result was a scene Bernie had read so many times, with envious longing, in Enid Blyton books for older children. The village postman coming up the path, bearing an ivory-white envelope with a London postmark. A crested letter, thanking him for his poems and suggesting he should call in and see Ray Williams at Liberty Records, next time he happened to be in Albemarle Street, Mayfair.

To Reggie, the visit to Albemarle Street at first seemed just another dead end. Friendly and sympathetic as Ray Williams had been, he could offer no quick way out of the situation with Bluesology. In the immediate term, all he could offer was a sheaf of lyrics with mystifying titles like 'Sad-Eyed Queen of Laughing Lake', and 'Year of the Teddy Bear'. And a promise to put the lyricist, Bernie Taupin, and Reggie together as soon as possible.

The truth was that Williams's *NME* advertisement had produced other applicants of far more obvious potential than Reggie Dwight. The most obvious find was a group of modish eccentrics called the Bonzo Dog Doo-Dah Band, soon to enjoy a hit with the quasi-comic 'Urban Spaceman'. Two other young men originally signed by Ray

Williams to Liberty would go on to massive money-spinning chart success in the early Seventies. One was Jeff Lynne, later of the Move and Electric Light Orchestra. The other was Mike Batt, musical director to that whimsical goldmine, the Wombles.

Despite all these more colourful attractions and distractions, Ray Williams went out on a limb for Reggie Dwight as far as he could. He still felt certain there was 'something' in the voice and the stubbornly unfashionable piano style. He also felt strangely obligated to the forlorn figure who had confessed so readily to feeling lost and desperate, yet was also funny, unpretentious and engaging. Like many afterwards, Ray Williams took Reggie's part, most of all, because he liked him.

He played Reggie's audition tape to Liberty's European head, Bob Reisdorf, and the head of promotion, Andrew Lauder. Neither could see anything in the mournful mix of Jim Reeves and José Feliciano that would warrant putting it under contract. Williams's secondary hope was that Liberty's publishing company, Metric Music, might sign up Reggie on the basis of his songwriting alone. But Metric's boss, Alan Keane, also declined the opportunity.

It so happened this was not the first time Williams's instincts had been thwarted by his Liberty bosses. A few weeks earlier, he had unsuccessfully tried to interest Metric Music in a pair of young Midlands songwriters named Nicky James and Kirk Duncan. Rather than let them go, Williams had taken them on independently, quartering them in his Bruton Mews house, renting a piano for them and, in airy teenage tycoon style, promising to form a company to divide the proceeds of their songs when these should eventually materialise. The company name – an amalgam of Nicky, Ray and Kirk – was to be Niraki Music.

From there, thanks to his past life as a PR man, Ray Williams had been able to wheel a further deal. He was still on friendly terms with Graham Nash, Allan Clarke and Tony Hicks of the Hollies. Graham, Allan and Tony had their own acronymic publishing company, Gralto, which in turn was managed by Britain's most successful song publisher, Dick James. It was easy for Ray Williams to strike an agreement whereby Niraki's output would be published by Gralto, under the umbrella of its parent organisation, Dick James Music.

Hence Ray Williams's power to offer at least a crumb of compensation to Reggie Dwight for failing the Liberty audition. He introduced Reggie to Nicky James and Kirk Duncan, both of whom were adept at writing the lyrics Reggie could or would not. He also brought Reggie, at however distant an initial remove, into the orbit of Dick James.

Dick James's legendary luck did not show itself for the first three decades of his life. Born in 1919 of Polish parentage in London's East End, he began life as a dance-band crooner, changing his name from Isaac Vapnick to cut a more romantic figure at the microphone. Throughout the Forties and Fifties he earned a decent living with British bandleaders like Geraldo and Cyril Stapleton, but was never up in the big league like Dickie Valentine or Ronnie Hilton. Unluckily losing his hair, he was obliged to perform romantic numbers like 'Tenderly' in a 'rug'. His biggest moment on record came in 1955, with the launch of commercial television in Britain. An early children's series, *The Adventures of Robin Hood*, took him into the Top 20 with its memorably tacky theme song.

Fortune did not smile on Dick James until November 1962, after he had quit the dance bandstand and set up as a music publisher in a poky office in London's Tin Pan Alley. He was not doing well – was, in fact, doing very badly – when his friend George Martin, head of Parlophone Records, rang up to try to interest him in the work of an unknown pop group from Liverpool. The publisher gave a cuddly laugh into which was gathered twenty years of know-how and experience. 'Liverpool!' he echoed. 'So what's from Liverpool?'

Dick James's first stroke of luck was getting a second chance. George Martin kept badgering him until he agreed to see the new group's manager, Brian Epstein, and hear a just-pressed copy of their record, 'Please Please Me'.

It was on the day of his meeting with Brian Epstein, however, that James's luck grew gorgeous and glorious. Epstein had meant to see another publisher first but on arriving for this appointment was told the other man hadn't turned up. Instead, it was suggested he should play his group's new record to the office-boy. Stalking out in crimson-faced fury, he arrived at Dick James's half an hour early. By a last semiquaver of Heaven-sent fortune, James was already there, and amenable to seeing his flustered visitor without delay. That is how he became publisher of John Lennon and Paul McCartney, the most stupendously successful and profitable songwriting partnership ever.

Luck, of course, is nothing unless tempered with energy and vision. The vision of Dick James was not to absorb Lennon and McCartney into his own existing organisation on the traditional meagre 10 per cent royalty. Rather, he created a separate company, Northern Songs, to be managed by him on their behalf, the proceeds split 50–50. It was a genuine example of fair-mindedness prompted by James's own days as a vocalist, when he would be paid only a flat £15 studio fee even for recording an international hit. Hence the ancillary miracle of the Beatles, managed by Brian Epstein, recorded by George Martin and published by James. The biggest show-business phenomenon of all time was directed by three honest men.

Of these, Dick James was always the most universally liked. A sunny-natured man, older than his forty-odd years, he was the archetype of the avuncular impresario, bald, pear-shaped and bespectacled, with a voice that retained its woofly calm, whether ringing round his matchless business contacts or calming the neuroses of his youthful protégés. Happily married, with a lovely home, a lovely car and lovely friends, he lived each day in a state of visible pleasure and gratitude to Providence, often exuberantly breaking out into one or other of his old hits, 'Tenderly' or the theme from *Robin Hood*.

The brainwave he had for Northern Songs was ironically to spell the end of James's own Tin Pan Alley milieu. Writing and publishing their own work, it was not long before the Beatles also began supervising their own sessions in the recording studio. In the rush to emulate them, Denmark Street's cosy hierarchy of chainsmoking 'professional' songwriters, arrangers, pluggers and A & R men had been all but swept away. Only Dick James, the ultimate Tin Pan Alleyite, could be said, with his astounding luck, to have stayed ahead of the game.

In the hugely transformed music business of 1967, his name was still a synonym for heaven's most profligate bounty. Northern Songs had become a public company, reaping vast dividends for its managing director in exact proportion to its unstoppable creative partnership. His own organisation, Dick James Music – which published no Beatles material after 'Please Please Me' – had waxed powerful in its own right, with numerous other catalogue acquisitions that seemed to confirm an unfailing Midas touch.

The new, improved headquarters of Dick James Music at 71–75 New Oxford Street, situated symbolically above the Midland Bank, could lay some claim to being the powerhouse of British pop. In administering Northern Songs, it was the most visible adjunct of the Beatles' empire – not yet formalised into Apple Corps – a calling-place for individual Beatles with their retinues, and for all seeking to cover Beatle songs, from Peter and Gordon to the London Symphony Orchestra. James's partnership with Brian Epstein, a company called Jaep, published the million-selling Merseybeat hits of Cilla Black and Billy J. Kramer and the Dakotas, and brought further large helpings of glamour in through the doors of 71–75 New Oxford Street.

In the four years since his Northern Songs coup every young

songwriter who dreamed of becoming a Lennon or a McCartney had beaten a path straight to Dick James's door. No successful pop act who copied John and Paul and formed a publishing company felt it was quite complete without his name on its masthead. Dick James Music was a warren of such companies, run by James on the same triumphantly equitable split. He owned 50 per cent of the Hollies' Gralto company, of Gerry Marsden's Pacermusic and the Spencer Davis Group's Spencer Davis Music. He was a partner in Cookaway Music, formed by Roger Greenaway and Roger Cook (a duo later globally successful with songs like 'Home Lovin' Man' and the Coca-Cola theme, 'I'd Like to Teach the World to Sing'). He was the publishing side of impresario Larry Page's Page One organisation, so enjoying a share in contemporary chart smashes like the Troggs' 'Wild Thing'. To the young writers, performers and session musicians who daily thronged his premises he seemed like some great, bluff broody hen that, ever and again, would shift its grey worsted wings to reveal yet another golden egg or gold disc.

Large as the DJM operation had become, it still functioned in the comfortable way of old-fashioned family business. The only share-holders were Dick James and his old friend and accountant Charles Silver. The executive staff were mostly men of James's own age who had known him since the days of sheet music and Geraldo's orchestra. His only son Stephen, now aged twenty, had worked in the business since leaving school at sixteen, and was very obviously the apple of his father's eye. A former employee remembers the morning executive meeting in Dick James's office as a running dialogue with Mrs James on the telephone and Stephen at his right hand. 'Your mother says, "Is the new shirt all right?" He says, "The new shirt's fine."'

Though as inclined to arrogance as any boss's son of twenty, Stephen James had shown genuine flair for music publishing and management. He was a successful plugger of DJM songs, having matched 'I Can't Let Go' to the Hollies, 'Needles and Pins' to the Searchers and 'Wild Thing' to Larry Page's Troggs. As the Beatles and Northern Songs claimed more and more of Dick James's attention, he gave Stephen increased executive power, eventually entrusting him with the whole organisation's day-to-day running.

By 1966, Stephen James was growing impatient with the traditional empire his father ruled at 71–75 New Oxford Street. To him, the job of hawking songs around until they reached the right performer seemed a time-consuming, labour-intensive way of earning not very much. With the Beatles and so many other hit artists writing their own songs, it was becoming harder and harder to persuade anyone to record a number written by someone else. Just as ultimately unrewarding was DJM's 'umbrella' method of handling sub-publishing for American record labels like CBS and Liberty, whereby one sedulously built up a catalogue's value only to lose it at the end of a two- or three-year agreement.

The ascendancy of the singer-songwriter – like the American Bob Dylan and his English counterpart, Donovan – offered far more attractive economics. With such an artist under contract, DJM could bypass the whole time-consuming, low-profit rigmarole of matching material to performer. They could also look forward to publishing all ten tracks on an album, instead of just one or two. All this Stephen James successfully argued with his father – and also the immediate requirement for implementing it. The company had always had taping facilities for writers to put down basic outlines of voice and piano or guitar. Stephen urged that, to nurture singer-songwriter talent, Dick James Music must have its own in-house recording studio.

To carping onlookers this, of course, looked very much like adoring impresario father giving son a recording studio for his birthday. None could have dreamed it would bring Dick James his second piece of once-in-a-lifetime luck.

The studio was established in an empty space at the rear of DJM's first-floor executive suite. As in all DJM interior décor, thrift was the watchword. 'I bought a Studer four-track system secondhand from EMI, Abbey Road,' Stephen James remembers now. 'A guy I knew, who went on to build Neve mixing desks, put a little mixing outfit together for me in his garage.' The original plan had been to produce only demos – rough demonstration versions of new songs. But the guy in his garage built a mixing desk sophisticated enough to produce masters, or finished versions, ready for manufacture.

Along with the new studio, Stephen set up a production company to handle the in-house talent that might eventually evolve, named with a more than faint tinge of boss's-son arrogance. 'I called it This Record Co., because "this" is an anagram of "hits" and "shit".'

At that stage it was not a sufficiently grown-up studio to necessitate hiring a grown-up manager and technical staff. Instead, the job was given to a teenager whose father Dick James had known in the dance-band days and who'd just joined DJM from Paxton's sheet music wholesalers. It was Caleb Quaye, the same who used to tease Mills Music's office boy for looking so very much like Billy Bunter.

The studio was available to all the songwriters and musicians of whose companies DJM owned a part: Roger Greenaway and Roger Cook of Cookaway Music, Spencer Davis, Eddie Hardin and Peter York of Spencer Davis Music, Graham Nash, Allan Clarke and Tony Hicks of the Hollies' Gralto. With the Hollies came the two young songwriters whom Ray Williams had recommended to them: Nicky James and Kirk Duncan. Tagging along with Nicky and Kirk came Williams's other protégé, the forlorn piano player Reggie Dwight.

Nicky and Kirk had begun to do extremely well. Not only did the Hollies like their work; so did the man who owned 50 per cent of the Hollies' Gralto publishing company, and towered over the whole pop industry with his phenomenal luck. Dick James himself had put them each under a £10 weekly retainer in expectation of songs they would write, if not for the Hollies then for other performers serviced by Dick James Music. They also had virtual *carte blanche* at the in-house studio to produce demo versions of their work.

This facility they generously extended to their new collaborator, Reggie Dwight. Throughout the hot summer of 1967, all Reggie's time off from touring with Bluesology was spent with Nicky James and Kirk Duncan at the Dick James studio. A scratch band evolved, with him on piano, Dave Hinds on drums and Tony Murray – later of the Troggs – on bass.

They were producing only demos of the songs written by Reggie with either Nicky or Kirk, which Nicky and Kirk's Niraki company could then offer the Hollies' Gralto company for possible use by them or some other established pop artist. Reggie Dwight's vocals were no more than blueprints for how the song might eventually be worked out. Kirk Duncan remembers how little confidence he seemed to have in his singing voice. 'He was very quiet, very humble,' Duncan says. 'Whenever I mentioned he might be good enough as a vocalist in his own right, he just didn't want to know.'

It had not helped Reggie's confidence to realise the studio engineer was Caleb Quaye, his fellow messenger, and leg-puller, back in Mills Music days. The Bunter tag first attached to him by Caleb had dogged him ever since. The last thing he thought was that anyone would ever want to hear a song sung by the Fat Owl of the Remove.

If Caleb's first instinct had been to start teasing Reggie again, it changed on seeing the professional musician he had become. Even on this humble demo work, his approach was brisk and businesslike, sitting straight down, spreading his stubby fingers and getting on with it. When Caleb himself left the control room to sit in with the band on guitar, his attitude to Reggie changed from respect to downright admiration. 'It was so obvious he'd got something special,' Caleb says now. 'Every day, a little bit more of it would come out.'

Quiet and businesslike as he usually was, there were moments when he could become exuberant, extrovert, even slightly demented. 'I remember once, we'd been working non-stop,' Kirk Duncan says. 'Reg was leaning on the desk, and he started shouting like some mad Hollywood agent. "I'm going to make you a star, my boy! A star!" He ran outside, down the passage, through the cutting-room, back through the studio and out again, screaming at the top of his voice. And he'd sometimes do the same thing in the street.'

In the first-floor studio he met all the big names from the current Top 10 and his own Pinner record collection. Often, to his amazement, they were not the standoffish demigods he had imagined, but just friendly young men a little older than himself, interested in his work, unselfishly willing to offer help and advice from their own practical experience. Graham Nash of the Hollies – who were to publish Niraki's eventual output – became such an adviser and friend. Another was Roger Greenaway, who had formerly been a pop star with Roger Cook (David and Jonathan) and was now a successful songwriter and pioneer of ad hoc studio-only bands like White Plains.

Kirk Duncan gives a poignant picture of how unknown backroom boys like Reggie Dwight and himself were swept up into the entourages of heedlessly wealthy pop stars. 'We hardly ate, we hardly slept, we were paupers. And all night we'd be around with people like Graham Nash and Allan Clarke of the Hollies. We'd go to the Bag O'Nails. There'd be a bottle of Scotch, a bottle of brandy and a dozen Cokes on the table – and no food! We were in these swish places, literally starving, and down at heel. Graham Nash had to buy me a pair of shoes once.'

It was only a week or so after Reggie's unsuccessful audition at Liberty that Bernie Taupin, mustering every resource at his command, managed to 'happen to be' in Albemarle Street, Mayfair. To the innocent Lincolnshire farm boy, Ray Williams's airy suggestion that he should call in and 'have a word' about his lyrics seemed like the summons of Destiny. So he successfully portrayed it to his long-suffering parents, ex-colleagues at jobs he'd failed to hold down and cronies around the chained-up shoe-catalogue at Banger Hall's boutique. Like Dick Whittington, Pip in *Great Expectations* and every other worthwhile hero in his hundred favourite books, Bernie was off to London to seek his fortune.

It was arranged that, pending the making of this fortune, he should lodge with his father's brother, Uncle Henry, in Putney. His spinster aunt Tati, who lodged in the house and to whom he was very close, promised his mother to keep an eye on him. His departure brought a moment of closeness with his father, the taciturn farmer to whom he had latterly been such a trial. As Bernie's early morning train to Kings Cross left St Mark's station, something made him lean forward and kiss Robert Taupin hard on the cheek.

His first meeting with Ray Williams at Liberty Records was enough to convince Bernie that he'd jumped straight into the big time. 'As I went in, I saw Graham Nash of the Hollies on the stairs. Graham Nash of the Hollies! My mouth just fell open.'

Like other respondents to Williams's *NME* ad, Bernie was amazed by the youth and blond beauty of Liberty's A & R chief. An agreeable conversation ensued, in which Ray Williams broke it to him that his lyrics were of no immediate use to Liberty Records. However, there was a piano player, working indirectly for Williams, who needed someone who could write words. The unpromising name of that piano player was Reggie Dwight.

Ray Williams set up a meeting between Bernie and Reggie Dwight the next day, at Dick James Music. Bernie travelled up from Putney to New Oxford Street in the nearest his small, battered suitcase could muster to a 'trendy' outfit. 'I only had the one jacket – a hideous moth-eaten blue double-breasted thing that was much too small for me.' To hide his extreme nervousness, he sported thick sunglasses.

When he arrived at DJM, Reggie was busy in the in-house studio doing a piano overdub. Bernie sat and waited meekly in the control room. At one point, the engineer, Caleb Quaye, turned round and inquired 'Are you supposed to be here?' The sunglasses he had worn in an effort to be cool produced another disconcerting moment. 'Somebody said "Nice shades, man." And I had no idea what they were talking about.'

After a while, Reggie came out, noticed him there and said 'Hi, are you the lyricist?' Bernie admitted that he was. The two of them went for a cup of coffee at the Lancaster Grill in Tottenham Court Road.

The initial bond was between two pop music fans of equal fanaticism and encyclopaedic knowledge. Despite the three-year difference in their ages, they discovered they felt the same about everything that mattered: Tamla Motown, the Beatles, the words of Bob Dylan's 'Subterranean Homesick Blues', the Spanish guitar solo on Marty Robbins's 'Devil Woman'. Their mutual shyness vanished as they exchanged the lore and trivia they had soaked up for years from tinny record players in bedrooms a hundred miles apart. Reggie warmed at once to the slight, shabby boy whose extreme diffidence was tempered with flashes of gypsyish mischief. Bernie instantly liked the podgy piano player who, twitching his specs up on his nose, confessed to being not nearly the big shot he had initially seemed.

'Even though he was there on the scene, plugged right into the circuit,' Bernie remembers now, 'I got the feeling he was rather isolated from it all.'

The more they talked, the more their disparities drew them together. Their childhoods, blissful and miserable. Their fathers, loving and remote. Their homes, a suburban maisonette and a farm. Their most recent work experience, playing in a blues club and carting chicken corpses to the incinerator.

'We were complete opposites – town mouse and country mouse,' Bernie Taupin says. 'But the one thing we had in common was being mad about pop music. And both being desperate to write songs.' Over two cups of coffee in the Lancaster Grill, they decided to give it a try.

Bluesology's third and final attempt to be a hit band in their own right was recorded in August 1967. They had switched labels from Fontana to Polydor and put themselves in the hands of Kenny Lynch, a pop star turned producer (afterwards to become a well-known TV compère and comic). As well as producing them, Lynch co-wrote the A-side, 'Since I Found You, Baby', and the B-side, 'Just a Little Bit'. If Reggie Dwight had felt smothered before, he now felt wholly disinvented. Not only did Stuart A. Brown sing lead vocal on both sides, but the billing on the record was amended to 'Stu Brown and Bluesology'. The finished product was so lacklustre that Polydor sat on it for two months, finally releasing it in October, to deafening public apathy. Like Jack Baverstock at Fontana, Kenny Lynch cannot now remember anything about working with the future Elton in the studio.

In the travelling band that supported Long John Baldry, his life was more frustrating than ever. The hubristic Long John had now added a third singer to the backup line that kept Reggie in keyboard-pounding obscurity. The newcomer was an ebullient black girl named Marsha Hunt, later to achieve fame as the star of *Hair* and the mother of Mick Jagger's first daughter. Though visually stunning, she possessed but a marginal singing voice. 'She only knew one number – "Love Is a Many-Splendored Thing",' the future star would recall. 'She didn't know what key she wanted, so she had to do it unaccompanied. And she was really terrible. But looked amazing. So Baldry said "All right dear, you're in."'

In London Reggie had by now introduced his new collaborator to his two associates in Niraki Music. Nicky James and Kirk Duncan both leafed through Bernie Taupin's lyrics and agreed there could well be 'something' there. They did not at all object to Reggie's starting an additional songwriting partnership with the seventeen-year-old boy in absurdly cool 'shades' who made himself as small as possible in corners of the DJM control room.

The new team's first song came from a Bernie poem, redolent of his Lincolnshire farm background, called 'Scarecrow'. Reggie then made a demo version of it in Nicky and Kirk's studio time at Dick James Music. It never became a finished track either on a single or album, and has long since disappeared into the vaults of its composers' corporate past. Bernie Taupin still remembers the thrill of taking the first rough acetate back to Putney to show his Uncle Henry and Aunt Tati.

The idea had been that Reggie should write with Bernie in alternation with Nicky James and Kirk Duncan. 'But as soon as they got together, it was obvious that magic was starting to happen,' Kirk Duncan remembers. The song list that has survived shows what a dichotomy was instantly at work. With Kirk Duncan Reggie would write something called 'Who's Gonna Love You?'. With Nicky James he would write something called 'Where It's At'. With Bernie Taupin he would write something called 'A Dandelion Dies in the Wind'.

Neither Nicky nor Kirk objected to this either. They were happy to see Reggie and Bernie evolve as a separate partnership that would be a further asset to their nascent publishing company, Niraki Music. The deal with Dick James was that when Niraki accumulated £10,000-worth of song copyrights, it would become a full company within the Hollies' Gralto company, within Dick James Music. It would then be able to put Reggie and Bernie under contract and take a share of their earnings. Nicky James and Kirk Duncan accordingly gave Reggie and Bernie every encouragement.

Having nerved themselves to begin, they found they could work at phenomenal speed. Within a week or so, they had produced more than a dozen songs to add to Niraki Music's embryonic catalogue. In this initial phase, they worked together only intermittently. There were frequent breaks when Reggie was hauled reluctantly back on tour with Bluesology, and Bernie wrote on in isolation at his Uncle Henry's, or back home in Owmby-by-Spital. As each new set of lyrics poured from him, he would post them to Reggie out on the road.

The postal method was to continue in much the same way even after they had come within permanent earshot of one another. Shyness and embarrassment on both sides dictated the *modus operandi*. Bernie would arrive at the Dick James studio with a sheaf of words, which, at some point, Reggie would take off to a piano in another room. In ten minutes or so, the song would be delivered back to Bernie, parcelled up tight in robust, professional chords.

As each new song was written, Reggie would demo it in the Dick James studio. Caleb Quaye, the engineer, allowed virtually unlimited time for each to be worked on, less and less as a rough sketch for some future performer than as a refinement of Reggie Dwight's own, gradually more confident and distinctive version. With Caleb's indulgence, the sessions went on late into each night, using Dick James's electricity and amenities long after most lights had dimmed along that rather isolated stretch of New Oxford Street.

For a break, they would go to the nearby Gioconda coffee bar, a place now empty of its daytime Tin Pan Alley clientèle and more likely to be occupied by drunks and derelicts. Or to the Lancaster Grill, that businessmen's venue in Tottenham Court Road, where Reggie and Bernie first sealed their partnership. Or to a cheapo Indian restaurant, L'Orient, which football-mad, pun-mad Reggie renamed Leyton Orient.

It surprised the country mouse at first that the town mouse was willing to sing everything he wrote, without the slightest quibble or demur. He did not realise how glad Reggie was to be saved from any part of lyric-writing, that old, inexplicable blind spot. No lyric was too literary, fanciful or obscure for this process of instant ventriloquism. Reggie's part in the words was purely sub-editorial, switching a verse here, reprising one there, occasionally cutting one altogether. Nor did Bernie try to influence the tune beyond tentative suggestions that this might be a slow ballad, that an uptempo rocker. Not infrequently the slow ballad he had imagined would come back to him as an uptempo rocker, and vice versa. For almost all his life as a lyric-writer, he was never to be quite certain what the postman would bring.

4

Hits and Shit

ALL through that fabled 1967 Summer of Love, Reggie Dwight and Bernie Taupin were outsiders, looking on wistfully with noses pressed against the glass. They saw the coming of hippies, of kaftans, sandals, tinkly bells and smoking joss-sticks. They heard the siren-soft voice of Scott McKenzie, bidding them go to San Francisco, see the 'gentle people' and wear flowers in their hair, even though at the time they were hard put to raise a double bus-fare across London or the price of a toasted sandwich at the Gioconda. Like half Britain's young men, Reggie became a quasi-hippy, draping his cardboard Carnaby clothes with hopefully mystical necklaces, pendants, thongs and amulets. Bookish Bernie became swept up in the hippy craze for J.R.R. Tolkien's donnish fantasies, *The Hobbit* and *The Lord of the Rings*. Lyrics handed or posted to Reggie suddenly teemed with echoes of Bilbo Baggins, Frodo, Gollum and the Dark Lord of Mordor.

With the new 'underground' counterculture came billow after billow of new pop sound, transfixing to the two record fans, inspirational to the two incorrigible copycats. The nasal sneer of 'electric' Dylan, the brassy strut of Memphis soul, the acid blues of Cream, the shivery pyrotechnics of the Jimi Hendrix Experience, the accents, licks and riffs of Jefferson Airplane, Canned Heat, Pink Floyd, the Foundations, the Warm Sound, the Flowerpot Men, the Honeybus, all worked their way, somewhere or other into the late-night sessions in Dick James's demo-studio.

Above all, the Beatles continued to be a seven-league leap ahead of all competition. That June, they had released *Sgt. Pepper's Lonely Hearts Club Band*, their album masterpiece, combining high-fashion psychedelia and mysticism with the whimsical mateyness of a Liverpool variety show. *Sgt. Pepper* instantly set a new style for pop LPs with its narrative form, its elaborately in-joking cover, its cargo of giveaway novelties, paper sergeant's chevrons and false moustaches. It was no sooner in the shops than the Beatles embraced hippydom, chanting their simplistic anthem 'All You Need Is Love' via a world television hook-up that reached an estimated audience of 400 million.

That summer was the time of greatest-ever Beatles songs, 'She's Leaving Home', 'Lucy In The Sky With Diamonds', 'A Day In the Life'. All were handled by the world's luckiest publisher, Dick James, in blissful unawareness that, on his own premises after dark, two unknown songwriters were producing a parallel Beatle-cum-Tolkien repertoire: 'Regimental Sergeant Zippo', 'Year of the Teddy Bear', 'Mr Lightning Strikerman', 'The Tide Will Turn For Rebecca'.

Few now remember what a dark underside the Summer of Love often revealed or how, along with the feathers and bells, its recurring motifs were pitiless warfare, official vindictiveness, mob fury and profligate death. In America, as the hippies sunned themselves in Haight-Ashbury, northern cities erupted into racial violence. In Vietnam, the helicopter gunships spread their healing flame over thatched villages. In Egypt, Jordan and Syria, the tanks incinerated their trapped consignments of young men.

While half Britain was intoxicated by pop music, the other half railed against it with the ferocity of seventeenth-century witchfinders. Composite villain and martyr of the hour was Mick Jagger of the Rolling Stones, the band most condemned for turning young people to rebellion, immorality and drugs. In reality a negligible drug-user, Jagger had been 'exposed' as a boasting dope-fiend by the gutter-press *News of the World*. His attempt to sue for libel only turned the paper loose on a vigorous campaign to dig up some genuine dirt that could be passed on to an overtly receptive police force. The result was the famous 'Redlands' drug bust at Keith Richard's house, where Jagger was caught in possession of four innocuous amphetamine pills, subjected to a vicious show trial and clapped into jail amid audible public rejoicing.

Though Jagger was quickly freed – largely thanks to a courageous editorial in *The Times* – his mistake would stand as a lesson to all pop stars over the next twenty years. However gross the lies written about you in sensationalist newspapers, there was no point in trying to sue. The papers were too powerful, with their huge resources, their batteries of lawyers and teams of muck-raking spies and sneaks. Anyone who took them on could only get in deeper and deeper.

On the August Bank Holiday weekend of 1967, the Beatles left London by excursion train, accompanying their new-found Indian spiritual teacher, Maharishi Mahesh Yogi, for a course of transcendental meditation in Bangor, North Wales. That same weekend their manager Brian Epstein walked out of a dinner-party in Kingsley Hill,

Sussex, to return alone to his Belgravia house. Next morning, he was found dead of what a coroner would later describe as 'incautious drink and drug overdoses'.

Epstein's death increased the high public profile of the Dick James Organisation. Helpless without their all-protecting manager, the Beatles instinctively turned to those whom Brian had made part of the original, impermeable shield, their record-producer and their publisher. Had James wished, there is little doubt he could have assumed their management; temporarily perhaps, but for long enough to avert the huge financial and emotional chaos of their efforts to run their own affairs.

Dick James knew that, whatever short-term healing might take place, the deepening rift between John Lennon and Paul McCartney must inevitably finish the Beatles. His most urgent worry was as managing director of Northern Songs, the company he had created as a joint venture with Lennon and McCartney to publish their prodigious output. Northern had gone public in 1965 and now had 3,000 shareholders, to whom James owed as much duty as to his own large residual stockholding. The nervous souls of the Stock Exchange could not be expected to understand that, whatever happened, Lennon and McCartney's song catalogue would continue earning fortunes for ever. Any rumour of a Beatles breakup would be sure to send Northern's share price plummeting. With these and other Fab Four preoccupations filling his mind, Dick James had little attention to spare for goings-on at his own offices.

The goings-on might never have come to light but for DJM's position above the New Oxford Street branch of the Midland Bank. Though relaxed enough about daytime traffic up and downstairs, the Midland was understandably sensitive about activity near its strongrooms after dark. Anyone working late at DJM had to give due warning to the bank's security staff.

Late one night, DJM's office manager, a former dance-band drummer named Ronnie Brohn, chanced to be driving past 71–75 New Oxford Street. To his alarm, he saw a light in the first-floor executive corridor. Going up to investigate, he came upon Caleb Quaye, Reggie Dwight and the others at their usual after-hours work in the demo studio. An angry scene ensued in which Brohn accused Caleb of using office resources without authority, and said that the matter would be reported first thing the following morning.

Since Stephen James had charge of day-to-day office business, it was to him that Ronnie Brohn angrily complained. 'He came into my office fuming,' Stephen James remembers, 'saying Caleb had been letting all kinds of people come in and use the studio. "He'll have to go," Ronnie kept saying. "He'll have to go." '

Twenty-year-old Stephen – himself on less than good terms with Ronnie Brohn – was inclined to take a milder view of the matter. Summoning Caleb Quaye, he learned that a Reg Dwight had been making demo records on the basis of vague arrangements with Nicky James, Kirk Duncan and the Hollies' Gralto company. If this Reg Dwight did not exactly fit Brohn's outraged description of rag, tag and bobtail off the street, misusing DJM's electricity, sofa fabric, instant coffee and lavatory paper, he was hardly a bona fide studio musician either.

'My attitude was, I didn't mind people using our studio as long as we had the chance to hear what they produced,' Stephen James says now. 'I asked Caleb what the material was like. He said, "There are half a dozen songs, and they're not very good." ' The upshot was that Stephen asked to listen to the demos himself. 'I thought there was something interesting there,' he remembers. 'When my father came in, I took the material and played it to him. He thought there was something interesting there as well.'

A relieved Caleb Quaye was not sacked but asked to relay a message to Reg Dwight and his partner, Bernie Taupin, that Dick James himself desired their presence. 'I remember them both sitting outside Dick's office,' says Caleb, 'dead scared because they thought they were going to be hauled over the coals.' Instead to their astonishment, they were greeted with the utmost affability by James, motioned to chairs next to the great man's large executive desk and cross-questioned by him at length about their backgrounds, their musical ambitions and their immediate plans. Glancing with incredulity at the gold discs and sacred Beatle photographs around the walls, they realised they were not being reprimanded, but wooed.

Dick James, for his part, was pleasantly surprised to find that Reg and Bernie were not the uppish young street urchins he had expected, but a pair of shy middle-class boys whose extreme politeness was tinged with palpable hero worship. Especially did he warm to the plump, bespectacled one who, despite diffidence and confusion, was quick, sharp and funny in a way no young pop hopeful had been since the first days of John, Paul, George and Ringo. 'We always believed in Reg, and thought he had talent,' Stephen James says now. 'But the main thing was, we just liked him.'

To Dick James, the matter was trifling enough. He merely followed the instinct of a man with proven colossal luck, that anything new in the music business was worth taking 50 per cent of. Finding there were two young songwriters of promise rolling about loose inside his organisation, he merely shifted his weight on the nesting-box to envelop them, along with Gralto, Pacer, Cookaway and the rest. His offer was to put Reggie and Bernie under contract as songwriters with Dick James Music.

For the two awestruck figures in facing chairs, it was a moment that made the world suddenly tilt askew. Reggie, in one bound, saw his escape from the months of frustration with Long John Baldry and Bluesology. To silent Bernie it was simply beyond his wildest storybook fantasies. 'To actually be given money for writing songs! I couldn't believe they were really serious.'

In the general euphoria, a small point was overlooked. This was that Reggie and Bernie had been supposed to sign with Nicky James and Kirk Duncan's Niraki Music, when Niraki accumulated enough song copyrights to warrant its becoming a proper company.

To Nicky and Kirk, the signing of Reggie and Bernie direct to DJM was presented as a *fait accompli*. An angry Nicky James complained to Graham Nash of the Hollies, whose Gralto company was to have published Niraki's output. Nash and Ron Richards, the Hollies' producer, went in to see Dick James, leaving Nicky waiting outside the office-door.

James was, as ever, a reasonable man. A deal was struck with Nash and Richards wherein the songs that Reggie had written with Gralto's writers, or that Reggie and Bernie had written under Gralto's sponsorship, should be copyrighted to the Hollies' company, along with ten more still to come, a total of some two dozen songs in all. Since Dick James part-owned Gralto, he would, in any case, share those royalties.

'When Graham Nash came out of Dick's office, I was still sitting there waiting,' Nicky James remembers. 'He told me, "It's all right, everything's fixed."'

Everything was fixed, save for the partners in Niraki Music, on whom it rapidly dawned that they featured in these satisfactory arrangements not at all.

For Ray Williams – who had put not only Niraki but also Reggie and Bernie together – it was no great tragedy. In his job as A & R head at Liberty Records, he was now on to numerous other projects (among them recording Rolling Stone Brian Jones in a drugged-out band named Hapshash and the Coloured Coat). Little dreaming how history was destined to repeat itself, Ray Williams shrugged and accepted being cut out of the Reggie Dwight deal.

But for Nicky James and Kirk Duncan, poor and struggling as they were, the event proved terminal. Despite all the promises of their pop star friends, Niraki Music never did become a fully fledged company.

Shortly afterwards, for reasons they never understood, Nicky and Kirk even lost the weekly retainer they had been paid by Dick James Music via Gralto.

Both still maintain that Dick James ditched their whole future by spiriting Reggie and Bernie away from Niraki Music. 'We'd brought them on, given them our studio time, fixed up cover versions for them,' Kirk Duncan says now. 'If we couldn't have managed them, we were connected with people who could. Spencer Davis, I know, was talking about signing them and taking them off to work in America.'

After leaving DJM, Nicky and Kirk struggled on for a while, but met with so little success that both decided to quit the music business. Today they have only vivid memories, and an abiding bitter taste. Such tales are commonplace in the rising of a star.

Keenly as he had sought a singer-songwriter for DJM to nurture Stephen James at first did not recognise such an apparition in Reggie Dwight. The dumpiness, glasses and carrier bag were like nothing from even the weirdest echelons of the new counterculture. And Reggie himself expressed no ambition to be anything but the backroom boy he was at present.

All Stephen initially thought that DJM had acquired was a songwriting team with a strong line in melody and a fancy twist in words, whose songs might best suit one or other of the female singers who had at last broken through in the British charts. Reggie and Bernie accordingly were instructed to study the latest successful recordings of Sandie Shaw, Dusty Springfield and Lulu, and see if they couldn't come up with something similar.

On 7 November, 1967, they formally signed with Dick James Music. As they both were still under twenty-one, the signature of each had to be witnessed by a parent: in Reggie's case his mother and in Bernie's, his father. Under the publishing agreement, they assigned DJM world copyright of their songs, which were to comprise at least eighteen titles, over an initial, renewable three-year period. For this they would receive a £100 advance against royalties calculated at 10 per cent of the marked selling price of each copy (after the first 250 copies) and 50 per cent of proceeds from recording, live performance, radio and TV broadcasting and sub-licensing abroad. In addition to their £100 joint advance, Reggie and Bernie would each receive a weekly cash retainer of £10, to be set against future royalties. Since, on reflection, Reggie's job as singer and pianist as well as writer seemed somewhat the more onerous, his weekly payment was upped to £15.

On Stephen James's next round of the record company A & R men, he took with him a selection of the demos Reggie had made in the DJM studio. The product he had to sell was the songs themselves, the vocal only a rough sketch of what a real singer might do. An early call was on Johnny Franz at Philips, who recorded Reggie's boyhood pin-up, Dusty Springfield. While regretting the song was not quite Dusty, Franz expressed interest in the voice on the demo. The same interest was shown by Tony Hatch, writer of many hits, like Petula Clark's 'Downtown'. 'He said the songs were too original to be covered by other people,' Stephen remembers. 'But the demo singer might be good enough to record them on his own account. "The voice isn't terrible," Tony said. "It might need working on a bit." It was only then that I mentioned to Reg that he might do his own record. He told me he'd always wanted to, but he didn't think anyone would be interested.'

The murmurs of vague interest, on top of his own, prompted Stephen James to offer Reggie a recording deal with DJM's This Record Co. It would not be a very big deal, since TRC was but a small production company, licensed through Philips, the label on which Bluesology had already made two unsuccessful singles.

Still, if he were to record, he would also have to make live concert appearances. If he hadn't already got a manager, Dick James advised him, then he'd better get one fast. At which – so Stephen James recalls – Reggie gave Dick a look that was both despondent and appealing, and said 'Can't you do it?'

This slight surge of encouragement over his voice prompted Reggie to one last attempt to break the jinx inside Bluesology. To prepare for it, he starved himself and took Sheila Dwight's slimming pills until he had lost more than two stone. His face lost its Bunter roundness, growing gaunt and long, down to the cleft in a single chin. In place of owlish Buddy Holly frames, he bought rimless granny glasses like John Lennon's in the Beatles and Roger McGuinn's in the Byrds. His stripe-blazered torso was now as girlishly lean and flat as anyone's in the line-up. Only the legs and arms remained chunky, and the fingers that stretched over the organ keys.

Reggie and Bernie's partnership was interrupted again when Bluesology left on a short tour of Sweden. Reggie took his new figure with him, euphoric at having proved he could do anything he set his mind to. On his return, he resolved to tackle Long John Baldry yet again about singing with the band.

He might have managed it, but for a wholly unforeseen event. For some time, Long John had been anxious to exchange the impecunious blues world for the far more lucrative one of mainstream pop. In the winter of 1967, encouraged by his manager John Gunnell, he recorded a schmaltzy slow ballad entitled 'Let the Heartaches Begin'. To everyone's amazement – not least the vocalist's – it zipped into the Top 20, reaching number one on November 22. Long John Baldry was suddenly a teen heart-throb.

With this radical change of style came an equally radical change of audience. As a blues singer, playing the studentish pub-'n'-club circuit, Long John had been lucky to clear £100 a night. But with a number one hit, the hard-nosed Gunnell could book him into the cabaret and gambling clubs which now dotted the industrial north. As Gunnell's other protégés Georgie Fame and Alan Price already knew, a successful artist in the northern clubs could earn up to £20,000 a week.

Bluesology changed form yet again, losing Marsha Hunt from the backup vocal line and acquiring an extra guitarist in Caleb Quaye, DJM's studio engineer. Its bookers were the Marquee and Klooks Kleek no longer, but Batley Variety Club or the Bailey Organisation, whose bird-of-paradise venues sparkled amongst the pit-heap fogs of County Durham and Teesside.

To the management of Club La Bamba, Darlington, or the Flamingo, Billingham, all that mattered about Bluesology's set was that it should be short, allowing the punters to get back as quickly as possible to spending money on blackjack and roulette. 'I remember one club, in Southport,' Long John Baldry says. 'The owner told us to play for twenty minutes, no more. When I overran a couple of minutes, the curtains closed in front of us. Just as if someone had got a nasty shock and snatched their front-room curtains together.'

There was now no question of Long John's sharing the limelight, vocally – or even instrumentally if he could help it. 'Let the Heartaches Begin' had been recorded solo voice, with Mantovani-ish violin accompaniment. When Long John performed it in the clubs, his R & B sidemen were silenced in favour of a pre-recorded instrumental tape. Bluesology's horn section and organist would just stand there in their green Brummel drag, trying to look appropriately lovelorn.

For Reggie, the northern cabaret club circuit was the last straw. His mind was now firmly made up to quit Bluesology, return to London and take whatever chances there might be with Dick James. But there were still endless nights in the smoky Las Vegas dark of Stockton or Darlington, playing against a buzz of conversation or a clash of cutlery as people ate their basket meals of scampi and chips. His private rebellion began with ritual maltreatment of that symbol of frustration and imprisonment, his orange Vox Continental organ.

'It was all falling to bits. It used to fart and make terrible noises. I finally destroyed the amplifier, my Vox 80, by kicking it in during a Bingo session.'

He also nearly took another wrong turn, secretly auditioning for the Mike Cotton Sound, a former trad-jazz band now briefly cashing in on pop. Again, the hand of Providence intervened. When the Mike Cotton Sound faded into oblivion a few months later, Reggie Dwight was not among their number.

On 10 January he signed a five-year agreement with This Record Co. wherein he undertook to record 'at least four sides of seven-inch records in each year', the content to be specified by TRC. For this he would receive a royalty 'equal to 20 per cent of all net monies received by the company in respect of the master recordings, after the cost of musicians, singers, musical directors, orchestrations, copying, cartage of musical instruments, studio-rentals, technicians, tape-costs, editing, dubbing and re-dubbing and all like production expenses incurred by the company in respect of any of the master recordings shall first have been recouped by the company.' This did not, as might be thought, mean 20 per cent of what each record earned in the shops. It meant 20 per cent of This Record Co.'s income from its manufacturing licensee, Philips – that is, 20 per cent of 10 per cent, equivalent to only about 2 per cent of each record's retail selling price.

With the contract went what a future High Court judge would describe as an 'imposing' addendum, signed by Reggie's mother (though she herself would later admit she had barely understood a word of what she was ratifying). 'I, Sheila Eileen Dwight, being the parent/guardian of Reginald Kenneth Dwight (who is a minor) have carefully considered the provisions of the above agreement and have advised my child/ward thereon. I am satisfied that the agreement is for the benefit of my child/ward, who has entered into the agreement with my approval. In consideration of the company entering at my request into the agreement with my child/ward, I hereby guarantee the performance of my child/ward's obligations under the agreement.'

Her child/ward's farewell appearance with Bluesology was in December 1967, in Edinburgh. On the shuttle flight back to London, he canvassed the others for a professional name, in place of the clearly unsuitable Reg Dwight, to be signed on the pending management agreement with Dick James Music. Bluesology's tenor-sax player Elton Dean remembers Reggie coming along the aisle to see him shortly before the plane began its descent to Heathrow airport. 'He said "I'm leaving the band. To become a pop star. Is it all right if I call myself Elton Dean?" I said "That's a bit strong,

Reg." So he went away. Then he came back and said "OK, is it all right if I call myself Elton John?"' 'John' had been a flash of inspiration, looking over the seat-backs to Long John Baldry's conspicuous blond head.

Neither Dean nor Baldry objecting to this shotgun marriage of their Christian names, it was Elton John who stood on the concourse at Heathrow, waiting for his holdall on the baggage carousel.

During that crossover Christmas season, when every radio played Long John Baldry's misty-eyed hetero love lament, another wholly unexpected thing had happened. The newly named, newly slimline Elton had amazed his road companions by finally 'pulling' a 'bird'.

It happened in Sheffield, where Bluesology were appearing at a Bailey circuit cabaret-club, the Fiesta. Between sets, Long John Baldry got talking to a midget named the Mighty Atom who worked as a disc jockey at the city's Locarno ballroom. With him that night, the Mighty Atom had a girl almost six foot tall, blonde, skinny and vaguely upper class in manner. Her name was Linda Ann Woodrow.

During the evening, the Mighty Atom's companion and Bluesology's usually shy and unamorous organ player fell into conversation. In Long John Baldry's sardonic words 'young love blossomed'.

Linda, then aged twenty-four, came from a colourful background. Her father, Alexander Dane Woodrow, had been a drummer in the Cameron Highlanders, a standup comic on the variety halls, a promoter of all-in wrestling and a conjurer skilled enough for admittance to the Magic Circle. As Al Woodrow, he now owned and ran a Soho drinking club, the New Cottage, in Litchfield Street, a favourite watering-hole for traditional jazz musicians like Acker Bilk and Mick Mulligan. There 'Cottage Al' cut an impressive figure, whether demonstrating magic at the bar or robustly warning Soho hoods like Big Maltese Frank that if they didn't behave properly, they'd be thrown out on their necks.

The Woodrow family owned Epicure, an old-fashioned manufacturer of pickles and preserves. As a pickled-onion heiress, Linda had been educated at a select girls' academy in Reigate, then at finishing-school in Eastbourne. Provided with a generous trust fund, she lived a life of peripatetic leisure, tinged by 'Cottage Al's' show-business proclivities. In 1968, she was staying with her remarried mother in Sheffield and working as a disc jockey at a club above the Mecca skating-rink.

Until this point there seems to have been no doubt in Elton's mind – or anyone else's – that he belonged utterly to the sexual mainstream. His lack of overt interest in girls, save as friends, was easily explicable by his shyness and vulnerability. The one sure way never to be rejected is never to advance even one step. None the less, like nearly all young men of 1967, he supposed he would meet 'someone' sooner or later and, like everyone normal, in the pop business as well as outside it, be married by his early twenties. What there was to learn about sex and love would keep until that notional wedding night. To be a male virgin at twenty, while nothing to shout about, was nothing abnormal either.

Why did his usual buttoned-up reserve disappear so spectacularly when he met Linda Woodrow? The answer seems not to have been sexual so much as social. The elaborately dressed and coiffured girl – who towered over him scarcely less than over the Mighty Atom – spoke in a middle-class accent much like Elton's own. With her finishing-school manner she was, indeed, somewhat superior to Middlesex and Metroland. But their accents were alike enough for understanding to gel. After years as a social outsider around working-class pubs and clubs, he had finally found someone to talk to.

Elton himself was later to give a lurid account of his meeting with Linda, claiming she had been the Mighty Atom's girl-friend and that he – Elton – had spirited her away from frequent ill-treatment at the midget DJ's hands. One can understand the need to blot out with comedy what was to prove a confusedly traumatic period in his life.

The story as Linda now tells it is much more circumspect. She was never the Mighty Atom's girl-friend, only his companion that evening. Elton asked her to show him round Sheffield next day, then suggested she should follow Bluesology on to their gigs in the north-east. He was a 'perfect gentleman', reserving her her own separate room at the band's hotel. In Newcastle, they did nothing more scandalous than go roller-skating together.

They began to go steady, seeing each other in between Elton's final spells on the road with Bluesology. Linda would come and stay with Sheila and Derf in Pinner at the Frome Court maisonette – always decorously occupying her own room. When Elton quit Bluesology and returned to London for his new career with DJM, they decided to set up house together.

They found a basement flat in Furlong Road, Islington. Bernie Taupin also moved there with them, an arrangement Linda would later have cause to rue. In addition there were her two pet dogs – small, yapping specimens which deposited ordure freely along the entrance-hall. 'I used to go to my room singing the tune of "Old Macdonald",' Bernie remembers. '"Here a turd, there a turd, everywhere a turd-turd."'

Bernie was not the only one of Elton's London circle to wonder why he had chosen such a girl-friend, three years older than himself as well as inches taller, coiffed and dressed with a formality that seemed almost middle-aged. 'Everything about her seemed to be artificial – her hair, her eyelashes, her nails. When she went to bed at night, she used to totally disassemble.'

The explanation now looks fairly simple. Ashamed of his own long indifference to girls, Elton was ready and willing – if not determined – to fall for the first one who came along. He seems to have begun the affair with Linda in the spirit of a non-swimmer, plunging headlong with eyes shut and fingers pinching nose, hoping that, if he went straight in at the deep end, everything would somehow sort itself out.

Alas, the opposite was the case. Their first attempt to make love was a disaster, setting the tragi-comic tone of subsequent events. Linda remembers that, for some reason, Elton had taken her to stay at one of the ornate old Victorian hotels on the border of New Oxford Street and Bloomsbury. 'When we rolled into bed, he was clumsy and, frankly, didn't have a clue.' Linda, at the time, detected no malaise other than inexperience, shyness and nerves. 'He was a gentle person by nature, and he was that way in bed. I was so keen on him that I didn't really mind.'

In all sorts of other ways, domestic life in Furlong Road proved trying and traumatic. The only person Elton had lived with before was his mother, that doting, protective figure who cooked, washed, ironed and did everything for him. Linda vehemently refused to be a party to any such mollycoddling. Elton was forced to take his turn at cleaning and cooking and visiting the local launderette. The habit remained of consulting Sheila about everything and instinctively turning to her whenever he felt under stress. Linda's abiding memory of this time is how often he would be on the telephone home to Pinner.

For a time, on the outside at least, it seemed a thoroughly conventional romance. Linda took Elton to meet her father, 'Cottage Al' Woodrow, the club owner and magician. 'I remember her bringing him up to my flat in Ridgemount Gardens,' Cottage Al says. 'This apparition walked in, wearing a tatty old fur coat. Linda said to me "He writes wonderful songs, he's going to be an enormous star." "Oh yes," I said. "Pull the other one."'

Elton introduced Linda to trusted Pinner mates like his old school friend Janet Ritchie. Both attended Janet's wedding, Elton in a now rather worn Bluesology Brummel suit. After the reception, Janet and her new husband made a foursome with Linda and him, travelling back by train to London for a long night round the Soho music clubs.

In the second-hand Hillman Imp car which Elton's mother had lent him £25 to buy, they travelled to Newcastle, for Linda's brother Neil's twenty-first birthday, and to Lincolnshire to visit Bernie Taupin's parents. On the way they had quite a bad accident, in which Linda injured her arm. 'I thought at first that I'd broken it. But it was cured by putting it on an air-cushion.'

Bernie was an amiable sub-tenant, tolerant of Linda's little dogs, content to live on the household's diet of sausages, instant puddings and Indian or Chinese takeaways. He, too, had by now lost his virginity, to a girl named Tottie whom he had met up in Lincolnshire. To Bernie the main attraction of Furlong Road was a room of his own in which to continue these delightful experiments.

He admits he was 'shit-scared' of Linda, who, since she met most day-to-day expenses from her pickled-onion trust fund, ruled the basement ménage somewhat like a school matron. When Bernie wanted to put up a Simon and Garfunkel poster on his bedroom wall, Linda told him he mustn't.

Since Linda had a day job as a secretary, Elton and he spent long hours together, if not at Dick James Music, then watching their socks and underwear rotate at the local Washeteria. 'I remember once putting a new cashmere sweater into the machine, then bringing it out shrunk down to the size of a postage stamp,' Bernie says. 'Elton was laughing so much, he literally rolled on the floor.'

One thing they could not do at Furlong Road was work at their embryonic partnership. The basement did not have a piano. And besides, Linda had her own ideas of the way Elton's career ought to shape. She wanted him to model himself on Buddy Greco, the American cabaret star.

From time to time she would come with Elton to the Dick James Studio, raising incredulous eyebrows among all collected there. Caleb Quaye could not subdue his old propensity for tactless mirth. 'I remember one night we'd all been out to dinner and were on our way back to the studio. Elton was trotting along beside Linda in his fur coat, with one of her little dogs on its leash. He looked so ridiculous with her towering over him, I just rolled on the pavement, laughing.'

To Dick James, Elton John was the smallest, most insignificant part of his daily concerns. Now and again, amid vastly bigger deals, he would remember the £25 he paid out every week and ask his son Stephen how that little side project was going along. Even the name of the little side project sometimes eluded him, and he would absent-mindedly call Elton 'Elvis'.

To Elton, James was a figure of absolute awe, the man who had

helped discover the Beatles, intermediary of every glorious hit from
'A Hard Day's Night' to 'I Am the Walrus'. Elton's greatest pop
idols and exemplars hung like a golden halo around Dick James's
bald head. Merely to associate with the publisher of Lennon and
McCartney was privilege and achievement enough. Never mind if no
song he himself wrote for James ever made it into vinyl or manuscript.

Yet, long before Dick James brought any advancement to Elton,
or Elton represented anything like profit to James, a bond of genuine
warmth grew up between them. The former dance-band crooner and
the former pub pianist were not so very different, notwithstanding
the vast gap in their ages, prestige and background. Dick James's
former world of swing, boiled shirts and scalloped music-stands was
one that Elton had known and loved vicariously through valve
wireless sets in Metroland. As James's dulcet voice discoursed, Elton
loved to remember those same tones issuing from a cabinet TV, amid
the twang of synthetic longbows, on mid-Fifties Sunday afternoons.
It was a source of wholly unironic pleasure to him that his publisher
had sung the *Robin Hood* theme.

In all kinds of ways, Dick James was destined to fill the greatest
emotional void of Elton's childhood and adolescence. From the very
start, he reposed total faith and trust in James, turning to him for
advice on every problem, absorbing his pronouncements in reverential silence and following them to the letter. As time passed, their
relationship would become less that of entrepreneur and artist than
of increasingly indulgent father and increasingly dependent, and
demanding, son.

The first Elton John single was released by This Record Co. via
Philips in March 1968, the month of his twenty-first birthday.
Disregarding the pile of exotic works that already existed on demo,
Stephen James opted for safety and convention. 'I've Been Loving
You' was a routine Elton ballad whose routine lyrics also happened
to be his, though Bernie Taupin still received credit as joint composer.
It had been recorded before Christmas in the DJM studio, with Caleb
Quaye producing, and the usual modest in-house backup band. Elton
himself disliked the result, which seemed to him all too much like the
soupy effusions of Engelbert Humperdinck. But that was the one
Dick James liked, and who knew better the constituents of a hit?

Even for whimsical 1968, the Christian name of Philips' new
recording artist struck an incongruous note. Most who heard it then
instantly thought of Elton Hayes, a genteel folk performer whose
Olde English ditties were still ineradicably engraved on Fifties
childhood's inner ear:

Oh I'll sing a song, a rollicky song, as I roll along my way.
With a hey derry-dow and a herry di-doo
And a riddle-de-diddle-de-day-de-day
And a riddle-de-diddle-de-day.

'John' was not much better, seeming merely a weak imitation of earlier pop stars who'd used Christian names for surnames, like Cliff Richard and Keith Richard. There was also the point that in America 'John' meant 'toilet'.

The bearer of this unluckily twice-evocative name possessed few obvious attributes of a pop heart-throb. Even the sympathetic lens of Philips' publicity photographer could make him no more than marginally good-looking, with his newly-gaunt face and granny specs, his expression its usual mixture of self-conscious shyness and faint dread. With his hair now cropped short and combed down over his forehead, he looked more like some troubled young Roman tribune than the requisite arrogant Carnaby Mod. There being neither time nor budget for grander settings, he was shown, in his tab collar and creased little box jacket, posing against a corrugated iron fence.

Philips' publicity department did their stuff none the less, billing 'I've Been Loving You' in the trade press as 'the greatest performance on a first disc' by '1968's great new talent . . . You have been warned.' The warning was to no avail. 'I've Been Loving You' sailed out into a sea of silence just like Bluesology's two attempts on the same label. The sensation of 1968 was not to be Elton John. It was a group from Birmingham named the Move, whose outrageous publicity stunts had even got them into legal trouble with Prime Minister Harold Wilson. Elton remembers going to see a concert by the Move around this time and feeling his spirits lurch downhill again. 'I thought, "I'm still not getting anywhere."'

As 'I've Been Loving You' stayed firmly out of the charts, Elton and Bernie resumed their duties as in-house songwriters at DJM. And once again Dick James in his wisdom – and on the strength of the £25 he paid them each week – instructed them to forget the airy-fairy stuff they had been writing before, and produce some solid commercial tunes that other artistes could cover.

A cross-section of their efforts survives on a cassette-tape made from some of the studio demos by Elton's footballer cousin, Roy Dwight. The background is Sheila Dwight's tiny lounge at Frome Court, with Roy's small son, Stephen, occasionally chirruping in the background. 'This is the first of Reggie's recordings,' Roy's voice announces with stolid pride. 'He now goes under the name of Elton John . . .'

The main item is entitled 'I Can't Go on Living Without You', sung by Elton in Latin style, punctuated by cod cries of 'Yariba! Yariba!' 'A group named the Plastic Penny has just recorded this one,' DJ Roy continues earnestly. 'It's called "Turn to Me" . . . This one is called "Sorry to See Me Go".' 'If only you knew what I'd been through,' runs the tenaciously unimaginative refrain, 'you'd be sorry to see me go!' A solitary lyric in true Taupin style, 'Smokestack Children' – with one line about 'the tapestry of children's faces' – has been slipped in like a packet of dope in a suitcase of woollen underwear.

The DJM organisation was not totally hostile to these surreptitious 'non-commercial' efforts. Lionel Conway, the young head of DJM's publishing division, was an enthusiastic fan of Elton and Bernie's work, though, alas, possessing insufficient clout to change so firmly made-up a mind as Dick James's. With Conway's support, a number of their more poetic efforts were covered by other artists within the large DJM network. 'Turn To Me' was recorded by the Plastic Penny, a group belonging to Larry Page's affiliated Page One Music. 'Thank You for Your Loving' (a song credited to Elton John and Caleb Quaye) became the B-side of a single by a group called the Dukes Noblemen. 'When the First Tear Shows' was recorded as the A-side of a November release by a DJM solo protégé, Brian Keith. 'Taking the Sun from My Eyes' was the B-side of a single by a children's TV 'story lady' named Ayshea. A song from their very earliest batch, 'The Tide Will Turn for Rebecca' ended up as a curio single for another DJM acquisition, the actor Edward Woodward.

Most successful was 'Skyline Pigeon', the wistful song of a captive bird turned loose by a prisoner. Elton's demo version came to the notice of Roger Greenaway and Roger Cook, the prolific writing team whose Cookaway Music also was run by DJM. So enthusiastic were they about the song that they arranged with Dick James for Cookaway to publish it, plus two further John–Taupin titles. Roger Cook, a singer in his own right – soon to front a string of hits by Blue Mink – released 'Skyline Pigeon' as an A-side in August 1968. A second A-side cover appeared that same month by a singer named Guy Darrell.

For every glimmer of success in tiny print on a revolving record label, there were a dozen disappointments when big-name cover versions they had pinned their hopes on failed to materialise. 'I used to get more down about it than Elton did,' Bernie Taupin says now. 'Usually he'd be the one keeping both our spirits up. What used to bring him down was when I'd go off back to Lincolnshire for a time. I know he once wrote in his diary: "Bernie away. Very depressed."'

While grinding out songs to Dick James's specifications, they continued surreptitiously writing their own uncommercial material. Elton's studio demos of these forbidden tracks, like 'A Dandelion Dies in the Wind', now amounted to a full album's worth. But, under all the rules of pop, they knew it was hopeless. No one ever recorded an album without the prior achievement of at least one Top 10 single.

The one faint hope of changing their luck was that some influential music journalist might be persuaded to listen to their songs, and write a story about them eulogistic enough to change Dick James's mind. But the national music papers, *Melody Maker*, *New Musical Express* and *Disc and Music Echo*, though right on Tin Pan Alley's doorstep, all seemed remote and unapproachable as the music mandarins at the BBC. To date, they had met only one journalist, a girl named Nina Myskow who worked as a fashion-writer for *Jackie* magazine, published by the penny-pinching D. C. Thomson group from Dundee, Scotland. Fleeing down to London for stories as often as she could, Nina soon made contact with the varicoloured pop musical life around Dick James Music. Elton John, at that stage, was nowhere near big enough to rate a mention in *Jackie* magazine. But something about him compelled Nina Myskow's attention. 'For a start, he was so funny and entertaining to be with, even though he often seemed depressed about the way his career was going. Once he told me he didn't think the partnership with Bernie was working out, and asked if I'd ever thought of writing words to songs. Silly bitch that I was, I never took him up on it. Later on, he told me he'd written a song called "Nina".'

To supplement his weekly £15 retainer from DJM, he also began doing freelance session work, both as a pianist and backup singer. He became one of the network of hardy musical pros, sent in to studios like kamikazes to beef up the sound of this or that ephemeral Top 20 act. During 1968 he played anonymously on hits by two comedy groups, the Barron Knights and Scaffold. He was also an indistinguishable voice in the chorus behind Tom Jones's melodramatic number two smash 'Delilah'. For a time he had a second career as pianist in a pubbish group named the Bread and Beer Band with other DJM musicians: Caleb Quaye on guitar, Roger Pope on drums and Bernie Calvert on bass. They even released a single on Decca, 'Breakdown Blues', and cut an album that reached test-pressing stage before being mysteriously cancelled.

Even when not working at DJM, he and Bernie would hang around the office, soaking up all possible propinquity with the men who knew the Beatles. At the time, Dick James had just hired Geoffrey Ellis, boyhood friend of Brian Epstein and one of the last to see him before his lonely death. A solicitor, impeccably dressed and inscrutably respectable, Ellis now looked after contracts and artist relations at DJM. He first noticed Elton as a down-at-heel figure, sitting with Bernie outside Dick James's office, for all the world like two schoolboys waiting to see the headmaster.

Paul McCartney would sometimes drop in to use the DJM studio with his new Welsh protégée, Mary Hopkin. On one memorable occasion, Elton and Bernie saw him at EMI's Abbey Road studios, where the Beatles had lately recorded the White Album. 'We were there talking to the Barron Knights,' Bernie Taupin remembers. 'Suddenly Paul came in, sat down at the piano and asked us if we'd like to hear this new thing he'd written. It was "Hey Jude". God, we thought that was just so cool.'

Neither Elton nor Bernie could ever bear to be far from pop music and records. Their constant port of call was the Musicland record shop in Berwick Street, London's best place for American import discs. They would spend hours there, riffling through the boxes or squashed into an audio booth, soaking up ideas like hippy magpies for half a dozen new songs that Dick James would prefer them not to write. Elton became so well-known to Musicland's two assistants, Ian and John, that he was allowed behind the counter and even took turns at serving customers. Little in Elton's afterlife was ever to match the excitement of queuing up, amid Berwick Market's banana boxes and squashed cabbage-stalks, for the newest albums by Leonard Cohen or Soft Machine. The high spot of each week was Friday, when Musicland's new import stock came in. Bernie Taupin still remembers the ecstasy with which they first listened to *Music from Big Pink*, by Bob Dylan's former backing group, the Band.

Bernie's weekly £10 was mostly going on rent, and buying successive volumes of Tolkien's *Lord of the Rings*. Often he couldn't afford to buy the record he wanted. 'So Elton always used to say "Never mind. I'll buy it and we'll share it."'

The early relationship between Elton and Bernie Taupin has often been speculated on. It was a bond of pure brotherly love. Throughout his solitary childhood, Elton had often wished he had a brother. In gregarious country mouse, with his warm family background and two brothers, town mouse found – or seemed to find – everything that was missing. 'I loved Bernie,' he would admit. 'Not in any physical way. It was just fantastic to know that someone else knew how I felt.'

For Bernie also, the relationship was utterly natural. His country upbringing had made him quite accustomed to living at close quarters with brothers and school mates. Elton and he worked, travelled, drank, ate and roomed together as uncomplicatedly as if they were going through school, college or military service.

Innocent and platonic as their relationship was, it brought Elton face to face with his true nature for the first time. For, whatever he still did not know about himself, one thing he knew beyond any shadow of doubt. He could not face marrying and settling down with Linda Woodrow.

In the basement flat in Furlong Road, Islington, the old psychologist's axiom had come true, that whenever three people are together, two will invariably turn against the third. On one side were Elton and Bernie, their hopes and disappointments, their similar musical tastes and shared LPs. On the other was Linda with her hairpiece, her false eyelashes, her two little dogs and her hope that her fiancé would cultivate the suave piano and vocal style of Buddy Greco.

Bernie Taupin remembers how they would gang up on Elton's supposed loved one behind her back like a pair of naughty schoolboys. 'One night, I remember, the two of us made a treacle sponge pudding. When we brought it out of the oven, we accidentally dropped about half of it into the sink and it got mixed up with gunge and Ajax powder. As we scraped it up, Elton said, "We'll give her this bit."'

Elton was afterwards to give semi-farcical accounts of the relationship, claiming that Linda so dominated and intimidated him, he dared not even try to end things with her. To one magazine, half a dozen years later, he described Linda habitually beating him up; a too perfect comic reversal of her own earlier alleged ill-treatment by the midget Mighty Atom. Bernie's more ordinary recollection is of rows in which the much taller female party would frequently lash out, and make contact. Linda herself denies even that. 'I never hit him, or any other fellow I went out with. If I had, I know I'd remember it.'

The truth is that Linda did not coerce him nearly so much as he coerced himself, further and further down the path where it was impossible for him to go. Like H. G. Wells's Mr Polly, he longed for escape, yet was powerless to stop the social forces he had set in motion.

It tormented him that, in almost nine months of living with Linda, he had found it difficult to establish any successful physical relationship with her. Linda's own relative tolerance and forbearance on this front could not remove the cloud that lay over their happiest domestic moments, the inward question, asked by so many young men in that same bewildered darkness: 'What's wrong with me?'

Yet he had asked Linda to marry him and she had accepted, buying her own engagement ring at a jeweller's in the Holloway Road. The Dwights of Peckham and Pinner were to unite with the Woodrows of Scotland, Soho and pickled eggs. The grip of the lofty, periwigged girl was vice-like on his arm, her two small dogs tying him ever tighter with their leashes. There seemed no way of wriggling out.

He was also in a trough of depression about his career, the failure of his first single, the endless false hopes and disappointments of trying to sell his songs to other performers. Bernie Taupin remembers how his initial buoyancy changed to dull resignation, as no chart action registered, and yet another big-time cover version failed to materialise. 'He got really down about it. I remember him often saying "Why doesn't anything ever work out for us?"'

Nobody realised the extent of his gloom and desperation until one afternoon at the Furlong Road flat. 'The three of us were supposed to be taking a nap,' Linda remembers. 'I came out of my room and Bernie came out of his, both thinking we'd heard a noise. We went into the kitchen, and there was Elton lying with his head in the gas oven.'

A few telltale clues suggested that his decision to end it all was somewhat less than wholehearted. 'He'd only turned the gas on to "low", and left the kitchen window open,' Bernie Taupin says. 'And he'd thought to take a cushion to rest his head on.'

Bernie pulled him clear of the unfatal jets – a succour that would one day be celebrated in a song. Linda took a more sceptical view, merely remarking on the waste of good gas.

Everyone around Elton strove to dissuade him from rushing into marriage with Linda. His mother, Sheila, in particular, said that if he went through with it, she'd never speak to him again. Fervently as he might agree with them all, the arrangements still went forward with deadly inexorability. A local registry office had been booked for a civil ceremony. Linda and he had already been out choosing furniture, and looking for a new flat in the middle-aged suburb of Mill Hill. A wedding cake was on order. Long John Baldry was to be best man.

The wedding date was only three weeks away when Elton and Bernie went out drinking with Long John at a Soho club called the Shazz. Linda had also been invited but, providentially, said she preferred to stay home that night.

At the Shazz, and later at the Bag O'Nails, Elton's friends rejoined battle to save him from his impending nuptials. 'Baldry kept on at him all evening,' Bernie Taupin remembers. 'It's absurd, you don't really love her, you're just being a damned fool...' Other music figures joined the discussion like supernumerary agony aunts, among them P. J. Proby and Cindy Birdsong of the Supremes, who had once gone out with Bluesology's lucky vocalist, Stuart Brown.

By the time the Bag closed in the early hours, Elton's resolve to end it with Linda had been stiffened. 'We were both pretty drunk,' Bernie says. 'We walked back up Furlong Road arm in arm, to give ourselves courage. On the way, I fell against a car and set its burglar alarm ringing.

'When we got to the flat, Elton said "I'm going to tell her." I said, "I'm going into the bathroom to throw up." Then I bolted straight into my room and shut the door, with all hell breaking loose on the other side. A little while later, there was a knock, and Elton's voice said "I'm coming in there with you." I think he spent the rest of the night on the floor.'

The next morning, in contemporary parlance, was 'heavy'. Linda announced she was pregnant, and threatened dire consequences if Elton called the wedding off. 'She locked herself in the bathroom and shouted out she was going to commit suicide by injecting an air bubble into her vein,' Bernie Taupin says. 'I remember the two of us outside, saying, "She can't, can she? She hasn't got a syringe."'

For Elton, there was now only one possible way out. He got straight on the telephone with an SOS to his mother.

Shortly before noon, a van drew up outside. In it was faithful Derf Farebrother, a one-man Dunkirk fleet for the evacuation of Elton, his household effects, his record collection and his songwriting partner. In little more than an hour, the wrathful Linda and her two little dogs were left behind. Elton and Bernie sat in the safety of Derf's van, heading home to 30a Frome Court, Northwood Hills.

The idea had been to seek sanctuary with Sheila and Derf just for a week or two, until the Linda furore had died down and they could find another flat in London. Little did Bernie Taupin realise they were destined to remain out in leafy Metroland for something like the next year and a half. Until well past the point when Elton John had taken the pop world by storm, he would still be living at home with his mum.

The only vacant space in the 1930s maisonette was the bedroom where Reggie Dwight had spent so many solitary hours. With Sheila's indulgence, this was now converted into a self-contained bedsitter for Elton and Bernie, with its own oil heater and television set. Their two fun-fur coats hung behind the door, where Reggie's solitary school cap and blazer used to be. The room was too small even for two single beds, so they had to go out and buy themselves metal-framed bunk beds, the kind that small boys sometimes have to share at seaside holiday hotels.

Both town and country mouse, fortunately, were neat and methodical and able to coexist quite happily in the tiny space. On one side were their records, scrupulously marked with an 'E' or a 'B', and the stereo system they were buying together on the instalment-plan. On the other was a cabinet with doors, housing the leather-bound volumes from the book club to which Elton subscribed.

The weeks of monastic seclusion at Frome Court brought one great benefit to Elton and Bernie. Their songwriting – in virtual abeyance during Elton's domestic traumas – now hit full stride, in the form it was to retain henceforth. Bernie would sit on the lower bunk bed, scribbling lyrics on a pad on his knee. He would then take them along the minuscule hallway and into the living room, where Elton sat at the upright piano. Back in the bedroom, a few moments later, he would hear chords begin to vibrate through the wall.

Sheila Dwight would come home from her job with the Ministry of Defence, cook Elton and Bernie an evening meal and listen to the day's compositions. Frequently, the audience would be swelled by Sheila's sister, Win, and her next-door neighbour, Mavis.

True, it was not the most convenient address from which to pursue a career as Tin Pan Alley tunesmiths. Each morning, wearing their mousy fun-fur coats, they had to walk up Pinner Road, turn left at the traffic roundabout and go along the parade of shops to Northwood Hills tube station, opposite the gloomy hotel-pub where Elton's performing career had begun. Thence on the Metropolitan Line, winding through Pinner, Harrow-on-the Hill, Northwick Park and Wembley, with its distant view of the stadium's towers, and finally Baker Street, with a change to the Bakerloo Line, then another to the Central Line for Tottenham Court Road, Tin Pan Alley and DJM. The last train home left Baker Street before midnight just as things were hotting up in their favourite Soho haunts, the Shazz and the Bag O'Nails.

Surprisingly enough, it was this tedious journey on the Metropolitan Line, rather than hanging around DJM, that gave Elton and Bernie's career its next nudge forward. Returning home alone one day, Elton spotted a familiar face in the commuter crowd. It was 'Muff' Winwood, elder brother of Stevie, the teenage vocal star of the Spencer Davis Group, with whom Bluesology had often shared gigs. Muff had now left the group to become a producer with the new progressive Island record label and, with his wife Zena, lived only a mile or so from Northwood Hills.

Elton began playing tennis, in his fiercely competitive way, with Muff Winwood. He also played him some of the demos of 'non-commercial' songs he had made illicitly at DJM. Like Lionel

Conway, Muff thought them brilliant. He couldn't understand why
Dick and Stephen James kept such songwriters on a treadmill of easy-
listening and Europop, nor why Elton wasn't being more adven-
turously launched as a solo performer. Muff Winwood's suggestion
was that he should approach Island's whiz-kid young boss, Chris
Blackwell, to see if Blackwell would take over Elton's contract from
DJM.

Meantime, Elton and Bernie had a friend and adviser, living only
minutes by car from Frome Court. 'We used to go over and see Muff
regularly every week,' Bernie Taupin remembers. 'We always took
his wife, Zena, a box of Black Magic chocolates and a bottle of
Mateus Rosé, and spent the evening playing table football. Muff used
to give us this really great advice about what to do when we finally
did make it and became famous. "Remember," he'd say, "a concert
promoter will give you anything you ask for, but you'll always end
up paying for it in the end."'

The meticulous day-by-day diary that Elton kept – and still keeps
– records this era in capital letters, often with the flavour of a
prototype Adrian Mole:

January 7, 1969. STAYED AT HOME. WROTE EMPTY SKY, FLOWERS WILL
NEVER DIE.

January 12. WENT TO LJB'S [Long John Baldry] BIRTHDAY PARTY, HAD
ROW WITH BERNIE.

April 10. RECORDING AT OLYMPIC – IT'S ME THAT YOU NEED. SESSION
WAS GREAT. HELPED IN MUSICLAND TODAY.

April 12. CAUGHT THE 9-30 TRAIN AND WENT IN TO MUSICLAND. GOT
'DUFFED UP' ON WAY HOME. WENT STRAIGHT TO BED.

May 28. PINNER FAIR. WENT UP TO GET PAID. WENT TO THE FAIR WITH
MICK AND PAT. I WON A COCONUT AND TWO GOLDFISH – JOHN AND
YOKO!!

May 29. MY GOLDFISH DIED TONIGHT. VERY UPSET!!

May 30. WENT TO GET SOME MORE GOLDFISH – GOT A TANK AND FOUR
FISH. PLAYED TENNIS WITH TONY'S FRIEND, MARK. WON 6-2, 6-4, 2-6,
4-6, 6-0.

August 14. DIDN'T WAKE UP UNTIL 3-0. BERNIE WENT TO THE

DENTIST . . . GOT DRUNK ON MERRYDOWN. BERNIE VERY ILL.

August 30. GOING TO THE I.O.W. TO SEE BOB DYLAN. TOO MUCH!!

To Bernie as well as to her natural son, Sheila Dwight was endlessly good-natured, cheerful and encouraging. He still does a fond impersonation of her, chain-smoking and nodding vigorous approbation for a 'nice ballad'. Her one domestic stricture was in throwing out his fun-fur coat, which, especially in wet weather, used to smell like an unhygienic woolly dog.

For Elton – especially after what had gone before – it was a happy, if not carefree time. Bernie and he were like nothing so much as study chums in some safe, cosy tale of Greyfriars school. Sharing prep and talking after lights-out, the darkness friendly and familiar – what more could anyone need in a relationship?

Bernie remembers moments of high farce, like the time Elton's glasses exploded on one morning train journey to Baker Street. 'It was his first pair of John Lennon glasses. He'd bought them at a shop in Charing Cross Road. As I watched him, they just spontaneously flew apart on his nose.

'There was another time when Sheila had gone away and we had to cook dinner for ourselves. We tried to cook sausages, chips, peas and make Instant Whip. Everything got spoiled, excepting the peas. While I'm burning the sausages, Elton's mixing up the Instant Whip with one of these gun-type mixers. When he tries to look at what I'm doing, he takes the gun out of the bowl and starts spraying Instant Whip all over the ceiling. "Look what you're doing!" he's shouting, and I'm shouting "No! Look what you're doing!"'

On quiet evenings in, Bernie would read *The Lord of the Rings* and Elton would sit watching football on television. The last thing country mouse would see before going to sleep each night was the rail of the bunk bed, with town mouse's hippy chains and amulets draped over it.

In September 1968 Dick James had persuaded a moustachioed young song-plugger named Steve Brown to leave EMI and join the expanding operation at DJM. The son of a Salvation Army officer, Brown had started out as a musician, playing baritone sax in Emile Ford's group, the Checkmates. Naturally ambitious, he saw the DJM job as a means of advancement from plugging to full-blown record-producing. His true niche in pop music, however, was to be as one of its very few genuine altruists.

Among the first assignments given to Steve Brown was the

motivation of DJM's two in-house songwriters. He accompanied Elton John and Bernie Taupin into the studio and listened to all their material, both the 'commercial' songs they had been forced to write, and the non-commercial ones they had gone on mutinously producing for the album no one would sanction. Then he delivered a verdict which lifted both their hearts. The uncommercial stuff was far superior to the commercial, Steve Brown told them. They should waste no more time in trying to ape other styles and voices. From now on, they must write only what they felt from the heart. 'It was a very brave thing for Steve to do,' the star would afterwards acknowledge. 'He was only an employee. He was telling us "Don't take any notice of the boss."'

Among the elderly Tin Pan Alleyites at DJM, Steve Brown came as a bright ray of salvation. Though only slightly older than Elton and Bernie, he seemed an omniscient figure, combining the knowhow of big-time commercial pop with hippyish sensibility and sympathy. His encouragement of them to be themselves had instantly positive results, rousing both to the challenge of being commercial without necessarily selling out.

It began, as usual, with Bernie, who came up with a lyric entitled 'Lady Samantha', combining his favourite image of a medieval damsel with a highly fashionable Sixties name. This Elton wrapped in piano chords and a vocal performance which began in the sad cypress bleakness Bernie had meant it to, but then dissolved into a gutsy chorus, as if the Lady of Shalott were suddenly revealed in black net stockings and a red garter. On Steve Brown's strong recommendation, Dick James accepted 'Lady Samantha' as Elton's long-delayed follow-up to 'I've Been Loving You'. It was also agreed a suitable opportunity for Brown to make his first essay as producer. 'Lady Samantha' and a B-side, 'All Across the Havens', were recorded in the DJM studio on 18 October, 1968.

The session got off to an uncomfortable start. Elton's hired Wurlitzer piano had a key out of tune, which prevented his playing a crucial note in the 'Lady Samantha' arrangement. Though Steve Brown and everyone else pronounced the finished track excellent, he still worried and fretted about that missing note. Attempts at reassurance did nothing but bring on one of Reggie's Little Moments. He said he hated 'Lady Samantha', and didn't want it released. Brown's diplomatic suggestion was that he should go away for a few days, then listen to it again to see if he still felt the same. After two or three days, Elton listened again, and gave in. '"Okay", I said. "Release it. You know, it can't do me any harm."'

'Lady Samantha' was released by Philips on 10 January, 1969. It did not reach the Top 20, or even the Top 50. But it received good notices everywhere that mattered. The *New Musical Express* called it 'professional and musicianly'. *Disc and Music Echo* thought the lyrics 'sensible and worthwhile' and the singer 'a promising talent'. The all-important *Melody Maker*, which gave ratings rather like a musical *Michelin*, commended a 'sturdy voice' and 'an interesting, guitar-ridden sound that could create waves of interest. Very good, and a gold star.'

More importantly, the song-plugging team of Stephen James and Steve Brown secured reasonable airplay on the BBC's new pop network, Radio One. To harassed BBC producers, fending off the druggy and the free-loving on every side, a quasi-Arthurian ballad, wherein no one spoke of 'turning on' or 'getting high', came as a welcome relief. Every major disc jockey, like Tony Blackburn and Johnny Walker, made room at least once among the Move, the Herd and Vanity Fair for 'Lady Samantha'. The cerebral John Peel gave it a special mention on his late night show, which in those days ran as late as almost midnight.

Though sales amounted to barely 4,000 copies, Elton was on the map as a performer at last. The BBC called him in for audition by its production panel, to determine if he was good enough to perform live on Radio One. He played 'Lady Samantha', 'Skyline Pigeon' and 'All Across the Havens' in a trial session which its producer, Aidan Day, called 'highly original and inventive', even though Elton had previously warned he was suffering from 'a migraine'. Not all the six-man BBC tribunal were so impressed. 'Male vocal in the 1969 feeling,' ran one report. 'Thin, piercing voice with no emotional appeal. Don't think this singer doing his own weird material is right for radio at present.' 'Writes dreary songs and sounds like a one-key singer,' another said. 'I suppose he must be available for anyone who wants his four-minute numbers, but I do not . . .'

With three votes for him and three against, Elton received the benefit of the doubt. He performed the same three numbers on a Radio One Saturday-morning session and afterwards was briefly quizzed by Britain's senior disc jockey, Brian Matthew. 'Any plans for personal appearances?' Matthew asked, in evident surprise there had as yet been none. 'I'm getting a band together at the moment,' Elton answered, in a voice both strained and shy. 'I've got a partner, who writes the lyrics to my songs. I've been very lucky. Well, I haven't had a hit yet, but I've still been lucky.'

One 'turntable hit' under their belt, Elton and Bernie now enjoyed further mild success via one of the 'commercial' numbers they had churned out to appease Dick James. It was a song called 'I Can't Go on Living Without You', composed with an ear half-cocked to the sub-Bacharach style of the barefoot chanteuse Sandie Shaw. Thanks to vigorous lobbying by Dick James, musical unoriginality and banality reaped the highest possible reward. 'I Can't Go on Living Without You' was chosen as a British candidate for the Eurovision Song Contest.

The annual satellite-linked event in which Europe's nations compete to produce execrable pop music was not quite so vomit-inducing two decades ago. In those days, established performers rather than gawky newcomers sang Britain's entry. Established songwriters did not practise the boycott that afterwards arose. Elton and Bernie were in highly respectable musical company.

'I Can't Go on Living Without You' was one of six potential British entries sung by the Scots star Lulu in successive editions of her weekly BBC TV variety show throughout January and February of 1969. She then reprised all six in a special *Song for Europe* programme on 1 March. A viewer's vote selected the one to go to the Eurovision final in Madrid on 29 March.

Despite a spirited performance by Lulu, the viewers did not choose 'I Can't Go on Living Without You'. Nor did they choose 'Come September', co-written by the prestigious lyricist Don Black. Their overwhelming choice was Peter Warne and Alan Moorhouse's 'Boom-Bang-a-Bang', a song destined, weirdly, to tie with three others for first place in the Eurovision final, and usher in a tradition of Esperanto-ish nonsense titles that continues to this day.

For Elton and Bernie, the only consolation was a brief TV walk-on appearance as writers on the *Song for Europe* programme. When their big moment came, Michael Aspel, the compère, announced them as 'Elton John and Bernie Poppin'. Bernie's local paper up in Lincolnshire subsequently carried the headline LINCS BOY WRITES A SONG FOR LULU.

During late 1968 and early 1969, the affairs of the Beatles loomed over Dick James Music like a mop-topped mushroom cloud. Elton's career, in both short and long term, was to be crucially affected by Fab Four fallout.

Over the past three years, James's relationship with the Beatles had dramatically deteriorated. The syndrome is a familiar one in show business, experienced by almost all those fortunate enough to sign up phenomenal talent on the ground floor. Financial arrangements that seem fair and equitable on the ground floor tend to look somewhat different after the talent has shot through the roof.

So had it become with the 50–50 deal Dick James had made with John Lennon and Paul McCartney for publication of their music through a jointly owned company, Northern Songs. To two unknown boys in 1963 it had seemed almost unbelievably generous. But to history's most successful songwriters in 1969 it seemed a wholly unwarranted and excessive portion of themselves. The 23 per cent of Northern which James had kept after public flotation loomed large in their growing sense of being exploited and trammelled by what John Lennon bitterly called 'the men in suits'.

Nor was Dick James any longer the impressive figure he had seemed to John and Paul in their naïve early days. Instead, he represented a brake on creativity with his grey suit and bald head, his pleas, as the White Album took its avant-garde course, to send Northern Songs more nice, tuneful numbers like 'Michelle' and 'Yesterday'.

To James must be ascribed a certain lack of intuition and tact. Sure of his own integrity – as he had always been and would be – he could not see how 'the boys' could have any cause to resent him. Nor could his amiable nature comprehend the pressures within them as they fought to find a saviour from the chaos of their business venture, Apple Corps, and reach some basic consensus on musical policy. That January of 1969 found the Beatles on a freezing sound stage at Twickenham film studios, near-paralysed with anger and misery over what would become their final album, *Let It Be*. Matters were not helped by Dick James's cheery visits and his Christmas gifts of plastic playing-cards bearing the DJM monogram.

The great worry to James was his responsibility as managing director of Northern Songs, and the adverse effect on 3,000 shareholders (among whom he was himself a major one) in this season of virtually nonstop anti-Beatle press coverage. Worse even than the Apple business fiasco had been John Lennon's public affair with Yoko Ono, their conviction for drug-possession and the series of headline-grabbing performance-art stunts on which they were now embarked. Each time John and Yoko crawled under a giant paper bag, planted symbolic acorns for peace, or issued pictures of themselves as full-frontal nudes, Dick James would give another gulp and turn to Northern's share quotation in the *Financial Times*.

With the appointment of Allen Klein, a tough New York accountant, to sort out the chaos at Apple, Dick James decided his nerves could stand no more. Early in 1969 – taking advantage of a moment when both Lennon and McCartney were abroad – he sold out his 23 per cent of Northern Songs to Lew Grade's ATV organisation for something over one million pounds. ATV then set about acquiring the other stock (beginning a chain of ownership that would end, two decades later, with the boy wonder Michael Jackson).

Though DJM continued to administer Northern Songs, and would do so for the next three years, a great personal incubus was lifted from Dick James. His immediate thought – so his son Stephen remembers – was that, in building up and running Northern, he had not paid enough attention to his own company. He was thus prepared to put unusual effort into developing DJM's one and only home-grown talent.

With only nominal protest, therefore, Dick James yielded to the pleas of his young assistant Steve Brown that Elton John and Bernie Taupin should be given their creative heads. The 'turntable' success of 'Lady Samantha' proved that their non-Eurovision music might not be so uncommercial after all. They could go ahead and make the album they had been dying to for almost a year.

From a music mogul as traditionally minded as Dick James, the concession was enormous. Record albums in the late Sixties were nothing like the gargantuan self-contained business they are today. Performers who sold albums still tended to be those with a large residual singles following, like the Beatles, Bob Dylan and the Beach Boys. 'Album only' artists, like Leonard Cohen and Leon Russell, were still almost wholly a transatlantic oddity. To advance an unknown singer into this rarified company showed an extraordinary degree of faith and indulgence.

Not that Elton's first album mobilised anything like the spendthrift resources of a *Sgt. Pepper* or *Pet Sounds*. The venue was the DJM studio, with its second-hand Studer four-track. The band was the usual rake-up of session mercenaries, led by Caleb Quaye on guitar. Steve Brown was producer, still very much feeling his way. By using in-house facilities, and cutting every corner possible, the final cost was barely £2,000.

All but one of the tracks had been written by Bernie, sitting on the lower bunk at Frome Court, then carried, postman-like, along the tiny hallway to Elton at the piano in the lounge. Sheila Dwight, her sister Win and her next-door neighbour Mavis had received sneak previews of most, while the composers' dinner simmered on the kitchenette stove.

The two daydreaming fans and inveterate mental hoarders poured forth a motley magpie cache. From Bernie came two- and three-minute storylines drawn from the literature and mass culture he had devoured since childhood, echoes of Walter Scott, Macaulay and Alfred, Lord Tennyson, of Kenneth Grahame, C. S. Lewis and

J. R. R. Tolkien, of *Buffalo Bill's Annual* and *Eagle* comic books, of BBC Monday-night radio plays and Technicolor screens on Saturday afternoons. From Elton came melodies just as instantly assembled from the years of playing he already had behind him, chords and progressions formed in each long epoch from the Royal Academy of Music to the Twisted Wheel Club, thrown into an instant stew of all his keyboard heroes from Russ Conway to Stevie Wonder, from J. S. Bach to Winifred Atwell.

The titles were a highly self-conscious mixture of poesy, sub-Kerouac parody and laboured *Goon Show* pun. 'Empty Sky' returned to one of Bernie Taupin's favourite themes, a prisoner bemoaning lost liberty. 'Val-Hala' rang with echoes of torch-lit Viking sagas starring Kirk Douglas. 'Western Ford Gateway' celebrated the American frontier landscape Bernie Taupin had yet to see. 'Hymn 2000' was a Joe Ortonesque fable of maternal incest, church and chocolate. 'Lady, What's Tomorrow?' was a lament for vanishing rural beauty in the voice of a child evacuee. 'Sails' was an unconscious reworking of John Masefield's poem, 'Cargoes'. 'The Scaffold' had a feel of Spanish conquistadors, invoking both Eldorado and the Minotaur. 'Skyline Pigeon' – Elton's belated version of a song already twice covered – returned to yearnings from the prison cell. 'Gulliver' was about one of the dogs on Bernie's father's Lincolnshire farm. All these far-sighted visions of country mouse, myopic town mouse wreathed about him in the light, clear, angst-ridden voice that still reminded its listeners most of José Feliciano.

The album took the title of its opening song, 'Empty Sky'. In contrast with the tortuously self-indulgent studio epics of Beatles or Beach Boys, it was completed in a few days during February 1969, at the astoundingly low cost of £150 per track. When the sessions ran late and the composers missed their last train back to Pinner, Steve Brown took them to sleep on the floor of his father's flat above the Salvation Army centre in Oxford Street.

The finished master was then handed to Dick James's son, Stephen, for release through This Record Company's distribution label, Philips. Much as Stephen liked what he heard, he could see the problems ahead. Since *Sgt. Pepper*, British record companies were just about reconciled to the theme or concept album. *Empty Sky* had no detectable theme, save perhaps the amount that could be borrowed from every rack at Musicland. From conventional acid rock, it swung to Olde English roundelay; from country and western to Afro-Caribbean; from Procol Harum to Jimi Hendrix; from the Rolling Stones to the Band. Poetically introspective, it still contrived to end on a note of saloon-bar cheeriness. The play-out track, 'Hay

Chewed', a tortuous pun on 'Hey Jude', featured Elton and saxophonist Don Fay in an extended jazz-boogie duet.

Stephen James's misgivings proved well founded. Johnny Franz, the Philips A & R head, would not consider releasing so 'strange' an album by someone who had not yet made a proper hit single. Stephen's nettled response was to invite him to tear up This Record Co.'s contract with Philips, which Franz obligingly did. In a bravura show of youthful confidence, Stephen announced he would put out *Empty Sky* on a wholly independent DJM record label. Rather than merely employing the resources of its distribution label, DJM took on the whole creative and marketing process excepting actual manufacture (a job passed from Philips to Pye). As well as its studio, 71–75 New Oxford Street now also needed an expanded publicity and promotions office and an art department to design record-sleeves. Large corporate steps, all on behalf of little Elton and Bernie.

To design *Empty Sky*, Steve Brown brought in a young graphic designer friend of his named David Larkham, who worked freelance for various magazines and newspapers like the London *Evening Standard*. Larkham produced the simple dark blue sleeve on which Elton John confronted his listeners for the very first time. An unrecognisable figure, sidewhiskered like a Victorian paterfamilias, leaned back from its keyboard against a vista of psychedelic cloud. Stubby fingers rested on the keys, just as in every such pose back to the age of six. His herringbone tweed jacket was only one step on from the hairy ginger job of the Northwood Hills Hotel. On unseen pedals below, one could almost visualise the Hush Puppies.

Overleaf on the sleeve was a facsimile note in Elton's neat music-student hand, thanking the various helpers and 'Auntie' BBC, one of whose disc jockeys, David Symonds, provided some modish gobble-degook by way of testimonial:

> Elton John plays and pleases on this album but . . . he does not confine himself to the brighter side of life. The runcible has since changed to the smouldering crucible of a million injustices. It's a sign of the times. I too want to hear the pealing bells of distant churches sing. When it does happen, it will be a sign of tomorrow. And Elton will have a song about that as well.

Elton's first publicity launch also owed a debt to Beatle fallout. The new DJM label's promotions man was Alistair Taylor, who had worked in Brian Epstein's Liverpool record shop, subsequently becoming personal factotum to Paul McCartney. With Allen Klein's appointment as the Beatles' manager, Taylor found himself summarily and brutally fired. Hearing of his predicament, Dick James had good-naturedly offered him a job.

Alistair Taylor hyped *Empty Sky* almost as if it were a Beatles album, booking advertisement space on what are called the 'back earpieces' of 100 red London double-decker buses. For some days in June 1969 puzzled Londoners beheld pairs of receding posters on which a bespectacled face was outlined in silver dots against a background psychedelically purple. In true enigmatic Sixties style, no copy appeared but the name 'Elton John'.

Despite this bold gesture, *Empty Sky* ended up by selling fewer than 4,000 copies. Its best review, in the London *Evening Standard*, said it was 'nicely recorded but unadventurous . . . While the music is sweet, the lyrics seem to be a bit self-consciously cultured and "poetic" in a highly fanciful style. To be fair, though,' the *Standard*'s critic patronisingly continued, 'he has talent. When he gets less fanciful and less pretentious he will, I'm sure, have a worthwhile contribution to make.'

5

'If you'll distribute him,
I'll give him to you'

NO decade ever ended as slowly and reluctantly as the 1960s. As a rule when each ten-year span draws to a close, there is a rush of excitement, a quickening interest and curiosity as to what the unfamiliar numeral will bring. So it had been when the Sixties approached with their illusory promise of realism and sleek modernity. By their utterly transformed end, to their millions of youthful beneficiaries, they had grown as mellowly comfortable as some old over-laundered, patched and darned denim jacket. Everything that was happy and easy had come to be identified with the number six. And suddenly, with a feeling of cold queasiness, one was having to think about sevens.

No other last year of a decade can have contained so many of its quintessential events. Nineteen-sixty-nine was the apogee of hippydom, with the Blind Faith and Rolling Stones' free concerts in Hyde Park, the festival which brought Bob Dylan to the Isle of Wight, and the half-million strong blue-denim bivouac at Woodstock. Other things happened, too, including the opening shots of terrorism and inflation, and man's first bouncy, tedious footstep on the moon. The abiding picture, however, is of millions of young people lying all over the earth, as if their blessed sunlit season truly could be spun out to eternity.

With winter came a growing dread, symbolised by that dread which emanated from a white Georgian house in Savile Row, Mayfair. The Beatles were breaking up, so how could the Sixties not follow? All the sadness of a fading golden age seemed gathered into Paul McCartney's great cow eyes as he sang the valedictory hymns of the *Let It Be* album.

The first bleary, hung-over day of 1970 was a stricken one for multitudes, all over the world, whose every impulse for joy and celebration since 1964 had been dictated by the Beatles. Suddenly they looked, and there was nothing.

*

And what of the person destined to soak up almost all that empty sea of fan-worship? As his *annus mirabilis* begins, we find him in yet another low-rent studio, trying to forget he is Elton John or ever possessed style or material of his own. Shutting his eyes like a heretic under torture, he swallows his natural voice and pulls down the shutter in his throat. From his grimacing lips there emerges a thin, reedy note, filled with the tremulous angst of a pullet about to have its neck wrung. All present agree it to be horrendously like Robin Gibb of the Bee Gees.

Times being tougher than tough, Elton could not afford to turn down any kind of freelance session-work. He would appear even on the cut-price LPs, sold mainly by Woolworth's stores, whereon anonymous artists produced wobbly counterfeit versions of current smash hits. During late 1969 and much of 1970, his talent for mimicry earned him at least as much as did his true persona.

Copying Robin Gibb on a pseudo-Bee Gees 'Saved By The Bell' was the most punishing of these vocal masquerades. For bargain-basement labels like Avenue or Ace of Clubs, he also impersonated Stevie Wonder singing 'Signed, Sealed, Delivered'; Mungo Jerry singing 'In the Summertime'; and Andy Fairweather-Low singing 'Natural Sinner'. He was there, singing or playing backup, on 'Woolies' 'versions of the Beach Boys' 'Cottonfields', Christie's 'Yellow River' and Creedence Clearwater Revival's 'Up Around the Bend'. He even recorded with the treacly Mike Sammes Singers and participated in a cover version of 'Back Home' as originally sung, with lumpen unmelody, by the England World Cup football squad.

As a Motown child prodigy, a crewcut surfer, a Mississippi swamp rocker, even an English footballer with the vocal range of a tired moose, he was utterly convincing. The only characterisation that continued obstinately not to gel was that of Elton John.

After *Empty Sky*, his first single on DJM, 'It's Me That You Need', had belly-flopped. His only sniff of the Top 10 had been as session man on two '69 winter hits, the Hollies' 'He Ain't Heavy (He's My Brother)' and the Scaffold's remake of a Wolf Cub camp-fire song, 'Gin Gan Goolie'.

Out of the studio, he bore only the most superficial resemblance to a would-be pop star. He and Bernie Taupin were still living at his mother's flat in Pinner, sleeping in little-boy bunk beds, hammering out songs in two-minute bursts on the living-room's upright piano. Every free day was still spent hanging round the reception area at Dick James Music, scrounging cups of tea or coffee and watching glumly as not only a new year but a new decade rolled off the blocks without him.

Nineteen-year-old Sue Ayton became the junior of Dick James's two secretaries late in 1969. Her first sight of Elton was when he and Bernie came in with a greetings card for her departing predecessor. As the plump, good boy in Metroland had been, so did the fiercely slimmed-down pop musician remain punctilious about remembering birthdays, writing thank-you notes and buying flowers.

'One day I was walking through Reception with a tray of dirty teacups,' Sue remembers. 'He was sitting there with Bernie, as always. As I went by, he put his foot out and tripped me up. Not viciously; just to get a laugh from everyone else. I was furious, and hit him. He hit me back, just in a jokey way. I told him what I thought of him, and stormed off to the tea-making room. He followed me in there, looking really worried. "Don't be cross with me," he said.'

Sue Ayton's duties included the issuing of Elton and Bernie's weekly retainer cheques, and receiving their formal receipts, for £15 and £10 respectively. She also looked after the cupboard where file copies of records by the Beatles and other DJM-affiliated artists were kept. 'I used to let them go through everything that came in and take what they wanted – until I found out I wasn't supposed to.'

To Sue and the other office staff, Elton was still a figure utterly without conceit or arrogance, courteous, considerate, almost painfully grateful for anything they did for him. At the end of the day, a whole group of them, singer, lyricist, producer, musicians and secretaries, used to adjourn to a pub round the corner. 'Elton always used to wear the same old tweed jacket and cords. A black trilby hat. A herringbone maxicoat with big lapels if it was cold. Another thing he lived and died in was a rainbow-coloured waistcoat his mother had knitted him. But he always looked businesslike. He always carried a briefcase.'

Bernie she remembers as an almost invisible figure, tagging on Elton's maxicoat-tails, more often than not moonstruck with love for some girl he had just met or daydreaming of new comic-book epics to compress into a song-lyric. 'We were all going along once, and Bernie walked straight into a lamp post. It was quite a nasty cut. I remember his Lincolnshire accent saying "It 'urts". Next day when he came into the office, he told everyone he'd been in a fight.'

At the same time, DJM's launch of Elton John the live performer was under way, despite some dogged resistance from the performer. The frustrations and discouragements of the past four years had flattened the confidence of the one-time keyboard showman and extrovert. He had developed a psychological block against going out on stage, in case someone told him to shut up and pushed him out to the sidelines again.

Better the life of a backup singer, where he need not be noticed even in the most public situation. Paradoxically, in this period of greatest reluctance to show himself, Elton made two separate appearances on BBC TV's *Top of the Pops* show. With Roger Cook and a female session trio, the Ladybirds, he was an indistinguishable part of the studio decor behind Brotherhood of Man singing 'United We Stand'. Another night, he was a face in the backup vocal crowd for a group named Pickettywitch.

When money was really short he would reluctantly return to his old frustrating role of backup musician. His journalist friend Nina Myskow never expected to run into him on her beat for *Jackie* magazine around Dundee, Scotland. But she got a surprise when she went to see a fading one-hit group called Simon Dupree and the Big Sound perform at a club in the remote Scots fishing port of Arbroath. 'There on the stage behind Simon Dupree was Elton, playing piano. When I talked to him afterwards, he said, "Is there any way I can get a game of tennis up here?" I had to take a day off work to play tennis with him.'

Stephen James remembers feeling deep dismay on first seeing Elton face an audience on his own. 'He seemed to have terrible problems communicating. He'd just sit at the piano, play six to eight songs, then say "There it is. That's it." For a long time, I don't remember him saying more than two words at a time during his set. My father and I had to go on and on at him about loosening up and projecting.'

Even the James organisation's entrepreneurial muscle could not secure him more than a sparse handful of bookings at obscure clubs, mostly in the London area. He would appear with all or some of the *Empty Sky* session musicians, Caleb Quaye on guitar, Roger Pope on drums, Dave Glover on bass. A contingent from the office would always be there – Bernie Taupin, Steve Brown, and Sue Ayton – fervently clapping, cheering, whooping and whistling. 'He went on stage to play in the same old tweed jacket and cords he always wore,' Sue Ayton says. 'I remember one night he'd bought a pair of jeans to wear, but when he tried to put them on, he just couldn't get into them. So he went out and played in his old cords again.'

Within the safety of the group, Elton began to take an interest in nineteen-year-old Sue, who was both his enthusiastic fan and a robustly down-to-earth character. The Linda Woodrow disaster had by no means ended his hopes of finding conventional happiness. Sue Ayton and he would go out on dates together, as well as with the office group. 'He was a very warm, loving person. We'd hold hands or have a bit of a kiss and cuddle. But it was all very innocent.

Anyway, I was still living with my mum, and he was living with his.'

The truth is that both sides in the Elton John project were rapidly running out of hope. DJM had spent more than two years in trying to launch him, an effort not devoted to the Beatles, the Rolling Stones or any other pop newcomer. He had been pushed with maximum force down every possible music avenue, from Europop composer to progressive singer-songwriter. Yet still the breakthrough refused to come.

Elton, for his part, had passed through the phase of dumb wonder and gratitude at that patience and indulgence, and was now at the more querulous stage of asking why the man who had harnessed the Beatles seemed able to do so little for him. In his deepening gloom, as one false dawn followed another, he had even started to wonder how much better he might do under management less celebrated but more go-getting. As far back as January 1969, when 'Lady Samantha' failed to chart, he had gone to his old Mills Music boss Cyril Gee and asked for help in getting out of his DJM contracts. Though Gee, as a friend of Dick James, preferred not to be involved, he gave Elton the name of a solicitor who might act for him. But Elton – in the new exhilaration of recording *Empty Sky* – decided to let the matter drop.

His feelings of discontent were exacerbated by the fact that another record company was by now actively trying to poach him from DJM. His friend Muff Winwood, the young producer for Island Records, had kept his promise to play Elton's demos to Island's charismatic boss, Chris Blackwell. Blackwell loved them and immediately offered a £10,000 advance, provided the existing agreements with DJM could be legally circumvented. On reading through these, he told Elton that, in his opinion, there were holes in them, and that Elton could easily get out of all or part of them. 'Most of my contracts void,' Elton jotted in his diary.

In the crusade to prise Elton away from DJM, Muff Winwood had joined forces with Lionel Conway, who had now left his job with DJM publishing to pursue impresarial ambitions of his own. During 1969, on four separate occasions, Muff Winwood and Lionel Conway approached Dick James with schemes for Island to take over Elton's recording contract. James firmly resisted these overtures, though he said he would be willing to sell Elton's management contract. A new agreement between Muff, Conway and Elton was drawn up – and signed by Elton – one night at the Speakeasy Club. But then Muff Winwood baulked at a manager's role, saying he would rather 'stay friends'.

That July of 1969, after *Empty Sky* had come out and flopped,

Elton's spirits nosedived again. He told Stephen James he was fed up with failure after failure, and definitely wanted to leave DJM. A meeting with Dick James hurriedly took place, at which James was able to mollify, reassure and reinvigorate him.

Much as the Jameses liked Elton, they could not ignore the large sums of money already uselessly spent on his advertising, promotion and, most of all, enough studio time to produce almost a hundred finished 'masters' as well as innumerable demos. Altogether, Stephen James calculates, Elton's development cost DJM about £70,000, a sum reckonable as close to half a million today. 'We were getting to the point where we knew we had to say "That's it."'

It was Steve Brown's urgent contention that Elton must make another album, to build on the undoubted creative development of *Empty Sky*. Dick James agreed to this further investment late in 1969, though with an emphasis which none present could fail to notice. Elton's second album was to be, in other words, his last chance.

Steve Brown, that singular altruist, laboured to ensure that, if this were indeed the final throw of the dice, then it would be a good one. For the album sessions he persuaded Dick James to let him quit the severely limited DJM recording facility and, instead, book time at a modern, well-equipped West End studio, Trident. In a further burst of selflessness, he declared that he himself was not an experienced enough producer to bring Elton to full potential. Instead, a top-flight man should be brought in from outside.

Brown's first choice was George Martin, the Beatles' producer, now running his own studio, AIR-London. Martin was amenable, but insisted on arranging as well as producing, and Steve Brown preferred that the two jobs remain separate. His nominee as arranger was Paul Buckmaster, who had dreamed up the eerie orchestration for David Bowie's 1969 hit, 'Space Oddity', the first (but not last) pop song about a disenchanted astronaut. Buckmaster agreed to participate after hearing two piano and vocal demos by Elton intended for the new album, a historical minidrama called 'The King Must Die', and a ballad called 'Your Song'. Buckmaster, in turn, introduced Brown to Gus Dudgeon, who had produced 'Space Oddity' as well as albums for the Bonzo Dog Doo-Dah Band. As an established and highly fashionable producer, Dudgeon at first was not keen to take on a virtual unknown like Elton John. What swayed him was the undoubted promise on the two demos, plus a handsome royalty cut and Steve Brown's promise of *carte blanche* at the sessions.

Elton himself was intimidated by the resources mustered for his final attempt to make good. In addition to the usual backing band,

Paul Buckmaster's arrangements called for a full symphony orchestra, complete with harp. As the star later recalled, it was like suddenly being projected backwards to the time of Royal Academy concerts and frowning teachers named Stoupe. 'All the notes were written down, even the rhythm notes. I had to play live with everything. I mean, they had all these brilliant musicians standing there, and if I made a mistake, they all went.'

The main part of the album was recorded in January 1970, in conditions as different as they could possibly be from the late-night indulgence of Beatles or Stones. The musicians kept office-hours, breaking for coffee, tea and the occasional Chinese lunch in nearby Wardour Street. Elton himself set the prevailing tone of good humour and dogged professionalism. Nevertheless, it quickly became clear to Gus Dudgeon that Dick James's budget of £6,000 would not nearly finance all the further instrumental flourishes Paul Buckmaster had in mind. Midway through the recording, Dudgeon had to go and beg a £1,500 extension. When this, too, was rapidly spent, he went to Dick James again, taking some of the half-completed tracks. After listening to what was there, James nodded and said 'Finish it.'

Even to those who saw it develop layer upon layer, the completed album was a revelation. The raw material was essentially the same as on *Empty Sky*, a motley of images from Bernie Taupin's favourite stories, poems and films, welded together with chords from pudgy, capable hands. Again, the song-titles mixed elaborate literariness with throwaway pun: 'No Shoe Strings on Louise', 'First Episode at Hienton', 'Sixty Years On', 'Take Me to the Pilot'. Again, the only sexual tone was blushing chivalry, in 'I Need You to Turn To', and 'Your Song'. Again, the style was utterly eclectic, glancing off Shakespeare and Mary Renault in 'The King Must Die', colliding with Dixie gospel in 'Border Song', punching up every and any musical influence, from Chopin études learned ten years previously to the latest Friday night stop-press import at Musicland.

The difference was all in the recording: the depth and perspective lent by Paul Buckmaster's chamber music arrangements, the masterly blending by Gus Dudgeon of poetic introspection with acid-edged rock, the constant, artful switch of moods from the manic to the sensitive, from regicidal rabble-rousing to bashfully tongue-tied charm. The difference, above all, was in the voice, performing with a new energy and confidence down all the pinball zigzag of its emotion. By the time the last switch was thrown, Elton had delivered his first virtuoso performance.

Though Dudgeon and Steve Brown knew they had something very special, the great fear was that Dick James – faced with a bill now nearer £10,000 – would simply shake his bald head in bafflement. But James also was instantly captivated. Sue Ayton remembers the day the full album was first played, from one DJM executive suite to the other. 'Everyone said how brilliant it was. No one could talk about anything else.'

For Elton, it meant an immediate change of role. No longer was he just the kid who had monopolised the demo studio and camped out in reception. Every door was open to him, every executive sofa his to command as the inspired mosaic was reviewed again and again. From Dick James came a new tone of respect as he declared the album was 'out of the area of experimentation', and 'quite outstanding'. Not only that, he told Elton it 'deserved the distinction of a worthwhile recording agreement'. In March 1970 the 1967 recording agreement was cancelled and a new one took its place, binding Elton to DJM for five years, with an undertaking to make six, instead of the previous four, album sides each year. Instead of 20 per cent of This Record Co.'s receipts from Philips, he would get 40 per cent – that is, 40 per cent of 10 per cent, a sum equivalent to roughly 4 per cent of the record's retail selling-price. In two years, this would be increased to 60 per cent – or 6 per cent of the retail selling-price.

Great time and expense were devoted to a sleeve that would do justice to the album within. David Larkham's front-cover design showed half Elton's face and one outsize spectacle lens emerging from the black of some latter-day Rembrandt. In the same mood of definitive talent classily understated, it bore no title but the small, white-lettered name 'Elton John'. Overleaf, the principal players stood in line – Paul Buckmaster, Bernie Taupin, Gus Dudgeon, Caleb Quaye, Steve Brown, some in wide-brimmed hats, like Wild West outlaws on identity parade. Elton here was just one of the band, slimmer and more bushy-haired than he would ever look again, in cherry-red trousers and the rainbow-striped waistcoat his mother had knitted him.

Pleasant arguments raged back and forth about which of so many different strong and varicoloured tracks should be released as a single in advance of the album. No one at that stage even considered the modest little ballad that began side one with a note of diffident infatuation: 'It's a little bit funny, this feeling inside . . .' The vote was for 'Border Song', a quasi-spiritual, more than somewhat reminiscent of the Edwin Hawkins Singers' 'Oh, Happy Day'.

'Border Song' was released on 20 March. Though it did not reach the charts, enough impact was made to get Elton a booking on BBC TV's *Top of the Pops*. Brotherhood of Man's backup singer made it to his own podium at last, set about by jigging girls in maxiskirts, razor-cut pageboy hair and sateen lace-up boots. Backstage at Television Centre, he finally met Dusty Springfield, his teenage pin-up bouffant and pink taffeta dream. Dusty's enthusiasm for 'Border Song', the star would afterwards say, 'made my year'.

Top of the Pops was recorded a day in advance of its Thursday transmission. 'We all watched it at the office, on Dick's colour television,' Sue Ayton remembers. 'I could see Elton sweating as he saw himself on the screen.'

Dick James was now in a free-spending mood. To promote the album, he engaged DJM's first full-time press and publicity officer, a girl named Helen Walters, who had just quit her job as a schoolteacher in Croydon. With no previous music industry experience, she found herself responsible for organising a lavish press launch on 26 March, at London's most fashionable club, the Revolution. Its climax was James's presentation to Elton of a tape deck for his twenty-third birthday, the day before. A photographer afterwards snapped smiling mogul and side-whiskered protégé in one of the Revolution's Louis XIV-style banquettes, enjoying a cup of tea together.

The *Elton John* album was far more successful than its maker ever realised. In later years, he would remember it as a critical triumph but a chart disappointment that barely scraped into BBC Radio's Top 50 albums. In fact, it reached number 11 in the newly instituted nationwide chart compiled by the British Market Research Bureau. It stayed in the chart for fourteen weeks, through May and June 1970, competing with giants like the Beatles' *Let it Be*, Simon and Garfunkel's *Bridge Over Troubled Water*, Bob Dylan's *Self Portrait*, Paul McCartney's eponymous first solo album, and *Led Zeppelin II*.

The reviews were as good as they could possibly be. The *New Musical Express* called Elton 'a big talent . . . who sounds as if he has lived in Nashville all his life.' On *Melody Maker*'s page of album notices, he received billing above Grand Funk, Blodwyn Pig, Toe Fat and Nirvana, only losing the lead slot to Lord Sutch's Heavy Metal Friends. The reviewer's initials RW belonged to Richard Williams, soon to emerge as Britain's best writer on pop and jazz, and one of the earliest to recognise Elton's potential. Williams called *Elton John* 'a truly great record', citing 'brilliant production' and 'superbly crafted songs'. He followed this up with a full-page feature interview, detailing Elton's tortuous history from Mills Music to Bluesology, giving thanks for his 'Border Song' appearance as a breath of fresh air on *Top of the Pops*, and quoting his hero-worshipping but articulate enthusiasm for other artists like Van Morrison, Neil Young, the Band, especially 'people like Jagger and [Frank] Zappa, who don't give a — '. The piece was headed IS THIS THE YEAR OF ELTON JOHN?

The album's sale of 10,000 copies was excellent in that market at that time. More important, everyone throughout the tight-knit British music business had now heard of Elton John as a singer, the John–Taupin songwriting partnership, the DJM record label and a new phase in the career of pop's luckiest man.

What was still lacking, however, was the breakthrough to the mass singles market in which Dick James had invested so heavily. A third Elton single on DJM, 'Rock and Roll Madonna', was released in June to capitalise on the first flush of the album's success. Like every other Elton single for the past four years, it vanished without trace. So did an American single, 'From Denver to LA', used – unrecognisably – on the soundtrack of a Michael Winner movie, *The Games*. Cult success though Elton John might be on fashionable stereos, his face was still virtually unknown. In this period he made a further television appearance, playing piano for the American singer Lou Christie on BBC2's *Disco Two* programme. Throughout the number only his back was visible in an embroidered coat, pounding the keys like some frenzied, shadowy eighteenth-century highwayman's ghost.

Dick James's diagnosis was simple. Elton could not expect to work like Bob Dylan or Leonard Cohen, releasing albums every now and then and otherwise remaining shrouded in poetic mystery. He must go on the road and work all-out at acquiring a following that would look for his records in the shops. It was the last thing that Elton, with his caved-in confidence, wanted to do, and he has admitted he fought against it 'tooth and nail. But I suddenly decided it was the only way if the records were going to sell.'

As a live performer, his most pressing short-term need was for a full-time manager. Dick James was doing the job only with reluctance, leaving his day-to-day supervision to Steve Brown, the selfless A & R man. Brown, with his hippy wisdom and subtle powers of persuasion, would have suited Elton to perfection. But he was married, with a baby daughter, and did not want to be constantly off on the road.

Elton himself racked his brains for a candidate among his contacts in the music industry. One person he approached was Don Black, the songwriter who had just won an Oscar for his movie theme, 'Born Free'. Black also was published by Dick James and, in addition, managed the ballad singer Matt Monro. Though a fan of Elton's work, Don Black was too busy with his own songwriting to take on another client. However, he referred Elton to his long-time business partner, Vic Lewis, who – in the industry's endless game of musical chairs – had recently taken charge of Brian Epstein's old agency, NEMS.

Though NEMS and Dick James Music had long ceased their old intimate relationship – and now, indeed, ran competing record labels – Vic Lewis and Dick James remained very old friends. Rather than poach Dick's boy, Vic Lewis agreed that NEMS should take on his agency work, though with one major proviso. If Elton were to go on the road, he could not do it as a soulful solo pianist. He must have his own full-time band.

Dick James agreed to this further investment, although with a sharp eye to thrift and making do. 'Band' is, in fact, far too grand a term. Elton was launched on the road as a trio, backed by drums and bass, doing the instrumental donkey work himself as well as singing. Both his new sidemen were from the pool of musicians awaiting fame or oblivion at 71–75 New Oxford Street. Dee Murray, the bass player, had been in Mirage, on Larry Page's Page One label. Nigel Olsson, the drummer, had been in Plastic Penny, for whom Elton and Bernie had once been hopeful songwriters.

Against their reluctant piano-leader, the two long-haired newcomers provided strong visual counterpoint. Nigel Olsson was elfin and dark, like some clever foreign girl in an Enid Blyton school story. Dee Murray was large, fair and cheery-looking, like the same school's hockey or lacrosse captain. But, makeshift though they might be as a unit, their playing gelled right from the start. 'As soon as we got together, everything felt right,' Dee Murray remembers. 'It was just like magic. Elton was great to play with because he gave you complete freedom. Other people might not like you to improvise – they'd cut you out as soon as you stopped playing right on the beat. Elton would always discuss what you were doing, and might suggest you did it a different way. But he'd never ever try to cramp you.'

It was arranged they should split the concert proceeds, 60 per cent to Elton, 20 per cent each to Nigel and Dee. Dick James also provided a van and a single roadie, Bob Stacey, who had formerly been with the Spencer Davis Group.

The tie-up with Vic Lewis proved fortuitous in another way. NEMS, at the time, had just bought up the business of a rock band agent named Bryan Morrison. As part of the deal, Morrison joined the parent company, bringing with him a young associate with Nordic blond hair, china-blue eyes and almost ludicrous good looks. It was Ray Williams, whose want ad for Liberty records, two years before, had first brought Elton and Bernie Taupin together.

The thwarting of his plan to sign Elton to his Niraki company had scarcely checked Williams's easy ascent through the London music scene. After a successful term as head of A & R at Liberty, he had gone on to manage Jeff Lynne's band, the Idle Race, precursors of Lynne's subsequent creation, the Electric Light Orchestra.

Ray Williams met up with Dick James and Elton again just at the moment he was on the lookout for an act to manage that would strengthen his rather tenuous standing at NEMS. With his sharp ears and blue eyes he quickly recognised his opportunity. Neither James nor Vic Lewis, in their middle-aged eminence, wanted the bother of being a full-time manager. Elton himself, moreover, still felt grateful to the personable young man who had shown him a first way out of feeling 'lost' with Long John Baldry and Bluesology. As Williams remembers it, Elton came to him with a straightforward entreaty – 'Manage me.'

The initial plan was that Bryan Morrison and Ray Williams should buy out Elton's management contract from DJM. But the price that Dick James set was more than Vic Lewis felt NEMS should pay. 'Vic said "For that money, his gigs would have to average £75,000 a year",' Williams remembers. 'When I said they could do that, everyone else just laughed.'

When no deal could be made through NEMS, Dick James came up with an alternative plan. This was that Williams should manage Elton on behalf of DJM, working in-house for a 50 per cent share of the management commission. The arrangement was incorporated into a new three-year management agreement, dated 11 May, 1970, assigning DJM 20 per cent of Elton's earnings in the entertainment field, excluding songwriting. Ray Williams's share was to be 50 per cent of 90 per cent of that (10 per cent being deducted for the office facilities he would receive). He would draw a salary of £40 per week on account, with £5 per week in advance expenses.

Williams's arrival coincided with Elton's launch, or relaunch, as a reluctant stage performer. The opening gigs were for £50 a night at provincial universities or day jobs at the fag-end of the free festival era. The band travelled round in a single van, much like early Bluesology: Williams, Elton, Nigel, Dee and Bob Stacey the roadie, humping the rather basic equipment that had been financed by Dick James. 'Dick bought them about £1,000-worth of stuff, which I think he got wholesale,' Ray Williams says. 'I had the most terrible job getting him to pay to insure it.'

Only Dee and Nigel had their own equipment. Elton played whatever piano was available, however beaten-up or hideously out of tune. At one early northern gig, the piano he was supposed to use had both its foot pedals missing.

In performance, the trio's star quality was anything but apparent. Concert audiences by then had grown used to band ensembles numbering anything up to seven or eight. Huge spaces seemed to yawn between Elton at the piano and two sidemen who barely redressed the sense of physical oddity. Elfin Nigel Olsson all but disappeared behind an outsize kit that would eventually expand to thirteen amplified drums. Dee Murray was an amiable but scarcely charismatic figure, picking at his bass with a leisurely index finger and smiling his lacrosse captain's smile.

And, indeed, their first big chance on an international stage ended in total disaster. Vic Lewis at NEMS had booked them as warm-up act on a European tour by Sergio Mendez and his Latin-American orchestra. On opening night in Paris, an all-too-typical French audience booed them off stage. Bernie Taupin – watching in the wings with a bottle of Courvoisier brandy – also remembers bits of hot dog being thrown.

Almost as traumatising in a different way was an appearance in Belgium, at something called the Knokke Festival. This was not, as they had supposed, a pop-music event but a competitive television festival. Elton – whose Belgian following none had suspected – found himself performing in an elaborate set, surrounded by a troupe of dancing girls. To the amazement of its subject, 'Portrait van Elton John' was judged the festival's winning entry.

During these up-and-down weeks between Paris and Halifax, Ray Williams saw Elton's huddled shyness at the keyboard gradually break down, to be replaced by a revived energy and relish for taking on an audience. He also began to show the personal flamboyance that had been virtually buried since Janet Ritchie visited his bedroom at Pinner to try on his new fun fur.

A decisive sartorial moment occurred on a further short European foray when – with the sublime bad taste of old-fashioned pop – Elton and his band posed for publicity pictures against a background of the Berlin Wall. They also visited Sweden, to play at Stockholm University, and a local club. 'Afterwards, the club owner took Elton and me into this boutique,' Williams remembers. 'Elton was just in the denim jacket and jeans he always wore. They showed him an enormous jockey cap, three or four times normal size, blue with white polka dots. When he said he liked it, the club-owner bought it for him. He also liked the look of some men's handbags they had in the shop. Suddenly, there he was, camping it up in his jockey cap, swinging a handbag over his shoulder.

'I was the last one to get on the plane back to London. As I walked out across the tarmac, I could see Elton in one of the plane windows, wearing this stupid great jockey cap. When I went into the cabin, he was sitting there, grinning at me, and everyone else obviously thinking we were a couple of you-know-whats.'

That summer's most prestigious booking was at the Roundhouse, an old north London tram shed, then enjoying its brief season as hippydom's Albert Hall. Elton's trio appeared in one of the regular Roundhouse 'Pop Proms', warming up for the stars of the evening, Tyrannosaurus Rex. Performing for 2,000 promenading longhairs under the soot-black industrial rafters brought another victory over Elton's performing block. 'While he was playing, he accidentally kicked his piano-stool over,' Ray Williams remembers. 'It got a terrific reaction from the audience. So, at the next gig, he kicked it over on purpose.'

As Britain was brought round to Elton John by sweated labour and infinitesimal degrees, America remained steadfast in not wanting to know him.

Of no help at all was the fact that DJM Records had an American licensee, the Bell label in New York. Despite the close bonds implied, American licensee labels were historically reluctant to pick up on talent submitted by their British counterparts. Dick James himself could all too well remember how EMI's American outlet, Capitol, had blithely turned down the first three British hit singles by the Beatles.

Bell, likewise, turned down Elton John's 'Lady Samantha' in January 1969, oblivious of its status as a British 'turntable hit'. Several other New York labels having passed on it, the only course was to put it out on an American DJM label, whereafter it vanished without trace. When *Empty Sky* was released that June, Dick James sent it over to Bell's Larry Uttal, with a personal plea to recognise a unique new talent. But – like Johnny Franz at British Philips – Uttal could see no future in releasing an album by someone who had yet to make a hit single.

The year 1969 was, in any case, a bad time to be sending British music to America. The phenomenal mid-Sixties 'British Invasion' of Beatles, Stones, Herman's Hermits et al., had long since sputtered out. American bands, like Buffalo Springfield, the Flying Burrito Brothers and Creedence Clearwater Revival, now laid decisive claim on the native idioms which British boys had temporarily borrowed. America's most successful British musician was Graham Nash, formerly of the Hollies, now manifestly the junior partner in an amalgam of American group talent, Crosby, Stills, Nash and Young.

No less propitious moment could be imagined for a British solo performer, playing so unhip a thing as a piano. *Empty Sky* went the rounds of other East Coast labels, and received a universal thumbs-down.

The West Coast record companies were bound to be even more xenophobically fixated on bands of West Coast flavour. None the less DJM's New York representative, Lennie Hodes, thought he had better try. Leaving on a short business trip to Los Angeles that summer, Hodes packed a copy of *Empty Sky* and one of 'Lady Samantha'.

It happened that Roger Greenaway, Elton's fellow DJM songwriter and long-time supporter, was also in New York, preparing to go on to Los Angeles. He and Lennie Hodes travelled on the same flight and checked into the same hotel, the Continental-Hyatt on Sunset Boulevard.

The Hyatt was a rendezvous for music people from home and abroad. Breakfasting together in its coffee shop, Hodes and Greenaway spotted two familiar faces. One was the songwriter Don Black, currently enjoying a US number one with his theme song for the movie *To Sir with Love*. The other was Russ Regan, lately appointed head of Uni Records, a small offshoot of the giant MCA corporation.

'Lennie Hodes told me he'd got this terrific guy that no one in New York wanted to sign,' Russ Regan remembers. 'I said "How much do you want for him?" Lennie said, "Nothing. If you'll distribute him, I'll give him to you."'

Regan agreed to listen to the album and single that everyone on the East Coast had turned down. As Hodes went to fetch them, Don Black added his own warm recommendation of Elton. 'If Don Black likes him,' Regan said, 'that's good enough for me.'

When Lennie Hodes went to Uni Records for Regan's verdict, Roger Greenaway accompanied him. 'Russ Regan played about four tracks of *Empty Sky* as we sat there,' Greenaway remembers. 'Then he said, "I don't think this is for us. It's too introverted." He asked me what I thought of Elton. I said, "Well, I'm biased because I've seen him play live" – which I hadn't actually. I told Russ "This is someone who's going to be really huge and if you don't grab him, you'll be a very unhappy A & R man."'

Regan, it turned out, was far more interested in another DJM act, a new band called Argosy. Lennie Hodes's offer – relayed from Stephen James in London – was that if Uni records would take on Elton, they also could have Argosy. For Argosy, a band destined to sink without trace, Russ Regan paid DJM an advance of $10,000. For

Elton John, under the quid pro quo arrangement, he paid nothing.

Uni at first would do no more than rerelease 'Lady Samantha' – coupled with Elton's earlier flop, 'It's Me That You Need' – on its Congress label in January 1970. 'Border Song' followed the same cautious route in June, and made similarly little impact save, for some reason, in Memphis, Tennessee.

By then, however, much had changed in America's musical climate. The Beatles' slow motion smash-up had refocused attention on Britain, albeit via bizarre rumours that Paul McCartney was now dead. The Rolling Stones had made their first American tour for four years, its mounting mayhem climaxed by the murder of a spectator at the ghastly Altamont festival. It was clear that no American band could yet claim to surpass either of these phenomena from the country of Dickens and Shakespeare.

In the California brain of Russ Regan, similar mystical changes had taken place. When Regan received *Elton John* – an album better produced, but essentially no different in tone or style from the 'too introverted' *Empty Sky* – his ecstasy rivalled Pilgrim's at the gates of Paradise. 'I just flipped! I couldn't believe my good fortune. I kept saying to myself "How lucky can I get, to be given such a great piece of product!" I called the whole staff of Uni into my office, about thirty people. We put all the phones on "hold" and I played them the album through. Everybody fell in love with it.'

Regan's overjoyed message of acceptance to Dick James was accompanied by an urgent *cri de coeur*. When Uni released *Elton John*, late that summer, it was imperative that the artist himself be in America to help with promotion. Dick James's largesse, however, did not run to paying Elton's transatlantic air fare merely for the odd press or TV interview. If he were to go – and, indeed, attract the notice required – it must be on the basis of a proper concert tour.

Vic Lewis at NEMS then contacted his American associate, the agent Jerry Perenchio – and the familiar story began again. Perenchio could make no worthwhile concert bookings for an unknown English singer-pianist. Lewis, in exasperation, decided to bypass Perenchio and see what he could do off his own bat. He had previously sent a group named Pentangle to a successful appearance at Los Angeles' famous folk club the Troubadour. Contacting the Troubadour's owner, Doug Weston, he talked Weston into giving Elton's trio a week-long engagement, opening on 25 August. The clincher was Lewis's promise that, if Doug Weston gave this chance to a British unknown, he would be sure of 'a club full of stars'.

Money was of minor importance against the Troubadour's reputation as a showcase for quality rock talent and a listening-post for the West Coast music industry. Far more important was that Elton's trio would headline over David Ackles, a folk singer who, it happened, was among his and Bernie's chief American influences. For the whole week's engagement, Doug Weston offered only $500. Built into the contract was a booking at Weston's other Troubadour club, in San Francisco, plus an obligation to play return dates at the LA Troubadour over the next two years.

The exciting news filled Elton with something like horror. He had only just ventured back on the road, with a wholly untried band; now they were trying to shoot him off to America. He protested to Dick James that it was 'too early': he should not attempt America until better established in Britain, say in a year or so. Nor could he see how one week at a small folk club could possibly 'break' his album as DJM's American people suggested.

He agreed to go simply because it would be a nice trip, both for him and his indispensable lyricist, to the very seat of the culture both had worshipped since early boyhood. If the performer baulked, the pop fan and inveterate record-buyer was eager. 'We thought we might as well go over,' Bernie Taupin says, 'just to check out the record shops.'

Elton's doubts and forebodings persisted, however, to such a degree that the Elton John Trio almost did not keep its appointment with destiny at the Troubadour. And he himself was only prevented in the nick of time from consigning himself to the same outer darkness as Reggie Dwight in Bluesology.

Playing the Speakeasy club with Dee and Nigel one night, he was approached by Jeff Beck, formerly of the Yardbirds, now Britain's most famous guitarist after Eric Clapton. Beck was so impressed with the trio, he asked to sit in at one of the rehearsals they were currently holding at Hampstead Town Hall. After a session miraculously enhanced by Jeff Beck wizardry, he offered to join up with them permanently.

For a heady time, it seemed that the Elton John Trio had struck paydirt. Beck had a large following in America as well as in Britain, and would ensure them far better things over there than gigs at West Hollywood folk clubs for rates below the Musicians' Union minimum. Indeed, Beck's first advice was that they should immediately cancel the Troubadour engagement. He also wanted to bring in a 'name' drummer, Cozy Powell, to replace the elfin Nigel Olsson.

Elton was all for the plan, even though Beck clearly saw himself as both lead instrumentalist and vocalist. Dick James's efforts to talk him out of it only brought on one of Reggie's Little Moments. 'I heard them having a terrible row about it,' Sue Ayton remembers. Elton was shouting, "I want to do this. I've worked my arse off and got nowhere . . ."'

His enthusiasm waned when Jeff Beck's agent came on the phone and said that Beck would expect 90 per cent of the new group's earnings. The argument was that even Elton's one-third share of 10 per cent would amount to far more than he currently made. If they toured in America, Jeff Beck's name out front might pull in as much as $25,000 per night. Dick James then made a pronouncement that seemed grandiose. 'In six months' time, Elton John will be earning $25,000 a night on his own.'

Another problem now confronted Elton, one that can blight the most hopeful journey (which this one was not). When he opened at the Troubadour on 25 August, what was he to wear? Obviously, his old cords, his home-knitted rainbow waistcoat and badge-bespattered denim Levi suit would not do for Los Angeles. Yet, apart from an outsize jockey cap, blue with white polka dots, he possessed almost nothing else. Right back to the ginger tweed jacket he had worn while singing Ray Charles to Northwood Hills drinkers, clothes had never really been the point.

The only London clothes boutique that attracted him was Mr Freedom's shop at the bottom of Kensington Church Street. Mr Freedom in real life was an ebullient Cockney named Tommy Roberts whose clothes designs reflected both his irrepressible swagger and his almost circular shape. He was outrageous in designing for leisure only, and with blithe disregard for his customers' height, age or silhouette. After the pinched, winklepicker Sixties look, boys and girls alike plunged with relief into Mr Freedom's outsize T-shirts, emblazoned with appliqué Old Masters, his bright red or yellow lie-around boiler-suits and his range of roomy though wacky boots and shoes, some embellished with little Mercury wings.

Mr Freedom well remembers Elton's first tentative visit to the Kensington Church Street shop. 'He didn't wear anything way-out then. Just a donkey duffel and a college scarf. I used to have a room where special customers could change, and have a drink if they wanted one. Everyone used to go in there and whip the clothes on and off without worrying. But Elton didn't like taking his trousers down in public. I remember seeing him over in a corner, fumbling.

'He came in one day and said he wanted a few things to take with him to America. I remember I made him a yellow boiler-suit with a grand piano appliquéd on the back. And some white boots with green wings. Just normal-size heels, those first ones had.' Elsewhere he acquired a floppy tweed cap, a hipster belt with two outsize metal Texan stars and a T-shirt inscribed ROCK 'N' ROLL.

At the DJM office, much banter went on about the forthcoming trip. Looking at Elton as he helped with mail-outs or photocopying, or put on the kettle in the tea-making cubicle, no one could see a transatlantic conquerer to follow the Beatles, the Stones or Herman's Hermits. Much leg-pulling went on about the fact that he'd started to grow a rock star-ish beard. Sue Ayton told him jokily to watch out for the Plaster Casters, two American groupies so named for their unique method of memorialising rock stars' penises.

Ray Williams, as Elton's personal manager, was put in charge of the trip. Eight in all flew to Los Angeles on TWA, economy class: Elton, Bernie Taupin, Williams, Steve Brown, the musicians Nigel and Dee, the designer David Larkham and the roadie Bob Stacey.

Behind them Elton and Bernie left the tiny room with bunk-beds which they had continued sharing at Sheila Dwight's maisonette in Northwood Hills. Sue Ayton subsequently received a note from Sheila:

'Have only just got in. Was at work when they went. Reg has left the whole place full of flowers.'

Uni Records' publicity consultant, a frenetic man called Norm Winter, had been assigned to bring Elton John to the attention of Los Angeles. Winter is the kind of hyper who will tell you he loathes hype – unless, of course, the product to be hyped really and truly merits hyping. Elton's album fell as such a precious rarity into Norm Winter's life, causing him to forget all normal instincts towards understatement and decorum. 'I knew it was special as soon as Russ Regan played me some of the tracks. I knew this was something you took your pecker out for, and put it on the table.'

The first taste of Winter's PR style was shown to Elton and his seven companions when they emerged from the arrivals hall at Los Angeles International Airport. Tired and rumpled after the eight-hour economy flight, they had looked forward to sinking into some restful air-conditioned record-company limousines. Instead, Norm Winter proudly showed them to the mode of transport he felt most eye-catchingly suitable for new young music stars from Swinging London. This was a red double-decker bus, filled with rollicksome Uni staff and hung with banners in the same typeface as the album, saying ELTON JOHN HAS ARRIVED.

The arrival photograph speaks eloquent volumes about Norm Winter's coup. Every English face ranged against it shows what a world-shattering thrill was the concept of being greeted by a London bus. By symbolic accident, Ray Williams seems the centre of the group with his gold hair and sideburns and his air of creativity, arrested in flight. Elton, on the extreme left, in dungarees and glasses, his arms resignedly folded, might be just another supernumerary roadie.

Grinding down the freeway to the City of Angels on hard bench seats, surrounded by reminders of a life Elton and Bernie thought they had left behind – '6 Passengers Standing', 'Used Tickets', 'Press Bell Once to Stop' – could not be called a promising start. And, indeed, things were to get a lot worse before becoming even faintly better.

The bus stopped first at the Troubadour Club, at 9079 Santa Monica Boulevard, and Elton was shown the unspectacular-looking 300-seat space where he would open in two nights' time. Thence to their hotel, the Hyatt, on an unglamorous uphill stretch of Sunset Boulevard. To be well in time for the Troubadour's Tuesday opening night, they had arrived on a weekend. Once Norm Winter's enthusiastic patter had faded and the London bus engaged its noisy gears and pulled away, there was nothing scheduled for approximately the next thirty-six hours.

As team leader, Ray Williams volunteered to get on the phone to see what entertainment he could find. It happened that none of the party had remembered to bring a hair-dryer, essential for the shampooing of apostle-length hippy hair. Williams called an old girl-friend of his named Joanne, to see if she had a hair-dryer. Joanne had gone abroad, but her sister Janice was at home. Janice had a hair-dryer, and volunteered to bring it right over. With her she also brought a girl friend named Maxine Feibelman, at the sight of whom Bernie Taupin's dark eyes immediately kindled.

With Janice and Maxine, Ray Williams hatched a plan for the following, free day. They would all take a trip down to Palm Springs in Janice's car. Six out of seven in the party accepted the idea eagerly. Only one – Elton – said he didn't want to go. 'At the time, I didn't think I was dealing with a star,' Ray Williams says now. 'To me, we were just a group of mates away on a trip together. So I told Elton, "The majority want to go to Palm Springs – see you when we get back". The six of us went off for the whole day in this girl Janice's car. I was getting on very well with Janice, and Bernie was getting on very well with Maxine. We spent the day in Palm Springs, and all got quite pissed.'

When he met up with Elton again that night, Ray Williams saw at once that something was seriously amiss. 'Elton was very very weird. I realised that being left alone all day had put him in some kind of bad mental state. He was sulking – and petrified. I heard later that he'd been on the phone to Dick James in London, and Dick had had to calm him down. The next morning at breakfast he was even worse. He said he wasn't going to play the Troubadour date, and was getting on the first plane home. I basically had a fight with him. I said, "You've got to do it, you can't spend all this money for nothing." He said "I don't give a fuck, I'm going."'

It was one of Reggie's Little Moments in excelsis. It was, indeed, the first of Elton's Little Moments. All Ray Williams's efforts on the spot and Dick James's over the transatlantic phone were needed to mollify the attack of mingled peevishness and terror, and stop him calling a cab for the airport.

Meanwhile Norm Winter, Uni Records' PR man, had been working at fever-pitch. All the main LA record stores displayed posters of Elton and piles of his funereally black-covered album. Every important disc jockey had been primed with free copies and press kits. When the cost outran what Uni were prepared to spend on an unknown British act, Winter approached Elektra Records, whose artist, David Ackles, was second on the bill to Elton. Elektra agreed to pay for half the hype, even though none of it was destined to benefit Ackles.

This latter gambit had to be carefully kept from Elton, himself a long-time fan of David Ackles via Musicland's imports box. While Winter laboured deviously to throw Ackles into the shade, Elton worried because his name appeared in bigger letters than Ackles's on the Troubadour's marquee. He and Bernie Taupin both thought it 'terrible' that idiosyncratic folk talents like Ackles, Tim Buckley and Tom Paxton enjoyed so little status and respect in their own country.

For the Tuesday first night, Norm Winter and Vic Lewis between them had succeeded in giving Doug Weston his 'club full of stars'. Winter had enticed in a galaxy of 'serious' rock stars: singer-songwriters Gordon Lightfoot, Mike Love of the Beach Boys, David Gates of Bread. Supporters from England included the two songwriters who had done so much to promote Elton, Roger Greenaway and Don Black. Working on Vic Lewis's behalf, Black brought along the arranger Quincy Jones, the composer Elmer Bernstein and the conductor Henry Mancini. The greatest coup of all had been to persuade Neil Diamond, then the hottest American pop troubadour – and, by happy chance, also a Uni artist – to introduce Elton onstage. Many of the industry people, press and radio disc jockeys arrived under the mistaken impression that they were to witness a performance by Neil Diamond.

Waiting in the tiny backstage area, Elton was almost incoherent with nerves. As well as the audience of his musical heroes out front, there were reviewers from every important West Coast publication, from underground papers like *Rolling Stone* and the *Los Angeles Free Press* to the stodgy but all-powerful *Los Angeles Times*. Robert Hilburn, the *Times*'s rock writer, had meant to go to the Coconut Grove that night, but Norm Winter had persuaded him instead to give an ear to this obscure import from London.

The moment of walking out before this glittering assembly was awesome. Yet it also was strangely familiar. It had happened nine years before, when the crop-headed schoolboy played his first Friday night at the Northwood Hills Hotel. Then he had looked out at olde oak walls, brown lino and tin ash-trays. Now, it was darkness lit by glass-cupped candle flames. Then he had worn a ginger Harris tweed sports jacket. Now he wore dark glasses, a grimy growth of beard and a T-shirt inscribed ROCK 'N' ROLL. But, just as at George Hill's cavernous pub, there was a yawning pit in front of him. And once again, to the boy nurtured on timidity and caution, the only possible way out was to take the plunge.

Robert Hilburn was not initially impressed when Elton struck up on a nod to his two sidemen. 'He started going through his songs in a somewhat distant, businesslike manner. He looked scared, keeping his eyes on the piano and microphone in front of him.

'I don't remember now what the first song he did that night was. I think it was from the *Elton John* album. But I do remember it had the kind of distinctiveness and personal vision you look for in a new pop act. The really impressive thing was that the strengths of the songs were all different. The songs, for instance, that hit me hardest that night were "Your Song", a gentle tale of romantic affection, "Sixty Years On", a touching look at the loneliness of old age, "Country Comfort", a country-flavoured sentimental song about going home, and "Burn Down the Mission", a raucous, straight-ahead rocker.'

Not everyone was as attentive as Robert Hilburn. This was, after all, a totally unknown British act, and the conventions of West Coast 'cool', besides, forbade overt enthusiasm about anything. The Troubadour audience therefore carried on their usual habit of lingering at the bar, greeting their friends and talking noisily among themselves. To Elton, it wasn't much better than playing with Bluesology in a Tyneside cabaret club while people marked their bingo cards and ate their chicken-in-the-basket.

Around the third or fourth number, his volatile temper snapped. 'He got really furious,' Don Black remembers. 'He stood up, kicked away his piano-stool and shouted "Right! If you won't listen, perhaps you'll bloody well listen to this." Then he started pounding the piano like Jerry Lee Lewis.'

The Troubadour crowd was taken utterly by surprise. On the evidence of the album-sleeve's shadowy face, they had supposed they were in for a rather serious set from some sombre, introspective British folkie. What they got was totally American – Greenwich Village coffee-house poems of Bob Dylan in the chicano wail of José Feliciano, pounded out in the torn-up keyboard riffs of the 'Killer' at his most recklessly manic. Of all the people Elton surprised that night, none was more astonished than himself. In his temper, he had come upon stores of passion and pazzazz not seen since breaktimes at Pinner County Grammar and nights at Northwood British Legion Hall.

The frosty cool of the Troubadour vanished like mist from a Martini glass. Instead of the usual polite applause, there were cheers, whistles and whoops of welcome back to the glorious disreputable old ghosts of rock 'n' roll. During 'Take Me to the Pilot', the huge silhouette of the soul singer Odetta became visible at the back, like a wildly frugging dreadnought in the night. By the finale of Bernie Taupin's new Western epic, 'Burn Down the Mission', Elton was playing down on his knees, just Reggie Dwight, at the very start with the Corvettes.

Britishness broke through only when he had finished his selection from *Empty Sky*, *Elton John* and his imminent new album, *Tumbleweed Connection*, and started a run of Little Richard and Jerry Lee oldies much as he might once have settled down to 'The Old Bull and Bush' or 'Bye Bye Blackbird'. Then the bearded owl gave his audience a smile that was pure Winnie Atwell, and told them they were welcome to join in the choruses if they liked.

Afterwards, so many people wanted to meet him that Norm Winter had to set up an almost royal receiving line. The piano-kicking showman became a fan once more, shaking his heroes' hands with dumb reverence, uncomfortable amid their accolades, wanting far more to talk about great things they had done. Arranger Quincy Jones (the future mentor of Michael Jackson) brought his whole family backstage. 'He seemed to have about 900 children,' the star was to remember. 'I just kept on shaking hands coming through the door.' A rash Uni PR man introduced him to Quincy Jones as 'a genius'. Elton was thrown into an anguish of embarrassment and stormed at the PR man, 'Never do that to me again.'

The next morning brought a flood of congratulatory phone-calls from those who had witnessed Elton's triumph, and those who wished they had. Among the latter was Bill Graham, America's foremost rock promoter, begging to put Elton on at his Fillmore East in New York. Graham offered $5,000, the largest sum that a first-time performer at the Fillmore East would ever have received.

The second night at the Troubadour brought a further influx of stars, not attracted by PR hype this time, but by excited word of mouth. Among them was Leon Russell, rock's prototype singer-pianist, an eerie-looking silver-haired man, as sour and cynical in appearance as his voice sounded on record. 'I didn't see him until the last number,' Elton remembers. 'Thank God I didn't, because at that time I slept and drank Leon Russell. When I saw him, I just stopped. He said "Keep on."

'I lost my voice during the next day, and he invited me up to his house. I thought he was going to tie me to a chair and say, "Listen, motherfucker, this is how you play piano." But he was so nice. He gave me a gargling potion that I continue to use to this day.'

Bernie Taupin went along, too, a star-struck back-seat passenger. 'It was the first time I'd ever seen a rock star's house. It was a huge place, completely empty but for some beds, instruments and stereo. For some reason, all rock stars' houses were exactly the same.'

He and Elton were given a grand tour of LA rock society by Danny Hutton from Three Dog Night, a band that had covered 'Lady Samantha' and 'Your Song' in America. Hutton took them to call on Brian Wilson, their ultimate pop idol, founding genius of the Beach Boys. The man who had hymned the open-faced, crew-cut joys of sun and surf was by then a neurotic recluse. 'I'll never forget arriving at Brian Wilson's house,' Bernie Taupin says. 'Danny Hutton rang at this big security gate and said, "I've got Elton John and Bernie Taupin here." Suddenly a voice on the intercom started singing, "I hope you don't mind . . . I hope you don't mind . . ." It was Brian Wilson, singing "Your Song".

'When we got inside, he insisted we had to see his kids, even though it was the early hours of the morning. He took us into a nursery, picked up each of these sleeping children and waved them under our noses. Then he started playing us marvellous tapes he'd made, that had never been released. But as soon as he started playing one, he'd take it off and start playing another. Both of us wanted to scream, "Let's hear all of it!"'

Elton was now, understandably, on top of the world, thrilled to have met Brian Wilson and Leon Russell, additionally excited to hear that, during his appearance at the San Francisco Troubadour, the tenth anniversary convention of the Tamla-Motown label would also be going on up there.

His one discontent, paradoxically, was on behalf of David Ackles, the pensive folk-poet he was nightly blasting off the Troubadour's stage. As a fortune now came within his own grasp, Elton was scandalised to hear that Ackles's whole year's income could be as little as $5,000. He watched Ackles play each night, an enraptured fan, furious with the audience for talking and fidgeting through the set. Ackles himself was philosophical, buying Elton half a bottle of whisky and saying it had been a pleasure working with him. 'Do you know,' the superstar would say, 'that meant most of all to me.'

He had apparently got over his anger with Ray Williams, pushing Williams into the Hyatt swimming pool to symbolise – as Williams thought – a return to friendly relations. 'I bought him a kimono,' Williams remembers. 'As far as I was concerned, everything was back to normal between us.'

In his punctilious way, Elton sent postcards to everyone at home, including the DJM office staff. '. . . Have not encountered any Plaster Casters yet . . .' he wrote to Sue Ayton. 'Having a great time . . . seem to be going down really well so far . . . Love, Reg.'

To lift his spirits further there was the discovery of Tower Records, a store many times larger than London's largest, the HMV shop in Oxford Street. More exciting even than his Troubadour début was that first journey with a supermarket trolley through aisle after aisle of albums that would not be at Musicland for weeks yet. A friend in London remembers an excited phone call, totally unconnected with having become the toast of LA. 'Hey,' Elton's voice said, in almost hushed reverence, 'I've just got Neil Young's new one, *After the Goldrush*.'

There was also a trip to Disneyland, arranged by Uni Records, a fleet of limos mercifully replacing the London bus. 'We were VIPs by this time,' Ray Williams says. 'They virtually gave us the key to Disneyland. We were loaded with souvenirs, ushered to the front of every line.'

That moment, posing in paper Mickey Mouse ears under the perma-pressed spires of Snow White's Castle, Reggie Dwight was finally laid to rest and Elton John was born. Marvellous, the feel and scent of this land without horizons or nosy neighbours, where 'good taste' did not exist, jumbo and outsize were normal scale and a bit of outrage was everyone's God-given right. He wore the ears onstage that night, together with a pair of baggy shorts, and went down even better. He had broken Squadron Leader Dwight's dress-code for good and all.

On Thursday 27 August – by the grace of Norm Winter's persuasive tongue and a fortuitously less enticing attraction at the Coconut Grove – Robert Hilburn's rock column in the *Los Angeles Times* was devoted to Elton's Troubadour opening. The headline was ELTON JOHN NEW ROCK TALENT. The opening sentence was a single word: 'Rejoice.'

Rock music, which has been going through a rather uneventful period recently, has a new star. He's Elton John, a 23-year-old Englishman, whose debut Tuesday night at the Troubadour was, in almost every way, magnificent.

. . . His music is so staggeringly original that it is obvious he is not merely operating within a given field (such as country or blues or rock) but, like Randy Newman and Laura Nyro among others, creating his own field . . . He has, to be sure, borrowed from country, rock, blues, folk and other influences, but he has mixed them in his own way. The resulting songs are so varied in texture that his work defies classification . . .

While his voice most often resembles José Feliciano, there are at times touches of Leon Russell and Mick Jagger . . .

John's songs are co-written by lyricist Bernie Taupin, whose lyrics often capture the same timeless, objective spirit of the Band's Robbie Robertson . . .

Beyond his vocals, melodies and arrangements there is a certain sense of the absurd . . . that is reminiscent of the American rock stars of the mid-1950s . . .

By the end of the evening, there was no question about John's talent and potential. Tuesday night at The Troubadour was just the beginning. He's going to be one of rock's biggest and most important stars.

There were similar eulogies in the *LA Free Press* ('a marvelous and very resourceful songwriter-performer'), the *Chicago Sun-Times* ('a major star before the end of his first set'), the *San Francisco Chronicle* ('interesting, offbeat and sympathetic to life'), and the *Hollywood Reporter* ('spectacularly exciting'). A local FM radio station, KPPC, took out a full-page press advertisement, thanking Elton for coming to America. But Robert Hilburn's piece eclipsed all. For its message was one irresistible to that tawdry town throughout fifty years of movie-making, the same message even now that the Sunset Boulevard billboards showed Janet Gaynor and Judy Garland no longer, but Diana Ross and the Jackson Five. The one idea guaranteed to wake up Hollywood from its romantic heart to its greedy head. A star is born.

Elton was 'broken' on the West Coast – and much more. By the strange magic that transmits any novelty coast-to-coast at a thousand miles an hour, all America now knew that the Seventies had a new rock star. Within only two weeks of his Troubadour opening, the *Elton John* album had sold 30,000 copies. In Philadelphia in a single day – to quote Russ Regan's ecstatic argot – 'six thousand units were popped loose'.

What had begun as a low-budget flying visit had become a fully fledged tour, going on from the San Francisco Troubadour to additional concert dates in Boston, the Electric Factory in Philadelphia, and a press reception in New York at the Playboy Club. Dick James was contacted in London, and agreed to put up more travelling money.

In Los Angeles, every FM rock station up and down the Strip now played tag with *Empty Sky* and *Elton John*. It is Roger Greenaway's memory of driving to the airport to catch his London plane: the sun, the smog, the scabby palms; a disc jockey's voice, in almost sacerdotal hush, saying 'The New Messiah is here.'

II
LORD CHOC ICE

6

'Dylan digs Elton'

A FEW weeks after the New Messiah's return to London, he was to be seen in concert at the Royal Albert Hall. The recent headliner in San Francisco and Boston now appeared merely as warm-up act for a folk-rock band named Fotheringay. On opening night Sue Ayton arrived by taxi, bringing Sheila Dwight and Derf Farebrother. They found the New Messiah waiting for them at the Albert Hall's main entrance, unnoticed by anyone in the crowd.

Such was the anticlimactic bump with which Elton returned to his native land in September 1970. In America, he was the biggest English coast-to-coast sensation since the Beatles in 1964. But back in Britain, he reverted to being just another semi-famous pop name among many. Over there, the second coming. Over here, still only second feature.

When the Beatles returned home in 1964, they were greeted by cheering crowds, orgies of celebration in the media and, ultimately, an MBE each for enhancing national prestige and aiding the export drive. Six years later, Britain exported long-haired musicians with as little emotion as safety pins or soap. The pop industry's routine hyperbole all but exhausted belief in genuine success or achievement. None but a tiny handful of people around the British music scene realised just what Elton had pulled off.

The few scanty press reports of his American triumph were confined to music papers. ELTON STORMS THE STATES, *Melody Maker* announced, though deeming Richard Williams's story of sufficient interest only for an inside page. To Williams, Elton gave a typically modest, humble and grateful account of the LA expedition, paying tribute to Dick James for the finance, owning up to near paralytic stage fright at the Troubadour, especially when Leon Russell appeared in the audience.

The effect was of a level head, totally unaffected by all the West Coast hype and adulation. 'Of course, some of the reviews have been ridiculous. But I know how good I am and what I'm capable of. You simply can't sit back and believe everything people say about you, or you'd get terrible ego problems. I do believe that we write good songs, but I get very embarrassed when people say so.' He added that among his American souvenirs was a gold lamé tail coat, which he planned to wear onstage at the Albert Hall. 'It's from a Thirties Busby Berkeley musical,' he told Richard Williams, adding cryptically, 'I may sew some sausages on it.'

In fact, as he admitted to another journalist, coming back down to earth in Britain, after that wild three-week American roller-coaster ride, had left Elton feeling 'depressed and shattered'. He also worried that the rave reviews had often overlooked Bernie Taupin's importance to the music. Bernie, however, was more than happy with the trip. He had fallen in love with Maxine Feibelman, the girl with whom he'd spent an idyllic hot afternoon in Palm Springs. Elton too, as it happened, had 'met someone'. But this could not be admitted for a long time yet.

So, for the present, life resumed a humdrum course, barely enlivened by the release of *Tumbleweed Connection*, his third album, completed the previous August. For this he had still been drawing on the huge cache of material written at Frome Court, though, fortuitously, the feel was totally different from the *Elton John* album's torchlit paganism. As its title suggests, *Tumbleweed Connection* celebrated Bernie Taupin's childhood love of the American West. Almost all the tracks had a cowboy or Mexican border feel: 'Country Comfort', 'Ballad of a Well-Known Gun', 'My Father's Gun', 'Burn Down the Mission'. The lyrics teemed with references to trains, riverboats, hellfire preachers and rocking chairs, mixed with memories from Bernie's own far frontier in Lincolnshire – the cow sheds, cornfields, squirrels and nightjars; the Angel Tree where he would sit and daydream; even his farmer father, 'the herdsman with his torch'. The mood throughout was folksy and down-home, punctuated with yodels and rebel yells, culminating in Elton's bravura honky-tonk finale to 'Burn Down the Mission' which had already knocked them dead at the LA Troubadour.

Only two tracks were not narratives cribbed straight out of *Buffalo Bill's Annual*. 'Amoreena' was an idyll touched with the spirit of a Renoir cornfield. 'Love Song' – a cover version of Lesley Duncan's ballad – charmed with its gentle persuasiveness, and words that might seem to have been prophetic:

Love is the opening door.
Love is what we came here for.

David Larkham's sepia album sleeve showed what an unreal world America had still been to both composers when the songs were recorded. Elton, in Lenin cap, floral shirt and cowboy boots, sat with his back to the wall on a Victorian station platform covered with enamel signs for Sunlight soap and Mazawattee tea. The shot continued overleaf, Bernie Taupin lounging near a sign for Swan Vesta matches, like some anonymous foot soldier photographed after Gettysburg. Inside was a twelve-page booklet with the lyrics expensively printed amid mock-Victorian woodcuts and cameos. There was also a dedication: 'With love to David' [Ackles].

Tumbleweed Connection was released on 30 October. Despite excellent reviews and steady sales, it made no immediate showing in the UK album charts. Elton was reluctant to put out any of the tracks as a single, and Dick and Stephen James agreed with him that none was 'commercial' enough. Workaholic as ever, he plunged into a fresh project, recording a soundtrack album for a movie, *Friends*, directed by Lewis Gilbert.

In lifestyle Elton remained as unassuming as before conquering America. New Messiah or not, he continued living at home with his mum in Northwood Hills, sharing the tiny bedsit with Bernie Taupin, hanging his hippy chains neatly over the rail of their little-boy bunk beds last thing every night. The only difference was that now Sheila Dwight's telephone rang at crazy early-morning hours with calls from Maxine Feibelman, Bernie's new Californian love.

To the public at large, Elton John still represented upmarket, even esoteric pop, the kind heard late at night on BBC Radio One, announced in the dour, deadpan Liverpudlian voice of John Peel. 'Now here's another incredibly wonderful track from *Tumbleweed Connection . . .*' Gratifying though it might be to have the track played all through, without interruption, it was not the way to mass sales. The way to mass sales was to be on Tony Blackburn's early-morning show, competing with cheeky boy puns and the electronic woof-woofs of Arnold, the dog.

Only a small band of initiates yet could confirm Richard Williams's assertion that 'despite the sombre quality in his recorded work, Elton is nothing if not a raver onstage.' They included the audiences who went to see Fotheringay at the Royal Albert Hall, ready for an evening of whimsical folk-rock songs about dragons, fairies and witches' spells. The opening act, in his gold Busby Berkeley tail coat, stole the show every night. 'He was determined about that,' Sue Ayton remembers. 'He was going to blow Fotheringay off the stage.'

In America, meanwhile, waves of excitement and interest continued to swirl around in his wake. The combined effect of four minuscule dates and Robert Hilburn's review was to propel the *Elton John* album to fourth position in *Billboard* magazine's chart. When *Tumbleweed Connection* was released, it too went into the *Billboard* chart, eventually reaching number five. Everyone in the music business, East and West Coast, was talking about this bespectacled Great White Hope for the Seventies who had come, briefly shone his light, then departed again, still on TWA economy class.

Clearly, it was imperative for Vic Lewis, his British agent, to send him back on a full-scale tour as quickly as possible. The complication was Doug Weston of the Troubadour, who, in return for Elton's matchless exposure at his club, had obliged Ray Williams to sign a contract stipulating two further appearances, at the same knock-down fee. 'In the end, we had to give Weston $100,000 to buy the contract out,' Vic Lewis says. 'Dick James and I paid it between us.'

This left Lewis and his US counterpart, Jerry Perenchio, free to set up a coast-to-coast itinerary for Elton, from mid-November to early December. For the major dates, he would open for his great idol, Leon Russell. The climax was the two-night booking in New York at Bill Graham's Fillmore East. Graham, typically, had no doubt where the future lay. At the Fillmore, Elton's and Russell's names were to be displayed with equal prominence.

The moment was well caught in a *New Musical Express* headline, ELTON JOHN, SHY EXTROVERT. The writer, Gillian Saitch, happened to be with Elton when the Fillmore East news came in, and so witnessed his mixture of excitement and anguish even to be mentioned in the same breath as Leon Russell. To Gill Saitch, he came over as sensible, courteous, straightforward, in every way a blessed relief from the mumbling poseurs that were a pop interviewer's usual lot. 'I get embarrassed by all the publicity,' he admitted. 'It's very flattering, but it can do more harm than good, because the kids who listen to music these days want to form their own opinion and not be hyped into liking something.'

As usual he talked of other people as much as of himself: Leon Russell, Quincy Jones, Graham Nash, and his latest pop fan enthusiasms, Joni Mitchell and James Taylor. Remembering what had happened in America, he took special pains to emphasise Bernie Taupin's vital role in the composition process. 'Without Bernie, there'd be no songs. I get very annoyed when people ignore him.'

'Interviewing Elton John must be one of the most relaxing occupations around,' wrote Gillian Saitch. 'Although quiet and retiring in some ways, once he starts talking he makes you feel how dedicated he is to his music, and he has very definite ideas about how things should be done.'

The same serious, low-key feel came from his first major performance on British television. This was a thirty-minute *In Concert* programme on BBC2, recorded the previous May but not transmitted until the end of October, just after Elton had left for the States again.

Apart from *Top of the Pops*, BBC TV in those days allowed pop music only if it could be given the guise of a serious, subclassical form. Elton's *In Concert* therefore was subtitled 'The Songs of Elton John and Bernie Taupin', as if part of some ongoing musico-anthropological study. Compounding the sense of upmarket exotica, it went out at the almost inconceivably late hour of 10.30 pm.

Seen now, the programme is a little classic of 1970 earnestness. The title appears in fairground carousel letters of psychedelic red, to the opening chords of 'Your Song'. The letters enlarge and simultaneously grow transparent, revealing Elton at a grand piano with a full string orchestra conducted by Paul Buckmaster. Watching in the round are sixty-odd teenagers handpicked for their fashionable but sensible and mature BBC2 look: girls with madonna-length hair and microskirts, and Indian-smocked, side-whiskered boys. Here and there, over the hirsute young heads and the balding ones of the middle-aged orchestra, hang long Oriental-looking mobiles of tinkly white.

Four months as this was before his Troubadour triumph, Elton gives off few signals of either showman or star. His knitted rainbow waistcoat, salmon-pink T-shirt and pale blue jeans are getting perilously close to shabbiness. Near-blond hair is combed down close as a helmet around squared granny specs. Only the stubby hands have changed, being now covered with chunky silver rings.

With the confident, impassioned singing comes a bare minimum of talk. His main concern seems to get through everything in the time allotted: 'Border Song', 'Sixty Years On', 'Take Me to the Pilot', 'The Greatest Discovery', 'I Need You to Turn To'. To the sedate applause his response is a brief 'Thank you', a gap-toothed grin and 'This next one's called . . .' In frequent arty cutaways we see Paul Buckmaster, like an elegant dervish, playing cello; the sheet music of the violinists; the hands of a lady harpist; the tuba-player's bulb-inflated cheeks; the solemn young audience listening with no movement but occasional flicks of hair from their faces; the ivory-white mobiles winking and shimmering overhead.

The longest pause between songs is for Elton to introduce Bernie Taupin, sitting in the audience; a shy Cherokee face and a fawn T-shirt. 'He's my partner . . . Actually he's more important than me because he writes the words. This next one, I think, is the finest lyric he's ever written . . .'

On the 'front board' where a recorded TV show's production details are chalked, 'The Songs of Elton John and Bernie Taupin' was classified for BBC archives as 'Folk'.

The Los Angeles trip had done permanent damage between Elton and Ray Williams, his personal manager. It was all the fault of that unfortunate initial free day, when Williams had taken Bernie and the band for a trip to Palm Springs with two girls, leaving Elton alone at the hotel.

Like many good-looking people, Ray Williams was somewhat lacking in imagination. He assumed Elton would treat the episode as just one of those things that happen when you're abroad with a group of mates. He did not realise that, in Elton's new but fast-developing concept of affairs, he was now no longer a mate, but a functionary. Still less did he realise that, to Elton, that day alone on Sunset Boulevard was rejection and abandonment akin to being tied with a label and put on a cattle train across Siberia.

Back in London, the Palm Springs episode continued to reverberate. Dick James made no secret of his view that, by going AWOL and stirring up Elton at that crucial moment, Williams could easily have ruined the whole American trip. In the political circles that now existed around Elton himself, opinion began to run against the blond-haired Adonis. It began to be whispered that in other management matters, too, he had been less than brilliant, lackadaisical in the organisation of Elton's gigs, and too reliant on the power of his looks and easy-going charm.

On the other hand, his vast importance to Elton and Bernie couldn't be denied. Not only had he found them both, with his want ad at Liberty Records, and put them together as songwriters, he also had brought them to Dick James Music, via his publishing company, Niraki.

At first the problem seemed amiably resolved. After their return from Los Angeles in September, Elton told Williams over lunch that he thought the management arrangement 'wasn't working'. 'I totally agreed with him,' Williams says. 'I could see the kind of manager he needed, and it wasn't someone like me. What he needed was the person who eventually did wind up managing him. Another thing was that, with his success, he was starting to get away with murder. He was very quick, very witty, very funny, and people just let him get away with anything. I'd been standing up to him and that hadn't been going down well. It was also the time he was starting to find himself sexually. I found that another pressure on our relationship.'

According to Ray Williams, Elton and he agreed informally to sever their association at the end of Williams's current one-year contract with DJM, in May 1971. The share of the management commission Dick James was contracted to pay him – 50 per cent of 90 per cent – would be substantial recompense. 'There was the tour coming up, and another one in spring-summer of '71. There were going to be albums, live concerts . . . I was looking at a lot of money.'

In mid-November, Elton and the band left for America again. Shortly afterwards, Ray Williams was summoned to Dick James's office. 'Dick just said "I'm tearing up your agreement. You can sue me. Or you can accept £500 settlement." I was totally amazed. I said "I've got an arrangement with Elton, which, after all, has only got about six months more to run." Dick said, "I don't care. I'm tearing it up."'

Williams's first reaction was to try to contact Elton on the road in America. 'As far as I was concerned, we were still friends. He was godfather to my daughter, Amoreena. But now when I called him up, I could never get through to him. Each time, Steve Brown or some other member of the organisation answered the phone and said Elton wasn't available. To this day, I don't know if he ever knew what was going on.'

There was very little else that Ray Williams could do. Despite the grandeur of his 'personal manager' title, he was no more than a salaried employee at DJM, not even privy to the various contracts between Elton and Dick James. His finances entirely dependent on the commission to come, he was living from hand to mouth with a wife and five-month-old baby. He approached a couple of lawyers, hoping one might take his case on the American system of a share in the proceeds, but none ethically could. Meanwhile, his weekly retainer from DJM was stopped. He fell behind with the rent on his Islington house, and was even running out of money to buy food. 'It may sound dramatic now, but that's the way things were.'

In a series of meetings with Dick James the compensation offer was laboriously winched up from £500 to £750, and finally to £1,500. 'Dick was quite vicious about it,' Williams says. 'All the time he was saying, "You can sue if you want", knowing full well that I couldn't.'

Williams saw he had no alternative but to accept £1,500. For that, the contract he had in no way breached was torn up, and his unspecified thousands in commission melted away. He also had to agree to the deduction of what he had already received in weekly salary. This meant his payoff finally boiled down to around £1,100. 'At least it was enough to pay my back rent and put some food in the fridge. I wasn't even allowed to take my files out of DJM.'

True to past form, Ray Williams landed on his feet. Shortly afterwards, he formed a partnership with the Kinks' manager, Robert Wace. They discovered a Scots band named Stealer's Wheel, destined to enjoy major chart success in the mid-Seventies and to spin off a solo singer-songwriter talent in Gerry Rafferty.

Today, his blond good looks intact, Williams has a successful company handling soundtrack music for mega-movies like *The Last Emperor*. He does not brood too much over business manoeuvres twenty years ago which bumped him out of a multimillion-pound property, not once but twice. It is only now and again – when Dick James is described in his hearing as the straightest man who ever walked Tin Pan Alley – that a sardonic grin appears on Ray Williams's handsome face.

The new Elton, for the present, was just a wild rumour, wafted home from 5,000 miles away. 'I remember when these pictures started to arrive of him on tour in the States,' Sue Ayton says. 'Everyone back in the office said "What on earth's going on?" But Steve Brown said, "No, it's great. This is the way it's going to be." '

There was, for instance, the picture of Elton clad in striped drawers and ankle socks, to set off his winged Mr Freedom boots, caught in an onstage paroxysm with mouth agape, fists clenched against his sides, sturdy knees turned in, for all the world like some fractious small boy howling because it's bed- or bath-time. The shot was by a young *Rolling Stone* photographer named Annie Leibovitz, who would afterwards build a great career from persuading rock stars to adopt unlikely or unflattering poses. With this one, she had no trouble from the start.

The Elton that burst forth on this second American tour began as a purely defensive measure. He knew that, in all outward manifestations of a 1970 rock star, he was totally deficient. He had no girlish physique, no spindly legs and tiny behind, no long, pale face or long, lank hair to toss to and fro in multi-spotlit ecstasy. He knew he was short and square and squat and all too solid. In Britain, the best way of diverting attention from this was to retreat into shyness and Rembrandt semi-dark. In America – so an infallible instinct prompted – his best disguise was to go all out and over the top, acknowledging and satirising his own shortcomings before anyone else had the chance.

Becoming outrageous was a conscious decision by someone who had been a pro since the age of six. America demanded spectacle; therefore he'd be spectacular in America. Britain preferred seriousness, therefore he'd be serious in Britain. Each time he passed through US Customs and Immigration, Dr Jekyll would turn into Mr Hyde.

This second American visit also began on the West Coast, though in surroundings very different from 300-seat folk clubs in West Hollywood. On 15 November, after a short holiday, Elton opened as top of the bill at the 6,000-seat Santa Monica Civic Auditorium. So great was the ticket demand that four more major concerts had to be scheduled in the Los Angeles area, at San Bernardino, Riverside, Anaheim and UCLA.

It was Santa Monica that saw the new Elton in full flight for the first time. Third on stage after Ry Cooder and Odetta, he appeared in a brown leather top hat, a blue velvet cloak over a jump suit, and high silver boots decorated with stars. His face, now shorn of stubbly beard, now sported outsize Afrika Korps-style sunglasses. Pinned to his chest was a Donald Duck badge. At the top of the gusset where his fly should have been was a smiling ceramic face in a miniature bowler hat.

The run of elegiac songs from *Elton John* and *Tumbleweed* was accompanied by slapstick striptease. First the blue velvet cloak went, then the top hat, then the jump suit to reveal a second jump suit beneath. This, too, was soon cast off, Elton popping from its sheath dressed only in a Fillmore West souvenir T-shirt, silver boots and what *Rolling Stone*'s critic incredulously described as 'purple panty-hose'. (They were, indeed, women's tights, worn as a dare for Bernie Taupin's girlfriend Maxine.) In the Jerry Lee Lewis finale, having kicked away his piano-stool, he played standing up, crouching, performing Tiller Girl kicks, even prone under the keyboard, somehow reaching to pound on it with one hand strainingly crab-wise.

Rolling Stone's critic noted the range of grimaces and facial contortions that accompanied all this. 'Sometimes he would stick out his lower lip like Stan Freberg used to do, or grit his teeth or pucker up his face like Alvin Lee. Sometimes he would recoil from the keyboard, his mouth falling open in horror as if his ass had been shot full of lightning.'

At the backstage party, *Rolling Stone*'s reporter, David Felton, noticed the great contrast between Elton onstage and off. 'Compared to the Little Richard–Jerry Lee Lewis acrobatics he went through during "Burn Down the Mission", his demeanour . . . seemed oddly subdued. He was extremely friendly, but seemed shy, almost fragile, rarely even looking at the person he's addressing . . . While scores of writers and industry people consumed tons of champagne and catered goodies, Elton stood off to the side, alone, costumed and silent.'

Despite all the plaudits, Elton still resolutely refused to consider himself a star. In his own eyes he was just a member of a trio that had miraculously found top form, and somehow kept on hitting it, night after night. 'In all the time Elton, Nigel and I were on our own, I never remember us ever doing a bad concert,' Dee Murray says now. 'Sure we used to have fun, but there was never that rock thing of being out of your head onstage. The music was always the number one priority.'

Elton made no demand for special accommodation in their hotels or backstage, and was perfectly happy to rough it, if need arose, just as in old touring days with Bluesology. 'I remember, there was a bit of the tour we had to do by road,' Dee Murray says. 'Bob Stacey drove the van with the equipment and I drove the station wagon with Elton and Nigel in it. Once, we had to drive all through the night. But it was still all good fun, a laugh. I think there was only one small row on the whole tour.'

In rest periods, Elton's main interest was adding to his record collection, faithfully detailed in *Rolling Stone* as '5,000 albums, 2,500 forty-fives, 100 EPs, 60 seventy-eights, 500 eight-track cartridges and 300 cassettes'. His musical knowledge amazed his American interviewers, covering as it did the whole spectrum of pop, country, soul, blues and jazz, even extending back to the barely mentionable eras of Doris Day and Pat Boone. In one typical buying spree in San Francisco, he picked up albums by Albert King, Leon Russell, Gordon Lightfoot and the Flamin' Groovies, plus cassettes by Spirit, John and Beverly Martyn, the Velvet Underground, Santana, Harry Nilsson, Marvin Gaye, David Crosby, the Voices of East Harlem and Seatrain.

On the road, his constant companion was the diary in which in his neat handwriting he recorded each day's events meticulously, the venue he had played, the probable size of the audience and the box-office gross. Driving away from a stadium, bathed in sweat and festooned in towels, he would at once reach for the diary and begin scribbling.

All the time, the plaudits of celebrated music figures continued to rain down. Al Kooper, Bob Dylan's organist and the founder of Blood, Sweat and Tears, described *Elton John* to the *Melody Maker* as 'the perfect record'. When Elton reached Boston, Kooper made a special trip to see him there, and afterward hired a limousine to give Bernie and him a day out in Massachusetts.

Still greater accolades waited in New York, where Elton was to play two nights with Leon Russell at the Fillmore East and also do a concert session over WABC radio. Goodwill messages included one

from the group of musicians most influential of all to Elton and
Bernie in their odyssey through the imports rack at Musicland. It was
the Canadian group whose brilliant history, first with Ronnie
Hawkins, then with Bob Dylan, glowed through a name of absurd
simplicity: the Band. The Band were also in New York, that week,
and sent word that they'd like Elton and Bernie to come over to their
hotel.

The thought of actually meeting his ultimate heroes, from *Music
from Big Pink* and 'Rag Mama Rag', made Bernie Taupin's knees
almost buckle with awe. In person, however, the Band were full of
the same easy unpretentiousness that made their music the first fully
grown-up rock. Especially agreeable was lead guitarist Robbie
Robertson, who had taken to the road as a boy even more innocent
than Bernie, after his first employer promised, 'You won't make much
money, kid. But you'll get more pussy than Frank Sinatra.'

'Robbie was really sweet,' Bernie remembers now. 'He invited us
up to his room, and we sat there talking the whole night. He gave us
lots of advice in that very sage way he has. He paid me the most
tremendous compliment as well. He said he couldn't believe the songs
on *Tumbleweed* had been written by someone who'd never been to
America or travelled through America.'

The new friends parted in opposite directions, Elton to play the
Electric Factory in Philadelphia, the Band to do a concert in upstate
New York. But when Elton came off stage in Philadelphia that night,
the Band were in his dressing room. To catch his performance, they
had put their own show forward a couple of hours and travelled
down by charter plane. They asked Elton and Bernie to write a song
for their next album, and Elton to record with them at their studio
in Woodstock.

On the first night at the Fillmore East, Bernie Taupin felt his knees
turn to blancmange again. 'Elton came up to me and said "Taupin,
there's someone I want you to meet." I followed him to this booth
where Leon Russell was sitting, and Leon said "Bernie Taupin –
Bob Dylan".'

It was, indeed, the great poet and recluse of rock, hawk-beaked,
bearded and savage-looking as some master of the Spanish Inquisi-
tion. 'I can't remember now what I said to him, or what he said to
me,' Bernie admits now. 'Something about liking one of the songs. I
was too overwhelmed. I just couldn't take it in.'

Back in Britain, the music press set up a hearty patriotic cheer.
DYLAN DIGS ELTON! screamed *Melody Maker*, in whose purist eyes
conquering America was of less significance than impressing the man
who wrote 'Subterranean Homesick Blues'. Almost the entire front

page was occupied by a picture of Elton, albeit in his last summer's beard and T-shirt, banging a tambourine at the Troubadour. 'Elton, his lyricist Bernie Taupin, bassist Dee Murray and drummer Nigel Olsson are blowing the States apart,' a column in bold type reported. 'His success is such that his manager estimates he will be a dollar millionaire within a year.'

Below were details of his first major British tour, from January to March 1971, playing thirty-eight dates from the south of England to the north of Scotland. Also of a third American tour in April and May, and a fourth – covering fifty-five cities and so guaranteeing his dollar millionaire status – from September through November.

Inside was a telephone interview with Elton, bubbling over with his excitement at meeting the Band and Al Kooper and jamming with Leon Russell at the Fillmore. 'We did a great gig in Philly . . . San Francisco audiences are a little cool at first, like those in London, because they've seen everything, and one night it was like pushing over a brick wall very slowly, but they went in the end. Los Angeles is like home to us, and Philly and Boston are great, too. Every audience is good if you get at them the right way . . .'

Not since the earliest Fab Four days had life on the road sounded so exciting, so wholesome or so much fun.

It wasn't until nearly Christmas that the conqueror returned, and Mr Hyde reverted once more to Dr Jekyll. But a Dr Jekyll whose taste for the loud and flamboyant there was now money enough to gratify. A few months earlier, Elton's idea of a luxurious present to himself had been a leather-upholstered Roberts portable radio. Now – thanks to a cash advance from Dick James – it was an Aston Martin sports car, sprayed pale mauve. He had bidden farewell for ever to the Metropolitan Line.

The DJM office staff, who had cheered him across America, at first found him little changed. He was as thoughtful as ever about bringing home little gifts; as punctiliously grateful as ever to people for doing things for him while he was away. Especially Sue Ayton, who had kept in touch with his mother and carried out other small personal commissions like sending a birthday greetings telegram to 'a bloke named John Reid'.

'We only really understood what had happened to him when it came to the office Christmas party,' Sue Ayton says. 'The previous year, he and Bernie had been the first to arrive. But this year he came late and made a big entrance in a long coat with a fur collar, looking like Greta Garbo.'

Dollar millionaire as he soon would be, Elton's life style clearly had to change. And with that material change – though none realised it yet – came the profoundest of emotional ones. The brotherly love affair between Bernie Taupin and him had reached a natural, amicable end. Bernie was head-over-heels in love with Maxine Feibelman, the California girl he'd met during the Troubadour trip (another debt owed to the luckless Ray Williams). Maxine had joined him on the second tour and afterwards followed him back to London. Bernie had no further use for the lower bunk in that tidy little bedsit at 30a Frome Court. There was not – and never would be – any diminution in their mutual affection and regard. But town mouse and country mouse were now embarked on very different voyages of discovery.

The task of finding Elton a flat 'in Town' devolved on Sue Ayton. She came up with 384 The Water Garden, a brand-new apartment block just off Edgware Road, with a central court full of tropical palms. The property belonged to the Church Commissioners, who required that prospective residents be interviewed by their estate agent, Chestertons.

A dubious Elton went for the interview, accompanied by Geoffrey Ellis, the immaculate lawyer from DJM. 'We were seen by a very snotty young estate agent, who clearly couldn't believe Elton had the money to buy the place,' Ellis remembers. 'Poor Elton went away very much with his tail between his legs. But then Dick James contacted his solicitor, who knew someone at Chestertons, and the deal went through that way.'

An early visitor to the new flat was *New Musical Express*'s reporter, Gillian Saitch. Elton talked to her euphorically of his imminent British and European tour, the 'tightness and funkiness' of his band, the show they had played on WABC radio in New York. 'We had an audience of about a hundred and we got such a buzz, we played for an hour and a half. They stopped the news, commercials, everything . . .'

Gill Saitch also mentioned the brand new pale mauve Aston Martin that stood in the Water Garden's precincts, adding the enigmatic observation that Elton had given his previous car 'to his flatmate'.

Paradoxically, the chief interest of the British record press in Elton was how stupendously well he was doing across the Atlantic. For a British act to break in America before Britain was almost unprecedented, not only in pop music but in any sphere of entertainment. Apart from Charlie Chaplin, there had been the child singer Laurie London with one freak single in 1958. Only a trivia hound like Elton himself now even remembered its name.

The down-at-heel London session musician of January 1970 was, by December 1970, the toast of New York radio, with two American top five albums and an impending gold disc, acknowledging $1 million sales of the *Elton John* album. Any American promoter who wanted to book him had now to be thinking ahead to 1972. In Britain, by contrast, he was merely another prominent new attraction, along with Dave Edmunds, Mungo Jerry, Pickettywitch, Hawkwind and Ashton, Gardner and Dyke. For all the BBC2-ish critical success of his albums, only one had left the faintest mark on the charts. Nor had he yet made the hit single by which, in Britain, pop success was still ultimately judged.

The disparity between abroad and home was underlined by the American and British record press end-of-year popularity polls. In American *Record World* magazine's poll, Elton was named Top Male Vocalist. On the basis of several important US cover versions – notably Aretha Franklin's of 'Border Song' – Elton and Bernie were named Best Composers of 1970 by the New York-based Circle of International Music Critics. Yet in the annual *New Musical Express* popularity poll, Elton was rated only number 14 in the categories for World Male Singer and World Musical Personality, behind obvious giants like Elvis Presley, Cliff Richard, Tom Jones and Paul McCartney, and less obvious ones like Andy Williams and Glen Campbell. Even in the British Vocal Personality section, he was rated only ninth. His solitary win was in the New Disc Singer category, pipping Dave Edmunds, Cat Stevens, Gilbert O'Sullivan and Led Zeppelin's Robert Plant.

What had eluded him in Britain for almost three years happened in America, almost while nobody was looking. As part of the run-up to his second tour, Uni Records unilaterally put out another track from the *Elton John* album. It was 'Your Song', the pensive ballad whose lyric Bernie Taupin had written in fifteen minutes around the breakfast table at 30a Frome Court. Though an integral part of Elton's stage show, and charming to all who heard it, no one at DJM had ever considered it remotely chart material.

'Your Song' was released in America in October 1970 and at first attracted little notice. The impact of Elton's second tour, however, pushed it into the Top 40 in time to be a farewell present on his return to London in mid-December. By January 1971, it was number eight.

Though Elton badly needed to put out a British single – not having done so since the disastrous 'Rock and Roll Madonna' six months earlier – Stephen James still balked at 'Your Song'. For it seemed no part of current taste with its quiet mood, its downcast eyes and tone of tongue-tied bashfulness. Elton has always claimed it was about a rather serious girl with glasses whom Bernie briefly worshipped from afar in Lincolnshire. Bernie himself insists he had no one specific in mind. 'It was just an idea that came to me one morning at Elton's mum's place. I remember writing it in the kitchen, after a plate of bacon and eggs, with Elton in the bath in the next room. The original lyrics have got an egg-stain on them.'

The song had been among a batch of album tracks sent out by Stephen James to the various BBC radio disc jockeys. There was an instant and surprising response from Tony Blackburn, host of Radio One's hugely influential breakfast show. Blackburn said that, if DJM put out 'Your Song' as a single, he would make it his Record of the Week.

The uphill work was in convincing Elton who, with such a stack of failed British singles behind him, still did not believe this could be the one. Dick James prevailed, and 'Your Song' was released in Britain on 8 January. Tony Blackburn kept his word and made it Record of the Week. On 23 January – a year and a day after its recording – it entered the British Top 50. By early February, it was number seven.

The overlooked little track would turn out to be Elton and Bernie's longest-lived success, their equivalent to the Beatles' 'Yesterday', and one notable exception to a later unwritten rule that other performers did not cover Elton John material. Over the next two decades it would generate some forty-five cover versions by, among others, Andy Williams, the New Seekers, Cilla Black, Lena Horne, Jack Jones, Sacha Distel, Roger Whitaker and even (as if to appease the departed Linda) Buddy Greco.

Few songs have so perfectly suited their moment. After the long era of psychedelic pretentiousness, Bernie Taupin's simple lyric was a breath of fresh air that seemed almost revolutionary. So, indeed, the greatest of all pop revolutionaries considered it. John Lennon later remembered hearing 'Your Song' in New York, where he had sought refuge from the Beatles' terminal lawsuits and Britain's persecution of Yoko Ono. Lennon was typically open and generous to the new performer who, in future years, would prove a staunch friend. 'There was something about his vocals that was an improvement on all the English vocals till then. When I heard it, I thought "Great! That's the first new thing that's happened since we [the Beatles] happened."'

Many other people shared this sense that a new musical era was taking shape at last. No longer clanging guitars, but a quiet piano. No longer clichés in chorus, but individual, intelligible thoughts. No longer outsize paper butterflies and Lenin posters on bathroom doors, but potted palms, Laura Ashley prints and lamps that could be pulled up and down over kitchen tables of stripped pine.

Albeit by pure coincidence, 'Your Song' ushered in a new pop musical genre. From then on, the sound of piano keys, a quiet voice in an empty room, became a recurring feature of both British and American charts. By the end of 1971, John Lennon had released his own piano soliloquy, 'Imagine'. The songwriter Carole King had emerged from Brill Building anonymity with her solo album *Tapestry*. An Irish Dead End Kid, burdened with the name Gilbert O'Sullivan, was tinkling a lugubrious ballad called 'Nothing Rhymed'. The age of Semprini and Winifred Atwell had begun anew.

Another consequence of 'Your Song' was to give Bernie Taupin his first serious public recognition. It intrigued the music press to discover that the shy hits did not spring direct from the head of their shy-sounding vocalist, but from a separate lyricist with a name almost as unhip as Reg Dwight. Up until now, the do-it-yourself geniuses of pop had always written words and music. Not since the days of Lorenz Hart and Ira Gershwin had there been someone famous for writing lyrics only. And neither Hart nor Gershwin had ever been taken round by the performers they supplied, and proudly shown off as '50 per cent of the music'.

Bernie's circumstances had become as different as they possibly could from study-chum days with Elton at 30a Frome Court. He was now engaged to Maxine Feibelman, and making plans for their wedding with all the heady haste of his twenty years.

Maxine was, indeed, a catch: blonde and willowy, with the warm-voiced cool of the classic 'Valley girl'. Her father was an inventor, responsible for such scientific breakthroughs as a microphone that worked by 'ear-tones'. Like many a California girl then, she had a barefoot, earth-mother folksiness that was bound to appeal to Bernie's romantic nature. An accomplished needlewoman, she was always on hand to do running repairs on badly stitched rock-'n'-roll clothes, and conform to the general chauvinistic idea of a 'chick', even though her tongue could occasionally be sharp. Some, indeed, who knew the sensitive Bernie felt vague forebodings on his behalf. 'I remember one day they were looking at some wedding presents together,' an ex-DJM girl says. 'Bernie made some comment and Maxine said "No, dummy!" I thought it was a funny expression to use to someone you were going to marry.'

Thanks to Dick James's largesse, Bernie also now owned a car, though somewhat more modest than a pale-mauve Aston Martin. 'It was a silver Mini, which I loved. The trouble was, I hadn't yet passed my driving test. Maxine used to have to drive me around.'

The interest in Bernie's writing, allied to his Lincolnshire burr and gypsy good looks, had given Dick James a further bright idea. Why not dress him in a dinner jacket and get him onstage reading his poems as an opener to Elton? Though Bernie was too shy – and possessed too much innate taste – for that, he had no objection to trying his hand at recording on his own. Moreover, he had a cache of lyrics which, for one reason or another, had proved unsuitable to become Elton songs. It was agreed he should make an album for DJM, reading his poems with an instrumental accompaniment in the tradition of W. H. Auden, Dylan Thomas and John Betjeman.

No such lofty pretensions are evident in the figure interviewed by *NME*'s Roy Carr in February 1971. The accompanying picture shows Bernie in Levi jacket and sweatshirt, looking less like latter-day Auden than some student thumbing a lift beside the M1. For most of the piece he talks to a not wholly comprehending interviewer about the many books and authors that have inspired him. It could be the first-ever mention in *NME*'s columns of C. S. Lewis, J. R. R. Tolkien and what a printing error unfortunately renders as 'Winnie-the-Poo'.

As Elton has ceaselessly pushed him, so Bernie now springs to Elton's defence against American critics who have taken to condemning the bizarre stage outfits as an unnecessary gimmick. 'What particularly annoys me is that the so-called in-crowd who were continually predicting great things for Elton are knocking him since he became big . . . People say why does he have to do rock 'n' roll and wear all those funny clothes? But that's Reg. He's an eccentric in the nicest possible way.'

Despite the impending poetry album, Bernie tells Roy Carr he has no desire for fame or limelight. He says he lives 'in a fantasy world. I'm not very realistic. I never read papers or listen to the news. To be honest, I can't take politics and violence.'

Bernie and Maxine were married early in 1971, back on his home territory of Market Rasen, Lincolnshire. Elton was best man, and a large party travelled up from Dick James Music by charabanc. For their honeymoon, they joined Elton on tour in Hawaii.

Even crossing and recrossing the continent in Elton's baggage train had not exhausted Bernie's infatuation with America. Accompanied by Maxine, he made his own long pilgrimage through the Far West, visiting famous Wild West sites like Dodge City and Tombstone, and Civil War battlefields in the South.

After that, his ambitions were simple. All he wanted to do was take his Californian bride back to live in the Lincolnshire countryside he had so loved as a child, and spend the rest of his life there, reading, writing and imagining.

In those days, Elton's dealings with journalists were all of the very happiest. To a record-company publicist, he was a 'dream client'. Helen Walters, still feeling her way in the job at DJM, never had a moment's difficulty with him. Whatever interview he was asked to do he did, cheerfully and generously. Female writers, like *Disc*'s Penny Valentine and *NME*'s Gillian Saitch, seemed to find him specially *sympathique*. En route to concerts, he would often call for Gill Saitch in his mauve Aston Martin, creating the natural, widespread assumption that they were walking out together.

The music press now recognised a prize interviewee, articulate and funny as no pop star had been since John Lennon. His air of normality, of health and wholesomeness, was something quite new in a world where the prevailing fashion had always been tubercular skinniness, sickly pallor, sunken cheeks, smoker's coughs and hair hanging in greasy rat's tails. Here was a musician of day rather than night, who didn't mumble cosmic gobbledegook, didn't smoke dope or screw six groupies a night, who got up and went to bed at normal hours, who had wind enough left to turn out on cricket pitches and tennis courts, and whose great passion, after music, was his local football club, Watford.

Throughout early 1971, Elton performed as tirelessly in print as on stages throughout Britain and mainland Europe. *Melody Maker* launched a four-part 'Elton John Story', featuring him in detailed question-and-answer with Richard Williams, tracing his career back to Long John Baldry and Bluesology. *New Musical Express* soon afterwards began its own three-part 'Chat-in With Elton John'.

The music papers took to using him as a commentator on any and every aspect of pop, from new American bands like Bread to Phil Spector's controversial production of the Beatles' farewell album, *Let It Be*. Elton possessed the gift of plain speech without sour grapes, neither mincing his words nor being gratuitously offensive. His background knowledge of the business was frequently more illuminating than any professional reporter's. 'I think [Phil Spector] did a bloody good job for the Beatles, because he made an album out of nothing. If you'd heard the original tapes, you'd know what Spector did for them. The only thing I can really get against him is 'The Long and Winding Road', which was beautiful without strings and all the other rubbish.' A typical *NME* foot-of-page trailer reads: NEXT WEEK ELTON TALKS ABOUT ROCK 'N' ROLL, CRITICISM, COPYING, PRESS RECEPTIONS, HYPES, MICK JAGGER.

In *Melody Maker*'s Face-to-Face session Richard Williams asked how he reacted to the critical backlash which now condemned the *Elton John* album as precious and overproduced. Elton replied that a bit of knocking would probably do him good. 'Own up – people are getting sick of reading about Elton John, the Wonder Human Being. I'm a bit cheesed off with it myself . . . Yeah, I've had a ball, but if it all ended tomorrow I could go out and get a job.'

At the same time, there were inklings that the cheery, voluble new star had a less robust, more troubled and vulnerable side. On 23 January, *Melody Maker*'s lead story reported that Elton had 'narrowly missed a nervous breakdown' through starting his British tour too soon after returning from America. With two more American tours in prospect, his doctor had faced him with the stark choice of slowing down or 'burning himself out'. As a result, three British concerts had had to be cancelled, at Southampton, Loughborough and Hull.

It happened at the moment Elton was due to fly to Cannes, to appear in the prestigious MIDEM international music convention. *Melody Maker* reported that he arrived there 'on a diet of vitamin pills'. To make things worse, MIDEM proved a total disaster. Elton, representing Britain, was scheduled to play after Eric Burdon, ex-vocalist with the Animals, representing America with his new band, War. However, Burdon refused to leave the stage after his allotted fourteen minutes, and continued blasting with War for almost an hour and a quarter. Elton was reported to have 'stormed out of the theatre'.

That week's *Melody Maker* loyally took Elton's part, reproaching Eric Burdon for a 'staggering display of selfishness'. Elton himself was ruefully apologetic, as always after one of his Little Moments. 'I've been feeling so rough, and I can only think it's been the strain of all the work . . . We've been travelling too much for any sort of comfort, and last week I felt really rotten. I was exhausted. It's funny, but I never even wanted to go on the road. All I ever wanted to do was make records and maybe produce. Now look at me.'

Dick James's bland communiqué – that Elton had merely been over-excited about receiving his second gold disc, for *Tumbleweed* – underlined the continuing chronic deficiency in his life. He had a music publisher who was the best in Britain, an inspirational songwriting partner and an agent of infinite experience. He had a top-flight record producer, a distinguished arranger, an excellent band. He also now had an accountant and a solicitor. What he did not yet have, and needed more desperately each day, was a manager.

The overpowering sense one gets from these first frenetically famous months is a lack of any firm voice or steady hand on the tiller. Elton is being worked into the ground, flung back and forth around Britain and Europe as a prelude to two more, almost consecutive American tours. His public image became oddly unfocused and contradictory as plans were made and bookings accepted with a fine disregard for overall strategy. In March alone, he could be seen at totally opposite ends of the pop-music spectrum. Here he was, one night, back in élitist BBC2 mode, playing the Royal Festival Hall with Paul Buckmaster, a full symphony orchestra and chorus. Here he was another night on BBC1, joining a Las Vegas-style finale with Ray Charles on the *Andy Williams Show*. Here he was, on yet another night, sweating it out in a basement blues club in West Hampstead. Everyone on every side was saying 'Yes' for him. Somebody should have been there, but wasn't, saying 'No' for him.

His career on record was in a similarly overwrought state. By May 1971, two more albums had joined *Tumbleweed* and *Elton John* in the British and American shops. One was the movie soundtrack album *Friends*, whose arrangement had been among Ray Williams's last managerial acts. At the time, Paramount Pictures had turned down the offer of a full Elton album, taking only five John–Taupin compositions to be interspersed with theme music from Lewis Gilbert's unmemorable tale of teenage romance.

Finding *Tumbleweed Connection* in the US chart, however, Paramount rush-released *Friends* ahead of the movie, in a drab pink sleeve showing boy kissing girl, like the cover of a cheap contact magazine. *Friends* reached only number 36 in the US chart and did not register at all in Britain. The title track did little better as a single, charting only in America at number 34. Paradoxically, the album was to earn Elton another American gold disc, having reached $1 million worth of sales to record outlets. No account was taken of the sale-or-return system, whereby an album that went out gold might come back cardboard. Such an inveterate visitor of record stores as Elton was all too painfully aware how quickly it was remaindered. 'I mean,' he commented wryly afterwards, 'you can go into any record store in the States now and find *Friends* for $1.98 with a hole punched through it.'

Also out was the live album he had made in New York, titled after its performance date, 17 November, 1970. A beady-eyed manager might have talked Elton out of the workaholic insecurity which turned a one-shot session on WABC radio into the follow-up to *Tumbleweed Connection*. The result was another odd mishmash, mixing a new John–Taupin song, 'Can I Put You On', with the Beatles' 'Get Back', the Stones' 'Honky Tonk Women' and Arthur 'Big Boy' Crudup's 'My Baby Left Me'. It made 11 in the *Billboard* chart but, like *Friends*, sank without trace in Britain.

Elton himself realised the absurdity of having four albums simultaneously on sale. 'I was getting more and more unhappy about it,' he recalled later. 'I thought "We've worked so bloody hard to get this far, and now we're blowing it."'

His management agreement was still the three-year one signed in June 1970 when Ray Williams had been drafted in to look after him. On Williams's departure that September, a rider had been added to the agreement, reallocating managerial duties to Dick James, his son Stephen and Steve Brown, the A & R man. But it was an arrangement that could never work satisfactorily. Dick James was far too grand to get involved in the daily minutiae of management work and Stephen was too busy, running This Record Co. Steve Brown was primarily a DJM employee, powerless to make major decisions on his own, and, besides, did not want to leave his wife and daughter too much to accompany Elton on tour.

In addition there were still managerial nibbles of interest from Island Records, via Muff Winwood and Lionel Conway, resulting in yet another pressure on Elton's time and a further odd refraction of his image. Under Conway's aegis, he went into the studio to record a non-Bernie Taupin song called 'Honey Man', in duet with Island's biggest artist, Cat Stevens. But, Island and DJM being unable to agree on a royalty split, the track was never released.

By early 1971, the need was growing desperate for someone to be with Elton around the clock, seven days a week; someone strong enough to protect him from outside pressures and also, on occasion, from himself. Stephen James remembers how, in that disorganised spring, Elton himself came up with yet another candidate. 'He said it was a friend of his named John Reid, who was label manager at Tamla-Motown.

'I went and asked Steve Brown if he knew this John Reid. "Oh yeah," Steve said. "Elton's a big Tamla-Motown fan. He goes over to John's office to hang out, and gets records out of the cupboard."

'"Elton wants him to be his manager," I said. "Do you know anything about it?"

'"Oh yeah," Steve said. "They're living together. John has moved in with Elton at the Water Garden."'

7

'At least he'll have someone to get him up in the morning'

BEFORE colour entered British men's clothes, their only touch of colour – only touch of class – came from Paisley. For businessmen or father at Christmas there was the Paisley tie in muted red or blue silk, printed with that inexplicably traditional pattern of large or small amoebas under a microscope. For sports car types, in gauntlets and Kangol caps, there was the yellow and red Paisley scarf. For men-about-town or would-be Noël Cowards, there was the green and red Paisley dressing-gown.

Few products have so little resembled their place of manufacture. Paisley lies a few miles to the west of Glasgow, in the industrial conurbation that straggles down the Scottish Central Lowlands next to the River Clyde. There is not much fine silk about the drab town with its looming Victorian mills and threadbare streets. Not many clothes-conscious dandies can be found, there or in the council estates that spread outward to merge into the colourless suburban weave of Dumbarton, Renfrew, Rutherglen, Motherwell and East Kilbride.

Aside from its contribution to the male wardrobe, Paisley can point to nothing remarkable. It suffers an identity problem common to all medium-sized towns in the hinterland of a great and notorious city. What Birkenhead, Wallasey and New Brighton are to Liverpool, so Paisley, Renfrew and Motherwell are to Glasgow, that most luridly notorious city in the United Kingdom. Glasgow of the great rail terminus and Sauchiehall Street. Glasgow of shipyard cranes along the Clyde, and fiery union demagogues. Glasgow of the Gorbals, where razor gangs reconstituted the clans, under chieftains with names like Red Rory of the Eagles. Glasgow, epitomising all that most worries the lowland Briton about the Scot's impulse to aggressiveness and uncontrollable violence.

John Reid became an entrepreneur at the age of eleven. He had the idea of collecting up the old newspapers which neighbours put out for the dustman, and selling them to a local greengrocer as wrappers for vegetables. The scheme turned such a quick profit that he soon could subcontract other children to collect the newspapers for him, paying them a percentage of what the greengrocer paid him. Thus did he simultaneously increase his dividend and remove the need to get his hands dirty.

The story is one of very few Reid would tell about himself in later years, when he ran a business empire worth £40 million and controlled the decade's greatest entertainment phenomenon. Generally, he has no need to be his own biographer. There are people enough to tell John Reid stories from all over the world, in tones varying from warm affection to bitter hatred, and from amusement to outright terror.

Little of his remarkable future could be prophesied for the boy born in Barshaw Hospital, Paisley, on 9 September, 1949. His father, John senior, was a thread-reeler in one of the mills that gave the town its purpose and the very thoroughfares their names. John and Elizabeth Reid lived at number 1 Thread Street. Betty Reid, née King, whom John had married two years earlier, was a vigorous woman with a temper he had learned to respect. She bore him two sons, Bobby and John, a year younger. John was easily the brighter and better-looking of the two, slight and dark with large liquid eyes and a face whose pointed alertness seemed more Latin than Celt. Take away the acrid Clydeside accent and he could easily have been some little French boy named Georges or Armand.

His modest upbringing contained one exotic interlude. John senior had abandoned mill work to become a welder with Crittle Ltd, a local engineering firm. In 1959, when John junior was ten, Crittle shut down their workshops in Paisley and transferred the whole of their workforce to Auckland, New Zealand. The Reids emigrated under the old neocolonial system, paying a nominal £10 each for a lengthy sea voyage out via the Panama Canal. John and Bobby found themselves in an easy-going land of sunshine and lushness at the furthest possible extreme from Scottish rain and fog.

Then, as now, New Zealand was famous for its Maoris, to be seen most spectacularly performing ceremonial war dances on state visits by the Queen. Who could have guessed that, one far distant day, Maoris would mass to dance in honour of John Reid, or that he would round off the occasion by spending a month in jail?

Despite the charms of New Zealand, Betty Reid became homesick for Scotland. In 1961 the family returned to Paisley, settling in a small house in Gallowhill, on the main road between Renfrew and the Firth of Clyde. John senior became a welder at the Chrysler car plant in nearby Linwood. Bobby and John junior were enrolled at St Mirin's

Academy, the Catholic grammar school that lay just a couple of hundred yards from their house.

At St Mirin's John Reid proved a model pupil. Though a year younger than the other boys of his class, he came consistently near the top in every academic subject. His demeanour was bright and co-operative, his blazer of blue and gold always immaculate. Outgoing and personable, he took a leading part in the school's social life, music, amateur dramatics, 'anything that was going', according to his former chemistry teacher, John Clews. After school he would return to his home a little way along Renfrew Road and, shortly afterwards, be seen out walking the family's large Alsatian dog.

In the fifth form he became a school monitor, responsible for supervising younger boys in the playground at break. This he did with a conscientiousness which, to the supervised ones, naturally seemed more like bossiness and oppressiveness. Among the boys under his jurisdiction was one named John Harvey. 'He used to come and try and catch me and my pals when we were in the smokers' corner,' Harvey remembers. 'He was always nosing after us. We used to call him Wee Alsatian-Face.'

Though nowhere near the scale of Glasgow, Paisley had its tough quarters and its gangs. Ferguslie Park (later mentioned in a Gerry Rafferty song) was one place where the prudent did not venture at night. Wars went on intermittently between local triads with names like the Young Disciples and the Gallowhill Team.

John Reid had little – although not nothing – to do with such things. His adolescence was utterly typical for a working-class Scottish boy in that Beatle and beat-boom era. With his friends he went to dances at St Peter's youth club and pop shows at Paisley ice rink. His main social stamping ground was a coffee bar called the Sherwood Café. He was popular with the opposite sex and had several girl-friends, though not one particular steady one. As an old schoolfriend, Charles Palmer, remembers, 'He went through them all.'

In his mid-teens he got a Saturday and holiday job working at a menswear shop called Stylecraft in Moss Street, Paisley. Stylecraft specialised in fashionable knitwear and the – for Scotland – slightly *outré* Ben Sherman style of button-down poplin shirt. The sharp-faced, dapper grammar-school boy quickly proved a natural salesman. John Palmer, the shop's proprietor, remembers him enthusiastically as 'brilliant'.

Like almost everyone his age, he got involved in amateur pop music, joining various unsuccessful folk groups with his elder brother, Bobby. The impresarial streak in him first showed itself when he offered to manage two other St Mirin's pupils, a pair of singing brothers named McBride. The relationship brought painful consequences, however, after the McBrides had managed to offend some or other element in Paisley's teenage gangland. One school lunchtime, as John Harvey remembers, a gang member appeared in St Mirin's playground, and began systematically beating up both McBride brothers. When John Reid tried to go to their aid, he too was badly beaten.

'I knew that scene so well from the movies,' Harvey says now. 'The fight in the school playground with everyone ganging round, shouting and cheering. But the chilling thing, when the McBrides and John got beaten up by this heavy, was that it all happened in total silence.'

Reid left St Mirin's in 1966, at the age of sixteen, with an exemplary tally of eight passes in the Scottish General Certificate of Education. His original ambition – fostered by the long sea voyages to and from New Zealand – was to become a marine engineer, and he began a diploma course at Stow Hill engineering college in Glasgow. Show business, however, was starting to claim more and more of his attention. He joined the amateur dramatic company centred on the Glasgow Pantheon Club and appeared in several musicals, once attaining the third lead in *Kiss Me, Kate*. He also spent a brief period as a vocalist with the house band at the Glasgow Locarno ballroom, singing not very good cover versions of current hits like 'There's a Kind of Hush'.

The decisive influence on his career was a Scots friend named David Bell, later to become head of light entertainment at London Weekend Television. In Bell's view, the job in which John Reid could best combine his passion for music with entrepreneurial push would be as song plugger for one of the London music publishers. He therefore abandoned his Glasgow engineering course, moved down to London and 'knocked on a lot of doors', but could find no openings. To tide him over, he got a job in the shirt department of Austin Reed, the Knightsbridge menswear shop. From his department there was a back view across to the pale cream luxury of Montpelier Square, Belgravia. A particular large, elegant town house in the square always caught John Reid's eye, and he vowed to himself that one day he'd own it or one like it.

After a few weeks at Austin Reed, his big break came. He was offered a job with Ardmore and Beechwood, a small publishing company owned by the giant EMI record company, based above their HMV record store in Oxford Street. It was with Ardmore and Beechwood that Brian Epstein's luck had finally changed after having the Beatles turned down by every major London label. And for seventeen-year-old John Reid, four years later, they brought a similar transformation of fortune. One week, he was selling shirts in Knightsbridge; the next he was responsible for plugging the catalogue of an exciting new American singer-songwriter called Neil Diamond.

His new employer, EMI, was in those days Britain's largest and most prestigious record company. On its namesake label, or equally famous subsidiaries like Parlophone, it mustered the élite of British recording talent from Cliff Richard to the Beatles. Through an agglomeration of licensing deals with American companies like Capitol, Bell and Motown, it imported such transatlantic money-spinners as Frank Sinatra, the Four Tops, Stevie Wonder and the Supremes.

Despite its huge success, EMI was an organisation of archaic stuffiness, run on bureaucratic lines close to those of the BBC. At its headquarters in Manchester Square, young producers and promo men were still not allowed to come to work in jeans or have stereo equipment in their offices. Secretaries were forbidden to wear trousers. Employees who arrived after 9am had their names entered in a penitential 'late book'.

In these surroundings, John Reid rapidly prospered. His short hair, smart suits and Austin Reed salesman's manner gave him an affinity with EMI's middle-aged command structure. At the same time, he worked with ferocious zeal to acquire all possible knowledge and expertise about music publishing, selling, accounting and contracting. It was not long before he came to the attention of Ken East, EMI's managing director. East and his wife Dolly took up the pleasing young man socially.

In 1969, a vacancy occurred for label manager of EMI's hottest American franchise, Tamla-Motown. Berry Gordy's Detroit-based company at the time was on its great winning streak, pumping out hits by Marvin Gaye, the Miracles, the Supremes and the Temptations with the consistency of an auto-factory conveyor-belt. To be Motown's man in London was a plum job for any would-be record executive.

Among the applicants were John Reid and a young man named David Croker, then manager of a progressive London record store, One Stop. Neither Reid nor Croker was given the coveted job. But about a year later it fell vacant again, and this time John Reid got it. He was still only nineteen.

David Croker had then just joined EMI as label manager for the American Bell label. Among the contacts he brought with him from One Stop was a producer named Gus Dudgeon, an A & R man named Steve Brown and a struggling singer-pianist, still called Reggie Dwight, whose passion for records surpassed even Croker's own.

He recalls Reid's arrival to take over Tamla-Motown, amid some dissension from people who felt that a more experienced person should have got the job. 'I remember a sort of a groan – "Oh, oh, John Reid's coming." A feeling that he'd only got it because of who he knew in the company.'

Managing an American label within EMI was generally a one-person operation. The label manager decided which tracks should be released in Britain, supervised publicity and promotion, and looked after his American artists when they visited London. The comparatively low salary was offset by abundant perks: free records, entertaining expenses, constant parties and receptions, the chance to mingle with the famous and, in that idyllic late Sixties time, virtual freedom from stress, insecurity or fear.

John Reid's job was particularly congenial thanks to Tamla-Motown's current run of enormous British chart hits. Under EMI's bureaucratic paternalism, label managers received points for each successful release, accruing to a cash bonus. An early glimpse of Reid's celebrated ferocity came when it was suggested that he might share his bonus points with his colleagues.

David Croker remembers him as a figure apart from the other label managers, short-haired and dapperly suited, tidy and meticulous, with an air of sophistication unusual for a 19-year-old, especially in that sub-hippy milieu. Whatever rough corners he had brought down from Paisley were now entirely rubbed away. He was socially graceful, knowledgeable about literature and art, a lover of good food and expensive restaurants. Where other young EMI executives did their entertaining at the local pub or trattoria, Reid preferred ultra-smart places like Inigo Jones in Covent Garden.

He possessed a talent for knowing bizarre as well as important people. One of them was Barbara Windsor, the blonde, busty ingénue star of the *Carry On* films. Reid met her while he was still a record-plugger, and impressed her with his 'dark, very French' looks, and the number of times he had attended her stage show, *Come Spy with Me*. 'He kept coming to the theatre to see me,' she recalls in her memoirs. 'Even though young, he had a good head on him. There was nothing he didn't know about show business. I found this young man very exciting.'

He became an escort to Barbara Windsor, in between her highly publicised involvements with tough characters from the East End. They must have made an arresting couple: the sleek Scots teenager and the pneumatic peroxide Cockney sparrow, some two decades his senior. Windsor remembers how it was said of him then that he wanted to be a millionaire and drive a Rolls-Royce by the time he was twenty-one.

She was aware at the time of an uncharitable construction which some people put on Reid's interest in her. 'John himself once said to me, "I hope you don't think I'm using you as a stepping-ladder." But that was not the case at all. I never introduced him to anyone or gave him a step up. I just loved him. But there again, John was so loved by his pals that they didn't want him going out with me. There were always little spokes being put into our relationship.'

Throughout this period, Reid knew Elton only vaguely as someone often seen around the EMI corridors or in David Croker's adjacent office. Some of Elton's early compositions with Bernie Taupin had been covered by EMI bands, like the repellently named Toe Fat. He had got to know David Croker via Gus Dudgeon and One Stop records, and Croker had watched some of the sessions for the *Elton John* album. Everyone at EMI knew him, both as an old pro session man and a hopeless record-collecting freak who would come in to cadge new American products from the various label managers. John Reid's first sight of him, so Reid himself would later say, was 'a dumpy little guy in a funny jumpsuit who put his head round the door and asked to borrow some records.' Croker subsequently gave him a white label pressing of *Elton John* but Reid put it aside without even playing it.

In August 1970, a few days before his twenty-first birthday, John Reid was in San Francisco, attending the tenth anniversary celebrations of Motown Records. Elton had just scored his triumph at the Los Angeles Troubadour club, and arrived in San Francisco to play the newly opened second Troubadour there. 'He rang me up,' Reid later recalled. 'He was bubbling over with what the critics had said, and dying to tell someone about it. I was the nearest Englishman – or nearest thing to an Englishman.' It was a day or so later that Sue Ayton in London got a request from Elton to send a birthday telegram to 'a bloke named John Reid'.

To most people, the situation presented nothing out of the ordinary. Thus far in Britain the sexual revolution had been an almost entirely heterosexual one. There was as yet no general notion of a 'closet' and consequent need or pressure to come out of it. London in 1971 was full of paired young men, unexceptionably living in flats together.

For quite a long time, therefore, close friends of both Elton and John Reid – and even friends they began to make in common – suspected no more than that. Two young bachelors of like mind, if wildly unalike appearance, happened to be sharing a modern apartment near Marble Arch after a metropolitan tradition familiar from Dickens down through Muriel Spark. As well as flatmates they were close companions who increasingly seemed to prefer one another's company to the girlfriends each was presumed to have. In literal-minded 1971, that could still be the beginning and end of it.

Besides which, these particular two bachelors possessed several additional layers of camouflage. John Reid wore a short haircut, a smart suit, a collar and a tie, all in those days definitive emblems of utter normality. And, to add still more concealing foliage and mottled paint, Elton was a pop star. The medium which, more than anything else, had unloosed Britain's heterosexual revolution was also mainly responsible for its general blindness to any alternative. Pop music had seldom been about anything other than boys chasing girls. The essence of the vicarious excitement in any pop star's rise to fame was how many dozens of girls he would now find at his disposal. Even a pop star who looked like Elton John must surely now be enjoying those same conventional delights.

Why did the most radical of all human changes happen to Elton? Why at this particular moment? Why with so unlikely seeming a person as John Reid? One can never know exactly why, any more than they themselves knew exactly why. One can only weigh the evidence.

Elton's twenty-three years had been spent in varying degrees of loneliness. Locked away in his room in Metroland, he had had all the solitary child's usual fantasies of idealised happiness. Sometimes the fantasy was a father who would love and care about him as his own real life one seemed not to. Other times, it was a younger brother whom he could lead, teach things to, indulge and protect. As infinite as his capacity to be hurt was his capacity both to receive and give affection. Only a very little had so far leaked out, via flowers, presents and birthday cards. The huge residue was still waiting for its trigger to be touched.

The change came about much less traumatically for Elton than for many other young men. His three-year relationship with Bernie Taupin had been, as it were, a quiet waiting-room. Not until he was famous – and so, to some degree, protected – did the decisive encounter occur. And occur, moreover, in that very same euphoric week when he first discovered the rewards of daring.

In character they were the total opposites that seldom fail to attract. Elton, in his purple and silver rock-'n'-roll drag. John Reid, in his low-key clerical grey. Elton chunky and wispily pale. Reid small and sleekly dark. Elton the soft-hearted and self-effacing. Reid the hard-headed and self-aggrandising. Elton the seasoned veteran. Reid the newcomer and junior who, for all that, possessed immeasurably greater stores of knowledge, cultivation and *savoir-faire*. Someone, in other words, who could be both kid brother and father.

John Reid entered Elton's complex social circle shyly and diplomatically. He was especially chary of Bernie Taupin, the most visible long-standing attachment in Elton's life. Elton, too, was worried lest Bernie should feel any way superseded or slighted, even though their relationship was plainly quite different and separate. 'I think Elton was more concerned than I was about us not being as close as before,' Bernie says now. 'When John would come and meet him, I'd usually get up and disappear, just to leave them alone. And Elton would always say "Oh, you don't have to leave", which I think made John feel that I didn't like him.'

In fact Bernie says he found Reid 'very personable' and did not feel in the least offended by the new arrangement. 'Elton and I had solidified our relationship early on. We knew we were very different in certain areas and that it was impossible to have continued in such close proximity. It was healthier that way, too. Otherwise we'd just have got sick and tired of each other. My basic attitude towards the whole thing was "Good luck."'

For the present, all most people could see was the instant and enormous change in Elton's lifestyle. With John Reid's advent, he seemed to step up an entire social class.

Their flat in the Water Garden was a world away from bedsitter life at 30a Frome Court. With a total redecoration job by Derf Farebrother, and several hundred pounds-worth of contemporary furniture, the place was a model of a modern bachelor pad. Every surface quickly became covered by the ornaments, toys, souvenirs and keepsakes that Elton acquired everywhere he went. On the shag-pile living-room rug stood his precious record collection, with his two framed gold discs in pride of place above. From the spotless bathroom came the expensive reek of his favourite after-shave lotion, Aramis.

Gone, too, was his Pinner diet of chips, peas and Instant Whip. Reid was an accomplished and ambitious cook. 'I remember going there for dinner, and John serving poussins,' David Croker says. 'There were six of us, and he brought out three poussins. I was thinking to myself "How on earth am I going to get through half of one of these?" Then he brought out three more. We were expected to eat a whole poussin each. The other thing I remember was that John was one of those people who start doing the washing up before the guests have left.'

Reid established an instant rapport with Elton's family, getting on especially well with the down-to-earth Sheila. She and Derf were frequent visitors to the Water Garden flat, as were Elton's aunt, Win

Robinson, and his young cousin, Paul. 'I remember there being gold discs on the wall,' Paul Robinson says now. 'And getting terribly drunk, for the first time in my life, on vodka and lime.'

All the Pinner relations took to this personable new friend of Elton's who seemed to be organising his life in such a satisfactory manner. Sheila and Derf would frequently go there to visit Reid while Elton was on the road. Indeed, in the first hectic months of 1971, it was Sheila Dwight who first floated the idea that Reid might become his manager.

At Dick James Music it had finally percolated through that Elton and John Reid were 'together'. It caused dumbfounded surprise, not least to the several girls there who had looked at the former Reg Dwight, in his shabby maxicoat, and wondered if they mightn't one day take him in hand. Sue Ayton, the only one he'd actually dated, was, paradoxically, the least surprised by the revelation. 'I think I may have had an inkling, because our relationship was so very innocent,' she says now. 'Anyway it made no difference at all to how I felt about him.'

With Sue, as with Bernie Taupin, Elton seemed anxious to show that the huge change did not alter long-standing attachments. 'I went to a party they gave at the Water Garden flat, and Elton was still just the same Reg. When I had to go, he called me a taxi, terribly apologetic because he couldn't drive me home himself. "I should do, Sue," he said, "But I can't leave the other guests." He was almost getting upset about it.'

So the news eventually reached Dick James that Elton and the young label manager of Tamla-Motown Records were living together, and that Elton wanted his new friend to become his manager.

James was hardly new to such things, having known Brian Epstein, Larry Parnes and the host of other major music industry figures whose proclivities the teenage record-buying public never suspected. His response was a tolerant shrug which he – and, even more, his son Stephen – would have cause to regret.

'Oh well,' Dick James said. 'If he's living with his manager, at least he'll have someone to get him up in the morning.'

John Reid was at first not at all sure he wanted to be Elton's manager as well as closest friend. 'I was quite happy doing what I was doing,' he recalled later. 'And it was generally accepted at EMI that I would be moving onwards and upwards there, so I wouldn't have gone to Dick James on that basis, except that I was being kind of nudged by Elton and his mother. I wasn't the only person who was approached.

There were a lot of American managers who were being very pushy.

'I went to America with Elton for a holiday, because he wanted me to go with him to meet all these managers. When we came back, he said "I don't see why I should go with any of them. Why don't you come and do it?" So I gave my notice in at EMI, and [they] went bananas, saying "How can you do this, we were getting you ready for great things?" so I withdrew my notice again. Then, after a month, I thought "Oh shit! I really should do it." I was pretty scared because I'd no management experience, no legal experience, no financial experience.'

The plan could not come to fruition for several more months, since Reid had to work out his notice with EMI. In the meantime, Elton's business affairs continued to be divided among many hands, sometimes making anything but light work.

In late 1970, when it became clear that he stood to earn large sums of money, Dick James had advised him to appoint a solicitor in addition to his accountant, Barry Lyons. James's associate Geoffrey Ellis had recommended his own solicitor, Michael Oliver of Berger, Oliver and Co. Michael Oliver played a large part in the subsequent complex refinements to Elton's agreements with the James organisation that John Reid was to spend so many subsequent years challenging and attacking.

On 21 September, 1970, DJM had exercised its option to extend the publishing agreement, made with Elton and Bernie in 1967, for a further three years. Dick James proposed three alternative new arrangements. (1) Elton and Bernie could extend the period of the agreement by two further years, with a rise in composers' royalties from 50 to 70 per cent. (2) They could keep to the present three years, with a royalty rise only to 60 per cent. (3) They could form a company in partnership with James (his well-tried formula) in the ratio 1–1–3, to which they would be bound for a further ten years.

Michael Oliver's discussions with Dick James raised a subject which would have repercussions fourteen years hence. Elton was now becoming a star, not only in Britain and America, but throughout the world. What could he and Bernie Taupin expect to earn from the many other countries where their songs were heard?

The practice as it stood was as old-fashioned and comfortable as Tin Pan Alley cigar smoke. The British music publisher licensed sub-publishers in North America, in major European capitals and elsewhere over the globe where his works found a public. In each country, the appointed sub-publisher collected royalties on the works, and then himself deducted a royalty. From the percentage of the income paid over by the sub-publisher, the main publisher then paid the performer his percentage.

Dick James Music operated a cat's cradle of such foreign arrangements and affiliations. In America it had a wholly owned subsidiary, DJM USA, with a separate staff and office in New York. It also had wholly owned subsidiaries in Australasia and in France, covering territories from Luxembourg to Morocco, Algeria and Tunisia. These, however, were not DJM offices, but local publishers, managing for a fee. In addition, there were copyright-policing and royalty-collecting agreements with independent (or third-party) publishers in West Germany, the Netherlands, Italy and Scandinavia.

The system was explained to Elton and Bernie in terms of relative benefit to themselves. The foreign wholly-owned subsidiaries of DJM paid a royalty of 50 per cent to British DJM. The foreign third-party publishers paid 50 per cent on recordings made within their territories, but on recordings made outside their territories, 75 per cent (or 85 per cent in the case of Beatles product). Thus Elton and Bernie earned 50 per cent of 50 per cent from their song publishing in the USA, Australasia and France, with the compensating advantage of direct control from DJM London. But under the third party arrangements in West Germany, the Netherlands, Italy and Scandinavia, they would earn 50 per cent of 75 per cent.

Oliver's advice to Elton and Bernie was to accept the second of Dick James's three new proposals on publishing: that they should keep to the prescribed three-year term, with a royalty increase from 50 to 60 per cent. Elton was said to have 'gratefully accepted' the increase, which demanded no quid pro quo from the composers, but was an expression of Dick James's 'goodwill'.

At this point, the topic was first raised that would cause even greater repercussions in the future. Under the publishing agreement, Dick James held the copyright in Elton and Bernie's work for the full copyright term, that is, for the rest of their lives and until fifty years after their deaths. Through Michael Oliver he was asked if he would allow the copyrights to revert to them.

The question touched on one of the few regrets in James's life at that point. Though publisher of John Lennon and Paul McCartney, he had never held their song copyrights, other than two early, insignificant ones.* True, the company he had set up for John, Paul and himself had reaped him large rewards. But how much larger still if he himself had kept title to such evergreens as 'Michelle', 'Penny Lane' and 'Yesterday'? So Dick James would not consider letting Elton and Bernie have their song copyrights back. To do so, he said,

*'Please Please Me' and 'Ask Me Why'

would make him 'just an agent'.

Elton's agreements with This Record Co. – through which he recorded on the DJM label – had undergone similar refinement and elaboration. In March 1970 he had signed a new five-year agreement with TRC – the 'worthwhile' agreement which Dick James said was merited by the still-unreleased *Elton John* album. In June 1971, with his music booming all over America, DJM made a new deal for him with his US record company, MCA. This, too, ran for five years, for a basic royalty of 15 per cent (of each record's retail price). This Record Co. undertook to supply MCA with seven Elton John albums at specified intervals. A $1-million advance would be paid, with a further $1 million to follow in May 1972.

As a result of the MCA deal, This Record Co. made a further improvement to Elton's recording agreement. In respect of all net proceeds received from MCA after January 1971, his share would rise from 40 to 50 per cent, as it would in respect of the album currently in production, *Madman Across the Water*. For all future master recordings supplied to America, Elton's share would be 60 per cent. TRC also undertook to pay him 60 per cent of MCA's $1-million advance. Fourteen years later, these figures would be produced in support of the argument that, if his British record royalties were on the meagre side, his American ones more than compensated for them.

A further elaboration was necessitated by British income tax, then reaching a maximum rate of 83 per cent. Another lesson was well learned from the Beatles, who had ended their career amid horrendous tax problems, both collective and individual.

To mitigate Elton's tax liabilities a scheme was drawn up separating his overseas earnings from his domestic ones and routing each through a company with which he himself had an 'employment contract'. Overseas earnings were to be received by a company named Sackville, of which Elton's solicitor, Michael Oliver, was a director. Domestic earnings were to be received by a company called Rencey, whose name was subsequently changed to William A. Bong Ltd.* A corresponding scheme was drawn up for Bernie Taupin, whose overseas earnings would now be paid through Sackville and his domestic ones through his own company Vanwall.

The simplest agreement was the management one, which Elton had re-signed in May 1970, extending for a further three years. Under this, DJM initially received 30 per cent of his earnings in every field except composing. By the rider agreed after Ray Williams's departure, DJM's commission was reduced from 30 to 20 per cent, and

*a tortuous pun on billabong, or Australian water hole

Elton's recording activities were also excluded from the agreement.

It might be asked why Dick James, that tireless accumulator of musical property, so readily gave up 20 per cent of Elton John to the totally unknown and inexperienced twenty-two-year-old John Reid. The answer is that he felt he controlled quite enough of Elton already, and didn't want the 'aggravation' of being his manager also. For the first time in many years, Dick James had made a decision that would not reap bountiful good luck.

The plan was for Reid to come on board initially as an employee of DJM, acting as a liaison man between Elton and the company, much as Ray Williams had formerly been supposed to do. But unlike Williams he was to be paid the, for then, handsome salary of £4,000 a year. And it was clearly understood that, in March 1973, when DJM's management agreement with Elton ran out, John Reid was to manage him exclusively.

In retrospect, the arrangement seems incredibly benevolent. A bloodier-minded man than Dick James might well have kept Reid waiting in the wings for the next two years, then contentedly sat back to see how he might botch the job through inexperience, lack of contacts or any of the other entrepreneurial handicaps he then possessed. As it was, he was being given the chance to learn the ropes at salaried leisure within DJM before spiriting away their greatest prize.

While John Reid worked out his final weeks at EMI, Elton was dispatched on another American tour, his fourth in eight months. This time he took his own warm-up act, Hookfoot, a band containing familiar faces from DJM demo days. Among them was Caleb Quaye, the ex-studio engineer, but for whose generosity with Dick James's tape none of this might be happening.

It was the ten-week, fifty-five-city tour that took Elton to dollar millionaire status and, among other things, put him for the first time on the cover of *Rolling Stone*. There he is in the issue of 10 June, 1971, filling the magazine's original tabloid front, from which broadsheet pages used to unfold like a road map. Annie Leibovitz's portrait shows him sitting on the ground, wearing one of the stage outfits that still suggest some wacky Disneyland tourist: shorts, a long-sleeved T-shirt inscribed 'Bernie Taupin' and silver boots with stars over white woolly athletics socks. His hair is mod-crop short. His glasses are normal size and serious. The issue's two main inside stories are billed together: 'Kent State One Year After. Elton John One Year On'. The early Seventies counterculture saw nothing incongruous in juxtaposing the massacre of Kent State University students by National Guardsmen with the rise of a pop star.

His fifty-five-city itinerary took Elton to New York, Boston, Philadelphia, Detroit, Baltimore and San Francisco. It took him for the first time into the American South: to Houston, San Antonio, Dallas, Fort Worth, New Orleans, Memphis and Atlanta. It took him to Oklahoma City and Omaha in the Midwest, Denver and Boulder in the far west, Seattle in the north-west, and over the Canadian border to Vancouver. It took him out across the Pacific to Honolulu; to Miami, Tampa and Jacksonville, Florida; to Sacramento, Fresno and Anaheim, California. It took him to Ashbury Park, New Jersey, where Bruce Springsteen was still a grimy loiterer on the boardwalk. It took him to Cincinnati, Cleveland and – twice – to Providence, Rhode Island.

As if on some evangelical crusade, the frantic little tourist, who sometimes also resembled a dumpy wing-booted Mercury and an astrological Wolf Cub, spread tidings of joy. There truly was life after the Beatles. Boys and girls would climb on to the stage to try to hug him as he played. Now and again he would stop and make an announcement, as politely as of yore in Pinner British Legion Hall. 'Look – you'd really better get off the stage, or the police will beat your heads in.'

His growing success with the crowd brought an inevitable highbrow backlash. Even more than on the previous tour, serious rock critics tut-tutted at the yellow jumpsuit, Mr Freedom boots and top hat. Where was the earnest troubadour of 'Sixty Years On' and 'First Episode at Hienton'? His climactic rock-'n'-roll medley was discussed with the gravity of some liturgical outrage at a church synod. Elton himself was becoming so used to this kind of thing, he even made an announcement before his rock-'n'-roll finale. 'This is for those of you who don't mind theatrical things. For those critics who don't like it, you can leave now. We're just here to have a good time.'

On 8 May *Melody Maker* struck a more seriously negative note in a report by its Los Angeles correspondent Jacoba Atlas. 'Elton John seems to be having a problem with the middle part of the USA,' Atlas wrote. 'His concerts have not been selling out, and, in the words of one observer, "He's dead in New York. And everyone knows New York is the centre of popular opinion."'

Rebuttal came swiftly, from no less an authority than Bill Graham, owner of the New York Fillmore East. 'The report that Elton John was dead in the USA is not true,' Graham wrote to *Melody Maker*. 'Elton John was alive and well at the Fillmore East. He played to five packed houses in April, which were sold out five weeks in advance, and we returned 6,000 mail-order envelopes. I consider

Elton one of the truly great entertainers working today.' He had, indeed, upstaged all competition at the Fillmore East, including the British band Wishbone Ash, one of whose members was seen to goggle incredulously from the wings as Elton launched into his piano handstands. 'He can't do that,' the Wishbone Ash man protested. 'He's too fat.'

Rolling Stone's cover story minutely examined the individual whose failure to meet all normal rock-star specifications was endearingly ludicrous, rather as if Britain had sent over another Charlie Chaplin, rather than another Fab Four.

He had just come from Maui and a week in the sun, and his forehead was peeling and blotchy, giving his face a prisoner-of-war quality. His knees were bruised and dirty from scampering round the stage that night.

Elton's still single. He almost got married once, but it turned out the girl wasn't pregnant. So I asked him the usual smutty questions about groupies.

'I don't have any trouble with groupies. I couldn't stand that sort of thing. Nigel has a groupie in every town, but there's no sort of plague. Anyway, they seem to be more sophisticated now. They've become – how should I put it? – they've become less sluttish.

'Bernie and I do seem to attract weirdos. I don't know why, because we're not really weird ourselves. People give me pineapples. And some girl gave me her knickers. Yeah, in Scotland some girl took off her knickers and threw them onstage. Along with a bowler hat. Can you get that one together?

'What upsets me are people who are really spaced out. Like last night there was this guy as we were driving out, he was clinging onto the car, shouting, "I must go home with you! Let me be a person!" What can you do, you know. You can't be rude to people. I couldn't say anything to him because he would have completely . . . we left him sobbing on the ground.'

Elton began rubbing his forehead where it was peeling. He looked tired and dazed.

'I've got no time for love affairs. You wake up in the morning – even if you have a day off – and the phone will ring. Your solicitor will phone you up, or your accountant or your manager or your publicist. Then you have the day-to-day things to worry about, like your car will go wrong, or the stove will blow up. It's amazing how many things go wrong in life.

'I've got about eight close friends and that's it. I haven't got any hangers-on. I couldn't bear that. I don't go to clubs. I sit at home and listen to records mostly. I hate parties.'

In future, Elton himself would say of such tours, 'They just kill you. They physically kill you.' It was not only the endless travel, the monotonous Holiday Inns and arid coffee shops, the bad diet, lack of sleep, and perpetual motion, varied by the boredom of an occasional rest day somewhere like Omaha. The grimaces that were becoming his trademark arose from real physical pain. His knees were perpetually bruised and scraped from his Little Richard kneelings and pratfalls. Banging the piano as he did for over an hour, night after night, broke fingernails, at times made his hands actually bleed. By half-way through each tour, he would have developed the calluses of a trapeze flier.

In New York he played Carnegie Hall, making the pictures of Brahms and Beethoven jog on the vestibule wall, just as John, Paul and Co. had in 1964. He also became the first rock star in history, so far as is known, to be joined on tour by his mother.

The arrangements to bring Sheila Dwight and Derf over were made by Elton's New York promoter, Ron Delsener. They were there to see him play Carnegie Hall, appear on the Dick Cavett TV show and receive his third gold disc, for the *Friends* soundtrack album, backstage at the Fillmore East. They were also with him at the gates of Disneyland, to witness a small sartorial contretemps. 'Elton John was the latest in a series of freaks to be refused admittance to Disneyland,' *Rolling Stone* reported aggrievedly. 'Despite his short hair and the company of his mum and dad, Elton was turned out because of numerous patches on his jeans. But John convinced the guards that the Disneyland concessions sold patches, and was let back in.'

Sheila wrote to Sue Ayton at DJM on her return, saying how great the trip had been and how happy Reg was to have her there. Among other news in her note, from the Frome Court kitchenette, was that he had just bought Derf and her a 'gorgeous' three-bedroom house ('Isn't he just too much!') and that John Reid would be starting as his manager in August.

'Have just got in from work,' Sheila ended, 'and am just trying to boil up some of Reg's washing to try to whiten it up a bit. Have just let it boil over (silly moo!). Must close now and get mopped up.'

From British rock critics that summer, the feeling was not of backlash so much as ceremonial flogging around the fleet.

ELTON BORES 'EM AT THE PALACE announced *Melody Maker*'s 'Caught in the Act' column on 7 August. The venue was not a Royal

Command Performance – yet – but Crystal Palace, former south London site of the cast iron and glass edifice which once housed Queen Victoria's Great Exhibition. Here, in 1971, hippydom tried to reassure itself that nothing had changed with a series of rock 'garden parties'. The freaks stripped off to their sallow torsos to hang out in the variable sun or dip in an artificial moat filled with flaccid rubber fish. Beyond the moat was a stage, where Elton featured in rotation with Hookfoot, Fairport Convention, Rory Gallagher and Yes.

At Crystal Palace, Elton faced a backlash of a completely different kind. What the beery British freaks wanted wasn't complex tracks like 'Levon' and 'Rotten Peaches' from his imminent new album. What they wanted – and threw beer cans if they didn't get – was plain old rock 'n' roll. By the time Nigel and Dee had joined the red jumpsuited figure on stage, and 'Whole Lotta Shakin'' was belatedly underway, hundreds could be seen drifting out of the ground. 'It was all somewhat sad,' wrote *Melody Maker*'s Roy Hollingworth, 'this man and living myth, darling of America, the ultimate of local boys making good, struggling like a pygmy centre-half with just several thousand of his own people.'

Elton was paying the pop industry's customary price for going too far too fast. A single bad gig – not that it was so very bad – instantly wiped away the memory of a hundred good ones. It was a classic case of performer overkill. There were too many albums on release, too many tours on the go, too many rapturous noises from across the Atlantic. The British music press, quite simply, was growing bored. Critics who had so recently hailed Elton John as the hope of a new decade now began to write him off as just a nine-day wonder, a publicist's invention, without real consistency or staying power.

Elton was now by no means the only new thing to be found in British pop. After the 1970 hiatus, 1971 had seen a whole crop of rival contenders to define the new decade. Two great names from the Sixties were born again and flourishing under the alien numeral. The Rolling Stones had re-launched themselves with their own eponymous record label and a new, spare, stripped-down sound, to match the stripped pine. George Harrison had stepped from his underdog role with the Beatles to release a hugely successful solo album, *All Things Must Pass*, in which Radha Krishna temple chant met Laura Ashley print. With his new-found confidence, Harrison had gone on to organise the spectacular New York concert when he, Bob Dylan, Leon Russell and assorted fellow superstars performed in aid of the starving millions in Bangladesh, so giving pop music its first faint breath of altruism and dignity.

As Elton's first success had prophesied, the time had come for singers without bands. There was Cat Stevens with his Florentine beard and songs of Mabel Lucie Attwell mildness (little hinting at the Muslim who would one day condone the *fatwah* against Salman Rushdie). At a rival piano, there was Gilbert O'Sullivan, in his orphan boy's cloth cap and hobnailed boots a more bizarre-looking figure than Elton would be for quite a long time yet.

There was also a youth with a long anteater face, combining Cockney and Scots ancestry, whose sandpaper scrub of a voice had been heard in semi-famous bands right back to Long John Baldry's Steampacket. After years of obscurity on the blues club circuit, Rod Stewart had joined with the rump of a Sixties teenybop band, the Faces, to score the biggest hit for a British vocalist in America since Elton's in 1970. Stewart's 'Maggie May', a morning-after lament to some backstage hag, foreshadowed every staple in Seventies pop. Pleasure to the point of boredom. Glamour to the point of squalor. Sex to the point of needing vitamin-A pills.

In the music papers where all these new phenomena were noted, Elton John now tended to draw only adverse criticism, if he was not ignored altogether. The general view was that his first great flush of fame would probably turn out to be his last. As 1971 drew to a close, one columnist acidly remarked that the best song for him to release next might be 'Death of a Clown'.

It was hardly the best moment for Elton's hitherto shy and private lyricist to step boldly forth into the limelight. Bernie Taupin's words had also begun to attract criticism for what was now seen as deliberate obscurity and pretentiousness. And when his solo poetry album, *Taupin*, was released on DJM Records in September, it shared in the same harvest of disenchantment.

Bernie's chief concern about the album was that it should not in any way exploit his association with Elton. He would not let Elton play on any of the sessions, and only one track, 'The Greatest Discovery', had previously been released as an Elton song. When *Taupin* was picked up by Elektra Records in America, Bernie stipulated that Elton's name must not be mentioned in any of the publicity.

The reviews were at best condescending, at worst downright horrid. Even critics who acknowledged Bernie to be a fresh and original voice among pop lyricists declared that he had absurdly overreached himself. Allan Richards, writing in *Crawdaddy* magazine, put it most brutally. 'Taupin is hardly a great poet, more a better-than-average storyteller, and his interpretations are tediously monotonous. His chosen musical accompaniment also drags like a horse with a lame hoof . . . I walk away from this recording a better man for never having to hear it again.'

The experience seemed to have cured Bernie of any further desire for individual celebrity. With advances against royalties from DJM, he had bought a tiny stone cottage in Tealby, a picturesque village near Market Rasen, Lincolnshire. There, he told everyone, he would be content to spend the rest of his life with Maxine and his collection of Wild West memorabilia, writing songs and poetry among the shades of his literary influences, Tolkien, Kenneth Grahame and A. A. Milne. In honour of Milne, and of Winnie-the-Pooh's equally famous, faithful sidekick, Bernie named the cottage 'Piglet-in-the-Wilds'.

John Reid's arrival within the Dick James Organisation initially made no great waves. The 21-year-old possessed all the canniness of his native land. He knew he was just a learner, and that unlimited scope to learn was being handed him on a plate. He therefore kept a low profile, with eyes and ears avidly open.

To begin with he seemed little more than Ray Williams and Steve Brown had been before him, a liaison man between Dick James and Elton on the management side, and between Stephen James and Elton on matters of recording. This function he performed with the same quiet diligence previously seen at St Mirin's Academy and the Knightsbridge branch of Austin Reed. His position was somewhat like that of an articled clerk in legal chambers, studying the vast case law of contracts and percentages, songs that had sold a million and acts that had stormed the world.

His zeal to learn found a ready response in Dick James, who had always been more than willing to share the fruits of thirty years' experience with anyone who'd listen. 'John used to spend a lot of time in my father's office,' Stephen James says now. 'I believe my father taught him a very great deal.'

Reid's arrival, in August, coincided with the wave of critical backlash against Elton, but no let-up in his treadmill work schedule. In September he was to make his sixth tour of America, going on from there to Japan and Australia. He was also still recording tracks for his sixth album, *Madman Across the Water*, due to be released in November. It was therefore a great relief for Elton's puppet masters to know there was someone with him all the time, both selflessly devoted to his welfare and with enough influence over him to ensure he always did what he was supposed to. As far as Dick James was concerned at that point, John Reid came as a boon and a blessing.

Yet Reid's advent did bring immediate change, most obviously in the relationship between Elton and James himself. Though still cordial on both sides, it now lacked a vital central element. For Elton now had no need of a father figure.

Stephen James is emphatic about the degree to which his father filled that seeming void in Elton's life. 'They used to have long, long talks behind closed doors, not just about music but about personal subjects, too. I think my father was one of the very few people in whom Elton confided about his private life and the difficulties he'd been having with girls. I know that if I was there, my father would sometimes ask me to go out of the room so that they could talk in complete privacy.'

Even after Elton became a big enough star to argue with James, their association had still been basically that of omniscient parent and wilful but fundamentally dutiful and grateful son. 'There'd be rows between them,' Stephen James says. 'Elton might get into a paddy and storm out of my father's office. But it never lasted long. A few minutes later he'd put his head round the door and say "Can I have a cup of tea?"'

Now that personal dimension greatly diminished. Elton's wishes were conveyed to Dick James by John Reid. And, in his own obvious power to influence those wishes, Reid also became a power to be reckoned with.

Between Stephen James and him there was almost instantaneous mutual antipathy. Stephen, too, had been used to dealing with Elton on a one-to-one basis on recording matters, and did not care for the new complexity of communication that John Reid introduced. 'Elton and This Record Company had always worked together very simply, as a team,' Stephen says. 'Now, suddenly, it was a matter of us and them. John was supposed to be our employee, but it quickly became obvious, his loyalty was only to Elton – and to himself. I think my father was very tolerant. If it had been up to me, I would have thrown him straight out.'

Elton's backing musicians, Nigel Olsson and Dee Murray, also quickly felt the difference John Reid made, travelling on that sixth tour, to America, Australia and Japan. 'We'd always been equals, like brothers,' Dee Murray says. 'Now, for the first time, Elton started seeming like a big star. You couldn't go straight to him any more. There was somebody else in the way. And it was pretty obvious that John didn't rate Nigel and me that much. At press conferences, it was all Elton. Nigel and I would just sit and not say a word. I said to John once, "Do we really need to be here at all?" He just said, "Aah, don't be so pedantic."'

On the road, Nigel and Dee had been used to only minimal 'management'. 'Steve Brown just used to let us get on with it,' Dee

Murray remembers. 'Russ Regan, from Uni Records, used to come to concerts, but all he ever did was hug us and shout, "This is a marriage." With John Reid around, suddenly there was a whole lot more going on. John would comment on the position of the microphones, or say the piano had to be moved.'

Both Dee and Nigel also became aware of a marked change in Elton himself. With John Reid, he seemed to grow moodier, more prone to sulks or his occasional, tempestuous Little Moments. To them – and to many others – it would even appear that, as well as calming Elton's Little Moments, Reid could also bring them on and greatly aggravate them.

The tour itself was a further mixture of critical wincing and huge popular sell-out. When Elton played the Greek Theater, Los Angeles, in September, even his press archangel Robert Hilburn commented adversely on his over-marketing (it was his fourth LA appearance inside a year) and sensed the desperation of a career on the decline. More flak flew at his 'costume gimmicks', even though these still embraced only such items as sleeveless T-shirts, dungarees with braces, badges pinned to his thigh or embroidered on his knee, and winged Mr Freedom boots.

From Los Angeles the party flew to Tokyo, a city bound to fascinate Elton with its phantasmagoric gadgetry and neon-crazed kitsch. The Japanese promoter presented them with kimonos and outsize paper umbrellas, and introduced them to the pre-cholesterol delights of Kobe beef.

Elton's concert in Osaka brought the nearest to a riot he had yet caused. 'In the hall, the kids were behind this long barrier,' Dee Murray remembers. 'They went so wild at one point, we thought the barrier was going to go. Some of them jumped on to the stage, after souvenirs. We finished the performance with about 150 of them up there with us. But it was still all perfectly friendly and polite.'

Thence to Australia, where Elton was to spend some of his very best and very worst times. Back in 1971, it gave little sign of becoming his future second home. 'When he arrived, Elton had dyed his hair orange, with little green bits behind the ears,' Dee Murray says. 'As we were queuing up for Customs, I heard a woman shout "What's this? A bloody travelling circus?"'

It is pure coincidence, but a poignant one, that the first tour that John Reid accompanied also happened to be the first with any faint whiff of offstage controversy. 'We were invited to a reception by the Dean of Perth,' Elton later remembered. 'We were so tired after the flight, we rang him and asked if we could make it the next day. That night on TV there's a big story: "Elton John snubs the Dean of Perth.

He says he's in a mood."'

Australia, he announced on returning, had been 'a nightmare'. 'We played at one football stadium, two racetracks and a speedway track – and it was in the middle of winter! The stage blew away on one gig, and we literally played in overcoats. It was raining on the piano ... New Zealand is nice, though. It's lovely and green, and the people are great. But Australia ... The band had five days off in Adelaide, and they went mad with boredom. If Mary Hopkin can run into trouble there, well, it gives you some idea ... But we'll go back again. Why not?'

The year ended on a confused note which one comes to recognise as peculiar to Elton: of euphoria pulled down by anxiety, and disappointment lightened by resolute optimism.

In Britain, his big moment seemed to have come and almost gone. The popularity poll run by *Melody Maker* in September suggested that Elton John was already growing passé. In the British Male Singer category he came fourth, after Rod Stewart, Robert Plant and Robert Chapman. In the Top British Single category – won by George Harrison's 'My Sweet Lord' – 'Your Song' managed only sixth place. In the International Pianist/Organist section, he was third, after Keith Emerson and Leon Russell. In the International Composer section, he was sixth. In the International Male Vocalist section, he did not even make the top ten.

To redress the balance, DJM took out a display advertisement pointing to American achievements that might otherwise have gone unnoticed. In *Billboard*'s year-end analysis of album sales, both by individuals and groups, Elton ranked an amazing sixth, beaten only by domestic monsters like Grand Funk Railroad, Chicago and the Partridge Family. In the solo singer category, he came joint first with James Taylor.

With his sixth album, *Madman Across the Water*, Elton hoped to silence for all time the critical chorus which dismissed him variously as a publicist's hype, a late-night BBC2 fad and a hula-hoopish American flavour of the month. Indeed, while working on it, he had described it to more than one person as 'make or break time'. Nothing would do but that he should come up with something his highbrow critics would pronounce every bit as fresh and exciting as the original *Elton John* album.

Madman, therefore, returned to the style of lushly dramatic orchestral settings, arranged by Paul Buckmaster. But now the songs had an edge which the two untravelled music fans of 1970 could never have given them. When Bernie Taupin wrote about America, it was no longer mere yearning over the open pages of a cowboy comic. When Elton played country or cajun piano, it was no longer just guessing how it might be done in the deep South. Their music had ceased to be mere Technicolor dream, and become first-hand Technicolor experience. 'What that album still reminds me of most is simply being in America,' Bernie Taupin says now. 'Driving down the freeways in LA, listening to the car radio.'

The lyrics were suffused with American tour life, mostly as experienced by Bernie from the wings of arenas or the back seats of cars. 'Tiny Dancer' was a love-song for his wife Maxine, 'Blue jean jean baby, LA lady', who'd 'married a music man'. 'Holiday Inn' was a country-and-western satire on endless domestic flights, with hot towels before landing, and the cheerless motel rooms into which they were decanted each night. Most of the songs were written in the first person, obliging Elton to assume a bewildering array of voices and characters. In the hillbilly-style 'Rotten Peaches' he was a fugitive from a Southern chain gang, who'd 'had my fill of cocaine and pills.' In the melodramatic 'Indian Sunset' he was a full-blooded brave who'd 'read the writings of the smoke . . . learned to hurl the tomahawk and ride the painted pony'. In the mournful 'Razor Face', he was a young wino looking out for a broken-down old one. In 'All the Nasties', he swiped back at the 'sacred cow' music critics who'd been harrying him all year.

Today, *Madman* seems a *tour de force* of shivery English violins and elegant American steel guitars, shot through with a dark cynicism and apocalyptic pessimism for which Leon Russell clearly must take much credit. Two tracks stand out for their utter, wonderful uncommerciality in any age. One is 'Levon', Bernie Taupin's own 'A Day in the Life', about a man born 'on the day the *New York Times* said "God is dead".' The other is 'Madman Across the Water' itself, soliloquy of a lunatic on visiting-day, played by an orchestra schizophrenically uncertain whether it is funeral dirge or slow-motion funk.

The sleeve design was again entrusted to David Larkham, and immediately became involved in acrimonious complications. Larkham's idea this time was to have no pictures on the sleeve, merely the title, hand-embroidered on blue denim. The work was done by his American wife, Janice, on a panel torn from one of his own Levi jackets. Packaged with the album was another expensive booklet with the lyrics in full, the running time of each track, portraits of Elton and Bernie and Victorian photographs with cod captions.

Stephen James considered the process unnecessarily complex and time-consuming. 'I asked the people in our art department, and they told me that exactly the same blue denim effect could be got photographically,' Stephen remembers. 'But no, Elton's people had to have it laboriously done by hand. And on specially expensive matt paper. I was all for good, original design, but what I was most concerned about was making our release date and getting the records into the shops.'

Alas, *Madman* barely measured up to all the effort, hope and stitchery invested in it. True, it reached number eight in the American album chart. But the place where Elton most wanted to prove and justify himself was Britain. *Music Week*'s album chart showed it no higher than number 41. The old problem of penetrating the singles market seemed as insoluble as ever. All the tracks were thought too long to be singles, and Elton would not hear of cutting them. In America, 'Levon' and 'Tiny Dancer' were released uncut, but neither made it into the *Billboard* Top 20. In Britain, nothing was thought worth even trying. Disappointed, and dazed from a year of overproduction and continual motion, Elton experienced yet another of those momentary compulsions to do utterly the wrong thing. 'I thought of quitting. I really thought I'd gone as far as I was going to.'

Instead, he managed to rally and give interviews, looking forward with a good show of brightness to 1972. There was to be another British tour, with American stars England Dan and John Ford Coley. He planned to make a new album in the Rolling Stones' mobile studio at their tax haven on the French Riviera. He also planned to augment his stage line-up with a guitarist whose name he could not yet divulge. The impression was of keeping his chin up and bravely smiling through.

On 8 December, he recorded a BBC TV *Sounds for Saturday* concert, apparently restored to seriousness and decorum, dressed in a conventional high-collared floral shirt, and remaining seated at the piano throughout. Only the occasional grimace of staring eyes and puffed-out cheeks hinted at the past year's wild transatlantic excursions. Between tracks from *Madman*, he did little more than smile shyly, twitch his square sunglasses up his nose, and sip from a BBC paper cup. It truly seemed as though, in the inner war of his two stage personae, Dr Jekyll finally had prevailed.

That very same day, as if to prove to himself there was no going back, he changed his name by deed poll. For a middle name, he looked both to the strong man of classical mythology, and to the broken-winded cart horse in his favourite TV comedy, *Steptoe and Son*. Now Reginald Kenneth Dwight was Elton Hercules John, legally and for ever.

8

'Can you help me?
How do I acquire taste?'

TURNING up copies of the *Melody Maker* or *New Musical Express* for early 1972, one is struck by how little everything seems to have changed in twenty-four months under the alien numeral. The big names in stories are still Dylan, Stones, Who and Beatles (albeit as individual performers), plus psychedelic giants like Pink Floyd and Led Zeppelin. New albums and singles are still reviewed at earnest length, in minuscule black type. Forthcoming tours are still announced in screaming full-page ads like the *New York Daily News*'s front page after Hiroshima. Everywhere one looks, one finds the Sixties generation still firmly in charge. The idea that there might be such a thing as a Seventies generation has barely yet risen above a whisper.

The Seventies generation were nothing like a generation younger. They were, in truth, only the young brothers and sisters of the Sixties generation, children in that magical time, and so excluded from the joys, excitements and indulgences. They were the ones who had been just too young to choose between Beatles and Stones. They had been just too young for hipster trousers, Cardin jackets, Courrèges boots and Op-Art PVC macs. They had been just too young to go to the Marquee, the Ad Lib, the Speakeasy or the UFO, or to strip naked and frolic in mud or foam at open-air festivals. They had been just too young for kaftans, gurus, teach-ins, love-ins, sit-ins, bed-ins, the I Ching, the *International Times* or *Hair*.

They were finally old enough, possessed of economic power and ready for the spree now established as youth's birthright. But the Sixties generation, their elder brothers and sisters, continued to obstruct them. The Sixties generation still held all vital installations: *Melody Maker*, *New Musical Express*, the Royal Albert Hall, the Roundhouse, Radio One, BBC2's *Old Grey Whistle Test*. Advancing into their twenties, with husbands, wives, babies and mortgages, they still could not imagine any manifestation of youth more vital and colourful – more definitive of the state of being young – than themselves.

The Seventies generation were first manifest in fashion rather than music. As might well be expected, it was a fashion rejecting all the Sixties style for which they had once longed, but been just too young. Out went long hair, washed at home and ironed on ironing-boards. In came shorter hair, professionally styled, razored, curled and permed, dyed scarlet, blonde or ash. Out went long, loose clothes in Oriental prints. In came short, tight clothes in chain-store versions of heavy English tweed or Fair Isle knit. Out went round-necked Indian shirts and collarless jackets. In came collars and lapels as high, broad and floppy as bucks' in the Regency. Out went pointed shoes with Cuban heels. In came squared-off shoes with wedge-shaped heels. Out went mysticism and wisdom. In came kid brother and sister cheek and *faux naïveté*. Out went designs of pentangles and Aquarius. In came designs of Bugs Bunny, Superman and Rupert Bear.

Out, in short, went the whole Sixties look of earthiness and naturalness, of lisping love and peace under a smiling sun. In – almost by way of revenge – came a new look of night-time artificiality and decadence; of whitish powder, brownish rouge and wine-dark lipstick; of slashes, flares, raised seams and gaping pleats; of shoulders extended, lapels sculpted and swaggered, sleeves puffed out and waists nipped in; of embellishments plundered from grandmother's needlework basket, trimmings of jet, diamanté, spangles and sequins.

The Seventies generation had been told by their elder brothers and sisters that pop's golden age could never come again. They therefore applied their economic power to making it do just that. Pop in the early Seventies thus suddenly ceased going forward, and began to replay itself. The songs and styles of the Fifties and early Sixties underwent wholesale revival. Rock 'n' roll, as once performed by Bill Haley and the Comets, Jerry Lee Lewis and Little Richard. A cappella and 'Doo-Wop', as once performed by Frankie Lymon and the Teenagers, the Platters, the Penguins and the Zirkons. Surfer songs, as once performed by the Beach Boys, Jan and Dean and the Surfaris. Ballads of puppy love, as once performed by Fabian, Bobby Vee, Bobby Vinton and Bobby Rydell. Not only the music of teenagers ten years before, but also their fashions – upswept, greased hair, sideburns and DAs; drape jackets, string ties and brothel-creeper shoes; circular skirts, hula-hoop earrings and ponytails. In the Sixties, every American kid had tried to look like a British one. In the Seventies, every British kid would try to look like an American one.

All these things had once been signs of youth's rebellion. Now they were signs of youth's emancipation, confidence, huge affluence, and the growing tendency among all age groups, as the modern world grew ever uglier, to wallow in nostalgia for the more and more recent past. Where Sixties pop had been almost wholly innovative, Seventies pop would be almost wholly derivative. The dominant mood of hit recordings became one of pastiche and parody. No longer did young people's music reflect, or have the slightest bearing on, social issues, war, famine, politics. The Seventies generation wished only for escapism. Their greatest idols would be those most adept in turning music into froth, fantasy, glitter and pantomime..

Looked at now, those early Seventies phenomena seem a bizarrely ill-assorted bunch. Today, who can fathom the mass hysteria engendered by a family of singing Mormons, as emptily wide-eyed and inanimately dimpled as Cabbage Patch Dolls? Or by the boy star of an American children's TV series, *The Partridge Family*? Or by an ageing warm-up singer for *Ready Steady Go!*, perennially unsuccessful under his former pseudonym, Paul Raven? Or by a group of pre-punk Scots in tartan trews, singing surf ballads with a power and attack that made Pinky and Perky, by contrast, seem Wagnerian? Yet the Osmonds, David Cassidy, Gary Glitter and the Bay City Rollers all would enjoy their stupendous hour in the Seventies generation's revenge.

Among the three runners-up to the ultimate crown, there was little of the conventional teenage heart-throb. David Bowie, white-faced and ambiguous of gender, his voice only marginally trendier than Anthony Newley's . . . Rod Stewart, long of beak and sly of smile, rumpling his slept-in thatch and kicking soccer balls around the stage . . . Marc Bolan, lowered on a cradle before his pre-pubescent fans, with his Clara Bow eyes and Theda Bara scowl, singing words so unintelligible that they might just as well have been Serbo-Croat or Esperanto . . .

And as to the crown itself, who ever would have guessed? The teen sensation of the new age, a former pub pianist from Pinner, of stocky build and thinning scalp, already famous beyond his wildest dreams, and more than half convinced this must be the limit of it.

Elton was as keen as anyone to know what the next pop wave would bring. The incorrigible record buff scanned each week's crop of releases for new directions and trends, sublimely unconscious that the new trend and departure to beat all would, very shortly, be himself.

'I wish the scene would change, and people would get young idols,' he told *Melody Maker* in another of his pop pundit interviews, late in 1971. 'I mean . . . it's crazy. Rod Stewart's in his mid-twenties, Dylan and Lennon are thirtyish. Elvis is an old man – and even I'm twenty-four! Where *are* they? Where are the new Beatles and Stones who are going to come along and shake us all out of our complacency? It's all become so static, so solemn. I don't want another Archies to come up, but things are just terrible as we stand. I can see Lennon still a teenage idol at forty!'

Certainly, the first idols of the Seventies generation all had a distinctly second-hand feel. Marc Bolan, the biggest thing in the British singles charts of 1971 and 1972, had been around since the mid-Sixties, as a male model, flower-power poet and leader of the hippy cult band Tyrannosaurus Rex. It was the first notable pop retread when Bolan collapsed the skeleton of Tyrannosaurus Rex and came back as T-Rex, producing records with names like 'Get It On' and 'Hot Love', aimed specifically at the new 'teenybopper' market.

Elton had opened for the old Tyrannosaurus Rex at the Round-house, and had often told interviewers how much he hated the hippy pretentiousness of their former style. Then one day he met Marc Bolan by chance in a record shop, and immediately took to him. Despite his look of kohl-eyed decadence, Bolan, too, was essentially normal, married and living in suburban Barnes. 'Marc and his wife, June, came to my wedding,' Bernie Taupin remembers. 'He was an incredible egomaniac, but so sweet that you couldn't help liking him. Anyway, that was what made him a star. The little that he had, he flaunted to the ultimate. For someone who was a limited guitarist, and maybe a limited songwriter, *Electric Warrior* is one of the great albums of that time.'

A more erratic relationship grew up with Rod Stewart, the other chart sensation of the hour, who had been around even longer than Elton before finally breaking through. Elton, indeed, could remember seeing him while still at school in Pinner, when Stewart appeared with Long John Baldry's Steampacket at a local Conservative club. 'Afterwards, I went to the pub, and went up to him and said "Excuse me, Mr Stewart, can I have your autograph?" Wild! He used to come on stage with a scarf around his neck, and sing "Good Morning Little School Girl" . . . I thought he was great.'

The two former Long John Baldry apprentices could hardly have been more different. While Elton shunned the excesses of pop-star life, Stewart embraced them all with avidity. He was, indeed, soon to become an early subject of tabloid newspaper headlines for taking snapshots of groupie orgies with his Polaroid camera.

What Elton and he had powerfully in common was their passion for football – in those days, still a fairly novel thing for pop stars to like. Stewart's concerts with the Faces already were more like games at Wembley or Ibrox Park, with fans turning up in colours of Celtic

FC, balls intermittently kicked or headed from the stage, and appreciation signalled by thousands of tartan scarves waving between upstretched arms as in a darkened grandstand.

Elton and Rod Stewart also became friends, though their liking for each other was masked by heavily affected rivalry and bitchery. 'Good piano player,' Stewart would concede whenever Elton's name came up. 'Pity his barnet's* falling out.'

What they also had in common was concern over their old mentor, Long John Baldry. Since breaking into the mainstream with 'Let the Heartaches Begin' – and sending Elton off to Liberty Records in despair – Baldry's career had gone into steep decline. He was now managed by Rod Stewart's manager, Billy Gaff, who phoned Elton in New York, asking for help in giving Long John a leg-up. Elton, typically, forgot his unhappy eclipse in Bluesology, preferring to remember how Baldry's acid tongue had helped stop him marrying Linda Woodrow. It was agreed that Elton and Rod Stewart should co-produce an album for Baldry, taking responsibility for one side each.

Baldry's album, *It Ain't Easy*, came as a welcome gear change for Elton in the frenetic summer of 1971. After so long in the spotlight, it was enjoyable to become a session man again, using his vast magpie store of styles and ideas unselfishly for Long John's benefit, and playing piano anonymously in a studio ensemble with guitarist Caleb Quaye and backup singers Roger Cook and Lesley Duncan. It was also a hilarious return to old times at the Marquee and Klooks Kleek, with Baldry as caustically camp as he had always been. The sessions created Baldryesque nicknames that would stick for ever, Elton becoming Sharon, Baldry himself Ada and John Reid Beryl, after the actress Beryl Reid.

Alas, neither this album nor a second Elton–Rod co-production, *Everything Stops for Tea*, early in 1972, was sufficient to restore Long John's British fortunes. Touring with Stewart and the Faces subsequently, he found those 'Woolworth's shopgirls' more disinclined to listen than ever. After sundry other relaunches through the Seventies, he decided to emigrate to Canada. At the time of writing, he was enjoying a new career in TV voice-overs, and had just finished playing Captain Hook in a touring production of *Peter Pan*.

As for Elton, his disappointment and chagrin over *Madman Across the Water* soon evaporated. The workaholic album-maker itched to get busy on his own account in a studio again – though which studio it would be was somewhat problematic. Trident, which had served

*Barnet fair – hair

him so well since the *Elton John* album, was now to be written out of the picture. His accountants advised that, for tax reasons, it would be better if future albums were made outside Britain.

Though modern recording studios existed throughout Europe, almost no British performers had ever thought to make use of them. European pop in the early Seventies was generally thought a joke, exemplified by the annual travesties of the Eurovision Song Contest. Greatest joke of all was France, with its garbled rock-'n'-roll parodies, endless Piaf impersonators and ubiquitous piano-accordions.

France had acquired some chic, however, after the Rolling Stones fled to tax exile on the Riviera, taking with them a fully equipped mobile studio. Elton had been supposed to use it first thing in 1972, but at the very last moment – in true Stones style – word came through that it wasn't available. Hasty inquiries then had to be made by Gus Dudgeon about other possible studios in France or just across its frontiers.

The most promising idea Dudgeon came up with was a studio named Strawberry, established in the seventeenth-century Château d'Hierouville in the countryside 40 kilometres north of Paris. It was a place already known among top American bands, and had recently been used by Jerry Garcia and the Grateful Dead. Elton went over to look at the château, and instantly fell in love with it. 'It had an atmosphere all its own,' he recalled later. 'It was in the middle of nowhere, with a swimming pool, tennis court. You could record in a room with a thirteenth-century chandelier, overlooking nothing but fields.'

With the booking of Strawberry, he could finally name the guitarist he had found to augment his two-man backup band. The newcomer was Davey Johnstone, a blond, lanky Scot who at the time played in an acoustic band named Magna Carta, as well as writing fiddly-diddley folk songs with titles like 'Sponge'. Elton's producer Gus Dudgeon also produced Magna Carta, and had brought Johnstone in on Bernie Taupin's album, playing sitar, banjo, mandolin and lute. Elton was 'knocked out' by his playing, and saw at once what a dimension might be added by translating his flowery acoustic technique to electric rock 'n' roll lead. 'It's a good time to extend the band,' Elton told *Melody Maker*'s Ray Coleman. 'You get an inner feeling that this is the moment to do something. For the past year, too much has been focused on me – I've been lead instrument, rhythm instrument and voice. I'd gone as far as I could with three men. It was either change completely, or split.'

This came as something of a surprise to Elton's two existing sidemen, Dee Murray and Nigel Olsson. The first Dee knew of it was when Davey joined them en route to record for the first time in France. 'Don't get me wrong – we both got on great with Davey from the start. He was a terrific player, and great for the band. It's just that we had no idea he was coming in.'

To Dee Murray, the affair was another example of how life with Elton changed after John Reid's arrival. 'Before John was around, I'm sure Elton would have discussed the whole thing with us. Now it was as if we just weren't worth consulting – and didn't really matter at all. Before Davey came in, Nigel and I were getting 40 per cent of the concert money between us, and Elton got 60. With Davey in, we just divided it three ways, thirteen and a third per cent each. I was usually the spokesman, so I went to John and asked him if we could get a bit of a raise on that. His answer was no, "and if you don't like it, you know what you can do".'

Recording at Strawberry studio proved an ideal arrangement. The setting of the half-ruined château was breathtakingly beautiful, and wonderfully free of all normal recording distractions. The musicians occupied basic but comfortable rooms, meeting for meals in a communal dining-area with a piano at one end of it. In the morning, they could get straight up from their breakfast coffee and *biscottes* and start rehearsing. From there it was a walk of only a few yards across a courtyard to the excellently equipped recording complex. 'It was literally like a music factory,' Bernie Taupin remembers. 'I'd be upstairs in my bedroom, writing at top speed. I'd give each set of lyrics straight to Elton at the piano.' With the chords that flowed naturally from the stubby hands, a song could be written in twenty minutes, rehearsed by the band in an hour and recorded that same afternoon.

Creature comforts, however, were not neglected. The château provided first-class cuisine and owned its own vineyard. The studio was run by a young Frenchwoman named Catherine Philippe-Gérard who, like many powerful, authoritative females, became devoted to Elton. He took to her just as strongly, making her part of the inner circle with John Reid, Bernie and Gus Dudgeon, even announcing that the finished album would be dedicated to her.

Such was the energy and euphoria of the Strawberry sessions that in barely three weeks, all ten tracks were finished and ready for mixing in London. The fun atmosphere even extended to Elton's asking his unofficial stepfather, Derf Farebrother, to contribute to one track by playing the spoons on his knee. When Derf could not make it, Elton called over 'Legs' Larry Smith of the Bonzo Dog Doo-Dah Band to simulate the noise of tap-dancing. (It was a poignant twist of fate, since the Bonzos had passed that same long-ago Liberty Records audition which Reggie Dwight had so hopelessly failed.)

There was also a song whose first line had occurred to Bernie Taupin complete, while driving alone in Lincolnshire. 'The words just came into my head: "She packed my bags last night, pre-flight. Zero-hour is nine am." I remember jumping out of the car and running into my parents' house, shouting "Please don't anyone talk to me until I've written this down."'

The song was 'Rocket Man' and, like so much of the best of Taupin and John, was anything but original. David Bowie's 'Space Oddity', in 1969, had explored precisely that same theme of a lonely, disenchanted astronaut. As burrowers through Musicland's import box, Elton and Bernie were aware of an even earlier prototype. In 1967, the American cult band Pearls Before Swine had recorded a song actually called 'Rocket Man', written by their leader Tom Rapp.

None of this was to matter in April 1972, when Elton John's 'Rocket Man' came out as a single in Britain and America. Elton had not wanted to release it, thinking it 'too slow', but the instinct of his producer Gus Dudgeon, fortunately, prevailed. By further happy chance, space happened to be in the headlines with the launch of America's latest three-man moon probe, *Apollo 16*. In Dudgeon's masterly production, it was as if Elton's voice also echoed down vast black freeways of hyper-space. The very last spot in the universe you would have imagined him to be was a château 40 kilometres from Paris.

It was the instant hit single Elton had longed and sweated for since 1967. More significantly still, it went to number two in Britain while reaching only six in America. From the space capsule whose interior still so much resembled a bedsitting-room in Pinner, Rocket Man might have observed the continents shifting into alignment at last.

One day early in 1972, a young man pushed open the door of a small bookshop in Virginia Water, Surrey. The proprietor who glanced up had a foxy face familiar to anyone raised on British black-and-white war movies of the mid 1950s. He was Bryan Forbes, actor-turned-director and, until lately, head of Britain's last major film studio, EMI. Keeping a bookshop was but one thread in a multistrand life that also encompassed screen- and novel-writing, magazine publishing and frequent appearances in showbiz, society and even royal circles, accompanied by his actress wife, Nanette Newman.

Of the young man browsing in his shop that day, Forbes noted only that he wore spectacles and 'a fur coat which looked as if it had just died. I'd heard that the Bee Gees were supposed to be living in the neighbourhood. My first thought was that he might be one of the Bee Gees. The funny thing was that, though I knew almost nothing about pop music, I happened to be going to a pop concert that very night. I was on the Council of the National Youth Theatre, and we were doing a fund-raising concert at the Shaw Theatre, where they'd got Elton John to appear. I'd heard of Elton John, of course, though I had no idea what he looked like at that stage.

'So to this young man, who I thought was a Bee Gee, I said, "I'm going to a pop concert tonight." "That's funny," he said. "So am I." And that was how I first met Elton.'

They met again that night, and afterwards had dinner together. Elton revealed that he'd just moved to Virginia Water and was living in a bungalow not far from Forbes's house, Seven Pines. Though the star of the night, he was far more absorbed in talking to the man responsible for such British movie classics as *I'm All Right, Jack* and *The League of Gentlemen*. Still more fascinated was he to hear of Forbes's vast circle of movie friends, especially his own idol, the arch Goon Peter Sellers.

A few days later, he paid the first of many neighbourly visits to Bryan Forbes and Nanette Newman at Seven Pines. Having bought the house as a shell in the Fifties, they had made it an opulent showplace, filled with desirable books and excellent art. Elton was deeply impressed. 'He took in every detail of the house,' Bryan Forbes remembers. 'He said "You've got a complete home here, haven't you?"'

He talked in a desultory way about his own new home, the bungalow down the road, and how he was thinking of decorating and furnishing it. Then he turned to Bryan Forbes with a beseeching look – one that Ray Williams, of Liberty Records, would have found all too familiar.

'Can you help me?' he said. 'How do I acquire taste?'

The choice of Surrey's stockbroker belt as a place to live was a familiar one among newly rich British pop stars. Since John, George and Ringo had shown the way, it was almost a *sine qua non* of making one's first million to buy a mock-Tudor mansion or Bel Air-style bungalow out in Weybridge, Esher, Roehampton or Sheen. Pop people even more than stockbrokers appreciated the combination of nearness to London with rural peace and tranquillity, and a lifestyle that was the nearest southern England could offer to the Hamptons or Beverly Hills.

The inhabitants of Weybridge, Esher, Roehampton and Sheen tended to be somewhat less than welcoming. This was because wherever pop people went, so as a rule did thunderous hi-fi, slamming car-doors, revving motorbikes, parties that went on seventy-two hours at a stretch, regular guitar and drum-practice, audible wife- and girlfriend-battering, neglected children with slatternly nurses, villainous-looking servants and hangers-on, public drunkenness and lasciviousness, periodic police swoops for drugs, chaos, neglect and a squalor that could carry a quarter of a mile on clear summer air. Stockbrokers and their families learned to tremble when neighbouring properties fell vacant, chauffeur-driven Austin Princesses appeared in the drive, long hair bobbed between the topiary work and laid-back voices grew audible, ominously talking about 'good vibes'.

Even sedate Virginia Water, where Elton concentrated his search, had its own resident Minotaur. Among properties for sale was the house of the Who's drummer Keith Moon, aka Moon the Loon, where the eventual purchaser found interior walls peppered with gunshot blasts, the kitchen awash with baked-bean tins, the glass wall to the living room in fragments and a Rolls-Royce Corniche standing submerged in the swimming pool.

Elton eventually found what he wanted in Abbots Drive, part of the exclusive estate surrounding Wentworth golf course. It was a modern split-level bungalow, with a large rear garden and swimming pool, costing £50,000. He moved there with John Reid early in 1972. Commemorating his new identity, and Steptoe's carthorse, the bungalow ceased to be 14 Abbots Drive and became Hercules.

To begin with, it was very much a standard pop-star home, with large Tiffany lamps, vermilion leather buttonback couches, coffee tables, ceiling-high gilt mirrors, framed reproduction Victorian posters, and the hundred-and-one knick-knacks presented for achievement in the record industry. There was the obligatory games room, with ping-pong table, hand-operated football game, fruit machine, golf balls and putter. Along with the stacks of albums in shiny covers and piles of singles in paper ones, there was also now a Fifties jukebox, filled with Elton's personal selection.

Outside on the short, sloping drive stood a thicket of expensive cars: a Rolls-Royce Corniche hardtop, a Rolls Phantom VI, used for touring, a Ferrari Boxer and a Mini GT. In the boot of one Rolls was a moped, which Elton would occasionally whip out and mount if brought to a standstill in London traffic.

The great difference from other pop-star domiciles was noted by *Melody Maker*'s Roy Hollingworth. Instead of the usual jumble and squalor, fastidious cleanliness and order prevailed. 'From the neatly folded face-flannel in the bathroom to the suit of armour guarding the stairway, all is a kind of tidy perfection one would expect to see at the Ideal Home Exhibition. In fact, Elton's house makes the Ideal Home Exhibition look like a display of Nissen huts shortly before demolition by squads of sanitary engineers. It seemed almost offensive to flick cigarette-ash into the glittering ashtrays.' Hollingworth went on to describe how the interview came to an embarrassing halt when his photographer, Barrie Wentzell, accidentally slopped some Dom Perignon champagne on to Elton's brand-new living-room carpet. Reporter and photographer watched, bemused, as Elton knelt between them with a bowl of water and a cloth, feverishly scrubbing at the mark.

An early use of the house was as an address on the marriage certificate of Elton's mother, Sheila. In May 1972, she married Fred Farebrother, whose surname she had adopted by deed poll some years earlier. Two witnesses' signatures appear on the certificate: that of John Reid's mother, Elizabeth, and a boldly-inscribed 'Elton Hercules John'.

Despite all the massive changes and upheavals in Elton's life, Sheila remained as central and vital a figure as ever. Only now, in his twenties, did he fully appreciate the struggle she had had, as a single parent, to raise and educate him, and the unquenchable vigour with which she had jollied him along since that day, in Pinner Hill Road, when he hesitantly pecked out the first notes of 'The Skaters' Waltz'. It was among the earliest satisfactions of his new wealth to persuade Sheila to quit her job as a government clerk, move out of the tiny maisonette where they had rubbed along so many years together, and move into the 'gorgeous three-bedroom house' he bought for her in Ickenham, Middlesex.

Sheila's decision to make Derf his official stepfather at last gave Elton huge pleasure, though in truth it made no real difference to their relationship. The genial painter and decorator – who had first delivered him and his PA system to George Hill's pub, and rescued him and his LPs from Linda Woodrow – had always been and would always be 'My Dad'.

At Hercules, Sheila and Derf were fixtures from the beginning. Derf supervised the redecoration and became responsible for the hanging of Elton's growing collection of pictures. When Elton and John Reid were away on tour, Sheila and Derf would move in as caretakers and to look after Elton's spaniel, Brian, and his Alsatian, Bruce.

Sheila, to be sure, was no liability to have around, still only in her late forties, as petite and darkly attractive as ever. She was even starting to take on a little pop style, with blue jeans, big jewellery and baggy T-shirts bearing details of her son's last US tour. Elton made no secret of his attachment to her, nor of his continuing reliance on her plainspoken good sense. 'She's just straight about everything, and she can smell a rat for a mile. She'll say "Don't bloody well trust him. He'll run off with all your money." She's always been right.'

The mother of Elton John was now newsworthy in her own right. A *Daily Mail* writer, Jane Gaskell, visited Sheila while she and Derf were holding the fort at Hercules during Elton's spring 1972 American tour. Both of them chatted freely about his childhood as Reggie and the way their lives had changed since he'd made it into the big time. Derf admitted undergoing some ragging from fellow builders when he wore the scarlet platform-heel shoes his stepson had recently given him. 'But we both feel younger. I expect I look younger, too.'

Sheila talked of Elton's generosity; the £15,000 'gingerbread house' he had bought her at Ickenham, the white MGB sports car he'd insisted she have instead of her old Mini. 'He loves paying out – and he loathes the feeling of owing anyone any money. The first thing he'll do when he gets home is sit down at that desk and write out a dozen cheques. There's been less contact between us, of course, since he became so busy. But he still rings at times and says "I've got the day to myself, Mum – come on over and spend it with me."'

The first parties to be held at Hercules were strictly family ones. Elton's grandmother, Ivy, his Aunt Win, his Uncle Reg, his cousins Paul, Cath and John, all often gathered there for the kind of jolly knees-ups that had always gone on at Frome Court or in Pinner Hill Road. The thoughtful small boy remained just as thoughtful now that he was a star. Chauffeur-driven cars would be sent to fetch everybody and take them home again. Exquisite food would be served by top-class caterers. When Elton's Aunt Win remarried, he insisted both on being best man and holding the wedding reception at his house. 'He organised everything – the cars, the food,' his cousin, Paul Robinson, remembers. 'We had a marvellous party afterwards, next to the swimming pool.'

He was just as pleased to see his Dwight relations, from Kent. His cousin Roy, the ex-soccer star, remembers dropping by one day with his wife, and getting a huge welcome. 'Elton had just come out of the shower,' Roy remembers. 'He took us into the living room still wearing just his bathrobe. It was just a skimpy little thing and, the way he was sitting, you could see everything. But he didn't mind, and we certainly didn't. He sat there, pleased as punch, talking to my wife eyeball to eyeball.'

Otherwise, the main visitors were pop landed gentry who lived in the vicinity: Keith Moon, Rod Stewart, the hippy poet Donovan. There was also a constant stream of interviewers from music papers, to whom Elton described a social life of Jane Austenish variety. 'Donovan's having a party next week, and he's invited the whole world. Keith Moon says he doesn't want any galactic fairy dust, he wants a good booze-up. Rod says he's not much into mushrooms and toadstools, but he'll go . . . David Bowie was just here. I really liked what Mott the Hoople did with his song ['All The Young Dudes'] so I rang him up and invited him for a meal.'

His major new friend in the business was Marc Bolan of T-Rex, whose singles, 'Get It On', 'Hot Love' and 'Ride A White Swan', now stocked the jukebox in his rumpus room. Towards so massive a rival, jealousy and condescension would have been more than understandable. But such things simply were not in Elton's nature. He recognised Bolan's songs as perfect pop music, expertly tailored to their market. When Elton played the Fairfield Hall, Croydon, late in 1971, Bolan walked onstage as a surprise guest, and they finished the show together, upstaging and outcamping one another like some spangly latter-day Laurel and Hardy.

Bolan lived in Barnes, only a few miles from Wentworth, and often drove over with his wife, June. To Elton, he was the perfect caricature of a pop idol, with his black eyes and pre-Raphaelite hair; transparently vain, ambitious and exploitative. Yet under the huge ego lay genuine charm, and a healthy root of self-mockery. A tongue-in-cheek contest developed between Elton and Bolan to see which could display the greater hubris and conceit. On Bolan's birthday, he received a life-size photographic blow-up of Elton. On Elton's next birthday, a furniture-removal pantechnicon drew up outside Hercules. In it was the silver disc Bolan had received for 'Jeepster', and a blow-up photograph of himself, 27 feet high. It was, indeed, higher than the house, and had to be put outside in the garden.

Elton and Bolan even tried to write something together, though the partnership did not progress much further than an ad libbing of 'Jeepster' around the grand piano at Hercules. Clive Banks, a young newcomer to Dick James Music, remembers the occasion as poignantly illustrative of Sixties- versus Seventies-style talent. 'Elton had a brilliant natural voice, but Marc's was all put together in the studio. In real life, it wasn't much more than a little squeak. You'd got Elton playing 'Jeepster' and doing a great vocal, and this squeak going on on top of it. Horrible!'

Elton still did not have the smallest notion of himself as a competitor to Marc Bolan. In his own eyes, he was an oldie from 1971 whose career was experiencing a wholly unlooked-for second wind. With 'Rocket Man' in the British and American charts, he could afford to be indulgent towards new young teenybopper crazes like David Cassidy, the Osmonds and Slade. His tone was that of elder statesman with heart in right place, insisting that youth must always have its say. As he often said, from the encrusted eminence of his twenty-four years, 'It's a sign of people getting old when they start grousing about the groups.'

Big name though he had indubitably become, he was still first and foremost a besotted fan – of rock-'n'-roll stars, film stars, theatre stars, anything with that thrilling golden aura of legend. As he had once made a pilgrimage to Batley Variety Club to see Dusty Springfield, he now went incognito to the London Palladium to see Marlene Dietrich. 'I was totally bowled over by her,' he recalled afterwards. 'As I came out afterwards, a girl saw me and said, "Can I have your autograph?" When I'd signed her book, she said, "Here what's this?" I looked, and I'd signed it "Marlene Dietrich".'

His main worry about his new album, released a month after 'Rocket Man', was whether sufficient time had elapsed since the absurd overproduction of 1971, and the somewhat dull thud of *Madman Across the Water*. After *Madman*'s design indulgences, this was a low-profile affair in a custard-coloured cover showing a plain head shot of Elton with his Troubadour beard. The tracks were those recorded at Strawberry studio, amid the unlikely grandeur of the Château d'Hierouville. The title – mixing street jive talk with snob French – was *Honky Château*.

Other than 'Rocket Man', the feel was country and western, with the accent on country. Bernie Taupin had written the idyll of his new life with new-found love, in a thatched cottage named Piglet-in-the-Wilds. The tone was set by 'Honky Cat', an opening track of Zip-a-de-doo-dah jauntiness, with piano chords such as Winifred Atwell might have played in 'Chinatown, My Chinatown'. The space man was also a farm boy after the Huck Finn style, in plantation hat and rolled-up dungarees.

It was an incarnation which seemed to please his audience more than any so far. By early summer 1972, *Honky Château* stood at number two in every British album chart. In America, it became Elton's first number one, earning him his fourth US gold disc for $1 million sales. 'Honky Cat' was afterwards released as a single, making eight in America but, oddly for so evergreen an Elton track, only 31 in Britain.

The blending of Bernie Taupin's thoughts with Elton's voice had produced a curious synthesis. Bernie's words were more important than mere song lyrics, each time inventing a wholly new version of their singer's character and psyche. But in another way, they scarcely seemed to register at all. Pop lyrics in the Sixties and Seventies were subject to rigorous vetting, both by the BBC, their all-important British outlet, and by American radio stations, especially those morally hypersensitive ones throughout the Southern Bible Belt. The list of banned records ranged from Screaming Jay Hawkins's 'Constipation Blues' to the Beatles' 'I am the Walrus'. The Rolling Stones had caused international scandal merely by naming a song 'Let's Spend the Night Together'. John Lennon's 'A Day in the Life', a masterpiece by any reckoning, had been outlawed for one marginally drug-flavoured line, 'I'd love to turn you on'.

Yet 'Rocket Man', with its far more narcotically explicit 'I'm gonna be high as a kite by then', blasted unchecked from the transistor radios of two continents. And on *Honky Château*, several even more blatant naughty bits were to be found. 'Slave' cast Elton in the role of Southern abolitionist, vowing, 'I swear one day I'm gonna burn that whore-house down'. 'Mellow' was a cameo of energetic sex: 'wreckin' the sheets real fine'. The Legs Larry tap-dancing track was a cheerful little thing called 'I Think I'm Going to Kill Myself', on which Elton light-heartedly sang of 'buying a forty-four' and 'causing a little suicide'.

It was not that he did not take on his ever-changing roles with total passion, sincerity and conviction. But something in that Latin-inflected voice – the way words were framed by that wide, narrow-lipped mouth – purged the darkest sentiment whiter than white. He was not androgynous so much as genderless, devoid of sexual charge as no male performer had been since the banjo-strumming George Formby. His songs of killing and arson might just as well have been sung by a Teddy bear with a ribbon round its neck; his songs of lust by a castrato from a medieval cathedral school.

As is usually the case with born fans, Elton was also a born collector. Like the urge to follow and worship heroes, the urge to acquire, to hoard and stroke and cherish inanimate objects can become an almost perfect substitute for true happiness. The solitary boy in his Pinner bedroom had long ago learned to draw from toys and possessions the companionship and warmth that human relationships seemed unable to give.

Such taste as he had at the beginning merely reflected the general one. This was 1971 and 1972, when all fashionable interiors lay under the same thrall of nostalgia and whimsicality. Having exhausted London's stocks of Victoriana, the second-hand dealers were now picking over the domestic remnants of Edwardiana, the Great War, the Twenties and Thirties. The craze was Art Nouveau and, at a cheaper level, Art Deco, that cosy Ovaltiney interwar look whose scalloped furniture, dadoed teacups and plaster flying ducks, still current in Metroland, now filled the smart Portobello stalls and Kensington hypermarkets. It was a time rivalling Queen Victoria herself for domestic clutter, when for every one useful household object, fifty would be on show that were useless but 'fun', when no modish mantelpiece could fail to display a set of W. D. and H. O Wills's cigarette cards, a golliwog in Boer War khaki, a postcard from a soldier in Flanders, a photograph of Jack Buchanan and a menagerie of W. Britain's lead zoo animals and scratched Dinky cars.

With his new pop star wealth, fulfilling his schoolboy dreams, Elton bought on an epic scale. But he possessed nothing casually or haphazardly. The great example was his record collection, still organised meticulously into categories and subsections, with neatly written index cards, even now when trips through Tower Records with a shopping trolley might increase it by 300 albums at a time. His mind was that of an archivist or librarian, cataloguing and cross-referencing all that he acquired, down to the smallest Pinocchio badge from Disneyland. What he lacked was discrimination, or any sense of the dictum 'less is more', a quality he had in common with Elvis Presley. The same rule applied at Hercules in Virginia Water as at Graceland in Memphis, Tennessee. However small, cheap, insignificant or ephemeral the acquisition, once in Elvis's or Elton's possession it stayed there.

By 1972, the bungalow at Wentworth already housed a dozen different collections in progress. There was one of Art Nouveau lamps, supported by streamlined nymphs in every attitude of flowing-robed endeavour. There was another of reproduction posters for such nineteenth-century happenings as *Exposition Internationale de Madrid, 1893–94* or 'Rudge's Rotary Tandem'. There was another of onyx eggs, graded in every size from ostrich to plover. There was another of Pop Art, including Andy Warhol's signed silk-screen print 'Last Suite of the Electric Chairs'. There was another of stuffed animals, including a bear, a cheetah and (*Melody Maker* assured its readers) a warthog. Plus the vast, unclassifiable collection of hypermarket impulse buys and tailor-made technological novelties, from a Victorian cash register to a neon sign spelling Hercules.

There was also the ever-growing and diversifying collection of Elton's clothes and accessories. The down-at-heel denim pirate of 1969 had become the ultimate shiny Seventies fashion plate. No new look could have been kinder to someone of his short and dumpy build. The new platform shoes, with their clubfoot toes and heels stacked up and variegated as layer-cake, added three or four inches to his height. The new trousers, with their gaucho flares, concealed the bulkiness of his legs. The new rigid, nipped-in jackets broadened his shoulders and gave him the appearance of a waist.

His suits, jackets, coats and cloaks, the finest fruits of Granny Takes a Trip in King's Road and Nudie the Rodeo Tailor, filled closet after closet, with pair upon pair of platforms from the Chelsea Cobbler ranged like flotillas of painted sampans beneath. An entire portmanteau was needed for the pairs of spectacles he brought home from every trip to America. A shop in Hollywood made them up to his specifications, with prescription lenses tinted every conceivable shade, and frames of ever-increasing fancifulness. One pair had orange-tinted lenses and white rims. Another had hexagonal rims of translucent blue. Another had heart-shaped rimless lenses, tinted in lateral stripes of red, white and blue. Another had little hoods that could be pulled down over their lenses like supernumerary eyelids.

In Reggie Dwight's Sixties schooldays, pop stars had been identifiable by their fringes and elastic-sided boots. The great star of the Seventies first became identifiable via outsize glasses, allied to footwear so precarious and cumbersome, he could walk only with the slow, measured tread of the circus stilt artist. En route to America in April 1972, four pairs of his platform boots and one pair of his shoes were impounded by US Customs officials who suspected that their eight-inch heels might conceal smuggled narcotics or jewels.

Elton could not claim to be first in what was now officially styled 'glitter rock'. The trend had been in evidence since 1970, with white British bands like T-Rex, Slade, Sweet, even the Rolling Stones, and black American soul groups like the Jackson Five, the Temptations and the Chi-Lites. If the style had any one progenitor it was David Bowie, another Sixties survivor, who had brilliantly seen how his marginal singing voice might be projected through a persona of androgynous high fashion and stage shows utilising every dramatic device from Marcel Marceau mime to schlock Hollywood sci-fi.

The difference between David Bowie and Elton John was that between *haute couture* and the rag trade. What Bowie created on the catwalk, Elton rushed post haste into the high street chain stores.

For him, glitter was no more than blessed camouflage. In the stage outfits it was now possible to wear, his physical shortcomings simply melted away. More crucial was the way Glitter Rock abolished the solemnity he had always so hated in live performance, replacing it with whoops and cheers for excesses of flamboyance and kitsch that would have made the Sixties generation wince. He loved it that the newest British chart sensation was a Fifties Teddy-boy caricature actually named Gary Glitter, whom Elton and his circle could remember as an office boy at the *Ready Steady Go!* programme.

In interviews, he constantly stressed that his stage acts were just 'a bit of fun', not to be taken in any way seriously. One music press reporter who called him 'showbizzy' provoked an eloquent tirade. 'It's glamour, but I refuse to say it's showbizzy. I'm sending show business up. I hate show business. I mean, Rod Stewart is exactly the same; he's very flamboyant and wears pink satin suits and that's showbiz, and yet it's not. You can't say I'm showbizzy. I'm so bloody clumsy, and there's nothing graceful about me with a pair of flying boots on. I just like to get up and have a lark. I do it tongue in cheek – with an 'up yours' sort of attitude. It's like an actor getting into his costume for his part. I don't really feel the part until I'm into what I'm going to wear.

'It's a reaction against everything I wasn't allowed to do as a kid. I wasn't allowed to wear winklepicker shoes in case they hurt my feet. I wasn't even allowed to wear Hush Puppies, can you imagine that? Not having had a real teenage life, I'm living all those thirteen to nineteen years now. Mentally I may be twenty-five, but half of me is still thirteen.'

Almost as nettling was the frequent music press insinuation that he worked in obedience to some Svengali-like manager behind the scenes. 'It's incredible – people have the impression that there's someone behind me with a great big button, saying, "You must wear this and you must wear that." I think it was Roy Carr who said they're pushing the Destruct button. Well, that's me, if anyone, because there's nobody behind me.'

Elton's first British tour of 1972 marked his first major foray into glitter rock. He came on in a silver-striped tail coat, red velvet trousers with knee-high green silk turn-ups, multi coloured Lurex socks and silver platform boots, one with a large red 'E' on its side, the other with a 'J'. His hair had changed hue from orange and green to silver. The turning of his scalp into Killing Fields had begun.

It was part of a conscious – indeed, conscientious – effort to get on terms with a British public which, with his concentration on American tours, he felt he had never really understood. 'In the States, I have no qualms,' he told *New Musical Express*'s Julie Webb. 'But I really don't know what people think of me in this country. I go out and think "What are they expecting?"'

Previously his stage clothes had been a random assembly of things bought at Mr Freedom, picked up at Disneyland or borrowed at the last minute from Bernie Taupin's wife, Maxine. But in this new competitive field of visual extravagance, the way to maintain his edge was clearly to start having performance outfits custom-made.

It happened that Steve Brown's brother Pete had married a girl named Annie Reavey, a freelance designer of shoes for trendy firms like Moya Bowler and Richard Smith's Chelsea Cobbler. Highly gifted and original in approach, she was herself the acme of early Seventies style, from her topply metallic boots to hair that changed colour, or parti-colour, even more often than did Elton's.

For Elton's twenty-fifth birthday, Steve Brown asked Annie Reavey to design and make him a special party outfit. She made him a fur cloak embroidered with palm trees, and a tall quilted hat from which the EJ monogram dangled on a string. Elton loved the ensemble so much that she was asked to start making him clothes to wear onstage.

Annie Reavey remained his chief couturière for the next three years. To begin with, her designs were relatively simple siren-suit affairs of pink and green woven Lurex, with ELTON in pink across the chest and HERCULES down the side of the right leg. Elton was especially fond of quilted satin, despite the crippling heat it generated during his performances. Another typical Reavey production was a yellow quilted satin suit, its short-sleeved jacket embroidered across the back with a scene of turquoise sea, violet sky, sand, a palm tree, musical notes, a cherry-red transistor radio and a pair of spectacles.

She quickly learned to camouflage the shortcomings of Elton's figure, broadening his shoulders with pads like an American football quarterback's, pluming his trousers like an Argentinian gaucho's to hide the bulkiness of his legs. She also learned that his measurements were seldom constant. If Elton was passing through a period of stress, his waistline could expand alarmingly between the first fitting and the final one. Though prone to indulgence in food and alcohol, he also possessed an ability, given to very few, to know when enough was enough. 'I've got an iron will,' he frequently observed of himself. 'If I want to lose weight, I can just lose it.' Having tactfully let everything out, Annie Reavey would sometimes have to take it all in again.

She also learned there was nothing she could dream up that was too wild, way-out or lacking in all normal masculine dignity for Elton to wear onstage. 'One outfit I made him for St Valentine's Day, I thought he'd never stand for. It was pink and gold Lurex brocade, trimmed with gold lace; it had a pink and gold heart embroidered on it. And short pants. But he loved it.'

The object was over-the-top ostentation and extravagance – but only up to a point. At an Elton John concert, his audience knew they could expect an entrance of surpassing fancy-dress absurdity and self-mockery. But there the posing and posturing stopped. The performance that followed was the same exuberant, unpretentious rock-'n'-roll sweatshop it had always been. The figure punishing the piano was as little aware of its fantastic plumage as a baby is of the designer label on its romper suit.

Not that his acquisitive eye failed to note the increasing use of stage theatrics in Britain by David Bowie and in America by the first male rock star to use a woman's name: Alice Cooper. Elton had attended an early Alice concert, and been overwhelmed by its *grand guignol* inventiveness. 'It was incredible, with the helicopter, the shower of panties, the fireworks. It was the best-produced show I've ever seen. I was caught up in it myself, scrambling for a pair of panties. You can't do anything like that in Britain. You'd get jobsworths backstage, saying "You can't do that here. Who's going to clean up the mess?"'

His belief in value for money onstage was almost Calvinistic in its fervour. He even lambasted his own supreme teenage idol, Jerry Lee Lewis, for giving short measure to concert audiences. 'They asked me to play on his album, but I said no. He was so disappointing when I saw him at the Palladium, and as far as I'm concerned he was the best rock-'n'-roll pianist ever. I went in my drape jacket, and got jeered at by all the Teds. He could have wiped the audience out, but he just sat there and played country and western numbers as if to say "Fuck you". And calling himself the Killer! I could kill more people with one finger than he did when I saw him.'

It is possibly the only instance of Elton being asked to appear on a record and refusing. The ex-session man remained a session man to the core. Even now, on his impossible treadmill of concerts and recording, he could always somehow find time to help out if a fellow musician was in need. He played piano on the debut album of Lesley Duncan, a backup singer and writer whose talent he had always been keen to promote. Not content with co-producing Long John Baldry's second album, *Everything Stops for Tea*, he volunteered to play piano and sing backup vocals, with Rod Stewart, when Baldry made it, once more, to *Top of the Pops*.

He agreed to be in Marc Bolan's film *Born to Boogie*, though predicting, correctly, that Bolan would monopolise most of the action. For Elton, the thrill of the occasion was meeting Ringo Starr, whom Bolan had also persuaded to play a bit part. They had something to talk about since Ringo still hung on in Surrey, living beside the river Wey in Peter Sellers's former house (where, with Liverpudlian practicality, the sixteenth-century oak doors had cat flaps cut into them).

Thereafter, Elton frequently dropped in to see Ringo at the Apple office in London. He was inside the empire of his ultimate heroes at last, even though that empire was now all but extinct, transferred from its Georgian house in Savile Row to a small administrative office in St James's. The general manager, Tony King, had originally worked for George Martin's AIR organisation out of an office at Dick James Music, and had known Elton since his days as struggling Reg. 'He told me I was to call him Elton officially now, but I just couldn't,' Tony King remembers. 'I didn't call him Reg either. I just called him nothing. For about the next two years, I'd say "Phone for you, er . . . " followed by this awful blank.'

His Aunt Win's son, Paul Robinson, was now sixteen and desperate to follow in Elton's footsteps to the music business. For his young cousin Elton did what his own elder cousin, Roy, had done for him at Mills Music, seven years earlier. He used his influence at Apple to get Paul taken on there as a messenger boy.

'I remember Elton coming in all the time, to see Ringo or Tony King,' Paul Robinson says now. 'Ringo had a furniture business then – selling things like glass-topped coffee tables mounted on Rolls-Royce grilles. I was always loading stuff like that into the car for Elton. It was when I first properly realised what a big star he'd become. He told me I oughtn't to be cheeky to him any more.'

He was, indeed, becoming famous on a national scale, rather than just in the closed, parochial world of young people's music. National papers then took little interest in pop musicians unless they figured in the expected scandals arising from drug use, insanitary hair or displays of public disrespect. But awareness was growing of this new, very different pop star: not mumbly and sneery, but clear-spoken and polite; not working-class but middle-class; not against the establishment like others of his kind, but happy, even anxious, to become a part of it.

Early in 1972, Elton and his music were the subject of an article by Michael Wale on the 'op-ed' page of *The Times*, a slot which Lennon and McCartney in their glory never attained. That same month, at the other journalistic extreme, he quite defeated the obvious scepticism of the *Sunday Mirror*'s showbusiness editor:

For star quality in the accepted sense, I wouldn't pick him out of a crowd of two. His appearance doesn't help – receding hair, desperately combed forward, stilt-heeled shoes raising him only to medium height, dark glasses that are not so much groovy, more a necessity.

Yet this is Elton John, multi-million disc seller, just back from a triumphant tour of the US. How does he do it? All I can assume is that his music is as honest as he seems to be as a person. It was Elton himself who drew my attention to his defects.

'Can't grow my hair long – it's too thin. The dark glasses I started to wear when I was thirteen, trying to copy Buddy Holly. Now my eyes are weak, with or without them. So if the fans are thinking about copying me, I advise them to forget it.'

In his private life, too, Elton is scarcely superstar material. There are no groupies either outside his fifty thousand pound house, clamouring for autographs, or inside, begging for bed.

'I live on my own, without servants,' he told me. 'I do my own housework, ironing, cooking and the rest of it. I like doing these chores. And that way, I know they've been done to my satisfaction. I can't stand tattiness and dirt.'

In America, the good impression was fortified by effective appearances on general TV chat shows, like Dick Cavett's and David Frost's, and by manifest respect and admiration for the American Way. While playing Houston on his spring 1972 tour, with 'Rocket Man' riding high, Elton asked to be allowed to visit the NASA space centre. It was no mere publicist's photo-opportunity. He and the band spent four hours at NASA, lunching with Al Worden, the *Apollo 15* pilot, even trying out a flight simulator.

The National Youth Theatre concerts, through which he met Bryan Forbes, belonged to this same period of social entrenchment. Though not previously a theatre enthusiast, Elton was persuaded by his lawyer, Michael Oliver, to attend the NYT's current production of *Good Lads at Heart*, a hard-hitting play about Borstal boys. The production turned him on to theatre in general and the underfinanced plight of youth theatre in particular. He gave three fund-raising concerts for the NYT at the Shaw Theatre, one at £1 a head, one at £5 a head, which Princess Margaret attended, then one which NYT members could attend free. He subsequently did a fourth show, and was invited to become one of the Theatre's vice presidents. After that, he kept up with all NYT productions and would even sometimes look in at rehearsals.

His plea to Bryan Forbes to help him acquire taste has the classic Elton note. Unpretentious, honest, trusting and ever so slightly forlorn. The selfsame note as 'I feel lost' and 'Can't you manage me? Please.'

He became a regular caller at the Forbes's bookshop in Virginia Water, frequently buying every book in its window display. 'He loved books,' Nanette Newman remembers. 'He wanted to have them, like we did, all through the house. But not just for show. When you talked to him, you realised how amazingly well-read he was.'

Hercules was only a short walk from the Forbes's house, Seven Pines. Elton became a frequent caller there, too, to the amazement of their two small girls, Sarah and Emma. 'I can see him standing in the hall, holding a couple of gigantic Easter eggs, which he'd brought over for the girls,' Nanette Newman says. 'One of them was a huge pink thing, like something out of Barbara Cartland, which I've still got. One couldn't get rid of it. An Easter egg like that only comes along once in any lifetime.'

He was fascinated by the Forbes's world of movies and studios, and their vast circle of friends in the film business. Bryan Forbes was, in any case, a gifted raconteur, especially on the subject of his close friend, and Elton's *Goon Show* hero, Peter Sellers. 'Once, when Peter and I were coming back from Paris, we told the press we'd discovered a pop singer named Turk Thrust. It even got into the papers that we were going to manage this nonexistent pop star, and we kept the gag going for quite a long time. Elton loved that story. He couldn't get over it.'

Nanette Newman remembers how unassuming and straightforward he was, despite his obvious pop-star eminence and the platform-wobbly weirdness of his clothes. 'He struck me as someone who was totally without conceit. Of course, he had a proper idea of his own worth. If a record was in the charts, he'd tell you, 'Hey, guess what – it's done so-and-so . . .' But underneath it all he was truly modest. And it wasn't the affectation of modesty some people put on. With Elton it was completely genuine.'

The Forbeses coached Elton in aesthetics, as far as they were able. They put him in touch with several reputable West End picture and antique dealers and also introduced him to Bryan Organ the portrait painter who had recently painted Nanette. Elton loved Organ's work, with its Pop Art record album feel, and immediately began to sit for his own portrait.

'Another thing he said he wanted to do was go to Cartier's,' Nanette Newman remembers. 'I said I'd take him, because I knew a couple of the people there – but first of all I had to go to Harrods to buy a new washing machine. So I'm there in Harrods' electrical department, trying to choose a washing machine, with this apparition next to me, in amazing clothes, murmuring "Boring, bor-ing!"

'When we finally did get to Cartier's, the first thing Elton did was to pick up an enormous ring. "God, this is really vulgar!" he said. "It's awful. It's just like some blue-rinsed old woman in Palm Beach or Miami would wear – I love it." While all these terribly smart and correct Cartier people watched, he went round the whole shop, picking things up and buying them. It was as if he was going round

Safeway's with a trolley. He spent money like Monopoly money. And everyone else had to have presents as well. He bought Bryan a Cartier watch. I certainly didn't want him to buy me anything, and didn't think he had. But when we got into the car afterwards, he said "That's for you", and there was a piece of jewellery on the seat that I hadn't even seen him buy.'

Elton and John Reid became regulars at the Forbeses' parties over at Seven Pines. Nanette Newman remembers them as an attractive couple, openly affectionate with one another. 'John was much more in the background, of course – the fixer who kept things running and made things happen. But he was tremendous company, too, and could be hysterically funny in his own right. I remember him telling us once that he'd been mixed up with Barbara Windsor, somehow or other, and was having terrible trouble with one of her ex-husbands or boy-friends.'

The Forbeses, in turn, would go over to Hercules for Sunday lunch, cooked by John Reid. 'It was always very traditional,' Nanette Newman says. 'Roast beef with roast potatoes. And the house was immaculate. Elton did the housework himself, and was incredibly houseproud. I remember one day they'd been over to us for lunch, and we were going back to the bungalow for tea. Elton rushed off in the car ahead of us. When we got there, he was frantically Hoovering the living room.'

As they got to know Elton more, they discovered the hectic range of his emotions. More than once, he reminded Bryan Forbes of the star he was most avid to hear about: Peter Sellers. 'They were similar in sometimes being able to get on a roll and be hysterically funny for an incredibly long time at a stretch. I remember once seeing Elton compose a whole impromptu operetta, with lyrics and music, about all the shopkeepers in Virginia Water, especially Mr Batty, the grocer. It went on and on, and was totally brilliant. Sellers would have done exactly the same kind of thing, without the music.

'And their temperaments were very alike, too. Either up at the peak or down in the valley.'

He was down in that valley, though soon to be up again, and scaling still higher, shinier peaks.

In June 1972, due to record a second album in France, Elton once more succumbed to the nervous exhaustion that could drop over him like a sack. He cancelled an Italian tour at the last moment, throwing himself into an even worse state at the thought of having let people down. 'It was the second time we were supposed to go there, but pulled out, cancelling the same promoter!' he recalled later. 'In Italy they were holding a competition. "Is he going to turn up or isn't he?"'

On gathering with band and technicians at Château d'Hierouville, he told his producer, Gus Dudgeon, that he couldn't face the work ahead. Dudgeon philosophically suggested postponing the album until September. Then Elton had another lightning change of mood. 'I thought, "I'm going on holiday in July, and it'd be nice to have it all over with by then. It'd be terrible to have come all the way over and not do it." So we did it, although I was very ill.'

He was in fact suffering from glandular fever, and in the very worst possible physical and mental state to begin composing a dozen new songs from scratch. To add to the pressure, Bernie Taupin had provided him with only one finished lyric. Bernie himself was in America, writing to short order and posting each set of words off as he finished them. Then he suddenly turned up at the château, materialising with a flower-child insouciance that Elton, in his overwrought state, found highly provoking. 'He'd been phoning up every night from Los Angeles, and one morning I walked out on the lawn and there he is, behind a bloody bush! In France! Nearly drove me round the bend!'

Iron willpower prevailed. And, once the stubby fingers were spread on the piano keys, ideas began crowding in with their usual facility. Going from bottom to top form in a blink, Elton wrote twelve new songs in two days, seven on one day, five on the other.

Among the lyrics Bernie had produced was a piece of pure Fifties rock-'n'-roll pastiche called, not 'See You Later, Alligator' but 'Crocodile Rock'. Another popped into his head after reading a story in an American news magazine. 'I forget now if it was *Time* or *Newsweek*. It was about this guy who'd been wounded in the Vietnam War and had gone back to his home town, just wanting to forget it all and get on with his life. But the people there wanted him to be a hero, and wouldn't leave him alone. In the end, this guy had become so disillusioned, he'd decided the only way out was to leave America altogether.'

The Vietnam veteran's story prompted one of the quickest pieces of lyric-writing by Bernie since 'Your Song'. 'I got out of bed one morning at the château and wrote this thing, called "Daniel", in about half an hour, and took it down to Elton. Elton got up from the breakfast table, went over to the piano and finished it in about fifteen or twenty minutes, then said to the band "Hey, guys. Let's cut this." We'd done the track by the end of the day.'

The whole of July had been set aside for Elton's first real holiday since becoming a full-time musician. John Reid, Bernie, Maxine and he were to share a rented house in Malibu with Bryan Forbes and

Nanette Newman and their little girls, Sarah and Emma.

When Elton arrived at Los Angeles airport from France, he was in anything but a holiday mood. 'As soon as I got off the plane, people said to me "Hey – you're having a nervous breakdown." I was on the verge of a crack-up. Personality-wise, I was unbearable – moody and shouting at people. I'd had bouts of exhaustion before, but had never been in a nervous state like this.'

By the time the Forbeses flew in from London, everything was different again. The glandular fever had subsided, the black moods and screaming Little Moments melted into the Malibu ozone. Elton was back on a roll.

To welcome Bryan Forbes he staged an elaborate joke, partly based on Forbes's old running pop-star gag with Peter Sellers, and partly on his own first inglorious arrival in Los Angeles. 'Elton met us at the airport,' Forbes remembers. 'While we were walking out through the concourse, I knew there was something going on. Outside he'd got a Greyhound bus with LA WELCOMES TURK THRUST written on the side. And a troupe of drum majorettes all twirling and chanting "Hip-hooray – Turk Thrust is in LA."'

The rented house was a rambling affair with a central courtyard, standing right on the beach. With other visitors, like Elton's friend Tony King, there could be as many as twelve people in residence. 'The whole month was like one of those holidays you remember from childhood,' Bryan Forbes says. 'I don't think any of us ever stopped laughing.'

What made the holiday for Elton were the Forbeses' numerous friends in the Hollywood film colony. Every movie star he had ever ogled in *Photoplay* magazines in the foyers of Middlesex Odeons seemed to be on first-name terms with Bryan and Nanette and available for visits or to visit. For most of that month, the pug face bore a look of blank bedazzlement.

One of the first Hollywood legends he met was Mae West. 'We were all taken into this room that was totally white,' Bernie Taupin remembers. 'We sat down on this big white couch, on this white shag-pile carpet. At the end of the room there was a sort of butler figure, standing in front of a curtain. "Gentlemen," the butler said, "Miss Mae West." The curtain was drawn back, and there she was. She looked at Elton and me on the couch and said, "Well! Wall-to-wall men."

'She came to my birthday party, too; she sat there all evening at the end of the room, not moving or saying anything. It was just like having a stuffed dummy of Mae West at your party.'

Another night, the Forbeses took them to a friend's house where a

Groucho Marx movie was being privately screened. When they got there, they found Groucho himself among the audience. On being introduced, he complained that Elton's name was the wrong way round, and thereafter always called him 'John Elton'.

'On the way back, we decided to stop and have a meal in a diner,' Nanette Newman remembers. 'It was one of those places where everything on the menu was "home-style this" and "corn-fed that". When our orders arrived, somehow we'd managed to get more chips than a whole army could eat in a year. Elton took his glasses off – a sure sign with him that something was about to happen. He picked up a handful of these chips and put them in a napkin. "I don't have to eat in places like this!" he said, "I could have been a famous brain-surgeon" – and he jammed all the chips down on top of his own head. There was nearly a riot in this place. Bryan got the bill, gave them a huge tip and got us all out before someone called the police.'

A few nights later, an elaborate outing was arranged. Groucho Marx would come to the house for dinner, then the whole party would go on to a performance of the Andrew Lloyd-Webber musical *Jesus Christ Superstar*.

Erroneously warned in advance that his guest was a frail and delicate old man, Elton took the precaution of lighting a roaring fire. Groucho arrived in a long overcoat and beret, both of which he declined to remove. He gave Elton such a general ribbing about his name being back to front that Elton at one point held up both hands in mock surrender and said, 'Don't shoot me, I'm just the piano player', so naming the new album he had just made.

Also among the company were Clive Banks from DJM in London, and Strawberry studio's manageress, Catherine Philippe-Gérard. As often happened with Elton, his former obsessive enthusiasm for Catherine had given way to boredom and covert mockery. 'She had rather large breasts,' Nanette Newman remembers. 'While she was out of the room, Elton used to imitate her with two grapefruit under his shirt.'

Unluckily, on the night Groucho Marx came to dinner, Catherine had announced she would prepare a typically French meal. 'But everything in the kitchen started to go wrong,' Clive Banks remembers. 'We're all sitting round the table with Groucho Marx, waiting to eat, and there's this sound of terrible panic going on offstage.'

The subsequent outing with Groucho to see *Jesus Christ Superstar* proved equally memorable, as Bryan Forbes describes it. 'In between leaving the car and getting to our seats, Groucho managed to pick up two teenage girls. So I'm sitting there with Elton in his rock-star gear on one side and Groucho Marx in his beret on the other, about to see *Jesus Christ Superstar*. As the performance began, Groucho's voice suddenly rang out: "Does this have a happy ending?" In the Crucifixion scene, it rang out again: "This is sure to offend the Jews."'

Forbes's birthday happened to fall during the month, prompting Elton's most ambitious stunt of all. 'He asked me what sign that meant I was born under, and I said "Leo". On my birthday, when I woke up and looked out of the window, there was a full-grown lion down in the courtyard. Elton had somehow got in touch with a zoo and arranged for one to be delivered, along with a trainer, who was standing there, pointing a gun at its head.'

Groucho Marx returned to the house several times, evidently fond of his new acquaintance, 'John Elton'. 'He'd sometimes sing to us,' Bernie Taupin remembers. 'He used to call up Marvin Hamlisch, who was hardly known then, to come over and accompany him on the piano.' Another visitor was Don Bachardy, Christopher Isherwood's artist lover, who made sketches of Elton, Bernie and Sarah and Emma Forbes.

They also met David Cassidy, the boy actor from the *Partridge Family* TV show, then enjoying his brief reign as teenybop's number one heart-throb. It was evidently a far from pleasant predicament, and it brought out all Elton's best qualities of elder-brother sympathy and rationality. 'Poor guy – we took him to the Troubadour to see a group, and it was the first time he'd been out for two and a half years. He gets up every morning at six, goes to the TV studio, makes an LP, gives a concert. He's like a robot. He asked Bernie and me to write a song for his next album, and I wouldn't mind that at all. People like him get written off. Beause it's the Osmonds, for example, everyone says "Ooh, terrible!" But records like "Crazy Horses" are really good.'

The constant, recuperative pleasure Elton remembered from that month's house party was shopping, acquiring and collecting:

'We used to get up in the morning and say "Right, here we go, looting." Bryan would go with Bernie to a bookshop, and I'd go to a tablecloth shop. We're such great looters, Bernie, Maxine and I. There were sixty-seven cases, and there must have been thirty-two trunks – you know, those Newberry's trunks with the American flag on them. They needed a Greyhound bus to take us to the airport.'

So far in 1972, Elton had done only one short American tour, at the time of 'Rocket Man', playing small college-type dates in far-flung places like Oxford, Ohio, and East Lansing, Missouri. To redress the intercontinental balance, a tour on the old gargantuan scale was scheduled for November and December, returning to big-city venues like Carnegie Hall, New York, and also opening up such new territories as Baton Rouge, Louisiana, College Station, Texas, and – perhaps the ultimate Elton conquest – Normal, Illinois.

Learning the lesson of 1971, his new album, *Don't Shoot Me, I'm Only the Piano Player*, was held back from release until *Honky Château* had run its course in the shops. His only new release in late 1972 would be a single from the new album, to create advance interest and also follow up the global success of 'Rocket Man'. Whatever might later be said about John Reid's influence, Elton's career can be seen here assuming a logical pace and strategic intelligence it had hitherto totally lacked.

The choice of a first single from *Don't Shoot Me* provoked what had by now become an almost traditional wrangle between Elton and his record company. Dick and Stephen James were for 'Crocodile Rock', the Fifties pastiche whose carefree sound was so very far from what its performer had been feeling at the time. Elton wanted to put out Bernie's song about the Vietnam veteran, 'Daniel', but the Jameses insisted it would stand no chance as a single. They said it was too slow, too slight, too quiet. It simply wouldn't be understood.

On this occasion, Elton gave in. 'Crocodile Rock', at least, was totally unlike 'Rocket Man', and the first real proof to his album audience (if they hadn't heard 'Rock and Roll Madonna') that he could play fast and furious as well as mournful and slow. With self-immunising pessimism, he wrote off its chances in advance, not least because on its release date, 27 October, he would still be in Britain. He had developed a superstition that no record could be successful if released in a country where he happened to be at the time.

The Jameses' instinct seemed more than vindicated. 'Crocodile Rock' went to number one in America and five in Britain. Bernie Taupin's lyric perfectly caught the breaking wave of teenage nostalgia. The song was like a tour bus crowded with the shades of all Elton and Bernie's favourite jukebox heroes, Bill Haley, Eddie Cochran, Neil Sedaka, Bobby Vee, the Beach Boys. The chorus was a joke falsetto, which the writers of Pat Boone's 'Speedy Gonzales' afterwards claimed had been plagiarised from them. Likewise, Don McLean spotted strong affinities, to put it no more strongly, with his prototype nostalgia hit, 'American Pie'. Elton himself admitted he had plundered ideas for 'Crocodile Rock' with the same enthusiasm that he threw albums into shopping trolleys at Tower Records. 'I wanted it to be a record about all the things I grew up with. Of course it's a rip-off. It's derivative in every sense of the word.'

The three-month American tour of late 1972 included another

major British group, Family. It also included Legs Larry Smith of the Bonzo Dog Band, who had provided tap-dancing effects on *Honky Château*, and in whom Elton discovered a kindred soul.

With the spindly shanks that gave Legs Larry his name went Apache-style hair, a long hatchet face, a military moustache, genteel speech and almost unlimited stores of camp whimsicality. On the American tour, when Elton sang 'I Think I'm Going to Kill Myself', Legs Larry came on and tap-danced in American football player's costume of knickerbockers, shoulderpads and silver helmet, topped by a miniature bride-and-groom ornament from a wedding cake. Later he and Elton donned trench coats and fedoras, put up umbrellas and did 'Singin' in the Rain' while dancing-girls high-kicked behind them and glitter was showered over them by a midget, borrowed from a TV frankfurter commercial. The finale consisted of Elton, Legs Larry and Bernie Taupin, playing toy guitars and flinging handfuls of confetti and sweets into the audience.

Elton and Legs Larry also went out 'looting', though this time the object was further idiotic bric-à-brac to incorporate into their stage routine. In a Montreal Woolworth's, they found a picture of Doris Day which had been on display so long, it was covered in dust. Elton bought it to put on his piano that night. It stayed there as a mascot for the rest of the tour.

Despite ecstatic audiences everywhere, the tour went anything but smoothly. Before one gig, Family's stage equipment got lost, and the girl-friend of one of them, the singer Linda Lewis, had to go on in their place. There were also some nasty moments on aeroplanes. 'Larry and I used to hold hands on every flight,' Elton later recalled. 'He used to wind me up by saying "The engine's on fire." One day I looked out, and the engine *was* on fire!'

To add to the strain, half-way through the thirty-odd date itinerary Elton had to return to England. He had been chosen to appear in the annual Royal Command Variety Performance in the presence of the Queen and the Duke of Edinburgh. The invitation had been issued before the tour, but was only finally confirmed as Elton, Legs Larry and the others were working their way through the American Midwest. Though it would mean cancelling his Phoenix concert, flying back to London overnight, rehearsing and performing virtually without sleep and flying straight out again to pick up the tour in Tulsa, Oklahoma, Elton did not hesitate. As he explained later, 'I've always done everything the Queen asked me.'

He arrived back at Heathrow airport early on a Sunday morning, to be greeted by hundreds of agitated teenage girls. It transpired they were not waiting for him but for the Jackson Five, who were also in the Royal Command Performance and whose flight arrived a few minutes after his. True to the endless replay of the Beatles' story, radio broadcasts had been saying that 200 free T-shirts would be given away: 'a stupid thing,' Elton commented angrily. 'They should give all the kids T-shirts or none at all. It's such a hype.'

He had been almost forty-eight hours without sleep, and was already far from his bonniest. His mood grew still more frayed during the naturally extensive and anxious rehearsals for the show which was to be held at the London Palladium and go out on television to some 25 million viewers. Elton had been asked to do two numbers. The organisers suggested 'Rocket Man' followed by 'Your Song' as most suitable for royal ears. But Elton insisted on doing 'Crocodile Rock', followed by 'I Think I'm Going to Kill Myself', complete with the Legs Larry camp tap-dance routine. Amazingly enough, this was agreed.

Nor did an impromptu press conference he gave during rehearsals strike a totally loyal note. He announced that breaking off his American tour to obey the royal command had cost him £25,000 – 'or it might be £15,000. It's a lot of money, anyway.' Why had he done so? 'Because 25 million people will be able to listen to my latest record, and this is the only chance I've got to plug it.'

The bill was the usual weird mishmash that Her Majesty customarily suffers in the name of charity. Among the other performers were Liberace, the Jackson Five, the crooner Jack Jones and the musical comedy star Carol Channing. There were almost two full days of pernickety TV setups and sound checks over the London Palladium's notoriously poor microphone system. Elton afterwards described it as 'the most horrendous two-day stretch I've ever had'.

The dressing rooms were as crowded as Bombay tenements. Elton shared one with Jack Jones and Liberace, whose jewel-encrusted costumes made a glitter rocker's simple shiny suit seem as modest as the garb of a minister of the kirk. 'He was great,' Elton remembered afterwards. 'He just kept wheeling trunks of clothes in. I just sat there, watching him. He kept calm through the whole thing. All these people were badgering him all the time for autographs and he always did the most ornate autographs, and drew a grand piano around them. He was really nice. He was the most professional person on that show.'

Those who remembered the Beatles' cheekily deferential Royal Command Performance in 1963 were to receive a vivid demonstration of how both times and pop music had changed. Since the Queen herself makes no comment about the show, it will never be known what she made of the shiny-suited figure, in heels several inches higher than hers, pounding a grand piano covered with a pink satin quilt on the hem of which little coloured Christmas lights winked on and off. Nor whether she grasped the import of the second song in which a tall, moustachioed man in a crash helmet tap-danced to and fro, letting off balloons whose farting noises, fortunately, were inaudible to 25 million viewers at home.

Press reviews of the Royal Command Performance are seldom kind. One highbrow Sunday critic said that Liberace had made Elton John 'look like the musical dwarf he is'. No one could have agreed more fervently than the 'musical dwarf' himself. 'Well, I think he did. I think he was the only decent thing on that show. I don't mind. I don't find that offensive at all.'

Elton could afford to disregard such little jibes. His American concerts were sell-out sensations, coast to coast. His records evaporated from stores: not only those currently in the charts but everything he had produced since his first overhyped advent in August 1970. Previous dissatisfactions and disappointments were swept away as questionable gold discs changed into unchallengeable brilliant white ones. By the end of 1972 *Honky Château*, *Madman Across the Water*, *Tumbleweed Connection* and the original *Elton John* album all had gone platinum in the US for sales of more than a million copies each. He was no longer a British rock star famous in America. He was America's most famous rock star.

There could have been many ways of marking this moment. Elton celebrated it by going back to Metroland, Pinner and school.

On 7 December he returned to Pinner County Grammar, whose streamlined façade he had not seen since 1965, when he left ingloriously to become an office boy at Mills Music. The school's sixth form Stag Society had asked him to play at one of their social gatherings. Elton agreed and, with his usual punctiliousness, kept to the appointed date, even phoning the school while on tour in America to reassure them that the visit was still on.

It is always agreeable to return to one's old school as a wealthy celebrity, especially if one has conspicuously failed to shine there as a pupil. Elton made the most of it, arriving by Ferrari in a purple satin suit and red-tinted spectacles with white frames.

Though Jack Westgate Smith was no longer headmaster, many of the staff remained from Reggie Dwight's time. Among them was Bill Johnson, the history master, who'd said that at forty Reggie would be either an assistant in a record shop or a millionaire. Mr Stoupe, the music master who had so often reproached Reggie for wasting his talents, was also still there. A photograph was taken of visiting rock star warmly shaking his hand as a guide, mentor and friend.

Elton gave a ninety-minute performance, playing 'Rocket Man' and 'Crocodile Rock' on the same Steinway grand he had once used to practise Bach and Brahms and illicit Jerry Lee Lewis licks. Only Stag Society members and teachers were allowed into the hall, even the new head's own children being excluded. 'Security' was provided by the school caretaker and heftier members of the rugby XV, while a low-key police presence kept watch outside. In between numbers, Elton confessed that he was more nervous playing before his old teachers than he would be performing for 15,000 people in America.

Afterwards he looked round the school, stopping to examine a group photograph from which Reggie Dwight looked out resignedly in buttoned-up blazer and Buddy Holly specs. He then kept up with the Stag Society's after-meeting tradition of adjourning to the local pub. 'There was only room for one other person in his Ferrari,' Bill Johnson recalls. 'So naturally he went off in it with the prettiest girl sixth-former in the school. We thought that was completely natural pop star behaviour.'

A few days later – wholly unannounced this time – Elton returned to Pinner County Grammar again. With him he had a colour TV set for the Stag Society's common room. 'He arrived right in the middle of the Second Year Christmas party,' Bill Johnson remembers. 'Of course, the whole lot of them surrounded Elton, going wild. I and some of the other staff had to form a human chain to protect him.'

The headmaster's summary of that term's events mentioned the visit in due context and characteristic style:

Mr and Mrs Pelzer and Miss Young took a party of 19 senior pupils on a skiing holiday to Macugnaga Staffa, Northern Italy, during the half-term break . . .

The Parks Department has recently removed the rubble from the old air-raid shelter and have finished off the area with a layer of top soil . . .

I have already reported to the appropriate committee through the Director of Education the theft on the night of November 3rd/4th of three transistor radios, a typewriter and 30 pence from the dinner float . . .

Meetings of Stag have included talks on 'Forensic Science in Detection', 'The Soviet Union', 'Local History', 'On Being An Air Pilot' and a never-to-be-forgotten visit of ex-pupil Elton John who delighted the younger membership with his songs and pleased the older members with the very real charm and common sense which lies behind the gimmickry of his profession.

It had taken ten years, and untold thousands of miles, but R. K. Dwight of Downfield House was going home with a good report at last.

9

Rocket Men

JOHN Reid had made the most of his time on the inside at Dick James Music. Like a good St Mirin's boy, swotting for his GCE, he had pored over the contracts and schedules that applied to Elton: the recording agreements with This Record Co. and MCA in America; the publishing agreement between Elton, Bernie Taupin and Dick James Music; and the cat's cradle of sub-publishing deals with DJM's overseas subsidiaries and licensees by which royalties on their songs were collected worldwide.

He also obtained detailed statements from Elton's accountants of sums so far received as Elton's share of record sales and in publishing royalties. The High Court, thirteen years later, would hear of his immediate 'concern' at the 'low' publishing royalties being received, especially from American 'mechanicals' (ie radio play). To one of the accountants, Mr Lawrence, he queried whether the James organisation's wholly owned American subsidiary, DJM USA, was making deductions of perhaps as much as 40 per cent before accounting to DJM UK.

His behaviour angered Stephen James, who felt that Reid owed loyalty to DJM for as long as it employed him. An awkward moment – also mentioned in the High Court thirteen years later – occurred when Reid was discovered photocopying Elton's recording and publishing agreements with the apparent intention of taking them out of the office for lengthy examination.

In mid-August 1972, John Reid handed in his notice at DJM. On 20 September, eleven days after his twenty-third birthday, his own company John Reid Enterprises was incorporated. The starting capital was £5,000, which Reid borrowed from Barclays Bank's Brook Street branch, using his management contract with Elton as collateral. There were two directors, Reid and his father, John Reid senior.

Long before Reid had any thought of acting for Elton, he knew what business matter was uppermost in Elton's mind. It was the publishing agreement which Bernie and he had signed as minors in 1967, making over the copyright in their work to Dick James Music. A syndrome with which Dick James was already familiar – what might be called the John and Paul Syndrome – was getting into gear again. To two unknown youths in 1967, it had seemed wonderful that a famous music-publisher should wish to put his name on their songs. In 1972, with those songs turning gold and platinum all over the world, the composers saw no reason why anyone but themselves should own them.

It was fortuitous that, in July 1972, a High Court action, Instone versus A. Schroeder Music Publishing Co. Ltd, had caused reverberations throughout the British music industry. The judge, Mr Justice Plowman, set aside a ten-year exclusive agreement between a songwriter and a music publisher, ruling that its terms were 'so unfair as to be oppressive and contrary to public policy'. He said the contract had implied that the publisher would not 'unfairly, unjustifiably or artificially diminish' the income of the songwriter, but that foreign sub-publishing arrangements breached that undertaking, so in effect negating the entire agreement.

On leaving DJM, one of John Reid's first business meetings was with Elton's solicitor, Michael Oliver of Berger Oliver, and the barrister who had successfully represented the plaintiffs in the Schroeder case. Shown Elton's publishing agreement with DJM, the barrister said it seemed 'entirely unobjectionable', but added that a publisher had a duty not to deplete royalties unfairly. He recommended that an audit be made at both DJM USA and DJM UK, that all sub-publishing agreements and relevant documents be examined, and that for the time being Elton should sign no further new material over to DJM. Among notes taken of the conference by Berger Oliver was one that 'Dick James must somehow justify the situation whereby his companies take 70 per cent of the sale proceeds in the United States, leaving Elton and Bernie with only 15 per cent each. This may be the basis for a settlement rather than litigation.'

On 20 October, John Reid met Dick James as his entrepreneurial equal. He complained that Elton's publishing agreements were unfair, particularly with regard to the USA, and that the DJM group was withholding more than its proper share of royalties. Even the emotionless legal document that records this encounter gives off a whiff of Dick James's chagrin at seeing the John and Paul Syndrome breaking out again.

In his own estimation, he had treated Elton magnificently, and his own estimation was very largely true. He had spent three years and an enormous sum in launching Elton, allowed him unlimited indulgence to make the music he wanted, acted not merely as his publisher but also his manager, even his father confessor, and steered him right on occasions when Elton's own instinct had been to steer himself wrong. For Elton, indeed – such was James's belief in him – standard procedures had been waived all along the line. One can only imagine the tension of that moment when fifty-two-year-old music mogul stared at twenty-three-year-old Scotsman, little suspecting how terminal bad luck would set in from here.

Dick James responded with the injured dignity one would expect. He denied that royalties were being unfairly withheld from Elton, and said that 'no fresh ground' existed for renegotiating the publishing agreement. As to the audit recommended by counsel, his company's books were open for inspection at any time.

The history of the Beatles continued to be an insistent subtext to Elton's career. Late in 1972, John Reid consulted John Eastman, the New York attorney, brother of Paul McCartney's wife Linda. Eastman had been McCartney's nominee to sort out the Beatles' finances: his rejection by the others in favour of Allen Klein can be said, as much as anything, to have brought on their final dissolution.

Having looked over Elton's contracts with DJM, John Eastman said that the only one which, perhaps, might be challenged was the publishing agreement. It was felt expedient however, not to press Dick James further, for the present. His co-operation was needed in negotiations with the US Internal Revenue Service, who were withholding a portion of Elton's earnings pending a decision on his tax status in America. Subsequently, John Eastman wrote to John Reid that in his view there was 'a strong case' for claiming DJM had failed to account to Elton satisfactorily, and that the practice of using wholly owned foreign subsidiaries like DJM USA to reduce royalties payable to him was 'not a proper one'.

On 10 May, 1973, DJM's management agreements with Elton, via the two income-receiving companies William A. Bong and Sackville, officially expired. Two months later, new contracts were signed between Bong and Sackville, on Elton's behalf, and John Reid Enterprises.

It was, as few doubted, the beginning of the end between Elton and the Dick James Organisation. The publishing agreement expired the following November and, clearly, was unlikely to be renewed. There remained only the five-year recording agreement with This Record Co., signed in 1970, which meant that Elton John product would continue to be released by DJM until 1975.

But the spirit of Elton – a benign shade in shabby herringbone, haunting the tea kettle and record cupboard – was gone from Dick

James Music. In its place was a small but exceedingly active Scots poltergeist that seemed to delight in its power to turn everything upside down, alter the temperature of rooms and make short hairs rise on the backs of necks.

The Beatles were not the first musicians to try owning their own record company. The practice was established in America in the early Sixties by such artist-owned labels as Frank Sinatra's Reprise and James Brown's JB. It was a well-known desire of those who made it big in music to break away from the companies that had originally nurtured them, and gain total artistic control of their own output. There was a time in almost every major performer's life when he wanted to be an entrepreneur, using his wealth and influence to give new talent the encouragement and financial backing he himself might have lacked. Generally linked to that was an ambition to try producing records rather than merely performing, and a desire to show the industry how a totally different kind of business organisation could be created by someone whose heart was in the right place.

The Beatles' Apple Corps had taken such altruism to its ultimate. John Lennon and Paul McCartney had hoped to institute 'a kind of Western communism' under which Beatle money would subsidise not only new recording talent but also new writers, poets, painters, sculptors, inventors and anyone else who turned up at 3 Savile Row with hand outstretched in the regulation manner. The result had been a freeloaders' free-for-all in which the Beatles had seen £2 million of their money wasted, their offices deluged by unusable material, their food and liquor gorged, their fitments, furniture and secretaries' handbags stolen, and, when all else was consumed, the very lead stripped from their eighteenth-century roof.

Though no one ever again went as far as Apple, artist entrepreneurism still flourished throughout pop music. In America, the Grateful Dead now recorded for their own Grateful Dead company, and Jefferson Starship (formerly Airplane) for their own label, the charmingly named Grunt. The Rolling Stones had their Rolling Stones label, Deep Purple their Purple label, the Moody Blues their Threshold label. Two ex-Beatles even nerved themselves to post-Apple business forays, Ringo Starr with Ring O' Records and George Harrison with his Dark Horse label. The fashion waxed equally strong among impresarios: Andrew Loog Oldham with his Immediate label, Kit Lambert and Chris Stamp with their Track label, Jonathan King with his UK label, Gordon Mills with his MAM label and Mickie Most with his Rak label.

Britain's record industry was altogether in a state of bountiful confidence and expansiveness. The huge fortunes trapped in each major company could be sensed by the most casual visitor. In cork-lined outer foyers, gold discs grew in double and triple rows, and overstuffed black leather sofas creaked under the leather coats of those sprawling on them. In twilit inner suites, music burbled softly from giant speakers, underlining an atmosphere of limitless prerogative and perpetual play. New artists were casually acquired, and launched with uniform extravagance. Every night of the week, there was a party to hype someone or other, at Ronnie Scott's Club, Maunkberry's or Les Ambassadeurs. Journalists and disc jockeys were wooed with every kind of favour and gift: free records, cases of Scotch, first-class air tickets, girl companions or, if need be, boy companions.

A new term had been invented, 'ligger', for those many whose whole lives were sustained by the record industry's undiscriminating largesse. Whatever PR launch was going on, liggers by the hundred would always be there, grabbing up peanuts and promo-packs, destroying the rice salads, scraping strawberries from the tops of cream gâteaux, filling the free flights, coaches and hotel rooms, stealing the shampoos, tooth glasses and bathrobes, drinking the minibars dry. A classic liggerfest was the party given by Jonathan King to mark his tenth year as a performer, record producer and all-purpose hypester. From Westminster Pier a riverboat set off up the Thames, packed with champagne-drinking liggers. Near Richmond they transferred to a second riverboat with an open-air barbecue. As the barbecue was ligged, a third riverboat steamed up, letting off fireworks.

All the time Elton had been rising as a performer, he had felt a reciprocal tug towards entrepreneurial roles for which he was equally well fitted. Long John Baldry's two albums had proved him a born producer, imaginative and meticulous. His catholic taste and openness to acts newer and younger than himself made him a habitual talent-spotter. He was filled with idealistic desire to give others the helping hand he himself had so sorely needed: both new performers and established but under-appreciated ones like Lesley Duncan and David Ackles. At moments of greatest hubris, it occurred to him that even idols whom he had worshipped as a teenager, and who were now fallen from fashion, might not disdain a boost from somebody like him. The A & R man manqué was curious to see what he might accomplish on behalf of someone else. The fan was ready, and anxious, to pay his dues.

Recording giant that he had become, he was still bound to a tiny label whose logo was an unexciting wiggly DJM monogram, and whose power over his artistic output was total. From earliest days, he had chafed intermittently against Dick and Stephen James's decisions about what he should release. Now, for the first time, chafing became open war.

As a single to follow 'Crocodile Rock', Elton wanted to release 'Daniel'. But Dick and Stephen James both said no. They thought it unwise to put out another track from the new album, due to be released in only another couple of weeks. Much as they both admired 'Daniel' (James *père* called it 'beautiful and fantastic') they could not see how a song about a blind war veteran could possibly succeed in the teenage glitter market where 'Crocodile Rock' had sold almost half a million.

The ensuing row was loud enough to spill over into the music press. ELTON SLAMS RECORD COMPANY announced *Melody Maker*. DISPUTE OVER DANIEL said *New Musical Express*. When Elton reached an impasse with Dick James, he began his own crusade in the music press, playing 'Daniel' to friendly interviewers like Roy Hollingworth and railing against 'the business' that was trying to stifle it. Dick James also went on record, saying that Elton's US record company, MCA, and even his 'personal co-ordinator' Steve Brown, agreed that releasing it was 'not a good marketing decision'.

Under intense pressure from Elton, and against MCA's wishes, Dick James agreed to release 'Daniel'. But he refused to pay anything to promote or advertise it. Elton retorted that if necessary he'd take out full-page ads in the trade press himself. James then said, with what was meant to be a restoration of joviality, that if it made the Top 10, he would pay for the advertising. 'Christ, isn't that nice!' Elton commented with scathing irony.

'Daniel' (coupled with that oldest of oldies, 'Skyline Pigeon') was released on 12 January, 1973. Its first major British TV exposure came a few days later, when Elton appeared on Michael Parkinson's BBC1 talk show. The now familiar bespectacled figure, clad in one-piece silver like the table ornament of some regimental mess, clumped down the entrance stairway on stilt-like heels, amid applause that was genuinely welcoming. Having talked to Parkinson in his usual fluent, modest fashion, he stilt-walked across to a tripod-mounted electric piano. From the first gently popping notes (very much like Stevie Wonder's intro to 'You Are The Sunshine of My Life'), it was obvious he had a gigantic hit.

Bernie Taupin had intended a straightforward narrative song, as clear and hetero as 'Devil Woman' or 'El Paso'. Daniel, the war veteran, was fleeing America, seen off by his brother at the airport. Unfortunately, most of the details came in a pay-off last verse which

Elton, as was sometimes his wont, had arbitrarily cut out at the composition stage. What remained was just the valediction to Daniel by his brother, watching 'the red tail-lights, heading for Spain'.

Sung by the silver-plated figure, with its owlish face and preposterous heels, 'Daniel' turned into something else. It became a love song of man to man, as platonic and unselfconscious as Elton and Bernie's own love had been. The foil-flashy astronaut sang in phrases as down-to-earth as a chat between stops on the Metropolitan Line.

Elton's every instinct about the song was triumphantly vindicated. It went to number two in America and four in Britain. Nor did it have any noticeable adverse effect on the album, released a fortnight later, on 26 January. *Don't Shoot Me, I'm Only the Piano Player* was hailed as an unqualified triumph, not only for 'Crocodile Rock' and 'Daniel' but also for darker, more complex tracks like 'High-Flying Bird,' 'Have Mercy on the Criminal', and 'I'm Going to Be a Teenage Idol', a satire inspired by Marc Bolan. The album sold as much on its cover, a perfect piece of glitter-rock pastiche showing Elton's name outside a 1950s movie-house with a James Dean boy and ponytailed girl buying tickets at the paybox. Image, jokey title and two proven hit tracks made reviews irrelevant. *Don't Shoot Me* became the first Elton album to go to number one in both America and Britain.

Annoyed as he was about 'Daniel', Elton still recognised that DJM under Stephen James was 'a damned good little record company', which handled him in a more personal and indulgent way than any large company could hope to do. He could record where he liked, hire what musicians he liked, have what album artwork and internal fripperies he liked. Though Dick James had dug his heels in over paying to advertise 'Daniel', he was not usually stingy in that regard. Elton's albums back to *Tumbleweed Connection* had been advertised on British television, not a usual thing for pop records then, and a further £7,500 was currently being spent on TV spots for *Don't Shoot Me*.

The same could not be said of his American record company, the giant multimedia conglomerate MCA. For all his albums until now, Elton had been on MCA's Uni label, a small and relatively personal operation under its ebullient chief, Russ Regan. With *Don't Shoot Me* he was transferred to the main MCA label, a move designed to compliment the music division's biggest profit-earner. Instead, Elton found himself marketed with heavy-handed incomprehension in trade ads and promotions that frequently made him cringe with embarrassment. On the week that *Don't Shoot Me* reached number one in America, MCA ran an ad billing it as the 'Latest Adventures of Elton and Bernie in France'. To add insult to injury, it was not even displayed on its own, but lumped into a composite page with such desperately unhip names as Dobie Gray and the country-and-western queen Loretta Lynn.

Chafing as he was against both his English and American record companies, Elton had every selfish reason for starting a label of his own. Paradoxically, what propelled him to the final decision was a desire to help someone else. Davey Johnstone, his guitarist, wanted to make a solo album, but had been unable to find a company in London willing to back it. Elton, Davey, John Reid and Steve Brown were at Château d'Hierouville late one night, drinking the château's home-produced wine and debating how the problem might be solved. Elton said they should start their own label and bring Davey Johnstone's album out on that. 'We all said "Yeah" and went to bed,' he recalled later. 'Next morning, we all got up and said "Was everybody serious?" We decided that we were.'

Firm intent established, the arrangements quickly fell into place. The new record company would be called Rocket, in honour of 'Rocket Man'. It would be controlled by Elton, John Reid, Bernie Taupin, Steve Brown and Gus Dudgeon. John Reid would oversee it in parallel to his management of Elton through John Reid Enterprises.

The objectives, as outlined by Elton, were familiarly straight-forward, sensible and sound. 'We want to start a company that's for the artist, both creatively and money-wise. I got tired of people who aren't in it for the music – just for the money from album sales. There must be room for a company where people don't feel they're being ripped off – or forgotten because five hundred other new albums are also coming out that week. We want to be a friendly record company. We'll pay a good advance and a decent royalty, and when we sign anybody, we'll work our bollocks off for them. It'll be like a family.'

Rocket would be different, too, from creations like Threshold and Purple which existed mainly for the benefit of their performer-proprietors. Elton took pains to emphasise that he himself would not record on the new label, being contracted to DJM until 1975. 'Me not being on it is what's good about it,' he said. 'It would dampen everyone else. It'd be like "Elton John is on Rocket – and so is Davey Johnstone."' His role would be purely entrepreneurial, fostering new talent and producing it, as also would Bernie Taupin.

The spirit of the whole enterprise was summed up in the logo soon designed for it. A toytown goods train puffed over an arc of track, its cheeky-faced engine winking one eye, as if to say 'Right on!'. It was, in fact, a virtual duplicate of Thomas the Tank Engine in the children's stories by the Reverend Wilbert Awdry. Amazingly, for all the millions of books it had sold, the design had never been copyrighted. From here on, Thomas the Tank Engine technically infringed the legal rights of Rocket Records.

Behind the nursery-wall whimsy, hard-headed economics went to work. To the lesson of Apple Corps were added John Reid's native prudence and thrift. One thing Rocket Records would not be, above all, was a faucet that could drain away Elton's own fortune. Of the original launch capital, most was provided by American MCA. With Elton's current contract running out in less than two years, MCA's president, Mike Maitland, suddenly awoke to the need to show vision and imagination. In return, Elton agreed to distribute Rocket product through MCA in America, as it would be distributed by his old friends Island Records in Britain. 'MCA aren't so bad,' he had conceded. 'They just need a good kick up the arse every now and then.'

A six-room suite of offices was leased at 101 Wardour Street in the heart of Soho's film district, just a stone's throw from the Marquee Club, where Elton used to play, and the old Bag O'Nails, where Long John Baldry had saved him from premature matrimony. Annie Reavey, his clothes designer, was called in to the room that would be Steve Brown's office, to paint a mural of trains, fields, trees and cows around the wall.

The new label already boasted two signings. One was Davey Johnstone who could now go ahead and make the solo album he wanted. The other was a teenage band named Longdancer, whose personnel included Nigel Olsson's younger brother Kai and a Scots guitarist named Dave Stewart.

On 3 February, 1973, a full page in *Melody Maker* announced the official formation of the Rocket Record Company, with its jolly, winking train puffing over the track and its directorial roster of John, Taupin, Reid, Dudgeon and Brown. Below was a pledge from Elton to the new label's prospective signings that editorial decency could not render without some dilution. 'What we are offering is undivided love and devotion, a f***ing good royalty for the artist and a company that works its b****cks off.'

The new company's personnel were lifted more or less complete from the team which had run Elton at Dick James Music: Steve Brown, the A & R man; Gus Dudgeon, the producer; Clive Franks, the sound engineer; and crucial technical people like the head of the art department. John Reid was even able to woo away Maureen, the personal secretary who had worked for Stephen James for the past seven years. Relations between Stephen and Reid thereafter did not improve.

*

It was on Elton's first British tour of 1973 that the unlikeliest of all phenomena revealed itself. *Melody Maker*'s front page for 31 March was filled by a huge photograph taken from rear-stage during his concert at the London Sundown theatre. In the foreground, Elton crouched at his keyboard, pummelling with stout, bare washer-woman's arms. Beyond him was what seemed a sheer wall of juvenile faces, clapping hands and open mouths. The accompanying banner headline could scarcely disguise its writer's incredulity: NOW ELTON'S A TEENAGE IDOL!

'Crocodile Rock' had taken him straight to the top of the same teenybopper market as T-Rex, the Osmonds, the Jackson Five and David Cassidy. That he himself bore not the slightest resemblance to these school-age objects of desire was irrelevant. The *raison d'être* of teenyboppers was to scream; and, as was now being proved, they could scream for anything. At Elton's concerts, the first five or six rows would be filled by girls of fourteen or even younger, shrieking on that curious long, whistling note, like ceremonial bosuns' pipes at a naval funeral. With the screaming frequently went its allied occupation, fainting. At closely packed venues, like those of the new Sundown chain, the only way to remove those who fainted was to lift them on to the stage, past Elton, and off through the wings.

The screams were detectably different, however, from those which greeted David Cassidy or Donny Osmond. 'Elton's fans don't want to go to bed with him,' *Melody Maker* commented. 'They want to mother him or hug him like a friendly Santa Claus after the show.' For corroboration there were cheerfully self-deprecating comments from the new idol himself. 'It's a bit funny to be screamed at, because I'm not your actual sex idol, am I? The only way I ever thought people would scream for me was in horror.'

It all pointed to a remarkable coup which *Melody Maker* – not dreaming any ironic *déjà vu* – headlined THE SECOND COMING OF ELTON JOHN. 'Those who thought Elton had burned himself out through his gruelling work-rate have been proved mistaken . . . In the fluctuating world of pop, he has made a dramatic come-back, to answer the doubters. It has turned him into a teen-idol pin-up as well as a respected musician. Few artists these days can wear both crowns, and wear them with such elegance.'

Teenybop hysteria was not confined to London; on the contrary, it seemed to grow stronger the further north Elton went. In Newcastle, the concert-promoter, Peter Bowman, suffered a broken ankle in attempts to protect him from a keening mob. Elton's glasses were snatched from his nose, and he had to bolt down the street with no idea where he was going. In Glasgow it took him an hour to escape from the theatre. Decoys had to be sent out first, and even then the back of his limousine, as it drove away, bore a latticework of prostrate, tearful girls. 'I'd rather they lined up for two hours and I signed autographs for them,' Elton said 'But they just don't want to do that. There were times when I thought they were going to rip me apart.'

Throughout every performance, girls would jump up on to the stage and fling their arms round his neck like so many skinny pink feather boas. He was forced to carry spare glasses everywhere to replace the pairs continually ripped from his nose or trampled under lurching platform heels.

He himself was at a loss to explain the hysteria. 'It's all very flattering, and it might be something to do with the clothes. They all seem to want to cuddle and mother me, like they're saying "Ooh, isn't he lovely!" I'd get worried if they were screaming all the way through, but they do seem to listen as well. I don't think they're the David Cassidy types, because they know all the songs. When I do something like "Mona Lisa and Mad Hatters" or "Your Song", I can hear them all singing along.'

As well as in the grown-up *NME* and *Melody Maker*, he now found himself the star of teenybopper fan magazines, vying with conventional heart-throbs like David Cassidy and Donny Osmond. His friend Nina Myskow, the fashion writer on *Jackie*, arranged for him to feature in one of its Life Story romantic cartoon strips. 'Elton loved posing for the drawings,' Nina remembers. 'He couldn't believe *Jackie* actually wanted him as a pin-up in that way.' *Jackie*'s publishers, the D. C. Thomson company, were later persuaded to break a lifetime policy and sell the strip's original drawings to John Reid.

With the astuteness peculiar to their kind, Elton's teenybopper fans quickly discovered where he lived. His bungalow in Wentworth, at that time, possessed no security as such. Only a grass verge separated the front door of Hercules from the road. On quiet Sunday afternoons in his living room, he would look up and see red, weeping faces pressed to the big picture window.

A typical example was Linda Mallarkey, then aged fifteen and going to school in Downham, near Bromley, Kent. A dark, tomboyish girl of partly Irish parentage, Linda possessed that calm air of purpose which so many pop fans bring to their apparent dementia. She had started liking Elton at the time of 'Rocket Man', and stayed loyal to him despite the more obvious attractions of T-Rex and the Jackson Five. 'I don't really know why I liked him so much,' she admits now. 'I knew he wasn't really good-looking. But he seemed a funny kind of person. I mean, sort of fun. Nice.

Natural. Just ordinary.'

With a friend, Marie Thacker from Rotherhithe, Linda became the most familiar among the little knot of girls perennially waiting for Elton outside his London ports of call, like DJM and Capital Radio. 'He'd always stop and talk and have pictures taken, and be really nice to us,' she remembers. 'After a while, he recognised us, and even looked for us. When we knew he was coming back from tour, we'd go out to Heathrow and meet him. We'd just find an electric point in the concourse, plug in our cassette recorders and settle down. We waited two days out there for him once.'

On his birthday, Linda and Marie combined with two other girls to get him a cake and deliver it to Wentworth in person. 'We took it down all the way on the train. We got him a Buddy Holly book as well, because we'd read that he liked Buddy Holly. When we got there, we were amazed that you could just walk right up to the front door and knock. His mum answered the door and when we told her who we were she was really nice as well. Elton invited us in and showed us his gold discs, and the pictures of him with the astronauts, and we all had a bit of the birthday cake each.

'Afterwards, we read that he liked Dom Perignon champagne, so we decided to buy him a bottle of that. We bought it in Shepherd's Bush because you could get it there for £12 a bottle; everywhere else, it cost about £18. We gave it to him when he was at Lord's playing in a charity cricket match.'

The girls' reassuring reports to their parents that Elton lived with his mum, in utter normality and respectability, were very nearly true. Sheila Farebrother was constantly at Hercules, serving tea to interviewers, looking after the two dogs, even posing for pictures with Elton beside the Bel Air-size swimming pool. It is said that a mother can never be truly shocked by anything her child may do. Certainly, Sheila seems to have accepted the situation between Elton and John Reid with perfect equanimity, making Reid a part of the warm Harris family as much as Bernie Taupin had formerly been. Only the closest members of Elton's circle ever detected a faint note of ambivalence in her attitude. 'For Christmas, she always used to give John an electric carving knife,' a former Rocket Records employee says. 'I used to wonder if there was any significance in that.'

In 1973, Elton moved Sheila and Derf from their Ickenham house into one of the properties immediately adjoining Hercules. Having his mother literally at the bottom of his garden was practically a return to the closeness of Frome Court days. At night, Sheila's house used to be bathed in anti-burglar floodlight which reminded Bryan Forbes of the prison camps he had often tried to escape from in black-

and-white British films.

Derf's picture-hanging duties continued unremittingly. Bryan Organ had completed his portrait of Elton, at an open window in a T-shirt printed with Andy Warhol's Marilyn Monroe. The portrait started Elton on a craze for Bryan Organ, as he would afterwards have crazes for Geoffrey Proud, Robert Young, Paul Wunderlich, Edouard Cortes, L. S. Lowry and Rembrandt. By 1973, he already owned two Rembrandt etchings, bought – surprisingly – at Harrods, one for £5,000, the other for £7,000. 'I never dreamed there were Rembrandts still to buy. I thought they were all in museums.' The same Knightsbridge shopping trip netted him a Dürer engraving of a coat of arms and a skull. The piquant fact also emerged that Harrods allowed its customers to buy even precious works of art on the instalment plan. Though Elton did not require this service, the provident John Reid decided to make use of it. 'John bought a Rembrandt etching two inches by one inch on the HP!' Elton kept telling people in amusement.

To other members of his family, he had been just as munificently generous. For his maternal grandmother, Ivy, he bought a house conveniently close to her daughter, his Aunt Win, in Ruislip, Middlesex. On his cousin Paul Robinson's eighteenth birthday, Elton turned up on the doorstep. 'He said "I've got you a present, but it's a bit too big to carry indoors",' Paul remembers. 'I went outside – and there was this brand-new white Mini.'

His Dwight relatives in Kent, while following his career with enormous pride, scrupulously distanced themselves from any semblance of 'cashing in'. Finally, his cousin Roy, the ex-footballer to whom he owed his first-ever job, decided to ask for a loan to start a clothes boutique called Lady Samantha. 'I said, "You can say no, and it'll be forgotten, but here's the proposition." The money was there straight away. "And," Elton said, "I'll even come down and open it for you."'

His care and concern for his family had prompted Elton to try to repair the one gaping hole in it. Sure beyond a doubt who he was, and that he could be, and wear, what he liked, he had resumed relations with his father.

Since divorcing Sheila in 1962, Stanley Dwight had moved far away from Metroland. Still only in his late fifties, he had long since left the RAF and taken an executive job with Unilever in Port Sunlight, Cheshire. By his second wife, Edna, he had four young sons, Stanley, Simon, Robert and Geoffrey.

Watching Elton's rise, Stanley had had painfully ample time to reflect on his first marriage and the dejected boy for whom he had thought the best course was a desk job with British European Airways. To see audiences go mad for Elton's wild outfits was an everlasting reproach to Stanley's strict dress code: the conventional blazers and grey flannels, the forbidden Hush Puppies. As he had admitted many times to his nephew, Roy Dwight, 'I was wrong.'

Yet Elton seemed to harbour no lasting bitterness. He would visit Stanley and 'Aunt Edna' at their house in Upton, near Liverpool, and play football with the four small boys who had displaced him. He would send them postcards from his tours, and a regular Christmas card. For Christmas 1972, he sent Nanette Newman's book of children's sayings, *God Bless Love*. Inside was written: 'To Dad and Aunt Edna, Robert, Stanley, Geoffrey, Simon. With love for a happy Xmas (yes, this is my card) Love, Elton', followed by a row of kisses.

Early in 1973, when Elton was appearing in Liverpool, he spent the day with Stanley and Edna, playing the piano with the four boys and kicking a football around the garden. He asked Stanley what his ideal car would be, and Stanley said it would be a Peugeot, because there'd be enough room for the children. Elton then handed him a cheque for £2,000 to buy one. Stanley refused to take it, but Elton managed to slip it into a pocket of Edna's cardigan.

He was deeply involved with setting up Rocket Records and creating a roster of deserving artists for whom to 'work his b****cks off'. After Davey Johnstone and Longdancer more acquisitions quickly followed, reflecting Steve Brown's hippyish stamp and Elton's feeling for talent hitherto undervalued or misprojected. So Rocket also signed Stackridge, a band well known on the pub-and-club circuit, and two solo singers, Mike Silver and Maldwyn Pope.

Rocket's crusading ideals were never better expressed than when Kiki Dee became its first female signing. For Kiki was the industry's outstanding example of someone who should have made it. Born Pauline Matthews in Sheffield, she had been around since the mid-Sixties, one of those almost-famous female names like Elkie Brooks and P. P. Arnold. Her voice was spectacular; indeed, she had been the only white female performer ever signed to Berry Gordy's Motown label. But even Motown had been unable to do for her what it had for Mary Wells, Gladys Knight and Diana Ross. For some reason, perhaps connected with her rather solid looks, stardom had always refused to come.

Kiki Dee became Elton's special project and protégée. It was not just that he considered her voice second to none among current British female performers. About the sturdy Sheffield girl there was some of the same mixture of smoky soul and total unsexiness that had once drawn him so powerfully to Dusty Springfield. Whatever else Rocket might do, he was determined Kiki would see her name in the Top 20 at last.

He acquired a further influential friend and supporter through the interview he gave to *Rolling Stone* early in 1973, just before his long-postponed Italian tour. The magazine had recently adopted a detailed question-and-answer format after the style of *Playboy* interviews, and to be chosen as a subject denoted election to rock's premier echelon. Interviewing Elton was the idea of Paul Gambaccini, a young American who freelanced for *Rolling Stone* in England while studying at Oxford University. For his enterprise, Gambaccini was rewarded with what stands among the best of *RS* interviews for its articulateness, forthrightness and humour. He himself became Elton's closest media confidant during a subsequent highly successful career as disc jockey and TV interviewer.

Outside the business, Elton's closest friends continued to be his Wentworth neighbours, Bryan Forbes and Nanette Newman. 'He was always dropping over,' Nanette Newman remembers. 'In this spirit of complete normality that was also utterly mad. So this apparition all in silver, with green hair, would sit in the kitchen and drink eighty-seven cups of tea. You'd say "Goodbye" and see him set off that little distance back to his house. Then you'd hear afterwards that on the way home he'd managed to buy a Ferrari.'

The Forbeses were by now well accustomed to Elton's fondness for extravagantly-staged practical jokes. After Turk Thrust, the drum majorettes and the lion came one inspired by Nanette's decision, just before Christmas, to change her car. 'I'd had a Mercedes, and was changing it for a Ford. Elton was horrified. "You can't have a Ford," he kept telling me. Then he said "I think you're exactly the sort of person who should have a Ford – with a nodding dog on the back shelf."

'That Christmas morning, we heard the most terrible commotion outside. Up the drive came this awful old Ford, with Elton behind the wheel. He'd sprayed "Happy Christmas" in fluorescent paint all over it, and on the rear shelf was a nodding dog. He'd gone to so much trouble . . . and, of course, then we were stuck with the old Ford. We had no idea how to get rid of it.'

He loved the two little girls, Sarah and Emma, and showered them with expensive presents that frequently alarmed their parents. 'When Emma was six, he'd give her a pint of Chanel No. 5,' Bryan Forbes remembers. 'One Christmas, he gave her a diamond and sapphire bracelet from Cartier. We put it away for her, but she managed to get hold of it somehow. One day she came home from school and said "Look what I've got. A fountain pen." She showed us this cheap little fountain pen, which she said she'd swapped at school for something else. "What did you swap it for?" we asked her. "That bracelet Elton gave me," she said. A Cartier diamond and sapphire bracelet for a piddly little fountain pen worth about eighty pence! We never did dare tell Elton.'

'We couldn't compete with presents like that,' Nanette Newman says. 'So I used to get the girls to make him things that were special and personal to him. Sarah made him a cushion with a Rolls Royce on it, and the numberplate EJ 1. It took her a year to do. Whenever we went to see him after that, at the bungalow and the big house in Windsor, that cushion was always there.'

Bryan Forbes's stint as a movie tycoon having ended, and his career as a blockbuster novelist not yet having begun, he was in a quiet period professionally. This he decided to occupy by producing, writing and directing two television documentaries. The first was about the doyenne of British stage actresses, Dame Edith Evans. The second was about Elton. Forbes financed it himself, and spent much of the spring and summer of 1973 with a film crew, watching Elton at work and play. A company named Companion Films was set up by John Reid and Forbes to divide the eventual proceeds from TV syndication.

Elton welcomed the project, tickled beyond words to be filmed by the man who had made all those black-and-white classics of his childhood. Some photographs by Bryan Forbes were even used inside the album-sleeve of *Don't Shoot Me, I'm Only the Piano Player*.

He was as dumbfounded as ever by the big star names whom Bryan and Nanette regarded as old friends. On hearing that Katharine Hepburn was to be their house guest, he begged Nanette to bring her over to Hercules for tea.

Hollywood's earliest and most stylish eccentric had lost none of the habit in beautiful old age. Though wafted everywhere by limousine, her preferred method of transport was the bicycle. 'I don't remember if she brought her own bike in the boot of the car, or borrowed one of ours,' Nanette Newman says. 'I remember she biked all around Virginia Water that week, with people gaping and clutching one another and saying, "That can't be Katharine Hepburn!" So when we went over to Elton's for tea, Bryan and I went in the car and Kate went on her bike.'

She arrived at Hercules to find Elton and a magnificent tea waiting, but a painful crisis in progress. A frog had somehow found its way into the swimming pool. Elton was afraid of frogs, and could not face trying to fish it out.

Katharine Hepburn responded with a decisiveness worthy of every brisk heroine she had ever played, in films from *Pat and Mike* to *The African Queen*. She dived into the swimming pool and retrieved the frog.

'That was fantastic,' Elton gasped. 'How did you manage to do that?'

'Character, dear boy,' Ms Hepburn replied. 'Character'.*

The Rocket Record Company was launched on 30 April, 1973, in a style appropriate to its Toytown railway emblem and the golden age of ligging. A special train was chartered to introduce the music press to Rocket's directors and a selection of its new signings, bands Longdancer and Stackridge, and solo singers Mike Silver and Kiki Dee. The train ran from Paddington to the quiet and beautiful Cotswold village of Moreton-in-Marsh. There a brass band greeted the 200-odd guests and marched with them in noisy procession to the village hall, a sumptuous buffet and performances by Mike Silver and Longdancer, with Elton, Bernie, John Reid and other Rocket executives getting up on stage, to sing the 'oohs' and 'aahs'. In its mixture of whimsicality and gluttony, the occasion was a liggerfest as notable as any the early Seventies recorded. On the return journey, the train's chief steward reported that his entire stock of champagne, wines, spirits and beer had been drunk. As an extra little memento of the occasion, Elton treated himself to L. S. Lowry's painting *Moreton-in-Marsh*, a work later put up for auction at a reserve price of £15,000.

The office at 101 Wardour Street then settled down to serious business. Steve Brown managed it from his office with a mural of steam trains, fields and cows. To Rocket Records, Brown would be much the same omniscient guru-like presence that the talented Derek Taylor was at Apple Corps. His younger brother Pete worked under him, as did a hippyish couple named David and Lindsay, two secretaries and a telephonist. John Reid commuted back and forth from the separate office he had established for John Reid Enterprises in South Audley Street, Mayfair.

One of Reid's earliest coups for Rocket was to persuade a well-known music journalist, Penny Valentine, to join the fledgling company as its first press and public-relations officer. Valentine was, in fact, London's best-known female music journalist, a columnist on

*Asked for corroboration of the story, Katharine Hepburn replied, 'I'm not afraid of frogs, and I've always enjoyed upsetting people, but I have no recollection of this incident.'

Disc, sometime panellist on *Juke Box Jury* and a personal friend of many leading pop stars, including Elton's first pin-up idol, Dusty Springfield.

Penny Valentine had followed Elton's career from the beginning and, like other women journalists, had seemed to develop a special rapport with him. Before even knowing of Elton's fixation on Dusty Springfield, she had noticed a strong similarity between them. 'As performers both of them had the same quality – I can only call it complete lack of sexuality. And both of them were obsessed with the trivia and minutiae of show business.'

The job of Rocket's press and PR officer was hardly an onerous one. Everyone in the music press wanted to write about the new company, its new acts and crusading aims. The Rocket office was also a convenient place for Elton to give the interviews he still poured out unstintingly. Journalists were entertained regally, lunched, dined, chauffeured and, if necessary, flown first class to Los Angeles and put up at the Bel Air Hotel.

Rocket's generosity to outsiders was as nothing compared with Elton's generosity to Rocket. Like his friends, his employees were showered with gifts: hampers from Fortnum and Mason, chocolates from Charbonnel and Walker, jewellery and watches from Cartier. Those small gold watches, with old-fashioned square faces and Roman numerals, became almost small change in Elton's circle, so many each year did he give away. 'At Christmas, he'd arrive with a cardboard box and go round the office, doling things out,' a Rocket executive remembers. 'Just an ordinary cardboard carton, full of Cartier watches and pens. He said it was easier that way.'

Rocket, to Elton, was a family – a further source of cameraderie, approval and affection to fill up the bottomless wells of his insecurity. On his birthday, if he was in America, it was not uncommon for the whole Rocket staff to cluster around the transatlantic phone chorusing 'Happy Birthday to you'. Even cynical Penny Valentine found herself drawn against her will into the atmosphere of protective babying. 'I remember shouting at him several times, "I'm not your mother, you know!" One day, just before a press interview, the hems of his trousers came unstitched, and he got me to sew them up for him. I found myself kneeling down on the floor with a needle and thread. "What's happening to me?" I said. "Why am I doing this?"'

When Elton was not there, the atmosphere at Rocket could be less idyllic. John Reid was in charge, and now need show no Austin Reed deference to anyone. London's music community was soon made aware that the most amiable of all pop stars now had a manager who could not be described in anything like similar terms. 'I met John

Reid with Elton at a poll winners' concert,' the former editor of a music paper remembers. 'I thought I'd never encountered anyone so unpleasant in my life.'

Working with Reid was Penny Valentine's first introduction to a quality hitherto unrecorded: his explosive and violent temper. As he quickly demonstrated, he was capable of outbursts that made Elton's Little Moments by contrast seem the merest trifles. 'You could always tell when he was going to explode. He'd suddenly go bright red in the face. He'd got one of those tempers that, for a moment or two, are totally uncontrollable. What upset him could be something as small as not getting the number he wanted on the phone. Bang! the whole thing would go flying across the room.

'I'd come in in the morning and find him sitting on the stairs with his head in his hands. "What shall I do?" he'd say. "I've fired the whole staff." "Why?" I'd say. "Oh," he'd say. "None of them was in to work on time. Now all the phones are ringing and there's no one to answer them. What am I going to do?" "Ring them all up and get them all back again," I'd say.'

The benign engine face of the Rocket Record Company little hinted at its wobbly, unpredictable steam valve. 'The whole place was in fear of John,' Penny Valentine says. 'But whatever happened, no one ever blamed Elton. Even if Elton might be behind some of what John did, no one ever thought badly of him. Elton was above it all.'

Bryan Forbes's documentary vividly recalls that '73 summer of idyllic hot weather and still-spiralling fame. As a friend, Forbes was given access to his subject's innermost court, in Britain, America and France. He himself acted as narrator and also appeared on camera, metamorphosed from British POW officer's duffel-coat to pale blue Rocket T-shirt, hipster trousers and cowboy boots.

An early sequence in the film alternates scenes of Elton onstage with one of him walking out to bat at Lord's cricket ground. From the wild night creature of silver and gold, we cut to a sedate noontide figure, fully and correctly attired in white flannels, pads, gloves and cap. He is playing in a charity match, part of a celebrity eleven, raised by his agent Vic Lewis, that also includes David Frost, Peter Cook, Michael Parkinson and Wes Hall. The only departure from tradition is the knot of long-haired boys and girls who leap towards this particular batsman with open arms and autograph books.

'Elton John plays cricket as he plays the piano,' says Bryan Forbes. 'Dressed to kill, and as if his life depended on it. For in his book the greatest sin is to be boring.'

Forbes then establishes his subject in a quick-cutting medley of images. Here is Elton walking onstage, flashing and caped like the most outrageous heavyweight champion all-in wrestling ever knew. Elton half-naked and showing much body hair, beating his chest at his audience like a myopic King Kong. Elton transferred to the Surrey countryside, jogging with his band, a squat, almost waddling figure against their beanpole flares. Elton, short-haired in one scene and, in the next, with hanks of green-patched orange obscuring his ears as stiffly as stale candy-floss. Elton, alone with his grand piano at Hercules, playing 'Daniel' as a Brahms nocturne, then suddenly turning it into 'She's a Lassie from Lancashire . . .' Elton demonstrating how he used to play 'The Skaters' Waltz' at the age of four in Pinner Hill Road, and doing 'The Poor People of Paris' in the style of Winifred Atwell. Elton, opening the drawer of an old-fashioned cash register whose compartments are stuffed with jewellery. Elton, with orange hair, tartan trews and red, white and blue glasses, drinking Rombouts coffee in a kitchen spotless enough to feature in a Domestos ad. Elton in his bath, holding up a soggy length of washcloth and talking like Colonel Bloodnock from *The Goon Show*. Elton, asked what he'll be like in twenty-five years and guffawing, 'Bald, I expect.' Elton deliberately and slowly squashing a cream doughnut into his own face.

'At twenty-six, he walks confidently on five-inch heels where lesser angels fear to tread,' Bryan Forbes continues. 'Sometimes as bright and unyielding as the diamonds he wears on his fingers: sometimes plunged into self-critical gloom . . . A child with every toy in the shop, and not a key to wind them with . . . As much an enigma to himself as to his friends . . . Now possessing no inhibitions: now totally inhibited . . . Seeking fame one minute: determined to reject it the next . . . The life and soul of the party: the party-destroyer . . . Jealous of his privacy: hating to be private . . . Arrogant, contrite . . . occasionally practising an infant's tyrannies among other infants . . . Gifted, lonely . . . the superstar who does his own Hoovering . . .'

Close-up of the face – in pale blue hexagonal glasses now – with its cleft upper lip, its pugnacious chin, its voice of utter reason and modesty. 'I'd like to become a legend,' Elton says. 'I'm hung up with legends. I'd like to become a Mae West, or someone like that. But I don't think I will be, because those people are so very, very special.'

We see Bernie Taupin up in Lincolnshire, walking alone over the hills, a simple, plaid-coated figure like some poetic young journeyman in a novel by Hardy. The next scene shows Bernie in less pastoral mode, wearing a white Stetson, accompanied by Maxine in platform boots with her name written in silver down the sides, walking along the village street in Tealby and entering the garden gate of Piglet-in-the-Wilds. 'He and his American wife live, snug as country mice, in a Beatrix Potter dolls' house,' says Bryan Forbes. 'A gentle, unassuming figure, he has perfected the art of remaining anonymous in a crowd, the Cartier-Bresson, as it were, of the pop world.'

As usual, Elton takes pains to stress that Bernie's is the more toilsome job. 'He just comes down to London and hands me a batch of lyrics. I potter around, and find a chord sequence I like. Usually it takes me about half an hour a song. I've just written twenty new songs, and they're my favourites. I think songs should be disposable. I can't even remember some of the words or chords of albums we did two years ago, like *Tumbleweed Connection*. To me songs are like postage stamps. You lick them, put them on a letter, and never see them again.'

The people closest to Elton appear in telling vignettes. John Reid, a blandly doll-faced figure in a batik shirt, recalls their first meeting and subsequent 'gude friendship'. 'He has a Jekyll and Hyde character,' Reid says, in the quiet voice of one who enjoys total emotional repose. 'You never know what he's going to do next.' Dick James smiles through thick sunglasses on a rooftop somewhere, son Stephen standing uncomfortably by. 'He's a parydox,' James says. 'He's very sincere. He can be very brash as well. He's bringing back to show business what show business very badly needs. And this is genuine showmanship.' This wholly predictable remark is followed by a flash of genuine old showman's wisdom. 'The artist on his way up lives with failure, magnificently. I've never yet met one who could live with success.'

His mother, Sheila, is innocently forthright. 'He's had darker moods since he made it in the pop world than he ever did before. He's always been a very quiet boy, never been the sort of boy to have the gay life. I know when he's in a mood, but I never expect him to be over the moon any time. He's just not that nature.'

The album destined to surpass all others he had made, or would make, began in troubled circumstances. Elton had planned to record it in May, at the place that was now like a lucky talisman, the Château d'Hierouville. But a legal dispute had broken out concerning the ownership of the château; as a result, the studio was closed indefinitely.

Instead, he decided to record in Jamaica, a place highly fashionable since the commercial popularity of reggae music and the migration there of Chris Blackwell's Island label. Two weeks were booked at Byron Lee's Dynamic Sounds studio in Kingston where the Rolling Stones had recently recorded *Goat's Head Soup*. Gus Dudgeon put in an extensive order for special sound equipment and band amenities including a tabletop football-game like the one at Hercules.

Elton's party arrived in Jamaica at the worst possible moment, on the day after the world heavyweight championship fight between Joe Frazier and George Foreman. Every hotel was jammed to capacity, and the streets pulsated with aggression. By an administrative mix-up, Elton had been booked into the Pink Flamingo in the middle of Kingston while everyone else was staying across the island in the resort area of Ocho Rios.

Terrified even to set foot outside his hotel, he had nothing to do but work on the new batch of lyrics Bernie Taupin had given him. Closeted in his room with an electric piano, he beat even his *Don't Shoot Me* record, writing the music to twenty-one songs in three days. Fortunately, the hotel's resident entertainer was one of his favourite jazz pianists, Les McCann. 'That was a saving grace,' Elton recalled. 'I just used to go and watch him every night.'

Byron Lee's Dynamic Sounds also proved a severe letdown. The studio was situated in one of the worst parts of Kingston, and fortified like a Belfast police station with barbed-wire fences and heavily armed guards. Almost none of the promised special equipment had arrived, not even a grand piano for Elton. The sessions that usually flew by were painfully slow and unproductive. 'We decided "the vibes just weren't right, man",' Bernie Taupin remembers. 'It's hard to see how they could have been with guards holding machine guns outside the door.'

Elton flew into a grand sulk, not moderated even when news came through that *Don't Shoot Me* had made number one in America. While the band held a celebration dinner at the Pink Flamingo, he remained in his room. Suddenly, the others heard a wild shriek. 'This centipede, about fourteen foot long, had crawled over me,' Elton recalled. 'I rushed down into the dining room with just a sheet covering me.'

It was decided to abort the Dynamic Sounds session, fly to New York and reconsider the situation there. But leaving the West Indies proved almost as traumatic for Elton's party as leaving Manila did for the Beatles in 1966. A dispute arose over payment for hotel accommodation. 'Things got so heavy, they even impounded our cars,' Bernie Taupin says. 'We were never so glad to get out of anywhere in our lives.'

In New York, however, there was better news. The legal dispute over Château d'Hierouville had been settled or, at least, suspended. The studio would be available to Elton after all.

The session that ensued forms the most idyllic part of Bryan

Forbes's documentary. We see the château looking good enough to
be painted by Monet, with shady cloisters and heat-hazed gardens
where clouds of midges whirl and dance. At the wide-open main gate,
a knot of French teenagers waits politely, like so many concièrges,
one of them holding an old-fashioned milk churn. We see the
monastic bedrooms, the YMCA-like communal living room, the high-
ceilinged refectory, where long-haired beanpoles in floral shirts sit at
breakfast with their *baguettes* and *biscottes*. After the horrors of
Kingston, a holiday atmosphere prevails.

Bryan Forbes walks through the grounds towards camera, looking
like a British officer in Colditz, even with his thumbs tucked into the
patch pockets of hipster flares. 'There's a scent of new-mown grass
outside,' he says. 'But not a suspicion of it inside' – an observation
which caused some little merriment when the film was finally shown.
For grass was in as widespread use here as in all pop music circles
of 1973. Only Elton and Bernie Taupin were consistent in refusing it.

With the songs already written and rehearsed in Kingston, all there
was to do was plunge straight into the studio and record them. In
twelve days in May, Elton completed twenty-one tracks.

The material was as eclectic as always, with veers of mood as
sudden and schizophrenic as Elton's could be in real life. One of the
first into the can was 'Saturday Night's Alright for Fighting', a rave-
up rocker, inspired by Bernie Taupin's disreputable teenage years
around tough dance halls in Lincolnshire. 'I'd started to feel I was
writing too much about American culture and American things,'
Bernie says now. '"Saturday Night" was my first attempt to write a
rock-'n'-roll song that was totally English.'

By contrast, 'Funeral for a Friend' was an instrumental piece,
almost Wagnerian in tone, bringing out all that was strange and
melancholic on the other side of that wild Saturday-night bopper.
'Gus Dudgeon had always said I should do an instrumental,' Elton
recalled later. 'One day, I was feeling really down, and said to myself
"What kind of music would I like to hear at my own funeral?" I'd
always liked funeral music anyway. I like very sad music of any
kind.'

There were lyrics sexier and seamier than Bernie had ever put into
Elton's mouth before: 'Bennie and the Jets', about a sci-fi female rock
star in 'electric boots and mohair suits'; 'Dirty Little Girl', about an
unhygienic nymphet; 'Sweet Painted Lady', about a seafarers' whore;
'Social Disease', about an alcoholic who humps his landlady;
'Jamaica Jerk-Off', about 'honky-tonkin' in the sea'. Nearest of all
to the knuckle was 'All the Girls Love Alice', a ballad about a teenage
lesbian with a line about 'two dykes in a go-go' which by rights

should have sent it straight to the top of every 'banned' list.

Other tracks were steeped as never before in nostalgic yearning for the Wild West, Hollywood and childhood innocence. 'The Ballad of Danny Bailey' was about a heroic gangster shot down by G-men. 'Roy Rogers' was a homage to the squeaky-clean buckskin hero, galloping his horse Trigger across a fourteen-inch TV screen in some Metroland living room. 'Goodbye Yellow Brick Road' found Bernie plundering imagery from the first film he, Elton and virtually every other postwar child had ever seen, at the same time giving it a back-spin of cynicism and disillusionment. In *The Wizard of Oz*, Judy Garland as Dorothy follows the Yellow Brick Road to her heart's desire. But Bernie has already been there, and found it wanting. His dream is to return from his 'penthouse' and 'vodka-and-tonics' to country simplicity, 'back with the howlin' old owl in the woods . . . huntin' the horny-back toad . . .'

There was also a heartfelt song on a theme which, even then, could hardly be called new. Marilyn Monroe had been an icon of pop culture since the late Sixties, when Andy Warhol turned her into a poster image almost as famous as the Campbell's soup can. Bernie had long been struggling with the problem of writing a song about Marilyn that would express both the tragedy of her death and the fascination she continued to exert. 'I wanted to say that it wasn't just a sex thing. That she was someone everybody could fall in love with, without her being out of reach.'

Even the title he chose was not original. It had earlier been said of the rock star Janis Joplin, also doomed to early death from drugs, that she was 'a candle in the wind'.

The subject had equal appeal to Elton, with his love of glamorous legends and his developing understanding that fame could produce despair. 'When I think of Marilyn, I just think of pain,' he says in Bryan Forbes's film. 'I can't ever imagine her being that happy.'

With seventeen out of twenty-one finished tracks clamouring to be used, the obvious course was to follow current fashion among prolix LP superstars and issue a two-record album. Elton resisted the idea, fearing that a double album would be too expensive for his new teenage fans to afford. In addition, both DJM and MCA in America had said they would treat it only as a single work under his contractual obligation to deliver two albums per year.

What persuaded him was the sheer weight of good things this double album would offer. Naming it after its most evocative track, *Goodbye Yellow Brick Road*, suggested further parallels with his great exemplars, the Beatles. '*Revolver* lifted them on to a higher plane, and *Honky Château* did the same for us. *Sgt. Pepper* was their most popular one, and *Don't Shoot Me* was ours. Then they did the White Album, and now we'll have a double, too.' To coincide with its release on 5 October, an American tour was planned, taking Elton for the first time to the country's two ultimate concert venues: Madison Square Garden in New York, and the Hollywood Bowl.

As a foretaste, 'Saturday Night's Alright for Fighting' was released as a single on 29 June. Proving that Bernie Taupin had succeeded in writing a 'totally English' rock-'n'-roll song, it reached number seven in the UK as against only twelve in America. Elton was cast in his most unlikely incarnation of all, a leather-clad rocker, whose favourite sounds were 'a switchblade and a motorbike'. Once again, the ears of the banning brigade seemed fortuitously blocked with wax. What made the song was its incantatory chorus, 'Saturday, Sat-urday', and the feeling of frantic stage performance created in that tiny French studio. At long last, Elton had a finale wild enough to hammer even Little Richard into the ground.

In the weeks before *Goodbye Yellow Brick Road* was released, he made his main concern the new artists signed to Rocket, in particular his personal protégée Kiki Dee. She has since recalled the selfless hours Elton spent with her as A & R man, building up her confidence and looking for the right song to break her five-year professional jinx. Rejecting the upbeat Motownish things she had previously done, he settled on a dramatic French torch-song called 'Amoureuse'. This Kiki duly recorded – albeit with some Yorkshire misgivings – in a session co-produced by Elton and his sound engineer, Clive Franks.

Rocket had by now also launched an American office, in Los Angeles. A small building was rented in Holloway Drive, just off Sunset Boulevard, literally over the road from Tower Records, Elton's favourite spot of all for 'looting'.

To help organise Rocket USA – and, in particular, work on the forthcoming Elton tour – John Reid hired a self-possessed girl named Sharon Lawrence. Originally a journalist with UPI, she had gravitated into music PR, somewhat against her will, become a close friend of many rock stars, notably Jimi Hendrix, and ended up working for Elton's frenetic publicist, Norm Winter.

Sharon Lawrence had met Elton through Winter at the beginning of 1973. 'I wasn't such a big fan of his at the beginning,' she remembers. 'But I always liked him very much as a person. He was so fresh, so humorous, so enthusiastic – so totally different from the other types of people you had to meet in that business. I'd go with him to Tower Records on his buying sprees. It always impressed me that he refused to take free records: he always insisted on paying for what he had. He'd buy hundreds of albums, and try to buy hundreds for me, too.'

She developed a special rapport with Elton, and gained the reputation of being able to deal with him during his tempestuous Little Moments. John Reid's advent did not remove the need for this. 'I realised the relationship between Elton and John was chaotic. You had a manager that one day seemed to control his artist completely and another day didn't seem able to control him at all. John would call me sometimes and say, "He's being hateful. He's supposed to do a radio spot, and now he won't." I'd be brought in to talk him into it.'

She agreed to head Rocket USA, fired by the idealistic zest which Elton had for the whole project. 'He cared about the music so much. He'd studied its history. Even after he became so big, he was still in awe of people he considered the great figures of rock 'n' roll. And he cared about them so much as people. If anyone he admired was going wrong, Elton would always try to help them. I've seen him take people aside and say "Look, I've always admired you . . . don't do this to yourself."'

What would go down in pop history as the Yellow Brick Road Tour reached the first of many climaxes before an audience of 16,000 at Hollywood Bowl on 7 September. The two concerts at the Bowl had sold out weeks earlier, fuelled by carefully placed rumours that for his first US appearance in almost a year, Elton intended to surpass all previous displays of excess showmanship. As a teaser, an enormous billboard on Sunset Boulevard had shown him as a Fred Astaire figure in top hat and white tie, winking suggestively from a vista of top-hatted and net-stockinged chorus girls.

The Bowl's scallop-shell stage was furnished as for one of Busby Berkeley's more ambitious dance routines. First, the audience beheld an enormous backcloth of Elton in his Fred Astaire guise, with top-hatted Elton cut-outs flourishing canes and white gloves in a long row beneath. The raising of the backcloth revealed a mass of potted palms and a precipitous, glittering staircase. At the bottom of the staircase were five grand pianos in pale airbrushed hues, one yellow, one orange, one blue, one grey and one mauve.

The commère for the evening was Linda Lovelace, whose book *Deep Throat* had lately become a sub-pornographic best-seller. 'Ladies and gentlemen,' she began. 'In the tradition of old Hollywood, let me introduce you to . . . the Queen of England.' Down the staircase came a lookalike of the monarch whose hand Elton had recently shaken at the London Palladium. More look-alikes followed of idols and current friends, among them Groucho Marx, Mae West, Batman and Robin, the Frankenstein Monster and four counterfeit

Seven-year-old Reggie
with his father at cousin
Roy Dwight's wedding,
1954

Roy Dwight (left)
playing for Fulham
against Liverpool in 1956

Co-lead singer in Bluesology. 'Stu Brown always took a bit of time to get going. But Reg just had to open his mouth, and there it was.'

Reggie (extreme right) with Bluesology at the time of their signing to Fontana

The newly named Elton with new partner, Bernie Taupin. 'We were total opposites. Town mouse and country mouse.'

Dick James (left), 'the luckiest man in pop music', with Elton and Vic Lewis, 1970

The Elton John Band:
Clockwise l to r Dee Murray, Davey Johnstone, Elton, Nigel Olsson

Elton and John Reid: 'the opposites that seldom fail to attract'

Elton and Bernie take a break between unarduous composing sessions. 'To me, songs are like postage stamps. You lick them, put them on a letter and never see them again.'

Elton and Bryan Forbes's
daughters, Sarah and
Emma

Elton with John Lennon
onstage at Madison
Square Garden,
Thanksgiving, 1973

Dodger Stadium, 1975

Relaxing at Hercules, 'the superstar who does his own Hoovering'

Captain Fantastic's in-flight boudoir

Elton and *Starship 1*

New-look Elton with Watford players fresh from the bath

Elton with Kiki Dee when the road was starting to get tougher

The study at Woodside: a place for everything and everything in its place

Wedding day, 1984

With 'Phyllis', aka Rod Stewart, at a football match

'He's not just Jekyll and Hyde. He's Jekyll and Hyde and about 20 other people, too.'

At his lowest physical ebb

Left: 'Being married has had me so much calmer. I'm less argumentative now, and more reasonable.'

Bernie Taupin in 1988

The Nehru look, 1989

The superstar in middle age: everybody's Uncle Reg

Beatles.

Elton himself was introduced by a freight train of superlatives, 'the biggest, most colossal, gigantic, fantastic . . .' and the 20th Century-Fox Cinemascope fanfare. Wearing huge white feathery breeches and a white-feathered toque, a cross between Bat Masterson and Queen Mary, he descended the staircase, nodded regally to the kowtowing effigies of Groucho and Batman, stepped on to the lid of the blue airbrushed piano, then platformed gingerly over the hedge bordering the stage proper. As he did so, the lids of all five pianos were raised, revealing the silver letters E L T O N, and 400 white doves were released into the Hollywood night.

Watching this orgy of ego in Bryan Forbes's documentary, it is interesting to see the moment when the last doves flutter away and Elton doffs his feathery bonnet to reveal a somewhat less feathery thatch, tinted scarlet above the ears. Despite the 20th Century-Fox trumpets and the roar of 16,000 voices, what we see is still no more or less than Reggie Dwight, getting down to business in the saloon bar.

Theatrics continued throughout the two-hour show, which suffered somewhat from the Hollywood Bowl's notorious open-air acoustics. While Elton played 'Crocodile Rock', a cloaked figure with a papier-mâché crocodile head backed him on electric organ. (It was Clive Franks, the sound-engineer.) Halfway through, he disappeared to exchange his white feathers for a purple jumpsuit scored with outsize musical notes, and his white-framed glasses for a pair that lit up on his face like the rings of an electric stove.

Melody Maker's report of the concert was headlined ELTON'S FINEST HOUR. In Bryan Forbes's film, the superstar himself describes the sensation of holding so enormous an audience in his grasp. 'I like to lift them up, drop them down, lift them up again. It's the same as having sex. You try to save the very best bit till last. It's like two hours of . . . I don't know. It's like fucking for two hours and then suddenly finding out there's nothing you can do after that. It's so emotional and so physical, you don't ever want to do anything else.'

Gone was the era of all-night drives between gigs in rattletrap station wagons. For this American tour, MCA Records provided Elton with his own personalised Boeing 707 airliner, allowing him to establish a central base and fly to and from his concerts each day. The Boeing's interior was so large, and Elton's entourage so small, he said he often felt like playing inflight hide-and-seek.

Out of his feather bonnet and space rodeo suit, he remained the simplest, healthiest, most clean-living performer rock had ever known. At 8 am, when most other stars were just closing gummy eyes, Elton would be exposing his sturdy legs out on the hotel tennis court. At night, he was scarcely less wholesome than in the morning. Pop concert audiences then were accustomed to seeing their idols punctuate each number with copious swigs from vodka or bourbon bottles and beercans, arrayed like a squalid bar along amplifier tops. Through all of Elton's dehydrating two-hour shows, his only refreshment came from a small bottle of Perrier.

Other touring stars were famous for misbehaviour in hotels, which could include the destruction of TV sets or telephones – sometimes even the entire room. 'That never went on around Elton,' Penny Valentine remembers. 'He was into property. He wasn't into smashing it up.'

Those not in the know marvelled, too, at his self-control where groupies were concerned. With willing female flesh to be had on every side, his hotel suite appeared as chaste as a Trappist monastery. In fact, Sharon Lawrence remembers, the crowds of attractive women who thronged through Elton's dressing rooms occasionally brought a definite gleam into his eye. 'I always felt that he could easily have married and had children – something he often said he wanted to do. Once or twice, I tried to encourage him in that direction. I told him "Don't get stuck with choices now that you'll regret for the rest of your life."'

She was impressed, like many before her, by the neat, meticulous habits that prevailed even amid the whirl of this biggest-ever tour. Driving away after a concert, his first act was still to reach for his diary and jot down his impressions of the place he had just played, the audience size and possible box-office gross. 'At the centre of all that excess and craziness, he was completely self-contained and self-reliant. I always thought if Elton had to do a gig and all the big star support systems broke down, he'd still get there, even if he had to hitchhike and carry his piano on his back.'

This time there had been no argument over which of the new album's tracks should precede it as a single. 'Goodbye Yellow Brick Road' was released at the tour's outset, in September. Within only days, it was number two in America and six in England. The full two-record collection followed early in October, launched by an elaborate TV link-up to the British press from Elton in Los Angeles. He had never released an album while on tour before, and, with his usual superstition, wondered what this might portend. The answer came before the tour's end: number one on both sides of the Atlantic.

Like the Beatles' *Revolver*, though for utterly different reasons, *Goodbye Yellow Brick Road* was an album exactly suited to its moment. One has only to hear that Wagnerian overture of Moog synthesiser and wind whistling round artificial crags to conjure up late 1973 with gruesome clarity. In London, Edward Heath is at 10 Downing Street, about to take on the coal miners and plunge the country into powercuts and a three-day working week. At the White House, Richard Nixon sits in the Oval Office, still wishing to make it 'perfectly clear' he knows nothing about Watergate. In the Middle East, Sadat holds desperately on to his 'pre-emptive strike' against Israel, and Saudi oil ministers double and redouble the price per barrel. In Belfast, Northern Ireland, and Beirut, Lebanon, terrorist murder in the name of religion becomes an almost daily commonplace. Groups of three or four psychopaths call themselves Liberation Fronts. Psychopaths who blow up children or milk roundsmen call themselves Popular Liberation Fronts. Psychopaths define innocent bystanders as 'legitimate targets' and, having murdered, issue statements claiming 'responsibility'. The word of the decade is 'security', meaning insecurity. Airport concourses become war zones. Inflation bites. Money shrinks. Rules break. Language lies. Scruples vanish.

The result is a desire for escapism as never before in all branches of mass entertainment, movies, television and pop music. Onscreen fires and explosions more cataclysmic than those of everyday life; onscreen murders more vicious and violent than those enacted daily in the street; cars piling up in smashes more demented than on real roads and freeways; shotguns blasting louder; bones crunching more sickeningly; blood spurting redder from super-jumbo exit wounds. And with the cathartic sadism, cathartic sentimentality; a deep hankering for the imagined stability, safety and kindliness of the past. Nostalgia ceases to be the resort of an affected few and becomes the opiate of all classes and age groups. Nostalgia for the Twenties, the Thirties, the childhood idylls of Beatrix Potter and Mabel Lucie Attwell, the 'great days' of Hollywood, the rock-'n'-roll Fifties.

Goodbye Yellow Brick Road perfectly mirrored this mood with its nostalgia and whimsy and, no less, its total lack of concept or focus. Long had the Seventies generation waited for an album so lushly, complicatedly, portentously and passionately adding up to nothing.

Even what little explicitness was there went over the heads of most of its audience. Scarcely anyone noticed the song about the sailors' whore, the unclean nymphet or the teenage lesbian. All that millions upon millions of pop fans wanted to hear were the vague, glowing echoes of childhood and fan-worship: Lucie Attwell, the *Beano* and Saturday-morning pictures; Fred Astaire, Roy Rogers and Judy Garland; Elton not rejecting the Yellow Brick Road, as Bernie Taupin had meant, but linking hands with the Cowardly Lion and the Tin Man, and dancing in high platforms over the rainbow. The production gave his singing a distorted quality, like a sentimental chorale by massed chipmunks. Through that neutral and neuter double voice, Bernie's words were clipped and flattened almost into a foreign language:

> Back with the howlin ol' owlinthewood.
> Huntin' the hawny black tauwd . . .

No other Elton album was to stay in the charts so long (more than a year in the American Top 40) or spin off so many single hits. 'Candle in the Wind' was only released in Britain, reaching number eleven ironically in a time of epidemic power cuts. Most extraordinary was what befell 'Bennie and the Jets', Bernie's song about a butch sci-fi rock goddess, to which Gus Dudgeon had added the sound effects of a live performance. As well as making number one in the US pop charts, 'Bennie' became a crossover hit on black soul and R & B radio stations across America. A trifling track named 'Harmony', written and recorded in half a day, achieved cult status among the chain of FM stations operated by RKO. In a 'battle of the hits' contest run by the New York station, listeners voted 'Harmony' the winner twenty-three times in succession.

The Yellow Brick Road tour's closing weeks saw Elton raised to a new, dizzy plateau of fame in America. Sharon Lawrence, who was often with him on the road, remembers how the ovations, the adulation and backstage mobbing seemed to surpass themselves each night. 'In Memphis, Al Green came to the concert, which really thrilled Elton. Afterwards, something went wrong with the security, and about 4,000 people seemed to get backstage. Elton was amazed. "My God," he said. "This is really like the Beatles, isn't it?" He was so proud.'

Back at the Rocket office, Sharon's most important job was to tell him his chart placing as soon as the lists were published each Wednesday. 'I'd call him up and say, "Well, I'm afraid I gotta tell you – you're number one again." It was that way week after week after week. One day when I told him, Elton said, "It's going to be terrible to be number two, isn't it?"'

His buoyant mood could always change, and did so more often and unexpectedly as months of travel and performance started to tell. 'He'd stand at the side of the stage sometimes and say, "Fuck it, I'm not going on",' Dee Murray, his bass-player remembers. 'But he always would – and usually give a killer of a performance. Onstage, I was the one who had most eye-contact with him. For the first few numbers, he'd refuse to look at me at all. Then, at a certain point, I'd meet his eye, and he'd grin. Whatever had been bugging him was all over.

'The thing was, you never knew when he was going to throw a wobbler. And when he did, everyone got it. We were all having dinner one night, in this really smart place, when Elton suddenly got up, said, "You're all nothing but a load of bastards", and walked out. A minute later, he came back and stood there and had another go at us.'

Sharon Lawrence witnessed still worse outbreaks, the kind that, for some reason, only women were ever allowed to see. The biggest rock star in America, whom all show business wanted to meet and court, would lie face down on the king-size bed in his emperor-size suite, mumbling, 'No one gives a damn about me.'

If his spirits were not to take these fearful dips, they had to be kept at a constant hyperactive high. During his appearance in Atlanta, Sharon discovered that the cult star Iggy Pop was appearing at a local club named Richard's. She suggested to Elton that he join Iggy onstage, unannounced, wearing a hired gorilla costume. 'He loved doing that – even though the suit was so hot, he almost suffocated in it.'

For a short hop in the Boeing between New York and Boston, Sharon arranged an equally elaborate surprise. Elton's great hero among black singers was Stevie Wonder, the ex-Motown child prodigy who had recently suffered a serious car crash and was only now inching back to performance. When Elton boarded the plane, Stevie would be at the portable piano in its rear cabin, singing 'Crocodile Rock'.

'But when Elton came out to get on the plane, he was in a terrible mood,' Sharon remembers. 'He hadn't gotten his chart placings that morning, or something. He didn't even see or hear Stevie. He just went straight into the front cabin and sat there, fuming. Stevie carried on playing and singing, and still Elton had no idea. In the end I had to go to him and say, "For God's sakes, Stevie Wonder's back there."

'He and Stevie played together that night, and were wonderful together. Stevie said afterwards that it was the start of things really getting back to normal for him after the auto crash. Elton was on top of the world again.'

The terrible moment was when the machine suddenly stopped. The forces that had kept you pinned to the whirling wall of the rotor-ride gave up their hold. You plunged down and landed with a sickening bump on earth again.

Sharon Lawrence remembers being rung up by Elton on the first night in more than three months when there was no plane ride to take, no white ostrich feather bonnet to don, no two-hour workout to do on callused fingertips, no piano top to strut, above the plantations of waving arms.

'He sounded totally lost. "It's all over," he said. "Where do I go now?"'

10

*'This is your song,
Your Majesty'*

I N late November 1973, mass interviews were held at London's Inn
on the Park hotel to bring the British press up to date with pop
music's most multi-faceted success. For favoured reporters, like the
NME's Charles Shaar Murray, a special bonus was laid on, owing
something to recent close encounters with Groucho Marx. Arriving
in a luxurious panelled suite above Hyde Park, Murray was puzzled
to find a room lavishly furnished with drinks and snacks but only
Elton's chauffeur in attendance. The chauffeur then pressed a button
on the wall, a panel swung around and a folding bed tipped out. Off
the bed rolled a mirthful Elton in white suit, white boots and red,
white and blue spectacles.

It was a fittingly euphoric end to a year that even the most hype-
hardened journalist could only call stupendous. Elton John was now,
undisputedly, the biggest pop star in the world, which by immutable
reckoning meant as big as, or bigger than, the Beatles. Like the
Beatles in the Sixties, he was pop's uttermost peak; the dictator,
inventor and pioneer to whom millions looked for their next era of
fantasy and joy. He had achieved what only Elvis Presley and the
Beatles had – what even the Rolling Stones and Bob Dylan never
could – that ultimate, colossal fame, expressed in affectionate
familiarity. As there had been just 'Elvis', just 'John, Paul, George
and Ringo', now there was just 'Elton'. After his appearance at Belle
Vue, Manchester, the *Melody Maker* could put only one possible
headline above Roy Hollingworth's ecstatic review: HAIL ELTON!
ROCK SAVIOUR!

American superstar or not, he was still the favourite clown of
Britain's music press with his slapstick stunts in folding beds, his first-
class quotes in Goon-accented voices – above all, his good-humoured
tolerance of the tradition that praise for his music and showmanship
be invariably accompanied by criticism of his personal appearance.
He would himself repeat the worst insults with apparent enjoyment:
'indubitably lunkish', 'a head like a coconut with a joke-shop mask

attached', 'Godzilla in drag', 'a bald, bespectacled plumpoid', 'a pasty little troll'.

The biggest pop star in the world remained defiantly normal and down-to-earth, even about recognising himself as the biggest pop star in the world. 'You can't be famous and be totally available to the public,' he told Charles Shaar Murray. 'I don't mean that in a snobbish sense at all, but if I walked about London all the time, people would go, "Hmm, he shouldn't do that." They don't want to see you in Camden Town, buying your vegetables. They don't associate you with going to the toilet or buying fruit or having trouble with your plumbing at home. You wouldn't expect the royal family to go out and buy budgie seed. "Oh yes, saw her yesterday, walking the corgis."

'If I'm walking down the road and someone says, "Can I have your autograph?" – sure, that's fine. There's never been a publicity machine behind me. I'd hate it. There's no image to go with me. I don't break thousands of girls' hearts at airports. If there's one photographer there, I'm lucky. I've not got attractive features. I'm plain.'

Though most journalists now understood the situation between John Reid and him, none made even the most oblique reference to it. Seventies pop might visually flaunt the homosexual, bisexual and 'unisexual' but there were still no words to express such a thing in *NME* or *Melody Maker*. For propriety's sake Elton would himself occasionally provide a token alibi. 'When I have kids, I'm going to call my little girl Umbrella. Umbrella John is a beautiful name. Poor little girl, she'll really have the piss taken out of her. "Umbrella – stand over there."'

To his triumphs as a performer he was restlessly adding fresh achievements as an entrepreneur, talent scout and Svengali. In December, Rocket Records had its first Top 20 hit with Kiki Dee's 'Amoureuse', the sexy torch song which Elton had matched to the stolid Sheffield girl, against all appearances. Though 'Amoureuse' made only 13, the haunting production Elton had given it ensured its future as a minor British non-feminist classic. Kiki at long last had the success and recognition she deserved. Here, as everywhere else, the Elton touch seemed to be infallible.

A further burst of high spirits took him back into the studio to record his first-ever purpose-made single, albeit in a corny tradition hallowed since the era of Bing Crosby. 'Step into Christmas' was completed in a single day at Trident, London, using all the electronic flimflam of Phil Spector's 'Wall of Sound'. 'I'd like to thank you for the year,' sang Elton dutifully as a substitute for a Basildon Bond notelet to his global audience. Though hardly meant seriously, 'Step into Christmas' reached number 24 in Britain before settling into the Yuletide radio repertoire. As a further seasonal bonus, Elton played four concerts in London at the Hammersmith Odeon, inaugurating what would become a Yuletide tradition in Santa Claus costume and beard, pounding and pratfalling amid swirls of polystyrene snow.

The new year took off, powered by the euphoric overdrive of the old. *Goodbye Yellow Brick Road* had only just been displaced as number one in the American album chart. 'Candle in the Wind' was released as a British single in February, making number eleven. At the same time in America, its intended B-side, 'Bennie and the Jets', slow-handclapped out of soul-music stations from Watts to Detroit, eventually crossed over to become number one in the mainstream pop chart.

Elton's clean living and conventional virtues had by now chalked up another amazing first. Not only was he the first Seventies pop star to play tennis before breakfast, and bat on the wicket at Lord's. He was also the first Seventies pop star to have become vice president of a football club.

It is the nature of all such football fanatics to support their local team or club with total loyalty, however small or inglorious that local team or club may be. For a boy growing up in Pinner, the local club was Watford, five stops north on the Metropolitan Line. Throughout Reggie Dwight's childhood, Watford football team had been little more glamorous than Watford town. Small and penurious, stuck permanently in the middle reaches of the Third Division, the club possessed no great players, attracted no great managers, won no great victories, always seemed an infinity away from the yearly Cup Final at Wembley. Yet Reggie had rooted for 'the Hornets' with all his devout fan's nature. He had plotted Watford's unspectacular gains and losses minutely on his League chart; sported Watford's black and yellow colours; cheered from the stands at every possible home game on the modest ground in Vicarage Road.

The club's ailment was nothing that couldn't be cured by money to purchase star players from bigger clubs and pay a charismatic manager to galvanise the team out of its apparent death wish. The days were ending when British sport seemed to run on invisible and bottomless funds. Elton, even so, might never have become involved but for a girl named Julie Webb, who contributed articles to *New Musical Express* and was also a passionate football fan. In late 1973, while interviewing Elton, she mentioned that Watford was making a concerted effort to arrest its long decline and, to this end, was actively seeking new sources of investment and sponsorship. Maybe he could help out by giving them a benefit concert.

The lifelong fan jumped at this chance to help Watford, with both his money and his name. At the same time, embarrassed misgivings all but overcame him. The club's board of directors, in his eyes, was still an august and imposing body. What if they should be embarrassed to receive approaches from a pop star? What if they should regard it as just some publicity stunt? What if they should think his interest merely temporary and feckless instead of profoundly from the heart? A faint, diffident ghost of Reggie Dwight suddenly saw all manner of reasons not to do what he most wanted to.

Enquiries to Vicarage Road banished such fears. The Watford directors would be delighted to have him as an investor, and also grateful for any publicity accruing from his association with the club. In return for the promised benefit concert, and buying a block of shares, he would receive the honorary title of vice-president.

Purely cosmetic though the title was, Elton took it as seriously as if just appointed vice-president of America. Determined to prove his involvement and dedication, he attended all Watford's matches, home and away, missing only a stray one or two from pressure of performing or recording. Though soon to leave Britain and begin globetrotting again, he promised he would stay in constant touch with how Watford was faring in the League.

Self-effacing as he usually was in interviews, he seldom could resist mentioning this honour, outweighing all his heaped-up gold and platinum discs. 'There's nothing to publicise about me,' he insisted to Charles Shaar Murray, 'except that I'm vice-president of Watford.'

On his last American tour, Elton had heard of a recording studio even more appealingly novel than the Château d'Hierouville. This was Caribou, a studio on a ranch 9,000 feet up in the Colorado mountains. The owner was Jim Guercio, an American rock prodigy of background not unlike Elton's own. Trained in classical composition at Chicago University, Guercio had gone on to play guitar with Frank Zappa's Mothers of Invention, to produce Blood, Sweat and Tears and then create the hugely successful brass-rock band Chicago. He also had close managerial ties with Elton's greatest of all American musical heroes, the Beach Boys.

Elton visited Caribou by helicopter and there and then booked time to make an album at the ranch, first thing in 1974. Talking to Jim Guercio filled his mind with plans for zingy brass effects like Chicago and Blood, Sweat and Tears. He also had expansive ideas for backing vocals and asked a large group of musician friends to participate, among them Bruce Johnston and Carl Wilson of the Beach Boys, Danny Hutton of Three Dog Night, and Dusty Springfield.

The album introduced a fourth, highly idiosyncratic figure into Elton's permanent backup band. Rather than a predictable new guitarist or keyboard player, he chose to bring in percussionist Ray Cooper, ex-stalwart of the studio band Blue Mink. Tall and thin, with the censorious face of some stern Baptist elder, Cooper was almost as much of an onstage extrovert as Elton himself. To his classical ensemble of cymbals and tympani he added sound effects à la Spike Jones: whistles, rattles and Donald Duck quacks. Elton adored him, perhaps taking some subliminal comfort from the fact that Ray Cooper, too, was noticeably sparse on top.

The *Caribou* album – so it would eventually be titled – was squeezed into the smallest time frame yet. Only ten days could be spared, in mid-February, before Elton and the band started a tour of Japan, Australia and New Zealand. From there, Elton and John Reid were due in Los Angeles for final negotiation of a new recording contract with MCA.

Seven months of perpetual motion since *Goodbye Yellow Brick Road* had left little time for Bernie Taupin and Elton to write new material, let alone anything as strong as 'Candle in the Wind' or 'Bennie and the Jets'. The songs they took with them into the Colorado wilderness were little more than hasty ad libs. There was, for instance, the time just after their last US tour when Bernie had been at Hercules, listening to Elton in a cross mood, badmouthing everyone he could think of. Maxine Taupin had entered the room at that moment, nodded knowingly and said, 'Oh-oh. The bitch is back.' The line sparked off an instant Bernie lyric that the 'bitch' in question indulgently set to a frantic rock-'n'-roll beat.

The session began with Elton on top form, charging round the ranch's snowy slopes on a Snowmobile as frenetically as his fingers found chords for Bernie's words. But unfortunately, no one had taken into account the totally different process of recording an album in America. It took two precious days at Caribou to adjust to the studio's unfamiliar monitor system. Repeated technical hitches threw Elton into a 'moody', lasting a day and a half. The entire album therefore had to be finished in barely a week, before he and the band left for their Far East tour.

The most troublesome track was an emotional ballad called 'Don't Let the Sun Go Down on Me'. 'When Elton sang the vocal track, he was in a filthy mood,' Gus Dudgeon remembers. 'On some takes, he'd scream it, on others he'd mumble it. Or he'd just stand there, staring at the control room. Eventually, he flung off the cans [earphones] and said "Okay, let's hear what we got." When I played it to him, he said "That's a load of fucking crap. You can send it to Engelbert Humperdinck and, if he doesn't like it, you can give it to Lulu as a demo."'

This tour of Japan, Australia and New Zealand was among the last to be set up for Elton by Vic Lewis at the NEMS agency. Elton's agreement with Brian Epstein's old firm was a subsidiary of his expiring agreements with the Dick James Organisation. John Reid had made it clear that, like Dick James, Vic Lewis belonged to the bad old days, and was to be shaded from the picture as soon as legally possible.

It was cavalier treatment for a man who had played almost as crucial a part as James in Elton's early development. Vic Lewis was the one who had largely coerced him from his songwriter's obscurity, forcing him to raise his original band and go back out on the road. Nor might there have been any miraculous American breakthrough in 1970 but for Lewis's fortunate contacts with the Los Angeles Troubadour Club.

The ex-bandleader, with his little matinée-idol moustache, had hitherto enjoyed the warmest possible relations with Elton. Both were avid sports fans, with kindred obsessions about tennis, football and cricket. Vic Lewis ran his own celebrity cricket team, and had put on the charity match which allowed Elton to bat at Lord's the previous summer. He also shared Elton's fondness for Goonish high spirits and comical accents. 'I used to do Peter Sellers as an Indian, going "oh dear, goodness gracious me", that Elton always adored.'

Numerous gifts from Elton underlined their special rapport. 'The year he first appeared at the Troubadour, he arranged for a television set to be delivered to my home, so that I'd come home and find it working. I had a gold Parker 51 pen set from him, specially inscribed "To Vic". Another time, he came round and said, "I've got something for you" in an Indian voice. It was a gold ring in the shape of a turban, and the turban part was set with diamonds.'

Traditional married man that he was, Vic Lewis had been pained by the later developments in Elton's private life. He disliked John Reid and considered Reid's influence on Elton wholly deleterious. Nonetheless, he was still Elton's agent and, as such, flew out to join the tour for its concerts in Australia and New Zealand.

The concerts themselves were spectacular sell-out successes. Australia by the mid-Seventies had awoken from its long cultural trance and become a market for pop as demandingly up-to-date as America and Britain. Elton was the continent's number-one pop star, a fact in itself reflecting the huge change in public mores. He, in return, liked Australia for its blissfully predictable climate, its American luxury without American stress, above all the sense of being as far as one possibly could from England's littleness and nosiness. In Australia, he always felt his freest and happiest. Australian audiences, consequently, saw him on a roll that even America seldom did.

Backstage, however, there was tension from the beginning. The opening concert was in Perth, at the ground of the West Australia Cricket Club. John Reid got into a dispute with the promoter, Christopher Cambridge, over the box-office take. As a result, Vic Lewis found himself with Cambridge in a room at Perth Town Hall, having to count out all the ticket stubs and check them against the takings.

Any pop-star manager worth his salt will always keep a sceptical eye on concert promoters, to ensure the maintenance of standards for his client, both onstage and off. But to Vic Lewis, John Reid's behaviour throughout the five days of Australian concerts was counterproductively aggressive and challenging. 'Chris Cambridge was an excellent promoter. I'd booked all my other acts with him, like Cilla Black. All the time, John seemed to be doing his best to be difficult and obnoxious. To show that he controlled Elton, so he called the shots.'

Similarly, problems with Elton – those sudden, unpredictable prima donna tantrums and sulks – were things that, in Vic Lewis's view, only seemed to happen when John Reid was around. In Reid's rare absences, he reverted to the straightforward, well-brought-up young man of old. In Melbourne, Reid went off to visit friends, leaving Vic to take Elton to dinner. They discussed sport throughout the meal, starting with cricket, working round to football. Elton talked of his passionate desire to help Watford and his ambition to be more at the club than just an honorary vice-president. His ultimate dream, he said, was to join the club's board of directors. In the light of subsequent evenings, Vic Lewis was to remember this one with nostalgia as 'wholly pleasant'.

Their rapprochement was cemented by revival of a favourite mutual joke. 'Elton was having guests up to his hotel suite for drinks, so we decided to do my Indian gag. I'd got a terrific tan anyway. I put a red spot on my forehead, wrapped a white sheet round my body and head, and sat cross-legged on Elton's bed. When the guests arrived, they thought he had a real Indian guru praying in his bedroom.'

Elton's single concert in New Zealand was to be his biggest ever in Australasia. On 28 February he was to appear at the 34,000-seat

Western Springs Stadium just outside Auckland. The plan then was for Elton, John Reid, the band and Vic Lewis to go to Tahiti for a week's holiday before Reid and Elton flew back to negotiate the new MCA recording contract in Los Angeles.

The party flew out of Australia on 27 February – coincidentally on the same day that the Queen flew in to perform the state opening of Parliament in Canberra. Their spirits, already good, lifted still higher as New Zealand's North Island materialised like a patch of rural Surrey in the ocean. Elton was especially buoyant, remembering what a haven New Zealand had been after his bumpy Australian tour of 1971. Those who did not know already were apprised of the interesting fact that John Reid had spent three years there as a small boy.

New Zealand was to welcome back its favourite rock star with almost royal ceremony. On the afternoon of Elton's arrival – the day before the concert – his Australasian record company, Festival, had organised a lavish press reception at an Auckland park, the Parnell Rose Garden. When the tour party arrived, they were to be greeted by massed Maoris performing a ceremonial war dance.

Every available Rolls-Royce in the North Island had been hired to take them from their hotel to the park in open-topped cavalcade. But, as the Rolls-Royce fleet awaited, a crisis suddenly blew up. John Reid was found not to be at the hotel. Urgent enquiries by Vic Lewis could produce only the vague explanation that he'd gone 'yachting'. Elton flatly refused to leave for the reception without him.

By the time Reid reappeared and the procession reached the park, the Maori dancers were almost ready to wreak carnage in earnest. The situation was saved by Elton, who entered wholeheartedly into the spirit of things, pretending to recoil in terror as the chanting natives advanced with levelled spears. Good humour apparently restored, the party then moved indoors to the press reception.

The press's long wait had made heavy depredations on the bar provided for the occasion. John Reid asked for some whisky, and was told that supplies had run out. What was later described as a 'heated' argument took place between Reid and the party's organiser, Kevin Williams, with Reid accusing Williams of incompetence. Offered a glass of champagne instead, Reid threw the contents of the glass at Williams, and stormed out of the room.

About ten minutes later – according to subsequent courtroom testimony – he returned to the bar. Sitting there was a woman friend of Williams's, a journalist named Judith Baragwanath, who, in forthright antipodean fashion, rebuked Reid for his earlier behaviour. Reid then hit her, knocking her to the floor.

Neither Elton nor Vic Lewis witnessed the incident. 'I was right on the other side of the room,' Lewis remembers. 'The first I knew of it was when one of the organisers came up and tugged at my elbow. "Get Elton John and your whole party out of here as quickly as possible," he said. "A woman reporter says Elton's manager has just hit her in the face."' Star and entourage were hurriedly shepherded out to the Rolls-Royce fleet and back to their hotel.

That evening, there was a concert by David Cassidy at Auckland Town Hall. Elton, Reid and Vic Lewis attended the concert and afterwards went on to a party for Cassidy at a local night club. Among the journalists present was one David Wheeler, a friend of Judith Baragwanath's. During the party, Wheeler spoke to one of Elton's entourage about that afternoon's episode at Parnell Rose Garden. He was alleged to have said that, because of what had happened to Baragwanath, Elton and his party were 'all marked men'.

The supposed threat was communicated to Elton, who reacted with unwonted truculence, marching up to David Wheeler, grabbing him by the shirt front and asking him whom he thought he was threatening. John Reid then intervened, knocking Wheeler down and kicking him as he lay on the floor.

To hit one person in the course of a day may be considered unfortunate. To hit two – especially in a foreign country, under a foreign legal system – exceeds even Lady Bracknell's definition of carelessness.

The immediate effect was to put Elton's whole party – bar Vic Lewis, who had left early – in imminent fear of retaliatory beatings-up. 'We left the club post-haste,' Elton later remembered, 'and were all physically threatened that anyone to do with the Elton John tour had better watch it. Then when we got back to the hotel we got a phone call [from David Cassidy's security manager] saying, "There's a carload of people on the lookout for you, so just stay inside your hotel."'

Next day – the day of Elton's giant concert at Western Springs – a posse of police arrived at the tour hotel. An agitated John Reid had been concealed in an outlying bungalow, leaving Vic Lewis with Elton. 'The police said they were looking for Elton John's manager,' Lewis remembers. 'At first they thought it was me they were looking for. I had to work quite hard to explain the difference between a manager and agent, and convince them I hadn't thrown champagne or hit anyone. But they finally realised I couldn't possibly fit the description they'd got.'

A strenuous effort was made to smooth matters over. John Reid apologised to Judith Baragwanath and offered to pay out-of-court damages to both her and David Wheeler. But the Auckland police were not to be mollified. Reid was arrested and charged with assaulting Baragwanath at the Maori reception and Wheeler at the night club. Elton, too, though he had merely grabbed the reporter's shirt-front, was arrested and charged with assaulting Wheeler.

Later that same day, John Reid was arraigned before Auckland magistrates. After a short preliminary hearing, the case was adjourned until the following day. Reid's application for bail was denied and he was remanded overnight to Mount Eden prison.

Thursday 28 March, 1974 was a day of the highest drama Australasia had known for some years. In Canberra, Australia, while the Queen performed the state opening of Parliament, an armed aboriginal demonstrator held four people hostage in the nearby Department of Aboriginal Affairs as a protest against alleged racial discrimination in its policies. That evening in Auckland, New Zealand, 34,000 Elton John fans converged on Western Springs Stadium, blissfully unaware that both their idol and his manager were facing trial for assault, and that the concert itself was within an inch of being cancelled.

Elton had been released from police custody, but was distraught at Reid's imprisonment and would not contemplate going on stage without him. The only hope was to go to New Zealand's Supreme Court and appeal the magistrates' refusal to grant bail. Frantic lawyer activity finally located a Supreme Court judge, Mr Justice Mahon, who was willing to sit for the appeal. The hearing took place at the judge's house, just ninety minutes before the concert's scheduled starting time. Mr Justice Mahon accepted that Reid was indispensable to the concert and granted bail on condition he surrendered his passport. The feathered space cowboy took to the boards that night as advertised.

Next day, when they should have been en route to Gauguin's island paradise, superstar and manager stood in the dock at Auckland magistrates court.

Elton's trial for assaulting David Wheeler was but a token official slap on the wrist. To such a lifelong good boy, it was none the less awful for that. Wearing a beige bolero suit with laterally-striped lapels, an open-neck striped shirt and yellow glasses, he said nothing in court, other than admitting the charge. His counsel, I. W. Brown, QC, submitted that the offence had been a minor one. Elton had only grabbed Wheeler by the shirt front, and had taken no further part in the assault. He was, his counsel said, 'non-aggressive, sensitive, sensible and concerned for other people, especially the young'. His conduct had been 'totally uncharacteristic of a person who is essentially a gentle individual'. As evidence of his character and public standing, a letter was produced from Princess Margaret, thanking him for work on behalf of her charity, the Invalid Aid Association. Thanks in part of this royal testimonial (which he evidently valued highly enough to carry around the world with him) Elton was discharged without conviction, and ordered to pay $50 NZ in costs.

To John Reid, no such leniency and latitude would be given. Photographs of Judith Baragwanath were produced, showing 'an injury above one of her eyes'. The attack on David Wheeler was said to have caused 'a cracked tooth, a chipped tooth, a black eye and bruises'.

His counsel, R. I. Maclaren, said that Reid admitted the two assaults, but that both had been the result of provocation. He had been under great pressure from supervising Elton's tour of Australia, and had arrived in New Zealand in a state of exhaustion. At the Maori park reception, Judith Baragwanath had used 'foul and derogatory language' to him. Baragwanath herself admitted she had called Reid 'a rotten little bastard' for throwing champagne at her friend Kevin Williams. But, under cross-examination, she denied that her remarks had included the word 'poof'.

David Wheeler said that, at the David Cassidy party, he had expressed 'a little bit of concern' over that afternoon's incident with Baragwanath, who was a friend of his. But he denied he had said, as Elton's side claimed, 'We have planned to get Elton John tonight. If not tonight, tomorrow night.' A few minutes later, he had been 'completely baffled' to be confronted by Elton, Reid and two other people, and accused of having threatened Reid.

In the witness box, Reid said he had struck Judith Baragwanath 'as a reflex action' when she confronted and abused him. In retrospect he thought it 'a despicable thing' to hit a woman, and now felt 'very bad' about it. He had attacked David Wheeler at the night club, thinking a fight was about to start. Menaced, as he believed, by several people, his instinct had been to protect Elton. As Wheeler had fallen, Reid was turning to go and had kicked him once, he thought, on the shoulder.

Reid's counsel said that the assaults were 'completely out of character', and that Reid had already been considerably punished by the publicity the case had received. But the Auckland stipendiary magistrate, H. Y. Gilland, was unmoved. He said he was prepared to accept that Reid was 'apparently not a violent man'. But the two assaults in one day must be considered more than an aberration

brought on by strain or misunderstanding. Reid had shown 'an ill-
mannered, arrogant indifference to people in the way he dealt with
them', which could not be punished simply by a fine. He was
sentenced to a month's imprisonment for assaulting Wheeler and a
further seven days for assaulting Baragwanath, the sentences to be
concurrent.

Reid's application for bail pending an appeal was refused by the
magistrate but later allowed by a Supreme Court judge in chambers.
The appeal was set down for hearing in the Supreme Court the
following Tuesday, 3 March. Meanwhile, the *New Zealand Herald*
reported, Elton and Reid had checked out of their hotel and gone into
hiding.

Urgent overseas phone calls to high-powered lawyers – including
Paul McCartney's brother-in-law John Eastman – produced little
comfort. New Zealand law would have to take its course. Vic Lewis
and the band dispersed for their holiday in Tahiti, leaving Elton
behind in Auckland with Reid. In pop-music lore, it is usually stars
who get into trouble on tours, and have to be protected by their
managers. Here, the manager had caused the trouble with conduct
that the most unruly star would have found it hard to equal.

Reid's appeal to the New Zealand Supreme Court, four days later,
was dismissed outright. The judge, Mr Justice McMullin, ruled that
the two assaults could 'only be branded as cowardly'. He was
unimpressed by Reid's payment of $2,500 to Judith Baragwanath and
$3,000 to David Wheeler, as well as a sum into court to cover a
possible fine. Nor was he moved by pleas that Reid had to be in Los
Angeles in five days' time to conclude a new worldwide recording
deal for Elton with MCA. He agreed with the prosecutor's submission
–ironic in the light of Reid family history – that the appellant should
not be treated as a celebrity, but 'just like any other New Zealand
citizen'. The sentence was upheld.

Back in Britain, the case received only minimal publicity. Elton's
light-hearted account, quoted in *New Musical Express*, said that
things 'just got out of hand' at a badly run reception. Later, one of
the roadies had been threatened with a beating-up. 'We asked who
was doing the threatening . . . I went up to him, seized him by the
collar and muttered, "You no-good son of an Irish leprechaun, what
do you think you're doing?" and was just about to clock him round
the face – me of all people! – when my manager stepped in and hit
him for me.' He added that the trial had been 'a farce'. 'The
magistrates just didn't believe any of us had been provoked. It was
all over in twenty minutes without any of us having witnesses. It was
a joke.'

At the Rocket Records office in London, where Steve Brown had held the fort, John Reid's restoration to liberty was awaited with deep trepidation. Penny Valentine felt she, at least, could look him squarely in the eye, having made heroic efforts to keep details of the affair at a minimum in the British papers.

'John amazed me, as always,' Valentine remembers. 'The first thing he said when he walked back into the office was, "Where are my press cuttings?"'

The Cartier-Bresson of pop, meanwhile, preferred not to be excluded any longer from the photograph. Bernie Taupin had realised that twenty-three was perhaps too young an age to settle down for good in the Lincolnshire countryside. 'I had this romantic view of myself as still being a country boy whose heart was in the land,' he says now. 'But it was only a romantic view, because of the great childhood I'd had. I was trying to go back and recreate a chapter that was past.'

Having an American wife meant that, while living his country idyll in Tealby, Bernie also made constant trips out to California, staying in a succession of rented or borrowed houses and apartments. While the A. A. Milne side of him loved Lincolnshire, the besotted Western fan longed to put down permanent roots in America. In 1972 he bought a second home in Los Angeles, paying $170,000 for a house on North Doheny Drive, next door to the film director George Cukor.

Soon afterwards, he sold Piglet-in-the-Wilds, and moved down with Maxine to join Elton in the Surrey stockbroker belt. 'I went from the sublime to the ridiculous. We'd been living in a tiny four-room cottage. Now we'd got a house in LA and this other enormous place called Bourne Lodge right on the Wentworth Golf Course – a Tudor hunting lodge with, I think, a bit of Georgian thrown in – just down the road from Elton at Hercules. Far grander than his place. I mean, he was just living in a bungalow. I was living in a hunting lodge. I think he was a bit put out by that.'

Bernie and Maxine were quickly absorbed into the social circle that revolved round Bryan Forbes and Nanette Newman at Seven Pines. 'They came to all our parties,' Nanette remembers. 'And, of course, Bernie was an even better customer at the bookshop than Elton. What I noticed about him and Maxine was how incredibly neat and meticulous they both were. And their house was as neat and perfect as a doll's house.'

Living at a distance from Elton, meeting only in the studio and on tour, Bernie had not realised the vast change in his old roommate's acquaintanceships. His first inkling was the charity concert Elton gave at the Royal Festival Hall for Princess Margaret's Invalid Aid

Association. Afterwards, Elton, Bernie and the band were invited to dinner with Princess Margaret and Lord Snowdon at Kensington Palace.

The Queen's younger sister had had a penchant for unconventionality since marrying a society photographer, the former Anthony Armstrong-Jones, at the start of the Sixties. She was still the most glamorous 'royal', a faintly raffish, as well as faintly tragic, figure, known to be atypically interested in the arts, fond of music and musicians – especially pianists – at times seeming less like a princess of the blood than a performer manquée. Still, it was stretching even Princess Margaret's bohemian lifestyle to invite a bunch of pop people back for a meal after a show.

'The whole night was very odd,' Bernie Taupin remembers. 'The thing that amazed me was that there didn't seem to be any kind of security at Kensington Palace, other than a policeman at the gate. You just rolled up, knocked at the door and were let in. The other thing I remember is that, getting out of the car, I split my trousers at the crotch. I had to borrow one of Lord Snowdon's dressing gowns while a lady-in-waiting sewed them up for me.'

The occasion was anything but formal. Two photographer earls were present, Snowdon and the Queen's cousin Lord Lichfield, both – Bernie Taupin remembers – 'getting plastered in a back room'. Nigel Olsson's girl friend, Josie, who collected celebrity telephone numbers, took the opportunity of copying down the palace's. Princess Margaret herself richly lived up to her reputation for earthy eccentricity. As the pop people stood in line to meet her, they noticed the evidently essential accoutrements of gin and tonic and wreathing smoke. At one point, mislaying her pack of American cigarettes, Her Royal Highness turned to a footman and demanded, 'Where are my fucking Winstons?'

Bernie Taupin's position in the mid-Seventies seemed an enviable one, perhaps even more so than Elton's. For Bernie could enjoy the fruits of their phenomenal success while experiencing almost none of its pressures. The tours that racked and crucified Elton were for him just free rides on a switchback of parties, receptions and room service. The album sessions, when Elton would scourge musicians and studio staff like Simon Legree, were for Bernie just pleasant interludes in France or the Colorado mountains. The closest he came to stress was those four weeks in every year when thirty-odd new lyrics must emerge. For the other forty-eight weeks, he need do nothing but sit and watch the figures change in his bank-balance.

He had undertaken a few extracurricular projects; recording his solo poetry album; producing an album, *American Gothic*, for David

Ackles; toying with various literary schemes including a children's book. Motivation was not strong when ten minutes work could earn him a sum greater than most poets saw in their whole lifetime.

Bernie, too, was now seriously rich, though with none of Elton's zeal to acquire sophistication and aesthetic sense. 'I had no notion of taste in those days,' he admits now. 'What I had in the cottage at Tealby was just like any other pop *nouveau riche* – black walls, lava lamps and sand candles. Heavy Victorian furniture everywhere. Orange couches, covered with Liberty prints. No co-ordination whatever. The things I wore were just as bad – denim jackets, covered in patches, fringed buckskin jackets, Navajo jewellery. I'd go to shops like Take Six and buy those awful three-piece suits with the big, wide lapels. Only, being me, I'd buy twelve of them at a time.

'In my most flash period, I had a magenta Rolls-Royce, and a friend working for me as a driver and personal assistant. I even had a phone put in the Rolls – one of the very earliest type, when you still had to ask an operator for the number. I never called anyone on it because of all that hassle of going through the operator. One night, we were sitting in the car outside the BBC, and we suddenly heard a beep but had no idea what it was. Then I realised. "My God! It's the car phone! Ringing for the very first time!" I rushed to answer it, but before I could pick it up, it stopped. I never discovered who the call was from. And it never rang again.'

While Elton rose steadily up the social register, Bernie preferred to stay among the street urchins of Britain's rock biz. He became a habitué of Tramp, the celebrity discothèque in St James's. As in boyhood, he took to running round with a gang. 'There was me, Rod Stewart, Ringo, Gary Glitter. Others came and went, but Rod, Gary and I were the nucleus. You'd see our picture in *Melody Maker* with a caption saying, "Yes, it's the same old crew again."'

With Rod Stewart, he developed somewhat the same love-hate relationship as had Elton. 'Rod lived at Ascot, only a couple of miles from Wentworth, so if I'd fallen out with Maxine, I'd go back and sleep on his floor. He was always fighting with his girl, Dee, so another night he'd come back to my place. We used to have a thing about copying one another's clothes. If I got a tuxedo from Yves St Laurent, Rod had to go and have one made exactly the same. Then I'd try to get shirts made the same as his.'

Gary Glitter – then at the height of his transmogrification from obscure warm-up man to camp teenybop heart-throb – was the gang's clown and occasional fall guy. 'He used to wear that terrible fur coat and that awful toupee,' Bernie remembers. 'Part of it was a toupee, anyway. I remember we pulled it off his head one night and threw it out of the car in the Cromwell Road.

'It was just like still being schoolboys, really. You did the same thing every night – went to some club and got legless while your car waited outside. Then drove around, pulling people's shoes off in the car and throwing them out. We took some poor guy's trousers off one night outside Tramp, threw them over a pawnbroker's sign and left him there – drove off and when we came back half an hour later, he was in a doorway without them, shivering. Silly, cruel things like that.

'I'd end up so wasted, I wouldn't even know which of the cars outside the club was mine. I put Harry Nilsson into what I thought was my car one night, and told the driver to take him back to his hotel. Next day, I found it hadn't been my car at all, but some Arab sheikh's. He comes out of the same club later with two hookers – and it's gone!'

In spring 1974 Elton became a director of Watford Football Club. Vic Lewis had arranged it for him as a memento of that pleasant dinner in Melbourne, before the Auckland nightmare set in. On returning to London, Lewis contacted Watford's chairman, Jim Bonser, and told him of Elton's passionate desire to graduate from mere honorary vice-president. With the club still problematically short of cash and good publicity, Bonser was only too glad to commend the idea to his fellow directors. As a gesture of appreciation, and to be company for Elton at matches and meetings, Vic Lewis also was invited to join the Watford board.

Probably no other moment in Elton's career, past or to come, gave him quite such elation as this. 'The day I took him along to finalise the details, he was over the moon,' Vic Lewis says. 'With a grin which spread from ear to ear and back again, he told me, "This has to be the happiest day of my life."'

His new appointment, for the moment, drove all other thoughts from Elton's mind. The music papers were suddenly full of football-oriented Elton John interviews, carrying headlines like THE STACK-HEELED STRIKER. Julie Webb in *New Musical Express* described him on the way to a game, waving a yellow and black Watford scarf in determinedly proletarian manner from the buzzed-down automatic rear window of his Rolls-Royce Corniche. His tone had the exhilaration of one thankfully regaining touch with roots: 'I've got such pleasure, mixing with ordinary people again. You do lose the value of things when you're racing around all the time on tour. Your lifestyle changes, your standard of living changes. And your appreciation of things lessens to a degree. You forget how much joy you can give by giving an autograph to a person who is actually knocked out at getting it – or a record, and you think "Christ, it's only a bloody record!" '

Mixing with ordinary people, as opposed to adoring fans, did have one slightly disagreeable consequence. As a resplendent Elton took his seat in the Watford directors' box, he realised that not all humanity was involved in the conspicuous camp of glitter rock. Amid the cheers and whistles from adjacent terraces, a lone voice made itself heard like the soothsayer in some classical tragedy. 'You great poof!' it shouted.

On 5 May, Elton gave Watford their promised benefit concert, performing at the Vicarage Road ground where he had, for so many years, been a faithfully star-struck spectator. A crowd of 40,000 – more than Watford had drawn in living memory – saw him all in yellow and black, like some astral traffic warden, hammering out his stadium repertoire with one extra item, the Beatles' 'Lucy in the Sky with Diamonds'. There was also a surprise guest artist, Rod Stewart, swathed in a rival tartan supporter's scarf. After Stewart's four numbers, a violent rainstorm began. Elton came back and led the dampened 40,000 in a chorus of 'Singin' in the Rain'.

The Watford benefit concert and Elton's fund-raiser for Princess Margaret were all his British fans were destined to see of him until the end of 1974. A British and European tour, meant to take him through the summer and reach its climax at Wembley Arena, was cancelled two weeks after being announced. A communiqué from Vic Lewis's office said that Elton and the band were suffering from 'severe strain', and could take on no further commitments outside London. The disappointed fans were mollified by Elton's assurance that there was no serious trouble within that democratic family group. 'I'm very close to them, and they more or less said, "We can't do it any more" and, "Can we relax a bit?" and I think we all deserve a break. But we're not going to become hermits – it's just so that everyone can sit down and plan things a bit better.'

'Serious strain' also flavoured *Caribou*, the album which Elton had virtually abandoned in Colorado the previous January. The rushed sessions with hastily written, inferior songs had caused a serious upset with his perfectionist producer, Gus Dudgeon. 'Until *Caribou*, I thought Elton had never sunk below a certain level,' Dudgeon says now. 'Generally speaking, whatever pressure he was under, the standard stayed incredibly high. But on this one, for me, he suddenly went. It was the first time I ever had a serious quarrel with him.'

The album was largely made in post-production, Dudgeon adding extra vocal tracks by the Beach Boys' Carl Wilson and Bruce

Johnston, and brass arrangements by the black soul band Tower of Power. The most inspired reworking had been on a slow ballad, 'Don't Let the Sun Go Down on Me', which Elton, before disappearing to Japan, had said was 'fuckin' crap', worthy only of Engelbert Humperdinck or Lulu. To this Dudgeon had added coolly soaring vocal tracks by Carl Wilson, Bruce Johnston and Toni Tennille, soon to find fame as half of Captain and Tennille. The result had an almost religious air, as if Elton were pleading for his happiness to some higher authority in the clouds.

'There was one bit of Elton's vocal I really wanted to bury,' Gus Dudgeon says. 'When he sang the line "Don't discard me", he put on this really ridiculous American accent, so it came out "Don't discord me". But Toni Tennille said, "No, leave it. It sounds good." ' 'Don't discord me', indeed, was the hook that made the hit: number two in America, though only 16 in Britain.

Despite its advance hit single, however, everyone around Elton knew *Caribou* to be a disastrously inferior product, especially as a follow-up to *Goodbye Yellow Brick Road*. The air of haste, indifference and compromise extended even to David Larkham's cover. No over-the-rainbow artwork this time; just a rather banal colour snap of Elton, in marcasite-framed red glasses and tiger-skin bolero, posing with husky swagger against a studio backcloth of mountains and lake. On the reverse, he and Bernie Taupin were shown perched on two stools, stiff and unsmiling, as if almost apologetic for the listing of forgettable doodles like 'Grimsby', 'I've Seen the Saucers', 'Stinker', 'You're So Static', and the impenetrable 'Solar Prestige à Gammon'.

The rock critics generally agreed the whole thing was makeshift and substandard. But who any longer gave a damn what rock critics said? Within a fortnight of release, *Caribou* was in the American top five. By mid-June, it had followed *Don't Shoot Me* and *Goodbye Yellow Brick Road* to number one simultaneously in America and Britain. The only faint hint of censure was the comparatively brief time it spent there: four weeks in America, two in Britain. Gus Dudgeon was later nominated for an award as producer of the year's best album.

With John Reid's release from prison in New Zealand, negotiation of Elton's new American recording contract could belatedly recommence. No trace of that hot-headed Auckland brawler could be seen in the immaculate young man who sat across the table from MCA's president, Mike Maitland, a model of composure and diplomatic level-headedness. With Reid at various times during the negotiations were Rocket's UK press officer, Penny Valentine, and Sharon

Lawrence, from the LA office. Though scarcely admiring Reid for his 'chaos' in other directions, Sharon Lawrence could not help but be impressed here. 'He was very proper, very considered, very much in command all through. He never let the other guys rile him, but also never let them take an inch more than they should.'

On 22 June, *Billboard* reported that Elton had arrived in New York to sign what Mike Maitland, with that wonderful vagueness that can come over corporate men, preferred to describe merely as 'the best deal anyone ever got'. Full-page advertisements in both the *New York Times* and *Los Angeles Times* subsequently announced his re-signing to MCA for the US and Canada. The terms were not disclosed, but were widely reported to be $8 million for five albums – the largest sum ever paid to a recording artist. According to John Reid later, trade gossip erred on the side of caution, and the MCA deal was worth 'appreciably more' to Elton than $8 million. With the advance went a hefty increase in his US royalty-rate: from 15 to 17.5 per cent on records already released, and 20 per cent on all product released in future.

With the handshakes and champagne went a proviso, albeit soaked in the honey of American executive-speak. Delighted as MCA were to have yet another number one album, the adverse comments about *Caribou*'s quality could not be ignored. Mike Maitland told Elton that two albums per year were too many and that he should slow down his frantic production rate. Elton's not specially mature reaction was to defend the album by slagging off the critics. 'I'm the big cheese at the moment, so everyone feels bound to have a go at me. I read a good piece by John Tobler in *Zig-Zag* which said the reviews of *Caribou* were probably written before it even came out.' It is revealing that, even with a number-one UK album, he thought he was once again 'cold sick in Britain'.

What he did concede was that *Caribou*, the Australasian tour and its aftermath had left him 'a physical wreck'. His weight had shot up alarmingly again, helped by heavy drinking that now ran at 'about a pint of whisky a day'. His solution was, as usual, to pull down all the shutters, give up spirits and go on a crash diet. He also – for an interlude at least – gave up John Reid, booking himself in singly at a tennis ranch in Arizona. 'It was the first time I'd been on my own for four and a half years. I spent a month doing nothing but hitting a ball around, seven hours a day, and lost twenty-eight pounds.' The tireless competitor could not relax: he won the mixed doubles tournament once and the men's singles twice.

His unexpected holiday from the road was also spent in writing songs for other people: 'Let Me Be Your Car' for Rod Stewart,

'Snookeroo' for Ringo Starr. He spent several months working on a new song for the Beach Boys, agonising about whether they'd even like it when he finally managed to finish it. He 'got into' the falsetto style of new black soul groups like the Stylistics and talked of making a cover version of their hit, 'Rock 'n' Roll Baby'. At the same time, he longed to write material for some traditional, Motown-oriented group like Gladys Knight and the Pips.

Caribou's other spin-off hit was 'The Bitch Is Back', that sardonic tribute of Maxine Taupin's to Elton in waspish mood. Released on 30 August, it reached number four in America, despite some local difficulties. For 'bitch', though a term of mildest chaff in Britain, has an almost Oedipal charge to American ears. Around this innocent rock-'n'-roll shouter swirled a moral furore that all Bernie Taupin's lyrics about murder, arson and lesbianism had not been able to arouse. Many radio stations insisted on bleeping the offensive word. Since it occurs approximately thirty times throughout the song, the result was ludicrous: 'I'm a [bleep!] I'm a [bleep!] Yeah the [bleep!] is back. Stone cold sober as a matter of fact. I can [bleep!] I can [bleep!] I can, better than you. It's the way that I do. The things that I do . . .'

One further performance was added to Elton's schedule, at the behest of his newest fan. Princess Margaret had been greatly taken by his concert for the Invalid Aid Association and, not long afterwards, got in touch with their mutual friends Bryan Forbes and Nanette Newman. 'She said she'd been telling the Queen Mother about Elton,' Nanette Newman remembers. 'The Queen Mother was terribly keen to see him as well.'

This first of many private command appearances took place at the Queen Mother's out-of-town residence, Royal Lodge, Windsor, which happens to be located conveniently only a mile or two down the road from Virginia Water. At dinner beforehand, a nervous Elton picked up what he took to be a silver salt cellar and found himself sprinkling sugar over his hors d'oeuvres. There was further embarrassment when he went into an adjoining room to change from black tie into his cream canvas suit, embroidered with the chinoiserie artwork from the cover of *Goodbye Yellow Brick Road*. He was standing there with his trousers off when the door suddenly opened and the ever-unpredictable Princess Margaret looked in.

The Queen Mother enjoyed the subsequent recital, much as she seems to enjoy everything. 'Elton just did it perfectly,' Nanette Newman remembers. 'In "Your Song", when he got to the line "I'd buy a big house", he changed it to "I'd buy Windsor Castle, Your Majesty".'

The performance over, Her Majesty announced there would now be general dancing. With that, she went to the gramophone, put on her own top pop favourite – a military air called 'Slattery's Mounted Foot' – then seized Elton and vigorously partnered him around the room.

In mid-1974, Steve Brown left his job as general manager of Rocket Records. The ostensible reason was a disagreement with John Reid over the direction the company should take. As another ex-Rocket man remembers, there was a falling-out between them when Reid returned from his enforced stay in New Zealand to find the office, under Brown, not functioning to his satisfaction.

The loss to Elton, in personal terms, was enormous. More than anyone else, Steve Brown had been responsible for putting Bernie Taupin and him on the right creative track. Instead of selfishly commandeering them to further his own career as a producer, he had built them a matchless studio support system that included the indispensable Gus Dudgeon and the brilliant Paul Buckmaster. For more than five years, his enthusiasm, wisdom, judgement and calm had been unshakeable. But in a superstar's life, even the most valued and trusty friend cannot expect to last for ever.

As well as leaving Rocket, Brown left the music business altogether, to pursue a vocation long hinted at by his rustic hippy garb and the mural of fields and cows around his Soho office wall. He became a farmer.

David Croker, his replacement as boss of Rocket, was an almost equally long-standing Elton supporter and friend. Croker had run the Harvest label at EMI when John Reid was running Tamla-Motown and could claim much of the credit for first bringing Elton and Reid together. Indeed, it was always said in their circle that Croker had grown tired of the shabby youth who kept coming to plunder his record cupboard, and had tactfully steered him down the hall to John Reid.

Another new Rocket recruit was Clive Banks, the young promotion man whom John Reid had long been trying to woo away from Dick James Music. That meant that almost everyone important to Elton in his DJM days had now transferred allegiance to Rocket.

By the time Croker and Banks arrived, Elton's concept of the perfect record company had come true, up to a point. Rocket, in its first year, had signed eight acts, solo singers and bands, paying nothing like $8 million in advances, but guaranteeing each a generous royalty when success should finally come. The problem was that, try as he might to distance himself from it, Rocket was indivisibly linked with Elton's own stupendous success. Kiki Dee's breakthrough had to a very large extent been due to his personal endorsement and involvement. Having seen that great result, Rocket's other acts expected similar involvement and similar success – a hope, in every case, doomed to bitter disappointment.

They were an oddly mixed bag, reflecting the disparate tastes of the company's talent-spotting directors. Two solo singers, Mike Silver and Tony Bird, had been Steve Brown protégés, and did not long survive Brown's departure. There was a band named Longdancer, containing Nigel Olsson's younger brother and an obscure Scots hippy guitarist named Dave Stewart. There were bands named Stackridge, Casablanca and the Hudson Brothers, the latter of whom Bernie Taupin was to produce. There was also a teenage Welsh singer, Maldwyn Pope, who might have suspected his ultimate destiny when, at an early press conference, Elton absent-mindedly referred to him as 'Blodwyn Pig'.

The saddest case was a singer-pianist named Frankie Fish, who joined Rocket as a gofer on a small weekly retainer, very much as Elton and Bernie had originally joined Dick James Music. 'Frankie worshipped Elton – and it was obvious he wanted to be another Elton John,' Clive Banks remembers. 'He'd do his best to dress outrageously – like go around wearing one red sock and one green. He was very sweet, and Elton had a bit of a soft spot for him, kind of like "This is me five years ago". He was given demo time, and mastering time, and more demo time and more mastering time, but nothing really ever came of it. No one knew what to do with him, and no one had the heart to let him go.'

Most of the Rocket signings accepted their failure to ignite with resignation. One who did not was Longdancer's guitarist Dave Stewart, a scruffy, dejected figure, unimaginable as today's charismatic co-star of the Eurythmics. 'I'd go into my office,' David Croker remembers, 'and Dave Stewart would be sitting on my desk with his guitar, waiting to play me his new songs. Sitting on my desk crosslegged! He'd got some kind of job at a record shop in an Underground station, and he'd ring me up from there and stay on the phone for hours.' Stewart himself has since admitted that, thanks to drug-use, the mid-Seventies were a 'blank' period in his life.

Despite Elton's dreams, the sponsorship of new, young talent was not to be Rocket's forte. Aside from Kiki Dee – and Elton himself, in due course – the label's greatest success would come in boosting the careers of two established stars and early Reg Dwight heroes, Neil Sedaka and Cliff Richard. The changeless record fan could thus pay some dues at last for those hours of Dansette joy in his bedroom in Metroland.

Neil Sedaka, in 1974, was suffering the eclipse common to so many early-Sixties jukebox idols. The prototype singer-songwriter, along with Paul Anka, his bubbly dual-tracked hits, like 'Oh, Carol' and 'Happy Birthday, Sweet Sixteen', were regarded as no more than dusty relics in America. His British fans remaining loyal, he had moved with his family to London and was enjoying a revival in the British charts with new songs like 'Standing on the Inside'. Yet he still had no American recording deal, nor any prospect of one.

When Neil Sedaka met Elton that summer, his single 'Laughter in the Rain' had just gone to number 15 in Britain. 'One of the first things Elton said to me was "What's doing with you in America?"' Sedaka remembers. '"Don't ask!" I told him. "Over there, they think I'm a ghost!"'

The two quickly became good friends, finding they had much in common. Sedaka, too, had been classically trained, at New York's Juilliard school, and would still include the odd piece of Bach or Brahms in his stage performances. Happily married for many years, he had two young children, to whom Elton immediately became an unofficial uncle. Hero-worshipped as he was by Elton, Sedaka's friends urged him to seek a contract with Rocket. But he was embarrassed to presume on their friendship.

In August, Sedaka and his wife Leba gave a party at their service flat in Mayfair. Elton came along and played 'Daniel' as a duet with Sedaka, apologising that it was 'just an oldie'. During the evening, Sedaka plucked up courage, took Elton and John Reid into another room and offered his British hits to Rocket for release in America. Elton immediately jumped at the idea. '"My God!" he said. "Why didn't I think of this? You're handing us gold bricks."'

Neil Sedaka's 'Laughter in the Rain' was released on American Rocket in October 1974. Twelve weeks later, it was number one, Sedaka's first hit in his native land since 1963 and only the second US number one in his career. It stayed in the American Top 40 for fifteen weeks, also becoming his only single other than 'Breaking Up Is Hard to Do' to sell a million copies.

The result was a Neil Sedaka revival in America, a sold-out appearance at the LA Troubadour and a Rocket album, *Sedaka's Back*, containing his recent British hits, which went gold late in 1975. To complete his triumph, Sedaka subsequently reached number eight with a slow ballad version of 'Breaking Up Is Hard to Do', so becoming the first artist ever to chart with two interpretations of the same song.

No hungry A & R man ever worked for an artist as Elton worked on the relaunch of Neil Sedaka. 'He even wrote the liner notes for the album cover,' Sedaka remembers. 'He went on radio and promoted it, as EJ the DJ. Here was the most successful recording artist in the world, being the best PR man anyone could have.'

For a time the Sedakas with their children Dara and Mark became another of Elton's surrogate families. Sedaka himself was a thorough-going fellow pro, more satisfying to talk to than most in the superstar's growing entourage. 'He'd call me up from the road sometimes, saying things like he was worried about his voice and whether it would stand up to all the strain,' Sedaka remembers. 'I'd tell him he had to take care of it. Drink tea with honey. Avoid smoky discos.' Leba Sedaka grew fond of him, despite a healthy scepticism about most people in her husband's profession. 'He was extraordi-narily sweet and generous. And I don't mean generous in the Elvis Presley way: "You want this ring? Here, take it." For example, he knew that, at that time, I was collecting antique silver picture frames. He went to the trouble of buying me some, finding the right shop, choosing exactly the right pattern.'

The Sedakas also spent time at Caribou ranch during the planning of Neil's American renaissance. Returning with Elton from Denver to Los Angeles produced a scene that Leba has never forgotten.

'We were due to fly out of Denver at something like eight o'clock in the morning. The night before, I said to Elton, "We're travelling real early tomorrow, so please don't wear anything outrageous." "I won't," he said. "I've got nothing to wear anyway. I've just been on a diet."

'Next morning, we're waiting for him at the airport. Down the concourse that's full of redneck Colorado types comes Elton dressed all in white – white suit covered in rhinestones, white shoes with rhinestones, a white bowler hat and a cane.

'The next thing is, he has to go up to the airline desk to collect a ticket that's been prepaid for him. The girl at the desk is one of those who hardly even bother to look up. "Surname?" she asks Elton. "John," he tells her. "Initial?" she asks. "E," Elton says. Then she asks him, "Do you have any means of identification?" "My God!" we all said. "Are you joking? Don't you realise who this is?" "I'm sorry," the girl says. "To issue a prepaid ticket I have to have identification." All that Elton's carrying in this white suit is the diary that he carries everywhere with him, and some cash. There's no way we can get the girl to accept that he's E. John without a formal ID. The only way he can get the ticket is to pay out all the cash he has on him.'

Among all the teenage heroes Elton's fame allowed him to meet, none meant more to him than John Lennon. They had been introduced by Tony King, the ex-DJM song plugger who went on to become an executive at Apple in its final days. Friendship did not immediately blossom, for Lennon was by then in exile in New York, and in their spasmodic encounters Elton was too consumed by adulatory shyness to establish much of a rapport. 'I nursed the friendship along for quite a time,' Tony King says now. 'I knew that, once they did get to know each other, they'd be friends for life.'

Distant though Elton now was from Dick James, the Beatles and their vast folklore remained an insistent subtext to his life. Tony King's secretary at Apple was a girl named Margo Stevens, a Beatles fan who had found her way inside after a vigil of years on the front doorstep. Margo got to know Elton well on his many visits to Tony King's office. When Apple folded as a record company late in 1974, it was easy for King to get her a job with Big Pig Music, the publishing division of Rocket.

Across the Atlantic, John Lennon had been going through troubled times. His marriage to Yoko Ono – that power supposedly greater than the Beatles – seemed to have broken down. In addition, he was fighting attempts by US Immigration, backed up by the CIA, to deport him as an 'undesirable alien'.

In 1973, Lennon had left Yoko and their New York apartment, and gone to Los Angeles for the year on the loose he would subsequently call his 'lost weekend'. It was during these months of rediscovered bachelorhood that he and Elton properly became friends. A sequence in Lennon's posthumous movie autobiography, *Imagine*, shows them together in some nameless velvet-curtained West Coast dive, waltzing with a manly figure in drag, their mutual friend and intermediary Tony King.

Hero-worship was not all on the younger musician's side. Lennon was amazed by Elton's stage act, especially remembering what used to be expected of him in the Beatles' performing days. 'We only had to do twenty minutes – and that still used to seem like an hour to me,' he told Elton. 'There were four of us, but you do two and a half hours on your own. How the fuck do you do it?' He would often say that the pressure on the Beatles in the Sixties seemed minuscule compared to what Elton had to endure.

Bernie Taupin, who also was in Los Angeles for much of that time, thinks the stories of Lennon's lost weekend mostly exaggerated. 'Everyone likes to make out that in that time away from Yoko, he was terrible and unhappy and drunk all the time, getting thrown out of the Troubadour with Harry Nilsson and sticking Kotex on his head. All I know is that every time I went around with him he was perfectly normal. I remember going with him to see Bob Marley at the Roxy, and we had a great night.'

To Bernie, Lennon was always the same generous enthusiast who had given that vital early accolade to the lyrics of 'Your Song'. 'He was always very sweet, and totally encouraging. He made a point of telling me he liked the things I wrote, which always meant a huge amount to me. And always incredibly modest about the fantastic things he'd done. He'd say things like, "Er, I wrote this song called 'Across The Universe', I don't know if you've heard of it, but anyway . . ."'

Elton's next single was planned both as a homage and a boost to Lennon's caved-in self-confidence. The ultimate Seventies star plunged off on another new way by covering the ultimate Beatles Sixties song, 'Lucy in the Sky with Diamonds'. The session took place at Caribou ranch in July, with help from Lennon himself, characteristically billed as 'the Reggae guitars of Dr Winston O'Boogie'. Those who had thought no one but Lennon could ever sing the song were to be charmed by Elton's version, modern in its reggae lilt but also perfectly mirroring that 1967 'summer of love' when Reggie Dwight used to wander round London, a forlorn Tiny Tim with his plastic carrier bag.

The following month, Elton was in a New York studio doing backup vocals for Lennon's new album, *Walls and Bridges*. The result was 'Whatever Gets You Thru the Night', a scattergun rocker which Elton's simplicity and energy helped to make more accessible than any Lennon song since 'Imagine'.

In the euphoria of the session, Elton asked Lennon if he'd also do the song with him live onstage – an enormous question. Since leaving the Beatles, Lennon had refused all attempts to get him to perform, bar one charity show in 1972. As far as millions of adoring fans were concerned, he had not been seen singing with a guitar since the Beatles' farewell concert on the Apple roof. His stage fright, always chronic, had become something like psychosis in the years of New York hermitage. In a spirit of pure banter he replied to Elton that if 'Whatever Gets You Thru the Night' made number one, they would perform it onstage together.

Elton's arrival back at Caribou studios for the second time in six months was not quite what MCA meant by 'slowing down'. For a follow-up to *Caribou*, it had been decided merely to release a compilation album, *Elton John's Greatest Hits*. But a new album for early 1975 had to be written and recorded before he began his traditional grand autumn tour of America.

The attacks on *Caribou* had chastened Bernie, perhaps even more than Elton. In atonement he planned a *tour de force* – no grab-bag of borrowed styles and characters this time, but a concept album, as none before had been, recreating his and Elton's early partnership and life together in the half-childlike, half-mythic style of C. S. Lewis or J. R. R. Tolkien. For Elton he chose the pseudonym 'Captain Fantastic', evoking caped superheroes of Fifties comic books. Bernie himself, simple country boy with head full of Wild West dreams, would be 'the Brown Dirt Cowboy'.

For the first time, the lyrics were not dashed off and fired at Elton in eight-minute bursts, but worked on all together, as if stanzas in a narrative poem like the Macaulay that Bernie's grandfather used to read to him in Owmby-by-Spital. One stanza was to be a portrait of Elton as Reggie Dwight, that day Bernie had first met him at the DJM studio. Another was to recall their early vicissitudes as songwriters and all-night vigils in Oxford Street coffee bars. Another was to describe the ménage at the Furlong Road flat with Linda Woodrow, when a wedding all but took place, and Brown Dirt Cowboy had been obliged to pull Captain Fantastic's head out of the gas oven.

It was an ambitious project and Bernie, for the first time in his literary career, found himself rewriting, recasting, agonising and rubbing things out. Elton, however, underwent no such creative agonies. He wrote the music for the entire epic while crossing to New York on the final voyage of the French luxury liner SS *France*. 'I'd tried to book the ship's music-room, but an opera singer had got it for the whole five days. The only time she wasn't there was when she scoffed her lunch for two hours. So every lunchtime I'd nip in there and grab the piano just for those two hours.'

The recording at Caribou – each stanza in the order Bernie had written it – took longer than any in the John–Taupin oeuvre to date. As Elton himself remarked in some awe, 'It's the first time we ever took a month to make an album.'

The breach was now healed with his producer, Gus Dudgeon. For Dudgeon considered that these new songs more than made up for the sloppiness of *Caribou*. 'The whole thing is perfect, it's absolutely perfect,' he told a music magazine. 'I can't fault it. I've managed to get the best sound I've ever got, and it's the loudest album I've ever cut, despite its being twenty-five and a half minutes long on one side. It's the best the band have ever played, it's the best Elton has ever played and it's the best collection of songs. He sings better than he's ever sung. There's not one song on there that's less than incredible.'

The simple private Boeing airliner of last year had been refitted in a style better suiting MCA's $8-million property. It was now *Starship 1*, a purpose-built flying palace for rock royalty in transit. The original space for 138 people had been converted to accommodate only forty in a luxurious den with couches, armchairs, cocktail bar, gourmet kitchen, hi-fi and movies on video. For the monarch himself, there was a master suite, complete with fur-covered bed that Hugh Hefner might have envied. The red, white and blue fuselage was embellished with stars and (to prove how democratic kings can be) the legend ELTON JOHN BAND TOUR 1974.

Thirty-three people assembled for a group photograph before *Starship 1* took to the skies. There was Elton, in turquoise and white jumpsuit and Somerset Maugham panama, leaning on a thin ebony cane. There was Bernie Taupin, and Kiki Dee, the warm-up act. There were Nigel and Dee and their consorts, and Davey Johnstone, who now went out with Kiki, and the clerkly percussionist Ray Cooper. There were the four-man Muscle Shoals Horns, augmenting the stage line-up. There was John Reid in a décolleté blue boilersuit, holding a clipboard. There was Howard Rose, the American booking agent. There was Elton's original media champion from the *LA Times*, Robert Hilburn. There were Rocket people, roadies, sound and lighting men, personal assistants, gofers: truly a kingly court of straggled hair, fitted plaid shirts, flared jeans, clogs and peep-toed platforms.

The group also included one pair of newlyweds. Rocket's young promotion man Clive Banks had recently married Moira Bellas, a press officer with Warner Bros Records. Elton had attended their wedding – and shown more than a passing interest in the bride's Chrissie Walsh dress. 'It had a winter theme,' Moira remembers. 'It was white, covered with a mass of blue appliqué icicles. When everyone else saw it, they said, "Mm, lovely dress." When Elton saw it, he said, "Mm, have to get one of those."'

His insistence that Clive Banks should go on the tour, and bring Moira as well, was typical Elton generosity. 'He made you feel that, however huge he'd become, you were a part of it,' Banks remembers. 'At that time, I'd never even flown in a plane before. Suddenly here I am on the other side of the world, travelling round in this massive private jet which had showers and beds in it, and cocktail bars and a piano.'

Starship 1 drastically reduced the fatigue of constant travel between one-night stands. For the tour's opening Southern leg, Elton could base himself in New Orleans, flying out each day to his concerts in Dallas, Houston, Mobile and Tuscaloosa. The short afternoon hops were beguiled by games of backgammon and pool, and brand-new movies like *The Exorcist*. Robert Hilburn remembers that, for some reason possibly connected with high altitude, the movie's famous scenes of revolving heads and squirting green bile reduced everyone to hysterical laughter.

John Reid, working with Howard Rose, had produced the smoothest tour organisation yet. 'It was like some presidential thing,' Clive Banks remembers. 'We'd fly in to a private airstrip. There'd be a fleet of limos waiting. We'd be taken into town with a police escort, driving down the wrong lane of the freeway. The entourage would be shoved in right at the front of the audience. Fifteen or twenty minutes later, Elton would be onstage. A couple of numbers before the end, we'd get the nod to go back to the limos. Elton would come out, get into the back of his, straight out to the airstrip again, and an hour later we'd be back in New Orleans.'

There were, inevitably, some hitches. In Dallas, when *Starship 1* landed, the limo fleet was waiting at the wrong end of the airstrip and had to race down the runway, as Robert Hilburn said, 'like cowboys trying to catch up with lost cattle'. In Mobile, the stage sound monitors gave such trouble that Elton furiously kicked one over, and refused to do an encore until the tumultuous clapping, stamping and whistling changed his mind. Though the concerts were usually miracles of mass good humour, the occasional security man would be seen mishandling boys or girls in the traditional rush to the stage during 'Saturday Night's Alright for Fighting'. This always enraged Elton – and also enraged John Reid, beyond any seeming care for his personal safety. 'John used to go berserk if the security men turned on the kids,' Dee Murray remembers. 'I've seen him do some incredible things – launch himself off a lighting tower to mix it with some huge Texan bouncer built like an all-in wrestler. You couldn't fault the guy for guts.'

The staging was the most extravagant yet, with Elton's name and each of the band's spelt out in neon above them. Elton's new stage costumes also touched new heights of the asexually bizarre. One was a black lurex bodystocking from which dozens of coloured balls sprouted on tendrils of piano wire. Another – by Hollywood designer Elizabeth Courtney – was a pink and silver sequinned catsuit worn with an outsize Edwardian dowager duchess hat, trailing huge white and pink ostrich boas. Another was mingled green, yellow and scarlet plumes, with a collar of pheasant feathers, two feet long. Another was a jumpsuit and cloak of diamanté-sewn orange and gold, worn with the jewelled skullcap of some fourteenth-century French dauphin. There was also a multicoloured cloak that spread over half the stage behind him, and a top hat trimmed with further snatchings from a giant pheasant's tail. To set these off, there were spectacles framed by feathered whorls, Odeon palm trees or thick circles of cuddly white mink.

Robert Hilburn was amazed to see how, even as the most fantastical apparition, Elton still drove himself unmercifully through every second of his two-and-a-half-hour set. The Aztec winged god, dowager duchess or French dauphin seldom lasted more than minutes in the frantic exertion and crippling heat. Feathered bonnet, skullcap, cloak or boa would be thrown off, leaving a spangled, half-naked figure whose abundant body hair contrasted ever more painfully with his monkish tonsure. 'The whole point of touring is to strive for something better,' he told Hilburn. 'Forget about the costumes and staging – it's the music that counts. If you don't keep improving, you're wasting your time. I've said it before: I don't want to end up like Chuck Berry or Little Richard – and I don't mean to degrade those people. But I couldn't stand the thought of coming on and playing "Crocodile Rock" ten years from now. That would be a nightmare.

'Sure, you can get excited about your own success, but that doesn't mean you're satisfied. I may have a number one record, but then I'll see someone on television and think, "God, I wish I could play like that." There's always something to strive for.'

Hilburn was used to world-weary rock superstars who toured only as an act of supreme condescension, treating their audience with indifference or disdain, refusing to sign autographs or pose for pictures, finding every excuse to delay their final, ungracious appearance on stage. Compared with these dilatory oiks, Elton's punctuality, civility – most of all, his undiminished enthusiasm – seemed marvellous. 'I can't understand people who say they don't like doing concerts. It's the greatest thing in the world to stand on a stage and see people in the front rows smiling, and know they came to see you. That's why I get so upset if I play badly. There's nothing worse than knowing thousands of people have gone away, thinking "Oh boy, what a drag." That's what you struggle against every night.'

Even Elton's own London staff had not grasped the full magnitude of his American fame. 'Nowadays when someone like Michael Jackson comes to London, you can avoid him, because there are other things going on,' Clive Banks says. 'But when Elton was on that tour in 1974, the whole of America knew he was there. When he came in to each city to play, there literally was talk of nothing else. In Los Angeles especially it was impossible to get away from him. You'd go into a shop – just a grocery – and you'd hear his name, Elton, Elton, Elton . . . "Have you got your tickets?" "Is he doing an extra show?" "You're English, you must know him." It was a buzz totally all over town.'

In Los Angeles Elton had been booked for three consecutive nights at the 18,500-seat Forum arena in Inglewood. A fourth show was hastily added when all 55,500 tickets were sold within six hours of the box office opening. Elton confessed to Robert Hilburn that when people told him things like that, he still had difficulty believing them. The fretful, pessimistic ghost of Reggie Dwight would never quite go away. 'I keep ringing them up and saying, "Are you sure we're sold out? Are you sure?"'

His opening night back in LA was the now traditional celebrity-studded night, attended by Elizabeth Taylor, Barbra Streisand, Ringo Starr, David Cassidy and Harry Nilsson. During the finale Elton lost his temper again, this time with ushers who were blocking the fans' surge to the stage. Rushing to a side mike, he shouted at the ushers to 'get the fuck out of it'.

Based in Malibu, in a beach-front house rented from Olivia Newton-John, he spent the time between concerts in his favourite LA pastime, 'looting'. As usual, he bought with equal prodigality for whomever happened to be with him. Like others of his entourage with scruples, Clive Banks grew adept at sidestepping the ludicrous generosity. 'He'd go into some store to buy an eight-track player, which were quite novel things then. There'd be three or four other people with him, and he'd buy one for each of them – "five eight-track players, please", like ordering a round of drinks or ice cream. You felt there was a bit of guilt there, like he felt he really ought not to be buying these expensive things just for him.'

It was a generosity that made no distinction between a superstar friend and a relatively junior member of his entourage. Hearing that Clive Banks's birthday fell in the LA week, Elton organised a surprise party for him at Chasen's restaurant. 'I didn't even want to go out that night,' Banks remembers. 'I was complaining because, it being Chasen's, I had to borrow a jacket and a tie to wear. I walk in, and there's this huge table with everyone round it, and Elton's at the piano, playing "Happy Birthday to You". Cheech and Chong are at the table, and Fred Astaire's sitting downstairs. I remember, Fred Astaire said "Hello" to Elton.'

He was, once again, in his almost predictable place at the top of American and British charts – this time with both an album and a single. The compilation *Elton John's Greatest Hits*, released in November, not only went to the number-one spot faster than any of its predecessors, but also stayed there longer: eleven weeks in Britain, ten in America. 'Lucy in the Sky with Diamonds' was number one in America and ten in Britain. He ate up the airwaves with new songs, with old songs back to 1970, with his fan's cover version of a song previously thought unrepeatable.

Whatever he touched, however incidentally, seemed to grow golden wings and fly. His protégée Kiki Dee, making her first American tour in his retinue, now also had her first American Top 20 single, 'I've Got the Music in Me' – a hit that owed its hilarious energy to drastic intervention by Elton. 'Kiki had a bit of a studio complex, and couldn't seem to get the vocal together,' Gus Dudgeon, the producer, remembers. 'While she was doing it, Elton crept in through a back door, hid behind a screen, took off all his clothes and suddenly streaked across the studio, stark naked. Kiki nearly freaked, but kept on singing. That's why the vocal came out so great.'

Best of all was the fillip he had given to his backup guitarist on Lucy, Dr Winston O'Boogie. For, with Elton singing backup vocals, 'Whatever Gets You Thru the Night' had pushed John Lennon back into the pop mainstream. In November, it went to number one in America – Lennon's only number-one single outside the Beatles in his lifetime.

Elton had gleefully contacted Lennon and reminded him of his promise to repeat their duet onstage if it made the top spot. Whether Lennon would keep that promise was far from certain, however. The obviously perfect time would be the climactic moment of Elton's present tour, his New York concert at Madison Square Garden on Thanksgiving night, 28 November. But the curse of the Beatles remained strong. The man for whom the world had screamed its heart out, ten years before, was more frightened than the newest novice of facing an audience with a guitar. And, even if he could nerve himself to go on, he genuinely doubted whether anyone would be that interested.

His life, anyway, was still in chaos, torn between his Chinese girlfriend May Pang and pleadings with Yoko to resuscitate their marriage. Thus far, Yoko had remained impervious. 'I'd been married twice before, and divorced,' she says now. 'For me, that was what happened to marriages. They ended.'

Even when Lennon agreed to rehearse with Elton, there still were doubts about whether he would really go through with it. 'They'd booked a little studio in New York to run through some numbers with the band,' David Croker remembers. 'When I got there, they were leaving – it was all over. They couldn't have been rehearsing longer than about an hour and a half.'

Meanwhile the word was out, in New York and London. There was, at least, a strong chance that Elton John's Thanksgiving concert at Madison Square Garden would include an appearance by John Lennon. With or without Lennon, it was to be a gala occasion, crowning a still more stupendous tour, attended by a large British media contingent flown to New York at Rocket Records' expense.

Among the party was Margo Stevens, secretary to Elton's friend Tony King, the girl who had spent literally years of her life waiting on Beatle doorsteps. Margo naturally had longed to see John Lennon onstage again, but could not afford the fare to New York. Hearing of this, Elton bought her a first-class air ticket and reserved a room for her at the Sherry-Netherland hotel. 'He rang me up out of the blue and said, "Is your passport in order? Can you be at Heathrow airport first thing tomorrow morning?"'

At Heathrow airport, she joined Rocket's VIP group, among them Sheila and Fred Farebrother and Alan Freeman, the veteran disc jockey, whom Elton had asked to do a walk-on at the concert. 'I went through the security check with Alan Freeman, which was a mistake,' Margo remembers. 'He was covered with chains and medallions, which set off all the anti-terrorist alarms.'

In New York, someone else was taking a strong interest in Elton's Thanksgiving concert and its attendant rumour. Yoko Ono contacted Tony King and asked him to arrange tickets for her and her current man-friend. As she admits now, she did not know with what precise objective. 'I asked for a seat where I could see the stage, but where I couldn't be seen.'

Up until the very last minute, Lennon himself seemed to be looking for a chance to duck out. Margo Stevens, who talked to him only hours before the concert, remembers him still doubting and havering. When he turned up at Madison Square Garden, it was in a plain black suit and dark glasses, as if trying to resist the notion he had ever been a rock-'n'-roll performer. Backstage he was so nervous, he went into the men's room and vomited. He even momentarily forgot the order of the strings on his guitar, and had to ask Davey Johnstone, from Elton's band, to tune it for him. Just before showtime, a messenger delivered two identical gift boxes, one for him, one for Elton. Inside each was a white gardenia and a note: 'Best of luck and all my love, Yoko.' 'Thank goodness Yoko's not here tonight,' Lennon said. 'Otherwise I know I'd never be able to go out there.'

No one was completely certain it would happen until halfway through the concert, when Elton paused at the piano, in his huge pheasant-feathered top hat. 'Seeing as it's Thanksgiving,' he said, 'we thought we'd make tonight a little bit of a joyous occasion by inviting someone up with us on to the stage . . .'

In the wings, still hesitating, Lennon suddenly turned to Bernie Taupin. 'He said, "I'm not going on unless you go on with me",' Bernie remembers. 'So I just went forward a little way with him, then he sort of hugged me, and I said, "You're on your own."'

The moment when Lennon's black-suited figure appeared will never be forgotten by anyone who saw it. The whole Madison Square Garden audience, 18,000 people, rose to their feet as one, with a roar far and away above the routine adulation of pop. House lights were turned full on, showing him the full scale and expression of the delight at every point. 'I'd heard of applause literally making a place shake, but I'd never seen it before,' David Croker says. 'That night, though, it was true, You could feel the floorboards quivering under your feet.'

The roar went on and on, Lennon trying to hide his bewilderment by pulling faces and pretending to loll against the piano, while Elton looked on and beamed like some proud parent at prize day. Even now, Lennon did not realise that Yoko was in the audience. 'I knew he was getting a wonderful reception,' she says now. 'But when he bowed, it was too quickly and too many times. And I suddenly thought, "He looks so lonely up there."'

The set was brief and, progressively, brilliant. Lennon sang 'Whatever Gets You Thru the Night' as promised, with Elton's backup vocal like a friendly instructor, keeping him on track. Elton sang 'Lucy in the Sky with Diamonds', backed, with evident high approval, by John. The thin-nosed face then shifted its gum, looked around and smiled with a gleam of its old subversiveness. 'We thought we'd do a number of an old estranged fiancé of mine, called Paul . . .' he said. The song was 'I Saw Her Standing There', from days when Beatles songs were as perfect in their way as primitive paintings, and Reggie Dwight used to sit in his bedroom, dreaming, as the yellow and black Parlophone label flicked round and round.

'Everybody around me was crying,' Margo Stevens remembers. 'John was hugging Elton, and Elton seemed to be crying, too. What was really incredible was how, when the audience finally let John go off, Elton managed to pick up his own performance and carry on again. When he did 'Candle in the Wind', it was the first time I'd seen everybody strike lighters and matches in the darkness. He finished with 'The Bitch Is Back', and John came on again, so did Bernie. By that time you as a spectator were completely wrung out and drained, so God knows what it must have felt like for Elton.'

Afterwards, Yoko and her date for the evening came backstage to visit John and his date for the evening. 'We immediately started talking, each of us totally forgetting the person we were supposed to be with,' Yoko says. 'After that, John invited me to an art show. We started dating all over again.' Their marriage tested and found durable, they settled down in the Dakota Building to have a child and – so they thought – to grow old together.

As for Elton, clasped in John Lennon's hug, with 18,000 voices blessing his loyalty, respect and unselfishness, all he could stammer out was, 'This has been a very emotional night for me . . .' Thanksgiving, 1974, indeed, was to prove his career's uttermost high-water mark. And on that authentically historic night, the same could be said of him as nearly always. He had been a very, very good boy.

11

'My God! It's all going to crumble and go to Hell!'

EARLY in 1975, Sue Ayton returned to the Dick James organisation. Elton's friend, and almost-girlfriend, of the late Sixties had left her job as Dick James's secretary to get married, three years earlier. Now divorced and seeking a job back in the music business, she happened to meet Stephen James, who by then was largely running Dick James Music on his father's behalf. Happy to regain such a valued employee, Stephen offered her the job of managing DJM's international division.

Back in her old surroundings, Sue Ayton quickly noticed the huge change in DJM's relationship with Elton. 'When I'd left in 1972, he'd still been coming in all the time, to see Dick or talk about the next album with Stephen. But now you hardly ever saw him. In all that second time I was there, I think he came in about twice.'

Little now remained of the edifice which Dick James had constructed around Reggie Dwight in 1967. His management had been relinquished to John Reid in May 1973. The publishing agreement, for Elton and Bernie Taupin together, had ended in November that same year, and had not been renewed. All that was left was Elton's four-year recording agreement, due to expire in February 1975.

Though reconciled to losing Elton's management and publishing (the latter bearable, since his pre-1973 songs remained copyright of DJM), James naturally had no wish to lose the world's biggest recording star. Nor was it yet a foregone conclusion that he would. Despite their recent estrangement, Elton was unswerving in acknowledgement of his professional debt to DJM and his affection for Dick James personally. His own Rocket label, so he constantly stressed, was not a vehicle for himself, but for new young talent. It was with some hope, therefore, that Stephen James approached John Reid in 1974 and asked if the recording contract could be renewed.

Reid did not refuse outright, especially since, in addition to an increase in future royalties, DJM also offered to boost the percentage on product already released. What Stephen James describes as 'quite meaningful' discussions took place between John Reid and him towards the end of 1974. The sticking point was Reid's insistence that DJM should put money into Rocket and that a £30,000 advance be paid on future British albums, which were then to be released unconditionally. 'He was saying we had to release stuff whether we liked it or not,' Stephen James remembers. 'That was the point when I decided to back out.'

Elton's recording agreement would thus terminate with his next album, *Captain Fantastic and the Brown Dirt Cowboy*. But that did not quite sever all links with the James organisation. Over the past two years, he had fallen behind with the annual quota of albums he was contracted to deliver to DJM. After *Captain Fantastic* he still owed two more – a studio-made one and a 'floater', the contractual term for a live album or compilation of past hits. Though legally separated, artist and record company had to continue in harness for at least another year.

This uncomfortable situation was made more so by the extreme personal hostility which now existed between Stephen James and John Reid. To Stephen, Reid was the viper who had betrayed his father's trust, using everything James senior had taught him to steal away and alienate DJM's most priceless asset. To Reid, Stephen was a pampered boss's son, contemptibly unaware of the tooth-and-claw struggle others had to go through to attain success. Things had got so bad between them that the simplest negotiation took on the character of fight to the death. 'I remember once trying to arrange a meeting for them at MIDEM,' Sue Ayton says. 'Each of them had set a time that didn't suit the other, and I couldn't get either of them to back down.'

Captain Fantastic and the Brown Dirt Cowboy provoked the most spectacular ructions yet. The sleeve concept had been masterminded by Bernie Taupin, whose idea it was to commission Alan Aldridge, the leading Pop Art illustrator of that day. Aldridge's design matched any of his famous reinterpretations of *Alice in Wonderland* or *The Butterfly Ball*. On the front cover, Elton as metropolitan Captain Fantastic, in top hat, silver goggles, mauve pompoms and spats, bestrode an Aldridge phantasmagoria of humanoid fish and birds in pierrot ruffles and jester's caps. On the back, Bernie Taupin as rural Brown Dirt Cowboy floated in a bubble, surrounded by pensive farm animals and insects. Two smaller bubbles contained the Elton John Band; in a third, tiny one sat a figure in a pink tie looking suspiciously like John Reid.

The Aldridge design was presented to Stephen James along with a bill far exceeding DJM's budget for album artwork. Faced with such costly *faits accomplis* in the past, Stephen had always swallowed his annoyance for the long-term aim of keeping Elton happy. But now no such constraints applied. He therefore told Reid that the design was too expensive – as well as 'too introverted and indulgent' – and that DJM would not pay for it. If Elton insisted on using it, the cost would have to be met by his own organisation.

Hours of battle finally produced a compromise, symbolising what a gulf now lay between Captain Fantastic and those who had launched him. The Alan Aldridge design would be used, but would not be paid for by DJM. The copyright would belong to Rocket, who would lease it to DJM for the lifetime of the album.

'Philadelphia Freedom', released on 28 February, was inspired by Elton's latest bout of fan-worship. In his tennis jag the previous summer, he had been thrilled to meet several Wimbledon champions, past and present, including Jimmy Connors and Billie Jean King. He was now an ardent supporter of Billie Jean's World Tennis League team, the Philadelphia Freedoms, and, for a stupefying few minutes, had even been allowed to play against her on court. In return he told Bernie they must write a song dedicated to Billie Jean King, Philadelphia and the general notion of striving against odds and winning through.

Philadelphia at the time was emerging as a music city to rival New York, with orchestral-backed vocal groups like the O'Jays, the Three Degrees and Harold Melvin and the Blue Notes. To add that modish dimension to 'Philadelphia Freedom', a string arrangement was commissioned from Gene Page, the man behind the sexually charged ballads of Barry White. The B-side was the version of 'I Saw Her Standing There' recorded live with John Lennon at Madison Square Garden. Further underlining the democracy among Elton and his stage partners, both sides carried a collective credit, 'the Elton John Band'.

'Philadelphia Freedom' went to number one in America – Elton's third there in twelve months – but only to twelve in Britain. Its home sales were not helped by a dispute between Elton and BBC1's *Top of the Pops* show, still the most important means of exposure for any new single. A new ruling by the British Musicians' Union required that any song performed on television must have its orchestral track specially pre-recorded. Elton protested that Gene Page's string effects could not be reproduced by British session men and, instead, offered his own tape of Page's arrangement. When this was not acceptable to the Musicians' Union, he refused to appear on *Top of the Pops*.

The first months of 1975 brought an extended lull in Elton's touring and recording schedule. His bass player Dee Murray remembers Elton coming up to him at a party the previous Christmas and jubilantly saying, 'Guess what! We don't have to tour next year!' 'Ah, that's great, man,' Murray replied with an enthusiasm he was afterwards to regret.

Without the customary year-opening British tour there was nothing on the diary until *Captain Fantastic*'s release in May, and the subsequent new album sessions at Caribou. Nor was there to be a summer tour but, instead, one single gigantic Elton concert at Wembley Stadium, with a supporting bill including the Beach Boys. Its future thus comfortably mapped out, basking in the collective kudos of 'Philadelphia Freedom', the Elton John Band dispersed for an extended holiday.

Only Elton himself, as usual, found it chronically difficult to relax or be still. In March he turned up on BBC Radio One, in his other incarnation as EJ the DJ, playing new releases and old favourites in a seventy-five-minute programme interspersed with Goon voices and football jokes. The show's producer remembers standing outside Broadcasting House in Portland Place, waiting with some trepidation for superstar and retinue to arrive. 'This Rolls-Royce came along, and Elton got out of it on his own. I said, "Is someone bringing the records you're going to play?" "No," he said. "They're in here", and he opened the boot of the Rolls. There was a great big cardboard carton full of records inside. He just hauled it out and carried it up to the studio.'

He could also be seen in a film, performing yet another cover version of a classic rock song. The previous year he had been asked to appear in the screen version of *Tommy*, the Who's 'rock opera', directed by the explosive Ken Russell. He hummed and hawed endlessly until offered the role of the Pinball Wizard, singing unarguably the best song Pete Townshend ever wrote. His costume included a pair of monstrous Doc Marten bovver boots on which he had to learn to walk stiltwise, attached by metal callipers. In his three days on the set, Ken Russell remembers, he was 'no problem whatever'. The omnivorous hoarder's only stipulation was that he be allowed to take the giant boots home afterwards.

In early May, he returned to America to promote an album already known to be the most successful of his career. For on advance orders alone *Captain Fantastic and the Brown Dirt Cowboy* had already sold a million copies, going gold two days after its US release and so being guaranteed instant entry at number one in every trade paper's album chart.

Serious rock critics, too, were looking forward to an Elton John album as they had not done since the teenybop market claimed him. Even from normally taciturn sources, like Gus Dudgeon, word of mouth buzzed with epithets like 'brilliant', 'perfect' and 'masterpiece'. The title could scarcely have been bettered as a piece of advance hype, with its image of Elton as caped crusader, punching aside past disappointments like *Caribou* and soaring to new heights. The critics, in any case, realised that, even at his most frothily insubstantial, Elton spoke for the half-completed decade like no one else across the whole pop spectrum from hard rock to easy listening. *Captain Fantastic* thus was the most eagerly awaited new album since *Sgt. Pepper's Lonely Hearts Club Band*.

It certainly was like no Elton album ever before, a suite of songs as sequential and vividly personal as his previous ones had been fragmented and oblique. Bernie Taupin had written the story of their early friendship and beginnings as songwriters, in episodes as clear as the allusive magpie poet could contrive. Elton sang the saga that was half his autobiography with a new passion, involvement, sarcasm, bitterness, and occasional triumph when some old score or other was finally paid off.

As with *Sgt. Pepper*, the most sophisticated sounds of contemporary pop were mixed with everyday words, to constantly arresting and charming effect. Captain Fantastic, in the opening track, was easily recognisable as the anything-but-fantastic Reggie Dwight, in fur coat and spectacles, circa 1967: 'hardly a hero . . . Someone his mother might know . . .'. 'Tower of Babel' evoked the inhospitable London that town and country mouse tramped round together in their cheap little fun furs. 'Bitter Fingers' remembered their frustration as the Tin Pan Alley Twins, trying to turn out 'a hit and run' at Dick James's behest for Tom Jones or the Eurovision Song Contest. 'Writing' was about the process of composition itself, and the equality of the partnership trying 'to instigate the structure of another line or two'. 'Tell Me When the Whistle Blows' was an echo of vaulted Kings Cross station on Friday nights, when Brown Dirt Cowboy would catch his 5.15 pm train back up to Lincolnshire. 'Curtains' was a lament for 'Scarecrow', the first of their songs that Elton ever put on demo in DJM's four-track studio, afterwards letting Bernie take the acetate home to show his Uncle Henry and Aunt Tati in Putney.

Here and there, memory probed deeper than their life of 'cornflakes and classics' and 'waking up to washing up'. 'We All Fall in Love Sometimes' was a discreet acknowledgement of the brotherhood that had sustained them in their tiny bunk bedsitter out in Pinner and past every stop along the Metropolitan Line. In deeper confessional vein,

'Someone Saved My Life Tonight' was Elton's thank-you note, partly to Bernie for pulling his head from the gas oven, and partly to Long John Baldry for bullying him out of marrying Linda Woodrow. 'You almost had your hooks in me, didn't you dear?' he sang with more than a shadow of a jeer at the long-departed Linda.

Packaged with each album was a giveaway miscellany also put together by Bernie: one book of printed lyrics and another of Elton memorabilia – old snapshots, extracts from his diary, Bernie's original handwritten words and extracts from *Jackie* magazine's Elton John strip cartoon.

The design caused something like marketing mayhem. In America, MCA's president, Mike Maitland, jibbed at the profit-shaving represented by two elaborate giveaway books, of which, on advance orders alone, a million copies must be manufactured. A further small but vital detail was that Alan Aldridge's cover had neglected to include the customary list of tracks. In American stores, prospective customers would rip open the wrapper to read the tracks on the disc itself, scattering the giveaway booklets heedlessly on the floor.

In Britain, DJM manufactured the sleeve without protest – not having had to pay for it – but then caused further upset by pricing it as if it were a double not a single LP. 'It's their decision, not mine,' Elton told *Melody Maker*, evidently seething with annoyance. 'There's only one album left to do in the DJM contract,' he added. 'After that I'm free.'

Captain Fantastic was played to the international press at two lavish receptions, one at Media Sound Studios in New York, the other, decidedly more memorable, at the Universal Pictures complex in Los Angeles.

'I flew over for the LA launch,' Stephen James remembers. 'There were about sixty of us, MCA executives, press and radio people, in this private cinema on the Universal lot. They'd laid on an audiovisual thing, with a slide show to watch as you listened to each side of the album. And while we were listening to the first side, it was obvious that something had gone wrong with the sound.

'When the first side ended, the house lights went up. John Reid got out of his seat and stormed down to the engineer who was in charge of the hi-fi monitors. John screamed at this guy, something like "The sound's a fucking shambles!" The guy turned to John and said, "Sorry, it's the best I can do." John kept screaming at him, really violent, "The whole fucking album's being ruined, and it's your fault!" This engineer was pretty laid back, considering he's about six foot two and John's only about five eight. He says, "I'm doing the best I can", and John says, "It ain't fuckin' good enough", and he swung at this guy and hit him straight in the mouth.

'The guy tried to walk away, but John kept hitting him; then everyone rushed forward and got hold of John, and this engineer finally could walk away, blood streaming from his mouth. It took about half an hour to calm things down.

'The whole episode really scared me. I thought, "The next time I'm in a meeting with John and I say no to him, is he going to do that to me?"'

Dee Murray was spending his time off on a scuba-diving holiday in the West Indies. One day, a phone call for him came through from London. The sun-worshipping bass player picked up the receiver, not supposing that he had a care in the world.

'It was Elton,' Murray remembers. 'I could tell right off that he was embarrassed about something. He said, "I've decided to change the band. I think you, Nigel and I have gone as far as we can together."' Nigel Olsson had already received a similar call, summarily firing him.

The decision came as a total shock to both, especially after so many recent signs – including the personalised neon ones above their heads – that the Elton John Band was an indestructible democracy. Elton subsequently revealed that he'd been brooding about personnel changes since just after the 1974 American tour. 'When I got back home afterwards, I was depressed for about two weeks. At first I didn't know why – I thought I was just unhappy. Then I realised: I had to change the band.'

The change was only a partial one. Lead guitarist Davey Johnstone and percussionist Ray Cooper stayed in the new, expanded line-up recruited from both Britain and America. To replace Nigel Olsson on drums, Elton brought in Roger Pope, who had been a session player on his first album, *Empty Sky*. Another face from the past was Caleb Quaye, his fellow Tin Pan Alley messenger boy, afterwards DJM's studio engineer, and guitarist with Pope in the mildly famous Hookfoot. Elton's idea was to use Caleb as a second lead guitarist, counterpointing Davey Johnstone's technical wizardry with a more visceral bluesy sound. To take over from Dee Murray on bass he brought in Kenny Passarelli, a young American with Afro hair and a handsome Latin face, who had co-written a country-rock hit, 'Rocky Mountain Way'. Like Dee's firing, Passarelli's hiring was effected by a single phone call. 'I just decided he was right,' Elton remembered. 'So I rang him and said, "We've never spoken before, but would you like to be in my band?"'

The most novel part of the new blueprint was a second keyboard player to supplement Elton's own piano playing both with organ and the Moog synthesisers that now dominated recorded pop. He was, quite simply, fed up with doing all the onstage keyboard work himself. A second player would give him more freedom to move round the stage, sing away from his piano, even feature on alternative instruments, like lead guitar. But finding a keyboard player to play in the shadow of Elton John wasn't easy. Three major names he approached all turned him down flat. Finally Howard Rose, his American agent, came up with James Newton Howard, an American synthesiser wizard, then to be heard on a Top 10 single by Melissa Manchester.

There was little time for Elton and his new musicians to mesh in with one another. Their first public appearance was to be on 21 June, at the giant Wembley Stadium concert with Elton headlining over the Beach Boys. For this, his single major British appearance of 1975, he planned a *tour de force*. *Captain Fantastic and the Brown Dirt Cowboy* was to be played in its entirety before the 72,000-strong Wembley audience.

A crash course of rehearsals took place in Amsterdam throughout the week before the concert. Fit and bouncy from his Arizona tennis ranch, Elton took the new line-up through thirty-five numbers, with the added unfamiliarity of a three-member backup vocal group. That the city sweltered in an early summer heatwave was no brake to his frenetic energy. Between rehearsals, instead of relaxing with cold beer as they would have liked, the band found themselves being organised by Elton into running races beside the canals.

Melody Maker's choice of interviewer to talk to him in Amsterdam was a portent of the change soon to engulf music journalism. Instead of the bonhomious Chris Charlesworth or Alan Hollinghurst, the job went to Caroline Coon, a countercultural celebrity, mainly known for her work with the drug charity Release. Tall and beautiful, with immaculate liberal credentials, she appealed strongly to Elton, and for most of that week was granted the freedom of his inner circle, and almost total confidence.

Coon describes him at the Amsterdam Hilton, sprawling on his bed in a tracksuit, enthusing about the new band, with no word of regret over the dumping of Nigel and Dee. 'I've always wanted to be part of a good driving rock-'n'-roll band. The old band never used to drive – we just used to rattle on. Whenever we played anything live, it was always twice the tempo of the recording, and that was always a bit off-putting to me. I want to chug rather than race.'

He is full of respectful praise for his new colleagues, especially the 'inspiration' of James Newton Howard, and Roger Pope and Caleb, both 'amazing musicians'. 'With Kenny and James, it's worked out that I'm literally the worst musician in the band. I've got to work to keep up with them, which is going to make me play harder and better.'

Caroline Coon deftly catches Elton's own attitude to his success, that mixture of disbelief, bemusement, excitement, pessimism, even occasional irritation that nothing on earth seems able to make it stop. 'In America I've got "Philadelphia Freedom" going up the charts again. I wish the bloody thing would piss off. And "Pinball Wizard" is being played to death. I can see why people get sick and tired of it. I know that in America for the next three or four years I could get a gold on my name alone. As Pete Townshend said, I could shit bricks and people would go out and buy them ... On the other hand, you can't force people to buy garbage. I just have to keep being very, very self-critical.'

'Someone Saved My Life Tonight' – now out as a single – had unleashed intense music press speculation as to who saved Elton's life, on which night and from what. To Caroline Coon he gives a brief version of the Linda Woodrow story and his eleventh-hour rescue by Long John Baldry. Why hasn't he settled down with any woman since Linda, Coon boldly inquires. 'I haven't settled down with anyone,' Elton replies. 'And the reason is because I haven't met anyone who I want to settle down with. And touring on the road is fun for me. I've seen so many musicians' marriages going through difficulties on the road. You can't take your old lady with you all the time because it's a bore and you want a little bit of freedom – that's a rock-'n'-roll musician's outlook on life. So I don't want to get settled down for a while yet.'

Coon – whose questions are becoming subtly more and more pointed – asks if he likes women enough to want that kind of relationship at any time.

'Oh yeah, of course. I find it easier to get to know ladies in America, though. English ladies put up so many fronts. American ladies are very bold, and that breaks the ice for me. I can never say boo to a goose to anyone. I'm very shy. I need someone to help me out.'

Caroline Coon clearly suspects an entirely different dimension, though her point of inquiry is 'We All Fall in Love Sometimes', the song about Elton's early times with Bernie Taupin. Did he, she asks, 'find it difficult to reveal the extent of his love for Bernie?'

'Oh, not at all. He loved me. We hit rock bottom together so many times, and at that point in my life he was the only person I could really call a friend. We found a spark together, and a way of writing that's still with us.'

The interview, spread over four pages in *Melody Maker*'s pre-Wembley extravaganza, was the most confessional Elton had ever given. If the final revelation was still a year off, ample hints were there for anyone who cared to look.

To Caroline Coon's seductive questioning, he responds almost like a patient under psychotherapy, talking freely about his childhood inferiority complex, his feeling of being unloved by his father, and sense of rejection when Stanley Dwight had four children by another wife. 'I'm very self-destructive,' he says at one point. 'I get terribly, stubbornly depressed. It's my desperate craving for affection coming out. I'll get in a mood and I'll sit at home for two days in bed, getting more and more depressed, wondering if it's all worth it.

'My manager can't help me when I'm depressed because, since he's my manager, I fight him. But Muff Winwood or Tony King will ring up and say "Run out of Pledge, have we?" Because, you see, I Hoover and dust. I used to love ironing, too. It soothed me. I'm one of those people who go around emptying ashtrays, washing them and putting them back. And so, as soon as I get depressed, one of my friends has only got to phone and send me up a bit about something like that, and I'll come out of it.

'I don't know why I get depressed. I never can figure it out. I can be very happy and then all of a sudden I'm on a come-down . . . I consider myself slightly insane, in a funny way.'

The Elton John Wembley festival on 21 June was one of very few Seventies rock events that could be called wholly pleasant. The fate that seldom smiles on British open-air gatherings decreed a day of balmy, unbroken sun. With the good weather went an equally miraculous good mood in both spectators and organisers, banishing the usual incipient violence of one and paranoia of the other. Seventy-two thousand people packed round the Art Deco oval, shirtless, topless and happy, made Wembley Stadium look more like a crowded Blackpool beach on some prewar bank holiday.

Even without its two headline stars, the programme of music – selected by Elton – would have been a generous one. First onstage, in mid-morning, were Rocket's group Stackridge, followed by the black funk band Rufus, the country-rock singer Joe Walsh, and a little-known California band, the Eagles. Some time in mid-afternoon, the Beach Boys would make their second-on-the-bill appearance. Elton and his new, augmented band would not appear until sunset, playing the whole of *Captain Fantastic* as a two-and-a-half-hour climax.

He was at Wembley for most of the day, nevertheless, watching from a VIP box with his numerous rock-star, showbiz and sporting guests. Snapshots by Terry O'Neill show him here with Candice Bergen; there with Jimmy Connors, brandishing a tennis racket; here with Ringo Starr, pretending to balance a pineapple on his head; there in a group shot, wearing bathrobe and socks, surrounded by Paul and Linda McCartney, Billie Jean King, Harry Nilsson and Martina Navratilova.

Outside, meanwhile, the huge, impacted mass of bare skin and blue denim seethed with rising pleasure and excitement. In early afternoon, the Eagles came onstage to demonstrate the sweetly cynical laid-back country rock that Elton had already predicted would make them the cult band of the late Seventies. By the end of their set, the Wembley crowd was not only delighted, but very nearly satisfied. Four hours before the main attraction was due to appear, his third on the bill had all but stolen the show.

That coup was left, however, to the second on the bill. At around six o'clock, the Beach Boys massed onstage: Carl and Dennis Wilson, Mike Love, Bruce Johnston and supernumerary musicians, all in Bermuda shorts, like so many bearded lifeguards. The absence of their founding genius Brian Wilson, after years of rumoured mental trouble, had aroused fears that the ultimate happiness band might no longer sound the same. But they sounded as coolly carefree as ever, pouring out all their Sixties surf hits in brilliant sunshine, to the utter joy of that congested urban beach.

By the time the Beach Boys had played their final encore, the best of the perfect day was over. A lengthy pause then ensued, as the sun sank behind the stadium rim and the stage was elaborately reset, not just with amps and drum-kits, but also with fairy lights, music stands and potted plants. This sudden atmosphere of pretentiousness and fuss produced a restless stirring in the audience. When Elton and the new band finally took their places amid the foliage, under a neon sign reading FANTASTIC, hundreds of people were trickling out of the stadium.

It was a moment when all Elton's accumulated stagecraft seemed to desert him. Following the Beach Boys need not have been disastrous if he had given his usual performance, crazily costumed and spring-heeled, countering their greatest hits with equally great hits of his own. Instead, he had opted to play the whole of *Captain Fantastic*, sombrely dressed – for him – and scarcely even rising from the piano. After 'Surfin' USA', 'Little Deuce Coupe', 'Fun Fun Fun' and 'Good Vibrations', the last thing his listeners felt disposed to hear were long, introspective tracks whose autobiographical nuances were mostly lost in the deepening dark. The recital proceeded in a spirit best described as dogged, with cheers in real volume only for his latest single, 'Someone Saved My Life Tonight'. But that night, nobody could.

The music critics were merciless, totally forgetting that the bands who'd stolen Elton's show had been sponsored by him in the first place. *Melody Maker's* headline put it all too vividly: BEACH BOYS' CUP RUNNETH OVER. ELTON LEFT TO PICK UP THE EMPTIES.

His career was starting to wane in Britain, though none would realise it for a long time yet. Enormous ships, holed below the water-line, can still steam bravely ahead for miles as if nothing has happened.

Signs of malaise had been manifest even before Elton's Wembley Stadium flop. His last two American number-one singles, 'Lucy in the Sky with Diamonds' and 'Philadelphia Freedom', had risen no higher than 10 and 12 respectively in the UK charts. 'Someone Saved My Life Tonight', now number four in America, did not even make the British Top 20. Indeed, for all the sweated triumphs of conquering his native land, there was one final accolade that Britain obstinately withheld. In all these phenomenal five years, Elton John had never had a UK number-one single.

In America – by familiar contrast – the great ship appeared to steam on as unstoppably as ever. Elton was by far and away America's most listened-to recording artist, not only on his monster new album or on his nose-to-tail hit singles, but on everything else he had recorded back to *Empty Sky* in 1969. In album sales he had surpassed the Beatles a dozen times over; added to the backlog of gold and platinum was now his *Greatest Hits* album which, a year after release, had sold 5 million copies, grossing $8 million. By mid-1975 in America, it was pretty well impossible to turn on any radio anywhere across the continent without hearing classics like 'Daniel', 'Crocodile Rock', 'Your Song', 'Honky Cat' and 'Bennie and the Jets'; cult favourites like 'Burn Down the Mission', 'Levon', 'Tiny Dancer' and 'Take Me to the Pilot'; cover versions like 'Pinball Wizard', 'I Saw Her Standing There', 'Get Back' and 'My Baby Left Me'; revived rarities like 'Honey Roll', 'Razor Face' and 'Mona Lisa and Mad Hatters'. The writer Greg Shaw conducted an experiment, spinning his radio dial for six hours and finding an Elton track, on average, once every two minutes. Many stations sold themselves to their listeners on his name alone, calling themselves 'your number-one Elton John station', 'the station that plays more Elton John than anyone' or 'your official Elton John spot on the dial'.

'If you ever die,' John Lennon once told him sardonically, 'I'm gonna throw my radio out of the window.'

He was now back in the land that appreciated him most, making an album with the new band at Caribou. The customarily brief sessions were interrupted by a trip to Denver, where the Rolling Stones' current tour happened to be passing through. After playing a guest number with the Stones, Elton was aggrieved to read in *Rolling Stone* that his matey walk-on style had not gone down well with the supersnobs of rock. 'Mick Jagger asked me to sit in on "Honky Tonk Woman", which I did, and then left the stage to watch the show,' he explained later. 'Then this roadie tells me Billy Preston wants me back to join them, so I go. Then I read how Keith is pissed that I wouldn't split the stage. I'm fed up with all the damned fucking lies.'

25 August was the fifth anniversary of his first triumphal American appearance at the Los Angeles Troubadour club. To mark the occasion, Elton returned to the Troubadour for a three-night charity appearance whose few hundred tickets were so desperately over-subscribed, they had to be allotted by prize draw. It was not quite an altruistic gesture, since his original contract with the Troubadour's canny owner, Doug Weston, had contained a clause binding him to a return date exactly five years hence. The opening night was a Hollywood gala occasion, with tickets at $250 each, attended by celebrities like Tony Curtis, Mae West and Cher. The six perform-ances raised $150,000 for the Jules Stein Eye Institute at UCLA.

Covering the event for the *Los Angeles Times* was Robert Hilburn, whose original ecstatic review had touched off Elton's American landslide. To Hilburn, the excitement of that début night in 1970 was scarcely recaptured now. 'There'd been so much excitement at the thought of seeing Elton back at the Troubadour, and fighting for tickets, that when he finally walked onstage, it was almost an anticlimax. He had that big band, which sounded deafening in a small place; people were pressed tight up against the stage; the whole effect, with all those celebrities and VIPs, was overpowering. But not so magical any more.'

With the Troubabour dates went a souvenir book entitled *Five Years of Fun*, with pictures of Elton at great performing moments and backstage with all his celebrity friends. Here he was with Elizabeth Taylor; with Steve McQueen; with *Hawaii Five-O* star Jack Lord. Here he was letting Richard Chamberlain and Tatum O'Neal try on pairs of his glasses. Here he was being simultaneously photographed by Terry O'Neill, Annie Leibovitz and Tim Hine. Here he was sitting on a male acrobat's shoulders, a female acrobat seated on his shoulders. No one would have guessed that at the time he was suffering from what he subsequently termed 'a mini-nervous break-down'.

His absence in America for almost all that remained of 1975 was interpreted by some British papers as pique following the Wembley flop. The reason was somewhat more pragmatic. Difficulties had arisen with the US Internal Revenue Service over Elton's tax liabilities on an American income conservatively estimated at $7 million per year. On record royalties alone, DJM USA had recently received an assessment of $620,000, for which his overseas employment company, Sackville, was asked to provide indemnity. Part of a labyrinthine tax strategy worked out by John Reid and his accountants was that Elton should spend the next few months resident in Los Angeles.

For so short a time, a rented mansion would have sufficed but, instead, Elton decided he would buy one. After viewing several superstar properties, he found what he thought he wanted in the remoter reaches of Benedict Canyon, Beverly Hills. This was a $1-million Moorish-style folly, built by the silent-screen star John Gilbert and later owned by David O. Selznick and his wife Jennifer Jones. In the courtyard was a fountain and a gazebo where another former occupant, Greta Garbo, was said to have spent much time.

Few who visited Elton there could see the charm of the place, with its gloomy wood panelling and musty ghosts of old Hollywood ruin and loneliness. 'There was a darkness about that house,' an ex-Rocket employee remembers. 'You felt like you wouldn't care to be alone there at night.' Elton, destined to be much alone there at night, might have been a conduit for every melancholy spirit that lingered there.

The Selznick house never felt much like a home. To begin with, John Reid was there only intermittently. Elton and Reid had by now almost ended the domestic phase of their relationship. Close and interdependent as they remained, each had his own separate life and lifestyle. The imbalance grew with Elton anchored to Los Angeles but Reid still able to fly off to London and around Europe with the frenetic energy that almost equalled his charge's.

Living in an LA canyon house had never felt quite comfortable since the Manson murders of 1969. As a further uneasy dimension, Elton's property backed on to that of Alice Cooper, a shrine to every spaced-out weirdo who'd ever bitten off a chicken's head or tattooed himself with a blunt breadknife. One night, in what seemed entirely appropriate fashion, Alice's house burst into flames. Elton was disturbed by a succession of longhairs ringing his bell to ask if they could park in his drive and watch the conflagration.

As a precaution against importuning fans, if nothing worse, his own address was kept a closely guarded secret and his telephone number changed every two weeks. His security, even so, proved easily breachable. One night, he awoke to find a completely strange girl sitting on his bed. 'I'm a bit blind without my glasses . . . I said "Who are you?" and she said, "Oh, don't you know me?" She'd gotten in without a key, and was just sitting there. Christ, it could have been someone with a fucking gun.'

Not that John Reid's absences left him short of company or diversion. Bernie Taupin was in Los Angeles, as were various members of the band, looking forward to the short American tour scheduled for October. There was his agent, Howard Rose; his PR man, Dick Grant; his personal co-ordinator, Connie Papas. There were his musician friends, flying in from New York or London, and his movie-star friends, venturing out from their Moorish or Spanish follies in the Hollywood Hills. Every night at Chasen's or Le Restaurant, he was the centre of a group seldom numbering less than a dozen.

No other city provides new friends as lavishly as Los Angeles, and on his previous visits Elton had acquired an entourage as large and competitive as Elvis Presley's Memphis Mafia or Mick Jagger's mini-Versailles. Feeling lonely, even abandoned, there, cut off from all his normal, commonsensical English roots, exacerbated that monarchical rock star compulsion to have people constantly on hand, running his errands, laughing at his jokes, participating in his puns, reassuring him by word and gesture at every second that he was totally and utterly wonderful. There are people all over the world who derive a handsome livelihood from doing this. But in Los Angeles it is practically a vocation.

The acquisition of an entourage always has one important side effect. This is to alienate, and usually drive out, genuine friends, unwilling to join in the prevailing sycophancy. One such in Elton's case was Sharon Lawrence, from Rocket's LA office. She quit at the end of 1974, feeling that the original, hard-working and motivated Rocket US team had been infiltrated by people of more doubtful value. 'I used to call them the *nouveau riche*. They were the ones who'd say they wanted a Porsche and half an hour later, Elton would have bought them one. I could see a lot of trouble coming, tax trouble coming. The end for me was when I found out some people were doing drugs in the office. I said, "I want nothing more to do with this."'

Having been a close friend of Jimi Hendrix, Sharon knew only too well how a fragile soul could be destroyed by parasitic hangers-on, tempting him into alcoholism and drugs. But she had always believed

Elton's character too robust to run such a risk. She remembered him as the clean-living rock star, up playing tennis before breakfast, immune to temptation by the softest drug, horrified to see any of his idols on that fatal downward path. Many was the time she had seen him in a corner with someone he admired, fervently begging them, 'Don't do this to yourself.'

Since Elton's return to Los Angeles, Sharon Lawrence had purposely kept away from him. 'I wasn't working for Rocket any more, and I didn't want to be drawn back into that circle of dependence that Elton creates. I knew that if I sat down with him, we'd end up agonising about his life back to the age of two. He'd have me involved up to the neck in every one of his troubles and anxieties in the same way as always.

'Mutual friends who had seen him kept telling me about the awful things he was doing to himself. People who weren't of the entourage, who genuinely liked and respected Elton, were appalled at what was going down. "Can't you talk to him?" they kept saying to me. "Even if it's only a phone call or letter? He always used to listen to you."'

Finally, Elton himself telephoned. 'It was three in the morning,' Sharon remembers, 'which in itself was an abnormal thing for Elton. He said, "Reid's out of town. Please come over. I want to play you the new album, and I really need to talk to someone."'

Next day, putting aside other engagements, Sharon drove to the Alhambra folly in Benedict Canyon. 'As soon as I walked into that house, I thought, "My God! This is no place for anyone to be." There was an enormous formal drawing-room, full of inglenooks, that you couldn't imagine anyone sitting in. The only daylight seemed to be at the back, as you got nearer the garden. If you were feeling in any way down or depressed, that house would sure finish you off.'

The sight of Elton filled her with horror. 'I remembered this person who was mildly temperamental, who could be a bit neurotic and difficult, but who was basically happy and organised. Now he looked ghastly, he was incredibly strung up, anxious and panicky. In the few months since I'd seen him, he seemed to have become a complete wreck.'

He played her the new album, to be released in October as *Rock of the Westies*. 'He seemed most panicked about that,' Sharon remembers. 'He put it on at full volume and sat there staring at me, waiting for me to say it was brilliant. I didn't think so, but I said it was because he seemed to need that so desperately. While I was still at the house, John Reid came back. I realised that Elton had been in a real snit because John had gone away, and had got me over there to prove he could get along without him. It was like, "There you are

– other people care about me, too." '

Various factors were to blame for Elton's condition. The rotor-ride had stopped again, flinging him to earth with a still more sickening thud. After months of giddy motion, when audiences provided every stimulus he needed, the concertless days stretched ahead with terrible tedium. There was nothing to do but put on expensive clothes, go to superb restaurants, eat fabulous food, drink marvellous wine, be courted and flattered and sit among all his myriad, well-dusted possessions. Exhaustion and anticlimax combined to produce the mood where buoyant Elton vanished and glum, pessimistic Reggie Dwight returned. These were the black plunges that took him, as well as everyone round him, totally by surprise; when all his gold and platinum discs seemed to crumple to ash; when the same thought came as years ago, in the background of Bluesology or making cut-price LPs for Woolworth's: I'm still not getting anywhere.

At such a vulnerable moment, he should have been in Virginia Water, with its support system of family and real friends. Instead, he was in Los Angeles where 'life in the fast lane', as the Eagles' song had it, frequently meant driving at 100 mph, blindfolded, with both hands off the wheel.

'There always was that strange dichotomy in Elton,' Sharon Lawrence says. 'Part of him adored and treasured his success, but another part seemed to want to do its utmost to destroy it. I've seen it with other big stars who start to take risks, knowing they have everything to lose. It's like they're consciously saying, "If people love me, then how much do they love me? How far can I go and still get away with it?" Elton and John Reid were alike in that respect. There was something in both of them that liked walking on the very edge.'

Whatever the circumstances, Elton John was still the best value any press interviewer could get. While living in LA, he did one of *Playboy* magazine's famous interviews, submitting to the same earnest question-and-answer format as had such international figures as Albert Schweitzer, Martin Luther King, Malcolm X and Marshall McLuhan. Articulate and spontaneous as ever, he revealed more than *Playboy* had ever expected to learn about the pains and anxieties of being the world's number-one rock star.

The interview, *Playboy* reported, took place beneath 'a Bedouin-style canopy' overlooking Greta Garbo's gazebo. Elton, on one of his periodic slimming benders, arrived fresh from several sets of tennis. Paradoxically, at this time of mental stress he was physically fitter than he had been for months.

Topics covered a wide spectrum, from Elton's annual income (he did not seriously quibble at $7 million) to Art Nouveau and the 'boringness' of most people he met in the rock business. There was an early, highly prophetic exchange about American tabloid papers, like the *National Star* and *National Enquirer*, which had taken to printing the bizarrest rumour and speculation about show-business celebrities in the guise of genuine news. 'When Evel Knievel jumped that canyon, I was supposedly sitting by his side, singing the National Anthem. And I'm in my house, going "Oh yeah?" ... When I read something in the *National Star* which is absolute rubbish, I say, "Well, how dare they print that?" Then I'll turn to the next page and read about someone else, and go "Hm – did they really do that?" I mean, I'm the first person to get sucked in.'

He was even prepared to talk about that old poisoner of happiness, his disappearing hair. '[It's] a real drag, because it didn't happen to the rest of my family. It must be because I was a silly cunt, and dyed my hair a lot. So, since I've discovered I don't want to be bald, I might have a hair transplant. It's just a matter of going down there with the courage to say, "I want some more hair please."'

Playboy asked in all innocence if he suffered from fear of failure or rejection. 'Sure. I think how, suddenly overnight, my records could stop selling. In this business, nothing's for certain. I'm constantly saying, "This is ridiculous. It can't go on for ever." But really I'm quite ready for the time when record sales level off or decrease, and I know that around the corner the next "biggest something" is lurking.

'I like the struggle to stay at the top. It's what keeps me going. I don't begrudge anyone else his success. You have to pay attention to what others are doing, keep listening to what's happening in order to grow. For example, Stevie Wonder can eat me for breakfast as far as musicianship goes, but that doesn't make me angry or jealous or up-tight. I'd give anything to have his talent, but that doesn't make me paranoid.'

Playboy, too, hovered around a question that could not yet be asked outright. Instead, it was wrapped in a comment about David Bowie's and Mick Jagger's increasing androgyny, and Led Zeppelin's recent appearance at an LA party in drag. Did Elton 'get off on the bisexuality scene'?

'I really don't know what to say about it,' Elton replied, smoothly turning the topic to who, of either gender, could enter a room and make him gasp. 'Jagger, Sinatra, Elvis, probably. Also people like Noël Coward, Edith Piaf and Katharine Hepburn.'

To a question about drugs, his reply was equally non-committal. 'I've got a completely split personality. One minute I'm up, then I just change like the wind. I'd like to take LSD to find out what it's like but ... it's like going into the unknown with a paranoid attitude.

One half of me would love to do it, but the other half owns up to the fact that it might be a bit of a disaster.'

A routine question about childhood prompted the interview's most remarkable passage. Elton's reply was to unlock the store of loneliness and pain that had almost been Reggie Dwight's second nature. He described his solitary schooldays, his 'introverted nature' and 'terrible inferiority complex'. In particular, he launched into a diatribe against his father, opening up scar tissue all the way back to his birth. He repeated the untrue assertion – though, presumably, as it had always been told to him – that Stanley Dwight had been abroad on RAF duty when he was born, and had not troubled to see him 'for about two years afterwards'. On to the Garbo vista were suddenly superimposed pictures of an unhappy little house in Potter Street, Pinner. 'My father was so stupid with me, it was ridiculous. I couldn't eat celery without making a noise. It was just pure hate . . .'

Playboy readers, expecting the lowdown on a swinger, instead saw that lonely boy in his bedroom, pouring into gramophone records all the love his father seemed to reject. 'I grew up with inanimate objects as my friends, and I still believe they have feelings. That's why I keep hold of all my possessions. I'll look at them and remember when they gave me a bit of happiness – which is more than human beings have given me.'

Most bitter of all was he about his parents' divorce, and the way he believed Stanley had treated his mother. 'She had to bear all the costs. She more or less gave up everything and had to admit to adultery, even though he was doing the same thing behind her back. He was such a sneak. Then he went away and four months later got married to this woman and had four kids in four years. My pride was really snipped, 'cause he was supposed to hate kids. I guess I was just a mistake in the first place.'

That particular part of the *Playboy* interview was widely reported by British newspapers. It caused total astonishment to Stanley Dwight, whose recent relationship with Elton had given no hint of such smouldering resentment. Though steadfastly unwilling to discuss the matter with reporters, he did unbend to a *Daily Mail* writer, Sally Brompton, who tracked him to his house in Cheshire. To her Stanley confirmed that he had not missed Reggie's birth, and had kept a home RAF posting until his son was eighteen months old. He had not met Edna Clough until after finally parting from Sheila, nor had he forced her to pay the costs of the divorce. His solicitor was even prompting him to sue *Playboy* over the allegations, but Stanley would not. 'I don't want to do anything that would alienate Reggie. I just don't understand why he's started saying all these awful things.'

He recalled their apparently amiable last meeting, two years before, when Elton had played football in the garden with his four young stepbrothers and later slipped a two-thousand-pound cheque for a new car into his 'Aunt Edna's' pocket. Since then Stanley had detected a sea-change in his attitude, but was at a loss to understand why. He no longer sent the family Christmas cards or replied to the boys' letters. Stanley had tried to ring him once on his ex-directory number, but had been unable to get through.

'He doesn't seem very happy to me,' Stanley told the *Daily Mail*. 'Last time we saw him I asked him who his friends were, and he said Elvis Presley and Billie Jean King. But when he was a child, they were his idols. How can someone you've only just met be described as a friend? There are friends and friends. And I think Reggie has to buy his friendships.'

The new album took its name from that autumn's short US and Canadian tour whose thirteen venues all happened to lie west of the Rocky Mountains. Elton being unable to resist any wordplay – and his entourage unable to resist hailing any Elton wordplay as comic genius – West of the Rockies became *Rock of the Westies*.

Recorded at Caribou the previous July, it was earmarked as the studio album Elton had to deliver to Dick James Music in final settlement of his contract. Elton, however, liked the finished album too much to use it merely as kiss-off to DJM. 'I heard he wanted to get out of giving it to us,' Stephen James remembers. 'I even had to threaten to sue him if he didn't honour the agreement we had.'

Elton's enthusiasm for *Rock of the Westies* is difficult to fathom. After the inventiveness and soul-baring of *Captain Fantastic*, it was a relapse into mainstream pop at its most predictable, even cynical. The meaningless pun introduced a meaningless miscellany in which one obvious chart hit – the Hawaiian-flavoured 'Island Girl' – was placed like a single bright red maraschino cherry among listless tinned grapefruit. The remaining titles have long since been consigned to the John–Taupin slush pile: 'Dan Dare (Pilot of the Future)'; 'Street Kids'; 'Hard Luck Story'; 'Billy Bones and the White Bird'; 'I Feel Like a Bullet (in the Gun of Robert Ford)'. If you care, Robert Ford was the assassin of the Western outlaw hero Jesse James. It says much for Bernie Taupin's own far from bucolic state in this era that he should have fallen back on the five-year-old style of *Tumbleweed Connection*.

Yet the huge ship steamed on regardless. Like *Captain Fantastic*, *Rock of the Westies* went gold on advance orders of a million plus, entering the American album charts at number one. 'Island Girl' went to number one in the singles chart, remaining there for three weeks. Back in Britain, meanwhile, the album made only number five; the single only number 14. Again, that barely perceptible wrench below the water-line.

For Elton, the Rock of the Westies tour was punishing in a way none had ever been before. Exhilarated as he was to have created a new band that worked, the thought of sitting down and playing filled him with increasing weariness and dread. 'We were having a great time – but something inside me was so revolted by the thought of constant touring that I just wanted to say, "I've had enough". Apparently my memory went as well. I used to go to rehearsals and then, for no reason, I'd just blow up, walk out and come back three hours later. I can't remember things I said or things I did. I think, "My God! Did I really do that?"'

The tour was to end with an event symbolising the special relationship between Elton and Los Angeles. At the end of November, he was to play two consecutive nights at the LA Dodgers' baseball stadium, to a total audience of 100,000. That week was to be designated Elton John Week in Los Angeles and to include the ceremonial laying of his name among the stars on the sidewalk outside Grauman's Chinese Theater.

While millions envied the star, one or two worried about the person, shut away in his gloomy Alhambra in Benedict Canyon. Chief among them was Sharon Lawrence to whom he had made that uncharacteristic 3 am call. Determined as she was not to be drawn back into Elton's 'circle of dependence', Sharon could not subdue an alarm and foreboding that felt horribly familiar. 'I'd spent all that earlier time around Jimi Hendrix. I knew that when a person's in a vulnerable state, anything they say can be a signal that should make you feel nervous.'

Even some of Elton's fellow rock stars now felt worried about the course he was taking, though few had the will or words to try to talk him out of it. One who did was a person to whom Elton himself had been a staunch friend in a similar period of drift. 'I know John Lennon tried to help him,' Sharon Lawrence says. 'He took Elton aside, and used just the same words Elton once had to him: "Look – I always admired you. Don't do this to yourself."'

It seemed that nothing anyone said could help. The robustly sensible character Lennon and Sharon Lawrence remembered was being drawn inexorably out of the sun, into a shadowy, murky netherworld. 'I had one other totally chaotic phone call from him,' Sharon remembers. 'He could hardly talk. "I'll bet you never thought you'd get a call like this from me," he said.' Not long afterwards, she heard from Elton's housekeeper that he had tried to commit suicide by swallowing a bottle of sleeping-pills.

His two Dodger Stadium concerts, and the ancillary celebrations of Elton John Week, were marked by the biggest display so far of Rocket Records' fun and largesse. A specially chartered Boeing 707 flew the entire London office staff out to LA for a week, together with Elton's and John Reid's parents and VIP friends like Bryan Forbes and Nanette Newman, the footballer Rodney Marsh and chat-show host Russell Harty, accompanied by a London Weekend Television film crew. For the journey over, each guest received a Rocket monogrammed flight bag of inflight goodies including an Instamatic camera and a *Beano* comic.

Rocket's staff now included Linda Mallarkey and Marie Thacker, the two diehard fans who had waited so many hours for Elton at airports and cricket matches. Linda ran his British fan club while Marie was a general office junior. They had originally planned to follow the tour under their own steam, blueing every penny of their savings. When John Reid found out, he paid for their plane tickets and hotels and, in not uncharacteristic fashion, sent a car to bring them to the concert at Oakland Coliseum. Afterwards, they were put into Elton's limousine and allowed to accompany him back to LA on one of the two Boeing 707s he had on standby that week.

The London party was put up on unlimited tab at the Westwood Holiday Inn. An elaborate programme of amusements included trips to Disneyland and a party on *Madman*, the 65-foot boat that had been Elton's last birthday present to John Reid. For the ceremonial laying of Elton's name on the sidewalk outside Graumann's, Hollywood Boulevard had to be closed – the first time in over 1,500 such ceremonies that such a thing had been known. There was also a party to launch Neil Sedaka's new album, when Elton appeared dressed as the Lone Ranger, black mask on top of his glasses.

Few of the assembled liggers noticed what an air of strain underlay their £50,000 junket. Nor did they notice that, for most of Elton John Week, Elton himself was a strangely fleeting presence. His usual music press interviewers like Steve Clark and Charles Shaar Murray were surprised to be curtly denied their usual access. Few even among his favourite celebrity guests were invited to visit him up at his Garbo mansion. Among those who did manage to cross the threshold was Margo Stevens, the Rocket secretary. Margo's eyes – sharpened in her former years of vigil outside Beatles' houses – were quick to spot something seriously amiss. 'Elton looked terribly pale and drawn,' she remembers. 'We were told that he'd been very ill.'

Whatever the illness, it could not be allowed to show in the figure, dressed in a sparkly lurex version of an LA Dodgers baseball suit, that played to its first steeply tiered 50,000 faces in the evening sunshine of 26 November. Bryan Forbes, standing in the wings, noticed a phenomenon unchanged since early switchback tours in ramshackle station wagons. By the end of Elton's two-hour performance, his finger-ends were streaked in blood.

It should have been his zenith, down there in Dodger Stadium's roaring bowl. But to Sharon Lawrence the sound of the rotor-ride seemed frightening. 'It suddenly came to me: "My God, all this is going to crumble and go to Hell!"'

12

'Christ! I wish I had someone to share all this with'

FINANCIALLY, the most sensible course for Elton at the end of 1975 would have been to become permanently resident in America. As a high-earning Briton living temporarily abroad, he was caught between two tax systems. The huge dollar sums he had grossed in America were still the subject of protracted wrangling with the Internal Revenue Service. Something like $3 million in concert earnings, back to 1973, had been frozen pending the outcome of negotiations over his US residential status. To this unreachable reserve had been added the proceeds of his last tour, including $1.1 million for his two Dodger Stadium concerts. If and when Elton moved the money to Britain, he risked being taxed on it a second time at the Wilson Labour government's top rate of almost 90 per cent, so losing the whole amount and a great deal more besides.

Several major British pop stars had already fled into tax exile, following the early lead of the Rolling Stones. Tom Jones lived permanently in Hollywood, in a Tudor-style hacienda to whose poolside he had nostalgically exported the red telephone kiosk from the street where he grew up in Tonypandy, Wales. Elton's old friend Rod Stewart was now also in California, living with Peter Sellers's ex-wife Britt Ekland, his every purchase minutely computed on her omnipresent pocket calculator.

Had Elton himself opted to settle in America in 1976, a very different story would remain to be told. With his immaculate social record, US Immigration would readily have granted him H-1 status as a person likely to improve the nation's cultural fabric. Spared the coming musical cataclysm in Britain, he would doubtless have become an American entertainment institution midway between Frank Sinatra and the Grateful Dead. Whatever else he might have lost, he would have gained the complete privacy that being colossally rich in so large a country allows. Very likely, the only 'revelation' to come would have been a tour of his house by some TV programme like *Lifestyles Of The Rich And Famous*.

But to a tax exile even after the shortest time, Britain begins to look alluring; a tiny green island in the Atlantic, to which phone calls peal quaintly, as in the hallway of a quiet country hotel. One can easily forget all about British income tax, British weather, British envy and the unspeakable elements of the British press.

To symbolise his homecoming there was the now traditional Elton John Christmas show at the Hammersmith Odeon, with dry-ice clouds pumped over the front-row spectators like a vaporous form of champagne toast. Soon afterwards, *Melody Maker*'s lead story announced his first British tour in more than two years, with venues ranging from Earls Court arena to Bailey's night club, Watford. The days of Garbo reclusiveness in Hollywood seemed over. Reg, clearly, was doing everything possible to get back in touch with his roots.

The clearest sign of patriotic intent to grit his teeth and pay British income tax was purchase of an English stately home. Hercules, his Virginia Water bungalow, now could barely contain the myriad possessions stuffed into it and, in addition, had to be protected from marauding fans by an electronic security fence. Elton had long since tired of Hercules and, in early 1976, put it up for sale at £125,000, a sum thought reasonable for exotic fixtures like gold taps in the bathroom. When no buyer could be found, he was forced to drop the price to £80,000.

In May 1975, he had reportedly been about to pay £800,000 for Wargrave Manor, former home of property magnate Nigel Broackes, a Thames-side Georgian mansion on a 78–acre estate that included a farm, assorted tenantry and a herd of Friesian cattle. At the last moment, however, the deal fell through, and Elton went off to Beverly Hills, leaving the search to be carried on by his mother.

To help her, Sheila enlisted Margo Stevens, the deeply sane as well as quite crazy girl who had joined Rocket after years as the most tenacious Beatle fan ever known. Though strictly speaking just an assistant at Big Pig, Rocket's music-publishing division, Margo had a warm personal relationship with Elton and his parents. It was therefore no surprise to her to be rung up by Sheila and asked to go out househunting for Elton.

Together they found Woodside in the Berkshire village of Old Windsor. A redbrick Queen Anne-type house of no outstanding architectural beauty, it stood on a 37–acre estate and was provided with every amenity a rock-star millionaire could demand: private cinema, interior lift, stabling, staff cottage and swimming pool. From the rolling, three-lake garden, it was possible to see Windsor Castle and the flagstaff which denotes whether or not the Queen is in residence. The price – a mere bagatelle after Wargrave Manor – was just under £400,000.

Elton himself was by now in Barbados, holidaying at a rented mansion in the exclusive St James enclave with a predominantly male group including John Reid, Bernie Taupin, Gus Dudgeon and the photographer David Nutter. The resultant portfolio shows him heavily engaged in water sports, skiing and para-gliding as ferociously as he played piano onstage. His spirits buoyant again, he chafed at the formality of his black butlers and maids, and kept urging them unsuccessfully to 'loosen up' and 'join in the fun'. 'There was one girl in particular who'd never even smile,' Gus Dudgeon remembers. 'One day when we were eating, Elton said, "I'm really going to get through to her." So, when a big bowl of custard was brought in, he plunged his head straight into it. Then he let out an awful scream. He'd thought the custard was cold, but it was boiling hot.'

Back in England, the purchase of Woodside settled, Sheila asked Margo Stevens to leave her job at Rocket and become Elton's live-in housekeeper. Though inexperienced in domestic work beyond a little children's nannying, Margo agreed to give it a try. Elton rang her from Barbados to say how delighted he was that she'd taken the job.

In the spring of 1976 came still more conclusive proof that, far from intending to migrate overseas, Elton was as committed as he possibly could be to Britain and the British way of life. He was elected chairman of Watford Football Club.

It was an ambition that Elton had cherished, though scarcely dared articulate, from the day Vic Lewis had arranged for him to join the Watford board. As expected, his public support had benefited the club enormously, though still not enough to improve its abysmal standing in the Football League. The 1974–5 season had seen it drop out of the Third Division and into the Fourth. The 1975–6 season, just ending as Elton's chairmanship began, found Watford at eighth place in that ignominious bottom echelon, with no visible prospect of ever hauling itself out again.

For Vic Lewis, the association with Elton and Watford was to end even more sourly than his years as Elton's booking agent. On delivering Elton to the club as a director and obvious vast potential asset, Lewis, too, had been given a seat on the board. The following season, Elton announced he wanted John Reid to become a Watford director also. By then his wishes could not be ignored and, to create the requisite vacancy, Vic Lewis was asked to resign. The man whom Elton had to thank for batting at Lord's – as well as persuading him to go on the road with a band – calls this episode 'the worst blow I ever received'.

Elton's acceptance of the chairmanship seemed the answer to all Watford's prayers. The club was in deep financial trouble, compounded of its disastrous match record and benign, old-fashioned management. In the season just past it had made a trading loss of £80,000. Despite Elton's benefit concert, and various loans from other directors, its bank overdraft stood at £100,000. Among the new chairman's first official duties was to preside at a serious of crisis financial meetings. The club's bank manager had called in the directors and warned that the deficit could not be allowed to run on.

Elton, however, quickly dispelled any idea of himself as Watford's golden goose. 'This won't be just a happy little bandwagon, with me picking up the bills,' he said. As with Rocket Records, the last thing he intended to do was splash out millions regardless. The idea was to make Watford financially stable and self-sufficient by exploiting its own neglected or unrealised natural assets. He was equally anxious to reassure those who might think his involvement merely a rock superstar's passing whim. He pledged '100 per cent effort' in working with the board to solve Watford's budget crisis and restore it to respectable standing in the League. If necessary, he said, he would cut back on touring to have more time for the club.

Everything was to be played fair and square, businesslike and dignified, without undue reliance on his own huge capacity to attract crowds. 'If Elton John being chairman puts 2,000 on the gate, I shall be happy. But I don't believe in gimmicks, and I'm not doing anything drastic until I settle in. I'm in the hot seat now.'

The first new player signed under his tenure certainly felt no hint of multimillionaire munificence. In May 1976, Watford paid Leyton Orient £3,000 for their striker Tommy Walley – a sum more akin to transfer fees 20 years earlier when Elton's cousin, Roy Dwight, was a professional. But, with Watford's bank manager on the warpath, even that small outlay required justification. 'It's ridiculous that a club of Watford's potential should be in this position,' Elton said. 'We feel that Tommy's experience will give us the character we require.'

He was by now touring Britain again, in conscious parallel with the supersonic airliner that had lately made its inaugural flight. 'Louder than Concorde', proclaimed the tour T-shirts, ' . . . but not quite as pretty'. The witticism came from an exalted source. After one of Elton's private royal command performances, Princess Margaret had told him, 'This tour of yours sounds as if it'll be louder than Concorde.'

The tour continued a habit, still rare among rock stars, of

performing in aid of charity and good causes. As well as taking on the Watford chairmanship, he had become involved with the Sports Aid Foundation, a government-backed body set up to provide financial support for British athletes in every field. One of Elton's two concerts at Earls Court arena was a benefit for the Sports Aid Foundation, raising £40,000. From the stage, he spoke passionately about the need to encourage young sportsmen and women, and said that other musicians, too, should be rallied to the cause: 'No one knows what sport means to people in this business.' Afterwards, he received an award from Labour's Sports Minister, Denis Howell. Rock music and government had never consorted so openly before.

He was still the same old Reg, though to discover this one had to penetrate many layers of superstar protection. Even so old and close a friend as Sue Ayton, from Dick James's office, found herself brusquely fended off by those who now arranged Elton's social programme and screened all those seeking audience with him. Sue, however, persisted in wanting to see him and, when he played Earls Court, managed to get backstage on a pass given her by the sound engineer, Clive Franks. 'I got a lot of very black looks, like "Who does this girl think she is?"' she remembers now. 'Then, finally, I caught sight of Elton. He was standing at the end of this long concourse, with minders all round him.

'As soon as he saw me, it was all right. He came hurrying over, got me a drink, was as sweet as ever. "Do ring Sheila," he said. "She'd love to hear from you. I'll give you her number." Then, because Elton had been nice to me, suddenly everyone else was being very nice to me, asking if I was all right, showing me to my seat. I'd have loved to keep in touch with him and see his mother again, because we'd all been such friends before. But now there was all this other stuff one had to go through, I decided I just couldn't be bothered.'

The 'Louder Than Concorde' tour more than wiped away his Wembley Stadium flop ten months before. Besieged box offices from Taunton to Dundee told the same story. As a crowd puller, a surreal clothes horse, stage acrobat and marathon man, Elton John was still without peer.

On record, however, the position was less clearcut. In Britain, Elton had not had a Top 10 single since 'Lucy in the Sky with Diamonds' just got in, a year earlier. He was used to chart rebuffs in his native land and, up to now, had always been able to turn away from them to his constantly escalating American success. But early in 1976, his US chart ratings also began to slip.

The tireless record buyer had always been keenly aware of the competition he faced, on both sides of the Atlantic. Now he was aware of a fundamental change in the trend that had carried him to the top. After five years of chart dominance by solo singers, the fashion once again was for bands. In Britain, the chief agents were the Bay City Rollers, a gruesomely underpowered Scottish Beach Boy parody who, none the less, created enough hysteria among teenyboppers for the term 'Rollermania' to be coined. By mid-1976, almost all the names with whom Elton competed for chart access were bands. In Britain there was Queen, a group first of all remarkable for bare-faced nerve in choosing such a name, their singer Freddie Mercury a camp white satin waif with the vocal range of a choirboy who had sold his soul to Satan before matins. There was 10 cc, a confederation of session wizards whose songs were an anti-American comic strip: 'Rubber Bullets', 'Wall Street Shuffle', 'I'm Mandy, Fly Me.' There was the leering country band Dr Hook, the warm-cocoa-bland Hot Chocolate, the Sixties rip-off band Darts. There was Roxy Music, Supertramp, Thin Lizzy, Sad Café and Be Bop Deluxe. In America, there was the new age of country rock, combining old-fashioned pedal-steel and bottleneck blues guitar with modern lyrics about trans-American life, freeways, truckstops, diners and motels. There was Poco, Little Feat, Lynyrd Skynyrd, the Allman Brothers, the Doobie Brothers and the Eagles. There was the jazz-oriented Weather Report and the sex-oriented Steely Dan, named after a dildo in William Burroughs's *The Naked Lunch.*

With the change to bands went a change in content, away from solo plaintiveness, pensiveness and *faux naiveté*, towards the grown-up, the jaded and cynical. In fairness, the lyrics Bernie Taupin had fed to Elton had often been quite as mordant and strange as the Eagles' 'Hotel California' or Steely Dan's 'Haitian Divorce'. But the abiding Elton images were of whimsy and nostalgia. His world-conquering hits suddenly seemed like just another set of the W. D. and H. O. Wills cigarette cards that everyone was now throwing away.

He had left the avant-garde, and was moving, slowly but inexorably, to the middle of the road. The audiences that flocked to his shows were no longer kids on the cutting edge, but people with a past, looking for excuses to remember it. The fact was brought home in an American poll to find the country's three most popular musical acts. One was Elton. Another was the anodyne country singer John Denver. The third was the orchestra leader Lawrence Welk. 'Lawrence Welk!' Elton repeated incredulously. 'It's like being compared with Mantovani!'

As usual, he fretted endlessly over the problem, and how to solve it. He concluded that he had released too many singles that were slow ballads, and would do better in the charts with more hard-edged rockers, like 'Crocodile Rock' and 'Saturday Night's Alright for Fighting'. The approach of his twenty-ninth birthday – panic time in every young man's life – sharpened his desire not to be consigned to some easy-listening geriatric home.

He had chosen two tracks to make a second single from *Rock of the Westies*. One was the cumbersomely named Western love song 'I Feel Like a Bullet (in the Gun of Robert Ford)'. The other was 'Grow Some Funk of Your Own', a rocker with the same kind of hammering chorus as 'Saturday Night'. Elton, even so, suddenly grew keen on putting out 'Robert Ford' as the A-side. It proved a disastrous decision: the song was laboured as well as obscure, and many US radio stations, notably WABC in New York, rejected it outright. WABC's programme director later recalled the pressure that Elton exerted to try to push the single on to his play list. 'An enormous cake arrived at my office, about half the size of my desk surface. On top of it was a decoration in the shape of a gun, and the message, "Give Robert Ford a shot". But we still didn't play the single. A week later, another cake arrived, this time as big as my desktop. With it was another message: "Disregard previous cake. Grow Some Funk is the A-side."'

The change of plan brought only minor comfort. 'Grow Some Funk of Your Own' – merely frenetic where 'Saturday Night' had been compulsive – rose no higher than number 14 in America. In Britain, it did not even make the Top 50.

Hits still happened, but they were hits of yesterday rather than tomorrow. In April, DJM put out a live album compilation named *Here And There*, the non-studio 'floater' to which they were entitled before finally letting Elton go. Side A featured a long-ago Elton performance at the Royal Festival Hall, London; side B was a selection from his Thanksgiving 1974 concert at Madison Square Garden. Second-hand and blurred concert oldies like 'Border Song', 'Take Me to the Pilot' and 'Bennie and the Jets' still proved golden enough to take him to number four in the US and six in Britain. That same month, he had his first British Top 10 single since 'Lucy in the Sky with Diamonds'. But it was with his two-year-old version of 'Pinball Wizard', from the Who's five-year-old rock opera, *Tommy*.

Even when hits became harder to find for Elton himself, they kept on happening for the performers he had encouraged and promoted. Late in 1975, Neil Sedaka had a second US number-one single on Rocket with 'Bad Blood', an exuberant rock-'n'-roll number, featuring Elton on backup vocals. Despite his turbulent private life, the session man proved as reliable as always. 'I was nervous that he wouldn't show,' Neil Sedaka remembers. 'Then, right at the end of the session, a limo drew up, and Elton walked in. In seven takes he'd got the whole background vocal down.'

'Bad Blood' became Sedaka's biggest-ever US and Canadian hit, selling 2 million copies. Rocket's promotion was as efficient as it could be. 'I'd been downhearted because my last single, "That's Where the Music Takes Me", hadn't been getting airplay on a certain chain of radio stations,' Neil Sedaka remembers. 'When "Bad Blood" came out, I called John Reid and said I was nervous these same stations would pass on it. John called me back and told me it had been taken by the chain, and was already on twenty out of the thirty stations. Within four weeks, it was number one.'

Still more remarkable was the renaissance that Rocket Records gave Cliff Richard, a performer who, in almost twenty years of consistent British chart success, had never achieved more than the faintest pinprick in the American market. Early in 1976, Richard's manager, Peter Gormley, sent John Reid tapes of two new songs, 'Miss You Nights', and 'Devil Woman'. Reid's instant response was to sign the Peter Pan of British pop on Rocket US, with a vow to get him the American hit he had been looking for since 'Move It' in 1958.

For Elton, a devout Cliff fan all that time, breaking him in the US became a matter of personal honour. Sharon Lawrence was lured back to Rocket to organise a publicity tour and introduce Richard to the right media people. It helped that the songs were excellent, in particular 'Devil Woman', a number far sexier than its vehemently Christian vocalist had permitted himself before. In the summer of 1976, 'Devil Woman' went to number eight in America, staying in the Top 40 for twelve weeks and earning a gold disc for sales of one million plus.

Elton's own biggest single to date was to come in the form of a dividend for unselfish work on another's behalf. He was now contractually free of DJM, and at liberty to sign with any of the other British record companies that clamoured for him. Instead, he had decided to do what he had previously said he would not, and record on his own Rocket label. A distribution deal for Britain was signed with EMI, the company of which both John Reid and Rocket's managing director David Croker were alumni.

Elton's debut on the Rocket label caused consternation within the company. He announced he wanted it to be a duet with Kiki Dee, the singer he had laboured so long to reinspire and establish. The song was 'Don't Go Breaking My Heart', a love duet in the Motown style of Marvin Gaye and Tammi Terrell. Reinforcing a suspicion that he was winding people up as he loved to do, it did not bear the usual John–Taupin byline, but was credited to 'Ann Orson and Carte Blanche'.

Various people came to David Croker, Rocket's managing director, and said that such a début for Elton on the label would be disastrous. 'I didn't really know either way,' Croker says now. 'I just thought it was a rather up-market form of pop. And duets just weren't fashionable.'

In July 1976, 'Don't Go Breaking My Heart' became Elton's first-ever British number-one single – a triumph he was not to know again for fourteen years. The breezy pledge of undying love to Kiki even prompted some speculation that they might be more than friends. That was how generally safe his secret still remained.

When Margo Stevens became Elton's housekeeper at Woodside, she received one crucial piece of advice from her Rocket colleagues. 'Everyone said the same thing. "If he gets in a mood, leave him alone. Don't try to talk to him or reason him out of it. He gets that way sometimes, and there's nothing anyone can do about it. He'll come out of it on his own if you leave him, and be quite all right." It struck me at the time it was the way grown-ups might talk about a difficult child.'

Elton's move to his new house, early in 1976, was accompanied by one other major change. John Reid did not go to Old Windsor with him. Their domestic relationship had ended, by mutual consent, apparently without recrimination or pain on either side. There was no question but that Reid should continue as Elton's manager nor that, by the curious role reversal their life together had evolved, Elton should be somehow responsible for Reid. Close as they still were, and would always be, they now had different lives, different friends and different addresses. With the considerable wealth he had amassed, and barely spent, since 1971, Reid had bought a new house of his own in London. It was one of the elegant white houses in Montpelier Square that he had coveted as a humble assistant at Austin Reed's menswear store.

Elton was elated by his move to Woodside, seeing it as a real home whereas Hercules had ended up merely a base camp and storehouse. 'I'm basically a home-loving person,' he told Paul Gambaccini in a radio interview. 'I'm tired of wandering round the world. It's time to put down some real roots. I've been having a really good time, walking through the fields, looking at the cows. It may sound corny, but there you go.'

Extensive as the house was, every newly decorated room was at once crowded with Elton's possessions, the crimson buttonback sofas, the Art Nouveau lamps, the pot plants, the jukeboxes, the Rembrandts, the neon signs, the big boots from Tommy, the rail after rail of clothes. The first room to be finished was his record library, an infinity of vertical spines, dimly lit and vaguely sinister, like some data centre at MI5 or the Pentagon.

The domestic layout comprised six self-contained suites, one Elton's own, another kept for John Reid, the rest allotted to aides and friends who came to stay. There was also an office used by Elton's mother Sheila, his day-time châtelaine. When no guests happened to be there, he occupied the main house alone. Margo Stevens's quarters were a self-contained flat in a lodge building called the Orangery. Another outlying cottage was given to Elton's chauffeur, Bob Halley, and his wife, Pearl.

As housekeeper, Margo's duties were not onerous. She had to cook Elton's breakfast, look after his dogs, Bruce and Brian, and his cockatoo, Ollie, an excitable bird whose flappings sometimes set off the house burglar alarms. The rest was housework, taking care to observe the ritual pristine cleanliness and immutably fixed place of everything Elton owned. 'There was a big Casa Pupo rug on the floor in the front hall. I remember Sheila telling me that he liked all its tassels to point in the same direction.'

Elton's habits, when alone, were exceedingly simple. Off the road, he seldom bothered to dress up, spending whole days in nothing more elaborate than a tracksuit and sneakers. The meals that Margo had to prepare for him would be beans on toast, bacon sandwiches, a slice of bread coated with the beef dripping that was permanently kept in the larder. Another proletarian passion was ordinary brown HP sauce, cases of which had to be shipped to him wherever he happened to be on tour. He drank endless cups of tea, had a ragingly sweet tooth and, like a good boy, would eat anything put in front of him, with the single exception of eggs. 'He hated the yolks or the whites. I can't remember now which it was.'

Margo was surprised by how little lavish entertaining went on at Woodside. 'I can only remember one party. Cliff Richard was there, so were Dave Clark and Cathy McGowan. Another time, Freddie Mercury, of Queen, came to dinner. I didn't have to cook for that: it was all catered by Friends, the restaurant John Reid started. And Princess Margaret came to tea, with her two children. When Elton sat down to play for them afterwards, he completely forgot the words of "Candle in the Wind".'

Despite all the people serving and protecting him, he often seemed a lonely figure to Margo, cast adrift in the cluttered, spotless rooms of his Queen Anne labyrinth. 'The house would be full of people;

then, suddenly, there'd be no one there but Elton. A lot of nights, he didn't seem to have anywhere to go or anyone to be with. He'd say to me, "Do you feel like coming over and watching TV for a while?" One time in the kitchen, we had a food fight. We did it just like you see in films – emptying jars of coffee over each other's heads, squirting Fairy liquid, pushing cake into each other's faces. It was something I'd wanted to do all my life. Elton said he had, too.'

At other times he would appear totally self-sufficient, as the boy in Metroland had been, poring over the record albums that now needed an entire library to house them. 'And he'd get spasms of building bonfires and burning things,' Margo Stevens remembers. 'I can see him now, trooping out into the garden in a woolly hat, boots and this bright green Teddy-boy drape jacket.'

The combustibility of his emotions was not revealed to Margo until the night of the party attended by Cliff Richard and Cathy McGowan. 'After everyone had gone, Elton and I were in the kitchen with Bob and Pearl Halley. Something or other was said about the party that upset Elton. He picked up this heavy glass ashtray and flung it across the kitchen. It hit the rail of the café curtains along the window, and smashed. Elton stormed out of the room and up to his suite.'

The procedure for such moments had been firmly impressed on Margo, as on everyone else present. 'They all said, "Leave him alone, he has these Little Moments, he'll get over it." But I thought that was stupid. If someone's upset, you ought at least to try to find out what's wrong.

'So I went upstairs and knocked on the door of Elton's suite. He opened it, still furious, but obviously wanting someone to pour out his heart to. "What the fuck do they all expect me to be?" he said. "What do they want from me?" I just went and hugged him, until he'd calmed down. "I bet they're all talking about me down there," he said. "Let's go and listen." So the two of us crept down the back stairs and listened, and everyone *was* talking about him.

'I think that all his life, whenever he got angry or upset or hurt, people had just backed off and left him alone. I don't think anyone had gone up to him, hugged him and said, "What is it? Do you want to talk?"'

The 1976 American tour likewise was billed as 'Louder Than Concorde' – ironically since, having spent untold fortunes on a supersonic transatlantic plane, Britain now learned that America was refusing to admit Concorde into its airspace.

No hint of any such rejection now greeted that other British export who, in performance terms, had long ago exceeded Mach 3. His live album *Here And There* had reached number four in April; 'Don't Go Breaking My Heart', with Kiki Dee, had been a number-one single in August. His concerts sold out fast enough to raise smoke from the Ticketron computers. Mainstream FM radio still provided a basic Elton John diet, varied by odd, aberrant bites of Linda Ronstadt, Jim Stafford, George McCrae and the Hues Corporation. Despite all misgivings, his American fame was still there intact, huge, inexplicable and comfortingly ridiculous. The *Melody Maker* journalist Chris Charlesworth arrived to cover the tour with an Elton John sticker on his inflight satchel. As he waited to claim his baggage in transit, a young man came up and asked for his autograph.

For all that, the tour was a weary and bleary affair, its atmosphere progressively like those hangovers which set in before the binge is quite over. It had been the most colossal six-year binge. Corks had not yet ceased to pop, nor streamers to fly. But the bubbly now had an acrid taste. Elton was terminally bored with going on the road. In Britain that spring he had tried to regain enthusiasm by leaving the superstar tour circuit of great halls in regional capitals, playing instead to smaller crowds in out-of-the-way places he had not seen since Bluesology days. David Nutter's photographic portfolio shows him travelling almost as a tourist, inconspicuous in parka and tracksuit, visiting Scottish castles, sitting among grubby ashtrays in roadside pubs, queuing at village shops for mundane English ice cream, huddled in the rain next to amusing road signs, eating fish and chips from newspaper and posing on Blackpool promenade in front of the Tower.

America permitted no such relaxation. Here it was just like last year, the year before and the year before that, the same giddy rotor-ride through heart-sinkingly familiar terrain. The same hotel suites of soulless Versailles luxury. The same private Boeing, *Starship 1*, with its cocktail bar and fur-covered kingsize bed. The same police motorcyclists, outriding the same air-conditioned stretch limousines. The same hustle through backstage areas of breeze blocks and chicken wire. The same dressing rooms, filled with flowers and well-wishing celebrities. The same walk out on to huge indoor or massive outdoor stages, to discover the same infinities of faces, adoring voices and upstretched arms.

Besides, there was now a greater preoccupation than music on Elton's mind. Earning a fortune in America seemed small by comparison with his chairmanship of Watford Football Club and his responsibility to help save the club from financial disaster. He even interrupted the tour to fly back and preside at the Watford board's annual general meeting.

His stage wardrobe reflected this new state of mind. His American fans, to their disappointment, beheld no feathered space cowboy, no beplumed Edwardian dowager, no walking mass of coloured balls, no glittery Venetian doge. Most nights, he performed in plain tracksuit and sneakers, the same outfit that the Watford first team would be wearing across the time zones in practice sessions at Vicarage Road. To these were added a miscellany hastily scooped up from his sartorial back catalogue: the matador jacket, seen on several previous tours, with big bars down its lapels; baseball caps, striped T-shirts, ski overalls, a fluffy duck suit, a straw boater, his old Uncle Sam top hat. To complete the ragbag ensemble, a dangling outsize carrot or strawberry. More than once, going out to greet the adoring continent, Elton looked a downright mess.

Different, too, was his view of the audience whose welcome had once been able to lift him from the blackest misery and self-doubt. Now, instead of 'smiling faces', he saw only a prison wall whose seething bricks happened to be human. Instead of renewing love, he felt pressure, even danger. Into his fathomlessly pessimistic mind popped a thought which, in 1976, still seemed laughable. Suppose that, in some nameless fan, adoration should metamorphose into hate? Suppose that, on some or other tropic stadium night, somebody should take a shot at him?

One fact weighed heavily, above all. In six months would come his thirtieth birthday, the formal end of youth. Unequipped as he was for an idol, he had at least always possessed that one fundamental qualification. He could pass, just about, as a balding young pop star. What was the world to make, though, of a balding, ageing pop star?

The exhaustions of touring, which youth had always thoughtlessly shrugged off, now began to take visible toll. One of David Nutter's photographs shows Elton aboard *Starship 1*, not drinking, playing piano, opening presents or looning as usual, but stretched on a sofa, dead to the world. Another picture shows him slumped in a chair, in striped lapels, striped socks and sparkly shoes, an outsize banana dangling on his chest. His face looks worn away with fatigue. The eyes, through the joke glasses, are glazed and uncomprehending.

For Bernie Taupin, even more than Elton, *ennui* was growing intolerable. He had been on virtually every American tour since 1970, watching from the wings, night after night, week after week. Elton always insisted on having him there, to emphasise that the music was 50 per cent his and give him his rightful share of the applause. All these years, touring had seemed like the most wonderful free ride from luxury jet to hotel suite, from room service to party. But Bernie, too, was starting to feel the years.

He insisted that he was happy just to be around, listening to Elton sing his words and seeing their effect on audiences. He was an eternal VIP in his security badge giving 'Access to all backstage areas'; a star with no role but to socialise in dressing rooms, pick his way over the ramps protecting electric cables, and watch for the signal to take his place in the limo before Elton's finale began. His was an odd blend of fame and obscurity, a back-room boy without whom the front-of-curtain man could not function; Boswell to Elton's piano-pounding Johnson. So reticent had he been about personal publicity that few of the millions who knew his lyrics by heart had any clear idea of what he looked like, or even how to pronounce his surname. At twenty-six, he was just as famous and just as obscure as he had been at twenty-two. His collected lyrics had just been published as an opulent book, with cover by Alan Aldridge and each song interpreted by a leading pop illustrator. Bernie's title for it echoed his caustic view of himself: *The One Who Writes the Words for Elton John.*

His private life was now very different from that early country idyll at Piglet-in-the-Wilds. His American wife, Maxine, had left him after barely four years of marriage. To compound the injury, Maxine started an affair with Elton's bass player Kenny Passarelli, who had formerly been Bernie's closest crony on the road.

He himself was now dating various people, including the singer Lynsey de Paul, and living mostly in his Los Angeles house. 'The place was virtually empty,' he remembers. 'All that was there were a couple of beds and some hi-fi equipment. Just like the rock-star houses I remembered seeing when Elton and I first came to America.'

The shy Lincolnshire poet was scarcely visible in David Nutter's picture of Bernie backstage, wearing a Stetson and sunglasses and swigging beer from a bottle. He had put on weight, thanks to heavy drinking, and, like many musician friends, had acquired a cocaine habit. With the ritual self-effacement went an ego, he himself admits, that rivalled any to be found on the public rock stage. These were the high days of contractual riders, special clauses under which rock superstars compelled promoters to provide Byzantine dressing-room amenities, from Can-Can girls and vintage brandy to Smarties with all the red ones taken out. Bernie's personal rider on tour with Elton was that he must always be provided with Coors beer. Budweiser would not do, nor Miller, nor Schlitz, nor Michelob, nor any of the other myriad American brews with their barely distinguishable tastes. If Coors were not available for Bernie where the tour happened to be, special supplies had to be airlifted in.

Kenny Passarelli continued to play in the band, which was unchanged but for the absence through illness of percussionist Ray Cooper. To show how Elton valued Cooper, a life-size dummy of him stood onstage until he was well enough to fly from Britain for the tour's final dates. Kiki Dee also appeared in the New York shows, to sing the hit duet with Elton that some still took to signal more than friendship.

It was, to outward appearance, the usual triumphal trans-American journey, magnetising the usual throng of backstage celebrities: Shirley MacLaine, Don Covay, The Jacksons, Queen, Frankie Valli from the Four Seasons, Leonard Nimoy, from TV's *Star Trek*. In Atlanta, Elton met Mayor Maynard Jackson. In Philadelphia, he met Mayor Frank Rizzo. The readers of *Playboy* magazine had voted Elton world's number-one vocalist and keyboard player, and Bernie and him world's number-one song-writers. To receive the awards, they were invited to Hugh Hefner's Playboy mansion in Chicago, that fabled pleasure grotto where the Rolling Stones, a few years before, had caroused in whirlpools with compliant Bunnies, but where Elton and Bernie now just played pinball with Hefner and his new centrefold love, Barbi Benton. In David Nutter's photographs, the occasion has an oddly tired and passé feel, Elton and Bernie in their flared, waisted suits with shirt collars open over butterfly lapels; even Hefner hippyish now, in a horrid little denim safari suit. Seventies fashion is already dead though, alas, it will never, ever quite lie down.

There was only one great American idol that Elton had not yet met, and on this tour he finally got to meet Elvis Presley. But by now little resemblance could be seen to the marvellous young punk who had revolutionised the posture, intonation and wet dreams of postwar British youth. In 1976, just a year before his death from narcotics abuse, 'the King' was a walking mummy, encrusted with Seventies tomb-ornaments, obese, incontinent and almost blind. 'We went to see him do a show,' Bernie Taupin remembers, 'but it was absolutely pitiful. He was so drugged, he could hardly sing – he just stood there, handing out scarves. Then we were taken backstage to see him. There was this dressing room, full of Memphis Mafia, with Elvis in the middle of them on a stool, wrapped in towels. He looked awful, he was sweating, with the dye from his hair running down his face. And all these guys in suits around him in a kind of huddle. I don't think he even knew who we were. As we walked away afterwards, Elton said, "He's not long for this world."' The awful spectacle of a great star, falling apart among servants and minders, shocked Elton to the core.

In New York in August, Elton broke the box-office record for a rock act at Madison Square Garden, playing seven consecutive nights to a total of 137,900 people. The last night's finale included Kiki Dee, Alice Cooper, Billie Jean King and the burly drag queen Divine. Its climax was Elton's appearance dressed as the Statue of Liberty, authentic in every detail but the white-framed glasses and stuck-out chin. That selfsame aureoled maiden, with torch aloft, had beckoned Reg Dwight from *New Musical Express* in the summer of 1967, when Liberty Records advertised for new talent.

At the start of the tour, MCA had announced to the US media that Elton would not be giving any press or TV interviews this time. The tireless provider of good copy was weary of doing that, too. Exceptions were made only for the two most serious music papers in Britain and America respectively, *Melody Maker* and *Rolling Stone*. Much as the obligation might bore him, when Elton gave an interview, he still could not help but give a good one. In this case, each of the lucky recipients was to find itself sitting on a world scoop.

To *Melody Maker*'s Chris Charlesworth, inflight on *Starship 1*, Elton revealed that the present tour would be his last for the foreseeable future. 'I've done it for six years, and I'm fed up with it,' he said. 'Not fed up with playing so much as with having no base and constantly roaming around. I don't want the pressure of having to tour for another two years or so.'

The idea had been fermenting in Elton's mind for many months. What had clearly brought it to a head was his meeting with Elvis Presley in Washington. He had suddenly seen with awful clarity how he himself might end like Elvis. 'I mean . . . I used to like walking round New York, but I can't do it any more. I can't go out of the hotel without someone causing a fuss, and, no matter how hard I try, I can't disguise myself. I can't live my life in a shell, like Elvis Presley or whoever. I have to do something positive, and getting associated with a soccer club is my way of doing it. I'm still dealing with people, but in a much more human situation. It won't be quite so insane as the music business.'

He stressed this wasn't permanent retirement, just a lay-off to give him leisure at his new house and time to devote to Rocket and Watford. His stage band was not to be broken up, but put on ice until he needed them again. 'I want to carry on being involved in music and sport together,' he told Chris Charlesworth. 'I want to be chairman of Watford, even if they are in a precarious position. I have wild ambitions for them because their ground can hold thousands, unlike most Fourth Division clubs. I dream about standing there in the directors' box on the night they win promotion. All the time, that's my one dream.'

Rolling Stone won its access despite having recently upset Elton with its story about Mick Jagger and him. The magazine had championed him since his earliest days and, in much lively, honest coverage, had only rarely given offence. Elton's 1973 *Rolling Stone* interview was considered one of the best with its rollicking tales of bedsitter life in Tin Pan Alley and Islington. To sustain another cover story, however, something more than recycled family and musical history would be needed. This, true to form, Elton provided in spades.

The last unrevealed detail about himself, though widely known and generally suspected, had never been officially confirmed. Everything about Elton John's public persona and private lifestyle suggested that he was homosexual. In fact, he was bisexual, capable of relationships both with women and men; prone to that capricious weather vane of the psyche that, without warning, can blow to totally opposite compass points. Most males, if they would admit it, pass through a bisexual phase at some time in their lives, but only for a tiny minority does the irresolution become permanent. As a rule, the immature homosexual phase moves on of its own accord to a mature and conclusive heterosexual one. The condition, where we can study it – in E. M. Forster's *Maurice*, or the modern, courageous writings of Colin Spencer – commonly shows male bisexuals ending up happily married, with children. For those tormented or perplexed by their condition, there was that ray of hope.

The secret that Elton had kept so sedulously through the early Seventies seemed of dwindling importance in 1976. Such had been glitter rock's blurring of gender that to be – or seem to be – bisexual was almost a requirement for chart-success. This was the time when David Bowie filled stadia across the world with his androgynous posturing; when the Rolling Stones wore Victorian sailor suits with full make-up; when Gary Glitter moved ever closer to the stage techniques of Danny La Rue; when Freddie Mercury flaunted a sateen ballet dancer's bottom in front of a band named Queen; when even so ravening a heterosexual as Rod Stewart found profit in coming onstage decked out in frills and turquoise satin tights like the fairy from atop some whorehouse Christmas tree.

Seventies fashion seemed to have swept away all former notions of macho masculinity. The least chic figures, from businessmen to trade union leaders, now wore their hair straggly-long, their sideburns to the extremities of their cheeks, their clothes in the flared, waisted and scalloped style which hinted, however vaguely, at the Regency fop.

The dourest northern England industrial town now had at least one pub that put on lunch-time drag shows to huge, appreciative stag audiences, and at least one hairdresser's window displaying the word 'Unisex'. The very construction workers now wore floral patterns with prissy shades of pale green and plum, sported small gold rings in their ears and used tall canisters of hair lacquer to tint their ashen pompadours.

How Elton's secret had not leaked out into the British press – even then notoriously more sensationalist than the American – must count as a minor miracle of news management, and self-management. Certainly, it was known to every national journalist who covered pop, like David Wigg of the *Daily Express*. Again we find a parallel with the Beatles, whose human and fallible aspects were resolutely ignored by Fleet Street for the first three years of their career. The stories that sold papers were about cuddly mop-tops, and so these were provided, whatever evidence might crop up to the contrary. Similarly with Elton now, the story that sold papers was of Mr Nice Guy: the rock star like no other in his clean-living ways, who put off his wild outfits to reveal a paragon, quiet, virtuous and devoted to his mother – 'The Cliff Richard of rock' as Elton himself wryly put it. Few such media efforts to maintain a reputation had been mounted since the days of Edward VIII and Mrs Simpson.

Elton himself, honest to the core, did not enjoy lying even by omission. More than once in the past year, he had teetered on the edge of confessing all, prompted by interviewers like Caroline Coon or *Playboy* magazine. What had chiefly restrained him was his new role as chairman of Watford, and the very different standards that applied in the world of football. Here his mother had been powerfully influential, urging him to cut down the camp when he attended Watford functions in his official capacity, and to do nothing that might harm the image of the club.

John Reid was extremely anxious that Elton should not come clean, even though their personal relationship had now ended. His reasons were hard-headed business ones. David Bowie had admitted to being homosexual in 1972; otherwise, through all the primping, pouting, drag-queenly world of glitter rock, there was not one performer who owned himself other than 100 per cent normal in the Victorian sense. Besides, Bowie had come out at a time when pop musicians received almost no coverage in the British and American press. Elton, by contrast, was a world figure, with connections to high society, even to royalty, and a reputation for having a positive influence on the morals of the young. However permissive and tolerant the climate might seem, no one could predict the effect of such news on his record sales and concert drawing power.

All this had been impressed on Elton many times, but – as Reid was well aware – one never knew what he might do on the spur of the moment. Accordingly, Rocket's press officer, Caroline Boucher, had orders to eavesdrop on his interviews, and to act whenever revelation seemed to be trembling on the horizon. Harder-nosed Fleet Street men, like the *Sun*'s Bob Hart and the *Mail*'s Mike Housego were by now vying with each other to nail the story. 'I came into the room just in time to stop Hart getting it,' Caroline Boucher remembers. *The Sun* being then still a paper that required genuine quotes to prop up its stories, Bob Hart remained in hot pursuit.

Caroline Boucher, alas, was not on hand when Elton met *Rolling Stone*'s interviewer, Cliff Jahr. By now, at the end of his tour, the quiet Dr Jekyll who had discussed football and normality with Chris Charlesworth had turned into a hyper and mischievous Mr Hyde. Earlier, he had appeared on WNEW radio, goosey on Dom Perignon, and intemperately attacked the *New York Times* for its review of him at Madison Square Garden. 'If you're listening, asshole,' he said to the *Times*' pop critic, John Rockwell, 'come down here, and I'll destroy you. I'll rip you to pieces on the air . . . I bet he's about four foot one. I bet he's got bogeys up his nose. I bet his feet smell.'

In New York – where homosexuality was now a familiar part of everyday life and gay pride a strong social movement – far more pressure existed to come out. David Bowie seemed to be pointing the finger, saying in a recent *Playboy* interview that Elton was 'the Liberace, the token queen of rock . . . I consider myself responsible for a whole new school of pretensions – they know who they are. Don't you Elton?' Elton seemed to be relaxing his usual discretion, talking campily on WNEW radio, using a drag queen in his stage show, even letting Divine take him to Crisco Disco, a leading gay night spot (named after the frying oil that was a popular sexual lubricant).

The interview destined to break the mould took place in the hotel suite, normally used by Elizabeth Taylor, where Elton had spent two weeks virtually a prisoner between concerts. To make it more homey, it had been stuffed with things from his LA house: potted trees, Teddy bears, piles of records and two pinball machines, respectively lighting up the names Captain Fantastic and Goodbye Yellow Brick Road. Cliff Jahr was initially somewhat dismayed by the tired, shy figure who sat opposite him, seldom meeting his eyes. Only later did he realise how consummately Elton had played to the tape recorder.

After some initial stonewalling about what David Bowie might have meant, and a fracas that had occurred at the door of Crisco

Disco, Jahr came right to the point. What happened when Elton came home at night? Did he have 'love and affection'?

'Not really. I go home and fall in love with my vinyl,' Elton replied. 'I suppose I have a certain amount of love and affection as far as "affection" goes. From friends and stuff. My sexual life? Um. I haven't really met anyone I'd want to have any big scenes with. It's strange that I haven't. I know everyone should have a certain amount of sex, and I do, but that's it, and I desperately want to have an affair. I crave to be loved. That's the part of my life I want to have come together in the next two or three years, and it's partly why I'm quitting the road. My life in the last six years has been a Disney film, and now I want to have a person in my life.

'I don't know what I want to be exactly. I'm just going through a stage where any sign of affection would be welcome on a sexual level. I'd rather fall in love with a woman eventually because I think a woman probably lasts much longer than a man. But I really don't know. I've never talked like this before. Ha ha. But I'm not going to turn off the tape. I haven't met anyone I would like to settle down with – of either sex.'

No press officer rushing in, with a stop-watch, Jahr was free to ask on the record, 'You're bisexual?'

'There's nothing wrong with going to bed with someone of your own sex,' Elton said. 'I think everyone's bisexual to a certain degree. I don't think it's just me. I think you're bisexual. I think everyone is.'

He'd never said so in print before?

'Probably not. It's going to be terrible with my football club. It's so hetero, it's unbelievable. But I mean, who cares? I just think people should be very free with sex – they should draw the line at goats.'

Had his first experience been with a man or woman?

'Um, when I was twenty-one, with a woman. The famous one.'

And how soon after that the first man?

'Um. The famous woman frightened me off sex for so long that I don't remember really. I think it was probably a good year or two.'

Had he and Bernie Taupin been lovers?

'No, absolutely not. Everybody thinks we were, but if we had been, I don't think we would have lasted so long. We're more like brothers than anything else. The press probably thought John Reid and I were an affair, but there's never been a serious person the whole time.'

Was he afraid that, on reading these disclosures, *Rolling Stone* readers would go 'Wow!'

'Well, I don't think so. There shouldn't be too much reaction . . . Nobody's had the balls to ask me about it before. I would have said something all along if someone had asked me, but I'm not going to come out and say something just to be – I don't want to shove it all over the front pages like some people I could mention. To be on the front of newspapers with my tongue down somebody's throat. That's really appalling.

'I'd like to have children, but I don't know if the time is right. I just want to settle down and sort of be lazy for a while. There are a couple of people back in England. I do have a crush on someone, but I can't say who it is – someone I met two or three times, who is American . . . I go for older women. Listen, Shirley MacLaine would do me fine . . .'

Only now was there an interruption. John Reid entered from the next room, where he had been playing pinball. But even this did not inhibit Elton, who – Jahr afterwards wrote – seemed relieved to have the whole thing out in the open at last.

'As soon as anyone tries to find out about me or to get to know me, I turn off,' he continued. 'I'm afraid of getting hurt. I was hurt so much as a kid. I'm afraid of plunging into something that's going to fuck me up. It's reached a point in my life where I get to my house and my animals and think, "Who am I going to . . .?" I'm certainly not going to bed with my horse. Ha ha. And I think, "Christ, I wish I had someone to share all this with." '

ELTON'S FRANK TALK: THE LONELY LIFE OF A SUPERSTAR was *Rolling Stone*'s principal cover line on 7 November, 1976. With it went a picture of Elton, lounging cheerfully enough in his big white specs and a sweater decorated with striped-shirted footballers. Inside was a more suitably sombre portrait, in straw boater, with heart-shaped spectacles. 'My life in the last six years has been a Disney film,' ran the subheading. 'Now I have to have a person in my life.'

The treatment could not have been more tasteful and sympathetic and *Rolling Stone*'s liberal young readership, for the most part, responded in kind. Next issue, half the magazine's correspondence column was given to readers' letters on the subject, aptly headed 'Dear Johns'. 'This is undoubtedly the best interview with Elton John I've ever read,' wrote Kathryn Cwikla, of Wethersfield, Connecticut. 'It is very sensitive and in parts touching.' 'He has opened my mind completely,' wrote C. Deley of Lima, Ohio. 'I'm never going to judge anyone by what they are physically, but instead by what an individual is inside . . .' A few were negative. 'My disgust is matched only by my disappointment, which are both overshadowed by pity,' wrote Lisa Crane of Provo, Utah. 'I pity him for his sexual illusions and perversions . . .' 'Elton John, leading proponent of fungus rock, is no more artistic than articulate,' wrote Bryan Johnson of Saginaw,

Michigan. 'Life is real, Elton and what will you do with yours? You're a commercial success, and that's about it.'

In Britain, the story broke in the mildest possible way. The mass-circulation dailies, *Mirror*, *Mail* and *Express*, reported Elton's confession on inside pages, merely as pick-ups of the *Rolling Stone* interview, in tones of no surprise and with no attempt to mount a wolf-pack-style follow-up. *The Sun*, amazingly, did not think it worth mentioning at all. The big fear was the Sunday tabloids, especially the *News of the World* with its voyeuristic relish for stories of sex and rock 'n' roll. But even in the 'News of the Screws', treatment was downbeat. ELTON: MY LOVE LIFE ISN'T SO STRANGE said a headline in lower-case white reversed on black. The *News of the World*'s reporter had caught Elton as he arrived with the Watford team to play an away match in Rochdale, Lancashire. Elton – 'wearing a check suit with orange trimmings, and pink-framed spectacles' – was as forthcoming as always.

'I don't see why people should be so surprised,' he was quoted as saying. 'The only reason I hadn't spoken about it before was that no one asked me. It's not important, nor is it a big thing in my life. I don't see why it should affect the fan worship I've got. It hasn't hurt David Bowie, and I don't see why it should hurt me.'

Even the *News of the World* was content merely to repeat the relevant parts of the (uncredited) *Rolling Stone* interview, and Elton's denial that he'd ever had an affair with Bernie Taupin. Beside the headline was one of Bernie's infrequent photographs, with the caption: 'Elton denied gossip about him'.

All in all there was not a fraction of the harassment and persecution that would attend a far less legitimate story about Elton eleven years later. Apart from a call to his father (who had heard the news with blank bewilderment) Elton's family was left in peace. Not until some time afterwards did his mother give her response. 'I was upset at first,' Sheila admitted. 'But I think it was a brave thing for him to do. I would still like to think he can find happiness with a male or female – I don't care.'

Elton's great fear, as he admitted to Cliff Jahr, was the response of Watford, his fellow directors and, even more, the team he was trying to inspire to League promotion. All at Watford, too, diplomatically expressed total astonishment, from the club secretary, Ron Rollitt, to Keith Mercer, the twenty-year-old forward who had joined Elton in practice kick-arounds with Rod Stewart. The consensus, among fellow directors and in the changing-room, was that it should make no difference. Elton was by now more than just Watford's only possible path to salvation. He was also liked and respected. The revelations about a private life he had kept far from Vicarage Road changed nothing.

The wider world of football, however, was to show no such forbearance. Nor did it recognise any fine distinction of terms. Throughout the Football League, Watford now found itself stigmatised as the club led by a 'poof'. Under football-crowd logic, that made Watford players, too, by association, 'poofs'. The team had to endure being so called, both by spectators and by their opponents on the field of play. Elton's own appearance in the Rochdale directors' box was to begin an era calling on every possible reserve of chin-jutting doggedness. Shouts of 'poof' and 'queer' from rival supporters would prove the least among such public ordeals. At one later match he attended, the crowd spent twenty minutes chanting 'Elton John's a homosexual' to the tune of 'John Brown's Body'.

An unfortunate postscript was supplied by the cover of Elton's new album, *Blue Moves*. For this he had chosen a painting from his own, now impressive, collection, 'The Guardian Readers' by Patrick Procktor. Hawk eyes in Fleet Street noted that in Procktor's delicate group, every figure was that of a young man.

As part of the album's promotion, fifty copies were to have been given away as prizes for a readers' competition in *The Sun*. This was cancelled because, as the paper disingenuously explained, the album cover 'didn't have a woman on it'.

Blue Moves was Elton's first album for Rocket and as such was intended to be a blockbuster. He insisted it must be a double album, the first since *Goodbye Yellow Brick Road* in 1973. His new distributor, EMI, acceded to his wishes, even though double albums were far trickier things to sell in the price-sensitive record market of 1976.

Blue Moves turned out to be anything but the bright herald of a new era. Bernie Taupin's new lyrics had a downbeat, pessimistic tone, the consequence of his breakup with Maxine and his general feeling of uncertainty and drift. 'Between Seventeen and Twenty', for instance, mourned the absurdly young age at which he had married, believing that everything would be House at Pooh Corner-perfect. Nor did other titles, like 'Cage the Songbird', 'Somebody's Final Song', 'If There's a God in Heaven (What's He Waiting for?)' and 'Sorry Seems to Be the Hardest Word', point to a happy or optimistic viewpoint. To lighten the tone, there were two instrumentals: one by Elton's guitarist Caleb Quaye; the other, redolent of Elton humour, entitled 'Theme From a Non-Existent TV Series'.

Gloomy or not, *Blue Moves* almost joined the great range of Elton album peaks, climbing to number three in both Britain and America. It was in fact not the start of an era, but the end of one. The days of looking down from those twin summits – fearing the moment when he might slip to number two – were gone for ever.

Choosing 'Sorry Seems to Be the Hardest Word' as the first single from the album could hardly have been more appropriate. Unhappy love lament though it was, it came across more as a polite note, from that usually well-behaved Metroland boy, to anyone whose sensibilities he might recently have offended. 'It's a sad sad situation' he sang in a moment of unconscious physiological truth, the superstar suddenly as forlorn and vulnerable as Reggie Dwight had ever been. He seemed to be asking for mercy and, in general, receiving it.

13

'There's a lot more to me than being on the road'

IN July 1976, the British pop tycoon Richard Branson threw a lavish garden party at the country house he used as a studio for his record organisation, Virgin. Among the guests was Caroline Coon, the liberal activist turned music writer, accompanied by a blond youth who seemed ill at ease among all the Seventies rock aristocrats. By day, the youth was an electrician at Barclay's brewery, a job involving so little work, he had to be paid extra for being bored. By night, he played drums in a new band, the Sex Pistols.

Six months later, the Sex Pistols were the terrorists of British pop. A group stupendously lacking all natural ability, they had come together in a Chelsea boutique called Sex, owned by the designer Vivienne Westwood. Their manager was Westwood's boyfriend, Malcolm McLaren, a shock-headed elf who combined aspirations to be a rock-'n'-roll Svengali in the Larry Parnes mould with vague theories about music as a tool of radical politics. The Sex Pistols, for McLaren, reincarnated the primeval state of rock 'n' roll, twenty years earlier. They were as musically inept as the Fifties establishment had considered Elvis Presley. Their performances unleashed the same chaos and destruction that Bill Haley's Comets had wrought in clubs, theatres and cinemas. Their discordant voices fell on Seventies ears as terribly as had Little Richard's first 'awopbopaloobopalopbamboom'.

In his quartet of talentless Cockney youths McLaren brilliantly focused the Seventies' twin propensities, for pastiche and mindless violence. Their lead singer was named Johnny Rotten, antithesis of all smiling idols at the mike, a shambling teenage heap with shabby clothes, filthy, spiky hair and green teeth, who sang in a demented whinge, in the intervals swearing at his audience, spitting at them, throwing bottles or lashing out with his fists. The bass player was named Sid Vicious, a genuine psychopath who would publicly cut bits off himself with knives or broken glass.

As exponents of 'punk rock' – a term hijacked by McLaren from the era of Lou Reed and the Velvet Underground – the Sex Pistols blazed a trail that made the Rolling Stones' Sixties outrages seem tame by comparison. They preached 'anarchy in the UK', encouraged brawling and bloodshed at their gigs, insulted the Queen, spat vodka at press photographers, destroyed toilets at the office of their record company and vomited in the public concourse at Heathrow airport. They inspired a new dance, 'pogoing', and a new form of audience appreciation, 'gobbing'. Their apotheosis was a family talk show on Thames Television when Johnny Rotten, the self-proclaimed 'Antichrist', repeatedly shouted four-letter words at his boggling middle-aged interviewer.

Even Malcolm McLaren, however, did not realise how perfect were his creation to be heroes in 1977. For the first time in twenty years, a generation was coming to teenagerdom in a world where it was not so very wonderful to be young. The former perquisites of youth – garish clothes, extravagant hair, wild music and feckless hedonism – now belonged to all age groups under the woozy make-believe Seventies sun. In both America and Britain, youth shared the same realities as everyone else: spiralling inflation, fear of terrorist bombs, decaying infrastructure and inner-city slums. In Britain in this year, one in every two school-leavers could expect to go straight into the unemployment line. Yet the music they heard was still glittery flimflam, played by complacent, ageing longhairs on acoustic guitars or fiddly mandolins.

Johnny Rotten's spit of Luddite rage was the signal for instantaneous general revolt. Like Steven Spielberg gremlins, punk rock bands started popping out everywhere, with similarly uninviting names – the Damned, the Clash – similar lack of melodic talent and similar huge juvenile audiences. The unifying factor was furious contempt for Seventies rock culture in all its forms, the huge arenas, the four-hour delays, the million-pound light shows and house-size amps, the permed yellow hair, the frilly shirts, the dobros and mandolins, the harmony, the clarity, the dexterity, the vanity, the snobbery, the hype. So punk-rock bands sang off key and struggled to find three-finger chords in claustrophobic clubs on gimcrack stages within spitting distance – literally – of the audience. It was not music so much as a kind of mass satire, taunting the rock status quo with cacophonous parodies of itself, mocking its supposedly ageless gods as preposterous dinosaurs.

With the music that negated music came fashion negating fashion – a look drawn from horror movies and the wardrobe of the sadomasochist, including cactus-spiked green hair, rubber trousers incapacitatingly tied together at the knee, shirts and coats deliberately rent into shreds and large safety pins worn as ornaments by being driven through nose or cheek. From here on, the way to show oneself past youth, or at the nadir of style, was to wear anything structured, anything waisted or – God forbid! – anything flared.

Re-enacting the 'British Invasion' of ten years before (in every particular but charm) punk rock spread to New York, then Los Angeles, then all points in between, turning an entire industry on its head and consigning millions who had believed themselves trendy to premature middle age. The flower children's young brothers and sisters, who had seized power in 1972, and replaced Bob Dylan with Gary Glitter, now themselves fell victim to an even more comprehensive revenge.

A prescient few in the rock establishment did not join the general chorus of horror and disgust. Among them was a 'dinosaur' who could be presumed at the very top of the punks' extermination list. Elton had always said, 'It's a sign of people getting old when they start grousing about the new groups.' In his thirty-first year, he was not about to slip into that habit.

He had always been remarkably free from musical prejudice, able to stand back and see how even tinselly nine-days wonders like the Osmonds or Bay City Rollers perfectly satisfied their particular audiences. To Elton, punk rock was like turning back the clock to mid-Fifties skiffle days, when anyone could pick up a guitar and have a bash. He was also fascinated by the implications for the record industry, as the major companies were forced to recognise the huge following of punk music, and back-street labels, run by boys with safety pins through their faces, suddenly became a force in the marketplace.

He could congratulate himself on perfect timing, having got out of the rock-idol business just a split second before it dissolved into bloody revolution. The sensible and realistic side of him knew, and was reconciled to the fact, that his incredible reign over mass musical taste was over. 'He was no way giving up,' David Croker, Rocket's then general manager, remembers. 'He was going to carry on putting out records and being himself, no matter which way the business went. But he wouldn't be King of the World any more.'

At Rocket, as at all record companies of the old order, life went on, shaken but still resolute, rather like that of tsarist aristocrats after the Bolsheviks had captured the streets. Elton was amply fulfilling his promise to use retirement for the development and production of Rocket's smaller in-house talents. He worked on a second album for Kiki Dee, and helped bring on two new bands, China and Blue, whose names, six months before, had seemed the very height of fashion.

He was further involved in the colourful and diversifying activities of John Reid Enterprises. For, now that there was no longer an Elton John road show to steer around the world, Reid was busily extending his entrepreneurial empire. As well as his first and paramount client, he now managed Queen, with the competitively flamboyant Freddie Mercury. Under Reid's tutelage, Queen had had a massive single hit with 'Bohemian Rhapsody', a six-minute operetta for which many people – Elton included – had predicted failure. What chiefly sold the single was a video film, made specially for television, showing Mercury and his band in a narcissistic kaleidoscope. The age of pop video started here.

Reid's enterprises, however, now extended far beyond the world of pop. In 1976, he had acquired an interest in the Edinburgh Playhouse theatre – hence its choice as venue for Elton's supposed farewell UK performance that September. Pursuing his long-time interest in food and cookery, Reid also opened a restaurant called Friends in London's Covent Garden. Elton put money into Friends, and – gossip writers were promised – might even occasionally turn up there, playing piano for the customers.

Something else was on John Reid's back burner, coming slowly but inexorably to the boil. This was the matter of Elton's contracts with the Dick James Organisation, which, although now expired, still regulated his publishing income up to 1973 and his recording income up to 1975. Reid had first queried these agreements in 1971, when he took over Elton's management on DJM's behalf. He had been probing around the matter ever since, constrained from open challenge by the need to keep Dick James co-operative while the contracts remained in force. Now that all had ended, the gloves could finally come off.

In 1976, he poached another key executive from DJM, persuading the solicitor Geoffrey Ellis to come across to John Reid Enterprises. Ellis was soon involved in Reid's efforts to prove that Elton's DJM contracts had not been fair and that, in the years since 1967, he and Bernie Taupin had received less than their due share of publishing royalties.

The matter was already being pursued by Reid's accountants, Shears and Co., who, in mid-1976, conducted an audit of DJM's books with regard to royalties due to Elton and Bernie Taupin up to December 1975. Geoffrey Ellis could provide further information relating to their publishing royalties from overseas. In 1975, DJM had made changes in the network of sub-publishers who collected royalties on their behalf throughout Europe. Barry Lyons of Shears accordingly wrote to DJM, asking for details of their foreign sub-publishers and licensees, and relevant contracts and agreements. DJM replied that the new arrangements were for internal convenience only, and that the contracts were based on 'normal commercial practice'. Since Elton and Bernie had 'a privileged form of agreement' with DJM's This Record Co., which guaranteed them a fixed percentage of its income, their royalty earnings would not be affected.

In October 1977, Shears finally obtained details of the new European sub-publishing arrangements. They were passed to an accountant named Alan Feigenbaum, whose reading of them suggested that, on the contrary, Elton and Bernie's income was adversely affected, possibly by as much as 50 per cent. Geoffrey Ellis reported these findings to John Reid, who instructed Feigenbaum to compute the full total of the presumed losses.

Geoffrey Ellis was too distinguished and discreet a figure ever to bear the brunt of Reid's temperament. But he was, several times, a fascinated spectator. Life with Brian Epstein had been placid by comparison.

'There was one occasion when John had been in Los Angeles, and was expected back in the office that day. We were very much involved in negotiations about income tax and on the day of his return, I had to go to a meeting with a leading tax counsel. A phone call was put through to me at the chambers. It was John, asking me to come back to the office. "When?" I said. "This is an extremely important meeting." "As soon as you can," he said. "I've fired all the staff."

'When I got back to South Audley Street, it was like the aftermath of an explosion. There was an eerie silence . . . every desk deserted. John had come back from Los Angeles in a temper, and told everyone to go. "There were too many hangers-on," he said. "You and I can run this place just between the two of us." I walked through the building, and found a couple of girls huddled together in the telephone-room.

'"All right, John," I said. "But we do need secretaries. And we do need people to answer the telephone." Within a few days, everyone had trickled back and was working normally again.'

Explosive as Reid was, he still managed to inspire loyalty, even affection, among the Rocket staff. 'He could be quite sweet as well, though he did his best not to show it,' Margo Stevens remembers. 'There was one time when he'd been in Paris, and came back, steaming through the office the way he always did – like the Road-Runner. Some of us were sitting on the floor, putting together stuff to mail out. As John came past, he threw something at me. It was a bottle of perfume.'

In almost schizophrenic contrast with the fear that Reid inspired at Rocket were the magnificent perks its employees received, like being flown to Los Angeles by chartered jet for a week. Christmas was a time of Dickensian largesse as Elton made his arrival with the traditional cornucopia from Cartier. 'He went around the whole office, handing out Cartier watches and pens,' Geoffrey Ellis remembers. 'Everyone got something – not just me but my secretary as well. And every single one had a personal card attached.'

He was equally generous at Watford, throwing parties for individual players who did well in matches, sending piles of new albums in an attempt to improve the team's generally abysmal pop musical taste. He took pains to get to know everyone at the club, not only the team and the office and ground staff but also their wives and children. One of his great pleasures was to be the summer garden party he organised for Watford employees and their families at Woodside, with sports events and games and everything else that Reggie Dwight used to miss in summers long ago, shut indoors at his eternal piano practice.

There was more to Elton's chairmanship of Watford, however, than simply being Mr Nice Guy. He had decided early on that the club's existing manager, Mike Keen, was not the person to lift it from the doldrums. After a further lacklustre season, when Watford managed to rise by only one place in Division Four, from eighth to seventh, Keen was ousted from the managership in favour of Elton's personal nominee.

He had long had his talent spotter's eye on Graham Taylor, the young player-manager who had spectacularly revived the fortunes of another moribund Fourth Division club, Lincoln City. In June 1977, he phoned Taylor and offered him the Watford job. Taylor, who had recently turned down an offer to manage First Division West Bromwich Albion, saw little to tempt him initially. 'I thought it was the last thing I wanted,' he says now. 'To go back into the Fourth Division, managing some southern club, with an outrageous pop star messing around as chairman.

'What impressed me was Elton's reaction when I rang him to say no. I expected him to try to hustle me with big talk about money and potential. But he didn't argue, didn't try to change my mind. Just wished me all the best at Lincoln, and said he hoped he might see me one day. By the time I rang off, I wanted to meet him.'

Several other candidates for the Watford job were mooted, including former England team captain Bobby Robson. Elton, meanwhile, waited for Graham Taylor's return from summer holiday, then approached him again. This time Taylor agreed, won over by the simplicity of Elton's dream for Watford. 'He said he wanted to take them to the top, and into Europe. I said, "Do you have an idea what that will cost?" and he said no. I told him, "Well, you ought to say a million to start with."'

Taylor's diagnosis of Watford's problem was brutally frank. He told the board and the players that their club was sloppy and run-down, and that, regardless of Elton's money, any success could only by attained by single-minded dedication and hard work. On this, and every other point, Elton and he found themselves in total sympathy. Both agreed, above all, that, rather than spending money on flash new players, Watford's primary need was to build up its support within the local community. A programme of improvements began at Vicarage Road with the emphasis on facilities to encourage parents to bring their children to matches.

Graham Taylor also took a firm line with Elton himself, whose chief pleasure as chairman had been to fraternise with the players, kicking around with them at practice or posing for zany photographs in the changing room. All that must stop, Taylor decreed. Football at Watford from here on was to be a totally serious business.

By only a few weeks into the 1977–8 season, Taylor seemed to be justifying his £125,000 contract. Two of Watford's home games drew more than 11,000 spectators each, a respectable tally for any Second Division side. They looked set fair to end up as Fourth Division champions and win their longed-for promotion back into the Third.

Pictures of Elton with Graham Taylor in the Watford directors' box showed him wearing an outsize tweed eight-piece cap like some gangster extra from Bonnie and Clyde. Out of the performing limelight, he had finally nerved himself to the last possible remedy for his vanishing hair. In September, the *Daily Express* reported that he had flown to Paris to consult plastic surgeon John Reed about a transplant operation – similar to that recently performed on Frank Sinatra – whereby hairs with healthy follicles were removed from abundant growth at the back of the neck and sewn in individual plugs over the denuded crown. Mr Reed had delivered his predictable opinion that such an operation would 'take'.

The cloth cap, and a large collection like it, concealed a crop of freshly grafted hair plugs and resultant, uncomfortable scar tissue. Elton had been told he must wait six months to see if the transplant operation had been a success; in the meantime, he should expose his scalp to the air as much as possible. He paid as much attention to that as to earlier advice that drenchings of gold, silver, scarlet or green dye could not possibly do his cursed hair follicles anything but harm.

Elton's housekeeper Margo Stevens was dusting the banisters at Woodside one day when she overheard a conversation between his mother and his chauffeur's wife. 'Well, she won't like it,' Sheila said, 'but there it is . . . she's got to go.'

Shortly afterwards, Margo was given notice. The official reason was that the house was about to be reinsured, and the insurance company objected to a single girl living alone in the Orangery. But, via her old boss, Elton's great friend Tony King, Margo heard a different story. She was thought to have become too officious in her duties, for instance locking up Elton's private suite in his absence and keeping the key jealously to herself. It was even alleged that she'd stolen some money and jewellery.

Both charges Margo indignantly denies. 'The only reason I locked his suite was because there were builders in the house at the time, and you didn't know who might walk in there and pinch something. As for stealing money, the only thing I can imagine they meant was one time when Elton had lost his piano ring, and I had to go through all his clothes searching for it. As I looked, I kept finding wads of dollars in pockets, and jewellery still pinned to lapels. I took the whole lot down to Sheila, who had an office in the house, and handed it all over to her.'

Many people knew Margo as the besotted Beatle fan who, in former years, would climb into Paul McCartney's house and walk through the rooms, looking but never stealing so much as a piece of lavatory paper. Among those who testified to her utter trustworthiness was Charlie Watts, the Rolling Stones' drummer, for whom she had often babysat.

None the less, the slur remained. Not only was Margo asked to leave Woodside; she also heard that her old job at Rocket was no longer open to her. Instead, she received compensation of £500.

'I still don't really know what happened,' she says today. 'All I can think is that Sheila got it into her head that I had some designs on Elton. I remember one day when he came into the house, and we were both standing there. He came straight up to me and said, "I've just bought some new furniture. You're going to love it." Maybe Sheila was a bit put out by that.

'Elton himself was away when they got rid of me. Just before he left, I remember, he came into the kitchen where I was working, and gave me some money. So perhaps he knew what was going to happen. I've no idea whether he did or not.'

That reduced Elton's domestic staff to just the chauffeur, Bob Halley, and his wife, Pearl. Subsequently, Bob and Pearl's marriage broke up, and Bob served Elton alone, sometimes waiting in his Rolls for seven hours at a stretch outside Friends in Covent Garden or the Rainbow on Sunset Strip.

To the fifty or so other Elton John employees, in early 1977, a stern edict went out. Elton had cut himself loose from all normal pressures, performing, writing, recording or giving interviews. He would stay at home in Old Windsor, being quiet and private. Underlining the point, only three people in the whole organisation had the Woodside telephone number: his mother, John Reid and Reid's secretary. A telex machine at the house handled all other communication. Anyone wishing to reach Elton must speak to the office, which would then – or not as the case might be – telex Elton at home. The flaw in this perfect plan was that Elton found telexes exciting; every fifteen minutes or so, he would go to the machine to see if anything new had come through on it, and feel disappointed if nothing had.

There were other signs that, much as he might ostensibly crave quiet and seclusion, Elton could never succeed in maintaining a totally low profile. In this period, *The Times*'s Personal Column contained two items, enigmatic even by its time-honoured standard. One said:

Pauline from Sheffield would like to announce it is a year since she last had a man.

The other said:

Lord Choc Ice would like to announce it is 10 years since he travelled on a bus.

Pauline from Sheffield was, of course, Pauline Matthews, aka Kiki Dee, whose sex life had always been of brotherly concern to her sponsor and producer. And even those who had not travelled with him on his last bus journey – with Uni Records into Los Angeles – had no trouble in guessing the identity of Lord Choc Ice. John Reid happened to be travelling abroad when the ads appeared but, on seeing them in his airmail *Times*, instantly knew whose little joke they were.

Less than a year previously, Lord Choc Ice had had the top-selling single in Britain and America. Now he seemed unable to gain the slightest toehold in either chart. His two 1977 singles were each trampled to invisibility by the punk rock horde. 'Crazy Water', released only in Britain that February, stalled at number 27. 'Bite Your Lip (Get Up and Dance!)', four months later, reached the same low-water mark on both sides of the Atlantic, stiffing at 28.

His only 1977 album was a second volume of past hits, compiled by DJM from the later material under their copyright, with the surprise addition of 'Don't Go Breaking My Heart' and 'Sorry Seems to Be the Hardest Word'. Fearing another substandard compilation, Elton instructed Rocket to lease the track to DJM. From here on, his only contact with his old mentors would be via accountants and lawyers.

The rise of *Elton John's Greatest Hits Volume II* to number six in Britain and 21 in America only seemed to confirm what a back number he now was. While punk mobs howled and looted, the aristos in their tattered flares huddled for comfort around 'Philadelphia Freedom', 'Island Girl' and 'Bennie and the Jets'.

For eleven months Elton steadfastly kept up his retreat, breaking it only at one, irresistible command. In May 1977, he was part of the Royal Windsor Big Top Show, a circus and variety spectacular given for the Queen as part of her Silver Jubilee celebrations. His confession of bisexuality had made no difference to his acceptability as a royal entertainer nor to his involvement in prestigious charity. That same month, the *Daily Telegraph*'s Court Circular reported that Princess Alexandra and the Honourable Angus Ogilvy had 'attended a gala performance by Elton John in aid of the Queen's Silver Jubilee Appeal at the Rainbow Theatre, Finsbury Park. Lady Mary Fitzalan-Howard was also in attendance.'

The Rainbow concert, though successful, had an embarrassing sequel. Introducing one number, Elton could not resist a mischievous ad lib to amuse the rock-business cognoscenti: 'This one's for Charlie – he's doing well tonight.' It was evidently explained to Princess Alexandra that, in certain circles, 'Charlie' referred to something other than her cousin, the Prince of Wales. On meeting Elton at the backstage party later, Her Royal Highness decided to get to the bottom of the matter. 'How do you play for two and a half hours at a stretch?' she asked him. 'Do you take some sort of drug? Do you take cocaine?'

An astonished Elton told reporters what the Princess had said, then was obliged to apologise for repeating royal remarks made privately. 'I very much hope I have not embarrassed the Princess. I thought it was very amusing, and that's why I repeated it. Of course I do not take cocaine . . . it [the in-concert reference to "Charlie"] was only meant as a light-hearted comment.'

That November brought another unbreakable commitment. Earlier in the year, he had become one of the sponsors of Goaldiggers, a charity set up to provide football pitches and equipment for deprived children. The climax of a Goaldiggers fund-raising drive was to be a gala concert at Wembley Arena, jointly organised with the Variety Club of Great Britain. Elton, who had already made a special promo record for Goaldiggers, agreed to be top of the bill.

He appeared alone at the piano, still in the cloth cap that covered his hair transplant – as multifarious types of headgear would for ever after. Though given a huge welcome by 8,000 embattled Seventies children, his thirty-minute solo spot seemed subdued, even melancholic. David Croker, for one, could see he wasn't enjoying himself. 'He hadn't played a huge venue like this for over a year, and he thought it was going to feel great to be doing it again. But, you could see, it still felt like shit.'

He seemed to revive and become the old manic, acrobatic Elton when Davey Johnstone, Ray Cooper and Rocket's band China joined him onstage for a thunderous version of Marvin Gaye's 'I Heard It Through the Grapevine'. Then, rippling the intro to 'Don't Let the Sun Go Down on Me', he came out with an announcement even his closest followers had not known he meant to make:

'I haven't been touring for a long while. It's been a painful decision for me, whether to carry on touring or not. But I've made the decision – and this is going to be the last show. There's a lot more to me than being on the road.' To anguished gasps and cries of 'No', he replied, 'Thank you very much. I really enjoyed tonight. But it's the last one.'

'If this was a wake, it will not be forgotten by any of the 8,000 present,' wrote the *Daily Telegraph*'s John Coldstream. 'It was a glorious way to go, but the concert stage will be a less colourful place even if Watford FC is the richer.'

III
HERCULES

14

Mr Cheveux

NINETEEN seventy-eight was rock music's Year Zero. The old
order, its labyrinthine structures, customs and refinements, had
been wiped from existence as totally as the era of music hall, silent
movies, harpoon whaling or steam trains. The new order, Eighties
children two years premature, controlled everything.

Punk rock in its impurest form was a fairly short-lived British
phenomenon. From that generalised shrieking and jeering, the
eternal 2 per cent of true talent soon emerged as, thankfully, it
always has and always will. A few months were sufficient to separate
the talentless opportunists from bands of manifest ability and
originality: the Police, the Jam, the Boomtown Rats. Out of the
'gobbing' rabble, names like Elvis Costello, Paul Weller and Sting
began to be recognised as songwriters and showmen to rival any
gone before. The spirit of aggressive egalitarianism quickly produced punk-influenced reggae, from bands that mixed black and
white personnel as democratically as did the dole queues of the
outside world. The most notable, indeed, called themselves
UB40, after the harsh government form issued to all applying
for unemployment benefit. One needs no better example of how
welded to real life rock had become, and how redundant now seemed
the tinsel age of *Captain Fantastic* and *Goodbye Yellow
Brick Road.*

Nowhere was the revolution more visible than in Britain's weekly
music press. The *New Musical Express*, *Sounds* and, finally, even
the illustrious *Melody Maker* dropped their conventional newspaper
format, substituting the garish asymmetry of post-punk publications
like *Blitz* and *The Face.* The once straightforward, literate feature
articles were replaced by tracts of teenage free association, sprayed
on to the page with the same wild predicability as the graffiti now
infesting public walls, buildings and underpasses. There was no point
any longer in being an articulate rock musician since no articulate
rock writers were there to take note of the fact.

Meanwhile, the megastars who had been eclipsed were exiles in their own land, holed up on their country estates, seldom daring to venture forth with their horribly outmoded silhouettes. For many, the blow was compounded by serious drug and alcohol problems, produced by long years of heedless excess. From their common predicament, one might have expected to see evolve a spirit of mutual sympathy and support. But rock stars – all except one – had never been very good at keeping in touch.

Eric Clapton, the nonpareil of British rock guitarists, was one major star whom the late Seventies found in a rough patch, both professionally and personally. He had never been a particular friend of Elton's, but Elton possessed the knack of keeping even peripheral friendships in good repair. 'Suddenly, out of the blue, you'd get a Fortnum and Mason hamper at Christmas, with a label on it, "Love from Elton",' Clapton remembers. 'Or you'd get a note, or a message with a hotel operator, or you'd hear he'd dedicated a tune to you onstage. Some little thing was always turning up to make you feel good.'

Whatever complex new twists Elton's life might be taking, the indestructible good boy in him seldom forgot a friend's birthday. 'It was my fiftieth,' Bryan Forbes remembers. 'We were having a big party in the garden at Wentworth. Elton wasn't in the country at the time, but I knew I'd be bound to hear from him in some way or another.

'But my birthday arrived – and no word from Elton. As we were having our party on the lawn, I suddenly heard something that sounded like a Welsh miners' brass band coming up the drive. It *was* a Welsh miners' brass band! Wherever Elton was, he'd got in touch with them, booked them and bussed them all the way up from the Rhondda Valley to Surrey. They played to us for the rest of the afternoon.'

One Watford match Saturday, during drinks in the club boardroom, Elton spotted a familiar face. It was George Hill, landlord of the pub where Reggie Dwight had got his first break as a solo performer, for £1 10s a night back in prehistoric 1962. George was still running the Northwood Hills Hotel, and, after the game, invited Elton over to see his wife, Ann, and look round the old place again. Elton stayed a couple of hours, reminiscing about those days when fifteen-year-old Reggie would sing mournful Jim Reeves songs in a ginger tweed sports jacket, undeterred by showers of ash-trays and empty crisp packets.

The Hills' son Andrew, just a toddler back then, was now about to leave school and begin an engineering course at Loughborough College. Andy Hill, too, was a Watford fanatic, and frequently ran into Elton during or after matches at Vicarage Road. One day in the spring of 1977, the superstar came up with a proposal that left the eighteen-year-old school-leaver speechless. 'You oughtn't to go straight from A-levels to college,' Elton told him. 'You should take some time off first, to have fun and broaden your outlook. Be my personal assistant for a year, and see the world.'

So Andy Hill, with experience of nothing but pub and school life in deepest Metroland, went straight to the number-one spot in Elton John's entourage, at a salary of £100 per week. His first duty was to be Elton's sole travelling companion on a six-week trip, taking in Washington, Los Angeles and Maui. 'Elton turned up for the Concorde flight trip in white shorts,' Andy Hill remembers. 'And each of his socks was a different colour, and each of his shoes was a different pattern.'

After a family gathering at Elton's LA house, master and personal assistant flew on to Maui for two weeks' intensive tennis coaching. Andy Hill soon discovered his fiercely competitive nature. 'I said I could beat him at squash, so we played; he was determined to beat me, and he did. It was the same with tennis. When Elton played anything, even if it was only pinball, he played to win.'

At tennis school on the loveliest Hawaiian island, Andy saw Elton at his most carefree and relaxed. 'He wasn't recognised. No one bothered him. He could go round just like an ordinary person. So he, in turn, was very open and friendly to everyone. I remember, one day some people came round collecting for "Save the Whale". Elton knew this guy who ran one of the local bars, and he said "Why don't we do a gig for Save The Whale?" So one night he just went and played the piano on his own in this bar. By the time he'd finished, of course, the word was out, and there were hundreds of people in the street, waiting for him.

'I discovered his sense of humour, as well, when we were leaving, and went to say goodbye to the tennis pro who'd been coaching him for the two weeks. When we arrived at this bloke's bungalow, he wasn't there. Elton said, "Why don't we take every bit of furniture out of his bedroom?" So we took out everything – his bed, the tables, chairs, lamps – and arranged them in exactly the same position in the garden.'

Another duty for the awestruck 18-year-old was to accompany Elton to his Paris hair-transplant clinic. The initial operation, performed by France's leading trichological surgeon Dr Pierre Pouteaux, followed a new and allegedly superior method called 'square grafting'. Sections of hair-bearing scalp were taken from the back of the neck, then cut into tiny squares and punched over the barren crown as in a checkerboard design. The advantage was that, if the grafts took, growth would be faster and the covering denser than from patches transplanted at random. The disadvantage was that several further uncomfortable operations were necessary until all the white cranial squares had been filled in.

Elton's first transplant experience bore his familiar imprint of mingled farce and pain. Emerging from the clinic, head bound in lint and gauze, he was ushered by Andy Hill to a waiting limousine. As he went to get in, he struck his vulnerable cranium an almighty blow on the rim of the car door. 'He thought he might have knocked some of the hair-plugs loose,' Andy remembers. 'So we had to go back into the clinic and have them checked out. I thought it was funny at the time. But I can see now he must have been in agony.'

It was in this second retirement period that Elton adopted the habit of travelling under elaborately comic aliases. An early alter ego – in tribute to his French trichological experiences – was Mr Cheveux. 'A lot of the time, people still knew who he was,' Andy Hill says. 'But sometimes they didn't. Once we were on a flight where first class had been overbooked, and, seeing this Mr Hill and Mr Cheveux, the airline just put us on the list to be downgraded to economy. Elton nearly went barmy! Luckily, at the last minute they realised who he was, and managed to find us a couple of seats in first.'

In the political swirls and eddies that surrounded Elton, Andy seemed to bear a charmed life. John Reid, for some reason, had no objection to his employment. Apart from one wobbly moment at Wembley, when Elton's hats failed to arrive backstage, he never found himself on the receiving end of a Reid explosion. 'Being so young, I didn't realise what a powerful figure John was. I wasn't in awe of him, which he seemed to like. I could sometimes even be a bit cheeky to him.' The only edge of animosity came from Elton's chauffeur, Bob Halley, who clearly had himself hoped to be promoted from mere driving to Andy's privileged place at the sovereign's right hand.

Though officially termed 'personal assistant', Andy Hill's administrative duties were of the lightest. Virtually all arrangements on Elton's behalf were made through John Reid's office at 40 South Audley Street, where he was nominally based. As weeks passed in unstrenuous, peripatetic luxury, in Los Angeles, Hawaii and Seattle, Andy realised what was the true and exclusive nature of his job. It was simply to go with Elton everywhere, and keep him company, day and night.

Like others before him, he was amazed to see how much of the superstar's life was unglamorous, funless and solitary. 'Everyone else in the organisation had a circle of friends that they could call on at the end of the day. Elton had good friends, but they didn't make any kind of structure around him. I couldn't believe how this incredible figure, who was the envy of millions, used to go back to an empty house most nights, and just be there on his own.'

At Woodside the main social events were squash or tennis tournaments, with Elton in obsessive combat against Andy Hill, Bryan Ferry or the more athletic members of Rod Stewart's new stage band. 'He was seeing quite a lot of Rod, and Rod's manager, Billy Gaff, who was a big friend of John Reid. Elton and Rod had this incredible love–hate relationship. They were terrific friends, but couldn't be together without continually trying to put each other down and score off each other. Like, Rod would buy some really horrible, cheap plonk, then stick expensive labels on it and say to Elton, "Hey I've got some incredible wine here: you ought to try it."'

They continued to call each other the camp nicknames dating from the Long John Baldry era. To Rod, Elton was Sharon; to Elton, Rod was Phyllis. When Rod was on tour with his album *Blondes Have More Fun*, Elton had a big banner hung outside Olympia: 'Blondes may have more fun, but brunettes have lots more money. Happy Xmas, love, Sharon.' It was taken down rather hastily by Rod's roadies.

Apart from Concorde trips abroad, Andy's chief duty was to accompany Elton to Watford matches, home and away. Throughout that season, 1977–8, they did not miss a single one, travelling by helicopter if the venue was too far in the chilly north for Bob Halley to pilot the long-distance Daimler.

In this sphere, at least, Elton's spirits were soaring. The inspirational management of his protégé Graham Taylor had transformed the sleepy, sloppy Watford team into an enthusiastic, highly motivated unit that was now scything through its Fourth Division opponents. By the end of Taylor's first full season, Watford's goal tally had earned them 71 League points, a club record. They finished as Division Four champions, winning promotion to Division Three with a 2–0 away win over Bournemouth. The result, said a rhapsodic Elton, was 'better than having a record at number one'.

The ground and its terraces also had been transformed with new fencing, bright new paint and a staff outfitted in blazers of canary yellow. The run-down adjoining greyhound track had been closed, without protest or regret. New amenities were constantly being added, underlining Elton's wish for a 'family club', free of the male macho mayhem that usually cursed English football. The most telling innovation was a 500-seat family enclosure in front of the directors' box, where parents with children had their own catering and toilet facilities and personalised seats. Child members received a gift at every match and, on their birthdays, a card signed by all the team. Every player had written into his contract an obligation to meet and talk to young supporters. There was a Christmas party each year, and before the home match nearest Easter, Elton would personally distribute up to 750 chocolate eggs.

Especially at away matches in northerly towns like Rochdale and Scunthorpe, the opposing supporters were still apt to chant disagreeable things about Elton and his sexuality to improvised tunes of pop songs or hymns. But Watford's fans now had an answering chant to characterise themselves in their ever more consistent triumph: 'Elton John's Taylor-made Army!'

With Watford on its feet and running, signs of the chairman's personal munificence began to appear. Two record transfer fees were paid to buy in outside players, Ray Train for £50,000, then Steve Sims for £170,000. What was his club's aim for 1979? the *Daily Express* asked Elton. 'Third Division champions, and promotion again,' he replied. 'There's no point in just consolidating. You've got to be positive in football.'

One revealing photograph from this era shows Elton in his floppy tweed cap, grinning proudly amid Watford's victors, towel-wrapped and steamy from the after-match communal bath. Another photograph shows him actually in the bath with them. 'You could always tell how much he himself would have loved to be a footballer,' Andy Hill remembers. 'There was one testimonial match where, in fact, he did turn out to play for Watford. I think it was probably the proudest moment of his life.'

From his inside vantage point Andy Hill saw how there were two Eltons in constant, unpredictable alternation: one brash and buoyant, the other shy and self-conscious; one hectically happy, the other bleakly morose; one decent, considerate and civilised, the other prone to explosive moods and Georgy-Porgy tantrums. 'I saw him in the dressing room at Wembley, the night he announced his retirement, throwing flower arrangements around, shouting, "I'm not bloody well going on!" It was just to get attention, because he thought no one cared about him and the pressure he was under, having to go out in front of all those people and perform. Most of the time, he really needed people. If there was a big match on TV, he'd ring me and say, "Do you want to come to the house and watch it with me? And can you pick up some smoked salmon from Harrods on the way?"

Another time, I'd go to the house and Bob Halley would say, "Elton doesn't want to see anyone at all for two days."'

Even the fabled Elton generosity, that splashed out Cartier watches, jewels, even cars on the most casual acquaintances, was counterpointed by an innate shrewdness. 'I've seen him bet £100 on the toss of a coin,' Andy Hill says. 'He could be the easiest touch in the world sometimes, and at other times watch the pennies just like anyone who didn't have his kind of money. I remember, while we were rehearsing with Davey Johnstone's band, China, at Shepperton studios, everybody got hungry and Elton gave me £20 to go out and fetch some hamburgers. When I got back, the first thing he said to me was "How much were they?" and, when I told him, "Where's the change?"'

His constant saving grace was a sense of humour that could usually pull him back from Elton number two's black abyss with a healing draught of Elton number one's rational and self-mocking laughter. Nor was the tireless practical joker lacking in humour when, as sometimes happened, the joke was turned back on him. 'While we were in Los Angeles, he got a message saying there was a fancy-dress party at the Rocket office,' Andy Hill remembers. 'Elton got really dolled up for it, in a woman's frock, a huge wig and roller skates. But it was all a big leg-pull. When he arrived there, in this incredible get-up, on skates, everyone there was in suits, holding the annual general meeting.'

Elton's interest in Andy Hill was entirely circumspect. Taking him on as personal assistant had been no more than a kind of long-belated thank you to George Hill for that first chance at the Northwood Hills Hotel. As well as being good-looking, Andy was a thoroughly presentable, intelligent and articulate boy, whose Metro-land innocence brought out all Elton's latent elder-brotherliness. 'His attitude to me was always very free. It was always "Enjoy yourself, do what you like." But once, he did give me a talking-to. Once, while we were in LA, I was with some people on a boat at Malibu. We'd been drinking, and we dived off the boat to get to shore and see some actor who was supposed to have draught Guinness in his garden. When Elton found out, he was furious. "Don't you realise how dangerous that was?" he said to me. "You're never ever to do it again!"'

None the less, Andy Hill was privy to the seamy side of rock superstar life, which now went on behind closed doors as if in hiding from the punk thought police. At parties, cocaine was still provided as copiously as sherbet powder, arranged into neat ploughman's lines with golden razor blades and sniffed up through spills of tightly rolled brand new £10 notes. Whatever the horrors of the Top 20 and this week's *NME*, 'Charlie' was still doing just fine.

Andy also had to deal with the succession of temporary companions who had passed through Elton's life since parting, domestically, from John Reid. These companions, usually of the American blond surfer type, were each taken up with an enthusiasm that seldom convinced Elton's nucleus of true, loving friends, like Nanette Newman. 'With Elton, there were never half-measures,' she says now. 'Whenever he started a relationship, it was always the one; the love of his life.'

The liaisons rarely lasted longer than a day or two. 'They usually weren't very bright,' Andy Hill remembers. 'Elton would get bored, and embarrassed by the whole thing, and want to get rid of them as quickly as possible. There was one named HG who stayed around some time. Elton told me to buy him a car, so I took him to a Ford showroom. But this guy wasn't interested in Fords; he wanted a Ferrari. I told Elton, and Elton said, "OK. Get him a Ferrari."'

For all that Elton's sexual nature was now public knowledge, he remained utterly discreet. When the growing horde of tabloid paparazzi sighted him, it would invariably be with John Reid, in the conventional mode of star and guard-dog manager. Separate as their lives were, they still saw each other constantly, even took the occasional holiday together. July 1977 found them in the south of France, revisiting the St Tropez waterfront where Elton had played the Papagayo club with Bluesology – and, one night, almost electrocuted himself. There was a John Reid-style contretemps after a local club refused to admit them. Reid tried to climb over the back wall and fell off, breaking his right foot in three places.

When Watford held a formal dinner or reception, the club chairman would arrive escorted by a female employee of Rocket Records or John Reid Enterprises. This was not entirely diplomatic artifice. Elton was still strongly, if spasmodically, attracted to women. Digress as he might, he always carried a clear mental picture of his ideal type. She would be American, some years older than himself, experienced and understanding enough to untie all the knots, accept all the conundrums and so, finally, bring him into line. His mother cherished much the same hopeful vision, as was revealed in a rare interview with *People* magazine. 'Deep, deep down, I know he would love to get married and have a family,' Sheila said. 'The sort of woman he'd marry would understand [the bisexuality] anyway.'

For a while, it seemed that he might be about to start a relationship with Melanie Green, the pretty seventeen-year-old daughter of a well-known London investment banker. They met in 1976, at a charity dinner attended by Prince Charles; thereafter Melanie became a noticeable fixture backstage and at post-concert parties. When Andy Hill arrived in 1977, she would still occasionally fly over to see Elton from Switzerland, where she was at finishing school.

'There's no doubt in my mind that Elton was born to be straight,' Andy Hill says. 'If he hadn't gone into the music business and met all those other people, he'd be living in Pinner now, happily married, surrounded by kids.'

Ceasing to perform was not the only great change in Elton's life during this era of massive general upheaval and uproar. He was also without the collaborator representing 50 per cent, if not more, of his artistic self. Bernie Taupin and he had ceased to write songs together.

Their last album, *Blue Moves*, though commercially successful, had been anything but the euphoric short-distance gallop to which both were accustomed. Bernie, in particular, had felt under immense pressure. 'By that point, we seemed to have achieved everything there was to achieve. Elton had filled every major stadium in the world. We'd written strings of number ones – eventually, things that went straight into the charts at number one. You couldn't fart without hearing Elton John. At that point, it felt like there was no way we could go any further. There was only one way to go from here.

'*Blue Moves*, Elton always says, was the doom-and-gloom album, and that's pretty much how I felt at the time. My marriage had broken up; I had a lot of negative thoughts about everything. For instance, 'Someone's Last Song' is about committing suicide. For the first time, when we began work, I found myself thinking, "I don't know if I've got it in me. I don't know if I want to do this any more."'

There was little resemblance now to the shy farm boy who had come down from Lincolnshire with his pockets full of wistful poems. Bestubbled and overweight, he looked more like one of the Mafia hoods who populated his new homeland. His drinking had reached the problem stage, though Bernie himself did not yet realise it. 'I used to wake up in the morning in my house on North Doheny Drive – the rock star's empty house – and the first thing I'd do would be to reach over to the refrigerator by my bed. I'd take out a beer, empty half of it away, then fill it up with vodka. I'd drink that every morning before I got up. When I went anywhere in a limo, I'd take a gallon jug full of vodka and orange juice. People were starting to say, "Hey, you've got a problem", but I wouldn't believe them. I said, "No, I'm just having a good time."

'I was doing drugs, too – though the funny thing was, I never smoked dope. It was basically cocaine, and dabbling in smack a couple of times. But not through a needle; always ingesting it. I went through my period of hallucinations, too – magic mushrooms, acid, stuff like that.'

In the post-*Blue Moves* period, two things happened to Bernie. He began a relationship with a high-powered Californian woman named Loree Rodkin. And he visited a doctor for treatment for a routine ailment. After examining him, the doctor told him his liver was in terrible shape and that if he didn't do something soon, the consequences might be disastrous.

'I'd started this new relationship, which seemed promising, so I took it on myself to go away and dry out. I went to Acapulco and lived on my own for three months. I had this big house at a place called Horseshoe Bay, and I stayed there, just getting the sun, and thinking about other forms of writing that I might do. Loree came back and forth, but basically I was alone there. I kept a diary and as I wrote it, gradually, I could feel my mind unfogging and clearing, and it was beautiful. In the evening, I could look over the bay and see the stars and the night lights, and I began to realise the world wasn't such a bad place after all.'

There was never any kind of falling out between Elton and Bernie, nor even formal acknowledgement that they had ceased collaborating. It simply happened that when the album-making feeling next came over Elton, as it did in late 1977, Bernie was 5,000 miles away, with little on his mind but the daily struggle against wanting a drink.

Coincidentally, Elton had also parted from Gus Dudgeon, the producer who had supervised all fourteen of his albums since the breakthrough one in 1970. The reasons, Dudgeon says, were manifold. 'I remember, at the time of *Blue Moves*, I rang up America to see how Kiki was doing with "I Got the Music in Me". My wife said, "You never even asked how Elton was doing." I said, "Oh I know he's all right." And I suddenly realised, the challenge there used to be in producing Elton had gone. We just assumed we were a team with a magic touch.'

As producer, Dudgeon had always enjoyed a unique measure of independence in Elton's highly political circle. 'I was only contracted album by album, which meant I worked directly for Elton. At the same time, because I had other projects, like Joan Armatrading, I was apart from all the political stuff. When Elton wanted to record, he called me, and we recorded. I didn't have to belong to all the Yes men, telling him that everything he said was wonderful and marvellous.'

Dudgeon's chief discontent was in his capacity as a director of Rocket. 'The problem was that, with Elton and John Reid travelling all over the world, and Bernie Taupin away in America, you could hardly ever get all the directors in one place for a meeting. I was getting fed up because I didn't think we were signing the people we had a chance to. I'd wanted to sign Dave Edmunds, but wasn't allowed to. "Oh no," they said. "He'll never have another hit." Another person I wanted to sign was Barry Humphries. "No," they said. "He's an actor." "But he's in this great show, *Housewife, Superstar*. He's going to be enormous," I said, but they still wouldn't listen.

'There was going to be this one board meeting when I had a lot of complaints to bring up. Neil Sedaka was very unhappy with the label, and thinking of signing somewhere else, but no one was even trying to keep him. And I was very dissatisfied with the way the accounts were being kept. I said, "Things have really got to be a lot better, or I'm quitting." I realised that no one was saying, "Don't go, Gus" – and I was out.'

It was cavalier treatment for the man who had masterminded Elton's career on records and had very often produced hits from shit. Subsequently he sold out his Rocket shares to John Reid, and continued his highly successful career with other artists, among them Elkie Brooks and Chris Rea.

Elton was on fire with enthusiasm for a project requiring neither Gus Dudgeon nor Bernie Taupin. His first studio sessions in more than a year were to be produced by Thom Bell, creator of the Philadelphia sound, lightweight orchestral soul music which had dominated the mid-Seventies charts. As well as producing, Bell was to supply the songs and arrangements in the pattern of his earlier huge successes with Harold Melvin, the O'Jays and the Three Degrees. The album was made at Bell's Sigma Sound Studios in Philadelphia and the Kay Smith Studio in Seattle. Andy Hill, who sat in on the Seattle sessions, remembers them as 'outstanding'. But when Thom Bell delivered the finished album, Elton decided it was overproduced and the orchestration 'too sweet'. The whole project was then peremptorily shelved.

From easy-listening soul music, he switched abruptly to the idea of meeting the new, dark forces of rock music head on. In March 1978, he released a one-off single called 'Ego', a stockpile Bernie Taupin song, recorded at the Mill Studios, Cookham, Berkshire, with production jointly credited to Clive Franks and Elton himself.

With it came images of a new-look Elton, hopefully more in accord with the stark, grainy tastes of punk. Gone was the familiar bespectacled face, with its air of intense anxiety or its manic gap-toothed grin. Instead, a dramatic, chiselled countenance, minus glasses and so artfully lit and retouched as to be barely recognisable, scowled forth from under beetling brows. After years of spectacle-wearing, he had taken to contact lenses, enduring the fiddles with eyelids, tiny containers and distilled water for the sake of a hopefully vast improvement in his personal attractiveness. Gone with the specs was the floppy tweed cap, revealing a manifest miracle. Where there had formerly been weak strands of thinning blond there was now dark hair, not thick but apparently firm and all-enveloping.

Elton was determined that 'Ego' should be launched with every proper modish marketing device. With the single came a video film showing the new unspectacled, hair-lined Elton, seated in an ornate room, receiving a large crowd of reverent courtiers. He explained it was meant to satirise 'the type of people you can meet in this business, with over-inflated ideas and big talk. The type of people I loathe.' But to many, the ego in question seemed to be Elton's own as he motioned people to this or that side of the room like some latter-day, wigless Sun King. Forty thousand pounds was spent on the video, as against the £4,000 that Queen's 'Bohemian Rhapsody' one had cost only two years before. Elton may be said to have single-handedly started the trend of pop videos with budgets as big as feature films.

There was instant massive media interest, though little of it in the new single. All that any Fleet Street news editor wanted to know was the exact nature and consistency of the dark substance under Elton's tweed cap. The fact that he resolutely kept his cap on for the video's West End cinema première and through all pre-release interviews added to the feverish speculation. During his talk with disc jockey Kenny Everett on London's Capital Radio, a listener phoned in to say she'd donate £10 to charity if Elton would remove the cap. This Elton briefly did, giving Everett and his studio staff as much newsworthiness as if they had witnessed some landing by Martians. 'There was hair, filmy hair, but hair all over as far as I could see,' Kenny Everett later testified to the *Daily Mail*. Studio engineer Keith Muirhead got into the story for having missed the revelation. 'It happened so quickly and I was so busy, I didn't even see it.'

Alas, the record was a resounding flop which did not even approach the Top 20 in either America or Britain. To compound the snub, Elton's costly video promo film was refused by BBC TV's *Top of the Pops*, whose policy was to feature only songs that had made the British Top 30.

Previous failures had been greeted by Elton – in public at least – with resigned good sportsmanship. But, when 'Ego' stiffed at 34, his response was to launch a bitter attack on the 'inaccuracy' of the chart which the British Market Research Bureau supplied to the BBC.

Complaining that alternative charts, notably the *NME*'s, showed 'Ego' in the lower 20s and even rising, he threatened to withdraw Rocket's advertising from papers carrying the BMRB's lists. Rocket's managing director David Croker and promotion manager Arthur Sherriff were bitterly blamed for the video's non-appearance on *Top of the Pops*. 'John Reid rang me up and screamed abuse at me,' Croker remembers. 'Told me I was fired on the spot.' ROCKETS FLY AS ELTON'S EGO FLOPS said Nigel Dempster's *Daily Mail* diary, reporting that Arthur Sherriff had been dismissed by John Reid through the company lawyer, and was now having to sign on the dole.

On Elton's next album, Bernie Taupin's place as lyricist was taken by Gary Osborne, an ebullient blond character who had been the monarch's attentive friend since the time of his Wembley Stadium Beach Boys show. Osborne had written the lyrics to Kiki Dee's 'Amoureuse' though he was slightly better known as a writer of TV jingles for a bank, a building society, a brand of toothpaste and the health drink Lucozade.

Elton's decision to team with Gary Osborne was not based on any serious idea that he'd found a rival to Bernie Taupin. Whereas Bernie was always different, and could often be brilliant, Osborne at his best was only very adequate. It was his personality that appealed to Elton: whatever they might produce, at least they could do it with ease and the necessary quota of laughs. 'Gary was such a character, with his flowing blond hair, his big coats and his great long fingers,' Andy Hill remembers. 'Elton had always wanted more hair, and longer fingers. I think he just wished he was Gary Osborne.'

On the allusively named *A Single Man*, released in October 1978, all but one of the tracks bore a Gary Osborne lyric; bread and butter where Bernie Taupin would have provided sherry trifle. The exception was an instrumental written by Elton alone, deriving from his love of the sombre and funereal. During the album sessions, a seventeen-year-old Rocket messenger named Guy Burchett was killed in a motorcycle crash. Elton had known and liked the boy and, on the day of the accident, sat down and produced 'Song for Guy', a lachrymose piano piece with no vocal beyond a vague accompanying murmur. Two songs, 'Georgia' and 'Big Dipper', had backup vocals by the Watford team, bussed in to the Mill Studio as if to an away match.

Though nominally the chief product of his own organisation, Rocket, Elton now began what would be an extended pass-the-parcel progress around the major companies that handled manufacture and distribution for independent labels. With *A Single Man*, Rocket severed its British distribution deal with EMI, who, naturally, had come in for some of the blame for the 'Ego' flop. A new contract was signed with the Dutch-based Phonogram company, previously Philips. Elton was thus back, indirectly, with the people who had first signed him up in Bluesology.

The advance single was 'Part-Time Love', a Gary Osborne pensée set to a tune that, as usual, had sprung in a few seconds from Elton's meandering fingertips. If banal by *Captain Fantastic* standards, it was at least catchy, unpretentious, and endowed with enough of Elton's old charm to break his two-year chart jinx. Within a week or two, it had made the British Top 30, finally entitling Elton to appear on *Top of the Pops* amid the punk riffraff in his floppy hat, his face oddly rigid and embalmed-looking, like some tight-lipped housewife out shopping in a neighbourhood gone to the dogs.

In late November, when 'Part-Time Love' was still clambering towards its eventual 15th place in the British charts, a second Elton single was suddenly lobbed out after it. The approach of Christmas had brought the customary crop of Christmas records, hoping to cash in on seasonal sentiment. 'Song for Guy', his piano requiem for the young Rocket messenger boy, seemed an ideal contender.

The funereal piece was scarcely in the shops when it took on an unpleasant real-life dimension. Elton collapsed at home, complaining of acute chest pains and unable to get his breath. The doctor who was called suspected a heart attack, and had him rushed by ambulance to the special coronary unit at the London Clinic. The trouble was subsequently diagnosed as 'exhaustion', brought on by the rigours of promoting his new album and playing five-a-side football in a charity match for Goaldiggers. David Croker, who had known Elton for years, made a more pragmatic diagnosis. 'It was an anxiety attack.'

The medical emergency, however, proved more effective than any amount of expensive promotion and hype. News that Elton John was in hospital after a suspected heart emergency prompted an immediate, rather ghoulish clamour for his new single with its well-publicised theme of mourning and death. 'Song for Guy' shot to number four in Britain. It would probably have reached number one but for a pre-Christmas manufacturing decision by Elton's new British distributor, Phonogram. 'They'd got two big hits – "Song For Guy" and "YMCA" by Village People,' David Croker remembers. 'They decided to give the final big retail push to Village People.'

The London Clinic's advice to Elton to cut down on anxiety and take things easier fell on unresponsive ears. Less than a month after his 'funny heart thing', as he continued to call it, Rocket Records announced that his retirement was over. He would begin playing live concerts again early in 1979.

The change of heart came suddenly that December, when Elton accepted an invitation to perform at the British music industry's annual equivalent to the Oscar ceremony. The huge welcome he received – plus seeing *A Single Man* now at number eight in Britain and 15 in America – convinced him there truly was life after punk rock.

At the outset, all was meant to be modest, low-profile and small-scale. The mad, manic Elton of the mid-Seventies, he announced, had been laid to rest for ever. There would be no more huge stadium shows; no more stages crowded with people; no more Hollywood stairways, flashing neon or pouring dry ice. He would play only intimate venues, to small audiences, not even using the band he had kept in cold storage for almost two years. There would be just him on piano and Ray Cooper on percussion. And no more gallivanting round the world. England, his England was the only place to be. The Northwood Hills saloon-bar entertainer would come back into his own.

But over lunch with the British rock promoter Harvey Goldsmith, everything suddenly changed yet again. 'Elton said he didn't want to do another European tour, because it was too boring,' Goldsmith remembers. 'He said he'd do a couple in Paris, but he wanted to play somewhere "interesting". I said, "Like where?" He said, "Russia." I said, "OK".'

The attitude of Russia to rock throughout its first twenty-five years had been a steadfast and stony-faced 'Nyet'. Born as it had been at the height of the Fifties Cold War, it figured almost top of the Kremlin's list of contemptible capitalist vices. From the Elvis Presley era onward, *Pravda*, the official newspaper, and Tass, the offical news agency, had regularly fulminated against the 'decadent' and 'primitive' music, and its power to turn young people's thoughts away from healthy pursuits, like building dams, driving combine harvesters and manufacturing safety pins.

In this, as much else, *Pravda* and Tass were wilfully blind. Russian youth was as besotted by rock music as youth everywhere, even though forced to hear it illicitly via overseas radio services and hugely expensive black market records. So great had the interest become, there had even been a few tentative concert appearances in Moscow by anodyne European acts, like Cliff Richard and Boney M. But in the eyes of the regime, the music simply did not exist.

'I decided the only way to go was strictly by the book,' Harvey

Goldsmith says. 'So I went through all the proper official channels at the Foreign Office. They said they'd pass on the request to the Russian Ministry of Culture, but they had no idea what the response would be.'

Goldsmith's approach came at a fortunate moment. Though nowhere comparable with today's *perestroika* under Gorbachev, Russia in the Brezhnev era had been gradually unbending to Western culture and consumerism. The men in the Kremlin realised the passion of young Russians for rock music, and saw the wisdom of providing it under official auspices, rather than seeing it grow as an underground movement. An additional factor was that the 1980 Olympic Games were due to be held in Moscow, prompting a major push in national PR and a determined thaw in the country's traditional image of frozen joylessness. Rock music was thus to be officially recognised and, for the right kind of Western rock star, every door would be opened.

There had long been in existence an Anglo-Soviet cultural treaty, under which Russian ballet troupes or balalaika players could perform in Britain, and Britain would send over corresponding amounts of opera, Shakespeare plays and readings from Charles Dickens. In January 1979, an official of the Soviet Ministry of Culture, Vladimir Kokonin, flew to London to renew this treaty for the next two years. During his visit, he attended one of Elton's new-style intimate shows in Oxford, flanked by Foreign Office minders and Soviet Embassy staff. 'There was a lunch at Lancaster House, which I went to,' Harvey Goldsmith says. 'At the end, this Russian got up and said the treaty would be renewed, there'd be more opera, Dickens and Shakespeare, "and we shall provide music for the masses." Everyone turned round and started toasting me, and I suddenly realised we were in.'

It was arranged that Elton should go in late May, when the Russian winter had finally ended, giving a total of eight concerts in Leningrad and Moscow. To complete the cultural tie, there would be an unprecedented live hook-up with BBC Radio One, and the tape of the broadcast would be released by the Soviet record label Melodiya. Five days before departure, Harvey Goldsmith was approached by the comedy scriptwriters Dick Clement and Ian La Frenais with a plan to make a film documentary of the trip. The deal agreed, extra visas had to be provided for a film crew. 'Normally, visas took ages to come through, but these appeared like lightning,' Goldsmith remembers. 'That was how much the Russians wanted us.'

The fee was a purely nominal one of £4,000. But in addition the Russians offered flights and first-class hotel accommodation for twelve people. Elton, once again, made it a family trip, inviting his mother and stepfather. The party would also include John Reid, Ray Cooper, Clive Franks, Harvey Goldsmith and Geoffrey Ellis, Reid's legal adviser, somewhat bemused to be taking his first-ever Rocket 'freebie'.

Thus, Elton's intended small-scale and semi-private return from retirement materialised in an eleven-country tour, beginning in Stockholm, Sweden, moving on to Paris and the Theatre Royal, Drury Lane in London and then – at yet another superstar whim – Tel Aviv, Israel. The new-style show featured Elton alone at the piano for its first hour, then augmented by Ray Cooper's percussion for a further hour and a half.

The sell-out success of this trans-European comeback was matched by that of the football team he had unwillingly left behind. Again, under Graham Taylor, Watford contrived a leap forward in the dying moments of the season, winning promotion from Division Three to Division Two in their very last match. Subsequently they reached the semi-final of the Football League Cup, losing 3–1 on aggregate to Roy Dwight's old team, Nottingham Forest. Elton was ecstatic and, on leaving for Russia, presented Taylor with the gold disc he had just received for sales of *A Single Man*.

On Sunday 20 May he arrived at Moscow airport, suitably attired in worker's cloth cap, satin anorak and pantaloons tucked, Cossack-style, into patent leather boots. With him and his twelve-person entourage also came Ian La Frenais, a film crew and a large contingent of British and American reporters, pens and mini-recorders poised for every utterance of what the *Daily Mail* had already dubbed 'the bizarre Czar of rock'. Appropriately, the press group included Robert Hilburn, whose review in the *Los Angeles Times*, nine years before, had given Elton the key to another, seemingly impenetrable continent.

Expecting frozen wastes, he found an 88-degree-Fahrenheit heat-wave, which forced him to doff his cap as immigration officials scrutinised his passport and stared at his Cossack outfit. Quotable quips came nineteen to the dozen. 'I don't know if they've heard of Watford in Russia, but they soon will. Mind you, this could be the last time you see me. If they don't like you in Moscow, you end up down a salt mine.'

From the airport, he and his entourage were driven to Moscow railway station, to board the midnight Red Arrow express for the eight-and-a-half-hour journey to Leningrad. A special de-luxe carriage had been provided to shield the superstar from normal Soviet railway experiences, such as dirt, acrid tobacco smoke, sleeping compartments shared by men and women, and washroom taps emitting nothing but liquid rust.

Elton's four Leningrad concerts were to be at the 3,800-seat Bolshoi Concert Hall, close to the square containing the tsars' Winter Palace and the Hermitage. All four had sold out as soon as they were announced, and eight-rouble ($8 or £4.50) tickets were now changing hands on the black market for almost twenty times their face value. One boy to whom Robert Hilburn talked had travelled from Kiev, 1,000 miles away, but still had been unable to get in to any of the concerts.

As promoter and liaison man, Harvey Goldsmith's chief concern was that Goskoncert, the government booking agency, still did not fully appreciate the kind of show Elton did, or the effect it might have on young members of its audience. 'I tried to put it all up front. "Look, the kids may get into the aisles and dance. And if there's any problem with the material he's going to do, tell me now." But none of it seemed to be a problem.'

In fact, most tickets had gone to the privileged élite whose lives have little to do with the familiar Russian images of shabbiness, shortage and queuing. Ninety per cent of the first night's audience were Party officials, their wives and families, filling the front rows, with the lucky few genuine Elton fans crammed in far to the rear. British journalist Paul Donovan sat between a twenty-one-year-old girl, the height of fashion in her scalloped early Seventies jacket, and two nervous boys in the blue jeans that were, and still are, Russia's most prized contraband. Before the performance, in true Soviet fashion, there was a lengthy broadcast address, including biographical sketches of Elton and Ray Cooper. Out in the street, meanwhile, thousands of teenagers who had been unable to get tickets were held back by massed police, militiamen and bobble-hatted sailors from the Baltic Fleet.

Taking the stage in another variant of his cloth-capped worker-cum-Cossack outfit, contact lenses once again replacing glasses, Elton said, *'Dobriy vecher'* (good evening) then sat at a solitary Steinway grand piano to play old hits now as well known in Russia as anywhere else: 'Your Song', 'Daniel', 'Don't Let the Sun Go Down on Me' and 'Rocket Man' (translated in the programme as 'Cosmonaut').

It was anything but easy work. As the Leninesque leprechaun toiled at his keyboard, the front rows of Party officials, deserving bureaucrats and hand-picked members of obedient 'youth leagues' all watched in stolid silence, occasionally turning round, puzzled by the stubborn cheering and clapping from the real rock fans at the back. Not even the heartbroken sincerity of 'Candle in the Wind' could dispel the atmosphere of some village Women's Institute talk, going subtly but disastrously wrong. Robert Hilburn felt an eerie *déjà vu* of that other uneasy overture at the Troubadour. 'When Elton kicked away the piano bench à la Jerry Lee Lewis and fell to his knees during "Bennie and the Jets",' Hilburn wrote, 'it was easy to imagine he was really praying for help.'

He persevered, however, in the best tradition of Reggie Dwight, projecting over the rigid official heads to the far-away but persistent signs of life. And, in the second hour, aided by Ray Cooper's percussive pyrotechnics, everything suddenly ignited. The genuine fans broke out of their rearward ghetto, surging down the aisles, clapping, whistling, dancing, making peace V-signs, flinging carnations and tulips on to the stage. The dozens of ushers, guards, invigilators and name-takers made no move to intervene. In a society founded on iron crowd control, it was an incredible moment.

The finale was a home run through all his old bourgeois rabble-rousers, 'Saturday Night's Alright for Fighting', 'Pinball Wizard', 'Crocodile [or, as it might be, Krokodil] Rock' and, as an audacious farewell touch, the Beatles' borscht Beach Boy parody, 'Back in the USSR'. 'I never meant to do that song,' Elton admitted later. 'It just popped into my head. I didn't know the chords, or any of the words except the title. So I just kept singing that over and over again.'

Unprecedented scenes continued for half an hour after Elton and Ray Cooper had left the tulip-strewn stage, with teenagers refusing to disperse, standing firm against officialdom with chants of 'Elton, Elton'. Outside, hundreds more broke through the police barriers to press around the exits, buttonholing those who emerged with cries of 'What was he like?' and entreaties to buy their official programmes. In his third-floor dressing-room, Elton could hear the same kind of desperately adoring cries that had once fallen on deaf Romanoff ears. 'These kids are really incredible,' he said, genuinely moved. 'They're starved of music. I hope I'm just the first of many who come here to play for them.' At the time, he had no idea that the 2,000 filling the tram-lined street were those who had not been able to watch him perform.

The American and British press, next morning, were as jubilant as if Russia had given up communism overnight. ELTON JOHN, SUPER-CZAR, ROCKS THEM BACK IN THE USSR, said the London *Daily Mail*. ELTON JOHN STUNS SOVIET ROCK FANS, said the *Daily Telegraph*. ROCK STAR RISES OVER RUSSIA, said the *Los Angeles Times*. LENIN-GRAD'S YOUNG PEOPLE MOB ELTON JOHN, said the *New York Times*.

Even the Russian press was indulgent, after its own peculiar fashion. *Pravda*'s story about Elton seized on his many public references to his unhappy boyhood, clearly deducing rock to be a by-product of decaying family values in the West. A piece in Russia's nearest approach to a teenage magazine noted, with Tolstoyan innocence, that Elton's style was marked by its 'gay originality . . . While some people like this style, others find it excessively naughty.'

None the less, there were some attempts at censorship. At the three remaining Leningrad concerts, the fans were checked from rushing down to the stage front. Elton was asked not to finish with 'Back in the USSR' – though he did so, anyway. But he agreed to a request that he shouldn't kick his piano stool over, nor offend Russian sensibilities by attacking the Steinway grand quite so hard.

He was, for the most part, the model of politeness and diplomacy, taking a keen interest in all things Russian, laughing off the dreary 'international' cuisine and snail's-pace restaurant service, standing still for endless pictures with his arm round his mum's shoulders or sportingly getting down in the traditional Cossack pose of crouch-and-kick. The only slight wobble occurred on the third day, after a night of much Russian champagne mixed with tinned mandarin juice, and high jinks with the film crew, which climaxed in Elton's throwing a full glass of vodka into Harvey Goldsmith's face.

The next morning, he was to make a specially arranged tour of the Winter Palace and Hermitage museums, which would also serve as a sequence in the film by Dick Clement and Ian La Frenais. He had been eager to see the museums' imperial treasures and collection of French Impressionist paintings but, when the time came, was unable to haul himself out of bed. He arrived at the Hermitage two hours late, still deeply hung over, and, after only two minutes, walked off in a sudden tantrum, leaving his film crew with no footage and his Russian guides staring in mystification and pique. ELTON SNUBS RUSSIANS IN WINTER PALACE REVOLT, the *Daily Mail* duly reported.

His four Moscow concerts were in the Rossiya Concert Hall, overlooking the onion domes of St Basil's Cathedral and the cobbled expanse of Red Square, where soldiers mount goose-stepping guard on Lenin's tomb around the clock. Once again, the bulk of the tickets had gone to Party officials and favourites, leaving only a few hundred to be fought for by hungry young rock fans. Many occupants of the front rows arrived in the chauffeur-driven Chaika limousines available only to senior Politbureau members. The running order was the same as in Leningrad, including 'Back in the USSR', but with one curious addition. Halfway through his first solo hour, Elton suddenly switched from Steinway grand to Yamaha electric piano and struck up 'He'll Have to Go', the same mournful Jim Reeves ballad with which fifteen-year-old Reggie Dwight had begun his uphill residency at the Northwood Hills Hotel.

As at his Leningrad first night, the beginning was muted and the end spectacular, with hundreds of young Russians forgetting Party decorum and rushing down the aisles to the stage front. Presents were continually handed up to Elton aides: a cuddly toy, flowers, books and numerous handwritten notes. At one point, a string of pearls landed on the stage. Elton returned for three encores, even though his throat had been giving him trouble. 'It started to go dodgy at the sound check,' he said afterwards. 'But somehow I shouted and screamed and gargled my way through.'

The second night's concert was beamed live to BBC Radio One, available throughout the United Kingdom and in many European countries as well. No rock star before had reached so many people at once, over so many cultural and political divides.

Between concerts, he, Sheila and Derf, pursued by their constant semicircle of snapping photographers, strolled round the red-walled Kremlin precincts and attended a performance of *Swan Lake* in the sumptuous Bolshoi Theatre. Elton was also shown the extensive building preparations for the following year's Olympic Games, an event which excited him so much that he offered to write a theme song to accompany the official Games logo of a cuddly little cartoon Russian bear. Another afternoon, he went to a football match between Moscow Dynamo and the Red Army, was presented with a football autographed by the Red Army team, and promised to try to organise some friendly matches between them and Watford.

At one of his press conferences, a Russian journalist asked in halting English whether he was against apartheid in sport. 'Yes,' he replied. 'I object to apartheid, whether it's because of colour, class or sexual preference.' In Russia at that time, as everyone present knew, the punishment for homosexuality was five years' imprisonment.

A *Daily Telegraph* leading article struck the only sceptical note, accusing Russia of using Elton's concerts to placate its young in the time-honoured dictatorial tradition of 'bread and circuses'. What had happened in Moscow and Leningrad, the *Telegraph* said, was that rock music had been detached from Western democracy and been remoulded as part of a new, subtler communism. But even the *Telegraph* leader writer had only benign feelings towards the performer whose music had proved so international and ideologically malleable.

For everyone on the Russian side, the enterprise had been a phenomenal success. Normally po-faced and cautious diplomats at Britain's Moscow embassy were openly calling it the biggest step forward in East–West understanding since Mr Khrushchev visited Hollywood. The ultimate sign of Soviet capitulation occurred after the third concert, when Tass filled its office display windows with publicity material and posters of Elton.

He arrived back at Heathrow airport on 31 May, 'knackered' but exhilarated, still wearing his big cap and Watford scarf. Pinned to his anorak was a badge reading 'Lend us a quid', stressing how unmercenary had been the purpose of the trip. With him came Harvey Goldsmith, carrying the blue bag in which the Russians had paid out £4,000 in notes so ancient, they had to be taken to the Bank of England and exchanged for new ones.

Sipping restorative Lucozade, Elton told his airport press conference the tour had been 'one of the most memorable and happy I've ever been on. We took along the Ludo, the Monopoly and the backgammon, thinking we'd be locked up in our hotel all night. But the country isn't dark, grey, grim or drab – it's beautiful, and the people are very warm. Leningrad is a marvellous city, and the hospitality was tremendous.'

So was he now a convert to communism and totalitarianism? 'I'm against bigotry and prejudice and persecution,' he replied. 'But if that stopped me playing my music, I wouldn't play it here, because of the National Front or the campaign against homosexuality. You don't go in with guns blazing, saying, "I want this and that." You've got to approach things gently. I'd be very presumptuous to consider myself an ambassador of any sort, but I'm glad to do my bit.'

Ignoring press pleas to take off his cap, he was then ushered to his Rolls-Royce and driven off to satisfy pent-up cravings for an Indian curry and a cup of tea brewed in a pot, not a samovar.

He kept his promise and wrote a song for the 1980 Moscow Olympic Games. But by that time, the cuddly little cartoon bear had sent tanks to invade Afghanistan, and the Games were subject to an international boycott. At the Foreign Office's 'suggestion', Elton's song never found its way to his new friends in Moscow.

The spent force and yesterday's man was back in his old niche as the world's most talked-about rock star. As in 1971, when his professional demise also was confidently predicted, Elton had contrived to reinvent himself.

The autumn of 1979 found him on top form again, both as performer and communicator, taking time off from a new American tour (headlined 'Back in the USSA') to hold court in a $1,000-per-day suite at the New York Waldorf Towers. An extravagant centre spread in the *Daily Mirror* shows him in décolleté silk pyjamas, posing in exaggeratedly camp style, cheeks drawn in and lips puckered, one hand archly patting the back of his head. An adjacent mirror reflects the new hair transplant, dark, patchy and vague, like sandbars seen through the shallow waters of Scapa Flow.

The new non-glitter, contact-lens look is accompanied by a new honesty and plain-spokenness about himself. He is now completely open about his bisexuality, and will talk about it to any interviewer, freely and without embarrassment. 'I realise it's not everyone's cup of tea, and I try not to dwell on it too much,' he tells the *Mirror*'s Alasdair Buchan. 'But I had to get it off my chest. That's the way I am, and it's no good hiding it.'

The camp pose, however, is pure parody, showing not what he is but what he isn't. His point is that not all men with homosexual tendencies conform to the mincing stereotype of current gay comedians like Larry Grayson and John Inman. 'A lot of them are just very confused, frightened people. I know it was far easier for me to come out than for many others. They go through a hell of a lot of pain, and I would support anyone who was totally frank, because it's never easy. I've had a lot of letters from people who think they're gay, but live in small communities where it would be very hard to say so. I rarely write back to anyone, but I wrote back to every one of those people and said, "If you ever get down in the dumps, write again."'

He also speaks for the first time about his mother's feelings on the subject. 'From the beginning, she always said, "Listen. Don't ever be deceitful to me. Tell me, even if you think I won't like it." I never thought I'd go to bed with someone of my own sex. When I did, she was the first person I phoned and told. I said "You told me never to be deceitful, so this is what happened."'

So tasteful and sympathetic was his treatment by the British tabloids that Sheila herself gave two lengthy interviews, confiding to the *Daily Express* WHY I WORRY ABOUT MY YOUNG ELTON, and telling the *Daily Mail* about THE JEKYLL AND HYDE THAT IS MY SON ELTON.

Tactfully prompted by the *Express*'s David Wigg, she admitted the shock of Elton's telephone call, but said she had long ago come to terms with what he was. 'A lot of people didn't admire him for saying it. Some used to shout odd names after him. But he was strong enough to come out of the closet when there's thousands more that won't. Half the people who look at him and say, "Oh, he's a queen" are the same way, if they'd be honest with themselves. But I don't think he'd ever have been if it wasn't for show business. Show business did it, definitely.

'Loneliness – that's what I worry about for him more than

anything else. I think he's desperate. He's got all the possessions you could wish for, but that doesn't make him happy. He hasn't anyone to share it with, and that's what he needs. He says he'd like to have a family. Unfortunately, his lifestyle doesn't allow him to meet anybody. And he won't allow himself. It's as if he holds back all the time. I feel that he's got everything – but nothing.'

Also back at full strength was the studio workaholic, keen as ever to release twice as much product as the market could stand. That April, three tracks from the abandoned Thom Bell album project had been resurrected, remixed and issued as a new-style twelve-inch single. Though none was a hit in Britain, the Beatle-echoey 'Mama Can't Buy You Love' reached number nine in America, firing up Elton's enthusiasm for a still bigger comeback in the land that had originally made him.

Straight after touring Europe, Israel and Russia, he was off making another album, commuting between Musicland studios in Munich and Rusk Sound Studios in Hollywood. His style flew in yet another direction, flavoured now by the disco sound that had been in vogue since John Travolta's movie *Saturday Night Fever*. For the new album, *Victim of Love*, he teamed with songwriter-producer Pete Bellotte, the man behind new disco stars like the erotic Donna Summer. In his keenness to fit the new mould, Elton left all the songwriting on *Victim of Love* to Bellotte and other lyricists, bizarrely miscellaneous. There was even a version of the Chuck Berry classic 'Johnny B. Goode'.

The words might have served as an admonition to Elton's manager. For in this period, as the superstar regained the ascendant in every possible constructive and positive way, John Reid was at his most unruly and controversial.

In 1978, Reid had astounded his and Elton's joint circle by becoming engaged to Sarah Forbes, Bryan and Nanette's eighteen-year-old daughter. The eleven-year difference in their ages might have mattered less had Reid not known Sarah as a little girl in the Wentworth days, and had she not known him in his apparently permanent domestic relationship with Elton. The engagement caused particular discomfort to Elton, for whom Sarah was still the little girl who had presented him with a Rolls-Royce-embroidered cushion. Reid was apparently quite serious, even phoning Nina Myskow, who had just joined *The Sun* from *Jackie* magazine, to give her the story exclusively. To general relief, however, the engagement was called off after a few weeks. Sarah Forbes went on to marry the actor John Standing – also some years her senior – and has remained on friendly terms with Reid.

In October 1979, Elton's disco album, *Victim Of Love*, was released, quickly stiffing at number 35 in America and 41 in Britain. Its namesake single did no better, making only 31 in America but not even registering in Britain's charts. John Reid's enraged response was another mass sacking of Rocket Records staff, including the managing director David Croker, whom he had sacked a year previously for the 'Ego' flop but afterwards reinstated.

'The pathetic sight of a small group of colourfully dressed people locked out on a Mayfair pavement is the latest evidence of pop millionaire John Reid's increasing eccentricity,' Nigel Dempster's *Daily Mail* diary reported. 'Passers by in South Audley Street were treated to the vision of Rocket staff being unceremoniously bundled out on to the pavement . . . A victim of last year's screaming match, former promotions manager Arthur Sherriff, tells me, "These sackings are an annual event at the very least."'

Like Elton, Reid was a walking weather-house rotation of Jekyll and Hyde. The public shrieker and punch-thrower also hankered for respectability and social standing and, for a time, even contemplated entering politics. In 1979, he got involved with the Conservative Party, just as it was preparing to fight its first general election under Margaret Thatcher's leadership. He cultivated the acquaintanceship of several Tory MPs and let it be known that, if offered a Parliamentary seat, he would willingly stand. The party responded to these overtures, seeing in him the kind of thrustful young self-made man it needed for its new meritocratic image. Reid underwent serious grooming and self-grooming as a prospective candidate, absorbing policy, attending cocktail parties, even speaking at one or two dinners to test his oratorial gifts.

Three weeks before the election, he was asked to stand for the far northern seat of Orkney and Shetland, but refused, deciding that, after all, pop managership and politics did not mix. Certainly, the career of a bright young Thatcherite MP would hardly have been compatible with stories like this, from the 1 October issue of *The Sun*:

ELTON'S MANAGER IS ARRESTED AFTER 'HITTING DOORMAN'

Superstar Elton John's manager has been arrested for allegedly attacking a hotel doorman with a walking stick.

Police said that John Reid, 30, lost his temper over a car parked outside the posh Fairmont Hotel in San Francisco's Nob Hill. The doorman, John Figuero, asked Reid to shut the car door because it was blocking other traffic.

Mr Charles Sandovic, the police spokesman, said yesterday: 'Reid is said to have become very abusive, and attacked the doorman with the black, silver-tipped cane he was carrying.

'He allegedly struck Figuero several times on the back and has been charged with battery.'

Figuero had to have medical treatment to his back and is considering suing Reid.

Because Reid is a Londoner and his only identification was his British passport, he was charged at the city's central jail, but bailed in his own recognisance.

15

The Sun Also Rises

LONG before the Seventies had limped to an end, they were
commonly agreed to have been an unmitigated disaster. The
whole decade seemed little but a long hangover from the Sixties, in
which the carried-on ideals of 'love' and 'peace' had looked
increasingly fatuous and futile. Though public pressure had finally
ended the Vietnam war, other nasty little wars raged unchecked, and
largely forgotten, in Nicaragua, Cambodia, Northern Ireland, the
Lebanon. Notions of human brotherhood had barely alleviated the
problem of world famine, or the plight of untold political prisoners
under innumerable repressive regimes. Across Europe, terrorist
murder was an almost daily fact of life, very often committed by
young men whose long hair, blue denim and 'Have a nice day'
patches were identical with those of the fraternal multitudes at Sixties
rock festivals.

America's election of a wholly liberal, wholly moral president,
Jimmy Carter, had brought about only chronic financial instability
and a ghastly dip in national pride, epitomised by the taking hostage
of an entire embassy in Teheran. In Britain, under successive Labour
governments, the welfare state was running amok, with millions
apparently preferring unemployment benefit to work, inflation out of
control and trade union tyranny rampant. In Britain, 1979 was the
so-called Winter of Discontent, when strikes paralysed public
transport, schools and hospitals, and rubbish sacks festered in
mountains on the streets. Different indeed from the winter of 1969,
with its golden, regretful afterglow. In 1979, no one could get out of
the old decade fast enough.

The decade ahead glowed with compensatory allure. After those
ten long years of dragged-out whimsy and illusion, the Eighties
approached Britain in a heady aura of cool realism. Science and
technology, fifteen years at the nadir of chic, suddenly made a
remarkable comeback. The fashionable rage was 'high tech', a gaunt
modernity of design in furniture and decor, sweeping away pine

floors, Victorian dressers, Art Deco ducks and Portobello Road bric-a-brac. Personal computers appeared in thousands of homes, no longer a vaguely sinister appendage to government, but a miraculously labour-saving, 'user-friendly' domestic pet. Cars lost their Seventies flimsiness and hollowness, growing chunky and soft-bumpered, full of user-friendly dials, lights, even voices, to assist and reassure their drivers. Movies like *Star Wars*, *Buck Rogers* and *Battlestar Galactica* made science fiction more popular than it had been since the mid-Fifties. New pop stars, like Gary Numan, all seemed to be rocket men, singing in the flat, jerky automaton voices from studios apparently located somewhere in inner space.

That long-delayed miracle, 'the Future', seemed ready to dawn at long last. One could hardly wait to kick away the Seventies' useless husk, and cross into the Eighties' vista of chaste black rooms, house-trained robots, bright chromium and cosy red indicator lights.

By coincidence, at this pivotal point between epochs, America and Britain each acquired a new leader. In both cases, the national choice was one which, a very few years before, would have seemed inconceivable. America's was a former actor in Hollywood B-pictures, already so aged and bewildered that he was unable to frame the simplest utterance without help from teleprompters and cue cards. Britain's was a nondescript Tory woman whose shrill voice rose and fell curiously out of sync' with her words, like an imperfectly dubbed foreign film.

Outwardly dissimilar as Ronald Reagan and Margaret Thatcher might seem, there was – as they would soon reveal – a profound kinship between them. For both were creations of publicity and marketing campaigns, so stupendously resourced as to make even the hype machine of rock music seem moderate by comparison. And both, lacking any sense of the absurd or embarrassing, were perfect mouthpieces for their respective parties' promise to the electorate. An end to the woozy liberalism and *laissez-faire* chaos of government in the Sixties and Seventies. A new atmosphere of purpose, efficiency and hard work. A new spirit of enterprise, self-help, national pride and feeling good about oneself.

Like the Sixties and Seventies, the Eighties had to run a couple of years before revealing their true character. In 1982, Margaret Thatcher sent a naval force to recapture one of Britain's last colonial territories, the Falkland Islands, from an Argentinian invasion force. A few months later, Ronald Reagan dispatched troops to crush an alleged communist coup on the West Indian island of Grenada. What will engross future historians may not be the cause or necessity of these operations so much as the way each was successfully used to sell leader to nation by their respective marketing organisations. To America, in the invasion of Grenada's undefended beaches, Reagan had magically wiped away the agony of Vietnam. To Britain, for mowing down the Argentinian boy-conscripts, Margaret Thatcher became Winston Churchill born again. Thus was the seal set on the two most astonishingly successful Western leaders of modern times.

Mrs Thatcher's transformation was accomplished with the help of one wholly unlooked-for ally. For fifty years, Britain's only significant mass circulation tabloid newspaper had been the left-wing *Daily Mirror*. In 1969, the Australian press tycoon Rupert Murdoch had bought the *Mirror*'s ailing broadsheet stablemate *The Sun*, turning it into a tabloid identical in every respect save that on its third page every day, flouting all Fleet Street convention, there appeared a bare-breasted young woman. For all the resultant controversy among moralists and feminists, *The Sun* had remained a conventional product, vying with its competitors first and foremost in the retailing of news. But with the Falklands war, its hour – as well as Margaret Thatcher's – had come.

Though Argentina had always been the most anglophile of Latin American countries, *The Sun* instantly characterised its people with primitive racism as 'Argies'. It declared itself 'the Paper Behind Our Boys', following the government line in tones of hysterical chauvinism not heard in Britain since August 1914. Broadcasters who questioned the conduct of the war were denounced in *Sun* editorials as 'traitors'. The quintessential moment occurred when pictures came back of Argentina's archaic cruiser *General Belgrano* being blown apart by British missiles. *The Sun*'s headline, displaying all the humane sensibility of a football thug putting the boot in, was GOTCHA!

So for Britain, once again, the Future failed to arrive. Overnight, the 1980s leapt back to the 1880s, our dreadnoughts masters of the seas again, our jolly tars triumphant and the dagoes licked. Instead of that high-tech vista came a landscape testifying to our regained glory as a great war-making power. In the microchip age, the great buzzwords turned out to be 'traditional', 'original' and 'classic'. Pubs transformed themselves into semblances of Boer War gin palaces or Dickensian coffee rooms. Fortunes were made in the mass-production of bogus nineteenth-century goods, from 'Victorian villager' soap-on-a-rope to 'Victorian country house' chutney and mustard foot-soak. Such things had existed, of course, in the Sixties and Seventies, but were always recognised as pastiche. In the Eighties, they began to be believed. Mrs Thatcher herself spoke of restoring 'Victorian values' and in this, at least, spoke the truth. For the values that returned were the Victorian ones which the previous two decades, for all their faults, had seemed to diminish: class snobbery, social cruelty, racism and blind prejudice.

All this was faithfully reflected in *The Sun*. Even before GOTCHA! the paper had adopted a formula uniquely blending the nationalistic and moral fervour of the new age with the reality of its tastes and appetites. News, in the form of daily political and social happenings, had little place in *The Sun*. Its world was the fantasy one of show business, television soap opera, royal tittle-tattle and its own daily bingo game and mammarily remarkable but airheaded 'Page Three girls'. The all-time classic *Sun* story illustrates the paper's huge distance from any traditional purposes of journalism. In 1986, the ex-girl-friend of a TV comedian named Freddie Starr gave it an anecdote, already three years old. Feeling hungry one night in 1983, Starr had picked up her pet hamster, jokily put it between two pieces of bread and pretended to bite into it. By any sane news value, the tired little tale barely rated mention at the foot of some show-biz gossip column. In *The Sun* it made front-page splash in three-inch headlines, FREDDIE STARR ATE MY HAMSTER!

Even by the dubious standard of Fleet Street, the paper's ethics and practices were unique. People whom it wished to feature in its 'stories', whether famous or obscure, were pursued and harassed with utter ruthlessness, into their homes, into hospital, even on to the very mortuary slab. On two infamous occasions, both connected with the Falklands war, 'interviews' were fabricated with people who had refused to speak to the paper. Its editorials – written in kindergarten English, for an imagined attention span of about eight seconds – combined slavish pro-Thatcherism with rabid xenophobia. Not only its prejudices but also its language echoed that of the construction site. To *The Sun*, French people were 'Frogs', Germans 'Krauts', Japanese 'Nips', and homosexuals 'poofs'. Each day's 'soaraway' edition competed with the last in plainly cynical effort to strike the basest, blindest and most brutish human note.

The result was a commercial triumph, selling over 4 million copies and claiming to reach 13 million readers daily, to the near-eclipse of the essentially decent and ethical *Daily Mirror*. The *Mirror*'s response was to ape *The Sun* – a lead quickly followed by its other daily rival, the *Star*, and the *Sunday People* and *News of the World*. Even so-called quality papers – two of which were now also owned by Murdoch – joined the headlong stampede downmarket. Britain's press in the Eighties could therefore sink to its all-time low with all-powerful justification, the plea of the pornographer through the ages: 'It's what people want.'

*

The change of tone where Elton was concerned happened as the decades revolved. In November 1979, he was talking about his bisexuality to a *Daily Express* whose editorial tone was as sympathetically restrained as some social worker or therapist. In August 1980, the same paper's William Hickey diary carried this ominously unpleasant item:

The only woman in Elton John's life has left him.

His mother.

After nursing her gay little lad through the rigours of stardom for the past 10 years, Mrs Sheila Farebrother has decided to make a go of it on her own.

She has bought a house in Brighton, miles away from her son's Windsor mansion. And no longer will she be popping in every day to make sure her superstar son's smalls are laundered.

Of course, Elton is 33, and it's high time he and his mum went their separate ways.

But the two have relied on each other for so long that it comes as a surprise.

Indeed, whenever there was a handbag fight between Elton and his diminutive manager John Reid, Sheila used to come into the offices to sort it out . . .

There's only one problem now that Sheila is moving on. Who will water Elton's newly-transplanted thatch?

At the beginning, ironically, few seemed likelier to prosper in Mrs Thatcher's Golden Age. Almost the first image we have of Elton in the Eighties is his black-windowed Rolls turning into the gateway of the Houses of Parliament. The occasion was a party to launch the *Guinness Book of Hits of the Seventies*, compiled by Elton's chief media mouthpiece Paul Gambaccini, and attended also by lesser hit-makers such as Freddie Mercury and Gary Glitter. Elton upstaged all, arriving – with Kiki Dee – in a schoolboy's cap and striped blazer, to set off £400,000-worth of jewellery including a diamond-encrusted watch. During the reception in a panelled Commons committee-room, he was seen chatting with Norman St John Stevas, then Leader of the House. 'I'm trying to make him into a Tory,' St John Stevas quipped.

A small kerfuffle subsequently broke out when it was alleged that, on a conducted tour of the Commons Chamber after the party, Elton had been allowed to sit in the Speaker's Chair. A Conservative MP, John Carlisle, wrote to Norman St John Stevas, complaining it was 'a gross breach of respect'. But the Cartier-encrusted schoolboy remained uncensured.

His apparently secure place in the national pantheon seemed confirmed by his inclusion in a 1980 BBC TV series *Best of British*, singling out those who had most enhanced Britain's international prestige in recent years. Again the interviewer was Paul Gambaccini, whose on-camera arrival at Woodside gives a vivid picture of the state in which Elton now lived. We see Gambaccini's car turn off the Old Windsor road into a tree-lined precinct, guarded by police, slalomed by traffic cones and punctuated by signboards warning 'Trespassers Will Be Prosecuted' and 'Guard Dogs On Patrol'. A quarter of a mile on, we reach the iron main gate, its electronic entryphone to be buzzed by 'Authorised Callers Only'. Thence down the long drive, past its signpost 'Elton Road', bumping over 'sleeping policemen' with the caution of an armoured convoy in Belfast. Here, finally, is the chunky Queen Anne house and its occupant, as well-guarded and sequestered as ever Elvis was at Graceland.

We see Elton at his piano, surrounded by the same vermilion leather buttonback sofas he had at Hercules. Both his face and waistline have noticeably filled out again. His transplanted hair is apparently so abundant that a loose strand can even be made to fall carelessly down over his forehead. He wears a plain white sweater with the sleeves pushed up, and almost no jewellery. He could be any young businessman showing off the fruits of the Thatcher enterprise culture.

His view of the decade just past is characteristically forthright. 'Great from a career point of view but from a personal point of view, terrible. A lot of the time, I was a complete mess. Around 1975, especially, I started acting like a real spoiled brat. There are parts of it I can't even remember.'

He describes the effort he has made – in his own estimation, at least – to come down to earth and join the human race again. 'I'd go away on my own, following the England football team; I'd check into a hotel, then ring my mother and say, "Well! I made it!" She'd say, "So? A grown man feels proud because he's unpacked his own suitcase?"' With due apology, he yet again mentions what a beneficent stabilising influence Watford has been. 'There, people don't treat me as anything special. I can just be myself. It's wonderful.'

The programme also fascinatingly demonstrates Elton's ability to produce a convincing pop melody almost instantaneously from any words handed to him. In this case, the words are some of the most resounding ever written in English, John Donne's famous 'No man is an island . . .' The scrap of paper from Paul Gambaccini is briefly

studied. The pudgy fingers reach and press. In five or six seconds, the
voice has found the hook. A new track is nearly ready for the guys
in the band:

> No man is an Island
> Entire of it self
> Every man is a peece of the Continent
> A part of the maine . . .
>
> Any man's death diminishes me
> Because I am involved in Mankinde.
> And therefore, never send to know for whom the bell tolls.
> It tolls for thee.

The *Daily Telegraph*'s TV critic, Sylvia Clayton, wasn't impressed. 'The
cadences he produced, rather like a syncopated hymn, put me in mind of
Oscar Wilde's Canon Chasuble, who had a sermon adaptable for any
occasion.' She felt it was wrong to present so interesting and articulate a
personality in the Japanese or Irish mode of 'living national treasure'.

Professionally, he was back from the wilderness. Pop had passed
through its punk holocaust and was moving forward again, which, as
ever, meant circling back and back. For up-and-coming bands, the *sine
qua non*, once more, was skill, together with an eclecticism pop had
never seen before. New line-ups featured saxes, trumpets, even
trombones, experimenting with idioms traditionally excluded from the
genre, Latin American, even jazz and bebop. Stage clothes made the
same total about-face, from punkdom's tatters and knee-manacles to
a revival of the mid-Sixties Mod style, embellished by floppy haircuts,
frills, cloaks and enough similar poetic flourishes to label a new
movement, the New Romantics. Most of its musicians had been small
boys in the early Seventies, and enjoyed the glitter and froth of music
then, much as earlier small boys had enjoyed comic books and Saturday
morning cinema. The new chart sensation Adam Ant performed in
bizarre period clothes amid extravagant settings, all much like
those which had first established Elton John. The New Romantic
band Spandau Ballet unashamedly acknowledged him as their chief
inspiration. An international genre of singer-songwriters, like Billy Joel
and Barry Manilow, produced hits as prolifically as he had done in the
mid-Seventies, accompanying themselves on piano in the same high,
passionate register. It was even revealed that Simon Le Bon, blond
heart-throb of Duran Duran, had grown up in the same Middlesex
suburb as Elton, and even attended the same school. Pinner was a pop
powerhouse at last.

Elton's 1980 album, *21 at 33*, took its title from the supposition that his thirty-third birthday coincided with his twenty-first LP. It was, in fact, counting compilations, only his eighteenth, but what did that matter except to mathematical pedants? *21 at 33* proved a commercial success, which restored Elton to the musical foreground in America and Britain, as well as restoring an irreplaceable element to his psyche. For Bernie Taupin and he were back writing songs together, as of old.

Bernie, too, felt he had survived the previous decade, and all its extravagant gifts to him, only by the skin of his teeth. 'The last thing I want to do is glorify the way I was,' he says now. 'I hate that press cliché of calling you a survivor just because you've got through binges of drink and drugs, and making a hero out of someone like Jim Morrison, who kills himself with sheer excess. There's nothing heroic in being a fall-down drunk. It's pathetic – and I was pathetic.'

Drying out in Acapulco, in the post-*Blue Moves* period, had dealt with only part of Bernie's problem. Despite the fortune he had earned in song royalties since 1970, his finances were in a chaotic mess. 'For years, I'd spent money without thinking, and borrowed it without thinking. I hadn't cared about anything but getting wasted and having a good time. And suddenly came the day I realised it wasn't a bottomless coffer. The reserves were running dry.'

In 1978, he acquired a new manager, Michael Lippman, who set about the long process of putting his business affairs in order. At the same time, his affair with the celebrated Loree Rodkin came to a painful – though, alas, not final – conclusion. Ten years later, Rodkin would still be pointing to Bernie's scalp, among others, on her belt in an interview with an American magazine.

Not long after splitting up with Loree Rodkin, he went to a friend's birthday party at the Beverly Hilton hotel. 'I was still feeling pretty sad about life, and hadn't wanted to go to this thing, but I was persuaded to. Standing at the bar there was the most stunning girl I'd ever seen. It sounds silly, but as soon as I looked at her, I thought, "That's the woman for me."'

He discovered her name was Toni Russo, and that her sister was Renée Russo, the top American fashion model of that time. For all his incurably romantic ardour, that seemed as far as Bernie was destined to get. 'I tried to set up a date with her, but she didn't want to know about me. I sent her flowers, but it was still no good. Then she started working as manageress at Lou Adler's club, and, when I walked in one night, there she was behind the bar. So I started talking to her again, and from there we just evolved into a relationship.'

Marrying Toni Russo, in 1979, was Bernie's final salvation from the Seventies. 'She was the one who put everything back together for me. I don't think anyone in my life, apart from my parents, has done more for me, physically and mentally. I'd always dreamed of writing other things, outside the things I did with Elton. I'd talked about it so much, but Toni was the one who really played hardball with me, and said, "Well, don't talk about it all the time. Do it."

'The really phenomenal thing she did was to pull everything together on the financial front. The people I'd had looking after my affairs were very lax, mainly because I couldn't be bothered, and there was no one sitting on top of them, saying, "What's going on?" Toni was the one who got my new manager, Michael Lippman, to go in and find out what was there, and put together a whole new crew to invest it properly.'

The gulf between Elton and him closed as wordlessly as it had opened. In the summer of 1979, while Elton was recording at Superbear Studios in Nice, he asked Bernie and Toni over to stay at the house he had rented in nearby Grasse. As part of the pleasant reunion, Bernie wrote three songs for *21 at 33*, including a memoir of his Acapulco exile called 'Two Rooms at the End of the World'.

The way was not yet open to their old total collaboration. Gary Osborne was still around, contributing three tracks, including the album's hit single, 'Little Jeannie'. In addition – to prove he could keep up with the times – Elton had tried writing with two lyricists of the new generation. One was Rocket Records' expensive new artiste, Judie Tzuke. The other was Tom Robinson, a performer admirable in many respects, not least his sane, plain-spoken declaration that one should be 'glad to be gay'.

Again, the album was co-produced by Elton with his former engineer Clive Franks. Bringing Bernie over was part of a conscious wish to reassemble as many as possible of the team who had made so many hits so easily in carefree days at Château d'Hierouville. The band he put together included his stalwart lead guitarist Davey Johnstone, and even his original bass player and drummer, Dee Murray and Nigel Olsson. In true Seventies longhair style, neither bore any grudge for their unceremonious sacking, five years before. 'I got a call when I was in Los Angeles,' Dee remembers. 'It was the office, the way it always used to be. "Elton's recording, would you like to do some sessions?" I said, "Yeah, great." We seemed to pick up just where we'd left off.'

21 at 33 was Elton's best received album internationally since *Blue Moves*, reaching number twelve in Britain and thirteen in America. The real astonishment was 'Little Jeannie', Gary Osborne's routine ballad, which reached only thirty-three in Britain, but flew to number three on the American singles charts.

Having a US hit album and single meant more to Elton now than it had ever done. His confession of bisexuality, while seeming to cause little backlash at the time, had done long-term damage to his popularity in Godfearing and straitlaced Middle America. To be permitted back to the top of *Billboard*'s and *Cashbox*'s charts seemed to indicate that the whole thing had finally blown over, on both sides of the Atlantic. 'Talking about it affected my popularity far more in the States than in Britain,' Elton himself acknowledged, adding what was to prove the unhappiest false prophecy of his career. 'There are far more maniacally religious people, who care about that sort of thing, in America. The British public, on the other hand, like you to be more upfront. They don't make such issues into big deals.'

His total rehabilitation in America was confirmed by that autumn's sell-out tour, backed by the *21 at 33* studio band, including Dee Murray and Nigel Olsson, and featuring an array of new stage outfits in his most extravagant Seventies styles. One was a sequinned cowboy outfit, another a floppy-capped chauffeur's uniform with two piano keyboards down its front like crisscrossed black-and-white bandoliers. His new publicity picture showed him in a New York policeman's wired cap and uniform tunic, embellished by a double lion's-head brooch at the throat. His face also appeared on an issue of novelty $1 bills, a distinction granted only to select VIPs like President Reagan, Frank Sinatra and the late Elvis Presley.

The climax of the 1980 tour was a free concert in New York's Central Park, with Elton performing to his largest-ever audience, an estimated 400,000. It was a glorious Fall afternoon, as much symbolising the reclamation of the park itself from muggers and fear by cyclists, joggers and skateboarders. The high point was Elton's appearance in a Daisy Duck costume, shaking his yellow beak, stomping webbed feet and wagging the tail that Nature had already started, back in those illicit rock-'n'-roll sessions on the school Steinway.

Among the songs from eighteen albums was a cover version specially relevant to Central Park, with its red-gold trees and skinny-tailed grey squirrels. Striking up John Lennon's 'Imagine', and looking away to the dark cupolas of the Dakota Building, Elton simply said, 'This one's by a friend of mine.'

In 1980, Elton's close-knit executive team lost a key member. David Croker resigned his managing directorship of Rocket Records to join the Hansa production company, handling rival attractions like Japan and Boney M. He subsequently embarked on a totally new career, one for which life with John Reid – being regularly screamed at, fired and rehired – might seem not unsuitable preparation. After years of taking heat in a metaphorical kitchen, David Croker became executive chef with a London catering company.

His successor at Rocket was a go-ahead young man named John Hall, who had arrived as promotions manager a year earlier, having previously owned his own label, Ebony. Hall's task was to reinvigorate an organisation from which all the Seventies champagne fizz seemed to have evaporated. The original roster with its outmoded names – Longdancer, Stackridge, China – was moribund. Neil Sedaka, the great hitmaker for Rocket USA, had been allowed to drift away to another label. Apart from Elton and Kiki Dee, no Rocket act had come near a chart hit for years. The company which its co-founder had committed to 'working its b****cks off' seemed flat, dispirited and no way ready to face the challenge of a brand new decade.

The main hope was Judie Tzuke, a David Croker signing, who combined songwriting abilities with a bruised and melancholy aura much like Kiki Dee's. Her second single for Rocket, 'Stay With Me Till Dawn', was indeed a torch song virtually identical to 'Amoureuse', and an almost exactly similar medium British hit. Elton's label seemed to make a speciality of girl singers prone to extravagant pillow-talk.

During the next couple of years, under John Hall, Rocket enjoyed more hits than ever in its history. The successful artistes were a strangely assorted bunch, reflecting the chaos and caprice of charts in those post-punk days. After Judie Tzuke, a band called the Lambrettas, signed by Hall himself, had a British number seven single with the old Coasters song, 'Poison Ivy'. The surprise number six hit to end them all was an ageing country-and-westerner named Fred Wedlock, singing a lament for all beer-bellies stuffed into blue jeans, called 'The Oldest Swinger in Town'.

Elton was delighted with these several successes, on top of his own resurgence in the British and US charts. One night at the Plaza Athenée Hotel in Paris, he impulsively offered John Hall a substantial share in Rocket. 'He said, "Got a pen, Beryl?" to John Reid, and wrote it out there and then inside a matchbook that I was to get something like 40 per cent of the company,' Hall remembers. 'I could see John sweating while it was going on, and feel pairs of eyes boring into this matchbook, like some slowed-up scene in a Clint Eastwood movie. Elton made me take it, so I just handed it to John and said, "If you want to give me this, fair enough." And he didn't.'

The operation that John Hall ran through the dawning Eighties was very different from what had begun, back in that seemingly boundless early Seventies sunshine. The days of 'looning' and 'ligging', of special trains to Moreton-in-Marsh, of lavish buffets torn apart and champagne bars drunk dry, of office outings to LA by charter jet and block bookings at the Beverly Hilton, of Cartier watches distributed by the carton and £50 notes pinned to Christmas cards, were gone for good. In the less than immortal words of Mrs Thatcher herself, there was to be 'no more free lunch'.

The rude awakening for Rocket came in 1979, when John Reid suddenly dismissed the company's accountants, Shears and Company. The ostensible reason was disappointing performance in a matter that obsessed the fiscally avid Scot. He remained convinced that, for all the millions Elton had earned in the Seventies, millions more might have been improperly witheld from him.

For almost six years, he had been engaged in guerrilla warfare with Elton's old mentors, Dick James Music, who held copyright on his songs up to 1973 and his record output up to 1975. The claim – backed up by divers expert legal and commercial opinions – was that DJM's network of foreign sub-publishing arrangements took too big a slice of the royalties Elton and Bernie earned from the playing of their songs worldwide.

On Reid's instructions, Shears and Co. had conducted an audit of DJM's books and examined its sub-publishing contracts, but with markedly little result. In October 1977, DJM had written to Geoffrey Ellis at Rocket, offering £6,687 in final settlement of the alleged shortfall in Elton's and Bernie's overseas royalties up to December, 1975 – a sum clearly nowhere near that which John Reid had in mind. Shears then began a further audit at DJM for the period 1976–78. This was still in progress when Reid lost patience, dismissed Shears and appointed the firm of Arthur Andersen and Company to look after Rocket, John Reid Enterprises and Elton.

Andersen's advice was a complete restructuring both of Rocket's corporate finances and Elton's personal ones. 'The message was that the silly times were over,' John Hall says now. 'People had to grow up and realise more money was going out than was coming in. Elton had to realise it, too, for the very first time in his career.'

Rocket, henceforward, was run on a tight rein, belied by the 'Help yourself' smile still on the face of its Thomas Tank-engine logo. And Elton, too, while not actually forced to economise, was encouraged to think twice before buying Ferraris for acquaintances or going round Cartier with his Safeway trolley. 'I don't spend as much money as I used to,' he admitted on his 1980 American tour. 'It used to be Rembrandts at Christmas for friends, which was a bit stupid.' (He had, in fact, given Rembrandt's etching 'The Adoration of the

Shepherds' as a thirtieth-birthday present to that noted connoisseur Rod Stewart.)

The other factor crucial to Rocket's health at the turn of the decade was negotiating a new recording deal for Elton in America. John Hall flew over with John Reid for this purpose, returning with a Reid story fit to join the classics of the genre.

Elton's $5-million deal with MCA, negotiated by Reid in 1974, was at that time the biggest and best ever made for a recording star. But now, at the end of its five-year span, the terms no longer seemed munificent. The putting of armlocks on to rich record companies, so ably pioneered by Reid, had become standard practice for managers throughout the music industry. Advances of $1 million per album, which once only Elton could command, were routinely paid out, to stop established stars from defecting or snap up potential money-spinners. In capital-investment terms, he rated as only a middle-sized fish in the pool.

The explosive additional factor in the affair, as always, was John Reid's personal hubris. Merely securing his client a right and proper increment was not enough for Reid. Nothing would do but that he make Elton an American deal as phenomenal for 1980 as the MCA deal had been for 1974.

'John went in to see the board of MCA,' John Hall remembers. 'They were pretty paranoid about losing Elton. Even though he wasn't hot at that time, he still accounted for an incredible amount of their turnover. They would probably have taken him on as a loss leader, just for the sake of his back catalogue.

'So John presents them with this phenomenal deal he's already boasted all around LA that he's going to do for Elton – I think it was $25 million for five albums. And having told the whole world he'd get it, he had to get it. The MCA people said, "Well, we're prepared to consider this, but for that sort of money, we'd need the rights for the whole world . . ." At that, John threw one of his massive tantrums and walked out of the room.

'I was at the meeting, but I'd already left. I heard later that John had come storming out of the boardroom into the main office, where all these secretaries were sitting, and the walls were covered with gold and platinum discs, mostly earned by Elton. John shouted something like "I made this fuckin' company, they can stick their fuckin' records" and got hold of one of the gold discs to tear it off the wall. But it was screwed on tight. He's standing there, with all the secretaries looking on, wrenching at this thing and cursing, but it just won't budge.'

Reid now found himself in serious difficulty. Having told the MCA board they were 'assholes', no channel existed for reopening negotiations. Nor could he take his deal to any of the other international companies capable of paying a $25 million advance. EMI and RCA had already featured in Elton deals ending less than happily for both sides. To go to PolyGram, Rocket's European distributor, would mean giving worldwide rights in Elton to a single company, with resultant loss of power both to artist and manager.

The one company willing and eager to do a deal on Elton in America only was a brand-new and largely untried label, Geffen Records. Its owner, David Geffen, had run the hugely successful Asylum label in the early Seventies, rising to still greater eminence after Asylum's merger with Warner and Elektra to form WEA. Setting up on his own, he had quickly wooed several major artists from other labels, compensating for the absence of enormous sums by a promise of imaginative and sympathetic handling. His great coup had come with the news that John Lennon was out of domestic retirement in New York, and recording tracks for a new album, *Double Fantasy*. After reviewing multimillion dollar offers from every major record company, Lennon – and Yoko – plumped for Geffen.

John Reid knew Geffen well, moving as they did in the same social circle. Geffen had already approached him about signing Elton, but – with the MCA superdeal supposedly imminent – had been scathingly rebuffed. No deal with MCA, or any other giant, having transpired, Reid's only option was to eat humble pie with David Geffen. 'I was involved in it,' John Hall remembers. 'We had to call Geffen and say, "Oh, gee, David – John's really sorry he hasn't got back to you before now, but he hasn't been feeling very well . . ."'

A deal was made with Geffen, saving Reid's face at the eleventh hour, though at some little cost. Instead of the much-trumpeted $25 million advance, Geffen paid essentially what MCA had under the 1974 deal, $1 million per album. The plus side, supposedly, was that Elton would be handled with a flair and sensitivity MCA could never match. 'What John had been going for was simply money,' John Hall says. 'And that, really was the right approach. With an artist of Elton's size, sensitive handling isn't the first priority. What you need first of all is massive cash investment to market him properly.'

To Elton, money was of less importance than sharing a label with his greatest idol and – now – great friend. 'Lennon and I are both on Geffen now,' he told people proudly on that summer 1980 tour. 'So we may do an album together one day. I'd love that.'

In Lennon's long hermitage at the Dakota Building, indeed, Elton had been one of the few welcome regular visitors. He was godfather to Sean, the son Yoko had borne after three traumatic miscarriages.

The baby, with his Lennon face and Japanese eyes, in many ways became a surrogate for the child Elton himself still longed to have.

Liking and admiring Lennon did not blind Elton to his many foibles and inconsistencies. The man who had engraved 'Imagine no possessions' on the mind of a generation now owned a vast property empire, including a farm and a prize herd of Holstein cattle. Yoko was an acquirer who put even Elton into the shade. 'I couldn't believe it,' he said after visiting the biggest of their three apartments at the Dakota. 'Yoko has a refrigerated room just for keeping her fur coats. She's got rooms full of those clothes racks like you see at Marks and Spencer. She makes me look ridiculous. I buy things in threes or fours, but she buys them in fifties. The funny thing is, you never see her wearing them. She's always got up in some tatty old blouse.'

For Lennon's fortieth birthday that October, Elton sent him a card, poking gentle fun at the words of his best-known song:

> Imagine six apartments.
> It isn't hard to do.
> One is full of fur coats,
> The other's full of shoes.

On the night of 8 December, Lennon returned home after an evening at New York's Hit Factory recording studio. As he and Yoko got out of their car and walked under the Dakota's Gothic arch, a young man, for whom Lennon had earlier autographed an album, stepped forward and fired five shots from a .38 handgun at point-blank range into his back. He managed to stagger into the Dakota vestibule, but died before an ambulance could get him to Roosevelt Hospital.

Other murders of modern times may have aroused similar worldwide grief and shock. But for no one else was universal grief more deeply personal. It would have astonished Lennon himself, who was convinced that the Beatles meant little to people any more, and, a few days before his death, had asked a British disc jockey if there might be 'any interest' in his appearing onstage again, as at Madison Square Garden in 1974.

The grief was greatest among the dozens of musicians, both British and American, who counted Lennon among their earliest inspiration. In a special memorial issue, *Rolling Stone* sought professional tributes from Ray Charles, Chuck Berry, Mick Jagger and a host of others. But, surprisingly, not from that once-upon-a-time Beatle fanatic in Pinner, who would prove Lennon's only rival in the command of mass personal friendship.

For Yoko, the shock included a reaction common among bereaved partners. In the days immediately after John's death, some of his characteristics seemed to transfer to her. Her eyesight, formerly excellent, suddenly became as bad as his. She also found herself developing his craving for chocolate.

Despite the vast outpouring of sympathy, very few people could find anything practical to do for her. One exception was an outsize chocolate cake, delivered to the Dakota Building with a card saying 'Love from Elton'.

In 1981, Elton's appearance changed yet again. The Cossack urchin look, of eight-piece caps and pantaloons tucked into boots, abruptly vanished. So did the contact lenses, the hollow face and bushy eyebrows. So did any further chance to monitor progress, or lack of it, in the hair-plugs checkered over his scalp. From here on, apart from a few involuntary unveilings, the transplant would remain permanently covered, like the Lord's wicket awaiting the end of rain.

The new Elton was a figure much attuned to the Eighties spirit of new Victorianism. It wore striped blazers, wing-poke collars with bow ties or cravats and over its bombarded cranium a straw boater tilted in the rakish style of Maurice Chevalier. Its torso – chunky once again – assumed a little parallel sideways twist, creating a silhouette that ultimately would be as recognisable as Chevalier's or Chaplin's. The eyes, that had so urgently wanted to meet others head on, hid away again behind dark glasses. In the right earlobe, a plain gold ring continued to make its small but unabashed self-declaration.

For most of 1981, Britain's press had little time to spare for Elton, or any rock star. Fleet Street was plunged into an obsession with royalty that even the Victorians might have considered excessive. The thirty-two-year-old Prince of Wales had announced his imminent marriage to Lady Diana Spencer, nineteen-year-old daughter of Earl Spencer. The royal choice, unprecedently, was a stunner, tall, buxom and blonde, with the legs of a fashion model. This 'fairy tale' romance roused the tabloids to outpourings of gush not seen in print since Nannie Crawford blew the whistle on Princess Lillibet.

The advent of Princess Diana – who would rollerskate around Buckingham Palace listening to pop on a personal stereo – was but one sign of greatly increased trendiness in the House of Windsor. Both the Queen's younger sons, Prince Edward and Prince Andrew, were now young men, of character very different from the circumspect Prince Charles. Andrew, in particular, was emerging as a hero of the new 'hooray Henry' class with his fondness for squirting soda siphons, and an indiscreet love life that led the tabloids to dub him 'Randy Andy'.

There remained, even so, only one rock performer with the equivalent of a royal 'By appointment' warrant. For Prince Andrew's twenty-first birthday party at Windsor Castle, Elton was invited to provide the cabaret. Six hundred guests, including Mrs Thatcher and her husband, watched him perform against a backdrop of castle walls, on which laser beams projected the word CONGRATULATIONS. The thank-you letter afterwards sent to Rocket Records was signed 'Diana Spencer'.

Otherwise, the year found him in another professional trough, following a pattern that Rocket's yong boss, John Hall, was quick to identify. 'It was always the same with Elton. He'd do one or two bad albums, and everyone would think that was the finish – he'd finally played himself out. Then he'd suddenly pull another great one out of nowhere.'

His album for 1981 was *The Fox*, a further *mélange* of collaborations with Gary Osborne, Bernie Taupin and Tom Robinson, co-produced by Chris Thomas, who had previously worked with the Sex Pistols, Paul McCartney and the Pretenders. It did respectably in Britain, reaching number twelve, but, as his first US release on Geffen, made only a disappointing twenty-one. Around it came a meteor shower of unsuccessful singles: 'Nobody Wins' and 'Just Like Belgium' from *The Fox*, plus DJM's opportunistic release of his three live tracks with John Lennon onstage at Madison Square Garden.

John Hall is almost unique among ex-Rocket employees in remembering his time there as happy and his treatment as generous and appreciative. 'I never got any of the fabled presents. I tried to distance myself from all that – even bought my own Cartier watch. But Elton was always great to me, and to my family. He adored my two kids, and they adored him. I remember when I took them to the Central Park gig, Elton had just landed by helicopter, and was in the middle of this huge entourage. But when he saw my kids, he came straight over, sat down and started talking to them.'

The sovereign's inner circle had lately taken on a new complexity. Bob Halley, his former chauffeur, was now the principal person in his life, a twenty-four-hour-a-day 'personal assistant'. As Rocket Records' head, John Hall had to deal with the ticklish emotional triangle formed by Elton, Halley and John Reid. 'Bob was the closest person to Elton on a day-to-day basis. But John and Elton still had something incredibly strong between them. They might have screaming rows and throw things at one another, or deliberately not call one another for weeks on end. But you knew there was something between them that no other relationship either of them might have could ever affect.'

Hall, despite himself, was drawn into what an earlier member, Sharon Lawrence, had called 'Elton's circle of dependence'. 'He seemed to have all these celebrity friends, and be hanging out with top musicians, like Rod, and Freddie Mercury. But I'd still find myself sitting up with him into the small hours. He could be incredibly funny, because he'd got this total recall of stories and the way people talked. And the more he drank, the sharper he got. He could drink brandy all night, and be totally fresh when everyone else was dropping dead.

'He loved to play cards as well, though he hated to lose, and never paid you what he owed you. He'd just go on doubling the stakes until he started winning by the law of averages. I think it was Gary Osborne who told him one night he'd got to pay up. "All right, what do you want?" Elton said. "I want that," Gary said, pointing to one of his cars. So Elton just gave him the car.'

Hall saw the total meticulousness that Elton could bring to bear, even in the staging of his characteristic little jokes. In March 1981, at a Christie's auction, he paid £14,000 for the original scripts of BBC Radio's *Goon Show*, to which he had been addicted since boyhood. Six thousand pages of script, with notes by Spike Milligan and Peter Sellers, were added to the dustless treasure house at Old Windsor. The Rocket spokeswoman who gave out Elton's press statement was instructed to speak in the accent of his favourite *Goon Show* character, Bluebottle: 'I have boughted dem because I loved dem.'

'The thing you had to recognise about Elton was that he was totally unpredictable,' John Hall says. 'I've had private planes waiting at Heathrow to take him to international conferences, with PolyGram executives waiting. At the last minute, there's a phone call: it's Bob Halley. "He's not coming. He doesn't feel well."

'A lot of the time, it was sheer stress – not just what other people put on him but also what he put on himself. He'd be on one of his awful diets, not eating anything at all. Or not drinking anything except water. Or he'd be in a depression because he thought he'd overeaten, or about his hair. Nobody really knew what he went through with those transplants. I've seen his head raw and bleeding.

'But the one area where you could totally rely on him was live performance. I've seen him blow out network TV shows – just turn round and say, "I'm not going to do it." But in all those hundreds of live gigs all over the world, he's never, if he could help it, let anyone down. Ever.'

*

Dick and Stephen James had long been braced to the idea that John Reid might sooner or later bring some kind of legal action against them. Virtually from the day Elton left DJM in 1975, Reid had been on their tail, questioning the terms of agreements they had allowed him to study at leisure as their employee. Stephen James had many times regretted what he considered his father's early indulgence of Reid, and his own failure to throw the importunate Scot neck and crop into the street.

The primary claim from Reid repeated that painful syndrome that Dick James had already experienced as publisher of John Lennon and Paul McCartney. Under the agreement Elton and Bernie Taupin had signed in 1967, all their songs up to 1973 remained the copyright of Dick James Music. Reid's assertion was that, however much 'standard practice', it had been unfair to allow two inexperienced teenagers thus to sign away their work. Likewise, the recording agreements Elton had signed with DJM, in 1968 and 1970, had not given him a nearly big enough share of the £200 million his records had earned worldwide. He, not DJM, should own the master recordings of all those gold-mine albums and singles. In addition, he should be paid the difference between his past record income and what he would have received under a 'fair' contract.

The second prong of Reid's attack centred on changes DJM had made to the network of foreign sub-publishers through whom overseas royalties were collected. According to DJM, the changes had been purely for administrative convenience. Reid, however, remained convinced that these new DJM foreign satellites were deducting a greater, and unjustified, proportion of Elton and Bernie's overseas publishing income.

The Jameses, on their side, pointed to the large capital sum they had sunk into launching Elton, an investment which, for three years, seemed unlikely to be recouped. In their view, they had been generous over his contractual obligations. At the end of the recording agreement he had, by their reckoning, still owed them a further studio album, but had nevertheless brought out *Blue Moves* on Rocket. 'We could have sued him to get *Blue Moves*, which turned out to be a big hit,' Stephen James says. 'But my father didn't want to get into a legal fight with Elton. All we finally got to settle the contract was two tracks licensed to us by Rocket for our second *Elton John's Greatest Hits* album.'

Dick James, by this time, was one of the most distinguished figures in the British entertainment industry. He had been chairman of the Music Publishers Association, and vice chairman of the Performing Right Society. His company had three times earned the Queen's

Award for industry for its export record, and James himself had received an Ivor Novello Award for services to entertainment. A mild heart attack in 1973 had forced him to stop smoking but otherwise he had scarcely slackened pace, still actively running the publishing side of DJM while Stephen ran the recording.

In manner and appearance, he remained as amiable and cuddly as ever. In 1980, he gave two long interviews to the present writer about his years with the Beatles and the acrimonious end of that publishing arrangement. 'But then we found Elton John,' he said, still evidently regarding it as a second instalment of stupendous luck. Ever ready to oblige a Fifties nostalgic, he even warbled a few lines of his own most unforgettable hit as a professional singer:

> Feared by the bad,
> Loved by the good,
> Robin Hood!
> Robin Hood!
> Robin Hood!

Reid's discharge of arrows at Dick James was sporadic – ceasing, for instance, when he needed DJM's co-operation at the time of Elton's tax difficulties in America. By 1980, the question of the song copyrights had receded against that of the alleged shortfall in Elton's royalties via DJM's reconstructed overseas subsidiaries. However, lengthy auditing of DJM's books by Rocket's accountants, Shears and Co., had found no discrepancy anywhere near the scale Reid had hoped for. For the years 1976–9, the figure Shears finally came up with was £12,178 pounds – mere small change, not worth a single day's court costs.

The galvanising factor was Reid's 1980 change of accountants to Arthur Andersen. A partner at Andersen's, Julian Lee, reactivated the question of the song copyrights in John Reid's mind. The opinion of a QC, Gerald Butler, was sought, both on that matter and the question of Elton's overseas royalties. The QC's opinion was that Elton's publishing agreements with DJM were 'valid and not open to attack', and he did not advise suing for the recovery of the song copyrights. The only feasible claim was for loss of royalties, and this would depend on expert testimony as to whether DJM's new overseas sub-publishing arrangements were 'commercially reasonable'.

Julian Lee's advice to Reid was to 'push harder'. To Reid, however, the stumbling-block was Elton, who remained very fond of Dick James and would only sue if the sums were large enough, and he became 'sufficiently aggrieved'. Arthur Andersen then began a fresh audit of the DJM group's books.

In 1981, Dick James's heart trouble recurred, and he underwent quadruple bypass surgery to forestall what might have proved a serious heart attack. His doctor's orders were that from now on he should take things much more easily. He therefore stepped down as managing director of DJM, handing the whole company over to Stephen while remaining its chairman. His plan henceforward was to come into the office only for an hour or so each day and to enjoy retirement with his wife at their penthouse in St John's Wood and their luxurious flat in Cannes.

Wounding as the various skirmishes with John Reid had been, they did not seriously undermine James's equanimity, nor unsettle his conviction that all his dealings with and on behalf of Elton had been utterly straight and above board. It was just the 'John and Paul Syndrome' all over again; an artist once grateful and thankful, now carpingly discontent. However microscopically the original agreements with Elton might be examined, there was one thing of which Dick James was righteously and securely certain. They had followed faithfully the standard practice throughout the industry.

In 1982, however, standard practice throughout the industry was turned totally on its head. The singer Gilbert O'Sullivan began legal action against his former manager and publisher Gordon Mills, on grounds precisely the same as John Reid's dispute with Dick James Music. O'Sullivan had joined Mills's company, MAM, on terms remarkably like Elton's at DJM, receiving a £10 per-week retainer as a combination in-house songwriter and odd-job boy. His string of huge Seventies hits, like 'Nothing Rhymed', 'Clair' and 'Alone Again (Naturally)', had grossed £14.5 million pounds for MAM, of which O'Sullivan claimed to have received barely half a million.

The O'Sullivan case was heard in the High Court during May 1982. It resulted in total victory for the singer-songwriter against the manager and publisher who claimed to have invented him. The judge, Mr Justice Mars-Jones, ruled that the agreements between Gordon Mills and O'Sullivan took unfair advantage of O'Sullivan's youth and innocence, and therefore could be said to constitute a 'restraint of trade'. Mills was ordered to relinquish all Gilbert O'Sullivan copyrights, deliver up all master recordings of his songs and pay him massive back royalties, with interest.

When Dick James read the verdict in the Gilbert O'Sullivan case, he knew it could not be long before an exactly similar lawsuit was launched against him by John Reid. In an effort to head it off, he phoned Reid and asked him to lunch, intending to make a conciliatory proposal. 'We agreed we'd offer to sell back the masters of Elton's records to him,' Stephen James says. 'If that went well, we'd also discuss selling back the song copyrights. John agreed to meet us for lunch, but at the last minute he rang up and cancelled.'

Three weeks later, DJM received formal notice of court action from Reid's solicitors. The full claim, when it arrived, corresponded almost word for word with Gilbert O'Sullivan's against Gordon Mills.

If Lord Choc Ice was in another temporary trough, the chairman of Watford Football Club was starting the biggest roll of his career. Under Graham Taylor's management, the 1981–2 season had been Watford's best yet, with bigger and bigger crowds cheering the emergence of gifted young players like John Barnes, Kenny Jackett and Nigel Callaghan. The rising tide of success reached its first climax when the club's youth team won the FA Youth Cup. Then, on 4 May, 1982, in front of 20,000 home fans, Watford beat Swansea City 2–0, so winning promotion to Division One for the first time in its ninety-year history.

The extent of Elton's support was revealed in the 1982 accounts, which showed he had so far provided a total of £1.2 million in interest-free loans. Currently he was suffering less frustration from dud singles than from Watford's local planning authority, which had mysteriously opposed the building of a new grandstand to accommodate the greatly increased numbers at Vicarage Road. He was also spearheading a somewhat implausible plan to turn Watford, the town, into a tourist attraction. The club had affiliated itself with a hotel chain, which now offered weekend package tours, including a VIP seat at a Watford home game, for less than £20 per head.

The euphoria of Watford's Division One debut, that autumn, might have been expected to flavour Elton's first British concert tour for five years. He was determined to do it, despite a year as slow on record as Watford's young strikers had been quick to the opposing goalmouth. His 1982 album, *Jump Up!*, had been a disappointment, reaching number thirteen in Britain and seventeen in America. Recorded at George Martin's AIR studios in Montserrat, it was a further uneasy mix of words by Bernie Taupin and Gary Osborne, with a stray track oddly provided by the *Evita* lyricist Tim Rice. Its only successful single was 'Blue Eyes', a Gary Osborne love song at near-standstill tempo, which made number eight in Britain and twelve in America. When Elton sang 'Baby's got blue eyes', then and ever afterwards, it seemed like nothing so much as a longing for fatherhood.

Most disappointing was what befell 'Empty Garden', an elegy for John Lennon which Bernie Taupin had written in a haze of grief the day after his great friend's death. At a time when cheap and tawdry 'tributes' to Lennon were still coining fortunes, this right and tasteful one – as angrily sad as 'Candle in the Wind' – reached only thirteen in America and fifty-one in Britain. Another hopefully topical track, 'Princess', issued in Britain only as a single, did not even get into the Top 50.

The pre-tour photograph showed Elton in a uniform of mitre-shaped cap, gold-epauletted hussar tunic, sash, frogged breeches and tasselled topboots, looking rather like one of the Argentinian generalissimos who had launched the Falklands invasion. THE GAY HUSSAR! chortled a *Daily Mirror* picture spread, whose caption of barely a hundred words managed to make two further nudge-nudge references to homosexuality.

It was to be an Elton tour in traditional style, winding up at his old London Yuletide home, the Hammersmith Odeon. The act was fundamentally the same as had packed them in by the million through the Seventies. New songs first, then album evergreens and, finally, the ceremonial kicking away of the piano stool for his time-honoured stand-up rock-'n'-roll finale.

Again his stage band mixed new blood with old stalwarts Davey Johnstone, Dee Murray and Nigel Olsson. Unluckily, British winter took its toll and just before the Hammersmith first night, Olsson succumbed to influenza. Elton was not told of his absence until minutes before going onstage. As a result, the gold-laced general faced his cheering fans in the very worst possible mood.

His ill-humour mounted throughout the show, reaching a crescendo when he kicked away his piano stool for the rock-'n'-roll climax. As a rule, Hammersmith Odeon had a conventional parapet stage, with a deep pit below, into which objects hurled from the stage could tumble harmlessly. For this week, however, unknown to Elton, a fabric slope had been built from the stage edge almost to the front row of the audience. The piano stool – whacked away with extra, peevish force – skidded over this ramp and hit a spectator on the shoulder.

The piano stool's victim, twenty-four-year-old Seana Connolly, suffered bruising on her cheek and the top of her right arm. 'She was one of those real die-hard Elton fans,' John Hall remembers. 'She'd got every album and loved him since she was ten. So I said, "Look, we're very sorry, it was an accident, please come back and meet Elton after the show." I took her to the dressing room, and Elton apologised to her, and gave her a bottle of champagne and a leather jacket. "To show you how really sorry I am," he said, "I'd like to buy you a dress as well."

'So the next day, someone from the office took this girl out, and she bought the world's most expensive dress. That night, we were having a big end-of-tour party at Xenon, and I'd also invited her along to that. We sent the limo for her and, of course, she turned up in the dress Elton had bought her. And it's one of those with a cutaway at the top of the arm, to highlight the bruise she got from the piano stool. After all the trouble we'd gone to to keep the thing quiet, there she is parading round Xenon, showing her bruise off to everyone.'

Those two Hammersmith concerts brought a flurry of tabloid headlines which made rock's good boy sound more like some latter-day Johnny Rotten. Some reports claimed that, after the flying piano stool incident, he had snapped at Seana Connolly, 'If you're so bloody hurt, call an RSPCA man.' *The Sun* alleged that a group of stage-door fans had seen him afterwards, still in his banana republic generalissimo's outfit, banging his head 'at least six times' on the bonnet of his Rolls-Royce. 'It was like watching a child throwing a temper tantrum because he can't get his own way,' one of the purported witnesses said. 'He yelled at someone, "Right, you're fired! I don't want to see you again!" [and] was then whisked away in another car.'

Nor had his mood much mellowed twenty-four hours later, when he arrived at the lavish end-of-tour party at Xenon. According to the ever-watchful *Daily Mail*, he did not show up until 1 am, and then 'brushed aside the good wishes of friends like David Essex, Pamela Stephenson, Billy Connolly and Lulu . . . Elton refused to mix with guests, and sat in a corner, surrounded by aides. After fifteen minutes, he left, saying, "I've had enough of this."'

16

'Good on yer, poofter'

THE 'party-destroyer', who could wipe out festivity with almost ectoplasmic emanations of black rage, might just as bafflingly switch back to being the life and soul of the party.

In April 1983, he accepted an invitation to what should have been only effortless, unadulterated luxury. It came from Cartier, the French jewellery house of whose products he was among the world's foremost bulk buyers. Cartier were launching a new range of 22-carat gold sunglasses and, to celebrate, flew a party of VIPs from all over Europe to a party at the luxury Tunisian resort of Monastir. Elton and John Reid were asked to join the British contingent, along with the Queen's cousin Lady Elizabeth Shakerley, the Countess of Lichfield, actor Christopher Cazenove, singers Hazel O'Connor and Lynsey de Paul, and assorted Fleet Street gossip columnists.

Unfortunately, none of the gold watches at Cartier had registered the fact that April is typhoon season in Monastir. Arriving after an uncomfortable four-hour flight, the VIPs found gale-force winds and driving rain. The beach marquee in which the glamorous sunglasses were to be launched had already partly collapsed and blown into the sea. At the resort's luxury Hannibal Palace Hotel, as much chaos reigned as if its namesake's war elephants had lately passed through. Some of the celebrities found that no rooms had been booked for them, and had to be decanted into a neighbouring, inferior establishment. Cries of agony from practised 'liggers' arose on discovering that room service and phone calls were not included in Cartier's hospitality. A grand gala 'welcome' dinner, cooked to be served at 9-30 pm, did not start reaching the tables until almost midnight.

Among those present was the *Daily Express*'s William Hickey diarist, Christopher Wilson. 'By about 1 am, when this pretty awful dinner had been served, everyone was pretty pissed off,' Wilson remembers. 'The only chance of rescuing the whole ghastly occasion was that Elton John might play something. No one was quite sure if he would, because he looked just as pissed off as everyone else. But in the end, he did go up to the piano and start to play.

'I've never seen anyone turn a room full of people around so totally. In about twenty minutes, he had everyone clapping, singing, standing on tables. It was an incredible performance, that seemed to come from absolutely nowhere. And once he got going, there was no stopping him. As a finale, he led all these quite starchy jet-set types, in their evening dress and jewellery, in a Pied Piper line out of the hotel and down to the beach, where the remains of this marquee were still standing. He grabbed Hazel O'Connor and danced with her among the ruins, then he dropped his trousers and wagged his bare arse. Which, everyone felt, summed the whole thing up perfectly.'

Any royal gala by now put Elton John automatically at the top of the A-list. Early in 1983, the Queen visited America, welcomed thither by President and Mrs Reagan with all the taste and restraint of their Hollywood B-movie background. The climax was a dinner in Tinseltown itself, organised and hosted by the First Lady and attended by movie greats such as James Stewart, Bette Davis, Fred Astaire and Gene Kelly. Elton was chosen to sit at Nancy Reagan's own top table, along with the Queen, Prince Philip and a miscellany of British stars like Michael Caine, Julie Andrews and Jane Seymour.

It was an occasion with all the hallmarks of Reagan taste, taking place on a movie sound-stage normally used for filming TV series like *M.A.S.H.* The cabaret – introduced by Johnny Carson's straight man – featured Dionne Warwick, and a duet between Frank Sinatra and Perry Como. The evening's longueurs made Elton once again forget politeness and protocol. To *The Sun*'s Los Angeles correspondent he said the royal dinner had been 'so boring, I almost fell asleep'. He thought it 'a shame' that, fenced around by Britishers like himself, the Queen had had no chance to meet the real stars of Hollywood. About the cabaret he was equally scornful, saying that Sinatra and Como had been under-rehearsed and Dionne Warwick, too, was 'boring'. ELTON RAPS QUEEN'S HOLLYWOOD PARTY, *The Sun* said with a wink to its four million initiates.

Most of 1983 was spent jetting around the world in search of the perfect party, or in retreat from it. Two months after baring his bottom at the Tunisian hurricane, he was standing on the Great Wall of China. Though China would soon succumb to rock music, as Russia had done, Elton was not this time to be the catalyst. He was there only as chairman of Watford, watching the club play two exhibition matches in Beijing and a third in Shanghai.

In China, Elton John the rock star was still virtually unknown. He could walk around as he pleased, conspicuous to Chinese eyes only as a foreigner. 'This is one of the few places in the world I can go without being recognised,' he said. 'It's a terrific feeling not to have people staring at you. I haven't known it for thirteen years.'

He visited tourist spots, as incognito as a man could be dressed in an Edwardian boater, a wing-poke collar and three-piece checked suit, and surrounded by footballers and photographers. At the tomb of Mao Tse Tung he respectfully removed his hat, giving the assembled press a collective world scoop. 'Elton John doffed his hat in memory of Chairman Mao . . . and revealed a costly failure,' the *Daily Mail* reported. 'Six hair transplants, for which he paid £1,800, have left him with only some fine wisps to cover his baldness.' There was a picture of an undeniably bald-looking Elton, boater pressed to chest, with Chairman Mao, above, seeming to look tactfully in the other direction.

Watford won all three of their friendly matches against Chinese teams, the third against the national side in Bejing's Workers' Stadium, watched by a crowd of 70,000 plus an estimated 400 million on television. Afterwards, there was a banquet in the club's honour on the Great Wall of the People. Elton confessed to being 'covered with goosepimples the whole time'.

Standing on the Great Wall, surrounded by 2,000 years of history, he sucked an ice lolly and gave thanks to Watford yet again for helping him not to be a rock ego monster. 'I was carried away with my own importance,' he told his circle of busily scribbling scribes. 'I've used my status wrongly in the past. But this club has done so much for me, because nobody there will put up with all that. In my business, it was luxury jets, the best hotels and shows in front of 20,000 people. Then I'd walk into Watford, and the washing-up lady would toddle across and say, 'I don't like your new record.' I needed that. They may have sniggered behind my back, but they've tolerated me until I've had time to mature.'

Especial thanks went to the club's manager Graham Taylor for keeping him on the rails with a bluntness none of his rock entourage would have dared. 'Three years ago, I was very unhappy, and drinking a lot of brandy. The team were playing Luton on Boxing Day, and I turned up in a coat that had cost £300 but looked like a dressing gown. The next morning, Graham called me round to his house. He put a bottle of brandy on the table and said, "Here you are. Are you going to drink that? What the hell's wrong with you?" He brought me to my senses.'

There was an impromptu concert at the team's hotel, and a visit to an antiques export store, where Elton spent £50,000 on Chinese artefacts including a set of stone lions weighing six tons each. The

Watford players received their first sight of his Safeway trolley shopping method. 'He just went in and said, "I'll have that, that and that",' one of them reported incredulously.

His frequent, well-publicised absences from home brought an inevitable consequence. Despite its electronic gates, roaming guard dogs and labyrinthine defences, Woodside was burgled in March 1983. The thief or thieves got into Elton's private suite, making off with a diamond and sapphire ring worth £50,000, a £6,000 Cartier watch and £100 in cash. Since none of the house's internal alarms had been triggered, and there was no sign of forced entry, the police suspected an inside job. 'But that just cannot be,' a spokesman for Elton said. 'All the people around at the time were trusted colleagues and friends.' In a separate but equally unsettling incident, one of the guard dogs went missing and was later found dead in a stream at Egham, a few miles away.

Two months after returning from China, he was off again, flying to South Africa to make a guest appearance with Rod Stewart at the Sun City leisure complex in Bophuthatswana. Though later to join the anti-apartheid boycott in Sun City, Elton at this time thought its Superbowl stadium was 'wonderful', and made tentative plans for a £700,000 concert season there the following October.

His stage appearance with Rod Stewart reactivated the carping, camping friendship that had existed since the early Seventies. Plans were announced for them to make a world tour together, and also co-star in a film as modern counterparts of Bing Crosby and Bob Hope in the old 'Road' pictures. The tour's opening was set for Sydney, Australia, early in 1984. But that autumn, appearing on Channel 4's American football programme, Elton suddenly announced that it was all off. Nor was any more heard of the film, with its putative female star Liza Minnelli.

In September, he flew to West Germany to see Watford play their first-ever UEFA Cup match. Despite losing to FC Kaisersläutern, they were 'not bad', the *Sunday Telegraph* said, 'for a club who six years ago were restricted to lunge and bash matches in the Fourth Division against teams like Rochdale'. Their famous young striker John Barnes had been picked for Bobby Robson's England squad, and the million-pound sale of Luther Blisset to AC Milan had bought another potential star, eighteen-year-old Walsall defender Lee Sinnott. Elton watched every moment of practice and match, and signed autographs tirelessly.

On 17 November, he was due to fly to Los Angeles to give a benefit performance for the American Cancer Society at the Beverly Hilton. His Steinway grand was already set up onstage when word came that he'd gone down with glandular fever, and was too ill to leave Old Windsor.

George Martin's AIR Studios were the means by which history's most successful record producer finally made some personal profit. As a label head for EMI, Martin masterminded the Beatles' multibillion-pound recording career for a salary that, at its highest, only just cleared £3,000 per year. Though far from mercenary, he frequently had cause to chafe against EMI's institutional meanness. At the end of 1963, a year in which Beatles hits had stuffed the British charts, George Martin received a memo telling him he did not qualify for the staff's Christmas bonus.

The result was AIR – Associated Independent Recording – founded by Martin and three partners in 1965, happily anticipating a new era of independent record production companies. A few years later, seeking further capital, Martin considered selling out to Dick James, but withdrew when James's offer proved less than favourable. So small is the British record world, and so abiding the fall-out from the Beatles.

By the early Eighties, AIR was the brand-leader among British independent production companies. To its studios in London, it had added a second complex on the West Indies island of Montserrat, where artists could work with total concentration in congenial surroundings. AIR-Montserrat became the in-place to record for everyone from Paul McCartney and Eric Clapton to Phil Collins and the Police.

Elton had first gone there in 1982, to record his rather static and unenergised *Jump Up!* album. He returned the following summer to make *Too Low for Zero*, a production equally nothing like its implied nadir of despair. Dismissing Gary Osborne and all his other part-time and would-be collaborators, he went into the studio with a full set of Bernie Taupin lyrics for the first time since *Blue Moves* in 1976. 'I told Elton, "We've got to collaborate totally, or it's never going to be any good",' Bernie says now. 'To me, our songs had always worked in total, with a feeling of continuity between them. I didn't want to keep on doing odd or obscure tracks on albums of other people's work. We had to try to get back to that complete closeness and understanding we had when we started out.'

Bernie himself was back on form, steadied by his new marriage, and writing with a simplicity and subtlety that made all former competitors redundant. *Too Low for Zero* contained two classic Elton tracks that carried him triumphantly back to the singles charts in both Britain and America. 'I Guess That's Why They Call It the

Blues' was a love letter from Bernie to his new wife, Toni, borrowed by Elton's voice with the usual purging of all lascivious intent. When he sang of 'rolling like thunder under the covers', he could as well have meant a game of sardines after lights out in a school dormitory. 'I'm Still Standing' was Brown Dirt Cowboy's overt tribute to a surrogate brother who, like himself, seemed to have weathered the Seventies intact, and to be bound now for sunny and mellow uplands. A third single from the album did much less well, but deserves mention for its eerily prophetic title: 'Kiss The Bride'.

On returning from Montserrat, Elton had to go into AIR's London studios to finish off some vocal overdubs. Working as tape-operator on these final sessions was a girl named Renate Blauel.

Tape op or second engineer in a recording studio is a subordinate job, generally combined with fetching coffee and phoning for taxis. This tape op was slightly unusual, in being female and German, in her late twenties, with dark curly hair and the kind of dimply, pointed face usually associated with frilly-sleeved serving wenches in Bavarian bierkellers.

Even so, the people around Elton had little cause to notice Renate at the beginning. 'She was very nice,' John Hall remembers. 'Quiet. Unassuming. Usually wearing jeans and a sweater or T-shirt. To my mind, she always looked a bit masculine. But none of us took any real trouble to talk to her or get to know her. She was just a nice girl, who was a very unimportant part of what was going on. Then we noticed that whenever Elton came in, he'd say something to her. She'd laugh. They've suddenly got this little relationship going. And when the album comes out, there's a dedication: "Special thanks to Renate Blauel".

'It was a time when Elton was coming back with Top 30 singles, and being asked to do *Top of the Pops* again. The rule there was still that you had to pre-record a special version of your backing instrumental and vocal tracks. Elton would say, "No, fuck it! I'm not going to do it." I'd say, "You've got to do it, or you can't be on *Top of the Pops*." He'd say, "All right, I'll do the backing tracks at AIR – and can you get that Renate girl there as well? I'm not going to do it unless she's there."

'Then it comes time for the next album, *Breaking Hearts*, which he's going to do in Montserrat again. We've booked the studio, the band, everything's lined up. Then Elton suddenly says, "I'm not going." Total consternation! "I'm not going," he says, "unless Renate goes out there, too." So the whole million-dollar production comes to a standstill unless we can get this tape op to Montserrat for him.'

The *Breaking Hearts* sessions flowed into Christmas 1983. Elton's journalist friend Nina Myskow – now TV critic of the *Sunday People* – also happened to be staying on the island. 'I'd no idea Elton would be there,' she remembers. 'Not till I arrived at Antigua airport and met John Reid also on his way out. He was in the duty-free shop, serving behind the counter.'

No sign of a romance was yet visible, even to Nina Myskow's practised eye. 'Renate was just one of the boys, in her usual jeans and T-shirt. Elton didn't seem to be taking any special notice of her. One night, I remember, she wore a dress – the first time I'd ever seen her in one. The change was extraordinary. She looked really sweet and terribly pretty.'

After seeing in the New Year on Montserrat, Elton was due to fly to Sydney to begin a tour of Australia and New Zealand. Again, the mystifying ultimatum was given. Renate Blauel had to be taken along.

Three weeks later, the tour party were at the Sebel Town House hotel, Elton's usual Sydney hideaway. His bass player Dee Murray and some others were having a late-night drink in the bar. Elton and Renate had gone out to dinner by themselves.

'I looked up and there they were in the doorway, holding hands,' Dee remembers. 'Elton said, "Guess what, man. I'm engaged."'

Why he did it should have been no mystery to anyone who had ever seen him with Bryan Forbes's little girls, or presenting Easter eggs to Watford junior members, or talking to John Hall's kids in Central Park, or with Sean Lennon, or a small Chinese boy who presented him with a painting near the Great Wall. Every friend and employee to whose children he was a doting godfather or uncle knew how desperately he wanted a family of his own.

The analogy of poor serving girl swept off her feet by millionaire Prince Charming was not wholly apt. Renate came from a respectable, even well-to-do West German background. Her father was a Munich publisher, Joachim Blauel. She had emigrated to London at twenty-two, partly as an act of rebellion against her parents, and drifted into the music business after various jobs including a spell with Lufthansa, the German airline. That dimpled, rather impersonal face might well be imagined above a trim Lufthansa blue jacket, scanning the aisle before take-off to ensure no tray tables were down and all seats were in the fully upright position.

In the male-dominated world of recordings studios, she had done remarkably well. Even today, only one in a hundred second engineers is likely to be a woman. Her superiors at AIR thought highly of her. 'She was more than good, she was very good,' remembers Bill Price, the engineer she assisted on *Too Low For Zero*. 'She was totally capable and reliable, and she had that peculiar Teutonic thoroughness.'

Outside work, her life was so low-profile as to be almost invisible. She lived alone in a £34-per-week flat in a Victorian house in Kilburn, north London. She had no boyfriend that her AIR colleagues ever saw. Her invariable dress of jeans and T-shirt suggested rather limited interest in men. She unbent to her fellow engineers only in revealing she could play piano a little, and had ambitions one day to produce records in her own right.

In one sense, she was the perfect person for Elton to woo. Much as he craved affection, he had always recoiled and withdrawn from anyone who came too precipitately close. The gulf in status between Renate and him gave him absolute control over the relationship. He could advance by whatever cautiously infinitesimal steps he chose.

It was further significant that they should have met in a recording studio, the one place in the world, other than onstage, where Elton felt completely at home. Almost their entire courtship was conducted over a control desk, in their common element of dead air, teacups, echo chambers, red lights and reverbs. He would make a joke. She would press a switch and smile. And suddenly the weather-vane swung from its wavery south-west back to strong due north.

One night in Montserrat they disappeared to have dinner together at an open-air restaurant called the Chicken Shack, where fried chicken was served in paper, like English fish and chips. Renate afterwards said that this was the first occasion on which Elton proposed to her.

The affair proceeded with as much propriety as if they were teenage virgins. In Sydney, even after their engagement, they continued to occupy separate rooms. Elton was constantly attentive and chivalrous. He would make jokes. She would smile. He seemed as delighted and excited as a person could be.

'Rock on! Here comes the bridegroom,' said the *Daily Mail*, in one of the kinder British press comments on the affair. 'The pop world was rocked last night by news that millionaire superstar Elton John is to marry next week . . . Last night, the 36-year-old singer and composer who has admitted to being bisexual, and once said he wanted to marry "but I don't care if it's a boy or a girl", was said to be over the moon with joy.'

His family and closest associates had already heard the news from Elton on the phone from Sydney. Clive Franks, his recording engineer, Graham Taylor, his football-club manager, Kiki Dee, his long-time token girlfriend, each listened to the bashful voice across the world in utter astonishment. The least surprised was Bernie Taupin, who had of course witnessed an almost exactly similar frantic courtship of Linda Woodrow, fifteen years earlier. 'It was unexpected, but it wasn't in the least out of character,' Bernie says now. 'I always knew that if Elton suddenly got a bee in his bonnet about wanting a family, it was likely to happen pretty suddenly.'

The great fascination within Elton's circle was how John Reid would react. Especially fascinated were those who remembered Elton's discomfiture, a few years earlier, when Reid had announced his own deeply unsuitable engagement to Bryan Forbes's daughter Sarah. 'John's attitude over the whole thing was quite weird,' an ex-Rocket employee says. 'He obviously didn't think much of Renate, and he was likely to be against anyone who threatened his power over Elton. But he seemed to regard the whole thing as terribly funny.'

The death of Soviet premier Yuri Andropov was relegated to out-of-the-way pages as Britain's tabloids fought for exclusive insights into the woman who had brought about this amazing transformation. *The Sun*'s first picture of 'vivacious brunette Renate Blauel', unfortunately, showed a girl who was not Renate laughing by Elton's side. Sunday's *News of the World* printed two pictures of the correct 'leggy brunette Renate Blauel', plus a good proportion of the few remarks she was ever destined to make on the record. She admitted she had 'heard all kinds of stories about Elton, that he's supposed to be bisexual. But that doesn't worry me at all . . . He's wonderful, the nicest guy I've ever met. He makes me laugh and he's very considerate. I'm feeling just fabulous. This is the greatest day of my life.'

The *Mail on Sunday* tracked down the Indian restaurant where Elton had proposed, and quizzed its assistant manager, Mr Debu Benerjee, for his observations of the climactic moment. 'It was very romantic,' Mr Benerjee recalled. 'I could see they were in love. We put them at a corner table and had some nice sitar music wafting softly over them. Perhaps that is what did it.

'They ordered tandoori chicken, beef curry, kebab and pilau rice and poppadums. They seemed totally preoccupied with each other. Mr Elton John didn't even notice another diner who came up to the table to ask for his autograph. The lady with him was very beautiful, and dressed in a beige-coloured dress. I couldn't hear the conversation, but it was obvious they were discussing something very serious. He kept reaching over and touching her hand. Then, when the meal was over, they sat back and smiled at each other a lot over coffee.'

Back in London, equally frantic newshounds were turning over the details of Renate's career as an AIR Studios tape operator and her modest, solitary home life in Kilburn. The *News of the World* quoted an unnamed female friend whom Renate had rung from Australia with the news. 'I thought it was a joke, and I said to her, "Put Elton on the line." I asked him if it was true, and he said, "Yes" . . . [She's] obviously very keen to marry Elton. She told me, "I really do love him very much."' Before announcing the engagement, Elton had phoned Renate's father, Joachim, in Munich, and had asked for her hand 'in a nice old-fashioned way'.

At her new home near Brighton, Sheila Farebrother appeared as enthusiastic as a mother could be who had never laid eyes on her prospective daughter-in-law. From what Elton had told her, Sheila felt 'instinctively' that Renate was the right choice. 'She's thirty, not some slip of a girl, which was what I first feared. She seems the kind of girl who'll keep Elton in his place.' His eighty-four-year-old grandmother, Ivy Harris, added, 'I'm thrilled. I had to take a tablet to calm myself down.' But there had been no call to his father, Stanley Dwight, now retired and living in Ruthin, north Wales. 'I don't hear from him any more,' Stanley told the *News of the World* bleakly. 'We live in two different worlds.'

The first anti-gay catcall came from the *Daily Express*, whose William Hickey diary on 13 February was headed 'Elton John and the boys he leaves behind':

As close friends around the globe reel from the shock of self-confessed bisexual Elton John's wedding announcement, what about the lads? Probably none is more startled than his personal assistant and live-in companion of more than eight years, Bob Halley.

. . . Halley, who started life with Elton as his chauffeur, has faithfully followed him almost everywhere, to the collapse of his own marriage in the 1970s, when he split from his wife, Pearl.

He and his boss even wear His and His earrings, one each of a pair of diamond solitaires. And he was in Montserrat when Elton met Renate at Christmas while recording there.

Elton, Halley and a blond Australian friend called Gary lived a few miles from the recording studio in a villa, to which the pop star retired early from a New Year's Eve party.

. . . Halley, in his early thirties, is also in Sydney, at the Sebel Town House hotel, where John and Renate have adjoining suites. The poor chap was apparently still mute with shock yesterday, refusing all telephone calls to his own room.

The *People* even succeeded in tracking down the only previous Elton John fiancée, Linda Woodrow. Twice married since, with four children, Linda now lived with an American serviceman in the village of Hilton, near Cambridge. She had not seen or heard from Elton since he and Bernie had fled from their Islington flat in 1969. She was aware of Elton's many satirical references to her in interviews – as well as in 'Someone Saved My Life Tonight' – and, after hearing for the umpteenth time that she was to blame for putting him off heterosexuality, had resolved to sue for libel. 'I went to a solicitor in Huntingdon, who said he'd take the case. I paid this guy £1,500, but then nothing ever came of it.'

ELTON JILTED ME, screamed the *People*'s front page, above a picture of Linda in her Cambridgeshire garden: 'He was lousy lover says star's old flame.' There followed a reprise of their nine-month romance and its sudden end, thickly planted with signposts to Elton's bisexuality. Linda recalled that, although 'not openly gay', he had 'worn a lot of jewellery and perfume' and had been a 'Mother's boy', constantly phoning home. 'I'm not a bitter woman,' she was quoted as saying. 'I really hope he makes a success of marriage . . . If Renate is expecting romance, though, she's picked the wrong guy. He was lousy in bed.'

The marriage was to be on 14 February, St Valentine's Day. The couple wanted a traditional white wedding, and had chosen St Mark's, an Anglican church in the aptly named Sydney suburb of Darling Point. Normally, under New South Wales law, applicants for a marriage-licence were subject to a thirty-day wait. Elton was granted a special waiver after explaining that concert commitments would not allow him to get married in Australia any later this tour.

In the preceding twenty-four hours, Elton stayed in his hotel suite while Renate shopped for clothes, displaying what would be a consummate skill in avoiding paparazzi. Unloosed on Sydney's expensive boutiques with a blank cheque from her husband-to-be, a second latent skill began to reveal itself. 'The jeans and T-shirts we'd always seen Renate in suddenly just went,' Dee Murray remembers. 'Suddenly, each time you saw her, it was in another nifty little designer number.' Elton emerged only once, furiously pushing through a crowd of reporters, one of whom asked whether he'd bought Renate a ring yet. 'No – and I don't intend to,' he shouted over his shoulder.

A hundred wedding guests were specially flown in from Britain and America, among them Olivia Newton-John, Michael and Mary Parkinson and Barry Humphries. Renate's parents did not attend, and even Sheila and Derf Farebrother decided they would rather share the occasion via a special TV hook-up. To the *Daily Mail*, Sheila revealed that her wedding present to Elton would be a pram. 'He's sensible and likes home life, and most of all he loves children,' she said. 'And I don't think he'll waste any time making sure he gets some.'

Tradition and old-world charm held sway throughout. Just before the wedding it was suggested to Elton that, following recent superstar precedent, Renate should be asked to sign a 'pre-nuptial agreement', defining her claim on his fortune in the event of a divorce. But, despite all that he had to safeguard, Elton thought a pre-nuptial agreement would be callous and unromantic, and refused to consider it.

Two thousand people stood outside St Mark's to see him arrive, seventeen minutes early, in a white tailcoat, a striped shirt with bow tie and his trademark boater. Renate wore a high-necked gown of white silk and Swiss lace and Elton's wedding gift, a heart-shaped gold pendant set with sixty-three diamonds. Bernie Taupin and John Reid were joint best men, and Toni Taupin was one of three pink-clad female attendants. The newlyweds posed at the church door to the strains of 'Kiss the Bride', from *Too Low For Zero*, played through the open window of an adjacent house. In their most-reproduced wedding picture, bride inclines her face to kiss her marginally shorter, boatered bridegroom, somewhat like the famous Buckingham Palace balcony shot of Prince Charles and Princess Diana.

Afterwards, there was a £50,000 reception in an apricot-coloured assembly-room at the Sebel Town House. The guests ate lobster, king prawns, oysters, scallops, smoked salmon, mud crabs, trout, lamb, venison, loin of beef, stuffed quail glazed with honey, pork, turkey and lemon chicken, washed down with Roederer's Cristal champagne, 1959 Puligny Montrachet, 1976 Château Latour and schnapps. Music was provided by a seven-piece string orchestra. Below the obligatory Commonwealth member's portraits of the Queen and Prince Philip stood two giant ice-blocks spelling ER – not for Elizabeth Regina but for Elton and Renate.

The bridegroom made a warm and funny speech, admitting that, left to him alone, the wedding might never have come off. Having asked Renate to marry him at breakneck speed, he had immediately started worrying about how they could possibly find a church and clergy, and order a cake in time. 'It isn't that unpleasant – like going to the dentist,' Renate had reminded him. He could even laugh at the comment from one Australian onlooker as he and his bride had emerged from St Mark's. 'Good on you sport, you old poof! You finally made it!' this well-wisher had shouted. 'It just goes to show

how wrong you all were,' Elton had shouted back.

Next morning's British papers all carried the same post-nuptial picture of Elton and – in the *Daily Mirror*'s gracious phrase – his 'Prussian possum'. The prize, however, went to *The Sun*. Picking up the remark of the church-door barracker as repeated by Elton, altering it to make it more offensive, and leaving off quote marks – so that quote imperceptibly became editorial comment – *The Sun*'s headline to Elton's wedding was GOOD ON YER, POOFTER.

The day after it appeared, John Reid spotted the *Sun*'s Sydney correspondent, Nick Ferrari, in the lobby of the Sebel Town House. What happened next Ferrari told in a second dispatch which, for all that he had not written the offending headline, was still somewhat overweening in its tone of innocent astonishment:

ELTON'S TOUGH MINDER BEATS UP SUN MAN

I was savagely beaten up yesterday in an astonishing attack by Elton John's tough-guy manager, John Reid.

He thumped me in the face and dragged me through a crowded hotel lobby after exploding with rage over yesterday's *Sun* headline on Elton's wedding. Furious Reid claimed the headline . . . was '****ing disgraceful'.

Short, stocky Reid, who had been drinking with friends in the bar of the luxurious Sebel Town House hotel, Sydney, suddenly lurched across the lobby towards me.

CRASH! He hauled me from my seat and ripped my shirt.

BANG! He dragged me through the lobby before stunned guests.

WALLOP! Reid hit me in the face and slammed my head against a lift door before staff dragged him away.

I made no attempt to fight back. I just tried to restrain him and talk quietly.

All I said was that I had reported what Elton said in an amusing speech at his wedding reception . . .

The tabloids kept up the pursuit to New Zealand, where Elton and Renate were to honeymoon between his three sold-out concerts. 'I can definitely predict we'll be starting a family,' Elton announced on arrival at Christchurch. In Auckland, there was a different kind of disturbance outside their hotel. Anti-apartheid groups staged an angry protest over Elton's recent appearance with Rod Stewart in South Africa.

The newlyweds' return to Heathrow airport, a month later, showed how rapidly Renate was settling down to her new life. With them off the plane came thirty suitcases, half gold-monogrammed 'EHJ', the other half 'RB'. Their similar garb, of rather medical-looking overalls, gave spice to a rumour sent ahead from the antipodes. Was Renate already pregnant? 'No way,' Elton replied, also scotching a claim that his honeymoon had been marred by an attack of chickenpox.

Larger Australian purchases were shipped home separately. They included a Sydney tram to which Elton had taken a fancy and bought for $10,000, paying a further $22,000 for its journey from one side of the world to the other. Since it would not pass through Woodside's front gates, the only method of delivery seemed to be to fly it in dangling from a pair of Chinook helicopters. This plan had to be abandoned because of the nearness of Heathrow airport, and Elton's mental visions of some headline like JUMBO JET COLLIDES WITH TRAM. In the end, the main road outside was closed, and the tram heaved through a gap in the security perimeter. A ten-foot concrete runway was specially built to display it among the flowerbeds and topiary work.

Elton was as explicit as always about the kind of marriage he hoped this would be. 'We're not going to be the type of couple who go out to discos – I'm tired of them anyway – and dinner parties. We just want to spend some time together. We want to have a home life. I simply want to be a family man – and I'm not getting any younger.'

To all such *gemütlich* ideas, Renate signified agreement with her dimply smile. Even so, she made it clear she would not be content with the merely decorative role of rockbiz wife. 'Just because I'm getting married to a famous superstar, it doesn't mean I'm going to give up my job as a recording engineer,' she announced at their wedding reception. To underline the point, Elton's new album, *Breaking Hearts*, bore the credit line 'Engineered by Renate', the verb in this case seeming to imply much more than mere operation of switches and winding-back of tape.

Despite all he had said, domestic life with Elton was not something Renate was ever to experience in abundance. In early April 1984, he brought her to her new home. Less than a week later, he departed on a European tour. Renate did not accompany him.

Two further absentees were conspicuous in the band he took with him. Nigel Olsson and Dee Murray, his original drummer and bass player, dropped in the mid-1970s and reinstated in the early 1980s, now found themselves dropped again, in Dee's case without warning or explanation. 'The *Breaking Hearts* tour went well, and ended very happily. Elton presented a Cartier watch to everyone who'd been with him on the road. I went off on vacation – same as I had in '74

– expecting a call from the office when I got back about where to meet up with the band again. But – same as in '74 – the call never came.'

His diplomatic triumphs in Russia and China, understandably, had rather gone to Elton's head. He saw himself now less as rock star than roving ambassador, with a gift of communication no diplomat had ever possessed to bridge the chasms between West and East. His spring 1984 European tour included three appearances in Poland, where the Gdansk shipyard workers' Solidarity trade union still waged its pioneering struggle against Russian-prescribed totalitarian rule. On Elton's arrival, with two private aircraft, it was announced he would also be visiting Solidarity's embattled leader, Lech Walesa. They met in Walesa's Gdansk flat, to sip tea from glasses under a portrait of the Pope. Walesa – who bore an eerie likeness to the DJ Paul Gambaccini – tried on Elton's cowboy hat, accepted two cassettes of his music and, later, was guest of honour at the Gdansk concert. 'Visits from people like you are a great help to me,' Walesa told him, adding, perhaps too modestly for a Nobel Peace Prize winner, 'It shows that I have not been forgotten.'

In Munich, joined by Renate, he paid what would be his one and only visit to his new German parents-in-law. Joachim and Gisela Blauel entertained him to dinner at their bungalow in the respectable suburb of Gauting. According to Elton later, 'Everything went well, just great. They are lovely people.' *The Sun*'s most faithful tabloid imitator, the *Daily Star*, published a picture of him with Renate after the meeting. Above was a headline transforming the Blauels' quoted opinion of him into yet another anti-homosexual jeer. HE'S A NICE BOY!

There was another, larger distraction from simple conjugal bliss. From midway through Watford's second season in Division One, the possibility had been growing that, for the first time in history, the FA Cup might be within their grasp. On top of Graham Taylor's inspired management, they had received a magical 'draw', matching them against easily trounced opponents like Second Division Charlton and Brighton, and relegation-doomed Birmingham. Their luck held when, reaching the barely conceivable heights of the semi-final, they found themselves facing only Third Division Plymouth. That 1–0 victory guaranteed what, even a year before, would have been unthinkable. Watford were through to the FA Cup Final, playing the Merseyside stars Everton.

Flying back from Berlin for the big occasion, at Wembley Stadium on 19 May, Elton found himself elevated to still greater heights of ambassadorial conciliation. Football in the 1980s had been increasingly plagued by violence, both among spectators and on the field. Merseyside supporters in particular enjoyed a Europe-wide reputation akin to that of Attila's Huns. To lessen the chance of crowd mayhem at Watford's Cup Final, Elton agreed to make a special pre-match appearance, driving round the Wembley pitch before kick-off with Everton's chairman, Philip Carter, in an open-top vintage car.

That day at Wembley expunged two stains from the Dwight escutcheon. Not only his own concert flop here in 1975, but also his cousin Roy's broken leg in 1959, were more than redeemed as Elton sat with Renate in the royal box, just a few places from the Duchess of Kent, who was to present the trophy. Hatless and dressed in a comparatively sober checked suit, he still had to face what the *Sunday Times* called 'good-natured mockery' from the Everton crowd. He was clearly overcome with emotion and during the traditional singing of 'Abide With Me', was seen to brush tears from his eyes. All that spoiled the dignity and spontaneity of the occasion was an outsize plug for his latest single, an electronic scoreboard lit up with the words 'Sad Songs (Say So Much)'.

Alas, Watford's dreams were to end with the drive up the stadium's triumphal avenue. Two weeks earlier, their captain Wilf Rostron, had been sent off in a match against Luton, and so was barred from appearing at Wembley. Against a giant side like Everton, Graham Taylor's only strategy could be to score first, and carry the game on sheer audacity. Though several openings for Watford occurred, the only goal in the first half came from Everton. Next to Elton, Renate was seen to smile in delight, then grow abruptly serious again as her husband explained it was not their side who had scored. A further blow came after half-time when the referee allowed a suspect goal by Everton striker Andy Gray. Try as they might, Watford could do no better than hold the score at 2–0.

On the credit side, thanks chiefly to Elton, it was a Cup Final of unusual good humour, from which the game's general morale received a desperately needed boost. Not one single player was booked for a foul, nor one flurry of kicks and punches noticed on the terraces. Some Watford and Everton fans were even seen sharing cans of lager.

After the final whistle, Elton ran out on to the turf to commiserate with Taylor and his team, especially goalkeeper Kenny Sherwood, the victim of that second, questionable goal. Win or lose, it had been a stupendous day for the club he had almost single-handedly reinvented. Later, there was a grand welcome home parade through Watford, followed by a lavish party for 230 guests at John Reid's house. The chairman switched roles again, getting up with Kiki Dee to sing their old hit 'Don't Go Breaking My Heart'. Shortly afterwards, Graham Taylor signed a further six-year managerial contract. As Elton, at his most sportsmanlike and philosophical, kept saying, there was always another year.

However lofty and dignified a personage he became, there was no escaping a perennial note of Reggie Dwight. Back on tour, his aides were now exercised by a tricky problem. So rapid was the progress from one capital to the next, no hotel had time to wash and dry the superstar's underwear. In Prague, with a backlog of twelve days' Elton undies, the American embassy had to be begged for a loan of its spin-dryer. No such high-level help could be found in Paris, where pairs of Calvin Klein briefs were spotted hanging over the balcony of Elton's suite at the Ritz. There was evident need for Sheila to be still there, doing Reg's washing and, in her own special way, 'whitening it up a bit'.

For Dick James, the music industry's luckiest man, things could hardly have turned out more unfortunately. After his quadruple bypass heart surgery, his doctor had warned him to cut right down on work and stress. A few months later, here he was, plunged into feverish preparation to fight a lawsuit which, if successful, would deal him and his organisation a crippling financial blow.

The writ which had taken John Reid nine years to unloose was, when finally received, a formidable document, covering every aspect of Elton's former involvement with Dick James Music. It challenged the publishing agreement he and Bernie Taupin had signed in 1967, and the recording deals he had signed in 1967 and 1970. It disputed the overseas sub-publishing arrangements by which Elton and Bernie's 'mechanical' royalties were collected. It even attacked the short-lived management agreement between Elton and Dick James, claiming that as manager, obligated to get his client the best possible deal, James should never have allowed the publishing and recording agreements to stand.

The remedies sought were the same as in Gilbert O'Sullivan's trailblazingly successful action against Gordon Mills and MAM, two years earlier. Elton and Bernie should receive back copyright in the 144 songs published during their six-year contract with DJM, including their greatest hits, 'Your Song', 'Daniel', 'Candle in the Wind' and 'Goodbye Yellow Brick Road'. Elton, not DJM, should own the masters of his huge cache of Seventies hit singles and perennially in-demand albums, including *Elton John*, *Honky Château* and *Captain Fantastic*. DJM also should give up the thirty-six unpublished songs and twenty-four unreleased tracks it held in its vaults. In addition, Elton and Bernie should be paid as damages the difference between what they had received under their DJM agreements and what it was alleged they ought to have received, plus compound interest for the intervening years.

English lawsuits, unlike American ones, are not valued in advance. But estimates were that a victory on all fronts, and a judgment like that awarded Gilbert O'Sullivan, could cost DJM as much as £30 million. Small wonder that, against all medical advice, Dick James devoted every possible moment to preparing and worrying about his company's defence.

In the time-consuming and costly pre-trial months of meeting lawyers, giving statements and ferreting out papers, DJM acquired an unexpected ally. This was their former executive Geoffrey Ellis, whom John Reid had wooed away in 1976. No longer with John Reid Enterprises, Ellis felt strongly enough about Dick James's integrity to assist DJM in the case on an advisory basis. Ever correct, he stipulated he could reveal nothing he had learned during his years with Reid. Great reliance also was placed on Sidney Goldwater, the company accountant and Dick James's old and close friend, who had been instrumental in drawing up the foreign sub-publishing arrangements at the centre of the dispute.

Confident as James was that all in his organisation could bear the minutest legal scrutiny, he was far from his old, calmly ebullient self. It wounded him enormously that Elton's lawsuit named him personally, along with his companies DJM and This Record Co. 'He felt they'd always had this special relationship, almost like father and son,' Stephen James remembers. 'He couldn't understand why Elton had turned on him.' He was convinced that, if Elton and he could sit down and talk together as of old, everything could be sorted out without recourse to litigation. But Elton, as ever, was an elusive pimpernel, jetting all over the world in apparent contradiction of his desire for a home life with Renate. August 1984 found him dangling from a helicopter in the south of France for a video to accompany his new single, 'Passengers'. By autumn, he was back on another American tour, so strenuous that he collapsed onstage with a 'virus infection', this time in Charlotte, North Carolina. Next he was reported in New York, in an incident revealing how much changed was the wide-eyed fan of yore. Emerging from a Madison Avenue store, he encountered Doris Day, the freckled *chanteuse* whose films, like *Calamity Jane*, he used to soak up on Technicolor afternoons in Metroland. 'Hello,' she said. 'I'm a fan.' But Elton walked past, not even recognising her.

That winter, Dick James finally succeeded in contacting Elton and arranging to meet him privately and discuss the lawsuit. 'We arranged to see him in a hotel, one afternoon at two o'clock,' Stephen James says. 'We got there at 1-30 and had a sandwich in the coffee shop. At about 1-45, we were paged and told there was a phone call for us. It was John Reid. He said he and his solicitor had talked Elton out of coming to see us.

'I still bitterly resent the fact that my father was never allowed to talk to Elton personally before going into court. I'm convinced that if they'd sat down on their own, they could have sorted it all out. Because we were willing to sell him back the master recordings, and discuss selling back the song copyrights. And I don't think Elton wanted to go through with it, and what it did to my father.'

After several delays, the case opened in the Chancery Division of the High Court, before Mr Justice Nicholls, on 4 June, 1985. Elton, Bernie and Elton's two companies, William A. Bong Ltd and Happenstance Ltd, were represented by Mark Littman QC, and three junior counsel. Dick James and his organisation were represented by George Newman QC, and two juniors. DJM contested the suit on all counts, and Dick James denied personal responsibility for the disputed contracts. Into court with both sides came a huge volume of paperwork, drawn from forty separate files. The plaintiffs' statement of claim alone ran to 100 pages, and the bundle of pleadings to more than 400. The giving of oral evidence took thirty days and the full hearing something like fifty. For much of that time, Elton's straw boater lay on a table in court, giving the dry, dusty, pedantic proceedings its rakish Edwardian signature.

Mark Littman's opening address quickly set the tone of the proceedings. He portrayed Dick James as an unscrupulous predator who had taken advantage of Elton and Bernie's extreme youth and inexperience to bind them to 'onerous' and 'one-sided' contracts and, in addition to having a stranglehold on their work, had systematically siphoned their royalty earnings off into a network of overseas 'shell' companies. In other words, a picture conforming to every stereotype and caricature of the cigar-chewing, swindling pop mogul. 'The whole suit was obviously aimed personally at my father,' Stephen James says. 'Elton himself never seemed comfortable about that. During the whole time in court, I never once saw him look at my father – not even when my father was in the witness box. At the end of each day, Elton was hustled off through a far door, so there was no chance of them meeting outside.'

A few days into the case, a meeting was set up with John Reid to see if, even at this late stage, some agreement might be hammered out. 'I went by myself to meet him at their solicitors, Frere Cholmeley,' Stephen James says. 'My father at that stage said he couldn't bear to be in the same room as John Reid. The offer from John was basically that, if we gave up the song copyrights and record masters, he'd give us a million dollars to go away. I said, "Why are you talking about dollars? We should be thinking in pounds. And, anyway, you left a nought off there." John told me to eff off, and I left.'

The James side suffered an early blow, both strategically and to morale. Sidney Goldwater, Dick James's accountant and a crucial witness on the sub-publishing question, was found to be suffering from cancer and so could not be expected to appear in court. The cancer proved inoperable and, only a few weeks after its diagnosis, Goldwater was dead. This sudden loss of his old friend caused Dick James further distress and stress.

Elton's side had been diligent in tracing figures from his earliest past who could present James in an unfavourable light. Among the first to be contacted was Ray Williams, who had discovered Elton, via *New Musical Express* back in 1967, had first teamed him with Bernie Taupin, but had ended up with zilch per cent of the eventual goldmine. Though not called as a witness, Williams added background to the picture of Dick James as ruthless mogul, recalling how James had arbitrarily terminated his contract as personal manager in 1970, and how, in his short tenure, he had never been allowed to see any of Elton's agreements with DJM.

The case against the publishing contract was a reprise of days long ago in Tin Pan Alley and Frome Court, Pinner. Sheila Farebrother told how she had backed her son in his desire to become a musician, allowing him to drop out of school before A levels; scraping up £25 to buy him an old car when he began at Mills Music; even helping him draft his fateful reply to Ray Williams's *NME* advertisement. She said she had signed the first publishing agreement on his behalf as a minor, having no real idea what it meant. 'It was just like the others he came home with and said, "Sign this, Mum", and I would sign it. I didn't carefully consider it. I don't even understand them now.'

Another figure from the distant past was Muff Winwood, the A & R man for Island Records who had befriended Elton and Bernie during their Pinner exile in 1969. Winwood recalled how frustrated Elton had been over the failure of his early singles, and how he had wanted to quit DJM for Island and let Winwood and Lionel Conway take over his management from Dick James. He described how Island's owner, Chris Blackwell, had offered him a £10,000 advance and, in looking over his DJM contracts, had opined there were 'holes' in them. The question had then been dropped, thanks chiefly to James's agreement that Elton and Bernie could write what they chose and that Elton should be allowed to make his first album, *Empty Sky*.

John Reid made an impressive witness. In his calm, quiet, orderly Scots voice, he told how he had become 'suspicious' about the overseas royalty earnings just after leaving DJM's employ to become Elton's independent manager in 1972. He recalled, at that early stage, consulting Paul McCartney's brother-in-law John Eastman, and Eastman's view that there was 'a strong case' against Dick James for not accounting properly and levying a 50 per cent retention rate on American mechanical royalties. Reid's pursuit of the matter via two firms of accountants over eight years earned the only compliment to come from Mr Justice Nicholls, who, in the eventual judgment, described him as 'a young man both astute and tenacious'.

Evidence from a solicitor named Charles Levison, whose firm Harbottle and Lewis had drawn up John Reid's management contract with Elton, gave some insight into Reid's own earnings in commission since 1972. He himself agreed that, under his entitlement to 10 per cent of Elton's record income, he had received £579,136 between 1973 and 1976, and a further £676,733 up to December 1982. It was the only faint allusion to the fact that a massive payout for Elton also would mean a proportionate payout for John Reid.

Bernie Taupin had flown in for the hearing from Los Angeles, a dapper, urbane, suntanned figure, very different from the shy country boy frequently referred to in evidence. He described how many of the songs in the £30 million jackpot had been written by him in that tiny shared bedsitter at 30a Frome Court, then carried, postman-like, along the tiny hall to Elton at the living-room piano. On the complex business matters under dispute, however, Bernie could shed little light. Ever bookish and vague, he had taken in virtually nothing of the papers he'd signed with Elton down the years; of meetings with lawyers and accountants, employment companies and tax shelters. 'It got a bit monotonous,' he remembers now. 'To question after question, I could only give the same reply. "I'm sorry, I just don't remember."'

Elton himself, soberly dark-suited, his exiguous new hair scraped back into a ponytail, took the stand at the start of the second week. Throughout his evidence, he was treated with noticeable deference by Mr Justice Nicholls, who, at several points, seemed worried that the proceedings might be overtiring him.

He recalled the day in 1967 when Bernie and he had been summoned to Dick James's office over the illicit use of DJM's studio, not knowing that their demos had already found favour with James.

Sitting outside the great man's room had been 'very frightening', Elton said: 'a bit like waiting for your O-level results'. James's offer to sign them both as writers had been 'unbelievable, like a dream come true'. The subsequent agreements, publishing, recording and management, had seemed 'heaven-sent'. 'I was very young. It was a very exciting period. I didn't think of going to a solicitor. I just trusted Mr James. I was very naïve and wet behind the ears. Anything anyone told me to sign, I signed. Everything was done on trust.'

To him, in those days, James's terms had often seemed munificent. Receiving a £50 advance and £15 a week to write songs was 'the big time' for two boys who had previously been paid nothing. Likewise, being allowed to make the *Elton John* album as an unknown, at a cost of £7,000 to £8,000, had come 'like manna from Heaven'. The resultant hike in his record royalty rate from 20 to 60 per cent – i.e. 2 per cent of retail sale price to 6 per cent – at the time had seemed like 'a shot in the arm'.

His assertion that 'vast sums' of his royalties had been 'whittled away' brought a sharp counterattack from DJM's counsel, George Newman QC. Balance sheets were passed to Elton, showing that up to December 1982, he had received £13.4 million from record sales. In publishing royalties he had received a further £1.16 million and Bernie Taupin just over £1 million. Over the same period, This Record Co. had made profits of £7 million and DJM Records £1.5 million. Would Elton care to comment on these figures? 'I can't comment on them,' he replied. 'I'm not a chartered accountant. My lawyers told me there had been mishandling of money, and I just told them to get on with it [the lawsuit]. I was led to believe that vast sums were involved.'

Never in question was the perseverance of the James Organisation in launching Elton's career nor that, in the most adverse judgement, DJM would be entitled to a reasonable return on palpable long-term faith and investment. The same balance sheets showed that, if it had taken three years to establish Elton John as an international star, it had taken five to see any profit back from him. In 1972, the year of *Honky Château*, 'Daniel' and 'Crocodile Rock', he still represented a deficit of £197,000. Only in 1973, the year of *Goodbye Yellow Brick Road* and the Hollywood Bowl, had he shot to a £236,000 profit.

The disputed recording agreement also showed how what had once been faith in an unknown artist looked like rank exploitation with the hindsight of that artist's global success. In 1967, when Philips refused to release an album by Elton, DJM had set up its own DJM record label, handling all aspects of production bar actual manufacture. DJM Records then paid its production company, This Record

Co., a 10 per cent royalty, on which Elton's royalty was calculated. This 10 per cent UK rate had never been increased even though the going rate – for performers far smaller than Elton – quickly rose to around 16 per cent.

The two-tier system of This Record Co., the production company, and DJM, the record label, had at the time seemed flattering to Elton, a way of ensuring total artistic control over his records. However, his contract entitled him only to a share of profits from This Record Co. The DJM label also generated profits from manufacture, distribution and sales, of which he was entitled to not a farthing. It was alleged that this side of the arrangement had never been explained to him, and that even John Reid had been ignorant of it until Geoffrey Ellis suggested broadening the audit from publishing to recording.

Even more serious allegations were made about the DJM foreign subsidiaries which, after 1975, had collected Elton and Bernie's song royalties in Australia, Japan, France, Scandinavia, the Netherlands and Italy. Elton and Bernie were by now on a 60–40 publishing split with DJM, but that was not as straightforward as it sounded. First, an administrator, responsible for collection in each territory, deducted a 15 per cent charge. Thirty-five per cent then remained in the overseas subsidiary while 50 per cent came home to be split 40–60 between DJM and the writers. According to their counsel, it was not just that DJM failed to explain the system and the full impact of its deductions to Elton and Bernie. There had been a deliberate cover-up of 'the critical factors which showed the diversion to be wrongful'.

Stephen James spent four days in the box, an ordeal for which there can be no adequate preparation. 'I'd been coached a bit by our lawyers in what to say, but it wasn't of much help. Up there, you're totally on your own. You're not even supposed to look at your own counsel. They can ask you anything they like, and you never know where it's coming from next.' He was cross-examined by junior counsel, often on matters of detailed accountancy that lay outside his knowledge. To him, as head of This Record Co., the crucial question was put. Why had Elton's UK royalty rate been permanently pegged at a beginner's 6 per cent of retail? Stephen replied that it had been more than compensated for by the higher than average rate that DJM had obtained for him throughout the rest of the world, especially with MCA in America. To have raised his UK royalty to the going rate, and lowered his American rate commensurately would have reduced his income by something like £2 million.

Dick James himself was in the box for five days. Despite recent traumas, he gave a relaxed performance in the face of hard and hostile questioning by Mark Littman QC. He recalled how, having 'a minute or two to spare', he had interviewed Elton and Bernie, divined their talent and signed it up for a £100 advance, which was, for those days, 'on the right side of generous'. The original 50–50 publishing split had been standard practice then and, indeed, still was today. Elton's royalty rate from This Record Co. might seem small in modern terms, but it had been generous at the time – Elton himself had freely admitted thinking so. DJM had done him proud, given that the chances of ever breaking him had been so remote for so many years.

Only once did James become ruffled. This was when Mark Littman suggested that DJM's Swiss subsidiary had merely been a front for him personally to siphon Elton and Bernie's royalties into a Swiss bank account. 'My father was terribly upset, and terribly annoyed,' Stephen James says. 'He thought it was a disgraceful suggestion.'

In July, Britain's legal system went into its summer recess and the case had to be adjourned for two months. The Jameses were cautiously optimistic, sensing that the judge inclined to their version of the evidence. Dick James felt he had acquitted himself well in the witness box, and began to think this aberrant stretch of bad luck might finally be nearing an end.

It had taken twenty-five years, but social conscience was taking root in pop music at last. Late in 1984, BBC television showed a horrifying report on the famine in Ethiopia, and the impotence of government and relief agencies in combating it. Among many shocked and outraged by the pictures was Bob Geldof, Irish lead singer with the Boomtown Rats. Mobilising his many friends in the music business, Geldof organised the making of a special ensemble single to raise funds for Ethiopian famine relief. 'Do They Know It's Christmas?', featuring performers like Boy George, Spandau Ballet and Big Country under the collective name Band Aid, was a massive British hit in December; the first 'Christmas record' ever deserving the name. There quickly followed an American counterpart, 'Feed the World', with a still more impressive artist roster, from Michael Jackson and Cyndi Lauper to Bruce Springsteen and Bob Dylan. What had been the most selfish and self-centred of all media suddenly transformed itself into the most community-minded and caring.

The past year in Britain had been one of extreme ugliness, as a misconceived and badly led miners' strike tested Margaret Thatcher's avowed intent to smash trade union power. TV images from home also became horrific, with a new-style paramilitary police force sealing off whole counties, and ferocious baton charges against those whom Mrs Thatcher repellently termed 'the enemy within'. Among the miners' few public supporters were young left-wing pop musicians like Paul Weller, Jimmy Somerville and Billy Bragg. There was a rebirth of the mid-Sixties 'protest song'. Even pop's latest teenybop sensation, the two-man group Wham!, gave a concert to raise money for wives and families hit by the strike.

In May 1985, football thuggery wrought its worst mayhem yet. A mindless riot by British supporters at the Heysel stadium in Brussels caused thirty-nine deaths from crushing and led English clubs to be banned from all matches in Europe for the next five years. The chairman of Watford was specially depressed to think how all his cleaning-up and peacemaking initiatives had been set back.

The brightest spot of the year – indeed, of the Eighties so far – came on 13 July. From Bob Geldof's Band Aid record had grown the concept of Live Aid, a giant concert for the Ethiopian famine, televised simultaneously from Wembley Stadium in London and JFK Stadium in Philadelphia, and featuring every major American and British pop name in a marathon eight-hour bill: Bob Dylan, the Rolling Stones, David Bowie, Tina Turner, Phil Collins, Sting, U2, Madonna, Queen, Paul Young, Geldof himself with the Boomtown Rats, and scores of others.

Such an occasion could not possibly leave out the performer who had pioneered these sensibilities fifteen years in advance of everyone else. Elton was allotted an unprecedented thirty-minute spot at the end of the day's marathon from Wembley, playing bespangled antiques like 'Rocket Man' and 'Bennie and the Jets' in a striped lamé frock coat and Queen Mary toque, backed by an augmented band and a vocal quartet including Kiki Dee.

In his role as Big Daddy to the new glitter rockers, he also introduced George Michael of Wham!, whose potential as a writer and solo performer he had spotted well ahead of the crowd. Michael then sang 'Don't Let the Sun Go Down on Me', a dual tribute to Elton's influence and his special way of bestowing public compliments. It was all a far cry from the High Courts of Justice, from writs, depositions, statements of claim, dusty robes, grey wigs, pink ribbon and green sealing-wax.

To build up strength for the second part of the case, Dick James went away with his wife to their flat in Cannes. After only three or four days there, they went to bed one night, leaving the doors to their balcony open. At about 1 am, Mrs James awoke to find a burglar standing over her. The burglar hit James in the face, then jumped over the balcony, which was six storeys high. It afterwards transpired he was a thief famous up and down the Riviera, a trained acrobat, able to perform near-impossible climbs and leaps from balcony to balcony.

'That was the last straw for my father,' Stephen James says. 'He was so distressed by the whole thing, he couldn't sleep without sedation for about three weeks afterwards. And he said he never wanted to go back to that flat. He felt his luck had turned so bad that it could never turn back again.'

Proceedings in the High Court resumed on 1 October. In his closing speech for the defendants, George Newman QC submitted that there was 'not a scintilla of evidence' that Dick James had used 'undue influence' to make Elton and Bernie sign away their song copyrights. 'There is no evidence of browbeating, persuasion or use of muscle in any way. The fact that they might have been in awe of Dick James and his position is neither here nor there. You might be in awe of your bank manager. Elton John simply has never had a complaint about his career and about what was done for him in the way of exploitation and promotion. In fact, he is very fond of Dick James, and is grateful to him in many ways. He has amassed a considerable fortune because of what Dick James has done for him.'

Closing for the plaintiffs, Mark Littman QC denied that Elton and Bernie had brought the case merely at the suggestion of lawyers. 'As long as these agreements remain in respect of this very large body of master recordings and songs – a third of them unissued – it is very reasonable to bring such a claim.' Though their confidence in Dick James had naturally been 'shaken' over the alleged siphoning of royalties abroad, they were 'more concerned with the future than with the past'.

On 29 November, Mr Justice Nicholls delivered his verdict in a four-hour judgment. Essentially, he found against DJM on almost all counts, but at the same time awarded Elton and Bernie only a fraction of what they had claimed. Clearing Dick James of all personal blame or liability, he was nevertheless to use words that wounded James to the quick.

The crux of the judgment was that, in dealings with their two protégés, especially as minors, DJM's prime duty had been that of a 'fiduciary', or trustee. The onus on Dick James throughout had been to secure Elton and Bernie the fairest possible terms rather than to do smart business on his own company's account. It was a piece of brand-new law, with obvious far-reaching consequences for the whole British music industry.

On this principle, the 1967 publishing agreement, assigning Elton and Bernie's entire songwriting output for the next six years to DJM, had been 'an unfair transaction'. Though James had not consciously sought to take advantage of them, and had acted in good faith and according to standard music-business procedure, this did not fully answer the claim of undue influence. 'One can obtain an unfair advantage by the exercise of a dominant influence without intending to be unfair.' In the same way, while similarly acknowledging Dick James's good faith, the 1968 recording agreement, with its fixed low royalty rate, had also been unfair. The amended agreement of 1970, increasing the royalty rate, had not been unfair, given that at the time Elton still had to make a hit record. But it had been 'not generous'.

The judge's harshest words were directed at the internal structure of Dick James Music and its adverse impact on Elton and Bernie's income as writers and Elton's as a recording artist. The way in which DJM's own record label paid its production company a systematically low royalty, as the basis of Elton's UK record royalty, 'could not stand scrutiny' as a discharge of fiduciary duty. Nor could the fact that the record company earned profits of which Elton received nothing. Under his contract, he should have received a share in all proceeds from the licensing and exploitation of his records.

Most damning was Mr Justice Nicholls about DJM's overseas subsidiaries, and the two separate bites taken out of Elton and Bernie's foreign royalties before they reached London. In the judge's view, it was not right for subsidiaries with neither offices nor staff to deduct 35 per cent on top of the 15 per cent already taken by the outside administrator. He refused to accept Stephen James's assertion that even subsidiaries without offices incurred expenses from such things as promotion, advertising and business travel.

Dick James, as 'an able businessman' had realised what John Reid would say about such a system, and so it had been kept dark in successive royalty statements and in all correspondence and discussion about sub-publishing. Elton's side had not known the full story until after the start of the present action. All this had been 'unconscionable' behaviour on DJM's part.

Three factors, however, militated against the setting aside of the publishing and recording agreements, despite their breaches of fiduciary duty. The first was DJM's undoubted success in marketing Elton and Bernie's work, which, even on unfair terms, had given them undreamed-of fame and wealth. The second was that throughout Elton's time with DJM, he had had a good relationship with Dick James, and felt he had 'no particular axe to grind'. The third was that so many years had been allowed to elapse between the signing of the agreements and the decision to bring a lawsuit. 'The balance of justice', therefore, was against rescinding either. The song copyrights and record masters would remain with DJM.

Damages were granted on two counts. First, on Elton's UK record royalty, where the judge ruled he should have received 12 per cent, not 5.4 per cent of the retail sale price, and that DJM must make good the difference, with interest. Second, on foreign sub-publishing, where 35 per cent had been improperly witheld from the calculation of his and Bernie's overseas royalties. These were now to be recomputed as 60 per cent, not of 50 but 85 per cent. In addition, the retention rate of DJM-USA was retroactively lowered from 50 to 25 per cent.

Dick James was absolved of all personal responsibility or liability on every count. There was no order as to which side should pay the costs of the action – by then estimated at between £1 million and £1.5 million.

In interviews with the trade paper *Music Week*, both sides claimed victory. John Reid said that, although Elton had not won back his song copyrights, 'a moral victory' had been won on the UK royalty rate and sub-publishing. Dick James's riposte was that DJM had 'lost a battle but won the war'. Each expressed regret that the action had ever been brought and said it need not have dragged on so long, enriching lawyers along the way, if the other had been prepared to see reason. Dick James added a heartfelt lament on behalf of all music publishers now likely to be hit by the John and Paul, or Elton and Bernie, syndrome. 'It seems rather incongruous that you can go back with a contract after seventeen years and expect to renegotiate. We never heard in the past that Cole Porter, Jerome Kern or George Gershwin disputed the contracts they'd made with their publishers.'

No one denied that the lawsuit had redrawn the ground rules for British music publishers and their writers. To Elton, personally, however, only marginal benefits had accrued. Copyright in his greatest hits still remained in other hands. The hoped-for fortune in damages had nowhere near materialised. Initial estimates of the royalty repayment went as high as £5 million. But, according to Stephen James, it ended up as 'a six-figure sum – less than a million', not enough to justify lodging an appeal.

But if Dick James Music was preserved, James himself had been devastated. He could not get over the fact that Elton, his surrogate son, had turned on him, nor that, even though cleared of personal blame, his cherished business integrity had come under repeated attack in court. The word 'unconscionable', in particular, returned again and again to haunt him. For the rest of his life, he believed his fabulous luck had turned bad, and would never turn good again.

His heart trouble, amazingly, had not recurred during the protracted strain of the lawsuit, the death of his friend Sidney Goldwater or the incident with the burglar at his flat. But, as heart specialists know, there can often be more danger to a serious cardiac condition when pressure ceases and adrenaline is suddenly shut off. Barely three months later, on 1st February, 1986, James suffered a massive heart attack at his St John's Wood home and died before he could be taken to hospital.

Stephen James has no doubt where the blame lies. 'I'm sure that if it hadn't been for the strain of the court case and the impugning of his reputation, which hurt him so much, he would never have had the attack, and might still be alive today. I still feel so furious that something so unimportant by comparison with my father's life should have caused that. It hadn't been the way I'd expected him to go.'

Elton was shocked and distressed by his old mentor's death, and patently troubled by thoughts that the lawsuit might have played a part in bringing it about. His lawyers were ordered to reach a settlement as rapidly as possible with DJM over the royalty repayments. Since Dick James had been absolved of personal liability in the case, Elton also agreed to meet his legal costs, paying them into an estate eventually valued at £6.8 million.

However, there was one touch that the punctilious, good boy of old might have managed a little better. 'After my father died, I got a message that Elton was very upset, and wanted to send his condolences,' Stephen James remembers. 'It was phoned through to me by someone at John Reid's office.'

17

Gotcha!

THE first reports, around 1982, were merely of another bizarre American invention. New York, that unique repository of dirt and germs, had created a brand-new disease. It was a virus which attacked antibodies in the bloodstream, destroying the body's immune system and causing death from the torrent of infection which then rushed in. Weirdly, it was thought to occur in only four social groups, haemophiliacs, Haitian immigrants, intravenous drug users and male homosexuals, among whom it was communicated by sexual and oral contact. Its cumbersome name, Acquired Immune Deficiency Syndrome was shortened to a computer-style acronym, AIDS.

In a short time, the haemophiliacs, junkies and Haitians had been cast off like so much ballast from a rising balloon. AIDS was reported primarily as a disease of homosexual males, endemic among New York's huge gay population, especially at Lower East Side pick-up joints and 'bath houses', where up to twenty casual promiscuous encounters per person per night might take place. A spate of deaths followed among figures prominent in the art and fashion world and in Hollywood, some of them men never dreamed to be other than totally hetero. This was a new and ghastly version of 'coming out'.

The first British AIDS cases made even worse impact on a society which prided itself on having virtually eliminated sexually-transmitted disease. That the figures were still infinitesimal, especially compared with those of cancer or heart disease, brought little comfort from the medical authorities. The lethal virus had been found to act with horrible leisureliness, taking up to eight years to incubate in a body which for all that time might think itself quite healthy. From the few dozen at present, future cases were projected in the thousands, even the millions. Late twentieth-century Europe was suddenly looking at another medieval Black Death.

The growing incidence of victims among heterosexuals – and those whose sexuality was irrelevant, like newborn babies and nuns – continued to make little general impression. To the public at large,

AIDS was a disease of homosexual men, one which seemed to confirm everything ever alleged about their promiscuity and predatoriness. In the rising panic, all final traces of Seventies liberal tolerance disappeared. A brush fire of homophobia swept through Britain, fanned by the Victorian voices that were once again in the ascendant. Several prominent Christians, in and out of the pulpit, went so far as to suggest that AIDS was more than a medical catastrophe. It was nothing less than God's will; a Heaven-sent scourge on all those guilty of 'unnatural' acts, whom a too-tolerant society by now almost recognised as legitimate human beings.

So the young men wasted away. The modern Pecksniffs told them it was their own fault for being so disgusting. And tabloid newspapers began to scent circulation in what *The Sun*'s headline writers, with their usual matchless accuracy and humanity, had already termed 'the Gay Plague'.

There was never any doubt that Elton genuinely loved Renate. Months after their wedding, he was still talking about it in wonderment to his long-time friend Nina Myskow. 'He told me that when he turned round in that church and saw Renate coming down the aisle towards him, he thought she was the most beautiful thing he'd ever seen in his life. And there were tears in his eyes when he said it.'

The myths that have grown up around Renate can be quickly disposed of. She was no mere gold-digger, taking advantage of a momentary mad whim on Elton's part to plug into his millions. Nor was she, as would also be alleged, a lesbian, conniving in a mutually convenient show marriage. She loved Elton back, with a wholehearted simplicity that very nearly overcame the handicaps of their relationship. There was probably no one in his life who ever got closer to him, or was finally rejected with such anguish.

Renate's rather wooden exterior proved to have been deeply misleading. 'She was a really intelligent, lively girl,' Nina Myskow says. 'She had a great sense of humour, and she was one of the most thoughtful people you could ever meet. Even as this big-time pop star's wife, she had a quality that was totally modest and unassertive. And she knew just the way to get along with Elton. When they were together, they were good together.'

Those who had seen the romance grow in half-smiles over a studio control desk wondered if it could ever have a sexual side. It did and, to begin with at least, it was totally successful. Two people equally shy and uncertain can often bring about miracles together. 'I know they had a physical relationship,' Nina Myskow says. 'Elton used to talk a lot about having children. Though, being him, in the next breath he'd say, "Ah, you've only got to sit next to a crying baby on a plane to be put off them for life."'

On one level, being married suited him perfectly. He called Renate 'the wife' as naturally as if they had settled in a mock-Tudor semi in Pinner, Northwood or Dollis Hill. He would write letters and cards to 'Wifey' signing them 'Hubby'. It amused him to picture them as Darby and Joan, with mugs of Bournevita, in tartan pompom slippers, seated on either side of a Magicoal fire.

No other rock star's wife was ever treated with such old-world chivalry. 'Whenever they were together, Elton paid attention to Renate all the time,' Nanette Newman remembers. 'He'd always be leaning over to kiss her or squeeze her hand. He always seemed worried that she might feel neglected or left out.'

It was wonderful to him to have someone in his life whom he could spoil, publicly and legitimately. His lavishness with Renate passed all previous bounds. He showered gifts on her, jewellery, flowers, clothes and still more clothes for her stupendously expanded wardrobe. Her great weakness, like his own, was chocolate. At Easter, Harrods would be ordered to send its most prodigious chocolate egg for 'the wife'.

Thoughtful and sensitive on that same level, he realised the problems Renate faced in integrating into his environment. In particular, he wanted her to feel at home at his Old Windsor mansion. When they returned there after their wedding in Australia, he told her to do anything she wanted that would make the house nicer for her.

The difficulty was that every room was packed with fifteen years'-worth of Elton's bulk-bought treasures, the mazes of Bugatti furniture, the labyrinths of Asprey's silver, the phalanxes of Lalique glass, the forests of many-hued and candled Tiffany lamps, the seraglios of Art Nouveau dancing girls and nymphs, all in their places like exhibits in a museum. From the model of Pharoah Tutankhamun's throne across the vista of mock-Renaissance sideboard, brass palm trees and Majorelle marquetry card tables to the Victorian clubman's chair with attached jockey-weighing scales, nothing that met Renate's eye could be called remotely lived-in or homey. 'She was totally bemused by the place,' an ex-Rocket employee remembers. 'She didn't know where she was supposed to sit or not to sit. She hardly liked to turn round unless something got knocked over or broken.'

Renate's influence was confined to the kitchen, which she began to have completely rebuilt, and the master bedroom suite, where she and

Elton shared a carved wooden bed modelled on that of Empress Josephine. So worried was Elton by her lack of territorial demands that he insisted she should have one of the five remaining suites as her private domain, decorated and furnished just as she wanted it.

One of the few journalists permitted into Woodside after Renate's arrival was David Wigg of the *Daily Express*. The perennially 'safe' Wigg duly reported on a wild man of pop, calmed and mellowed by a good woman's love. 'I had everything but I had nothing,' Elton told him. 'I needed the challenge of changing my life, making it more fulfilling and sharing. I could see myself ending up as an eccentric, living alone and being incredibly fussy, rather like Quentin Crisp, except that I dust and he doesn't. I didn't want that.'

His verdict on marriage so far? 'Fabulous. I'm so happy, and very much in love. Being married has made me so much calmer. I'm less argumentative now, and more reasonable. I don't get my own way any more, but it's so nice to come home and actually share things.' Even so, he admitted that he could be a terrible person to live with. 'I'm so set in my ways. I've got certain methods of doing everything. Like, I can't speak at breakfast. I've got to have total silence. When you share a house with someone else, that can be a problem, but so far it hasn't been. The wife's got her own suite of rooms that she can go to if she wants to, but otherwise we share most things in the house. She's taking over, and making it more of a home than it was before. She just adds little things to the place, like flowers, and the way she puts things together make it more homely. It's a woman's touch, and I like that.'

He returned constantly to the theme of having children, always stressing the plural. 'I was an only child, and I didn't enjoy that much. Ideally, I'd like to have two, but you never know. Please God that we can have one. We've been trying for children, but it hasn't happened yet. If we find we can't have them, we'll consider adoption. There are so many kids who don't have a home. I think adoption is wonderful.'

So why, if he was so calm and happy with Renate, did he plunge right back into his old frenetic and frequently miserable way of life? Why, longing for children so much, did he embark on the one course that guaranteed he would never have any? Why, with happiness within his grasp, did he almost immediately fling it away?

It seems clear that Elton had hoped marriage to Renate would stamp out his homosexual side and that, within a very short time, he realised that had not happened. Plenty of marriages have worked in such circumstances, and Renate evidently possessed sufficient understanding and patience to give this one a more than healthy chance, on any terms Elton chose. But he himself was too conventional for any kind of open relationship à la Sackville-West and Nicolson. 'It wasn't enough for Elton that the marriage should work,' Nina Myskow says. 'It had to be seen to work. So being apart, with the excuse he had to go off on tour, was better than being together in any way that could cause comment or criticism.'

Renate was not left completely alone. A live-in couple ran the house, and there were frequent callers, from Elton's business organisation and family. His grandmother Ivy Harris had by now been installed in the Orangery, and Sheila often drove up from Sussex to see her, sometimes bringing along Ivy's other daughter, Win. No evidence exists of specially warm relations between Renate and her British in-laws.

The curious feature of her months at Woodside is how little she used its magnificent facilities. Private cinema, swimming pool, squash court and games room had no allure to her, and she seldom even went out into the 38 acres of perfectly manicured grounds. Apart from one or two visits to health farms, she preferred not to leave the house. Much of her time – even in the most brilliant summer weather – was spent lying on an expensive sunbed Elton had bought her. She became fascinated by computers, and would spend all day, and all night as well, up in her private suite rattling the keys of a VDU. Almost the only pastime she and Elton shared outside a recording studio was watching video films, which he would bring home from his trips in huge quantity. With a meticulousness he warmly approved, Renate set herself to cataloguing the videos in a set of expensive leather-bound ledgers.

Even from a distance, Elton remained hugely protective of her. He was specially concerned to shield her from the politics that always raged inside his court, and told her that when she wanted something, she must always come straight to him, rather than speaking to Bob Halley or John Reid. The woman who, a year ago, had possessed only jeans and a few T-shirts now had need of a personal assistant to catalogue her clothes. 'John didn't think she ought to have one,' Nina Myskow remembers. 'So she had to go to Elton about that. He got very annoyed that she shouldn't immediately have been given what she asked for.'

He relied on John Reid to be supportive of her in his absence, and bristled extremely if ever Reid proved dilatory in the job. 'John was supposed to be coming over to dinner one night while Elton was away,' Nina Myskow remembers. 'At about five-thirty, the phone goes. Typical John – he's cancelling. Then Elton rings up from the States and asks "How are things going for the dinner party tonight?"

"John's not coming," Renate says. "Oh, isn't he!" Elton says. "Just you wait and see!" Half an hour later, the phone rings again. It's John. He is coming after all.'

A curious sense of the relationship leaked into Elton's album, *Ice on Fire*, released in 1985 while the court battle with DJM was just drawing to an end. That the marriage had already hit trouble was obvious to close friends like Nina Myskow. 'I remember being at the house for dinner one awful night. Renate was away at a health farm, and Elton wouldn't get up. I just saw these trays being brought out of his room, covered with Mars-bar wrappers and sandwich crusts.'

Ice on Fire marked the return to the fold of his best-ever record producer, Gus Dudgeon. Seven years after being peremptorily dropped, Dudgeon got a phone call from Elton out of the blue. 'He said, "There never was a team like you and me. You've got to produce my next one." I said, "All right, but I've got to hear the songs first." He said, "Christ! It can't still be like that!" I said, "That's the way it always was." '

The album included a duet between Elton and George Michael whose title, 'Wrap Her Up', was all too apt a summary of Renate's situation. Still more unconsciously evocative was 'Nikita', in which Elton sang to a lonely Russian girl 'in your little corner of the world', but as bleakly as if he meant a West German girl at home in Old Windsor, painstakingly listing video films in a leather-bound book.

The accompanying video was directed by Ken Russell, British cinema's white-haired *enfant terrible*, who had cast Elton in his screen version of *Tommy*. Underlining the new hetero image, Russell made Nikita a blonde East German guard on the Berlin Wall and Elton her wooer from a capitalist Rolls-Royce. A dream sequence followed in which Elton was seen with Nikita at a Watford game, strapped to the gigantic Doc Marten boots Ken Russell had originally made him wear as the Pinball Wizard.

'Nikita' was his biggest single for years, reaching number three in Britain and seven in America and more than answering the long-time demand of an enormous public for 'another song like Daniel'. For what not even Ken Russell realised at the time was that Nikita is actually a man's name.

By early 1986, British gossip columns were routinely describing Elton's marriage as 'shaky'. There was constant hammering on about his 'gay past', and scarcely veiled speculation that Renate might be hiding something similar. The solitary former boyfriend to be dredged up from her Kilburn bedsitter days reported that on their nights together, she slept in the bed while he occupied the sofa. 'Renate didn't want a passionate relationship,' complained this conveniently anonymous voice. 'She only wanted to live like brother and sister.'

Elton's former lifestyle was more specifically and damagingly under the spotlight. In 1985, police had charged a man with stealing the £6,000 gold and diamond Cartier watch which had gone missing from his bedroom at Woodside two years earlier. It had been recovered in a dawn raid on the West Croydon home of twenty-one-year-old Cornelius Culwick, who had at first tried to hide it in his pyjama trousers. Asked where he got the watch, Culwick had allegedly replied, 'I'll give you a clue – the Pinball Wizard. Now work it out.'

Culwick denied stealing the watch, claiming it had been a gift from a bisexual friend named Tommy Williams, who had been given it by Elton himself. The case went for trial at the Old Bailey, and Elton was obliged to appear as a prosecution witness. He said that on the night the watch disappeared, he had come home with Tommy Williams and 'two other men', and had changed into a bathrobe, taking off the watch and a sapphire ring. 'At about 1 am, my friends came to my suite, and we then went to the video room until about 4 am. I fell asleep on the sofa until about 9 am.'

The theft charge was amended to one of 'dishonest handling', and the case dragged on over several months, Culwick alleging along the way that he'd had 'a gay fling' with Elton. He was eventually acquitted and also given back the watch, since Elton had not attempted to reclaim it. 'EX-LOVER' CAN KEEP ELTON'S WATCH was the *Daily Express* headline.

Elton met the ceaseless media probing and digging with his usual total unpredictability. February 1986 found him celebrating his second wedding anniversary on a French TV programme called *The Truth Game*, in which celebrities were invited to bare their innermost souls to phone-in questioners.

An early caller asked with Gallic forthrightness if his marriage to Renate wasn't just camouflage for his homosexuality. He replied with all his old winning frankness and good humour. 'I'm not trying to hide my homosexuality at all. It was just that I met someone whom I liked a lot and wanted to marry. It happened at a moment when I was tired of my old style of living. But I don't regret anything I did, nor my style of life before. I have nothing to hide. I regret nothing.'

Another caller said he remembered once seeing Elton on a beach in St Tropez 'surrounded by beautiful boys'. 'Before, he saw me with a beautiful boy,' Elton replied. 'Now I'm with a beautiful woman . . .'

He was just as forthcoming on *The Tube*, a new British TV rock show, hosted by Bob Geldof's girl-friend, Paula Yates. Though guests on *The Tube* were expected to speak only in ten-second sound bites, Elton gave them an extended confessional. 'When I announced I was gay in 1976, it really hurt me a lot. In America, a lot of radio stations stopped playing my records. I even thought about committing suicide. If I hadn't had Watford, I might have become a very big casualty. But I had to learn to take defeat well. If you take your seat at a football ground and 20,000 people are singing, "Elton John's a homosexual", you learn fairly quickly.'

Nor was he afraid to stand up and be counted in the growing horror of the AIDS epidemic. Three years on, only minimal government resources had been allotted to fight the disease, and sufferers were still cast out of society like lepers. Pop music, in its new humanitarian mood, offered one of the earliest pleas for compassion and charity. On the Band Aid principle, a special fund-raising single, 'That's What Friends Are For', was recorded by Dionne Warwick, backed by three 'friends', Gladys Knight, Stevie Wonder and Elton.

His charity performances continued, though less noticeable now in the general mania of rock stars for doing good works. He gave an open-air concert in St James's Park to raise funds to help young drug addicts, and became a stalwart of the Prince's Trust, Prince Charles's youth charity, appearing in its giant Wembley gala with Tina Turner and Phil Collins. Once, Elton had been the only pop figure within miles of royalty. Now you could barely see him in the throngs of them, bowing stiffly to the Prince of Wales or whispering discreet designer-stubbly jokes into Princess Diana's scrumptious little ear.

Yet where was Mrs John? people continued to ask. He seemed to bring her out only on the most formal public occasions, in his capacity as Watford chairman or when receiving some ceremonial accolade from the music industry. In February 1986, he collected a belated BPI award for his 1979 Russian tour, handed over with an unconvincing warm smile by the Conservative Party chairman, Norman Tebbit. Infuriated by both occasion and presenter, Elton was believed to have smashed the statuette to pieces. In April, Renate appeared again as he received two Ivor Novello Awards, one for 'outstanding' services to music, the other for 'Nikita' as the 'year's best song'.

A media invitation he could hardly refuse, affording maximum prestige with zero controversy, was appearing on BBC Radio's *Desert Island Discs*. The plodding old radio fantasy, in which a famous 'castaway' chooses his or her eight favourite records, has become a mark of recognition only just short of the Queen's honours list. To obtain Elton, the strict rule was waived that castaways, even if royal, must make their selection from a studio at Broadcasting House. The interviewer, Michael Parkinson, travelled specially down to Old Windsor.

Elton's *Desert Island Discs* remains among the best ever broadcast. As well as choosing music from Thelonius Monk through Elgar's 'Nimrod' to Nina Simone's 'I Put a Spell on You', he was at his most winningly lucid, modest and funny. In the biographical interludes, he deftly summed up his career and performing rationale, talked of Watford and John Lennon and, with no trace of mawkishness, remembered cuddling a boy with incurable cancer on a Barbados beach. *Desert Island Discs* has an enormous audience. This focusing of Elton at his best in the public mind could not have come at a more timely moment.

Michael Parkinson was a reliable old friend. The one indirect mention of Renate occurred when Elton chose 'Abide With Me' to remind him of Watford's Cup Final. 'Apart from getting married,' he said, 'that was the happiest day of my life.'

The tabloids had been quick to spot his seeming fascination with George Michael of Wham!. That June, Wham! gave a giant concert at Wembley Stadium, in brilliant summer weather recalling another spectacular, long ago, starring the Beach Boys. Elton was among the backstage guests, holding court to young acolytes like Simon Le Bon of Duran Duran and Holly Johnson of Frankie Goes to Hollywood. With him he brought a 60-foot mobile trailer stuffed with food and liquor, an expanse of synthetic lawn and a portable swimming pool. He joined Wham! onstage, playing piano in a Ronald McDonald orange wig, red nose and clown suit while George Michael sang 'Candle in the Wind'. In the finale Elton came back again, wearing a fluorescent pink tracksuit and a matching Marie-Antoinette wig.

In July, Britain was convulsed by its second royal wedding of the decade. Prince Andrew, aka Randy Andy, took unto himself Sarah Ferguson, daughter of Prince Philip's polo manager, a jovial redhead whom the tabloid press instantly dubbed 'Fergie'. Even this regal occasion brought Elton and Renate's marriage back into the spotlight.

Like Randy Andy, Fergie was an avid Elton fan. She also became a personal friend, unhampered by the constraints of royalty. Her favourite Elton track was 'Song for Guy', so he recorded a special new piano-only track for her as a wedding gift. She in return was to join his long line of sympathetic female listeners.

Elton and Renate were among the highly unconventional wedding guests invited to join the Queen, the Queen Mother, the Prince and Princess of Wales, the Princess Royal and Princess Margaret at

Westminster Abbey. Elton in addition attended Prince Andrew's stag party at the Guards Polo Club, which Fergie and Princess Diana attempted to gatecrash, disguised as policewomen.

On his wedding morning, the Queen gave her boisterous second son the more dignified title of Duke of York. During the Abbey service, many eyes wandered to a morning-suited figure whose doffed grey top hat revealed wispy zigzags of transplanted hair. Renate sat close, in a couture outfit of suit, pillbox hat and veil, cosily gripping his arm. It was said in the gossip columns that their marriage had got its second wind, and that their new friends 'the Yorks' had been instrumental in providing it.

Renate was with Elton when he travelled to New York in early September for a four-night appearance at Madison Square Garden. An American Elton fanatic named Wayne Newton, surreptitiously backstage at the Garden, observed the rather curious way in which husband and wife arrived. 'I heard this voice singing, and then Elton walked past me, totally alone. About ten minutes later, there was the slam of a car door, and Renate came in with Bob Halley, Elton's bodyguard and another man. She came only for the first and third nights. She'd stay in the dressing room until after the show started, then be ushered up to the wings. And she'd leave well before the end of the show.'

The four Madison Square Garden nights were the first sign that something might be going wrong with Elton's voice. 'I heard that before the first night, he hadn't been able to speak at all,' Wayne Newton says. 'He'd made a joke of it by arriving backstage dressed as Harpo Marx, and running through honking a motor horn. Another night, I was there before the show at around 6 pm when no one was onstage but Elton and his piano tuner. He played for about five minutes, and then his voice completely cut out. They were four great shows that week, but in every one there'd be moments when his voice just went. On the last night, the audience were virtually singing the words because he couldn't. I heard he was due to go to Australia, then coming back to the States in January. I couldn't see how he was going to make it.'

On 17 October, he was back in London to do BBC TV's Terry Wogan show, hosted in the great Irishman's absence by Esther Rantzen. He made his appearance in a huge yellow Tina Turner wig and a silver lamé teagown, topped by enormous silver angel wings. 'I'm forty next year,' he explained in a voice noticeably lower and huskier than usual. 'I'm having a great time onstage, and I feel just in the mood to put on all this kind of stuff just once more. People expect me to make a fool of myself, and I always do.'

For his Australian tour, he had gone back to his old Seventies designer Bill Mackie, and ordered a wardrobe as preposterous and obliteratingly heavy as anything seen by the glitter age. As well as the Tina Turner gown, there was a Mephistopheles costume with a four-foot-high scarlet ruff, a bespangled Ali Baba turban and bloomers, and a Mozart suit, worn with cascading white wig and beauty spot. Before Elton on the coffee table was a Mohican wig in fluorescent pink, trimmed with a Fergie-style black velvet bow.

He took the opportunity to stress again that he and Renate were truly happy, and all the gossips were wrong. 'When we were in America there were all these headlines that our marriage was on the rocks, and we were having private conversations with the Duke and Duchess of York. I mean, can you imagine it? "She threw a sausage at me, Your Highness . . ." The press over here are unbelievable.'

As if in confirmation of marital harmony, his new album, *Leather Jackets*, included a track written by Renate under the pseudonym Lady Choc Ice. There was also a credit line: 'Special thanks to Lady Choc Ice for being a continued source of inspiration.'

However, when he left for Australia in November, Renate did not accompany him. And within a week or so, rumours of a rift between them had broken out again. Q magazine published an interview with Elton, insisting that they were still happy and his marriage had not been 'a cover-up'. This was enough for the *Daily Star* to headline its pick-up story ELTON SLAMS GOSSIP ABOUT RENATE and for *The Sun* to tag its even shorter précis ELTON IN GAY 'COVER-UP' ROW.

Renewed tabloid interest in his family life was swelled by the unluckiest of coincidences. On 5 November, his half-brother Geoffrey Dwight – one of the four sons from his father's second marriage – was sentenced to a term of youth custody by a court in Mold, north Wales. It was said that twenty-year-old Geoffrey and an older accomplice had broken into a lonely farmhouse and robbed the young couple there after tying them up and terrorising them with pickaxe handles. Both accused pleaded guilty, explaining in mitigation that they had thought the house belonged to a local drugs dealer. Since Elton had last seen him, Geoffrey had evidently gone downhill, giving up university to become a timber salesman, then falling in with the worst possible company. Despite the long silence between Elton and his father and half-brothers, a message was sent, asking him to attend court as a character witness for Geoffrey. But he was on tour on the other side of the world.

With his Seventies wardrobe, the Australian tour saw a stage format harking back to even earlier. The first half of each show was all-out rock, with Elton leading his thirteen-piece band as Mohican, Mephistopheles or Tina Turner taking tea at the Ritz. The second half featured him in his Mozart suit, white wig and beauty spot, playing antique album-tracks like 'The King Must Die' and 'Madman Across the Water', accompanied by the Melbourne Symphony Orchestra. There were to be twenty-seven separate shows, ending with a climactic Christmas season at the enormous Sydney Entertainment Centre. The Sydney concerts were to be filmed by American ABC television and also recorded for a double live album to be released in 1987.

By the end of the first week in Australia, Elton's voice had started breaking down again. Gus Dudgeon, arriving to supervise the live album, was shocked by its sudden deterioration. 'He did two concerts in Perth that went fine, then on the third night, he was sitting in his dressing room beforehand, and suddenly found he couldn't speak at all. The concert had to be cancelled, and Elton was told by a doctor not to speak at all for four days. He had to go around with a little blackboard, writing down everything he wanted to say.'

The tour had been specially timed to allow Elton to follow the winter Test cricket series between England and Australia. He became the England touring team's unofficial mascot, supporting them at all their matches, joining their group pictures in baggy T-shirt, pads and cap. It was worth the whole trip to see them win back the Ashes from Australia after a tense final day's play in Melbourne. At the celebration party that night, he presided over a hired mobile disco as voluntary DJ.

Even his well-known hero worship of great sportsmen was now turned round to provide winks and nudges in the British tabloids. He had long been friendly with England's captain Ian Botham, a figure fully as controversial as any rock star. Euphoric after the Melbourne Test he gave an interview to a *Sun* journalist, chiefly for the purpose of answering back Botham's numerous attackers in the media. 'It's not just Ian's cricket I adore – it's his love of life, his generosity, his complete openness. I've only ever met one other person like him, and that was John Lennon.' *The Sun*'s double-page spread was headlined WHY I LOVE BEEFY BOTHAM, BY ELTON.

The approach of Christmas was celebrated with his usual expansiveness. All eighty-eight of his temporary colleagues in the Melbourne Symphony Orchestra received £500 Cartier watches. Ian Botham, recovering from an onfield injury, inspired a typical Elton jape. A Cartier bag was delivered to Botham, containing a cricketer's genital-protecting box. The *Daily Star*'s subsequent gossip paragraph should by rights have drawn the earliest libel writ. '. . . As for Elton, it is a box upon whose contents he will never be permitted to gaze. Still, it is the thought that counts.'

He was by now at Sydney Entertainment Centre, playing nightly to 12,000 people, with 101 musicians round him on the special set built for ABC's end-of-week telerecording. Gus Dudgeon stood by to mix the sound for ABC and also record tracks for the projected double live album, though increasingly alarmed by the worsening throat problem. 'After about a number and a half, it would start. It was just as if he'd got a faulty mike that kept cutting out, then coming on again. You'd see him singing with all his might, but there'd be no sound coming out. By the end of the first half of the show, it would seem to be all right. Then after the interval, when he came back as Mozart, it would start going again.'

After a third night of problems in Sydney, Elton was persuaded to forget about theatre doctors and honey-and-lemon remedies and consult a serious throat specialist. 'We were all in the bar at the Sebel Town House when he came back,' Gus Dudgeon remembers. 'He said, "They think it might be throat cancer." It was a terrible moment. Elton just stood there in the crowded bar and burst into tears. John Reid shut down the place there and then. He went round turfing everyone out, saying, "I'm sorry, the bar's closed", like a little Scots bouncer. What I remember was how totally supportive of Elton everyone was, from the band right down through the road crew. People might gripe about him and say, "He's a right little asshole" but as soon as he was in trouble, everyone was behind him all the way.'

Pending further examination and tests, the specialist's advice was to cease performing immediately. Elton, however, said he would finish the week's concerts in Sydney, do the ABC telerecording and make the live album.

By the end, no one close to him knew how he was managing to carry on. 'He was having these awful coughing fits right there onstage,' Gus Dudgeon says. 'Coughing up green stuff, red stuff, God knows what. When it got really bad, the lighting man had to turn the spotlights off him, so that the audience wouldn't see. By the end of each show, he'd be literally knee-deep in used Kleenexes.'

On the very last night, his resolution almost broke. He announced he wasn't going on – but then thought of the 12,000 audience, ABC's film and the live album. Strangely enough, that show, in his idiotic lamé teagowns and wigs, with the terror of cancer hanging over him, was the most brilliant of the whole tour. When Gus Dudgeon later came to choose album tracks from several nights'-worth of performance, almost all the best proved to be from the last night.

His duty done, Elton's only thought was to get back to England as fast as possible and seek a second opinion from a Harley Street specialist. He was warned, however, that going from Australian heat into London's December cold might make the trouble even worse. Instead, he flew to Canberra, to see John Tonkin, Australia's leading ear, nose and throat surgeon. Tonkin's examination revealed the presence of several tiny lesions, or nodules, clustered around Elton's vocal cords. If they proved malignant, he could expect to have his larynx removed and – at the most hopeful – be unable ever to sing or speak properly again.

He faced the prospect with all his deepest reserves of dogged Dwight courage. His chief concern was that, after the operation, he should be told immediately if it was cancer, and the full extent of the danger he would then face. He telephoned his mother in England, cheerily telling her he was fine and not to worry, and that he'd phone her again after his surgery, as soon as he was allowed to talk. He spent the last hours before going into hospital with conspicuous *sang-froid*, watching a one-day cricket match in Perth between England and the West Indies. 'I'm not in the least bit worried,' he said. 'It's a relief to have found a doctor who can help.' Only to a few close friends did he break down in tears and confess, 'I'm scared. I'm so scared.'

The operation was performed by John Tonkin at a private Sydney clinic on 6 January, 1987. The nodules proved to be benign, and easily and permanently cauterised by surgical laser-beam. On regaining consciousness, Elton was told he would make a full recovery and that, after a period of strict convalescence, his singing voice would not be affected.

He was inundated by get-well messages and telegrams, including one from Fergie, Duchess of York. It was reported in one paper that both Fergie and the Princess of Wales had written to Elton, begging him to have the operation. His Australian publicist, Patti Mostyn, dismissed the claim as 'ridiculous'.

He was no sooner discharged from hospital than rumours about his marriage erupted afresh in the British tabloids. A man facing an operation for suspected cancer would be expected to have his wife constantly at his bedside. But Renate, throughout the whole crisis, had remained 8,000 miles away, in Los Angeles.

'Superstar Elton John's marriage is on the rocks because of his bisexual lifestyle,' said the *Sunday People*, with the tabloid's usual blithe lack of any named source, on 11 January. 'Friends say he is now determined to get a divorce after spending just three days with his wife Renate in the past four months. Self-confessed bisexual Elton has been married nearly three years, but has always bluntly refused to give up his male friends.

'. . . A friend in Australia said last night, "Renate realised from the start what Elton was about, but she never realised he would completely shut her out. The crunch came when Elton demanded she come to Australia to be with him during his surgery. He only wanted her because the press thought it strange that she was in America while he was ailing. He exploded when she refused to come and is now more than ever determined to get a divorce . . . Renate, 31, has reportedly gone to great lengths to save her marriage, but over recent months Elton has shut her out of his life. He has admitted privately that he married her because he wanted children, but the couple haven't had any success. The friend added: "Elton realised he can't go on living a lie."'

It was unlucky that, just as the tabloids began quarrying into Elton's private life yet again, his name should be dragged into a particularly sordid Australian sex trial. A former policeman named David Moore, convicted at Brisbane Supreme Court for seducing teenage boys, was said to have boasted that Elton had once been a friend of his. According to the prosecution, Moore had used Elton's name merely to impress his victims, and there was no evidence they had ever met. None the less, a juicy footnote was provided to every insubstantiated press claim that 'flings' with men were what had fatally undermined Elton's marriage.

Next from *The Sun* was a 'world picture exclusive', showing Elton, in the aftermath of his throat surgery, aboard a boat cruising in Sydney Harbour. Seated beside him, as if in corroboration of everything ever alleged, insinuated or suspected, was – a man! 'Troubled rock star Elton John found a shoulder to cry on yesterday, as his best pal flew in to cheer him up,' *The Sun* reported with its usual meticulous choice of words. 'The friend in need is hunky bachelor Peter Ikin, who helped organise Elton's wedding to his now-estranged wife, Renate . . . And Elton needs a friend more than ever at the moment, as he reels from his MARRIAGE breakdown, his THROAT operation and being named in a sordid SEX case . . . Peter, a record company boss, took the lonely rock star for a three-hour boat trip around Sydney Harbour yesterday . . . David Brown, who shares a Sydney home with Peter, said "Whenever Elton is in town, he always spends time with Peter."'

The *News of the World*, on 18 January, claimed to have reached the heart of the matter: GAY ELTON WED TO PLEASE HIS MUM. The story that followed was a little masterpiece of the stilted police-court language which tabloid newspapers invent on their victims' behalf.

'Elton John sat down with his mother and frankly confessed the bad news. "I'm gay," he said. But then came the good news. "I'll still try to make you a grandma," he pledged.

'Now, as part of that amazing pact with his mum, the superstar will beg his estranged wife, Renate: "Let's stay married and try for the baby I crave." . . . For Elton is trapped between two women. WIFE Renate refuses to start a family unless Elton drops his self-confessed bisexual lifestyle. MUM Sheila Farebrother accepts her son has had male lovers, but is desperate for a grandchild . . . '

Renate, in Los Angeles, had succeeded in totally eluding the scores of journalists pursuing her. 'She has shunned the reflected limelight in a way that would be worthy of Greta Garbo,' *Today* admitted with a touch of grudging admiration. 'She is said to be working but on what is a mystery, even to her publicist, Sarah McMullen. All she will say is that Renate plans to fly to Sydney on January 22.'

Her father Joachim, in Munich, reportedly corroborated this intention. Elton was said to be spending £200,000 on chartering Sir Justin Hickey's luxury yacht *Lady Patricia* – 'a floating Paradise with mirrored master suite, bedroom ceiling included' – to take her on a cruising second honeymoon.

Instead, Renate flew back to Britain and, with an unpredictability worthy of her spouse, gave an exclusive interview to the *Daily Express*. Far from contemplating divorce, she said, Elton and she were planning a second marriage ceremony. 'I really don't know where these awful rumours started,' she told the *Express*'s Roger Taverner in the kitchen at Woodside. 'The truth is, we are as close as we ever were, and this is very close. The reason we are apart at the moment is that I must get on with my own career. Elton knows that and wants it that way.'

She revealed she had become a record producer in her own right, and was working on a single with her friend Sylvia Griffin, former lead singer with a band called Kissing the Pink and now another client of John Reid. Ms Griffin, a wide-awake blonde, was pictured with her at the studio control desk. Roger Taverner was even allowed to hear the demo they had made, a song called 'Lonely Heart', co-written by Elton and Gary Osborne.

Why had Renate not been at his bedside during the cancer scare in Australia? 'We talked about it for a long time before he went to the hospital for the tests. I had been told by the doctors that it was not serious. Elton said there was no need for me to be there. We agreed we would speak on the phone every day, which we do.'

In Australia, meanwhile, Elton joined Lionel Ritchie onstage, playing piano only, since still forbidden either to sing or speak. One

TV news report followed him through his hotel lobby, in a black satin suit and zebra-skin Nehru cap, clutching the child's scribbling board that was his only means of communication. 'Thanks for everything' he wrote on it to his audience, before giving a forced little smile and a thumbs-up sign and slipping through a half-opened door. His poorest and most ill-dressed fans were already starting to feel fortunate by comparison.

We can see, therefore, that what *The Sun* was shortly to unloose on Elton did not happen in isolation. For five or six years already, he had been the target of anti-gay smears and sneers in Britain's tabloid press, a public whipping-boy for the growing phobia about AIDS. The unwritten law that rock stars never sue allowed things to be written about him that in any other context would instantly have drawn libel writs. The *Express*, the *Star* the *People* and *News of the World* had all, at one time or another, had their knives into Elton. It was just that, true to form, *The Sun* sank lowest.

Early in 1987, the paper had received a tip-off from one of its network of paid spies and informers. The tip-off led to a nineteen-year-old male prostitute, or rent boy, named Stephen Hardy, who told a story calculated to make any *Sun* man salivate. He claimed to have attended gay parties at the home of Rod Stewart's manager, Billy Gaff, in Finchampstead, Berkshire, and to have been involved in drug-taking and homosexual orgies there with Elton John.

No one can object to a tabloid publishing an exposé, however nasty, if sufficient informed sources have been found to corroborate it. Behind the screaming headlines of old-fashioned scandal sheets could always be found the most meticulous delving and triple-checking. To *The Sun*, however, the word of Stephen Hardy was basis enough for another great coup in the tradition of GOTCHA! and FREDDIE STARR ATE MY HAMSTER. Hardy was paid £2,000 for his revelations, with further regular sweeteners of £250.

ELTON IN VICE BOYS SCANDAL was *The Sun*'s four-deck front page splash on 25 February. There followed the 'confession' of Stephen Hardy under the alias Graham X. He claimed to have been the pimp who had recruited teenage rent boys for parties at Billy Gaff's house, specifically as sexual partners for Gaff and Elton. Over a period of months, he said he had supplied 'at least ten youngsters, who were each paid a minimum of £100 each, plus all the cocaine they could stand'. According to Graham X, aided by *The Sun*'s distinctive typography, Elton 'LOVED his boys to be tattooed skinheads or punks with spiky hair, SNORTED cocaine throughout the orgies, which lasted up to four days, and BEGGED the teenagers to indulge in his bondage fantasies. The sordid rent-boy sessions began just eighteen months after Elton's highly publicised Valentine's Day marriage to German bride Renate Blauel.'

The story was presented not as an exultant soft-porn feast, but as a solemn moral duty, with Graham X, in the bosom of *The Sun*, now reformed and penitent. 'I am ashamed of what I did . . . I am speaking out to show how widespread this sort of thing is and to warn other gullible young kids to steer clear of people like these.'

Inside, hammering home the moral message, was a double-page spread, ELTON'S LUST FOR BONDAGE, in which Graham X 'confessed' to his own sexual encounters with Elton at Billy Gaff's house. He said that on the first occasion, Elton had been lying on a bed in a pair of skimpy leather shorts, 'looking like Cleopatra and twirling a sex aid between his fingers'. He claimed he had been shown bondage accessories, and that Elton had fantasised about tying him to a tree in the woods before making love to him. On a later occasion, he said, he had witnessed a foursome between Elton, Billy Gaff and two rent boys, which had ended with them swapping partners.

Ironically, it was none of this spun-out sleaze, but the spurious attempts to give it social uplift, which would prove *The Sun*'s undoing. In a foot-of-page 'box' story, Graham X told how he had repented his rent-boy life after falling in love with a girl, but had carried out one final pimping mission to pay for their engagement ring. So 'he took two youngsters to Gaff's home on 30 April last year. It was the last time he saw Elton.'

It was the only specific date mentioned in the whole story, and in *The Sun*'s own office there was someone who recognised it as deeply unsafe. Nina Myskow had returned to the paper a few months earlier after a stint as TV critic for the *Sunday People*. Knowing she was a long-time friend of Elton, *The Sun*'s legal adviser showed her the Graham X copy a couple of weeks before publication. Nina still kept up with Elton intermittently and was sure she remembered that on 30 April, 1986, he and his assistant Bob Halley had both been out of Britain. 'I said, "If you're going to go with this stuff, for God's sake make sure you check and double check that date."' Her advice fell on deaf ears.

In fact, on 30 April, 1986 – as many more of his friends, like Bryan Forbes, remembered – Elton had been in New York, staying at the Carlyle Hotel. He had had lunch with his old confidant Tony King, then gone to see his costume designer, Bill Mackie. Any number of people could confirm that he had remained in New York one further night, flying home, with Bob Halley, by Concorde early on 1 May.

That one slip, if nothing else, opened up *The Sun* to a massive libel suit. Even so, there were those around Elton who urged him in the strongest terms not to sue. Mick Jagger, in particular, phoned to warn against it, citing his own experience with the *News of the World* twenty years earlier. That, too, had arisen from the grossest of factual errors. Jagger had been accused of boasting about his drug consumption in an interview with two *News of the World* reporters who did not realise they were actually talking to another Rolling Stone, Brian Jones. Jagger had issued a libel writ, only to be followed and spied on by the paper until finally set up for the Redlands drug bust that led to his and Keith Richard's imprisonment. If Elton tried to fight *The Sun*, even on this seemingly winnable count, what campaign of still dirtier tricks could be expected before the case finally came to court? In Jagger's view, the best course was to follow rock-star precedent since 1967, and just take it until it stopped.

Elton disagreed. On the day of *The Sun*'s first Graham X stories, a writ for libel arrived from his solicitors, Frere Cholmeley. So full of confident glee was the paper at this stage that its second front-page Elton John 'world exclusive', next morning, bore an additional come-on tag: 'The story they're all suing over'.

In this instalment, ELTON'S KINKY KICKS, Graham X claimed that Elton would snort cocaine through rolled-up $100 bills 'to set himself up for orgies with rent boys', and that he insisted his youthful partners also be 'drugged with vast amounts of coke before they were brought to his bed'. A second inside spread, ELTON'S DRUG CAPERS, alleged, through Graham X, that Elton would take as many as three 'lines' of cocaine in an hour, sometimes dividing it up with an American Express Gold credit card, and throwing the $100 bills away after he'd used them. Here, too, the nineteen-year-old uneducated rent boy expanded into psychological analysis. 'It was as though he needed the drug as a crutch because he believed in some strange way that the boys wouldn't talk to him if he wasn't stoned on drugs.'

A bold-type side bar announced, on a note of palpable triumph, that Elton was suing over the first day's story and that his lawyers had unsuccessfully sought a High Court injunction to halt the series. Continuing the public service motif, it was said that Scotland Yard had begun an investigation into the whole matter, and were preparing to interrogate Graham X. 'Tomorrow . . .' a streamer at the bottom promised, 'Elton's Pink Tutu Party'.

The Sun's chief rival, the *Daily Mirror*, had by now also thrown its hat into the ring. The *Mirror* still retained some shreds of its old decency, and had not gone quite as far as other tabloids in the recent spate of gay-bashing. It would, besides, do anything in its power to wound, insult or embarrass *The Sun*. So, on 26 February, as ELTON'S

KINKY KICKS hit the streets, the *Mirror* came trumpeting to his defence. A page-five story set out the evidence that Elton could not possibly have attended a homosexual orgy in Berkshire on 30 April, 1986, because at the time he was 5,000 miles away in New York.

A 'detailed examination of the star's diary' – which only Elton's own office could have made possible – reconstructed almost his entire day's itinerary. There were confirmed sightings of him all around Manhattan, from the *New York Daily News*, his clothes designer, Bill Mackie, even a restaurant that had turned him away for refusing to remove his hat. There was also a statement from Billy Gaff, who not only denied that Elton had ever been at his house but could prove that at the time of the alleged orgy, he, too, had been out of Britain. That day, Gaff said, in one of the saga's more delectable touches, he had been flying home from the Philippines 'after meetings with the vice president to discuss a new national anthem'.

The *Mirror* was not about to let *The Sun* off the hook. Next morning, it produced a second story, THE BIG LIE, offering documentary proof that Elton had not returned from New York to Britain until 1 May, 1986. The *Mirror* had found his and Bob Halley's names on the passenger list for Concorde's 9.30 am flight, and obtained a copy of the invoice from the limousine company that took them to JFK Airport. On the Concorde manifest, Elton's name bore a special notation, 'famous singer', in case he should not be recognised. The airport limo had been driven by a man named Walt.

The Sun, meanwhile, had adopted the time-honoured voice of editorial courage, and was 'standing by' its story. Instead of the promised revelations about a 'pink tutu party', its third Graham X instalment was the rent boy's retort that 'Elton can say what he likes, but deep in his heart he knows I'm telling 100 per cent the truth [*sic*]. I know why he is saying he has never met me or been to bed with boys I supplied for him and Billy Gaff. He wants to protect his image as the Royal favourite, loved by millions of fans. I'm sorry to have to tell his wife, but he did have sex with the teenagers I brought to Gaff's home . . .' The front-page headline – that familiar *Sun* device of turning quote into editorial comment – was YOU'RE A LIAR, ELTON!

The slip-up over the date was certainly unfortunate. But *The Sun* had infinite faith in its own power as a newsprint bludgeon. It believed that if it kept hitting Elton, he would eventually cave in, the way people always did. The chance of eventually winding up in court would be of little account against the damage suffered meantime, not just by the victim himself but also by his family, business associates and friends.

Elton was aware of all the risks. He knew what a drawn-out battle with a ruthless tabloid might do to his mother and stepfather, and the many other respectable, inoffensive members of his family. He knew what it might do to the football club in whose junior enclosure he had often appeared, presenting children with Easter eggs. He knew what it might do to his social life and cherished royal connections. Above all, he knew what it might do to his already strained and vulnerable marriage. His biggest fear, Nina Myskow remembers, was that Renate would be hurt.

None the less, the dogged Dwight chin was firmly stuck out. ELTON'S KINKY CAPERS brought a second libel writ. YOU'RE A LIAR, ELTON brought a third. Estimates of the damages he would be seeking rose from £5 million to £20 million. His solicitor, Frank Presland, said that as long as the Graham X series continued, the writs would keep on coming.

Elton himself, still in Australia, put on a light-hearted front. Acting as MC at a record-awards ceremony, he was defiantly full of his usual camp one-liners. A female guest admired a brooch he was wearing. 'You get one of those when you sleep with a queen,' Elton told her. To a male guest he said he'd always thought 'bondage' was a surfers' beach in Sydney. His hair had become platinum blond, cut in a star shape high above the ears. 'Blondes have more fun,' he explained.

The only press interview he would give was to John Blake, who had written the *Daily Mirror*'s BIG LIE story. This time there was no joking. 'I have travelled the world and seen a lot of things, but I have never even heard of any orgies with underage boys. And I swear I have never, ever seen anything like the things that were described. The outfits I was supposed to have worn, and all of the rest of it, were just plain ridiculous.

'No matter what happens, I will go into court, swear on the Bible and tell the truth about everything. I'm going to nail the paper that wrote all those lies. I'm doing it to clear my name, not for the money. But £50 million would not be enough to compensate for all the harm they have done me . . . I don't care what comes out in court about my life. They can throw every single thing at me, and I'll still nail them.'

He said he would be returning to Britain to face up to *The Sun*, and celebrate his fortieth birthday on 25 March. 'And it's also about time I saw the wife again . . . We've had to put up with an awful lot of nonsense during our time apart. But the fact is, our marriage is fine. I love her, she loves me, and we are happy . . . It was arranged before Christmas that we would have to spend these months apart . . . Renate has been in the studio with a girl singer, and she's been working very hard. If you are in the Air Force, you are often away from your wife for six or seven months at a time. And, really, it's pretty much the same for me.'

One had to know about Elton's father, and how his absences in the Royal Air Force during the Fifties helped create a lonely, obsessive, insecure small boy, to relish the full poignancy of that.

18

Reg Strikes Back

ELTON'S fortieth birthday party was held at Lockwood House, a ten-bedroomed Georgian mansion which John Reid had lately acquired, near Rickmansworth, Hertfordshire. NATO-style security surrounded a bash as munificent as any thrown by Rocket in the spendthrift Seventies. Guards with Doberman pinscher dogs checked passes before allowing access to the lit-up house and the five marquees in its grounds. The 350 guests included rock superstars George Harrison, Ringo Starr, Eric Clapton, Phil Collins, Bob Geldof, and Lionel Ritchie, designer Zandra Rhodes, actor Sir John Mills, actresses Hazel O'Connor and Britt Ekland, film directors Ken Russell and Michael Winner, impresarios Richard Branson and Mickie Most, local MP Tristan Garel-Jones and the entire Watford football team. Just before midnight, the Duke and Duchess of York arrived, racing up the drive in a chauffeur-driven Jaguar, followed by a car full of armed Special Branch men. 'The Yorks', at least, seemed unworried by what *The Sun* said.

The party was also expected to be a grand public reunion for Elton and Renate. He arrived alone, however, and before long it became painfully obvious that Renate would not be joining him. Friends who asked after her were told that she'd gone down with flu.

Elton seemed in good spirits none the less, cutting his sarcophagus-sized birthday cake and pulling pink ribbons from the £80,000 Ferrari Testarossa sports car that was John Reid's present. A chorus of 'Happy birthday to you' from an ad hoc supergroup including two ex-Beatles showed how solidly behind him were all his music business friends. In his speech he apologised for Renate's absence, showing off an antique diamond and ruby watch which he said she had given him. His only allusion to other current troubles was to sing a few bars of 'My Way'.

Afterwards there was a firework display which awoke patients in nearby Mount Vernon Hospital and brought two fire engines racing to the scene. Police received over a hundred calls from disturbed local residents, some of whom believed the nearby air base at Northwood to be under attack.

Renate's non-appearance on such a night could lead to only one conclusion. It was confirmed next day by a press announcement from John Reid's office. Elton and Renate had decided to 'continue living apart', though there were no plans at present for a divorce and they remained on 'very good personal terms'. In particular it was emphasised that the separation had nothing to do with *The Sun*'s rent-boy claims, which had come after their decision to part and which both found 'deeply distressing and intrusive'.

Fleet Street's wolf pack were not long in providing background details. Renate had already left Woodside and was to move into a £300,000 flat, bought and decorated for her by Elton, in Adam and Eve Mews, Kensington. Lawyers were said to be at work on a divorce settlement after Renate had turned down Elton's original offer of £2 million.

All the stories mentioned Renate's friendship with Sylvia Griffin, clearly implying a lesbian relationship. Though neither could be found, it was safe to assume, in kindergarten tabloidese, that Elton's fugitive wife was being 'comforted' by her 'close pal'. The *News of the World* claimed the marriage had latterly become a *ménage à trois*, with Elton lavishing expensive gifts on Sylvia, even allowing her to accompany Renate and him on holiday. '. . . A close friend of Sylvia believes that Renate turned more and more to her as the strain of marriage to bisexual Elton took its toll . . . Now she and Renate are believed to be planning a get-away-from-it-all break together, probably in California . . .' A second *News of the World* 'exclusive', ELTON WEEPS ON FERGIE'S SHOULDER, said he had spent much of his fortieth birthday party pouring out his marital troubles to a sympathetic Duchess of York.

The Sun's coverage managed to combine voyeuristic relish at the split with sycophantic slavering over Fergie's presence at the party, and further stabs at Elton on the rent-boy question. The front-page splash, ELTON ENDS SHAM MARRIAGE, made it all seem the inevitable result of Graham X's revelations, and promised a further 'dossier' linking Elton with teenage boys 'back to the 1970s'. The centre spread, A MARRIAGE BUILT ON LIES, listed all Elton and Renate's previous press quotes about their marriage, each with the word LIE beside it. The implication was that his word about rent-boys could not be believed either. On the same page, schizophrenically, was ROYAL RAVER! FERGIE'S NIGHT OF STAR MAGIC. (Completing the flavour of that day's edition, one could turn to a story about Japanese imports to Britain, headed HOW THE NIPS DO US DOWN.)

Outwardly, *The Sun* appeared as brassily confident as ever. But behind the death-dealing three-inch heads and white-on-black thunderbolts, things were starting to go awry. In particular, twinges of scepticism were tardily being felt about that 'world exclusive's' one and only source. It was finally borne in on *The Sun*'s great editorial brains that a hard-up rent boy might not be the most reliable or truthful person.

To stop rival papers getting to Stephen Hardy, a task force of *Sun* heavies had smuggled him, his girlfriend and their baby out of Britain, keeping them for a month at secret addresses in Paris, Malaga and Gibraltar. All this effort and expense was wasted, however, when the *Daily Star* found a gay picture magazine named *Vulcan* for which Hardy had posed three years earlier. EXPOSED! THE WORM THAT TURNED ON ELTON, chortled the *Star*. The two unedifying pictures of a scrawny nude boy were accompanied by character notes that caused further wincing over at *The Sun*'s Wapping fortress. 'When he walked through the door, we knew he was trouble,' said a man who had been at the *Vulcan* photo session. 'He is capable of doing anything for money.'

The obvious urgent need, if Graham X could not be trusted, was to find other rent boys able to tell the same tale. In earlier times, such work would have been entrusted to hard-digging reporters. *The Sun*, however, chose as its investigator a young Scot named John Boyce, a former rent boy who professed nine criminal convictions for fraud and one for attempted murder. Boyce was offered £1,750 for every signed affidavit he could deliver from a rent boy claiming to have slept with Elton. Of this, the rent boy would receive £500 while Boyce pocketed the remainder. He later described his work method in a television interview: 'We used to bring people to hotel rooms and they would tell us that they had an affair with Elton John and, you know . . . I mean it was all pure crap.'

Besides which, the game plan against Elton, mysteriously, wasn't working. *The Sun* was hitting him with everything it had, but he still wasn't turning tail and running. Every new 'world exclusive' that was expected to produce a hasty climb-down instead produced a further libel writ. The more people urged him to give in and cut his losses, the more resolute Elton became. He would repeat what he had said on the phone to Mick Jagger's advice that it wasn't worth it. 'They can say I'm a fat old sod, they can say I'm an untalented bastard, they can call me a poof, but they musn't lie about me because I'm going to fight. And I'm determined to be a winner.'

On 13 April, *The Sun* struck again with ELTON PROBE: HEAVY MOB MOVE IN. The story was that gay men who had agreed to co-operate in the 'Elton John investigation' were now suffering 'vicious attacks and threats of violence'. One 'gay couple' had had their house broken into, their furniture smashed and dog excrement smeared on the walls, and a message for the *Sun* informant had been left behind: 'It will be his kneecaps, not the furniture next time'. A second 'witness' was said to have been warned via a phone call to his elderly mother to 'keep his nose out of other people's business or we'll cut it off for him'. A third had been menaced by 'heavies' in a pub and 'several more' had received threatening phone-calls.

'There is no evidence to suggest that Elton is aware of these attacks,' *The Sun* continued magnanimously. 'But it is known that certain violent elements of the pop-gay community [*sic*] are incensed by our revelations.' Readers were left to draw their own conclusions from a picture of Elton in gangster-looking dark glasses, over a sub-head SINGING TO BEAT A KILLER which only close inspection revealed to be unconnected with the criminal underworld. 'Elton sings at Wednesday's AIDS fund-raising concert in London,' the caption noted in a miniature classic of weasel prose. 'Friends say he would be horrified to think people were threatening gays in revenge for *The Sun*'s revelations about his escapades with rent boys.'

With libel writs out, both sides were under legal obligation not to comment further on the case. *The Sun*, however, showed no sign of honouring the *sub judice* rule. And pressure was growing on Elton to make some kind of public statement about the torrent of accusations against him.

Television was clearly the only medium that could hope to equal *The Sun*'s massive daily circulation. It was, besides, the medium in which Elton had always most excelled. He therefore turned to his old friend Michael Parkinson who, though no longer a prime-time chat-show host, was still among Britain's best-liked TV interviewers. It was agreed that he should appear on Parkinson's Yorkshire Television show *One to One*. The programme was recorded before a studio audience on 14 April for network transmission on 2 May.

The Sun, meanwhile, was still straining every muscle and resource to trawl up further filth on Elton. At one point, a tip-off came that he was to meet his mother for lunch at an out-of-town restaurant. *The Sun* sent so many spies to eavesdrop that there was no room in the restaurant for their quarry, who had to be put into an overflow establishment down the road. In any case, the target proved to be only Sheila Farebrother and someone from John Reid's office. Elton himself was not even in the country at the time.

In mid-April, the operation seemed to strike paydirt. A person was found who claimed to be an ex-lover of Elton's, but who this time offered evidence in the form of three Polaroid photographs. In a hush-

hush operation that would have done credit to John le Carré, *The Sun* bought the Polaroids for £10,000.

Before publishing them, as a cat might toy with a mouse, it made sure that Elton himself received copies. His lawyers at the time had been seeking a High Court injunction to prevent any further 'revelations' from appearing. To *The Sun*'s added triumph, this was now abandoned.

ELTON PORN PHOTO SHAME hit the streets on Thursday 16 April. With the splash headline went a fuzzy nude shot of Elton in sunglasses, cropped at the waistline. Inside was a somewhat clearer head and shoulders shot of him in a striped football shirt, his arm round the shoulders of a boy cuddling what seemed to be a pillow. The third polaroid allegedly showed him 'having sex with a young man'. This, *The Sun* breathtakingly said, was 'too disgusting to be printed in a family newspaper'.

The treasure trove was not quite what it had first appeared. As Elton's physique and, even more, his hairline showed, the Polaroids had been taken years earlier, possibly as long ago as 1976. In those far-off liberal times, several famous gay men had posed as full frontal nudes, most famously the painter David Hockney. In the unpublished sex-shot, the other participant was someone clearly old enough to be acceptable under the law as a 'consenting adult'. As to the boy Elton was shown cuddling, *The Sun*'s own caption readily admitted: 'There is no suggestion of any sexual liaison between them'.

The polaroids, however embarrassing, were merely evidence of the bisexuality which Elton had freely admitted eleven years before. They had no connection with Graham X or rent boys and, in particular, none with the patently untrue claim that Elton had attended a cocaine and rent-boy orgy at Billy Gaff's house on 30 April, 1986.

In this issue a new informant, 'Malcolm M', described as a '19-year-old artist', claimed he had been involved in 'a sordid five-day gay sex and cocaine orgy' with Elton and another man at Woodside during 'the early Eighties'. In *The Sun*'s familiar typographical style, Malcolm M claimed that Elton 'PLIED him with massive amounts of cocaine, cannabis and champagne, PERSUADED him to perform horrible gay perversions, COMMITTED other degrading sex acts on him, FLEW in another gay lover to take part in a three-in-a-bed homosexual session, and INVITED the teenager to fly to Paris to continue the orgy.' The 'five-day bash', with a Californian surfer named as Vance, was said to have happened at a time when Elton was filming at Shepperton studios. 'I had to control my laughter,' Malcolm M was quoted as saying. 'Elton John was the biggest pop star going and all he wanted to do was to be degraded. He looked pathetic, stretched out there on the green carpet.'

The ELTON'S FIVE-DAY ORGY centre spread featured a new departure – a *Sun* editorial, denouncing Elton and praising the paper's own courage and steadfast championing of truth and light:

> Elton John is a pop star of great talent.
>
> His gifts have earned him riches and the adulation of millions.
>
> But he is not entitled to live above the law.
>
> In February, *The Sun* published a series on his lifestyle. It was not a pretty story.
>
> ### Threatened
>
> It involved drug-taking and illegal homosexual exploits with young boys.
>
> Elton's reply was volcanic. It was LIES he said, and he threatened to sue *The Sun* for £20 million.
>
> Other newspapers, less concerned with the truth than with their dreadful circulation figures, tried to take advantage by supporting his campaign against us. The singer assembled a battery of lawyers to muzzle us. Then we received fresh evidence in the shape of porno-graphic pictures showing Elton involved in sex with a young man.
>
> The lawyers dropped their action as eagerly as a patron saint denounces sin.
>
> *The Sun* has no hard feelings towards Elton John. We wish him no ill. Certainly, we shall never pursue him maliciously.
>
> But he must stop telling LIES about *The Sun*.
>
> In return, we shall stop telling the TRUTH about him.

Next day, 16 April, came I RAN COKE FOR ELTON. A twenty-seven-year-old 'showbiz executive', codename John D, claimed to have taken Elton supplies of cocaine, for which he was sometimes so eager that he 'tore at the packet with his teeth'. John D was said to have worked as an office boy at Rocket Records, and there to have witnessed 'much drug-abuse and homosexual activity' between Elton and various young men. Like Graham X and Malcolm M, John D was now a reformed character, speaking to his tabloid father confessor only for the greater public good. 'I very much regret getting involved with drugs and the Elton John scene. I'm lucky to be alive.'

Overleaf on page six could be found a fine example of *Sun* cartoon humour. A crudely drawn fat figure in straw boater and large spectacles was shown vanishing into a cupboard labelled 'Closet'. 'I'm not coming out again 'til this lot's all over,' the caption read.

With public interest in the affair at its height, Yorkshire TV had hastily brought forward transmission of Elton's interview with Michael Parkinson from 2 May to 18 April. *The Sun* knew in advance much of what he would say and, that morning, spoke in another editorial:

> *The Sun* urges its 12 million readers to sit down tonight and watch Elton John's performance on the Michael Parkinson show.
>
> Not since Vivien Leigh in *Gone With the Wind* has there been such an extraordinary piece of acting.
>
> For Mr John is lying through his back teeth. HE knows it, his MANAGEMENT knows it and his FRIENDS know it.

> Sickening

> But in a desperate attempt to bamboozle fans and family alike, he claims our sex and drug allegations are all lies.
>
> His public denials are as sickening as his private perversions.
>
> If you believe Elton, you'll believe in fairies.

Onscreen that night, Michael Parkinson faced a haggard and dejected-looking figure. Since last seen in public, Elton had acquired a thick growth of beard. He was, for him, drably dressed, in a shapeless flying suit and red Watford FC baseball cap. None would have recognised the silver-clad Rocket Man who used to trip forth on four-inch platforms in Parkinson shows of the happy Seventies.

It was the gentlest possible interrogation by a plainly sympathetic old friend, but Elton still put up an impressive performance. He repeated that *The Sun*'s allegations were 'all lies', and he intended to prove so in court, no matter what the toll on him and his family. He revealed that Sheila, 'at the end of her tether' with scandal and press harassment, had decided to emigrate to Spain. He himself was being followed and spied on and, during a recent trip to America, had actually found an electronic bug in his hotel suite. There had even been attempts to persuade Renate's doctor to reveal confidential medical details about him. 'They probably want to examine my sperm,' Elton said. 'You would have thought they had buckets of the stuff.' The studio audience, and viewers at home, loved it.

He said he would be going to Los Angeles for a few months, but denied he intended to settle there permanently. He also denied recent press reports that he intended to sell Watford. 'The reason I would never sell . . . is because they are people who would fight and die for me.'

The real revelation, however, was that he had spent the past week with Renate, who would be awaiting him afterwards back in Old Windsor. 'We're really good friends,' Elton said. 'The marriage isn't over *per se*. We've just separated for a little while ... We're known as the Odd Couple, apparently. That's fair enough. But we still get on very well with each other. I still love her. She still loves me.'

I STILL LOVE MY RENATE! was *The Sun*'s headline, under a white-on-black flash STRANGE BUT TRUE.

Lady Choc Ice had, indeed, come back, as an announcement from John Reid's office confirmed soon afterwards. She had kept in constant touch with Elton in their month apart, making it clear she did not believe a word of *The Sun*'s stories. 'The lady's dignity throughout the whole thing taught me a hell of a lot,' Elton admitted. 'Her faith in me never wavered for a minute. So something good came out of it.'

Renate was resolutely by his side once more at Watford that May, as he watched the closing games of the 1986–87 football season. He was determined that *The Sun*'s campaign should not drive him into hiding and, in particular, not spoil his life's chief pleasure and pride.

Watford's attitude to his troubles gave Elton much heart. *The Sun*'s soccer-thug taunts found few echoes on the Vicarage Road terraces. Scores of letters came in from ordinary supporters whose young sons and daughters used the family enclosure. Their message was nearly always the same. What Elton did in his private life was his business so long as he continued to behave with dignity as chairman of Watford.

Nor did all this ghastly personal publicity seem to have any adverse effect on Watford's performance or morale. The Vicarage Road ground now boasted a new £2.2 million west grandstand – largely paid for by Elton – and attendance and receipts were at an all-time high. In 1986, Watford had made a second bid for Wembley glory, reaching the quarter-final of the FA Cup before losing to mighty Liverpool. This year, they had won right through to the semi-final, going down at last 4–1 to Tottenham Hotspur.

A double blow to Watford and Elton personally came in May, when Graham Taylor resigned his managership to join Second Division Aston Villa. His explanation was that, after ten triumphant years with Elton at Watford, it was time to move on to a fresh challenge. Elton was magnanimous over the loss of a partner as important to him, in many ways, as Bernie Taupin had once been. Though three years of Taylor's Watford contract remained, no compensation was sought from Aston Villa. So Graham Taylor left

Vicarage Road and embarked on the route which, three years later, would lead him to managership of England.

Elton maintained his deliberately high profile with Watford, welcoming Taylor's replacement, Dave Bassett, and announcing that he would accompany the team on their second tour of China that August. At the welcome party for Bassett, he joked that he'd thought of standing in the imminent general election, but 'after all the recent publicity, my chances might not have been too great'. Some tabloid photographers shouted to him and Dave Bassett, a good-looking young Cockney, to move closer together. 'Now come on, don't start that,' Elton snapped.

Interspersed with scandal and smear were Elton stories that could still raise the old familiar smile. In August he took another step from his Pinner origins by acquiring a coat of arms. Two years had been spent by an artist at the College of Heralds on focusing all things associated with Elton John into a heraldic device. A shield with a black-and-white piano keyboard top was surmounted by a figure of Pan playing blue pipes (for Bluesology) with a golden football caught under one hoof. The shield's lower part was 'gules and or', ie Watford's colours of red and gold. The motto beneath was a pun in Spanish, *El Tono es bueno*: The Music, or Elton, is good.

In Beijing with the Watford touring team, he announced that his vocal chords had totally recovered from their recent surgery. 'At one point, about two months after the operation, I was very frightened because I couldn't get any falsettos. I think my voice is lower in pitch, but I've got my falsettos back.' He said he would be giving his voice 'at least a year and a bit off' and meanwhile planned to write music, for stage or screen. He had already been asked to score a film about Peter Wright, the former MI5 man whose book *Spycatcher* was currently embarrassing the Thatcher government.

His only record releases for 1987 were the *Live in Australia* album and, as a single, the stage version of 'Your Song' he had managed to perform in his Mozart wig and beauty spot before his voice totally collapsed. Having pulled off another brilliant technical production for him, Gus Dudgeon was astonished to be dispensed with yet again. 'I remember, I went to Renate's birthday party, and Elton was really friendly,' Dudgeon says. ' "You and I are a team," he told me. "We'll always work together." As I was leaving, I saw John Reid give me a peculiar look. I said to my wife, "I've been dropped." And sure enough, I had.'

Elton seemed overjoyed to be with Renate again, showering her with expensive presents and splurging on exotic fitments for the home that was going to work this time. John Reid's managerial acquisitions now included Princess Margaret's son Viscount Linley, who had emerged as a fashionable Chelsea furniture designer. The viscount was commissioned to build a new marital bed for Elton and Renate to replace their Empress Josephine replica. Delivered in October, the Linley bed was a sumptuous affair, with towered and battlemented half-screens and E and R initials entwined on its headboard. With it came an equally regal bill for £75,000.

They seemed a united and even carefree couple early that month, when Elton received a special award from the American Society of Composers, Authors and Publishers for twenty years' achievement in music. Renate was pictured kissing him over his Golden Note statuette, both of them looking as bemusedly happy as on their wedding day.

In private, however, Elton's battle with *The Sun* was taking a heavy toll. After publication of the Polaroid pictures, and the allegations of Malcolm M and John D, his lawyers had issued two more libel writs. Two had also been issued against the *Daily Star*, for repeating the alleged defamation. With the pile of writs already against *The Sun*, that brought the grand total to twelve.

Since February, he had received hundreds of letters from friends and fans alike, sympathising with his ordeal and expressing revulsion at what *The Sun* was doing. The punctilious good boy wrote back to everyone personally, often sending flowers along with his note. He was continually amazed to discover how much he was loved, and what little difference smearing headlines made to that.

None the less, some of the mud was sticking. Just before *The Sun*'s onslaught, Elton had made a series of television commercials for Cadbury's chunky chocolate bars. Britain's chocolate companies were almost all founded by Quakers, and the possible effect of ELTON'S KINKY KICKS on chunky bar family sales had the Cadbury's men quaking in their boots. The TV ads were cancelled forthwith.

Though other papers dared not join *The Sun*'s frontal attack, there was constant sniggering and swiping from the sidelines. One gossip columnist managed to inject homophobia even into a report that Elton and John Reid had visited the White House, and had tea with President Reagan. 'I wonder who was mother?' the writer concluded archly. Another vicious little paragraph noted that Elton was looking for a new house in Los Angeles, and commended the one formerly owned by Rock Hudson. It was just a few months since Hudson's death, ravaged by AIDS.

Cruellest of all was a *News of the World* story that, but for the rent-boy allegations, Elton would have received a knighthood in the Queen's Birthday Honours. He himself was said to have confided to 'friends' that the scandal had 'destroyed his close friendship with the Royal Family'. Prince Andrew, Fergie and the other pop-loving 'young Royals' had allegedly been banned from mixing socially with him ever again. 'The Yorks' had defied this ban by attending his fortieth birthday party and in so doing, had 'infuriated' the Queen and Prince Philip. But 'kind-hearted Fergie did accept a phone call from the tormented singer last week. He called her at a villa in Barbados, where she was on holiday, and cried down the line about his troubles while she tried to reassure him . . . The Duchess told him she did not believe [the] allegations . . . But she admitted that she could not see him in the near future, and had no plans to do so . . . A member of the Royal Household said: "It's quite inconceivable that any member of the family could recognise Elton John after this . . . I can't think that the Queen could give him any honour now, though he was certainly in line for one." '

There were those around Elton who seriously doubted whether he could survive all this punishment. Especially fearful were those who remembered two suicide attempts, at moments of far less extremity. As an unnamed 'friend' gloomily put it in one interview: '*The Sun* might just as well have sent him a rope and told him to get on with it.'

Much of the time, he was resolutely upbeat. He knew that at the end of the road, as things stood, was a massive court case that would inflict incalculable further damage on himself and his family. He would be obliged to go into the witness-box and allow his private life to be dissected for days on end by some ruthless, supercilious QC. Whatever the personal and financial cost – and whatever the pragmatic legal advice – he was determined not only to survive but come out a winner.

On other days, his resolve would collapse, and engulfing despair come flooding in. 'I hardly went out, because I couldn't stop crying,' he later admitted. 'One minute I'd be fine, the next – "waaaa". I'd get up, have breakfast, then go back to bed. Eat ice lollies and watch TV all day.' In his depression, he was eating 'six times what I should have' and drinking more heavily than ever in his life. 'I started drinking vodka martinis. You're supposed to sip them . . . but I used to just woosh them back. I would need three or four before I went out in the evening. Then I'd go on to red wine.'

Bernie Taupin recognised the danger signs, having been through his own bout of runaway drinking ten years before. After a party for John Reid's father, at which Elton was scarcely coherent, Bernie told him what no one else would dare. 'I've never seen you so embarrassing as you were last night. If I'd had a tape recorder with me, you'd never drink again.'

At the nadir, he locked himself in his suite and remained there for almost a week, refusing all entreaties to open the door. Alarm grew that he might be about to do something desperate. The situation was saved by Renate, who ran outside, got a ladder, climbed up to his window and tapped on it. Elton was instantly shaken out of his black mood. 'He thought it was wonderful that someone cared enough about him to do that,' Nina Myskow remembers. '"And she's scared of heights," he kept saying. He couldn't get over it.'

On Remembrance Sunday, 1987, IRA terrorists bombed a church parade at Enniskillen, Northern Ireland. Among those fatally injured was a young nurse named Marie Wilson. Her father, Gordon Wilson, later gave a moving TV interview in which he described holding her hand in the rubble and talking to her as she lay dying.

Seeing and hearing Gordon Wilson was what brought Elton conclusively round from his glooms, forebodings and despair. 'That man was so forgiving, so gracious . . . I thought, "Christ, this is what courage is about. Elton, just shut up, will you. Shut up immediately and get back to work."'

Meanwhile, within the barbed-wired compound at Wapping, all was far from well. *The Sun* had believed its gamble on the rent-boy story would be justified by huge rises in circulation. But its marketing people reported a strange phenomenon. On days when it ran an Elton John exposé, circulation actually fell. On *pièce de résistance* issues like ELTON PORN PHOTO SHAME the fall could be as much as 200,000 copies. When no Elton John story occupied the front page, sales returned to normal once more.

The fact was that even *Sun* readers, who otherwise seldom balked at their daily dose of brute prejudice and leering smut, did not like seeing Elton on the rack. Seventeen years of being publicly decent, sane and positive – as well as adding immeasurably to life's fun – paid off for him now in spectacular dividends. Even those whom the 'revelation' had titillated at first, soon wearied of their grinding overkill. *The Sun* had lost what credibility it ever had as a moral crusader, and merely seemed to be pursuing a vendetta.

The paper's proprietor Rupert Murdoch – whom Elton described as 'a praying mantis' – had always hitherto allowed it to rampage unchecked. But even Murdoch was becoming concerned that the exposés could do him more harm than good. His media empire in America and Australia included many TV stations that could well suffer retaliatory withdrawal of Elton concert films and videos. As a rule, libel actions against his newspapers represented the merest small change to Rupert Murdoch. But he seems to have had a premonition, long before any of his hapless minions, that this one would cost him dear.

In July 1987, the stakes in the game were raised dramatically. The novelist Jeffrey Archer had sued the *Daily Star* for a story alleging he was involved with a London call-girl. A drawn-out and spectacular High Court trial found against the *Star* and, by bizarre custom, left the amount of Archer's damages to be set by the jury. They awarded him half a million pounds, the largest libel damages in British legal history. Those at Wapping who had felt uneasy twinges about the Elton John affair began feeling them with redoubled force.

Yet the 'investigators' were still allowed to go about their business. And on 28 September, as surely as one of its own much-derided 'Japs', the paper took a long curved knife and publicly disembowelled itself.

Its reporter in the Thames Valley, covering Old Windsor, filed a story that two Rottweiler guard dogs on Elton's estate had had their 'voice boxes sliced through' to prevent them barking. With the story – a revealing insight into *The Sun*'s editorial procedures – came a note from the reporter saying he was 'not 100 per cent sure' it was true.

MYSTERY OF ELTON'S SILENT DOGS led the next day's paper none the less, under a thin guise of concern for dumb animals. RSPCA officials were said to be 'furious' at the 'evil and outrageous operation' on the Rottweilers. The only quoted source was 'one of Elton's staff', who claimed to have seen the dogs in the Woodside grounds, being walked by a guard on a long lead. 'They looked frightening,' the source had allegedly said, 'but all they could do was snarl and whimper. Afterwards, one of Elton's men said they couldn't make any noise because they'd had their voice boxes cut. Nobody in the grounds would know the dogs were there until it was too late. They're like silent assassins.'

With the spread went a large picture of an open-mouthed Rottweiler, and a reminder that 'the most savage breed in the world . . . will not release their jaws when locked on a victim.' The clear insinuation was that the dogs had been mutilated to make their attacks on trespassers even more terrifying.

The story was nonsense, as *The Sun* found out within hours of running it. One of its photographers, dispatched to Old Windsor to get pictures of the 'silent assassins', reported back that he could find only two Alsatians, both with barks in working order. As a spokesman for Elton confirmed soon afterwards, those were the only dogs he owned. His solicitors, meanwhile, had issued his seventeenth libel writ.

Its entrails all over its desert boots, *The Sun* still kept on slugging.

October 15 brought a new front-page splash, in which only trained eyes could detect signs of desperation: YARD BID TO GRAB SUN FILE ON ELTON. Scotland Yard detectives were said to have demanded access to the paper's 'dossier' on 'Elton's sordid sex-life', believing it of 'substantial value' in long-term investigations into the corruption of young boys. The dossier, 'gathered during months of inquiry into London's sordid vice trade', was said to contain testimony from 'dozens of rent boys . . . along with pals and former associates of Elton'.

Next day came news of one legal action, at least, in which *The Sun* could claim unequivocal victory. A judge at the Old Bailey had refused the police a court order to seize the dossier. Its contents, whatever they might be, enjoyed full legal privilege, having been collected in defence of a libel action.

The unkindest cut of all for *The Sun* was that its original rent-boy informant, Stephen Hardy, had now fallen into the hands of its arch-rival, the *Daily Mirror*. On 6 November, the *Mirror* administered the *coup de grâce*, an interview with Hardy under the heading MY SEX LIES OVER ELTON. 'It's all a pack of lies,' Hardy was quoted as saying of *The Sun*'s original 'world exclusive'. 'I made it all up. I only did it for the money, and *The Sun* was easy to con. I've never even met Elton John . . . I've never been to one of his concerts or bought one of his records. In fact, I hate his music.'

The process of wholesale divestment had begun, though it would not be noticeable for some little time yet.

In November 1987, the Rocket record company finally reached the end of the line. Its once proud roster had run down to a few obscure names like Anya and Splash, and, apart from Elton, it had not registered a hit for several years. Its two last supporting acts were told their contracts would not be renewed and that from here on, Rocket would exist only as a vehicle for Elton John product. Just what he had always said he didn't want, back in those idealistic Seventies days of smiley tank-engine logos, give-away tote bags and office trips to Los Angeles.

Less than a week later, an even bigger dream seemed to have reached its end. Elton announced he was resigning as chairman of Watford and selling his 95 per cent stake in the club for £2 million.

His reason was that he could not go on being Watford's sole financial support. 'I love the club passionately, but I'm no longer touring, so there's no cash flow coming in. It would be difficult to provide cash for Watford, and the club has reached a stage where it needs financial security. I could continue as chairman, but I don't want to destroy what's been achieved, by an act of folly on my part. As much as it hurts me to step down, I know I leave the club having done a lot for it. Now I cannot go on. I don't want to burn myself out.'

The buyer was press and publishing tycoon Robert Maxwell, who had lately diversified his interests with the purchase of two other First Division clubs, Derby County and Oxford United. Elton was initially doubtful about Maxwell, but was won over by the fact that his company, BPCC, had its headquarters in the Watford area and, as large local employers, would have an interest in maintaining a 'family' club. Since Maxwell was already chairman of Derby and his son Kevin of Oxford, BPCC's chief executive John Holloran was appointed to take over at Vicarage Road. Elton would receive the Papa Doc title of Life President and retain a seat on the board.

However, the Football Association opposed the sale under its regulation 60, which prohibited the control of more than one club by any individual or family. A High Court injunction was successfully sought, preventing the transfer of Elton's shares to BPCC. For a time, pop star and press tycoon formed a weird alliance, the latter implausibly sporting an Elton-style baseball cap. The FA agreed to drop its ban if Maxwell would balance his takeover of Watford by selling his interests in Oxford United. But in late December, Elton called the whole deal off. For the present anyway, that part of his life was too precious to throw out.

For Christmas cards that year he commissioned a series of cartoons designed to show how happy Renate and he still were, despite everything. On one card, Renate sat on a couch, wrapping presents and asking, 'What are you wearing for Christmas, Elton?' Behind her stood Elton, dressed as a laden and lit-up Christmas tree.

The Watford sale saga rumbled on into 1988. In January, the strip-club king Paul Raymond offered to match Robert Maxwell's £2 million offer for Elton's shares. To add to the turmoil, Dave Bassett had resigned after only half a season as manager, and the club's poor showing that year had doomed it to Division Two in 1988–9. Elton had found a successor to Bassett in Steve Harrison, Watford's former full back and coach. But Harrison would not sign unless given assurances that the club had a stable future. Elton pledged to spend half a million pounds, if necessary, to restore Watford to Division One, and promised he had no intention of making it the adjunct to Raymond's Revuebar. 'I'm not going anywhere,' he said. 'I will not be selling my soul to the devil.'

On 16 January, *The Sun* mustered a last full front-page assault, ELTON JOHN QUIZZED BY VICE POLICE. Elton was said to have been questioned 'for THREE HOURS' by the head of Scotland Yard's Vice Squad, Chief Superintendent Bill Carnie, and two other senior detectives at his solicitor's office in Lincoln's Inn. But, by previous standards, the reporting was almost eerily circumspect. 'At 9-06 pm, the Vice Squad men left, but Mr Carnie would only say: "There is no statement." Elton . . . was escorted to the waiting car by his lawyers. The star shook their hands, then smiled briefly for a *Sun* photographer, saying "Thank you, gentlemen."' The only result of this meeting – if, indeed, it took place in the way *The Sun* claimed – was to eliminate him from any police inquiries on any subject whatever.

Elton's public restraint towards *Sun* representatives was not emulated by his manager. A few weeks later, in a West End night club, John Reid spotted Elton being buttonholed by a *Sun* reporter named Rick Sky. What happened next was retailed next morning in the paper's familiar gobsmacked typography: 'Reid shouted abuse as he GRABBED our man and SHOOK him. Then he BASHED Rick's head against a pillar five times and PUSHED him out of the club while punching him on the chest. Rick was taken to hospital with blood streaming on to his shirt . . . [he] suffered a deep cut on the back of his head, and doctors put three stitches in the wound.' A paparazzi picture showed the superstar, in tasselled smoking cap, being ushered from the scene by his manager with checked jacket rumpled and tie askew.

Reid was charged with assault, and subsequently appeared in the dock at Bow Street Magistrates' Court. He was fined £150 after telling magistrate William Robbins, 'I'm very sorry. I'd had a few drinks.' ELTON THUG FINED, *The Sun* noted with righteous satisfaction. Elton was furious over the incident, and stormed at Reid to remember that such outbursts always rebounded directly on to him. 'It's always "Elton Aide Beats Up *Sun* Man". And they do like to get the letters AID next to my name.'

But *The Sun* had not finished, either with Reid or the letters AID. Next week came a story dredged up from the fortieth birthday party that 'bully-boy pop supremo John Reid' had given for Elton at his Hertfordshire house, more than a year earlier. It was alleged that the noise of the fireworks had frightened a neighbour's pregnant mare into premature labour and the foal had been born dead. The mare's owner had intended taking Reid to court, but at the last minute he had sent her £2,753 in compensation. ELTON AIDE'S WILD PARTY KILLED MY HORSE, apart from its satisfactory arrangement of capitals, had a resonance akin to FREDDIE STARR ATE MY HAMSTER.

In March, Elton returned to AIR Studios in London to make his first album since the throat surgery, and so discover whether or not he still had a singing voice. To lend moral support, producer Chris Thomas had assembled a squad of star helpers, including Pete Townshend on acoustic guitar and Carl Wilson and Bruce Johnston of the Beach Boys to do backing vocals. Another track featured vocals by Elton's two original band musicians, the perennially forgiving Dee Murray and Nigel Olsson. The sessions took longer than expected, owing to the accidental wiping of several half-completed songs; immediately afterwards Elton flew to Los Angeles to celebrate his forty-first birthday. There was no sign of Renate.

In early April he had been scheduled to join Ian Botham on the latter's sponsored walk in aid of leukaemia research. The plan was to follow Hannibal's invasion route across the Alps to Italy, leading a symbolic elephant. The event was cancelled, however, and instead Elton flew to Hawaii, where George Michael was on tour. Checking in to a £1,000-per-night suite at the Honolulu Hilton, he spent a week sunbathing with George Michael and cheering him on from the front row of his concert audience. There was still no sign of Renate.

Almost exactly twenty years earlier, he had bolted from his first fiancée, summoning his stepfather's van to take away his records, cushions and books. And now – albeit on an infinitely more opulent and elaborate level – history was to repeat itself.

A press release from Sotheby's, the international auction house, announced that Elton was to dispose of his entire collection of antiques and art. The reason given was that he planned to sell Woodside and to move to a smaller house further into the country where Renate and he could live a more secluded life. The auction, at Sotheby's New Bond Street salesrooms, later that summer, was expected to realise as much as £3 million.

Coming so soon after his attempt to sell Watford, the announcement aroused speculation that Elton might be running short of cash. However, a recent survey in *The Sunday Times Magazine* had rated him Britain's 95th richest person, with an estimated fortune of £42 million. The same survey had rated John Reid 176th, with an estimated £12 million.

Elton's story was that, at 41, he had suddenly lost his lifelong mania for collecting, and his reliance on inanimate objects as the sole dependable source of happiness. He had woken up one day at Woodside and realised the full enormity of his two-decade shopping spree. 'It was like Harrods' warehouse. There was stuff sitting unopened in crates, which was preposterous. Literally everything was covered. Every wall, every surface. It was suffocating me.'

He still talked resolutely about 'us' and 'our home' and making the fresh start that selling everything would allow. But by this stage, few who knew him believed in that quieter new place in the country where married life would finally begin. 'Clearing out the house was a typical Elton way of going about things,' Nina Myskow says. 'What he was really clearing out was Renate.'

During Renate's final days at Woodside, in March or April of 1988, she invited Nina there for the weekend. Elton was still away, in Los Angeles or Hawaii. The Sotheby people were soon to arrive with their rescuing vans, like Derf Farebrother, twenty years earlier, to strip the place bare.

Renate by now spent almost all her time in the one part of the house she could call her own. This was a screened-off alcove at one end of the 'private suite' Elton had insisted she should have. It contained her computer, her clothes and some furniture in her own modest, tentative taste. 'It was a bit like a bedsitter,' Nina Myskow remembers. 'Very feminine. Flowered covers and pot-pourri. Almost Biba feathers kind of style.'

Nina herself slept at the top of the house in the Bugatti Suite, named for its collection of quasi-Egyptian spiked and tasselled furnishings by Carlo Bugatti. Nearby were rooms of Elton's stage costumes and of artworks never unpacked from their delivery crates.

She spent a curious couple of days, sitting with Renate in her screened-off little bedsit, or downstairs in the sumptuous newly rebuilt kitchen. 'The fridge alone was like a room in its own right. You could walk in and find anything you wanted. All the facilities were magnificent. But all the time one felt slightly illicit. As if having been invited by Elton's wife wasn't really sufficient excuse to be there.'

Lying around, as always, was a large selection of the newest hardback books. Nina picked up Kitty Kelley's biography of Frank Sinatra and was leafing through it when a piece of paper slipped from between the pages. 'It was a note from Renate to Elton. I tried to put it back without reading it, but couldn't help seeing a few words. It said she really loved him, but didn't want to stand in his way or be a problem to him. And she didn't want anything from him.'

Already this year, the treasure troves of two other noted materialists had come under the auctioneer's hammer, attracting huge publicity and fetching bonanza prices. In Los Angeles, Liberace's furs, jewellery and mink-lined, chandelier-hung limousines had gone for $2 million. Then in New York, Andy Warhol's collection of art and kitsch had made an unbelievable $25 million. Warhol and Liberace had followed convention, at least, in being dead before their estates were sold off. It was something new for a superstar publicly to dispose of his own valuables, as if he were about to take a vow of poverty and become a wandering friar.

This new phenomenon, the 'celebrity sale', had made even dignified auction houses see the value in pop-style hype and razzmatazz. Both Sotheby's and their arch rival Christie's had courted Elton for his business as avidly as any record company of yore. Sotheby's won the day in a presentation combining talk-'em-up pre-sale showmanship with reverent good taste. The firm's senior director Marcus Linell, accompanied by its 'Head of Collectibles' and its jewellery and fine art experts, then paid an exploratory visit to Woodside. Having seen the hoard – which by that time had overflowed even into the squash court – they came away marvelling that anyone could actually live there.

Elton's overriding stipulation was that everything must go. Not only the art treasures and costly antiques, the 150 Art Nouveau lamps and 200 Art Deco nymphs, the jukeboxes and pinball machines, but all his other possessions, down to the most private and personal. The clothes he had worn onstage since 1970, his jewellery, his shoes, his collected spectacles, his massed gold discs, even his luggage, were put out to be assessed, graded and priced. Every expensive toy, and every cheap one, that had ever caught his looter's eye, every relentlessly hoarded and obsessively dusted ornament, conversation piece, souvenir, knick-knack and keepsake was dismissed without a backward glance. He was disposing not simply of assets but of his whole past. Taking him at his word, Sotheby's even removed the soap dish from Bob Halley's bathroom. Three days were needed to transport the hoard in a fleet of pantechnicons from Old Windsor to Old Bond Street.

Sotheby's success with Elton had much to do with its chairman, the former Tory arts minister Lord Gowrie. They had met ten years earlier, when Gowrie was a dealer in contemporary art, and sold Elton an important portrait by Francis Bacon. This 'great masterpiece' he persuaded Elton to hold back from the sale, along with a handful of other paintings. Nor, finally, were the superstar's fourteen cars included, or his prodigious record library, or his Goon Show scripts, or his £75,000 marital bed.

Characteristically, the grand sell-off was no sooner announced than Elton started buying once more, abetted by his new friends in aprons of green baize. In July, Sotheby's held a sale of works by Russian avant-garde painters who, until Gorbachev, had been unable to exhibit even in their own country. Elton paid £44,000 for two works by the husband-and-wife team Igor and Svetlana Kopystianski.

The Elton John sale was scheduled for four days early in September. Meanwhile, lavish picture spreads of the merchandise to be auctioned appeared in every major newspaper and magazine, with Elton posing in their midst like an opulent Albert Steptoe. Selected items were taken on tour to New York, Los Angeles, Tokyo and Sydney. The Victoria and Albert Museum mounted a special summer exhibition of 500 lots, including pictures by Magritte and L. S. Lowry, Bugatti Furniture, Art Nouveau figures, jewellery, spectacles and stage costumes. It was another notable 'first' for glam rock sequins and glasses spelling 'Elton' to be given the same historical weight as cabinets of royal armour and Iron Age axe-heads.

The catalogue ran to four volumes, contained in a white slip case and costing £40. Volume 1, 'Stage Costume and Memorabilia', showed Elton perched on the edge of a pinball machine, flanked by his hussar and aquamarine feather outfits and wearing the stole of artificial bananas from his Bob Mackie pirate suit. Volume 2, 'Jewellery', showed him in close-up under his boater brim, displaying a large diamond and sapphire ring, a diamond and sapphire double wrist band and an onyx and diamond brooch with a tassel as long as a fly switch. Volume 3, 'Art Nouveau and Art Deco', showed him holding the spike of a Bugatti chair, surrounded by mottled glass and ethereal figurines. Volume 4, 'Diverse Collections', showed him with a gold palm tree, Warhol's 'Marilyn', Magritte's blue fish swathed in pearls, a replica of Tutankhamun's state throne, a jewelled papier-mâché cabinet, an umbrella stand and a stool on two legs clothed in checked trousers and white shoes.

Everything received the same scrupulous description and provenance. Thus: '1163. Rembrandt Harmensz Van Rijn. Self-portrait . . . Etching, a very good impression of the second state . . .' Thus: '1851. A Smoky Plastic Musical Guitar, modern, revolving on a spigot and playing "Love Me Tender".' Thus: '782. A Salon Suite with Decorative Aubusson Tapestry Coverings, designed by Raoul Dufy, *circa* 1925–30.' Thus: 1853. A Cutey-Doll Radio, modern, wearing a see-through negligée, with dual controls, her body containing the works.' Thus: '119. A Presentation Platinum Disc for the Album *Rock of the Westies*.' Thus: '88. Pinball Wizard movie prop boots from the film *Tommy*, the fibre-glass giant Doc Marten lace-up boots with platform supports above and metal callipers and leather supports for attaching to the legs.' Thus: '215. A Camisole belonging to Judy Garland in *Meet Me In St Louis*.' Thus: '281. Multi-coloured Jockey Cap, by Interstellar Propellors, with twin-bladed propellor mounted on the crown.' Thus: '76. A pair of 'sun-blind' novelty spectacles, the yellow frames stamped 'Roma' with unfolding semi-circular fabric sun-blinds.'

Thus the original lounge suite he had brought for Hercules ('of slightly concave outline, upholstered in red leather'); his monogrammed Louis Vuitton cases and cabin trunks ('each with traditional tan leather and brass-bound exterior'); his long-ago blue Levi suit 'applied with commercially produced embroidered patches'); his John Lennon lithographs ('inscribed "To Elton/Let's hope it's a good one/ Love Yoko and Sean"'); and his souvenir programme 'signed in black ball pen by Elvis Presley'.

The lots jammed Sotheby's storerooms, spilling into corridors and even Lord Gowrie's own office. They included a selection of footwear, like '144. 'A pair of monogrammed high platform boots, the silver-leather zippered boots lettered E and J in scarlet with leather stacked heels and silver and scarlet platform soles.' His lordship's Sloaney secretary, too young to remember glam rock, asked Elton if he'd really worn such things on stage. 'They were for day wear, darling,' he said. 'I used to run for taxis in those.'

The great Woodside turn-out also made a cover for Elton's new album, which showed his stage costumes on their manikins, massed like a small army beyond a foreground heap of feathers, glasses, boaters, bananas and Minnie Mouse ears. Its title, too, reflected his disinvention of two decades as well as his continuing firm resolve against *The Sun*. Recognising a self cast off in 1968, but never really lost, the album was called *Reg Strikes Back*.

Any other rock star passing through such ordeals would have shown his anger and anguish in his music. But Elton, as always, was singing Bernie Taupin's words, and Bernie's horizons were quite clear. *Reg Strikes Back* was no furious thunderbolt but a cheery miscellany on topics far from home, whose references to Elton's current state were only of the most accidental kind. Elton had found great solace in recording it, especially since it showed his voice to be not only unimpaired but even improved. One particular track, 'Since God Invented Girls', yet another homage to Brian Wilson and the Beach Boys, found him making notes as high and harmonies as complex as Wilson ever had. Only the straining eye could see any emotional subtext in titles like 'Poor Cow' and 'I Don't Wanna Go on with You Like That', and lines like 'This overload is edging me further out to sea / I need to put some distance between overkill and me.'

It was clear by now that *The Sun*'s onslaught had had no effect whatever on Elton's career. Despite a large Murdoch media presence there, America had remained indifferent to *The Sun* saga. In January 1988, as the world was crashing round his ears, he had had a surprise single hit with his live Australian concert version of 'Candle in the Wind', which made number five in Britain and six in America. *The Sun*'s so-called corrupter of youth was hard to reconcile with his video image, Mozart-wigged and husky-voiced, impassionedly singing of Marilyn Monroe as 'something more than sexual'.

Reg Strikes Back proved that his public had not ostracised him, reaching seventeen in the UK and eighteen in America, while its best single, 'I Don't Wanna Go on with You Like That', was an American number two. Any idea that he had lost his royal friends was also quashed when, in June, he appeared in a gala concert for the Prince of Wales's Prince's Trust with Eric Clapton, Rick Astley, Joe Cocker and Leonard Cohen.

Feeling 'like a man who's taken a cleansing shower' after the Woodside purge, he plunged into a variety of new projects, none of them leading to a smaller, quieter house in the country. He agreed to appear in Ken Russell's film version of *The Rainbow* by D. H. Lawrence, playing the cameo role of Uncle Henry. He got involved in a compact-disc version of Dylan Thomas's *Under Milk Wood*, writing new music for Polly Garter's song, to be sung by Bonnie Tyler. He dropped out of *The Rainbow* – just before he was due to appear on camera – but was then mooted to play Liberace in an American TV movie.

The 2,000 lots on preview in five rooms at Sotheby's brought him his first reviews in salesroom columns rather than musical ones. 'His collection . . . is the opposite of a connoisseur's choice,' said the *Daily Telegraph*. 'It is two decades of impulse-buying, done with a splendid sense of humour, but its interest in excellence is incidental. It is not a "collection" in any disciplined sense; it is an assemblage, a magpie's nest piled high with glamour and glitz. What there is, as art, starts with Art Nouveau glass, chosen to be big, colourful, ritzy and flamboyant. The 20th-century furniture is more impressive and better-chosen. The jewellery . . . oddly mixes the tastes of a conservative duchess and a mid-Thirties flapper.'

In the Warhol sale, even insignificant trinkets had commanded huge prices thanks to the great artist's personal imprimatur. To give the Elton sale a 'Warhol factor', each lot came with a special label warranting it to be of the Elton John Collection and stamped with a logo of straw hat and spectacles.

The four-day sale, when it came, was conducted more like a rock concert, with police and crash barriers in New Bond Street, and Elton fans packed among the dealers and collectors. Six hundred people, in six separate rooms, competed for the treasures, with telephone bids coming in from others all over the world. Even Elton's mother had a representative there to snap up some mementos of her boy's past. He himself did not attend the sale, being on tour again in America.

From the first day's business, on 6 September, it was obvious that prices were going wild. The Magritte gouache, 'Hommage à Alphonse Allais', went to a Brussels buyer for £70,200, twice the anticipated price. Three Lowrys, 'The Beach at Penarth', 'Moreton-in-Marsh' (Elton's souvenir of Rocket Records' inauguration) and 'A Yacht at Lytham' went respectively for £46,200, £41,800 and £17,600, again roughly double the estimates. An Allen Jones 'kneeling nude' glass table, expected to make up to £7,000 went to a Japanese buyer for £20,900. Furnishings and glass were equally astonishing. The Dufy Aubusson suite made £90,200, again doubling Sotheby's prediction, as did a Morris and Co. carpet, designed for Merton Abbey in 1900, which fetched £71,500. A Daum vase with applied red glass tulips went for £56,100. Two Tiffany lamps went for £37,400 and £36,300. The jewellery fetched £400,000, its prize piece a diamond and onyx Cartier watch, which went to a Japanese department store for £25, 300, twelve times the catalogue estimate.

Of the £14.8 million made in four days, more than £1 million came from Elton's personal effects, showing what frantic desire now existed to invest in pop music memorabilia. A collector from Nashville paid £44,000 for eleven of his stage costumes. His Dodger Stadium suit, thought to be worth £1,800, went for £6,200 and his 'Eiffel Tower boater' for £4,000, ten times the estimate. His 1939 Wurlitzer jukebox fetched £17,600, his light-up 'Elton' glasses £9,900, his mink-framed Dior ones £950 and his signed picture of Elvis Presley £2,500, five times as much as expected. The giant Pinball Wizard boots, expected to make under £2,000, went for £11,000 to a director of the Doc Marten company. The propellor baseball cap, expected to fetch £40, went for £800. A straw boater, which could be bought new in Oxford Street for £20, went for £825, and a painted mirror, $5 on any Venice Beach stall, for £285. A white-haired woman unsuccessfully bid £3,600 for the silver E and J platform boots, which went to America for £4,950. A cushion like the *Madman Across the Water* album-sleeve went to Gus Dudgeon, the album's producer, for £2,950. Even the ELTON JOHN SALE banners hanging outside were added as extra lots, and fetched £550.

No break-up ever happened with more sad amicability. All through the final months, Elton kept in daily touch with Renate on the mobile phone he now carried everywhere. The smallest upset or piece of news still made him instinctively turn to her. One day she found a message on the answering machine from Elton in a hotel room somewhere in America. He said he'd awoken to find a small earthquake going on, but it had stopped now and he was going back to sleep again.

The end was officially confirmed on 18 November. Elton and Renate were to divorce 'by mutual consent . . . and with no fault attaching to either party'. He was especially emphatic on that point, remembering his own parents' divorce and the way his mother had been named as the guilty party.

A bleakly formal statement from Renate was issued via John Reid's office: 'Both of us have been and will be so busy with our own work commitments that we are seeing too little of each other. And for that reason it seems unavoidable that we are growing apart. We are, however, parting on the most amicable terms and genuinely intend to remain best friends. Moreover we are both confident that all personal matters will be resolved without any animosity. I am obviously saddened to see our marriage end, and I wish Elton all the happiness in the world and I know that he wishes me the same.'

The orgy of tabloid headlines was generally sympathetic in tone. With each one went the wedding-day picture of boatered, wing-poke bridegroom and bewildered bride, as unreal now as figures under glass in a shake-up snowstorm. *Today*'s full colour extravaganza used an all-too-inviting simile: ELTON'S MARRIAGE FLICKERED AND WENT OUT LIKE A CANDLE IN THE WIND.

The Sun called them BRIDE 'N' DOOM, surrounding the words with a broken heart-shape. Two inside pages explained WHY THE ODD COUPLE WERE DESTINED TO GET DIVORCED, helped by one picture of Elton giving a kiss to Phil Collins, another of him with his arm round George Michael and a third of him dressed as a pantomime dame. Significantly, however, there was no mention of cocaine, orgies or escapades with rent boys.

The only interview Elton gave was to his old friend Nina Myskow, for the *Mail on Sunday*. 'I gave it my best shot,' he said. 'And it's certainly not Renate's fault. She's done nothing wrong. That's what makes it so hard. I feel this terrible guilt because she was so supportive when things were going badly for me. She was absolutely wonderful.'

He admitted to Nina that at the time of the worst *Sun* stories, he'd thought of seeking psychiatric help. 'Lots of my friends say it's wonderful to be able to unburden yourself. But I think I should overcome my own problems.'

Though Renate had made no pre-nuptial agreement, there was speculation that her divorce settlement might be as high as £10 million. Her only visible acquisition, however, was a seventeenth-century cottage in Godalming, Surrey. 'She chose it just because she liked its name,' Nina Myskow says. 'It was called Cobblers.'

Ever unpredictable, having refused interviews to all network TV shows, Elton suddenly agreed to talk to Thames, London's local channel, in the huge, perfect, empty garden of Woodside. The inevitable questions about Renate were fielded with deft grace. 'I'd rather not say anything about the marriage situation. It's only fair to my wife, who's been so dignified throughout this whole thing.' That evidently meant most of all to him.

Elton apart, there had been signs all through 1988 that the tide was turning against *The Sun*. Its persecution of the dying TV star Russell Harty, another 'self-confessed' homosexual, aroused widespread protest and brought a memorable denunciation by Alan Bennett from the pulpit at Harty's memorial service. More flak flew when, in reporting the horrific Ealing Vicarage rape case, it ignored all conventions of decency and identified the victim. Then in October, it went too far with the royal family, ending a long-standing convention that the Queen never answers back. To obtain a first sight of Fergie's new baby daughter, *The Sun* hijacked a royal family group photograph destined to be the Queen's next Christmas card. The Queen brought proceedings for breach of copyright and Scotland Yard's Serious Crime Squad began an investigation into how the picture had been misappropriated. *The Sun* was forced to pay £100,000 to four Palace-nominated charities and publish a grovelling front-page apology.

To add to all this, its bully-boy muscle had been resisted in unprecedented fashion. The 'poofter' pop star had not turned tail and run. Its Elton John exposé must be defended in court, using a chief witness who had already confessed, in the columns of its greatest rival, that he'd told 'a pack of lies'.

In the libel action over Graham X's allegations against Elton, *The Sun* knew it stood no chance whatever. What it still could do was make that trial a personal nightmare for Elton, bringing forward its other witnesses to smear him and reporting everything under the protection of full legal privilege. If the paper was going down, it would have the consolation of taking Elton with it.

At this point, Elton's lawyers pulled off a coup that can only be called dazzling. They arranged that the first libel case into court was the subject of Elton's seventeenth and last writ – the instantly disprovable allegation that he owned Rottweiler dogs whose barks had been silenced. *The Sun* was thus faced with an action in which its muck-raking would be useless, one which it had to lose and which would, moreover, unleash hysterical laughter up and down Fleet Street. The case of the voiceless Rottweilers was set to begin in the High Court on 12 December, before Mr Justice Michael Davies. But lawyers from Wapping were already talking to lawyers from Lincoln's Inn.

Later that week, Nina Myskow was invited to dinner with Elton and John Reid at Reid's house. 'When I got there, Elton took me outside into the drive,' Nina remembers. 'He said, "I've won. *The Sun* are going to pay me a million pounds." Then he burst into tears.'

On December 12, the morning that the Rottweiler libel action was due to open in the High Court, *The Sun*'s splash headline was two words: SORRY ELTON. As a rule, in British papers apologies are minuscule paragraphs in legalese, buried at the foot of inside pages. Never before had one appeared this way as a lead story in house-style prose, every word of it approved in advance by the plaintiff's lawyers:

> *The Sun* last night agreed to pay megastar Elton John £1 million libel damages.
>
> The settlement followed allegations published in *The Sun* last year about his private life.
>
> A delighted Elton said last night: 'This is the best Christmas present I could wish for.
>
> 'Life is too short to bear grudges and I don't bear *The Sun* any malice.'
>
> Later a *Sun* spokesman apologised to Elton for running the stories which they acknowledge to be completely untrue.
>
> The spokesman said: 'We are delighted that Elton and *The Sun* have become friends again and are very sorry that we were lied to by a teenager living in a world of fantasy.'
>
> Elton said: 'Now I welcome the fact that my name has been cleared.'
>
> The settlement included *The Sun* paying damages concerning an article about Elton's alleged cruelty to dogs.
>
> The spokesman said: 'We accept that he loves his pets and we are very sorry we suggested otherwise.'
>
> *The Sun* is paying Elton's legal costs.

Inside was a centre spread in which Elton repaid the compliment by giving *The Sun* an exclusive interview. The Rottweiler of Fleet Street was transformed to fawning puppy dog as it proudly told how its late quarry was 'fighting fit and ready for action', having lost twenty-eight pounds in less than two months. 'He has completely changed his lifestyle by cutting out BOOZE and his DIET of stodgy food and going on a rigid training EXERCISE . . .' The interview itself was presented in a manner verging on the schizophrenic. 'Things hadn't gone well for me in 1987, and I was feeling desperately depressed . . .' Elton was quoted as saying. 'I needed to get fit and healthy again after the worst year of my life . . .' A second instalment retailed his views on current pop hits, under the strapline WHEN STARS MAKE FRIENDS, THEY MAKE FRIENDS WITH THE SUN. Having failed to pierce his jugular, the paper now seemed intent on licking Elton to death.

The damages doubled Jeffrey Archer's record jury award a year earlier, and *The Sun* was estimated to be liable for about as much again in costs. Elton had in addition received what few thought he ever could, 'an apology to match the smear'.

But not everybody was thrilled. The judge who had been due to sit in the Rottweiler case, Mr Justice Michael Davies, complained the court had been 'manipulated' by *The Sun*'s 'pre-emptive strike' in announcing the settlement before it had been formally put before him. 'Reading it, one would think that Elton John and the newspaper had formed a mutual admiration society,' the judge commented acidly. Recording 'extreme disapproval and distaste', he pointed out that courts of law were a forum for trials and disputes. They were not 'a supine adjunct to a publicity machine for pop stars and newspapers'.

But in nailing *The Sun*, Elton had done a service to the whole nation. Though still an odious tabloid, it never quite regained its old contemptuous arrogance. Its coverage of the Hillsborough soccer stadium tragedy, a year later, produced another major boycott by its customers. Not long afterwards, it appointed an ombudsman to adjudicate in reader complaints.

Nor was it ever fully appreciated how much Elton had *The Sun* over a barrel. In the original apology headline dictated by his lawyers, SORRY ELTON was followed by an exclamation mark. Between editions, for aesthetic reasons, the editor decided to drop the exclamation mark. But before even this could be done, it had to be cleared with Elton's lawyers.

Epilogue
'I just want to smell a few roses'

ON 28 August, 1989, Elton appeared in a special bank holiday one-to-one edition of *Wogan*. It was the British television public's first chance to see him since his victory over *The Sun*, and the total change he had announced in every department of his life. Goodwill still waxed strong, if the studio audience was anything to go by. Congratulatory applause, whistles and whoops greeted him as he walked out on to the gimcrack chat-show set.

This born-again, new-look, low-key Elton wore modest rimless glasses, an unadorned dark blue Gianni Versace suit and lavender turtleneck shirt. Over the platinum blond hair strands curved a purple bead-trimmed Nehru cap. He might have been the leader of some Rajneeshi-style religious sect who had just purchased an entire American state for his disciples. Lounging on the coach next to Terry Wogan, his coat sleeves slipped up his forearms and one silk sock-top disclosed a band of white shin. Almost all the two stone, euphorically sweated off in late 1988, seemed to have found its way back again.

He was as good-humoured and fluent as ever, responding to Wogan's clueless Irish blarney, which included an observation that his 'old bones' must by now be feeling the strain of performing and going on tour. He contrived to keep smiling even through a photo and film montage containing scenes of his wedding to Renate and blow-ups of the worst rent-boy stories from *The Sun*.

'In all these years, you've never had a British number-one single,' Wogan reminded him at one point. 'Does that rankle at all?'

The lavender Nehru twitched his glasses up his nose, in the mannerism all interviewers had noted, right back to Cyril Gee at Mills Music in 1965.

'No, not really,' he answered – and, ever the record trivia hound, could instantly list all those bizarre or unlikely names who had achieved what he, somehow, never could. 'Laurel and Hardy had one, Richard Harris, even Arthur Mullard's had a British number one. It would have been nice, but it doesn't bother me. I don't suppose I ever will have one now.'

Rupert Murdoch's million pounds had been poured into a life that seemed totally dismantled. Not only had wife and possessions gone from Woodside but the mansion itself had now been gutted, pending total renovation and refurnishing. Its owner spoke vaguely of a new 'traditional' look, replacing the Art Deco labyrinth with chaste vistas of Laura Ashley print, quiet furnishings and open fires. Meanwhile, for the foreseeable future, the only residents were his ninety-year-old grandmother, Ivy, whom he'd installed in the Orangery, and his servants and security staff.

Throughout that spring, summer and autumn, Elton was back onstage – 'the only place where I feel safe' – pushing himself to constant new extremes of self-flagellating celebration. While playing Bercy stadium, near Paris, he collapsed from heat exhaustion and had to be revived with damp towels and water before continuing. Two nights later, he spent a reported £200,000 on a party to celebrate his forty-second birthday, bringing over 200 guests including Tina Turner, Ringo Starr and Viscount Linley, all of whom were put up at exclusive hotels and ferried by fleets of limousines to the château hired for the occasion. Food and drink were served by footmen in powdered wigs and, after cutting his cake, a nine-foot-high replica of the Eiffel Tower, Elton sat down at the piano and belted out number after number. 'He was more like a man celebrating his twenty-first birthday than his forty-second,' one guest commented. 'The Romans couldn't have done it better. There was champagne by the bucketful, and a snap of fingers brought a host of flunkeys to your table.'

In August, he was reported to have spent £6,000 on wines at a single dinner for himself and a fourteen-strong party at a restaurant in Dallas, Texas. In September, he cancelled his two concerts in Tampa, Florida, after going down with influenza. In October, he was said to have 'keeled over with exhaustion, which called off his final US show, in Worcester, Massachusetts, and caused speculation that he might be suffering from the 'yuppie virus', myalgic encephalitis. That same week, an 'ailing' and 'burned-out Elton' checked into a £560-per-night suite at the Ritz Hotel, Paris, under orders to take a month's complete rest before going on to tour the Far East, Australia and New Zealand. In November, he was due to top the bill at a music festival in Antwerp, Belgium, and also receive a Diamond Career Award for services to music. This performance, too, was cancelled when Elton's people notified the festival organisers that he was 'not yet fully fit'.

There were intermittent rumours that, after his trials with the British press, he intended to live permanently overseas. The *Daily Star* claimed he had already paid £4.5 million for an enormous estate in Palm Beach, Florida. An aerial photograph was provided, showing the high tower from which Elton would allegedly gaze at the Atlantic like a muezzin in a minaret. The story brought an instant denial from his lawyers – a force now held in awe throughout Fleet Street. This time there was no writ, only a complaint of inaccuracy to the Press Council. But the *Star* was still rattled enough to print a fulsome retraction within days. None could doubt that Elton's battle with *The Sun* had fundamentally changed the way in which tabloid newspapers went about their business.

He admitted that, in the darkest days of *The Sun*'s onslaught, he had often been tempted to take permanent refuge abroad. 'But I couldn't just run away. I had to stay and take it until I'd totally cleared my name. Anyway, Britain's my home. It always has been and it always will be.'

His mother and stepfather now lived, safe from tabloid harassment, on the Spanish island of Minorca. But his remaining close family, on Sheila's side, were still in Britain, around the mock-Tudor fringes of Metroland. The millionaire gypsy kept in touch as conscientiously as his whirlwind schedule would allow. His Aunt Win and his younger cousin Paul – now married with a baby daughter – both lived on the same modest street in Ruislip, Middlesex. Every so often, Paul would get a phone call from his mother to come along quickly as Elton had looked in for a few minutes en route across the world. He was devoted to his grandmother, who, even though living in his mansion grounds, made no distinction between him and her other grandchildren and great-grandchildren. It meant much to him that, when the Duke and Duchess of York attended one of his huge parties, Fergie made a special point of talking to his 'Nan'.

With his paternal relations, the Dwights, he was less close. His older cousin Roy, the ex-pro footballer, remained a huge fan of his music and was first in line to book seats and coach-tickets up to his first night's concert at Wembley. To Roy's relief, Elton's attitude to his father had noticeably softened, especially since Stanley Dwight had been stricken by serious heart trouble. 'Both my parents were strict with me,' he told Terry Wogan, modifying the story he had always given out. 'I'm glad now that they were. And both of them made a sacrifice in staying together for the sake of my education.'

Fractured and frenzied as his existence might seem, it maintained its perennial fixed points of normality and sanity. He still played tennis like a podgy whirling dervish, in early mornings after the heaviest carousing. He was as much a football fan as ever, timing his latest world circumnavigation to end in time for the 1990 Cup Final. But his days as Watford FC's saviour and bottomless piggy bank were definitely over. In December 1989, he tried for the second time to sell his 92 per cent stake in the club, this time to a London-based leisure company, Wrighton Enterprises. As with the abortive Robert Maxwell deal, the sale was to bring him £2 million, removing the club's drain on his finances while leaving him its figurehead life president. But a month later, it was announced that the negotiations had 'failed to come to fruition'.

The social connections that meant so much to him proved to have been unharmed by *The Sun*'s muck-raking. He remained on the guest list for parties at Windsor Castle when, it was said, the Queen relied on him as a jiving partner to Bill Haley's 'Rock Around the Clock'. At a luncheon he gave at Woodside before its shutdown for refurbishment, the Queen Mother was among the guests. 'I sat next to her,' Bernie Taupin remembers. 'We talked about gardening – and summer pudding. While we were out in the garden, we could see the tower of Windsor Castle, where the flag was flying. "Oh," the Queen Mother said. "My daughter's at home."'

Despite these social triumphs, the company Elton relished most was still that of musicians, especially his fellow time-travellers through the Sixties and Seventies: Eric Clapton, Ringo Starr, George Harrison, Freddie Mercury. His favourite pastime was still hanging out into the small hours, behind a myriad of bottles and glasses, reminiscing about the vast lengths of road that stretched behind. Despite his wealth and freewill, he remained the music industry's biggest workaholic, never really happy unless head-clamped between cans in some airless underground booth. He was still a tireless accumulator of records, tapes and compact discs, an omnivorous hoarder of record trivia, an astrological porer over Top 20, 40 and 100 charts, a forensic dissecter of any new sound that might be turned to his own purposes. For all his global fame, he remained at heart a session man, always willing to sing or play backup anonymously for others, just as in the long-ago days of Marble Arch and Picketty-witch. In 1987, he played piano and electric piano on George Harrison's album *Cloud Nine*. In 1988, he co-produced the title track of Olivia Newton-John's album, *The Rumour*, as well as contributing piano tracks and vocals. In 1989, he duetted with Aretha Franklin on her single, 'Through the Storm'. In 1990, he played piano on new albums by Jon Bon Jovi and his undiminished idol, Bob Dylan.

Advancing into middle age, he was still utterly without musical prejudice, able to find something to praise as well as much to damn in every new era of commercial pop. Madonna he damned, in typically waspish style, for not singing live at her concerts. But, just as he once had liked the Osmonds, he now liked the milk-fed puppets of Stock, Aitken and Waterman's Hit Factory studio. Rick Astley, in particular, he said, had 'a terrific voice'. He liked the peroxide Goss twins, natural heirs to the Bay City Rollers. He believed George Michael to be a virtuoso ranking with any of his own time. There was no one with whom he wouldn't share a stage, and none who did not jump at the chance to share one with him.

He continued unique among his species as a mixture of egomaniacal arrogance, infantile petulance, punctilious chivalry, sensitivity, gener-osity and the fine-tuned thoughtfulness of that good boy at Pinner County Grammar School. In 1989, the comedienne Marti Caine was found to be suffering from cancer. Returning one day to her theatre dressing-room, she found it full of white flowers sent by Elton. That same year his old journalistic friend Nina Myskow – now herself a considerable celebrity – was 'turned over' by the *News of the World* in a miniature version of what Elton had gone through with *The Sun*. He immediately sent her an enormous bouquet and a sympathetic cheer-up note. In 1990, burglars ransacked the house of his young cousin Paul, making off with the TV set, the stereo and other valuables. When Elton heard of it, he paid for every lost item to be replaced.

For someone who had ended so many eras and made so many fresh starts, his life possessed a remarkable degree of continuity. His close friends and associates in 1990 were fundamentally the same as in 1970. There was Tony King, his long-time confidant and accomplice in outrage, now living in New York and working for Mick Jagger. There was Steve Brown, Elton and Bernie's original saviour and mentor at Dick James Music, now reclaimed from agriculture and back in his old crucial role as co-ordinator of albums and tours. There was Bob Halley, who had survived fourteen years with Elton, first as chauffeur, then as live-in companion and finally as selfless twenty-four-hours-a-day personal factotum.

Continuity, above all, was represented by John Reid, his manager for almost twenty years and still impregnably so, despite regular rumours of terminal rifts between them. The relationship between them in some ways resembled that of Elvis Presley and Colonel Parker, in others that of Richard Burton and Elizabeth Taylor. They were like old marrieds, endlessly divorced and reconciled, unable to live with one another or survive longer than a few months apart. They still could have rows rivalling the big scene in *Who's Afraid of Virginia*

Woolf, and thereafter refuse to communicate except through their respective courtiers. Then one would throw a stupendous party for the other, or present him with some breathtaking new toy, and harmony would be restored. In 1990, *Music Week* published one of the very few pictures ever seen of Reid and Elton together. Superstar's puggy face looks down on manager's foxy one with that old paradoxical elder brother smile. Little seems to have changed since the days at the Water Garden, when streetwise John first taught innocent Reggie to eat poussin instead of Instant Whip.

The peculiar, unstable, indestructible chemistry between them was best observed by John Hall, the young head of Rocket Records to whom Elton once almost signed away something like 40 per cent of the company. Hall did well enough without, going on to found the Filmtrax organisation and, eventually, to sell it for $95 million.

John Hall dissents from the view that Reid was the worst thing ever to happen to Elton. 'There's a strength about him that Elton always needed, and still needs. He's the one who fights battles for Elton. He'll go out into the playground and bash big boys up. He doesn't care. And he'll protect Elton until the last drop of blood is spilt. You can say he's only looking after his own interests, but there's always been much more to it than that. What's between them is a love, a mutual need; you simply couldn't have one without the other. Elton is the prize and John Reid is the keeper of the gate.'

He retained his oldest associate of all, his original surrogate brother, country mouse to his town mouse, Brown Dirt Cowboy to his Captain Fantastic, Piglet to his Winnie-the-Pooh. Twenty-two years on, when stubby fingers stretched on piano keys, there was still only one person who could fill in the empty bubble overhead.

Bernie Taupin, now aged thirty-nine, lived permanently in Los Angeles. He, too, had gone through the Eighties couture mill, no longer dressing in Take Six flares and Navajo amulets, but in luminous grey Versace suits, cream silk blouses and string ties clasped by pieces of designer silverware. His dark hair remained intact, flattened back with gel and slung in a modish ponytail. He was a figure of mature sophistication who these days, grandly, preferred to be known as plain 'Taupin'. Yet, tanned by California life, his face still had the shy yet faintly dangerous good looks of some uppish young Indian brave.

Despite his blissful childhood in Lincolnshire, Bernie felt little nostalgia for England. His faint East Midland burr was now larded with Americanisms – 'Sir', for instance, when calling a waiter. He had lately brought his parents over to live in LA, severing the last link with Market Rasen and Owmby-by-Spital. Having so long absorbed America through every pore, he had decided to exchange his resident-alien status for full US citizenship.

His place in pop music remained unique. Twenty years had produced no other megastar musician with a lyric-writing partner who received equal credit. The great Elton John evergreen hits, 'Your Song', 'Goodbye Yellow Brick Road', 'Daniel', 'Crocodile Rock', 'Candle in the Wind', all were universally acknowledged to be as much Bernie's as Elton's. The supreme accolade for him had been to attend a Frank Sinatra concert, and hear Sinatra perform 'Your Song' alongside the best of Cole Porter, Ira Gershwin and Sammy Cahn. And at the intermission, a Sinatra bodyguard tapped him on the shoulder and croaked, 'Frank wants to see ya.'

Bernie's career in the Eighties had considerably diversified. He had released two albums as a vocalist in his own right, and made his first essay as a director of pop videos. He also had formed an extra-mural partnership with the British musician Martin Page. Together they had written two number one US singles, 'We Built This City' for Jefferson Starship, and 'These Dreams' for the female rock band Heart. The possibility that Bernie Taupin might be on the open market had produced a flood of offers, some from young bands like Level 42 and Curiosity Killed the Cat. Though much flattered, Bernie politely declined, preferring to save himself for the voice and the psyche he knew best.

He lived quietly with his second wife Toni in the house on North Doheny Drive which he had bought in 1972. His main interest was his library, divided between English literary first editions and rare volumes about the American West. The former hard-drinking lie-abed had become a fitness fanatic, rising early to work out for several hours each day, taking alcohol only moderately, in the form of good-quality wines. Even more than in the Seventies, personal publicity was abhorrent to him. He received an unwelcome dollop of it in 1988 when his former girlfriend Loree Rodkin gave disparaging details about their time together in an interview with *Vanity Fair*. The next issue carried a dignified riposte from Bernie, calling Rodkin a 'primal diva', interested only in her social career and dental bridgework. There may have been the makings of a new lyric here.

He had long wanted to write narrative prose, rather than irresistible half-line hooks, and, encouraged by Toni, finally squared himself to the task. The result was an autobiography called *A Cradle of Haloes*, recreating his Lincolnshire childhood and adolescence after the style of Laurie Lee's *Cider with Rosie*. With his own odd mixture of star ego and sensitive consideration, he gave Owmby-by-Spital another name, fearing that crowds of reverential pop fans might descend on the place and give annoyance to his parents' former neighbours. *A Cradle of Haloes* was not critically praised. But Bernie continued undaunted, working on a book of poems, provisionally called *The Devil at High Noon*, and a movie screenplay about an offbeat Western desperado named Sam Bass.

In late 1988, he was in London, doing publicity for *A Cradle of Haloes* before joining Elton at sessions for a new album in Denmark. He appeared on Radio Two's Gloria Hunniford programme, answering questions about their exploits together with the gravitas of an Auden-in-exile. At the same time, he made no attempt to conceal how instantaneous and painless their collaboration had been, nor how many sources they had blithely plundered over the years.

'Like "Rocket Man",' Gloria Hunniford ventured. 'Didn't the idea for that one come from David Bowie?'

'Oh no,' Bernie replied. 'We didn't steal that one from Bowie. We stole it from another bloke, called Tom Rapp.'

He might have added that he was about to join Elton in Denmark to produce the most derivative song collection of their entire career. The idea came from Elton, remembering black vocal groups like the Drifters, with whom he had toured as a humble keyboard player twenty-five years earlier. He would make his twenty-sixth album a homage to the Drifters, the Impressions, the Miracles, with their smiles in unison, their shape-drawing dance routines, their easygoing French-fried world of 'Saturday Night at the Movies' and 'Under the Boardwalk'. At the same time, there would be an edge of modern pastiche, like the Billy Joel album which contained 'Uptown Girl'.

Elton named this 1989 album *Sleeping with the Past*, despite the probability of much unfriendly sniggering. With pre-emptive chutz-pah, he joked to Terry Wogan that he had half thought of issuing it with an illustrated catalogue. Any sexual charge, however, was instantly defused by the cover, which showed just his face, asleep in its granny specs, as innocent as the Ovaltine moon over Metroland.

The first track issued as a single was 'Healing Hands', a rousing neo-spiritual about love as a redemptive power, 'a light where the darkness ends'. With it went a high-fashion black-and-white video, featuring Elton in wide-brimmed Zorro hat and gale-blown cloak, intercut with yearning faces clasped between hands that might have modelled for Velasquez. It was, by the highest Taupin–John standards, a very good song. Against 1989's chainsaw drill of hip-hop, it seemed as old-fashionedly ingenious and well made as a Cecil B. de Mille movie or a Terence Rattigan play. Its tone of heartfelt thanks for a good woman's love was unhappily ironic; not long afterwards, Bernie Taupin and Toni were to separate.

Elton played 'Healing Hands' as a finale to his Wogan appearance, seated in Nehru cap before a digital piano, with a back-projected light show which the BBC must have been hoarding since his *Sounds for Saturday* concert in 1971. Though *Sleeping with the Past* made both the British and US album Top 20, the old jinx remained. 'Healing Hands' failed to become a hit single. So did its follow-up, 'Sacrifice'. The impression – as so many times down the years – was of a career gently but inexorably in decline.

The Seventies may have seemed a formless, aimless jumble at the time. But here, on the threshold to the Nineties, they were starting to look better and better. It was like some magic-mushroom-induced dream to remember a time when Britain was governed by the liberal Left rather than the repressive Right; when the rich did not grow constantly richer at the expense of the poor; when social snobbery seemed extinct; when public utilities were not in the hands of private speculators; when tabloid newspapers published news; and when the destiny of youth was to have fun, not to sleep rough on the streets and be liable for the poll tax.

As 1990 dawned, however, there were signs that the garish greed and philistinism of the Thatcher decade might have run their course. Hype now governed everything, and the Nineties received heavy advanced hype as a new era of social reconciliation and 'caring'. Since no one could have 'cared' less than Mrs Thatcher, any small step in that direction by her successors was bound to be highly conspicuous. Those in government now at least acknowledged the problems – for instance, that of endemic homelessness, most shamingly in the nation's capital. Blind eyes ceased to be turned on the cardboard cities around Waterloo and the Strand.

One area where compassion definitely had increased was with regard to AIDS sufferers. The disease was now known to be the scourge not only of junkies and gays but of every sexually active man and woman throughout the world. Through the medium of infected blood, it had been transmitted to celibate haemophiliacs, nuns, children, even unborn babies. The few thousand who suffered its terminal disintegration represented but a fraction of this ghastly spread. Hundreds of thousands, possibly millions, unknowingly carried the HIV virus as a ticking time bomb inside them. No one who had slept with anyone over the past decade could feel entirely easy, now or for half a dozen years to come.

Thanks to his freely admitted bisexual past, Elton clearly was in a high risk category. He owned up to being terrified of AIDS, characteristically, during a 1988 interview for *Woman's Own* magazine. 'Sure, the AIDS problem worries me – it should worry everyone,' he said. 'People ask me if I've ever had an AIDS test. Well, I have. I have blood tests all the time.'

That fear was bound to increase as AIDS plied its knife ever wider through the once carefree, careless world of show business, media and the arts. In four or five years, it had cut down the Hollywood star Rock Hudson, the clothes designers Willie Smith and Perry Ellis, the photographer Robert Mapplethorpe, the actor Ian Charleson, not to mention innumerable celebrity lovers, ex-lovers and friends of friends. Among its saddest victims was Liberace, Elton's great exemplar in piano showmanship and sartorial excess. He was personally grieved, and John Reid still more so, by the death of David Bell, an influential figure in British television and an *éminence grise* to both throughout their careers.

Most public figures at personal risk from AIDS maintained a careful silence on the subject. Elton, however, was among the most visible supporters both of research into finding a cure and of the charities set up to shelter and counsel AIDS victims. It was in large part his doing that rock music's new conscience now embraced the problem, drawing millions into awareness of it via multi-star fund-raising concerts and charity records like his pioneering one with Dionne Warwick and Stevie Wonder. Even now, no one could rival Elton for the grand gesture. In June 1990, he re-released his year-old 'Sacrifice', announcing that all its British royalties would be donated to four AIDS charities: London Lighthouse, Body Positive, Jefferies Research Wing Trust and the Terence Higgins Trust.

That same month, he appeared at a huge charity concert in the grounds of Knebworth Hall, Hertfordshire. The good cause was Music Therapy, a system of using music to teach handicapped children which Elton had already supported for more than a decade. At Knebworth, he contrived to make his old show-stopping impact, even against the massed talents of Eric Clapton, Phil Collins, Cliff Richard, Paul McCartney and Pink Floyd. He later complained that the bill had featured too many 'dinosaurs' like himself, and not enough new young talent.

Not the least factor in changing public attitudes to AIDS had been the courage shown by many of its sufferers. Among the most notable in America was a teenage boy named Ryan White, one of the blameless multitude accidentally infected via blood transfusion. The subsequent story of his parents' ostracism by neighbours and Ryan's own persecution at school, until the family was obliged to flee from its home in Indianapolis, represented the very worst anti-AIDS ignorance and prejudice. Though already terminally ill, Ryan thereafter became an indefatigable campaigner for the rights and dignity of other AIDS sufferers. His bravery won him a nationwide audience and earned a personal commendation from former president Ronald Reagan.

Elton, in America at the time, was deeply moved by the Ryan White story. Like several other celebrities, he travelled to see the dying boy and pay public tribute to his spirit and fortitude. But this was no big-star flying visit. He remained with Ryan until the end, and even then still stayed around, comforting the White family, taking responsibilities off their shoulders, attending the funeral and helping carry the coffin. It was as if a miraculous elder brother had descended out of the blue, just a few days too late.

Willing as British pop fans now were to help AIDS sufferers, and warmly as they esteemed Elton John, what befell his 'charity single' still defies explanation. On its first release, a year previously, 'Sacrifice' had seemed no more than a pleasant period piece, unfashionably slow, heart-searching and tuneful. Reissued in June 1990 – a double A-side with the equally unsuccessful 'Healing Hands' – it suddenly took fire. After twenty-two years' trying, long after having given up hope, Elton suddenly received his heart's desire. He had a British number-one single.

'Sacrifice'/'Healing Hands' stayed at the top for five weeks, finally selling more than 600,000 copies. Adding the proceeds from a follow-up single, 'Club at the End of the Street', Elton was able to present a cheque for £328,000 to his four nominated AIDS organisations. Back on the Terry Wogan show that summer, he announced that in future all royalties from his British singles would be donated to charity.

By the end of 1990, further remarkable things had happened. His *Sleeping with the Past*, a respectable British number six a year earlier, also now leapt back, on the strength of its hit single, to become his first British number-one album since 1977. A few weeks later, he was back in that top spot a second time, with a new compilation album, *The Very Best of Elton John*. Two number-one albums and a smash number-one single made him PolyGram Records' only million-seller in 1990 and, ultimately, Britain's highest-grossing artist on record during the whole year. He had not been so big since Captain Fantastic soared up in silver-winged boots, accompanied by the faithful Brown Dirt Cowboy.

To have been Elton John seems, at the last, strangely unsatisfactory. He has sold records by the billion, amassed walls full of platinum and gold discs, filled great arenas from the Royal Albert Hall to

Madison Square Garden, earned the love of a worldwide audience, the affectionate respect of his peers, the good opinion of pretty well everyone. He has written and sung music which, as much as any other, establishes pop music's fitful claim to be a modern art form. But, even at its unbelievable apogee, his success never seemed enough. And all these years later, he still fusses on, ignoring the piled-up achievement behind him, endlessly worrying whether this or that next one will go Top 20, Top 40 or, horror of horrors, only Top 100. The eras of his glory seem no more substantial than so many courses in a Chinese banquet. There is always the fretful, dyspeptic hunger for more.

A recent survey of Britain's wealthiest people by the *Sunday Times* estimated Elton's personal fortune at £100 million. Whether that can buy him happiness is doubtful. It certainly has not bought him a luxuriant head of hair, a controllable waistline, a stable temperament or a resting place for the heart.

For all those Captain Fantastic years, there is now a heavy price to be paid. In April 1990, John Reid was reported to have entered a detoxification clinic at the Cedars Sinai Medical Center, Los Angeles. A 'source close to Reid' was quoted as saying, 'John has always been a big party man. He likes to go over the top in every way [but] even he now accepts that his dabbling with drugs and drink has gone too far.' Not long afterwards, Elton himself was said to be undergoing treatment at a clinic specialising in 'eating disorders'.

In the autumn of 1990, he returned to *The Sun*'s front page in a story claiming he had joined Alcoholics Anonymous. Despite the paper's obsequious care in calling him 'brave Elton', and praising him editorially for his courage in trying to kick a destructive habit, it was widely speculated that more thunderbolt writs might be hurled towards Wapping. However, none was. And an AA member subsequently reported seeing Elton regularly at two London group sessions, one in Hinde Street, Marylebone, the other in Earls Court. He was said to be throwing himself into the spirit of the thing, testifying frankly about his addiction and joining with enthusiasm in the frequent, mutually supportive group hugs.

From people who met him or talked to him during late 1990, the reports were uniformly good. With Woodside still under renovation, he had moved into a large rented house in London's Holland Park. He had finally done a deal over Watford, selling out to a London property and hire-car magnate named Jack Petchey, while retaining the title of life president. His two British number-one albums seemed to have temporarily sated even his addiction to work, and he had announced he would take the whole of 1991 off. To his oldest friends and associates – Steve Brown, Bernie Taupin, Clive Banks – he seemed at last to have put all his troubles and traumas behind him. Brown, indeed, told an interviewer that, in twenty years, he had never seen Elton happier, more positive about the future or personally at ease.

All this seemed confirmed in December 1990, when he agreed to appear on Jonathan Ross's Channel 4 talk show. He had become a great fan of Ross, whose manager, Gary Farrow, started out as a Rocket Records messenger boy. Both were constant guests at his regular round-table soirées at Mr Chow's restaurant in Knightsbridge.

Jonathan Ross's show unveiled yet another brand-new Elton, lighter by two stone, wearing a wide-brimmed fedora and triumphantly loose-hanging green Versace suit. The Ross show is 'live', and in the dressing room beforehand there was a brief Little Moment, with Elton threatening to walk out because his spot was a few minutes delayed. But once before the cameras, he was his usual candid and lucid self, willing – even anxious – to talk about this further absolutely fresh beginning to his life. He had lost the weight, he said, by giving up sugar and white flour, and by a regimen of abstinence that was for keeps. 'I used to get depressed; I'd overeat and overdrink, and it used to get ridiculous. Because I always wanted too much. Whenever I had a hit record or met someone, I was never happy with just that. I always wanted more. I never gave myself time to stop and smell the roses. Well, now I can stop and I'm going to. I just want to smell a few roses.'

He said the great change had been brought about by the ten days he'd spent with the dying AIDS victim, Ryan White, and his family. 'God, what those people went through. And they had such dignity. Such grace. For all they'd suffered, they bore no grudge towards anyone. They never complained. And I was someone who'd go into a hotel suite and complain because I didn't like it. And I've had such blessings in my life. After that, I'm never, ever going to complain again . . .'

Postscript, 1992

T HE street is one of the least grand to be found in London's white and leafy Holland Park district. On the corner is a down-to-earth pub with a blackboard of bar-food and a beer-garden behind a latticework fence. Opposite runs a terrace of plain-fronted two-storey villas, built in the early 19th-century as servants' quarters for mansions in the neighbouring squares. Though prettified and gleaming, they are still very far from millionaire residences. Only one, half-way along, stands out from its neighbours. Grafted on to its narrow façade is a mock-Georgian pedimented doorway that seems to belong to some much larger and grander establishment. It is also the only house in the row with an illuminated security buzzer, and a pale green Rolls Royce parked outside.

The buzzer's soft electric chord sets off a frantic barking behind the outsize front door. At the same moment, an unmistakable bodyguard figure walks rapidly across the road from the pub's beer-garden.

The barking proves to come from no Rottweiler or Alsatian but from a rangy grey-and-white mutt with good-natured eyes and a silly, bearded face, frisking and worrying around the striped trousers of a black American major domo. 'Thomas thinks everyone comes here to see him,' the major domo explains, leading the way down a narrow, dusky hall. To the left is a polished sideboard, bearing many silver-framed photographs of the same multi-hatted celebrity, hobnobbing with royalty, sports personalities and movie stars. To the right is a small sunken drawing room with primrose-coloured walls and chintzy armchairs. And here, at long last, stands Elton John.

For more than two years, I have been his unauthorised biographer, resigned to his management's firm refusal of all access to him. My book is now on sale in the UK, replete with the anecdotes of friends, business colleagues, even close family; packed with musical, historical and sartorial detail, but, alas, containing not one first-hand quote from its subject. Two afternoons ago, while I was drowsing on my office couch in post-publication tristesse, the telephone rang. I picked it up, expecting to hear my wife. 'Hi,' a familiar light, rapid voice said. 'This is Elton. I'm reading the book. It seems pretty accurate so far. Maybe you'd like to come round for a cup of tea.'

It is the strangest experience, after one has chronicled someone's whole life at second hand, finally to meet him face to face. It is like shaking hands with a character from a novel. The physical details I have tenaciously highlighted and emphasised over 500 pages dwindle to the minor key of real life. In person he is taller than I expected; paler and much thinner. He is wearing a blue baseball cap, a creased T-shirt, striped buccaneer pants and purple pointed shoes, intricately cross-laced. One trait, at least, is as the novelist recorded. As he talks, a jumpy forefinger constantly points up to twitch his glasses straight on his nose.

What follows is not an interview. In an interview, one asks questions, hoping to tease or startle the information out. Here it is understood that I know every twist and cranny of Elton's life during its first forty-three years. We begin *in medias res*, where my biography ended in late 1990. There are next to no questions. He talks for two hours as if dictating a supplementary chapter; at times, as if to his psychiatrist.

'I just wanted to explain why I couldn't co-operate while you were writing the book. It was nothing against you personally. It was just that two years ago when you asked me, I was so totally fucked up I couldn't have done anything like that. But I'm okay now. I've found someone I really love. I'm so in love, it's wonderful. I'm quite comfortable about being gay. I've finally resolved every one of the problems that I had. I'm really happy and optimistic, for the first time ever.'

Even to his biographer, all this is pure revelation. For two years ago, when Elton Hercules John went into semi-retirement, he seemed to have no more problems left to overcome. As he says now, 'There was still one thing I hadn't sorted out. That was me.'

'I was cocaine-addicted. I was an alcoholic. I had a sexual addiction. I was bulimic for six years. It was all through being paranoid about my weight but not able to stop eating. So in the end I'd gorge myself, then deliberately make myself sick. For breakfast I'd have an enormous fry-up, followed by 20 pots of Sainsbury's cockles and then a tub of Häagen-Dazs vanilla ice cream, so that I'd throw it all up again. I never stood still. I was always rushing, always thinking about the next thing. If I was eating a curry, I couldn't wait to throw it up so that I could have the next one.'

Drugs, drink and his stupendous fame had turned him into a monster of ego and megalomania rivalling any in the rock pantheon.

The difference with Elton was that a normal, sensible part of him could always stand back and watch it happening. 'I could be unbelievably horrible and stupid. On tours, I'd get on a plane, then get off it, maybe six or eight times. I'd walk out of a hotel suite because I didn't like the colour of the bedspread. I remember looking out of my room at the Inn on the Park one day and saying, 'It's too windy. Can someone please do something about it?'

His famous tantrums used to astonish him as much as any of their victims. 'What you call "Elton's Little Moments" in the book is spot-on. I never knew where they came from. At one time, I even started having seizures.' (This bears out an American source who told me that, in the late Seventies, she became worried that Elton might be suffering from epilepsy.)

He himself now puts much of the blame on his unhappy, repressed childhood, growing up as Reginald Kenneth Dwight in the Art Deco tedium of Pinner. 'My father never showed me any affection, and that made me keep everything in.* I was always held up by my family as the paragon of what a child should be, which, I think, never left me. I wish I'd had the courage to really express my feelings – like not going onstage and performing when I felt I couldn't face it. But I always made myself do it. I was too afraid of letting people down.'

Without prompting, he describes his second suicide attempt, at the very zenith of his fame, in November 1975. It was 'Elton John Week' in Los Angeles. His footprints had joined those of the movie immortals on Hollywood Boulevard. He was playing sold-out nightly concerts at Dodger Stadium and living in David Selznick's old mansion in the Hollywood Hills. One day, when his proud relations were gathered around his swimming pool, Elton swallowed sixty Valium tablets. 'I jumped into the pool in front of my mother and my seventy-five year-old grandmother, screaming "I'm going to die!" I always remember that, as they pulled me out, I heard my gran say "I suppose we've all got to go home now."'

His excesses gradually estranged him from his mother, that once tireless ally and champion. 'My mum had always supported me and never reproached me, even when I went on record and said I was bisexual. But by the mid-eighties, even she'd had enough. She and my stepfather left England and went to live in Minorca.'

The first straw at which he clutched was having to leave his Old Windsor house during a post-marital gutting and refurbishment that would eventually take almost three years. Lodged in Elton's mind was the awful memory of having met Elvis Presley in 1977, only weeks

*Stanley Dwight died in January 1992.

before Presley's death, in a similar, suffocating mansion. 'He looked terrible – all bloated, with hair-dye trickling down his forehead. He had dozens of people round him, supposedly looking after him, but he already seemed like a corpse. I knew that if I didn't do something now, I could end up in exactly the same way.'

The solution was to rent this small house in Holland Park and make one last, desperate stab at a 'normal' existence. 'My whole life, I'd never lived on my own. First I lived at home with my mum, then I lived with John [Reid], then I was on tour with people constantly around me. In the morning I'd get up, wash, get ready for the day and from then on there were dozens of people to do everything for me. I decided I was going to live alone here, and do everything for myself – make my own phone-calls, pack my own bags to go away. For weeks I stayed in my bedroom, too scared to go out, just doing *The Times* crossword puzzle. In the end, I could do the whole thing in about ten minutes.'

Much of the time his only companion was Thomas, the lanky grey and white mongrel now sprawling untidily on the designer carpet. 'I decided I'd have a dog, so I went to find one at Battersea Dogs' Home. All the dogs in the cages were barking like mad – only one was just lying there, looking as miserable as I felt. I said "that's the one for me."'

He had already met Hugh, the young American he now unabashedly calls 'the love of my life'. In almost twenty years of covert relationships, on and off the road, nothing remotely like it had ever struck Elton before. 'I had a sexual addiction as bad as any of the others. For the first time, I knew someone I wanted to be totally monogamous with. Before, I only took hostages.'

The blight on their love affair was Elton's cocaine addiction, and the drug's deadly illusion of sharpening, not destroying, the user's faculties. 'After I'd had a line of coke I could set the whole world to rights. I'd say to people "You want to do this and that..." It never occurred to me that I was the one who needed help most of all. Finally, it was Hugh who said to me, "You've got to get straight. Love has to be a two-way relationship. At the moment it's a three-way relationship – you, me and coke."'

Hugh also had a drug problem and begged Elton to accompany him into 'detox''. For initial therapy, each had to make a list of what he considered the other's worst faults. 'Hugh's list started "Elton does drugs, he's alcoholic, he's bulimic, he has terrible fits of rage..." My list began "Hugh never puts his CDs away tidily..."'

When Hugh began detoxification in earnest, Elton's first thought was that their relationship was over. 'I went to see him in hospital, and it was awful. I came back to this house and wrecked the whole place, tore up all his photographs. Then I realised it was him I loved, there was no one else. If we were going to have a future, I had to get myself properly back on the rails.'

The problem was finding a rehabilitation programme that could help someone so comprehensively self-abused. All the big-star clinics turned Elton away, saying he had too many addictions for them to handle. The only detox' centre that would take him was at the Parkside Lutheran Hospital in Chicago. Inmates had to endure a spartan regime, living two to a room in army-style beds and doing their own laundry. 'I had to take all these little packets of detergent in my luggage. On the journey there, the one thing that terrified me was that I wouldn't be able to work the washing-machine. When I saw the place, I almost checked out. But then I thought, "Elton, there's nowhere else to go."'

Part of his therapy at Parkside was to write a letter to cocaine, bidding it a formal and conclusive farewell. He fetches the letter, on neatly handwritten yellow sheets, and reads it aloud. It is Elton John's *De Profundis*, a beautifully composed elegy, as if the wicked white powder were some beautiful, heedless woman. 'I have sent cars – even planes – to pick you up...' One wonders afresh why someone so literate and articulate has always been afraid to write lyrics for his own songs. When he read the cocaine letter to Bernie Taupin, it made Bernie cry.

During the treatment in Chicago, Elton and his mother became reconciled. 'She'd write to me. I'd cry when I read her letters. She's told me she'd cry when she read mine. Now that I'm okay, she's come back to live in England again. The funny thing is, while she was in Minorca her health got bad. Since she got home, she's been perfectly well. It must have been all psychological, because of worrying about me.'

He also began attending AA meetings in Los Angeles and at two centres in London. 'It was wonderful, the way they just accepted me. They didn't care who I was. For the first time in twenty years I could feel totally anonymous. The incredible thing about AA is that, whatever your addiction has made you do, there's never any blame, only sympathy and love. At one meeting, we all had to confess to something in our pasts that we were really ashamed of. I confessed that I'd only got married to please my mother. Then a young woman got up and confessed to something so tragic and traumatic that I thought I ought to do better with my confession, so I told them about something really really bad that I'd once done.'

Though never conventionally religious, he now makes frequent reference to the 'Higher Power' which AA encourages its members to invoke in their battle against self. The group's emphasis on human contact, hand-holding and hugging, has been no less revelatory to someone who always found difficulty with giving and receiving affection. 'After one meeting, this boy came up to me very shyly and said "Do you mind if I speak to you?" He wanted to confess to me that he was gay. After that, he slipped – what we call going back on the booze. We didn't see him for a while and when he next came to a group, he'd been sleeping rough, and looked it. I hugged him, and sat and held his hand through the whole meeting.'

The former Nero-gorging bulimic now follows a healthy regime of three meals per day with no snacking in between, no sugar or white flour. His major domo and a maid enter with a silver tray of tea, smoked salmon sandwiches sprinkled with cress, and a dark chocolate cake under a glass dome. The new self-help Elton pours my tea, adds milk to it and cuts me a slice of the 'chocky cake' he himself is forbidden. He tips forward his baseball cap, giving a brief glimpse of the crown where hair-transplant surgeons have worked as long and intricately as embroiderers on the Bayeux Tapestry. All in vain, it would appear. There are just a few dark strands floating in parallel, like seaweed on an ebb tide.

Now completely settled and monogamous, he divides his time between his London house and Hugh in America. 'We do ordinary things together that I've never done in my whole life. We go to Paris like ordinary tourists, and go up the Eiffel Tower. I'd never been up the Eiffel Tower before. We go to Hawaii and swim in the ocean. I'd been to Hawaii about nine times on tours, but never thought of going in the ocean.' When travelling alone, he asks a fellow AA group member to accompany him. Under AA rules, only two people are needed to constitute an official meeting.

He speaks fondly of Renate, whom he certainly married for love if also to please his mother. It remains miraculous to him that Renate was not after his millions, but genuinely wanted the relationship to work on any terms Elton chose. He still appreciates her dignity and restraint, during their drawn-out public separation, and a loyalty to him which never wavered. 'When *The Sun* came out with their rent-boy stories, Renate was ready to go into court and speak for me. And we'd already decided to split up by that time.'

Around him today there are few signs of the impulse-buying sprees that once crammed Woodside, his country house, to the roof. On the walls hang one or two paintings of quietly manifest quality. In a raised recess stands an electric piano and a multi-coloured jukebox of compact discs. His one remaining addiction is buying clothes. 'I still do it at incredible speed. It's all a hangover from childhood, when my mum would bring me up to London to look at a coat she wanted to buy. "I don't know," she'd always say. "We'd better come back next week and have another look..."'

He acknowledges that, while his fame has brought huge problems, it also brought moments undreamed by a boy named Reg from suburban Middlesex. 'Like playing for Prince Andrew's 21st birthday party at Windsor Castle. When I arrived, there was no one there but the dance band and Princess Diana. We danced the Charleston alone on the floor for twenty minutes. Then Princess Anne came up to me and said "Would you like to dance?" What am I going to say? "No – fuck off"? We went into this disco where the music was so quiet, you could hardly hear it. As we're bobbing up and down, the Queen comes up with an equerry and says "Do you mind if we join you?" Just at that moment, the music segues into Bill Haley's *Rock Around The Clock*. So I'm dancing to *Rock Around The Clock* with the Queen of England.'

After almost three years, Woodside is nearly ready for him to move back. In place of the former Art Nouveau, Lalique and Bugatti warehouse there is now a mature country squire's residence, all quiet colours, understated prints and open fireplaces. In the grounds is a new ornamental lake containing three million gallons of water. Thomas, the mongrel, will be introduced to Elton's other pet dogs, two German shepherds and two Irish wolfhounds. One corner of the garden is kept as a cemetery for his dogs down the years. 'There are all these little headstones with names like Bruce and Brian. Anyone looking at them might think they were old boyfriends I'd bumped off.'

He is as interested as ever in the contemporary music scene, as acerbic as ever in his comments about it. He detests rap and the post-uring and laziness of young bands who think the only key to success is making a trendy video. 'The way to get on isn't any different from when I started in the early Seventies. You've got to go out there and grab the audience; travel America coast to coast as number two on the bill; build up your following in Europe. Nothing beats working your ass off.'

Since the triple surprise success of 1990 – his first UK number one single and two number one albums – his name has stayed up there among pop's young lions and lionesses. A boxed four-CD set, *To Be Continued...*, includes rarities like his first recorded vocal, *Come Back Baby*, with Bluesology. Also in 1991 came *Two Rooms*, an album breaking the convention that Elton John/Bernie Taupin songs are seldom, if ever, covered by other artists. Assorted British and

American superstar friends paid tribute to the partnership with original and oddball cover-versions – Eric Clapton, for instance, doing *Border Song*, and Kate Bush an eccentric squeezebox version of *Rocket Man*.

Now, the only remaining problem for Elton is 'what next?' For years, people have been saying that he and Bernie should develop their colossally successful partnership by writing a stage musical. Elton says he's sometimes tempted, just to pay out Andrew Lloyd Webber for all those shows without tunes. 'The trouble is, I'm not really that keen on musicals. To be honest, I've no idea what I'll be doing over the next few years. It could just as well be something charitable.'

His parting words are about my biography: 'Thanks for all the dedication.' Before I leave, he writes my name and phone number carefully in his neat little self-help Filofax. 'I'm off to the States in a few days. But I'll let you know what I think of the book when I finish it. I'll call you and maybe we can go to dinner...'

Since then, nothing.

Discography
by Mark Lewisohn

The following discography charts Elton John's entire career, spanning UK record releases from his first session with Bluesology in 1965 to early 1991.

All compositions are by Elton John and Bernie Taupin, unless denoted by one of the following symbols:

[1] composed by Elton John only
[2] composed by Elton John and Bernie Taupin with one or more other writers
[3] composed by Elton John and Gary Osborne
[4] composed by Elton John and Gary Osborne with one or more other writers
[5] composed by Elton John with one or more other writers but not Taupin or Osborne
[6] composed by neither Elton John nor Bernie Taupin
[7] composed by Reg Dwight only (pre-name-change to Elton John)
[8] composed by Reg Dwight with three other writers.

'Don't Go Breaking My Heart' and 'Hard Luck Story' were written by John–Taupin under the pseudonyms Ann Orson–Carte Blanche. 'Cartier Commercial' was written by John–Taupin under the pseudonyms Dinah Card–Carte Blanche. 'Choc Ice Goes Mental' was written by Elton John only, under the pseudonym Choc Ice.

In the USA, 'Sartorial Eloquence' was called 'Don't Ya Wanna Play This Game No More?' and 'Screw You' was retitled 'Young Man's Blues'.

Unless otherwise stated, the artist credit on all singles and albums is Elton John.

Singles

July 1965	'Come Back, Baby'[7]/'Times Getting Tougher Than Tough'[6] (*Bluesology*)
February 1966	'Mr Frantic'[7]/'Everyday (I Have the Blues)'[6] (*Bluesology*)
October 1967	'Since I Found You Baby'[6]/'Just a Little Bit'[6] (*Stu Brown & Bluesology*)
March 1968	'I've Been Loving You'/'Here's to the Next Time'[1]
January 1969	'Lady Samantha'/'All Across the Havens'
February 1969	'The Dick Barton Theme (The Devil's Gallop)'[6]/'Breakdown Blues'[8] (*The Bread and Beer Band*)
May 1969	'It's Me That You Need'/'Just Like Strange Rain'
March 1970	'Border Song'/'Bad Side of the Moon'
June 1970	'Rock and Roll Madonna'/'Grey Seal'
January 1971	'Your Song'/'Into the Old Man's Shoes'
April 1971	'Friends'/'Honey Roll'
April 1972	'Rocket Man (I Think It's Going to Be a Long, Long Time)'/'Holiday Inn', 'Goodbye'
August 1972	'Honky Cat'/'It's Me That You Need', 'Lady Samantha'
October 1972	'Crocodile Rock'/'Elderberry Wine'
January 1973	'Daniel'/'Skyline Pigeon'
June 1973	'Saturday Night's Alright for Fighting'/'Jack Rabbit', 'Whenever You're Ready (We'll Go Steady Again)'
September 1973	'Goodbye Yellow Brick Road'/'Screw You'
November 1973	'Step into Christmas'/'Ho! Ho! Ho! (Who'd Be a Turkey at Christmas?)'
February 1974	'Candle in the Wind'/'Bennie and the Jets'
May 1974	'Don't Let the Sun Go Down on Me'/'Sick City'
August 1974	'The Bitch Is Back'/'Cold Highway'

November 1974   'Lucy in the Sky with Diamonds'[6]/'One Day at a Time'[6]

February 1975   'Philadelphia Freedom'/'I Saw Her Standing There'[6] (*A-side credited to the Elton John Band; B-side to the Elton John Band featuring John Lennon & the Muscle Shoals Horns*)

June 1975   'Someone Saved My Life Tonight'/'House of Cards'

September 1975   'Island Girl'/'Sugar on the Floor'[6]

January 1976   'Grow Some Funk of Your Own'[2]/'I Feel Like a Bullet (in the Gun of Robert Ford)'

March 1976   'Pinball Wizard'[6]/'Harmony'

June 1976   'Don't Go Breaking My Heart'/'Snow Queen'[2] (*duets with Kiki Dee*)

September 1976   'Bennie and the Jets'/'Rock and Roll Madonna'

October 1976   'Sorry Seems to Be the Hardest Word'/'Shoulder Holster'

February 1977   'Crazy Water'/'Chameleon'

June 1977   'Bite Your Lip (Get Up and Dance!)'/'Chicago'[6] (*Double A-side. 'Chicago' performed only by Kiki Dee*)

March 1978   'Ego'/'Flintstone Boy'[1]

October 1978   'Part-Time Love'[3]/'I Cry at Night'

December 1978   'Song for Guy'[1]/'Lovesick'

April 1979   'Are You Ready for Love (Part 1)'[6]/'Are You Ready for Love (Part 2)'[6] (*Other format also includes* 'Three Way Love Affair'[6], 'Mama Can't Buy You Love'[6])

September 1979   'Victim of Love'[6]/'Strangers'[3]

November 1979   'Johnny B. Goode'[6]/'Thunder in the Night'[6]

May 1980   'Little Jeannie'[3]/'Conquer the Sun'[3]

August 1980   'Sartorial Eloquence'[5]/'White Man Danger'[3], 'Cartier Commercial'

November 1980   'Dear God'[3]/'Tactics'[1] (*Other format also includes* 'Steal Away Child'[3], 'Love So Cold')

March 1981   'I Saw Her Standing There'[6]/'Whatever Gets You Thru the Night'[6], 'Lucy in the Sky with Diamonds'[6] (*The Elton John Band featuring John Lennon & the Muscle Shoals Horns*)

May 1981   'Nobody Wins'[6]/'Fools in Fashion'

July 1981   'Just Like Belgium'/'Can't Get Over Getting Over Losing You'[3]

March 1982   'Blue Eyes'[3]/'Hey Papa Legba'

May 1982   'Empty Garden (Hey Hey Johnny)'/'Take Me Down to the Ocean'[3]

September 1982   'Princess'[3]/'The Retreat'

November 1982   'All Quiet on the Western Front'/'Where Have All the Good Times Gone?'

April 1983   'I Guess That's Why They Call It the Blues'[2], 'Choc Ice Goes Mental'[1] (*B-side artist credit: Lord Choc Ice, pseudonym for Elton John*)

July 1983   'I'm Still Standing'/'Earn While You Learn'[1] (*B-side artist credit: Lord Choc Ice, pseudonym for Elton John*)

October 1983   'Kiss the Bride'/'Dreamboat'[4] (*Other format also includes* 'Ego'/'Song for Guy'[1])

November 1983   'Cold as Christmas'/'Crystal' (*Other formats also include* 'Don't Go Breaking My Heart'/'Snow Queen'[2] (*duets with Kiki Dee*) *and* 'J'veux d'la Tendresse'[6])

May 1984   'Sad Songs (Say So Much)'/'A Simple Man'[3]

August 1984   'Passengers'[2]/'Lonely Boy'[3]

October 1984   'Who Wears These Shoes?'/'Tortured' (*Other format also includes* 'I Heard It Through the Grapevine'[6] *live*)

February 1985   'Breaking Hearts (Ain't What It Used to Be)'/'In Neon'

June 1985   'Act of War (Part 1)'/'Act of War (Part 2)' (*duet with Millie Jackson*)

October 1985   'Nikita'/'The Man Who Never Died'[1] (*Other formats also include* 'Sorry Seems to Be the Hardest Word' *live*/'I'm Still Standing' *live*)

November 1985   'Wrap Her Up'[2]/'Restless' *live* (*A-side duet with George Michael*)

February 1986   'Cry to Heaven'/'Candy by the Pound' (*Other format also includes* 'Rock and Roll Medley' *live*: 'Whole Lotta Shakin' Going On'[6]/'I Saw Her Standing There'[6]/'Twist and Shout'[6])

September 1986   'Heartache All Over the World'/'Highlander'[1]

November 1986   'Slow Rivers'/'Billy and the Kids' (*A-side duet with Cliff Richard. Other format also includes* 'Lord of the Flies')

July 1987   'Your Song' *live*/'Don't Let the Sun Go Down on Me' *live* (*Other format also includes* 'I Need You To Turn To' *live*, 'The Greatest Discovery' *live*)

January 1988	'Candle in the Wind' (*live*)/'Sorry Seems to Be the Hardest Word' (*live*) (*Other formats also include* 'Your Song' *live*, 'Don't Let the Sun Go Down on Me' *live*)
May 1988	'I Don't Wanna Go on with You Like That'/'Rope Around a Fool'
August 1988	'Town of Plenty'/'Whipping Boy' (*Other format also includes* 'My Baby's a Saint', 'I Guess That's Why They Call It the Blues'[2])
November 1988	'A Word in Spanish'/'Heavy Traffic'[2] (*Other format also includes* 'Song For Guy'[1], 'Blue Eyes'[3], 'I Guess That's Why They Call It The Blues'[2])
August 1989	'Healing Hands'/'Dancing In the End Zone'[2] (*Other formats also include* 'Sad Songs (Say So Much)')
October 1989	'Sacrifice'/'Love is a Cannibal'[2]
June 1990	'Sacrifice'/'Healing Hands'
August 1990	'Club at the End of the Street'/'Whispers'[6] (*Other formats also include* 'I Don't Wanna Go on with You Like That' *live*)
October 1990	'You Gotta Love Someone'/'Medicine Man'
November 1990	'Easier To Walk Away'/'I Swear I Heard the Night Talkin'' (*Other formats also include* 'Made For Me')
February 1991	'Don't Let the Sun Go Down on Me'/'Song For Guy'[1] (*Other formats also include* 'Sorry Seems To Be The Hardest Word')

Albums

June 1969   *Empty Sky*
A: 'Empty Sky', 'Val-Hala', 'Western Ford Gateway', 'Hymn 2000'
B: 'Lady, What's Tomorrow?', 'Sails', 'The Scaffold', 'Skyline Pigeon', medley: 'Gulliver'/'Hay Chewed'[1]

April 1970   *Elton John*
A: 'Your Song', 'I Need You to Turn To', 'Take Me to the Pilot', 'No Shoe Strings on Louise', 'First Episode at Hienton'
B: 'Sixty Years On', 'Border Song', 'The Greatest Discovery', 'The Cage', 'The King Must Die'

October 1970   *Tumbleweed Connection*
A: 'Ballad of a Well-Known Gun', 'Come Down in Time', 'Country Comfort', 'Son of Your Father', 'My Father's Gun'
B: 'Where to Now, St Peter?', 'Love Song'[6], 'Amoreena', 'Talking Old Soldiers', 'Burn Down the Mission'

April 1971   *17–11–70*
A: 'Take Me to the Pilot', 'Honky Tonk Women'[6] 'Sixty Years On', 'Can I Put You On?'
B: 'Bad Side of the Moon', medley: 'Burn Down the Mission'/'My Baby Left Me'[6]/'Get Back'[6]

May 1971   *Friends* (Original Soundtrack Recording)
A: 'Friends', 'Honey Roll', '*Variations on 'Friends' Theme (The First Kiss)*'[6], 'Seasons', '*Variations on Michelle's Song (A Day in the Country)*'[6], 'Can I Put You On?'
B: 'Michelle's Song', '*I Meant to Do My Work Today*'[2], '*Four Moods*'[6], 'Seasons (Reprise)'
                                                        (*Italicised titles not performed by Elton John*)

November 1971   *Madman Across the Water*
A: 'Tiny Dancer', 'Levon', 'Razor Face', 'Madman Across the Water'
B: 'Indian Sunset', 'Holiday Inn', 'Rotten Peaches', 'All the Nasties', 'Goodbye'

May 1972   *Honky Château*
A: 'Honky Cat', 'Mellow', 'I Think I'm Going to Kill Myself', 'Susie (Dramas)', 'Rocket Man (I Think It's Going to Be a Long, Long Time)'
B: 'Salvation', 'Slave', 'Amy', 'Mona Lisas and Mad Hatters', 'Hercules'

January 1973   *Don't Shoot Me, I'm Only the Piano Player*
A: 'Daniel', 'Teacher, I Need You', 'Elderberry Wine', 'Blues for My Baby and Me', 'Midnight Creeper'
B: 'Have Mercy on the Criminal', 'I'm Going to Be a Teenage Idol', 'Texan Love Song', 'Crocodile Rock', 'High-Flying Bird'

October 1973   *Goodbye Yellow Brick Road*

A: medley: 'Funeral for a Friend'/'Love Lies Bleeding', 'Candle in the Wind', 'Bennie and the Jets'

B: 'Goodbye Yellow Brick Road', 'This Song Has No Title', 'Grey Seal', 'Jamaica Jerk-Off', 'I've Seen That Movie Too'

C: 'Sweet Painted Lady', 'The Ballad of Danny Bailey (1909–34)', 'Dirty Little Girl', 'All the Girls Love Alice'

D: 'Your Sister Can't Twist (but She Can Rock 'n' Roll)', 'Saturday Night's Alright for Fighting', 'Roy Rogers', 'Social Disease', 'Harmony'

June 1974   *Caribou*

A: 'The Bitch Is Back', 'Pinky', 'Grimsby', 'Dixie Lily', 'Solar Prestige à Gammon', 'You're So Static'

B: 'I've Seen the Saucers', 'Stinker', 'Don't Let the Sun Go Down on Me', 'Ticking'

May 1975   *Captain Fantastic and the Brown Dirt Cowboy*

A: 'Captain Fantastic and the Brown Dirt Cowboy', 'Tower of Babel', 'Bitter Fingers', 'Tell Me When the Whistle Blows', 'Someone Saved My Life Tonight'

B: '(Gotta Get a) Meal Ticket', 'Better Off Dead', 'Writing', 'We All Fall in Love Sometimes', 'Curtains'

October 1975   *Rock of the Westies*

A: medley: 'Yell Help'[2]/'Wednesday Night'[2]/'Ugly'[2], 'Dan Dare (Pilot of the Future)', 'Island Girl', 'Grow Some Funk of Your Own'[2], 'I Feel Like a Bullet (in the Gun of Robert Ford)'

B: 'Street Kids', 'Hard Luck Story', 'Feed Me', 'Billy Bones and the White Bird'

April 1976   *Here and There*

A: 'Skyline Pigeon', 'Border Song', 'Honky Cat', 'Love Song'[6], 'Crocodile Rock'

B: medley: 'Funeral for a Friend'/'Love Lies Bleeding', 'Rocket Man (I Think It's Going to Be a Long, Long Time)', 'Bennie and the Jets', 'Take Me to the Pilot'

October 1976   *Blue Moves*

A: 'Your Starter for . . .'[6], 'Tonight', 'One Horse Town'[2], 'Chameleon'

B: 'Boogie Pilgrim'[2], 'Cage the Songbird'[2], 'Crazy Water', 'Shoulder Holster'

C: 'Sorry Seems to Be the Hardest Word', 'Out of the Blue', 'Between Seventeen and Twenty'[2], 'The Wide-Eyed and Laughing'[2], 'Someone's Final Song'

D: 'Where's the Shoorah?', 'If There's a God in Heaven (What's He Waiting for?)'[2], 'Idol', 'Theme from a Non-Existent TV Series', 'Bite Your Lip (Get Up and Dance!)'

October 1978   *A Single Man*

A: 'Shine on Through'[3], 'Return to Paradise'[3], 'I Don't Care'[3], 'Big Dipper'[3], 'It Ain't Gonna Be Easy'[3]

B: 'Part-Time Love'[3], 'Georgia'[3], 'Shooting Star'[3], 'Madness'[3], 'Reverie'[1], 'Song for Guy'[1]

October 1979   *Victim of Love*

A: 'Johnny B. Goode'[6], 'Warm Love in a Cold World'[6], 'Born Bad'[6]

B: 'Thunder in the Night'[6], 'Spotlight'[6], 'Street Boogie'[6], 'Victim of Love'[6]

May 1980   *21 At 33*

A: 'Chasing the Crown', 'Little Jeannie'[3], 'Sartorial Eloquence'[5], 'Two Rooms at the End of the World'

B: 'White Lady White Powder', 'Dear God'[3], 'Never Gonna Fall in Love Again'[5], 'Take Me Back'[3], 'Give Me the Love'[5]

May 1981   *The Fox*

A: 'Breaking Down the Barriers'[3], 'Heart in the Right Place'[3], 'Just Like Belgium', 'Nobody Wins'[6], 'Fascist Faces'

B: medley: 'Carla'[1]/'Etude'[1]/'Fanfare'[5]/'Chloe'[3], 'Heels of the Wind', 'Elton's Song'[5], 'The Fox'

April 1982   *Jump Up!*

A: 'Dear John'[3], 'Spiteful Child', 'Ball & Chain'[3], 'Legal Boys'[5], 'I am Your Robot', 'Blue Eyes'[3]

B: 'Empty Garden (Hey Hey Johnny)', 'Princess'[3], 'Where Have All the Good Times Gone?', 'All Quiet on the Western Front'

June 1983   *Too Low for Zero*

A: 'Cold as Christmas', 'I'm Still Standing', 'Too Low for Zero', 'Religion', 'I Guess That's Why They Call It the Blues'[2]

B: 'Crystal', 'Kiss the Bride', 'Whipping Boy', 'My Baby's a Saint', 'One More Arrow'

June 1984 *Breaking Hearts*
A: 'Restless', 'Slow Down Georgie (She's Poison)', 'Who Wears These Shoes?', 'Breaking Hearts (Ain't What It Used to Be)', 'Li'l 'Frigerator'
B: 'Passengers'[2], 'In Neon', 'Burning Buildings', 'Did He Shoot Her?', 'Sad Songs (Say So Much)'

November 1985 *Ice On Fire*
A: 'This Town', 'Cry to Heaven', 'Soul Glove', 'Nikita', 'Too Young'
B: 'Wrap Her Up'[2], 'Satellite', 'Tell Me What the Papers Say', 'Candy by the Pound', 'Shoot Down the Moon' (*Compact disc and cassette versions also include* 'Act of War')

November 1986 *Leather Jackets*
A: 'Leather Jackets', 'Hoop of Fire', 'Don't Trust That Woman'[6], 'Go It Alone', 'Gypsy Heart'
B: 'Slow Rivers', 'Heartache All Over the World', 'Angeline'[2], 'Memory of Love'[3], 'Paris', 'I Fall Apart'

September 1987 *Live in Australia*
A: 'Sixty Years On', 'I Need You to Turn To', 'The Greatest Discovery', 'Tonight'
B: 'Sorry Seems to Be the Hardest Word', 'The King Must Die', 'Take Me to the Pilot', 'Tiny Dancer'
C: 'Have Mercy on the Criminal', 'Madman Across the Water', 'Candle in the Wind'
D: 'Burn Down the Mission', 'Your Song', 'Don't Let the Sun Go Down on Me'

July 1988 *Reg Strikes Back*
A: 'Town of Plenty', 'A Word in Spanish', 'Mona Lisas and Mad Hatters (Part Two)', 'I Don't Wanna Go on with You Like That', 'Japanese Hands'
B: 'Goodbye Marlon Brando', 'The Camera Never Lies', 'Heavy Traffic'[2], 'Poor Cow', 'Since God Invented Girls'

September 1989 *Sleeping with the Past*
A: 'Durban Deep', 'Healing Hands', 'Whispers', 'Club at the End of the Street', 'Sleeping with the Past'
B: 'Stones Throw from Hurtin'', 'Sacrifice', 'I Never Knew Her Name', 'Amazes Me', 'Blue Avenue'

Other Recordings

June 1969
This was the month in which the début album by the Bread and Beer Band was set for release, although it was withdrawn before issue and did not exist beyond test pressings and sample covers. The band – consisting of Reg Dwight (keyboards), Bernie Calvert (bass), Caleb Quaye (guitar), Roger Pope (drums) and two Jamaican percussionists, Rolfo and Lennox – taped two songs at EMI Studios, Abbey Road, on 2 December, 1968, a version of 'The Dick Barton Theme (The Devil's Gallop)' and 'Breakdown Blues', the latter jointly written by all four band members. These formed two sides of an unsuccessful single, issued by Decca in February 1969.

Undaunted by the failure, the Bread and Beer Band taped cover versions of ten more songs in two further Abbey Road sessions, on 19 March and 9 April, 1969. These were produced by Chris Thomas who, in the 1980s, would produce several Elton John albums. The ten songs were compiled into an album and test-pressings were made but the project went no further, and it remains commercially unreleased to this day. Had it appeared, the album would have contained the following.
A: 'Woolly Bully', 'Mellow Yellow', 'If I Were a Carpenter', 'Zorba's Dance', 'The Letter'
B: 'Quick Joey Small', 'Needles and Pins', 'God Knows (A Bit of Freedom)', 'Billy's Bag', 'Last Night'

April 1970
A recording of Elton John singing 'From Denver To LA' appeared on the film soundtrack album *The Games*, released only in the USA. He did not compose the song. Backed by an altogether unrelated film piece, it was also issued as the A-side of a US single, his artist credit erroneously reading 'Elton Johns'.

March 1975
The first release of Elton John's cover of the Who's 'Pinball Wizard', included on the soundtrack album of the film *Tommy*. Elton released it as a single in March 1976.

April 1977
'The Goaldiggers Song'/'Jimmy, Brian, Elton & Eric' was a special Rocket Records single, recorded to raise funds for Goaldiggers, a British football charity. It was not released commercially and only 500 copies were pressed. The A-side features an otherwise unissued Elton John solo composition and recording. The B-side consists of spoken messages from Elton, the football commentators Jimmy Hill and Brian Moore, and the comedian Eric Morecambe, then a director of Luton Town FC.

February 1980
Numerous compilation albums of Elton John recordings have been issued over the years, mostly collections of hits. One particularly interesting model was *Lady Samantha*, first issued on record at this time but available on cassette since September 1974, which brought together fourteen of the more obscure releases from Elton's early recording career, many of which were no longer available in their original format.
A: 'Rock and Roll Madonna', 'Whenever You're Ready (We'll Go Steady Again)', 'Bad Side of the Moon', 'Jack Rabbit', 'Into the Old Man's Shoes', 'It's Me That You Need', 'Ho! Ho! Ho! (Who'd Be a Turkey at Christmas?)'
B: 'Skyline Pigeon', 'Screw You', 'Just Like Strange Rain', 'Grey Seal', 'Honey Roll', 'Lady Samantha', 'Friends'

February 1981
Elton John recorded two songs in the French language with France Gall, one of the leading female vocalists in France, and the original singer of 'J'veux d'la Tendresse' (see below). The songs were 'Les Aveux' (meaning 'avowal') written by Elton John with Michel Berger (Gall's husband), and 'Donner Pour Donner' (meaning 'giving for giving'), written by Berger with Bernie Taupin. In that order, as A- and B-sides, the songs were issued as a February 1981 single in France by Atlantic Records.

May 1981
'J'veux d'la Tendresse' – the original French version of 'Nobody Wins', written by Jean-Paul Dreau, meaning, literally, "I want tenderness" – was recorded by Elton John in that language, and released as a single by Rocket Records in France. (The B-side, 'Fools in Fashion', was in English.) The French-language recording also replaced its English counterpart on local pressings of Elton's album *The Fox*, issued in May 1981. 'J'veux d'la Tendresse' was not released in Britain until December 1983, as a bonus track on the twelve-inch single of 'Cold as Christmas'.

July 1981
The B-side of the US-only single release 'Chloe' (from the album *The Fox*) was the song 'Troubled', yet to be issued in Britain.

May 1983
'Take Me Down to the Ocean', composed by Elton John and Gary Osborne and otherwise available only as the B-side of the May 1982 single 'Empty Garden (Hey Hey Johnny)', was included on the soundtrack album of the film *Summer Lovers*.

April 1987
Elton appeared on *The Prince's Trust 10th Anniversary Birthday Party*, the album of the Wembley Arena show on 20 June, 1986, singing 'I'm Still Standing'. He was also pianist in the all-star band which perform several numbers backing guest vocalists.

August 1987
Elton appeared on *The Prince's Trust Concert 1987*, the double album of the Wembley Arena show on 6 June, 1987, singing 'Saturday Night's Alright for Fighting' and 'Your Song'. He was also pianist in the all-star band which perform several numbers backing guest vocalists.

October 1988
A BBC Radio session recording of the *Tumbleweed Connection* album track 'My Father's Gun' was included on the various-artists compilation album *21 Years of Alternative Radio 1*. It was recorded for broadcast in 1970.

February 1989
Between *Reg Strikes Back* and *Sleeping with the Past*, MCA Records in the USA issued a six-track album, *The Complete Thom Bell Sessions*, featuring the full complement of songs Elton recorded in Seattle and Philadelphia in the autumn of 1977. Three of the titles ('Mama Can't Buy You Love', 'Are You Ready for Love' and 'Three Way Love Affair') had been issued as a single in April 1979. The other three were previously unreleased: 'Nice and Slow' (composed

Elton John–Bernie Taupin–Thom Bell), 'Country Love Song' (cover version) and 'Shine on Through' (Elton John–Gary Osborne). The album was originally scheduled for full international release in autumn 1982 but had been withheld.

May 1989
Elton John contributed 'I'm Ready', a new exclusive cover-version recording, to the various artists' concept album *Rock, Rhythm & Blues*.

August 1989
'Love is a Cannibal', otherwise available only as the B-side of the October 1989 single 'Sacrifice', was first released on the soundtrack album of the film *Ghostbusters II*.

July 1990
'Medicine Man', otherwise available only as the B-side of the October 1990 single 'You Gotta Love Someone', was first released on the Romanian Angel Appeal charity album *Nobody's Child*.

August 1990
Elton appeared on *Knebworth – The Album*, the double-album of the celebrated charity concert which took place there on 30 June, 1990, singing 'Sad Songs (Say So Much)' and 'Saturday Night's Alright for Fighting'.

August 1990
Some non-UK European pressings of the single 'Club at the End of the Street' featured as a bonus track a previously unissued December 1988 Elton John studio performance of Lennon–McCartney's 'Give Peace A Chance'.

August 1990
'You Gotta Love Someone', issued as a single and as part of the boxed-set *To Be Continued . . .* in October 1990, was first released on the soundtrack album of the film *Days Of Thunder*.

October 1990
Elton John's 25th anniversary as a recording artist was celebrated in the USA by the release of a four-CD (also four-cassette) boxed set, *To Be Continued . . .* No better summary of John's career is available. There were several rarities among the 68 tracks, such as 'Come Back, Baby', his début composition and the début single by Bluesology, the original (1970) version of 'Grey Seal' and 'Donner Pour Donner', one of his two duets with France Gall; six others were previously unavailable: a solo demo of 'Your Song', live versions of 'I Feel Like a Bullet (in the Gun of Robert Ford)' and 'Carla'/'Etude', and three more new (July 1990) recordings, 'Made For Me', 'I Swear I Heard the Night Talkin'' and 'Easier to Walk Away'. The full list of 68 tracks lined up as follows:
CD/Cassette 1: 'Come Back, Baby', 'Lady Samantha', 'It's Me That You Need', 'Your Song', 'Rock and Roll Madonna', 'Bad Side of the Moon', 'Your Song', 'Take Me to the Pilot', 'Border Song', 'Sixty Years On', 'Country Comfort', 'Grey Seal', 'Friends', 'Levon', 'Tiny Dancer', 'Madman Across the Water', 'Honky Cat', 'Mona Lisas and Mad Hatters'.
CD/Cassette 2: 'Rocket Man (I Think It's Going to Be a Long, Long Time)', 'Daniel', 'Crocodile Rock', 'Bennie and the Jets', 'Goodbye Yellow Brick Road', 'All The Girls Love Alice', 'Funeral For a Friend'/'Love Lies Bleeding', 'Whenever You're Ready (We'll Go Steady Again)', 'Saturday Night's Alright for Fighting', 'Jack Rabbit', 'Harmony', 'Young Man's Blues', 'Step Into Christmas', 'The Bitch Is Back', 'Pinball Wizard', 'Someone Saved My Life Tonight'.
CD/Cassette 3: 'Philadelphia Freedom', 'One Day At A Time', 'Lucy in the Sky with Diamonds', 'I Saw Her Standing There', 'Island Girl', 'Sorry Seems to Be the Hardest Word', 'Don't Go Breaking My Heart', 'I Feel Like a Bullet (in the Gun of Robert Ford)', 'Ego', 'Song For Guy', 'Mama Can't Buy You Love', 'Cartier Commercial', 'Little Jeannie', 'Donner Pour Donner', 'Fanfare', 'Chloe', 'The Retreat', 'Blue Eyes'.
CD/Cassette 4: 'Empty Garden (Hey Hey Johnny)', 'I Guess That's Why They Call It the Blues', 'I'm Still Standing', 'Sad Songs (Say So Much)', 'Act Of War', 'Nikita', 'Candle in the Wind', 'Carla'/'Etude', 'Don't Let the Sun Go Down on Me', 'I Don't Wanna Go on with You Like That', 'Give Peace A Chance', 'Sacrifice', 'Made For Me', 'You Gotta Love Someone', 'I Swear I Heard the Night Talkin'', 'Easier to Walk Away'.

January 1991
Elton John contributed 'The Measure of a Man', a new cover-version recording, to the soundtrack album *Music from the Film Rocky V*.

May 1991
Elton John contributed a recording of 'The Pacifier', a solo instrumental composition, to the Pediatric AIDS Foundation charity album *For Our Children*, issued in the USA.

The Songwriting
Compositions never released by any artist, 1967–73

Many of these songs were originally recorded by Reg Dwight/Elton John in rough demonstration form, acetate pressings of which are beginning to surface in auction and on the collectors' market. There even exists a demonstration-use-only album containing ten of the songs, including 'Regimental Sgt Zippo' and 'Watching the Planes Go By'.

All songs are Elton John (or Reg Dwight) and Bernie Taupin compositions, unless otherwise stated. The dates indicate month of copyright registration.

September 1967
'Can't You See It' (Reg Dwight solo composition)
'Scarecrow'
'A Dandelion Dies in the Wind'
'If You Could See Me Now' (Reg Dwight solo composition)
'A Little Love Goes a Long Long Way' (Reg Dwight solo composition)
'Mr Lightning Strikerman'
'Onetime, Sometime or Never'
'Watching the Planes Go By'
October 1967
'Where It's At' (Reg Dwight–Nicky James composition)
'Countryside Love Affair' (Reg Dwight solo composition)
'I Could Never Fall in Love with Anybody Else' (Reg Dwight solo composition)
'I Get a Little Bit Lonely' (Reg Dwight solo composition)
'Who's Gonna Love You' (Reg Dwight–Kirk Duncan composition)
'Witch's House' (Reg Dwight solo composition)
'Year of the Teddy Bear'
November 1967
'Nina'
December 1967
'I Want to See You Smile' (Elton John–Caleb Quaye composition)
January 1968
'The Angel Tree'
February 1968
'Tartan Coloured Lady'
April 1968
'And the Clock Goes Round'
'When I Was Tealby Abbey'
'Trying to Hold on to a Love That's Dying'
'Reminds Me of You'
'I'll Stop Living when You Stop Loving Me'
May 1968
'Regimental Sgt Zippo'
'You'll Be Sorry to See Me Go' (Elton John–Caleb Quaye composition)
June 1968
'Cry Willow Cry'
'If I Asked You'
'There Is Still a Little Love'
September 1968
'Smokestack Children'
'Two of a Kind'
'The Girl on Angel Pavement'
'Baby I Miss You'
October 1968
'Bonnie's Gone Away'
'Just an Ordinary Man'
'Going Home'
'There's Still Time for Me'
December 1968
'Digging My Grave'
February 1969
'Child'

April 1969
'Last to Arrive'
July 1969
'I'm Going Home'
August 1969
'Big Circle of Stone' (Elton John–Bernie Taupin–Caleb Quaye composition)
October 1969
'She Sings Rock and Roll'
'In the Morning'
December 1969
'All the Way Down to El Paso'
'Thank You Mama'
February 1970
'Rolling Western Union'
April 1970
'Scales' (Elton John solo composition; featured in the film *Friends*)
May 1972
'Tell Me What the Doctor Said'
December 1972
'Gotta Get Back to England'

In addition to the above, another early Elton John–Bernie Taupin composition is 'Velvet Fountain', copyright registration date unknown.

Compositions released only by other artists

Most notably before his own-name career became successful, but also on a few subsequent occasions, Elton John has authored songs which have been released only by other artists, not by Elton himself. This is the complete list of such compositions, in alphabetical order. All have been written with Bernie Taupin unless otherwise stated.

'Breakdown Blues'
(composed by Caleb Quaye–Reg Dwight–Chris Jackson–Bernie Calvert)
First released as the B-side of a single by the Bread And Beer Band in February 1969. (Reg Dwight was a member of this group, which released just this one single.)

'The Flowers Will Never Die'
First released as the A-side of a single by Ayshea in January 1976.

'Get Out (of This Town)'
(composed by Elton John only)
First released as the B-side of a single by Mr Bloe in May 1971.

'Hey Lord You Made the Night Too Long'
(composed by Tony Macaulay–John Baldry–Reg Dwight)
This composition surfaced only as the B-side of an export issue of Long John Baldry's British hit 'Let the Heartaches Begin' (Pye 7N 17408), pressed in the UK expressly for the overseas market in November 1967, the same month that the UK version (Pye 7N 17385) entered the domestic chart. (The B-side of the British edition was entitled 'Annabella (Who Flies to Me When She's Lonely)'.)

'I Can't Go on Living Without You'
First released in Europe (but not in the UK) by Lulu in March 1969 as part of a four-track EP of songs which, with two others, were contenders for Britain's Eurovision Song Contest contribution that year. First released in the UK as the A-side of a single by Stuart A. Brown in March 1969. (Brown was a former member of Bluesology.)

'I Loved a Man'
(words by Dylan Thomas, set to music by Elton John)
First released on the album *Under Milk Wood*, sung by Bonnie Tyler, in November 1988.

'The Last Good Man in My Life'
First released as the B-side of a single by Kiki Dee in June 1973.

'Let Me Be Your Car'
First released on the album *Smiler* by Rod Stewart in September 1974.

'Lonely Heart'
(composed by Elton John and Gary Osborne)
First released as the third track on a twelve-inch single (A-side 'Love's a State of Mind') by Sylvia Griffin in May 1988.

'Lonnie and Josie'
First released as the A-side of a single by Kiki Dee in June 1973.

'The Man Who Loved to Dance'
Written by John–Taupin under the pseudonyms Tripe–Onions, this was first released as the B-side of a single by Kiki Dee in January 1977.

'Never Going to Fall in Love . . . (Again)'
(composed by Elton John and Tom Robinson)
First released as the A-side of a single by Tom Robinson with the Voice Squad in June 1979.

'Planes'
First released as the A-side of a single by Colin Blunstone in November 1976.

'Rock Me When He's Gone'
First released on the album *It Ain't Easy* by John Baldry in July 1971.

'Roll On'
(composed by Elton John and Gary Osborne)
First released on the album *Did He Jump . . . Or Was He Pushed?* by Garth Hewitt in October 1979.

'The Rumour'
First released on the album *The Rumour* by Olivia Newton-John in October 1988.

'Season of the Rain'
First released as the B-side of a single by Nite People in June 1970.

'71–75 New Oxford Street'
(composed by Elton John only)
First released as the A-side of a single by Mr Bloe in May 1971.

'Sing Me No Sad Songs'
First released as the A-side of an immediately withdrawn single by Guy Darrell in October 1969. Issued again in October 1974 on a DJM Records various-artists compilation cassette.

'Smile That Smile'
(composed by Elton John and Gary Osborne)
First released as the A-side of a single by Neil Bashan in May 1979.

'Snookeroo'
First released on the album *Goodnight Vienna* by Ringo Starr in November 1974.

'Supercool'
First released on the album *Loving and Free* by Kiki Dee in December 1973.

'Sweetheart on Parade'
(composed by Elton John and Gary Osborne)
First released on the album *Home Again* by Judy Collins in November 1984.

'Taking the Sun from My Eyes'
First released as the B-side of a single by Ayshea in February 1969.

'Thank You for Your Loving'
(composed by Caleb Quaye and Elton John)
First released as the B-side of a single by Dukes Noblemen in July 1968.

'The Tide Will Turn for Rebecca'
First released on the album *This Man Alone* by Edward Woodward in April 1970.

'Turn to Me'
First released on the album *Currency* by Plastic Penny in February 1969.

'When the First Tear Shows'
First released as the A-side of a single by Brian Keith in November 1968.

Compositions released first by other artists, then by Elton John

The following Elton John compositions, all subsequently released by him, were initially recorded and issued by other artists. All are Elton John–Bernie Taupin compositions, unless otherwise stated.

'Bad Side of the Moon'
First released as the A-side of a single by Toe Fat in February 1970.
 First released by Elton John as the B-side of the single 'Border Song' in March 1970.

'Country Comfort'
First released on the album *Orange Bicycle* by Orange Bicycle, and on the album *Gasoline Alley* by Rod Stewart, in September 1970.
 First released by Elton John on the album *Tumbleweed Connection* in October 1970.

'Empty Sky'
First released as the B-side of a single by Roy Everett in May 1969.
 First released by Elton John on the album *Empty Sky* in June 1969.

'Hard Luck Story'
First released as the A-side of a single by Kiki Dee in March 1974.
 First released by Elton John on the album *Rock of the Westies* in October 1975.

'Indian Sunset'
First released on the album *Mary* by Mary Travers in August 1971.
 First released by Elton John on the album *Madman Across the Water* in November 1971.

'Nice and Slow'
(composed by Thom Bell–Elton John–Bernie Taupin)
First released on the album *Don't Take Love for Granted* by Lulu in July 1979.
 First released by Elton John on the US album *The Complete Thom Bell Sessions* in February 1989, although recorded in late 1977.

'Sixty Years On'
First released as the A-side of a single by Hayden Wood in February 1970.
 First released by Elton John on the album *Elton John* in April 1970.

'Skyline Pigeon'
First released as the A-side of a single by Roger James Cooke (Roger Cook), and as the A-side of a single by Guy Darrell, in August 1968.
 First released by Elton John on the album *Empty Sky* in June 1969.

'Son of Your Father'
First released as the A-side of a single by Spooky Tooth featuring Mike Harrison in September 1969.
 First released by Elton John on the album *Tumbleweed Connection* in October 1970.

'Take Me to the Pilot'
First released as the A-side of a single by Orange Bicycle in January 1970.
 First released by Elton John on the album *Elton John* in April 1970.

The unreleased demos of other writers' compositions

From 1968, until achieving fame, Reg Dwight/Elton John supplemented his weekly wage from Dick James Music by recording demonstration versions of newly-written songs for this and other music publishing companies. Almost all were written by other composers, although it is conceivable that one or two of the following may be Elton John–Bernie Taupin songs, not registered as copyright. This list, the fullest yet compiled, is certainly incomplete. It is known, for example, that Elton recorded demos of many Roger Cook–Roger Greenaway compositions, and that he also recorded a demo for British comedian-singer-songwriter Lance Percival, yet these are not detailed below.

 Unless otherwise stated, none of the songs has been released commercially by any artist, and the composer details cannot be traced.

'Best Of Both Worlds', April 1968.
'Empty Hands', *circa* 1969.
'Hanging Upside Down', *circa* 1969.

'Hour Glass', autumn 1969. Written by Tony Collacott–Jack Mowbray–Breen Leoeuf and published by Dick James Music. The song was never released commercially.

'I Love You and That's All That Matters', 1968.
'Open Your Eyes to the Sun', *circa* 1969.

'Sarah's Coming Back', spring 1969. Written by Paul Raymond–Tony Murray and published by Dick James Music. The song was never released commercially.

'Say Hello to Mrs Jones', *circa* 1969. Written by Martin Hall and published by Belsize Music. The song was released as a single by Jigsaw in January 1971.

'She's Only Anne', 1968.
'Since the Poet Came', October 1968.
'Sitting Doing Nothing', 1968.
'A Slow Fade to Blue', *circa* 1969.

'United We Stand', late 1969. Written by Tony Hiller–John Goodison (the latter under the pseudonymous surname Simons) and published by Mills Music, the song became an international hit for Brotherhood of Man in spring 1970. Ironically, at that time, Elton then recorded the song again for an 'anonymous cover version' album (see below).

The anonymous cover version recordings

Before becoming a successful performer in his own right, Elton John supplemented his income with regular contributions to anonymous 'cover version' recordings. These discs, usually albums or special EPs, typically sold at budget price through multiple retail outlets such as Woolworths, presented sound-alike versions of current hit singles in Britain. In an effort to maintain the pretence, the sleeves did not name the decidedly unfamous singers and musicians who had worked to re-create another artist's sound.

No one has yet summoned sufficient resolve to research through these difficult to locate and often unlistenable-to albums to identify which recordings feature Elton. While some bear his easily recognisable lead vocal, he undoubtedly contributed backing vocals and perhaps even instrumental work to many other recordings less easy to identify.

The most surprising aspect of this work is that Elton continued to contribute to such recordings as late as August 1970, when his own third album was awaiting release and at the time of his important US concert début at the Troubadour in Los Angeles.

The list that follows comprises just some of Elton's work in the anonymous cover-version field, in approximate date order. Some feature his lead vocal, others his backing vocal or instrumentation. The artist whose work was being mimicked is named in parentheses.

August 1969:	'Saved by the Bell' (Robin Gibb)
March 1970:	'My Baby Loves Lovin'' (White Plains)
April 1970:	'United We Stand' (Brotherhood of Man)
May 1970:	'Back Home' (the England World Cup Squad)
June 1970:	'Cottonfields' (the Beach Boys)
June 1970:	'Yellow River' (Christie)
July 1970:	'In the Summertime' (Mungo Jerry)
August 1970:	'Natural Sinner' (Fair Weather)
August 1970:	'Signed, Sealed, Delivered (I'm Yours)' (Stevie Wonder)
August 1970:	'Up Around the Bend' (Creedence Clearwater Revival)

Other recordings

Like any prodigious recording artist, Elton John has recorded a number of songs that remain unissued. Since the mid-1970s, when his output switched to his own Rocket Records, information on such works has been kept confidential. From the preceding period, the following unreleased recordings are known.

'Honey Man', 1971. A duet recorded with Cat Stevens, which, it is believed, was kept unissued owing to differences of opinion between DJM (Elton's record company) and Island (Stevens's). The song was written by Cat Stevens and Ken Cumberbatch and was finally issued as a single in April 1972 by Brotherly Love and Sweet Salvation.

'Hi-Heel Sneakers', February 1972. A cover version of the 1964 hit by Tommy Tucker, written under his real name of Robert Higgenbotham.

Elton John's guest appearances

Since he first worked in recording studios, and particularly since he achieved international fame in 1970, Elton John has appeared as a guest performer on dozens of recordings by other artists. The list that follows is the most complete yet compiled, though owing to completely anonymous contributions it is probably incomplete. (Unless otherwise stated, none of the songs named in this section was composed by Elton John.)

Rick Astley
Elton John contributed piano to two tracks, 'Behind the Smile' and 'Wonderful You' on the February 1991 album *Free*.

Kevin Ayers
Elton John contributed piano to the song 'Circular Letter' on the March 1975 album *Sweet Deceiver*.

John Baldry
Elton John produced all four songs on side B of the July 1971 LP *It Ain't Easy*. These were: 'Let's Burn Down the Cornfield', 'Mr Rubin', 'Rock Me When He's Gone' (an Elton John–Bernie Taupin composition especially donated to Baldry and otherwise unissued) and 'Flying'. Elton also contributed piano to all four songs.

Elton John produced all five songs on side A of the May 1972 album *Everything Stops for Tea*. These were: 'Come Back Again', 'Seventh Son', 'Wild Mountain Thyme', 'Iko Iko' and 'Jubilee Cloud'. Elton also contributed vocal accompaniment to four of these, the exception being 'Seventh Son'.

The Barron Knights
Elton John contributed piano to the group's single 'An Olympic Record', issued in October 1968. Typical of the Barron Knights' singles, the track wove together parodies of contemporary hits, in this instance 'Lazy Sunday', 'I Pretend', 'Delilah', 'Cinderella Rockefella', 'Dream a Little Dream of Me' and 'Here Comes the Judge'.

Blue
Elton John and Clive Franks co-produced all ten tracks on the band's June 1977 Rocket Records album *Another Night Time Flight*. These were:
A: 'Another Night Time Flight', 'Fantasy', 'Women', 'The Shepherd', 'Strange Thing'
B: 'Bring Back the Love', 'I'm Alone', 'Tired of Loving You', '(Gonna) Capture Your Heart', 'I Understand'
   Elton John and Clive Franks co-produced 'Falling', the B-side of the single 'Another Night Time Flight' taken from the above album and issued in July 1977.
   Elton John and Clive Franks co-produced 'I'm Alone', the B-side of the single 'Women' taken from the above album and issued in November 1977.
   Elton John and Clive Franks co-produced 'Change in the Weather', the B-side of the Rocket Records single 'Stranger's Town' issued in February 1979.
   Elton John and Clive Franks co-produced 'Danger Sign' and 'Love Sings', two songs on the Blue album *Fool's Party*, released by Rocket Records in April 1979. Together with Clive Franks and Blue, Elton also jointly produced a third, 'Victim'.

Jon Bon Jovi
Elton John contributed to two tracks on the album *The Blaze of Glory: Young Guns II*, issued in August 1990: piano on 'Billy Get Your Guns' and piano and backing vocals on 'Dyin' Ain't Much of a Livin''.

Jackson Browne
Under the pseudonym Rockaday Johnnie, Elton John contributed piano to 'Redneck Friend', a song on Browne's January 1974 album *For Everyman*. The track was also issued as a single two months previously, in November 1973.

China
With Clive Franks and China, Elton John produced both sides of the Rocket Records single 'On the Slide'/'Save Your Soul', issued in September 1977. The A-side also appeared on the band's Rocket album (see below).
   With Clive Franks and China, Elton John produced all ten tracks on the band's October 1977 Rocket Records album *China*. These were:
A: 'On The Slide', 'Meet Me Halfway', 'Broken Woman', 'Hametheme', 'Savage'
B: 'Dear You', 'One Way Ticket', 'For A While', 'Shameful Disgrace', 'This Time (It's For You)'

Elton also received a credit for supplying backing vocals, though to which song(s) was not specified on the sleeve.

Kiki Dee

Both sides of Kiki Dee's June 1973 single for Rocket Records, 'Lonnie and Josie'/'The Last Good Man in My Life' were John–Taupin compositions especially donated to Dee and otherwise unissued. The former was on the album *Loving and Free* (see below), the latter only appeared on the single. Both were produced by Elton John–Clive Franks.

Elton John and Clive Franks co-produced Kiki Dee's entire December 1973 album *Loving and Free*, issued by Rocket Records. The content was:

A: 'Loving and Free', 'If It Rains', 'Lonnie and Josie', 'Travellin' in Style', 'You Put Something Better Inside Me'

B: 'Supercool', 'Rest My Head', 'Amoureuse', 'Song For Adam', 'Sugar on the Floor'.

Two of the songs, 'Lonnie and Josie' and 'Supercool', were John–Taupin compositions especially donated to Dee; Elton John also contributed musically to the album, playing keyboards on 'If It Rains', 'Lonnie and Josie', 'You Put Something Better Inside Me', 'Supercool', 'Rest My Head' (backing vocals too), 'Song For Adam' and 'Sugar on the Floor'.

Elton John and Clive Franks co-produced both sides of a Rocket Records single issued by Kiki Dee in March 1974. Side A was 'Hard Luck Story', a John–Taupin song written under the pseudonyms Ann Orson–Carte Blanche, given first to Dee and not issued by Elton John until October 1975. Side B was 'Everyone Should Have Their Way'.

Both sides of Kiki Dee's January 1977 single for Rocket Records, 'First Thing in the Morning'/'The Man Who Loved to Dance' were produced by Elton John and Clive Franks. The A-side was on the album *Kiki Dee* (see below) while the latter track, the B-side, was also a John–Taupin composition (although the composers' credit read Tripe–Onions) especially donated to Dee and released only here.

Elton John and Clive Franks co-produced the entire March 1977 album *Kiki Dee*, issued by Rocket Records. The content was:

A: 'How Much Fun', 'Sweet Creation', 'Into Eternity', 'Standing Room Only', 'Bad Day Child', 'Chicago'

B: 'Night Hours', 'Keep Right On', 'In Return', 'Walking', 'First Thing in the Morning'

Elton sang duet with Kiki Dee on 'Loving You Is Sweeter Than Ever', on the June 1981 album *Perfect Timing*. It was a hit single when issued in November 1981.

Elton John and Gary Osborne co-produced 'The Loser Gets to Win', issued as a single in September 1983.

Lonnie Donegan

Elton John contributed piano to two tracks on Donegan's January 1978 album *Puttin' on the Style*: 'Diggin' My Potatoes' and 'Puttin' on the Style'.

Lesley Duncan

Elton John contributed piano to one or more unspecified tracks on Duncan's eleven-song June 1971 album *Sing Children Sing*.

Bob Dylan

Elton John contributed piano to the track '2 × 2' on Dylan's September 1990 album *Under the Red Sky*.

Family Dogg

Elton John contributed piano to 'Way of Life', first released as a single in May 1969.

Aretha Franklin

Elton John sang duet with Franklin on 'Through the Storm', issued as a single in April 1989 and on the album of the same name one month later.

George Harrison

Elton John contributed piano to two songs on Harrison's November 1987 album *Cloud Nine*: 'Devil's Radio' and 'Wreck of the Hesperus', and electric piano to the title track 'Cloud Nine'.

The Hollies

Elton John contributed piano to 'He Ain't Heavy, He's My Brother', first released as a single in September 1969.

Elton John contributed piano to 'I Can't Tell the Bottom from the Top', first released as a single in April 1970.

Elton John contributed piano to 'Perfect Lady Housewife', first released on the November 1970 album *Confessions of the Mind*.

Davey Johnstone
Elton John played harmonium on 'Keep Right On', a track on Johnstone's May 1973 Rocket Records album *Smiling Face*.

Tom Jones
Elton John contributed backing vocals to 'Delilah', first released as a single in February 1968.
　　Elton John contributed backing vocals to 'Daughter of Darkness', issued as a single and on the album *I Who Have Nothing* in April 1970.

John Lennon
Elton John contributed piano, organ and backing vocals to two songs on Lennon's October 1974 album *Walls and Bridges*: 'Whatever Gets You Thru the Night' and 'Surprise Surprise (Sweet Bird of Paradox)'. The former became Lennon's first US number-one single as a solo artist.

Olivia Newton-John
Elton John co-produced and contributed digital piano and vocals to 'The Rumour', the title song on Olivia Newton-John's album released in October 1988, and an Elton John–Bernie Taupin composition especially donated to the singer. It was also issued as a single the previous month.

Hugh Nicholson
Elton John and Clive Franks co-produced 'Love's on Fire', the B-side of his February 1979 Rocket Records single 'How Beautiful'.

Nigel Olsson
Elton John played keyboards on 'Only One Woman', a track on the Rocket Records album *Nigel Olsson*, released in November 1975.

Maldwyn Pope
Elton John and Clive Franks co-produced his July 1977 Rocket Records single 'If I Wasn't There'/'A Child's Prayer'.

Jennifer Rush
Elton John sang duet with Rush on 'Flames of Paradise', a track on her April 1987 album *Heart Over Mind*. It was a hit single when issued that June.

Brian and Brenda Russell
Elton John contributed piano and backing vocals to Brian and Brenda Russell's cover version of his and Bernie Taupin's *Captain Fantastic* track 'Tell Me When the Whistle Blows', which appeared on their June 1976 Rocket Records album *Word Called Love*.

Mike Sammes Singers
Although precise details are not known, Elton John participated in numerous 1968–70 sessions with Sammes's in-demand troupe, principally adding vocals to other artist's recordings.

Saxon
Elton John contributed piano to 'Northern Lady', a track on Saxon's September 1986 album *Rock the Nations*. It was also released as a single in February 1987.

The Scaffold
Elton contributed uncredited backing vocals on several Scaffold recordings, *circa* 1968/69, including the October 1969 single 'Gin Gan Goolie'.

Neil Sedaka
Elton John sang harmony vocal on Sedaka's single 'Bad Blood', released in November 1974, also included on Sedaka's February 1975 UK album *Overnight Success*, titled *The Hungry Years* in the USA where Sedaka was signed to Rocket Records and 'Bad Blood' was a number-one hit single.
　　Elton John sang backing vocals on 'Steppin' Out', the title track on Sedaka's Rocket Records album issued in the USA in June 1976.

Ringo Starr
Elton John contributed piano to 'Snookeroo', a John–Taupin composition especially donated to Starr and otherwise unissued, which appeared on his November 1974 album *Goodnight Vienna*.

Rod Stewart
Elton John contributed piano and vocals to 'Let Me Be Your Car', a John–Taupin composition especially donated to Stewart and otherwise unissued, which appeared on his September 1974 album *Smiler*.

Bernie Taupin
See below.

Dionne Warwick
Elton John, Stevie Wonder and Gladys Knight all assisted Warwick with backing vocals on the AIDS charity song 'That's What Friends Are For', released as a single in November 1985 and as a track on Warwick's album *Friends* in December 1985

Bernie Taupin releases

To 1991, Bernie Taupin released three albums fully credited to himself, in which his poems or lyrics are set to music written by musicians other than Elton John.

September 1971   *Taupin*
A: *Child:* 'Birth', 'The Greatest Discovery', 'Flatters (a Beginning)', 'Brothers Together', 'Rowston Manor', 'End of a Day', 'To a Grandfather', 'Solitude', 'Conclusion'
B: 'When the Heron Wakes', 'Like Summer Tempests', 'Today's Hero', 'Sisters of the Cross', 'Brothers Together Again'; *Verses After Dark:* 'La Petite Marionette', 'Ratcatcher', 'The Visitor'

June 1980   *He Who Rides the Tiger*
A: 'Monkey on My Back (The Last Run)', 'Born on the 4th of July', 'Venezuela', 'Approaching Armageddon', 'Lover's Cross'
B: 'Blitz Babies', 'Valley Nights', 'Love (The Barren Desert)', 'The Whores of Paris'
Note: Elton John contributed musically to this album, although precise track information is not given.

August 1987   *Tribe*
A: 'Friend of the Flag', 'Corrugated Iron', 'Citizen Jane', 'Hold Back the Night', 'She Sends Shivers'
B: 'Billy Fury', 'I Still Can't Believe That You're Gone', 'Conquistador', 'The New Lone Ranger', 'Desperation Train'
Note: Elton John is credited for contributing 'voice' to this album, although on which track(s) he appears is not specified.

Bernie Taupin's other compositions

To date, more than two dozen songs written by Bernie Taupin with composers and musicians other than Elton John have been released.

Bernie Taupin co-wrote all ten tracks on the Alice Cooper album *From the Inside*, released in December 1978:
A: 'From the Inside', 'Wish I Were Born in Beverly Hills', 'The Quiet Room', 'Nurse Rozetta', 'Millie and Billie'.
B: 'Serious', 'How You Gonna See Me Now', 'For Veronica's Sake', 'Jacknife Johnny', 'Inmates (We're All Crazy)'.

'Broken Woman', first released by China on the album *China* in October 1977.

'The Burn', first released by Starship on the album *Love Among the Cannibals* in November 1989.

'Deal For Love', first released by John Waite on the film soundtrack album *Days of Thunder* in August 1990.

'Donner Pour Donner', first released by Elton John (in France) in February 1981.

'Guess I'll Always Love You', first released by Rod Stewart on the album *Absolutely Live* in December 1982.

'Hard Lesson to Learn', first released by Rod Stewart as the B-side of a 12″ (A-side 'Love Touch') single in June 1986.

'Hey Ricky (You're a Low Down Heel)', first released by Melissa Manchester as the A-side of a single in February 1983.

'I Engineer', first released by Animotion on the album *Strange Behaviour* in June 1986.

'If I Weren't So Romantic I'd Shoot You', first released by Derringer on the album *If I Weren't So Romantic I'd Shoot You* in September 1978.

'Into the Heartland', first released by the Motels on the album *Little Robbers* in February 1984.

'Love Rusts', first released by Starship on the album *Knee Deep in Hoopla* in December 1985.

'Never Give Up on a Dream', first released by Rod Stewart on the album *Tonight I'm Yours* in November 1981.

'No Tricks', first released by Alice Cooper on the B-side of the single 'How You Gonna See Me Now' in December 1978.

'Satisfied', first released by Rod Stewart on the album *Body Wishes* in June 1983.

'Savage', first released by China on the album *China* in October 1977.

'Sonny', first released by Rod Stewart on the album *Tonight I'm Yours* in November 1981.

'These Dreams', first released by Heart on the album *Heart* in November 1985.

'We Built This City', first released by Starship on the album *Knee Deep in Hoopla* in December 1985.

'When the Phone Stops Ringing', first released by Boomerang on the album *Boomerang* in August 1986.

Index